Stephen Coonts

Three Great Novels: The Pentagon

The Intruders
The Minotaur
Under Siege

ORION

The right of Stephen Coonts to be identified as the author of this work
has been asserted in accordance with the
Copyright, Designs and Patents Act 1988.

The Minotaur:
Epigraph reprinted from *Jomini's Art of War*,
by Brig. Gen. James D. Hittle, USMC Ret.,
with permission of Stackpole Books

Lines of poetry quoted in Chapters 19 and 31
are from *Darius and His Flying Machine*
by J. T. Trowbridge, a humorous mid-nineteenth
century poem about a young bumpkin who
tried to fly from his father's hayloft.

This collection first published in Great Britain in 2005 by
Orion
An imprint of Orion Books Ltd
Orion House, 5 Upper St Martin's Lane, London WC2H 9EA

A CIP catalogue record for this book is available
from the British Library

Typeset at The Spartan Press Ltd,
Lymington, Hants

Printed and bound in Great Britain by
Clays Ltd, St Ives plc

www.orionbooks.co.uk

Contents

The Intruders   1

The Minotaur   289

Under Siege   669

The Intruders

Author's Note

For their kindness in assisting with the technical aspects of this novel, the author wishes to thank Captain Sam Sayers, USN Ret., and Captain Bruce Wood, USN.

The in-flight emergencies featured in this novel are based on actual incidents. Where necessary I have simplified the complexities of cockpit switchology, emergency and air traffic control procedures in the interest of readability and pacing. I have also altered the outcome of some of the incidents. It was not my intent to write an aviation safety treatise or a manual on how to do it, but to entertain.

I also hope that you, the reader, develop a better understanding of the pride, skill, professionalism and dedication of the men and women of US Navy and Marine Corps Aviation. As you read these words, they are out there on the oceans of the earth working for all of us. This book is dedicated to them.

Eternal Father, strong to save,
Whose arm does bind the restless wave,
Who biddest the mighty ocean deep,
Its own appointed limits keep;
O hear us when we cry to thee
For those in peril on the sea.

– The Navy Hymn,
William Whiting

1

The huge ship towered above the pier that projected into the bay. The rain falling from a low, slate-colored sky made everything look dark and wet – the ship, the pier, the trucks, even the sailors hurrying to and fro.

At the gate at the head of the pier stood a portable guard shack where a sailor huddled with the collar of his pea coat turned up, his hands thrust deep into his pockets. There was no heater in the wooden shack so the air here was no warmer than it was outside, but at least he was out of the wind. Raw and wet, the swirling air lashed at unprotected flesh and cut like a knife through thin trousers.

The sailor looked yet again up at the projecting flight deck of the great ship, at the tails and wing butts of the aircraft sticking over the edge. Then his eyes wandered back along the ship's length, over a thousand feet. The gray steel behemoth looked so permanent, so solid, one almost had to accept on faith the notion that it was indeed a ship that could move at will upon the oceans. It looked, the sailor decided, like a cliff of blue-black granite.

Streams of water trickled from scuppers high on the edge of the flight deck. When the wind gusted these dribbles scattered and became an indistinguishable part of the rain. In the lulls the streams splattered randomly against the pier, the camels that wedged the hull away from the pilings, and the restless black water of the bay.

The sailor watched the continuous march of small swells as they surged against the oil containment booms, swirled trash against the pilings, and lapped nervously against the hull of the ship. Of course the ship didn't move. She lay as motionless as if she were resting on bedrock.

Yet she was floating upon that oily black wet stuff, the sailor mused. This 95,000 tons of steel would get under way tomorrow morning, steam across the bay and through the Golden Gate. All of her eighty aircraft were already aboard, all except the last one that was just now being lifted by a crane onto the forward starboard elevator, Elevator One. This past week had been spent loading bombs, bullets, beans, toilet paper – supplies

5

by the tractor-trailer load, an endless stream of trucks and railroad cars, which were pushed down tracks in the middle of the pier.

Tomorrow.

Carrying her planes and five thousand men, the ship would leave the land behind and move freely in a universe of sea and sky – that was a fact amazing and marvelous and somewhat daunting. The carrier would be a man-made planet voyaging in a universe of water, storms, darkness, maybe occasionally even sunlight. And on this planet would be the ants – the men – working and eating, working and sleeping, working and sweating, working and praying that somehow, someday the ship would once again return to the land.

And he would be aboard her. This would be his first cruise, at the age of nineteen years. The prospect was a little strange and a little frightening.

The sailor shivered involuntarily – was it the cold? – and looked again at the tails of the planes projecting over the edge of the flight deck. What would it be like to ride one of those planes down the catapult into the sky, or to come across the fantail and catch one of the arresting gear wires? The sailor didn't know, nor was it likely he would ever find out, a fact that gave him a faint sense of disappointment. He was a storekeeper, a clerk. The aviators who would fly the planes were officers, all older and presumably vastly more knowledgeable than he – certainly they lived in a world far different than his. But maybe someday. When you are nineteen the future stretches away like a highway until it disappears into the haze. Who knows what lies ahead on that infinite, misty road?

The sailor wasn't very interested in that mystical future: his thoughts turned glumly to the here and now. He was homesick. There was a girl at home whom he hadn't been all that serious about when he joined the Navy after high school, but the separation had worked its insidious magic. Now he was writing her three long letters per week, plus a letter to his folks and one to his brother. The girl . . . well, she was dating another guy. That fact ate at his insides something fierce.

He was thinking about the girl, going over what he would say in his next letter – her last letter to him had arrived three weeks ago – when a taxi pulled up on the other side of the gate. An officer stepped out and stood looking at the ship, a lieutenant, wearing a leather flight jacket and a khaki fore-and-aft cap.

After the cab driver opened the trunk, the officer paid him and hoisted two heavy parachute bags. One he swung onto his right shoulder. The other he picked up with his left hand. He strode toward the gate and the guard shack.

The sailor came out into the rain with his clipboard. He saluted the officer and said, 'I'm sorry, sir, but I need to see your ID card.'

The officer made eye contact with the sailor for the first time. He was about six feet tall, with gray eyes and a nose that was a trifle too large for his face. He lowered the bags to the wet concrete, dug in his pocket for his wallet, extracted an ID card and handed it to the sailor.

The sailor carefully copied the information from the ID card to the paper on his clipboard as he tried to shield the paper from the rain. LT JACOB L. GRAFTON, USN. Then he passed the credit-card-size piece of plastic back to the officer.

'Thank you, sir.'

'Okay, sailor,' the lieutenant said. After he stowed the card he stood silently for several seconds looking at the ship. He ignored the falling rain.

Finally he looked again at the sailor. 'Your first cruise?'

'Yessir.'

'Where you from?'

'Iowa, sir.'

'Umm.'

After a last glance at the airplanes on the flight deck above, the officer reached for his bags. He again hoisted one of the parachute bags to his right shoulder, then lifted the other in his left hand. From the way the bags sagged the sailor guessed they weighed at least fifty pounds each. The officer didn't seem to have any trouble handling them, though.

'Iowa's a long way behind you,' the lieutenant said softly.

'Yessir.'

'Good luck,' the lieutenant said, and walked away down the pier.

The sailor stood oblivious to the rain and watched him go.

Not just Iowa . . . everything was behind. The ship, the great ocean, Hawaii, Hong Kong, Singapore, Australia – all that was ahead. They would sail in the morning. Only one more night.

The sailor retreated to the shack and closed the door. He began to whistle to himself.

An hour later Lieutenant Jack Grafton finally found his new two-man stateroom and dumped his bags. His room-mate, a Navy pilot, wasn't around, but apparently he had moved into the bottom bunk.

Jake climbed into the top bunk and stretched out.

Just five months into his first shore tour – after three years in a fleet squadron with two combat cruises – his tour was cut short. Now he was going to sea again, this time with a Marine squadron.

Amateur hour! Jarheads!

How had he gotten himself into this fix anyway?

Well, the world started coming unglued about three weeks ago, when he went to Chicago to see Callie. He closed his eyes and half-listened to the sounds of the ship as it all came flooding back.

'Do you know Chicago?' Callie McKenzie asked.

It was 11 A.M. on a Thursday morning and they were on the freeway from O'Hare into the city. Callie was at the wheel.

Jake Grafton leaned back in the passenger's seat and grinned. 'No.'

Her eyes darted across his face. She was still glowing from the long, passionate kiss she had received at the gate in front of an appreciative audience of travelers and gate attendants. Then they had walked down the concourse arm in arm. Now Jake's green nylon folding clothes bag was in the trunk and they had left the worst of O'Hare's traffic behind.

'Thank you for the letters,' she said. 'You're quite a correspondent.'

'Well, thank you for all the ones you wrote to me.'

She drove in silence, her cheeks still flushed. After a bit she said, 'So your knee is okay and you're flying again?'

'Oh, sure.' Unconsciously Jake rubbed the knee that had been injured in an ejection over Laos six months ago. When he realized that he was doing it, he laughed, then said, 'But that's history. The war's over, the POWs are home, it's June, you're beautiful, I'm here – all in all, life is damn good.'

In spite of herself Callie McKenzie flushed again. Here he was, in the flesh, the man she had met in Hong Kong last fall and spent a bittersweet weekend with in the Philippines. What was that, seven days total? And she was in love with him.

She had avidly read and reread his letters and written long, chatty replies. She had told him she loved him in every line. And she had called him the first evening she arrived back in the States after finishing her two-year tour in Hong Kong with the State Department. That was ten days ago. Now, here he was.

They had so much to talk about, a relationship to renew. She was worried about that. Love was so tricky. What if the magic didn't happen?

'My folks are anxious to meet you,' she said, a trifle nervously Jake Grafton thought. He was nervous too, so nervous that he couldn't eat the breakfast they had served on the plane from Seattle. Yet here with her now, he could feel the tension leaving him. It was going to be all right.

When he didn't reply, she glanced at him. He was looking at the skyline of the city, wearing a half-smile. The car seemed crowded with his presence. That was one of the things she had remembered – he seemed a much larger man than he was. He hadn't changed. Somehow she found that reassuring. After another glance at his face, she concentrated on driving.

In a moment she asked, 'Are you hungry?'

'Oh, getting there.'

'I thought we'd go downtown, get some lunch, do some sightseeing, then go home this evening after my folks get home from the university.'

'Sounds like a plan.'

'You'll like Chicago,' she said.

'I like all American towns,' he said softly. 'I've never yet been in one I didn't like.'

'You men! So hard to please.'

He laughed, and she joined in.

He's here! She felt delicious.

She found a parking garage within the Loop and they went walking hand in hand, looking, laughing, getting reacquainted. After lunch with a bubbling crowd in a pub, they walked and walked.

Of course Callie wanted to hear an account from Jake's own lips about his shootdown and rescue from Laos, and they talked about Tiger Cole, the bombardier who had broken his back and was now undergoing intensive physical therapy in Pensacola.

When they had each brought the other up-to-date on all the things that had happened to them since they last saw each other, Callie asked, 'Are you going to stay in the Navy?'

'I don't know. I can get out after a year in this shore tour.' He was a flight instructor at Attack Squadron 128 at NAS Whidbey Island, Washington, transitioning new pilots and bombardier-navigators (BNs) to the A-6 Intruder. 'The flying is fun,' he continued. 'It's good to get back to it. But I don't know. It depends.'

'Oh what?'

'Oh, this and that.' He grinned at her.

She liked how he looked when he grinned. His gray eyes danced.

She thought she knew what the decision depended on, but she wanted to hear him say it. 'Not finances?'

'No. Got a few bucks saved.'

'On a civilian flying job?'

'Haven't applied for any.'

'On what then, Jake?'

They were on a sidewalk on Lake Shore Drive, with Lake Michigan spreading out before them. Jake had his elbows on the railing. Now he turned and enveloped Callie in his arms and gave her a long, probing kiss. When they finally parted for air, he said, 'Depends on this and that.'

'On us?'

'You and me.'

The admission satisfied her. She wrapped her hands around one of his arms and rested her head on his shoulder. The gulls were crying and wheeling above the beach.

The McKenzies lived in a brick two-story in an old neighborhood. Two giant oaks stood in the tiny front yard between the porch and the sidewalk. After apparently struggling for years to get enough sunlight, most of the grass had surrendered to fate. Only a few blades poked through last autumn's leaf collection. Professor McKenzie appeared to be as enthusiastic about raking leaves as he was about mowing grass.

Callie introduced Jake to her parents and he agreed that he could drink a beer, if they had any. The professor mixed himself a highball and poured a glass of wine for each of the ladies. Then the four of them sat a few minutes in the study with their drinks in hand exchanging pleasantries.

He had been in the Navy for five years, liked it so far. He and Callie had met in Hong Kong. Wasn't this June pleasant?

Callie and her mother finally excused themselves and headed for the kitchen. Jake surveyed the room for ashtrays and saw that there weren't any. As he debated whether he should cross his legs or keep both feet firmly on the floor, Callie's father told him that he and his wife taught at the University of Chicago, had done so for thirty years, had lived in this house for twenty. They hoped to retire in eight years. Might even move to Florida.

'I was raised in southwestern Virginia,' Jake informed his host. 'My dad has a pretty good-size farm.'

'Have you any farming ambitions?'

No, Jake thought not. He had seen his share of farming while growing up. He was a pilot now and thought he might just stick with it, although he hadn't decided for certain.

'What kind of planes do you fly in the Navy?' Professor McKenzie asked.

So Callie hadn't mentioned that? Or the professor forgot. 'I fly A-6s, sir.'

Not a glimmer showed on the professor's face. He had a weathered, lined face, was balding and wore trifocals. Still, he wasn't bad looking. And Mrs McKenzie was a striking lady. Jake could see where Callie got her looks and figure.

'What kind of planes are those?' the professor asked, apparently just to make conversation.

'Attack planes. All-weather attack.'

'Attack?'

'Any time, anywhere, any weather, day or night, high, low or in the middle.'

'You . . . drop . . . *bombs*?' His face was blank, incredulous.

'And shoot missiles,' Jake said firmly.

Professor McKenzie took a deep breath and stared at this young man who had been invited into his house by his daughter. His only daughter. Life is amazing – getting into bed with a woman is the ultimate act of faith: truly, you are rolling cosmic dice. Who would have believed that twenty-five years later the child of that union would bring home this . . . this . . .

'Doesn't it bother you? Dropping bombs?'

'Only when the bad guys are trying to kill me,' Jake Grafton replied coolly. 'Now if you'll excuse me, sir, maybe I should take my bags upstairs and wash my face.'

'Of course.' The professor gestured vaguely toward the hallway where the stairs were and took a healthy swig of his highball.

Jake found the spare bedroom and put his bags on a chair. Then he sat on the bed staring out the window.

He was in trouble. You didn't have to be a genius to see that. Callie hadn't told her parents *anything* about him. And that look on the old man's face! 'You drop *bombs*?'

He could have just said, '*Oh, Mr Grafton, you're a hit man for the Mafia? What an unusual career choice! And you look like you enjoy your work.*'

Jesus!

He dug in his pocket and got out the ring. He had purchased this engagement ring last December on the *Shiloh* and carried it with him ever since, on the ground, in the air, all the time. He had fully intended to give it to Callie when the time was right. But this visit . . . her parents . . . it made him wonder. Was he right for this woman? Would he fit into her family? Oh, love is wonderful and grand and will conquer all the problems – isn't that the way the songs go? Yet under the passion there needs to be something else . . . a *rightness*. He wanted a woman to go the distance with. If Callie was the woman, now was not the time. She wasn't ready.

And he wasn't if she wasn't.

He looked disgustedly at the ring, then put it back into his pocket.

The evening sun shone through the branches of the old oak. The window was open, a breeze wafted through the screen. That limb – he could take out the screen, toss down the bags, get onto that limb and climb down to the ground. He could be in a taxi on the way to the airport before they even knew he was gone.

He was still sitting there staring glumly out the window when Callie came for him thirty minutes later.

'What's wrong?' she asked.

'Nothing,' he said, rising from the bed and stretching. 'Dinner ready?'

'Yes.'

'Something is wrong, isn't it?'

There was no way to avoid it. 'You didn't tell me your Dad was Mr Liberal.'

'Liberal? He's about a mile left of Lenin.'

'He looked really thrilled when I told him I was an attack pilot.'

'Dad is Dad. I thought it was me you were interested in?'

Jake Grafton cocked his head. 'Well, you *are* better looking than he is.

Probably a better kisser, too.' He took her arm and led her toward the stairs. 'Wait till you meet my older brother,' he told her. 'He can't wait for the next revolution. He says the next time we won't screw it up like Bobby Lee and Jeff Davis did.'

'How would you rate me as a kisser?' she asked softly.

They paused on the top stair and she wrapped her arms around him. 'This is for score,' he whispered. 'Pucker up.'

That night when they were in bed Professor McKenzie told his wife, 'That boy's a killer.'

'Don't be ridiculous, Wallace.'

'He kills people. He kills them from the air. He's an executioner.'

'That's war, dear. They try to kill him, he tries to kill them.'

'It's murder.'

Mary McKenzie had heard it all before. 'Callie is in love with him, Wallace. I suggest you keep your opinions and your loaded labels to yourself. She must make her own decision.'

'Decision? What decision?'

'Whether or not to marry him.'

'*Marriage?*'

'Don't tell me you didn't know what was going on?' his wife said crossly. 'I swear, you're blind as a bat! Didn't you see her at dinner tonight? She loves him.'

'She won't marry him,' Professor McKenzie stated positively. 'I know *Callie!*'

'Yes, dear,' Mrs McKenzie muttered, just to pacify the man. What her husband knew about young women in love wouldn't fill a thimble. She herself was appalled by Callie's choice, believing the girl could do a whale of a lot better if she just looked around a little.

Callie was inexperienced. She didn't date until college and then couldn't seem to find any young men who interested her. Mrs McKenzie had hoped she would find a proper man while working for the State Department – apparently a futile hope. This Grafton boy was physically a good specimen, yet he was wrong for Callie. He was so . . . blue-collar. The girl needed a man who was at least in the same room with her intellectually.

But she wasn't going to say that to Callie – not a chance. Pointed comments would probably be resented, perhaps even resisted. In this new age of liberated womanhood, covert pressure was the proper way, the only way. One had to pretend strict neutrality – 'This is *your* decision, dear' – while radiating bad vibes. She owed her daughter maternal guidance – choosing a mate is much too important to be left to young women with raging hormones.

Secure in the knowledge that she was up to the task that duty had set before her, Mrs McKenzie went peacefully to sleep while her husband stewed.

At breakfast Professor McKenzie held forth on the Vietnam War. The night before at dinner he had said little, preferring to let the ladies steer the conversation. This morning he told Jake Grafton in no uncertain terms what he thought of the politicians who started the war and the politicians who kept the nation in it.

If he was expecting an argument, he didn't get it. In fact, several times Jake nodded in agreement with the professor's points, and twice Callie distinctly heard him say, 'You're right.'

After the senior McKenzies left the house for the university, Jake and Callie headed for the kitchen to finish cleaning up.

'You sure handled Dad,' Callie told her boyfriend.

'Huh?'

'You took the wind right out of Dad's sails. He thought you were going to give him a bang-up fight.'

She was looking straight into his gray eyes when he said, 'The war's over. It's history. What is there to fight about?'

'Well . . . ,' Callie said dubiously.

Jake just shrugged. His knee was fairly well healed and the dead were buried. That chapter of his life was over.

He gathered her into his arms and smiled. 'What are we going to do today?'

He had good eyes, Callie thought. You could almost look in and see the inner man, and that inner man was simple and good. He wasn't complicated or self-absorbed like her father, nor was he warped with secret doubts and phobias like so many of the young men she knew. Amazingly, after Vietnam his scars were merely physical, like that slash on his temple where a bullet gouged him.

Acutely aware of the warmth and pressure of his body against hers, she gave him a fierce hug and whispered, 'What would you like to do?'

The feel and smell and warmth of her seemed more than Jake could take in. 'Anything you want, Miss McKenzie,' he said hoarsely, mildly surprised at his reaction to her presence, 'as long as we do it together.' That didn't come out quite the way he intended, and he felt slightly flustered. You can't just invite a woman to bed at eight-thirty in the morning!

His hand massaged the small of her back and she felt her knees get weak. She took a deep breath to steady herself, then said, 'I'd like to take you to meet my brother, Theron. He lives in Milwaukee. But first let's clean up these dishes. Then, since you so coyly suggested it, let's slip upstairs in a Freudian way and get seriously naked.'

When Jake's cheeks reddened, Callie laughed, a deep, throaty woman's laugh. 'Don't pretend you weren't thinking about that!'

Jake dearly enjoyed seeing her laugh. She had a way of throwing her head back and unashamedly displaying a mouthful of beautiful teeth that he found captivating. When she did it her hair swayed and her eyes crinkled. The effect was mesmerizing. You wanted her to do it again, and again, and again.

'The thought did flit across my little mind,' he admitted, grinning, watching her eyes.

'Ooh, I want you, Jake Grafton,' she said, and kissed him.

A shaft of sunlight streamed through the open window and fell squarely across them in the bed. After all those months of living aboard ship, in a steel cubicle in the bowels of the beast where the sun never reached, Jake thought the sunlight magical. He gently turned her so their heads were in the sun. The zephyr from the window played with strands of her brown hair and the sun flecked them with gold. She was woman, all warm taut sleek smoothness and supple, sensuous wetness.

Somehow she ended up on top and set the rhythm of their lovemaking. As her hair caressed his cheeks and her hands kneaded his body, the urgency became overwhelming. He guided her onto him.

When she lay spent across him, her lashes stroking his cheek, her breath hot on his shoulder, he whispered, 'I love you.'

'I know,' she replied.

Theron McKenzie had been drafted into the Army in 1967. On October 7, 1968, he stepped on a land mine. He lost one leg below the knee and one above. Today he walked on artificial legs. Jake thought he was pretty good at it, although he had to sway his body from side to side to keep his balance when he threw the legs forward.

'It was in II Corps,' he told Jake Grafton, 'at the base camp. And the worst of it was that the mine was one of ours. I just forgot for a moment and walked the wrong way.' He shrugged and grinned.

He had a good grin. Jake liked him immediately. Yet he was slightly taken aback when Theron asked, 'So are you going to marry her?' This while his sister walked between them holding on to Jake's arm.

Grafton recovered swiftly. 'Aaah, I dunno. She's so pushy, mighty smart, might be more than a country boy like me could handle. If you were me, knowing what you know about her, what would you do?'

Both men stared at Callie's composed features. She didn't let a muscle twitch. Theron sighed, then spoke: 'If I were you and a woman loved me as much as this one loves you, I'd drag her barefoot to the altar. If I were you.'

'I'll think about it.'

'And what about you, Sis? You gonna marry him?'

'Theron, how would you like to have your throat cut?'

They ate lunch at a sports bar around the corner from the office where Theron worked as a tax accountant. After a half hour of small talk, Theron asked Jake, 'So are you going to stay in or try life on the outside?'

'Haven't decided. All I've got is a history degree. I'd have to go back to school.'

'Maybe you could get a flying job.'

'Maybe.'

Theron changed the subject. Before Callie could get an oar in, Theron was asking questions about carrier aviation – how the catapults worked, the arresting gear, how the pilots knew if they were on the glide slope. Jake drew diagrams on napkins and Theron asked more questions while Callie sat and watched.

'God, that must be terrific,' Theron said to Jake, 'landing and taking off from an aircraft carrier. That's something I'd love to do someday.' He slapped his artificial legs. 'Of course, I can't now, but I can just imagine!'

Callie glowed with a feeling of approaching euphoria. She had known that these two would get along well: it was almost as if they were brothers. Having a brother like Theron was hard on a girl – he was all man. When you have a real man only a year and a half older than you are to compare the boys against, finding one that measures up isn't easy.

Jake Grafton did. Her cup was full to overflowing.

'Is he going to stay in the Navy?' Mrs McKenzie asked her daughter. They were in the kitchen cutting the cherry pie.

'He hasn't made up his mind.'

Grafton's indecision didn't set well with Mrs McKenzie. 'He probably will,' she said.

'He might,' Callie admitted.

'The military is a nice comfortable place for some people. The government feeds and clothes and houses them, provides medical care, a living wage. All they have to do is follow orders. Some people like that. They don't have to take any responsibility. The military is safe.'

Callie concentrated on getting the pie wedges from the pan to the plates without making a mess.

'Would he continue to fly?' Mrs McKenzie asked. 'If he stayed in?'

'I suspect so,' her daughter allowed.

Mrs McKenzie let the silence build until it shrieked.

When Callie could stand it no longer, she said, 'He hasn't asked me to marry him, Mom.'

'Oh, he will, he will. That's a man working himself up to a proposal if ever I saw one.'

Callie told her mother the truth. 'If he asks, I haven't decided what the answer will be.'

Which was, Callie McKenzie suspected, precisely why he hadn't asked. Jake Grafton was nobody's fool. Yet why she hadn't yet made up her mind, she didn't know.

I love him, why am I uncertain?

Mrs McKenzie didn't know much about Jake Grafton, but she knew a man in love when she saw one. 'He's an idiot if he throws his life away by staying in the Navy,' she said perfunctorily.

'He's a pilot, Mom. That's what he does. He's good at it.'

'The airlines hire pilots.'

'He's probably considering that,' Callie said distractedly, still trying to pin down her emotional doubt. Had she been looking for a man like Theron all this time? Was that wise? Was she seeking a substitute for her brother?

Her mother was saying something. After a moment Callie began to pay attention. '. . . so he'll stay in the Navy, and some night they'll come tell you he's crashed and you're a widow. What then?'

'Mother, you just announced that some people stay in the military because it's safe, yet now you argue it's too dangerous. You can't have it both ways. Do you want whipped cream on your pie?'

'Callie, I'm thinking of you. You well know something can be physically dangerous yet on another level appeal to people without ambition.'

Callie opened the refrigerator and stared in. Then she closed it. 'We're out of whipped cream. Will you bring the other two plates, please?' She picked up two of the plates and headed for the dining room.

She put one plate in front of Jake and one in front of her father. Then she seated herself. Jake winked at her. She tried to smile at him.

Lord, if her mother only knew how close to the edge Jake lived she wouldn't be appalled – she would be horrified. Jake had made light of the dangers of flying onto and off of carriers this afternoon, but Callie knew the truth. Staying alive was the challenge.

She examined his face again. He didn't look like Theron, but he had the same self-assurance, the same intelligence and good sense, the same intellectual curiosity, the same easy way with everyone. She had seen that in him the first time they met. And like Theron, Jake Grafton had nothing to prove to anyone. Perhaps naval aviation had given Jake that quality – or combat had – but wherever he acquired it, he now had it in spades. He owned the space he occupied.

He *was* like Theron! She was going to have to come to grips with that fact.

'The most serious problem our society faces,' Professor McKenzie intoned, 'is the complete absence of moral fiber in so many of our young people.'

They had finished the pie and were sipping coffee. Jake Grafton let that pronouncement go by without bothering to glance at his host. He was observing Callie, trying to read her mood.

'If they had any sense of right and wrong,' the professor continued, 'young men would have never fought in that war. Until people understand that they have the right, nay, the duty, the obligation, to resist the illegal demands of a morally bankrupt government, we will continue to have war. Murder, slaughter, rapine, grotesque human suffering, for what? Just to line the pockets of greedy men.'

After the prologue, the professor got down to cases. Jake had a sick feeling this was coming. 'What about you, Jake? Were you drafted?'

Jake eyed the professor without turning his head. 'No.'

Something in his voice drew Callie's gaze. She glanced at him, but his attention was directed at her father.

'Wallace,' said Mrs McKenzie, 'perhaps we should—'

'You volunteered?'

'Yes.'

'You volunteered to kill people?' the professor asked with naked sarcasm.

'I volunteered to fight for my country.'

The professor was on firm ground here. He lunged with his rapier. 'Your country wasn't under attack by the Vietnamese. You can't wrap the holy flag around yourself now, Mister, or use it to cover up what you people did over there.'

Now the professor slashed. 'You and your airborne colleagues murdered defenseless men, women and children. Burned them alive with napalm. Bombed them in the most contemptible, cowardly manner that—'

'You don't know what the hell you're talking about.'

'Gentlemen, let's change the subject.' Mrs McKenzie's tone was flinty.

'No, Mary,' the professor said, leaning forward with his eyes on Jake. 'This young man – I'm being charitable here – is courting our daughter. I think I have a right to know what kind of man he is.'

'The war's over, Mr McKenzie,' Jake said.

'The shooting has stopped, no thanks to you. But you can't turn your back on all those murdered people and just walk away. I won't allow it! The American people won't—'

But he was orating to Jake Grafton's back. The pilot walked through the doorway into the hall and his feet sounded on the stairs.

Mrs McKenzie got up abruptly and went to the kitchen, leaving Callie alone with her father.

'You didn't have to do that, Dad.'

'He's not the man for you, Callie. You couldn't live with what he did, he and those other criminal swine in uniform.'

Callie McKenzie tapped nervously on the table with a spoon. Finally she put it down and scooted her chair back.

'I want to say this just right, Father. I've been wanting to say this for a long time, but I've never known just how. On this occasion I want to try. You think in black and white although we live in a gray world. It's been my experience that people who think the dividing line between right and wrong is a brick wall are crackpots.'

She rose and left the room with her father sitting open-mouthed behind her.

In the guest room upstairs Jake was rolling up his clothes and stuffing them into his folding bag. The nylon bag, Callie noticed listlessly, was heavily stained. That was the bag he had with him in Olongapo last autumn.

'I've called a cab,' he told her.

She sagged into a chair. 'My father . . . I'm sorry . . . why do you have to go?'

Grafton finished stuffing the bag, looked around to make sure he hadn't forgotten anything, then zipped the bag closed. He lifted it from the bed and tossed it toward the door. Only then did he turn to face her.

'The people I knew in the service were some of the finest men I ever met. Some of those men are dead. Some are crippled for life, like your brother. I'm proud that I served with them. We made mistakes, but we did the best we could. I won't listen to vicious slander.'

'Dad and his opinions.'

'Opinions are like assholes – everybody has one. At his age your father should know that not everyone wants to see his butt or hear his opinion.'

'Jake, you and I . . . what we have might grow into something wonderful if we give it a chance. Shouldn't we take time to talk about this?'

'Talk about what? The Vietnam War? It's *over*. All those dead men! For *what*? For fucking nothing at all, that's for what!' His voice was rising but he didn't notice. 'Oh, I killed my share of Vietnamese – your father got *that* right. They are dead for nothing. Now I've got to live with it . . . every day of my life. Don't you understand?'

He slammed his hand down on the dresser and the photo on top fell over. 'I'm not God. I don't know if we should have gone to Vietnam or if we should have left sooner or if the war was right or wrong. The self-righteous assholes who stayed at home can argue about all that until hell freezes. And it looks like they're going to.

'I took an oath. I swore to uphold the Constitution of the United States. So I obeyed orders. I did what I was told to the absolute best of my ability. Just like your brother. And what did it get us? Me and your brother? You and me? Jake and Callie – what did it get *us?*'

He took a ragged breath. He was perspiring and he felt sick. Slightly nauseated. 'It isn't your father. It's *me*. I can't just *forget*.'

'Jake, we must all live with the past. And walk on into the future.'

'Maybe you and I aren't ready for the future yet.'

She didn't reply.

'Well, maybe I'm not,' he admitted.

She was biting her lip.

'You aren't either,' he added.

When she didn't answer he picked up the folding bag and carry-on. 'Tell your mom thanks.' He went out the door.

She heard him descend the stairs. She heard the front door open. She heard it close.

Then her tears came.

Almost an hour later she descended the stairs. She was at the bottom when she heard her mother's voice coming from the study. 'You blathering fool! I'm *sick* of hearing you sermonize about the war. I'm *sick* of your righteousness. I'm *sick* of you damning the world from the safety of your alabaster pedestal.'

'Mary, that war was an obscenity. That war was wrong, a great wrong, and the blind stupidity of boys like Grafton made it possible. If Grafton and boys like him had refused to go, there wouldn't have been a war.'

'Boys? Jake Grafton is no boy. He's a *man!*'

'He doesn't *think*,' Professor McKenzie said, his voice dripping contempt. 'He *can't* think. I don't call him much of a man.'

Callie sank to the steps. She had never heard her parents address each other in such a manner. She felt drained, empty, but their voices held her mesmerized.

'Oh, he's a man all right,' her mother said. 'He just doesn't think like you do. He's got the brains and talent to fly jet aircraft in combat. He's got the character to be a naval officer, and I suspect he's a pretty good one. I know that doesn't impress you much, but Callie knows what he is. He's got the maturity and character to impress *her*.'

'Then she's too easily impressed. That girl doesn't know—'

'Enough, you *fool!*' said Mary McKenzie bitterly. 'We've got a son who did his duty as he saw it and you've never let him forget that you think he's a stupid, contemptible fascist. Your *only* son. So he doesn't come here anymore. He *won't* come here. Your opinion is just *your* opinion, Wallace – you can't seem to get it through your thick head that other people can honorably hold different opinions. And a great many people do.'

'I—'

His wife raised her voice and steamed on. 'I'm going to say this just once, Wallace, so you had better listen. Callie may marry Jake Grafton, regardless of our wishes. In her way she's almost as pigheaded as you are. Jake Grafton's every inch the man that Theron is, and he won't put up with your bombast and supercilious foolishness any more than Theron does. Grafton proved that here tonight. I don't blame him.'

'Callie won't marry that—'

'You damned old windbag, *shut up!* What you know about your daughter could be printed in foot-high letters on the head of a pin.'

She shouted that last sentence, then fell silent. When she spoke again her voice was cold, every word enunciated clearly:

'It will be a miracle if Jake Grafton ever walks through that door again. So I'm serving notice on you, Wallace, here and now. Your arrogance almost cost me my son. If it costs me my daughter, I'm divorcing you.'

Before Callie could move from her seat on the steps, Mrs McKenzie came striding through the study door. She saw Callie and stopped dead.

Callie rose, turned, and forced herself to climb the stairs.

2

After a miserable night in a motel near O'Hare, Jake got a seat the next day on the first flight to Seattle. Unfortunately, the next Harbor Airlines flight to Oak Harbor was full, so he had two hours to kill at Sea-Tac. He headed for the bar and sat nursing a beer.

The war was over, yet it wasn't. That was the crazy thing.

He had tried to keep his cool in Chicago and had done a fair job until the professor goaded him beyond endurance. Now he sat going over the mess again, for the fifteenth time, wondering what Callie was thinking, wondering what she felt.

The ring was burning a hole in his pocket. He pulled it out and looked at it from time to time, trying to shield it in his hand so that casual observers wouldn't think him weird.

Maybe he ought to throw the damned thing away. It didn't look like he was ever going to get to give it to Callie, not in this lifetime, anyway, and he certainly wasn't going to hang on to it for future presentation to whomever. He was going to have to do *something* with it.

He had been stupid to buy the ring in the first place. He should have waited until she said yes, then taken her to a jewelry store and let her pick out the ring. Normal guys got the woman first, the ring second. A fellow could avoid a lot of pitfalls if he did it the tried-and-true traditional way.

Water under the bridge.

But, God! he felt miserable. So empty, as if he had absolutely nothing to live for.

He was glumly staring into his beer mug when he heard a man's voice ask, 'Did you get that in Vietnam?'

Jake looked. Two stools down sat a young man, no more than twenty-two or -three. His left hand was a hook sticking out of his sleeve. His interrogator was older, pushing thirty, bigger, and stood waiting for the bartender to draw him a beer.

'Yeah,' the kid said. 'Near Chu Lai.'

'Serves you right,' the older man said as he tossed his money on the bar and picked up his beer. He turned away.

Jake Grafton was off his stool and moving without conscious thought. He laid a heavy hand on the man's shoulder and spun him around. Beer slopped from the man's mug.

'You *sonuvabitch!*' the man roared. 'What do you think you're doing?'

'You owe this guy an apology.'

'My *ass!*' Then the look on Grafton's face sank in. 'Now hold on, you bastard! I've got a black belt in—'

That was all he managed to get out, because Jake seized a beer bottle sitting on the bar and smashed it against the man's head with a sweeping backhand. The big man went to the floor, stunned.

Grafton grabbed wet, bloody hair with his right hand and lifted. He grabbed a handful of balls with his left and brought the man to his feet, then started him sideways. With a heave he threw him through the plate-glass window onto the concourse.

As the glass tinkled down Jake walked out the door of the bar and approached the man. He lay stunned, surrounded by glass fragments. The glass grated under Jake's shoes.

Jake squatted.

The man was semiconscious, bleeding from numerous small cuts. His eyes swam, then focused on Grafton.

'You got off lucky this time. I personally know a dozen men who would have killed you for that crack you made in there. There's probably thousands of them.'

Slivers of glass stuck out of the man's face in several places.

'If I were you I'd give up karate. You aren't anywhere near tough enough. Maybe you oughta try ballet.'

He stood and walked back into the bar, ignoring the gaping onlookers. The ex-soldier was still sitting on the stool.

'How much for the beers?' Jake asked the bartender.

'Yours?'

'Mine and this gentleman's. I'm buying his too.'

'Four bucks.'

Jake tossed a five-spot on the bar. Through the now-empty frame of the window he saw a policeman bending over the man lying on the concourse.

Jake held out his hand to the former soldier, who shook it.

'You didn't have to do that.'

'Yeah I did,' Jake said. 'I owed it to myself.'

The bartender held out his hand. 'I was in the Army for a couple years. I'd like to shake your hand too.'

Jake shook it.

'Well,' he said to the one-handed veteran, who was looking at his hook, 'don't let the assholes grind you down.'

'He isn't the only one,' the man murmured, nodding toward the concourse.

'I know. We got a fucking Eden here, don't we?'

He left the bar and introduced himself to the first cop he saw.

It was about four o'clock on Monday afternoon when a police officer opened the cell door.

'You're leaving, Grafton. Come on.'

The officer walked behind Jake, who was decked out in a blue jumpsuit and shuffled along in rubber shower sandals that were several sizes too big. He had been in the can all weekend. He had used his one telephone call when he was arrested on Saturday to call the squadron duty officer at NAS Whidbey.

'You're *where?*' that worthy had demanded, apparently unable to believe his own ears.

'The King County Jail,' Jake repeated.

'I'll be damned! What'd you do, kill somebody?'

'Naw. Threw a guy out of a bar.'

'That's all?'

'He went out through a plate glass window.'

'Oh.'

'Better put it in the logbook and call the skipper at home.'

'Okay, Jake. Don't bend over to pick up the soap.'

This afternoon he got into his civilian clothes in the same room in which he had undressed, the same room, incidentally, in which he had been fingerprinted and photographed. When he was dressed an officer passed him an envelope that contained the items from his pockets.

Jake examined the contents of the envelope. His airline tickets were still there, his wallet, change, and the ring. He pocketed the ring and counted the money in the wallet.

'Don't see many white guys in here carrying diamond rings,' the cop said chattily.

Grafton wasn't in the mood.

'Dopers seem to have pockets full of them,' the cop continued. 'And burglars. You haven't been crawling through any windows, have you?'

'Not lately.' Jake snapped his wallet shut and pocketed it.

'Bet it helps you get laid a lot.'

'Melts their panties. Poked your daughter last week.'

'Sign this receipt, butthole.'

Jake did so.

They led him out to a desk. His commanding officer, Commander Dick Donovan, was sitting in a straight-backed chair. He didn't bother watching as Jake signed two more pieces of paper thrust at him by the desk sergeant. One was a promise to appear in three weeks for a preliminary hearing before a magistrate. Jake pocketed his copy.

'You're free to go,' the sergeant said.

Donovan came out of his chair and headed for the door. Jake trailed along behind him.

In the parking lot Jake got into the passenger seat of Donovan's car. Donovan still hadn't said a word. He was a big man, easily six foot three, with wide shoulders and huge feet. He was the first bombardier-navigator (BN) to ever command the replacement squadron, VA-128.

'Thanks for bailing me out, Skipper.'

'I have a lot better things to do with my time than driving all the way to Seattle to bail an officer out of jail. An *officer!* A bar brawl! I almost didn't come. I shouldn't have. I wish I hadn't.'

'I'm sorry.'

'Don't shit me, Mister. You aren't *sorry!* You weren't even drunk when you threw that guy through that window. You'd had exactly half of one beer. I read the police report and the witnesses' statements. You aren't sorry and you've got no excuse.'

'I'm sorry you had to drive down here, sir. I'm not sorry for what I did to that guy. He had it coming.'

'Just who do you think you are, Grafton? Some comic book superhero? Who gave you the right to punish every jerk out there that deserves it? That's what cops and courts are for.'

'Okay, I shouldn't have done it.'

'You're breaking my heart.'

'Thanks for bailing me out. You didn't have to do it. I know that.'

'Not that you give a good goddamn.'

'It really doesn't matter.'

'What should I do with you now?'

'Whatever you feel you gotta do, Skipper. Write a bad fittie, letter of reprimand, court-martial, whatever. It's your call. If you want, I'll give you a letter of resignation tomorrow.'

'Just like that,' Donovan muttered.

'Just like that.'

'Is that what you want? Out of the Navy?'

'I haven't thought about it.'

'*Sir!*' Donovan snarled.

'Sir.'

Donovan fell silent. He got on I-5 and headed north. He didn't take the exit for the Mukilteo ferry, but stayed on the freeway. He was in no mood for the ferry. He was going the long way around, across the bridge at Deception Pass to Whidbey Island.

Jake merely sat and watched the traffic. None of it mattered anymore. The guys who died in Vietnam, the ones who were maimed . . . all that carnage and suffering . . . just so assholes could insult them in airports? So college professors could sneer? So the lieutenants who survived could fret about their fitness reports while they climbed the career ladder rung by slippery rung?

June . . . in the year of our Lord 1973.

In Virginia his dad would be working from dawn to dark. His father knew the price that had to be paid, so he paid it, and he reaped the reward. The calves were born and thrived, the cattle gained weight, the crops grew and matured and were harvested.

Perhaps he should go back to Virginia, get some sort of job. He was tired of the uniform, tired of the paperwork, even . . . even tired of the flying. It was all so absolutely meaningless.

Donovan was guiding the car through Mount Vernon when he spoke again. 'It took eighty-seven stitches to sew that guy up.'

Jake wasn't paying attention. He made a polite noise.

'His balls were swollen up the size of oranges.' The skipper sighed. 'Eighty-seven stitches is a lot, but there shouldn't be any permanent injuries. Just some scars. So I talked to the prosecutor. There won't be a trial.'

Jake grunted. He was half listening to Donovan now, but the commander's words were just that, words.

'The prosecutor walked out from the Chosin Reservoir with the Fifth Marines,' Donovan continued. 'He read the police report and the statements by the bartender and that crippled soldier. The police file and complaint are going to be lost.'

'Humpf,' Jake said.

'So you owe me five hundred bucks. Two hundred which I posted as bail and three hundred to replace that window you broke. You can write me a personal check.'

'Thanks, Skipper.'

'Of course, that jerk could try to cash in on his eighty-seven stitches if he can find a lawyer stupid enough to bring a civil suit. A jury might make you pay the hospital and doctor bill, but I doubt if they would give the guy a dime more than that. Never can tell about juries, though.'

'Eighty-seven,' Jake murmured.

'So you can pack your bags,' Donovan continued. 'I'm sending you to the Marines. Process servers can't get you if you're in the middle of the Pacific.'

With a growing sense of horror Jake realized the import of Commander Donovan's words. 'The *Marines?*'

'Yeah. Marine A-6 outfit is going to sea on *Columbia*. They don't have any pilots with carrier experience. BUPERS' – the Bureau of Naval Personnel – 'is looking for some Navy volunteers to go to sea with them. Consider yourself volunteered.'

'*Jesus H. Christ*, Skipper!' he spluttered. 'I just completed two 'Nam cruises five months ago.' He fell silent, tongue-tied as the full implications of this disaster pressed in upon him.

Shore duty was the payback, the flying vacation from two combat cruises, the night cat shots, the night traps, getting shot at, shot up and shot down. Those night rides down the catapults . . . sweet Jesus how he had hated those. And the night approaches, in terrible weather, sometimes in a shot-up airplane, with never enough gas – it made him want to puke just thinking about that shit. And here was Tiny Dick Donovan proposing to send him right back to do eight or nine more months of it!

Aww, fuck! It just wasn't fair!

'*The gooks damn near killed me over North Vietnam a dozen times! It's a miracle I'm still alive. And now you feed me a shit sandwich.*'

That just popped out. Dick Donovan didn't seem to hear. It dawned on Jake that the commander probably couldn't be swayed with sour grapes.

In desperation, Jake attacked in the only direction remaining. 'The jarheads maintain their planes with ball peen hammers and pipe wrenches,' he roared, his voice beyond its owner's control. 'Their planes are flying deathtraps.'

When Donovan didn't reply to this indisputable truth, Jake lost the bubble completely. 'You can't *do* this to me! I—'

'Wanna bet?'

There were three staff instructors seated at stools at the bar nursing beers when Jake walked into the O Club. The afternoon sun streamed through the tall windows. If you squinted against the glare you could see the long lazy reach of Puget Sound, placid in the calm evening, more like a pond than an arm of the sea. If you looked closely though, you could see the rise and fall of gentle swells.

Jake broke the news that he was on his way to the Marine squadron going aboard *Columbia*. He could see by the looks on their faces that they already knew. Bad news rides a fast horse.

Heads bobbed solemnly.

'Well, shore duty gets old quick.'

'Yeah. Whidbey ain't bad, but it ain't Po City.'

Their well-meaning remarks gave Jake no comfort, although he tried to maintain a straight face. Not being a liberty hound, the whores and whiskey of Olongapo City in the Philippines had never been much of an attraction for him. He felt close to tears. *This* was what he wanted more of – the flying without combat, an eight-thousand-foot runway waiting for his return, relaxed evenings on dry land with mountains on the horizon, the cool breeze coming in off the sound, delicious weekends to loaf through.

The injustice of Donovan's decision was like a knife in his gut. It was his turn, yet he was leaving all the good stuff and going back to sea!

'Lucky you aren't married,' one of the barflies said. 'A little cruise in the middle of a shore tour would drive a lot of wives straight to the divorce court.'

That remark got them talking. They knew four men who were in the process of getting divorces. The long separations the Navy required of families were hell on marriages. While his companions gossiped Jake's thoughts turned morosely to Callie. She was a good woman, and he loved her. He could see her face, feel her touch, hear her voice even now.

But her father! That jerk! A flash of heat went through him, then flickered out as he surveyed the cold ashes of his life.

'Things happen to Marines,' Tricky Nixon was saying when Jake once again began paying attention to the conversation.

Tricky was a wiry, dark, compact man. Now his brows knitted. 'Knew a Marine fighter pilot once. Flew an F-4. He diverted from the ship into Cecil Field one night. Black night. You guys know Cecil, big as half of Texas, with those parallel runways?'

His listeners nodded. Tricky took another swig of beer. After he swallowed and cleared his throat, he continued: 'For reasons known only to God, he plunked his mighty Phantom down *between* those parallel runways. In the grass. Hit the radar shack head-on, smacked it into a million splinters.'

Tricky sighed, then continued: 'The next day the squadron maintenance officer went into Cecil on the COD, looked the plane over pretty good, had it towed outta the dirt onto a taxiway, then filled it with gas and flew it back to the ship. It was a little scratched up but nothing serious. Things happen to Marines.'

They talked about that – about the odds of putting a tactical jet with a landing weight of 45,000 pounds down on grass and not ripping one or more of the gear off the plane.

'I knew a Marine once,' Billy Doyle said when the conversation lagged, 'who forgot to pull the power back when he landed. He was flying an F-4D.'

His listeners nodded.

'He went screeching down the runway with the tires smoking, went off the end and drove out across about a half mile of dirt. Went through the base perimeter fence and across a ditch that wiped off the landing gear. Skidded on across a road, and came to rest with the plane straddling a railroad track. He sat there awhile thinking it over, then finally shut 'er down and climbed out. He was standing there looking 'er over when a train came along and plowed into the wreck. Smashed it to bits.'

They sipped beer while they thought about forgetting to pull the throttle to idle on touchdown, about how it would feel sitting dazed in the cockpit of a crashed airplane with the engine still running as the realization sank in that you had really screwed the pooch this time. *Really* screwed the pooch.

'Things happen to Marines,' Billy Doyle added.

'Their bad days can be spectacular,' Bob Landow agreed in his bass growl. He was a bear of a man, with biceps that rippled the material of his shirt. 'Marine F-8 pilot was trans-Pacing one time, flying the pond.'

He paused and lubricated his throat while his listeners thought about flying a single-seat fighter across the Pacific, about spending ten or twelve hours strapped to an ejection seat in the tiny cockpit.

Landow's growl broke the silence. 'The first time he hit the tanker for gas, the fuel cells overpressurized and ruptured. Fuel squirted out of every orifice. It squirted into the engine bay and in seconds the plane caught fire.

'At this point our Marine decides to eject. He pulls the face curtain. Nothing happens. But not yet to sweat, because he has the secondary handle between his legs. He gives that a hell of a jerk. Nothing. He just sits there in this unejectable seat in this burning aircraft with fuel running out of every pore over the vast Pacific.

'This is turning into a major-league bad day. He yanks on the handle a couple more times like King Kong with a hard on. Nothing happens. Gawdalmighty, he's getting excited now. He tried jettisoning the canopy. Damn thing won't go off. It's stuck. This is getting seriouser and seriouser.

'The plane is burning like a blowtorch by this time and he's getting *really* excited. He pounds and pounds at the canopy while the plane does smoky whifferdills. Finally the canopy departs. Our Marine is greatly relieved. He unstraps and prepares to climb out. This is an F-8, you understand, and if he makes it past that tail in one piece he will be the very first. But he's going to give it a try. He starts to straighten up and the wind just grabs him and whoom – he's out – free-falling toward the ocean deep and blue. *Out,* thank God, *out!*

'He falls for a while toward the Pacific thinking about Marine maintenance, then decides it's time to see if the parachute works. It wasn't that kind of a day. Damn thing streams.'

'No!' several of his listeners groaned in unison.

'I shit you not,' Bob Landow replied. He helped himself to more beer as his Marine fell from an indifferent sky toward an indifferent sea with an unopened parachute streaming behind him.

'What's the rest of it?' Tricky demanded.

Landow frowned. There is a certain pace to a good sea story, and Tricky had a bad habit of rushing it. Not willing to be hurried, Landow took another sip of beer, then made a show of wiping his lips with a napkin. When he had the glass back on the bar and his weight lifter's arms crossed just so, he said, 'He had some Marine luck there at the end.

Pulled strings like a puppeteer and got a few panels of the rag to blossom. Just enough. Just enough.'

He shook his head wearily and settled a baleful gaze on Jake Grafton. 'Things happen to Marines. You be careful out there, Jake.'

'Yeah,' Jake told them as he glanced out the window at the reflection of small puffy clouds on the limpid blue water. 'I will.'

3

Jake Grafton was dressed in khakis and wearing his leather flight jacket when he stepped onto the catwalk around the flight deck. The sun was out, yet to the west a layer of fog obscured the higher buildings of San Francisco and all of the Golden Gate Bridge except the tops of the towers. The gentle breeze had that moist, foggy feeling. Jake shivered and tugged his ball cap more firmly onto his head.

The pier below was covered with people. The pilot rested his elbows on the railing of the catwalk and stood taking it all in, listening to the cacophony of voices.

Sailors, Marines, officers and chiefs stood surrounded by their families. Children were everywhere, some clinging to their mothers, others running through the crowd chasing one another, the smaller ones being passed from hand to hand by the adults.

A band was tuning up on Elevator Two, which was in the down position and stuck out over the pier like a porch roof. Even as Jake watched, the conductor got the attention of his charges and whipped them into a Sousa march.

On the pier near the stern another band was assembling. No doubt that was the Naval Air Station band, which tooted for every ship's departure. Well and good, but *Columbia* had a band too and apparently the ship's XO thought there couldn't be too much music.

Above Jake's head the tails of aircraft stuck out precariously over the edge of the flight deck and cast weird shadows on the crowded pier. Occasionally he could see people lift their gaze to take in the vast bulk of the ship and the dozens of aircraft. Then the people turned their attention back to their loved one.

Last night he had stood in line at one of the dozen phone booths on the head of the pier. The rain had subsided to occasional drips. When his turn for the booth came, he had called his folks in Virginia, then Callie. It was after midnight in Chicago when she answered.

'Callie, this is Jake.'

'Where are you?'

'On the pier at Alameda. Did you get my letters?'

'I received three.'

He had written the letters and mailed them from Oceana, where he had been sent to do field carrier qualifications with a group of students from VA-42. He had completed his field quals, of course, but didn't go to the ship. There hadn't been time. He would have to qual aboard *Columbia* after she sailed. He needed ten day and six night traps because it had been over six months since his last carrier landing.

'Another letter is on the way,' he told Callie, probably a superfluous comment. 'You'll get it in a day or two.'

'So how is the ship?'

'It's a ship. What can I say?'

'When do you sail?'

'Seven-thirty in the morning.'

'So when I wake up you'll be at sea.'

'Uh-huh.'

They talked desultorily for several minutes, the operator came on the line and Jake fed in more quarters, then he got down to it. 'Callie, I love you.'

'I know you do. Oh, Jake, I'm so sorry your visit was such a disaster.'

'I am too. I guess these things just happen sometimes. I wish . . .' And he ran out of steam. A phone booth on a pier with dozens of sailors awaiting their turn didn't seem the place to say what he wished.

'You be careful,' she said.

'You know me, Callie. I'm always careful.'

'Don't take any unnecessary chances.'

'I won't.'

'I want you to come back to me.'

Now Jake stood watching the crowd and thinking about that. She wanted him to come back *to her*.

He took a deep breath and sighed. Ah me, life is so strange. Just when everything looks bleakest a ray of sunshine comes through the clouds. Hope. He had hope. She wouldn't have said something like that unless she meant it, not Callie, not to a guy going on an eight-month cruise.

He was standing there listening to the two bands playing different tunes at the same time, watching the crowd, watching sailors and women engage in passionate kisses, when he saw the Cadillac. A pink Cadillac convertible with the top down was slowly making its way down the pier. People flowed out of its way, then closed in behind it, like water parting for a boat.

Cars were not allowed on the pier. Yet there it was. A man in a white uniform was driving, yet all of his passengers were women, young women, and not wearing a lot of clothing either. Lots of brown thighs and bare shoulders were on display, several truly awesome bosoms.

In complete disregard of the regulations, the car made its way to the foot of the officers' gangway and stopped. The driver got out and stretched lazily as he surveyed the giant gray ship looming beside the pier. The women bounded out and surrounded him.

It's Bosun Muldowski! Who else could it be? No sailor could get a car past the guards at the head of the pier and few officers under flag rank. But a warrant officer four? Yep.

Muldowski.

He had been the flight deck bosun on *Shiloh*, Jake's last ship. Apparently he was coming to *Columbia*. Now Jake remembered – Muldowski never did shore duty tours. He had been going from ship to ship for over twenty-five years.

Look at those women in hot pants and short short skirts!

Sailors to the right and left of Jake in the catwalk shouted and shrieked wolf whistles. Muldowski took no notice but the women waved prettily, which drew lusty cheers from the onlooking white hats.

With the bosun's bags out of the trunk of the car, he took his time hugging each of the women, all five of them, as the bands blared mightily and spectator sailors watched in awe.

'The bosun must own a whorehouse,' one sailor down the catwalk told his friends loud enough for Jake to hear.

'He sure knows how to live,' his buddy said approvingly.

'Style. He's got *style*.'

Jake Grafton grinned. Muldowski's spectacular arrival had just catapulted him to superstardom with the white hats, which was precisely the effect, Jake suspected, that the bosun intended. The deck apes would work like slaves for him until they dropped in their tracks.

All too soon the ship's whistle sounded, bullhorns blared and sailors rushed to single up the lines holding the great ship to the land. The men on the pier gave their women one last passionate hug, then dashed for the gangways. As seven bells sounded over the ship's PA system, cranes lifted the gangways clear and deposited them on the pier.

The last of the lines were released and the ship began to move, very slowly at first, almost imperceptibly. Slowly the gap between the pier and the men crowding the rails widened.

Sailors tossed their Dixie cups at the pier and children scurried like rats to retrieve them. The strains of 'Anchors Aweigh' filled the air.

When the pier was several hundred feet away and aft of the beam, Jake felt a rumble reach him through the steel on which he stood. The screws were biting. The effect was noticeable. The pier slid astern slowly at first, then with increasing speed.

Now the pilot climbed to the flight deck and threaded his way past tie-down chains toward the bow, where he joined a loose knot of men leaning into the increasing wind. Ahead was the Bay Bridge, then the Golden Gate. And the fog beyond the Golden Gate was dissipating.

The ship had cleared the Bay Bridge and was steaming at eight or ten knots past Alcatraz when the loudspeaker sounded. 'Flight Quarters, flight quarters. All hands man your flight quarters station.'

The cruise had begun.

Jake was in the locker room donning his flight gear when a black Marine in a flight suit came in. He had railroad tracks pinned to the shoulders of his flight suit, so he was a captain, the Marine equivalent of Jake's Navy rank of lieutenant. He looked Jake over, nodded to a couple of Marines who were also suiting up to get some traps, then strolled over to Jake.

'They call me Flap. I guess we're flying together.'

The BN had his hair cut in the Marine Corps' version of an Afro – that is, it stuck out from his head about half an inch and was meticulously tapered on the sides and back. He was slightly above medium height, with the well-developed chest and bulging muscles that can only be acquired by thousands of hours of pumping iron. He looked to be in his late twenties, maybe thirty at the most.

'Jake Grafton. You're Le Beau?'

'Yep.'

'How come you weren't at the brief?'

'Hey, man. This is CQ!' CQ meant carrier qualification. 'All we're gonna do is fly around this bird farm with the wheels down, dangling our little hook thingy. Where is *your* bag. You can hack it, can't ya?'

Jake decided to change the subject. 'Where you from?'

'Parris Island. Get it? Le Beau? French name? Parris Island?'

'Ha ha.'

'Don't let this fine chocolate complexion fool you, my man. It's French chocolate.'

'French shit,' said one of Le Beau's fellow Marines.

'Eat it, butt breath,' Flap shot back. 'I'm black with a seasoning of Creole.'

'Sorta like coffee with cream,' Jake Grafton remarked as he zipped up his torso harness.

'Yeah man. That's exactly right. There was a planter in Louisiana, Le Beau, with a slobbering craving for black poontang. After the Civil War he took personal offense when his former slaves adopted his last name. They did it 'cause most of them was his sons and daughters. But Le Beau didn't like the thought of being recognized in history as a patriarch, didn't want to admit his generous genetic contributions to improving a downtrodden race. Hung a couple of his nigger kids, he did. So all the blacks in the parish adopted the name. More damn black Le Beaus in that section of Louisiana than you could shake a stiff dick at. Now that redneck Cajun planter bigot was one of my many great-great-grand-pappys, of whom I am so very proud.'

'Terrific,' said Jake Grafton, who checked to see that the laces of his new G-suit were properly adjusted.

'We heard you were coming. The Nav just didn't think us gyrenes could handle all this high tailhook tech. So we heard they were sending an ace Navy type to indoctrinate us ignorant jarheads, instruct us, lead the way into a better, brighter day.'

Grafton didn't think that comment worth a reply.

'It'll be a real pleasure,' said Flap Le Beau warmly as he grabbed his torso harness from his locker, 'flying with a master hookster. Just think of me as a student at the fount of all wisdom, an apprentice seeking to acquire insights into the nuances of the arcane art, appreciate the—'

'Are you always this full of shit or are you making a special effort on my behalf?' Jake asked.

Le Beau prattled on unperturbed. 'It's tragic that so many Navy persons are dangerously thin-skinned in a world full of sharp objects! One can infer from your crude comment that you share that lamentable trait with your colleagues. It's sad, very sad, but there are probably gonna be tensions between us. None of that male-bonding horse pucky for you and me, huh? Tensions. Stress. Misunderstandings. Heartburns. Hard feelings. Ass kickings.' He sighed plaintively. 'Well, I try to get along by going along. That's the Cajun in me coming out. I am so very lucky I got this white blood in me, ya know? Lets me see everything in a better perspective.'

The Marine bent slightly at the waist and addressed his next comment to the deck: 'Thank you, thank you, Jules Le Beau, rotting down there in hell.'

Back to his locker and flight gear – 'Lots of the bros ain't as lucky as I am – they can't tell trees from manure piles, and—'

'Oh, for Christ's sake, Flap,' someone in the next row said. 'Turn off the tap, will ya?'

'Yeoww,' Flap howled, 'I feel *great!* Gonna get out there and fly with a Navy ace and see how it's *done* by the best of the best!'

'How did I wind up with this asshole?' Jake asked the major two lockers down.

'No other pilot wanted him,' was the reply.

'Hey, watch your mouth over there,' Flap called. 'This is my rep you're pissin' on.'

'Pissin' on, *sir!*'

'Sir,' Flap echoed dutifully.

The sun shone down softly through a high thin cirrus layer. The wind out of the northwest was heaping the sea into long windrows and ripping occasional whitecaps from the crests as gulls wheeled and turned around the great ship.

Two frigates and four destroyers were visible several miles away, scattered in a haphazard circle around the carrier. These were the carrier's escorts, an antisubmarine screen, faithful retainers that would attend the queen wherever she led.

On the eastern horizon land was still visible. It would soon drop over the earth's rim since the carrier would have to spend the next several hours running into the northwest wind, then the universe would consist of only the ships, the sea and the sky. The land would become a memory of the past and a vision of a hazy future, but the solid reality of the present would be just the ships and the men who rode them. Six small moons orbiting one wandering planet . . .

Jake's vision lingered on that distant dark line of earth, then he turned away.

The ship rode easily this morning, with just the gentlest of rolls, which Jake noticed only because he didn't have his sea legs yet. This roll would become a pitching motion when the ship turned into the wind.

Sensing these things and knowing them without really thinking about them, Jake Grafton walked slowly aft looking for his aircraft. There – by Elevator Four.

She was no beauty, this A-6E Intruder decked out in dull, low viz paint splotched here and there with puke green zinc dichromate primer. An external power cord was already plugged into the plane. Jake lowered the boarding ladder and opened the canopy, then climbed up and placed his helmet bag on the seat. He ensured the safety pins were properly installed in the ejection seat, let his eye rove over the cockpit switches, the gear handle, the wing position lever and the fuel dump switches, then checked the fuel quantity. Ten thousand pounds. As advertised. He toggled the seat position adjustment switches, noted the whine and felt the seat move, then released them. Jake climbed down the ladder to the deck and began his preflight inspection.

In Vietnam he had flown A-6As, the first version of the Intruder. This plane was an A-6E, the second-generation bomber, the state-of-the-art in American military technology. Most of the updates were not visible to the naked eye. The search and track radars of the A-6A had been replaced with one radar that combined both search and track functions. The A's rotary-drum computer had been replaced with a solid-state, digital, state-of-the-art version. The third major component in the electronics system, the inertial navigation system, or INS, had not yet been updated, so it was now the weak point in the navigation/attack system. The new computer and radar were not only more accurate than the old gear, they were also proving to be extraordinarily reliable, which erased the major operational disadvantage of the A-6A.

The E had been in the fleet for several years now, yet it had not been used in Vietnam, by Pentagon fiat. Had the updated E been used there, the targets could have been hit with greater accuracy, with fewer missions, thereby saving lives and perhaps helping shorten the war, but inevitably some of these planes would have been lost and the technology compromised, i.e., seen by the Soviets.

So lives had been traded to keep the technology secret. How many lives? Who could say.

As Jake Grafton walked around this A-6E looking and touching this and that, the raw, twisted Vietnam emotions came flooding back. Once again he felt the fear, saw the blood, saw the night sky filled with streaks of tracer and the fiery plumes of SAMs. The faces of the dead men floated before him as he felt the smooth, cool skin of the airplane.

It seemed as if he had never left the ship. Any second Tiger Cole would come strolling across the deck with his helmet bag and charts, ready to fly into the mouth of hell.

Jake felt his stomach churn, as if he were going to vomit. He paused and leaned against a main-gear strut.

No!

Six months had passed. His knee had healed, he had visited his folks, done a little flight instruction at Whidbey Island, visited Callie in Chicago . . . thrown that asshole through the window at Sea-Tac . . . why was he sweating, nauseated?

This is *car quals*, for Christ's sake! It's a beautiful day, a cake hop, a walk in the park!

He stood straight and, looking out to sea, took several deep breaths. He should have popped the question to Callie – should have asked her to marry him. And he should have resigned from the Navy.

He shouldn't even be here! On the boat again! He had done his share, dropped his share of bombs, killed his share of gomers.

For God's sake – another cruise – with a bunch of jack-off jarheads!

He took his hand off the strut and stood staring at the plane, his face twisted into a frown. Primer splotches everywhere, dirt, stains from hydraulic leaks . . . And it was a fairly new plane, less than a year old!

Camparelli would have come screaming unglued if they had sent a plane like this to *his* squadron. Screaming-meemy fucking *unglued!*

Somehow the thought of Commander Camparelli, Jake's last skipper in Vietnam, storming and ranting amused Jake Grafton.

'Looks like a piece of shit, don't it?'

Bosun Muldowski was standing there staring at the plane with his arms crossed.

'Yeah, Bosun, but I ain't looking to buy it. I'm just flying it this morning.'

'Sure didn't expect to find you aviatin' for the jugheads, Mr Grafton.'

'Life's pretty weird sometimes.'

The bosun nodded sagely. 'Heard about that shithead that went through the window at Sea-Tac.'

Jake nodded and rubbed his hand through his hair. 'Well, I guess I lost it for a little bit. I'm not the smartest guy you ever met.'

'Smart enough. Thanks.'

With that, the bosun walked forward, up the deck, leaving the pilot staring at his back.

'Hey, my man! Is this mean green killing machine safe to fly?' Flap. He came around the nose of the plane and lowered the BN's boarding ladder.

'We'll find out, won't we?'

'It's an embarrassing question to have to ask, I know, yet the dynamics of the moment and the precarious state of my existence here in space and time impel me to ponder my karma and your competence. No offense, but I am growing attached to my ass and don't want to part with it. What I'm getting at, Ace, is, are you man enough to handle the program?'

The pilot slapped the fuselage. 'This relic from the Mongolian Air Force is going off the pointy end of this boat in about fifteen minutes with your manly physique in it. That's the only fact I have access to. Will your ass stay attached? Will sweet, innocent Suzy Kiss-me succumb to the blandishments of the evil pervert, Mortimer Fuck-butt? Stay tuned to this channel and find out right after these words from our sponsors.' He turned his back on Flap Le Beau.

'I have no doubt this thing will go *off* this scow, but can *you* get it back aboard all in one piece?'

Jake Grafton shouted back over his shoulder: 'We'll fly together or die together, Le Beau. None of that macho male bonding crap for hairy studs like us.'

The bosun – he didn't have to say that. And it was a beautiful day, the sun glinting on the swells, the high, open sky, the gentle motion of the ship . . .

The plane would feel good in his hands, would do just as he willed it. She would respond so sweetly to the throttles and stick, would come down the groove into the wires so slick and honest . . .

As the sea wind played with his hair the pilot found himself feeling better.

4

Wings spread and locked, flaps and slats to takeoff, Roger the weight-board – it all came back without conscious thought as Jake followed the taxi director's hand signals and moved the warplane toward the port bow catapult, Cat Two. Flap didn't help – he didn't say or do anything after getting the inertial aligned and flipping the radar switch to standby. He merely sat and watched Jake.

'Takeoff checklist,' Jake prompted.

'I thought you said you could fly this thing, Ace.'

Jake ran through the items on his own as he eased the plane the last few feet into the catapult shuttle and the hold-back bar dropped into place.

The yellow-shirt taxi director gave him the 'release brakes' signal with one hand and with the other made a sweeping motion below his waist. This was the signal to the catapult operator to ease the shuttle forward with a hydraulic piston, taking all the slack out of the nose-wheel tow-launching mechanism. Jake felt the thunk as he released the brakes and pushed both throttles forward to the stops.

The engines came up nicely. RPM, exhaust gas temperatures, fuel flow – the tapes ran up the dials as the engines wound up.

The Intruder vibrated like a living thing as the engines sucked in rivers of air and slammed it out the exhausts.

'You ready?' Jake asked the bombardier as he wrapped the fingers of his left hand around the catapult grip while he braced the heel of the hand against the throttles.

'Onward and upward, Ace.'

The taxi director was pointing to the catapult officer, who was ten feet farther up the deck. The shooter was twirling his fingers and looking at Jake, waiting.

Oil pressure both engines – fine. Hydraulics – okay. Jake waggled the stick and checked the movement of the stabilator in his left-side rearview mirror on the canopy rail. Then he saluted the cat officer with his right hand. The shooter returned it and glanced up the cat track toward the bow as Jake put his head back into the headrest and placed his right hand behind the stick.

Now the cat officer lunged forward and touched the deck with his right hand.

One heartbeat, two, then the catapult fired. The acceleration was vicious.

Yeeeaaaah! and it was over, in about two and a half seconds. The edge of the bow swept under the nose and the plane was over the glittering sea.

Jake let the trim rotate the nose to eight degrees nose up as he reached for the gear handle. He slapped it up and swept his eyes across the instrument panel, taking in the attitude reference on the vertical display indicator – the VDI, the altimeter – eighty feet and going up, the rate of climb – positive, the airspeed – 150 knots and accelerating, all warning lights out. He took in all these bits of information without conscious thought, just noted them somewhere in his subconscious, and put it all together as the airplane accelerated and climbed away from the ship.

With the gear up and locked, he raised the flaps and slats. Here they came. Still accelerating, he stopped the climb at five hundred feet and ran the nose trim down. Two hundred and fifty knots, 300, 350 . . . still accelerating . . .

To his amusement he saw that Flap Le Beau was sitting upright in his ejection seat with his hands folded on his lap, just inches from the alternate ejection handle between his legs.

At 400 knots Jake eased the throttles back. Five miles coming up on the DME . . . and the pilot pulled the nose up steeply and dropped the left wing as he eased the throttles forward again. The plane leaped away from the ocean in a climbing turn. Jake scanned the sky looking for the plane that had preceded him on the cat by two minutes.

He had four thousand pounds of fuel – no, only three thousand now – to burn off before they called him down for his first landing, in about fifteen minutes.

Better make it last, Jake. Don't squander it. He pulled the throttles back and coasted up to five thousand feet, where he leveled indicating 250 knots in a gentle turn that would allow him to orbit the ship on the five-mile circle.

Flap sighed audibly over the intercom, the ICS, then said, 'Acceptable launch, Jake. Acceptable. You obviously have done this once or twice and haven't forgotten how. This pleases me. I get a warm fuzzy.'

There the major was, almost on the other side of the ship, level at this altitude and turning on the five-mile arc. Jake steepened his turn to cut across above the ship and rendezvous.

'I almost joined the Navy,' Flap confided, 'but I came to my senses just in time and joined the Corps. It's a real fighting outfit, the best in the world. The Navy . . . well, the best that can be said is that you guys try. Most of the time, anyway.'

He talked on as Jake got on the major's bearing line and eased in some left rudder to lower the nose so he could see the major out the right-side quarter panel. Rendezvousing an A-6 with its side-by-side seating took some finesse when coming in on the lead's left because the pilot of the joining aircraft could easily lose sight of the lead plane. If he let himself go just a little high, or if he let his plane fall a little behind the bearing line – going sucked, they called it – and attempted to pull back to the bearing, the lead would disappear under the wingman's nose and he would be closing blindly. This was not good, a situation fraught with hazard for all concerned.

This morning Jake stayed glued to the bearing. If Flap noticed he gave no indication. He was saying, '. . . the closest I ever came to being in the Navy was the wife of some surface warrior I met at MCRD' – Marine Corps Recruit Depot – 'O Club on a Friday night. She rubbed her tits all over my back and I told her she was going to give me zipper rash. She was all hot and randy so I thought, Why not. We went over to her place . . .'

When he was fifty feet away from the major's plane Jake lowered the nose and crossed behind and under. He surfaced into parade position on the right side, the outside of the turn. The BN gave him a thumbs-up.

Jake's BN talked on. '. . . I just put the ol' cock to her . . .'

After a frequency shift that the major's BN signaled and Jake had to dial in because Flap wasn't helping at all, they made two more turns in the circle, then started down.

'She had those nipples that are like strawberries, you know what I mean? All puffed up so nice and sweet and red and they're just made for sucking on? I like them the very best. Can't understand why God didn't equip more women with 'em. Only about one broad in ten has 'em. It's a mystery.'

They were descending through patches of sunlight interspersed with shadow. The occasional golden shafts played on the planes and made the sea below glisten, when Jake could steal a second from holding position on the lead plane and glance down.

His plane handled well. Slick and tight and responsive. He contented himself with moving his plane a few inches forward on the lead, then a few inches back, staying in absolute control. When he felt comfortable he moved in on the bearing line so that the wing tips overlapped. He stopped when he could feel the downdraft off the lead's wing and the tip was just two feet from his canopy. He held it there for a moment or two to prove to himself that he could still do it, then eased back out to where he belonged.

Flying is the best that life offers, Jake Grafton thought. *And carrier flying is the best of the flying. These day traps and cat shots are going to be terrific.* He fought back the sense of euphoria that suffused him.

'. . . as close as I ever came to being in the Navy, I'll tell you that.'

If Flap would just shut up!

But he won't. So no sense making a scene.

The two warplanes came up the ship's wake at eight hundred feet glued together. There were already two other planes in the pattern with their gear and hooks down, two A-7 Corsairs, so the major delayed his break. Then the BN kissed him off and the major dumped his left wing and pulled. Jake watched the lead plane turn away as he counted to himself. At the count of seven he slammed the stick sideways and pulled as he reached for the gear handle with his left hand and slapped it down. Then the flaps.

Turning level, three G's . . . gear coming, flaps and slats coming . . . seven thousand pounds of fuel.

Stable on the downwind he toggled the main dump and let seven hundred pounds squirt out into the atmosphere. He wanted to cross the ramp of the ship with precisely six grand.

Precision. That's what carrier flying is all about. That's the challenge. And the thrill.

'. . . just don't see why anybody would want to float around in the middle of the ocean on these bird farms. Eight months of this fun. The Navy is full of happy masturbators . . .'

Hook up for the first pass, a touch-and-go. Let the LSO get his look and learn that I'm not suicidal.

Coming through the ninety, on speed, exactly 118 knots with a three-o'clock angle-of-attack . . . there's the meatball on the Fresnel lens. Cross the wake, roll out, coming in to the angled deck, watch the lineup! There's the burble from the island . . . power on then off fast. Keep that ball in the center . . .

The wheels smacked into the deck and the nose came down hard as Jake Grafton shoved the throttles to the stop and closed the wing-tip speed brakes with the throttle-mounted switch. The Intruder shot up the angled deck and ran off into the air. He brought the stick back and got her climbing.

'The amazing thing is that the Navy finds so many of you masturbators to ride these floating aviaries. You wouldn't think there were this many jack-off artists in the whole world. Not if you just looked at the world casually. I mean, most people like their sex with *somebody else,* y'know? No doubt a lot of you guys are queer. Gotta be.'

On the downwind Jake lowered the hook and checked that his harness was locked. Normally he flew with it unlocked so that he could lean forward if he wished or wiggle in the ejection seat.

He toggled the seat up a smidgen and adjusted the rheostat that brightened the angle-of-attack indicator.

The interval between Jake and the major was good, and the major trapped on his first pass as Jake was reducing power at the 180-degree position. Down and turning, on speed, looking for the ball crossing the wake, wings level and reducing power, now power on for the burble, watching the lineup and flying that ball . . .

The Intruder swept across the ramp and slammed into the deck. As the throttles went forward the tailhook caught a wire and dragged the plane to a dead stop.

Then the plane began to roll backward. Jake jabbed the hook-up button and added power to taxi out of the gear. The director was giving him the come ahead as Flap said, 'The whole concept of having five thousand guys crammed together without women is unnatural. Everybody horny, jacking off in the shower, into their sheets – this boat is a floating semen factory! In nineteen seventy-three! My God, haven't we humans made any progress in understanding man's sexual needs in all these years of . . .'

Queued up waiting for Cat Two, checking the gear and flap settings, the fuel, then following the yellow shirt's signals as he brought the plane into the shuttle – Jake was doing the things he knew how to do, the things that made the hassles worthwhile.

Throttles up . . . the salute – and wham, they were off to do it again. This time Jake left the gear and flaps down. He flew straight ahead upwind until the major passed him on the left going downwind.

Jake banked for the crosswind turn. The plane entered a shaft of sunlight and the warmth played on his arms and legs. Inside his oxygen mask Jake grinned broadly.

After four traps Jake was directed to fold his wings and stop near the carrier's island with the engines running while the plane was refueled, a 'hot' turnaround. He opened the canopy and took off his oxygen mask. His face was wet with sweat. He swabbed away the moisture and watched the planes making their approaches.

Flap Le Beau also sat watching, silent at last.

Heavenly silence. Except for the howl of jet engines at full power and the slam of the catapult and an occasional terse radio message. The flight deck of an aircraft carrier was the loudest place on earth, yet oh so pleasant without Flap's drivel.

In a few minutes Jake had 6,500 pounds of fuel and gave the purple-shirted fuel crew the cut sign, a slice of the hand across his throat. Mask on, canopy closed, parking brake off, engage nose-wheel steering and goose the throttles a smidgen to follow the director's signals. Now into the queue waiting for the cat . . .

All too soon it was over. Jake had the ten day traps the law required and was once more day qualified as a carrier pilot. He shut the plane down on the porch near Elevator Four and climbed down to the deck still wearing his helmet. After a few words with the plane captain, he descended a ladder to the catwalk, then went down into the first passageway leading into the 0-3 level, the deck under the flight deck.

Flap Le Beau was behind him.

'You did okay out there this morning, Ace,' Flap commented.

'You didn't.' Jake stopped and faced the bombardier-navigator.

'Say again?'

'I got an eighty-year-old grandmother who could have done a better job in the right seat than you did today.'

'Kiss my chocolate ass, Ace. I didn't ask for your opinion.'

'You're going to get it. You flew with me. I expect a BN to help me fly the plane, to act as a safety observer at all times, to read the checklists.'

'I just wanted to see if you could—'

'I *can!* While you were sitting there with your thumb up your butt and boring me to tears with the story of your miserable life, you could have been checking out the computer and radar for the debrief. You never even brought the radar out of standby! Don't *ever* pull that stunt again.'

Flap put his face just inches from Grafton's. 'I ain't taking any shit from the Navy, swabbie. We'd better get that straightened out here and now.'

'Le Beau, I don't know if you're senior to me or I'm senior to you and I really don't give a rat's ass which way it is. But in that cockpit I'm the aircraft commander. You're going to do a solid, professional job – there ain't no two ways about it. If you *don't*, your career in the grunts is gonna go down the crapper real damn quick. You won't be able to catch it with a swan dive.'

Flap opened his mouth to reply, but Jake Grafton snarled, 'Don't push it.' With that he turned and stalked away, leaving Flap Le Beau staring at his back.

When Jake was out of sight Flap grinned He nodded several times and rubbed his hand through his hair, fluffing his Afro.

'Flap, my man, this one's gonna do,' he said. 'He's gonna do *fine*.' And he laughed softly to himself.

Jake was seated in the back of the ready room filling out the maintenance forms on the airplane when the air wing landing signal officer, the LSO, and the A-6 squadron LSO came in. The A-6 guy Jake knew. He was an East Coast Navy pilot who had been shanghaied like Jake to provide the Marines with 'experience.' His name was McCoy and by some miracle, he was Jake's new roommate. If he had a first name Jake didn't learn it last night, when the LSO came in drunk, proclaimed himself to be the Real McCoy, and collapsed into his bunk facedown.

'Grafton,' the senior air wing LSO said, consulting his notes, 'you did okay.' His name was Hugh Skidmore. 'Touch-and-go was an OK, then nine OKs and one fair. All three wires. You're gonna wear out that third wire, fella.'

Jake was astonished. OKs were perfect passes, and he thought he had five or six good ones, but nine? To cover his astonishment and pleasure, he said gruffly, 'A *fair*? You gave me a *fair*? Which pass was that?'

Skidmore examined his book again, then snapped it shut. 'Seventh one. While you were turning through the ninety the captain put the helm over chasing the wind and you went low. You were a little lined up left, too.' He shrugged, then grinned. 'Try a bit harder next time, huh?'

Skidmore went off to debrief the major but McCoy lingered. 'Geez, Real, you guys sure are tough graders.'

'Better get your act together, Roomie.'

'What did you do to rate a tour with the Marines? Piss in a punch bowl?'

'Something like that,' the Real McCoy said distractedly, then wandered off.

After lunch Jake went to his stateroom to unpack. He had gotten the bulk of his gear on hangers or folded when McCoy came in, tossed his Mickey Mouse ears on his desk, and collapsed onto his bunk.

'I threw a civilian through a plate glass window,' Jake told the LSO. 'Just what did *you* do?'

McCoy sighed and opened his eyes. He focused on Grafton. 'I suppose you'll tell this all over the boat.'

'Try me.'

'Well, I made too much money. I got to talking about it with the guys. Then I had the Admin guys draft up a letter of resignation. Before I could get it submitted the skipper called me in. He said a rich bastard like me could just count his money out on the big gray boat.'

'Too much money? I never heard of such a thing. Did you loot the coffee mess?'

'Naw. Nothing like that.' McCoy sat up. He rubbed his face. 'Naw. I just got to playing the market.'

'What market?'

'*The* market.' When he saw the expression on Jake's face, he exclaimed, 'Jesus H Christ! The *stock* market.'

'I never knew anybody who owned stock.'

'Oh, for the love of . . .' McCoy stretched out and sighed.

'Well, how much money did you make, anyway?'

'You're going to tell every greasy asshole on this ship, Grafton. It's written all over your simple face.'

'No, I won't. Honest. How much?'

McCoy regarded his new roommate dolefully. Finally he said, 'Well, I managed to save about sixteen thousand in the last five years, and I've parlayed that into a hundred twenty-two thousand three hundred and thirty-nine dollars. As of the close of business in New York yesterday, anyway. No way of knowing what the market did today, of course.'

'Of course,' Jake agreed, suitably impressed. He whistled as he thought about $122,000, then said, 'Say, I got a couple grand saved up. Maybe you could help me invest it.'

'*That's* what got me shipped out here with these jarheads! All the guys in the ready room wanted investment advice. Everybody was reading the *Wall Street Journal* and talking about interest rates and P/E ratios and how many cars Chrysler was gonna sell. The skipper blew a gasket.'

McCoy shook his head sadly. 'Ah well, it's all water under the keel. Can't do nothing about it now, I guess.' He looked again at Jake. 'Tell me about this guy you threw through the window.'

When they had exhausted that subject, Jake wanted to know about the officers in the squadron.

'Typical Marines' was the Real's verdict, spoken with an air of resigned authority since he had been with this crowd for three whole weeks. 'Seems like three months. This is going to be the longest tour of my life.'

'So how many are combat vets?'

'Everyone in the squadron, except for the three or four nuggets, did at least one tour in 'Nam. Maybe half of them did two or more. And six or eight of them did tours as platoon leaders in Vietnam before they went to flight school. Your BN, Le Beau? He was in Marine Recon.'

Grafton was stunned. Le Beau? The San Diego cocksman? 'You're pulling my leg.'

'I shit you not. Recon. Running around behind enemy lines eating snake meat, doing ambushes and assassinations. Yeah. That's Le Beau, all right. He's a legend in the Corps. Got more chest cabbage than Audie Murphy. He ain't playing with a full deck.'

Jake Grafton's face grew dark as he recalled Flap's rambling cockpit monologue. And that aura of bumbling incompetence that he exuded all morning!

Seeing the look, McCoy continued, 'God only knows why the Marines made him a BN. HE went back to Vietnam in A-6s. Punched out twice, the first time on final to DaNang. Walked through the main gate carrying his parachute and seat pan. The second time, though, was something else. His pilot got his head blown off and Le Beau ejected somewhere near the Laotian border. Maybe in Laos or Cambodia – I don't know. Anyway, nobody heard anything. Just nothing, although they looked and looked hard. Then seventeen days or so later a patrol stumbled onto him out in the jungle in the middle of nowhere. He was running around buck naked, covered with mud and leaves, carrying nothing but a knife. Was busy ambushing the gomers and gutting them. They brought him back with a whole collection of gomer weapons that he had stashed.'

From the look on Grafton's face, McCoy could see that he was not a happy man.

'That ain't the amazing part, Jake,' the Real McCoy continued. 'The amazing part is that Le Beau didn't *want* to get rescued. Two guys have told me this, so I'm assuming that there's something to it. He didn't want to come back because he was having too much *fun*. The grunts on that patrol almost had to tie him up.'

'Why me, Lord?'

'His last pilot didn't cut the mustard,' McCoy continued, 'not to Le Beau's way of thinking. Was having his troubles getting aboard. Oh, he wasn't dangerous, but he was rough, couldn't seem to get a feel for the plane in the groove at night. He might have come around, then again he might not have. He didn't get the chance. Le Beau went to the skipper and the skipper went to CAG and before you could whisper "Semper Fi" the guy was transferred.'

'*Le Beau* did that?'

'Whatever it takes to make it in the Corps, that dickhead has it. He just got selected for promotion to major. Everyone treats him with deference and respect. Makes my stomach turn. Wait till you see these tough old gunnies – they talk to him like they were disciples talking to Jesus. If he lives he's going to be the commandant someday, mark my words.'

'Strangers in a strange land,' Jake murmured, referring to himself and McCoy.

'Something like that,' the Real agreed. He pulled off his steel-toed flight boots and tossed them carelessly on the floor. 'This tour is going to be an adventure,' he added sourly.

'Uh-huh.'

'We've got an all-officers meeting in the ready room in about an hour. I'm going to get fourteen winks. Wake me up, huh?'

'Okay.'

McCoy turned over in his bunk and was soon breathing deeply.

Jake snapped off the overhead light, leaving only his desk lamp lit, the little ten-watt glow worm. He tilted his chair back against McCoy's steel foot locker and put his feet up on his desk.

Thinking about Le Beau, he snorted once, but his thoughts soon drifted on to Callie. The gentle motion of the ship had a tranquilizing effect. After a few moments his head tilted forward and sleep overcame him.

*

The skipper of the squadron was Lieutenant Colonel Richard Haldane. He was a short, barrel-chested, ramrod-straight man with close-cropped black hair that showed flecks of gray. In this closed community of military professionals his bearing and his demeanor marked him as an officer entitled to respect. He took Jake aside after the all-officers meeting – boring administrative details in a crowded, stuffy room filled with strangers – and asked him to sit in the chair beside him.

Haldane had Jake's service record on his lap. 'We didn't get much of a chance to talk last night, Mr Grafton, but welcome aboard. We're glad to have someone with your carrier experience.'

'Thank you, sir.'

'We're going to assign you to the Operations Department. I think your experience will be the most help to us there.'

'Yessir.'

'During this transit to Hawaii, I want you to put together a series of lectures from CV NATOPS.' CV NATOPS was the bible on carrier operations. The acronym stood for fixed-wing carrier naval air training and operation procedures. 'We've been through it several times while working up for this deployment,' Colonel Haldane continued, 'but I'd like for you to lead us through the book again in detail. I want you to share with us everything you know about A-6 carrier operations. Do you think you can do that?'

'Yes, sir.'

Richard Haldane nodded his head a millimeter. Even sitting down he exuded a command presence. Jake sat a little straighter in his chair.

'I see from your record that you have plenty of combat experience, but it's experience of the same type that most of the officers in this room have had – bombing targets ashore.'

'Single-plane day and night raids, some section stuff, and Alpha strikes, sir, plus a whole hell of a lot of tanker flights.'

'Unfortunately our combat experience won't do us much good if we go to war with the Soviets, who are our most likely opponent.'

This remark caught Jake by surprise. He tried to keep his face deadpan as Haldane continued: 'Our part in a war with the Russians will probably involve a fleet action, our ships against their ships. Mr Grafton, how would you attack a Soviet guided-missile frigate?'

Jake opened his mouth, then closed it again. He scratched his head. 'I don't know, sir,' he said at last. The truth was, he had never once even thought about it. The Vietnam War was in full swing when he was going through flight training, when he transitioned into A-6s, and during his three years in a fleet squadron. The targets were all onshore.

'Any ideas?'

Jake bit his lip. *He* was the naval officer and he was being asked a question about naval air warfare that in truth he should know something about. But he didn't. He decided to admit it. 'Sir, I think the answer to that question would depend on a careful analysis of a Soviet frigate's missile and flak envelope, and to be frank, I have never done that or seen the results of anybody else's look. I suspect the Air Intelligence guys have that stuff under lock and key.'

'So what weapons does a Soviet frigate carry?'

Jake squirmed. 'Colonel, I don't know.'

Haldane nodded once, slowly, and looked away. 'I would like for you to study this matter, Mr Grafton. When you think you have an answer to the question, come see me.'

'Aye aye, sir.'

'That's all. Good luck tonight.'

'Thank you, sir.' Jake rose and walked away, mortified. Well, hell, the stuff he had spent his career attacking was all mud-based. Of course he *should* know about ships, *but* . . .

What Haldane must think – a *naval* officer who doesn't know diddly-squat about *naval* warfare!

Congratulations, Jake. You just got your tour with the Marines off to a great start.

5

There was still a little splotch of light in the western sky and a clearly discernible horizon when Jake Grafton taxied toward the catapult that evening. This first shot would be a 'pinky,' without severe sweat. He needed six landings to attain his night qualification, which meant after this twilight shot there would be five more . . . in stygian darkness. A pinky first one was just dandy with him.

He carefully scanned the evening sky. The cloud cover was almost total, with the only holes toward the west, and low, maybe seven or eight thousand feet. Wind still out of the northwest, but stiffer than this morning. That was good. Tonight the ship could steam slower into the wind and yet still have the optimum thirty knots of wind over the deck. Since every mile upwind took her farther from the coast and the airfields ashore, the fewer of those miles the better.

Car quals are always goat-ropes, Jake thought, something going wrong sooner or later, so there is at least a fifty-fifty chance I'll have to divert ashore once tonight. And if my luck is in, maybe spend the night in the Alameda BOQ, call Callie . . .

No matter how long you've been ashore, after a half hour back aboard one of these gray tubs you're tired, hungry and horny. No way to cure the horniness, but a night ashore in a real bed would work wonders on the other syndromes, with real food and a long, hot shower and Callie's voice on the phone—

His reverie was interrupted by Flap Le Beau's voice on the intercom system, the ICS. 'Don't do nothin' cute tonight, huh? My internal table ain't so stable when we're out here flyin' through black goo.'

'You and Muhammad Ali. How about laying off the monologue. When I want comedy I watch TV.'

'Golden silence to practice your pilot gig. You got it. Just fly like an angel flitting toward paradise.'

'You do the radio frequency changes and I'll do the transmissions, okay?'

'Fine.'

'Takeoff checklist,' Jake said, and Flap began reading off the items. Jake checked each item and gave the appropriate response.

And soon they were taxiing toward the cat. Automatically Jake leaned forward and tugged hard on the VDI, the televisionlike display in the center of the instrument panel that functioned as the primary attitude reference. It was tight, just as it should be.

'Flashlight on the backup gyro, please,' Jake said to Flap, who already had it in his hand. If both generators dropped off the line, the little gyro would continue to provide good attitude information for about thirty seconds, long enough for Jake to deploy the ram-air turbine, called the RAT, an emergency wind-driven generator.

Of course a double generator failure was rare, and if it happened on a launch with a discernible horizon there wouldn't be a problem. Yet on a coal black night . . . and all nights at sea were coal black. Jake Grafton well knew that emergencies were quirky – they only happened at the worst possible time, the time when you least expected one and could least afford it. Then you would have to entertain two or three.

The A-7 on the cat in front of Jake was having a problem with the nose-tow apparatus. A small conference was convening around the nose wheel, but nothing obvious seemed to be happening.

Jake looked again at the sky. Darkening fast.

Automatically he reviewed what he would do if he got a cold cat shot – if the catapult failed to give him sufficient end speed to fly. From there he moved into engine failure. He fingered the emergency jettison button, caressed the throttles and felt behind him for the RAT handle. Every motion would have to be quick and sure – no fumbling, no trying to remember exactly what he had to do – he must just do it instinctively and correctly.

They were still screwing with the A-7. *Come on, guys!*

He felt frustrated, entitled to a pinky. These guys had better get with the program or this shot will be like being blasted blindfolded into a coal bin at midnight.

'Gettin' pretty dark,' Flap commented, to Jake's disgust. The pilot squirmed in his seat as he eyed the meeting of the board under the Corsair's nose.

'Why did you stay in the Navy anyway?'

What a cracker this Le Beau is! 'I eat this shit with a spoon,' Grafton replied testily.

'Yeah, I can see you're loving this. Me, I'm too stupid to make it on the outside. It's the Marines or starve. But you seem smarter than me, so I wondered.'

'Put a cork in it, will ya?'

Jake smacked the instrument panel with his fist and addressed the dozen men milling around the Corsair: 'For Christ's sake, let's shoot it or get it off the cat. We gonna dick around till the dawn's early light?'

And here came Bosun Muldowski, striding down the deck, gesturing angrily. 'Off the cat. Get it off.'

And it happened. The Corsair came off the cat and Jake eased the Intruder on. Into the hold-back, the thump as the shuttle was moved forward hydraulically, off the brakes and full power, cat grip up, cycle the controls, check the flaps and slats, now the engine gauges . . .

Time to go.

Jake flipped on the external lights, the nighttime equivalent of the salute to the cat officer. He placed his head back into the rest, just in time to catch Flap giving Muldowski the bird.

Wham!

As the G's slammed them back into their seats Jake roared into the ICS: '*Yeeeeoooow*,' and then they were airborne. A pinky! *All right!* Not very pink, but pink enough.

Engines pulling, all warning lights out, eight degrees nose up – his eyes took it all in automatically as he reached for the gear handle and slapped it up.

With the gear coming, the bird accelerating nicely, the pilot keyed the radio transmitter: 'War Ace Five One One airborne.'

'Roger, Five One One,' the departure controller said from his seat in front of a large radar screen in Air Ops, deep in the bowels of the ship. 'Climb straight ahead to six thousand, then hold on the One Three Five radial at sixteen miles. Your push at One Seven after the hour.'

'Five Eleven, straight up to Six, then hold on the One Three Five at Sixteen.' Jake moved his left thumb from the radio transmit button to the ICS key and opened his mouth. He wanted to say something snotty to Flap about the gesture to the bosun, but the bombardier beat him to the switch.

'Hey, I damn near ejected on the cat stroke. What in hell was that squall you gave back there?'

'I—'

'You damn fool! I came within a gnat's eyelash of punching out. I coulda *drowned!* If I got run over by the boat you wouldn't be so damn happy. Yelling on the ICS like a wildcat with a hot poker up your ass – that's the stupidest thing I ever . . .'

Jake Grafton waited until the flaps and slats were safely in, then he reached over and jerked the plug on Flap's mask.

Silence. Blessed silence.

Damn you, Tiny Dick Donovan. Damn you all to hell.

The night quickly enveloped them. The world ended at the canopy glass. Oh, the wing-tip lights gave a faint illumination, but Jake would have had to turn his head to see them on the tips of the swept wings, and he wasn't doing much head turning just now. Now he was flying instruments, making the TACAN needle go where it was supposed to, holding the rate-of-climb needle motionless, making the compass behave, keeping his wings level. All this required intense concentration. After five minutes of it he decided enough was enough and reached for the autopilot switch. It refused to engage.

Maybe the circuit breaker's popped. He felt the panel between him and the bombardier. Nope. All breakers in.

He punched the altitude-hold button three more times and swore softly to himself.

Okay, so I hand fly this monument to Marine maintenance, this miraculous Marine Corps flying pig.

He hit the holding fix, sixteen miles on the One Three Five radial, and did a teardrop entry. Established inbound he pulled the throttles back until he was showing only two thousand pounds of fuel flow per hour on each engine. This fuel flow would soon give him 220 knots indicated, he knew from experience, the plane's maximum conserve airspeed. Would as soon as the speed bled off.

Hit the fix, start the clock, turn left. Go around and around with the tailhook up, because this first one is a touch-and-go, a practice bolter.

The second time he approached the fix the symbology on the VDI came alive and gave him heading commands from the plane's onboard computer. Flap. He glanced over. The BN had his head against the black hood that shielded the radar scope and was twiddling knobs. Sure enough, the mileage readout corresponded with the TACAN DME, or distance measuring equipment.

'You plugged in?' Jake asked.

'Yep.'

'Thanks for the help.'

'No sweat.'

'Autopilot's packed it in.'

'I noticed.'

Just like an old married couple, here in the intimacy of a night cockpit. There are worse places, Jake thought, than this world of dials and gauges and glowing little red lights. Worse places . . .

At exactly seventeen minutes after the hour he hit the fix for the third time, popped the speed brakes and lowered the nose. This was the pushover. The A-7 that had been holding at five thousand feet was inbound in front of them a minute earlier.

Jake keyed the mike: 'Five One One is inbound at One Seven, state Seven Point Six.'

'Roger, War Ace Five One One. Continue.'

At five thousand feet Jake shallowed his descent as Flap called on the radio: 'Five One One, Platform.'

'Roger, Five One One. Switch button One Seven.'

Flap changed the radio frequency. Jake watched the TACAN needle carefully and made heading corrections as necessary to stay on the final bearing inbound. Soon he was level at 1,200 feet, inbound. At ten miles he dropped the gear and flaps. This slowed the plane still more. He checked the gear and flap indications and soon was stabilized at 120 knots. Flap read the landing checklist and Jake rogered each item.

Seventy-five hundred pounds of fuel. He toggled the main dump and let a thousand pounds bleed overboard into the atmosphere. If this worked out, he should cross the ramp with exactly six thousand pounds remaining, the maximum fuel load for an arrested landing.

Jake adjusted the rheostat on the angle-of-attack indexer, a small arrangement of lights on the left canopy bow in front of him. These lights indicated his airspeed, now a smidgen fast. One hundred eighteen knots was the speed he wanted, so he eased off a touch of throttle, then eased it back on. The indexer came to an on-speed indication. He checked his airspeed indicator. Exactly 118. Okay.

There – way out there – the ship! It appeared in the dark universe as a small collection of white and red lights, not yet distinguishable as to shape. Oh, *now* he could see the outline of the landing area, and the red drop lights down the stern that gave him his lineup cues. The ball on the left side of the landing area that would give him his glide slope was not yet visible.

The final approach controller was talking: 'Five One One, approaching the glide slope, call your needles.'

The needles the controller was referring to were crosshairs in a cockpit instrument that was driven by a computer aboard the ship. The computer contrasted the radar-derived position of the aircraft with the known location of the glide slope and centerline. It then sent a radio signal to a box in the aircraft, which positioned the needles to depict the glide slope and centerline. The system was called ACLS, automatic carrier landing system, and someday it would indeed be automatic. Right now it was just the needles. Jake had to fly the plane.

'Down and right.'

'Disregard. You're low and slightly left . . . Five One One, slightly below glide slope, lined up slightly left. Come a little right for lineup, on glide path . . . on glide path . . .'

At the on-glide path call Jake squeezed out the speed brakes and concentrated intently on his instruments. He had to set and hold a six-hundred-foot rate of descent, hold heading, hold airspeed, keep the wings level and this plane coming down just so delicately so.

'I've got a ball,' Flap told him at two miles.

The controller: 'Left of course. Come right.'

The pilot made the correction, then glanced ahead. Yes, he could tell from the drop lights he was left. When he was properly lined up again he took out most of the correction. Still his nose was pointed slightly right of the landing area. This correction was necessary since the wind was not precisely down the angled deck, which was pointed ten degrees left of the ship's keel. Except for an occasional glance ahead, he stayed on the gauges.

'Five One One, three-quarter mile, call the ball.'

Now Jake glanced out the windshield. There's the meatball, centered between the green datum lights. Lineup looks good too. Jake keyed the mike and said, 'Five One One, Intruder ball, Six Point Oh.'

'Roger, ball. Looking good.' That was the LSO on the fantail, Skidmore.

The ball moved in relation to the green reference or datum lights that were arranged in a horizontal line. When the yellow 'meatball' in the center moved up, you were above glide path. When it appeared below the reference line, you were low. If you were too low, the ball turned red, blood red, a stark prophecy of your impending doom if you didn't immediately climb higher on the glide slope. The back end of the ship, the ramp, lurked in red ball country, waiting to smash a plane to bits.

Yet as critical as proper glide slope control was, lineup was even more so. The landing area was 115 feet wide, the wing span of the A-6, 52. The edges of the landing area were defined by foul lines, and aircraft were parked with their noses abutting the foul lines on *both* sides of the deck. Landing aircraft were literally sinking into a canyon between parked airplanes.

And Jake had to monitor his airspeed carefully. The angle-of-attack indexer helped enormously here, arranged as it was where he could see it as he flew the lineup and glide slope cues. Any deviation from an on-speed indication required his immediate attention because it would quickly affect his descent rate, thereby screwing up his control of the ball. Running out of airspeed at the ramp was a sin that had killed many a naval aviator.

Meatball, lineup, angle-of-attack – as he closed the ship Jake's eyes were in constant motion checking these three items. Nearing the ship he dropped the angle-of-attack from his scan and concentrated on keeping properly lined up, with a centered ball. As he crossed the ramp he zeroed in on the meatball, flying it to touchdown.

The wheels hit and the nose slammed down. Jake Grafton thumbed the speed brakes in as he smoothly and quickly shoved the throttles forward to the stops. The LSO was on the radio shouting, 'Bolter, bolter, bolter,' just in case he forgot to advance the throttles or to positively rotate to a flying attitude as he shot off the edge of the angled deck.

Jake didn't forget. The engines were at full song as the Intruder left the deck behind and leaped back into the blackness of the night. Jake eased the stick back until he had ten degrees nose up and checked for a positive rate of climb. Going up. Gear up. Accelerating through 185 knots, flaps and slats up.

Now to get those six traps.

The radar controller leveled him at 1,200 feet and turned him to the downwind heading, the reciprocal of the ship's course. He was stable at 220 knots. Jake reached for the hook handle and pulled it. Hook down.

The controller turned him so that he had an eight-mile groove, which was nice. As soon as the wings were level he dropped the gear and flaps. Once again he concentrated intently on airspeed and altitude control, nailing the final bearing on the TACAN, retrimming until the plane flew itself with only the tiniest of inputs to the stick to counter the natural swirls and currents of the air. This was precision flying, where any sloppiness could prove instantly fatal.

'Five One One, approaching glide slope . . . Five One One, up and on glide slope . . . three-quarters of a mile, call the ball.'

'Five One One, Intruder ball, Five Point Six.'

Deep in the heart of the ship in Air Ops, a sailor wearing headphones wrote '5.6' in yellow grease pencil on the Plexiglas board in front of him and the time beside the notation that said 'Grafton, 511.' He wrote backward, so the letters and numbers read properly to the air officer, the air wing commander, and the other observers who were sitting silently on the other side of the board watching the television monitors and occasionally glancing at the board.

Just now the picture on the monitors was from a camera buried on the landing centerline of the flight deck, which pointed aft up the glide slope. As they watched the officers saw the lights of Jake's A-6 appear on the center of the screen, in the center of the crosshairs that indicated the proper glide slope and lineup. As the plane closed the ship the lights assumed more definition.

Up in the top of the carrier's island superstructure was Pri-Fly, the domain of the air boss. His little empire was pretty quiet just now since all the air traffic was being controlled via radar and radio from Air Ops, but two enlisted men behind the boss's chair were busy. One held a pair of binoculars focused up the glide slope. He saw the approaching Intruder, identified it, and chanted, 'Set Three Six Zero, A-6.' Regardless of a plane's fuel state, the arresting gear was always set at the maximum trap weight, in the case of the A-6, 36,000 pounds.

To his left, the other sailor made a note in his log and repeated into a sound-powered phone that hung from his chest, 'Set Three Six Zero, A-6.'

The air boss, a senior commander, sat in a raised easy chair surrounded by large bullet-proof glass windows. He could hear the radio transmissions and the litany of the sailors behind him, and noted subconsciously that they agreed with what his eyes, and the approach controller, were telling him, that there was an A-6 on the ball, an A-6 with a maximum trap weight of 36,000 pounds.

Under the after end of the flight deck in the arresting gear engine rooms, all four of them, sat sailors on the Pri-Fly sound-powered circuit. Each individually spun a wheel to mechanically set the metering orifice of his arresting gear engine to 36,000 pounds, then they sang out in turn, 'One set Three Six Zero A-6,' 'Two set Three Six Zero A-6,' and so on.

When the fourth and last engine operator had reported his engine set, the talker in Pri-Fly sang out, 'All engines set, Three Six Zero A-6,' and the air boss rogered.

On the fantail of the ship directly aft of the island, on the starboard side of the landing area in a catwalk on the edge of the deck, stood the sailor who retracted the arresting gear engines once they had been engaged. He too was on the Pri-Fly sound-powered circuit, and when the fourth engine reported set, he shouted to the arresting gear officer who stood above him on the deck, right on the starboard foul line, 'All engines set, Three Six Zero A-6.'

The gear officer looked up the glide slope. Yep, it was an A-6. He glanced forward up the deck. The landing area was clear. No aircraft protruded over the foul lines, there were no people in the landing area, so he squeezed a trigger switch on the pistol grip he held in his right hand.

This switch operated a stop-light affair arranged twenty feet or so aft of the landing signal officer's platform on the port side of the landing area. The LSO waving tonight, Hugh Skidmore, saw the red light go out and a green light appear.

'Clear deck,' he called, and the other LSOs on the platform echoed the call.

'Clear deck!'

This entire evolution had taken about fifteen seconds. The ship was ready to recover the inbound A-6. Now if Jake Grafton could just fly his plane into that little sliver of sky that would give him a three wire . . .

He was trying. He was working the stick and throttles, playing them delicately, when he slammed into the burble of air disturbed by the ship's island. The plane jolted and he jammed on some power, then as quickly pulled it off as he cut through the turbulence into the calm air over the ramp. On he came, aiming for that eighteen-inches-thick window where the third wire waited, coming in at 118 knots in an eighteen-ton plane, the hook dangling down behind the main gear, coming in . . .

Hugh Skidmore strode about five feet into the landing area, inboard of the LSO's platform. Against his ear he held a telephonelike radio headset connected with the ship's radios by a long cord. Forward of the LSO's platform was a television monitor, the PLAT – pilot landing assistance television – which he checked occasionally to ensure the plane in the groove was properly lined up. He could hear the approach controller and he could hear and talk to Jake Grafton. Yet there was nothing to say. The A-6 was coming in like it was riding rails.

Then it was there, crossing the ramp.

Jake still had a steady centered yellow ball as the wheels smashed home. The ball shot off the top of the lens as he slammed the throttles to the stops and the hook caught, seemingly all at the same time. The deceleration threw the pilot and bombardier forward into their harnesses.

The A-6 Intruder was jerked to a halt in a mere two hundred and sixty feet.

It hung quivering on the end of the arresting gear wire, then Jake got the engines back to idle and the rebound of the wire pulled the plane backward.

The gear runner was already twenty feet out into the landing area signaling the pilot with his wands: hook up. When he saw the aircraft's tailhook being retracted, the runner waved one of his wands in a huge circle, the signal to the arresting gear operator in the fantail catwalk to retract the engine.

Obediently the operator selected the lever for number-three engine and pulled it down. Since the lever was connected by a wire over three hundred feet long to a hydraulic actuating valve on the engine, this pull took some muscle. When he had the yard-long lever well away from the bulkhead, the sailor leaped on it with his feet and used the entire weight of his body to force the lever down to a ninety-degree angle.

By now the A-6 that had just landed was folding its wings as it taxied out of the landing area. By the time the tail crossed the foul line, the third engine operator said 'battery,' and the retract man got off the lever and let it come back to its rest position. As he did he heard the Pri-Fly talker sing out, 'Set Two Seven Zero A-7.'

On the LSO platform Hugh Skidmore leaned over to his writer, tonight the Real McCoy. 'Give him an OK three. Little lined up left at the start.'

McCoy scribbled the notation in his pocket logbook like this: 511 OK3 (LLATS).

Then both men turned their full attention to the A-7 in the groove as they waited for the clear-deck light to illuminate.

The second cat shot, into a sky as black as the ace of spades, went well. Jake leveled at 1,200 feet and turned downwind, as directed by the controller. He held 250 knots until the controller told him to dirty up, which he did at the same time he told Jake to turn base. So Grafton was turning as he changed configuration – slowing, retrimming and trying to maintain a precise altitude, all at the same time. He lost a hundred feet, a fact that Flap instantly commented upon.

Jake said nothing, merely kept flying his plane. *This is the big leagues. Gotta do it all here and do it well. Flap has a right to comment.*

A short, tight pattern left him still searching for a good steady start when he hit the glide slope. The secret to a good pass is a good start, and Jake didn't have it. He wasn't carrying enough power and that caused a settle. By the time he was back up to a centered ball he was fast, which he was working off when he hit the burble. He added power. Not quite enough. The ball was a tad low when the wheels hit the deck.

'A fair two-wire,' he told Flap as they rolled out.

Aviation Boatswain's Mate (Equipment) Third Class Johnny Arbogast enjoyed his work. He operated the number-three arresting gear engine, the one that got the most traps and therefore required the most maintenance. Still, Johnny Arbogast loved that engine.

During a slow, rainy day in port this past spring, the gear chief had worked out how much energy an engine absorbed while trapping an F-4 Phantom. The figure was nine million foot-pounds, as Johnny recalled. Nine million of anything is a lot, but *man!* Those planes make this engine sing.

Any way you cut it, an arresting gear engine was one hell of a fine piece of machinery. And Johnny Arbogast was the guy who ran *Columbia*'s number three, which was pretty darn good, he thought, for a plumber's kid from Cotulla, Texas, who had had to struggle for everything he ever got.

The engine consisted of a giant hydraulic piston inside a steel cylinder about thirty inches in diameter that was arranged parallel with the ship's beam. Almost fifty feet in length, the cylinder containing the piston sat inside a large steel frame. Around the piston were reeved two twelve-hundred-foot strands of arresting gear cable, one-and-five-eighths-inch-thick wire rope made of woven steel threads. These two cables ran repeatedly around sheaves at the head and foot of the main piston and squeezed it as the aircraft pulled out the flight deck pennant above Johnny's head. It was the metering of the fluid squeezed by the piston from the cylinder – pure ethylene glycol, or antifreeze – through an adjustable orifice that controlled the rate at which the aircraft was arrested. Johnny set the size of this orifice for each arrestment as ordered by the talker in Pri-Fly.

To maintain proper tension on the engine cable as the aircraft on the flight deck was pulling it out, two anchor dampeners that held the bitter ends of each cable stroked simultaneously. These fifty-foot-long pistons inside cylinders about twelve inches in diameter pulled slack cable off the back, or idle, side of the engine, thereby keeping the wire taut throughout the system.

When he first reported aboard *Columbia*, the arresting gear chief had impressed Johnny with a story about an anchor dampener that sheared its restraining nut during an arrestment. The suddenly free dampener, as big as a telephone pole, was forcibly whipped through the aluminum bulkhead of the engine room into the 0-3-level passageway, where it cut a sailor on his way to chow sloppily in half. The running cable whipped the dampener like a scythe. It sliced through a dozen officers' stateroom bulkheads as if they were so much tissue paper. When the dampener had accomplished a 180-degree turn, it reentered the engine room and skewered the engine like a mighty spear, exploding sheaves and showering the room, and the operator, with sharp, molten-hot metal fragments. All this took place in about a second and a half. Fortunately the plane on the flight deck was successfully arrested before the now-unanchored cable could run completely off the engine, but the engine room was a shambles and the operator went to the hospital with critical injuries.

As a result of this little story, Johnny Arbogast developed a habit of running his eyes over the anchor dampeners after each arrestment. Tonight, after setting the engine to receive an A-6, he saw something that he had never before seen. As the anchor dampeners stroked back into battery after the last engagement, the steel cable on one of them had kinked about six inches out from the connecting socket that held the bitter end of the cable to the dampener piston.

A kink, like a kink in a garden hose.

Johnny Arbogast stared, not quite sure his eyes could be believed.

Yep, a kink.

If this engine takes a hit, that cable could *break*, right there at the kink!

Johnny fumbled with the mouthpiece of the sound-powered phone unit hanging on his chest. He pushed the talk button and blurted, 'Three's foul. Three's not ready.'

'*What?*' This from the deck-edge operator, who had already told the arresting gear officer that all the engines were set. And he had delivered this message over a half minute ago, maybe even a minute.

'*Three's not ready,*' Johnny Arbogast howled into his mouthpiece. '*Foul deck!*'

And then Johnny did what any sensible man would have done: he tore off the sound-powered headset and ran for his life.

Up on the fantail catwalk the deck-edge operator shouted at the arresting gear officer, 'Three's not ready.'

The gear officer was still standing on the starboard foul line on the flight deck and he didn't hear what the operator said. He eyed the A-6 in the groove and bent toward the sailor, who was also looking over his shoulder at the approaching plane, now almost at the ramp.

'Foul deck,' the sailor roared above the swelling whine of the engines of the approaching plane.

The gear officer's reaction was automatic. He released the trigger on the pistol grip he held in his hand and shouted, 'What the hell is wrong?'

Across the landing area on the LSO's platform the green 'ready deck' light went out and the red 'foul deck' light came on.

Hugh Skidmore was looking intently at the A-6 Intruder almost at the ramp when he saw the red light on the edge of his peripheral vision. He was faced with an instant decision. He had no way of knowing why the deck was foul – he only knew that it was. A plane may have rolled into the landing area, a man may have wandered into the unsafe zone . . . any one of a hundred things could have gone wrong and all one hundred were bad.

So Hugh Skidmore squeezed the red button on the pistol grip he held in his hand, triggering a bank of flashing red lights mounted above the meatball. At the same time he roared into his radio-telephone, 'Wave-off, wave-off.'

The flashing wave-off lights and the radio message imprinted themselves on Jake Grafton's brain at the same time. His reaction was automatic. The throttles went full forward as he thumbed in the speed brakes and the control stick came aft.

Unfortunately jet engines do not provide instantaneous power as piston engines do: the revs can build only as fast as the burners can handle the increasing fuel flow, which is metered through a fuel control unit to prevent flooding the engine and flaming it out. The power builds with revs. Tonight the back stick and the gradually increasing engine power flattened the A-6's descent, then stopped it . . . four feet above the deck.

The howling warplane crossed the third wire with its nose well up, boards in, engines winding to full screech, but with its tailhook dangling.

From his vantage point near the fantail the arresting gear officer watched in horror as the tailhook kissed the top of the third wire, then snagged the fourth. The plane continued forward for a heartbeat, then seemed to stop in midair.

It was a lopsided contest. An 18-ton airplane was trying to pull a 95,000-ton ship. The ship won. The airplane fell straight down.

As he took the wave-off, Jake Grafton instinctively knew that it had come too late. The ship was *right there*, filling the windscreen. He kept the angle-of-attack on the optimum indication – a centered doughnut – by feeding in back stick while he tried to bend the throttles over the stops.

Somehow he found the ICS switch with his left thumb and shouted to Flap, 'Hook up!' but the aircraft was already decelerating. The angle-of-attack indexer showed slow and his eye flicked to the AOA gauge on the panel, just in time to see the needle sweep counterclockwise to the peg as the G threw him forward into his harness straps.

Then they fell the four feet to the deck.

The impact snapped his head forward viciously and slammed him downward into the seat, stunning him.

He got his head up and tried to focus his eyes as cold fear enveloped him. Are we stopped? Or going off the angled deck? Dazed, scared clear through and unable to see his instruments, he instinctively placed the stick in the eight-degree-nose-up position and kept the engines at full power.

The air boss exploded over the radio: 'Jesus Christ, Paddles, why'd you wave him off in close?'

On the LSO platform Hugh Skidmore was having trouble finding the transmit button on his radio. He fumbled for it as he stared forward at the A-6 straining futilely against the fourth wire with its engines still at full power. Miraculously the airplane seemed to be all in one piece. Here a hundred yards behind those two jet exhausts without the protection of a sound-suppression helmet the noise was awesome, a thunder that numbed the ears and vibrated the soul.

Unwilling to wait for Skidmore's response, the air boss now roared over the radio at Jake Grafton : 'We got you, son. Kill those engines! You aren't going anywhere now.'

Long seconds ticked by before the pilot complied. When he did, finally, the air boss remembered Skidmore:

'El Ss Oh, if you ever, *ever*, wave off another airplane in close on this fucking boat I will personally come down there and throw your silly ass into the goddamn wake. Do you read me, you mindless bastard?'

Skidmore found his voice. 'The deck went foul, Boss.'

'We'll cut up the corpse later. Wave off the guy in the groove so we can get this squashed A-6 out of the gear and clean the shit out of the cockpit.'

The plane in the groove was still a half mile out, but Skidmore obediently triggered the wave-off lights. As he did so he heard the engines of the A-6 in the gear die as the pilot secured the fuel flow.

Already the arresting gear officer had his troops on deck stripping the pennant from number-three engine. The rest of the recovery would be accomplished with only three engines on line.

Skidmore turned to the Real McCoy. 'I guess I screwed the pooch on that one.'

McCoy was still looking at the A-6 up forward. The yellow shirts were hooking a tow tractor to the nose wheel. He turned his gaze on Skidmore, who was looking into his face.

He had to say something. 'Looks like the boss is safety-wired to the pissed-off position.'

Skidmore nodded toward the stern. 'I thought he could make it. I didn't think he was *that* close.'

'Well . . .'

'Oh, hell.'

Jake Grafton stood rubbing his neck in Flight Deck Control, the room in the base of the carrier's island superstructure where the aircraft handler directs the movement of every plane on the ship. Flap Le Beau stood beside him. Someone was talking to the handler on the squawk box, apparently someone in Air Ops. The handler listened awhile, then leaned toward Jake and said, 'You need two more traps. The in-flight engagement was your fourth.'

'Yeah.'

'If you're feeling up to it, we'll give you another plane and send you out for your last two. Or you can wait until we get to Hawaii and we'll do the whole night bit again. It's up to you. How do you feel?'

Jake used a sleeve to swab the sweat from his forehead and eyes. 'What about tomorrow night?' he asked.

'The captain won't hold the ship in here against this coast just to qual one pilot. We have to transit to Hawaii.'

Jake nodded. That made sense. He flexed his shoulders and pivoted his head slowly.

The fear was gone. Okay, panic. But it was gone. He was still feeling the adrenaline aftershock, which was normal.

'I'm okay,' he told the handler, who turned to relay the message into the squawk box.

Flap pulled at Jake's sleeve. 'You don't have to do this tonight. There's no war on. It doesn't matter a whit whether you get qualled tonight or a week from now in Hawaii.'

Jake stared. The flippant, kiss-my-ass cool dude he had flown with all day was gone. The man there now was serious and in total control, with sharp, intelligent eyes. This must be the Flap Le Beau that was the legend.

'I can hack it. Are you okay?'

'I am if you are.'

'I am.'

'I gave you a load of shit today just to see if you could handle a little pressure. You can. You don't have anything to prove to anybody.'

Jake shook his head from side to side. 'I have to go now so the next time I'll know I can.'

A trace of a smile crossed Le Beau's face. He nodded, just the tiniest dip of the head, and turned toward the handler.

'What plane do they want us to aviate, Handler-man? Ask the grunts in Ready Four and have them send up the book.'

'Please, *sir!*'

'Of course, *sir*. Did I leave the please out? What's come over me? I must still be all shook up. You know, we came within two inches of being chocolate and vanilla pudding out there. If we'd fell another two inches you'd be cleaning us up with spoons. I'm gonna write a thank-you letter to Jesus. Praise *God,* that was a religious experience, Amen! I feel born again, Amen! The narrowness of our escape and my ecstasy must have made me the eensiest bit careless in my military manners. I apologize. You understand, don't you, sir?'

'Ecstasy! What crap! Go sit over there in that corner with your Amens and keep your mouth shut until your fellow jarheads get the maintenance book up here for your pilot to read. He can read, can't he?'

'Oh yes, sir. He's Navy, not Marine. He's got a good, solid, second-grade education. His mamma told me he did just fine in school until . . .'

Jake Grafton decided he was thirsty and needed to take a leak. He wandered away to attend to both problems.

He was slurping water from a fountain in the passageway outside the hatch to Flight Deck Control when he realized that Lieutenant Colonel Haldane was standing beside him. Haldane was wearing his uniform tonight, not his flight suit. His I-been-there decorations under his gold aviator wings made an impressive splotch of color on his left breast.

'What happened?' he asked Jake.

'They gave me a late wave-off, sir. I was almost at the ramp, or at it. Somebody said something about the deck going foul. Whatever, at the time all I knew was that the red lights were flashing and the LSO was shouting. So I did my thing. I was just too close.'

Haldane was watching his eyes as he spoke. When he finished speaking the colonel gave him another five seconds of intense scrutiny before he asked, 'Did you do everything right?'

Jake Grafton swallowed hard. This just wasn't his day. 'No, sir. I didn't. I knew we had passed the wave-off point, so I was concentrating on the ball and lineup. When the wave-off lights came on, I guess I was sorta stunned there for a tenth of a second. Then I reacted automatically – nose up, boards in, full power. I should have given her the gun and got the boards in, but I should have just held the nose attitude. Should have rode it into a bolter.'

Haldane's head bobbed a millimeter. 'Are you up to two more?' he asked.

'I think so, sir.'

'If you don't want to go I'll back you up. No questions asked.'

'I'd like to go now, sir, if we can get a bird.'

'How many carrier landings do you have?'

'Before today, sir, three hundred twenty-four.'

'How many at night?'

'One hundred twenty-seven, I believe.'

Haldane nodded. 'Whenever I have a close call,' he said, 'the first thing to go afterward is my instrument scan. I get way behind the plane, fixate on just one instrument. Really have to work to keep the eyeballs moving.'

'Yessir,' Jake said, and grinned. He liked the way Haldane used himself as an example. That was class. 'I'll keep it safe, Skipper,' Jake added.

'Fine,' said the colonel, and went into Flight Deck Control to see the handler.

'A thank-you letter to Jesus, huh?'

'That was the best I could do on the spur of the moment. Don't hold it against me.'

'Amen to that.' Jake sighed and tried to relax. They were sitting behind the jet-blast deflector for Cat One, waiting for the A-7 ahead to do his thing. Jake tugged at the VDI reflexively and wriggled to get his butt set in the seat.

He was still feeling the aftereffects of adrenaline shock, but he knew it, so he forced himself to look at everything carefully. Wings locked, flaps and slats out, stabilator shifted, roger the weight board, ease forward into the shuttle, throttles up and off brakes, cat grip up, wipe out the controls, check fuel flow, RPM, EGT . . . Lights on and bam! they were hurling down the catapult into the blackness.

Off the pointy end, nose up, gear up, climbing . . .

It went well until he got onto the ball, then he couldn't get stabilized. Too nervous. Every correction was too big, every countercorrection overdone. The plane wobbled up and down on the glide slope and went from fast to slow to fast again. He was waggling the wings trying to get properly lined up as he went across the ramp and that, coupled with not quite enough power, got him a settle into the two-wire.

The last one was more of the same. At this point Jake realized he was totally exhausted.

'Settle down,' Flap told him in the groove.

'I'm trying. Let's just get this fun over with, okay?' Crossing the ramp he lowered the nose and eased the power a smidgen to ensure he wouldn't bolter. He didn't. One wire.

He had to pry himself from the cockpit. He was so tired he had trouble plodding across the deck.

'Another day, another dollar,' Flap said cheerfully.

'Something like that,' Jake mumbled, but so quietly Flap didn't hear it. No matter.

'It was a late wave-off, and I'm sorry,' Hugh Skidmore told Jake in the ready room. The LSOs were waiting for Jake when he came in. The television monitor mounted high in the corner of the room was running the PLAT tape of the in-flight engagement, over and over and over. Colonel Haldane was there, but he stood silently without saying anything. Jake and the LSOs watched the PLAT tape twice.

'You owe me, Skidmore.'

'Other than that little debacle, your first one – the touch-and-go – was okay, the first trap okay, the second fair, the third okay. The fifth trap was a fair and the last one a no-grade. I almost waved you off. I don't want to see any more of that deck spotting—' After a glance at the skipper Skidmore ran out of words. He contented himself with adding, 'I think you were a little wrung out on the last one.'

Jake nodded. He had sinned there at the end and wasn't too proud to admit it. 'I spotted the deck on the last one. Sorry!' He tried to shrug but didn't have the energy. 'What about the in-flight?'

'Gave you a fair.'

'Fair? Now wait just a minute—' Jake knew the futility of arguing with the umpire, but that pass had cost him too much. 'I had a good pass going until everything went to hell.'

'Not all that good. You were carrying a little too much power in the middle and went fast. You made the correction but you overdid it. Approaching the ramp you were slow and settling into a two-wire when I waved you off.'

'How do you figure that?'

The Real McCoy spoke up. 'Jake, if you had been right on a centered ball when the wave-off came, you would have missed all the wires on the wave-off. Smacking on a big wad of power should have just carried you across the wires into a bolter. Hugh's right. You were a half ball low going lower when you gunned it. That pass would have been a fair two-wire. Look at that PLAT tape again. Carefully.'

Jake surrendered. 'I bow to the opinion of the experts.'

'Next time keep the ball centered, huh?'

Flap Le Beau spoke up. 'There had better not be a next time. If there is, you two asshole mechanics better swim for it before I get out of the plane.' He was apparently oblivious of the presence of Richard Haldane.

Jake glanced at the colonel to see how he was taking all this. Apparently without a flicker of emotion.

'No, I'm serious,' Skidmore said. 'If you ever get a wave-off in close like that, Jake, slam the throttles up and run the boards in, but don't rotate. Just ride her into a bolter.'

'But don't go into the water waiting for the wheels to hit,' the Real added.

Now Richard Haldane spoke. 'May I have a word with you gentle-men?'

Skidmore and McCoy went over to where the colonel was standing. Flap asked Jake, 'How are you supposed to know that it's an in-close wave-off if the LSOs can't figure it out?'

'The guy with the stick in his hand is always responsible,' Jake told the bombardier. 'He's the dummy who signed for the plane.'

After Jake and Flap debriefed both the planes they had flown that evening, Jake asked Flap if he wanted a drink.

'Yeah. You got any?'

'A little. In my stateroom. One drink and I'm into my rack. See you in a bit.'

Ten minutes later Flap asked, 'So Skidmore should not have waved us off, even though the cable might have parted on number three if we had caught it?'

'Yeah. That's right. The in-close position is defined as the point where a wave-off cannot be safely made. From that point on, in to touchdown, you are committed, like the pig. The LSO has to take you aboard no matter what. It's a practical application of the lesser of two evils theory.'

'Like the pig?'

'Yeah. A chicken lays eggs, she's dedicated. A pig gives his life, he's committed.'

'Where you from, anyway?'

'Virginia. Rural Virginia, down in the southwest corner. And you?'

'Brooklyn.'

'All that crap you gave me this morning about Louisiana and you're from Brooklyn?'

'Yep. Born in the ghetto to a woman who didn't know who my daddy was and raised on the streets. That's me.'

'So how did you get into the Corps?'

Flap Le Beau finished off his straight whiskey and grinned. He held up the glass. 'Got any more?'

'Help yourself.'

When he finished pouring, Flap said, 'Did you ever hear of a guy named Horowitz who funded scholarships for ghetto children?'

'No. Don't think so.'

'Well, it's sorta the in-thing for a millionaire to do these days. Publicly commit yourself to funding a college education for ten ghetto kids, or fifty, a hundred if you have the bucks. Sol Horowitz was the first. He promised to pay for the college education of a hundred first-graders in a public school in Brooklyn if they graduated from high school. I was one of the hundred. It's sort of amazing, but I actually got through high school. Then I got caught stealing some cars and the probation officer told the judge I had this college scholarship waiting, if I would only go. So the judge sentenced me to college. I kid you not.'

Flap sipped, remembering. Finally he continued. 'I screwed around at the university. Drank and came real close to flunking out, or getting thrown out. Miracle number two, I graduated. So somebody arranged for me to meet Horowitz. I don't know exactly what I expected. Some wizened old Jew with money sticking out of every pocket sitting in a mansion – I don't know. Well, Solomon Horowitz was none of that. He lived in a walk-up flat off Flatbush, a real dump. He looked me up and down and told me I was nothing.

' "You have learned nothing," he said. "You barely passed your courses – I hear you continued to steal cars. Oh yes, I have my sources. They tell me. I know." What could I say?

'Horowitz asked, "Who do you think gave you a chance to make something of yourself? Some oil baron? Some rich Jew asshole whose daddy left him ten million? I will tell you who."

'He rolled up his sleeve. He had a number tattooed on the inside of his wrist. He had been in Dachau. And you know something else? When he made the promise to send those kids to college, *he didn't have any money*. He made the promise because then he would have to work like hell to earn the money.'

'Why?' Jake asked.

'That was my question. I'll level with you, Jake. I was twenty-two years old and I'd never met anybody in my life who wasn't in it for himself. So I asked.

'Horowitz thought about it for a little bit and finally said he guessed I was entitled to know. The Nazis castrated him. He could never have any children. When he got out of Dachau after the war weighing ninety-one pounds, he came to America. He wanted his life to make a difference to somebody, he said, so he promised to send a hundred kids to college, blacks and Puerto Ricans who would never have a chance otherwise. He worked three jobs, seven days a week, saved his money, invested every dime. And he did it. Actually sent thirty-two, who were all of the hundred that finished high school and could read and write well enough to get into a college. Thirty-two. He paid board, room, books and tuition and sent a little allowance every month. Twenty-three of us graduated.'

Flap tossed off the last of the liquor and set the glass in the small metal sink jutting out from the wall.

'I thought long and hard about the interview. I decided I wanted my life to make a difference, to make Horowitz's life make a difference . . . you see what I mean. But I'm not Solomon Horowitz. All I knew how to do was drink, screw, do burglaries and fight. I wasn't so good at stealing cars – I got caught a lot. So I picked the fightin'est outfit of them all and joined up.

'They wouldn't send me to officer candidate school because of my record. I enlisted anyway. I was full of Horowitz's fire. I went to boot camp and finished first in my class, went to mortar school and came out first, so they made me an instructor. Got to be a pretty fair hand with a mortar and a rifle and led PT classes in my spare time. Finally they decided I might make a Marine after all, so they sent me to OCS.'

'How did you do there?' Jake asked, even though he thought he knew the answer.

'Number one,' Le Beau said flatly, without inflection. 'They gave me a presentation sword.'

'Going to stay in?'

'There's nothing for me in Brooklyn. My mother died of a drug overdose years ago. I've been in ten years now and I'm staying until they kick me out. The Corps is my home.'

'Don't you get tired of it sometimes?'

'Sometimes. Then I remember Horowitz and I'm not tired anymore. I've got his picture. Want to see it?' The Marine dug out his wallet.

Jake looked. Flap towered over Horowitz – a younger Flap togged out in the white dress uniform of a Marine officer. The old, old man had wispy white hair and stooped shoulders. His head was turned and he was looking up into the beaming face of the handsome black man. They were smiling at each other.

'Horowitz came to Parris Island for the graduation ceremony,' Flap explained. 'They gave me the sword and I walked over to where he was sitting and gave it to him.'

'He still alive?'

'On no. He died six months after this picture was taken. This is the only one of him I have.'

After Flap left, Jake slowly unlaced his flight boots and pulled them off. It took the last of his energy.

If the whole cruise goes like this day has, I'm not going to make it. Russian frigates, in-flight engagements . . . Jesus!

He eyed his bunk, the top one, and worked himself up to an effort. He didn't even pull off his flight suit. Sixty seconds after his head hit the pillow he was asleep.

6

The ships sailed across a restless, empty ocean. Jake saw no ships other than those of the task group whenever he went on deck, which he managed to do three or four times a day. Many sailors never went topside; they spent every minute of their day in their working spaces, their berthing areas, or on the mess deck, and saw sunlight only when the ship pulled into port. Jake Grafton thought he would go stir-crazy if he couldn't see the sea and sky and feel the wind on his face every few hours.

He would stroll around the deck, visit with Bosun Muldowski if he ran into him, chat with the catapult crews if they were on deck, and examine planes. His eyes seemed naturally drawn to airplanes. His destination on these excursions was usually the forward end of the flight deck, where he would stand between the catapults looking at the ocean. The wind was usually vigorous here. It played with his hair and tugged at his clothes and cleaned the below-decks smells from his nostrils.

The first morning he saw a school of whales to starboard. Knots of sailors gawked and pointed. The whales spouted occasionally and once one came soaring out of the water, then crashed down in a magnificent cloud of spray. Mostly the view was of black backs glistening amid the swells.

When he went below this first morning at sea, reentered the world of crowded passageways, tiny offices, and never-ending paperwork, the squadron maintenance officer cornered him. 'That plane you flew last night – well, we haven't found any airframe damage yet. Maybe we dodged the bullet.' If there was no damage there would be no official report assessing blame. 'The avionics took a helluva lot bigger lick than they're designed for, though. Radar and computer and VDI are screwed up.'

Jake threw himself into the problem assigned to him by Colonel Haldane. How would you attack a Soviet ship? Since the Soviets had all kinds of ships, he soon focused on the most capable, the guided missile cruisers that were the mainstay of their task forces, Kyndas and Krestas.

After preliminary research of classified material in the Air Intelligence spaces, he paid a visit to the EA-6B Prowler squadron in their small ready room on the 0-3 level, near the number-four arresting gear room.

This squadron had only four aircraft, but they were Cadillacs. A stretched version of the A-6, the Prowler held a crew of four: one pilot and three electronic warfare specialists. The airplane's sole mission was to foil enemy radars. The electronic devices it used for this task were mounted in pods slung on the weapons stations. Other than the pilot's instruments, the panels of the cockpit were devoted to the displays and controls necessary to detect enemy radar transmissions and render the information they gave the enemy useless. Since it was a highly modified version of the A-6, the plane was popularly referred to as a Queer Six.

The Prowler crews in Ready Eight greeted Jake with open arms. They too were stationed on Whidbey Island when ashore, and two or three of the officers knew Jake. When he finally got around to explaining his errand, they were delighted to help. The capabilities of Soviet warships were their stock in trade.

Jake had already known that Soviet ships were heavily armed, but now he found out just how formidable they really were. Radar capabilities were evaluated, weapons envelopes examined. Finally Jake Grafton gave his conclusion: 'A single plane doesn't have much of a chance against one of these ships.' This comment drew sober nods from the two electronic warfare experts at his elbows.

Nor, he soon concluded, did a flight of planes have much of a chance if the weapons they had to use were free-falling bombs, technology left over from World War II. Oh, free-falling bombs had been adequate in Vietnam when attacking stationary targets ashore – barely adequate – but modern warships were another matter entirely. Ships would detect the aircraft on radar while they were still minutes away. Radar would allow antiaircraft missiles to be fired and guided long before the attacker reached the immediate vicinity of the ship. Then, in-close, radar-directed guns would pour forth a river of high explosives.

If our lucky attack pilot survived all that, he was ready to aim his free-fall weapons at a maneuvering, high-speed target. Even if he aimed his bombs perfectly, the bombs were unguided during their eight to ten seconds of fall, so if the ship's captain reversed the helm or tightened a turn, or if the pilot had miscalculated the wind, the bombs would miss.

And now our frustrated aerial warrior had to turn his fanny to the fire and successfully avoid on the way out all the hazards he had penetrated on the way in.

What the attack pilot desperately needed was a missile he could shoot at the ship, Jake concluded, the farther away the better. Alas, the US Navy's antiship missiles were still in the development stage, victims of

Vietnam penny pinching, so the attack crews would have to make do with what they had. What they had were some short-range guided missiles like Bullpup, which unfortunately carried only a 250-pound warhead – enough to cripple a warship but not to sink it.

If the weather was good enough, the attacking planes could use laser-guided bombs, preferably two-thousand pounders. Although these weapons were unpowered, the laser seeker and guidance assembly on the nose of the weapon could steer it into the target if the attack pilot made a reasonably accurate delivery, and if the spot of laser light that the guidance system was seeking was indeed on the target. The weak point of the system was the beam of laser light, which was scattered by visible moisture in the air. Alas, over the ocean the sky was often cloudy.

With or without laser-guided bombs, the attackers were going to have to penetrate the enemy ship's radar-directed defenses. Here was where the EA-6B came in. The electronic warfare (EW) plane could shield the attack force electronically if it were in the middle of it or placed at the proper angle to the attack axis.

What about overloading the enemy's defenses with planes? Perhaps a coordinated attack with as many planes as we can launch, saturating the enemy's defenses with targets, one prays too many targets. Some would inevitably get through.

And our coordinated attack should come in high and low at the same time. Say A-6s at a hundred feet and A-7s and F-4s diving in from thirty thousand.

Jake made notes. The EA-6 crews had a lot of ideas, most of which Jake thought excellent. When he said his good-bye two hours after he came, he shook hands all around.

Back in his stateroom staring at his notes, Jake wondered what a war with the Soviets would be like. An exchange of intercontinental ballistic missiles would make for a loud, almighty short war, but Jake didn't think there would be much reason for the surviving warships to try to sink one another. Without countries to go back to, the sailors and the ships were all doomed anyway. Could there be a war without nuclear weapons, in 1973?

Really, when one is contemplating the end of civilization the whole problem becomes fantastic, something out of a sweaty nightmare. Could sane men push the button, thereby destroying themselves, their nations, most of the human race? He got bogged down at this point. The politicians would have to figure it out.

One thing he knew for sure – if there was a war without a nuclear Armageddon, the American admirals would go for the Soviet ships like bulldogs after raw meat.

It wouldn't be easy. He knew well that a strike on a single ship would be a fluke, an ambush of a straggler. Like every other navy, the Soviets would arrange their ships in groups for mutual support. Any attack would have to be against a task force.

Staring at his notes on detection ranges, missile and flak envelopes, Jake could envision how it would be. The ships would be rippling off missiles – the sky would be full of Mach 3 telephone poles. If that weren't enough, Soviet warships were covered with antiaircraft guns. American ships these days didn't have many, but then the Soviet Navy had no aircraft carriers to launch strikes against them. The flak from the Soviet ships would be fierce, would literally be a steel curtain the attacking planes would have to fly through.

An Alpha strike – everything the ship could launch, coming in high and low and in the middle, shielded by EA-6B Prowlers and coordinated as well as possible by an E-2 Hawkeye orbiting safely out of range a hundred miles away – that was the answer he would give Colonel Haldane.

Wouldn't ever happen, of course. America and Russia weren't about to fight a war. Planning an attack on a Soviet task force was just another peacetime military what-if exercise. Yet if it *did* happen, few of those planes would survive. And of those crews who successfully penetrated the cordon of missiles and flak, only the most fiercely determined would successfully drive the thrust home. For Jake Grafton knew that it was neither ships nor airplanes that won battles, but men.

Were there men like that aboard this ship? By reputation Flap Le Beau was one, but were there any more?

Disgusted with the whole problem, he began to think of home. He had visited his parents on their farm in southwestern Virginia this spring. In May, with the leaves on the trees coming out, the grass in the meadows growing green and tender, the cows nursing new-born calves.

His parents had been so glad to see him. Dad, well, his pride in his son had been visible, tangible. And Mother, smiling through her tears at her man-son come home.

He had helped his father with the cattle, once again felt the morning chill and smelled the aroma of warm bovine bodies, manure, sweet hay . . . Just the memory of it made him shiver here in his small stateroom aboard this giant steel ship. The dew in the grass that recorded every step, the sun slanting up over the low ridges and shining into the barn, his father's voice as he talked to the cattle, reassuring, steady . . . all of it came flooding back.

Why are you here, aboard this steel ship on this wilderness of ocean, worried about Russian flak and missiles, contemplating the ultimate obscenity? Why aren't you there, where you grew up, feeling the warmth of the sun on your back and helping your father in the timeless rituals that ensure life will go on, and on . . . as God intended? Why aren't you there to help your mother in her old age? Answer me that, Jake Grafton. You never hated

the farm as your elder brother did – you loved it. Loved everything about it.
Your parents – you love them. You are of them and they are of you. Why are
you here?

Why?

Life aboard ship quickly assumed its natural rhythm, which was the
rhythm dictated by two hundred years of naval tradition and regulations.
Everyone worked, meals were served, the ship's laundry ran full blast,
and every afternoon at precisely 13:30 the PA system came to life and
announced a general quarters drill. 'This is a drill, this is a drill. General
quarters, general quarters. All hands man your battle stations. Go up and
forward on the starboard side and down and aft on the port side. General
quarters.'

The aviators' battle stations were their ready rooms. While the damage
control parties fought mock fires and coped with flooding, nuclear,
chemical and biological attack, the aviators took NATOPS exams,
listened to lectures, and generally bored one another. It was during these
drills that Jake gave his lectures on shipboard operations. In addition to
the material in the CV NATOPS, he added every tip he could recall from
his two previous combat cruises. The lectures went well, he thought. The
Marines were attentive and asked good questions. To his amazement, he
found he actually enjoyed standing in front of the room and talking about
his passion, flying.

After secure from general quarters the officers scattered to squadron
spaces throughout the ship to do paperwork, to which there was no end
in this life. The evening of the second day at sea Jake found an opportunity to discuss his Soviet ship project with the skipper, Colonel Haldane,
who knew as much about the subject as Jake did. After they had spent
an hour going over the problem, the colonel took him to the air wing
spaces to meet the air wing ops officer, a lieutenant commander. Here the
subject was aired again. The upshot of it was that Jake was assigned to
help Wing Ops put together realistic exercises for the ship's air wing.

Officers could eat dinner in either of the two wardrooms aboard – the
formal wardroom on the main deck, right beside Ready Four, where
uniforms were required, or in the dirty-shirt wardroom up forward in the
0-3 level between the bow catapults where flight suits and flight deck
jerseys were acceptable. In practice the formal wardroom was the turf of
the ship's company officers who were not aviators, invaded only occasionally by aviation personnel on their best behavior. Here in the evening
after dinner a movie was shown, one watched with proper decorum by
congressionally certified gentlemen.

The aviators congregated in their ready rooms for their evening
movies, here to whistle, shout, offer ribald suggestions to the characters,
moan lustily at the female lead, and throw popcorn at the screen and each

other. If a flyer didn't like the movie in his ready room, he could always wander off to another squadron's, where he would be welcome if he could find a seat.

And in the late evening somewhere in the junior officers' staterooms there was a card game under way, usually nickel-dime-quarter poker because no one had much money. Although alcohol was officially outlawed aboard ship, at a card game a thirsty fellow could usually find a drink. Or several. As long as one didn't appear in any of the ship's common spaces drunk or smelling of liquor, no one seemed to care very much.

Of course, a junior officer could skip the movie and card game and retire to his stateroom to listen to music or write letters. Since a lot of the junior officers were very much in love, a lot of them did this almost every night, Jake Grafton among them. Of course the lonely lovers had roommates, which sometimes presented problems.

'It's so damned unfair,' the Real McCoy lamented. 'I could get more information about the markets if I were sitting in a mud hut in some squalid village in the middle of India. Anywhere but here.' He turned his woeful gaze on his roommate. 'There are telephones everywhere on this planet except here. Everywhere.'

Jake Grafton tried to look sympathetic. He did reasonably well, he thought.

'It's the not knowing,' the LSO continued. 'I bought solid companies, with solid prospects, nothing speculative. But I am just completely *cut off*. Condemned to the outer darkness.' He gestured futilely. 'It's maddening.'

'Maybe you should put your investments in a trust or something. Give someone a power of attorney.'

'Who? Anyone who can do as well as I have in the market is doing it, not fooling around with someone else's portfolio for a fee.'

'We'll be in Hawaii in a week. I'll bet you'll find that you're doing great.'

The Real McCoy groaned and glanced at Jake Grafton with a look that told him he was hopeless. The LSO took a deep breath, then exhaled slowly. He looked so forlorn that Jake decided to try to get him talking.

A question. He should ask a question. After thinking about it for a moment, Jake said, 'Hey, what's the difference between stocks and shares? In the newspapers they talk about stockholders and shareholders and—'

He stopped because the Real gave him a withering look and stomped for the door. He slammed it shut behind him.

Dear Callie,
   We are three days out of San Francisco on our way to Pearl Harbor.
We are making about twenty knots. We tried to go faster but the escorts

were taking a pounding in heavy swells, so we slowed down. The swells are being kicked up by a typhoon about fifteen hundred miles to the southwest. I got requalified on carrier landings, day and night, the first day out of port, but we haven't flown since.

My bombardier-navigator is a guy named Flap Le Beau. He's from Brooklyn and has been in the Marines for ten years. I'm still trying to figure him out. He appears to be a good BN and a fine officer. He wasn't too sure about me the first time we flew together and gave me a lot of gas to see if I could take it. What he didn't know is that I've learned to take gas from experts, so his little performance was just a minor irritation. I think he's a pretty neat guy, so I was lucky there. I think you'd like him too.

My roommate is a character, fellow called the Real McCoy. He is in a tizzy worrying about what is happening in the stock market while we are out of touch. He's made a lot of money in stocks and wants to make a lot more. If I knew anything about stocks I would too, but I don't. I couldn't make easy money if I owned the mint.

The skipper is a lieutenant colonel – same rank as a commander – named Richard Haldane. Don't know where he is from but he doesn't have an accent like I do. Neither does Flap, for that matter.

Jake didn't know he had an accent until Callie told him he did. She was a linguist, with a trained ear. Since she made that remark he was listening more carefully to how other people talked. Just now he said a few words to see if he could detect some flaw in his pronunciation. 'My name is Jake Grafton. I work for the government and am here to save you.'

Nope.

She wouldn't kid about a thing like that, would she?

Colonel Haldane has me giving lectures to the flight crews on flight operations around the ship. It's easy and sort of fun. It used to be that I didn't like standing in front of a crowd and saying anything, but now I don't mind it if I know the material I am going to talk about. I must have a little ham in me.

The colonel also has me doing some research on how to attack Soviet ships, just in case we ever have to. The research is difficult, especially when you realize that if the necessity ever arises, a lot of American lives are going to depend on how well you did your homework.

As I mentioned, the first day out of port I got requalified day and night. The day traps went okay, but the night ones were something else. On the fourth one I had an in-flight engagement, which means I caught a wire during a wave-off and the plane fell about four feet to the deck. The impact almost destroyed the airplane. It appears to have survived with only damage to the avionics, which is the electronic gear. Why a wheel didn't come off I'll never know.

Everyone says the in-flight wasn't my fault, but in a way it was. The LSO gave me a wave-off too late, and I shouldn't have rotated as much as I did when I poured the power to her. It's a technique thing. I did it by the book and got bitten, yet if I had deviated from approved wave-off procedure *in this particular case*, things would have probably worked out better.

All you can do is hope that when the challenge comes, you will do the right thing through instinct, training, or experience, or some combination of these. The one thing you know is that when the crunch comes you won't have time to think about how you should handle it. The hard, inescapable reality is that anyone who flies may die in an airplane.

I suppose I have accepted this reality on some level. Still, the in-flight shook me up pretty good. As the airplane decelerated, still in the air, we were thrown forward into the straps that hold us to the seat. At moments like that every perception is crystal clear, every thought arrives like a bell ringing. You are so totally alive that the events of seconds seem to happen so slowly that later you can recall every nuance. As I felt the plane decelerating, I knew what had happened.

In-flight!

I could feel her slowing, saw the needle of the angle-of-attack gauge swing toward a stall, saw the engine RPM still winding up . . . and knew that we were in for it. For an instant there we hung suspended above the deck. Then we fell.

The jolt of falling about four feet stunned me. I knew exactly what had happened, yet I didn't know whether or not we were safely arrested. I couldn't see too well. I didn't know if the hook had held, or if the cross-deck pennant had held together. Or if the airplane was in one piece – if the fuel tank had ruptured we were only seconds away from blowing up.

It was a bad scare.

I've had a few of those through the years and one more isn't headline stuff, but still, with the war over and all and me thinking about getting out, that moment was a hard, swift return to cold reality.

I have been thinking a lot about you these last few days. Our time together in Chicago was something very special. Although the visit didn't wind up quite the way I planned, everything else was super. Theron is a great guy and your folks seem like they would be very pleasant once I got to know them a little better.

He stopped and reread that last paragraph. That bit about the parents wasn't strictly true, but what could he say? *Your dad's a royal jerk but I like them like that.*

76

Diplomacy. This letter had some diplomacy in it.

When you stop and think about it, life is strange. Some people believe in preordination, although I don't. Still, you grow up knowing that somewhere out there is the person you are going to fall in love with. So you wonder what that person will be like, how she will look, how she will walk, talk, what she will think, how she will smile, how she will laugh. There's no way of knowing, of course, until you meet her. The realization that you have finally met her comes as a wondrous discovery, a peek into the works of life.

Maybe a guy could fall instantly in love, but I doubt it. I think love sort of creeps over you – like a warm feeling on a clear blue fall day. This person is in your thoughts most of the time – all the time, actually. You see her when you close your eyes, when you look off into the distance, when you pause from what you are doing and take a deep breath. You remember how her eyes looked when she laughed, how she threw her head back, how her fingers felt when they touched you . . .

The loved one becomes a part of you, the most valuable part.

At least it is that way with me when I think of you.

As ever,
Jake

7

Visual dive-bombing really hadn't changed much since the 1930s, even though the top speeds of the aircraft had tripled and their ordnance-carrying capacity had increased fifteenfold. The techniques were still the same.

Jake Grafton thought about that as the flight of four A-6s threaded their way upward through a layer of scattered cumulus clouds. The four warplanes, spread in a loose finger-four formation, passed the tops at about 8,000 feet and continued to climb into the clear, open sky above.

Perhaps it was the touch of the romantic that he tried with varying degrees of success to keep hidden, but the link to the past was strong within him. On a morning like this in June 1942, US Navy dive bomber pilots from *Enterprise* and *Yorktown* topped the clouds and searched across the blue Pacific for the Japanese carriers then engaged in hammering Midway Island. They found them, four aircraft carriers plowing the broad surface of that great ocean, pushed over and dove. Their bombs smashed *Kaga*, *Akagi* and *Soryu*, set them fatally ablaze and turned the tide of World War II.

This morning thirty-one years later this group of bombers was on its way to bomb Hawaii, actually a small island in the Hawaiian archipelago named Kahoolawe.

The oxygen from the mask tasted cool and rubbery. Jake eyed the cockpit altimeter, steady at ten thousand feet, and unsnapped the left side of his mask. He let it dangle from the fitting on the other side as he devoted most of his attention to holding good formation. His position today was number three, which meant that he flew on the skipper's, Colonel Haldane's, right side. Number four was on Jake's right, number two on Haldane's left.

He glanced at his BN, Flap Le Beau, who had his head pressed against the radar hood. He was using both hands to twiddle knobs and flip switches, but he never took his eyes from the radar. Excellent. He knew the location and function of every knob, button and switch without looking. When the going got tough there would be no time to look, no time to fumble for this or that, no time to think.

The colonel's BN, Allen Bartow, was similarly engaged. From his vantage point twenty feet out from the colonel's wingtip, Jake could see every move Bartow made in the cockpit, could see him pull his head aft a few inches and eye the computer readouts on the panel just to the right of the radar screen, could see him glance down occasionally, referring to the notes on his kneeboard.

He had gotten to know Bartow fairly well the last few days. A major with twelve years in the Corps, Bartow was addicted to French novels. He read them in French. Just now he was working his way through everything that Georges Simenon had ever written. He had books stacked everywhere in his stateroom and carried one in his flight suit, which he pulled out whenever he had a few minutes to kill.

'I'm retiring as soon as I get my twenty years in,' he told Jake. 'On that very day. Then I'm going to get a doctorate in French literature and spend the rest of my life teaching.'

'Sounds dull,' Jake said, grinning, just to needle him.

To his surprise Bartow had considered that remark seriously. 'Maybe. Academic life won't be like the Corps, like life in a squadron. Yet we all have to give this up sooner or later. I enjoy it now, but when it's over I have something else I'll enjoy just as much. Something different. So now I've got the flying and the guys and the anticipation of that something else. I'm a pretty rich man.' And he returned Jake's grin.

Bartow *was* rich, Jake reflected ruefully as he watched the bombardier sitting hunched over his scope. Richer than Jake, anyway. All Jake had was the flying and the camaraderie. He didn't even have Callie – he had screwed that up.

Le Beau – he apparently didn't want anything else. Or did he?

'You got a gal waiting for you?' Jake asked his bombardier without taking his eyes off the lead plane.

'You can fly this thing and think about women too?'

'I always have time to think about women. You got one stashed somewhere?'

'Dozens.'

'A special one?'

'Naw. The ones I want to get serious about don't want me after they've had a good look. I'm just tempered, polished steel, a military instrument. How we doing on fuel, anyway?'

Jake glanced at the gauges. He punched the buttons to get a reading on his remaining wing fuel, then finally said, 'We're okay.'

'Umph. We're only fifty miles out.' Le Beau went back to the radar. 'Don't embarrass me. Try to get some decent hits.'

The bombs hanging under the wings were little blue twenty-five-pound practice bombs. Each one contained a small pyrotechnic cartridge in the nose that would produce a puff of smoke when the bomb struck, allowing the hit to be spotted. Each A-6 carried a dozen of these things on their bomb racks.

The planned drill was for the pilot of each plane to drop the first half-dozen manually, using the visual bomb sight à la World War II, then the second six using the aircraft's electronic system. Jake carefully set the optical sight to the proper mil setting for a forty-degree dive with a six-thousand-foot release. Releasing six thousand feet above the target, the slant range was about nine thousand feet. To drop a bomb nine thousand feet from a target and hit it was difficult, of course – nearly impossible when you considered the fact that the wind would affect the bomb's trajectory throughout its fall. Yet *that* was the dive bomber's art.

Hitting the target was the payoff. Five thousand men at sea for months, the treasure spent on ships, planes and fuel, the blood spilled in training, all to set up that moment when the bomb struck the target. If the pilot could get it there.

Colonel Haldane expected his pilots to do their damnedest. Last night he taped a poster to the ready room bulkhead with the names of all his pilots on it. The poster was just as large, just as prominent as the one on the bulkhead that recorded each pilot's landing grades. You had to be able to get aboard ship safely to be a carrier pilot, but you weren't much use in combat unless you could hit the target when the chips were down. Haldane said as much. He went further:

'In this squadron, after the upcoming Hawaiian ops period, the pilots who are going to lead sections and flights are the pilots with the best bombing scores. I guarantee you, your bombing scores will appear on your fitness report. I expect each and every one of you to earn your pay on the bombing range.'

First Lieutenant Doug Harrison couldn't resist. 'Hey, Skipper. You can fly on my wing.'

'If you can out-bomb me, I will,' Haldane shot back.

Harrison was number four today, flying on Jake's right wing. You had to admire Harrison, for his chutzpah if nothing else. Haldane had spent years in Vietnam dive-bombing under fire and Harrison was just a year out of flight school. No fool, Harrison well knew how good the experienced professionals were and risked ignominy anyway.

Although he was less vocal about it, Jake Grafton took a backseat to no one when it came to pride in his own flying skills. He had seen his share of flak and dropped his share of bombs. His name would be at the top of that ready room poster if it were humanly possible to get it there.

Major Bartow pumped his fist at Jake, who scooted farther away from the lead plane. Number two, Captain Harry Digman, came under the lead, his canopy just a few feet below Haldane's exhausts, and surfaced where Jake had been. Now the formation was in right echelon.

Colonel Haldane did the talking on the radio. Cleared into the target area as a flight of F-4s were leaving, he led his echelon down in a gentle, sweeping left turn to 15,000 feet, then straightened out for the run up the bearing line. Over the target he broke to the left. Ten seconds later the second plane broke, and Jake ten seconds after that.

Around they came, now strung out, each pilot verifying his clearance from other airplanes, then concentrating on the target and flying his own plane.

The first essential for a successful run is to get to the proper roll-in point. This is that location in space from which you can roll in and arrive on the proper run-in heading at the preselected dive angle, today forty degrees. Practice targets, with run-in lines bulldozed into the earth and marks gouged out as reference points, help the pilots develop a feel for that correct, perfect place to roll in.

And 'roll in' describes the maneuver. Today Jake approached the bearing line obliquely, at about forty-five degrees off, waiting, watching the target get nearer and nearer as he ran the trim to one degree nose-down, the 500-knot setting, while he held the plane level with back stick.

Now!

He slaps the stick sideways and in a heartbeat has the A-6 past the vertical, in 135 degrees of bank. Now the stick comes sharply back and the G's smash them into their seats as the pilot pulls the nose of the aircraft to just below the target while he adjusts the throttles. Since he is carrying low-drag practice bombs today, Jake sets the throttles at about eighty percent RPM.

G off, stick right to roll her hard to the upright position.

Flap flips on the master armament switch and makes the radio call: 'War Ace Three's in hot.'

If the pilot has rolled in properly, the plane is now in a forty-degree dive, the pipper in the bombsight below the target and tracking toward it. This is where Jake finds it now, although just a little too far right. He corrects this instantly by forcing the stick to the left, then jerking the wings back level. This is no place to try to be smooth – it is imperative that he quickly get the lane into the proper dive with the pipper tracking so that he will have as many seconds as possible to solve the drift problem. Jake flies his dives with both hands on the stick, muscling the plane to the position he wants.

A glance at the airspeed – over 400 and increasing – now the altimeter. Flap is calling the altitudes: 'Fourteen . . . thirteen . . . forty-one degrees . . . twelve . . .'

The wind is drifting the pipper leftward. Jake rolls right and forces the pipper back to the right. He wants the pipper to the right of the bearing line and drifting left toward it, yet at the moment of release it must still be slightly right of the bull's-eye. The bomb will continue to drift during its fall.

And he is steep. He must release with the pipper just a smidgen short of the target to compensate for that.

'. . . Ten . . . nine . . . eight . . .'

Coming down with the pipper tracking toward the bull's-eye, today a painted white spot in the middle of a white circle, he glances at the G-meter. Steady on one. He releases his death grip on the stick so that he can feel the effect of the trim. Coming toward neutral, which means he is getting toward 500 knots true airspeed, 465 indicated. The briefest glance at the airspeed indicator – 445 and increasing . . .

'Seven . . .'

And since the target is several hundred feet above sea level and he has synchronized the movement of the pipper with the descent, he releases the bomb two hundred feet above six thousand feet with the pipper at a five o'clock position on the bull.

And pulls.

Wings level and throttles forward to the stops, pull until the G-meter needle hits four, then hold it there. He reaches for the master arm switch with his right hand – his arm weighs a ton with all this G on – and toggles it off.

Flap again on the radio: 'War Ace Three's off safe.'

With his nose passing the horizon Jake Grafton relaxes the G and scans the sky for the airplane in front of him. There! And farther around, the skipper. Okay. Nose on up and let her soar, converting that diving airspeed back into altitude.

The spotters on the ground are calling the hits. The skipper's first one was seventy-five feet at seven o'clock. His wingman gets a called score of a hundred-ten feet at twelve. Jack gets a score of fifty feet at five.

'Overcompensated for the wind,' he mutters to Flap, who has no comment.

Now they are back at 15,000 feet and he pulls the throttles back, steers a little wider as he makes his turn. He glimpses the flashing wings of the plane ahead as it rolls into its dive.

'War Ace Four, your hit seventy-five feet at nine o'clock.'

'Harrison's holding his own with the colonel,' Jake tells Flap, and chuckles.

He checks the drift of the puffs of smoke from the practice bombs. He eyes the clouds, glances behind to see where Harrison is, checks his fuel, checks the annunciator panel for warning lights, then eyes the target to see where he should go to get to the roll-in.

Master Arm switch on, roll and pull!

'Don't you just love this shit?' Flap says between altitude calls on their second dive.

'Bull's-eye,' the target spotter says as Jake soars upward after release, and he reaches over and slaps Flap on the thigh.

'With a spoon, Flapjack!' He slams the stick sideways and the aircraft spins on its longitudinal axis. He stops it after precisely 360 degrees of roll.

'Okay, okay, you're the best in the west,' Flap says. 'Just keep popping them in there.'

After their sixth dive, it was Flap's turn. He had the radar and computer ready. This time as Jake rolled he had to point the fixed reticle of the bombsight exactly at the target. Then he squeezed the commit trigger on the stick and began to fly the steering commands on the vertical display indicator, the VDI, in the center of the instrument panel in front of him.

Squeezing the commit trigger told the computer where the target was and told the radar to track it. While Flap monitored the velocities the computer was getting from the inertial, the computer providing steering commands, wind-compensated of course, to guide Jake to the proper release point, which was that point in space where the bomb could be released to fall upon the target.

Jake concentrated upon the steering commands and followed them as precisely as he could. When the computer gave him a pull-up command he laid on the G while concentrating fiercely on keeping the wings level. The computer released the weapon and he kept the nose coming up.

'Seventy-five feet at six o'clock.'

He went around to do it again.

'You know,' he said to Flap, 'it's like they invented a machine to hit a baseball.'

'Just follow steering, Babe Ruth. This gizmo is smarter than you are.'

'Yeah, but I'm an *artiste!*'

'We ain't dodging flak today, Jake.'

This was the eternal war – the pilot wanted to drop them all visually and the bombardier wanted to use the system every time. Both men knew the system was better and they both knew Jake would never admit it. Today at this practice target the pilot had ideal conditions: a stationary target with a known elevation, a plowed run-in line, visual cues on the ground, no flak, the luxury of repeated runs that allowed him to properly dope the wind. The system of this A-6E was a first-time, every-time sure thing.

But a machine is hard to love.

The four A-6s rendezvoused off target and Harrison, the number-four man, slid under the other three checking them for hung bombs. Then

Jake checked Harrison. Harrison and number two each had one little blue bomb still hanging on the racks.

The skipper led them up to 20,000 feet and Flap dialed in the ship's TACAN, a radio navigation aid. The mileage readout refused to lock – they were still too far out – but Flap soon had the ship on radar. One hundred thirty-two miles.

After checking the cockpit altitude – stable at 10,000 feet – Jake took his mask off and hung it on the left side mirror on the canopy rail. He swabbed the sweat off his face.

The planes were in parade formation, only about fifteen feet from the cockpit to the wing tip of the next man. Flying this close to another plane was work, but Jake Grafton enjoyed it. The restless air always affected the planes differently as they sliced through it, so constant adjustments were required from the wingman. The lead just flew his own machine.

If you were the wingman, you kept the wing tip of the lead plane just below and behind the canopy. This look must be maintained with continuous small adjustments of stick and throttles, occasionally rudder. If you did it right, you could hang here no matter what the lead plane was doing – flying straight and level, banking, climbing, diving, executing wingovers, loops; whatever.

Jake settled in and concentrated. Doing this on a sunny morning in clear, fairly calm air was merely drill. Doing it on a stormy, filthy night with the planes bouncing in turbulence over an angry ocean demanded a high level of skill and confidence. With an emergency and a low reading on the fuel gauge, your ability to hang on someone's wing became your lifeline.

Bartow was motioning him out. A pushing motion.

'We're opening it up,' he told Flap, who glanced at Bartow, then gave the identical signal to Harrison, on Jake's right wing.

When he had opened the gap to about sixty or seventy feet, Jake stabilized and checked Harrison. He looked at the skipper's wingman, on the skipper's left wing. Everybody about right. Okay.

Flap had written down all the scores and now he was tallying them, figuring each crew's CEP – circular error probable. He did this by finding the sixth best hit. Half the bombs would hit within a circle with this radius.

In the skipper's cockpit Bartow was looking at his radar. Jake glanced at the mileage readout on the radar repeater between his legs: 126. Then his eyes flicked across the instrument panel. Airspeed 295 indicated, altitude 20,040 feet, warning lights out, hydraulic pressures okay. Fuel – about 7,600 pounds remaining.

He looked straight ahead, saw nothing, then glanced again across that gap toward Bartow.

He had his eyes focused on Bartow when an F-4 Phantom crossed his line of vision. Between him and the skipper. Flashed by going in the opposite direction, and at the same time another Phantom went by the skipper's left side, between him and his wingman.

They were there only long enough to register on Jake's brain, then they were gone. The A-6 jolted as it flew into the edges of the wash of the Phantom's wings.

'What was that?' Flap asking, raising his head and looking around.

Jake grabbed his oxygen mask and snapped it on. 'You won't believe this,' he said on the ICS, 'but a Phantom just went between us and the skipper. And another went down the skipper's left side, between him and Digman.'

'What?'

'Yeah, a flight of Phantoms just went through our flight. I shit you not. The skipper went between the lead and his wingman and one of them went between us and the skipper. We missed by *inches*.'

Jake stared across the gap that separated him from Bartow. Bartow was looking back at him. Had he seen the F-4s?

'If we had been still in parade formation,' Jake told Flap, 'you and me would be tapping on the pearly gates right now.'

Say the fighters were also going 300 indicated – that's a closing speed of 600 knots indicated, over 800 knots true. Almost a thousand miles per hour!

He had looked straight ahead just a second or two before they got here – and seen nothing.

But they were *there*, coming head-on, like guided missiles.

And he didn't see them. Of course the distance was over a half mile two seconds before they arrived, but still . . . He should have seen something!

He broke into a sweat. His mouth and lips were dry. He tried to swallow.

At those speeds, if his plane had collided with that Phantom . . .

He wouldn't have felt a thing. Not a single thing. He would have been just instantly dead, a spot of grease trapped in the exploding fireball.

'Well, Ace,' Flap said, 'you will be delighted to hear we have a fifty-foot CEP.'

Jake tried to reply but couldn't.

'If World War III comes, you and I will be among the very first to die,' Flap informed him. 'How about them apples? We've earned it.'

Those Phantoms – he wondered if the pilots of the fighters had even seen the A-6s.

'Gives you goose bumps, huh? Ain't life something else?'

'Did anybody see those Phantoms?' Jake asked.

Silence. Blank looks. They were debriefing the flight in the ready room. Seven blank faces.

'You mean I was the only one to see them?'

Later, in the solitude of his stateroom, he thought about miracles. About how close to the abyss he had come, how many times. What was that quote – something about if you stared into the abyss long enough, the abyss stared back.

That was true. He could feel it staring back just now.

No one doubted his word when he told them about the fighters. But no one else had seen them.

To be told later that you had a close call was like learning that your mother had difficulty when you were born. It meant nothing. You shrugged and went on.

The Phantoms must have been from this ship. That was easy enough to check. He examined the air plan and found the fighter squadron that had the target time immediately after the A-6 outfit, then paid a visit to their ready room.

'Hey, did any of you guys have a near midair today? Anybody almost trade paint with four A-6s? On your way into the target?'

They stared at him like he was a grotesque apparition, a leering reminder of their own mortality. No one had seen anything. All must have been looking elsewhere, thinking of something else, because unless they were looking in exactly the right place, they would have missed it. Just as the other seven Intruder crewmen had.

Here in his stateroom he worked out the math. An F-4 was about fifty feet long. At a combined speed of 800 knots it would pass the eye in thirty-seven thousandths of a second. Less than an eye blink.

When death comes, she will come quick.

But you've always known that, Jake Grafton.

He got out of his chair and examined his face in the mirror over the sink. The face in the glass stared back blankly.

'A ship under way is a very difficult target,' Jake said.

Lieutenant Colonel Haldane didn't reply. He knew as well as Jake did that once free-falling bombs were released, a well-conned ship would turn sharply. Probably into the wind, although the attacker certainly couldn't count on that.

'Ideally we should drop as close to the ship as possible to minimize the time he has to turn,' Jake said. Such a choice would also minimize the effect of any errors in the computer, errors in velocity, drift angle, altitude, etc.

'That would be the ideal,' Haldane agreed, 'but it wouldn't be smart to get all our airplanes shot down trying for the perfect attack. We're going to have to pick an attack that maximizes our chances of hitting yet gives us a half-decent chance of getting to the drop point. Let's look again at the weapons envelopes we'll have to penetrate.'

Jake was briefing the skipper on the progress of the planning efforts under way in the air wing offices. He had been attending these meetings for several days. Now he spread out several graphs he had constructed and explained them to his boss, Lieutenant Colonel Haldane.

As the attackers approached a Soviet task force, the first weapons that they would face would be SA-N-3 Goblet missiles, which could engage them up to twenty miles away at altitudes between 150 and 80,000 feet. These Mach 2.5 missiles would probably be fired in pairs, the second one following the first by a few seconds. Then the launcher would be reloaded and another pair fired – each launcher had the capacity to shoot thirty-six missiles. The number of launchers present would depend on the makeup of the task group, but for planning purposes figure there were ten. That's a possible 360 missiles in the air.

The next threat would be encountered at a range of nine or ten miles, when the attackers penetrated the envelope of the Mach 3.5 SA-N-1 Goa missiles. The weak point in the Goa system was the fire control director, which could engage only one target at a time. Yet since the missiles were carried on twin launchers, presumably two would be fired at the target, then a second target could be acquired while the launcher was reloaded. The magazine capacity for each launcher was sixteen missiles. Unfortunately the Soviets placed these weapons on destroyers as well as Kynda and Kresta cruisers, so one could expect a lot of launchers. Plan for twenty and we have another possible 320 missiles to evade.

If our harried attack crews were still alive seven miles from the target, they would enter the envelope of the Mach 2+ SA-N-4. This weapon was also fired from twin launchers, each with a magazine capacity of twenty missiles. Figure a task group with twenty launchers and we have a possible 400 missiles of this type.

Finally, after a weapons release, the attacker could expect surviving ships to fire a cloud of SA-N-5 Grail heat-seeking missiles, the naval version of the Soviet Army's Strela. Grail carried a one-kilogram warhead over a slant range of only 4.4 kilometers and needed a good hot tailpipe signature to guide, but just one up your tailpipe would ruin your day. Within the Grail envelope the attacker could expect to see dozens in the air.

Yet missiles were only half the story. There would also be flak, an extraordinary amount of it. Soviet ships bristled with guns. The larger guns would fire first, as soon as the attacking force came in range. As the distance between the attackers and the defenders closed, the smaller calibers would open fire.

The smaller the gun, the faster the rate of fire, so as the range closed, the sheer volume of high explosive in the air would increase exponentially. In close, that is within a mile and a quarter, the attacker would fly into range of six-barreled 30-mm Gatling guns, each capable of firing at a sustained rate of a thousand rounds per minute or squirting bursts of up to three times that volume.

'Since I started putting this data together,' Jake told the colonel, 'I've become a big fan of attack submarines.'

'Why don't you say what you really think?'

'Yes, sir. Attacking a Soviet task group with free-fall bombs will be a spectacular way to commit suicide.'

'If the balloon goes up, we'll go when we're told to go, suicide or not.'

'Yessir.'

'So we had better have a realistic plan, just in case.'

'The air wing is planning Alpha strikes. Two strikes, Blue and Gold, half the planes on each one.' An Alpha strike was a maximum effort, with fighters escorting the attackers and the entire gaggle diving the target in close order. The ideal was to get all the bombs on target and everyone exiting the area within sixty seconds.

'Okay,' Colonel Haldane said.

'That will only work on a daytime, good weather launch,' Jake continued. 'In my opinion, skipper, we can figure on losing half our planes on each strike.'

Haldane didn't say anything.

'At night or in bad weather, they'll just send the A-6s. We're the only planes with the capability.'

8

Steam catapults make modern aircraft carriers possible. Invented by the British during World War II, catapults freed designers from the necessity of building naval aircraft that could rise from the deck under their own power after a run of only three hundred feet. So wings could shrink and be swept as the physics of high speed aerodynamics required, jet engines that were most efficient at high speeds could be installed, and airframes could be designed that would go supersonic or lift tremendous quantities of fuel and weapons. A luxury for most of the carrier planes of World War II, the catapult now was an absolute requirement.

The only part of the catapult that can be seen on the flight deck is the shuttle to which aircraft are attached. This shuttle sticks up from a slot in the deck that runs the length of the catapult. The catapult itself lies under the slot and consists of two tubes eighteen inches in diameter arranged side by side like the barrels of a double-barreled shotgun. Inside each tube – or barrel – is a piston. There is a gap at the top of each barrel through which a steel lattice mates the two pistons together, and to which the shuttle on deck attaches.

The pistons are hauled aft mechanically into battery by a little cart called a 'grab.' Once the pistons are in battery, the aircraft is attached to the shuttle, either by a linkage on the nose gear of the aircraft in the case of the A-6 and A-7, or by a bridle made of steel cable in the case of the F-4 and RA-5. Then the slack in the bridle or nose-tow linkage is taken out by pushing the pistons forward hydraulically – this movement is called 'taking tension.'

Once the catapult is tensioned and the aircraft is at full power with its wheel brakes off, the firing circuit is enabled when the operator pushes the 'final ready' button.

Firing the catapult is then accomplished by opening the launch valves, one behind each tube, simultaneously, which allows superheated steam to enter the barrels behind the pistons.

The amount of acceleration given to each aircraft must be varied depending on the type of aircraft being launched, its weight, the amount of wind over the deck, and the outside air temperature. This is accomplished by one of two methods. Either the steam pressure is kept constant and the speed of opening of the launch valves is varied, or the launch valves are always opened at the same rate and the pressure of the steam in the accumulators is varied. Aboard *Columbia*, the steam pressure was varied and the launch valves were opened at a constant rate.

Although the launch valves open quickly, they don't open instantaneously. Consequently steam pressure rising on the back of the pistons must be resisted until it has built up sufficient pressure to move the pistons forward faster than the aircraft could accelerate on its own. This resistance is provided by a shear bolt installed in the nose gear of the aircraft to be launched, to which a steel hold-back bar is attached. One end of the bar fits into a slot in the deck. The bolt used in the A-6 was designed to break cleanly in half under a load of 48,000 pounds, only then allowing the pistons in the catapult, and the aircraft, to begin forward motion.

The superheated steam expanding behind the pistons drove them the length of the 258-foot catapults of the *Columbia* in about 2.5 seconds. Now up to flying speed, the aircraft left the deck behind and ran out into the air sixty feet above the ocean, where it then had to be rotated to the proper angle of attack to fly – in the A-6, about eight degrees nose-up.

Meanwhile, the pistons, at terminal velocity and quickly running out of barrels, had to be stopped. This was accomplished by means of water brakes, tubes welded onto the end of each of the catapult barrels and filled with water. The pistons each carried a tapered spear in front of them, and as the pistons reached the water brakes the spears penetrated the open ends, forcing water out around the spears. Water is incompressible, yet as the spears were inserted the escape openings for the water got smaller and smaller. Consequently the deeper the spears penetrated the higher the resistance to further entry. The brakes were so efficient that the pistons were brought to a complete stop after a full-power shot in only nine feet of travel.

The sexual symbolism of the tapered spears and the water-filled brakes always impressed aviators – they were young, lonely and horny – but the sound a cat made slamming into the brakes was visceral. The stupendous thud rattled compartments within a hundred feet of the brakes and could be felt throughout the ship.

Tonight as he sat in the cockpit of an A-6 tanker waiting for the cat crew to retract the shuttle, Jake Grafton ran through all the things that could go wrong with the cat.

The launching officer, Jumping Jack Bean, was wandering around near the hole in the deck that contained the valves and gauges that allowed him to drag steam from the ship's boilers to the catapult accumulators. The enlisted man who always sat on the edge of the hole wearing a sound-powered telephone headset that enabled him to talk to the men in the catapult machinery spaces was already in his place, staring aft at the two planes on the cats. The luminescent patches on his helmet and flight deck jersey were readily visible in the dim red glow of the lights from the ship's island superstructure, almost a hundred yards aft.

If anything goes wrong with the machinery below-decks, Jake Grafton knew, the probable result would be less end speed for the plane being launched. A perfect shot gave the launching aircraft a mere fifteen knots above stall speed. A couple knots less and the pilot would never notice. Five off, the plane would be sluggish. Ten off, a ham-handed pilot could stall it inadvertently. Fifteen or more off, the plane was doomed.

Bad, or 'cold,' cat shots were rare, thank God. The catapult was very reliable, more so than the aircraft that rode it. They could have an engine flame out under the intense acceleration, dump a gyro, lose a generator, spring a hydraulic or fuel leak . . . or the pilot could just become disoriented during the sudden, intense transition from sitting stationary on deck to instrument flight fifteen knots above a stall, at night. The blackness out there beyond the bow was total, a void so vast and bleak that one wanted to avert his eyes. Look at something else. Think about something else.

The hell of it was that there was nothing else to look at – nothing else to think about. Tonight Jake was flying a tanker, which was going to be flung off the pointy end of the boat in just a few minutes right into that black void, climb to 5,000 feet and tank a couple Phantoms, climb up to 20,000 and circle the ship for an hour and a half, then come back and trap. That was it, the whole damn mission. Go around and around the ship. Orbit. At max conserve airspeed. On autopilot. The challenge would be staying awake.

No, the challenge was this goddamn night cat shot. The worst part of the whole flight was right at the start – the blindfolded ride on the rabid pig . . .

The cat crewmen were now taking the rubber seal out of the catapult slot. Steam wisped skyward from the open slot, steam leaking from some fitting somewhere in the cat. They kept the slot seal in between launches, Jake knew, to help maintain the temperature of those eighteen-inch tubes.

The handler had parked the tanker here on the cat, probably so that the miserable peckerhead pilot would have to sit in the cockpit watching the steam wisp up from the cat against the backdrop of the black void while he thought about dying young.

And his life wasn't going so good just now. First Callie's jerk father, then Tiny Dick Donovan, the in-flight engagement, that near-midair . . .

Maybe God was trying to tell him something.

Or maybe those Phantoms this morning hadn't been there at all.

What if he had just imagined them? Of course the planes passed each other quickly, but there were at least two Phantoms and four A-6s, two guys in each plane. A total of twelve men, and *he* was the *only* one who had seen the varmint.

Really doesn't make sense.

Does it?

'What are you staring at through that windshield?' Flap Le Beau asked.

'There's a naked woman out there. If you look real careful you can see her nipples.'

'You look like you're mentally composing your will. That isn't good leadership. You are supposed to be impressing me with *your* self-confidence, calming *my* fears. The stick's on your side, remember?'

'What if those F-4s weren't really there this morning? What if I just imagined it?'

'Are you still on that? You saw 'em. They were there.'

'How come no one else is in a sweat?'

'What do you want me to do, fill my drawers? Slit my wrists? Fate fired a bullet and it missed.'

'You could have the common courtesy to look nervous, sweat it a little.'

'You're making me nervous.'

'That'll be the day,' Jake Grafton replied disgustedly.

'Okay, I'm sweating. It's dripping out of my armpits. Every jerk pilot I ever met has tried to kill me. I'm waiting for you to give it a whirl.'

'How come you got into aviation anyway?'

'Jungle rot. Pretty bad case. They tell me I'm now a paragraph and photo in a medical textbook. Little did I know when I signed up for this glamorous flying life how much jungle I still had to visit.'

The brown-shirt plane captain standing beside the aircraft waved his wands to get Jake's attention, then signaled for a start.

Time to do it.

'It could have been worse,' Flap told Jake as he started the left engine. 'I could have made medical history with a spectacular social disease. Wouldn't that have been a trip? For a hundred years every guy going overseas would have had to watch a movie featuring my diseased, ulcerated pecker.'

Six minutes later Jake rogered the weight board and eased the plane forward into the shuttle. He felt the nose-tow bar drop into the shuttle slot and came off the brakes and added power at the yellow-shirt's signal.

The engines began winding up. Another small jolt as the hydraulic arm shoved the cat pistons into tension, taking all the slack out of the hold-back bar. Now just the shear-bolt was holding them back.

Full power, wipe out the controls, check the gauges, cat grip up . . . 'You ready?' he asked Flap.

'I'm really really ready.'

He could feel the vibration as the engines sucked air and blasted it out the exhausts against the jet black deflector, feel rather than hear the ear-splitting roar. He swept his eyes across the annunciator panel – all warning lights out. The exterior light master switch was on the end of the cat grip, right beside his left thumb. He flicked it on.

The cat officer took a last look at the island, looked up the cat at the void, then swept his yellow wand down in a fencer's lunge until he touched the deck, then he came up to a point.

The catapult fired. The G's slammed him back . . . and both fire warning lights illuminated.

They were big red lights, one on each side of the bomb-sight on the top of the instrument panel. Labeled L FIRE and R FIRE, both lights shone into his eyes like spotlights as the acceleration pressed him deeper into the seat back.

Oh, God, he thought, trying to take it in as the adrenaline whacked him in the heart.

His eyes went to the engine instruments, white tapes arranged vertically in front of his left knee. They looked—

The acceleration stopped and the plane was off the cat, the nose coming up. A glance at the airspeed – not decaying. Angle-of-attack gauge agreed. He grabbed the stick and slapped the gear handle up. Wings level, check the nose . . .

His left hand rose automatically toward the emergency jettison button above the gear handle. If he pushed it and held it down for one second the five drop tanks, each containing two thousand pounds of fuel, would be jettisoned from the aircraft. She would instantly be five tons lighter and could then fly on one engine. He was sorely tempted but he didn't push it. His hands came back to the throttles.

Which engine was it?

Both lights were screaming at him!

Which fucking engine?

Engine tapes still okay . . . airspeed okay . . . eight degrees nose up. He was squinting against the glare of the red fire lights. He had let the left wing sag so he picked it up. Climbing through two hundred feet, 160 knots . . .

Both fire lights – the book said to pull the affected engine to idle, but he had *both* lights on!

Fire!

Was he on fire? If he was it was time to eject. Jettison this fucking airplane. Swim for it. He looked in the mirrors. Black. Nothing to see.

He became aware that Flap was on the radio. '. . . both fire lights . . . declaring an emergency . . . Boss, can you see any fire?'

The reply was clear in his ears. 'Off the bow, you look fine. You say you have both fire lights on?'

Jake cut in on Flap. 'Both of them. We'd like a dump charley.'

'Your signal dump. It'll be about eight more minutes until we have a ready deck. We'll call you.'

'Roger.'

His heart was slowing. She didn't seem to be on fire. Thank you, thank you, thank you.

Accelerating through 185 knots, he raised the flaps and slats, then toggled the switches for the wing and main dump valves. They were carrying 26,000 pounds of fuel and the max he could take aboard the ship was 6,000. He needed to dump ten tons of fuel into the atmosphere.

And as he reached for the switch that would isolate a portion of the combined hydraulic system, he looked at the hydraulic gauges. For the first time. He had forgotten to look at the hydraulic gauges before. Now, squinting against the glare of the fire lights, he saw the needle on the right combined system pump flickering.

Uh-oh. A fire could be melting hydraulic lines. Hydraulic fluid itself was nonflammable, but the lines could melt.

'We have hydraulic problems,' he told Flap.

'How come those fire lights are so bright?' Flap asked. 'I can barely see the gauges.'

'Dunno.' Jake was too busy to cuss out that comfortable, anonymous bureaucrat who had specified the wattage of the bulbs in the fire warning lights. They were certainly impossible to miss. You are about to die, they screamed.

'Maybe you better stop dumping the main tank.'

Flap was right. Jake secured the main tank dump. Still 8,500 pounds there.

By now he had the plane at 2,500 feet headed downwind, on the reciprocal of the launch bearing, steady at 250 knots. When he pulled the power back the fire lights stayed on.

Did they have a fire? Modern jet aircraft utilized every cubic inch of space inside the fuselage for fuel, engines, pumps, switches, hydraulic lines, electronic gear, wires, etc., and the spars and stringers that held the whole thing together. A fire anywhere within the plane had to be burning something critical. And if it got to the tanks . . . well, the explosion would be spectacular.

Jake again checked the rearview mirrors for a glow. Nothing.

'Get out the checklist,' he told Flap as he turned off the cabin pressurization system. Unfortunately the ducts carrying bleed air from the engines had failed on a half-dozen occasions in the past: the resulting fires had cost the Navy men and airplanes. Jake had no desire to add his name to that list. If there was a leak downstream of the valve that controlled cabin pressurization, closing the valve should isolate it.

'Got it right here. You ready?'

'Yeah.'

Flap read the comments and recommended procedure over the ICS. One of the comments read, If a fire warning light stays illuminated, secure the affected engine.

He only had two engines and both fire lights were lit. So much for that advice.

The right combined hydraulic system gauge read zero. The needle on the left one was sagging, twitching. And a hydraulic leak was a secondary indication of fire! But did he have one?

'Marine airplanes are shit,' he groused to Flap, who shot back:

'Yeah, the Navy gives us all the crap they don't want.'

Flap got busy on the radio and reported the hydraulic failure. Soon he was talking to Approach. The controller put them in an orbit ten miles aft of the ship. Jake slowed to 220 knots and checked the fuel quantity remaining in the wings. Still a few thousand. In the glow of the left wing-tip light he could just make out the stream from the dump pipe gushing away into the slipstream.

Well, he had it under control. Other than the nuisance glare of the fire lights, everything would be fairly normal. He would blow the gear down, lower the flaps electrically and just motor down the glide slope. He could hack it.

He released the left side of his oxygen mask. He sniffed carefully, then swabbed the sweat from his face. His heart rate was pretty much back to normal and the adrenaline was wearing off. There was no fire – he was fairly confident of that.

Wing fuel read zero. OK. He would leave the dump open a moment or two longer to purge the tank, then secure it. He reached down and punched the button to make the needle on the fuel gauge register main tank fuel. And stared, unable to believe his eyes. Only 3,500 pounds.

Holy . . . !

Yes, the main dump switch was off. But the valve never closed! All the fuel in the main tank had dumped, right down to the top of the standpipe, which prevented the last 3,600 pounds from going overboard. And he had already burned a hundred pounds of that 3,600.

He slapped on the mask and spoke to the controller. 'Uh, Approach, War Ace Five Two One has another problem out here. The main dump valve didn't close. We're down to Three Point Five. How soon can you give us a charley?'

'Standby, War Ace.'

Flap leaned across the center consol and stared at the offending fuel gauge for several seconds, then straightened up. He didn't say anything.

'How far is it to Hickam Field?' Jake asked.

Flap consulted the notes on his kneeboard. 'About a hundred fifty miles.'

'We're almost to bingo!' Jake exclaimed, his horror evident in his voice. 'We've got to have a tanker *right now!*'

Flap Le Beau keyed the radio: 'Approach, War Ace Five Two One, our state is Three Point Five. We're eight hundred pounds above bingo. Apparently the fuselage dump valve stuck open. Request a tanker ASAP.'

'Negative, War Ace. We'll take you aboard in about eight or ten more minutes.'

A sense of foreboding seized Jake Grafton. They were in deep and serious trouble. 'How's the spare tanker?' he asked.

'We're still trying to launch it,' was the reply. 'We should have it off in a few minutes.'

Jake couldn't help himself. 'Is there some problem with the spare?' He felt like a condemned man asking if he could have one more cigarette.

'Yes.' One word.

'They're digging us a hole,' Flap told Jake.

The pilot glumly examined the instruments. What else can go wrong? Bingo was the fuel state that required he depart for the shore divert field on a max range profile flight. Bingo was a low fuel emergency. And he was eight hundred pounds above that state. He had to leave for the shore field before his fuel reached that level or he would flame out before he got there.

Without additional fuel which only a tanker could provide, Jake had to trap or eject. Well, he still had some time. Right now he was burning four thousand pounds of fuel per hour. When he blew the gear down he would be unable to raise them again. And his fuel consumption would immediately jump to six thousand pounds per hour in level flight. More in a climb. At this moment he had three thousand four hundred.

Why had he switched the fuel gauge from the fuselage tank to the wings? So he could monitor dumping. Of course, there was a totalizer there under the needle, but it was usually unreliable. Over the years he had developed a habit of ignoring it. What a fool he was! The lash stung and he laid it on hard.

He could stand the glare of the fire warning lights no longer. He took the L-shaped flashlight hanging on the webbing of his survival vest and pounded the offending lights until they shattered. The cockpit was darker, a lot darker, and that calmed him.

At least the weather was good tonight. Ceiling was high, maybe ten thousand feet, and the visibility underneath was ten miles or so. He could see the lights of the carrier eight miles away, just a little collection of red and white lights in the dark universe, and here and there, the little globs of light that were her escorts. At least he could fly alongside a destroyer or frigate when he had to eject. Then he and Flap wouldn't have to depend on the rescue helicopter to find them.

That was something. A straw to grasp.

Exasperated, his thoughts turned to Callie. It was four-thirty in the morning in Chicago; she was probably in bed asleep.

Thirty-one hundred pounds on the fuel gauge. A-6s had been known to flame out with as much as seven hundred pounds showing on the gauge. He could have as little as twenty-four hundred.

He got a pen from the sleeve pocket of his flight suit and did some figuring on the top card on his kneeboard, which as usual he wore strapped to his right thigh. The numbers told him he was burning sixty-seven pounds of fuel a minute, about ten gallons. Every six seconds a gallon of gas went into the engines. Twenty-four hundred divided by sixty seven – hell, he could dangle here twisting slowly in the wind for thirty-five more minutes. What's the problem? What's the sweat? Well, when he lowered the gear the power requirements would go up. He might bolter. The deck could stay fouled. The weather could go to hell. Something else could go wrong with the plane – like the gear might not come down or the hook might stay up. Or . . . He felt frustrated and outraged. The plane had betrayed him!

The second hand on the clock caught his eye. It swept around and around and around.

'Did I ever tell you about the time I stole a police car?' Flap asked.

'No, and I don't need to hear it now.'

'Stole a cruiser, with a bubble-gum machine on top, siren, police radio, even a shotgun on a rack in the front, the whole deal. Fellow in Jersey wanted it for a farm truck. He wanted to take the trunk lid off and weld up a pickup bed. Was gonna use it to haul manure. He was a retired Mafia soldier. Now I didn't know Mafia guys ever retired, but this one apparently had. He was out of the rackets and had him a little farm in north Jersey. A brother I knew told me there was five hundred bucks in it for me if I could come up with a police car. Luckily I knew another bro who was screwing a cop's daughter pretty regular, so I got to thinking. Five hundred bucks was real money to me back then. Anyway . . .'

Jake could hear pilots in other planes checking into marshal. It all sounded pretty normal. Well, the weather was good, no one was shooting . . .

'Ninety-nine planes in marshal, ninety-nine planes in marshal, this is Approach.' Ninety-nine meant 'all.' 'Your signal, max conserve. Add ten minutes to your commence times. Add ten minutes to push times.'

Now what?

Should he ask? He waited a minute, waited while another sixty-seven pounds of fuel went into the engines. Then he said, 'Approach, War Ace Five Two One. Does that ten minutes apply to me too?'

'Affirm.'

'Uh, what's the problem?'

Silence. Then, 'The nose gear collapsed on a Phantom on Cat Three. The deck is foul.' Cat Three was on the waist, in the landing area.

'War Ace Five Two One has Two Point Eight. Any word on Texaco?' Texaco was the tanker.

'We're working on it, War Ace.'

Flap left his story unfinished. Jake stared at the offending fuel gauge. Should he just say Bingo and go?

The ship was headed northwest, into the prevailing wind. Hickam was northeast. As the minutes passed they were getting no closer to Hickam, but on the other hand, they were getting no farther away. Without more fuel, what did it matter?

The minutes ticked by. Five, six, seven . . .

The needle on the fuel gauge passed twenty-four hundred pounds and kept descending. One pass – that was it. They would get one lousy pass at the deck. If he boltered for any reason, he and Flap were going to have to swim for it.

The crew fidgeted.

The hell of it was that they were betting everything on the emergency gear extension system. Compressed nitrogen would be used to blow the gear down since hydraulic fluid was no longer available to do the job. If any one of the three wheels failed to lock down, they could not trap aboard the ship. They would have to eject.

Betting your ass on any one system in an airplane with a variety of other problems is not the recommended path to a long and happy life.

Jake Grafton sat monitoring the instruments and thinking about the black ocean beneath him. At least the water was warm. With warm water came sharks. He hated sharks, feared them unreasonably. Sharks were his phobia. If he went into the water he would have to fight back the panic, have to keep functioning somehow.

He had never told anyone about the sharks. The thought of being down there with them made him nauseated. And at night, when he couldn't see. Of course he would be bleeding somewhere. Nobody ever ejected without getting cut somehow. Blood in the water, trying to keep from drowning . . .

'War Ace Five Two One, your signal charley.'

'Five Two One,' Jake acknowledged bitterly, then bit his lip. He should have told the brass to go to hell and bingoed.

First came ten degrees of flaps, which had to be lowered electrically. Linked to the flaps were the slats on the leading edge of the wing; they also came out. The flaps and slats changed the shape of the wings and allowed them to develop lift at lower airspeeds. They also added drag, slowing the plane.

Next came the hook. Jake merely pulled the handle and made sure the transition light disappeared.

The Intruder was slowing . . . 170 . . . 160 . . . 150 . . . 'Here goes nothing,' he told Flap as he lowered the gear handle to the gear down position, then rotated the knob on the end ninety degrees and pulled it out. The up-up-up indications on the panel barber-poled.

He waited. He could feel the drag increasing on the plane, could see his airspeed decreasing, and added power. The fuel-flow tapes surged upward.

C'mon, baby. Give me three down indications. Please!

The nose gear locked down first. Two seconds later the mains locked down. Seventeen hundred pounds of fuel left in the main bag.

'They're down,' he announced to Flap and God and whoever else was listening.

Approach controller was giving him a steer.

'Hell!' Flap exclaimed disgustedly between calls from the controller, 'it wasn't even close. We don't even have a low fuel light.' The low fuel warning light would come on at about 1,360 pounds.

'We aren't down yet,' Jake pointed out.

'Oh ye of little faith, take note. We're almost down.'

Jake concentrated on flying the plane, staying on speed, smoothly intercepting the glide path. He was carrying less power than normal since the speed brakes were inoperative after the hydraulic failure, and while this saved a few gallons of gasoline, it caused its own problems. If he got high, retarding the throttles would be less effective than usual – the plane would tend to float.

He saw the ball two miles out. At a mile he called, 'Five Two One, Intruder ball, One Point Four.'

'Roger ball. Paddles has you. Looking good . . . fly the ball!'

The meatball began to rise above the datums and he pulled power aggressively while watching that angle-of-attack needle.

Paddles was talking to him. 'Power back on . . . too much, off a little . . . No, little more . . . lineup . . .'

Any second would come the burble, the swirl of air disturbed by the ship's island. He anticipated it just a smidgen on the power and didn't have to slam on too much, then he was quick to get it off.

Coming across the ramp the airspeed decayed a tad and the ball began to sink.

'Power!' shouted the LSO.

Slam! The wheels hit. Throttles to the stops . . . and the welcome, tremendous jerk as the hook snagged a wire.

'Two wire, I think,' Flap told him.

Jake didn't care. A huge sigh of relief flooded through him.

Here came the yellow-shirts. He raised the flaps and slats electrically while they chocked the plane, then cut the engines.

They were back.

Walking across the flight deck with their helmet bags in their hands, with the warm sea wind on their wet hair, the firm steel deck beneath their flight boots, Flap repeated, 'It wasn't even close.'

No, Jake Grafton acknowledged to himself, it wasn't. Not tonight. But a man can't have luck all the time, and someday when he reached into that tiny little bag where he kept his luck, the bag would be empty. A hold-back bolt would break at the wrong time, a taxiing plane would skid into another, the airborne tanker would go sour, the weather would be bad . . . some combination of evil things would conspire against the man aloft and push him over the edge. Jake Grafton, veteran of more than 340 cat shots and arrested landings, knew that it could happen to him. He knew that as well as he knew his name.

The brass had taken the net from under the tightrope when they didn't let him bingo, and he was infuriated and disgusted with himself for letting them do it.

I think, Jake wrote to Callie that night, *that a man's fate is not in his control. We are under the illusion that we can control our destinies, that the choices we make do make a difference, but they don't. Chance rules our lives Chance, fate, fortune – whatever you wish to call it – sets the hook and pulls the string and we quiver and flail, jerk and fight. Maybe pray.*

I don't think praying helps very much. I do it anyway, just in case. I ask Him to be with me when I fall.

9

There are few things in life more satisfying than to be accepted as an equal in a fraternity of fighting men. Jake Grafton was so accepted now, and this morning when he entered the ready room he was greeted by name by the men there, who asked him about his adventures of the previous evening and listened carefully to his comments. They laughed, consoled him, and joked about the predicament he had found himself in last night. Several refused to believe, they said, that the main dump valve had failed: he had forgotten to secure it and was now trying to cover his sin by appealing to their naivete. All this was in good fun and was cheerfully accepted as such by Jake Grafton. He belonged. He was a full member of this aristocracy of merit, with impeccable credentials. His mood improved with each passing minute and soon he was his usual self.

He and his Marine colleagues inspected the board that recorded the pilots' landing grades. Jake's grades for his qualification landings were not displayed there, so like most of them, he had only two landings so far this cruise, an OK 3-wire and a fair 2-wire.

The bombing poster was more complicated, displaying the CEP of each crew, and to settle ties, the number of bull's-eyes. Jake ranked fourth in the squadron here. Today he was scheduled to go to the target with twelve five-hundred pounders, so perhaps he could better his standing.

He had a secret ambition to be the best pilot in the squadron in landings and bombing and everything else, but he shared that ambition with everyone so it wasn't much of a secret. Still, it wasn't a thing that you talked about. You tried your very best at everything you did, glanced at the rankings, fiercely resolved to do better, and went on about your business. The rankings told you who was more skilled – 'more worthy' was the phrase used by the Real McCoy a day or two before – than you were.

The LSO regarded intrasquadron competition with good-natured contempt. 'Games for children,' he grumped. But Jake noticed now that McCoy's name was in the top half of the rankings on both boards.

This morning there was mail, the first in six days. A cargo plane brought it out from Hickam Field, trapped aboard, then left with full mail sacks from the ship's post office. Two hours later the mail was distributed throughout the ship.

Jake got three letters from Callie, one from his folks, and something from the commanding officer of Attack Squadron 128 in an official, unstamped envelope. He shuffled Tiny Dick Donovan's missive – probably some piece of official foolscap from a yeoman third in the Admin Office – to the bottom of the pile. Callie's letters came first.

She was taking classes at the University of Chicago, working on her master's degree. Her brother and her parents were fine. The weather was hot and muggy. She missed him.

I think that it is important for you to decide what you wish to do with your life. This is a decision that every man must make for himself, and every woman. To make this decision because you hope to please another is to make it for the wrong reason. We each owe duties to our families, when we acquire them, but we also owe a duty to ourselves to make our lives count for something. To love another person is not enough.

I have thought a great deal about this these last few weeks. Like every woman, I want to love. I feel as if I have this great gift to give – myself. I want to be a wife and mother. Oh, how I could love some man!

And I want the man I love to love me. To have a man who would return the love I have to give is my great ambition.

I have dated boys, known boys of all ages, and I do not want to marry one.

I want to marry a man. I want a man who believes in what he is doing, who goes out the door every day to make a contribution – in business, in academia, in government, somewhere. I want a man who will love not just me, but life itself. I want a man who will stand up to the gales of life, who won't bend with every squall, who will remain true to himself and those who believe in him, a man who can be counted on day after day, year after year.

An hour later, after he had reread Callie's letter three times and lingered over the one from his parents, he opened the official letter. In it he found a copy of his last fitness report, bearing Donovan's signature. In the text Donovan wrote:

Lieutenant Grafton is one of the most gifted aviators I have ever met in my years in the naval service. In every facet of flying, he is the consummate professional. As a naval officer, Lieutenant Grafton shows extraordinary promise, yet he has not made the commitment to give of himself as he must if he is to fulfill that promise.

There was more, a lot more, most of it the usual bullshit required by custom and instruction, such as a comment upon his support of the Navy's equal opportunity goals and programs. Jake merely skimmed this treacle, then returned to the meat: '. . . has not yet made the commitment to give of himself as he must if he is to fulfill that promise.'

A pat on the back immediately followed by a kick in the pants. His first reaction was anger, which quickly turned to cold fury. He stalked from the ready room and went to his stateroom, where he opened his desk and seized pen and paper. He began a letter to Commander Donovan. He would write a bullet that would skewer the sun of a bitch right through the heart.

What kind of half-assed crack was that? Not committed to being a good naval officer? Who the hell did that jerk Donovan think he was talking about anyway?

Even before he completed his first sentence, the anger began leaking from him. Donovan had said nothing about the Sea-Tac adventure, didn't even mention that the promising Lieutenant Grafton had punched out a windy blowhard and thrown him ass over tea kettle through a plate glass window, then spent a weekend in jail. Perhaps his comments dealt strictly with the performance of Jake's duties at the squadron. No, he *must* have meant that comment to cover the Sea-Tac debacle in addition to everything else. Worse, Donovan was right – a more committed, thinking officer would not have done it. A wiser man . . . well, he wouldn't have either.

Jake threw down the pen and rubbed his face in frustration.

Were Callie and Dick Donovan talking about the same thing?

'Man, you should have seen ol' Jake last night,' Flap Le Beau told his fellow Marines. 'Both the you're-gonna-die lights pop on bright as Christmas goin' down the cat, and this guy handled it like he was in a simulator. Cool as ice. Just sat there doin' his thing. Me – I was shakin' like a dog shittin' razor blades. I ain't been so scared since the teacher caught me with my hand up Susie Bulow's skirt back in the sixth grade.'

There were eight of them, four crews, and they had just finished a briefing for another flight to the Kahoolawe target. This time they were carrying real ordnance, twelve five-hundred-pound bombs on each plane. After they had reviewed how the fuses and arming wires should look on the bomb racks, the crews stood and stretched. That was when Flap took it on himself to praise his pilot to the heavens.

Jake was embarrassed. He had been frightened last night, truly scared, and Flap's ready room bull puckey struck a sour note. Still, Jake kept his mouth shut. This was neither the time nor place to brace Flap about his mouth.

He got out of his chair and went over in the corner to check his mailbox. Nothing. He gazed at the posters on the wall as if interested, trying to shut out Flap, who was expanding upon his theme: Jake Grafton was one cool dude.

One of the pilots, Rory Smith, came over and dug a sheet of official trash out of his mailbox, something he was supposed to read and initial. 'Flap gets on your nerves, does he?' he asked, his voice so soft it was barely audible. He scribbled his initials in the proper place and shoved the paper into someone else's box.

'Yeah.'

'Don't sweat it. To hear him tell it, every guy he flies with is the best who ever stroked a throttle. He was saying that in the ready room about his last stick five minutes before he was down in the skipper's stateroom complaining that the guy was dangerous. You just have to take him with a grain of salt.'

Jake grinned at Rory.

'Everybody else does,' the Marine said, then wandered off toward the desk where the maintenance logs on each aircraft were kept. Jake followed him.

Smith helped himself to the book for 511, the plane Jake had flown into an in-flight engagement.

'Gonna fly it today, huh?' Jake said.

'Yeah,' Smith said. 'The gunny says it's fixed. We'll see.'

'It'll probably go down on deck,' Jake pointed out. 'Down' in this context meant a maintenance problem that precluded flight. 'Since I bent it,' he continued, 'I'll fly it if you want to trade planes.'

'Well, I'm one of the maintenance check pilots and they gave it to me.'

'Sure.'

Meanwhile Flap had progressed to his favorite subject, women. Jake looked up from the maintenance book on his plane when Flap roared, 'Oh, my *God*, she was *ugly!*'

'*How* ugly?' three or four of his listeners wailed in unison.

'She was *so* ugly that paint peeled off the walls when she walked into a room.'

'*How* ugly?'

'So ugly that strong men fainted, children screamed, and horses ran away.'

'*How* ugly?' This refrain had become a chorus. Even Rory Smith joined in from the back of the room.

'Women tore their hair, the sky got black, and the earth trembled.'

'*That's* not ugly.'

'I'm telling you guys, she was *so* dingdong ugly that mirrors cracked, dogs went berserk, fire mains ruptured and one man who had smiled at her at night dropped stone cold dead when he saw her in the daylight. That, my friends, is the gospel truth.'

It was a typical afternoon in the tropics – scattered puffy clouds drifting on the balmy trade winds, sun shining through the gaps. Hawaii was going to be wonderful. Two more days, then Pearl Harbor! Oh boy.

Jake inspected the Mark 82 five-hundred-pounders carefully. He hadn't seen deadly green sausages like this since the night he was shot down, seven months ago. Talk about a bad trip!

Well, the war was over, this was a peacetime cruise . . . He could probably spend another twenty years in the Navy and would never again have to drop one of these things for real. World War III? Get serious.

Up into the cockpit, into the comfortable seat, the familiar instruments arranged around him just so. The truth was he knew this cockpit better than he knew anything else on earth. Just the thought of never getting back into one bothered him. How do you turn your back on six years of your life?

Flap settled into the seat beside him as the plane captain climbed the ladder on Jake's side and reached in to help with the Koch fittings.

He had lived all this before – it was like living a memory.

And somehow that was good.

Rory Smith preflighted his aircraft, 511, very carefully indeed. That four- or five-foot fall couldn't have done this thing any good. The main concern was the landing gear. If anything cracked . . . Well, the airframes guys hadn't found a single crack. They had scraped the paint from the parts, fluoroscoped them and pronounced them perfect. What can a pilot doe? Just fly it.

The radar, computer and inertial were seriously messed up. All the component boxes of those systems had been replaced, as had the radar dish and drive unit in the nose. The vertical display indicator – the VDI – and the radio were also new.

When Smith and his BN – Hank Davis – were strapped in, they turned on each piece of gear and checked it carefully. The inertial was slow getting an alignment, but it did align. Make a note for the debrief.

They were the last A-6 to taxi toward a cat, number two on the bow. The others were airborne and in a few minutes, Smith would join them at nine thousand feet. That altitude should be well above the tops of this cumulus, he thought, taking three seconds to scan the sky.

Roger the weight board, check the wing locks, flaps and slats down, stabilizer shifted, into the shuttle, off the brakes and power up. Check the controls.

'You ready?'

'Yep,' Hank Davis told him cheerfully.

Rory Smith saluted and placed his head back into the headrest. He watched the bow cat officer give his fencer's lunge into the wind as his arm came down to the deck. Out of the corner of his eye he saw the catapult deck edge operator lower both hands as he reached for the fire button.

In the space of a second the launching valves dropped open, 450 pounds of steam hit the back of the pistons, and the hold-back bolt broke. The G's slammed Smith back into his seat as War Ace Five One One leaped forward. And the VDI came sliding out of the center of the instrument panel.

Rory Smith reached for the black box with both hands, but too late. The front of it tilted down and came to rest in his lap. Jammed the stick back. All this in the first second and a half of the shot.

Desperately Smith heaved at the box against the G. He had to free the stick!

And then they were off the bow, the nose coming up. And up and up as he struggled to lift the fucking box!

With his right hand he reached under and tried to shove the stick forward. Like pushing against a building.

He felt the stall, felt the right wing go down. He was trying to lift the box with his left hand and push the stick forward with his right when Hank Davis ejected. The horizon was tilting and the nose was slewing right.

Oh, *damn!*

On the bridge of *Columbia* the captain saw the whole thing. The nose of the Intruder off of Cat Two rose and rose to almost thirty degrees nose up, then her right wing dropped precipitously. Passing thirty or forty degrees angle-of-bank he saw a man in an ejection seat come blasting out. The wing kept dropping past the vertical and the nose came right and the A-6 dove into the ocean. A mighty splash marked the spot.

Galvanized, the captain roared, 'Right full rudder, stop all engines.'

The officer of the deck immediately repeated the order and the helmsman echoed it.

The captain's eyes were on the ejection seat. The drogue streamed as the seat arched toward the sea. The seat was past the apogee when the captain saw a flash of white as the parachute began to deploy. He blossomed, but before the man on the end of the shrouds could complete a swing he hit the water. Splat.

This 95,000-ton ship was making twenty-five knots. The A-6 went in a little to the right of her course, and the survivor splashed a little right of that. All he could hope to do was swing the stern away. The stern with its thrashing screws.

There, the bow was starting to respond to the helm.

The rescue helicopter, the angel, was already coming into a hover over the survivor. His head was just visible bobbing in the water as the carrier swept by, still making at least twenty knots.

Missed him.

'War Ace Five Oh Five, Departure.'

'Go ahead, Departure.'

'Five Oh Five, your last playmate will not be joining you. Switch to Strike and proceed with your mission, over.'

'Roger that.' Major Sam Cooley gave the radio frequency change signal by hand to Jake on his left wing and the Real McCoy on his right. He waited until the formation came around to the on-course heading, then leveled his wings and added power for the climb. They were on top of the cumulus layer. Above them was sunny, deep blue open sky.

So Rory Smith didn't get that plane airborne, Jake thought. He should have accepted that offer to switch planes. It's a good day to fly.

'Rory Smith's dead.'

They heard the news in the ready room, after they landed.

'He never got out. When Hank Davis punched Rory was sitting there wrestling the VDI. Hank's okay. He said the VDI came out on the cat shot. Came clean out of the panel right into Rory's lap. Jammed the stick aft. They stalled and went in.'

'Aww . . . ,' Flap said.

When Jake found his voice he muttered, 'He must not have checked to see that it was screwed in there.'

'Huh?'

'Yeah,' he told Flap. 'You gotta tug on the thing to make sure the screws that hold it are properly screwed in. Doesn't matter except on a catapult shot. If the VDI isn't secured right on a cat shot, it can come back into your lap. The damn thing weighs seventy pounds.'

'I never knew that.'

'I thought *everybody* knew that.'

'*I* never knew that. I wonder if Smith did.'

Jake Grafton merely stared in horror at the BN. *He* was the one tasked to cover everything these Marines needed to know about shipboard operations. He had forgotten to mention checking the VDI before the shot. Flap didn't know. Maybe Rory didn't either. And now Rory Smith was *dead!*

He sagged into a nearby chair. He had forgotten to tell them about the VDI on the cat! What else had he forgotten to tell them? *What else?*

The television camera on the ship's island superstructure had caught the whole accident on videotape. The tape was playing now on the ready room television. Jake stared at the screen, mesmerized.

The shot looked normal, but the horizontal stabilizer – the stabilator – was really nose up. Too much? Hard to tell. There he went, off the bow, nose up rapidly, way too high, the stall and departure from controlled flight, a spin developing as the plane went in. One ejection. The whole thing happened very quickly. The A-6 was in the water twelve seconds after the catapult fired.

Just twelve seconds.

The show continued. The angel hovered, a swimmer leaped from about four feet into the water . . . lots of spray from the rotor wash . . .

Jake rose and walked out. In sick bay he asked the first corpsman he saw, 'Captain Hank Davis?'

'Second door on the left, sir.'

The skipper came out of Hank's room before Jake got to the door. He told Jake, 'He doesn't need any visitors just now. He swallowed a lot of seawater and he's pretty shook.'

'I need to ask him a question, sir.'

'What is it?'

Jake explained about the VDI, how the screws might not engage when the box was installed, how the pilot must check it. 'I need to know, Colonel, if Rory tugged on the VDI to check it before he got to the cat.'

The colonel said nothing. He listened to Jake, watched his eyes, and said nothing.

'I'll ask him,' Haldane said finally, then opened the door and passed through.

Minutes passed. Almost five. When Haldane reappeared, he closed the door firmly behind him and faced the pilot, who was leaning against the bulkhead on the other side of the passageway.

'He doesn't remember.'

'Did he know about the possibility of the VDI coming out?'

'No. He didn't.'

Jake turned and walked away without another word.

He was sitting in his stateroom at his desk when the Real McCoy came in. The only light was the ten-watt fluorescent tube above Jake's desk. McCoy seated himself on his bunk.

'Take a hike, will ya, Real? I need some time alone.'

McCoy thought about it for a few seconds. 'Sure,' he said, and left.

Summer in Virginia was his favorite time of year. Everything was growing, the deer were lazy and fat, the squirrels chattered in the trees. The sun there would be hot on your back, the sweat would dampen your shirt. You would feel good as you used your muscles, accomplished tangible work that stood as hard evidence of the effort that had been put into it. The folks up and down the road were solid, hard-working people, people to stand with in good times and bad. And he had given that up for this . . .

Sitting in his stateroom Jake Grafton could hear the creaks and groans of the ship, the noises made by the steel plates as she rode through the seaway. And man-made noises, lots of them, trapping and hammering, chipping, pinging, clicking, grinding . . . slamming as doors and hatches were opened and closed.

Responsibility – they give you a tiny little job and you fuck it up and someone dies. In twelve seconds. Twelve lousy seconds . . .

And he had tried hard. He had taken the time, made the effort to do it right. He had written point after point, gone through the CV NATOPS page by page, paragraph by paragraph. He had covered every facet of carrier operations that he knew about. And had forgotten one item, a scintilla of information that he had heard once, somewhere, about an improperly secured VDI that slid four inches out of the tray in which it sat when the plane went down the catapult. Probably there were messages about it, several years ago, but the Marines didn't take cat shots then and the info apparently went in one official grunt ear and out the other. Now, when they needed to know that tidbit, he had forgotten to tell them.

Luck is really a miserable bitch. Just when you desperately need her to behave she sticks the knife in and twists it, leering at you all the while.

Rory Smith was dead. No bringing him back. All the teeth gnashing, hair pulling, hand wringing and confessions in the world won't raise him from the Pacific and breathe life back into his shattered body. The cockpit of War Ace 511 was his coffin. He was in it now, down there on the sea floor. The sea will claim his body and the airplane molecule by molecule, until someday nothing remains. He will then be a part of this ocean, a part of the clouds and the trade winds and the restless blue water.

Jake opened his safe and got out a bottle of whiskey. He poured himself a drink, raised it to Rory Smith, and swallowed it down.

The liquor made him sleepy. He climbed into the top bunk.

This guilt trip was not good. Yet at least it gave him the proper perspective to view the flying, the ship, the Navy, and all those dead men. Morgan McPherson, the Boxman, Frank Allen, Rory Smith, all those guys. All good dead men. All good. All dead. All dead real damn good.

He was going to get out of the Navy, submit a letter of resignation.

Never again. I'm not going to stand in the ready room any more helplessly watching videotapes of crashes. I'm not going to any more memorial services. I'm not packing any more guys' personal possessions in steel footlockers and sending them off to the parents or widow with any more goddamn little notes telling them how sorry I am. I'm not going to keep lying to myself that I am a better pilot than they were and that is why they are dead and I'm not. I've done all that shit too much. The guys that still have the stomach for it can keep doing it until they are each and every one of them as dead as Rory Smith but I will not. I have had enough.

10

Jake and Flap flew a tanker hop the next afternoon, which was the last scheduled flying day before the ship entered Pearl Harbor. They were in the high orbit, flying the five-mile arc around the ship at 20,000 feet, when Flap said, 'I hear you are putting in a letter of resignation.'

Since it wasn't a question, Jake didn't reply. He had talked to the first-class yeoman in the air wing office this morning, and apparently the yeoman talked to the Marines.

'That right?' Flap demanded.

'Yeah.'

'You know, you are one amazing dude. Yesterday afternoon you dropped six five-hundred-pounders visually and got four bull's-eyes, then did six system bore-sights and got three more. Seven bull's-eyes out of twelve bombs. That performance put you first in the squadron, by the way.'

This comment stirred Jake Grafton. In the society of warriors to which he belonged it was very bad form to brag, to congratulate yourself or listen placidly while others congratulated you on your superb flying abilities. The fig leaf didn't have to cover much, but modesty required that he wave it. 'Pure luck,' Jake muttered. 'The wind was real steady, which is rare, and—'

Flap steamed on, uninterested in fig leaves. 'Then you motor back to the ship and go down the slide like you're riding a rail, snag an okay three-wire, find out a guy crashed, announce it's all your fault because you knew something he didn't, and submit a letter of resignation. Now is that weird or what?'

'I didn't announce anything was my fault.'

'Horse shit. You announced it to yourself.'

'I didn't—'

'I had a little talk with the Real McCoy last night,' Flap explained. 'You were moping down in your room. You sure as hell weren't crying over Rory Smith – you hardly knew the guy. You were feeling sorry for yourself.'

'What an extraordinary insight, Doctor Freud! I can see now why I'm so twisted – when I was a kid my parents wouldn't let me screw my kitty cat. Send me a bill for this consultation. In the meantime *shut the fuck up!*'

Silence followed Jake's roar. The two men sat staring into the infinity of the sky as the shadow cast by the canopy bow walked across their laps. This shadow was the only relief from the intense tropic sunshine which shone down from the deep, deep blue.

'Hard to believe that over half the earth's atmosphere is below us,' Flap said softly. 'Without supplemental oxygen, at this altitude, most fit men would pass out within thirty minutes. You know, you've flown so many times that flying has probably become routine with you. That's the trap we all fall into. Sometimes we forget that we are really small blobs of protoplasm journeying haphazardly through infinity. All we have to sustain us are our little lifelines. The oxygen will keep flowing, the engines will keep burning, the plane will hold together, the ship will be waiting . . . Well, listen to the news. The lifelines can break. We are like the man on the tightrope above Niagara Falls: the tiniest misstep, the smallest inattention, the most minuscule miscalculation, and disaster follows.'

Flap paused for a moment, then continued: 'A lot of people have it in their heads that God gave them a guarantee when they were born. At least seventy years of vigorous life, hard work will earn solid rewards, your wife with be faithful, your sons courageous, your daughters virtuous, *justice* will be done, *love* will be enough – in the event of problems, the manufacturer will set things right. Like hell! The truth is that life, like flying, is fraught with hazards. We are all up on that tightrope trying to keep our balance. Inevitably, people fall off.'

In spite of himself Jake was listening to Flap. That was the problem with the bastard's monologues – you couldn't ignore them.

'I think you're worth saving, Grafton. You're the best pilot I've met in the service. You are very very good. And you want to throw it all away. That's pretty sad.'

Flap paused. If he was giving Jake a chance to reply, he was disappointed. After a bit he continued:

'I never had much respect for you Navy guys. You think the military is like a corporation – you do your job, collect your green government check, and you can leave any time you get the itch. Maybe the Navy *is* that way. Thank God, the Corps *isn't.*'

Stung, Jake broke his silence. 'During our short acquaintance, you haven't heard one snotty remark out of me about the Holy Corps. But if you want to start trading insults, I can probably think up a few.'

Flap ignored Jake. 'We Marines are all in this together,' he said, expanding on his thesis. 'When one man slips off the rope, we'll grab him on the way down. We'll all hang together and we'll do what we have to do to get the job done. The Corps is bigger than all of us, and once you are a part of it, you are a part of it forever. Semper Fidelis. If you die, when you die, the Corps goes on. It's sorta like a church . . .'

Flap fell silent, thinking. The Corps was very hard to explain to someone who wasn't a Marine. He had tried it a few times in the past and always gave up. His explanations usually sounded trite, maybe even a little silly. 'Male bonding bullshit,' one woman told him after he had delivered himself of a memorable attempt. He almost slapped her.

For you see, the Corps was *real*. The feelings the Corps aroused in Flap and his fellow Marines were as real, as tangible, as the uniforms they wore and the weapons they carried. They *would* be loyal, they *would* be faithful, even unto death. Semper Fi. They belonged to something larger than themselves that gave their lives a meaning, a purpose, that was denied to lesser men, like civilians worried about earning a living. To Marines like Flap civilians concerned with getting and spending, getting and spending, were beneath contempt. They were like flies, to be ignored or brushed away.

'I'm trying to explain,' he told Jake Grafton now, 'because I think you could understand. You're a real good aviator. You're gifted. You owe it to yourself, to us, to hang tough, hang in there, keep doing what you know so well how to do.'

'I've had enough,' Jake told him curtly. He had little patience for this sackcloth and ashes crap. He had fought in one war. He had seen its true face. If Flap wanted to wrap himself in the flag that was his business, but Jake Grafton had decided to get on with his life.

'Rory Smith knew,' Flap told him with conviction. 'He was one fine Marine. He knew the risks and did his job anyway. He was all Marine.'

'And he's dead.'

'So? You and I are gonna die too, you know. Nobody ever gets out of life alive. Smith died for the Corps, but you're gonna go be a civilian, live the soft life until you check out. Some disease or other is going to kill you someday – cancer, heart disease, maybe just plain old age. Then you'll be as dead as Rory Smith. Now I ask you, what contribution will you have made?'

'I already made it.'

'Oh no! Oh no! Smith made *his* contribution – he gave all that he had. You've slipped one thin dime into the collection plate, Ace, and now you announce that dime is your fair share. Like hell!'

'I've had about two quarts more than enough from you today, Le Beau,' Jake spluttered furiously. 'I did two cruises to the Nam. I dropped my bombs and killed my gooks and left my friends over there in the mud to rot. For what? For not a single goddamn thing, that's for what. You think you're on some sort of holy mission to protect America? The idiot green knight. Get real – those pot-smoking flower-power hippies don't *want* protection. You'd risk your life for them? If they were dying of thirst I wouldn't piss in their mouths!'

Jake Grafton was snarling now. 'I've paid my dues in blood, Le Beau, *my* blood. Don't give me any more *shit* about *my fair share!*'

Silence reigned in the cockpit as the KA-6D tanker continued to orbit the ship 20,000 feet below, at max conserve airspeed, each engine sucking a ton of fuel per hour, under the clean white sun. Since the tanker had no radar, computer or inertial navigation system, there was nothing for Flap to do but sit. So he sat and stared at that distant, hazy horizon. With the plane on autopilot, there was also little for Jake to do except scan the instruments occasionally and alter angle-of-bank as required to stay on the five-mile arc. This required almost no effort. He too spent most of his time staring toward that distant, infinite place where the sky reached down to meet the sea.

The crazy thing was that the horizon looked the same in every direction. In all directions. Pick a direction, any direction, and that uniform gauzy junction of sea and sky obscured everything that lay beyond. Yet intelligence tells us that direction is critical – life itself is a journey *toward something, somewhere . . .*

Which way?

Jake Grafton sat silently, looking, wondering.

Hank Davis was still in a private room in sick bay when Jake dropped by to see him. He looked pale, an impression accentuated by his black-as-coal, pencil-thin mustache.

'Hey, Hank, when they gonna let you out of here?'

'I'm under observation. Whenever they get tired of observing. I dunno.'

'So how you doing?' Jake settled into the only chair and looked the bombardier over carefully.

Davis shrugged. 'Some days you eat the bear, some days the bear eats you. He got a big bite of my butt yesterday. A big bite.'

'Well, you made it. You pulled the handle while you still had time, so you're alive.'

'You ejected once, didn't you?'

'Yeah,' Jake Grafton told him. 'Over Laos. Got shot up over Hanoi.'

'Ever have second thoughts?'

'Like what?'

'Well, like maybe you were too worried about your own butt and not enough about the other guy's?'

'I thought the VDI came out on the shot? Went into Smith's lap?'

'Yeah.'

'Hank! What could you do? The damned thing weighs seventy pounds.

Even with your help, Smith couldn't have got it back into its tray. No way. If you'd crawled across to help, you'd both be dead now. It's not like you guys had a half hour to dick with this problem.'

Davis didn't reply. He looked at a wall, swallowed hard.

Jake Grafton racked his brains for a way to reach out. *I should have told you guys about checking the VDI's security.* Although he felt that, he didn't say it.

Hank related the facts of his ejection in matter-of-fact tones. The chute had not completely opened when he hit the water. So he hit the water way too hard and had trouble getting out of his chute. The swimmer from the helicopter had been there in seconds and saved his bacon. Still, he swallowed a lot of seawater and almost drowned.

'I dunno, Jake. Sometimes life's pretty hard to figure. When you look at it close, the only thing that makes a difference is luck. Who lives or who dies is just luck. "The dead guy screwed up," everybody says. Of course he screwed up. Lady Luck crapped all over him. And if that's true, then everything else is a lie – religion, professionalism, everything. We are all just minnows swimming in the sea and luck decides when it's your turn. Then the shark eats you and that's the fucking end of that.'

'If it's all luck, then these guilt trips don't make much sense, do they?' Jake observed.

'Right now the accident investigators are down in the avionics shop,' Hank Davis told him. 'They are looking for the simple bastard who didn't get the VDI screwed in right. All this *shit* is gonna get dumped right on that poor dumb son of a bitch! "Rory Smith is dead and it's *your* fault." Makes me want to puke some more.'

Squadron life revolves around the ready room, ashore or afloat. Since the A-6 squadrons always had the most flight crewmen, they always got the biggest ready room, in most ships Ready Five, but in *Columbia*, Ready Four. The ready room was never big enough. It was filled with comfortable, padded chairs that you could sink into and really relax in, even sleep in, but there weren't enough of them for all the officers.

In some squadrons when all the officers assembled for a meeting – an AOM – chairs were assigned by strict seniority. In other outfits the rule was first come, first served. How it was done depended on the skipper, who always got a chair up front by the duty desk, the best seat in the house. Lieutenant Colonel Haldane believed that rank had its privileges – at least when not airborne – so seniority reigned here. Jake Grafton ended up with a seat four rows back. The nuggets, first lieutenants on their first cruise, stood around the back of the room or sat on metal folding chairs.

AOMs were social and business events. Squadron business was thrashed out in these meetings, administrative matters dealing with the ship and the demands of the amorphous bureaucracies of the Navy and the Marine Corps were considered, lectures delivered on NATOPs and flying procedures, the 'word' passed, all manner of things.

At these soirees all the officers in the squadron got to know each other well. Here one got a close look at the department heads – the 'heavies' – watched junior officers in action, here the commanding officer exerted his leadership and molded the flight crews into a military unit.

In addition to the legal authority with which he was cloaked, the commanding officer was always the most experienced flyer there and the most senior. How he used these assets was the measure of the man, for truly, his responsibility was very great. In addition to the aircraft entrusted to him, he was responsible for about 350 enlisted men and three dozen officers. He was legally and morally responsible for every facet of their lives, from the adequacy of their living quarters to their health, professional development and performance. And he was responsible for the squadron as a military unit in combat, which meant the lives of his men were in his hands.

The responsibility crushed some men, but most commanding officers flourished under it. This was the professional zenith that they had spent their careers working to attain. By the time they reached it they had served under many commanding officers. The wise ones adopted the best of the leadership styles of their own former skippers and adapted it as necessary to suit their personalities. Leadership could not be learned from a book: it was the most intangible and the most human of the military skills.

In American naval aviation the best skippers led primarily by example and the force of their personalities – they intentionally kept the mood light as they gave orders, praised, cajoled, hinted, encouraged, scolded, ridiculed, laughed at and commented upon whatever and whomever they wished. The ideal that they seemed to instinctively strive for was a position as first among equals. Consequently AOMs were normally spirited affairs, occasionally raucous, full of good humor and camaraderie, with every speaker working hard to gain his audience's attention and cope with catcalls and advice – good, bad, indifferent and obscene. In this environment intelligence and good sense could flourish, here experience could be shared and everyone could learn from everyone else, here the bonds necessary to sustain fighting men could be forged.

This evening Rory Smith's death hung like a gloomy pall in the air.

Colonel Haldane spoke first. He told them what he knew of the accident, what Hank Davis had said. Then he got down to it:

'The war is over and still we have planes crashing and people dying. Hard to figure, isn't it? This time it wasn't the bad guys. The gomers didn't get Rory Smith in three hundred and twenty combat missions, although they tried and they tried damned hard. He had planes shot up so badly on three occasions that he was decorated for getting the planes back. What got him was a VDI that slid out of its tray in the instrument panel and jammed the stick.

'Did he think about ejecting? I don't know. I wish he had ejected. I wish to God we still had Rory Smith with us. Maybe he was worried about getting his legs cut off if he pulled the handle. Maybe he didn't have time to punch. Maybe he thought he could save it. Maybe he didn't realize how quickly the plane was getting into extremis. Lots of maybes. We'll never know.'

He picked up the blue NATOPs manual lying on the podium and held it up. 'This book is the Bible. The engineers that built this plane and the test pilots that wrung it out put their hearts and souls into this book – for you. Telling you everything they knew. And the process didn't stop there – as new things are learned about the plane the book is continually updated. It's a living document. You should know every word in it. That is the best insurance you can get on this side of hell.

'But the book doesn't cover everything. Sooner or later you are going to run into something that isn't covered in the book. Whether you survive the experience will be determined by your skill, your experience, and your luck.

'There's been a lot of mumbling around here the last twenty-four hours about luck. Well, there is no such thing. You can't feel it, taste it, smell it, touch it, wear it, fuck it, or eat it. It doesn't exist!

'This thing we call luck is merely professionalism and attention to detail, it's your awareness of everything that is going on around you, it's how well you know and *understand* your airplane and your own limitations. We make our own luck. Each of us. None of us is Superman. Luck is the sum total of your abilities as an aviator. If you think your luck is running low, you'd better get busy and make some more. Work harder. Pay more attention. Study your NATOPs more. Do better preflights.

'A wise man once said, "Fortune favors the well prepared." He was right.

'Rory Smith is not with us here tonight because he didn't eject when he should have. Hank Davis is alive because he did.

'We're going to miss Rory. But every man here had better resolve to learn something from his death. If we do, he didn't die for nothing. Think about it.'

The best way to see Hawaii is the way the ancient Polynesians first saw it, the way it was revealed to whalers and missionaries, the way sailors have always seen it.

The islands first appear on the horizon like clouds, exactly the same as the other clouds. Only as the hours pass and your vessel gets closer does it become apparent that there is something different about these clouds. The first hints of green below the churning clouds imply mass, earth, land, an *island*, where at first there appeared to be only sea and sky.

Finally you see for sure – tawny green slopes, soon a surf line, definition and a crest for that ridge, that draw, that promontory.

Hawaii.

Jake Grafton stood amid the throng of off-duty sailors on the bow watching the island of Oahu draw closer and closer. She looked emerald green this morning under her cloud-wreath. The hotels and office buildings of Honolulu were quite plain there on the right. Farther right Diamond Head jutted from the sea haze, also wearing a cumulus buildup.

The sailors pointed out the landmarks to one another and talked excitedly. They were jovial, happy. To see Hawaii for the first time is one of life's great milestones, like your first kiss.

Jake had been here before – twice. On each of his first two cruises the ship had stopped in Pearl on its way to Vietnam. As he watched the carrier close the harbor channel, he thought again of those times, and of the men now dead whom he had shared them with. Little fish. Sharks.

He went below. Down in the stateroom the Real McCoy was poring over a copy of the *Wall Street Journal*. 'Are you rich enough to retire yet?'

'I'm making an honest dollar, Grafton. Working hard at it and taking big risks. We call the system capitalism.'

'Yeah. So how's capitalism treating you?'

'Think I'm up another grand as of the date of this paper, four days ago. I'll get something current as soon as I can get off base.'

'Uh-huh.'

'Arabs turned off the oil tap in the Mideast. That will send my domestic oil stocks soaring and melt the profits off my airline stocks. Some up, some down. You know, the crazy thing about investing – there's really no such thing as bad news. Whether an event is good or bad depends on where you've got your money.'

Jake eyed his roommate without affection. This worm's-eye view of life irritated him. The worms had placed bets on the little fish. Somehow that struck him as inevitable, though it didn't say much for the worms. Or the little fish.

'You going ashore?' McCoy asked.

'Like a shot out of a gun, the instant the gangway stops moving,' Jake Grafton replied. 'I have got to get off this tub for a while.'

'Liberty hounds don't go very high in this man's Navy,' McCoy reminded him, in a tone that Jake thought sounded a wee bit prissy.

'I really don't care if Haldane uses my fitness report for toilet paper' was Jake Grafton's edged retort. And he didn't care. Not one iota.

'Hello.'

'Hello, Mrs McKenzie? This is Jake Grafton. Is Callie there?'

'No, she isn't, Jake. Where are you?'

'Hawaii.'

'She's at school right now. She should be back around six this evening. Is there a number where she can reach you?'

'No. I'll call her. Please tell her I called.'

'I'll do that, Jake.'

The pilot hung up the phone and put the rest of the quarters from his roll back into his trouser pocket. When he stepped out of the telephone booth, the next sailor in line took his place.

He trudged away looking neither right nor left, ignoring the sporadic salutes tossed his way. The palm trees and frangipani in bloom didn't interest him. The tropical breeze caressing his face didn't distract him. When a jet climbing away from Hickam thundered over, however, the pilot stopped and looked up. He watched the jet until the plane was out of sight and the sound had faded, then walked on.

About a ship's length from the carrier pier was a small square of grass complete with picnic table adjacent to the water. After brushing away pigeon droppings, Jake Grafton seated himself on the table and eased his fore-and-aft cap farther back onto his head. The view was across the harbor at the USS *Arizona* memorial, which he knew was constructed above the sunken battleship's superstructure. *Arizona* lay on the mud under that calm sheet of water, her hull blasted, holed, burned and twisted by Japanese bombs and torpedoes. Occasionally boats ferrying tourists to and from the memorial made wakes that disturbed the surface of the water. After the boats' passage, the disturbance would quickly dissipate. Just the faintest hint of a swell spoiled the mirror smoothness of that placid sheet, protected as it was from the sea's turbulence by the length and narrowness of the channel. The perfect water reflected sky and drifting cumulus clouds and, arranged around the edge of the harbor, the long gray warships that lay at the piers.

Jake Grafton smoked cigarettes while he sat looking. Time passed slowly and his mind wandered. Occasionally he glanced at his watch. When almost two hours had passed, he walked back toward the telephone booths at the head of the carrier pier and got back into line.

'Hey, Callie, it's me, Jake.'

'Well, hello, sailor! It's great to hear your voice.'

'Pretty nice hearing yours too, lady. So you're back in school?'

'Uh-huh. Graduate courses. I'm getting so educated I don't know what I'll do.'

'I like smart women.'

'I'll see if I can find one for you. So you're in Pearl Harbor?'

'Yep. Hawaii. Got in a while ago. Gonna be here a couple days, then maybe Japan or the Philippines or the IO.' Realizing that she probably wouldn't recognize the acronym, he added belatedly, 'That's the Indian Ocean. I don't know. Admirals somewhere figure it out and I go wherever the ship goes. But enough about me. Talk some so I can to listen to your voice.'

'I got your letter about the in-flight engagement. That sounded scary. And dangerous.'

'It was exciting all right, but we lost a plane yesterday on a day cat shot. An A-6. Went in off the cat. The pilot was killed.'

'I'm sorry, Jake.'

'I'm getting real tired of this, Callie. I've been here too long. I'm a civilian at heart and I think it's time I pulled the plug. I've submitted a letter of resignation.'

'Oh,' she said. After a pause, she added, 'When are you getting out?'

'Won't be until the cruise is over.'

'Are you sure about this?'

'Yeah.'

He twisted the telephone cord and wondered what to say. She wasn't saying anything on her end, so he plunged ahead. 'The plane that went in off the cat was the one I had the in-flight engagement in, ol' Five One One. The in-flight smacked the avionics around pretty good, and when they reinstalled the boxes one of the technicians didn't get the VDI properly secured. So the VDI box came out on the cat shot, jammed the stick. The BN punched and told us what happened, but the pilot didn't get out.'

'You're not blaming yourself, are you?'

'No.' He said that too quickly. 'Well, to tell the truth, I am a little bit responsible. With better technique I might have avoided the in-flight. That's spilled milk. Maybe it was unavoidable. But I was briefing these Marines on carrier ops – everything you need to know to be a carrier pilot in four two-hour sessions, and I forgot to mention that you have to check the security of the VDI.'

'I see.'

'Do you?'

'Not really. But aren't these risks a part of carrier aviation?'

'Not a part. This is the main course, the heart of it, the very essence. In spite of the very best of intentions, mistakes will be made, things will break. War or no war, people get killed doing this stuff. I'm getting sick of watching people bet their lives and losing, that's all.'

'Are you worried about your own safety?'

'No more than usual. You have to fret it some or you won't be long on this side of hell.'

'It seems to me that the dangers would become hard to live with—'

'I can handle it. I think. No one's shooting at me. But see, that's the crazy part. The war is over, yet as long as men keep flying off these ships there are going to be casualties.'

'So what will you do when you get out?'

'I don't know, Callie.'

Seconds passed before she spoke. 'Life isn't easy, Jake.'

'That isn't exactly news. I've done a year or two of hard living my own self.'

'I thought you liked the challenge.'

'Are you trying to tell me you want me to stay in?'

'No.' Her voice solidified. 'I am not suggesting that you do anything. I'm not even hinting. Stay in, get out, whatever, that's your choice and yours alone. You must live your own life.'

'Damn, woman! I'm trying.'

'I know,' she said gently.

'You know me,' he told her.

'I'm beginning to.'

'How are your folks?'

'Fine,' she said. They talked for several more minutes, then said good-bye.

The vast bulk of the ship loomed high over the bank of telephone booths. Jake glanced up at the ship, at the tails of the planes sticking over the edge of the flight deck, then lowered his gaze, stuffed his hands into his pockets and walked away.

The problem was that he had never been able to separate the flying from the rest of it – the killing, bombing, dying. Maybe it couldn't be separated. The My Lai massacre, Lieutenant William Calley, napalm on villages, burning children, American pilots nailed to trees and skinned alive, Viet Cong soldiers tortured for information while Americans watched, North Vietnamese soldiers given airborne interrogations – talk or we'll throw you from the helicopter without a parachute: all of this was tied up with the flying in a Gordian knot that Solomon couldn't unravel.

He thought he had cut the knot – well, Commander Camparelli and the Navy had cut it for him – last winter in Vietnam. He had picked an unauthorized target, the North Vietnamese capitol building in Hanoi, attacked and almost got it, then faced some very unhappy senior officers across a long green table. They knew what their duty was: *obey orders from the elected government*. What they couldn't fathom was how he, Lieutenant Jake Jackass from Possum Hollow, had lost sight of it.

We're all in this together. *We must keep the faith*. Wasn't that what you and your friends were always telling one another when the shit got thick and the blood started flowing?

We do what we must and die when we must *for each other*.

The faith was easier to understand then, easier to keep. Now the war was over. Although some people want to keep fighting it, by God, it's *over*.

Now the Navy was peacetime cruises, six- to eight-month voyages to nowhere, excruciating separations from loved ones, marriages going on the rocks under the strain, kids growing up with a father who's never there; it's getting scared out of your wits when Lady Luck kisses your ass good-bye; it's seeing people squashed into shark food; it's knowing – knowing all the time, every minute of every day – that you may be next. The life can be smashed out of you so quick that you'll inhale in this world and exhale in hell.

Lieutenant Jake Grafton, farmer's son and history major, was going to get on with his life. Do something safe, something sane. Something with tangible rewards. Something that allowed him to find a good woman, raise a family, be a father to his children. He would bequeath this flying life to dedicated half-wits like Flap Le Beau.

Yet he would miss the flying.

This afternoon as Jake Grafton walked along the boulevard that led into downtown Honolulu, huge, benign cumulus clouds were etched against the deep blue sky, seemingly fixed. He would like to fly right now – to strap on an airplane and leave behind the problems of the ground.

We are, he well knew, creatures of the earth. Its minerals compose our bodies and provide our nourishment. Our cells contain seawater, legacies of ancestors who lived in the oceans. Yet on the surface man evolved, here where there are other animals to kill and eat, edible plants, trees with nuts and fruits, streams and lakes teeming with life. Our bodies function best at the temperature ranges, atmospheric pressures and oxygen levels that have prevailed on the earth's surface throughout most of the age of mammals. We need the protection from the sun's radiation that the atmosphere provides. Our senses of smell and hearing use the atmosphere as the transmitting medium. The earth's gravity provides a reference point for our sense of balance and the resistance our muscles and circulatory systems need to function properly. The challenges of surviving on the dry surface provided the evolutionary stimulus to develop our brains.

Without the earth, we would not be the creatures we are. And yet we want to leave it, to soar through the atmosphere, to voyage through interplanetary space, to explore other worlds. And to someday leave the solar system and journey to another star. All this while we are still trapped by our physical and psychological limitations here on the surface of the mother planet.

Sometimes the contradictions inherent in our situation hit him hard. Last fall, while he was hunting targets in North Vietnam as he dodged the flak and SAMs, Americans again walked on the moon. Less than seventy years after the Wright brothers left the surface in powered flight, man stood on the moon and looked back at the home planet glistening amid the infinite black nothingness. They looked while war, hunger, pestilence and man's inhumanity to man continued unabated, continued as it had since the dawn of human history.

It was a curious thing, hard to comprehend, yet worth pondering on a balmy evening in the tropics with the air laden with fragrant aromas and the surf flopping rhythmically on the beach a few yards away.

Jake Grafton walked along the beach, stared at the hotels and the people and the relentless surf and thought of all these things.

An hour later, as he walked back toward the army base with traffic whizzing by, the tops of the lazy large clouds were shot with fire by the setting sun.

The problem, he decided, was keeping everything in proper perspective. That was hard to do. Impossible, really. To see man and his problems, the earth and the universe, as they really are one would have to be God.

The officers' club was full of people, music, light, laughter. Jake stood in the entrance for several seconds letting the sensations sink in. He tucked his hat under his belt, then strolled for the bar.

He heard them before he got to the door.

'How ugly was she?' three or four voices asked in a shaky unison.

'She was ugly as a tiger's hairball.' Flap's soaring baritone carried clearly. People here in the lounge waiting to be called for dinner looked at each other, startled.

'How ugly?'

'Ugly as a mud wrestler's navel.' Eyebrows soared.

'How ugly?' Eight or ten voices now.

'Ugly as a pickled pervert's promise.' Women giggled and whispered to each other. Several of the gentlemen frowned and turned to stare at the door to the bar. Jake saw one of the men, in his fifties, with short, iron gray hair, wink at his companion.

'*That's* not ugly!'

'She was so damn ugly that the earth tried to quake and couldn't – it just shivered. So ugly that five drunken sailors pretended they didn't see her. The city painted her red and put a number on her – two dogs relieved themselves on her shoes before I got to the rescue, that's how ugly she was. She was so desperately ugly that my zipper welded itself shut. And that, my gentle friends, is the gospel truth.'

Jake Grafton grinned, squared his shoulders, and walked into the bar.

11

The air was opaque, the sun hidden by the moisture in the air. Two or three miles from the ship in all directions the gray sea and gray sky merged. *Columbia* was in the midst of an inverted bowl, three days northwest of Pearl laboring through fifteen-foot swells. The wind was brisk from the west.

From his vantage point in the cockpit of a KA-6D tanker spotted behind the jet blast deflector – the JBD – for Cat Three, Jake Grafton could see a frigate a mile or so off the port beam. Just ahead, barely visible on the edge of the known universe, he could make out the wake and superstructure of another.

Jake and Flap were standing the five-minute alert tanker duty, which meant that for two hours they had to sit in the cockpit of this bird strapped in, ready to fire up the engines and taxi onto the catapult as soon as the F-4 Phantom that was parked there – also on five-minute alert – launched. There was another fighter on five-minute status sitting just short of the hook-up area on Cat Four, and an airborne early warning aircraft, an E-2 Hawkeye, parked with its tail against the island. Sitting on the waist catapult tracks was a manned helicopter, the angel, which would have to launch before the catapults could be fired. A power unit with its engine running was plugged into each aircraft, instantly ready to deliver air to turn the engines. All five of the alert birds had been serviced and started, checked to make sure all their systems worked, then shut down.

The crews were strapped into the airplanes. The pilot of the Phantom on Cat Four was reading a paperback novel, Jake could see, but he couldn't make out the title.

On the deck behind the waist catapults sat two more fighters and a tanker on alert-fifteen status, which meant that their crews were flaked out in their respective ready rooms wearing all their flight gear, ready to run for the flight deck if the alarm sounded.

Alert duty kept flight crews busy any time that planes were not aloft. Except in waters just off the shore of the United States, it was rare for a carrier to be below alert-thirty status. Alert-fifteen was the usual status for the high seas, with alert-five reserved for the South China Sea during the war just ended or other locations where a possible threat existed. Today a possible threat existed. Intelligence expected the Soviets to try to overfly the carrier task group as it transited to Japan with land-based naval bombers from Vladivostok or one of the fields on Sakhalin Island or the Kamchatka peninsula.

The Russkis were going to have their work cut out for them overflying the ship in this low visibility, Jake thought, if they came at all. He sat watching the frigate on the port beam labor into the swells, ride up and then bury her bow so deep that white spray was flung aft all the way to the bridge.

Columbia's ride was definitely more pleasant, but Jake could feel her pitching and see the leading edge of the angled deck rise and fall as she rode the restless sea.

To Jake's right, in the bombardier-navigator's seat, Flap Le Beau was reading a book by Malcolm X. Every time he got to the bottom of a page, he lowered the paperback and glanced around, his eyes scanning several times while he turned the page.

On one of Flap's periscope sweeps, Jake asked, 'That book any good?

'Guy sure is interesting,' Flap said, and resumed his reading.

'What's it about?

'You don't know Malcolm X?'

'Uh-uh.'

'Hated honkeys. Believed the races should have their own enclaves, no mixing, that kind of stuff.'

'Do you believe that?' Jake asked tentatively. Flap was only the second or third black naval aviator Jake had ever met, and he had never discussed race with one.

'He had some good ideas,' Flap said, glancing at Jake. 'But no, I think the races should be integrated. America is for Americans – black, white, brown, yellow, green or purple. But what about you? You're from rural Virginia, nigger-hating redneck heaven, one-party bigot politics, pot-gutted klagel sheriffs – what d'ya think?'

'Ol' X should've had you writing his speeches.'

Jake Grafton wasn't stupid enough to proclaim himself a true believer in racial equality and brotherly love, certainly not to a black man probably capable of forcing him into the bigot cesspool with just a little effort.

'Who knows, if this Marine Corps gig goes sour, I might go into politics,' Flap allowed, then resumed reading his book.

His father had two black employees on his farm during the years Jake was growing up. They were both huge men, with hands like pie plates and upper arms larger than Jake's thighs. They were barely able to sign their names but they could work any four white men into the dirt. In their younger days they had worked on railroad track-repair gangs swinging sledge-hammers. 'Georgia niggers,' his father, Sam, had called them. How they came to end up on the Grafton farm Jake never quite understood, but Isaiah and Frank allowed from time to time that they had absolutely no intention of crossing the Virginia line south-bound. Then they would shake their heads and laugh at some private joke, creating the vision in the boy's mind of blood-thirsty southern sheriffs eager to avenge spectacular, unmentionable crimes.

His father treated the two blacks like the whites he hired occasionally, worked alongside them, shared food and smokes and jokes. Young Jake liked the men immensely.

Yet, like most of the boys of his generation in southwestern rural Virginia, he accepted racial segregation as natural, as unremarkable and logical as the deference men showed women and the respect accorded the elderly. That is, he did until 1963, the year he turned eighteen. One evening while watching the network news show footage of Negro children in Birmingham being blasted with streams from high-pressure fire hoses, his father had let out an oath.

'I guess it's a damn good thing that I'm not colored,' Sam Grafton declared. 'If I were, I'd get me a gun and go to Birmingham and start shooting some of those sons of bitches. And I'd start with that bastard right there!' His finger shot out and Jake found himself staring at the porky visage of Bull Connor.

'Sam!' exclimed his mother disgustedly.

'Martha, what the hell do they have to do to get treated decent by whites? The colored people have put up with a hell of a lot more crap than any Christian should ever have to deal with. Those sons of bitches laying the wood to them aren't Christians. They're Nazis. It's a miracle the colored people haven't started shooting the damned swine.'

'Do you have to cuss like that?'

'It's high time some white people got mad at those bigots,' Sam Grafton thundered. 'I wish Jack Kennedy would get his ass out of his rocking chair and kick some butt. The President of the United States, saying there's nothing he can do when those rednecks attack children! By God, if Bull Connor was black and those kids were white he'd be singing a different tune. He's just another gutless politician scared of losing the bigot vote. Pfft!'

That evening had been an eye-opener for Jake. He started paying attention to the civil rights protests, listening to the arguments. His father had always been a bit different than his neighbors, marching to a different drummer. And he was usually right. He was that time, too, his son concluded.

Remembering that evening, he sighed, then glanced around the flight deck. People were lying on the deck beside their equipment, napping.

He was in the middle of a yawn when he heard the hiss of the flight deck loudspeaker system coming to life. 'Launch the alert-five. Launch the alert-five. We have bogies inbound.'

The lounging men on the flight deck sprang into action. Jake Grafton twirled his fingers at the plane captain, received a twirl in response. He turned on the left engine-fuel master switch and pushed the start button. With a low moan the engine began to turn. When the RPM was high enough he came around the horn with the throttle, then sat watching the temperatures and RPMs rise while he pulled his helmet on.

By the time he got the second engine started and the canopy closed, the chopper on the cat tracks was engaging its rotors. The ship was turning – Jake could see the list on the flight deck – coming about forty degrees left into the wind. Now the deck leveled out. The *Columbia*'s rudder was centered. Thirty seconds later the angel lifted off. It left the deck straight ahead. When it was safely past the bow the chopper pilot laid it into a right turn.

Now the catapult shuttles were dragged back out of the water brakes into battery while the final checkers inspected the two fighters and gave their thumbs-up. Red-shirted ordnancemen pulled the safety pins from the missile racks and showed them to the pilots. The yellow-shirted taxi director gave the pilot of the plane in front of Jake a come-ahead signal and let him inch the last two feet forward onto Cat Three while the green-shirted catapult hook-up men crawled underneath with the bridle and two more greenies installed the hold-back bar, on the Phantom a ten-foot-long hinged strap with the hold-back shear-bolt attaching to the airplane's belly and the other end going into a slot in the deck. The weight-board man flashed his board at the pilot and got a thumbs-up, then showed it to the cat officer, who also rogered. The whole perform-ance was a ballet of multicolored shirts darting around, near and under the moving fighter, each man intent on doing his job perfectly.

As the taxiing fighter reached the maximum extent of the hold-back bar, the JBDs came up, three panels that would deflect the exhaust of the launching aircraft from the plane behind.

Now Jake saw the Phantom lower its tail – actually the nose-gear strut was extended eighteen inches to improve the angle-of-attack. He saw the cat officer twirl his fingers above his head for full power and heard the thunderous response from the Phantom, saw the river of black smoke blasted upward by the JBD, felt his plane tremble from the fury of those two engines. The fighter pilot checked his controls, and the stabilator and rudder waggled obediently. Thumbs-up flashed from the squadron final checkers.

The cat officer signaled for afterburners, an opening hand on an extended arm. The river of smoke pouring skyward off the JBDs cleared, leaving hot, clear shimmering gases. Incredibly, even here in the cockpit of the tanker the noise level rose. Jake got a good whiff of the acrid stench of jet exhaust.

My oxygen mask must not be on tight enough. Fix it when I'm airborne.

The last of the catapult crewmen came scurrying out from under the fighter. This was the man who swung on the bridle to ensure it was on firmly. He flashed a thumbs-up at the cat officer, the shooter.

The shooter saluted the F-4 pilot, glanced down the deck, and lunged. One potato, two potato, and wham, the fighter shot forward trailing plumes of fire from its twin exhausts. It hadn't gone a hundred feet down the track when the JBD started down and a taxi director gave Jake Grafton the come-ahead signal.

After he watched the Phantom clear the deck, the shooter turned his attention to the fighter on Cat Four, which was already at full power. He gave the burner sign. Fifteen seconds later this one ripped down the cat after the first one, which was out of burner now and trailing a plume of black smoke that showed quite distinctly against the gray haze wall.

Jake taxied forward and ran through his ritual as the wind over the deck swirled steam leaking from the catapult slot around the men on deck. Their clothes flapped in the wind.

Power up, control check, cat grip, engine instruments, warning lights, salute.

One potato, two pota – he felt just the tiniest jolt as the hold-back bolt broke, then the acceleration smashed him backward like the hand of God.

The strike controller told Jake to go on up to 20,000 feet. 'Texaco take high station.'

Flap rogered, then Jake said on the ICS, 'They must not be going to launch the alert-fifteen.'

'Why do you say that?'

'Surely they'll want us to tank the second section of fighters immediately after launch, if they launch them.'

'Maybe not.'

'Ours is not to reason why, ours is but to do or die.'

'Noble sentiment. But let's *do* today, not die.'

'Aye aye, sir.'

'Don't get cute.'

Jake Grafton gave a couple of pig grunts.

'I thought you said you weren't going to insult the Corps?' Flap sounded shocked.

'I lied.'

The sea disappeared as they climbed through 3,000 feet. Jake was on the gauges. There was no horizon, no sky, no sea. Inside this formless, featureless void the plane handled as usual, but the only measure of its progress through space was movement of the altimeter, the TACAN needle, and the rotating numbers of the distance measuring equipment – DME.

Jake kept expecting to reach an altitude where the goo thinned perceptibly, but it was not to be. When he leveled at 20,000 feet he could see a blob of light above him that had to be the sun, yet the haze seemed as thick as ever. Just what the visibility might be was impossible to say without another object to focus upon.

Flap reported their arrival at high station. The controller rogered without apparent enthusiasm.

Jake set the power at max conserve and when the airspeed had stabilized, engaged the autopilot. He checked the cockpit altitude and loosened one side of his oxygen mask from his helmet. Flap sat silently for a moment or two, looking here and there, then he extracted his book from a pocket of his G-suit and opened it to a dog-eared page.

Jake busied himself with punching buttons to check that the fuel transfer was proceeding normally. The tanker carried five 2,000-pound drop tanks. The transfer of fuel from these drops was automatic. If transfer didn't occur, however, he wanted to know it as soon as possible because he would have that much less fuel available to give to other aircraft or burn himself. Today the transfer seemed to be progressing as advertised, so he had 26,000 pounds of fuel to burn or give away.

They were almost eight hundred miles northwest of Midway Island alone in an opaque sky. Other than flicking his eyes across the instruments and adjusting the angle-of-bank occasionally, he had nothing to do except scan the blank whiteness outside for other airplanes that never came.

The fighters were being vectored out to intercept the incoming Russians, the E-2 was proceeding away from the ship to a holding station – those were the only other airplanes aloft. There was nothing in this sky to see. Yet if an aircraft did appear out of the haze, it would be close, very close, on a collision course or nearly so, a rerun of the Phantom incident a week ago. He sure as hell didn't want to go through *that* again.

In spite of his resolution to keep a good lookout, boredom crept over him. His mind wandered.

He had signed the letter of resignation from the Navy yesterday and submitted it to Lieutenant Colonel Haldane. The skipper had taken the document without comment. Well, what was there to say?

Haldane wasn't about to try to argue him into staying – he barely knew Jake. If Jake wanted out, he wanted out. What he could expect was a form letter of appreciation, a handshake and a hearty 'Have a nice life.'

That *was* what he wanted, wasn't it?

Why not go back to Virginia and help Dad with the farm? Fishing in the spring and summer, hunting in the fall . . . He would end up joining the Lions Club, like his father. Lions meeting every Thursday evening, church two or three Sundays a month, high school football games on Friday nights in September and October . . .

It would be a chance to settle down, get a house of his own, some furniture, put down roots. He contemplated that future now, trying to visualize how it would be.

Dull. It would be damn dull.

Well, he had been complaining that the Navy was too challenging, the responsibility for the lives and welfare of other people too heavy to carry.

One life offered too much challenge, the other too little. Was there something, somewhere, more in the middle?

'Texaco, Strike.'

'Go ahead.'

'Take low station. Buster.' Buster meant hurry, bust your ass.

'We're on our way.'

Jake Grafton disengaged the autopilot and rolled the Intruder to ninety degrees angle-of-bank. The nose came down. Speed brakes out, throttles back, shallow the bank to about seventy degrees, put a couple G's on . . . the rate-of-descent needle pegged at 6,000 feet per minute down. That was all it would indicate. A spiral descent was his best maneuver because the tanker had a three-G limitation, mandated by higher authority to make the wings last longer. He was right at three G's now, the altimeter unwinding at a dizzying rate.

Low station was 5,000 feet, but it could be lowered if the visibility was better below this crud. Maybe he should ask. 'Ah, Strike, Texaco. How's the visibility and ceiling underneath?'

'A little worse than when you took off. Maybe a mile viz under an indefinite obscuration.'

'Who's our customer?'

'Snake-eye Two Oh Seven. He's got an emergency. Switch to button sixteen and rendezvous on him.'

Jake was passing ten thousand feet, still turning steeply with G on. Bracing himself against the G, Flap changed the radio channel and called.

'Snake-eye Two Oh Seven, this is Texaco. Say your posit, angels, and heading, over.'

'Texaco, I'm on the Three One Zero radial at nine miles, headed inbound at four grand. Better hurry.'

Jake keyed the radio transmitter. 'Just keep going in and we'll join on you.'

The fighter pilot gave him two clicks in reply.

Jake eyed the TACAN needle on the HSI, the horizontal situation indicator, a glorified gyroscopic compass. He had a problem here in three-dimensional space and the face of the instrument was an aid in helping him visualize it.

He rolled the wings level and stuffed the nose down more. His airspeed was at 400 knots and increasing.

'Snake-eye, Texaco, what's your problem?'

'We're venting fuel overboard and the pull-forward is going to take more time than we've got.'

'Posit again?'

'Three One Zero at five, angels four, speed three hundred, heading One Three Zero.'

'Are you in the clear?'

'Negative.'

'Let's go on down to three grand.'

Jake was passing six thousand feet, on the Three Three Zero radial at nine miles. He was indicating 420 knots and he was raising the nose to shallow his dive. He thumbed the speed brakes in and added some power. 'We're going to join fast,' he muttered at Flap, who didn't reply.

The problem was that he didn't know how much visibility he would have. If it was about a mile, like the controller on the ship said, and he missed the F-4 by more than that margin, he would never see him. Unlike the Phantom, the tanker had no radar to assist in the interception.

He was paying strict attention to the TACAN needle now. The seconds ticked by and the distance to the ship closed rapidly.

'There, at one o'clock.' Flap called it.

Now Jake saw the fighter. He was several hundred feet below Jake, which was good, at about a mile, trailing a plume of fuel. Grafton reduced power and deployed the speed brakes.

Uh-oh, he had a ton of closure. He stuffed the nose down to underrun the Phantom.

'*Look out!*'

The wingman! His tailpipes were *right there*, coming in the windscreen! Sweet Jesus!

He jammed the stick forward and the negative G lifted him and Flap away from their seats. In two heartbeats he was well under and jerked the stick back. He had forgotten about the wingman.

Still indicating 350, he ran under the Phantom in trouble and pulled the power to idle. 'At your one o'clock, Snake-eye. We'll tank at two seventy. Join on me.'

At 280 knots he got the power up and the speed brakes in. He quickly stabilized at 270 indicated. After checking to ensure that he was level headed directly for the ship, Jake turned in his seat to examine the Phantom closing in as Flap deployed the refueling drogue.

The three-thousand-pound belly tank the F-4 usually carried was gone. Fuel was pouring from the belly of the aircraft.

'Green light, you're cleared in,' Flap announced on the radio.

Jake turned back to his instruments. He wanted to provide a stable drogue for the fighter to plug. 'What's your problem, Snake-eye?'

'Belly tank wouldn't transfer. We jettisoned it and now we are pumping fuel out the belly. The check valve must be damaged. We're down to one point seven.'

'Strike, Texaco, how much does Two Oh Seven get?'

'All he needs, Texaco. We should have a ready deck in six or seven minutes. Pulling forward now.' This meant all the planes parked in the landing area were being pulled forward to the bow.

The green light on the refueling panel went out and the fuel counter began to click over. 'You're getting fuel,' Flap told the fighter.

They were crossing over the ship now. Jake Grafton eased the tanker into a descent. If he could get underneath this haze he could drop the Phantom at the 180-degree position, only thirty seconds or so from the deck.

When the fuel-delivered counter registered two thousand pounds, Jake told the fighter pilot.

'Keep it coming. We're up a grand in the main bag. At least we're getting it faster than it's going over the side.'

At two thousand feet Jake saw the ocean. He kept descending. At fifteen hundred feet he spotted the carrier, on his left, turning hard. The ship was coming into the wind. From this distance Jake could only see a couple airplanes still to go forward. Very soon.

He leveled at twelve hundred feet and circled the ship in a left turn at about a mile.

Five thousand pounds transferred . . . six . . . seven . . . the ship was into the wind now and the wake was streaming straight behind her, white as snow against the gray sea as the four huge screws bit hard to drive her faster through the water.

'Snake-eye Two Oh Seven, this is Paddles. We're going to be ready in about two minutes. I want you to drop off the tanker on the downwind, dirty up and turn into the groove. Swells still running about fifteen feet, so the deck is pitching. Average out the ball and fly a nice smooth pass.'

'Two Oh Seven.'

Jake was crossing the bow now, the fuel counter still clicking. Eight thousand five hundred pounds transferred so far.

'Texaco, hawk the deck.'

'Roger.' Hawk the deck meant to fly alongside so that the plane on the bolter could rendezvous and tank.

This was going to work out, Jake told himself. This guy is going to get aboard.

The fuel-delivered counter stopped clicking over at 9,700 pounds. The fighter had backed out of the basket. Jake took a cut to the right, then turned back left and looked over his shoulder. The crippled fighter was descending and slowing, his hook down and gear coming out. And the fuel was still pouring from his belly in a steady, fire-hose stream. The wingman was well behind, still clean.

When the fighter pilot jettisoned the belly tank, Jake thought, the quick-disconnect fitting must have frozen and the plumbing tore loose inside the aircraft. There was a one-way check valve just upstream of the quick-disconnect; obviously it wasn't working. So the pressure in the main fuel cell was forcing fuel overboard through the broken pipe.

Jake slowed to 250 knots and cycled the refueling hose in and back out to reset the reel response. Now to scoot down by the ship, Jake thought, so that if he bolters, I'll be just ahead where he can quickly rendezvous.

He dropped to a thousand feet and turned hard at a mile to parallel the wake on the ship's port side.

The landing fighter was crossing the wake, turning into the groove, when Jake saw the fire.

The plume of fuel streaming behind the plane ignited. The tongue of flame was twice as long as the airplane and clearly visible.

'You're on fire!' someone shouted on the radio.

'In the groove, eject, eject, eject!'

Bang, bang, two seats came out. Before the first chute opened the flaming fighter went nose-first into the ship's wake. A splash, then it was gone.

'Two good chutes.' Another voice on the radio.

In seconds both the chutes went into the water. As Jake went over he spotted the angel coming up the wake.

'Boy, talk about luck! It's a wonder he didn't blow up,' Jake told Flap.

He was turning across the bow when the air boss came on the frequency. You always knew the boss's voice, a God-like booming from on high. 'Texaco, your signal, charley. We're going to hot spin you.'

Jake checked his fuel quantity. Nine thousand pounds left. He opened the main dump and dropped the hook, gear and flaps.

As advertised, the ball was moving up and down on the optical landing system, which was gyroscopically stabilized in roll and pitch, but not in heave, the up and down motion of the ship.

He managed to get aboard without difficulty and was taxied in against the island to refuel. He kept the engines running.

In moments the helicopter settled onto the deck abeam the island. Corpsmen with stretchers rushed out. The stretchers weren't needed. The two Phantom crewmen walked across the deck under their own power, wet as drenched rats, grinning broadly and flashing everyone in sight a thumbs-up.

Jake and Flap were still fueling five minutes later when two Soviet Bear bombers, huge, silver, four-engine turboprops, came up the wake at five hundred feet. The bombers were about a thousand feet apart, and each had an F-4 tucked in alongside like a pilot fish.

The flight deck crew froze and watched the parade go by.

'We could have done a better job up there today,' Jake told Flap. 'We should have had the second radio tuned into Strike. Then we would have known what Two Oh Seven's problem was without asking. And we should have asked about that wingman. Phantoms always go around in pairs, like snakes.'

'Those tailpipes in our windscreen,' Flap said, sighing. 'Man, that was a leemer.'

Jake knew what a leemer was – a shot of cold urine to the heart. 'We gotta get with the program,' he told the BN.

'I guess so,' Flap said as he tucked Malcolm X into his G-suit pocket and zipped it shut.

The air wing commander was Commander Charles 'Chuck' Kall, a fighter pilot. He was known universally as CAG, an acronym that rhymed with *rag* and stood for Commander Air Group. This acronym had been in use in the US Navy since it acquired its first carrier.

CAG Kall made careful notes this evening as he listened to the air intelligence officer brief the threat envelopes that could be expected around a Soviet task force. Lieutenant Colonel Haldane, his operations officer Major Bartow, and Jake Grafton were the A-6 representatives at this planning session. Jake sat listening and looking at the projected graphics with a sense of relief – The AI's presentation sounded remarkably like his homemade presentation for Colonal Haldane several weeks ago. An attacking force could expect to see a *lot* of missiles and stupendous quantities of flak, according to the AI.

'They aren't gonna shoot all those missiles at the first American planes they see,' CAG said softly. He always spoke softly so you had to listen hard to catch his words. 'It wouldn't surprise me to find out that half those missile launchers are out of service for lack of maintenance. Be that as it may, these numbers should dispel any notions anybody might have that smacking the Russians is going to be easy. These people aren't rice farmers – they are a first-class blue-water Navy. Putting them under with conventional, free-fall bombs is going to be really tough. We're going to lose a lot of people and airplanes getting it done.'

'We'll probably never have to,' someone said, and three or four heads bobbed in agreement.

'That's right,' Kall said, almost whispering. 'But if the order comes, we're going to be ready. We're going to have a plan and we're going to have practiced our plan. We're not going to try to invent the wheel after war is declared.'

There were no more comments about the probability of war with the Soviet Union.

'We'll plan Alpha strikes,' CAG said. 'When we get to the Sea of Japan we'll schedule some and see how much training we need to make that option viable. At night and in bad weather, however, the A-6s are going to have to go it alone. I'd like to have the A-6 crews run night attacks against our own destroyers to develop a profile that gives them the best chance of hitting the target and surviving. Colonel Haldane and his people can work out a place to start and we'll go from there.'

'Aye aye, sir,' Haldane said.

12

One morning when Jake came into the ready room the duty officer, First Lieutenant Doug Harrison, motioned to him. 'Sir, the skipper wants to see you in his stateroom.'

'*Sir!* What is this, the Marines?'

'Well, we try.'

Jake sighed. 'You know what it's about?'

'No, sir.'

'For heaven's sake, my name is Jake.'

'Yes, sir.'

'You try too hard. Let your hair grow out to an inch. Take a day off from polishing your shoes. Do twenty-nine pushups instead of thirty. You can overdo this military stuff, Doug.'

The skipper's stateroom was on the third deck, the one below the ready room deck. Entry to the skipper's subdivision was gained by lowering yourself through a watertight hatch, then going down a ladder.

Jake knocked. The old man opened the door. 'Come in and find a seat.'

The pilot did so. Colonel Haldane picked up a sheaf of paper and waggled it, then tossed it back on his desk. 'Your letter of resignation. I have to put an endorsement on it. What do you want me to say?'

Jake was perplexed. 'Whatever you usually say, sir.'

'Technically your letter is a request to transfer from the regular Navy to the Naval Reserve and a request to be ordered to inactive status. So I have to comment about whether or not you would be a good candidate for a reserve commission. Why are you getting out?'

'Colonel, in my letter I said—'

'I read it. "To pursue a civilian career." Terrific. Why do you want out?'

'The war's over, sir. I went to AOCS because it was that or get drafted. I got a regular Navy commission in 1971 because it was offered and my skipper recommended me, but I've never had the desire to be a professional career officer. To be frank, I don't think I'd be a very good one. I like the flying, but I don't think I'm cut out for the rest of it. I'll be the first guy to volunteer to come back to fight if we have another war. I just don't want to be a peacetime sailor.'

'You want to fly for the airlines?'

'I don't know, sir. Haven't applied to any. I might, though.'

'Pretty boring, if you ask me. Take off from point A and fly to point B. Land. Taxi to the gate. Spend the night in a motel. The next day fly back to A. You have to be a good pilot, I know, but after a while, I think a man with your training and experience would go quietly nuts doing something like that. You'd be a glorified bus driver.'

'You're probably right, sir.'

'So what are you going to do?'

'I don't know, Skipper.'

'Hells bells, man, why resign if you don't have something to go to? Now if you had your heart set on going to grad school or into your dad's business or starting a whorehouse in Mexicali, I'd say *bon voyage* – you've done your bit. That doesn't appear to be the case, though. I'll send this in, but you can change your mind at any time up to your release date. Think it over.'

'Yessir.'

'Oh, by the way, the skipper of the Snake-eyes had some nice words for the way you tanked Two Oh Seven and dropped him off on the down-wind. A quick, expeditious rendezvous, he said, a professional job.'

'Too bad Two Oh Seven caught fire.'

'As soon as he slowed to landing speed the gas seeped into the engine bays around the edges of the engine-bay doors. The engines ignited the fuel. From the time the fire first appeared visually, it was a grand total of two and a half seconds before the hydraulic lines burned through. The pilot punched when the nose started down. He pulled back stick and there was nothing there.'

Jake Grafton just nodded.

'This is a man's game,' Haldane said. He shrugged. 'There's no glamour, no glory, the pay's mediocre, the hours are terrible and the stakes are human lives. You bet your life and your BN's every time you strap on an airplane.'

The carrier and her escorts sailed west day after day. *Columbia*'s airplanes remained on deck in alert status as her five thousand men maintained their machinery, coped with endless paperwork, and drilled. They drilled morning, afternoon, and evening: fire drills, general quarters, nuclear, biological and chemical attack, collision, flooding, engine casualty, and flight deck disasters. The damage control teams were drilled to the point of exhaustion and the fire fighting teams did their thing so many times they lost count.

The only breaks in the routine came in the wee hours of the night when underway replenishments – UNREPS – were conducted. The smaller escorts came alongside the carrier every third day to top their tanks with NSFO – Navy standard fuel oil – from the carrier's bunkers.

Nowhere was seamanship more on display than during the hours that two or three vastly dissimilar ships steamed side by side through the heavy northern Pacific night seas joined by hoses and cables.

The destroyers and frigates were the most fun to watch, and Jake Grafton was often on the starboard catwalk to look and marvel. The smaller warship would overtake the carrier from astern and slow to equal speed alongside. The huge carrier would be almost rock-steady in the sea, but the small ship would be pitching, rolling, and plunging up and down as she rode the sea's back. Occasionally the bow would bite so deep into the sea that spray and foam would cascade aft, hiding the forward gun mount from view and dousing everyone topside.

As the captain of the destroyer held his ship in formation, a line would be shot across the seventy-five-foot gap between the ships to be snagged by waiting sailors wearing hard hats and life jackets. This rope would go into sheaves and soon a cable would be pulled across the river of rushing water. When the cable was secured, a hose would go across and soon fuel oil would be pumping. Three hoses were the common rig to minimize the time required to transfer hundreds of tons of fuel. Through it all the captain of the small boy stood on the wing of the bridge where he could see everything and issue the necessary orders to the steersman and engine telegraph operator to hold his ship in formation.

One night a supply ship came alongside. While Jake watched, a frigate joined on the starboard side of the supply ship, which began transferring fuel through hoses and supplies by high-line to both ships at once. Now both the frigate and carrier had to hold formation on the supply ship. To speed the process a CH-46 helicopter belonging to the supply ship lifted pallets of supplies from the stern of the supply ship and deposited them on the carrier's flight deck, a VERTREP, or vertical replenishment.

Here in the darkness on the western edge of the world's greatest ocean American power was being nakedly exercised. The extraordinary produce of the world's most advanced economy was being passed to warships in stupendous quantity: fuel, oil, grease, bombs, bullets, missiles, toilet paper, movies, spare parts, test equipment, paper, medical supplies, canned soft drinks, candy, meat, vegetables, milk, flour, ketchup, sugar, coffee – the list went on and on. The supply ship had a trainload to deliver.

The social organization and hardware necessary to produce, acquire and transport this stupendous quantity of wealth to these powerful warships in the middle of nowhere could be matched by no other nation on earth. The ability to keep fleets supplied anywhere on the earth's oceans was the key ingredient in American sea power, power that could be projected to anyplace on the planet within a thousand miles of saltwater. For good or ill, these ships made Washington the most import-ant city in the world; these ships made the US Congress the most important forum on earth and the President of the United States the most powerful, influential person alive; these ships enforced a global Pax Americana.

The whole thing was quite extraordinary when one thought about it, and Jake Grafton, attack pilot, history major and farmer's son, did think about it. He stood under a A-6's tail on the flight deck catwalk wearing his leather jacket with the collar turned up against the wind and chill, and marveled.

'I hear you're going to get out,' the Real McCoy said one evening in the stateroom.

'Yeah. At the end of the cruise.' Jake was in the top bunk reading his NATOPS manual.

McCoy had the stock listing pages of the *Wall Street Journal* spread across the floor, his cruise box, bunk and desk. He was sitting cross-legged on the floor with his notebook full of charts on his lap. He had fallen into the habit of annotating his charts each evening after the ship received a mail delivery. He leaned back against his locker, stretched out his legs, and sighed.

'I've thought about it,' he said. 'Getting exiled to the Marines got the wheels spinning. Being ten days behind the markets makes them spin faster. But no.' He shrugged. 'Maybe one of these days, but not now.'

Jake put down his book. 'What's keeping you in? I thought you really liked that investment stuff?'

'Yeah, makes a terrific hobby. I think my problem is I'm a compulsive gambler. Stocks are the best game around – the house percentage is next to nothing – just a brokerage fee when you trade. Yet it's just money. On the other hand, you take flying – that's the ultimate gamble: your life is the wager. And waving – every pass is a new game, a new challenge. All you have is your wits and skill and the stakes are human lives. There's nothing like that in civilian life – except maybe trauma medicine. If I got out I'd miss the flying and the waving too much.'

Jake was slightly stunned. He had never before heard flying described as a gamble, a game, like Russian roulette. Oh, he knew the risks, and he did everything in his power to minimize them, yet here was a man for whom the risks were what made it worth doing.

'If I were you,' Jake told the Real, 'I wouldn't make that crack about waving down in the ready rooms.'

'Oh, I don't. A lot of these guys are too uptight.'

'Yeah.'

'They think the LSO is always gonna save them. And that's what we want them to think, so they'll always do what we tell them, when we tell them. If they get the notion in their hard little heads that we might be wrong, they'll start second-guessing the calls. Can't have that now, can we?'

'Ummm.'

'But LSOs are human too. Knowing that you can make a mistake, that's what keeps you giving it everything you've got, all the time, every time.'

'What if you screw up, like the CAG LSO did with me? Only somebody dies. How are you going to handle that?'

'I don't know. That's the bad thing about it. You do it for the challenge and you *know* that sooner or later the ax will fall and you're going to have to live with it. That's why flying is easier. If you screw up in the cockpit, you're just dead. There's a lot to be said for betting your own ass and not someone else's.'

'Aren't many things left anymore that don't affect someone else,' Jake muttered.

'I suppose,' said the Real McCoy, and went back to annotating his stock charts.

Columbia and her retinue of escorts entered the Sea of Japan one morning in late July through the Tsugaru Strait between the islands of Hokkaido and Honshu. Transiting the strait, the five-minute alert fighters were parked just short of the catapults with their crews strapped into the cockpits, but a mob of sailors stood and sat around the edge of the flight deck wherever there was room between the planes. Some were off-duty, others had received their supervisors' permission to go topside for a squint, many worked on the flight deck.

Land was visible to the north and south, blue, misty, exotic and mysterious to these young men from the cities, suburbs, small towns and farms of America. That was Japan out there – geisha girls, kimonos, rice and raw fish, strange temples and odd music and soft, lilting voices saying utterly incomprehensible things. And they were here looking at it!

Several large ferries passed within waving distance, and the Japanese aboard received the full treatment – hats and arms and a few shirts. Fishing vessels and small coasters rolling in the swells were similarly saluted as the gray warships passed at fifteen knots.

This was the first cruise beyond America's offshore waters for many of these young men. More than a few sniffed the wet sea wind and thought they could detect a spicy, foreign flavor that they had never whiffed before in the nitrogen-oxygen mixture they had spent their lives inhaling back in the good ol' US of A. Even the homesick and lovelorn admitted this was one hell of a fine adventure. If the folks at home could only see this . . .

So steaming one behind the other, the gray ships transited the strait while the young men on deck soaked up impressions that would remain with them for as long as they lived.

Those men standing on the carrier's fantail saw something else: two thousand yards astern the thin sail of a nuclear-powered attack submarine made a modest bow wave. How long she had been there, running on the surface, no one on the flight deck was sure, but there she was. Those with binoculars could just make out a small American flag fluttering from the periscope.

Once through the strait, the ship went to flight quarters and the tourists cleared the flight deck. Except for the few pilots who had launched in the interception of the Russian Bears, most of the aviators had not flown for nine days. This layoff meant that they needed a day catapult shot and trap before they could legally fly at night. With this requirement in mind, the staff had laid on a series of surface surveillance missions in the Sea of Japan. These missions would also show the flag, would once again put carrier-borne warplanes over the merchantmen and warships that plied these waters just in case anyone had become bored listening to American ambassadors. By the time the carrier hurled her first planes down the catapults, the submarine had quietly slipped back into the depths.

Jake was not scheduled to fly today. He was, however, on the flight schedule – two watches in Pri-Fly and one after dark in the carrier air traffic control center, CATCC, pronounced cat-see. During these watches he was the squadron representative, to be called upon by the powers that be to offer expert advice on the A-6 should such advice become necessary. There was an A-6 NATOPS manual in each compartment for him to refer to, and before each watch he found it and checked it to make sure it was all there. Then he stood with observers from the other squadrons with the book in his hand, watching and listening.

In addition to ensuring the air boss and Air Ops officer had instant access to knowledgeable people, these watches were a learning experience for the observers. Here they could observe how the aircraft were controlled, why problems arose, and watch those problems being solved. In CATCC they could also watch the air wing commander, known as CAG, and their own skippers as they sat beside the Air Ops officer on his throne and answered queries and offered advice. Air Ops often conferred with the skipper of the ship via squawk box. Every facet of night carrier operations was closely scrutinized and heavily supervised. While the junior officer aloft in the night sweated in his cockpit, he was certainly not alone. Not as long as his radio worked.

During the day the seas became rougher and the velocity of the wind increased. By sunset the overcast was low and getting lower. Below the clouds visibility was decreasing. A warm front was coming into the area.

Jake watched the first night recovery on the ready room PLAT monitor as he did paperwork. The deck was moving and there were three bolters. The second night recovery Jake spent in CATCC with the NATOPS book in his hand. It was raining outside. Two pilots were waved off and four boltered, one of them twice. One of the tankers was sour and a flailex developed when the spare tanker slid on the wet catapult track during hook-up and had to be pushed back with a flight deck tractor. While this mess kept the deck foul, the LSOs waved off three planes into the already-full bolter pattern.

When the last plane was aboard – the recovery took thirty-eight minutes – Jake headed for his stateroom to work on a training report.

He was still at it half an hour later when the Real McCoy came in, threw his flight deck helmet and LSO logbook onto his desk and flopped into his bunk. 'Aye yei yei! What a night! They're using those sticks to kill rats in the cockpits and the weather is getting worse.'

'You were on the platform?' Jake meant the LSO's platform on the edge of the flight deck.

'Yep. I'm wavin' 'em. Another great Navy night, I can tell you. A real Chinese fire drill. Three miles visibility under a thousand-foot overcast, solid clag up to twenty-one grand, ten-foot swells – why didn't I have the sense to join the Air Force? The boys in blue would have closed up shop and gone to the club three hours ago.'

'The next war,' Jake muttered.

'Next war, Air Force,' McCoy agreed. 'So, wanna stand on the patform with me for the next act?'

Jake regarded his half-finished report with disgust, got out of his chair and stretched. 'Why not? I've listened to you wavers preach and moan for so long that I could probably do it myself.'

McCoy snorted. 'That'll be the day!'

Jake did a clumsy tap dance for several seconds, then struck a pose. 'He looked good going by me.'

McCoy groaned and closed his eyes. He was a self-proclaimed master of the short catnap, so Jake timed it. Sixty-five seconds after the LSO closed his eyes he was snoring gently.

They came out of the skin of the ship by climbing a short ladder to the catwalk that surrounded the flight deck, yet was about four feet below flight deck level.

The noise of twenty jet engines at idle on the flight deck was piercing, even through their ear protectors. Raindrops swirling in the strong wind displaced by the ship's structure came from every direction, seemingly almost at once, even up through the gridwork at their feet. The wind blew with strength, an ominous presence, coming from total darkness, black-ness so complete that for a second or two Jake felt as if he had lost his vision. This dark universe of wind and water was permeated by the acrid stench of jet exhaust, which burned his nose and made his eyes water.

Gradually his eyes became accustomed to the red glow of the flight deck lights and he could see things – the outline of the catwalk, the rails, the round swelling shapes of the life raft canisters suspended outboard of the catwalk railing, and in the midst of that void beyond the rail, several fixed lights. The escorts. Above his head were tails of airplanes. He and McCoy crouched low as they proceeded aft toward the LSO platform to avoid those invisible rivers of hot exhaust that might be flowing just above their heads. Might be. The only sure way to find one was to walk into it.

Somewhere aloft in the night sky, high above the ship, were airplanes. With men in them. Men sitting strapped to ejection seats, studying dials and gauges, riding the turbulence, watching fuel gauges march mercilessly toward zero.

Jake and the Real McCoy climbed a ladder to the LSOs' platform as the first of the planes on deck rode a catapult into the night sky. Both men watched the plane's lights as it climbed straight ahead of the ship. There – they were getting fuzzy . . . And then they were gone, swallowed up by the night.

'Six or seven hundred feet, a couple of miles viz. That's it,' McCoy roared into Jake's ear.

The petty officer who assisted the LSOs was already on the platform getting out the radio handsets, plugging in cords, checking the PLAT monitor, donning his sound-powered headset and checking in with the enlisted talkers in Pri-Fly and Air Ops.

The platform was not large, maybe six feet by six feet, a wooden grid that jutted from the port side of the flight deck. To protect the signal officers from wind and jet blast, a piece of black canvas stretched on a steel frame was rigged on the forward edge of the platform, like a wall. So the platform was an open stage facing aft, toward the glide slope.

Under the edges of the platform, aft and on the seaward side, hung a safety net to catch anyone who inadvertently fell off the platform. Or jumped. Because if a pilot lost it on the glide slope in close and veered toward the platform, going into the net was the only way for the LSOs to save their lives.

Jake Grafton glanced down into the blackness. And saw nothing. 'Relax, shipmate,' McCoy told him. 'The net's there. Honest Injun.'

The platform was just aft of the first wire, about four hundred feet away from the ship's center of gravity, so it was moving. Up and down, up and down.

As McCoy checked the lights on the Fresnel lens, which was several hundred feet forward of the platform, Jake watched. McCoy triggered the wave-off lights, the cut lights, adjusted the intensity of the lens. The lights seemed to behave appropriately and soon he was satisfied.

The Fresnel lens was, in Jake's mind, one of the engineering triumphs that made carrier aviation in the jet age possible. In the earliest days, aboard the old *Langley*, pilots made approaches to the deck without help. One windy day one of the senior officers grabbed a couple signal flags and rushed to the fantail to signal to a young aviator who was having trouble with his approach. This innovation was so successful that an officer was soon stationed there to assist all the aviators with signal flags, or paddles. This officer helped the pilot with glide slope and lineup, and since the carriers all had straight decks, gave the vital engine 'cut' signal that required the aviator to pull his throttle to idle and flare.

When angled decks and jets with higher landing speeds came along, it became obvious that a new system was required. As usual, the British were the innovators. They rigged a mirror on one side of the deck and directed a high-intensity light at it. The light was reflected up the glide slope. By rigging a set of reference lights midway up on each side of the mirror, a datum was established. A pilot making his approach would see the light reflected on the mirror – the ball – rise above the datum lights when he was above glide slope, or high, and descend below it when he was low. The landing signal officer was retained to assist the pilot with radio calls, and to give mandatory wave-offs if an approach became unsafe.

The Fresnel lens was the mirror idea carried one step further. The light source was now contained within five boxes, stacked one on top of the other. The datum lights were beside the middle, or third, box. Due to the way the lens on each light was designed, a horizontally wide but vertically narrow beam of light was directed up the glide slope by each box. Crossing the fantail, the beam from the middle box, the 'centered ball,' was a mere eighteen inches in height.

This was the challenge: a pilot must fly his jet airplane through turbulent air into an eighteen-inch-thick window in the sky. At night, with the deck moving as the ship rode a seaway, hitting this window became extraordinarily difficult, without argument the most difficult challenge in aviation. That anyone other than highly skilled, experienced test pilots could do it on a regular basis was a tribute to the training the Navy gave its aviators, and was the reason those who didn't measure up were ruthlessly weeded out.

You could do it or you couldn't – there was no in between. And yet, no one could do it consistently every time. The task was too difficult, the skills involved too perishable. So night after night, in fair weather and foul, they practiced, like they were doing on this miserable night in the Sea of Japan, eighty miles west of Honshu.

As Jake Grafton stood on the platform staring into the darkness as the wind swirled rain over him, he was glad that tonight was not his night. It felt so good to be *here*, not up *there* sweating bullets as the plane bounced around, trying to keep the needles steady, watching the fuel, knowing that you were going to have to fly that instrument approach to the ball, then thread the needle to get safely back aboard. To return to the world of the living, to friends, to food, to letters from loved ones, to a bunk to sleep in, to a world with a past *and* a future. There in that cockpit when you were flying the ball there was only the present, only the airplane, only the stick in your right hand and the throttles in your left and the rudder beneath your feet. There was only the *now*, *this* moment for which you had lived your whole life, *this* instant during which you called upon everything within you to do this thing.

Oh, yes. He was glad.

Other LSOs were climbing to the platform now, so Jake moved as far back as he could to stay out of the way. All these specialists were here to observe, to see another dozen landings, to polish their skills, to learn. This was normal. The platform was packed with LSOs on every recovery.

The last airplane to be launched was upon the catapult at full power when the lights of the first plane on the glide slope appeared out of the gloomy darkness astern. In seconds the catapult fired and the deck became unnaturally silent.

The Real was already three feet out onto the deck holding the radio headset against his ear with his left hand while he held the Fresnel lens control handle in his right over his head, a signal to his colleagues that he was aware the deck was foul. Jake leaned sideways and looked forward around the edge of the canvas screen. The waist catapult crewmen were working furiously to put the protector plate over Cat Three's shuttle and clear the launching gear from the flight deck. Until they were out of the landing area, the deck would remain foul.

'Come on, people,' the air boss roared over the flight deck loudspeaker. He seemed to believe that his troops worked best when properly stimulated. In any event, he didn't hesitate to stimulate them. 'We've got a Phantom in the groove. Let's clear the deck.'

The last flight deck tractor zipped across the foul line near the island, yet three cat crewmen were still struggling with the protector plate.

Jake lifted one side of his mouse ears away from his head. He heard McCoy roger the ball call.

The air boss on the loudspeaker again: 'He's called the ball. Let's get this deck clear *now*, people!'

There, the cat crewmen were running for the catwalk. Jake looked aft. The Phantom was within a half mile, about two hundred feet high, coming fast. On his nose-gear door was a stop-light arrangement of little lights, red, yellow and green, that was operated by the angle-of-attack instrument in the cockpit. Red for slow, yellow for on speed, and green for fast. The yellow light was lit, but even as Jake saw it, the red light flickered.

'You're going to go slow,' Real told the pilot. 'Little power.'

The red foul deck light went out and the green light came on.

'Clear deck,' shouted the LSO talker.

'Clear deck,' McCoy echoed, and lowered his right arm.

The jet was slamming through the burble causd by the island, his engines winding up, then decelerating. In seconds the Phantom crossed the ramp with its engines wailing, its hook reaching for a wire. Then the hook struck in a shower of sparks and the main gear thumped down. The hook snagged the second wire as the engines wound up to their full fury – a futile roar, because the big fighter was quickly dragged to a quivering halt. The exterior lights went out. The hook runner raced across the foul line with his wands signaling 'hook up.' Seconds later the Phantom was taxiing out of the landing area and the wings were folding.

Meanwhile McCoy was giving the grade to another LSO, who was writing in the log. 'Little slow in the middle, OK Two.'

McCoy glanced at Jake. 'Nice pass. Pitching deck and reduced visbility and he handled it real well. I bet I couldn't do as well on a shitty night like this.'

Then he was back out into the landing area listening to the radio. In seconds another set of lights came out of the goo. Another Phantom. This guy had more difficulty with the pass than the first fighter, but he too successfully trapped. The third Phantom boltered and McCoy waved off the fourth one. It was going to be a long recovery.

One of the LSOs handed Jake his radio. He put it to his ear in time to hear the RA-5C Vigilante call the ball.

The Vigilante was the most beautiful airplane the Navy owned, in Jake's opinion. It was designed as a supersonic nuclear bomber back when nuclear bombs were big. The weapon was carried in an internal bay and was ejected out a door in the rear of the plane between the tailpipes. The Navy soon discovered this method of delivery didn't work: the bomb was trapped in the airplane's slipstream and trailed along behind – sometimes for seconds at a time before it fell free. The weapon's impact point could not be predicted and there was a serious danger that the bomb would strike the aircraft while it was tagging along behind, damaging the plane and the weapon. So the Vigilantes were converted to reconnaissance aircraft. Fuel tanks were installed in the bomb bays and camera packages on the bellies.

With highly swept wings and empennage, a needle nose, and two huge engines with afterburners, the plane was extraordinarily fast, capable of ripping through the heavens at an honest Mach 2+. And it was a bitch to get aboard the ship. Jake thought the Vigie pilots were supermen, the best of the best.

Yet it was the guys in back who had the biggest *cojónes,* for they rode the beast with no control over their fate. Even worse, they rode in a separate cockpit behind the pilot that had only two tiny windows, one on each side of the fuselage. They could not see forward or aft and their view to either side was highly restricted. A-6 BNs with their seats beside the pilot and excellent view in all quadrants regarded the Vigie backseaters with awe. 'It's like flying in your own coffin,' they whispered to one another, and shuddered.

Tonight the Vigie pilot was having his troubles. 'I got vertigo,' he told McCoy on the platform.

'Fly the ball and keep it coming,' the LSO said. 'Your wings are level, the deck is moving, average out the ball. You're slightly high drifting left . . . Watch your lineup!' The Vigilante was a big plane, with a 60-foot wingspan – the foul lines were 115 feet apart.

'Pick up your left wing, little power . . . right for lineup.'

Now the Vigie was crossing the ramp, and the right wing dropped.

'*Level your wings,*' McCoy roared into the radio.

The Vigilante's left wing sagged and the nose rose. Jake shot a glance at the PLAT monitor: the RA-5 was way too far right, his right wingtip almost against the foul line.

His gaze flipped back to the airplane, just in time to hear the engines roar and see the fire leap from the afterburners, two white-hot blow-torches fifteen feet long. The light ripped the night open, casting a garish light on the parked planes, the men standing along the right foul line, and the ship's superstructure.

With her hook riding five feet above the wires and her left wing slightly down, the big swept-wing jet crossed the deck and rose back into the night sky. Only then did the fire from the afterburners go out. The rolling thunder continued to wash over the men on the ship's deck, then it too dissipated.

An encounter with an angry dragon, Jake thought, slightly awed by the scene he had just witnessed.

'A nugget on his first cruise,' McCoy told his colleagues, then dictated his comments to the logbook writer.

The motion of the ship was becoming more pronounced, Jake thought, especially here on the platform. When the deck reached the top of its stroke, he felt slightly light on his feet.

McCoy noticed the increased deck motion too, and he switched the lens to a four-degree glide slope, up from the normal three and one half. The talker informed the controllers in Air Ops.

In seconds there was another plane on the ball, this time an A-7 Corsair. 'Three One Zero, Corsair ball, Three Point Two.'

'Roger ball, four-degree glide slope. Pitching deck.'

This guy was an old pro. McCoy gave him one call, a little too much power, and that was all it took. He snagged a three.

The next plane was the Phantom that boltered, and this time he was steadier. Yet the steeper glide slope fooled him and he was fast all the way, flattened out at the ramp and boltered again.

The next plane, a A-7, took more coaching, but he too caught a wire. So did the Phantom that followed him, the one that had waved off originally. The next A-7 had to be waved off, however, because the deck was going down just before he got to the in-close position, while he was working off a high and slightly fast. If he had overdone his power reduction he would have been descending through the glide slope just as the deck rose to meet him: a situation not conducive to a long life.

An A-6 successfully trapped, then the Phantom came around for his third pass. Clear sky and the tanker were twenty-one thousand feet above, so the pressure was on. McCoy looked tense as a coiled spring as he stood staring up the glide slope waiting for the F-4's lights to appear out of the overcast.

There!

'One Zero Two, Phantom ball, Four Point Two, trick or treat.' Trick or treat meant that he had to trap on this pass or be sent to tank.

'Roger ball, four-degree glide slope, it'll look steep so fly the ball.'

A dark night, a pitching deck, rain . . . these were the ingredients of fear, cold, clutching, icy as death. A carrier pilot who denied he ever experienced it was a liar. Tonight, on this pass, this fighter pilot felt the slimy tentacles of fear play across his backbone. As he crossed the ramp he reduced power and raised the nose. The heavy jet instantly increased its rate of descent.

'No,' screamed McCoy.

The hook slapped down and the main mounts hit and the number one wire screamed from its sheaves.

'There's one lucky mother,' McCoy told the writer and the observing signal officers when the blast of the Phantom's two engines had died to an idling whine. 'Spotted the deck and should have busted his ass, but the deck was falling away. Another military miracle. Who says Jesus ain't on our side?'

More A-7s came down the chute. The first one got aboard without difficulty but the second announced he had vertigo.

'Roger that. Your wings are level and you're fast. Going high. Steep glide slope, catch it with power. More power.' He was getting close and the red light on his nose gear door winked on. He was slow. 'Power. Power! *Power!*'

At the third power call the Real McCoy triggered the wave-off lights, but it was too late. Even as the Corsair's engine wound up, the wheels hit the very end of the flight deck and there was a bright flash. With the engine winding up to full screech the plane roared up the deck, across all the wires, and rotated to climb away. McCoy shouted 'Bolter, bolter, bolter,' on the radio.

Now McCoy handed the radio and Fresnel lens pickle to the nearest LSO. He began running toward the fantail. Jake Grafton followed.

The dim light made seeing difficult. The deck was really moving here, 550 feet aft of the ship's center of gravity. The ship was like a giant seesaw. Keeping your knees bent helped absorb the thrusts of the deck.

McCoy took a flashlight from his hip pocket and played it on the ramp, the sloping end of the flight deck. The ramp dropped away at about a thirty-degree angle, went down ten or twelve feet, then ended. That was the back end of the ship. The flashlight beam stopped three feet right of the centerline stripe, at the deep dent.

'Hook strike,' Jake shouted.

'No, that's where his main mount hit.' Real scanned with the flashlight and stopped at another dent, the twin of the first. 'There's where the other wheel hit. His hook hit below the ramp.' Then McCoy turned and ran for the LSO platform, with Jake following.

Back on the LSO platform McCoy told the sailor wearing the sound-powered phones, 'His hook hit the back end of the ship and disintegrated. He doesn't have a hook now. Tell Air Ops.'

Without a hook, the plane could be trapped aboard only with the barricade, a huge nylon net that was rigged across the landing area like a giant badminton net. Or it could be sent to an airfield in Japan.

Air Ops elected to send the crippled plane to Japan.

McCoy got back to the business of waving airplanes. He had the Vigilante on the ball, with an A-6 and EA-6B behind him, then the E-2 Hawkeye and KA-6 tanker to follow.

This time the Vigie pilot drifted right of centerline and corrected back toward the left. He leveled his wings momentarily, so McCoy let him keep coming. Then, passing in close, the left wing dropped. The Vigilante slewed toward the LSOs' platform as McCoy screamed 'Wave-off' and dived to the right.

Jake had his eyes on the approaching plane, but McCoy was taking everyone on the platform with him. Jake was almost to the edge when the RA-5 swept overhead in burner, his hook almost close enough to touch. Instinctively Jake ducked.

That was close! Too close. Now Jake realized that he and McCoy were the only two people still on the platform. He looked down to his right. Two hands reached up out of the darkness and grabbed the edge by Jake's foot. *Everyone else went into the net.*

They clambered back up, one by one. The talker picked up his sound-powered headset where he had dropped it and put it back on.

McCoy leaned toward the talker. 'Tell Air Ops that I recommend he send the Vigie to the beach for fuel and a turnaround. Give that guy some time to calm down.'

And that is what Air Ops did.

The last plane was still two miles out when a sailor brought a lump of metal to the platform and gave it to McCoy. 'We found this down on the fantail. There's a lot of metal shards down there but this was the biggest piece. I think it's a piece of hook point.'

McCoy examined it by flashlight, then passed it to Jake.

It was a piece of the A-7's hook point, all right. About a pound of it. The point must have shattered against the structure of the ship and the remnants rained down on the fantail.

When the last plane was aboard, Jake followed McCoy down the ladder to the catwalk, then down another flight into the ship.

'That was exciting,' Jake Grafton told the LSO.

'You dum ass. You should have gone into the net.'

'Well, I didn't think—'

'That Vigie about got us. No shit.'

'Hell of a recovery.'

'That's no lie. Did you hear about the A-7 that had the ramp strike?'

'No.'

'The talker told me. The guy had a total hydraulic failure on the way to the beach and ejected. He's in the water right now.'

'You're kidding.'

'The rebound of the hook shank probably severed his hydraulic lines. He's swimming for it. Just another great Navy night.'

The pilot of the RA-5C Vigilante who had so much trouble with lineup on this recovery landed in Japan and refueled. He returned to the ship for the last recovery of the evening and flew a fair pass into a three-wire.

The A-7 pilot with the hydraulic failure wasn't rescued until ten o'clock the next morning. He spent the night in his life raft, buffeted by heavy seas, overturned four times, though each time he regained the safety of the raft. He swallowed a lot of seawater and did a lot of vomiting. He vomited and retched until blood came up. Still retching when the helicopter deposited him back on the carrier, he had to be sedated and given an IV to rehydrate him. He was also suffering from a serious case of hypothermia. But he was alive, with no bones broken. His shipmates trooped to sick bay in a steady procession to welcome him back to the company of living men.

13

The Soviet intelligence ship *Reduktor* joined the task group during the night and fell in line astern. At dawn she was two miles behind the carrier wallowing heavily. When the sun came up she held her position even though the task group raised its speed to twelve knots. When the sea state eased somewhat the Soviet ship rode steadier.

Jake came up on deck for the first launch of the day only to find that the AGI was dropping steadily astern. Her captain knew the drill. The carrier had been running steadily downwind, but to launch she would turn into the wind, toward the AGI. So now the Soviet ship was slowing to one or two knots, just enough to maintain steerageway.

At the brief the air intelligence officers showed the flight crews file photos of this Okean-class intelligence collector. She was a small converted trawler. Had she not been festooned with a dazzling array of radio antennas that rose from her superstructure and masts, one would assume her crew was still looking for fish.

So there they were. Russians. In *Reduktor*'s compartments they were busy with their reel-to-reel tape drives – probably all made in Japan – recording every word, peep or chirp on every radio frequency that the US Navy had ever been known to use. Doubtlessly they monitored other frequencies occasionally as well, just in case. These tapes would be examined by experts who would construct from them detailed analyses of how the US Navy operated and what its capabilities were. Encrypted transmissions would be turned over to specialists who would try to break the codes.

In short, the crew of *Reduktor* were spies. They were going about their business in a lawful manner, however, in plain sight upon the high seas, so there was nothing anyone in the US Navy could do about it. In fact, the American captains and watch officers had to make sure that their ships didn't accidentally collide with the Soviet ship.

There was one other possibility, not very probable, but possible. *Reduktor* might be a beacon ship marking the position of the American task group for Soviet forces. Just in case, American experts aboard the US ships monitored, recorded and analysed every transmission that *Reduktor* made.

Anticipating the coming of a Soviet AGI, the US task group had already reduced its own radio transmissions as much as possible. During the day the aircrews from *Columbia* operated 'zip-lip,' speaking on the radio only when required. Specialists from the Communications Security Group – COMSEGRU – had visited every ready room to brief the crews.

This morning Jake Grafton spent a moment watching the old trawler, then went on with his preflight. He would, he suspected, see a lot of that ship in the next few months.

After four days of operations in the Sea of Japan, *Columbia* and her escorts called at Sasebo and stayed for a week. *Reduktor* was waiting when they came out of port.

The first week of August was spent operating off the southern coast of Korea, then the task group steamed south and spent a week flying in the South China Sea. The Soviet AGI was never far away.

Here, for the first time, the air wing began flying the Alpha strikes that Jake had helped plan with CAG Ops. Jake didn't get to go on the first one, when Skipper Haldane led the A-6s. Due to his bombing scores, however, he was scheduled to lead the A-6s the next day. He and Flap spent half the night in Strike Planning with the other element leaders making sure they had it right.

CAG Kall sat in a corner and sipped coffee during the entire session. He didn't say much, yet when he did you listened carefully because he had something to say worth listening to. He also smiled a lot and picked up names easily. After an hour you thought you had known the man all your life. That night in his bunk the thought tripped through Jake Grafton's mind that he would like to lead the way Chuck Kall did.

Well, tomorrow he would get his chance. Six Intruders were scheduled to fly and the maintenance gunny said he would have them. The target was an abandoned ship on a reef a few miles off the western coast of Luzon, the northernmost of the Philippine Islands. Today's strike had pretty well pulverized the ship, but there were enough pieces sticking out of the water to make an aiming point. The water was pretty shallow there. To make sure there were no native fishing boats in the target area tomorrow before live bombs rained down, an RA-5C was scheduled to make a prestrike low pass.

Jake had so many things on his mind that he had trouble falling asleep. He took the hop minute by minute, the climb-out, the rendezvous, frequency changes, formation, airplane problems, no-radio procedures, the letdown to roll-in altitude . . . he drifted off to sleep and dreamed about it.

The morning was perfect, a few puffy low clouds but widely scattered.

The brisk trade wind speckled the sea with whitecaps and washed away the haze.

After a quick cup of coffee and check of the weather, Jake met with the element leaders for two hours. Then he went to the ready room for the crew briefs, briefed the A-6's portion of the mission, read the maintenance logbook on his assigned plane and donned his flight gear. By the time he walked out onto the flight deck with Flap Le Beau he had been working hard for four hours.

The escort ships looked crisp and clean upon a living blue sea. The wind – he inhaled deeply.

He and Flap took the time to inspect the weapons carefully. For today's mock attack they had live bombs, four Mark-84 two-thousand-pounders. A hit with one of these bombs would break the back of any warship that was cruiser-size or smaller. The multiple ejector racks that normally carried smaller bombs had been downloaded so the one-ton general purpose bombs could be mated to the parent bomb racks. There were two of these on each wing. As usual, the centerline belly station carried a two-thousand-pound drop tank. One of the bombs, the last one to be dropped, had a laser-seeker in the nose. The other three were fused with a mechanical nose fuse and an electrical tail fuse.

The mechanical nose fuse was the most reliable fuse the Navy possessed, which made it the preferred way to fuse bombs. A bare copper wire ran from a solenoid in the parent rack forward across the weapon to the nose, where it went through a machined hole in the fuse housing and then through the little propeller at the very front of the fuse. The wire physically prevented the propeller from turning until the weapon was ejected from the rack. The wire then pulled out of the fuse and stayed on the rack, which freed the propeller. As the bomb fell the wind spun the propeller for a preset number of seconds and armed the fuse. When the nose of the bomb struck its target, the fuse was triggered. After a small delay – one hundredth of a second to allow the weapon to penetrate the target – the fuse detonated the high explosive in the bomb.

If the mechanical fuse was defective, the electric tail fuse would set the bomb off. That fuse was armed by a jolt of electricity in the first two feet of travel as the bomb fell away from the parent rack, then its arming wire, an insulated electrical cable, pulled loose.

The BN's job on preflight was to check to ensure the ordnancemen had rigged bombs, fuses and arming wires correctly. Since any error here could ruin the mission, Jake Grafton always checked too. Today he and Flap stood side by side as they examined each weapon. Everything was fine.

The bomb with the laser-seeker in the nose was the technology of the future, the technology that had already made unguided free-fall bombs obsolete and would itself be made obsolete by guided missiles. One had to aim a laser-light generator at the target and hold the light on it as the bomb fell. If the bomb was dropped into the proper cone above the target, the seeker would guide it to the reflected spot of laser light by manipulating small canards on the body of the device.

In two or three years the A-6 would have its own laser-light generator in the nose of the aircraft. Now the generators, or 'designators,' were hand-held. Today a radar-intercept officer in the backseat of an F-4 orbiting high above the target would aim the designator while Intruders, Corsairs and other Phantoms dropped the bombs. This system worked. Navy and Air Force crews used it with devastating effect on North Vietnamese bridges in the last year of the war.

Due to the cost of the seekers, each plane had only one for today's training mission. Dropping three unguided weapons in addition to the guided one had an additional benefit – the pilot had to try for a perfect dive to put all four on the target. If one bomb was a bull's-eye and the other three went awry, he screwed up.

The plane looked good. Strapped in waiting for the engine start, Jake Grafton arranged his charts in the cockpit, then paused for a few seconds to savor the warmth of the sun and the wind playing with his hair. The moment was over too soon. Helmet on, canopy closed, crank engines.

The cat shot was a hoot, an exhilarating ride into a perfect morning. His airplane flew well, all the gear worked as advertised, none of the other A-6s had maintenance problems and all launched normally.

The A-6s rendezvoused at 9,000 feet. When Jake had his gaggle together, he led them upward to 13,000 feet and slowly eased into position on the right of the lead division, today four Corsairs. When all the other divisions were aboard, the strike leader, the CO of one of the A-7 squadrons, rolled out on course to the target and initiated a climb to 23,000 feet.

The climb took longer than usual. The bombers were heavily loaded. At ninety-eight percent RPM all Jake could coax out of his plane was 280 knots indicated. He concentrated on flying smoothly so his wingmen would not have to sweat bullets to stay with him.

The six-plane division was broken up into two flights of three. Jake had one wingman on each side. Out farther to the right flew another three-plane flight, but its leader was also flying formation on Grafton. Just before the time came to dive, the man on each leader's left would cross over, then the two flights would join so that there were six airplanes in right echelon. The plan was for Jake to roll in and the others to follow two seconds apart, so that all six were diving with just enough separation between the planes that each pilot could aim his own bombs. If they did it right, all six would be in the enemy's threat envelope together and divide the enemy's antiaircraft fire. And all would leave together. That was the plan, anyway.

Flap had the radar and computer fired up, so Jake was getting steering to the target. He was merely comparing it to the course the strike leader was flying, however.

The radio frequency was crowded. The strike leader was talking to the E-2 Hawkeye, the RA-5C was chattering about a fishing boat that he had chased away from the target and the cloud cover, someone had a hydraulic problem, the tankers wanted to change the poststrike rendezvous position because the carrier wasn't where it was supposed to be when this evolution was put together, and one of the EA-6s was late getting launched and was going to be late getting to its assigned position. Situation normal, Jake thought.

He checked the position of his wingmen regularly, yet he spent most of his time scanning the sky and staying in proper position in relation to the strike leader. When he had a spare second he brought his eyes back into the cockpit to check his engine instruments and fuel.

The cumulus clouds below thickened as the strike group approached the coast of Luzon. The bases were at 4,000 feet, but the tops were building. From 23,000 feet the clouds seemed to cover about fifty percent of the sea below.

Would there be holes over the target big enough to bomb through?

The twenty-six bombers and their two EA-6 escorts began their descent toward their roll-in altitude of 15,000 feet. The leader left his throttle alone, so the airspeed began to increase. The faster the strike could close a Soviet task group, the fewer missiles and less flak it would encounter. In aerial warfare, speed is life.

Now CAG was on the radio. He was at 30,000 feet over the target in an F-4. 'Where are the Flashlights?'

Flashlight was the F-4 that would illuminate the target with the laser designator. Actually there were two F-4s, both carrying hand-held laser designators. The pilots would have to find a hole in the clouds so the RIOs — radar intercept officers — could aim the designators, then they would have to maneuver to keep the target in sight and avoid colliding with one another. In a real attack on Soviet ships, the pilots would also be dodging missiles and flak.

'Uh, Flashlight is trying to find the target.'

The F-4's electronic system was designed to find and track other airborne targets, not find the remnants of a wrecked ship resting on a reef. The A-6s' systems, however, were working fine. Flap had the target and Jake was getting steering and distance. In the planning sessions he had argued that A-6s should carry the designators but had been overruled.

'Ten miles to roll-in,' Flap told Jake. The strike was passing 20,000 feet. Now the strike leader dropped his nose farther, giving the group about 4,000 feet a minute down. Three hundred twenty knots indicated and increasing.

Passing 18,000 feet Jake pumped his arm at the A-6 on his left side. Flap did the same to the man on his right. The Intruder formation shifted to echelon.

The tops of the clouds were closer. Still some holes, but the target wasn't visible through them.

The situation was deteriorating fast. Without holes in the clouds, the F-4s carrying bombs could not find the target. The A-7s might be able to, but not in formation since the pilots could not fly formation and work their radars and computers too. The A-6s could break off at any point and make a system attack on the target, individually or in pairs. This was the edge an all-weather, two-man airplane gave you.

The strike leader, Gold One, knew all this. He had only seconds to decide.

'This is Gold One. Let's go to Plan Bravo. Plan Bravo.'

Jake Grafton lowered his nose still farther. Now he wanted to descend below the formation. The A-7s were shallowing their dive, which helped.

Flap was on the ICS: 'Target's twenty degrees left. Master Arm on.'

'Kiss off,' Jake told him, and Flap took a few seconds to splay his fingers at the wingman on his right as Jake turned left to center steering and dropped his nose still more. Fifteen degrees down now, going faster than a raped ape, the plane pushing against the sonic shock wave and vibrating slightly, nothing but clouds visible in the windscreen dead ahead. The other A-6s would continue on course for four seconds each, then turn toward the target. All six would run the target individually.

'We're in attack,' Flap announced, and sure enough, the attack symbology apeared on the VDI in front of Jake.

'War Ace One's in hot,' he announced on the radio.

He took one more quick look around to ensure the other airplanes in this gaggle were clear.

Something on his left wing caught his eye. His eyes focused.

The bomb on Station One, the station nearest the left wing tip – *the propeller on the mechanical fuse was spinning!* The fuse was arming.

He gaped for half a second, unwilling to believe his eyes.

The propeller was spinning.

One bomb in a thousand, they say, will detonate at the end of arming time. The propeller will spin for 8.5 seconds to line up the firing circuit.

He could drop it now!

His thumb moved toward the pickle. The master armament switch was already on. All he had to do was squeeze the commit trigger and push the pickle. The bomb would fall away and be clear of the plane when the fuse finished arming. If it blew then . . .

He would still be within the blast envelope.

All these thoughts shot through his mind in less than a second. Even while he was considering he scanned the instruments to ensure he was tracking steering with his wings level.

He looked outside again. The propeller was stopped.

The bomb was armed! And it hadn't exploded. Okay, we've dodged the first bullet.

He pushed the radio transmit button as he retarded the throttles and raised the nose. 'War Ace One has an armed bomb on the rack. Breaking off the attack and turning north at . . .' He looked at the altimeter. He was descending through 12,000 feet. '. . . At twelve thousand.'

He grabbed the stick with his left hand and used his right to move the Master Arm switch to the safe position.

Everyone was talking on the radio – A-6s calling in hot, and A-7s breaking up for dives, F-4s looking for holes – probably no one heard Jake's transmission.

'Station One,' he told Flap on the ICS when he had his left hand back on the throttles, talking over the gabble on the radio. 'The bomb is armed.'

He concentrated on flying the plane, on getting the nose up and turning to the north. He was in the clouds now, bouncing around in turbulence. A northerly heading should take him out from under the strike gaggle, which was circling the target to the south.

'The arming wire pulled out of the fuse somehow,' he told Flap. 'I saw the propeller spinning. The fucking thing is armed.'

He looked again at the offending weapon. Now he saw that the thermal protective coating was peeled back somewhat. The Navy sprayed all its weapons with a plastic thermal coating after experiencing several major flight-deck fires in which bombs cooked off. The coating must have had a flaw in it, something for the slipstream to work on. The slipstream peeled the coating, which pulled the arming wire.

A two-thousand-pound bomb . . . if it detonated under the wing, the airplane would be instantly obliterated. The fuel in the plane would probably explode. So would the other three weapons hanging on the plane. Not that he or Flap would care. They would already be dead, their bodies crushed by the initial blast and torn into a thousand pieces.

And this turbulence . . . it could set off that fuse.

He retarded the throttles. Almost to idle. Cracked the speed brakes to help slow down.

'Let's climb out of this crap,' Flap suggested.

Jake slipped the speed brakes back in and raised the nose. He added power.

Finally he stabilized at an indicated 250 knots.

'Cubi?' Flap asked.

'Yeah.'

Flap hit a switch and the computer steering went right. Jake looked at the repeater between his legs. The steering bug was at One Six Zero degrees, eighty miles. Flap dialed in the Cubi TACAN station.

'It could go at any time,' Jake said.

'I know.'

'Let's get off this freq and talk to Black Eagle.'

Flap got on the radio as they climbed free of the clouds.

The turbulence ceased.

Left turn. Fly around the target and the strike group to seaward.

No. Right turn. Go around on the land side. The other planes would be leaving the garget to seaward. Maybe at this altitude. No sense taking any more chances than—

An F-4 shot across the windscreen going from right to left. Before Jake could react the A-6 flew into his wash. Wham! The plane shook fiercely, then it was through.

'If that didn't set the damned thing off, nothing will,' Flap said.

Like hell. The jolts and bumps might well be cumulative.

Jake concentrated on flying the plane. He was sweating profusely. Sweat stung his eyes. He stuck the fingers of his left hand under his visor and swabbed it away.

Black Eagle suggested a frequency switch to Cubi Point Approach. Flap rogered and dialed the radio.

They were at 18,000 feet now and well above the cloud tops.

Jake glanced at the armed bomb from time to time. If he pickled it the shock of the ejector foot smacking into the weapon to push it away from the rack might set it off.

If the bomb detonated he and Flap would never even know it.

One second they would be alive and the next they would be standing in line to see St Peter.

What a way to make a living!

Just fly the airplane, Jake. Do what you can and let God worry about the other stuff.

'Cubi Approach, War Ace Five Oh Seven. We have an armed Mark Eighty-Four hanging on Station One. We're carrying three more Mark Eighty-Fours, but they are unarmed. After we land we want to park as far away from everything as possible. And could you have EOD meet us?' EOD stood for explosive ordnance disposal.

'Roger live weapon. We'll roll the equipment and call EOD.'

Cubi Point was the US naval air station on the shore of Subic Bay, the finest deep-water port in the western Pacific. It had one concrete runway 9,000 feet long. Today Jake Grafton flew a straight-in approach over the water, landing to the northeast.

He flared the Intruder like he was flying an Air Force jet. He retarded the engines to idle, pulled the nose up and greased the main mounts on.

He held the nose wheel off the runway until the airspeed read 80 knots, then he lowered it as gently as possible. Only then did he realize that he had been holding his breath.

The tower directed him to taxi back to the south end of the runway and park on the taxiway. As he taxied he raised his flaps and slats and shut down his left engine. Then he opened the canopy and removed his oxygen mask. He wiped his face with the sleeve of his flight suit.

A fire truck was waiting when Jake turned off the runway. He made sure he was across the hold-short line, then eased the plane to a stop. One of the sailors on the truck came over to the plane with a fire bottle, a fire extinguisher on wheels. Jake chopped the right engine. On shutdown the fuel control unit dumped the fuel it contained overboard, and this fuel fell down beside the right main wheel. If the brake was hot the fuel could ignite, hence the fire bottle. The danger was nonexistent if you shut down an engine while taxiing because you were moving away from the jettisoned fuel. But there was no fire today.

One of the firemen lowered the pilot's boarding ladder. Jake safetied his ejection seat and unstrapped. He left the helmet and mask in the plane when he climbed down.

The thermal casing on the armed bomb had indeed been peeled back by the blast of the slipstream, pulling the arming wire and freeing the fuse propeller.

Jake Grafton was standing there looking at it when he realized that a chief petty officer in khakis was standing beside him.

'I'm Chief Mendoza, EOD.'

Jake nodded at the weapon. 'We were running an attack. I just happened to look outside for other planes just before we went into a cloud and saw the propeller spinning.'

Flap came over while Jake was speaking. His put his hands on his hips and stood silently examining the bomb.

'If you'd dropped it like that, sir, it might have gone off when the ejector foot hit it,' the chief said.

Neither airman had anything to say.

'Guess you guys were lucky.'

'Yeah.'

'Well, I gotta screw that fuse out. We'll snap a few photos first because we'll have to do a bunch of paperwork and the powers that be will want photos. I suggest you two fellows ride on the fire truck. You don't want to be anywhere around when I start screwing that fuse out.'

'I'll walk,' Jake said.

Flap Le Beau headed for the fire truck.

The chief turned his back on the weapon while the firemen took photos. He was facing out to sea, looking at the sky and the clouds and the shadows playing on the water when Jake Grafton turned away and began walking.

The pilot loosened his flight gear. He was suddenly very thirsty, so he got out his water bottle and took a drink. The water was warm, but he drank all of it. His hands were shaking, trembling like an old man's.

The heat radiated from the concrete in waves.

He wiped his face again with his sleeve, then half turned and looked back at the plane. The chief was still standing with his arms folded, facing out to sea.

As he walked Jake got a cigarette from the pack in his left sleeve pocket and lit it. The smoke tasted foul.

14

A week after Jake and Flap visited Cubi Point for three whole hours, *Columbia* maneuvered herself against the carrier pier.

Subic Bay, Olongapo City across the Shit River, the BOQ pool, the Cubi O Club with its banks of telephone booths and the Ready Room Bar out back – Jake Grafton had seen it all too recently and it brought back too many memories.

He got a roll of quarters and sat in a vacant telephone booth with a gin and tonic, but he didn't make a call. Callie wasn't in Hong Kong – she was in Chicago. Mail was arriving regularly but there were no letters from her; in fact, she hadn't written since he called her from Hawaii.

Somehow he had screwed it up. He sat in the phone booth smoking a cigarette and sipping the drink and wondered where it had gone wrong.

Well, you can't go back. That's one of life's hard truths. The song only goes in one direction and you can't run it backward.

Morgan McPherson, Corey Ford and the Boxman were gone, gone forever. Tiger Cole was undergoing rehab at the Naval Aeromedical Institute in Pensacola and working out each day in the gym where the AOCS classes did their thing, in that converted seaplane hangar on the wharf. Sammy Lundeen was writing orders at the Bureau of Naval Personnel in Washington, Skipper Camparelli was on an admiral's staff at Oceana. Both the Augies had gotten out of the Navy – Big was going to grad school someplace and Little was in dental school in Philadelphia.

And he was here, sitting in fucking Cubi Point in a fucking phone booth with the door open, listening to a new crop of flyers get drunk and talk about going across the bridge tonight and argue about whether the whores of Po City were worth the risk.

They're up there now near the bar, roaring that old song:

> '*Here I sit in Ready Room Four,*
> *Just dreaming of Cubi and my Olongapo whore,*
> *Oh Lupe, dear Lupe's the gal I adore,*
> *She's my hot-fucking, cock-sucking Olongapo whore . . .*

All his friends were getting on with their lives and he was stuck in this shithole at the edge of the known universe. The war was over and he had no place to go. The woman he wanted didn't want him and the flying wasn't fun anymore. It was just dangerous. That might be enough for the Real McCoy, but it wasn't for Jake Grafton.

He finished his first drink and began on his second – he always ordered his drinks two at a time in this place – and lit another cigarette.

He was just flat tired of it – tired of all of it. He was tired of the flying, tired of the flyers, tired of the stink of the ship, the stink of the sailors, the stink of his flight suit. He was tired of Navy showers, tired of floating around on a fucking gray boat, tired of sitting in saloons like this one, tired of being twenty-eight years old with not prospect one.

'Hey, whatcha doin' in there?' Flap Le Beau.

'What's it look like, dumb ass? I'm waiting for a phone call.'

'From who?'

'Miss June. The Pentagon. Hollywood. Walter Crankcase. The commissioner of baseball. Whoever.'

'Hmmm.'

'I'm getting drunk.'

'You look pretty sober to me.'

'Just got started.'

'Want any company, or is this a solo drunk?'

'Are you waiting for a call?'

'No. The only one who could conceivably want to talk to me would be the Lord, and I ain't sure about Him. But He knows where to find me if and when.'

'That's comforting, if true. But you say you're not sure?'

'No, I'm not.'

'Life's like that.'

'Come on up to the bar. I'll buy the next round.'

'Some of that Marine money would be welcome,' Jake admitted. He pried himself from the booth and followed Flap along the hallway and up the short flight of stairs into the bar room.

Flap ordered a beer and Jake acquired two more gin and tonics. 'Only drink for the tropics,' he told Flap, who cheerfully paid the seventy-five-cent tab and tossed an extra dime on the counter for the bartender. These Americans were high rollers.

'Miss June, huh?'

'Yeah,' said Jake Grafton. 'I wrote her a fan letter about her tits. Gave her the number of that booth. Told her when I was gonna be in Cubi. She'll call anytime.'

'Let's go play golf. We got enough time before dark.'

'Golf's a lot of work. Whacking that ball around in this heat and humidity . . .'

'Come on,' Flap said. 'Bring your drinks. You can drive the golf cart.'

> '*Oh Lupe, dear Lupe's the gal I adore,*
> *She's my hot-fucking, cock-sucking Olongapo whore . . .*'

There was a line of taxis in front of the club. Jake and Flap went to the one at the head of the line. Jake took huge slurps of both his drinks before he maneuvered himself into the tiny backseat, so he would be less likely to spill any.

And away they went in a cloud of blue smoke, the little engine in the tiny car revving mightily, the Filipino driver hunched over the wheel and punching the clutch and slamming the shift lever around like Mario Andretti.

The golf course was in a valley. Hacked out of the jungle were long, rolling fairways and manicured greens with sand traps and fluttering hole flags. Somewhere up there in the lush tropical foliage beyond the rough was the base fence, a ten-foot-high chain-link affair topped by barbed wire. Beyond the base fence were some of the world's poorest people, kept in line by a Third World military establishment and ruled by a corrupt, piss-pot tyrant. The native laborers who maintained this golf course, and were of course not allowed to play on it, were paid the magnificent sum of one US dollar a day as wages.

The whole damned scene was ludicrous, especially if you were working on your fourth drink of the hour. The best thing was not to think about it, not to contemplate that vast social chasm between the men running lawnmowers and raking sand traps and the half-tanked fool driving this shiny little made-in-Japan golf cart. Best not to dwell on the shared humanity or the Grand Canyon that sepraated their dreams and yours.

The heat and humidity made the air thick, oppressive, but it was tolerable here in the golf cart with the faded canvas top providing shade. Jake stuck to piloting the cart while Flap drove, chipped and putted.

'Hotter than hell,' Jake told Flap.

'Yeah. Fucking tropical rain forest.'

'Jungle.'

'Rain forest. Nobody gives a shit about jungle, but they bleed copious dollars over rain forest.'

'Why is that?'

'I dunno. I got a seven on that last hole.'

'That's a lot of strokes. You aren't very good at this.'

'When I play golf, I play a *lot* of it. The object of the game is whacking the ball.'

'Keep your own score. I"m just driving.'

'Driver has to keep score. That's the way it's done at all the top clubs.

Pebble Beach, Inverness, everywhere. Gimme a six on the first hole and a seven on this one.'

'You wouldn't cheat, would you?'

'Who? Me? Of course I'd cheat. I'm a nigger, remember?'

Jake wrote down the numbers and put the cart in motion. 'You shouldn't call yourself a nigger. It isn't right.'

'What do you know about it? I'm the black man.'

'Yeah, but I have to listen to it. And I don't like the word.'

'Bet you used it some yourself.'

'When I was a kid, yeah. But I don't like it.'

'Just drink and drive. It's too damn hot to think.'

'Don't use that word. I mean it.'

'If it'll make you happy.'

'I'm out of booze.'

'Well, you can get drunk tonight. Right now you can sit half-tanked and enjoy the pleasure of watching the world's greatest black colored Negro African-American golfer while you contemplate your many heinous sins.'

'It seemed like a good day for a drunk.'

'I've had days like that.'

The problem was, Jake finally admitted to himself, somewhere along the fourth fairway, that he had no dreams. Everyone needs dreams, goals to work toward, and he didn't have any. That fact, and the gin, depressed him profoundly.

He didn't want to be skipper of a squadron, or an admiral, or a farmer. Nor did he want to be an executive vice president in charge of something or other for some grand, important corporation, luxuriating in his new Buick and his generous expense account and his comfortable semi-custom house in an upscale real estate development and his blond wife with the big smile, big tits and purse full of supermarket coupons. He didn't want a stock portfolio and he didn't want to spend his mornings poring over the *Wall Street Journal* to see how rich he was. Just for the record, he also didn't give a damn about French novels and doubted if he ever could.

He didn't want *anything*. And he didn't want to *be* anything.

What in hell do people do who don't have any dreams?

True, he had once wanted to be a good attack pilot. To walk into the ready room and be accepted as an equal by the best aerial warriors in the world. He had achieved that ambition. And found it wasn't worth a mouthful of warm spit.

He had worked awful hard to get there, though.

That was something. He had wanted something and worked hard enough to earn it. And he was still alive. So many of them weren't. He was.

That was something, wasn't it?

He was still thinking about that two holes later when Flap dropped into the right seat of the cart after a tee shot and said, 'There's somebody in the jungle up by the next hole.'

'How do you know?'

'Two big birds flew out of there while I was in the tee box.'

'Birds fly all the time,' Jake pointed out. 'That's the jungle. There's zillions of 'em.'

'Not like that.'

Jake Grafton looked around. He and Flap were the only people in sight. There weren't even any Filipino groundskeepers. 'So?'

'So I'm going to hit this next one over into the jungle on that side, then go in there to look for the ball. You just sit in the cart and look stupid.'

'I've heard that some locals like to crawl under the fence and rob people on this course.'

'I've heard that too.'

'Let's get outta here. You don't need to play hero.'

'Naw. I'll check 'em out.'

'I hear they carry guns.'

'I'll be careful. Just stop up there by my ball and let me slap it over into the jungle.'

'Don't go killing anybody.'

'They're probably just groundskeepers working on the perimeter fence or something.'

'I mean it, Le Beau, you simple green machine shit. Don't kill anybody.'

'Sure, Jake. Sure.'

So Flap addressed his ball in the fairway and shanked it off into the rough. He said a cuss word and flopped into the cart. Jake motored over to the spot where the ball had disappeared into the foliage and stopped the cart. They were still sixty yards or so short of the green.

'I think this is the spot.'

'Yeah.'

Flap Le Beau climbed out and headed for the jungle, his wedge in his left hand.

Jake examined his watch – 5:35 P.M. The shadows were getting longer and the heat seemed to be easing. That was something, anyhow. Damned Le Beau! Off chasing stickup guys in this green shit – if there were any stickup guys. Probably just a couple of birds that saw a snake or something.

He waited. Swatted at a few bugs that decided he might provide a meal. Amazing that there weren't more bugs, when you thought about it. After all, this was the jungle, the real genuine article with snakes and lizards and rain by the mile and insects the size of birds that drank blood instead of water.

Jake had seen enough jungle to last a lifetime in jungle survival school in 1971, on the way to Vietnam that first time. They held the course in the jungle somewhere around here. He ate a snake and did all that Tarzan shit, back when he was on his way to being a good attack pilot.

For what?

That had been a stupid goal.

It had been a stupid war, and he had been stupid. Just stupid.

He was still sitting in the cart five minutes later trying to remember why he had wanted to be an attack pilot all those years ago when Flap came out of the jungle up by the green and waved at him to come on up. He was carrying something. As Jake got nearer he saw that Flap had a submachine gun in his right hand and his golf club in his left. The shaft of the club was bent at about a sixty-degree angle six inches or so up from the head.

He pulled the cart alongside Flap and stopped. 'Is that a Thompson?'

'Yeah. There were two guys. One had a machete and one had this.' Flap tossed the bent club in the bin in back of the cart.

'Is it loaded?'

Flap eased the bolt back until he saw brass, then released it. 'Yep.'

'Did you kill them?'

'Nope. They're sleeping like babies.'

Jake got out of the cart. 'Show me.'

'What do you want to see?'

'Come on, Le Beau, you moron. I want to see that these dumb little geeks are still alive and that you didn't kill them just for the fucking fun of it.'

Jake took three steps and entered the foliage. Flap trailed along behind.

The vegetation was extraordinarily thick for the first five or six feet, then it thinned out somewhat and you could see. For about ten feet.

'Well, where are they?'

Flap elbowed by him and led the way. One man lay on his face and the other lay sprawled ten feet away, on his back.

Jake rolled the first man over and checked his pulse. A machete lay a yard away. Well, his heart was still beating.

Jake picked up the machete and went over to the second man. He was obviously breathing. As Jake stood there staring down at him, taking in the sandals, the thin cotton shirt and dirty gray trousers, the short hair and brown skin and broken teeth, the man's eyes opened. Wide. In terror. He tried to sit up.

'Hey. You doing okay?'

His eyes left Jake and went behind him. Jake glanced that way. Flap was standing nonchalantly with the Thompson cradled in his left arm, peering lazily around. Yet his right hand was grasping the stock and his forefinger was on the trigger.

The man slowly got to his feet. He almost fell, then caught himself by grabbing a tree.

'Grab your buddy and get back across the fence.'

The Filipino worked on his friend for almost a minute before he stirred. When he had him sitting up, he looked at the two Americans. Jake jerked his head at the fence, then turned and headed for the fairway. Flap followed him.

Jake tossed the machete into the bin beside Flap's rented golf bag and the bent club. Flap dumped the Tommy gun there too and sat down in the passenger seat.

'You're really something else, Grafton.'

'What do you want to do? Play golf or discuss philosophy?'

'I've heard it said that golf is philosophy.'

'It's hot and I'm thirsty and a little of your company goes a hell of a long way.'

'Yeah. Tell you what, let's go see what the rest of this course looks like. Drive on.' He flipped his fingers and Jake pressed the accelerator. The cart hummed and moved. 'Just drive the holes and we'll ride along like Stanley and Dr Livingston touring Africa. Nothing like an evening drive to settle a man's nerves and put everything into perspective. When we get back to the clubhouse, I'll buy you a drink. Maybe later we can go find two ugly women.'

'How ugly?'

'Ugly enough to set your nose hair on fire.'

'That's not ugly.'

'Maybe not,' Flap said agreeably. 'Maybe not.'

15

The days at sea quickly became routine. The only variables were the weather and the flight schedule, but even so, the possible permutations of light and darkness, storms and clouds and clear sky and the places your name could appear on the flight schedule were finally exhausted. At some point you'd seen it all, done it all, and tomorrow would be a repetition of some past day. So, you suspected, would all the tomorrows to come.

Not that the pilots of the air wing flew every day, because they didn't. The postwar budget crunch did not permit that luxury. Every third day was an off day, sprinkled with boring paperwork, tedious lectures on safety or some aspect of the carrier aviator's craft, or – snore! – another NATOPS quiz. Unfortunately, on flying days there were not enough sorties to allow every pilot to fly one, so Jake and the rest of them took what they could get and solaced themselves with an occasional ugly remark to the schedules officer, as if that harried individual could conjure up money and flight time by snapping his fingers.

On those too-rare occasions when bombs were the main course – usually Mark 76 practice bombs, but every now and then the real thing – Jake Grafton managed to turn in respectable scores. Consequently he was a section leader now, which meant that when two A-6s were sent to some uninhabited island in the sea's middle to fly by, avoid the birds, and take photographs, he got to lead. He led unless Colonel Haldane was flying on that launch, then he got to fly the colonel's wing. Haldane *was* the skipper, even if his CEP was not as good as Jake's. Rank has its privileges.

Of course Doug Harrison reminded the skipper of his earlier commitment to letting the best bomber lead. Haldane's response was to point to the score chart on the bulk-head. 'When *you* get a better CEP than *mine*, son, I'll fly your wing. By then my eyes will be so bad I'll need someone to lead me around. Until that day . . .'

'Yessir,' Harrison said as his squadron mates hooted.

Jake had been spending at least half his time in the squadron maintenance department, and now the skipper made it official. Jake was to assist the maintenance officer with supply problems.

The squadron certainly had supply problems. Spare parts for the planes were almighty slow coming out of the Navy supply system. The first thing Jake did was to sit down with the book and check to see if the requisitions were correctly filled out. He found a few errors but concluded finally that the supply sergeant knew what he was doing. Then he sat down for a long talk with the sergeant.

Armed with a list of all the parts that were on back order, he went to see the ship's aviation supply officer, a lieutenant commander in the Supply Corps, a staff corps that ranked with law and medicine. Together they went over Jake's list, a computer printout, then sorted through the reams of printouts that cluttered up the supply office. Finally they went to the storerooms, cubbyholes all over the ship crammed with parts, and compared numbers.

When Jake went to see Colonel Haldane after three days of this, he had several answers. The erroneous requisitions were easily explained – there were actually fewer than one might expect. Yet the Marine sergeant was the odd man out with the Navy supply clerks, who were giving him no help. The system would not work if the people involved were not cooperating fully and trying to help each other.

The most serious problem, Jake told the colonel, was the shortages on the load-out manifest when the ship put to sea. Parts that should be aboard the ship weren't. Related to this problem was the fact that the supply department had stored some of its inventory in the wrong compartments, effectively losing a substantial portion of the inventory that was aboard. This, he explained, was one reason the clerks were less than helpful with the squadron supply sergeant – they didn't want to admit that they couldn't find spare parts that their own records showed they had.

Lieutenant Colonel Haldane went to see CAG, the air wing commander, and together they visited the ship's supply officer, then the executive officer. Jake didn't attend these meetings but he read one of the messages the captain of the ship sent out about shortages in the load-out manifest. Sparks were flying somewhere. Two chief petty officers in the supply department were given orders back to the States. Soon parts began to flow more freely into the squadron's maintenance department. One evening the supply sergeant stopped Jake in the passageway and thanked him.

It was a pleasant moment.

One day the flight schedule held a surprise. From the distant top branches of the Pentagon aviary came tasking for flights to photograph estuaries along the coast of North Vietnam. Told to stay just outside the three-mile limit, the aircrews marveled at these orders. They knew, even if the senior admirals did not, that even if the North Viets were preparing a mighty fleet to invade Hawaii and they managed to get photographs of the ships, with soldiers marching aboard carrying signs saying WAIKIKI OR BUST, the politicians in Washington would not, could not renew hostilities with the Communists in Hanoi. Still, orders were orders. In Ready Four the A-6 crews loaded 35-mm cameras with film, hung them around the BNs' necks, and went flying.

There were no enemy warships lurking in the estuaries. Just a few fishing boats.

It was weird seeing North Vietnam again, Jake told himself as he flew along at 3,000 feet, 420 knots, dividing his attention between the coast and his electronic countermeasures – ECM – alarms as Flap Le Beau busied himself with a hand-held 35-mm camera. The gomers were perfectly capable of squirting an SA-2 antiaircraft missile out this way, even if he was over international waters. Or two or three missiles. He kept an eye on the ECM and listened carefully for the telltale sounds of radar beams painting his aircraft.

And heard nothing. Not even a search radar. The air was dead.

The land over there on his right was partially obscured by haze, which was normal for this time of year. Yet there it was in all its pristine squalor – gomer country, low, flat and half-flooded. The browns and greens and blues were washed out by the haze. The place wasn't worth a dollar an acre, and certainly not anybody's life. That was the irony that made it what it was, a miserable land reeking of doom and pointless death.

Looking at it from this angle four miles off the coast, from the questionable safety of a cockpit, he could feel the horror, could almost see it, as if it were as real and tangible as fog. All those shattered lives, all those terrible memories . . .

They had fuel enough for thirty minutes of this fast cruising, then they planned to turn away from the coast and slow down drastically to save fuel. First Lieutenant Doug Harrison was somewhere up north just now, taking a peek into Haiphong Harbor. Grafton would meet him over the ship.

They were fifteen minutes into their mission when Jake first heard it – three different notes in his ears, notes with a funny rhythm. Da-de-duh . . . da-de-duh . . .

He reached for the volume knob on the ECM panel. Yes, but now there were four notes.

'Hear that?' he asked Flap.

'Yeah. What is it?'

'Sounds like a raster scan.'

'It's a MiG or F-4, man. Look, the AI light is illumin—'

He got no more out because Jake Grafton had rolled the plane ninety degrees left and slapped on five G's as he punched out some chaff.

When the heading change was about ninety degrees, Jake rolled out some of the bank and relaxed the G somewhat. The coast was behind him and he was headed out to sea. The Air Intercept light remained illuminated and the tone continued in their ears, although it was back to three notes, a pause, then the three notes again.

'We're on the edge of his scan, but he sees us all right,' Flap said.

'Hang on.'

Throttles forward to the stops, Jake lowered the left wing and pulled hard until he had turned another ninety degrees. Now he was heading north. He let the nose drop and they slanted down toward the ocean. Meanwhile Flap was craning his head to see behind. Jake was looking too, then coming back inside to scan the instruments. Outside again . . . too many puffy clouds. He saw nothing.

The adrenaline was really pumping now.

'See anything?' he demanded of Flap.

'You'll be the first to hear if I do. I promise.'

Probably a Phantom, but it could be a MiG! Out over the ocean, in international waters. If it shot them down, who would know?

Or care?

Goddamn!

This A-6 was unarmed. Sidewinders could be fitted but Jake had never carried one, not even in training. This was an *attack* plane, not a fighter. And there was no gun. For reasons known only to God and Pentagon cost efficiency experts, the Navy had bought the A-6 without any internal guns. Against an enemy fighter it was defenseless.

The raster beat was tattooing their eardrums. Now they had a two-ring-strength strobe on the small Threat Direction Indicator – TDI. Almost directly aft.

He did another square corner, turning east again, then retarded the throttles to idle to lower the engines' heat signature and kept the plane in a gentle descent to maintain its speed. The enemy plane extended north, then turned, not as sharply. Now it was at five o'clock behind them.

Jake looked aft. Clouds. Oh, sweet Jesus! Dit-da-de-duh, dit-da-de-duh, dit-da-de-duh . . . the sound was maddening.

He was running out of sky. Passing eleven hundred feet. The ocean was down here.

He slammed the throttles full forward. As the engines wound up he pushed the nose over to convert what altitude he had into airspeed. He bottomed out at four hundred feet on the altimeter with 500 knots on the airplane. He pulled, a nice steady four-G pull.

He was climbing vertically, straight up, when he entered the clouds. Concentrating on the gauges, trying to ignore the insane beat of the enemy radar, he kept the stick back but eased out most of the G. Still in the clouds with the nose up ten degrees, he rolled upright and continued to climb.

The sound of the enemy's radar stopped. The MiG must have sliced off to one side or the other, be making a turn to reacquire him. But which way? He had been concentrating so hard on flying the plane that he hadn't had time to watch the TDI.

'Right or left?' he asked Flap.

'I dunno.'

The clouds were thinning. Lots more sunlight. Then the A-6 popped out on top.

Jake looked left, Flap right.

The pilot saw him first, three or four thousand feet above, turning toward them. An F-4.

'It's a fucking Phantom,' he roared over the ICS to Flap.

Flap spun and craned over Jake's shoulder. Then he flopped back in his seat and held up middle fingers to the world.

Jake raised his visor and swabbed his face. Now the strobe reappeared on the TDI and the music sounded in his ears. He reached with his right hand and turned the ECM equipment off.

The plane was climbing nicely. He engaged the autopilot, then turned to watch the F-4. It tracked inbound for several seconds, then turned away while it was still a half mile or so out.

Jake took off his oxygen mask and helmet and used his sleeve to swab the perspiration from his face. He was wearing his flight gloves, so he used them to wipe his hair. The sweat made black stains on his gloves and sleeve. Then he took off one glove and used his fingers to clean the stinging, salty solution from his eyes.

'Think he did that on purpose?' Flap demanded when he had his helmet back on and could again hear the ICS.

'How would I know?'

One evening as Jake entered the stateroom, his room-mate, the financier, glanced at him and groaned. 'Not another haircut! For heaven's sake, Jake, why don't you just shave your head and be done with it?'

Grafton surveyed his locks in the mirror over the sink. 'What are you quacking about? Looks okay to me.'

'Is this the third haircut this week?'

'Well, I admit, watching these Marines parade off to the barbershop on an hourly basis has had a corrosive effect on my morals. I feel like a scuz bucket if I don't go along. What are you caterwauling about? It's my head and it'll all grow out, sooner or later.'

'You're ruining my image, Grafton. Already they are giving me the evil eye. I feel like a spy in the house of love.'

'You've been reading Anaïs Nin, haven't you?'

'Bartow loaned me an edition in English. Wow, you ought to read some of that stuff! Ooh la la. It's broadening my horizons.'

'What are you working on this evening?' The Real had paper strewn all over his desk, but there wasn't a stock market listing in sight.

McCoy frowned and flipped some of the pages upside down so that Jake couldn't see them. Then he apparently thought better of his actions and sat back in his chair surveying Grafton. The frown faded. In a moment he grinned. 'We're going to cross the line in two days.'

The line – the equator. The task group was heading south-east, intending to sail around the island of Java and reenter the China Sea through the Sunda Strait. Of necessity the ship would cross the equator twice.

'So?'

'I'm the only officer shellback in the squadron. Everyone else is a pollywog, including you.'

A pollywog was a sailor who had never crossed the equator. A shellback was one who had previously crossed and been duly initiated into the Solemn Mysteries of the Ancient Order of Shellbacks. It was easy enough to find out who was and who wasn't. In accordance with naval regulations, all shellbacks had the particulars of their initiation recorded in their service records – ship, date and longitude.

'Too bad you'll miss out on all the fun,' Jake said carelessly.

McCoy chuckled. 'I ain't gonna miss a thing, shipmate, believe you me. I'm coming to the festivities as Davy Jones. But if you're willing, I could use a little help.'

Jake was aghast. 'Help from a lowly pollywog?'

'We'll have to keep this under our hats. Can't have scandalous things like this whispered around, can we? This would be help on the sly, for the greater glory of King Neptune.' He picked up the documents on his desk that he had turned over to keep Jake from seeing and passed them to his room-mate.

The next two days passed quickly and pleasantly. Then the great day arrived. There was, of course, no flying scheduled. All morning people – presumably shellbacks – bustled around the ship on mysterious errands, with lots of giggling.

The pollywogs were given strict orders over the ship's loudspeaker system. They were to go to their staterooms or berthing compartments after the noon meal and remain there until summoned into the august presence of Neptunus Rex, Ruler of the Raging Main. Actually there were over two dozen Neptunes, selected strictly on seniority, i.e., the number of times they had crossed the line. Initiation ceremonies would be held simultaneously in ready rooms, berthing areas and mess decks throughout the ship, and each ceremony would be presided over by Neptunus Rex.

In his stateroom, Jake took off his uniform and pulled on a pair of civilian shorts. He donned a T-shirt and slid his feet into shower thongs. Then he settled back to wait for his summons.

It wasn't long in coming. The telephone rang. The duty officer. 'Pollywog Grafton, come to the ready room.'

'Aye aye, sir.'

Jake took off his watch and dog tags. After he checked to ensure that his stateroom key was in his pocket, he went out and locked the door behind him.

The ready room was rapidly filling with his fellow wogs. Jake slipped into his regular seat. Colonel Haldane was lounging in his seat near the duty officer's desk, chatting quietly with the executive officer. Alas, both officers were also wogs and were decked out for the festivities to come in jeans and Marine Corps green T-shirts. Standing everywhere around the bulkheads were officers from the air wing and other squadrons in uniform. Shellbacks. They immediately began to heckle the Marines, and Grafton.

'You're in for it now, wogs . . . Just you wait until King Neptune arrives . . . You slimy wogs are in deep and serious . . .'

The public address system crackled to life. Ding ding, ding ding, ding ding, ding ding, ding ding. Ten bells. 'Ruler of the Raging Main, arriving.'

A howl of glee arose from the onlookers, who laughed and pointed at the assembled victims, many of whom were making faces at their tormentors. Now Flap Le Beau stood in his chair, his arms folded across his chest. He was wearing a pillowcase on top of his head, held on with a band. His face was streaked with paint. As the onlookers hooted, he explained that he was an African king, ruler of the ancient kingdom of Boogalala, and he demanded deferential treatment from this Rex guy.

The shellbacks successfully shouted him down. Finally he sat, promising that he would renew his demands when the barnacled one arrived. One row behind him, Jake Grafton grinned broadly.

They didn't have long to wait. The door was flung open and the Real McCoy stalked in. 'Attention on deck,' he roared. The Marines snapped to attention like they were on parade. When everyone was erect and rigid, McCoy continued, 'All hail, Neptunus Rex, Ruler of the Ragin' Main.'

'Hail,' the assembled shellbacks shouted lustily.

Here they came, the royal party, led by the air wing commander, the CAG, who was decked out in a bedsheet. Behind him came Neptunus Rex, wearing a gold crown that looked suspiciously like it had been crafted of cardboard and spray painted. He wore swimming trunks and tennis shoes, but no shirt. His upper arms each bore a tattoo of a well-endowed, totally naked woman and on his chest was a screaming eagle in flight. A bedsheet cape flowed behind him. In his hand he carried a cardboard trident. As he seated himself on his throne – a chair on a platform so that everyone had a good view – Jake recognized him, as did half the men in the room. Bosun Muldowski.

The Real McCoy – Davy Jones – took his place at the podium and adjusted the microphone. He was wearing long underwear, which he and Jake had decorated with a bottle of iodine last night in a vain attempt to paint fish, octopi and other sea creatures. Alas, the outfit just looked like a bloody mess, Jake decided now. McCoy was enjoying himself immensely, and it showed on his face.

Flap Le Beau stood up again in his chair. 'Hey, King! How's it going?'

McCoy frowned, CAG frowned, Neptune frowned.

'Sit down, wog! Show some respect in the royal presence.'

'Uh, Davy, you don't seem to understand. I'm King Flap of Boogalala. Being a king my very own self, I shouldn't be here in the company of these slimy pollywogs. I should be up there on a throne beside ol' Neptune discussing the many mind-boggling mysteries of the deep and how he's making out these days with the mermaids.'

'Well pleaded, King Flap.' The onlookers seemed to disagree, and hooted their displeasure. Davy looked over at Neptune. 'What say you, oh mighty windy one?'

Neptune scowled fiercely at the upstart Le Beau. 'Have you wogs no respect? The dominions of the land are irrelevant here upon the briny deep, where I am sovereign. I suggest, Davy, that the loud-mouth pretender kiss the royal baby three times.'

'Wog Le Beau, you heard the royal wish. Thrice you shall kiss the royal baby. Now sit and assume a becoming humility or you will again face the awesome wrath of mighty Neptune.'

Le Beau sat. He screwed up his face and tried to cry. And almost made it. A gale of laughter swept the room.

It was good to be a part of this foolishness, Jake Grafton thought, good to have a hearty laugh with your shipmates, fellow voyagers on this journey through life. He and the Real had worked hard to get some laughs, and they succeeded. Many of the wogs were hailed individually before the royal court and their sins set forth in lurid detail. Major Allen Bartow was confronted with a book labeled *S'il Vous Plaît* – really a NATOPS manual with a suitable cover – from which spilled a dozen Playmate-of-the-Month foldouts.

'Reading dirty books, slobbering over dirty pictures . . . shame, shame!' intoned Davy Jones, and King Neptune pronounced the sentence: three trips through the tunnel of love.

After about an hour of this nonsense the wogs were led up to the hangar deck, then across it to an aircraft elevator, which lifted the entire Ready Four pollywog/shellback mob to the flight deck. There the remainder of the initiation ceremonies, and all of Neptune's verdicts, were carried out.

The tunnel of love was a canvas chute filled with garbage from the mess decks. All the wogs crawled through it at least once, the more spectacular sinners several times. At the exit of the tunnel were shellbacks with saltwater hoses to rinse off the garbage, but the wogs were only beginning their odyssey.

Next was the royal baby, the fattest shellback aboard, who sat on a throne without a shirt. His tummy was liberally coated with arresting gear grease. Victims were thrust forward to kiss his belly button. He enthusiastically assisted the unwilling, grabbing ears and smearing handfuls of grease in the supplicants' hair. After kisses from every three or four victims, able assistants regreased his gut from a fifty-five-gallon drum that sat nearby. A messy business from any angle . . .

A visit to the royal dentist was next on the list. This worthy squirted a dollop of a pepper concoction into his victim's mouths from a plastic ketchup dispenser. Expectoration usually followed immediately.

After a visit to the royal barber – more grease – and the royal gymnasium, the wogs ended their journey with a swim across the royal lagoon, a canvas pool six inches deep in water. No, Jake learned as he looked at the victims splashing along, the water was only about one inch deep. It floated on at least five inches of something green, something with a terrible smell. Shellbacks arranged around the lagoon busily offered opinions about what the noisome stuff might be. The wogs slithered through this mess to the other side, where shellbacks helped them out, wiped them down, and congratulated them heartily. Without hesitation Jake flopped down and squirmed his way through the goo while his squadron-mates on the other side – the ones who had beat him over – cheered and offered impractical advice.

Jake joined Flap Le Beau on the fantail, where they stood watching the proceedings and comparing experiences as they wiped away the worst of the grease with paper towels.

The ship wasn't moving, Jake noticed. She lay dead in the water on a placid, gently heaving sea. Around her at distances ranging from one to three miles her escorts were similarly still. All the ships were conducting crossing-the-line initiation ceremonies. Painted ships upon a painted ocean, Jake thought.

With a last glance at the sea and the sky and the merry group still cavorting on the flight deck, he headed below for the showers.

'Getting shot down was a real bad scene,' Flap le Beau told Jake. They were on a surface surveillance mission along the southern coast of Java, photographing ships. To their right was the mountainous island with its summits wreathed in clouds, to the left was the endless blue water. They had just descended to 500 feet to snap three or four shots of a small coaster bucking the swells westward and were back at 3,000 feet, cruising at 300 knots. The conversation had drifted to Vietnam.

Perhaps it was inevitable, since both men had been shot down in that war, but neither liked to talk about their experiences, so the subject rarely came up. If it did, it was in an oblique reference. Somehow today, in a cockpit in a tropic sky, the subject seemed safe.

'It was just another mission, another day at the office, and the gomers got the lead right and let us have it. I hadn't even seen flak that morning until we collected a packet. Goose was killed instantly – one round blew his head clean off, the left engine was hit, the left wing caught fire. All in about the time it takes to snap your fingers.'

'What were you doing?'

'Dive-bombing, near the Laotian border. We were the second plane in a two-plane formation, working with a Nail FAC.' A FAC was a forward air controller, who flew a small propeller-driven plane.

'We were on our second run. Oh, I know, we shouldn't have been making more than one, but the FAC hadn't seen any shit in the air and everything was cool during our first run. Then whap! They shot us into dog meat going down the chute. I grabbed the stick, pickled the bombs and pulled out, but the left engine was doing weird things and the wing was burning like a blowtorch and Goose was smeared all over everything, including me. Wind howling through the cockpit – all the glass on his side was mashed out. Real bad scene. So I steered it away from the target a little and watched the wing burn and told Goose good-bye, then I boogied.'

'How long did you wait before you ejected?'

'Seemed like an hour or so, but our flight leader told me later it was about a minute. All the time he was screaming for me to eject because he could see the fire. But we were at about six thousand feet at that point and I wanted a little distance from the gomers and I wanted the plane slowed down so I wouldn't get tore up going out. There was so much noise I never heard anything on the radio.'

Jake remembered his own ejection, at night, over Laos. Just thinking about it brought back the sweats. He didn't say anything.

'When I got on the ground,' Flap continued, 'I got out my little radio and started talking. Now I'd checked the battery in that jewel before we took off, but I could barely hear the FAC. I found a place to settle in where I could keep an eye on the chute. Then the rescue turned to shit. The gomers were squirting flak everywhere and it was late in the afternoon and darkness was coming. What I didn't know until way afterward was that the guy flying the rescue chopper got a case of cold feet and decided his engine wasn't right or something. Anyway, he never came. It got dark and started raining and I decided I was on my own.'

'So how'd you feel?'

'Well, I felt real bad about Goose. He was a good guy, y'know? Tough getting it like that.'

'I mean how did *you* feel?'

'Like I had never left Marine recon. At least my jungle rot wasn't itching. That was something. I skinned out of all that survival gear and kept only what I needed and decided to set up an ambush. What I really wanted was a rifle. All I had was the forty-five. And my knife.'

'Didn't you think they might catch you?'

'No way, man. I knew they wouldn't. Couldn't. Not unless they shot me or something. I was on the ground for two weeks and had people walk by within six feet of me and they never saw me.'

'So what did you do?'

'Do? Well, I found a guy who had a rifle and took it, and his food. Ball of rice, with a lot of sand mixed in. You sort of have to develop a taste for it.'

'Uh-huh.'

'Checked in on the emergency freq about once a day, when the gomers weren't close. Didn't want to overwork the batteries in that radio. But they never heard me. A patrol found me on the fourteenth day. It was a good thing, because my jungle rot was starting to itch by then. You can never really cure that shit, you know.'

'So how many gomers did you kill?'

'A dozen that I know about.'

'Know about?'

'Yeah. I kept busy building booby traps and such. With a little luck the traps got a few more of 'em. In a way, it sort of made up for losing Goose. Not really, I guess. But it helped.'

'Uh-huh.'

'A fucked-up war, that's what it was. A hell of a mess.'

'Yeah,' Jake said, and checked the fuel and the clock on the instrument panel. 'I think we're going to have to turn around.'

'Okay,' Flap Le Beau said. 'Boy, it sure is pretty out here today.'

'There's a decision point for every career officer,' Lieutenant Colonel Haldane said, 'one day when you wake up and decide that you want to make a contribution. And for pilots, that doesn't mean driving an airplane through the sky every day.'

He and Jake were sitting in the ready room. Jake had the duty and sat at the duty desk and Haldane was in his chair just behind it. There was only one other officer in the room, doing paperwork near the mailboxes. Haldane's voice was low so that only Jake could hear it.

'True, some officers merely decide to stay until retirement, and I suppose that's okay. We need those people too. But the people we want are those who dedicate themselves to making the service better, to being leaders, people who try to grow personally and professionally every day. Those folks are few and far between but we need them desperately.'

Jake merely nodded. Haldane had read the latest classified messages and handed the board back to Jake just before he began this monologue.

Apparently Jake's letter of resignation was on his mind, although he hadn't mentioned it.

Haldane went on, almost thinking out loud: 'In every war America fought before Vietnam, the people who led the military to victory were never the people in charge when the shooting started. US Grant and William T. Sherman weren't even in the army when the Civil War started. Phil Sheridan was a captain. Eisenhower and George Patton were colonels at the start of World War II, Halsey and Nimitz were captains. Curious, don't you think?'

Before Jake could reply, he continued, 'In peacetime the top jobs go to politicians, men who can stroke the civilians and oil the wheels of the bureaucracy. During a war the system works the way it is supposed to – men who can lead other men in combat are pulled to the top and given command. In Vietnam this natural selection process was stymied by the politicians. It was a political war all the way and the last thing they wanted was to relinquish the controls to war fighters. So we lost. And you know something funny? We could afford to lose because we didn't have anything important at stake in the first place.

'Someday America is going to get into a fight it has to win. I don't know when it will come or who the fight will be with. That war may come next year, or twenty years from now, or fifty. Or a hundred. But it *will* come. It always has in the past and evolution doesn't seem to be improving the human species anywhere near fast enough.

'The question is, who will be in the military when that war comes? Will the officer corps be full of glorified clerks, efficiency experts and computer operators putting in their time to earn a comfortable retirement? Or will there be some military leaders in that mix, men who can lead other men to victory, men like Grant, Patton, Halsey?'

Haldane rose from his chair and adjusted his trousers. 'Interesting question, isn't it, Mr Grafton?'

'Yessir.'

'The quality of the people in uniform – such a little thing. And that may make all the difference.'

Haldane turned and walked out. The officer doing paperwork had already left. Jake pulled out the top drawer of the desk and propped his feet up on it.

That Haldane – a romantic. Blood, thunder, destiny . . . If he thought that kind of talk cut any ice anymore he was deluding himself. Not in this post-Vietnam era. Not with the draft dodgers who didn't want to go and not with the veterans who weren't so quick.

Jake Grafton snorted. He had had his fill of this holy military crap! His turn expired when this boat got back to the States in February. Then somebody else could do it.

And if the United States goes down the slop chute someday because no one wants to fight for it, so be it. No doubt the Americans alive then will get precisely what they deserve, ounce for ounce and measure for measure.

What was that quote about the mills of the gods? They grind slowly?

16

Singapore lies at the southern end of the Malay peninsula, a degree and a half north of the equator. This city is the maritime crossroads of the earth. Ships from Europe by way of Suez and the Red Sea, India, Pakistan, Africa and the Middle East transit the Strait of Malacca and call here before entering the South China Sea. Ships from America, Japan, China, Taiwan, Korea and the Soviet Far East call here on their way west. The city-state is close enough to the Sunda Strait that it makes a natural port call for ships from the Orient bound for South Africa or South America via the Cape of Good Hope.

Although it is one of the world's great seaports, Singapore doesn't have a harbor. The open roadstead is always crammed with ships riding their anchors, except on those rare occasions when a typhoon threatens. There are few piers large enough for an oceangoing vessel, so the majority of the cargo being off- or on-loaded in Singapore travels to and from the ships in lighters. The squadrons of these busy little boats weaving their way through the anchored ships from the four corners of the earth and all the places in between make Singapore unique.

As befits a great seaport, the city is a racial melting pot. The human stew is composed mostly of Malay, Chinese, Thai, Hindu, Moslem, and Filipino, with some Japanese added for seasoning, but there are whites there too. British, primarily, because Singapore was one of those outposts of empire upon which the sun never set, but also people from most of the countries of Europe, Australia, New Zealand, and, inevitably, America.

Visitors who have always considered their place, their nation, as the zenith of civilization here receive a shock. Vibrant, cosmopolitan Singapore is a major vortex, one of those rare places where the major strains of the human experience come crashing together and swirl madly around until something new is created.

To the delight of visiting American sailors, the British still had a military base there, Changi, and shared it with those stout lads from Down Under, the Australians, who naturally came supplied with Down Under lassies. Australian women were the glory of Singapore. These tall, lithe creatures with tanned, muscular legs and striking white teeth that were forever being displayed in dazzling smiles somehow completed the picture, made it whole. You ran into them at Raffles, the old hotel downtown with ceiling fans and rattan chairs and doddery old gentlemen in white suits sipping gin. You ran into them in the lobbies and restaurants of the new western hotels and in the bazaars and emporiums. You saw them strolling the boulevards and haggling with small Chinese women in baggy trousers for sapphires and opals. You saw them everywhere, young, tan, enjoying life, the center of attention wherever they were. It helped that their colorful tropical frocks contrasted so vividly with the drab trousers and white shirts that seemed to be the Singaporean national costume. They were like songbirds surrounded by sparrows.

'If Qantas didn't bring them here, the United Nations should supply them as a gesture of good will to all human kind.'

Flap Le Beau stated this conclusion positively to Jake Grafton and the Real McCoy as they stood outside Raffles Hotel surveying the human parade on the sidewalk.

'I think I'm in love,' the Real McCoy told his companions. 'I want one of those for my very own.'

The three of them had ridden the liberty boat two miles across the anchorage an hour ago. They had walked for an hour, taking it all in and had developed a terrible thirst. Just now they were contemplating going into Raffles to see if their need could be quenched somewhat.

'After forty-five days at sea, everything female looks mighty good to me,' Flap Le Beau said, then smiled broadly at an elderly British lady coming out of the hotel. She nodded graciously in reply and seated herself in a waiting taxi.

'Well, gentlemen,' Jake Grafton said, and turned to face the white antique structure, 'shall we?'

'Let's.'

The temperature inside was at least ten degrees cooler. The dark interior and the ceiling fans apparently had a lot to do with that, but the very Britishness of the place undoubtedly helped. The heat and humidity could stay outside – it wouldn't dare intrude.

The American aviators went to the bar and ordered – of all things – Singapore slings. The waiter, a Chinese, didn't bat an eye. He nodded and moved on. He had long ago come to terms with the curious taste of liquor that seemed to afflict most Americans.

'You sort of expect to see Humphrey Bogart or Sidney Greenstreet sitting around under a potted palm,' the Real commented as he tilted his chair back and crossed his legs.

Jake Grafton sipped his drink in silence. Forty-five days at sea riding the catapults, night rendezvouses above the clouds, instrument approaches to the ball, mid-rats sliders, ready room high jinks, lying in his bunk while the ship moved ever so gently in the sea as he listened to the creaks and groans . . . then to be baptized with a total immersion in *this*. Cultural shock didn't begin to describe it. The sights and sounds and smells of Singapore were sensory overload for a young man from a floating monastery.

He sat now trying to take it all in, to adjust his frame of reference. He had been here once before, on one of his cruises to Vietnam. He tried to recall some details of that visit, but the memories were vague, blurred scenes just beyond the limits of complete recall. He had sat here in this room with Morgan McPherson . . . at which table? He couldn't remember. Morgan's face, laughing, he could see that, but the room . . . Who else had been there?

Oh, Morg! If you could only be here again. To sit here and share a few moments of life. We wouldn't waste it like we did then. If only . . .

So many of those guys were dead. And he had forgotten. That the moments he had spent with them were fuzzy and blurred seemed a betrayal of what they had been, what they had given. Life goes on, but still . . . All that any man can leave behind are the memories that this friends carry. He isn't really gone until they are. But if the living quickly forget, it is as if the dead man never was.

'. . . we oughta go buy some souvenirs,' the Real was saying. 'The folks at home would really like . . .'

Jake polished off the last of his drink and stood. He threw some Singapore dollars on the table, money he had acquired this morning from the money changers aboard ship. 'See you guys later.'

'Where are you going?'

He was going back to the ship, but he didn't want to say that. 'Oh, I dunno. Gonna just walk. See you later.'

Outside on the street he stuffed his hands into his pockets and turned toward the wharves. He walked along staring at the sidewalk in front of him, oblivious of the traffic and the sights and the human stream that parted to let him past, then immediately closed in behind him.

The next day Jake stood an eight-hour duty officer watch in the ready room. About two in the afternoon the Real McCoy came breezing in.

'Today's your lucky day, Grafton. You are blessed to have Flap and me for friends. Truly blessed.'

'I know,' Jake told him dryly.

'We met some Brits. What a bunch they are! How we ever kicked them out of the good ol' US of A is a mystery I'll never understand.'

'A military miracle.'

'These are *good* guys.'

'I'm sure.'

'They've invited us to a party at Changi this evening. A party! And they swore that some Aussie women would be there! Qantas stews. Can you beat that?' Without pausing to let Jake wrestle with that question, he steamed on. 'When do you get off?'

'Uh, two hours from now.'

The Real consulted his watch. 'I'll wait. Flap is taking the next boat in, but I'll wait for you. I've got directions. We'll grab a cab and tootle on over to *party hearty*. Maybe, just maybe, we'll get a glorious opportunity to lower the white count. Oooh boy!'

McCoy strode up the aisle between the huge, soft chairs, past the silent 16-mm movie projector, and blasted through the door into the passageway.

Jake sat back in his chair and opened the letter from his parents yet again. It had been two weeks since the last mail delivery, via a cargo plane out of Cubi Point, and this was the current crop, delivered this morning – one letter from his mother. She signed it 'Mom and Dad,' but she wrote every word. Nothing from Callie McKenzie.

Maybe that was for the best. It had been a hell of a romance, but now it was over. She was from one world, he was from a completely different one. Presumably she was doing her own thing there in Chicago, going to class and dating some long-haired hippie intellectual who liked French novels. What was it about French novels?

But he desperately wished she had written. Even a Dear John letter would be preferable to this vast silence, he told himself, wanting to believe it but not quite sure that he did.

Oh well. Like most of the things in his life, this relationship was out of his control. Have a nice life, Callie McKenzie. Have a nice life.

Darkness comes quickly in the tropics. Twilight is an almost instantaneous transition from daylight to darkness. Jake, Flap and the Real had just arrived at Changi by taxi and found the outdoor pavilion when the transition occurred. Whoom, and the lanterns in the pavilion were flickering bravely against the mighty darkness.

The Brit and Aussie soldiers had indeed not forgotten their invitation of the afternoon. They led the three Americans around and introduced them, but Flap was the only surefire hit with the ladies. Soon he had all five of the women gathered around him.

'The Aussies aren't used to black men wearing pants,' the Real whispered to Jake. 'Those stews will get over the novelty in a while and we'll get a chance to cut a couple out.'

Jake wasn't so sure. The soldiers seemed to be eyeing the crowd around Flap with a faint trace of dismay. Nothing obvious, of course, but Jake thought he could see it.

'Hey, mate. How about a beer?' The Australian who asked held out a couple of cold bottles of Fosters.

'Thanks. Real hard duty you guys got here.'

'Beats the outback. Beats that scummy little war you Yanks gave in the Nam, too. Saigon was a bit of all right but the rest of it wasn't so cheery. This is mighty sweet after that busman's holiday, I can tell you.'

'It was the only war we had,' the Real explained, then poured beer down his throat. Jake Grafton did the same.

Two beers later Jake Grafton was sitting at a table in the corner listening to Vietnam War stories from a couple of the Aussies when one of the stews came over to join them. 'Mind if I join you chaps?'

'Not at all, not at all. Brighten up the party. How long are you in for this time, Nell?'

'Off to Brisbane and Sydney tomorrow. Then back here via Tokyo the following day.' Nell winked at Jake. 'Girl has to keep herself busy now, doesn't she?'

Grafton nodded and grinned. Nell returned it. She was a little above medium height, with fair hair and a dynamite tan. Several gold bracelets encircled each of her wrists and made tiny tinkly noises when she moved her arms.

'My name's Jake,' he told her.

'Nell Douglas,' she said, and stuck out her hand. Jake shook it. Cool and firm. And then he looked around and realized the Aussies had drifted and he and Nell were alone.

'So what do you do for the Yanks?'

'I'm a pilot.'

'Oh, God!' Not another one. I've sworn off pilots for at least three months.' She smiled again. He liked the way her eyes smiled when she did.

'Better tell me about it. Nothing like a sympathetic listener to ease a broken heart.'

'You don't look like the sympathetic type.'

'Don't be fooled by appearances. I'm sensitive, sympathetic, charming, warm, witty, wonderful.' He shrugged. 'Well, part of that's true, anyway. I'm warm.'

Now her whole face lit up. Her bracelets tinkled.

'How long have you been flying with Qantas?'

'Five years. My father has a station in Queensland. One day I said to myself, Nell old girl, if you stay here very much longer one of these jackeroos will drag you to the altar and you'll never see any more of the world than you've seen already, which wasn't very much, I can tell you. So I applied to Qantas. And here I am, flying around the globe with my little stew bag and makeup kit, serving whiskey to Japanese businessmen, slapping pilots, giving lonely soldiers the hots, and wondering if I'm ever going back to Queensland.'

'What's a jackeroo?'

'You Yanks call them cowboys.'

This could be something nice, Jake thought, looking at the marvelous, open, tanned female face and feeling himself warmed by her glow. There are a lot of pebbles on the beach and some of them are nuggets, like this one.

'So a station's a ranch?'

'Yes. Sheep and cattle.'

'I was raised on a farm myself. Dad ran a few steers, but mainly he raised corn.'

'Ever going back?' Nell asked.

'I dunno. Never say never. I might.'

She told him about the station in Queensland, about living so far from anything that the world outside seemed a fantasy, a shimmering legend amid the heat and dust and thunderstorms. As she talked he glanced past the lanterns into the darkness beyond, at that place where the mown grass and the velvet blackness met. The night was out there as usual, but here, at least, there was light.

An hour or so later someone turned on the radio and several of the women wanted to dance. To Jake's surprise Flap 'Go Ugly Early' Le Beau proved good at dancing, slow or fast, so good that he did only what his partner could do. You had to watch him with three or four of the sheilas before you realized that he sensed their skill level almost instantaneously and asked of them only what they had to give. Nell pointed that out to Jake, who saw it then. She danced a fast number with Flap – she was very good – as the Aussies and Brits watched appreciatively. They applauded when the number ended.

Nell rejoined Jake and led him out onto the floor for the next slow number. 'I don't dance very well,' he told her.

'That's not the point,' she said, and settled in against him to the beat of the languid music.

It was then that Jake Grafton realized he was in over his head. The supple body of the woman against his chest, the caress of her hair on his cheek, the faint scent of a cologne he didn't recognize, the touch of her hands against his – all this was having a profound effect and he wasn't ready.

'Relax,' she whispered.

He couldn't.

The memory of his morning in bed with Callie four months ago came flooding back. He could see the sun coming through the windows, feel the clean sheets and the sensuous touch of her skin . . .

'You're stiff as a board.'

'Not quite.'

'Oops. Didn't mean it quite that way, love.'

'I'm not a very good dancer.'

She moved away a foot or so and looked searchingly into his face. 'You're not a very good liar either.'

'I'm working on it.'

She led him by the hand through the crowd and out of the pavilion into the darkness. 'Why is it all the good ones come with complications?'

'At our age virgins are hard to find,' Jake told her.

'I quit looking for virgins years and years ago. I just want a man who isn't too scarred up.'

She led him to a wall and hopped up on it. 'Okay, love. Tell Ol' Nell all about it.'

Jake Grafton grinned. 'How is it that a fine woman like you isn't married?'

'You want the truth?'

'If you feel like it.'

'Well, the truth is that I didn't want the ones who proposed and the ones I wanted didn't propose. Propose marriage, that is. They had a lot of things in mind but a trek to the altar wasn't on the list.'

'That sounds like truth.'

'It is that, ducky.'

The music floating across the lawn was muted but clearly audible. And she was right there, sitting on the wall. Instinctively he moved closer and she put an arm around his shoulder. Their heads came together.

Before very long they were kissing. She had good, firm lips, a lot like Callie's. Of course Callie was . . .

His heart was thudding like a drum when they finally parted for air. After a few deep breaths, he said, 'There's another woman.'

'Amazing.'

'I'm not married or anything like that. And I haven't asked her to marry me, but I wanted to.'

'Uh-huh.'

'I think she gave up on me. Hasn't written in a couple months.'

'You like your women dumb, then?' she asked softly, and put her lips back on his.

Somehow she was off the wall and they were entwined in each other's arms, their bodies pressed together. When their lips parted this time, a ragged breath escaped her. 'Whew and double whew. You Yanks! Sex-starved maniacs, that's what you are.'

She eased away from him. 'Well, that was my good deed for today. I've given another rejected, love-starved pilot hope for a brighter future. Now I think it's time for this Sheila to trek off to her lonely little bed. Must fly tomorrow, you know.'

'Going to be back in Singapore day after tomorrow?'

'Yes.'

'What hotel? Maybe I can stop by and take you to dinner.'

'The Intercontinental.'

'I'll walk inside with you.'

'No, just stay where you are, mate. I've had quite enough tonight. One more good look at you in the light and I might drag you off to my lonely little bed for a night of sport. Can't have that, can we, not with you pining your heart out for that other silly girl.'

With that she was gone. Across the lawn and into the crowd.

Jake Grafton leaned on the wall and lit a cigarette. His hands were trembling slightly.

He didn't know quite what to think, so he didn't think anything. Just inhaled the cut-grass smell and looked into the darkness and let his heart rate subside to its normal plodding pace.

At least half an hour passed before Jake went back into the pavilion. Three half-potted Aussies were huddled around the piano watching Flap dance with the three stews who were still there. Le Beau had them in a line and was teaching them new steps to the wailing of a Japanese music machine. Everyone else had left, including the Real McCoy. Tomorrow was a working day for most of them.

Jake decided one more beer for the road wouldn't hurt, so he picked a bottle out of the icy water of the tub and joined the piano crowd.

'Hey, mate.'

'How you guys doing tonight?'

'Great.'

'Sure nice of you fellows to invite us to your wing ding. Makes a good break after forty-five days at sea.'

'Don't know how you blokes manage.'

'Prayer,' Jake told them, and they laughed.

The biggest of them was a brawny man three or four inches taller than Jake and at least forty pounds heavier. Most of his bulk was in his chest, shoulders and arms. He hadn't said anything yet, but now he gestured to Flap. 'Wish your bleedin' nigger mate would pick his bird and let us at the other two.'

Jake Grafton carefully set his beer on the piano. This was getting to be a habit. The last time they had sent him to the Marines.

Wonder where they'll send me this time?

He stepped in front of the big Aussie, who still had one giant mitt wrapped around a bottle of beer.

'What did you say?'

'I said, I wish your bleedin' nigger mate would—'

As Jake drew back his right fist for a roundhouse punch he jabbed the Aussie in the nose with his left. This set the man momentarily off balance, so when the right arrived on his chin with all Jake's weight behind it, it connected solidly with a meaty thunk that rocked Jake clear to the shoulder. The Aussie went backward onto the floor like he was pole-axed. And he stayed there.

'Nice punch, mate, but you—' said the one to the left, but his words stopped when Jake's fist arrived. The man took it solidly on the side of the head and sent a right at Jake that connected and shook him badly.

Stars swam before Grafton's eyes. He waded in swinging furiously. Some of his punches missed, some hit. That was the lesson he had learned as a boy on the grade school playground – keep swinging and going forward. Most boys don't really like to fight, so when you keep swinging they will fall back, and ultimately quit. Of course, these soldiers weren't boys and worse, they *liked* to fight.

His attack worked for several seconds, then the third Aussie, who was now behind him, grabbed him and spun him around. Before Jake could get set he took a shot on the cheekbone that put him down.

Dazed, he struggled to rise. When he got to his feet it was too late. All three of the Aussies were asleep on the floor and Flap Le Beau was standing there calmly scrutinizing him.

'What was that all about?'

Jake swayed and caught himself by grabbing the piano.

'They insulted Elvis.'

Flap sighed. 'I guess we've worn out our welcome.' He took Jake's arm and got him started for the door. 'Ladies,' he said, addressing the three stews gaping at them, 'it's been a real treat. The pleasure of your company was sweeter than you will ever know.'

He beamed benignly at them and steered Jake out into the night.

The base was quiet. No taxi at the main gate. They waved at the sentry and kept walking. Jake's right hand throbbed and so did his head. The hand was the important thing, though. He rubbed it as he walked.

'What really happened back there?' Flap asked.

'The big stud called you a nigger.'

'You hit him for *that?*'

'Yeah. The asshole deserved it.'

Flap Le Beau threw back his head and laughed. 'Damn, Jake, you are really something else.'

'He was peeved because you were monopolizing the women.'

Flap thought this was hilarious. He roared with laughter.

'Want to tell me what's so damn funny?'

'You are. You nitwit! All of them are bigots. Even the women. I wasn't getting anywhere with them. Not a one of those women would have gone to bed with me, not even if I was the richest nigger in America and had a cock eighteen inches long. They'll go back to Australia and tell all about their big adventure, talking to and dancing with an American *nigger*. "Oh, Matilda, you won't believe this, but I even let him *touch* me."'

Jake didn't know what to say, so he said nothing.

After a bit Flap asked, 'Think you broke your hand?'

'Dunno. Don't think so. Maybe stoved it. Man, I got that big guy with a perfect shot. Had everything behind it and drove it right through his chin.'

'He never moved after you hit him. Bet it's the first time anybody ever knocked him out.'

'Thanks for coming to the rescue, Kemo Sabe.'

'Any time, Tonto. Any time. But you could have broken your hand hitting that guy that hard.'

'Had to. He outweighed me by forty pounds. If I had just given him a you-piss-me-off social punch he would have killed me.'

'You're a violent man, Jake.'

'I had a lot of trouble with potty training.'

The next morning he realized the dimensions of the quandary he faced. Nell Douglas was a fine woman, passionate, level-headed, intelligent, thoughtful . . . And Callie McKenzie was one fine woman, also passionate and level-headed, intelligent, educated, well spoken . . . He was in love with one and could easily fall in love with the other. But the woman he loved hadn't written in two months and had made it clear that he wasn't measuring up.

The woman he could love wasn't being quite so picky. No doubt when he knew her better she would get more picky – women were like that. But she wasn't being picky *now!* And if you couldn't take the heat there was always celibacy to fall back on.

Alas, celibacy didn't seem very attractive to Jake Grafton. Not when you are in your twenties, in perfect health, when the sight, smell and touch of a woman makes the blood pound in your temples and your knees turn to jelly.

He sat in his chair in his stateroom savoring the memories of last night. Of how her lips had felt against his, how her hot, wet tongue had speared between his teeth and stroked his tongue, how her breasts had heaved against his chest, how her thighs had pressed against his while her hands stroked his back. Gawd Almighty!

He liked the way she talked, too. That flat Australian twang was sexy as hell. Just made shivers run up your spine when you recalled how the words sounded as she said them. '. . . I might drag you off to my lonely little bed for a night of sport.' Well, lady, I wish . . .

I don't know what I wish! Damnation.

He was writhing on the horns of this dilemma when the door opened and the Real McCoy staggered through. He flopped into his bunk and groaned. 'Wake me up next week. I am spent. Wrung out like a sponge. That woman turned me every way but loose. There are hot women and there are *hot* women. That one was a thermonuclear.'

'Tough night, huh?'

'She was after me every hour! I didn't sleep a wink. Every *hour!* I'm so sore I can hardly walk.'

'Lucky you escaped her evil clutches.'

'Never in my born days, Jake, did I even contemplate that there might be women like *that* walking the surface of the earth. Australia is merely the greatest nation on the planet, that's all. That they breed women like *that* down there is the best-kept secret of our time.'

Jake nodded thoughtfully and flexed his right fist. It was sore and a little swollen.

'I'm getting out of the Nav, arranging to have my subscription to the *Wall Street Journal* sent to me Down Under, and I am going south. May the cold, blue light of Polaris never again meet my weary gaze. It's the Southern Cross for me, Laddie Buck. I'm going to Australia to see if I can fuck myself to death before I'm forty.'

With that pronouncement the Real McCoy turned on his side and curled his pillow under his head. Jake looked at his watch. The first gentle snore came seventy-seven seconds later.

Were the women bigots? Well, Flap should know. If he said those three stews were prejudiced, they probably were. But what about Nell?

And what about you, Jake? Are you?

Aaugh! To waste a morning in port fretting about crap like this.

He pulled a table around and started a letter to his parents.

The liberty boat for the enlisted men was an LCI – landing craft infantry – a flat-bottomed rectangular-shaped boat with a bow door that flopped down to let troops run through the surf onto the beach. Jake often rode it from the beach to the ship. This evening, however, he was dressed in a sports coat and a tie and didn't want to get soaked with salt spray, so he headed for the officers' brow near Elevator Two. The captain's gig and admiral's barge had been lowered into the water from their cradles in the rear of the hangar bay. In ten minutes he was descending the ladder onto the float, then he stepped into the gig.

Jake knew the boat officer, a jaygee from a fighter squadron, so he asked if he could stand beside the coxswain on the little midships bridge. Permission was granted with a grin and a nod. The rest of the officers went below into either the fore or aft cabin.

With the stupendous bulk of the carrier looming like a cliff above them, the sailors threw the lines aboard and the coxswain put the boat in motion. It stood out from the ship and swung in a wide circle until it was on course for fleet landing.

The water was calm this evening, with merely a long, low swell stirring the oily surface. The red of the western sky stained the water between the ships, gave it the look of diluted blood.

The roadstead was full of ships: freighters, coasters, tankers, all riding on their anchors. Lighters circled around a few of the ships, but only a few. Most of them sat motionless like massive steel statues in a huge park lake.

But there were people visible on most of the ships. As the gig threaded its way through the anchorage Jake could see them sitting under awnings on the fantails, sometimes cooking on barbecue grills, talking and smoking on after-decks crowded with ship's gear. Most of the sailors were men, but on one Russian ship he saw three women, hefty specimens in dresses that reached below their knees.

'Pretty evening,' the jaygee said to Jake, who agreed.

Yes, another gorgeous evening, the close of another good day to be alive. It was easy to forget the point of it all sometimes, easy to lose sight of the fact that the name of the game was to stay alive, to savor life, to live it day to day at the pace that God intended.

One of Jake Grafton's talents was to imagine himself living other lives. He hadn't been doing much of that lately, but riding the gig through the anchorage, looking at the ships, he could visualize sitting on one of those fantails, smoking and chatting and watching the sun sink closer and closer to the sea's rim. To go to sea and work the ship and spend quiet evenings in port in the company of friends – it could be very good. *I could live that way*, he reflected.

Maybe in my next incarnation.

The Intercontinental was a huge, modern hotel built on a slight hill. The lobby was a cavern seven or eight stories high. Marble floors accented with giant potted plants, a raised bar with easy chairs in the middle, all the accents a plush burgundy, polyester fabric glued to the walls – yuck!

Jake settled into one of the bar's overstuffed polyester chairs and tilted his head back. You could almost get dizzy looking up at the balconies, which were stacked closer and closer together until they met at the ceiling. Tropical plants hung from planters along each balcony, so the view upward was green. Dark green, because the lighting up there was very poor.

'Grotesque, isn't it?'

He dropped his gaze from the green canopy above to the young woman walking toward him. He stood and grinned. 'Yep.'

'The interior designer was obviously demented.' Nell Douglas settled into the chair opposite. A waiter appeared and hovered.

'Something to drink?' Jake asked her politely.

'A glass of white wine, please.'

'Scotch on the rocks.'

The waiter broke hover and disappeared behind a large potted leafy green thing.

'So how was your flight in?'

'Bumpy. Storms over the South China Sea. How's your hand?'

'You heard about that, huh?'

'The other girls were all atwitter. Your black friend really impressed them.'

'Flap can move pretty fast when he wants to. He's handy to have around.'

'If the necessity arises to knock people senseless. Is he lurking nearby now, just in case?'

Vaguely uneasy, Jake flashed a polite smile. 'No, I think he came ashore earlier today hoping to cheat some opal merchants. And my hand's fine.' He wiggled his fingers at her, pretending she cared.

Their drinks came and they sat sipping them in silence, both man and woman trying to sense the mood of the other.

After a bit Nell said, 'He's some kind of trained killer, isn't he?'

That comment was like glass shattering. Amazingly, Jake Grafton felt a tremendous sense of relief. It had been a nice fantasy, but this woman was not Callie.

'I guess everyone in combat arms is,' he said slowly, 'if you want to look at it that way. I deal in high explosives myself. I fly attack planes, not airliners.'

He took the plastic stir stick from his drink and chewed at it. Why do they put these damn things in a drink that is nothing but whiskey and ice? He took it out of his mouth and broke it between his fingers as he examined her face.

'I started the fight,' he continued, now in a hurry to end it. 'One of the soldiers referred to Captain Le Beau as a nigger. He happens to be my BN and a personal friend. He is also a fine human being. The fact that his skin is black is about as important as the fact that my eyes are gray. That word is an insult in America and here. The man who said it knew that.'

'The only black people in Australia are aborigines.'

'I guess you have to be an American to understand.'

'Perhaps.'

The waiter reappeared with his credit card and the invoice. Jake added a tip, signed it and pocketed the card and his copy.

Her face was too placid. Blank. Time to get this over with. 'Would you like to go to dinner?'

Nell Douglas looked this way and that, apparently searching for something to say.

Finally she sat her wineglass on the table and leaned forward slightly. She looked him in the eye. 'It was wonderful the other night, and I am sure you are a fine person, but let's leave it at that.'

He nodded and finished his drink.

'We grew up on opposite sides of the world.' She stood and held out her hand. 'Thanks for the drink.'

'Sure.'

Jake stood and shook. She threaded her way through the potted jungle and made for the elevators.

*

'Did you get laid?' the Real McCoy asked late that night in their stateroom aboard ship.

'She said we grew up on opposite sides of the world.'

'You idiot. You're suppose to fuck 'em, not discuss philosophy.'

'Well, it probably turned out for the best,' Jake said, thinking of Callie. He desperately wished she would write. She could write anything – if she would just put *something* in an envelope and stick a stamp on it.

He decided to write her.

He got a legal pad, climbed into the top bunk and adjusted the light just so. Then he began. He went through their relationship episode by episode, almost thought by thought, pouring out his heart. After eight pages he ground to a halt.

Every word was true, but he wasn't going to send it. He wasn't going to take the chance that he cared more than she did.

You aren't going to get very far with the fairer sex if you aren't willing to take some risks.

I'm tired of taking risks. Someone else can take a few.

Faint heart never won—

If she cared, she'd write. End of story.

The night before the ship weighed anchor Lieutenant Colonel Haldane asked Jake to come to his stateroom. According to the duty officer. Jake went.

Flap was already there sitting in the only chair. Jake sat on the colonel's bed and Flap passed him a sheet of paper. It was a letter from the commander at Changi. Fight in the pavilion. Jake scanned it quickly and passed it back to Flap, who handed it to Haldane, who tossed it on his desk.

'The skipper of the ship got this. He wants me to investigate, take action, and draft a reply for his signature. What can you tell me?'

Jake told the colonel about the incident, withholding nothing.

'Any comments, Captain Le Beau?'

'No, sir. I think Mr Grafton covered it.'

Haldane made a face. 'Okay. That's all. We're having a back-in-the-saddle NATOPS do in the ready room at zero seven-thirty. See you there.'

Both the junior officers left. Jake closed the door behind him.

Twenty frames down the passageway he asked Flap, 'Was that it? We aren't in hack or candidates for keelhauling?'

'Naw. Haldane will apologize profusely to our allies, tell them that he's ripped us a new one, and that's that. It was just a friendly little social fight. What more could there be?'

Jake shrugged. 'My hand's still sore.'

'Next time kick 'em in the balls.'

17

At dawn one morning the task group weighed anchor and entered the Strait of Malacca. With Sumatra on the left and the Malay peninsula on the right, the ships steamed at 20 knots for the Indian Ocean, or the IO as the sailors called it, pronouncing each letter.

In the narrows the strait was a broad watery highway with land on each horizon. The channel was dotted with fishing boats and heavily traversed by tankers and freighters. As many as a half dozen of the large ocean-going ships were visible at any one time.

As usual in narrow waterways, the carrier's flight deck and island super-structure were crowded with sightseeing sailors. Typically, Jake Grafton was among them, standing on the bow facing forward. With all of the great ship behind him the sensation was unique, almost as if one were a seabird soaring along at sixty feet above the water into the teeth of a 20-knot wind.

This morning Jake watched the steady stream of civilian ships and marveled. He had flown enough surface surveillance missions over the open ocean to appreciate how empty the oceans of the earth truly were. Often he and Flap flew a two-hour flight and saw not a single ship, just endless vistas of empty sea and sky. Yet here the ships plowed the brown water like trucks thundering along an interstate highway.

A hundred years ago these waters hosted sailing ships. As he stood on the bow watching the ships and boats this morning he thought about those sailing ships, for Jake Grafton had a streak of romance in him about a foot wide. Clipper ships bound for China for a load of tea left England and the eastern ports of the United States and sailed south to round the Cape of Good Hope on the southern tip of Africa. The sailors would have gotten close enough to land for a glimpse of Africa only in good weather. Then they crossed the vast Indian Ocean and entered this strait, where they saw land for the first time since leaving England or America. Months at sea working the ship, making sail, reefing in storms, watching the officers shoot the sun at noon and the stars at night when the weather allowed, then to hit this strait after circumnavigating half the globe – it was a great thing, a thing to be proud of, a thing to remember for the rest of their lives. Exotic China still lay ahead, but here the sailors probably saw junks for the first time, those flat-bottomed Chinese sailing ships that carried the commerce of the Orient. Here two worlds touched.

Jake looked at the freighters and tankers with new interest. Perhaps he should look into getting a mate's license, consider the merchant marine after the Navy. It was a thing to think on.

Standing on the bow with the moist wind in his hair and the smell of the land filling his nostrils as the task group transited this narrow passage between two great oceans, he was struck by how large the earth really was, how diverse the human life, how many truths there must be. The US Navy was a tiny part of it, surely, but only a tiny part. He had been confined long enough. He needed to reach out and embrace the whole.

The Indian Ocean lay ahead, beyond that watery horizon. The flying there would be blue water ops, without the safety net of a divert field ashore. The ship would be hundreds of miles from land, so when the planes burned enough fuel to get down to landing weight there would be no dry spot on earth they could reach with the fuel remaining in their tanks. They had to get aboard. Airborne tankers could provide fuel for another handful of attempts, but their presence would not change the scenario – every pilot would have to successfully trap or eject into the ocean.

Carrier aviation never gets easier. The challenge is to develop and maintain skills that are just good enough. In this war without bullets the stakes were human lives. Each pilot would have only his skill and knowledge to keep him alive in the struggle against the weather, chance, the vagaries of fate. Some would lose. Jake Grafton knew that as well as he knew his name. He might be one of them.

Thinking about that possibility as he stood here on the bow, he took a deep breath of the moist sea air and savored it.

A man never knows.

Well, he would do his best. That was all he could do. God had the dice, He would make the casts.

Jake was standing the squadron duty officer watch in the ready room one night when first Lieutenant Doug Harrison came in from a flight. He gave Jake his flight time figure and handed him the batteries from his emergency radio – the batteries were recharged in a unit above the duty officer's desk – then dropped into the skipper's empty chair as Jake annotated the flight schedule. Only then did Grafton turn and take a good look at the first-cruise pilot. His face was pasty and covered with a sheen of perspiration.

'Tough flight, huh?'

Harrison dropped his eyes and massaged his forehead with a hand. 'No . . . Got a cigarette?'

'Sure.' Jake passed him one, then held out a light.

After Harrison had taken three or four puffs, he took the cigarette from his mouth and said softly, 'After we landed, I almost taxied over the edge.'

'It's dark out there.'

'I've never seen anything like it. No light at all, the deck greasy, rain on top of the grease . . . it was like trying to taxi on snot.'

'What happened?'

'Taxi director took me up to the bow on Cat One, then turned me. Wanted me to taxi aft on Cat Two. It was that turn on the bow. Sticking out over the fucking black ocean. I was *sure* I was going right off the bow, Jake. I about shit myself. I kid you not. Pure, unadulterated terror, two-hundred proof. I have *never* had a feeling like that in an airplane before.'

'Uh-huh.'

'I was turning tight, I could feel the nose wheel sliding, the yellow-shirt was giving me the come-ahead signal with the wands, and the edge was *right there!* And there isn't even a protective lip. You know how the bow just turns down, same as the stern?'

'So what did you do?'

'Locked the left wheel and goosed the right engine. The plane moved about a foot. I could feel the left wheel sliding. To make things perfect I could also feel the deck going up and down, up and down. Every time it started down the vomit came up my throat. Then the yellow-shirt crossed his wands and had the blue-shirts chock it right where it sat. When I climbed down from the cockpit I couldn't believe it – the nose wheel was like *six inches* from the edge! It was so dark up there that I had to use my flashlight to make sure. There was *no way* the nose wheel was going around that corner. Even if it had, the right main wouldn't have made the turn – it would have dropped off the edge.'

Harrison took a greedy drag on his cigarette, then continued: 'My BN couldn't even get out of the cockpit. The plane captain didn't have room to drop his ladder. He had to stay in the cockpit until they towed the plane to a decent parking place.'

'Why'd you keep taxiing when you knew you were that close to the edge?'

Harrison closed his eyes for a second, then shook his head. 'I dunno.'

'I know,' Jake Grafton told him positively. 'You jarheads are spring-loaded to the yessir position. Doug, if it doesn't feel right, don't do it. You have only one ass to lose.'

Harrison nodded and sucked on the cigarette. The color was slowly coming back to his face. After a bit he said, 'Did you ever watch those RA-5 pilots taxi at night? The nose wheel is way aft of the cockpit. They are sitting out over the ocean when they taxi that Vigilante to the deck edge and turn it. I couldn't do that. Not in a million years. Just watching them gives me the shivers.'

'Don't obey a yellow-shirt if it doesn't look right,' Jake said, emphasizing the point. 'It isn't the fall that kills you, Doug, or the stop at the bottom – it's the sudden realization that, indeed, you *are* this fucking stupid.'

When Doug wandered off Jake went back to the notes of his talks on carrier operations. He was expanding and refining them so he could have them typed. He thought he would send them back to the senior LSO at the West Coast A-6 training squadron, VA-128 at Whidbey Island. Maybe there was something in there that the LSOs could use for their lectures.

Boy, if he wasn't getting out, it would sure be nice to go back to VA-128 when this cruise was over. Rent a little place on a beach or a bluff overlooking the sound, fly, teach some classes, kick back and let life flow along. If he wasn't getting out . . . If Tiny Dick Donovan was willing to take him back. Forgive and forget.

But he was getting out! No more long lonely months at sea, no more night cat shots, no more floating around the IO quietly rotting, no more of this—

Allen Bartow came up to the desk. 'When you get off here tonight, we're having a little game down in my room. We need some squid money in the pot.'

'I've still got a lot of jarhead quarters from the last game. I'll bring those.'

'The last of the high rollers . . .'

He wasn't going to miss it, he assured himself, for the hundredth time. Not a bit.

One of the most difficult tasks in military aviation is a night rendezvous. On a dark night under an overcast the plane you are joining is merely a tiny blob of lights, flashing weakly in the empty black universe. Without a horizon or other visual reference, the only way the trick can be done is to keep your instrument scan going inside your cockpit while you sneak peeks at the target aircraft. The temptation is to look too long at the target, to get too engrossed in the angles and closure rate, and if that happens, you are in big trouble.

On this particular night Jake Grafton thought he had it wired. He was rendezvousing on the off-going tanker at low station, 5,000 feet over the ship on the five-mile arc. There it was, its lights winking weakly.

'Ten o'clock,' Flap said.

'Roge, I got it.'

'He'll be doing two-fifty.'

Jake glanced at his airspeed. Three hundred knots indicated. He would have to work that off as he closed. But not quite yet.

The tanker would be in a left-hand turn. Jake cranked his plane around until he had his nose in front of it and was looking at it through the right quarter panel, across the top of the radar scope-hood. He eased in a little left rudder and right flaperon to help keep his plane in a position where he could see the tanker.

With the target plane on the right side the A-6 was difficult to rendezvous because the cockpit was too wide – the BN sat on the pilot's right. This meant that the right glareshield and canopy rail were too high and, as the planes closed, would block the pilot's vision of the target aircraft if he allowed himself to get just a little behind the bearing line or get a tad high. Jake knew all this. He had accomplished several hundred night rendezvous and knew the problems involved and the proper techniques to use without even thinking about it. Tonight he was busy applying that knowledge.

Yet something was wrong. Jake checked his instruments. All okay. Why was the tanker moving to the right? Instinctively he rolled more wings level, rechecked his attitude gyro, the altimeter, the airspeed . . . All okay. And still the sucker is moving right!

'Texaco, say your heading.'

'Zero Two Zero.'

Hell! Now Jake understood. He was still on the outside of the tanker's turning radius, not on the inside as he had assumed. He leveled his wings and flew straight ahead to cross behind the tanker, feeling slightly ridiculous. He had *assumed* that he was on the inside . . .

Now, indeed, he was on the inside of the tanker's turn. He turned to put the nose in the proper position and started inbound. Checking the gauges, watching the bearing, slowing gently . . . 280 knots would be perfect, would give him 30 knots of closure . . .

And the tanker was . . . Jesus! Coming in awful fast – *way too fast!* Power back, boards out, and . . .

'Look at your altitude.' Flap.

Jake looked. He was at ninety-degrees angle-of-bank, passing 4,500 feet, descending.

He leveled the wings and got the nose up. The tanker shot off to the left.

'I'm really screwed up tonight,' he told the BN.

'Turn hard and get inside of him, then close.'

Jake did. He felt embarrassed, like a neophyte on his first night formation hop. Yet only when he got to within two hundred yards and could make out the tanker's position lights clearly was he sure of the tanker's direction of flight. Only then was he comfortable.

He wasn't concentrating hard enough. Attempting to rendezvous on a single, flashing light, in a dark universe devoid of any other feature . . . it was difficult at best and impossible if you weren't completely focused.

Flap extended the drogue as Jake crossed behind the tanker and surfaced on his right side. 'You got the lead,' said the tanker pilot, Chance Malzahn. Jake clicked his mike twice in reply as Chance slid aft. He dropped slightly and disappeared from sight behind. Jake concentrated on flying his own plane, staying in this steady, twenty-degree angle-of-bank turn, keeping on the five-mile arc, holding altitude perfectly.

In seconds the green ready light on the refueling panel went out and the counter began to click off the pounds delivered. The refueling package worked.

'Five Twenty-Three is sweet,' Flap told the ship.

The green ready light appeared again. Malzahn had backed out of the drogue. Now he came up on Jake's left side.

'You got the lead,' Jake told him as Malzahn's drogue streamed aft.

The drogue looked like a three-foot-wide badminton birdie. It dangled on the end of a fifty-foot-long hose aft and slightly below the wash of the tanker. To get fuel, Jake would have to insert his fuel probe, which was permanently mounted on the nose in front of his windscreen, into the drogue and push it in about five feet. When the take-up reel on the tanker had turned the proper amount, electrical switches would mate and begin pumping fuel down the hose into the receiver aircraft.

The trick was getting the probe into the drogue, the basket. If the basket was new, with all the feathers in good shape, it was usually almost stationary and fairly easy to plug. If it was slightly damaged, however, it tended to weave back and forth in the windstream and present a moving target. Turbulence that bounced the tanker and receiver aircraft added to the level of difficulty. And, of course, there was the 'pucker factor' – extensive experience has proven that the tension of a pilot's sphincter is directly proportional to the level of his anxiety, ie, higher makes tighter, etc.

Tonight, needing only to hit the tanker to 'sponge' the excess fuel, Jake's anxiety level was normal, or even slightly below. He was fat, had plenty of fuel. And the air was fairly smooth. The only fly in the ointment was the condition of that Marine Corps drogue. Tonight it weaved in a small, erratic figure-eight pattern.

Jake stabilized his plane about ten feet behind the drogue and watched it bob and weave for a moment. Flap Le Beau kept his flashlight pointed at it.

'Little Marine bastard is bent.'

'Yeah.' Flap was full of sympathy.

Flopping drogues had cracked bullet-proof windscreens, shattered Plexiglas and fodded engines. Tonight Jake Grafton eyed this one warily, waited for his moment, then smartly added power and drove his probe in. Drove it at that spot where the drogue would be when he got there. He hoped.

Miraculously he timed it right. The probe captured the drogue and locked in. He kept pushing until the green light above the hose chute in the tanker came on. Now he was riding about fifteen feet below the tanker's tail and ten feet aft. As long as he stayed right here, held that picture, he would get fuel.

'You get twelve hundred pounds,' Chance Malzahn told him.

Two clicks in acknowledgement.

'Nice,' Flap said, referring to the plug, the flashlight never wavering.

When the last of the gas was aboard Jake backed out. He came up on Malzahn's left side and took the lead as Malzahn reeled in his hose. After a word with Tanker Control, Malzahn cut his power and turned away, headed down on a vector for an approach.

Jake and Flap were now Texaco. Soon two F-4s came to take a ton of fuel each, then they turned away and disappeared in the vast darkness.

Jake took the tanker on up to high station, 20,000 feet, and settled it on autopilot at 220 knots. Around and around the ship, orbiting. Flap got out a paperback book and adjusted his kneeboard light. Jake loosened one side of his oxygen mask and let it dangle.

'Do you ever see the faces of the men you killed?' Jake asked. They had been orbiting the ship at high station for almost half an hour.

'What do you mean?'

Jake Grafton took his time before he answered. 'I got shot down last December. We ended up in Laos. Had to shoot three guys before they got us out. They were trying to kill us – me and my BN – and one of them shot me. That's how I ended up with this scar on my temple.'

'Uh-huh.'

'Had to do it, of course, or they would have killed us. Still, I see them sometimes in dreams. Wake up feeling rotten.'

Flap Le Beau didn't say anything.

'Dropping bombs, now, I did that for a couple cruises. Bound to have killed a lot of people. Oh, most of the time we bombed suspected truck parks and crap like that – probably killed some ants and lizards and turned a lot of trees into toothpicks. That's what we called them, toothpick missions – but occasionally we went after better targets. Stuff where there would be people. Not just trees in the jungle and mud roads crossing a creek.'

'Yeah.'

'Toward the end there we were really pounding the north, hitting all the shit that Johnson and McNamara didn't have the brains or balls to hit six years before.'

'It was fucked up, all right.'

'One mission, close air support of some ARVN, they told me I killed forty-seven of 'em. Forty-seven. That bothered me for a while, but I don't see them at night. Forty-seven men with one load of bombs . . . it's like reading about it in a newspaper or history book . . . doesn't seem real now. I still see those three NVA though.'

'I still see faces too.'

Below them an unbroken cloud deck stretched away in all directions. The sliver of moon was fuzzy and there weren't many stars – they were trying to shine through a gauzy layer of high cirrus.

'Wonder if it'll ever stop? If they'll just fade out or something.'

'I don't know.'

'Doesn't seem right somehow, to lose fifty-eight thousand Americans, to kill all those Vietnamese, all for nothing.'

Flap didn't reply.

'I don't like seeing those faces and waking up in a cold sweat. I had to do it. But damn . . .'

He wanted to forget the past, forget all of it. The present was okay, the flying and the ship and the men he shared it with. Yet the future was waiting out there, somewhere, hidden in the mists and haze. He was reaching out for *something*, something that lay ahead along that road into the unknown. Just what it would be he didn't know. He was ready to make the journey though.

Under the overcast it was raining. At five thousand feet visibility was down to two or three miles and the oncoming tanker had trouble finding them, even with vectors from tanker control. It was that kind of night, with nothing going right. Once he was there Jake slipped in behind, eyed the basket, and went for it. He got it with only a little rudder kick in close and pushed it in.

Nothing. The green light over the hose hole did not illuminate.

'Are we getting any?' Flap asked the other crew.

'No. Back out and let us recycle.'

Jake retarded the power levers a smidgen and let his plane drift aft. The basket came off the probe. He moved out to the right and Flap told the other crew to recycle. They pulled the hose all the way in, then ran it out again.

This time Jake missed the basket on the first try. He stabilized and slipped in on his second attempt.

'Still no gas.'

'Tanker Control, this is Five Two Two, we're sour.'

'Roger, Two Two. Your signal is dump. Steer Two Two Zero and descend to One Point Two, over.'

'Five Two Two, Two Two Zero and down to One Point Two.'

'Texaco, Tanker Control, you steer Two Zero Zero and descend to One Point Two, over.'

Jake slid left and the other tanker went right. It was already streaming fuel from the main and wing-tip dumps. Nine tons of fuel would have to be dumped into the atmosphere. Too bad, but there it was.

Jake settled onto his desired course and popped his speed brakes. The nose went over. When he stabilized he looked to the right for the other A-6, which was already fading into the rain and darkness. He came back into the cockpit and concentrated on his instruments.

This little world of needles and dials illuminated by red lights had always fascinated him. Making the needles behave didn't seem all that difficult, until you tried it. And on nights like this, when he felt about half in the bag, when he was having trouble concentrating, then it was exquisite torture. Everything he did was either too little or too much. It was maddening.

The perverse needles taunted him. *You are too high,* they whispered, *too fast, off course, now you are low . . .* He had to work extremely hard to make them behave, had to pay strict attention to their message. The slightest inattention, the most minute easing of his concentration would allow the needles to escape his grasp.

The controller worked him into a hole in the bolter pattern, which was rapidly filling up. The voices on the radio told him the story as he struggled to make the needles behave. The weather was worse than forecast. Rain was ruining the visibility, the sea was freshening, and one of the F-4s had already boltered twice. Nearest land was 542 miles to the northwest. There were no sweet tankers in the air.

'Ain't peace wonderful?' Flap muttered.

'Landing checklist,' Jake said, and they went through it. They were too heavy so they dumped fifteen hundred pounds of fuel to get to landing weight. Crazy, that the only good tanker was dumping to land instead of hawking the deck to help that Phantom crew, but ours is not to reason why, ours is but to do or . . .

At a mile and a half he saw the ship, a tiny smear of red light enlivening the dead universe.

Flap called the ball at Six Point Oh.

'Roger Ball.'

Jake recognized the Real McCoy's voice, but just in case he didn't the Real continued. 'Deck's dancing, Jake. Watch your lineup.'

He had the ball centered, nailed there, and with just a little dip of the wings he chased the landing centerline to the right, working the throttles individually so as not to over-control. The rain flowed around the canopy in a continuous sheet, but the engine bleed air kept the pilot's windscreen clear.

There was an art to throttle-work on the ball, moving each individual lever ever so slightly, yet knowing when to move them both. Tonight Jake got it just right. The deck got closer and closer, the ball stayed centered, the lineup was good, the angle-of-attack needle behaved . . . and they caught a three-wire.

'Luck,' Jake told Flap as they rolled out of the landing area.

They taxied him to a stop abeam the island where a half-dozen purple-shirts – grapes – waited with a fuel hose. Jake opened the canopy as the squadron's senior troubleshooter climbed the ladder. The wind felt raw and the rain cold against his skin.

'We're going to hot pump you and shoot you again,' the sergeant shouted over the whine of the engines. 'This is the only up tanker.'

Jake stuck his thumb up to signify his understanding.

The sergeant went back down the ladder and raised it as Jake closed the canopy. Might as well keep the rain out. The sergeant flashed a thumbs-up and went around to the BN's side of the plane to watch the refueling operation. Jake moved the switch to depressurize the tanks.

Refueling took a while. They needed twenty thousand pounds for a full load and the ship's pumps could only deliver it at about a ton a minute.

He was tired and his butt felt like dead meat, yet it was very pleasant sitting here in the warm, comfortable cockpit. From their vantage point here beside the foul line they had a grandstand seat. The planes came out of the rain and darkness and slammed into the deck. The first two trapped, then a Phantom boltered, his hook ripping a shower of sparks the length of the landing area. This was the guy who had already boltered twice before.

Ah yes, this comfortable cockpit, with everything working just the way it was supposed to, the rain pattering on the Plexiglas and collecting into rivulets that smeared the light.

He was tired, but not too much so. Just pleasantly tired.

Jake unhooked his oxygen mask and laid it in his lap. He took off his helmet and massaged his face and head. He used his sleeves and gloves to swab away the perspiration, then pulled the helmet back on.

The minutes ticked by as the fuel gauges faithfully reported the fuel coming aboard.

They were still fueling when the errant F-4 came out of the gloom and snagged a two-wire. The pilot stroked the afterburners on the roll out. The white-hot focused flames poured from the tailpipes for about a second, then went out, leaving everyone on deck half-blinded.

Two minutes later an A-7 carrying a buddy store, a tanking package hung on a weapon's station under one wing, was taxied from the pack up to Cat Two and launched. Apparently the brain trust in Air Ops wanted more gas aloft.

At last Jake and Flap were ready. Pressurize the tanks. Boarding ladders up, refueling panel closed, seats armed, and they were taxiing toward Cat Two, the left bow catapult.

Spread the wings, flaps to takeoff, slats out, wipe out the cockpit, ease into the shuttle. There, the jolt as the hold-back reached full extension, then another jolt as the shuttle went forward into tension. Off the brakes, throttles up.

He watched the engines come up to full power as he pulled up the catapult grip and arranged the heel of his hand behind the throttles, felt the airplane tremble as the engines sucked in vast quantities of that rainy air and slammed it out the tailpipes into the jet blast deflector – the JBD. Fuel flow normal, temperatures coming up nicely, RPM at 100 percent on the left engine, a fraction over on the right. Hydraulics normal, everything okay.

Jake wiped out the cockpit, glanced at the panel, ensured Flap had his flashlight on the standby gyro . . . 'You ready?'

'Let it rip.'

He flipped on the exterior light master switch on the end of the cat grip with his left thumb.

The hold-back bolt broke. *He felt it break.* Then came the shot, a stiff jolt of terrific acceleration, which lasted about a quarter of a second. Then it ceased. *Sweet Jesus fucking Christ the airplane was still accelerating but way too god-damn slow!*

He was doing maybe 30 knots when he released the cat grip and closed the throttles. Automatically he extended the wing-tip speed brakes. He jammed his feet down on the top of the rudder pedals, locking both brakes.

They were still going forward, sliding on the wet, greasy deck. Thundering toward the bow, the round-down, the edge of the cliff . . .

Jake pulled the left throttle around the horn to idle cutoff, stopping the flow of fuel to that engine.

He released the left brake and engaged nose-wheel steering. Slammed the rudders to neutral, then hard right. That should capture the nose wheel and turn it right, if the shuttle wasn't holding it. But the nose wheel refused to respond.

Still going forward, but slower. The edge was there, coming toward them . . . only seconds left.

He released both brakes, and engaged nose-wheel steering and slammed the rudder full left. He felt something give. The nose started to swing left.

On the brakes hard. *Is there enough deck left, enough—?*

An explosion beside him. Flap had ejected. The air was filled with shards of flying Plexiglas.

Sliding, turning left and still sliding forward . . . he felt the left wheel slam into the deck-edge combing, then the nose, now the tail spun toward the bow, the whole plane still sliding . . .

And he stopped.

Out the right he could see nothing, just blackness. The right wheel must be almost at the very edge of the flight deck.

He took a deep breath and exhaled explosively.

His left hand was holding the alternate ejection handle between his legs. He couldn't remember reaching for it, but obviously he had. He gingerly released his grip.

The Plexiglas was gone on the right side of the canopy. Flap had ejected through it. Where his seat had been there was just an empty place.

Was Flap alive?

Jake closed the speed brakes and raised the flaps and slats, watched the indicator to make sure they were coming in properly, exterior lights off. Out of the corner of his eye he saw people, a mob, running toward him. He ignored them.

When he had the flaps and slats up, he unlocked the wings, then folded them. The wind was puffing through the top of the broken canopy . . . rain coming in. He could feel the drops on the few inches of exposed skin on his neck.

Was the plane moving? He didn't think so. Yet if he opened the canopy he couldn't eject. The seat was designed to go through the glass – if the canopy was open, the steel bow would be right above the seat and would kill him if he tried to eject. And if this plane slid off the deck he would have to eject or ride it into that black sea.

Now the reaction hit him. He began to shake.

A yellow-shirt was trying to get his attention. He kept giving Jake the cut sign, the slash across the throat.

But should he open the canopy?

Unable to decide, he chopped the right throttle and sat listening as that engine died.

Someone opened the canopy from outside. Now a sergeant was leaning in. 'You can get out now, sir. Safe your seat.'

'Have they got it tied down?'

'Yes.'

He had to force himself to move. He safetied the top and bottom ejection handles on the seat and fumbled with the Koch fittings that held him to the seat. Reached down and fumbled in the darkness with the fittings that attached to his leg restraints. There. He was loose.

He started to get out, then remembered his oxygen mask and helmet leads. He disconnected all that, then tried to stand.

He was still shaking too badly. He grabbed a handhold and eased a leg out onto the ladder, all the while trying to ignore the blackness yawning on the right side, and ahead. Here he was, ten feet above the deck, right against the edge. He felt like he was going to vomit.

Hands reached up and steadied him as he descended the boarding ladder.

With his feet on deck, he looked at the right main wheel. Maybe a foot from the edge. The nose-wheel was jammed against the deck-edge combing and the nose-tow bar was twisted.

Jake asked the yellow-shirt, 'Where's my BN?'

The sailor pointed down the deck, toward the fantail. Jake looked. He saw a flash of white, the parachute, draped over the tail of an A-7. So Flap had landed on deck. Didn't go into the ocean.

Now the relief hit him like a hammer. His legs wobbled. Two people grabbed him.

His mask was dangling from the side of his helmet, and he swept it out of the way just in time to avoid the hot raw vomit coming up his throat.

He started walking aft, toward the island and the parachute draped over that Corsair a hundred fifty yards aft. He shook off two sailors who tried to assist him. 'I'm all right, all right, okay.'

An A-7 came out of the rain and trapped.

There was Flap, walking this way. Now he saw Grafton, spread his arms, kept walking.

The two men met and hugged fiercely.

Lieutenant Colonel Richard Haldane watched the PLAT tape of the cat shot gone awry five or six times as he listened to Jake Grafton and Flap Le Beau recount their experience in the ready room.

They were euphoric – they had spit in the devil's eye and escaped to tell the tale. In the ready room they went through every facet of their adventure for their listeners, who shared their infectious glee.

Isn't life grand? Isn't it great to still be walking and talking and laughing after a trip to the naked edge of life itself?

After a half hour or so, Haldane slipped away to find the maintenance experts. He listened carefully to their explanations, asked some questions, then went to the hangar deck for a personal examination of 523's nose-tow bar.

Apparently the hold-back bolt had failed prematurely, a fraction of a second before the launch valves fully opened, perhaps just as they began to open. The KA-6D at full power had begun to move forward, creating a space – perhaps an inch or two – between the T-fitting of the nose-tow bar and the catapult shuttle. Then the shuttle shot forward as steam slammed into the back of the catapult pistons. At this impact of shuttle and nose-tow bar, the nose-tow bar probably cracked. It held together for perhaps thirty feet of travel down the catapult, then failed completely.

Now free of the twenty-seven-ton weight of the aircraft, the pistons accelerated through the twin catapult barrels like two guided missiles chained together. Superheated steam drove them through the chrono-graph brushes five feet short of the water brakes at 207 knots.

With a stupendous crash that was felt the length of the ship, the pistons' spears entered the water brakes, squeezed out *all* the water and welded themselves into the brakes. Brakes, spears, and pistons were instantly transformed into one large lump of smoking, twisted, deformed steel. Cat Two was out of action for the rest of the cruise.

Colonel Haldane was less interested in what happened to the catapult than the sequence of events that took place inside 523 after the catapult fired. Careful analysis of the PLAT tape showed that the plane came to a halt just 6.1 seconds later. Total length of the catapult was 260 feet, and it ended twenty feet short of the bow. The plane had used all 280 feet to get stopped. The bombardier ejected 3.8 seconds into that ride.

That Jake Grafton had managed to get the plane halted before it went into the ocean was, Colonel Haldane decided, nothing less than a miracle.

Seated at his desk in his stateroom, he thought about Jake Grafton, about what it must have felt like trying to get that airplane stopped as it stampeded toward the bow and the black void beyond. Oh, he had heard Grafton recount the experience, but already, while it was still fresh and immediate, Grafton had automatically donned the de rigueur cloak of humility: 'In spite of everything I did wrong, miraculously I survived. I was shot with luck. All you sinners take note that when the chips are down clean living and prayer pays off.'

Most pilots would have ejected. Haldane thought it through very carefully and came to the conclusion that he would have been one of them. He would have grabbed that alternate ejection handle between his legs and pulled hard.

Yet Grafton hadn't done that, and he had saved the plane. Luck, Haldane well knew in spite of Grafton's ready room bullshit, had played a very small part.

Should he have ejected? After all, the Navy Department could just order another A-6 from Grumman for $8 million, but it couldn't buy another highly trained, experienced pilot. It took millions of dollars and years of training to produce one of those; if you wanted one combat experienced, you had to have a war, which was impractical to do on a regular basis since a high percentage of the liberal upper crust frowned upon wars for training purposes.

Yep, Grafton should have punched. Just like Le Beau.

Sitting here in the warmth, safety, and comfort of a well-lit stateroom nursing a cup of coffee, any sane person would reach that obvious conclusion. Hindsight is so wonderful.

And the same person would be wrong.

Great pilots always find a way to survive. Almost by instinct they manage to choose a course of action – sometimes in blatant violation of the rules – that results in their survival.

The most obvious fact here was probably the most important: Jake Grafton was still alive and uninjured.

Had he ejected . . . well, who can say how that would have turned out? The seat might have malfunctioned, he might have gone into the ocean and drowned, he might have broken his neck being slammed down upon the flight deck or into the side of an airplane. Le Beau had been very lucky, and he freely admitted it, proclaimed it even, in the ready room afterward: 'I'd rather be lucky than good.'

Grafton was good. He had saved himself and the plane. Yet there was more. In the ready room afterward he hadn't been the least bit defensive, had stated why he did what he did clearly and cogently, then listened carefully to torrents of free advice – the what-you-should-have-done variety. He wasn't embarrassed that Flap ejected. He blamed no one and expressed no regrets.

Haldane liked that, had enjoyed watching and listening to a man whose rock-solid self-confidence could not be shaken. Grafton believed in himself, and the feeling was contagious. One wondered if there were anything this man couldn't handle.

Now the colonel dug into the bottom drawer of his desk. In a moment he found what he was looking for. It was a personal letter from the commanding officer of VA-128, Commander Dick Donovan. Haldane removed the letter from its envelope and read it, carefully, for the fourth or fifth time.

I am sending you the most promising junior officer in the squadron, Lieutenant Jake Grafton. He is one of the two or three best pilots I have met in the Navy. He seems to have an instinct for the proper thing to do in a cockpit, something beyond the level that we can teach.

As an officer, he is typical for his age and rank. Keep your eye on him. He has a temper and isn't afraid of anything on this earth. That is good and bad, as I am sure you will agree. I hope time and experience will season him. You may not agree with my assessment, but the more I see of him, the more I am convinced that he is capable of great things, that someday he will be able to handle great responsibilities.

I want him back when your cruise is over.

Colonel Haldane folded the letter and put it back into its envelope. Then he pulled a pad of paper around and got out his pen. He hadn't answered this letter yet, and now seemed like a good time.

Donovan wasn't going to be happy to hear that Grafton was resigning, but there wasn't anything he or Donovan could do about it. That decision was up to Grafton. Still, it was a shame. Donovan was right – Grafton was a rare talent of unusual promise.

When the adrenaline rush had faded and the ready room crowd had calmed down, Jake and Flap went up to the forward – 'dirty shirt' – wardroom between the bow cats. Flap had already been to sick bay and had several minor Plexiglas cuts dressed. 'Iodine and Band-Aids,' he told Jake with a grin. 'I've been hurt worse shaving. Man, talk about luck!'

In the serving line each man ordered a slider, a large cheeseburger so greasy that it would slide right down your throat. With a glass of milk and a handful of potato chips, they sat on opposite sides of a long table with a food-stained tablecloth.

'I didn't think you could get it stopped,' Flap said between bites.

'You did the right thing,' Jake told him, referring to Flap's decision to eject. 'If I hadn't managed to get it sliding sideways I would have had to punch too.'

'Well, we're still alive, in one piece. We did all right.'

Jake just nodded and drank more milk. The adrenaline had left his stomach feeling queasy, but the milk and slider settled it. He leaned back in his chair and belched. Yep, there's a lot to be said for staying alive.

Down in his stateroom he stood looking around at the ordinary things, the things he saw every day yet didn't pay much attention to. After a glimpse into the abyss, the ordinary looks fresh and new. He sat in his chair and savored the fit, looked at how the light from his desk lamp cast stark shadows into the corners of the room, listened to the creaks and groans of the ship, examined with new eyes the photos of his folks and Callie that sat on his desk.

He twiddled the dial of the desk safe, then pulled it open. The ring was there, the engagement ring he had purchased for her last December aboard *Shiloh*. He took it from the safe and held it so the light shone on the small diamond. Finally he put it back. Without conscious thought, he removed his revolver from a pocket of his flight suit and put that in the safe too, then locked it.

He was going to have to do something about that woman.

But what?

It wasn't like he had her hooked and all he had to do was reel her in. The truth of the matter was that she had him hooked, and she hadn't decided whether or not he was a keeper.

So what is a guy to do? Write and pledge undying love? Promise to make her happy? Worm your way into her heart with intimate letters revealing your innermost thoughts?

No. What he had to do was speak to her softly, tell her of his dreams . . . if only he had any dreams to tell.

He felt hollow. Everyone else had a destination in mind: they were going at different speeds to get there, but they were on their way.

It was infuriating. Was there something wrong with him, some defect in him as a person? Was that what Callie saw?

Why couldn't she understand?

He thought about Callie for a while as he listened to the sounds of the ship working in a seaway, then finally reached for a pad and pen. He dated the letter and began:

'Dear Mom and Dad . . .'

When he finished the letter he didn't feel sleepy, so he took a hot shower and dressed in fresh, highly starched khakis and locked the door behind him. There weren't many people about. The last recovery was complete. The enlisted troops were headed for their bunks and the die-hard aviators were watching movies. He peered into various ready rooms to see who was still up that he knew. No one he wanted to talk to. He stopped in the arresting gear rooms and watched a first-class and two greenies pulling maintenance on an engine. He stopped by the PLAT office and watched his aborted takeoff several more times, wandered through the catapult spaces, where greenies supervised by petty officers were also working on equipment. In CATCC the graveyard shift had a radar consol torn apart.

In the Aviation Intermediate Maintenance avionics shop the night shift was hard at repairing aircraft radars and computers. This space was heavily air-conditioned and the lights burned around the clock. The technicians who worked here never saw the sun, or the world of wind and sea and sky where this equipment performed.

Finally, on a whim, Jake opened the door to the Air Department office. Warrant Officer Muldowski was the only person there. He saw Jake and boomed, 'Hey, shipmate. Come in and drop anchor.'

Jake helped himself to a cup of coffee and planted his elbows on the table across from the bosun, who had a pile of paper spread before him.

'You did good up there on that cat.'

'Thanks.'

'Kept waiting for you to punch. Thought you had waited too long.'

'For a second there I did too.'

They chewed the fat for a while, then when the conversation lagged Jake asked, 'Why did you stay in the Navy, Bosun?'

The bosun leaned back in his chair and reached for his tobacco pouch. When he had his pipe fired off and drawing well, he said, 'Civilians' worlds are too small.'

'What do you mean?'

'They get a job, live in a neighborhood, shop in the same stores all their lives. They live in a little world of friends, work, family. Those worlds looked too small to me.'

'That's something to think about.' Jake finished his coffee and tossed the Styrofoam cup in a wastebasket.

'Don't you go riding one of those pigs into the water, Mr Grafton. When you gotta go, you go.'

'Sure, Bosun.'

18

A Soviet task group came over the horizon one Sunday in late November. *Columbia* had no flying scheduled that day, so gawkers packed the flight deck when Jake Grafton came up for a first-hand look. A strong wind from the south-west was ripping the tops off the twelve- to fifteen-foot swells. Spindrift covered the sea, all under a clear blue sky. *Columbia* was pitching noticeably. The nearest destroyer was occasionally taking white water over the bow.

Up on deck Jake ran into the Real McCoy. 'Where are they?'

McCoy pointed. Jake saw six gray warships in close formation, closing the American formation at an angle from the port side, still four or five miles away. The US ships were only making ten knots or so due to the sea state, but the Soviets were doing at least twice that. Even from this distance the rearing and plunging of the Soviet ships was quite obvious. Their bows were rising clear of the water, then plunging deeply as white water cascaded across the main decks and smashed against the gun mounts.

On they came, seemingly aiming straight for *Columbia*, which, as usual, was in the middle of the American formation.

Gidrograf, the Soviet Pamir-class AGI that had been shadowing the Americans for the last month, was trailing along behind the Americans, at least two miles astern. Her speed matched the Americans' and she made no move to join the oncoming Soviet ships.

'What do you think?' McCoy asked.

'Unless Ivan changes course, he's going to run his ships smack through the middle of our formation.'

'I think that is exactly what he intends to do,' McCoy said after a bit, when the Russians were at least a mile closer.

'Sure looks like it,' Jake agreed. The angle-of-bearing hadn't changed noticeably, which was the clue that the ships were on collision courses. He glanced up at *Columbia*'s bridge. Reflections on the glass prevented him from seeing anyone, but he imagined that the captain and the admiral were conferring just now.

'Under the rules of the road, we have the right of way,' McCoy said.

'Yeah.' Somehow Jake suspected that paper rules didn't count for much with the Russian admiral, who was probably on the bridge of his flagship with one eye on the compass and the other on the Americans.

The Soviet ships were gorgeous, with sleek, raked hulls and super-structures bristling with weapons and topped with radar dishes of various types. The biggest one was apparently a cruiser. A couple were frigates, and the other three looked like destroyers. All were armed to the teeth.

The American destroyer on the edge of the formation gave way to the Russians. On they came. Now you could see the red flags at their mastheads as dots of color and tiny figures on the upper decks, like ants.

'Big storm coming,' McCoy said, never taking his eyes off the Russians. 'Up from the southwest. Be here this evening.'

Jake looked aft, at the carrier's wake. It was partially obscured by parked aircraft, but he saw enough. The wake was straight as a string. He turned his attention back to the Soviet ships. About that time the collision alarm sounded on *Columbia*'s loudspeaker system. Then came the announcement: 'This is not a drill. Rig for collision portside.'

The Soviet destroyers veered to pass ahead and behind *Columbia* but the cruiser stayed on a collision course. Now you could plainly see the sailors on the upper decks, see the red flag stiff in the wind, see the cruiser's bow rise out of the water as white and green seawater surged aft along her decks, see that she was also rolling maybe fifteen degrees with every swell.

But she was a lot smaller than the carrier. The American sailors on the flight deck were well above the Russians' bridge. In fact, they could see the faces of the Russian sailors at the base of the mast quite plainly. The Russians were hanging on for dear life.

The Russian captain was going to veer off. He had to. Jake jumped into the catwalk so he could see better as the cruiser crossed the last fifty yards and the carrier's loudspeaker boomed, 'Stand by for collision portside. All hands brace for collision.'

The Soviet captain misjudged it. He swung his helm too late and the sea carried his ship in under the carrier's flight deck overhang. The closest the two hulls came was maybe fifteen feet, but as the cruiser heeled her motion in the sea pushed her mast and several of the radar antennae into the underside of the flight deck overhang. The Russian sailors clustered around the base of the mast saw that the collision was inevitable only seconds in advance and tried to flee. Two didn't make it. One fell to the cruiser's main deck, but the other man fell into that narrow river of white water between the two ships and instantly disappeared from view.

The top of the mast hit the catwalk forward of the Fresnel lens and ripped open three of the sixty-man life raft containers. The rafts dropped away. One ended up on the cruiser and the others went into the sea. The

Russians' mast and several radar antennae were wiped off the super-structure and her stack was partially smashed.

Then the cruiser was past, surging ahead of *Columbia* with her mast trailing in the water on her portside.

Jake bent down and stuck his head through the railing under the life raft containers so that he could keep the cruiser in sight. If the Russian captain cut across *Columbia*'s bow he was going to get his ship cut in half.

He did cut across, but only when he was at least six or seven hundred yards ahead, still making twenty knots.

The Soviet ships rejoined their tight formation and continued on course, pulling steadily away.

An American destroyer dropped aft to look for the lost Soviet sailor as the air boss ordered the flight deck cleared so he could launch the alert helo.

The helo searched for half an hour. The destroyer stayed on the scene for several hours, yet the Russian sailor wasn't found.

By evening a line of thunderstorms formed a solid wall to the south-west, a wall that seemed to stretch from horizon to horizon. As the dusk deepened lightning flashed in the storms continually. Jake was on deck watching the approaching storms and savoring the sea wind when the carrier and her escorts slowly came about and pointed their bows at the lightning.

The ships rode better on the new course. Apparently the heavies had decided to sail through the storm line, thereby minimizing their time in it. Unfortunately the weather on the back side of the front was supposed to be bad; heavy seas, low ceilings and lots of rain. Oh well, no flying tomorrow either.

When the darkness was complete and the storms were within a few miles, Jake went below. This was going to be a good night to sleep.

The ringing telephone woke Jake. The Real McCoy usually answered it since all he had to do was roll over in his bunk and reach, and he did this time. The motion of the ship was less pronounced than it had been when Jake and Real went to bed about 10 P.M., during the height of the storm.

'McCoy, sir.'

Jake looked at his watch. A little after 2 A.M.

After a bit, he heard his roommate growl, 'This had better not be your idea of a joke, Harrison, or your ass is a grape . . . Yeah, yeah, I'll tell him . . . In a minute, okay?'

Then McCoy slammed the receiver back on the hook.

'You awake up there?'

'Yeah.'

'They want us both in the ready room in five minutes, ready to fly.'

'Get serious.'

'That's what the man said. Must be World War III.'

'Awww . . .'

'If Harrison is jerking our chains he'll never have another OK pass as long as he lives. I promise.'

But Harrison wasn't kidding, as Jake and the Real found out when they went through the ready room door. The skipper and Allen Bartow were standing near the duty desk talking to CAG Kall. Flap Le Beau was listening and sipping a cup of coffee. All of them were in flight suits.

'Good morning, gentlemen,' CAG said. He looked like he had had a great eight hours sleep and a fine breakfast. He couldn't have had, Jake knew. Things didn't work like that in this Navy.

''Morning, CAG,' McCoy responded. 'So it's war, huh?'

'Not quite. Pull up a chair and we'll sort this out.'

Apparently the admiral and CINCPACFLT had been burning the airways with flash messages. The Soviet ambassador in Washington had delivered a stiff note to the State Department protesting the previous day's naval incident in the Indian Ocean, which he called 'a provocation.' The powers that be had concluded that the US Navy had to serve notice on the Russians that it couldn't be bullied.

'The upshot is,' CAG said, 'that we have been ordered to make an aerial demonstration over the Soviet task group, tonight if possible.'

'What kind of demonstration, sir?'

'At least two airplanes, high-speed passes, masthead height if possible.'

Eyebrows went up. McCoy got out of his chair and went to the television, which he turned to the continuous weather display. Current weather was three to four hundred feet broken to overcast, three-quarters of a mile visibility in rain. Wind out of the northwest at twenty-five knots.

CAG was still talking. '. . . it occurred to me that this would be a good time to try our foul weather attack scheme on the Russians. I thought we could send two A-6s and three EA-6Bs. We'd put a Hummer up to keep it safe. The admiral concurred. The Prowler crews and Hummer crews will be here in a few minutes for the brief. What do you think?'

'Sir, where are the Russians?'

'Two hundred miles to the east. Apparently the line of thunderstorms went over them several hours ago and they are also under this system.'

As he finished speaking the ship's loudspeaker, the 1-MC, came to life: 'Flight quarters, flight quarters, all hands man your flight quarters stations.'

In minutes the Prowler and Hawkeye crews came in and found seats and the brief began. CAG did the briefing, even though he wouldn't be flying. Forget the masthead rhetoric from Washington – the lowest any of the crews could go was five hundred feet.

The three senior pilots of the Prowler squadron would fly their planes, and the CO of the E-2 squadron would be in the left seat of the Hawkeye. Lieutenant Colonel Haldane and the Real McCoy would fly the go A-6s and Jake Grafton would man the spare.

'Uh, skipper,' Flap said, 'if I may ask, why McCoy?'

'He's got the best landing grades in the squadron. Grafton is second. As it happens, they have more traps than anyone else in the outfit and getting back aboard is going to be the trick. As for me, this is my squadron.'

'Yessir, but I was wondering about McCoy. Let's face facts, sir. When the landing signal officer has the best landing scores – well, it's like an umpire having the top batting average. There's just a wee bit of an odor, sir.'

Laughter swept the room as McCoy grinned broadly. He winked at Jake.

'What say you and I flip for the go bird,' Jake suggested to McCoy.

'Forget it, shipmate. If my plane's up, I'm flying it. Tonight or any other night.'

'Come on! Be a sport.'

The Real was having none of it. And Jake understood. Naval aviation was their profession. Given the weather and sea state, this would be a very tough mission. When you began ducking the tough ones, you were finished in this business. Maybe no one else would know, but *you* would.

In flight deck control Jake looked at the airplane planform cutouts on the model ship to see where his plane was spotted. Watching the handler check the weight chits as rain splattered against the one round, bomb-proof window and the wind moaned, Jake Grafton admitted to himself that he was glad he had the spare. He wasn't ducking anything – this was the bird the system gave him and he wasn't squawking.

All he had to do was preflight, strap in and start the engines, then sit and watch Haldane and McCoy ride the catapult into the black goo. After that he could shut down and go below for coffee. If he went to the forward mess deck galley he could probably snag a couple doughnuts hot from the oven.

The handler was a lieutenant commander pilot who had left the Navy for two years, then changed his mind. The only billet available when he came back was this one – two years as the aircraft handler on *Columbia*. He took it, resigning himself to two years of shuffling airplane cutouts around this model, two years of listening to squadron maintenance people complain that their airplanes weren't where they could properly maintain them, two years listening to the air boss grouse that the go birds were spotted wrong, two years checking tie-down chains and weight chits, two years listening to the hopes, dreams and fears of young, homesick sailors while trying to train them to do dangerous, difficult jobs, two years in purgatory with no flying . . . yet the handler seemed to be weathering it okay. True, his fuse was getting almighty short and he wasn't getting enough sleep, but his job performance was first-rate, from everything Jake had seen and heard. And behind the tired face with the bleary eyes was a gentle human being who liked to laugh at a good joke in the dirty-shirt wardroom. Here in Flight Deck Control, however, he was all business.

'Forty-six thousand five hundred pounds? That right, Grafton?' The handler was reading from Jake's weight chit. This would be his weight if he launched.

'Yessir.'

Savoring the hubbub in Flight Deck Control while surreptitiously watching the handler, Jake Grafton felt doubt creep over him. Was getting out a mistake? It had been for the handler. An eight-to-five job somewhere, the same routine day after day . . .

He turned for the hatch that led to the flight deck. The first blast of cool air laden with rain wiped the future from his mind and left only the present, this moment, this wild, windy night, this airplane that awaited him under the dim red island floodlights.

His bird was sitting on Elevator Four. The tail was sticking out over the water, so he checked every step with his flash-light before he moved his feet. If you tripped over the three-inch-high combing, you would go straight into the ocean to join that Russian sailor who went in yesterday. Poor devil – his shipmates didn't even stop to look for him. How would you like to go to sea in that man's navy?

Going around the nose he and Flap passed each other. 'What a night,' Flap muttered.

Both men were wearing their helmets. They had the clear visors down to keep the rain and salt spray out of their eyes. The wind made the raindrops hurt as they splattered against exposed flesh.

Jake took his time preflighting the ejection seat. He was tempted to hurry at this point so he could sit down and the plane captain could close the canopy, but he was too old a dog. He checked everything carefully, methodically while he used his left hand to hang tightly to the airplane. The motion of the ship seemed magnified out here on this elevator. The fact he was eight or nine feet above the deck perched on this boarding ladder and buffeted by the wind and rain didn't help. He pulled the safety pins, inspected, counted and stowed them, then he sat.

The plane captain climbed the ladder to help him hook up the mask, don the leg restraints, and snap the four Koch fittings into place. Then the plane captain went around to help Flap. When both men were completely strapped in, he closed the canopy.

Now Jake checked the gear handle, armament switches, circuit break-ers, and arranged the switches for engine start. He had done all these things so many times that he had to concentrate to make sure he was seeing what was there and not just what he expected to see.

When he had the engines started, Flap fired up the computer while Jake checked the radio and TACAN frequencies.

'Good alignment,' Flap reported, and signaled to the plane captain to pull the cable that connected the plane to the ship's inertial navigation system.

They were ready. Now to sit here warm and reasonably dry and watch the launch.

The E-2 taxied toward Cat Three on the waist. A cloud of water lifted from the deck by the wash of the two turbo-props blasted everything. The plane went onto the cat, the JBD rose, then the engines began to moan. Finally the wing-tip lights came on. The Hawkeye accelerated down the catapult and rose steadily into the night. The lights faded quickly, then the goo swallowed them.

'Uh-oh,' Flap said. 'Look over there at Real's plane.'

A crowd of maintenance people had the left engine access door open. Someone was up on the ladder talking to McCoy. In less than a minute a figure left the group and headed for Jake's plane.

The man on the deck lowered the pilot's boarding ladder while Jake ran the canopy open. Then he climbed up. The squadron's senior troubleshooter. 'Mr McCoy can't get his left generator to come on the line,' he shouted. Jake had to hold his helmet away from his left ear to hear. 'You're going in his place.'

'His tough luck, huh?'

'Right.'

'The breaks of Naval Air . . .'

'Be careless.' The sergeant reached for Jake's hand and shook it, then shook Flap's. He went down the boarding ladder and Flap closed the canopy.

'We're going,' Jake said on the ICS. 'In McCoy's place.'

'I figured. By God, when they said all-weather attack, they meant all-weather. Have you ever flown before on a night this bad?'

'No.'

'Me either. Just to send a message to the Russians, like the Navy was an FTD florist. Roses are red, violets are blue, you hit our ships and we'll fuck you. The peacetime military ain't what it was advertised to be. No way, man.'

The yellow-shirted taxi director was signaling for the blue-shirts to break down the tie-downs. Jake put his feet on the brakes. 'Here we go.'

It never gets any easier. In the darkness the rain streaming over the windshield blurred what little light there was and the slick deck and wind made taxiing difficult. Just beyond the bow the abyss gaped at him.

He ran through possible emergencies as he eased the plane toward the cat.

Total electrical failure while taking the cat shot was the emergency he feared the most. It wasn't that he didn't know what to do – he did. The doing of it in a cockpit lit only by Flap's flashlight as adrenaline surged through you like a lightning bolt would be the trick. You had just one chance, in an envelope of opportunity that would be open for only a few seconds. You had to do it right regardless or you would be instantly, totally dead.

'Why do we do this shit?' he muttered at Flap as they taxied toward the cat.

'Because we're too lazy for honest work and too stupid to steal.'

The truth of the matter was that he feared and loathed night cat shots. And flying at night, especially night instrument flight. There was nothing fun about it, no beauty, no glamour, no appeal to his sense of adventure, no sense that this was a thing worth doing. The needles and gauges were perverse gadgets that demanded his total concentration to make behave. Then the night flight was topped off with a night carrier landing – he once described a night carrier hop as sort of like eating an old tennis shoe for dinner, then choking down a sock for dessert.

Tonight as he ran through the launch procedures and ran the engines up to full power, rancid fear occupied a portion of his attention. A small portion, it is true, but it was there.

He tried to fight it back, to wrestle the beast back into its cage deep in his subconscious, but without success.

Wipe out the cockpit with the controls, check the engine instruments . . . all okay.

Jumping Jack Bean was the shooter. When Jake turned on his exterior lights, he saluted the cockpit perfunctorily with his right hand while he kept giving the 'full power' signal with the wand in his left hand. Jake could see he was looking up the deck, waiting for the bow to reach the bottom of its plunge into a trough between the swells.

Now Bean lunged forward and touched the wand to the deck. The bow must be rising.

The plane shot forward.

Jake's eyes settled on the altitude instruments.

The forward edge of the flight deck swept under the nose.

Warning lights out, rotate to eight degrees, airspeed okay, gear up.

'Positive rate of climb,' Flap reported, then keyed the radio and reported to Departure Control.

The climb went quickly because the plane was carrying only a two-thousand-pound belly tank and four empty bomb racks. But they had a long way to climb. They finally cleared the clouds at 21,000 feet and found the night sky filled with stars.

An EA-6B Prowler was already there, waiting for them. It was level at 22,000 feet, on the five-mile arc around the ship. Its exterior lights seemed weak, almost lonely as they flickered in the starry night.

The Prowler was a single-purpose aircraft, designed solely to wage electronic war. Grumman had lengthened the basic A-6 airframe enough to accept two side-by-side cockpits, so in addition to the pilot the plane carried three electronic warfare specialists known as ECMOs, or electronic counter-measures officers. Special antennae high on the tail and at various other places on the plane allowed the specialists to detect enemy radar transmissions, which they then jammed or deceived by the use of countermeasures pods that hung on the wing weapons stations. Tonight, in addition to the pods, this Prowler carried a two-thousand-pound fuel tank on its belly station. Although the EA-6B was capable of carrying a couple of missiles to defend itself, Jake had never seen one armed.

As expensive as Boeing 747s, these state-of-the-art aircraft had not been allowed to cross into North Vietnam after they joined the fleet, which degraded their effectiveness but ensured that if one were lost, the Communists would not get a peek at the technology. Here, again, America traded airplanes and lives in a meaningless war rather than risk compromising the technological edge it had to have to win a war with the Soviets, a war for national survival.

Jake thought about that now – about trading lives to keep the secrets – as he flew in formation with the Prowler and looked at the telltale outline of helmeted heads in the cockpits looking back at him. Then the Prowler pilot passed Jake the lead, killed his exterior lights, slid aft and crossed under to take up a position on Jake's right wing.

The Prowler pilot was Commander Reese, the skipper of the squadron. He was about five and a half feet tall, wore a pencil-thin mustache, and delighted in practical jokes. Inevitably, given his stature, he had acquired the nickname of Pee Wee.

Jake retarded the throttles and lowered the nose. In seconds the clouds closed in around the descending planes and blotted out the stars.

'Departure, War Ace Five Oh Two and company headed southeast, descending.'

'Roger, War Ace. Switch to Strike.'

'Switching.'

Flap twirled the radio channelization knob and waited for the Prowler to check in on frequency. Then he called Strike.

Flying in this goo, at night, wasn't really flying at all. It was like a simulator. The world ended at the windshield. Oh, if you turned your head you could see the fuzzy glow of the wing-tip lights, and if you looked back right you could see your right wing-tip light reflecting off the skin of the Prowler that hung there, but there was no sense of speed or movement. Occasional little turbulence jolts were the only reminder that this box decorated with dim red lights, gauges and switches wasn't welded to the earth.

The big plan was for each bomber and its accompanying Prowler to run a mock attack on the Soviet task group as close to simultaneously as possible. Jake would approach from the southwest, Colonel Haldane from the northwest. The E-2 Hawkeye, the Hummer, would monitor their progress and coordinate the attack. However, each A-6 BN had to find the task group on radar before they sank below the radar horizon. Then the bombers would run in at five hundred feet. In an actual attack they would come in lower, perhaps as low as two hundred, but not at night, not in this weather, for drill. The risks of flying that close to the sea were too great.

Flap started the video recorder, a device that the A-6A never had. This device would record everything seen on the radar screen, all the computer and inertial data, as well as the conversation on the radio and in the cockpit.

'Recorder's on,' he told Jake. 'Keep it clean.'

This electronic record of the attack could be used for poststrike analysis, or, as CAG had hinted in the brief, sent to Washington to show to any bigwigs or congressmen who wanted to know what, exactly, the Navy had done in response to the collision at sea.

Had the Soviet skipper intended to bump the carrier? Did he tell the truth to his superiors? These imponderables had of course been weighed in Washington, and orders had been sent to the other side of the earth.

It was midafternoon in Washington. The city would be humming with the usual mix of tourists, government workers anxious to begin their afternoon trek to the suburbs, the latest tunes coming over the radios, soap operas on television . . .

Jake wondered about the weather there. Late November. Was it cold, rainy, overcast?

All those people in America, finishing up another Monday, and he and Flap were here, over the Indian Ocean, passing ten thousand feet with a Prowler on their wing and a Soviet task group somewhere in the night ahead.

'See it yet?'

'No. Stop at eight thousand and hold there.'

As they flew eastward the turbulence increased. Jake had Flap arrange his rearview mirror so he could keep tabs on the Prowler. Pee Wee Reese seemed to be hanging in there pretty well. He had to. If he lost sight of the bomber, he would have to break off. Two planes feeling for each other in this soup would be a fine way to arrange a midair collision.

'The Commies aren't where they're supposed to be,' Flap said finally.

'You sure?'

'All I know is that the radar screen is empty. Rocket scientist that I am,

I deduce the Reds aren't where the spies said they would be. Or *Columbia*'s inertial was all screwed up and this is the wrong ocean. Or all the Reds have sunk. Those are the possibilities.'

'Better ask Black Eagle.'

It turned out the E-2 was also looking for the Soviets at the maximum range of its radar. It soon found them, steaming hard to the northeast, directly away from Jake and Flap and directly toward the line of thunderstorms that had just passed over them.

'They know something's up,' Jake said.

'Terrific. They're at general quarters expecting us and we'll have to go under thunderstorms to get to them. And to think we almost didn't get a date for this party.'

'Man, we're having fun now.'

Flap didn't reply. He was busy.

After a bit he said, 'Okay, I got 'em. Give me a few moments to get a course and speed and then we'll go down.'

While he was talking the electronic warfare (EW) panel chirped. A Soviet search radar was painting them. In addition to the flashing light on the panel when the beam swept them, Jake heard a baritone chirp in his headset.

So much for surprise.

The turbulence was getting worse. The bouncing was constant now. Rain coursed around the windscreen and across the canopy. 'Radar is getting degraded,' Flap muttered. 'Rain. I got them though, course Zero Five Zero at fifteen. Lots of sea return. Swells are big down there, my man.'

'Can we go down?'

'Yeah.'

Jake glanced over at the reflection of the Prowler in the mirror. Pee Wee was riding fairly steadily, cycling up and down as the planes bounced, but never slipping too far out of position. Jake carefully eased the throttle back and let the nose go down a half a degree. When he was sure the EA-6B pilot was still with him, he lowered the nose some more.

A pale green light caught his eye, and he glanced at the windscreen. Dancing tendrils of green fire were playing across it.

'Look at this,' he told Flap. 'Saint Elmo's fire.'

'This makes my night,' the BN said. 'All we need is for the Russians to squirt a missile at us and this will be a complete entertainment experience.'

'Will a lightning bolt do?'

'Don't say stuff like that. God's listening. You're passing five thousand.'

'Radar's altimeter's set.'

'Roger. Station one selected, master arm to go.'

They were up to four hundred knots indicated now. The EA-6B was right there, hanging on. Eighty miles to go.

Wasn't Saint Elmo's fire an indicator that lightning might strike? Wasn't that what the old sailors said? Even as he wondered the flickering green fire faded, then disappeared completely.

Black Eagle gave them a turn. Jake banked gently to the new heading. The steering to the target was forty degrees left, but the controller in the E-2 was trying to coordinate the attack. When he had one of the formations four miles farther from the target than the other, he would have them turn inbound and accelerate to five hundred knots. The pilots would call their distance to go on the radio every ten miles. The plan was for the bombers and their EA-6B escorts to pass over the Soviet task group thirty seconds apart. Neither formation would see the other, so this separation was required for safety reasons.

Jake eased his descent passing twenty-five hundred feet. He shallowed it still more passing a thousand and drifted slowly down to five hundred, keeping one eye on the radar altimeter. He adjusted the barometric pressure on the pressure altimeter so it matched the radar altimeter's reading exactly.

The turbulence had not let up, nor had it increased. The rain was heavier, though. The high airspeed kept the windscreen clear but the water ran across the top and sides of the canopy in sheets.

'War Aces, turn inbound.'

Jake came left to center the steering and fed the throttles forward until they were at ninety-eight percent RPM. Pee Wee stayed right with him.

'Five Oh Two, seventy miles.'

Fifteen seconds later he heard Haldane's voice: 'Five Oh Five, sixty miles.'

Each plane was inbound on a bomb run at eight and a third nautical miles per minute. They were a little over thirty seconds apart, but the extra margin was an added safety cushion.

'I should get them at about thirty miles, I think,' Flap said.

And when we can see them, they can see us.

Jake reached down and flipped the IFF, the transponder, to standby. No use giving the Reds an easy problem.

He glanced at the EW panel. Still quiet. When they rose above the Russians' radar horizon it would light up like a Christmas tree.

'Five Oh Two, sixty miles.'

The turbulence was getting vicious. The radar altimeter beeped once when Jake inadvertently dropped to four hundred feet. He concentrated on the instruments, on the altitude indicator on the VDI, on the needle of the rate-of-climb indicator, cross-checking the radar and pressure altimeters, all the while working to keep his wings level and steering centered. Every moment or two he glanced in the mirror to check on Pee Wee Reese, who was sticking like glue. No question, the guy was good.

'Five Oh Two, fifty miles.'

Rain poured over the plane, so much that a film of water developed on the windscreen even though they were doing five hundred knots.

'Five Oh Two, forty miles.'

A lightning flash ahead distracted him for several seconds from the instruments. When he came back to them he had lost fifty feet. He struggled to get it back as he wondered if Haldane had seen the lightning flash. Should they go under a thunderstorm? It was Haldane's call. Jake wasn't breaking off the run unless the skipper did.

'Five Oh Two, thirty miles.'

Twenty-nine, twenty-eight . . .

'They've turned,' Flap said. 'They're heading southeast. Follow steering.'

Even as Jake eased right to center the bug, the EW panel lit up and the tones assailed him. X-band, Y-band – the Russians had every radar they had turned on and probing, looking for a target.

Now the tones of the radars became a buzz. The bomber was so close to the EA-6B, which was jamming the Russian radar, that the bomber's EW gear was overwhelmed.

'Five Oh Two, twenty miles.'

'Master Arm on, we're in attack,' Flap reported.

The attack symbology came alive on the VDI.

Another lightning flash. Closer. Lots of rain.

'Five Oh Five, ten miles.' That was Haldane.

Fifteen miles . . . fourteen . . . thirteen . . .

'They're jamming me. Keep on this heading.'

Now Flap flipped on frequency agility, trying to change his radar's frequency to an unjammed wavelength long enough to get a look.

'Five Oh Two, ten miles.'

Three lightning flashes in a couple seconds. They were flying right under a boomer. The turbulence was so bad Jake had trouble concentrating on the instruments. Pee Wee was still hanging on, though.

Five miles.

Four.

Three.

Symbols marching down toward weapons release.

Lights. The Russian ships should be lit up. He should pass over them just after weapons' release. *But don't look!* No distractions. *Concentrate!*

Two.

One.

Release marker coming down. Steering centered. Commit trigger pulled.

Click. Flag drop on the ordnance panel and the attack light on the VDI went out.

If there had been a bomb, it would now be falling.

A searchlight split the night. Three or four, weaving.

Instantly he had vertigo. He stared at the VDI, forced himself to keep his wings level as he tugged the stick slightly aft to begin a climb.

And then the lights were behind. That quick.

More lightning ahead. Jake eased into a left turn, toward the north. The skipper went out to the southeast, so this direction should be clear.

He would climb away from this ocean, turn west to head for the carrier, get out of this rain and turbulence and lightning, and to hell with the Ivans!

Message delivered: fuck you very much, stiff letter to follow.

He had the power back to ninety percent and was up to two thousand feet, in a ten-degree angle-of-bank left turn passing north on the HSI when the lightning bolt struck. There was a stupendous flash of light and a sound like a hammer striking, then nothing.

He was blind. Everything was white. Flash blindness. He knew it.

He keyed the ICS and told Flap, 'Flashlight—' but there was no feedback in his headset. A total electrical failure. And he was blind as a bat, two thousand feet over the water, in a turn.

He *had* to see.

He blinked furiously, trying by sheer force of will to see the instrument panel.

But there was no light, no electricity.

He reached behind him with his left hand, found the handle for the ram-air turbine – the RAT – and pulled hard. Real hard.

The handle came out.

Perhaps four seconds had passed, not more.

The white was fading. He reached for his oxygen mask with both hands and unfastened the right side.

What the plane was doing he had no way of knowing, although he knew whatever it was, it wasn't good. But he couldn't fly blind. His seat-of-the-pants instincts were worthless. Oh, he knew *that*, had had it drummed into him and had experienced it on so many night carrier landings that he wasn't even tempted to try to level the wings.

The white was fading into darkness. He blinked furiously, then remembered his L-shaped flashlight, hanging by a hook on the front of his survival vest. He found it and pushed the switch on.

In the growing darkness he saw the spot the beam made on the instrument panel. Another few seconds . . .

But there was already a spot of light on the needle-ball turn indicator! *Flap!* He must have had his head in the scope when the lightning hit.

He could see. The VDI was blank. The standby gyro showed a thirty-degree left turn. Ten degrees nose-down.

Cross-check with the turn indicator!

Turn needle pegged left. He rolled right to center it, overdid it and came back left some. The standby gyro responded.

The altimeter! Going down.

Back stick. Stop the needle. Gently now. Coming down on eleven hundred feet. Stop it there, center that turn needle. Standby gyro disagrees by five degrees. *Ignore it!*

Flap was shouting and he caught the muffled words: 'Reese is still with us. He has his lights on. I think he wants to take the lead.'

Jake could see now. His vision was back to normal. How many seconds had it been?

He risked a glance in the rearview mirror. There was Reese, with his exterior lights on, bobbing like a cork on Jake's right wing. Reese must be the world's finest formation pilot, to hang on through that gyration.

Should he chance it? Should he pull the power and try to ease back onto Reese's wing without a radio call or signal?

Even as the thought shot through his mind, he was retarding the throttles. Reese's plane began to move forward.

Okay! Flap was flipping his flashlight at Reese in the EA-6B's cockpit.

Pee Wee knows. He wants me to fly on him. It's our only chance if the TACAN and radar are screwed up. We'll never find the ship on our own.

Now Reese was abeam him, the two planes flying wing tip to wing tip and bouncing out of sync in the turbulence.

Be smooth, Jake. Don't lose him. Don't let him slip away into this black shit or you'll be swimming for it.

He stabilized in parade position on Reese's left side, so that he was looking straight up the leading edge of the swept wing into the cockpit. Reese was just a dark shape limned by red light, the glow from his instrument panel.

No comforting red glow in this cockpit. This place was dark as a tomb.

The bouncing was getting worse. He had to cross under, get on Reese's right side so he wouldn't be looking across the cockpit at the other plane.

He tucked the nose down gently and pulled a smidgen of power. Now power back on and a little right bank while he wrestled the stick in the chop.

Right under the tail, crossing, surfacing on Pee Wee's right wing. Okay. Now hang here.

Another flash of lightning. He flinched.

Flap was shouting something. He concentrated, trying to make sense of the words. '. . . must've zapped us with a zillion volts. Every circuit breaker we got is popped. I'm going to try to reset some, so if you smell smoke, let me know.'

'Okay,' he shouted, and found reassurance in the sound of his own voice.

All he had to do was hang on to Reese. Hang on and hang on and hang on, and someday, sometime, Reese would drop him onto the ball. The ball would be out there in the rain and black goo, and the drop lights, and the centerline lights, and the wires, strung across that pitching, heaving deck.

All he had to do was hang on . . .

As Flap pushed in circuit breakers and the cockpit lights glowed, then went out, then glowed again, the planes flew into and out of deluges. The torrents of rain were worse than they had been coming in. Several times the rain coursing over the canopy caused Reese's plane to fade until just the exterior lights could be seen.

Jake concentrated fiercely upon those lights. Each time the rain would eventually slacken and the fuselage of the EA-6B would reappear, a ghostly gray presence in the blacker gloom.

Finally the clouds dissipated and a blacker night spread out before them. Far above tiny, cold stars shown steadily. They were on top, above the clouds. Behind them lightning strobed almost continually.

Jake eased away from Reese and put his mask to his face. The oxygen was flowing, cool and rubbery tasting. He lowered it again, then swabbed the sweat from his eyes and face with the fingers of his left hand.

When he had his mask fixed back in place he glanced at the instruments. The instrument lights were on – well, some of them. It was still dark on Flap's side. The VDI was still blank, but the standby gyro was working. The TACAN needle swung lazily, steadily, around and around the dial.

He pushed the button to check the warning lights on the annunciator panel. The panel stayed dark. Both generators were probably fried. Maybe the battery. He recycled each of the generator switches, but nothing happened. Finally he just turned them off.

Fuel – he checked the gauge. Nine thousand pounds. He pushed the buttons on the fuel panel to check the quantity in each tank. The needle and totalizer never moved. They were frozen.

Flap was still examining the circuit breaker panel with his flashlight.

'Hey, shipmate, you there?' Flap – on the ICS.

'Yeah.'

'A whole bunch of these CBs won't stay in.'

'Forget it.'

'We're gonna need—'

'We'll worry about it later.'

Later. Let's sit up here in the night above the storms and savor this moment. Savor life. For we are alive. Still alive. Let's sit silently and look at the stars and Reese's beautiful Prowler and breathe deeply and listen to our hearts beating.

19

The radome on the nose of the aircraft had a hole in it. Jake and Flap examined it with their flashlights. It was about the size of a quarter and had black edges where the Plexiglas or whatever it was had melted. They had shut down on Elevator Two so the plane could be dropped below to the hangar deck.

Now they stood looking at the hole in the radome as the sea wind dried the sweat from their faces and hair and the overcast began to lighten toward the east.

Dawn was coming. Another day at sea.

The hole was there and that was that.

'Grafton, you're jinxed,' Flap Le Beau said.

'What do you mean?' Jake asked, suddenly defensive.

'Man, things happen to you.'

'I was doing fine until I started flying with you,' Jake shot back, then instantly regretted it.

Flap didn't reply. Both men turned off their flashlights and headed for the island.

Lieutenant Colonel Haldane had rendezvoused with Pee Wee Reese and Jake had transferred over to his wing. An approach with a similar aircraft was easier to fly. Fortunately the weather had cleared somewhat around the ship, so when the two A-6s came out of the overcast with their gear, flaps and hooks down they were still a thousand feet above the water. There wasn't much rain. The ship's lights were clear and bright.

Jake boltered his first pass and made a climbing left turn off the angle. He and Flap had been unable to get the radio working again, so he few a close downwind leg and turned into the groove as if he were flying a day pass. He snagged a one-wire.

The debrief took two hours. After telling the duty officer to take him off the schedule for the rest of the day, Jake went to breakfast, then back to his bunk. The Real McCoy woke him in time for dinner.

Jake and Flap didn't fly again for four days. The skipper must have told the schedules officer to give them some time off, but Jake didn't ask. He did paperwork, visited the maintenance office to hear about the electrical woes of 502, did more paperwork, ate, slept, and watched three movies.

The maintenance troops found another lightning hole in the tail of 502. Jake went to the hangar deck for a look.

'Apparently the bolt went in the front and went clear through the plane, then out the tail,' the sergeant said. 'Or maybe it went in the tail and out the front.'

'Uh-huh.' The hole in the tail was also about quarter size, up high above the rudder.

'Was the noise loud?'

'Not that I recall.'

'Thought it must be like sitting beside a howitzer when it went off.'

'Just a metallic noise,' Jake said, trying to remember. Funny, but he didn't remember a real loud noise.

'You guys were sure lucky.'

'Like hell,' Jake told him. He was thoroughly sick of these philosophical discussions. 'Pee Wee Reese was on my wing and the lightning didn't hit him. It hit me. He didn't get a volt. *He* had the luck.'

'You were lucky you didn't blow up,' the sergeant insisted. 'I've heard of planes hit by lightning that just blew up. You were lucky.'

'Planes full of avgas, maybe, but not jet fuel.'

The sergeant wasn't taking no for an answer. 'Jets too,' he said.

Thanksgiving came and went, then another page was ripped off the ready room calendar and it was December.

Jake had that feeling again that his life was out of control. 'You just got to go with the flow,' the Real McCoy said when Jake tried to talk to him about it.

'It's a reaction to the lightning strike,' Flap said when Jake mentioned it to him. Jake didn't bother telling him he had had it off and on for years.

Yet gradually the feeling faded and he felt better. Once again he laughed in the ready room and tried to remember jokes. But he refused to think about the future. I'm going to take life one day at a time, he decided. If a guy does that there will never be a future to worry about. Just the present. That makes sense, doesn't it?

'What does it feel like to die?' Flap Le Beau asked.

He and Jake were motoring along at 350 knots at five thousand feet just under a layer of cumulus puffballs. Beneath them the empty blue sea spread away to the horizon in every direction. This afternoon they were flying another surface surveillance mission, this time a wedge-shaped pattern to the east of the task group. They were still on the outbound leg. They had not seen a single ship, visually or on radar. The ocean was empty.

All those ships crossing the Indian Ocean, hundreds of them at any one time, yet the ocean was so big . . .

'Did you ever think about it?' Flap prompted.

'I passed out once,' Jake replied. 'Fainted. When I was about fourteen. Nurse was taking blood, jabbing me over and over again trying to get the needle into a vein. One second I was there, then I was waking up on the floor after some nightmare, which I forgot fifteen seconds after I woke up. Dying is like that, I suspect. Not the nightmare part. Just like someone turned out the light.'

'Maybe,' Flap said.

'Like going to sleep,' Jake offered.

'Ummm . . .'

'What got you thinking about that, anyway?'

'Oh, you know . . .'

The conversation dribbled out there. Flap idly checked the radar, as usual saw nothing, then rearranged his fanny in his seat. Grafton yawned and rubbed his face.

The radio squawked to life. The words were partially garbled: the aircraft was a long way from the ship – over two hundred miles – and low.

'This is War Ace Five Oh Eight,' Flap said into his mask. 'Say again.'

'Five Oh Eight, this is Black Eagle. We'll relay. The ship wants you to investigate an SOS signal. Stand by for the coordinates.'

Flap glanced at Jake, shrugged, then got a ballpoint pen from the left-shoulder pocket of his flight suit and inspected the point. He scribbled on the corner of his top kneeboard card to make sure the pen worked, then said, 'War Ace is ready to copy.'

When he had read back the coordinates to the controller in the E-2 Hawkeye to ensure he had copied them correctly, Flap tapped them into the computer and cycled it. 'Uh-oh,' he muttered to Jake. 'It's over four hundred miles from here.'

'Better talk to the controller.'

Flap clicked his oxygen mask into place. 'Black Eagle, Five Oh Eight. That ship looks to be four hundred twenty-nine miles from our present position, which is' – he pushed another button on the computer – 'two hundred forty-two miles from the ship. We don't have the gas and we can't make the recovery.'

Grafton was punching the buttons, checking the wing fuel. They launched with a total of 18,000 pounds, and now had 11,200.

'Roger, War Ace. They know that. We're talking to them on another frequency. They want you to go look anyway. They only got about fifteen seconds of an SOS broadcast, which had the lat-long position as a part of it. The ship thinks you can get there, give it a quick look-over, then rendezvous with a tanker on the inbound leg on this frequency.'

Already Jake had swung the plane fifteen degrees to the right to follow the computer's steering command to the ship in distress. Now he added power and began to climb.

'Set up a no-rad rendezvous, just in case,' Jake told Flap.

He wanted to know where to find the tanker even if the radio failed. The only way to fix positions in this world of sea and sky was electronically, in bearings and distances away from ships that were radiating electronic signals that the plane's nav aids could receive. Unfortunately the A-6s radar could not detect other airplanes. And the tanker had no radar at all. Of course, Flap could find the carrier on radar if he were within 150 miles of it and the radar worked, and they could use the distance and bearing to locate themselves in relation to the tanker. If the radar kept working.

There were a lot of ifs.

The ifs made your stomach feel hollow.

Seventeen days had passed since their night adventure in the thunderstorm and here they were again, letting it all hang out.

Jake Grafton swore softly under his breath. It just isn't fair! *And the ship in distress might not even be there.* A fifteen-second SOS with the position. Sounded like an electronic program, one that could have easily broadcast the wrong position information. The ship could be hundreds of miles from the position they were winging they way to, and they would never find it.

The emergency broadcast might have been an error – a radioman on some civilian freighter might have inadvertently flipped the wrong switch. There might not be any emergency at all.

No doubt the bigwigs on the carrier had considered all that. Then, safe and comfortable, they had sent Jake and Flap to take a look. And to take the risks.

Finding the tanker would be critical. Jake eyed the fuel gauge without optimism. He would go high, to forty thousand feet, stay there until he could make an idle descent to the ship in distress, make a quick pass while Flap snapped photographs, then climb back to forty thousand headed toward the carrier. The tanker would be at 150 miles, on the Zero Nine Five radial, at forty grand. If it were not sweet, or this plane couldn't take fuel, they wouldn't be able to make it to the ship. They would have to eject.

At least it was daytime. Good weather. No night sweats. No need to do that needle-ball shit by flashlight. That was something.

Now Jake turned in his seat to look behind him at the sun. He looked at his watch. There should be at least a half hour of daylight left when they reached the SOS ship, but the sun would be down by the time they got to the tanker. Still, there would probably be some light left in the sky. Perhaps it would be better if the sky were completely dark, then they could spot the tanker's flashing anticollision light from a long distance away. But it would not be dark. A high twilight, that was the card the gods of fate had dealt.

One of these fine Navy days we're gonna use up all our luck. Then we two fools are gonna be sucking the big one. That's what everyone is trying to tell us.

'We won't descend unless you have a target on the radar,' Jake told Flap.

'Uh-huh.'

That was a good decision. No use squandering all that fuel descending to sea level unless there was a ship down there to look at. And if there was a ship, it would show on radar.

What if the ship had gone under and the crew was in lifeboats? Lifeboats wouldn't show on radar, not from a long distance.

'How far can you see a lifeboat on that thing?' he asked Flap, who had his head pressed against the scope hood.

'I dunno. Never looked for one.'

'Guess.'

'You were right the first time. We don't go down unless we see something.'

He leveled at forty thousand feet and retarded the throttles. Twenty-two hundred pounds per hour of fuel to each engine would give him .72 Mach. Only they had used four thousand pounds climbing up here. Seven thousand eight hundred pounds of fuel remaining. It's going to be tight. He retarded the throttles still farther, until he had only eighteen hundred pounds of fuel flowing to each engine. The airspeed indicator finally settled around 220 knots, which would work out to about 460 knots true.

Flap unfolded a chart and studied it. Finally he said, 'That position is in the channel between the islands off the southern coast of Sumatra.'

'At least it isn't on top of a mountain.'

'True.'

'Wonder if the brain trust aboard the boat plotted the position before they sent us on this goose chase.'

'I dunno. Those Navy guys . . . You never can tell.'

After much effort, Flap got the chart folded the way he wanted it. He wedged it between the panel and the Plexiglas so he could easily refer to it, then settled his head against the scope hood. After a bit he muttered, 'I see some islands.'

Land. Jake hadn't seen land in over a month, not since the ship exited the Malay Strait. *Columbia* was scheduled to spend three more weeks in the Indian Ocean, then head for Australia.

Rumors had been circulating for weeks. Yesterday they were confirmed. Australia, the Land Down Under, the Last Frontier, New California, where everyone spoke English – sort of – and everyone was your mate and they drank strong, cold beer and they liked Yanks . . . oooh boy! The crew was buzzing. *This* was what they joined the Navy for.

Those few old salts who claimed they had been to Australia before were surrounded by rapt audiences ready for just about any tale.

'The women,' the young sailors invariably demanded. 'Tell us about the women. Are they really fantastic? Can we really get dates?'

Tall, leggy, gorgeous, and they *like* American men, actually prefer them over the home-grown variety. And their morals, while not exactly loose, are very very *modern*. One story making the rounds had it that during a carrier's visit to Sydney several years ago the captain had to set up a telephone desk ashore to handle all the calls from Australian women wanting a date with an American sailor! Any sailor! *Send me a sailor!* These extraordinary females gave the term 'international relations' a whole new dimension.

That was the scuttlebutt, solemnly confirmed and embellished by Those Who Had Been There, once upon a time Before the Earth Cooled. The kids listening were on their first cruise, their first extended stay away from home and Mom and the girl next door. They fervently prayed that the scuttlebutt prove true.

The Marines in the A-6 outfit were as excited as the swab jockeys. They knew that, given a choice, every sane female on the planet would of course prefer a Marine to a Dixie cup. Australia would be liberty heaven. As someone said in the dirty-shirt wardroom last night, *Columbia* had a rendezvous with destiny.

All this flitted through Jake Grafton's mind as he flew eastward at forty thousand feet. He too wanted to be off the ship, to escape from the eat-sleep-fly cycle, to get a respite from the same old faces and the same old jokes. And Australia, big, exotic, peopled by a hardy race of warriors – Australia would be fun. He hummed a few bars of 'Waltzing Matilda,' then glanced guiltily at Flap. He hadn't heard.

Jake's mind returned to the business at hand. Hitting the tanker on the way back to the ship was the dicey part . . . Why did fate keep dealing him these crummy cards?

The fiercely bright sun shone down from a deep, rich, dark blue sky. At this altitude the horizon made a perfect line, oh so far away. It seemed as if you could see forever. The sea far below was visible in little irregular patches through the low layer of scattered cumulus, which seemed to float upon the water like white cotton balls . . . hundreds of miles of cotton balls. To the northeast were the mountains of Sumatra, quite plain now. Clouds hung around the rocky spine of the huge island, but here and there a deep green jungle-covered ridge could be glimpsed, far away and fuzzy. The late afternoon sun was causing those clouds to cast dark shadows. Soon it would shoot their tops with fire.

'There's something screwy about this,' Flap said.

'What do you mean?'

'Ships don't sink in fifteen seconds. Not unless they explode. How likely is that?'

'Probably a mistake. Radio operator hit the wrong switch or something. I'll bet he thought no one heard the SOS.'

'Wonder if the ship tried to call him back.'

'Probably.'

'Well, I say it's screwy.'

'You'd better hope we find that tanker on the way home. Worry about that if you want to worry about something. Extended immersion in saltwater is bad for your complexion.'

'Think it might lighten me up?'

'Never can tell.'

'Life as a white man . . . I never even considered the possibility. Don't think it would work, though. You white guys have to go without ass for horribly long periods. I need it a lot more regular.'

'Might cure your jungle rot too.'

'You're always looking for the silver lining, Grafton. That's a personality defect. You oughta work on that.'

The minutes ticked by. The mountains seemed closer, but maybe he was just kidding himself. Perspective varies with altitude and speed. He had noticed this phenomenon years ago and never ceased to marvel at it. At just a few thousand feet you see every ravine, every hillock, every twist in the creeks. At the middle altitudes on a clear day you see half of a state. And from up here, well, from up here, at these speeds, you leap mountain ranges and vast deserts in minutes, see whole weather systems . . . In orbit the Earth would be a huge ball that occupied most of the sky. You would circle it in ninety minutes. Continents and oceans would cease to be extraordinarily large things and appear merely as features on the Earth. The concept of geographical location would cease to apply.

At this altitude he and Flap were halfway to heaven. On his kneeboard Jake jotted the phrase.

He was checking the fuel, again, when Flap said, 'We're a hundred twenty miles out. I can see the area.' The area where the ship in distress should be, he meant, if it were really there.

Odd day for an emergency at sea. Most ships got into trouble in bad weather, when heavy seas or low temperatures stressed their systems. On a day like this . . .

'I got something on the radar. A target.'

'The ship?'

'The INS says it's about four or five miles from the position Black Eagle gave us. Of course, the inertial could have drifted that much.'

'Big ship?'

'Well, it ain't a rowboat. Not at this distance. Can't tell much more than that about the size. A blip is a blip.'

233

'Course and speed?'

'She's DIW.' Dead in the water, drifting.

He would pull the power at eighty miles, descend with the engines at eighty percent RPM initially to ensure the generators stayed on the line.

'It's about fifteen miles from the coast of Sumatra, which runs north-west to southeast. Islands to seaward, west and southeast. Big islands.'

'Any other ships around?'

'No. Nothing.'

'On a coast like that . . .'

'Maybe we'll see some fishing boats or something when we get closer.'

'Yeah.'

'I'll tell Black Eagle.' Flap keyed the radio.

They arrived over the ship at seven thousand feet, the engines at idle. Peering down between cumulus clouds, Jake saw her clearly. She was a small freighter, with her super-structure amidships and cranes fore and aft. Rather like an old Liberty ship. No visible smoke, so she wasn't obviously on fire. No smoke from the funnel either, which was amidships, and no wake. There was a smaller ship, or rather a large boat, alongside, right against the starboard side.

Jake put the plane into a right circle so Flap could get pictures with the hand-held camera and picked a gap in the clouds to descend through. The engines were still at idle.

They dropped under the clouds at 5,500 feet. 'Shoot the whole roll of film,' Jake told Flap. 'From every angle. We'll circle and make one low pass down the rail so you can get a closeup shot of the ship and that boat alongside, then we're out of here.'

'Okay.' He focused and snapped.

'Looks like the crew has been rescued.'

'Swing wide at the stern so I can get a shot of her name.'

Jake was passing three thousand feet now, swinging a wide lazy circle around the ship, which seemed to be floating on an even keel. Wonder what her problem was?

'Can you read the name?'

'You're still too high. It'll be in the photos though.'

Fuel? Sixty-two hundred pounds, over six hundred miles to *Columbia*. He shivered as he surveyed the drifting freighter and the small ship alongside. That small one looked to be maybe eighty or ninety feet long, a small superstructure just forward of amidships, one stack, splotchy paint, a few people visible on deck.

'There's people on the freighter's bridge.'

'About finished?'

'Yeah.'

'Here we go, down past them both.' Jake dumped the nose. He

dropped quickly to about two hundred feet above the water and leveled, pointing his plane so that they would pass the two stationary vessels from bow to stern. Jake adjusted the throttles. If he went by too fast Flap's photos would end up blurred. He steadied at 250 knots.

'They aren't waving or anything.'

Jake Grafton saw the flashes on the bow of the small ship and knew instinctively what they were. He jammed the throttles forward to the stops, rolled forty degrees or so and pulled hard. He felt the thumps, glimpsed the fiery tracers streaming past the canopy, felt more thumps, then they were out of it.

'*Flak!*' Now Flap Le Beau found his voice.

'Fucker's got a twenty-millimeter!'

They were tail on to the ships, twisting and rolling and climbing. The primary hydraulic pressure needles flickered. So did the secondary needles. The BACK-UP HYD light illuminated on the annunciator panel.

'Oh sweet fucking Jesus!'

Jake leveled the wings, trimmed carefully for a climb.

The plane began to roll right. The stick was sloppy. Jake used a touch of left rudder to bring it back.

Heading almost south. He jockeyed the rudder and stick, trying to swing the plane to a westerly heading. The plane threatened to fall off on the right wing.

It was all he could do to keep the wings level using the stick and rudder. Nose still a degree or so above the horizon, so they were still climbing, slowly, passing two-thousand feet, doing 350 knots.

'Get on the radio,' Jake told Flap. 'Talk to Black Eagle. Those guys must be pirates.'

He retarded the throttles experimentally, instinctively wanting to get down to about 250 knots so the emergency hydraulic pump would not have to work so hard to move the control surfaces. He trimmed a little more nose up. The nose rose a tad. Good.

'Black Eagle, Black Eagle, this is War Ace, over.'

They were in real trouble. The emergency hydraulic pump was designed to allow just enough control to exit a combat situation, just enough to allow the crew to get to a safe place to eject.

'Black Eagle, this is War Ace Five Oh Eight with a red hot emergency, over.'

And the emergency pump was carrying the full load. All four of the hydraulic pressure indicator needles pointed at the floor of the airplane, indicating no pressure at all in any of their systems.

'Black Eagle, War Ace Five Oh Eight in the blind. We cannot hear your answers. We have been shot up by pirates on this SOS contact. May have to eject shortly. We are exiting the area to the south.'

Just fucking terrific! Shot down by a bunch of fucking pirates! On the high fucking seas in *1973!* On a low, slow pass in an unarmed airplane. Of all the shitty luck!

'Squawk seventy-seven hundred,' Jake said.

Flap's hand descended to the IFF box on the consol between them and turned the mode switch to emergency. Just to be sure he dialed 7700 into the windows. Mayday.

'There's an island twenty miles ahead,' Flap said. 'Go for it. We'll jump there.'

The only problem was controlling the plane. It kept wanting to drop one wing or the other. Jake was using full rudder to keep it upright, first right, then left. The stick was almost useless.

He reached out and flipped the spin assist switch on. This would give him more rudder authority, if the loss of hydraulic pressure hadn't already made that switch. It must have. The spin assist didn't help.

When the left wing didn't want to come back with full right rudder, he added power on the left engine. Shoved the power lever forward to the stop. That brought it back, but the roll continued to the right. Full left rudder, left engine back, right engine up . . . and catch it wings level . . .

'Seventeen miles.'

'We aren't gonna make it.'

'Keep trying. I don't want to swim.'

'Those fuckers!'

Three thousand feet now. Now if he could just maintain that altitude when the wings rolled . . .

They were covering about four and a half nautical miles per minute. How many minutes until they got there? The math was too much and he gave up. And he could see the island ahead. There it was, green and covered with foliage, right there in the middle of the windscreen.

'Fifteen miles.'

The roll was left. Full right rudder, left engine up. The roll stopped but the nose came down. Full back stick didn't help. He ran the trim nose-up as he pulled the right engine to idle.

The nose was coming up. Yes, coming, so he started the trim nose-down. The wing was slowly rising, oh so slowly, rising . . .

They bottomed out at fifteen hundred but the plane began a very slow roll to the right, the nose still climbing.

He reversed the engines and rudder, played with the trim.

Slowly, agonizingly, the wings responded to the pilot's inputs. Now the nose fell to the horizon and kept going down.

Full nose-up trim! He held the button and glanced at the trim indicator on the bottom of the stick. Still nose-down! Come on!

They bottomed out this time at one thousand feet and the entire cycle began again.

'We won't make it the next time,' Jake told Flap.

'Let's jump at the top, when the wings and nose are level.'

'You first and I'll be right behind you.'

Nose coming down, right wing coming down, soaring up, up, to . . . to twenty-three hundred feet.

'Now,' Jake shouted.

An explosion and Flap was gone. Jake automatically centered the rudder as he pulled the alternate firing handle. Instantly a tremendous force hit him in the ass. The cockpit disappeared. The acceleration lasted for only an instant, then he began to fall.

20

The parachute opened with a shock. As Jake Grafton turned slowly in the shrouds the airplane caught his eye, diving toward the ocean like a wounded gull. The nose rose and it skimmed the sea, then began to climb. It soared skyward in a climbing turn, its right wing hanging low, then the wing fell and the nose went through and it dove straight into the sea. There was a large splash. When the spray cleared only a swirl of foam marked the spot.

The pirates! Where were they?

He got his oxygen mask off and tossed it away, then craned his head. He saw the other parachute, lower and intact with Flap swinging from it, but he couldn't see the pirate ship or its victim.

Oh, what a fool he'd been. To fly right over a drifting ship with another craft tied to it – and to never once think about the possibility of pirates! These waters were infamous . . . and the possibility never even crossed his mind. Son of a bitch!

The sea coming toward him brought him back to the business at hand. There was enough of a swell that the height was easy to judge – and he didn't have much time. He reached down and pulled the handle on the right side of his seat pan. It opened. The raft fell away and inflated when it reached the end of its lanyard. He felt around for the toggles to the CO_2 cartridges that would inflate his life vest. He found them and pulled. The vest puffed up reassuringly.

Good! Now to ditch this chute when I hit the water.

Amazingly, the thoughts shot through his mind without conscious effort. This was the result of training. Every time the ship left port the squadron held a safety training day, and part of that exercise involved each flight crewman hanging from a harness in the ready room while wearing full flight gear. Blindfolded, each man had to touch and identify every piece of gear he wore, then run through the proper procedure for ejections over land and sea. Consequently Jake didn't have to devote much thought to what he needed to do: the actions were almost automatic.

The wind seemed to be blowing from the west. He was unsure of directions. The way he wanted to go was toward that island – yes, that was south – and the wind was drifting him east. Somehow he also knew this without having to puzzle it out.

The raft touched the water. He felt for the Koch fittings near his collar bones that attached his parachute harness to the shroud lines and waited. Ready, here it comes, and . . . He went under. Closing his mouth and eyes automatically as the surge of cold seawater engulfed him, he toggled the fittings as he bobbed toward the surface. He broke water gasping for air.

The parachute was drifting away downwind. Now, where was that line attached to the raft?

He fumbled for it and finally realized it was wrapped around his legs or something. He began pulling toward the raft with his arms and finally grabbed the line. In seconds he had the raft in front of him.

All he had to do was get in.

The first time he slipped off the raft and went under on his back. Kicking and gasping, he managed to get upright and swing the raft so it was in front of him again.

This time he tried to force the raft under him. And almost made it before it squirted out and his head went under again.

The swells weren't helping. Just when he had the raft figured out, a swell broke over him and he swallowed saltwater.

Finally, after three or four tries, he got into the raft. He gingerly rolled so that he was on his back and lay there exhausted and gasping.

A minute or two passed before he realized he was still wearing his helmet. He removed it and looked for a lanyard to tie it to. He might need it again and everything not tied to him was going to be lost overboard sooner or later. He used a piece of parachute shroud line that he had tucked into his survival vest months ago.

Only then did he remember Flap and start sweeping the horizon for him.

The radio! He got out his survival radio, checked it, then turned it on. 'Flap, this is Jake.'

No answer.

Jake lay in his bobbing, corkscrewing raft looking at clouds and thinking about pirates and cursing himself. In a rather extraordinary display of sheer stupidity he had managed to get himself and Flap Le Beau shot out of the sky by a bunch of pirates. Yo ho ho and a bottle of rum. After the war was over! Not just any Tom, Dick or Harry can put an almost-new, squawk-free A-6E into the goddamn drink! Is that talent or what? The guys at the O Clubs were going to be shaking their heads over this one for a long long time.

Colonel Haldane was going to shit nails when he heard the happy news.

He looked at his watch. The damn thing was full of water. It had stopped. Perfect!

And his ass was six inches deep in water. Occasionally more water slopped in, but since the doughnut hole in which he sat was already full, the overflow merely drained out. Useless to try to bail it.

Luckily the water wasn't too cold. Sort of lukewarm. The tropics. And to think real people pay real money to swim in water like this.

He tried to radio again. This time he got an answer. 'Yo, Jake. You in your raft?'

'Yep. And you?'

'Nope. It's like trying to fuck a greased pig.'

'You hurt?'

'No. You?'

'No.'

'Well, nice talking to you. Now I gotta get into this sonuvabitching raft.'

'Pull the damn thing under you. Don't try to climb into it. Pull it under you.'

'Call you back after a while.'

A cigarette. He could sure use a cigarette. He made sure the radio was firmly tied to his survival vest, then laid it in his lap. The cigarettes and lighter were in his left sleeve pocket. He got them out. The cigarettes were sodden. The lighter still worked though, after he blew repeatedly on the flint wheel and dried it off somewhat. It was one of those butane jobs. He extracted a wet cigarette, put it to his lips and lit the lighter. The cigarette refused to burn.

He put the cigarette back into the pack and stowed the pack away. If he ever managed to get ashore he could dry these things out and smoke them.

Wait! He had an unopened pack in his survival vest. Still wrapped in cellophane, an unopened pack would be watertight.

He wanted a cigarette now more than anything else he could think of. He got the left chest pocket of the vest open and felt around inside, trying not to let the rest of the contents spill.

He found it. Thirty seconds later he had a cigarette lit and was exhaling smoke. Aaah!

Bobbing up and down, puffing away, he decided he was thirsty. He had two plastic baby bottles full of water in his survival vest. He got one out and opened it, intending to drink only a little. He drained it in two long gulps.

He almost tossed the empty away, but thought better of it and slipped it back into the vest pocket.

Something on top of a swell to his left caught his eye, then it was gone. He waited. Flap, sitting in his raft, visible for a second or two before the out-of-sync swells lowered Jake or Flap.

He checked the radio. He had turned it off. He turned it on again and immediately it squawked to life. 'Jake, Flap.'

'Hey, I saw you.'

'I've seen you twice. How far apart do you think we are?'

'A hundred yards?'

'At least. We've got to do some thinking, Jake. We're going to be out here all night. The ship won't be close enough to launch a chopper until dawn.'

Jake looked longingly at the island, the one he and Flap had been trying to reach when they ejected. He saw flashes of green occasionally, but it was miles away. And the wind was blowing at a ninety-degree angle to it.

'Let's try to paddle toward each other. If we could get together, tie our rafts together, we'd have a better chance.'

A better chance. The words sprang to his lips without conscious thought, and now that he had said them he considered their import. A night at sea in one of these pissy little rafts was risky at best. The sea could get a lot rougher, a raft could spring a leak, the pirates might come looking, sharks . . .

Sharks!

A wave of pure terror washed over him.

'Okay,' Flap said. 'You paddle my way and I'll paddle toward you. I don't think we can make it before dark but we can try. I'm going to turn my radio off now to save the battery.'

Jake inspected himself to see if he was injured, if he was bleeding. Adrenaline was like a local anesthetic; he had been far too pumped to feel small cuts and abrasions. If he were bleeding . . . well, sharks can smell blood in the water for miles and miles.

He felt his face and neck. Tender place on his neck. He held out his gloved right hand and stared at it: red stain. Blood!

For the love of God!

Must be a shroud burn or Plexiglas cut.

He got up on his knees in the raft. This was an inherently unstable position and he took great pains to ensure he didn't capsize. Crouching as low as he could, he began paddling with his hands, making great sweeping motions. Then he realized he didn't know where Flap was, so he forced himself to stop and look. There, just a glimpse, but enough. He turned the raft about sixty degrees and resumed paddling.

It was hard work. Every thread Jake wore was of course soaked, so even though the air was warm and humid, he stayed cool. Stroke for a while, pause to look for Flap, stroke some more, the cycle went on and on.

Finally he became aware that the sun was down and the light was fading. He got out his survival light, triggered the flash, and stuck it onto the Velcro that was glued to a spot on the right rear of his helmet. Then he put the helmet on. Three minutes later he saw that Flap had done the same thing. They were, at this point, maybe fifty yards apart.

Jake paused for a moment to rest.

What a mess! And if he had had a lick of sense, used an ounce of caution, they wouldn't be floating around out here in the middle of the ocean, at the ends of the earth.

He cussed awhile, then went back to work.

It was completely dark when they got the rafts together. Lengths of parachute shroud from their survival vests were quickly tied so the two rafts lay side by side. They arranged themselves so that Jake's feet were adjacent to Flap's head, and vice versa.

The two men lay inert in the rafts for minutes, resting. Then Flap said, 'This is a fine mess you got us into, Grafton. A very fine how-do-you-do.'

'I'm sorry.'

Flap was silent for several seconds. 'You really think this is your fault? I'm sorry I said that. It ain't. It's the fault of that asshole son of a bitch over there that smacked us with that twenty mike-mike. Talk about a cheap shot! I'd like to cut his nuts off and make him eat 'em.'

'Think Black Eagle heard any of our transmissions?'

'I don't know.'

'Boy, I hope so. I'd hate to think that that chicken-shit pirate cocksucker might get a free shot at somebody else tomorrow.'

'Turn off that flashing light on your helmet. Makes my eyes hurt.'

Jake did so. He took off the helmet. Then he got out his second baby bottle of drinking water and took a big slug. He held it out for Flap. 'Here.' Flap had to feel for it. The darkness was total. There were some stars visible, but the moon wouldn't be up for some hours yet.

'Shit. This is water.'

'What did you expect? Jack Daniel's?'

Flap drained the bottle and handed it back. Jake carefully screwed the top back on and stowed it.

'Want to try mine?'

Jake felt in the darkness. Another baby bottle. He sipped it. Brandy. The liquor burned all the way down. He passed it back. 'Thanks.'

'So what's for supper?'

'I got a candy bar in my vest someplace,' Jake told the Marine. 'Stuck it in here while we were in the Philippines, so it's only three months old.'

'I'll wait. I got one from Singapore. Maybe for breakfast, huh?'

'Yeah. You hurt any?'

'Scratched up in a couple places. Nothing bad.'

'I did a little bleeding from a cut on my neck. Maybe the sharks will come.'

Flap had nothing more to say, so Jake sat thinking about sharks. He hated the whole idea. An unseen terror that stalked and *ate* you – it was something from a horror movie, some poorly animated, low-budget monstrosity designed to make kids scream at the Saturday afternoon matinee.

But it was *real*.

Real sharks lived in these waters and they would come – of that he was absolutely certain.

Lying there in the darkness in this rubberized canvas raft with your butt in the water, shivering because the water kept wicking up your flight suit and evaporating, bobbing up and down, up and down, endlessly, up and down and up and down, your mind fixated upon sharks, on the giant predators with row upon row of huge, sharp teeth that even now were following the blood trail, coming closer, coming up from deep deep down towards this flimsy little raft that their teeth could slash through as if it were tissue paper, coming to rip and tear your flesh and *eat you!*

At some point he realized that he had his Colt automatic in his hand. He hadn't thumbed off the safety, thank God, but it was there in his hand and he couldn't remember pulling it from his shoulder holster.

He hefted it.

He had always liked the bulk of it, the thirty-nine ounces of smooth blued steel and oiled wood that promised deadly power if he ever needed it. Tiger Cole had given it to him. It held eight big .45 caliber slugs, any one of which would kill anything from a mouse to a moose. If he shot a shark with this thing, it was going to die quick.

The problem was that the sharks were under water and bullets don't go very far when fired into water. Certainly not these big slow lead slugs. It would be better if he had his .357, but life wasn't like that. If the shark would only stick his head out of the water and hold still . . .

His survival knife! It wasn't all that sharp and, to tell the truth, wasn't really much of a knife, but he could stick a shark with it. And probably get his hand ripped off.

He transferred the automatic to his left hand and got the knife from his survival vest.

The first thing the sharks would do was bump the raft. He would feel that, he hoped. They would bump it and rub it with their sandpaper hide and sniff the blood and finally use their teeth. If they punctured the raft he would go into the water. Then he was doomed. Sooner or later they would get a leg or foot and even if he killed the bastard that did it, the blood would draw more sharks that would finish the job, if he hadn't already bled to death.

He was living a nightmare. If only he could wake up.

He sat in the darkness listening to the slop of the water and waiting for the bump and shivering from the cold. Every sense was alert, straining.

How long he sat like that, half-frozen with fear, listening, he didn't know, but eventually the moon rose and a sliver of light came through a gap in the clouds. Flap saw him then.

'Hey, what's the knife and gun for?'

He was so hoarse that he had trouble with the word and had to clear his throat before he got it out. 'Sharks.'

'You stick that knife into your raft and you'll be swimming.'

Jake just sat shivering.

'Throw out some shark repellent. You got some in your vest, don't ya?'

'It don't work. Ain't worth shit.'

'Won't hurt. Throw it out.'

Now he had the problem of what to do with the gun and knife. 'Hold the gun, will ya?'

'Holster it. The knife too. Believe me, there'll be plenty of time if you need 'em.'

When he had tossed the shark repellent packets into the water, Jake felt better. It was crazy. The repellent – allegedly a mixture of noxious chemicals and ground-up shark gonads – was worthless: someone had done a study and said it had no noticeable effect on sharks and was a waste of government money to acquire. Even though Jake knew all that, throwing the repellent into the water still gave him a sense that he was doing *something*, so he felt better. Less terrorized and more able to cope.

The moonlight helped too. At least if he got a glimpse he could shoot or stab.

'Sorry I got you into this,' he told Flap.

'If this moonlight cruise causes me to miss Australia, Grafton, I'm going to kick your ass up between your shoulder blades. I've been sitting here thinking about Australia and those chocolate aborigine women who will think I'm Sidney fucking Poitier, and believe you me, this buck nigger is really really ready.'

'Those aborigine men may show you how to use a boomerang for a suppository if you mess with their women.'

Flap dismissed that possibility with an airy wave. He was shivering too, Jake noticed.

'Actually I ought to charge you a travel agent's fee,' Jake told the BN. 'You'll cadge free drinks on this tale for years. A silver moon, a tropical lagoon—'

'And you. I wouldn't pay ten cents Hong Kong money to go on a moonlight cruise with you. You got all the romance of a . . .'

They bantered back and forth for a while, then talked seriously about their situation. The US Navy would search until Jake and Flap were rescued or the heavies were convinced they were dead, no matter how long it took. Right this very moment the ships of the task group were making their best speed eastward, eating up the sea miles, their screws thrashing the black water into long foamy ribbons that stretched back under that pale slice of moon to the horizon. At dawn the carrier would pause in her eastward charge only long enough to veer into the wind and launch her planes.

Just in case someone was up there right now, Flap got out his radio and made a few calls. There was no answer, which didn't upset them.

In the morning. The carrier's planes would come in the morning. And if that pirate was anywhere around when the sun came up, he was going to Davy Jones's locker faster than the *Arizona* went to the bottom of Pearl Harbor.

Eventually the conversation petered out and exhaustion caught up with them. Both men dozed as their tiny rafts rocked in the long swells.

Jake woke up to vomit. The equilibrium of the raft was too precarious to stick his head over the side, so he heaved down his chest. He slopped some water over himself to wash the worst of it away.

Seasick. Fuck it all to hell!

He heaved until his stomach was empty, then retched helplessly as his stomach convulsed.

Flap was philosophical. He wasn't sick. 'These things happen in the best of families, even to swab jockeys. It won't kill you. You're tough.'

'Shut up.'

'Wait until I tell the guys in the ready room about this. Sailor Grafton, puking his guts like a kid on the Staten Island ferry.'

'Could you please—'

'It'll get worse. You'll see. You'll think you're gonna die. You're really in for it now.'

The convulsions had subsided somewhat when Jake felt the first nudge, just an irregularity in the motion of the raft. He almost missed it.

His seasickness was forgotten. He was reaching for the automatic when Flap said, 'Uh-oh. I think a shark bumped me.'

Now he scanned the water. His eyes were well adjusted to the moonlight. He glimpsed a fin break water, for maybe two seconds. Then it was gone.

'Shark,' he told Flap. 'I saw one!'

'See what you caused! All that moaning about sharks and you attracted the sons of bitches.'

Another bump, more aggressive this time. Jake thought he could feel the grinding from the rough hide rubbing against the fabric of the raft. They didn't have to bite it – if they rubbed it enough they would rub a hole through it.

Fear coursed through him, fear as cold as ice water in his veins. Automatically he had drawn his feet into the raft and tucked his elbows in, which drove his butt deeper into the water. And there was nothing between his butt and those teeth but a very thin layer of rubberized canvas.

He tried to see downward, into the depths where the predators were. Not enough light. It was like looking into a pot of ink.

'See anything?'

'If I scream,' Flap said, 'you'll know they got me.'

'You asshole! You stupid perverted Marine asshole!'

'They're just curious.'

Another nudge. Jake thought he saw something pass out to his right that was darker than the surrounding blackness, but he wasn't sure.

'You hope,' Jake muttered. 'Maybe they're hungry too.'

A fin broke water fifty feet or so away, slightly to the right of the way Jake was facing. He thumbed off the pistol's safety, leveled it and couldn't see the sights clearly! He squeezed off the shot anyway. The muzzle flash temporarily blinded him.

The report was strangely flat. There was nothing to echo or concentrate the noise. The recoil of the weapon in his hand felt reassuring though.

He blinked his eyes clear and looked at Flap. He had some kind of knife in his right hand and was watching the water intently. It wasn't a government-issue survival knife.

'What kind of knife is that?'

'Throwing knife. For stabbing.'

'What if you want to cut something?'

'Got another knife for that.'

'What are you, a walking cutlery shop?'

'Just look for sharks, will ya? Try not to shoot me or either of the rafts. If they get you I may need your boat.'

'Maybe they like dark meat. Can I have your stereo?'

'My roommate has first dibs.'

They sat staring intently at the water near them. Occasionally a shark nudged them, but the level of aggression didn't seem to increase.

Maybe they would get out of this with whole hides. Then again . . .

A fin broke water just ten feet to Jake's immediate right. He swung the pistol and squeezed the trigger in almost the same motion. The water seemed to explode.

Dimly he saw a tail slashing furiously and spray cascaded over them. The rafts rocked dangerously.

In seconds it was over. The shark sounded.

'Think that was the only one?' Flap asked, his voice betraying his tension for the first time.

'We'll see.'

For some reason the terror that had gripped Jake earlier was gone. He still had enough adrenaline coursing through his veins to fuel a marathon and his heart was thudding like a drum, but for the first time he felt ready to face whatever came.

Nothing came.

If there were any more sharks out there, they stayed away from the raft. After a while Flap tried his radio again. This time he got an answer. One of the E-2 Hawkeyes from *Columbia* was up there somewhere far above, the crew warm, dry and comfortable.

Flap told them of the pirates, of being shot down, of flying south trying to keep the A-6 airborne on the backup hydraulic system and finally ejecting into the sea.

'We're all right. Both of us are in our rafts, uninjured, and the rafts are lashed together.'

Jake had his radio out by this time and heard a calm voice say, 'We'll get planes off at dawn to look for you. You guys check in after sunrise about every fifteen minutes, okay?'

'Roger that. Keep the coffee hot.'

Jake Grafton spoke up. 'Black Eagle, tell the Ops guys that they need to arm the planes. If anybody shoots at them, they need to defend themselves vigorously.'

'I'll pass that along. Wait one while I talk to the ship on the other radio.'

They sat in the darkness with their radios in their hands. Finally the radio came back to life. 'Five Zero Eight Alpha, just how sure are you that you were actually shot at? Is there any way the hydraulic failure could have been a coincidence?'

The question infuriated Grafton. 'I've been shot at before,' he roared into the radio. 'I've been shot at and missed and shot at and hit. You tell those stupid bastards on the ship that we were *shot down*.'

'Roger. You guys hang tough. Talk to you again fifteen minutes after sunrise.'

His anger kept Jake warm for about five minutes. Then he was just cold and tired. With every stitch they wore sopping wet, Jake and Flap huddled in their rafts and shivered. After a time their thirst got the better of them and Flap broke out his two baby bottles full of water. He passed one to Jake, who drank it quickly, afraid he might spill it.

The moon rose higher and gave more light, when it wasn't obscured by clouds.

Eventually, despite the conditions, exhaustion claimed them and they dozed. Jake's mind wandered feverishly. Faces from the past talked to him – Callie, his parents, Tiger Cole, Morgan McPherson – yet he couldn't understand what they were saying. Just when he thought he was getting the message, the faces faded and he was half-asleep in a bobbing raft, wet and cold and very miserable.

Occasionally they talked. Once Jake asked Flap, 'If that attack last month against the Russians had been real, do you think we would have made it?'

'I dunno.'

'Think we would have hit the cruiser?'

'Maybe.'

'They said it was eighty percent probable.'

'I say maybe. I don't do numbers.'

'I think we would be dead.'

'Maybe,' Flap said.

Time passed too slowly, every minute seemed like an hour. The temptation to call Black Eagle to see if he was still up there was very strong and hard to resist. Jake got his radio out twice. Each time he stowed it without turning it on. He might need all the juice in those batteries tomorrow. Wasting battery power now would be stupid.

The worsening sea state brought them fully and completely awake. The swells were bigger and the wind was stronger.

At the top of each swell the rafts pitched dangerously, forcing each man to hang on tightly to keep from being thrown out. They made sure they still had a lanyard attached to each raft.

They had been hanging on to their seats in their frail craft for an eternity when Flap said, 'You shouldn't have called the heavies stupid bastards.'

'I know.'

'Someone will ream you out when we get back.'

'Give me something to look forward to.'

Gradually they became aware that the sky was lightening up. Dawn. It was coming.

Incredibly, the wind strengthened and began to rip spin-drift from the swells. Jake reeled in his helmet – it had fallen overboard at some point during the night – dumped out the water and put it on. He ran the clear visor down to keep the salt spray out of his eyes.

It worked. Incredibly, his head was also warmer. He should have been wearing this thing all night!

'Put on your helmet,' he shouted at Flap, who had his tucked under his thighs.

The clouds were just beginning to show pink when they saw the ship. It was almost bows on and coming this way. A little ship, one stack, coming with a bone in its teeth.

Jake pointed.

'Of all the fucking luck!' Flap Le Beau swore.

It was the pirate ship.

21

'They've seen us,' Flap shouted over the wind. 'They're coming this way.'

'Better ditch the guns and radios,' Jake told him. He drew the Colt .45 from its holster under his life jacket and survival vest and slipped it over the side. In a holster sewn inside a pocket of his survival vest he had a five-shot Smith & Wesson .38 with a two-inch barrel that he kept loaded with flares. He ditched that too.

The radio – he held on to the radio for a moment as he watched the bow wave of the oncoming small ship subside. They were stopping.

Son of a . . .

He used his survival knife to cut the parachute shroud line that tied him to the radio and lowered it to the water, then released it. Out of the corner of his eye he saw Flap slip his .45 over the side.

'The knife,' Flap told him. 'Dump it too. They'll just take them away from us.' Jake opened his hand and the knife made a tiny splash.

The small ship drifted to a stop on the windward side of the two rafts, about fifteen feet away. Her bulk created a sheltered lee. It was a nice display of seamanship, but Jake and Flap were in no mood to appreciate it.

Staring down from the rail were eight brown faces. Malays, from the look of them. They held assault rifles in their hands.

The sides of this little ship had once been blue, but now the blue was heavily spotted with rust. Where some of the paint had peeled glimpses of gray were visible. Apparently she had once been a patrol boat. Forward of the bow was a gun mount, now empty. That was where they had had the twenty millimeter. It must be stowed below.

The men on deck lowered a net and made gestures with their rifles. Jake and Flap slowly paddled over. Flap went up the net first. Jake followed him. The ship was rocking heavily in the swells. The net was wet, hard to grasp firmly. His foot slipped on the wet cordage and he almost went into the sea. When he was clear of the raft the people on deck began shooting bursts of fully automatic fire. He looked down. Holes popped everywhere on the inflated portions of the rafts and spray flew.

By the time he pulled himself up enough to grasp the rail, the rafts were completely deflated and sinking.

Hands grabbed him and pulled. He scrambled on up the net. As he was coming over the rail, someone hit him in the helmet with a rifle butt and he sprawled onto the deck. Flap was already lying there on his back looking upward.

Most of the crew were barefoot. A couple of them looked like teenagers. Their clothes were ragged and dirty. There was nothing half-assed about their weapons however, worn AK-47s without a fleck of rust. Several of them had pistols stuck into their belts or the tops of their pants.

One of them gestured toward a ladder with the barrel of his weapon. Up. Jake glanced at Flap. His face was expressionless. Grafton prayed that he looked at least half that calm.

At the top of the ladder was the bridge.

The man working the helm and engine was a bit larger than medium height, apparently fit, and had a wicked scar on his chin. The ship was already gathering speed and heeling in a turn. The captain, if captain he was, glanced at them, then concentrated on putting the ship on the course he wanted. When he had the helm amidships and had checked the compass, he said, 'Gentlemen, welcome aboard.'

Jake looked around. Two of the crew were behind them and the rifles were leveled at his and Flap's backs. He turned back to the captain.

'Take off all that . . .' He gestured toward their life jackets and survival vests. 'And the helmets. You look very silly in those helmets.'

Jake and Flap unsnapped their torso harnesses and let them fall into the puddle that was spreading away from each man. They got rid of the G-suits and helmets. Jake took off his empty shoulder holster and dropped it into the pile.

'Where's the pistol?'

Jake shrugged.

The captain took one step and slapped him, quickly and lightly. He stood with his hands on his hips in front of Jake, looking up at him. 'I think you will answer my questions. Where is the pistol?'

'In the ocean.'

The captain went back to the wheel and checked the compass. 'And your survival radios? Where are they?'

'Same place.'

'Where did you fly from?'

'USS *Columbia*.'

'Where is she?'

'West of here.' He toyed with the idea of lying for less than a heartbeat. 'Maybe two or three hundred miles now.'

'When will the planes come looking for you?'

'Shortly.'

'When?'

'I don't know. Sometime soon. After the sun comes up.'

'My men must learn to shoot better. Now we have this complication.'

'Must be a tough way to make a living.'

The captain continued as if he hadn't heard. 'The question is, do we need you alive? You disposed of your radios so you cannot talk to the airplanes on UHF. You could have warned them that you would die if they attacked us. Alas, we have only a marine band radio. It's a pity.'

'You speak English pretty well.'

The captain was scanning the ocean and glancing occasionally at the sky. He didn't bother looking at the two Americans. 'But I do not think they will attack. They will look us over and take many pictures. That is all.' His eyes flicked to their faces. 'What do you think?'

Unfortunately Jake thought he was right. He tried to keep his face deadpan but his turmoil probably showed. The captain apparently thought so. He said something to the guards and waved his hands. They prodded the aviators in the back and turned them around. As they left the bridge, Jake saw one of the crewmen opening the pockets of the survival vest and dumping the contents on the deck.

They were shoved into a tiny compartment below the main deck. There was a large hasp on the door.

'Can we have some water?' Jake asked the three men who pushed him inside right behind Flap. They ignored him.

The door swung shut and they heard the padlock snapping closed. The compartment was only slightly larger than a bedroom closet and had apparently been used for storage. There was no light and no electrical sockets, although there was one small, filthy porthole that admitted subdued light.

Flap leaned against the door and listened. After a bit he shrugged. 'They've gone, I think.'

'Maybe there's a bug.'

'Go ahead and look for it, James Bond.'

Jake sat against a wall and began taking off his boots. He took off his socks and wrung the water out, then put them back on. 'They'll probably shoot us after a while,' he said.

'Probably,' Flap agreed. He also sat. 'The captain ain't sure if he'll need us or not. The bastard has it figured pretty good. I'll bet he can get this thing to port before the US Navy can get a surface ship here to board him. He thinks so too. But he's saving us just in case.'

'What do you think they did with the freighter?'

'Sank her would be my bet. They were probably off-loading high-value items when we showed up.'

'And the crew?'

Flap shrugged.

'Then why in hell did these guys shoot at us?'

'Perhaps someone panicked. Or they didn't want their picture taken. The airplane overhead was a problem they hadn't figured on.'

'So you think this is some kind of local industry?'

'Don't you?'

'I don't know.'

'Well, look at it. Here we are on the southern coast of Sumatra, about the most out-of-the-way corner of the earth it's possible to imagine. In among these islands we're well off the shipping lanes, which go through the Sunda Strait or the Strait of Malacca. So these dudes from a local village sail out into the shipping lanes, board a ship – probably at night when only one or two people are on watch on the bridge – then bring it here and loot it. They probably kill everyone aboard and scuttle the ship. The high-value items from the cargo that can't be traced eventually end up in the bazaars in Singapore or Rangoon or even Mombassa. The ship never shows up at its destination and no one knows what happened to it. Say they knock off one ship a year, or one every two years. Be a nice little racket if they don't pull it too often and get the insurance companies in a tizzy.'

'But someone got off fifteen seconds of an SOS and we came to look.'

'To look and take pictures. They probably thought they had killed everyone on that ship, then the SOS burned their eardrums. They should have disabled the radio but they didn't. One mistake led to another. So instead of waiting to loot the ship after dark, they decided to try it in daylight. Then we showed up. You know as well as I do that a good photo interpreter could identify this ship sooner or later. The captain knows that too. So he fired when we gave him a golden opportunity. I'll bet he was the bastard at the trigger.'

'He's going to get photographed again today.'

'But the victim isn't tied up alongside. Now this is just a little ship going about its business in a great big ocean.'

Jake merely grunted. After a bit he said, 'It doesn't figure.'

'What doesn't?'

'That ship they stopped is an old freighter. Looked to me like a Liberty ship. Eight to ten thousand tons, no more than that. Why didn't these guys stop a big container ship? All the valuable electronic stuff gets shipped in sealed containers these days.'

'Beats me.' Flap sat and removed his boots and socks. After a while he said, 'The bastards could at least have given us water. I'm really thirsty.'

He had his boots back on when he said, 'Did you notice the captain's hands? The calluses on the edges of his palms? He's a karate expert. If you had even flinched when he slapped you he might have broken your neck.'

'Now you tell me.'

'You did fine. Handled it well. Be submissive and don't give them the slightest reason to think you might fight back.'

'I'm certainly not going to strap on a karate expert.'

Flap snorted. 'They're the easiest to beat. They're too self-confident.'

Jake didn't think that comment worth a reply. He retrieved his cigarettes from his flight suit shoulder pocket and carefully removed each one from the pack, trying not to tear the wet paper. He laid them out to dry. Then he rolled onto his side and tried to stretch out. The compartment was too small. At least his ass wasn't submerged.

A bullet in the head or chest wasn't a cheery prospect. All these months of planning for the future and now it looked as if there would be no future. Strange how life works, how precarious it is. Right now he wanted water, food and a cigarette. If he got those, then he would want a hot bath and dry clothes. Then a bunk. The wants would keep multiplying, and sooner or later he would be staring at a bulkhead and fretting about insubstantial things, like what the next ready room movie was going to be, his brush with death shoved back into some dark corner in the attic of his mind.

He had faced death before in the air and on the ground, so he knew how it worked. If you survived you had to keep on living – that was a law, like gravity. If you died – well, that was that. Those left behind had to keep on living.

Maybe in the great scheme of things it really didn't matter very much whether these two blobs of living tissue called Jake Grafton and Flap Le Beau died here or someplace else, died today or next week or in thirty or fifty years. The world would keep on turning, life for everyone else would go on, human history would run exactly the same course either way.

It mattered to Jake, of course. He didn't want to die. Now or any other time. Presumably Flap felt the same way.

Fuck these pirates! Fuck these assholes! Murdering and stealing without a thought or care for anyone else. If they get theirs, life is good.

As he thought about the pirates Jake Grafton was swept by a cold fury that drove the lethargy from him.

He sat up and looked at Flap, who had also curled up on the deck. He wasn't asleep either. 'We gotta figure out a way to screw these guys good.'

Flap didn't smile. 'Any suggestions?'

'Well, if they shoot us, we sure as hell ought to take a couple of them with us. I don't think they'll shoot us in here. Blood and bullet holes would be hard to explain if this ship were ever searched. I figure they'll take us topside, tie a chain around us and put us over the side. Maybe shoot us first.'

'And . . . ?'

'If we could kill a couple of the bastards we ought to give it a try.'

'Why?'

'Don't give me that shit!'

'What's a couple more or less?'

'You'd let them shoot you without a struggle?'

'Not if I have a choice. I'm going to take a lot of killing. But if they want us dead we're going to end up dead, sooner or later.

'That's my point. When I go to meet the devil I want to go in a crowd.'

Flap chuckled. It was a chuckle without mirth. 'What I can't figure out, Grafton, is why the hell you joined the Navy instead of the Marines.'

'The Navy is more high-toned.'

They sat talking for most of an hour, trying to plan a course of action that would kill at least one and hopefully two pirates.

Flap could kill two men in two seconds with his bare hands, Jake assumed, so it seemed that the only real chance they had was for him to cause enough commotion to give Flap those two seconds. He didn't state this premise, however Flap let it go unchallenged. They hadn't a chance of surviving, not against assault weapons. But if their captors relaxed, if only for an instant . . .

When they finally ceased talking, both men were so tired they were almost instantly asleep, curled around each other on the deck because there was no room to stretch out and rocked by the motion of the ship.

About an hour later a jet going over woke them. The thunder of the engines faded, then increased in volume. Then it faded completely and they were left with just the sounds of the ship. The plane did not come back.

The pirates came for Flap and Jake after the sun set. Both men stood when they heard the padlock rattle and assumed positions on opposite sides of the door. When the door opened two men were there with their weapons leveled, ready to fire.

One man motioned with the barrel of his rifle.

Jake went first, with Flap behind. They had discussed it and concluded a fight in the confined interior passageways was too risky. They shuffled along with their heads down, going willingly in the direction indicated.

When they came out on deck they saw land close aboard, just visible in the twilight. The shore was rocky, but the dark jungle began just inland from the rocks. Maybe three hundred yards. The water was flat, without swells. The ship was inside the mouth of a river headed upstream.

The two pirates wanted them to go aft. The deck here was probably only six feet wide. Flap was looking scared and had his hands up about head high. Two men stood on the dark fantail watching them come, their rifles cradled in their arms.

'Four,' Jake muttered. 'Jesus . . .'

They had just reached the fantail when they heard a jet running high. They looked up.

'Point,' Flap said, and Jake did, enthusiastically, as Flap shot a quick glance back over his shoulder.

What happened next happened so quickly Jake almost didn't react. Flap half-turned and his right arm swept down. The blade of a knife buried itself in the solar plexus of the gunman just behind him. This man staggered and looked down in stupefied amazement at the knife handle sticking out of his chest.

The man behind him had been looking up, trying to see the jet. He dropped his gaze in time to see Flap Le Beau hurtling across the ten feet of space that separated them. He swung the rifle, but too late.

With one vicious, backhand swipe, Flap cut his throat from ear to ear. Blood spouted from severed arteries as the man collapsed. In a continuation of his motion, Flap spun and rammed the knife into the left kidney of the first man, who was somehow still on his feet and trying to turn to bring his rifle to bear.

Meanwhile Jake Grafton had launched himself at the two spectators standing with their rifles cradled in their arms. They too had been looking up, which gave him just the break he needed. He took them both down in a flying tackle.

He got his hands on one of the rifles and used it as a club. He smashed the butt into one man's Adam's apple.

The other man had retained his rifle and now it fired, the muzzle just inches from Jake's ear. Deafened, with the strength born of terror, Jake dropped the weapon in his hands and seized the barrel of the other man's AK-47 as he drove a punch at his face. The blow glanced off his forehead, but the man struggled to hold on to the rifle, so Jake let fly again. This time his fist connected solidly and the man went to the deck, still holding on to the rifle. Jake ripped it from his hands and slammed the butt down on his throat with all his strength.

With the rifle coming up, he turned in time to see Flap inserting his throwing knife back into the sheath that hung down his back, inside his flight suit. The fighting knife had a triangular blade about four inches long – it went into the sheath worn on his left forearm, under the sleeve of his flight suit.

Le Beau picked up an AK-47, glanced at the action, then fired one round into each of the four men lying on the deck. Then he flashed a grin at Jake. 'Still alive, by God!'

Jake grabbed the rifle on the deck at his feet and removed the magazine. He stuck it into a chest pocket of his flight suit. 'I thought you ditched your knives.'

'I haven't been without a knife since I was thirteen.'

'Let's see if we can get to the bridge.'

'If it gets too hot we'll go over the side and swim for shore.'

'Okay.'

With his rifle at the ready, Flap went forward on the starboard side. Jake took the port.

The bridge stuck out over the deck. Someone appeared in the window and Jake snapped off a shot. The window shattered and the head disappeared. A miss.

An open hatch revealed a ladder that probably gave access to the engine room. Jake pulled the hatch shut and rotated the lever that dogged it shut. He looked around for something to block the lever so it couldn't be opened. Nothing.

He came to another open hatchway, a short passageway across the superstructure to the starboard side of the ship.

He paused, trying to decide what to do. Sweat was running into his eyes. And he was thirsty as holy hell. What he wouldn't give for one drink of water!

Flap's head popped around the corner on the starboard side. He saw Jake and came his way. 'What did ya shoot at?'

'Someone on the bridge.'

'There's at least five more guys on this tub, probably more.'

'How come they aren't coming after us?'

'We're probably pretty near their base. When they pull in, someone on the pier will take care of us.'

'We gotta get off this bucket.'

'They'll gun us in the water.'

Jake wiped the sweat from his eyes and tried to think. 'Somebody is probably in the engine room,' he said. 'The ladder down is here on the port side. What say you go up to the bridge and keep them occupied. I'll go to the engine room and try to disable this tub. Then we go over the side.'

'Which way?'

'Port side. In five minutes.'

'My watch isn't working.'

'*About* five minutes. Or if the engines stop.'

'Okay.'

Jake checked to make sure no one was in sight, then he moved back to the engine room hatch, opened it and latched it open. The ladder down was actually a steep stair.

Uh-oh. He wished he hadn't volunteered to do this.

What the hell! They were dead this morning when this pirate ship came over the horizon.

With the rifle at the ready and the safety off, he eased down the ladder, waiting for the inevitable bullet.

This is like committing suicide slowly.

The area at the bottom of the ladder was shielded by a large condenser. Jake paused behind it, wiped the sweat from his hands and gripped the rifle carefully. He eased his head out, so that he could look with one eye. He was looking aft along a narrow passageway between the ship's two diesel engines. He saw a leg, the back of a leg. He pulled his head back and turned so he could see forward. Ease the head out and peek. No one.

Okay. Someone aft, no one visible forward. He would step out, shoot the guy aft, then swing so he could shoot forward.

That was a good plan.

He was going to get shot. Sure as shit.

He took a deep breath, and exhaled slowly. His heart was pounding a mile a minute.

Now!

He leaped out and squeezed the trigger.

The man was using a pipe wrench on a valve. The bullets slammed him down. Jake spun. A man coming through the door shooting as Jake's bullets caught him, hammered him.

Something slammed into Jake's side, turning him half around.

He staggered, leaned back against the starboard engine and looked aft.

The man there wasn't moving. The man forward had taken at least three in the chest.

Jake dug the extra magazine out of his chest pocket and substituted it for the magazine in his weapon. His left side was numb. Shock. He staggered aft. The magazine of the AK-47 on the floor looked like it still held ten shells or so. He pocketed it.

Now he heard a racket from topside that he knew were shots. Flap. He peered through the open hatch that led forward.

Fuel valves. This guy had been opening or closing these valves. The main tank must be on the other side of this bulkhead.

Which ones were the feed lines? He picked two that looked like they went up over the engines to the fuel injectors. Holding the rifle in his left hand, he began screwing the starboard engine valve shut. Then he closed the one to the port engine.

The engines would take a minute or so to die. If he had picked the right valves.

Unwilling to wait, he spied a large red valve at the bottom of the bulkhead with a pipe that wasn't connected to anything. The valve had a rusty padlock on it. Must be the tank drain valve. He put one bullet into the lock. The lock broke, and diesel fuel began running out of the bullet hole.

Jake twisted the valve. It was rusty.

Desperate to be out of here, he laid down the rifle and used both hands. It opened. Fuel began running out, at first a trickle, then a steady stream. He kept twisting.

The steady throb of the diesels took on a new note. Several cylinders missed. The starboard engine died. By the time the port engine stopped he had the drain valve full open. He was getting splashed with diesel fuel.

The lights died to a dim glow when the port engine quit. With the generators off, the lights were using battery juice.

He grabbed the rifle and started aft through the engine room for the ladder. He heard more shots, quite clearly now that the engines were silent.

His left side was pretty bloody and the pain was fierce.

Well, if he was going to fuck these guys, he should do the job right. He went back to the second man he shot and ripped his shirt off. It was cotton. He went back to the drain valve and let some diesel fuel run onto the shirt. He squeezed the shirt to get rid of the excess and dug his lighter out of his pocket.

The plastic butane piece of shit refused to light. He blew several times on the flint wheel. Come on, goddamnit!

There. He held the flame under a corner of the shirt. It took. He waited until the shirt was going pretty well, then dropped it into the gap between the catwalk and one engine. The diesel fuel was running into the bilges there.

The fire lit with a whoof.

Jake eased his head around the corner of the ladder, and jerked it back just in time. Bullets spanged into the condenser.

The fire was spreading in the bilges. Already the smoke was dense, the lights barely visible.

This couldn't be the only ladder topside. The other ladder must be on the starboard side. Trying not to breathe the smoke, he hurried that way.

Coughing and gagging, he found the ladder.

Was there someone up here waiting for him?

'Come on, Jake.' Flap's voice.

He was having trouble breathing and his feet were getting damned hot. Somehow he lost the rifle. He scrambled up the ladder on all fours, slipped and slammed his head against a step and slid a couple steps before he caught himself.

Hands grabbed him and pulled. He kept scrambling and somehow they made the deck.

'I've been shot.'

'Let's get over the side or you'll get shot again. There's at least four of them forward.'

'Where?'

'We go off the fantail. Ship's sideways in the river.'

They went that way, Jake barely able to walk. He took deep breaths, trying to get enough oxygen. Spots swam before his eyes. 'They'll shoot us in the water.'

'It's our only chance. Come on.'

Flap tossed his AK-47 into the water, then jumped after it. Jake followed.

The darkness was almost total now. Jake was only able to swim with his right arm. His left side felt like it was on fire. Several times he got mouthfuls of water, so he swallowed them. It tasted good.

He was struggling. More water in his mouth and nose. He gagged.

'Just float. I've got you.' And Flap did have him, by the collar of his flight suit.

Jake concentrated on staying afloat and breathing against the pain in his side.

Flap was pulling him backward, so he could see the foreshortened outline of the ship, and smoke black as coal oozing out amidships. He could also see the glow of fire coming from a ladder well, apparently the one on the port side, since he could now see the top of the bow. All this registered without his thinking about it, which was good, since he needed desperately to concentrate on breathing and keeping his head above water.

They were maybe fifty yards from the ship when he saw muzzle flashes from the bow.

'They're shooting,' he tried to say, but he swallowed more water.

'Relax,' Flap whispered. 'Quit trying to help. Let me do this.'

Somehow they must have swum out of the main channel, Jake realized, because the ship was pulling away from them. The current must be taking her downstream.

The current and the darkness saved them. When the twenty-millimeter cannon on the bow opened up, the bullets hit downstream, abeam the ship. Bursts split the night for almost a minute, but none of the shells even came close.

22

'I never saw a knife like that before.'

'Designed it myself,' Flap said. 'Call it a slasher.'

Of course Jake couldn't see the knife now, since they were sitting in absolute total darkness under a tree in the jungle, but Flap had borrowed his lighter and gone looking for tree moss. Now he was back and was cutting up his and Jake's T-shirts to use as a bandage. He had inspected the wound in the glow of the lighter when they first got ashore. 'It's nasty but not deep. You are one lucky white boy. I think maybe one rib broke, and it ain't too bad.'

'Feels like one of your knives is stuck in there.'

Jake sat now holding the moss in place while Flap cut up the shirts. The moss was slowing the bleeding, apparently. He heard a motorboat coming down the river. They sat silently while it passed. When the sound had faded, Jake asked, 'So what are we going to do?'

'Not much we can do tonight. There's an overcast so there wouldn't be much light when the moon comes up. The jungle canopy will keep it dark down here. We're going to have to just sit tight until morning.'

'Think they'll come looking for us tonight?'

'In the morning maybe. Maybe not. I hope they come. We need some weapons. All we have are my knives. Be easier to ambush them here than around their village, wherever that is.'

'The stabber and the slasher.'

'Yep.'

'Where did you learn to throw a knife like that?'

'Taught myself,' Flap told him. 'It's a skill that comes in handy occasionally.'

Jake moved experimentally. He tried to stretch out and relax to ease the pain. After a bit he said, 'I don't think their village is far upriver. It was narrowing when we left that ship.'

'We'll work our way upriver in the morning. We need a boat to get out to sea.'

'Tell you what, Tarzan, is there any way you could rustle us up some grub? My stomach thinks my throat is cut.'

'Tomorrow. You like snake?'

'No.'

'Tastes like—'

'Chicken. I've heard that crap before. I ate my share at survival school.'

'Naw. Tastes like lizard.'

'I don't like them either.'

'Sit up and hold up your arms and let me wrap this thing around you.'

Jake obeyed. When Flap finished he eased his arms back into his flight suit and zipped it up. 'What about bugs?'

'They're okay as an appetizer, but you expend about as many calories gathering them as—'

'How are we gonna keep 'em from bleeding us dry tonight?'

'Smear your skin with mud.'

Jake was already encased in mud almost to his waist from wading through the goo to get ashore. He scraped some from his legs and ankles and applied it to his face and neck.

After a bit, Flap asked, 'How many guys were in the engine room?'

'Two. What happened topside?'

'They pinned me down. I needed a couple grenades and didn't have them. Got one of them, though.'

'We're lucky to be alive.'

'Grafton, you are the luckiest SOB I know. If that bullet had been an inch farther right you'd be lying dead in that engine room. It's scary – we're using up oodles of luck and we're still young men. We're gonna be high and dry and clean out of the good stuff before we're very much older.'

They lay down on the jungle floor and tried to relax. Lying in the darkness in the muck, swatting at mosquitoes as the creepy-crawlies examined them – Kee-rist! Well, at least they weren't sitting in seawater to their waist or huddled in a steel compartment waiting for an executioner to come for them.

After a while Jake said, 'Are you ever going to get married?'

'You read my mind. I was lying here hungry and thirsty and miserable as hell contemplating that very subject. And you?'

'Smart ass!'

'No, seriously – why don't you tell the Great Le Beau all about it. After all, before a man commits holy matrimony he should have the benefit of unbiased, expert counsel. Even if he plans on ignoring the pithy wisdom he will undoubtedly receive, as you most certainly will.'

'I *might* get married. If she'll say yes.'

'Ahh – you haven't queried your intended victim. Or you have and she refused in a rare fit of eminent good sense. Which is it?'

'Haven't asked.'

'Uh-huh.'

'Met her last year in Hong Kong.'

'I met a girl in Hong Kong once upon a time,' Flap replied. 'Her name was . . . damn! It was right on the tip of my tongue. Anyway, she worked at the Susy Wong whorehouse, a couple of blocks from the China Fleet Club. You know it? She was maybe sixteen and had long black hair that hung almost to her waist and exquisite little breasts that—'

'I met an American girl.'

'Umph.'

'I knew you'd be interested, seeing how we fly together and all, so I'll tell you. Since you aren't sleepy and we got nothing else to do.' And he did. He told about meeting Callie, what she looked like, sounded like, how he felt when he was with her. He told Flap about her parents and about Chicago, about getting out of the Navy and what she said. He had been talking for at least half an hour when he finally realized that Le Beau was asleep.

His side throbbed badly. He changed positions in the detritus of the jungle floor, trying to find one that would cause the least stress on his wound. The sharpness of the pain drove his mind back to the pirate ship, to the prospect of death in a few moments by execution.

Flap threw that knife into that one guy and sliced the other's throat in what – three seconds? Jake had never seen a man move so fast, nor had he ever seen a man butchered with a knife. Shot, yes. But not slashed to death with one swipe of the arm, his throat ripped from ear to ear, blood spurting as horror seared the victim's face.

Life is so fragile, so tenuous.

Luckily he had gotten into motion before the surprise wore off the other two.

And the engine room, the horror as that man came around the engine shooting and the bullet struck him. Now the scene ran through his mind over and over, every emotion pungent and powerful, again and again and again.

Finally he let it go.

He felt like he had that sticker of Flap's stuck in his side right now.

So those other guys died and he and Flap lived. For a few more hours.

It was crazy. Those men, he and Flap – they were like fish in the sea, eating other fish to sustain life before they too were eaten in their turn. Kill, kill, kill.

Man's plight is a terribly bad joke.

He was dozing when the sound of a motorboat going upriver brought him fully awake. Flap woke up too. They lay listening until the noise dissipated completely.

'Wonder what happened to the pirate ship?'
'Maybe it sank.'
'Maybe.'

After the sun came up the foliage was so thick that Jake had to keep his hand on Flap's shoulder so that he wouldn't lose him. Flap moved slowly, confidently and almost without noise. Without him Jake would have been hopelessly lost in five minutes.

Flap caught a snake an hour or so after dawn and they skinned it and ate it raw. They drank water trapped in fallen leaves if there weren't too many insects in it. Once they came to a tiny stream and both men lay on their stomachs and drank their fill.

Other than the noises they made, the jungle was silent. If anyone was looking for them, they were being remarkably quiet.

Jake and Flap heard the noises of small engines and voices for a half hour before they reached the village, which as luck would have it, turned out to be on their side of the river. It was about noon as near as they could tell when they hit the village about a hundred yards inland. Thatched huts and kids, a few rusty jeep-type vehicles. They could smell food cooking. The aroma made Jake's stomach growl. A dog barked somewhere.

They stayed well back and worked their way slowly down to the riverbank to see what boats there might be.

There were several. Two or three boats with outboard engines and one elderly cabin cruiser lay moored to a short pier just a couple of dozen yards from where Jake and Flap crouched in the jungle. Beyond the boats was a much larger pier that jutted almost to midstream. Resting against the T-shaped end of it was the hijacked ship. Above the ship numerous ropes made a latticework from bank to bank. Leafy branches of trees dangled from the ropes – camouflage. The freighter seemed to be held in place against the current mainly by taut hawsers from the bow and stern that stretched across the dark water to the river's edge, where they were wrapped numerous times around large trees.

From where they lay they could just see the ship's name and home port: *Che Guevara, Habana*.

Flap began to laugh.

'What's so funny?' Jake whispered.

'A Cuban freighter. We got shot down and almost killed over a Commie freighter. If that doesn't take the cake!'

'My heart bleeds for Fidel.'

'Ain't it a shame.'

The ship's cranes were in motion and at least a dozen men were visible. A large crate was lowered to the pier and six or eight men with axes began chopping it open. Apparently they didn't have a forklift.

Inside the box were other, smaller boxes. Pairs of men hoisted these and carried them off the pier toward the village.

'Weapons,' Flap said. 'They hijacked a ship full of weapons.'

'What do you think was in those little boxes just now?'

'Machine guns, I think. Look, aren't those ammo boxes?'

'Could be.'

'They are. I've seen boxes like that before. One time up on the Cambodian border.'

'Maybe this ship wasn't hijacked. Maybe those guys met it in midocean to put aboard a pilot.'

'Then why the SOS?'

Jake shrugged, or tried to. The pain in his side was down to a dull throb, as long as he held his shoulder still and didn't take any deep breaths.

'These dudes are ripping off a Commie weapons shipment,' Flap said slowly. 'Maybe one bound for Haiphong. Guns and ammo are worth their weight in gold.'

'That little cabin cruiser is our ticket out of here, if it isn't a trap.'

'Maybe,' Flap said shortly. 'We can't do anything until tonight anyhow, so let's make ourselves comfortable and see what we can see. I don't see any floodlights anywhere; these people won't be working at night. But that little boat is just too good to be true. The captain we met yesterday didn't impress me as the type of careless soul who would leave a boat where we could swipe it at our convenience.'

After a few minutes Jake muttered, 'I haven't seen the captain yet on the dock.'

'He's around someplace. You can bet your ass on that.'

'That ship we set fire to isn't here either.'

'Maybe they abandoned it. But remember that boat that went down the river last night, then came back hours later? It was probably that cruiser there, and it probably rescued everyone left alive. The captain is here. I can feel him.'

'Okay.'

'See that shack just up there on the left? From there a fellow would have a good view of the boat and the dock. Keep your eyes on that. I'm going to slip around and see what they're doing with all these weapons they're taking off that ship.'

'Leave me one of your knives.'

'Which one?'

'The sticker.'

Flap drew it from the sheath hanging down his back and handed it to Jake butt-first. Then he took two steps and disappeared into the jungle.

A throwing knife with a needle-sharp point and a slick handle, the weapon was perhaps ten inches long. Jake slipped it into his boot top, leaving just enough of the hilt exposed so that he could get it out quickly. He hadn't the foggiest idea how to throw it, but he had no qualms about jabbing it into somebody to defend himself. His throbbing side was a constant reminder that these people wanted him dead.

Lying under a tangle of vegetation, he rolled on his good side and gingerly unzipped his flight suit. The bandage was encrusted with old blood. Nothing fresh. He zipped the flight suit back up and rolled on his belly. He wormed his way forward until he could just see the shack and the pier beyond, then checked to ensure that he was completely hidden. He decided he was.

At least two hours had passed when Flap returned. It was hard to judge. Time passed slowly when you were lying in a jungle with bugs crawling around and flying critters gnawing at your hide. If you were short of sleep, so hungry that your stomach seemed knotted, suffering from a raging thirst and had diarrhea, every minute was agony. Jake dared not leave his post, so he shit where he lay.

Once he heard a jet. It was far away, the sound of its engines just a low hum.

'Jesus H. Christ!' Flap whispered when he crawled up beside Jake, startling him half out of his skin. 'What died?'

'That's shit, you bastard. Never smelled it before, huh?'

'For crying out loud, you could at least have dropped your flight suit.'

'There's someone over there in that shack. He stuck his head out twice and looked around. Seen smoke a couple times too, just a whiff, like he's standing right inside the door smoking a cigarette.'

'There's two of them in there. I looked in the back window.'

Jake had kept his eyes glued on that shack and hadn't once glimpsed Flap. For the first time he realized just how terrifically good Le Beau was in the jungle.

'Here, this is for you.'

Flap passed over an AK-47. 'It's loaded with a full clip. Safety is on.'

'Found this lying around, did you?'

'Relax. They won't find the guy who had it for quite a while. Maybe never. Gimme my sticker back. I feel kinda naked without it.'

Jake got the knife from his boot and handed it over.

'Lotta good that would have done you in your boot. You should have stabbed it into the dirt right by your hand, so you could grab it quick.'

'Next time. Until then I'll just stick to ol' Betsy here. Appreciate the gift. So what's the setup?'

The bad guys were stacking the weapons back in the jungle, out of sight from the air. Most of the stuff was still in crates. 'They got a hell of a pile out there but I don't think they got it all. Certainly not a shipload. There's no way of telling what's left on the ship.'

'I've been figuring,' Jake said. 'Seems to me that the first thing we have to do after dark is take out those two guys in the shack and check out that cabin cruiser.'

'It may be booby trapped.'

'I don't think so. That was the boat we heard last night. The guys in the shack are supposed to kill us if we try for it.'

'Can't start the engine here.'

'I know. We'll have to cast off and drift downriver. We can use one of your knives to cut us some poles to keep it off the banks. Then when we're a couple miles downriver, we'll start the engine and motor out to sea.'

'What if the engine won't start?'

'We just drift on out.'

'They'll follow.'

'Not if we blow up the ammo dump and sink all these little boats.'

Flap gave a soft whistle of amazement. 'You don't want much, do you?'

'So what's your plan?' Jake asked.

'Kill the guys in the shack and steal the boat. The Navy can come back any old time and bomb these dudes to hell.'

Jake snorted. 'Your faith in the system is truly amazing. Here we are in a foreign country – Indonesia, I think. Whatever. Assuming we manage to get rescued and tell our tale, the only thing the US Navy can do is send a polite note to the State Department. State is going to pass this hot tip to the National Security Council, which will probably staff the shit out of it. The fact that these weapons are going to be sold to revolutionary zealots in Asia, the Mideast or Africa who will use them to cause as much hell as humanly possible and murder everyone who disagrees with them won't cause one of those comfortable bureaucrats to miss a minute's sleep. When the nincompoops who brought you Vietnam get through scratching their butts, they'll give the US ambassador to Indonesia a note to give to whoever is running this country this week. That whoever may or may not do anything. After all, he's probably getting a cut of this operation. There's a whale of a lot of money to be made here: your karate expert captain friend is probably smart enough to spread it around a little.'

'A lot of the weapons are still on Fidel's freighter,' Flap pointed out.

'We'll have to blow it up too.'

'Just out of curiosity, what little army is going to do all this blowing up you envision?'

'You and me.'

Le Beau rolled over on his back and threw an arm across his face. In a moment he said, 'You got gall, Grafton, I'll give you that. You lay there with a bullet hole in your side, wearing your own shit and tell me that "you and me" are going to blow up a weapons cache and a ship! My ass.

They'll smell you fifty feet away. *You* want *me* to go do the hero bit and probably get myself killed.'

'We'll both go. But this is a volunteer deal. You're senior to me and we aren't in the airplane anymore. It's your call.'

'Thank you from the bottom of my teensy little heart. Ah me . . . My second command – I used to lead a whole platoon, you know. Now it's just me and one wounded flyboy with the shits. My military career is going up like a rocket.'

'Oh, cork it. What do you want to do?'

'You think you're up for this?'

'Yeah.'

'Well, you asked for it. Here's the plan.'

As Jake Grafton listened the thought occurred to him that Flap Le Beau had been thinking about screwing these pirates all afternoon. He got a warm feeling. Flap had let him suggest it. Flap Le Beau was one hell of a good guy.

'Not right after dark,' Flap said. 'They'll expect us then. After midnight, in the wee hours.'

'The moon will be up sometime after midnight,' Jake pointed out. 'The clouds will probably obscure it though.'

'It would be good if the clouds let the moonlight through. They'll relax and maybe sleep.'

They pulled back into the jungle to a small stream. Jake undressed and sat in it. The diarrhea was drying up, a little anyway, leaving him very thirsty. He drank and drank from the stream. Then he washed out his flight suit and underwear and put them back on.

Finally he and Flap stretched out in the damp, rotting leaves. The bugs were bad, but they were very tired and the muffled noise from the village and the pier lulled them to sleep. They were both emotionally wrung out from their experiences of the last two days and nights, so their sleep was dreamless. When they awoke the light was fading rapidly and the noise from the ship had ceased. They drank again from the stream, Jake relieved himself, then they crawled back to the vantage point where they could see the shack and the small boats.

The waiting was hard.

When you have finally crossed the threshold, left behind good meals, a comfortable bed, clean clothes and the relaxed company of friends, life becomes a mere battle for survival. The nonessential sinks out of sight.

They lay in the foliage, one man on his stomach watching, the other on his side or back napping. Fortunately there was a small electric light mounted on a pole near the boat dock.

The hours dragged. With nothing to look forward to but battle, and perhaps death, delay was painful. Yet they waited.

The guards in the shack were changed several hours into the night. Two new men came, the two inside left. All of them carried rifles.

No one approached the boats. Even when the rain came. At first it was gentle, then it increased in intensity. Still no one came to cover the boats or check their moorings.

All activity on the dark freighter ceased. From their vantage point the watchers caught occasional glimpses of cigarettes flaring, but the ship was just a blacker spot in the black night.

Finally activity in the village ceased.

The rain continued to fall.

Jake slept again.

When Flap shook him awake, the rain had slowed to a drizzle.

'Look,' he whispered so softly that at first Jake didn't understand. He had to inch around to see what Flap was pointing at. After several seconds he realized he was looking at the two men standing by the boat dock smoking. They were away from the light, but there they were, quite plain.

'They came out of the shack. I'm going now.'

'Okay.' Jake fumbled with the AK-47, made sure the action was clear of leaves, then eased it through the foliage in front of him and spread his feet. Only then did he realize Flap had disappeared.

Minutes passed as he watched the figures by the boat dock. He could hear the murmur of voices. They stood smoking and talking.

Jake waited. If Flap were discovered now, they had no choice but to try for the cabin cruiser.

Finally the men turned and ambled uphill for the shack. One of them paused while the other went on ahead. He was facing in this direction. Only when he turned toward the shack did Jake realize that he was zipping up his pants. He had relieved himself.

The first man was already inside. The second man paused in the doorway. Flap was inside. Jake stopped breathing and blinked rapidly, trying to see in the almost nonexistent light. If the man shouted or fired his weapon . . .

Then he turned for the door and merged with another shadow coming out. Now he disappeared within.

In less than a minute Flap Le Beau came across the open ground toward Jake's position. He was walking calmly, with a rifle in each hand. When he approached Jake's position he said softly, 'Come on. Let's look at the boat.'

Jake wormed his way straight ahead out of the brush, then struggled to his feet. Flap was already at the boat dock. Jake followed along, trying to look as nonchalant as the two guards had.

Flap got into the cabin cruiser. 'The battery works,' he reported.

'Any fuel?'

'There's a can here. Let me see.' A half minute passed. 'Well, it's gasoline. A couple of gallons. I'm going to pour it into the tank.'

This cabin cruiser – what if it were sabotaged? Maybe they should take one of the little boats. Jake looked in them for oars. Each of them had a set. They had outboard engines too, but the presence of oars seemed to indicate that the owners of the boats weren't brimming with confidence over the reliability of those engines. Or maybe they were just careful.

It was going to be a big gamble.

Jake turned his back on the cabin cruiser and stood looking at the village. A faint glow from three or four lights showed through the foliage.

Flap joined him on the dock. 'Decision time, shipmate. We can untie this scow and get out of here right now with a chance and maybe a future. They won't know this tub's gone until morning.'

'You're senior,' Jake told him. 'You make the decision and you live with it.'

'I'm giving you a choice.'

'This is ridiculous.' They couldn't stand here in plain sight arguing like two New York bankers waiting for a taxi. 'Lead the way, Le Beau. I'll be right behind you.'

Flap took one of the AKs and lowered it into the water, then released it. With the other rifle in his left hand, he turned and walked off the dock. Jake followed him.

They circled the village through the jungle. The weapons cache was on the side away from the sea, a hundred yards from the long pier. At least two guards were on duty.

Flap picked a vantage point and watched for a while with Jake beside him. The guards walked the perimeter alertly. After the second one passed, Flap told Jake, 'They're too alert. They know something's up.'

'Maybe they missed that guy you killed this afternoon.'

'Maybe.'

'What if there's someone inside the pile?'

'There is. Believe it.'

'Let's go around to the other side and get a look before we go in.'

Flap led the way with Jake behind him. Jake concentrated on following Flap, afraid that he might lose him, and let Flap worry about avoiding the opposition.

Flap halted on a little hill halfway between the ship and the cache. The village was directly opposite them. To get to the boat landing, however, they would have to either pass the village or retrace the route they had just traveled, circling both the weapons cache and the village.

'Has to be here,' Flap said. 'It's shitty, I know. But we'll need a side shot at the ship. From the boat landing we're looking at the stern.' After a bit he asked, 'Think you can get here on your own if you have to?'

'Yeah. Unless they turn off that streetlight across the way.'

'They won't. Let's go.'

They went back toward the cache and settled in fifty feet away, hidden in waist-high foliage. Flap waited until a guard went by and turned the corner, then he flitted across the gap like a shadow and disappeared into an aisle between stacks of boxes. He left his rifle with Jake.

One minute passed, then another.

The second guard came around the corner and walked by.

Flap had to find the man inside amid the aisles, if there was one, kill him, then come back to dispose of the guards outside. It was a tall order, yet these men had to be down before Jake and Flap could rip into the boxes, which could not be done noiselessly.

Several more minutes ticked by. Jake fingered his flooded, useless watch. Perhaps he should have thrown it away.

Okay, Flap. Where are you, shipmate?

Come on! Come on, Flap!

Oh, Jesus, don't let anything happen to Le Beau.

Little late to think about that, isn't it, Jake? You two could be on a boat going down the river right this very moment if you hadn't insisted on going through with this.

Well, something had gone wrong. Flap was in trouble.

Jake was torn by indecision. If he went inside looking he could blow this whole deal. Yet if Le Beau were injured he might die without assistance.

Here comes one of the guards. Walking and looking, his rifle held carelessly in the crook of his arm.

As the guard went by the aisle where Flap had disappeared, he hesitated. Jake stared at him across the sights of the AK. Now the guard took a step back and peered into the gloom as Jake's finger tightened on the trigger. *If he points his weapon he's dead.*

Hands reached for the guard and jerked him forward off his feet, into the aisle.

What were you worried about, Jake? Flap's the best, the absolute best, a fucking super-Marine.

More time passed.

Waiting was the hard part. If you didn't know what was happening.

Jake lifted his head and took a long, careful scan of the area. No one moving.

The other guard came around the corner. He was more alert than the first one. He held his rifle in both hands, the muzzle up. He looked puzzled.

Uh-oh, he didn't pass the other guy and now he's wondering where he is.

He stopped and looked about carefully, then turned and went back the way he had come. When he reached the corner an arm shot forward. The guard jerked away.

Even from this distance Jake could see the hilt of the knife protruding just below his chin. The rifle fell harmlessly as the man staggered, grabbing at his throat. Le Beau was right there, an arm coiling around the man's mouth to ensure he didn't scream. When he went down Jake hobbled forward.

Le Beau was bent over holding his side. Blood splotched his flight suit everywhere. The Marine jerked the knife from the man's throat and wiped it on his leg, leaving yet another streak on his filthy flight suit, then slipped it into his sleeve sheath.

'What happened?'

'Guy inside had a knife. He got me good.'

'Let's saddle up and get the fuck outta here.'

'No. They bought us tickets and we're taking the ride. Quick, let's drag this guy out of sight. Grab hold.'

They each took an arm.

'How bad is it?' Jake wanted to know.

'I don't know. Burns like fire.'

'Can you keep going?'

'We'll see.' As they dropped the body in a dark aisle, Flap muttered, 'Always knew I'd get it with a knife.'

He led the way down a gloomy aisle, almost feeling his way along. 'The stuff we want is down here. Fuses and wire. Found it this afternoon.'

They attacked the side of a box with Flap's throwing knife. The nails ripping loose sounded loud as gunshots.

'How do you know what's in each box?'

'Seen crates like these before, in Cambodia. This is all Russian stuff. The crates got symbols on them for the comrades who can't read Russian. Like me.'

The side of the crate came loose. Flap dug into it. He came out with a handful of primers and wire. After a little more digging they extracted a timer.

'Now all we gotta do is find the plastique.'

Jake was horrified. 'You don't know where it is?'

'Couldn't find it this afternoon.'

'Maybe it's still on the ship.'

'Maybe. Get out your lighter and look.'

They found a crate with the lid already open. Grenades. Each man stuffed four or five into his chest pocket, then they went on.

Time was dragging. The lighter got hot and flickered. It was about out of butane. Someone was going to come check on the guards any minute now.

Jake was about to give in to despair when they found the plastique. There were at least five crates of it, piled one on top of the other.

'Boost me up,' Flap said.

Lying on top of the crates, Flap pried at the lid of the topmost one with his knife. More groaning noises, as loud as fire sirens. Finally he said, 'Okay, pass up the primers and stuff.'

'How long do you want on the timer?'

'Thirty minutes.'

The timer was mechanical. Jake began winding it up as fast as he could. When the spring would go no tighter, he used the lighter. The clock face would take up to a twelve-hour delay. He set thirty minutes, then passed it up to Flap.

Two minutes passed before Flap asked for help to get down. His side was wet with warm blood.

'Those anti-tank rockets are down this way,' he murmured. He took four steps and fell.

Jake helped him up. 'Let's try to get a bandage on that.'

'With what?'

'Shirt off one of the corpses.'

'We don't have time. Come on!'

They took four of the rockets, two for each man. Flap was visibly weaker now, but in the spluttering light of the butane lighter he took the time to explain how to arm, aim and shoot. The lighter died for the last time before they were through and couldn't be relit. Jake dropped it and slung his rifle over his back. Then he hoisted two of the rockets.

He had to help Flap to his feet. Flap hoisted his two and let the rifle lay. He turned and led the way.

Two steps out of the aisle Flap froze. A figure stood in front of him with a rifle leveled.

The captain!

'You two! I knew you weren't dead.'

He took a step closer. 'You have caused me a great deal of trouble. Now I'm going to cause you a great deal of pain.'

Quick as thought he moved forward and smashed Flap in the head with the butt of his rifle. Flap collapsed.

The captain drove a kick at Jake Grafton that caught him right where his rib was broken. He almost passed out from the pain.

When he came to his senses he was lying almost across Flap. The captain was talking. 'Been into the weapons, I see. What else have you done?' He kicked Jake again, but he took the blow mostly on his shoulder.

Jake felt for Flap's left arm. He found it. The sleeve was loose. The knife came free in his hand.

Another kick. 'What have you done in there? Answer me!'

As the foot flashed out again Jake grabbed it and pulled. Off balance, the captain fell. Jake scrambled to his knees and went for him but the man was too quick. He was coming off the ground so Jake slashed with the knife, a vicious, desperate backhand.

The captain staggered back. Through all the kicks he had kept his rifle in his left hand. Now he dropped it and grabbed his stomach with both hands as a shriek of agony escaped him.

His guts spilled out.

The captain fell to the ground. Jake crawled toward him and stabbed, again and again and again.

When the captain went limp Jake slashed at this throat for good measure, then rolled over moaning. He couldn't breathe. His side!

The captain quivered. In a haze of pain, Jake stabbed the knife into his chest and left it there.

Somehow he got to his feet.

Le Beau seemed only partially conscious. Jake grabbed him by the back of the neck of his flight suit and heaved. The Marine slid about two feet.

Jake needed both hands.

The boat dock. He had to get Flap to the boat.

No way but to drag him.

In a haze of pain, struggling to breathe, he pulled. He paused occasionally to glance over his shoulder, because he was dragging him backward. Right by the lights of the village.

Someone would see him and shoot him.

He didn't care.

How he made the journey he didn't know. Flap stirred several times but he didn't come to.

Finally he had the Marine on the boards of the dock. In a supreme effort he got him over the side of the cabin cruiser onto its deck.

He paused, breathing raggedly, not getting enough air but sucking hard anyway.

Cast off. He had to cast off.

Somehow he remembered the other boats. He got out on the dock and fumbled with their ropes.

The knife! Damn, he had left it sticking in the captain.

He managed to untie all of the ropes except one, which was knotted too tight for his fingers. In his pain and anxiety he forgot all about the second knife that Flap carried.

The ropes for the cabin cruiser came loose easily.

Jake got aboard just as the current began to ease it away from the dock. Those other boats that were free from their moorings were already drifting.

The grenades.

He fumbled in his chest pocket for one. He pulled the pin and held it as the distance increased.

Now.

He let the spoon fly, gritted his teeth and heaved. It hit on the dock, bounced once, then rolled into the moored boat.

Jake sagged down just as it went off.

The noise would bring the pirates. Maybe this would be a good time to see if the engine in this boat can be started.

Fumbling with the switches by the helm, he found the one for the battery. A little light came on. There was a button just beside it. Here goes nothing!

Please, God.

The engine turned over.

He jabbed the button in and held it. Grind, grind, grind as he played with the throttle.

A choke. Maybe there was a choke. Desperately he felt around the panel.

He found it and pulled it out. The engine ground several more times, then caught. He inched the throttle forward from idle and spun the helm.

He had the boat headed downriver when the first bullets thudded in.

One man shooting. No, two.

He hunkered by the wheel and fed in full throttle.

The boat accelerated nicely. He slewed it and craned his head to see. The banks of the river were even darker than the water.

Stay in the middle.

More bullets whapping in. The windshield in front of Jake shattered. Then something hit him in the shoulder, drove him forward into the panel. Somehow he kept his feet under him.

The shooting stopped. He was rounding a bend. He got himself into the seat behind the wheel.

How far to the sea? Would the pirates follow?

He was worrying about that when he heard the explosion, a roar that grew and grew and grew, then died abruptly.

His head swam and he worked desperately hard to breathe. Somehow he stayed conscious and kept the boat in the channel.

Eventually the darkness of the trees on the riversides merged with the night and the boat began to pitch and roll. The ocean. They were out of the river.

There was a bungee cord dangling from the wheel. With the last of his strength Jake managed to hook the free end to the bottom of the chair where he had been sitting.

He rolled Flap over to check on him. He had a terrible knot on his forehead and the pupil of one eye was completely dilated. Concussion.

'Hey, Flap. It's me, Jake.'

The Marine moved. His lips worked. Jake put his head down to hear. 'Horowitz had a brother. Tell him . . . Tell him . . .'

Just what Jake was to tell him Flap didn't say.

Jake was so tired. He lay down beside Flap.

*

The boat ran out of fuel an hour later. It was rolling amid the swells of a sun-flecked blue sea when a pilot of an A-7 from *Columbia* spotted it. The crewman of the helicopter lowered found Jake Grafton and Flap Le Beau lying side by side in the cockpit.

23

Jake woke up in a room with cream-colored walls and ceiling, in a bed with crisp white sheets. A sunbeam shown like a spotlight through a window. An IV was dripping into a vein in his left arm.

Hospital.

His curiosity satisfied, he drifted off to sleep again. When he next awoke a nurse was there taking his pulse. 'Welcome back to the land of the living,' she said, and lowered his wrist back to the bed. She annotated a clipboard, then gave him a grin.

'Where am I?'

'Honolulu. Trippler Army Hospital.'

'Hawaii?'

'Yes. You've been here almost a day now. You're just coming out of the recovery room.'

'Le Beau? Marine captain. He here too?'

'Yes. He's still in recovery.'

'How is he?'

'Still asleep. He's had an operation. You've had one too, but yours didn't take quite as long.'

'When he wakes up, I want to talk to him. Okay?'

'We'll see. You take that up with the doctor when he comes around. He should be here in about thirty minutes. Is there anything I can do for you?'

'No.'

She busied herself arranging the sheets and checking that he had fresh water in a glass by the bed. He lay taking it in, enjoying the brightness and the cleanliness.

After a bit curiosity stirred him. 'What day is it?'

'This is Wednesday.'

'We got shot down . . . December nine. What day . . . is it now?'

'The sixteenth of December.'

'We missed Australia.'

'What was that?'

'Nothing,' he murmured, and closed his eyes again. He was very tired.

He was still pretty foggy when he talked to the doctor, either later that morning or that afternoon. The sunbeam had moved. He noticed that.

'We operated on your left side. Your lung collapsed. Lucky you didn't bleed to death. And of course you were shot in the shoulder. By some miracle the bullet missed your collarbone. Went clean through.'

'Uh-huh.'

'You're also fighting a raging infection. You aren't out of the woods yet, sailor.'

'Le Beau, how's he doing?'

'He's critical. He lost a lot of blood.'

'He gonna make it?'

'We think so.'

'When he wakes up, I want to see him.'

'We'll see.'

'Bring him in here. This room's big enough. Or take me into his room.'

'We'll see.'

'How'd we get here, anyway?'

'The ship medevaced you two to Clark and the Air Force flew you here.'

'I may not be out of the woods, but I'm out of the jungle.'

The next day Flap was wheeled into the room. His bed was placed beside Jake's. A bandage covered half his head. But he grinned when he saw Jake out of his one unobstructed eye.

'Hey, shipmate.'

'As I live and breathe,' said Flap Le Beau as the nurses hovered around hooking up everything. 'The neighborhood is integrating. Better put the house up for sale while you still can.'

'If you don't stop that racist stuff I'm gonna start calling you Chocolate.'

'Chocolate Le Beau,' he said, savoring it. 'I like it. They hung that Flap tag on me because I talk a lot. My real name is Clarence.'

'I know. Middle initial O. What's that stand for?'

'Odysseus. I picked it out in college after I read the Odyssey. Clarence O. Le Beau. Got a ring to it, don't it?' He directed the question to one of the nurses, who looked sort of sweet.

'It is very nice,' she said, and smiled.

'So how you feeling?' Jake asked.

'Like a week-old dog turd that's been run over by a truck. And you?'

'Not quite that chipper.'

When the nurses were leaving Flap told the sweet one, 'Come back and see us anytime, dearest.'

'I will, Clarence O.'

When they were gone, Flap told Jake, 'Don't worry. I'll get you one too. Trust me.'

'So what's wrong with your head?'

'Concussion and blood clot. They had to drill a hole to relieve the pressure. Another hole in my head – just what I needed, eh?'

'The captain laid you out with a butt stroke. I killed him.'

'I figured that or we wouldn't be here. But some other time, huh? I don't want to even think about that shit.'

'Yeah.'

'What's for lunch? Have they told you?'

'No.'

'I am really ready for some good grits.'

'Guess we missed Australia.'

'These things happen. Don't sweat it. You can make it up to me somehow.'

The following day they were visited by a Navy commander, an officer on the staff of Commander In Chief Pacific – CINCPAC. He interviewed both men, recorded their stories, then when they tired, left while they napped. He came back for another hour just before dinner and asked questions.'

'If I can do anything for you gentlemen, give me a call.'

He left a card with his name and telephone number on the stands beside each of their beds.

They had lost a lot of weight. When the nurses first sat Jake up he was amazed at how skinny his legs and arms were.

Improvement was slow at first, then quicker. By the fifth day Jake was walking to the bathroom. He bragged, so Flap got himself out of bed and went when the nurses weren't there. He had trouble with his balance but he made it to the john and back by holding on to things.

On the eighth day they went for a hike, holding on to each other, to see what they could see. A nurse caught them and made them retrace their steps.

The hospital was half-empty. 'Not like it used to be. You were the first gunshot victim we saw in two months,' one nurse told Jake.

'Not like the good old days,' he replied.

'They weren't good days,' he was told. 'Thank God the war is over.'

On the day after Christmas they demanded clothes. That afternoon an orderly brought them cardboard boxes containing some of their clothes that the guys on the ship had packed and sent. The orderly helped Jake open his. Inside he found underwear, uniforms, shoes, insignia.

As he was inspecting a set of khakis, the thought went through his head that he should discard this shirt and buy another.

Where had that thought come from? He was getting out – *out* of the Navy!

He sat on the edge of the bed holding the shirt, looking at it but not seeing it. *Out.* To do what? What could he conceivably do as a civilian that would mean as much to him as what he had spent the last six years of his life doing?

He was a naval officer. Lieutenant, United States Navy.

That meant something.

He was digging in the box when he found a letter. It was from the Real McCoy.

Hey Shipmate,

When you read this you will probably be getting spruced up to go to the club or chase women. Some guys will do about anything to get out of a little work.

This boat was like a damn funeral parlor the night you and Flap didn't come back. The mood improved a thousand percent when they announced that the chopper was inbound with both of you aboard. The captain and CAG and Skipper Haldane were there on the flight deck with the medicos when the chopper landed, along with a couple hundred other guys.

After the docs got you guys stabilized and you left in the COD, the captain got on the 1-MC and said some real nice things about you. It was pretty maudlin. I forgot most of it so I won't try to repeat it here, but suffice it to say that every swinging dick on this boat is glad you two clowns made it.

Australia is on. TS for you. We'll party on without you, but you'll be missed.

Your friend,
Real

Two days later Jake decked himself out in a white uniform and Flap selected a set of khakis. They strolled the grounds. The days were Hawaii balmy with clouds every afternoon. One day they took a taxi to the golf course and rented a golf cart.

Out on the fairways they went over the whole adventure again, little by little, a scene here, a scene there. Gradually they dropped it and went on to other subjects, like women and politics and flying.

One day Flap brought the subject up again, for what proved to be the last time. 'So *where* is my slasher?'

'I think I left it sticking in the captain. But I might have just dropped it somewhere. It's a little hazy.'

'That was my best knife.'

'Tough.'

'I designed it. It was custom-made for me. Cost me *two hundred* bucks.'

'Order another.'

Flap laughed. 'I can see you are oozing remorse over my loss.'

'To be frank, I don't give a shit about your knife.'

'You're as full of tact as ever. That's one of the qualities that will take you far, Grafton. Ol' Mister Smooth.'

'And the horse you rode in on, Clarence O.'

'It's my turn to drive this friggin' cart. You're always hoggin' the drivin'.'

'That's because *I'm* the pilot. Why don't you tell me about some of the ugly women you've run across in your adventures?'

'Well, by God, I just will.' And he did.

In the evenings there was little to do, so Jake wrote letters. His first was to his former roommate, Sammy Lundeen. He hit the highlights of this last cruise and devoted a whole page to crossing the line. In the finest traditions of naval aviation, he seriously downplayed his and Flap's role in the pirate adventure. Luck, luck, luck – he and Flap had survived due to the grotesque ineptitude of the villains and despite their own extra-ordinarily stupid mistakes, mistakes that would have wrung tears from the eyes of any competent aviator. All in all, the letter was quite a literary effort, first-class fiction. That thought didn't occur to Jake, of course, when he reread it before stuffing it into an envelope. His buddy Lundeen would chuckle, Jake knew, and shake his head sadly. Good ol' Sammy.

Instinctively he adopted a completely different tone when he wrote to Tiger Cole, his last BN during the Vietnam War. There was no bullshit in Tiger Cole, and no one who knew him would try to lay the smelly stuff on him. You gave it to that grim warrior straight and unadorned.

He ended the letter this way:

I have never thought of myself as professional. Never. I've been a guy who went into the service because there was a war and I've merely tried to do my best until the time came for me to go back to the real world. Still I have watched so many pros since I have been in the Navy – you included – that I think I'm beginning to see how the thing is done. And why. I hope so, anyway. So I've decided to stay in.

The decision hasn't been easy. I guess no important commitment is.

Whenever I get back to the mainland, I'll give you a call. I'll probably take some leave. Maybe swing by Pensacola if you're still there and we can swill a beer at the club.

Hang tough, shipmate.

Your friend,
Jake

One day Jake penned a letter to Callie. Then he put it in the drawer beside his bed. Each day he got it out, read it through and debated whether or not he should mail it.

She probably had another boyfriend. There was always that possibility. Jake Grafton had no intention of playing the fool, with this or any other woman. So he kept the letter formal, as if he were writing to a great-aunt. He omitted any reference to his adventure with the pirates or the fact that he was just now residing in a hospital room. But on the second page he said this:

I've decided to stay in the Navy. It has been a tough decision and I've had to really wrestle with it. The arguments for getting out are many and you know most of them. The Navy is a large bureaucracy; anyone who thinks the bureaucracy will miss them when they are gone is kidding himself.

Still, this is where I belong. I like the people, I can do the work, I believe the work is important. Of course the Navy is not for everyone, but it is, I believe, the best place for me. I know full well that there is nothing that I can do here that others cannot do better, but here I *can* make a contribution.

He closed with a few pleasantries and the hope that all was fine with her.

On New Year's Eve he got it out again to read it through carefully.

The tone was wrong, all wrong.

He added a PS.

As I reread this letter it occurs to me that I've made a very stupid mistake. The last few months I've been so busy worrying that you might not love me as much as I love you that I lost sight of what love is. Love by its very nature opens you up to getting burned.

I love you, Callie. You were a rock to hang on to the last year of the war, the one sane person in an insane world. And you've been a rock to hang on to these last six months. You've been in my thoughts and in my dreams.

If I love you more than you love me, so be it. I'm tough enough to love and lose. But I just wanted you to know how much I care.

As ever,

Jake

In the third week of January he and Flap moved to the BOQ. They continued to visit the hospital on an outpatient basis. Flap took daily physical therapy to overcome the effects of his head injury. The knife wound in his side drained slowly and healed stubbornly. Eventually it did heal, leaving a bad scar.

Jake merely needed a checkup occasionally. His collapsed lung and the resultant infection had been more serious than the bullet hole in his shoulder, which healed quickly, yet by now he was well on his way to a complete recovery. He went with Flap every morning anyway and kibitzed as the Marine went through his exercises. Then they went to the golf course and rode around in a golf cart.

One day they rented clubs. They merely slapped at the balls, since neither man could swing a club with any vigor. Slap the ball a hundred feet, using mostly arms and wrists, get in the cart and drive over to it, slap the thing again. It was crazy, but it felt fine.

After that they played daily. Gradually the shoulders and ribs loosened up and they swung more freely, but neither man had ever played much golf and neither was very good.

They were standing on the carrier pier at Pearl Harbor when *Columbia* arrived in early February.

'Look who has returned!' the Real McCoy shouted when they walked into the ready room. 'The prodigal sons are *back!*'

'We only came aboard for a change of underwear. It's been hell, golf every day, hot women every night . . .'

They were surrounded by people shaking their hands and welcoming them back. When the mob scene had subsided to a low roar, the Real asked Jake, 'By any chance did you bring a copy of the *Wall Street Journal?*'

'I hate to give you the bad news, roomie, but the market is down a thousand points this morning. They're talking about a depression.'

'Aah . . . ,' said the Real, searching Jake's face.

'Millionaires are leaping out of windows even as we speak.'

'You're kidding, right?'

After lunch Jake went to his stateroom with McCoy. He crawled into the top bunk and let out a long sigh. 'Feels so good.'

'Got something to show you,' the Real said. From his desk he brought forth a series of aerial photos. 'We took these before we smacked that hijacked Cuban freighter. See that big blast area – that's where the pile was that you and Flap blew up.'

'You guys bombed the Cuban ship?'

'Oh yes. The government of Indonesia thought those weapons might go to some of their own indigenous revolutionaries, so they asked for our help before we even offered it.'

'I never saw anything about it in the papers.'

'They never told the press.'

'I'll be darned.'

That night the entire squadron went to the O Club en masse. It was an epic party, complete with a letter the next day from the CO of the base to the captain of *Columbia* complaining about rowdy behavior and demanding damages. That night Jake and Flap slept in their bunks aboard ship.

Before the ship sailed, Jake spent a quiet moment with Lieutenant Colonel Haldane. 'I'd like to stay in the Navy, Skipper. I want to withdraw my resignation.'

Haldane smiled and offered his hand. Jake shook it.

'There's one other thing,' Jake said slowly. 'I hear that some of the guys are going to get some traps the first day out of port just in case they need to fly during the transit to the States. I'd need too many to get current, but I'd take it as a personal favor if you'd let me and Flap get one.'

'I need up chits from the flight surgeon.'

'That's the rub. I think I can get one but I don't think they'll give Flap an up. The doctors at Trippler want him to do more physical therapy. He still has some balance problems.'

'According to that report we received from CINCPAC, he took a rifle butt in the head.'

'Yessir. One hell of a butt stroke. He had lost a lot of blood by the that time and didn't have the reflexes to minimize the impact.'

'Well, you and Flap take your medical files to the flight surgeon and have him look you over. Then have him call me.'

'Aye aye, sir.'

Somehow it worked out. Jake and Flap rode the catapult two hours after *Columbia* cleared Pearl. By some miracle he didn't question he got a plane full of gas, so he had to burn down or dump before he could come back into the pattern.

They yanked and banked and shouted over the ICS as they did tight turns around the tops of cumulus clouds. Jake managed a loop and a Cuban eight before Flap begged for mercy. He was dizzy.

Jake smoked into the break at five hundred knots. The air boss never peeped. Better yet, Jake snagged a three-wire.

On the morning of the fly-off Jake took the Pri-Fly duty. All the planes of the air wing were to be launched: the crews were selected strictly on the basis of seniority. Tonight they would be home with wives and children and sweethearts. Jake and Flap were, of course, not flying off. They were riding the ship into port. Flap had an appointment at the Oakland Naval Hospital and Jake was catching a commercial flight to Oak Harbor via Seattle to pick up his car, then he was taking a month's leave. He thought he would head for Virginia by way of Chicago. Maybe look Callie up, see what she was up to. At the end of the month he would report again to Tiny Dick Donovan at VA-128.

The fly-off went well. One by one every plane on the ship taxied to the catapults and was shot aloft. They rendezvoused in divisions over the ship and headed east.

When the last plane was gone and the angel helicopter had settled onto the angle and shut down, the ship secured from flight quarters. Jake went down to the strangely empty flight deck and walked around one last time.

Not really. He would be back. If not this ship, then another. Once again he savored the oily aroma of steam seeping up from the catapults, felt the heat as it mixed with the salty sea breeze.

He was wandering the deck when Bosun Muldowski approached. He stunned Jake with a salute. Jake returned it.

'Hear you're staying in, Mr Grafton.'

'Yep. Your example shamed me into it.'

Muldowski laughed. 'It's a good life,' he said 'Beats eight to five anywhere. Maybe if I had found the right woman and had some kids . . . But you can't live on maybes. Didn't work out that way. You gotta live your life one day at a time. That's the way God fixed it up. Today do what you do best and let tomorrow take care of tomorrow.'

Jake was packing in his stateroom when the ship docked at the Alameda carrier pier. The Real McCoy had flown off with the Marines – he had earned it. McCoy's steel footlockers sporting new padlocks sat one atop the other by the door. His desk was clean and nothing hung in his closet. His bunk was stripped and the sheets turned in.

Jake had also turned in his sheets and blankets. Last night he had packed the suitcase he was taking on leave – now he was stuffing everything else into the parachute bags. The suitcase he had purchased in Hawaii. The padlocks for the bags lay on the desk. Net gain after one eight-month cruise: one suitcase and some new scars.

The engagement ring he had purchased for Callie oh those many months ago was the last item left in his desk safe. He held it in his hand and wondered what to do with it. The suitcase might get stolen or lost by the airline, shuffled off to Buffalo or Pago Pago or Timbuktu. For lack of a better option, he put the ring in his shirt pocket and buttoned the pocket.

The telephone rang. 'Lieutenant Grafton, sir.'

'Mr Grafton, this is the duty officer at the officers' brow. You have a visitor.'

'Me?'

'Yes, sir. You need to come sign her in and escort her.'

'Okay, but who is this pers—?' He stopped because he was talking to a dead phone. The duty officer had hung up.

There was obviously some mistake. He didn't know a soul in the San Francisco Bay area. He glanced at his new watch, guaranteed to be waterproof to a depth of three hundred feet or his money back. He had four hours to catch the plane from the Oakland airport. Plenty of time.

He grabbed his ball cap and headed for the ceremonial quarterdeck at the head of the officers' brow. It was on the hangar deck, which was the scene of hundreds of sailors coming and going on a variety of errands, most of them frivolous. Crowds of sailors stood on the aircraft elevators shouting to people on the pier below. Near the enlisted brow a band was tooting merrily.

He saw her standing, looking curiously around when he was still a hundred feet away.

Callie McKenzie!

As he walked toward her she spotted him. She beamed.

'Hello, Jake.'

He couldn't think of anything to say.

'You've lost some weight,' she said.

'Been sick.'

'Oh. Well, aren't you glad to see me?'

'Thunderstruck. I'm speechless.'

She looked even better than he remembered. As he stared her eyes danced with amusement and a smile grew on her face.

'I *never* expected to see you here,' he told her. 'Not in a million years.'

'Life is full of surprises.'

'Isn't it, though?'

He was rooted where he stood, unable to take his eyes off her and unsure what to do next. Why was she here? Why hadn't she written in five months? Then a thought struck him: 'Did you come with someone?' he asked, and glanced around, half expecting to see her mother, or even some man.

'No.' She reached out and touched his arm. 'All these sailors are staring at us. Can you sign me in so we can go somewhere and talk?'

Jake flushed. 'Oh, yes, sure.'

The officer of the deck and quartermaster of the watch grinned shamelessly, enjoying Jake's obvious discomfort. Jake scribbled his name beside Callie's in the visitors' log, then steered her away with two fingers on her elbow.

'Let's go up to the flight deck. Fine view of the bay area from up there.'

Indeed, the view from the flight deck was spectacular. The San Francisco skyline, Treasure Island, airliners coming and going at San Francisco International and Oakland – the panorama would have frozen most people who had spent the largest part of the last eight months looking at empty ocean dead in their tracks. However Jake Grafton was too acutely aware of the presence of Callie McKenzie to give the scene more than a glance.

'How are your folks?' he asked finally, breaking the silence.

'They're fine. And yours?'

'Okay. Almost called you a time or two.'

'And I almost wrote you. I should have. And you should have called.'

'Why didn't you write?'

'I didn't want to influence your decision. To stay in or get out, what to do with your life. This was your decision, Jake, not mine.'

'Well, I made it. I'm staying in.'

'Why?'

Jake Grafton ran his fingers through his hair. 'I was looking for something. Turns out I had it all along and just didn't realize it.'

'What were you looking for?'

'Something worth doing. Something that made a difference. The war was such a mess . . . I guess that I lost sight of what we're all about here. It's more than ships and planes and cats and traps. I realized that finally.'

'I always thought that what you did was important.'

'Your dad didn't.'

'Dad? I love him dearly but this is my life, not his.'

'So what are you going to do with your life?'

She didn't answer. She lowered her head and began walking slowly. Jake stayed with her. When she got to the bow of the ship she stood looking across the water at San Francisco with the wind playing in her hair.

'I guess I'm like most modern women. I want a family and a career. Languages have always fascinated me, and I have found I love to teach. That's the big plan, but some of it is contingent.'

'On what?'

'On you.'

'Well, I don't think that's very fair. After all, lady, you shoved me out into the cold to make up my own mind.'

'You were never out in the cold, Jake. There hasn't been an hour in the last eight months that I wasn't thinking about you. I've read and reread your letters until I almost wore out the paper. Especially that last letter. I think I was wondering too, wondering if you loved me as much as I loved you.'

'You were always with me too,' he confessed, and grinned. 'Maybe an hour or two now and then you slipped away, but most of the time you were there.'

Her hand found his. They began strolling along the deck. The breeze was fresh and crisp.

'So why did you come here?' he asked.

'I came to get married.'

He gaped. It was like a kick in the stomach. He had thought . . . He jerked his hand from her grasp.

'Who's the lucky guy?' he managed.

'You,' she said, her head cocked slightly to one side, her lips twisting into a grin.

'*Me?*'

'Who else could it be? I love you more than words can tell, Jacob Lee Grafton.'

'You want to marry *me?*'

She laughed. He had always liked her laugh. 'Do you want me to get down on one knee and propose?'

'I accept,' he told her, and seized both her hands. 'Where and when?'

'This afternoon. Anywhere.'

'My God, woman! This is sudden. Are you sure?'

'I've been thinking about this for a year,' she told him. 'I'm absolutely certain.'

'Well, I'll be . . .' He took off his cap and ran his fingers through his hair. Then he remembered the ring. He pulled it from his shirt pocket, looked at it, then put it on her finger.

Now she was surprised. 'You knew I was coming?'

'No. I bought that for you over a year ago. Been carrying it ever since.'

'Oh, Jake,' she said, and wrapped her arms around his neck. Her lips found his.

He finally broke the embrace and seized her hand. 'Come on. We'll need a best man. My BN is still aboard. He and I were going to have lunch together.'

The quickest way to Flap's stateroom was into the catwalk behind the island, then into the 0-3 level and down. On the catwalk Jake happened to glance at the pier. There was a pink Cadillac convertible parked at the foot of the officers' brow with four women in it.

Muldowski was walking across the brow. Now he turned and saluted the American flag on the fantail.

Jake cupped his hand to his mouth and shouted, '*Muldowski! Hey, Bosun!*'

The warrant officer looked up. He pointed.

'I'm getting *married,*' Jake Grafton roared. 'Will you give the bride away?'

'When?' Muldowski boomed.

'This afternoon. Wait for us. We'll be down in ten minutes.'

'Is that the bride?'

'Yes.'

'I may keep her my—' The rest of the bosun's comment was drowned by music as the band launched into another tune.

The women in the convertible were on their feet applauding. The bosun started clapping too, as did dozens of people on the pier.

Callie was grinning broadly. She looked so happy. What the heck! In full view of the world Jake swept her into his arms.

The Minotaur

Acknowledgements

The author received invaluable unclassified technical advice from numerous individuals who volunteered to assist in his education. Some of them wished to remain anonymous. Those who forgot to request anonymity are: Commander Robert Day, Commander Doug Hargrave, Captain Michael E. Kearney, Fred Kleinberg, Captain Richard E. 'Dick' Koehler, Captain Wayne Savage, Captain Karl Volland and Dr Edward Walsh. The author also referred extensively to Bill Sweetman's excellent works on low-observable technology aircraft. To all of these people the author extends his thanks.

Knowledgeable readers are advised that the intricacies and eccentricities of the bureaucratic maze within the Department of Defense forced the author to take liberties within this novel in the interest of readability. Some of the mind-boggling complexities of modern military hardware have been simplified for the same reason.

You've heard the story – it's old, they say –
how the queen of Crete took a bull for a lover
and in her time delivered the Minotaur.
Contriving to hide his shame, to banish
the hideous man-bull from the sight of men,
King Minos ordered Daedalus to construct a labyrinth.
The artist set the stone, captured conflict
in aisles and passages of confusion and deceit,
devious ways that twisted the mind and eye
of all who entered that prison of no escape,
wherein was placed the Minotaur.
Thus did Daedalus build his monument
to the betrayal of the king.

The means of destruction are approaching perfection
with frightful rapidity.

Baron Antoine Henri Jomini, 1838

1

Terry Franklin was a spy. This afternoon in February, in a small cubby-hole in the basement of the Pentagon, he was practising his trade. It was tedious work.

He adjusted the screen brightness on his computer monitor and tapped the secret access code of the user he was pretending to be tonight. Now the file name, also special access, a classification higher than top secret. He had to be careful, since the letters and numerals he was typing did not appear on the screen. A mistake here meant the computer would lock him out and deny him the file. And he was not a good typist. He worked with just two fingers.

Voilà! There it was. The ATA File, the Advanced Tactical Aircraft. He tapped some more and began examining the document list. Number 23.241, that's the first one. He slid one of his high-density, 5.25-inch floppies into the slot and hit the keys again. The little red light came on above the disk drive and the drive began to whir. Franklin smiled when he saw the light.

It was quiet here in the computer service shop. The only noise was the whirring of the disk drive and the tiny clicks of the keyboard. And the sound of Terry Franklin's breathing. It was ironic, he mused, how the computer silently and effortlessly reveals the deepest secrets of its owners. Without remorse, without a twinge of emotion of any kind, the screen lays bare the insights gained from man-years of research by highly educated, gifted scientists and the cunning application of that research by extraordinarily talented engineers. Pouring onto the floppy disk was a treasure more valuable than gold, more precious than diamonds, a treasure beyond the reach of most of the human race, still struggling as it was with basic survival. Only here, in America, where a significant percentage of the best brains on the planet were actively engaged in fundamental research into the secrets of creation, were these intangible jewels being created in significant quantity, gushing forth, almost too fast to steal.

Terry Franklin grinned to himself as he worked. He would do his best.

He called up the document list again, then changed floppies as he listened to the silence.

These three little floppy disks would earn him thirty thousand dollars. He had bargained hard. Ten thousand dollars a disk, whether full or partially full. Cash.

He had figured out a way to make computers pay. He grinned happily at this thought and stroked the keyboard again.

Terry Franklin had become a spy for the money. He had volunteered. He had made his decision after reading everything he could lay his hands on about espionage. Only then had he devised a plan to market the classified material to which he had access as a navy enlisted computer specialist. He had thought about the plan for months, looking for holes and weighing the risks. There were risks, he knew, huge ones, but that was the reason the compensation would be so high. And, he assured himself repeatedly, he enjoyed taking risks. It would add spice to his life, make a boring marriage and a boring job tolerable. So he recruited himself.

One Saturday morning five years ago Terry Franklin walked into the Soviet embassy in Washington. He had read that the FBI kept the embassy under constant surveillance and photographed everyone who entered. So he wore a wig, false mustache and heavy, mirrorlike sunglasses. He told the receptionist he wanted to see an intelligence officer. After a forty-five minute wait, he was shown into a small, windowless room and carefully searched by the receptionist, a muscular, trim man in his early thirties. A half hour later – he was convinced he was photographed during this period by an unseen camera – a nondescript man in his fifties wearing a baggy suit had entered and occupied the only other chair. Without a word, Franklin displayed his green navy ID card, then handed the man a roll of film. The man weighed it in his hand as Franklin removed the sunglasses, wig and mustache. The Russian left the room without speaking. Another half hour passed, then another. No doubt he was again photographed.

It was almost noon when baggy-suit returned. He smiled as he entered and shook Franklin's hand. Could he examine the ID card? Where was Franklin stationed? When had he exposed the film? Why? The Russian's English was good but slightly accented.

Money, Terry Franklin had said. 'I want money. I have something to sell and I brought you a free sample, hoping you might want to buy more.'

Now, as Franklin worked the computer keyboard, he thought back to that day at the embassy. It had been the most momentous day of his life. Five years and two months after that day he had $540,000 in cash in a storage locker in McLean, Virginia, under an assumed name and no one was the wiser. He was going to quit spying when that figure reached a million. And when his enlistment was up, he was going to walk out on Lucy and the kids and fly to South America.

It was typical of Terry Franklin that he intended to delay his departure until he received his discharge. When he entered his new life he would go free, clean and legal, with no arrest warrants anywhere. He would go in his fake identity. Petty Officer First Class Terry Franklin, the college kid from Bakersfield who had knocked up Lucy Southworth in the back seat of her father's station wagon at a drive-in movie, married her, then joined the navy – that Terry Franklin would cease to exist.

It was a nice bundle: $540,000, plus $30,000 for these three disks. A lot of money. But not enough. He wasn't greedy, but he had to have a stake big enough so that he could live on the interest.

He had been very, very careful. He had made no mistakes. He had never spent a penny of the money. The spying was going smooth as clockwork. These Russians, they were damn good. You had to take your hat off to them. They had never called or spoken to him after that last meeting in Miami almost three years ago, right after he received orders to the Pentagon.

The operation was slick, almost foolproof, he reflected as he inserted the third disk. The calls always came on an evening when his wife was out, sometimes with her bowling league, sometimes at a friend's house. The phone rang once, and if he picked it up there was no one there, merely a dial tone. One minute later it rang again, once. Then a minute after that it rang one, two, three or four times. The number of rings that third time was the message. He was to check dead drop one, two, three or four, and he was to do it as soon as possible. He usually left the house immediately, cruised for at least an hour in his car to ensure he wasn't being followed, then headed for the dead drop. And the information would be there. Spelled out in block letters on the back of an empty, torn cigarette pack would be the file name he was to photograph, the classified computer codes necessary to gain access and a telephone number to call the evening he was ready to transfer the disks, when the whole sequence would begin again. No one saw him, he saw no one, all very slick.

He chuckled. The cigarette packs on which he received his instructions were always Marlboro Gold 100s, and it had occurred to Terry Franklin that someone had a subtle sense of humor. As he worked now and thought about the money, he savored that sardonic twist.

They must be watching the house to see when he was home alone. Of course someone was servicing the drops. But how were they getting the computer codes and file names? Oh well, he was getting his piece of the pie and he wasn't greedy.

'Ask me no questions and I'll tell you no lies,' Terry Franklin muttered as he removed the final disk from its slot and tucked it into its own little envelope. He grinned at the monitor screen, then tapped keys to exit the file.

Now came the tricky part. Three years ago, when he had first been told by the Soviets that they wanted copies of documents from the computer system, he had written a trapdoor program for the software of the main computer. The job had taken him six months; it had to be right the first time – he would get no second chance. This program accomplished several things: it allowed Franklin to access any file in central memory from this terminal here in the repair shop, a permanent secret 'doorway,' thereby defeating the built-in safeguards that gave access to classified files only from certain specific terminals; it erased the record of his access from the 3-W file, which was a security program that automatically recorded who, what and when; and finally, it allowed him to access the 3-W file to see that his footprints were indeed not there.

This trapdoor program was his crowning achievement. He had once seen a written promise from the software designer that unrecorded access was an impossibility. What a load! It had been damn tough – he would give them that – but he had figured out a way in the end. There's *always* a way if you know enough. That contractor, he really sold the brass a sow's ear when he told that fib. Ah well, the contractor had gotten his and now Terry Franklin was making his own score.

He had loaded the trapdoor program in the main computer one day while fifteen technicians loafed and sipped coffee and watched him work on a sticky tape drive. Not a one of them saw what he was doing. Nor, he told himself with glee, would they have understood what he was doing even if they had noticed. Most of them were as ignorant as they were trusting.

Tonight, the 3-W file looked clean as a virgin's conscience. Franklin exited the program and turned off his terminal. He stood and stretched. He felt good. Very, very good. The adrenal excitement was almost like a cocaine high, but better since there was no comedown. He was living on the edge and it felt terrific.

After straightening up the office, he turned off the coffeepot and put on his coat. With a last glance around, he snapped off the lights and locked the door behind him.

Getting past the guards at the building exits carrying the disks was a risk, though a small one. The civilian guards occasionally selected people for a spot search and sooner or later he would be chosen. He knew several of the guards on sight and made it a habit to speak to them, but inevitably, sooner or later . . . It didn't happen this evening, but he was clean just now anyway. The disks were still back in the office, carefully hidden. He would bring them out some evening next week at the height of the rush-hour exodus when the probability of being searched was the smallest. Minimize the risk, maximize the gain.

As he rode the escalator up to the bus stop for Virginia suburban buses, Terry Franklin buttoned his coat tightly and turned the collar up behind his neck. From a pocket he extracted his white sailor's cap and placed it carefully on his head, exactly one finger width above his eyebrows.

The cold, wet wind at the top of the mechanical stairs made him cringe. He quickly climbed aboard the Annandale bus and made his way up to an empty window seat. He stared through the gathering dusk at the looming building. People in uniform and civilian clothes kept pouring from the escalator exit, trying to hide their faces from the wind, scurrying for buses. These poor snooks. What they didn't know!

Vastly content, Terry Franklin pursed his lips and began to whistle silently.

As the bus bearing Terry Franklin pulled away from the loading area, a senior naval officer, a captain, leaned into the wind as he crossed the lighted parking lot. He paid no attention to the buses queued for the freeway entrance and it was probable no one on the buses paid any attention to him. Terry Franklin was opening the sports section of a newspaper he had purchased during his lunch break. Franklin wouldn't have recognized the captain out there in the rapidly emptying parking lot anyway, not even if they had passed in a corridor. They had never met. But Franklin would have recognized the officer's computer security access password, for he had just finished using it.

Tonight the captain grimaced as the wind tore at his unprotected face and took the time to open the hatchback of his Toyota Corolla and toss his attaché case in. Then he fumbled with the key to the driver's door. Snuggled in with the engine running and waiting for the heater to warm up, Captain Harold Strong tried to relax. It had been another long week, as each and every one of them were in this gargantuan paper factory by the Potomac. He cast a bleak eye on the cars creeping toward the exit. Not too many now, well after quitting time. And he had wanted to get an early start this evening! God, he was tired.

He put the car in gear and threaded it toward the exit. He checked his watch. It was twenty-two minutes past six. At least the timing was right. He would reach the interstate just as the car pool restrictions ended.

On the freeway he headed north along the river, past the Arlington Memorial Bridge, under the ramps of the Teddy Roosevelt Bridge and out into the traffic snarl on I-66 westbound. Here at the tail end of the rush hour the traffic moved along fairly well at about forty miles per hour, only occasionally coming to a complete stop. Captain Strong listened carefully to an airborne traffic reporter tally the evening's casualties. I-66 westbound wasn't mentioned.

Nearing Falls Church he stopped beside the road for a moment and removed his bridge coat. With the car back in motion and the radio tuned to a soft-rock FM station, Strong chewed over the week's frustrations and disasters again. Oh crap, he thought, it's Friday night and you have the cabin all to yourself for an entire weekend, so forget it. It'll all keep until Monday, God knows.

Since the divorce he had spent most of his weekends in the cabin. His son was a junior in college this year, busy with school and girls. The captain wasn't interested in female companionship, which was perhaps a good thing since he lacked both the finances and the time.

They want too much from that airframe, he told himself as he drove, reviewing the arguments of the week yet one more time. You can't build a plane that will drop bombs, shoot missiles, hassle with MiGs, have a radar cross section so small it can't be detected – haul the President back and forth to Camp David on weekends when it isn't being used to save the free world – and still expect the goddamn thing to take a cat shot and make an arrested carrier landing. With so many design compromises it can't possibly do any mission well.

A fucking flying Edsel, assuming that one way or the other it can be made to fly. He had used precisely those words this afternoon to that simple sonuvabitch from SECNAV and that slimy political hack looked like his wallet was being snatched. And what had he said to Vice Admiral Henry after the meeting? 'It's almost as if those idiots want to buy just one ultimate do-everything flying machine and park it in the Rose Garden of the White House to scare the shit out of the Russian ambassador when he comes to call.' Henry wasn't happy with his blunt assessment. Well, he was right, whether Henry liked it or not. Those political clowns want to build something straight out of a Hollywood special-effects shop, a suborbital battlestar that will automatically zap anybody who isn't wearing olive-drab underwear.

Why is it, over eighty-five years after Orville and Wilbur showed the world how to build an airplane, that we have to keep explaining the basic laws of aerodynamics to these used-car salesmen in mufti?

Strong was still stewing when he reached the outskirts of Winchester. Raindrops began to splatter on the windshield. He turned on the wipers. The road looked slick and the wet night seemed to soak up his headlights, so he slowed down.

He was hungry. He turned into the drive-through lane of a McDonald's and was soon back on the road mechanically munching a burger as he headed west. The coffee was hot and black.

Passing through Gore he noticed headlights behind him. Not too close, but glued there. How long had that guy been back there? A cop clocking him? Well, he wasn't speeding, not on a night like this.

The road was a twisty two-lane and empty. Almost no traffic. That was one of the charms of coming up here. The glare of his headlights illuminated the black trunks of wet, naked trees as he cranked the wheel back and forth around the switchbacks up the mountain. The sign at the top said: 'Welcome to Wild, Wonderful West Virginia.' And the radio reception would go on the other side of the sign! Sure enough, on the second curve down the music faded to static. He switched off the radio. The headlights were still in the rearview mirror.

At the foot of the mountain he went through the village of Capon Bridge. Almost there, just a few more miles. He checked the mirror as they went by a sodium light on a pole by the little Shell station, which was dark and deserted at this hour of the evening. It was some kind of pickup with a huge steel bumper welded to the front. Not too new. Mid-seventies maybe.

Impossible to make out the color. Then a camper passed him headed east and, curious, he glanced in the mirror again. The guy behind – blue, I think. Maybe blue.

Leaving the village the road began to climb and he was again in switchbacks at twenty-five miles per hour. The glare of the headlights from the pickup behind him swept across the mirror going into and coming out of every curve, and he squinted. He turned the mirror so the lights wouldn't blind him. Should've got the day-night mirror, he told himself, but he had saved twenty bucks passing on that option.

Above the noise of his engine he could hear the rhythmic slap-slap of the wipers and the protests of his tires on the wet macadam.

He was almost at the top of this low mountain. He would build a fire in the fireplace when he reached the cabin in a few minutes. Maybe a shot of Irish whiskey while the fire was driving out the chill. Tomorrow he would—

He could hear the engine of the pickup behind roaring and the headlights spotlighted his dash and windshield. He squinted. What was that damn fool doing? Did he want to pass? We're right at that over-look—

The truck behind smashed into his rear bumper and pushed him. Strong fought the wheel. His vehicle was accelerating. He applied the brakes. Wheel lock-up. He released the brakes and jammed the throttle down. He was trying to steer but the wheels wouldn't bite on the slick pavement. Goddamn – the car was going across the road, straight for the overlook pullout!

In the gravel the car skidded sideways and Strong glanced over his shoulder, straight into the pickup's headlights. Then he felt the lurch as the pickup slammed on its brakes.

Panicked, he looked forward but saw nothing, still blinded from the headlights' glare. He felt the car's nose go down, then it began to roll, over and over and over.

The motion stopped suddenly with a terrific, smashing impact.

When he came out of his daze he was in darkness and the engine was silent. There was a little light, but it seemed to come from above and behind, from the road. Jesus . . . Something black and wet beside him. A tree trunk, where the passenger seat used to be.

The car was half wrapped around a tree. He had gone down over the edge and rolled several times and smashed into a tree. That asshole in the pickup . . . trying to *kill* him.

He wasn't hurt too bad. Thank God for seat belts. Blood on his face, minute pieces of glass everywhere. He was still groggy. What's that smell? *Gasoline!* A leak. He fumbled for the seat-belt release.

Someone was beside him, reaching in through the smashed window. 'Hey—'

He was being splashed with something wet. 'What—' Gas! It was *gas*! 'Please, you gotta—'

Out of the corner of his eye he saw the lighted match come floating through the broken window. The roar of the gasoline igniting was the last sound he heard.

2

The airplanes were shiny and brilliant in their bright colors of red, yellow and blue. They hung in the window suspended on wires, frozen in flight, the spring sunlight firing the wings and fuselages and emphasizing the sleek perfection of their forms.

Jake Grafton stood on the sidewalk and stared. He examined each one carefully, letting his eyes roam from tail to prop to gull-like wingtip. After a moment he pushed the door open and went into the warm shop, out of the weak sunshine and the cool breeze coming off the ocean.

As he stood and gazed at another dozen or so planes hanging from the ceiling, the shop proprietor behind the glass counter laid aside his newspaper and cleared his throat. 'Good morning.'

'Hi.' Jake glanced at the man. He was balding and bearlike and perched on a stool. 'You've got some nice airplanes here.'

'Sure do. You have a son interested in radio control?'

Jake let his eyes find the swooping, soaring forms above his head. 'No,' he said thoughtfully. 'Just looking.'

The proprietor began turning the pages of his newspaper as Jake moved deeper into the shop. He wandered slowly, examining the counter displays, fingering balsa from a wire bin, scanning the rack of X-acto knives and miniature drills, looking at the rows and rows of boxes with airplanes and cars on the covers that stood on shelves behind the counter. Finally, back at the door, he muttered his thanks to the shopkeeper and went out onto the sidewalk.

The sea breeze was brisk this morning and tangy with salt. Not many people on the street. This Delaware beach town lived on tourists and summer was a long way off. At least the sun was out after a week of low, scuddy clouds and intermittent drizzle. Standing there, Jake could faintly hear the gulls crying as they soared above the beach and boardwalk a half block away. He looked again at the airplanes in the window, then went back into the shop.

'Sell me an airplane,' he said as the proprietor looked up from his newspaper.

'Delighted to. Which one you want?'

Jake scanned the planes hanging from the ceiling. He began to examine them critically.

'You ever build an RC plane before?'

'Build? You mean I can't buy one already made?'

'Not any of these, you can't. My son built all these years ago, before he went to the air force. They're his.'

'Build one,' Jake said softly, weighing it. He hadn't figured on that. Oh well, the decision was already made. Now he wanted a plane. 'Let me see what you have.'

Forty minutes later, with a yellow credit card invoice for $349.52 tucked into his wallet, Jake Grafton left the hobby store carrying two large sacks and walked the block to his car. He walked purposefully, quickly. For the first time in months he had a task ahead that would be worth doing.

Fifteen minutes later he parked the car in the sand-and-crushed-seashell parking area in front of his house. He could hear the faint ringing of the telephone as he climbed the steps to the little wooden porch. He unlocked the front door, sat one of the paper sacks on the floor and strode across the living room for the phone on the wall by the kitchen table. The ringing stopped just as he reached for the receiver. He went back to the car for the other sack.

The airplane on the lid of the box looked gorgeous, mouth-wateringly gorgeous, but inside the box was sheet after sheet of raw balsa wood. At least the aircraft parts were impressed, stamped, into the wood. All you would have to do was pick them out and maybe trim the pieces. The instruction booklet looked devilishly complicated, with photos and line drawings. Jake studied the pictures. After a bit he began laying out the balsa pieces from the box on the kitchen table, referring frequently to the pictures in the booklet. When the box was empty he surveyed the mess and rubbed his temples. This was going to be a big job, even bigger than he thought.

He put coffee and water in the brewer and was waiting for the Pyrex pot to fill when the phone rang again. 'Hello.'

'Jake. How are you feeling this morning?' Callie, his wife, called twice a day to check on him, even though she knew it irritated him.

'Fine. How's your morning going?'

'Did you go out?'

'Downtown.'

'Jake,' she said, tension creeping into her voice as she pronounced his name firmly. 'We need to talk. When are you going to call that admiral?'

'I dunno.'

'You can't keep loafing like this. You're well. You're going to have to go back to work, or retire and find something to do. You can't just keep loafing like this. It isn't you. It isn't good for you, Jake.'

She emphasized the word 'good,' Jake noticed listlessly. That's Callie, instinctively dividing the world into good and evil. 'We'll talk about it this weekend.' She was driving over from Washington when she got off work this evening. Jake had driven over to the beach house two days ago.

'That's what you said last weekend, and Monday and Tuesday evenings. And then you avoid the subject.' Her voice was firm. 'The only way I can get your undivided attention is to call you on the phone. So that's what I'm doing. When, Jake?'

'This weekend. We'll discuss it this weekend. I promise.'

They muttered their goodbyes. Jake poured a cup of coffee and sipped it as he sorted through the piles of balsa again. What had he gotten himself into?

Coffee cup in hand, he went through the front door and walked past the car to the street. He turned toward the beach, which was about a hundred yards away. The house beside his was empty, a summer place that belonged to some doctor in Baltimore. The next house belonged to a local, a pharmacist whose wife worked nights down at the drugstore. He had seen their son on the beach flying a radio-controlled airplane, and didn't Callie say this week was spring break for the kids? He went to the door and knocked.

'Captain Grafton. What a pleasant surprise.'

'Hi, Mrs Brown. Is David around?'

'Sure.' She turned away. 'David,' she called, 'you have a visitor.' She turned back toward him, 'Won't you come in?'

The boy appeared behind her. 'Hey, David,' Jake said. He explained his errand. 'I need some of your expert advice, if you can come over for a little while.'

Mrs Brown nodded her approval and told her son to be back for lunch.

As they walked down the street, Jake explained about the plane. The boy smiled broadly when he saw the pile on Jake's kitchen table. 'The Gentle Lady,' David read from the cover of the instruction booklet. 'That's an excellent airplane for a beginner. Easy to build and fly. You chose a good one, Captain.'

'Yeah, but I can't tell which parts are which. They aren't labeled, as far as I can tell.'

'Hmmm.' David sat at the table and examined the pile. He was about twelve, still elbows and angles, with medium-length brown hair full of cowlicks. His fingers moved swiftly and surely among the parts, identifying each one. 'Did you get an engine for this plane?'

'Nope.'

'A glider is more difficult to fly, of course, more challenging, but you'll get more satisfaction from mastering it.'

'Right,' Jake said, eyeing the youngster at the table.

'Let's see. You have a knife, and the man at the store – Mr Swoze, right?

– recommended you buy these pins to hold the parts in place while you glue them. This is a good glue, cyanoacrylate. You're all set, except for a board to spread the diagram on and pin the parts to, and a drill.'

'What kind of board?'

'Oh, I'll loan you one. I've built three airplanes on mine. You spread the diagram on it and position the parts over the diagram, then pin them right to the board. And I'll loan you my drill if you don't have one.' Jake nodded. The youngster continued, his fingers still moving restlessly through the parts, 'The most important aspect of assembling this aircraft is getting the same dihedral and washout on the right and left wing components, both inner and outer panels. Be very careful and work slowly.'

'Okay.'

'I'll run home and get my board and drill. You won't need the drill for several days, but I might as well bring it over.' He bolted the door, leaving Jake to refill his coffee cup and stare at the actual-size diagram.

The house was quiet, with only the background murmur of the surf on the beach and the occasional burble of a passing car to break the solitude. The task assumed a life of its own; breaking the pieces out of the balsa boards, assembling them on the diagram, occasionally sanding or trimming with the razor-sharp hobby knife before pinning them into place. As he worked he occasionally glanced at the picture on the box, visualizing how the airplane would look soaring back and forth above the sand, trying to imagine how it would feel to fly it. This would be real flying, he knew. Even though his feet would not leave the ground, the plane would by flying free, and since he would be flying it, so would he. He carefully glued the rudder and vertical stabilizer parts together and began assembling the horizontal stabilizer.

The knock on the door startled him. He had been so intent on his task he had paid no attention to the sound of the car driving up. 'Yeah. Come on in.'

He heard the door open. 'Captain Grafton.'

'Yep.' Jake looked up.

The man standing there was in his late twenties, slightly above medium height, with short brown hair. 'Toad Tarkington! Come on in! What a surprise!'

The man's face split in a wide grin and he crossed the room and pumped Jake's hand. 'It's great to see you again. CAG. I thought for a while there you were dead.'

Grafton nodded and studied Lieutenant Toad Tarkington, today clad in jeans and rugby shirt and wind-breaker. He looked . . . just the same as he did the morning they went after Colonel Qazi in an F-14 five months ago. Last September. And here he was with that grin . . . quick, energetic, nervous. He was ready to laugh or fly, ready for a prank in the ready room or a night cat shot, fully alive. That's what Toad Tarkington projected – vibrant, energetic, enthusiastic life.

'I'm not a CAG now, Toad. I'm just a plain ol' sick-leave captain.' CAG was the title bestowed on an air wing commander, and was pronounced to rhyme with 'rag.'

Toad grabbed his hand and held it, that grin splitting his face. 'Have we got a lot to talk about! I tried to call you, sir, but your phone wasn't listed.'

'Yeah. Had to have the number changed. The reporters were driving me nuts.'

Toad pulled one of the kitchen chairs around and sat down. 'I was pretty damn happy last fall when I heard you were alive. What happened to you anyway, after we rammed that transport?'

'Some Greek fishermen pulled me out of the water. I don't remember a thing. Had a concussion. Lucky for me the life vests inflate automatically nowadays. Anyway, they pulled me out and I made it.'

'How come they didn't radio someone or head for port?'

'Their radio was broken and they were there to fish.' Jake looked away from Toad. He was back among the ordinary, everyday things. For a moment there . . . but he was *here*, at the beach house. 'They thought I was gonna die on them any minute and they needed the fish. I was in a coma.' His shoulders moved up and down. 'Too damned many Gs. Messed up my eyes. That's why I wear these glasses now.'

Jake removed the glasses and examined the lenses, as if seeing them for the first time. 'It's 20/100 now. It was 20/500. The Gs almost ripped my eyeballs out.' He placed the glasses back on the bridge of his nose and stared at the pieces of balsa on the kitchen table. 'I don't remember much about it. The docs say some blood vessels popped in the front part of my brain and I had some memory loss.'

'By God, sir, I sure as hell can fill you in.' Toad leaned forward and seized his arm. Jake refocused on that excited, expressive face. 'The Gs were something else and I couldn't get to the ejection handles, and I guess you couldn't either. Man, our bacon was well and truly fried when she broke up and spit us out. The left wing was gone and I figure most of the left vertical stab, because we were getting pushed around screwy. I—' He continued his tale, his hands automatically moving to show the plane's position in space. Jake stopped listening to the voice and watched the hands, those practiced, expressive hands.

Tarkington – he was the past turned into a living, breathing person. He was every youngster Jake had shared a ready room with for the past twenty years, all those guys now middle-aged . . . or dead.

Toad was still talking when Jake turned back to the pile of balsa on the table. When he eventually paused for air, Jake said mildly, 'So what are you up to these days?' as he used the X-acto knife to trim a protruding sliver from a balsa rib piece.

'My squadron tour was up,' Toad said slowly. 'And when you get a Silver Star you can pretty well call your next set of orders. So I talked it over with the detailer.' He looked around the room, then swivelled back to Jake. 'And I told him I wanted to go where you were going.'

Jake laid the knife down and scooted his chair back. 'I'm still on convalescent leave.'

'Yessir. I heard. And I hear you're going to the Pentagon as a division director or something. So I'm reporting there this coming Monday. I'll be working for you.'

Jake smiled again. 'I seem to recall you had had enough of this warrior shit.'

'Yeah. Well, what the hell! I decided to stay around for another set of orders. I can always pull the plug. And I've got nothing better to do right now anyway.'

Jake snorted and rubbed his fingertips together. The glue had coated his fingertips and wouldn't come off. 'I don't either. So we'll go shuffle paper for a while, eh?'

'Yessir,' Toad said, and stood. 'Maybe we won't get underway, but we'll still be in the navy. That's something, isn't it?' He stuck out his hand again, like a cowboy drawing a pistol. 'I'll be seeing you in the office, when you get there,' he said as Jake pumped the outstretched hand. 'Say hello to Mrs Grafton for me.'

Jake accompanied Toad to the door, then out onto the porch. There was a young woman in the car, and she looked at him curiously. He nodded at her, then put a hand on Toad's shoulder and squared around to face him. 'Take care of yourself, y'hear?'

'Sure, CAG. Sure.'

'Thanks for coming by.'

As Toad drove away Jake waved, then went back into the house. The place was depressing. It was as if Tarkington brought all the life and energy with him, then took it away when he left. But he was of Jake's past. Everything was past. The flying, the ready rooms, the sun on the sea as you manned up to fly, all of it was over, gone, finished.

It was after four o'clock. He had forgotten to eat lunch. Oh well, Callie wasn't going to get here until nine o'clock or so. The Chesapeake Bay Bridge shouldn't be crowded on Friday evenings this time of year. He could get some more of this plane assembled, then fix a sandwich or something. Maybe run over to Burger King.

He scratched at the glue caked on his fingertips. The stuff came off in flakes if you peeled it right. This plane – it was going to be a nice one. It was going to be good to fly it. When flying was all you knew and all you had been, you needed a plane around.

Oh, shit! As he looked at the pieces he felt like a fool. A fucking toy plane! He threw himself on the couch and lay there staring at the ceiling.

Toad Tarkington was silent as he drove from stoplight to stoplight on the main highway through Rehoboth Beach. The woman beside him finally asked, 'So how is he?'

'He's changed,' Toad said. 'The official report said he was in a coma for two weeks. It was a week before that Greek fishing boat even made port. It's a miracle he didn't die on the boat. He said the fishermen expected him to and kept fishing.'

'I would have liked to meet him.'

'Well, I was going to mention you were in the car, but he was busy working on a model airplane and he was . . . Anyway, you can always meet him later.'

The woman reached for the knob to turn the stereo on, then thought better of it. 'This new assignment – asking for it just because you like him . . .'

'It's not that I like him,' Toad said. 'I respect him. He's . . . different. There aren't many men like him left in this day and age. If Congress hadn't jumped into that incident with both feet and voted him the Medal of Honor, he would probably have been forced to retire. Maybe even a court-martial.' Toad smacked the steering wheel in his hand. 'He's a national hero and he doesn't give a damn. I've never met anyone like him before.' He thought about it. 'Maybe there aren't any more like him.'

The woman reached for the knobs again and turned the stereo on. She had known Toad Tarkington for three weeks and she was still trying to figure him out. He was the first military man she had dated and he was modestly famous after the attack last fall on *United States*. Her friends thought it was so exciting. Still, he was a little weird. Oh well, he made a decent salary and bathed and shaved and looked marvelous at parties. And he was a fine lover. A girl could do a lot worse.

'Where do you want to eat tonight?' she asked.

It was dark and spattering rain when Jake heard Callie's car pull in. He had completed assembly of the vertical and horizontal stabilizers, and rudder, and the wings, and had placed them on top of the bookcase and credenza to cure and was cleaning up the mess on the kitchen table. He raked the rest of it into the box the airplane had come in and slid the box up on top of the kitchen cabinets, then went outside to meet her. She was opening the trunk of her car.

'Hey, good-looking. Welcome home.' He pecked her cheek and lifted her overnight bag out of the trunk.

'Hello.' She followed him into the house, hugging herself against the evening chill. He closed the door behind her and climbed the stairs toward the bedrooms. 'What's this?' Callie called.

'I'm building an airplane,' he boomed as he dropped the bag on the bed. When he reached the foot of the stairs she was examining the wing structure without touching it. 'It's dry enough to pick up. How about coffee?'

'Sure.' Callie walked slowly around the living/dining area, her purse still over her shoulder, looking. She opened the door to the screened-in porch and was shivering in the wind, looking at the wicker furniture, when he handed her the coffee cup. 'This stuff needs to be painted again.' She slid the door closed and leaned back against it as she sipped the hot liquid.

'What kind of week did you have?'

'So-so.' She was halfway through her first semester as a language instructor at Georgetown University. 'They asked me to teach this summer.'

'What did you say?'

'That I'd think about it.' She had been planning on spending the summer here at the beach. Kicking her pumps off, she sat on the sofa with her legs under her. 'It all depends.'

Jake poured himself coffee and sat down at the kitchen table where he could face her.

'I went to see Dr Arnold this afternoon.'

'Uh-huh.' Jake refused to go back to the psychologist.

'He says if you don't get your act together I should leave you.'

'Just what does the soul slicer think my act is?'

'Oh, cut the crap, Jake.' She averted her face. She finished her coffee in silence, then rinsed the cup in the sink. Retrieving her shoes, she went upstairs.

The sound of water running in the shower was audible all over the downstairs. Jake spread the airplane diagram on the table and opened the instruction manual. Finally he threw the manual down in disgust.

He needed a drink. The doctors had told him not to, but fuck them. He rummaged under the sink and found that old bottle of bourbon with several inches of liquid remaining. He poured some in a glass and added ice.

The problem was that he didn't want to do anything. He didn't want to retire and sit here and vegetate or find a civilian job. He didn't want to go to the Pentagon and immerse himself in the bureaucracy. The Pentagon job had been the only one offered him when he was finally ready to be discharged from Bethesda Naval Hospital. The politicians had made him a hero and checkmated the naval establishment, but the powers that be had still been smarting from the way the official investigation had been derailed. Luckily he had been damn near comatose in the hospital and everyone in uniform knew he had nothing to do with the political maneuvering. So he was still in the navy. But his shot at flag rank had vaporized like a drop of water on a hot stove. Not that he really ever hoped to make admiral or even cared.

He lay down on the couch and sipped at the drink. Maybe the whole problem was that he just didn't care about any of it anymore. Let the other guys do the sweating. Let them dance on the tightrope. Let someone else pick up the bodies of those who fell. He put the glass on the floor and rolled over on his side. Maybe he was depressed – that soul doctor . . . Yes, depression, that was probably . . .

When he awoke it was two in the morning and the lights were off. Callie had covered him with a blanket. He went upstairs, undressed, and crawled into bed with her.

The wind whipped the occasional raindrops at a steep angle and drove the gray clouds at a furious pace as Jake and Callie strolled the beach. They were out for their usual morning walk, which they took rain or shine, fair weather or foul. Both wore shorts and were barefoot; they carried the flip-flops they had worn to traverse the crushed-seashell mix that covered the street in front of their house that led to the beach. Both were wearing old sweatshirts over sweaters. Callie's hair whipped in the wind.

Jake critically examined the contours of sand around the piles that supported a huge house some ignorant optimist had constructed on the dune facing the beach. The first hurricane, Jake suspected, would have the owner tearing his hair. The sand looked firm now. Shades obscured all the windows. The house was empty. Only three or four other people were visible on the beach.

Birds scurried along the sand, racing after retreating waves and probing furiously for their breakfast. Gulls rode the air currents with their noses pointed out to sea. He watched the gulls and tried to decide if the Gentle Lady could soar with them. The moving air had to have some kind of an upward vector over the sand. Perhaps if he kept the plane above the dune. The dune was low, though. He would see.

Callie's hand found his and he gave it a squeeze. He led her down into the surf, where the ice-cold water swirled about their feet. 'Toad Tarkington said to say hi.'

'He called?'

'Stopped by yesterday afternoon. He's going to the Pentagon too.'

'Oh.'

'If you teach summer school, we'll see more of each other this summer,' he said. 'We'll be together every evening at the apartment in Washington as well as every weekend here.'

Her hand gripped his fiercely and she turned to face him.

He grinned. 'Monday morning, off I go, wearing my uniform, vacation over—'

She hugged him and her lips made it impossible to continue to speak. Her hair played across his cheeks as the ebbing surf tugged at the sand under him.

3

It was almost 9 A.M. when the subway train – the Metro – ground to a halt at the Pentagon station. Jake Grafton joined the civilian and military personnel exiting and followed the thin crowd along the platform. Rush hour for the 23,000 people who worked in this sprawling five-story building was long over. The little handful that Jake accompanied seemed to be made up of stragglers and visiting civilians.

Just ahead of Jake a man and a woman in casual clothes led two small children. When they came to the long escalator, the kids squealed joyfully and started to run up the moving stair. Each parent grabbed a small arm, then a hand.

The sloping staircase was poorly lighted. As he looked at the dim lights, Jake noticed the plaster on the ceiling was peeling away in spots.

At the head of the escalator two corridors led in, one from either side, and more people joined the procession, which trudged ever upward on a long, wide staircase toward the lights above.

At the head of the stair was a large hall, and the stream of people broke up, some heading for the main entrance, some moving cautiously toward the visitor's tour area. The couple that Jake had followed led their progeny in that direction with an admonition to behave. Jake approached the two Department of Defense policemen scrutinizing passes at the security booth. 'I have an appointment with Vice Admiral Henry.'

'Do you have a building pass, sir?'

'No.'

'Use those phones right over there' – he pointed at telephones by the tour windows – 'and someone will come down to escort you.'

'Thanks.' Jake called and a yeoman answered. Five minutes, the yeoman said.

Jake stood and watched the people. Men and women wearing the uniforms of all four services came and went, most walking quickly, carrying briefcases, folders, gym bags and small brown paper bags that must have contained their lunches. People leaving the interior of the building walked by the security desk without a glance from the two armed DOD policemen.

'Captain Grafton?'

A small black woman in civilian clothes stood at his elbow. 'Yes?' he said.

'I'm your escort.' She smiled and flashed her pass at the guards and motioned Jake toward the metal detector that stood to the left of the security booth. He walked through it, nothing beeped, and the woman led him through the open doors into another huge hallway, this one lined with shops. Directly across from the entrance was a large gedunk – a store selling snacks, magazines and other sundries.

'I was expecting a yeoman.'

'The phone started ringing and he sent me down.'

As she led him along the corridor, he asked, 'How long did it take you to learn your way around in here?'

'Oh, I'm still learning. I've only been here five years. It's confusing at times.'

They went up a long ramp that opened onto the A-Ring, the central corridor that overlooked the five-acre interior courtyard. As they proceeded around the ring, Jake glanced through the windows at the grass and huge trees and the snack bar in the center.

'Have you ever been here before?' she asked.

'Nope,' said Jake Grafton. 'I've always managed to avoid it.'

After she had gone what seemed like a hundred yards or so, she turned right and ascended a staircase with a ninety-degree bend in it and at the top turned right. They were still on the A-Ring, but on the fourth level. After another fifty feet she veered left down a corridor, then right onto another corridor that zagged away at an angle. 'Now we're walking back toward the outside of the building,' she said. 'There are five concentric rings in the Pentagon. The inner is the A-Ring, and next is B, and so forth, with the outer being E. They are connected by ten radial corridors like the spokes of a wagon wheel. It's supposed to be efficient but it does confuse newcomers.' She grinned.

This corridor had little to commend it. It was lit by fluorescent lights, and over half the tubes were dark. The walls were bare. Not a picture or a poster. Dusty, tied-down furniture was stacked along one wall. It looked as if it had been there since the Eisenhower administration. Catching Jake's glance, the guide said, 'It's been there for three months. Some of the offices got new furniture. This is the old stuff.' The piles were composed of sofas and chairs and scarred and battered gunmetal-gray desks. 'These places on the ceiling where the plywood is?' Jake looked. 'The plaster was falling off from water seepage from the roof and asbestos was being released.'

At the end of the corridor stood a magnificent large painting of Admiral Dewey's flagship, *Olympia*, entering Manila Bay. Spots illuminated it. The guide turned right and Jake followed. The overhead blue mantel proclaimed: 'Naval Aviation.' Here the hallway was well lit, painted a yellowish pastel and decorated with pictures of past and present naval and marine aircraft. This straight stretch was long, a third as long as the outside of the building. Almost at the end, his guide turned left into a large office. The sign over the door said: 'Assistant, Chief of Naval Operations, Air Warfare.' Beside the door was a blue sign that read: 'OP-05.' This was the office of the senior U.S. Naval Aviator, Mr Naval Aviation.

The room was large and contained numerous windows facing south across the huge parking lot toward Arlington. Wooden desks, blue drapes, wainscoting on the walls.

A commander greeted Jake. 'I'm a little early,' Jake said, glancing at his watch.

'I'll see if the admiral's free.' He was. Jake was escorted in through a swinging double saloon door.

Vice Admiral Tyler Henry rose from his chair and came around his desk wearing a warm smile to greet Jake.

'Good to see you again, Captain.' The men had met on several occasions in the past, but Jake was unsure if Henry would remember. After he pumped Jake's hand the admiral motioned to a chair. 'Please, be seated. Have any trouble getting here this morning?'

'I rode the Metro this morning, sir,' Jake said as the admiral seated himself behind his desk. It was dark wood, perhaps mahogany. A matching table extended outward from the main desk, forming the leg of a T. It was at this table Jake sat.

'Good idea. Parking places are all for car pools and flag officers.' He pushed the button on his intercom box. 'Chief, did Commander Gadd sweep the office this morning?'

'Yessir,' was the tinny reply.

'Are the window buzzers on?'

'Yessir.'

'Please close my door . . . Window buzzers are little security gizmos to vibrate the glass. Supposed to foil parabolic mikes, but who knows?' the admiral explained. 'The damn things play waiting room music, and I can't hear noises like that anymore.' Jake listened hard. He could just hear the beat and a trumpet.

The admiral leaned back comfortably in his chair as the door to the office closed behind Jake. 'Soundproof,' he muttered, then smiled. 'You look surprised.'

Jake smiled, his embarrassment showing. 'Seems like a lot of trouble to go to just to talk to the guy who's going to be designing the new officer fitness report form.'

The admiral smiled broadly. 'That job has been floating around with no takers. No, we have another project for you that is going to demand expertise of a different sort.'

Jake was having trouble holding his eyebrows still. 'I thought,' he said softly, 'that I was a pariah around here.'

The smile disappeared from Admiral Henry's face. 'I'm not going to bullshit you, Captain. Last fall when you disobeyed a direct order from a vice admiral, you may have torpedoed any chance you had of ever getting promoted again. Now with hindsight and all, most people can see you did the right thing. But the military won't work if people go around telling flag officers to get fucked. For any reason, justified or not. And the congressmen and politicos from SECDEF's office who interfered with a navy investigation of that incident made you no friends.'

He raised his hand when Jake opened his mouth to speak. 'I know, I know, you had nothing whatever to do with that and you couldn't control the politicians even if you tried. No one can. They go any damn place they want with hobnail boots. Still, they raised hackles when they implied the navy couldn't or wouldn't be fair in its treatment of a naval officer.'

'I understand.'

The admiral nodded. 'I suspect you do. Your record says you're one of our best, which is why I asked for you. We need a shit-hot attack pilot with a ton of smarts and a gilt-edge reputation who can waltz a little project through the minefields. You're him.'

Jake flexed his hands and rearranged his bottom in his chair. 'I didn't think my reputation was quite that shiny. And I've never had any Pentagon duty before.'

Henry pretended not to have heard. 'Do you want to hear about the job?'

'I'm just a little surprised, sir. Shocked might be a better word. I'd thought . . .' He punched the air. 'What's the job?'

'You'll be working for Vice Admiral Roger Dunedin. He's NAVAIR.' NAVAIR was Naval Air Systems Command, the procurement arm of naval aviation. 'He needs a new program manager for the Advanced Tactical Aircraft, also known as the ATA. If and when we get it, it'll be the A-12.'

Jake Grafton couldn't suppress a grin.

The admiral laughed. 'The fact we have this project is unclassified. ATA, A-12, those are the only two things unclass in the whole program, and those two terms were just recently declassified. The project is black.' Jake had heard about 'black' programs, so highly classified that even the existence of the program was sometimes a secret.

The admiral rapped a knuckle on the desk. 'So far, it *appears* to be one of our best-kept military secrets.' His voice fell to a murmur. 'No way of being sure, of course.'

Henry fixed his eyes on Jake. 'The A-12 is our follow-on airplane for the A-6.' The A-6 Intruder was the aircraft carriers' main offensive weapon, an all-weather medium attack plane.

'But I thought the A-6 was going to remain in the inventory into the next century. That was the justification for the A-6G project – new graphite-composite wings and updated avionics.'

'The A-6 had to have the new wings just to stay in the air, and the A-6G avionics are going into the A-12. We were trying the new gee-whiz gizmos out in the A-6G, until they canceled it.' The A-6G had died under the budget cutters' knives. Henry smiled wickedly. 'The A-12 will have something even better. Athena. Do you know Greek mythology?'

'A smattering. Wasn't Athena the goddess of war, the protector of warriors?'

'Yep, and she had a quality that we are going to give to our new plane.' He paused and raised one finger aloft. When he grinned like that his eyebrows matched the curve of his lips. 'She could make herself invisible.'

Jake just stared.

'Stealth technology. The air force built a land-based fighter: that's first-generation stealth technology. Then came new paint and radar-absorbent materials and the flying-wing shape – that's second-generation.' His voice dropped conspiratorially. 'We're building an all-weather, go-anywhere anytime carrier-based attack plane that will equal or exceed the A-6 in range, speed and payload, and carry advanced sensors that will make the A-6 look blind as a cornfield scarecrow. These sensors – anyway, they're a whole new generation beyond the A-6. *And* the A-12 will have third-generation stealth technology – Athena – which will make it truly invisible to radar. A stealth Super-Intruder, if you will. That's the A-12.' Henry's eyebrows danced.

'And that, my friend, is the secret.'

The admiral smacked his hand on the desk. The gold rings encircling his sleeve attracted Jake's eye. 'The Russians don't know about it. Yet. If we can get this thing to sea before they steal the technology and figure out how to counter it, we've pretty well guaranteed that there won't be a conventional war with the Soviets for at least the next ten years. Their ships would be defenceless against a stealth Intruder.'

Admiral Henry sighed. 'We're trying to build one of these things, anyway. You're replacing Captain Harold Strong, who was killed in a car wreck a month ago. We had to wait to get you, but now, by God, your ass is ours.'

Jake Grafton sat stunned. 'But how – all the weapons will have to be carried externally and they'll reflect energy – how will you get around that?'

The corners of Henry's lips turned up until his mouth formed a V and his eyebrows danced. 'You're going to enjoy this job, Captain.'

'A real job,' Jake said, his relief obvious. 'And I thought I was just going to be designing fitness report forms.'

'Oh,' Henry boomed. 'If you want you can work on that in your spare time. Don't know when you'd sleep, though.' He turned serious. 'Things are really starting to move. We've got two prototypes about ready to fly – constructed by two different manufacturers – and we must get them evaluated and award the production contract. We've got to quit noodling and get this show on the road. We need airplanes. That's why you're here.'

After a glance at his watch, Henry reached for his intercom. His hand hovered near it. 'Start checking in,' he said hurriedly. 'Go get your paperwork done. They've got some orders for you someplace; you'll have to find them. Maybe at NAVAIR, which is over at Crystal City. Then you might go around the corner and introduce yourself to the project coordinator, Commander Rob Knight. He's here today, I think. I'll see you at nine tomorrow morning. And then I want to hear all about the attack on *United States* and how you started El Hakim on the road to Paradise.'

He keyed the intercom and started talking as he shooed Jake out with his left hand. Jake didn't even get a chance to say thanks.

Crystal City, Jake was informed by Henry's aide, was across the Pentagon's south parking lot, on the other side of the highway, southeast of the Pentagon. NAVAIR was in buildings JP-1 and JP-2, in the northern portion of the Crystal City office complex. He wandered out into the corridors and walked along slightly dazed. A real job! A *big* job!

Although the aide had suggested the shuttle bus, Jake decided to walk. After asking an air force officer in the parking lot which set of tall buildings was which and getting a careful sighting across a pointing finger, Jake began walking. The wind was chilly, but not intolerably so. Under I-395, across a four-lane boulevard dodging traffic, under US Route 1, the hike took about ten minutes. He accosted a pedestrian and building Jefferson Plaza 1 was pointed out. In he went, punched the elevator button and after waiting what seemed to be an inordinately long time, rode to the twelfth floor, the top one.

They did have a set of orders. It took the civilian secretary five minutes to find them, and in the interim Jake visited with three officers he knew from his shipboard days. With the orders in his hand, the secretary called a yeoman, who put the captain to work filling out forms.

Jake was eating lunch in Gus's Place, a commercial cafeteria on the ground floor of the complex, when Toad Tarkington spotted him. Toad came over, tray in hand. 'Saw you sitting over here by yourself, CAG. May I join you?'

Jake moved his tray and Toad off-loaded his food onto the table. A group of junior officers twenty feet away began to whisper and glance in their direction.

'How has your morning gone?'

'Same old stuff,' Toad announced as he placed his large brown manila envelope full of orders and forms on his chair and carefully sat on it. 'Got my picture taken for my permanent building pass, which I'm supposed to pick up this afternoon. I must have signed my name fifty times this morning. Every naval activity between here and Diego Garcia will soon receive notification in triplicate that I can be found sitting on the bull's-eye at this critical nerve center of the nation's defenses ready to save the free world from the forces of evil.' Toad made a gesture of modesty and slowly unfolded his napkin.

'I hear we're going to be putting that new officer fitness report form together, though just why the heck they got the two greatest aerial warriors of the age over here at NAVAIR to do that sort of beats me. Ours not to reason why . . .' He glanced at Jake to get his reaction as he smoothed the napkin on his lap.

Grafton sipped his coffee, then took another bite of tuna salad.

'But what the hey,' Toad continued cheerfully. 'Flying, walking, or sitting on my ass, they pay me just the same. Do you know there are 3.4 women in Washington for every man? This is *the* place. Bachelor city. Sodom on the Potomac. A sturdy young lad ought to be able to do pretty well with all these lonely females seeking to satisfy their social and sexual needs. Mr Accommodation, that's me. I figure with my salary—'

'The sexual revolution is over,' Jake muttered as he forked more tuna salad. 'You missed it.'

'I'm carrying on a guerrilla campaign, sir. Indomitable and unconquerable, that's the ol' Horny Toad, even in the age of latex. I just dress up like the Michelin man and go for it. A fellow could always spring a leak, I guess, but the bee must go from flower to flower. That's the natural order of things.' He chewed thoughtfully. 'Have you noticed how those people over there keep sneaking looks at us?'

'Yeah.' Jake didn't look around. Although the room was filled with civilians and uniformed men and women eating and carrying trays and visiting over coffee, the four junior officers two tables away had been glancing over and speaking softly since Jake sat down.

'It's been like that all day with me,' Toad said with a hint of despair in his voice, then sent another mouthful of food down behind his belt buckle. 'At first I thought I had forgotten my pants, but now I think it's the hero bit. Asked two admirers for dates this morning and got two yeses. Not bad for a Monday.'

'It'll pass. Next week you'll have to spell your name twice just to get into the men's head. How's your leg?'

'Got a couple girders in it, sir. One of them is a metal rod about a foot long. But I passed my flight physical. Those Israeli doctors did a good job. Aches some occasionally.'

'We were damned lucky.'

'That's an understatement,' Toad said, and proceeded to fill Jake in on how he had spent the last five months.

After lunch Jake hiked back across the streets and parking lots to the Pentagon. His temporary pass so excited the security cop that he nodded his head a quarter inch as Jake walked by.

Commander Rob Knight was several years younger than Jake and had more hair, although it was salt-and-pepper. He wore steel-rimmed glasses and beamed when Jake introduced himself.

'Heard about your little adventure in the Med last year, Captain. It's been pretty dull without El Hakim to kick around.' Knight grinned easily. He had an air of quiet confidence that Jake found reassuring. Like all career officers getting acquainted, Knight and Jake told each other in broad terms of their past tours. Knight had spent most of his operational career in A-6 outfits, and had been ordered to this billet after a tour as commanding officer of an A-6 squadron.

'I came by to find out everything you know about the A-12,' Jake said lightly.

Knight chuckled. 'A real kidder, you are. I've been soaking up info for a year and a half and I haven't even scratched the surface. And you see I'm only one guy. The A-6 coordinator sits here beside me, and on the other side of the room we have the F-14 and F/A-18 guys. One for each airplane. We don't have a secretary or a yeoman. We do our own mail. We make our own coffee. I spend about a third of my time in this office, which is where I do the unclass stuff and confidential. Another third of my time is spent upstairs in the vault working on classified stuff. I have a desk up there with another computer and safes. The rest of my time is spent over at NAVAIR, in your shop, trying to see what you guys are up to.'

'Just one guy.' Jake was disappointed, and it showed. He felt a little like the kid who met Santa for the first time and found he was old and fat and smelled of reindeer shit. 'One guy! Just exactly what is your job?'

'I'm the man with the money. I get it from Rear Admiral Costello. He's the Aviation Plans and Programs honcho. He tells me what we want the plane to do. We draw up the requirements. You build the plane we say we want, you sell it to me, and I write the checks. That's it in a nutshell.'

'Sounds simple enough.'

'Simple as brain surgery. There's an auditor that comes around from time to time, and he's going to cuff me and take me away one of these days. I can see it in his eyes.'

They talked for an hour, or rather Knight talked and Jake listened, with his hands on his thighs. Knight had a habit of tapping aimlessly on the computer terminal on his desk, striking keys at random. When Jake wasn't looking at Knight he was looking at the *Sports Illustrated* swimsuit girl over Knight's desk (April 1988 was a *very* good month), or the three airplane pictures, or the Farrah Fawcett pinup over the A-6 guru's desk. Between the two desks sat a filing cabinet with combination locks on every drawer. Similar cabinets filled the room. Twice Knight rooted through an open cabinet drawer and handed Jake classified memos to read, but not to keep. Each was replaced in its proper file as soon as Jake handed it back.

Then Knight took Jake up a floor to the vault, where he signed a special form acknowledging the security regulations associated with black programs. In this chamber, surrounded by safes and locks and steel doors, Commander Knight briefed him on the technical details of the prototypes, the program schedules and so on.

At three o'clock Jake was back on the twelfth floor of the Crystal City complex to meet with Vice Admiral Dunedin. His office was not quite as plush as Henry's but it was every bit as large. Out the large windows airliners were landing and taking off from National airport.

'Do you have any idea what you're getting into?' Dunedin asked. He was soft-spoken, with short gray hair and workman's hands, thick, strong fingers that even now showed traces of oil and grease. Jake remembered hearing that his hobby was restoring old cars.

'In a vague, hazy way.'

'Normally we assign Aeronautical Engineering Duty Officers, AEDOs, to be program managers. By definition, an AEDO's speciality is the procurement business. Harold Strong was an AEDO. But, considering the status of the A-12, we figured that we needed a war fighter with credibility on the Hill.' The Hill, Jake knew, was Capitol Hill, Congress. But who, he wondered, were the 'we' of whom the admiral spoke? 'You're our warrior. There's not enough time to send you to the five-month program manager school, so we've waived it. You're going to have to hit the ground running. Your deputy is GS-15 civilian, Dr Helmut Fritsche. He's only been here three years or so but he knows the ropes. And you've got some AEDOs, on your staff. Use them, but remember, you're in charge.'   .

'I won't forget,' Jake Grafton said.

Dunedin's secretary, Mrs Forsythe, gave him a list of the officers who would be under his supervision. She was a warm, motherly lady with silver-gray hair and pictures of children on her desk. Jake asked. Her grandchildren. She offered him a brownie she had baked last night, which he accepted and munched with approving comments while she placed a call to the Personnel Support Detachment. She gave him detailed directions on how to find PSD, which was, she explained, six buildings south. When Jake arrived fifteen minutes later a secretary was busy pulling the service records for him to examine.

He found an empty desk and settled in.

The civilian files stood out from the others. Helmut Fritsche, PhD in electrical engineering, formerly professor at Caltech, before that on the research staff of NASA. Publications: wow! thirty or forty scientific papers. Jake ran his eye down the list. All were about radar: wave propagation, Doppler effect, numerical determination of three-dimensional electromagnetic scattering, and so on.

George Wilson was a professor of aeronautical engineering at MIT on a one-year sabbatical. He had apparently been recruited by Admiral Henry and came aboard the first of the year. He would be leaving at the end of December. Like Fritsche's, Wilson's list of professional publications was long and complicated. He had co-authored at least one text book, but the title that caught Jake's eye was an article for a scientific journal: 'Aerodynamic Challenges in Low Radar Cross Section Platforms.'

Jake laid the civilians' file aside and began to flip through the naval officers'. Halfway through he found one that he slowed down to examine with care. Lieutenant Rita Moravia, Naval Academy Class of '82. Second in her class at the Academy, first in her class in flight school and winner of an outstanding achievement award. Went through A-7 training, then transferred to F/A-18s, where she became an instructor pilot in the West Coast replacement squadron. Next came a year at the Naval Postgraduate School in Monterey, California, for a master's in aeronautical engineering, and another year at Test Pilot School at NAS Patuxent River, Maryland, where she graduated first in her class.

There were three line commanders: an A-6 bombardier-navigator, an F-14 pilot and an EA-6B Electronic Countermeasures Officer – ECMO. Jake knew the A-6 BN and the Prowler ECMO. There was an aircraft maintenance specialist, whom Jake knew, and five AEDOs, all of whom wore pilot or naval flight officer wings. Except for the A-6 BN and the Prowler ECMO, the rest had fighter backgrounds, including Tarkington, who was one of only two lieutenants. The rest were commanders and lieutenant commanders.

If the navy wanted a stealth attack plane, why so many fighter types? The air force called all their tactical drivers fighter pilots, but the navy had long ago divided the tactical fraternity into attack and fighter. The missions and the aircraft were completely different, so the training and tactics were also different. And according to the amateur psychologists in uniform who thought about these things and announced their conclusions at Happy Hour, the men were different too. Either their personalities were altered by the training or the missions attracted men of certain types. According to the attack community, fighter pukes were devil-may-care, kiss-tomorrow-goodbye romantics who lived and lusted for the dubious glory of individual combat in the skies. The fighter crowd said the attack pukes were phlegmatic plodders with brass balls – and no imaginations – who dropped bombs because they didn't know any better. Most of it was good, clean fun, but with a tinge of truth.

When Jake finished going through the records he stacked them carefully and stared thoughtfully at the pile. Dunedin and Strong had assembled a good group, he concluded, officers with excellent though varied backgrounds, from all over tactical naval aviation. The test pilot was the only real question mark. Moravia certainly had her tickets punched and was probably smarter than Einstein, but she had no actual experience in fight-testing new designs. He would ask Dunedin about her.

Tomorrow he would meet them. That was soon enough. First he had to find out what was really happening from Henry or Dunedin.

Henry spoke of minefields – a grotesque understatement. The problems inherent in overcoming the inertia of the bureaucracy to produce a new state-of-the-art weapons system were nothing short of mind-boggling. Dunedin must feel like he's been ordered to build the Great Pyramid armed with nothing but a used condom and a fly swatter. And for God's sake, do it quietly, top secret and all. Aye aye, sir.

In the Crystal City underground mall he found a toy store and purchased a plastic model of the air force's new stealth fighter, the F-117. He also bought a tube of glue. Then he boarded the Metro blue train for the ride to Rosslyn.

When the subway surfaced near the Key Bridge, Jake stared gloomily at the raindrops smearing the dirt on the windows as the train rocked along under a dark gray sky, then it raced noisily back into another hole in the ground and like his fellow passengers, he refocused his eyes vacantly on nothing as he instinctively created his own little private space.

He felt relieved when the doors finally opened and he joined the other passengers surging across the platform, through the turnstiles, then onto the world's longest escalator. The moving stair ascended slowly up the gloomy, slanting shaft bearing its veterans of purgatory. Amid the jostling, pushing, hustling throng, he was carried along as part of the flow. This morning he had been a tourist. Now he was as much a part of this human river as any of them. Morning and evening he would be an anonymous face in the mob: hurry along, hurry, push and shove gently, persistently, insistently, demanding equal vigor and speed from every set of legs, equal privacy from every set of blank, unfocused eyes. Hurry, hurry along.

Rain was still falling when he reached the sidewalk. He paused and turned his collar up against the damp and chill, then set off for the giant condo complex four blocks away.

Most of the people scurrying past him on the sidewalk had done this every working day for years. They were moles, he told himself glumly, blind creatures of the dark, damp places where the sun and wind never reached, unaware that the universe held anything but the dismal corridors where they lived out their pathetic lives. And now he was one of them.

He stopped at the corner, the model in the box under his arm. People swirled around him, their heads down, their eyes on the concrete. Callie wouldn't get home to the flat for another hour.

He turned and walked back against the flow of the crowd toward the station exit. Right across the street from the exit was a Roy Rogers. He paid for a cup of coffee and found a seat near the atrium window where he could watch the gray people bent against the wind and the raindrops sliding down the glass.

The euphoria he had felt when he talked to Vice Admiral Henry this morning was completely gone. Now he had a job . . . a paperwork job, going to endless meetings and listening to reports and writing recommendations and trying to keep from going crazy. A job in the bureaucracy. A staff job, the one he had fought against, refused to take, pulled every string to avoid, all these years. In the puzzle palace, the place where good ideas go to die.

It could have been worse, of course. He could have been assigned to design the new officer fitness report form.

Like many officers who spent their careers in operational billets, Jake Grafton loathed the bureaucrats, held them in a secret contempt which he tried to suppress with varying degrees of success. In the years since World War II, the bureaucracy had grown lush and verdant here in Washington. Every member of Congress had twenty aides. Every social problem had a staff of paper pushers 'managing' it. The military was just as bad. Joint commands with a staff of a thousand to fifteen hundred people were common.

Perhaps it happens because we are human. The people in the military endlessly analyze and train for the last war because no one knows what the next one will be like. New equipment and technologies deepen the gloom which always cloaks the future. Yesterday's warriors retire and new ones inherit the stars and the offices, and so it goes through generations, until at last every office is filled with men who have never heard a shot fired in anger or known a single problem that good, sound staff work, carefully couched in bureaucratese, could not 'manage' satisfactorily. Inevitably the gloom becomes stygian. Future war becomes a profound enigma that workaday admirals and generals and congressmen cannot penetrate. So the staffs proliferate as each responsible person seeks expert help with his day-to-day duties and the insoluble policy conundrums.

Another war would be necessary to teach the new generation the ancient truths. But in the Pax Americana following World War II, Vietnam accelerated the damage rather than arrested it.

In its aftermath Vietnam appeared to many as the first inadvertent, incautious step toward the nuclear inferno that would destroy life on this planet. Frightened by the new technologies and fearful of the incomprehensible political forces at work throughout the world, citizens and soldiers sought – demanded – quantifiable truths and controls that would prevent the war that had become unthinkable, the future war that had become, for the generations that had known only peace, the ultimate obscenity. Laws and regulations and incomprehensible organizational charts multiplied like bacteria in a petri dish. Engineers with pocket calculators became soothsayers to the terrified.

All of this Jake Grafton knew, and knowing it, was powerless to change. And now he was one of *them*, one of the faceless savants charged with creating salvation on his desk and placing it in the out basket.

Over on the beach it was probably raining like this. The wind would be moaning around the house and leaking around the windowpanes. The surf would be pounding on the sand. It would be a great evening for a walk along the beach under a gray sky, by that gray sea. Suddenly he felt an overpowering longing to feel the wind in his hair and the salt air in his nostrils.

Oh, to be there and not here! Not *here* with the problems and the hassles and the responsibilities.

His eye fell upon the bag that the clerk had placed the F-117 model in. He ripped out the staple and slid the box from the bag. The artist had painted the plane black. It had twin vertical stabilizers, slanted in at the bottom, and flat sides all over the place, all of which he suspected were devilishly expensive to manufacture. The intakes were on top of the fuselage, behind the canopy. How would the engines get air when the pilot was pulling Gs, maneuvering? He stared at the picture. No doubt this plane was fly-by-wire with a flight control computer stabilizing the machine and automatically trimming. But what would it feel like to fly it? What would be the weight and performance penalty to get this thing aboard ship? How much were they going to cost? Could these machines ever be worth the astronomical sums the manufacturers would want to charge? The politicians would decide.

Jack drained his coffee and threw the cup in the trash can by the door. He pulled the bag up over the box and rolled the excess tightly, then pushed the door open and stepped out into the evening.

'Hi, darling,' Callie said brightly when she came home and found Jake assembling the model on the kitchen table.

'Hey, beautiful.' Jake looked up and grinned at her, then resumed his chore of gluing the landing gear into the wheel wells.

'So how was the first day back at the office?'

Jake laid the plastic model on the diagram and leaned back in his chair. He stretched. 'Okay, I guess. They didn't tie me to the wooden post where they shoot traitors, and nobody said anything about a court-martial, so I guess I'm still in the navy.' He winked at her. 'It's going to be all right. Don't sweat it.'

She poured a cup of coffee and blew across it gently, then took an experimental sip. She stood looking at him over the rim of the cup. 'Where will you be working?'

'It's a little shop, some cubbyhole that belongs to NAVAIR. I'll be working on the new Advanced Tactical Aircraft.'

'Oh, Jake.' She took the seat beside him. 'That's terrific.' For the first time in months, her voice carried genuine enthusiasm.

'That's about all I can tell you. The project is classified up the wazoo. But it's a real job and it needs doing, which is a lot more than you can say for a lot of the jobs they have over there.'

He shouldn't have added that last phrase. The muscles around her eyes tightened as she caught the edge in his voice. 'After all you've done for the navy, they owed you a good job.'

'Hey, Callie, it doesn't work like that. You get paid twice a month and that's all they owe you. But this is a navy job and Lord knows how it'll all turn out.' Perhaps he could repair the damage. 'I'd rather have a navy job than be president of a bank. You know me, Callie.'

Her lips twisted into a lopsided smile. 'Yes, I guess I do.' She put her cup on the coffee table and stood.

Uh-oh! Here we go again! Jake took out his shirttail and used it to clean his glasses as she walked into the kitchen. You'd better be cool now, he decided. Help her along. He called out, 'What say we go get some dinner? I'm hungry. How about you?'

4

The ringing of the telephone woke Jake Grafton. As he groped for the receiver on the stand by the bed he blinked mightily to make out the luminous hands of the alarm clock: 5 A.M. 'Grafton.'

'Good morning, Captain. Admiral Henry. I wanted to catch you before you got started this morning.'

'You did, sir.'

'How about meeting me on the steps of Lincoln Memorial about oh-seven-hundred in civilian clothes.'

'Aye aye, sir.'

'Thanks.' The connection broke.

'Who was that?' Callie asked as Jake cradled the phone and closed his eyes. The alarm wouldn't ring for half an hour.

'One of my many bosses.'

'Oh,' she muttered. In less than a minute he heard her breathing deepen with sleep. He wondered what Tyler Henry wanted to talk about that couldn't be said at the office. After five minutes he gave up trying to sleep and got out of bed. He tiptoed for the bathroom.

By the time the alarm went off he had showered and shaved and dressed. He had picked out dark gray slacks and long-sleeved yellow shirt. Over this he had added a tie, an old sweater and a blue blazer.

'Good morning,' he said as he pushed the lever in on the back of the clock to silence it.

'Come hug me.' She smelled of warm woman and sleep. 'It's so nice having you here to give me my morning hug.' She pushed him back so she could see his face.

'I love you, woman.' He cradled her head in his hands. 'You're going to have to quit trying to analyze it and just accept it. It's true.'

'Hmmm.' She flashed a smile and became all business as she moved away from him and got up. 'Why the civilian clothes?'

'I'm playing hooky with the boss.'

'And it's only your second day on the job. Lucky you,' she said as she

326

headed for the bathroom. With the door closed she called, 'How about turning on the coffeepot and toasting some English muffins?'

'Yeah.' He headed towards the kitchen, snapping on the lights as he went. 'You're a real lover, ace. One look at your sincere puss and they tighten up like an IRS agent offered a ten-dollar bribe.'

Vice Admiral Henry was sitting on the steps of the Lincoln Memorial when the taxi deposited Jake in front. He came down the steps as Jake approached and joined him on the wide sidewalk. 'Morning, sir.'

The admiral flashed a smile and strolled to the curb. As he reached it a gray Ford Fairmont sedan sporting navy numbers on the door pulled to a stop. Henry jerked open the rear door without fanfare and maneuvered his six-foot-three-inch frame in. Jake followed him. When the door closed the sailor at the wheel got the car in motion.

'Why the cloak and dagger?'

'I don't know who all the players are,' the admiral said without humor.

Jake watched the occasional pedestrians braving the blustery wind under a raw sky until he became aware that the admiral's attention was on the vehicles on the street behind them. Jake glanced over his shoulder once or twice, then decided to leave the spy stuff to Henry. He watched the sailor handle the car. The man was good. No wasted motion. The car glided gently through the traffic, changing lanes at the last moment and gliding around corners without the application of the brake, all quite effortlessly. It was a show and Jake watched it in silence.

'Could have picked you up at your place,' Henry muttered, 'But I wanted to visit the Wall.' The Wall was the Vietnam Memorial, just across the street from the Lincoln Memorial. 'It's been too long and I never seem to have any time.'

'I understand.'

'Turn left here,' Henry said to the driver, who complied. The car headed east on Independence Avenue. Henry ordered another left turn on Fourteenth Street and directed the driver to go by the Jefferson Memorial. 'I think we're clean,' he muttered to Jake after another careful look through the rear window. At the Jefferson Memorial, Henry asked the driver to pull over. 'Come back for us at nine.'

He led Jake toward the walkway around the Tidal Basin. Across the basin the Washington Monument rose toward the low clouds. Beyond it, Jake knew, but not visible from here, was the White House.

Jake broke the silence first. 'Does Admiral Dunedin know we're having this talk this morning, sir?'

'Yeah. I told him. You work for him. But I wanted to brief you personally. What do you know about stealth?'

'The usual,' Jake said, snuggling into his coat against the chill wind. 'What's in the papers. Not much.'

'The air force contracted for two prototype stealth fighters under a blanket of absolute secrecy. Lockheed got the production contract. They call the thing the F-117A. It's a fighter in name only; it's really an attack plane – performance roughly equivalent to the A-7 without afterburner but carries less than half the A-7 weapons load. Primary weapons are Maverick missiles. It's a little ridiculous to call a subsonic minibomber a fighter, but if they can keep the performance figures low-key they might well get away with it.'

'I thought that thing was supposed to be a warp-three killing machine.'

'Yeah. I suspect the congressmen who agreed to vote for a huge multibillion-buck project with no public debate probably did too. But even supersonic ain't possible. The thing doesn't even have afterburners. Might go supersonic in a dive – I don't know. Anyway, the air force got more bang for their buck with the stealth bomber, the B-2, which Northrop is building. It's also subsonic, a flying wing, but big and capable with a good fuel load. The only problem is the B-2 cost $516 million a pop, so unless you're sending them to Moscow to save the human race, you can't justify risking them on anything else. A B-2 isn't a battlefield weapon.'

'How are these gizmos going to find their targets?' Conventional bombers used radar to navigate and locate their targets, but the transmission of a radar beam from a stealth bomber would reveal its location, thereby negating all the expensive technology used to hide it.

Admiral Henry settled onto a park bench with his back to the Tidal Basin. His eyes roamed the sidewalks, which were deserted on this early-spring morning. 'You're not going to believe this, but the air force hasn't solved that problem yet. They're waiting for technology that's under development.'

Jake Grafton looked at Henry to see if he was serious. He appeared to be. 'How about a satellite rig like the A-6G was going to have? The Navstar Global Positioning System?'

'That's part of the plan, but the trouble with satellites is that you can't count on them to last longer than forty-eight hours into a major East-West confrontation. And there's only eight satellites aloft – the system needs twenty-eight. If they ever get all the birds aloft it should tell you your position to within sixteen meters anywhere on earth, but that's a big if, what with NASA's shuttle and budget problems. No, I think the answer is going to be a system made up of a solid-state, ring-laser gyro inertial nav system, passive infra-red sensors and a stealthy radar, one that powers up only enough to see what's necessary, has automatic frequency agility, that sort of thing. That's basically the A-6G and B-2 system. We'll use it on the A-12. It's still under development.'

Henry snorted and wiggled his buttocks to get comfortable. 'Congress isn't going to fund any significant B-2 buy. The way the whole budget process screwed up the buy, with inflation and predictable over-runs and underbuys, the last plane in the program is going to cost over a billion bucks. The manned strategic bomber is going the way of the giant panda and the California condor. We want to avoid the mistakes the air force made.'

'SAC will have more generals than airplanes.'

'The stealth concept has been around since World War II,' Henry continued, 'more as a curio than anything else. It really became a driving force in aircraft design after Vietnam when it became apparent that conventional aircraft were going to have a very rough time surviving in the dense electronic environment over a Western European battlefield. Conventional electronic warfare can only do so much. The spooks say there'll be too many frequencies and too many sensors. That's the conventional wisdom, so it's probably wrong.' He shrugged. 'But any way you cut it, the attrition rate over the battlefield would be high, which favors the Soviets. They have lots of planes and we can't match them in quantity. So we would lose. Ergo, stealth.'

'But we *could* match them in quantity,' Jake said. 'At least the air force could build a lot of cheap airplanes optimized for one mission, like fighter or attack. No room on carriers for that kind of plane, of course.'

'The air force doesn't want that. Their institutional ethic is for more complex, advanced aircraft with greater and greater capability. That's the whole irony of the stealth fighter. They've billed this technology as a big advance but in reality they got a brand-new tactical bomber with 1950s performance. But, they argue, it's survivable. Now. For the immediate future. Until and only until the Russians come up with a way to find these planes – or someone else figures out a way and the Russians steal it. Even so, the only thing that made first-generation stealth technology feasible was smart weapons, assuming the crew can find the target. These planes have little or no capability with air-to-mud dumb bombs.' Henry stared at his toes and wriggled them experimentally. 'Can you imagine risking a five-hundred-million buck airplane to dump a load of thousand-pounders on a bridge?'

'Does stealth ensure survivability?' Jake prompted, too interested to notice his continuing discomfort from the breeze off the river.

'Well, it all boils down to whether or not you think fixed air bases are survivable in the war the air force is building their planes to fight, and that is a war in Europe against the Soviets *which has escalated to a nuclear exchange.* If I were a Russian I wouldn't worry much about these airplanes – neither of which has any off-concrete capability – I'd just knock out their bases at the beginning of hostilities and forget about them.'

'What about conventional war with the Soviets?'

'If anyone has figured out a way to keep it from going nuclear, I haven't heard about it.'

'How many Maverick missiles are there? A couple thousand?'

'Twice that.'

'That's still no more than a week or two's supply. It'd better be a damn short war.'

The admiral grunted. 'The basic dilemma: without stealth technology the air force says planes can't survive over a modern battlefield; with stealth they must use only sophisticated weapons. And if the airplanes truly are a threat, the Soviets have a tremendous stimulus to escalate the war to a nuclear strike to eliminate their bases.' He chopped the air with the cutting edge of his hand. 'This stuff is grotesquely expensive.'

'Sounds like we've priced ourselves out of the war business.'

'I fucking wish! But enough philosophy. Stealth technology certainly deserves a lot of thought. It's basically just techniques to lower an aircraft's electromagnetic signature in the military wavelengths: radio – which is radar – and heat – infrared. And they're trying to minimize the distance the plane can be detected by ear and by eye. Minimizing the RCS – the Radar Cross Section – and the heat signature are the two most important factors and end up driving the design process. But it's tough. For example, to half the radar detection range you must lower the RCS by a factor of sixteen – the fourth root. To lower the IR signature in any meaningful manner you must give up afterburners for your engines and bury the engines inside the airplane to cool the exhaust gases, the sum total of which is less thrust. Consequently we are led kicking and screaming into the world of design compromises, which is a handy catchall for mission compromises, performance and range and payload compromises, bang-and-buck compromises. That's where you come in.'

Admiral Henry rose from the bench and sauntered along the walk discussing the various methods and techniques that lowered, little by little, the radar and heat signatures of an aircraft. He talked about wind and fuselage shape, special materials, paint, engine and inlet duct design and placement, every aspect of aircraft construction. Stealth, he said, involved them all. Finally he fell silent and walked along with his shoulders rounded, his hands thrust deep into his pockets.

Jake spoke. 'If the best the air force could get out of their stealth attack plane was A-7 performance, is it a good idea for the navy to spend billions on one? We can't go buying airplanes to fight just one war, and we need a sufficient quantity of planes to equip the carriers. Five gee-whiz killing machines a year won't do us any good at all.'

The admiral stopped dead and scrutinized Jake. Slowly a grin lifted the corners of his mouth. 'I *knew* you were the right guy for this job.'

He resumed walking, his step firmer, more confident. 'The first question is what kind of fighters are we going to get into in the future. And the answer, I suspect, is more of the same. I think the likelihood of an all-out war with the Soviets in Western Europe is pretty small – no way to prevent it from going nuclear and the Russians don't want that any more than we do. But we must prepare to fight it, prepare to some degree, or we can't deter it. I'd say it's a lot more likely we'll end up with more limited wars, like Korea or Vietnam or Afghanistan or the Persian Gulf or the Middle East or South Africa. So the capability to fight those wars is critical. We need planes that can fly five hundred miles through the high-density electronic environment, deliver a devastating conventional punch, and return to the carrier to fly again, and again and again. Without *that* capability our carrier battle groups are an expensive liability and not an asset. We need that plane by 1995, at the latest.'

'You're implying that our plane can't rely on pin-point missiles for weapons.'

'Precisely. The air force has a lot of concrete to park their specialized planes on; carrier deck space is damn precious. We can't build planes that can only shoot missiles that cost a million bucks each, then push them into the drink when we run out of missiles. We have to be able to hit hard in any foreseeable conflict with simple, cheap weapons, like laser-guided bombs.'

'So we can do something the air force couldn't with the F-117?'

Henry threw his head back and grinned, obviously enjoying himself. 'We aren't going to trade away our plane's performance or mission capability.'

'But how—'

'Better design – we learned a lot from the F-117 – plus Athena. *Active* stealth technology.' His mood was gloomy again. 'I think the fucking Russians have gotten everything there was to get out of the F-117 and B-2. Every single technical breakthrough, they've stolen it. They don't appear to be using that knowledge and they may not ever be able to do so. This stuff involves manufacturing capabilities they don't have and costs they can't afford to incur. But what they can do is figure out defenses to a stealthed-up airplane, and you can bet your left nut they're working their asses off on that right this very minute.'

He looked carefully around. 'There's a Russian mole in the Pentagon.' His voice was almost a whisper, although the nearest pedestrian was a hundred yards away. 'He gave them the stealth secrets. The son of a bitch is buried in there someplace and he's ripping us off. He's even been given a top secret code name – Minotaur.' He scuffed his toe at a pebble on the sidewalk. 'I'm not supposed to know this. It goes without saying that if I'm not, you sure as hell aren't.'

'How'd—'

'Don't ask. I don't want you to know. But if I know the Minotaur's there, you can lay money *he* knows we know he's there. So the bastard is dug in with his defenses up. We may never get him. Probably won't.'

'How do we know he gave them stealth?'

'We know. Trust me. We know.'

'So we have a mole in the Kremlin.'

'I didn't say that,' Henry said fiercely, 'and you had damn well better not. No shit, Grafton, don't even whisper that to a living fucking soul.'

They walked along in silence, each man occupied with his own thoughts. Finally Jake said, 'So how are we gonna do it?'

'Huh?'

'How are we going to build a stealth Intruder and keep the technology in our pocket?'

'I haven't figured that one out yet,' Henry said slowly. 'You see, everything the Russians have gotten so far is passive – techniques to minimize the radar cross section and heat signature. To build a mission-capable airplane like we want we're going to have to use active techniques, Project Athena. They haven't stolen Athena yet and we don't want them to get it.'

'Active techniques?' Jake prompted, unable to contain his curiosity.

'We're going to cancel the bad guys' radar signal when it reaches our plane. We'll automatically generate a signal that nullifies the echo, mutes it, cancels it out. The plane will then be truly invisible to the enemy. They'll never see it on their scope. They'll never receive the echo.' He thought about it. 'It's the biggest technological breakthrough since the Manhattan Project. Biggest by a mile.'

'I've heard speculation about cancelling radar signals for years. The guys who are supposed to know all laughed. Can it be done?'

'The party line is no. Impossible. But there's a crazed genius who wants to be filthy rich that has done it. That technology is the living, beating heart of the ATA. Now all we have to do is get an airplane built and keep the Minotaur from stealing the secret.'

Jake whistled. 'Can't we put this on all our ships?'

'No doubt we will,' Henry said sourly, 'and the Russians will steal it before our first ship gets out of the harbor. For now let's just see if we can get it in one airplane without someone stealing it. That'll be plenty for you and Roger Dunedin to chew.'

'Existing aircraft? How about retrofitting them?'

'Right now, as the technology exists, the best approach is to design the plane for it. The power output required to hide a stealthy plane would be very small. The device would be easy enough to put on a ship, when we get the bugs worked out. As usual there are bugs. Expensive, though.'

Admiral Henry glanced at his watch. 'Our work's cut out for us. The air force will want this technology when they get wind of it, and right now everything they see winds up in the Kremlin. It's not their fault, of course, but that's the way it is. The manufacturer of our plane will see it and from there it may end up in the Minotaur's clutches. Ditto the ship drivers. And the politicians who have been trick-fucked on the F-117 won't sit still for more stealth hocus-pocus; they're gonna want justification for the four or five billion dollars the ATA will require to develop, and there it goes again. So right now I'm sitting on a volcano that's about to erupt and my ass is getting damn warm. You see why I wanted you on board.'

'Not really,' Jake said, wondering how far he should push this. After all, who the hell was Jake Grafton? What could an over-the-hill attack pilot in glasses with four stripes on his sleeve do for a three-star admiral? Bomb the Pentagon? 'So what's your plan? How are you going to do this?'

Henry was so nervous he couldn't hold still. 'I'm going to hold the cards real close to my chest and catch the Minotaur peeking over my shoulder. Or that's what I'm going to try to do, anyway.'

'Admiral, with all respect, sir, what does CNO say about all this?' CNO was the Chief of Naval Operations, the senior uniformed naval officer.

Henry squared off in front of Jake. 'I'm not stupid enough to try to run my own private navy, Captain. CNO knows exactly what I'm doing. So does SECNAV and SECDEF. But you sure as hell didn't get it all in this little conversation.'

'Admiral, I'll lay my life on the line for you. I'm not going to do anything illegal or tell even one solitary little lie. I'm not a very good liar.'

Admiral Henry grinned. 'You just haven't had the experience it takes. I've been single for ten years, so I've done a good bit of it. Seriously, all I want you to do is play it straight. Do your job for NAVAIR. Just keep it under your hat that we have an active system we're going to put into this bird. Roger will tell you the same.'

'How many people know about this active system?'

'Here in Washington? Eight now. The Secretary of the Navy, CNO, SECDEF, NAVAIR, OP-50 – which is Rear Admiral Costello – me, you and Helmut Fritsche. And let's keep it that way for a while.'

'Have you tested this system? Does it work?'

Henry made a face. 'Fritsche's seen it work on the test bench. Your first job, after you look at the proto-types, is to put part of it into an A-6 and test it on the ground and in flight.'

Jake eyed the older man. He had this sinking feeling in the pit of his stomach. There was a hell of a lot he wasn't being told. 'So how do you know Fritsche?'

'He was a professor at Caltech when I was there for a master's. We became good friends. He did some consulting work for the inventor on some theoretical problems. He saw what the guy had and came to me. that was three years ago. It was coincidence that there was a deputy project manager job opening in the ATA program. I talked Fritsche into taking it. He wants to be a part of Athena. The theoretical problems intrigue him.'

'You said you didn't know all the players.'

Henry took his opportunity to look around again. 'Yeah. I don't. Your

predecessor, Harold Strong? Great guy, knew naval aviation from catapult to tailhook, everything there is to know, but he wasn't a politician,
not a diplomat. He was a blunt, brilliant, take-no-prisoners kind of guy.
Somebody killed him.'

'Why?'

'I wish I knew.' Henry described how he personally drove to West
Virginia on Saturday morning after the Friday-night automobile accident. He summarized the conversation he had had with the West Virginia
state trooper who investigated the accident. The trooper had served in the
marine corps and by a stroke of fortune Henry had been in uniform. The
trooper had been good; he knew murder when he saw it. He had taken
the admiral to see the local prosecuting attorney, who had been splitting
firewood in his backyard when the two of them arrived in the police
cruiser. After two hours of talking, Henry induced the prosecutor and the
trooper to a wording of the accident report that did not mention
homicide and yet would not preclude a homicide prosecution if the
identity of the murderer could ever be established.

'My theory' – Henry shrugged – 'I got no evidence, you understand –
my theory is Harold found out something, learned something somebody
didn't want him to know – so he got rubbed out.'

The navy Ford pulled up to the curb, but Henry put a hand on Jake's
arm. 'This is big, Jake. Real Big. You don't understand how big. The
Russians will figure out we're going to do something different and
wonderful with the A-12 and they'll pull out all the stops to get Athena.
And five billion dollars in development money is on the line, plus twenty
billion in production money – that much shit will draw every blowfly and
bloodsucker in the country. A lot of these people would kill for this
technology.'

'Maybe someone already has.'

'Just don't trust anybody.'

'I've figured that out, sir. I think there's a hell of a lot here you haven't
told me. So I don't trust you.'

Henry threw back his head and guffawed. 'I *knew* you were the right
man for the job. He became instantly serious. 'I don't give a damn
whether you trust me or not. Just do your job and keep your mouth shut
and we'll get the navy a good airplane.'

'By the way, did Strong know about the active system?'

'Yes.'

The admiral's driver dropped Jake at his office building. One of the few
benefits of working a black program was that he could come to work in
civilian clothes.

Vice Admiral Dunedin was finishing a conference, so Jake visited with
Mrs Forsythe. In fifteen minutes the door opened and people streamed
out, in a hurry.

'Good morning, Admiral,' Jake said.

'How'd your talk go with Admiral Henry?'

'Very well, sir.'

'Don't lie to me, Captain. I'm your boss.'

'Yessir.' Jake found a seat and looked straight at the blue-eyed Scotsman behind the desk. 'He told me what he wanted me to know and that was that.'

'How long you been in the navy?'

Long enough to know how to take orders, Jake thought. 'Yessir.'

'Let's talk about the A-12. It's now your baby.'

An hour later the admiral rose from his chair. 'Let's go meet the crew.'

Jake mentioned to the admiral that he had been looking at the personnel folders. 'Lieutenant Moravia. She's got platinum credentials but no experience. How'd she get on the team?'

'Strong wanted her. He was down at Pax River when she went through as a student. He said she'd one of a kind. Since he was a test pilot himself, I figured he had the experience even if she didn't, so I said okay.'

'I'm not a test pilot,' Jake said.

'I know. These people work for you. If you want someone else, just say so. That goes for any of them, except for Fritsche. If they stay it's because you think they can do the job and you trust them.'

'I read you loud and clear, sir.'

'Anybody doesn't pull his weight, or you get goosey about any of them, I'll have them sitting on the ice cap in the Antarctic so quick they won't have time to pack their long johns.'

The office in Crystal City where the A-12 program team worked was a square space with twenty metal desks jammed in. Five-drawer filing cabinets with combination locks on the draws had been arranged to divide the room into work areas. The scarred tops and askew drawers of the desks proclaimed them veterans of other offices, other bureaucratic struggles now forgotten. Office equipment was scattered all over the room: a dozen computer terminals, four printers, a copy machine, a paper shredder, and a fax machine linked to an encryption device. Jake's office would be one of the two small private offices. These two small offices each had an outside window and a blackboard, plus the usual filing cabinets with combination locks on the drawers.

But the security – wow! There were two entry doors, each with cipher locks, and a closed-circuit television that monitored the dead space between the doors. An armed security team was on duty inside twenty-four hours a day. Their business was to check each person entering the space against the master list and log them in and out. The windows had the music sound vibrators and could not be opened. The shades were permanently closed. The fire extinguisher system in the ceiling had plastic cutouts installed in the pipes so that they would not conduct sound.

'Every sheet of paper is numbered and accounted for,' the admiral told Jake. 'The phone numbers are unlisted and changed monthly. I can never find my number sheet, so I end up walking down here.'

After a quick tour, Jake stood in the middle of the room with the admiral. 'Where'd they get this carpet?'

'Stole it someplace. I never asked.'

'Sure would be nice to get a little bigger space. Thirty people?'

'This is all the space I have to give you. It takes the signature of an Assistant Secretary of the Navy to get space not assigned to NAVAIR. I haven't had time to kiss his ass. But if you can get his scrawl, go for it.'

'Nothing's too good for the boys in navy blue,' Toad Tarkington chirped cheerfully from his little desk against one wall, loud enough to draw a frosty glance from the admiral.

'You're Tarkington?' Dunedin said.

'Yessir.'

'I hear you suffer from a mouth problem from time to time. If it's incurable your naval career is about to hit the wall. You read me?'

'Yessir.'

Dunedin raised his voice. 'Okay, folks. Gather around. I want you to meet Captain Jake Grafton, the new program manager. He's your new boss.' Dunedin launched into a traditional 'welcome aboard' speech. When he was finished Jake told the attentive faces how pleased he was to be there, then he and the admiral shook hands. After a quick whispered word with Fritsche, Dunedin left the office.

Jake invited the commanders and civilian experts into his new cubbyhole. It was a very tight fit. Folding chairs were packed in and the place became stuffy in minutes. They filled him in on the state of the project and their roles in it. Jake said nothing about his visit with the admirals and gave no hint that he knew anything about the project.

He looked over Helmut Fritsche first, the radar expert from Caltech. About fifty, he was heavyset, of medium height, and sported a Hemingway beard which he liked to stroke when he talked. He had alert, intelligent eyes that roamed constantly, even when he was addressing someone. He spoke slowly, carefully, choosing his words. He struck Jake as an intelligent, learned man who had long ago resigned himself to spending most of his life in the company of fools.

George Wilson was at least five years younger than Fritsche and much leaner. He spoke slowly, in cadenced phrases, automatically allowing his listeners to take notes if they wished. When he used his third pun Jake finally noticed. Listening more carefully, he picked up two double entendres and another pun. At first blush Wilson seemed a man in love with the sound of his own voice, but Jake decided that impression didn't do justice to the fertile, active mind of the professor of aeronautical engineering.

The A-6 bombardier, Commander Les Richards, looked as old as Fritsche although he couldn't have been a day over forty-two or forty-three. Jake had met him years ago at NAS Oceana. They had never been in the same squadron together but had a speaking acquaintance. Richards' tired face contained tired eyes. Jake remembered that just a year or so ago Richards had commanded an A-6 squadron, so this assignment was his post-command tour. His eyes told whoever looked that the navy was no longer an adventure, if indeed it ever had been. The navy and perhaps life itself were experiences to be endured on this long, joyless journey toward the grave. If he caught any of Wilson's wordplay his face gave no hint. In spite of his demeanor, Jake knew, Richards had the reputation of being an aggressive, competent manager, a man who got things done.

Commander 'Smoke' Judy was an F-14 pilot. Like all the commanders, he had had a squadron command tour. Smoke was short and feisty. He looked like a man who would rather fight than eat. The joyous competitive spirit of the fighter pilot seemed incarnate in him. A fire-eater – no doubt that was the origin of his nickname, which had probably ceased to be a nickname long ago. Jake suspected that his wife and even his mother now called him Smoke.

Dalton Harris was an extrovert, a man with a ready smile. He grinned nervously at George Wilson's humor and glanced at him expectantly every time it seemed Wilson might become inspired. He was a lithe, compact man, as full of nervous energy as Judy. An alumnus of the EA-6B Prowler community, he was an expert in electronic warfare. He even had a master's in electrical engineering from the Naval Postgraduate School.

The other two commanders, Aeronautical Engineering Duty Officers, were equally interesting. Technical competence was their stock-in-trade.

An excellent group, Jake decided as the conversation wound down, good shipmates. Harold Strong and Admiral Dunedin had chosen well. He glanced at his watch with a start; they had been talking about the A-12 for two hours. In parting he told them, 'I want a complete inventory of the accountable classified material started tomorrow. Every document will be sighted by two officers and they'll both sign the list.'

'We did an inventory after Captain Strong died. Took two weeks.'

'You'd better hope I don't kick the bucket any time soon or you'll be doing it a couple more times.'

Jake spent five minutes with each of the other officers, saving Moravia and Tarkington for last. He saw them together. After the preliminaries he said, 'Miss Moravia, I'm going to be blunt. You don't seem to have any test-flying experience other than Test Pilot School.'

'That's right, sir. But I can do the job. Try me and see.'

Moravia was of medium height, with an excellent figure and a face to match. Subtle makeup, every hair in place. Her gold naval aviator wings gleamed above the left breast pocket of her blue uniform. Try me and see – that fierce self-confidence separated those who could from those who never would.

Tarkington seemed to treat her with deference and respect, Jake noted wryly. 'Ever flown an A-6?'

'About two hours or so at Pax River, sir.' Jake knew how that worked. During the course of his training at Test Pilot School – TPS – each student flew anywhere from twelve to seventeen different kinds of air-craft. The final examination to qualify for graduation consisted of writing a complete flying qualities and performance evaluation of an airplane the student had not flown before. The student was handed a manual, and after studying it, was allowed to fly the airplane for four flights or six hours' flight time, whichever came first. On the basis of this short exposure the student then wrote the report. Rita Moravia was an honors graduate of that program.

Try me and see!

'I want you and Tarkington to leave for Whidbey Island tomorrow morning. The folks at VA-128 are expecting you.' VA-128 was the replacement training squadron for A-6 Intruders on the West Coast. 'They're going to give you a crash course on how to fly an A-6. Report directly to the squadron skipper when you get there tomorrow. Mrs Forsythe in the admiral's office is getting you orders and plane tickets.' He looked again at his watch. 'She should have them for you now.'

'Aye, aye, sir,' Moravia said and stood up. 'Is there anything else, sir?'

'Remember that nobody at Whidbey has a need to know anything. You'll be asked no questions by the senior people. The junior ones will be curious, so just say the Pentagon sent you to fly. That's it. Learn everything you can about the plane and its mission. And don't crash one.'

Miss Moravia nodded and left, but Toad lingered.

'Uh, CAG,' Toad said, 'I'm a fighter type and this attack puke stuff—'

'The admiral says that anyone I want to get rid of can winter over in Antarctica. You want to go all the way south?'

'I'll take Whidbey, sir.'

'I thought you would.' He picked up some paper on his desk and looked at it, signaling the end of the interview. 'Oh,' he added, looking up again, 'by the way, you stay the hell away from Moravia. Absolutely no romance. Keep it strictly business. You'd mope around here like a whipped puppy after she ditched you. I haven't got the stomach for another sorry spectacle like that.'

The office emptied at 5:30. Jake stayed, sorting through the paper that had accumulated in Strong's in basket. Most of it he threw in the waste can under his desk. Memos and letters and position papers that looked important he saved for later scrutiny.

When he finished with the in-basket pile he began rooting through the desk drawers. Unbelievable! Here at the back of the wide, shallow drawer above his knees was an old memo on army stationery, dated 1956. Where had they gotten these desks? And what else was in here? Maybe he would find an announcement from the War Department that Japan had surrendered.

Alas, nothing so extraordinary. A two-year old date book, most of the pages blank. Some matchbooks from a restaurant – perhaps Strong liked to drop in there for a cup of coffee. Three envelopes addressed to Strong in a feminine hand: empty envelopes with the stamp canceled, no return address. One broken shoelace, a button that didn't look like it came from a uniform, two rubber bands, a collection of government pens and #2 lead pencils. He tried the pens on a scrap of paper. Most of them still worked. Some of the erasers on the pencils were pretty worn.

So Harold Strong had been murdered.

And Admiral Henry had throttled the investigation even before it started. Or so he said.

He shook his head in annoyance. Those problems were not his concern. His job was to run this project. With the A-12 still in the prototype stage, many major decisions remained to be made. Jake already knew he would throw his weight, what little he had. For too long, in his opinion, the military had been stuck with airplanes designed to accomplish so many disparate missions that they were unable to do any of them well. If they wanted an attack plane, then by God he would argue like hell for a capable attack plane.

Every aircraft design involved inevitable trade-offs: fuel capacity was traded for strength and maneuverability, weapons-carrying capacity sacrificed for speed, maneuverability surrendered for stability, and so on, because every aircraft had to have all of these things, yet it needed these things in degrees that varied with its mission. But with stealth literally everything was being compromised in varying degrees to achieve invisibility, or in the jargon of the trade, survivability.

For two hours this afternoon the commanders and experts had argued that a plane that could not survive over the modern battlefield was not worth having. Yet a plane that did survive but could not fight was equally worthless. Somewhere between these two extremes was a balance.

The other major consideration that had been tossed around this afternoon was a conundrum that baffled politicians and generals as well as aircraft designers. What war do you build your airplane to fight? World War III nuclear? World War III conventional? Vietnam? Anti-terrorist raids against Libya? The answer, Jake believed, had to be all of them. Yet achieving survivability over the European battlefield might well mean trading away conventional iron-bomb-carrying capacity that would be essential in future brushfire wars, like Vietnam. Megabuck smart missiles were currently in vogue but the nation could never afford enough of them to fight any war that lasted longer than two weeks.

This job was not going to be easy, or dull.

'She-it,' Jake Grafton said aloud, drawing the word out slowly. When you looked at Tyler Henry and listened to him he seemed okay. But if all you did was listen to the words – well, it sure did make you wonder. Spies? Murder investigations put on hold? Was Henry some paranoid wacko, some coconut schizo on the naked edge who ought to be locked in the bowels of St Elizabeth's without his belt and shoelaces?

The first thing I ought to do, Jake told himself, before I go see the ultimate war machine manufactured by some greedy Gyro Gearloose in a garage in California, is check out Henry. It would be nice to know that the big boss has all his marbles. It would be damn nice to know if he doesn't. Dunedin wanted Jake to salute and march.

'A fellow never gets very far marching in the dark, anyhow,' Jake said aloud. 'Too much stuff out there to trip over.'

He used one of the black government pens from Strong's hoard to write a note for the senior secretary's desk. What was her name? Mrs Pulliam. There were just two secretaries, both civilians.

The note informed all and sundry he would be in late tomorrow, after lunch. He had a moment of doubt. There was so much to be done here. Yet they had gotten along without a project manager for two months now: they could suffer through another day.

5

Toad Tarkington lowered himself into a seat against the window on the left side of the airplane, a Boeing 727. Three engines, he noted with satisfaction. Airliners made him nervous these days. He couldn't see the guys flying or monitor the instruments and he had no ejection seat, so he couldn't boogy on out if the clowns up front hamburgered it, which, from what he read in the newspapers, they had been doing lately with distressing frequency. Luckily this flight to Seattle was almost empty, so after the crash there wouldn't be any unsightly mob ripping out hair and eyeballs scrambling for the emergency exits.

He glanced across the four empty seats and the aisle at Rita Moravia sitting against the window on the right side. Now there was one cold, cold woman. She hadn't yet smiled in his presence or given any indication she ever would. The old Tarkington charm rolled right over her as if it had gone bad in the winter of '85, turned sour and rotten and gave off an evil odor.

The plane began to move. Backwards. They were pushing it out. Toad glanced at his watch. Twenty minutes late. They were always late. He tried to get comfortable in his seat. Reluctantly he picked up the copy of *The Washington Post* he had purchased at a news counter and scanned the headlines. Same old crap – it's absolutely uncanny how politicians can be relied upon to do or say something every single day that even Charlie Manson would think bizarre.

He sneaked a glance at Moravia. She was reading a paperback. He squinted. My God – it's a Jackie Collins novel! How about that? The ice queen deep into sex among the rich and stupid. Maybe her hormones are okay after all.

Toad leaned back and closed his eyes. He needed to work out some kind of approach, a line. First he needed to know more about her. This was going to take some time, but she looked like she'd be worth it and Jake Grafton had implied that they were going to be spending plenty of time together. That Grafton, he didn't just fall off a turnip truck. He knew the score.

Toad opened one eye and aimed it her way. Yep, a nice tight unit. Reading a romance novel. Who'd have guessed?

When the plane was safely airborne he reclined his seat and drifted off to sleep wearing a satisfied little smile.

Jake Grafton found a place to park the Chevy right on Main Street a block from the courthouse intersection, which sported the only stoplights in town. Actually there were three empty parking places all in a row and he took one on the end. Romney, West Virginia, was not a bustling place on a cold, breezy March morning.

The interior of the courthouse was massive and calm. The ceilings were at least fifteen feet high. Even the interior walls were thick, substantial, built to last. He examined the signs on the wooden doors and settled on the circuit clerk's office. Inside he asked, 'Where do I find the prosecuting attorney?'

'Across the street on the left end of the block. He has an office above the liquor store. Cookman's his name.' The lady smiled.

'And the state police?'

'Out of the courthouse, turn right and go three blocks, then another right and down about a half mile. The barracks is a nice little brick building. You can't miss it.'

Standing in front of the courthouse beside the statue of a World War I doughboy, Jake decided to walk to the state police barracks first. The first three blocks were along the main drag, by stores and empty display windows. The decay of the American Main Street had reached this little community too. When he turned right he left the commercial district and found himself in a quiet residential area. As he passed modest houses with trees in the lawns and pick-ups and motorcycles in the drive, he could hear dogs barking and occasionally a snatch of talk show from an open door.

The police barracks had American and West Virginia flags flying on large poles in front, beside an empty parking area festooned with signs and plastic barriers for driving tests. Inside there wasn't a cop in sight. The girl behind the desk looked like she was barely out of high school.

'Hi, I'd like to get a copy of an accident report from a couple of months ago.'

'Did it happen in the city or out in the country?'

'Outside the city.'

'You've come to the right place.' She smiled. 'I need the names of the parties involved, or at least one of them.'

'Harold Strong.'

'Just a moment.' She selected a drawer in a large file cabinet and began looking. 'All we have are copies, of course. The originals go to DMV in Charleston. We're not even required to keep copies but we do because the lawyers and insurance adjusters always want to see them. Are you a lawyer?'

'Uh, no. I was a friend of Captain Strong's.'

'Here it is.' She looked at it as she walked toward the counter. 'He was in the navy, wasn't he.'

Her comment was a statement, not a question, but he responded anyway. 'Yes, he was.'

She laid the report on the counter in front of him. 'That's our office copy and our copy machine is out of order. There's one up in the county clerk's office, where they keep the deeds and all?' He nodded. 'But you need to leave your driver's license with me.' She smiled apologetically. 'So many people forget to bring our copy back.'

He dug out his wallet and extracted his license. She didn't even look at it. 'Thanks. I'll be back in a bit.'

Very nicely done, he thought as he walked the half mile back toward the main street. No doubt before he got out of Romney he would be talking to a state trooper. He looked at the name on the report. Trooper Keadle.

There was an unpadded bench in the corridor outside the county clerk's office and he settled there. The report consisted of three pages. The first was a form with blanks to be filled in and a diagram where the investigating officer drew little cars and arrows to show what he believed happened. The next two pages were merely handwritten comments of the investigating officer. Keadle had a neat hand – he obviously hadn't ruined his penmanship with years of furious note-taking.

The report was straightforward, devoid of bureaucratese. Jake read it a second time slowly, studying the words. According to Admiral Henry the prosecuting attorney had had a hand in this report, which 'would not preclude a homicide prosecution.' That could only mean that none of the critical facts were omitted. A half-smart defense lawyer would raise holy hell if the prosecutor asked the trooper to testify about facts that he had 'forgotten' to put in the official report.

What was in the report? Marks on the highway where it appeared tires may have broken their regular grip with the pavement and spun under power. No skid marks: wet pavement prevented that. Deep trenches in the gravel, some of which went all the way to the edge, presumably from skidding tires. Marks in the earth where the Corolla went over the edge. Wooden guardrails had been chain-sawed several days before the accident, presumably by vandals or parties unknown; see previous report of sheriff's deputy. Fire in Corolla passenger compartment very intense, body burned beyond recognition and identified with help of FBI forensic lab. No mention of why or when the FBI was notified. Dents and scrape marks all over the vehicle. Finally, Corolla still structurally intact but gutted by fire.

No mention of the Corolla's fuel tank. But the trooper could certainly testify that the fuel tank, like the car's frame, was intact. No speculation on or estimate of how fast the Corolla would have had to be going up that mountain to slide all the way across the overlook area. Did he explain that the Corolla was ascending the grade? Yes, on page one.

No speculation about the cause of this single-car accident and no speculation anywhere that another vehicle might be involved.

He took the report into the office beside him and had it copied. They charged him thirty cents. He was tempted to use the car to return the original report but decided the exercise would be good for him. As he approached the police building, a trooper was parking his car in a reserved spot.

'Thanks,' he told the girl at the desk. She handed him his driver's license, which had been lying on the counter beside the police radio microphone.

The door behind Jake opened. 'Hi, Susie.' Jake turned. The trooper was clad in a green uniform and wore a short green nylon jacket. He was somewhere between thirty and thirty-five years of age, with a tanned, clean-shaven face and short military haircut. He stood several inches taller than Jake and was built heavier. On the left breast of his coat was a silver name tag: Keadle. 'Hello,' he said, addressing the greeting to Jake.

'Hi.'

'This is Mr Jacob L. Grafton of Arlington, Virginia,' the girl said. 'He was a friend of Captain Strong's.'

'Izzatso?' The trooper's eyes swept him again, more carefully. 'Why don'tcha step into this other room here for a minute. Susie, how about getting us both coffee. White or black?' he said to Jake.

'Black.'

'Black it is,' he said, and led the way behind the counter and through a door into an adjoining office. His big revolver swung freely below his jacket in a brown holster that hung halfway down his right leg.

'Captain Strong had a little cabin a few miles east of here for weekends and all,' the trooper said. 'I knew him to speak to. Helluva nice guy. Too bad about that wreck.'

Jake nodded and sank onto an old sofa with the stuffing coming through the cracks in the vinyl.

'You in the navy too?' the trooper said.

Jake took out his wallet and extracted his green ID card. He passed it across. The trooper looked it over, both sides, then handed it back. 'Why'd you come up here, Captain Grafton?'

'Were you ever in the service?'

'Marines, four years. Why?'

'Just curious.'

The door opened and Susie came in with coffee in Styrofoam cups. Both men thanked her and she pulled the door shut on her way out.

'Let's try it again. Why'd you come up here, Captain Grafton?'

'To get a copy of this report.'

Keadle thought about that for a bit, then said, 'Well, you got one. What do you think of it?'

'It was a strange accident.'

'How so?'

'Car going up a steep, curvy road on a rainy evening goes skidding off the pavement and across a fifty-foot-wide gravel turnout. Right over the edge. Then there's a furious fire in the passenger compartment.'

'What's strange about that?'

'He must have been flying low that night. Or else somebody pushed him over the edge. And an interior fire – I thought that stuff only happened in movies. Wrecked cars rarely explode or catch fire.'

'You don't say. If it wasn't an accident, who wanted Captain Strong dead?'

'I don't know. I dropped in to see if you did.'

'I'm just a rural peace officer, not some big-city detective. This county don't have much real crime. Seems that most of the scumbags just do their thing over in Washington. I'm not—'

'Let's cut the bullshit. Why aren't you investigating an apparent homicide?'

'Who says I'm not? I'm sitting here chinning with you, ain't I?'

Jake sipped on his coffee. Finally he said, 'Well, you got any more questions?'

'Gimme your address and phone number.' Keadle picked up a pad of paper and a pen from the desk. 'If I think of any I'll give you a call.'

Jake told him the number. 'Susie already gave you my address from my driver's license.' He stood and drained his coffee. 'Thanks for the coffee. I hope you catch him.'

Keadle looked at him with pursed lips.

Jake opened the door and walked out. He nodded at Susie as he went by.

The red flag was up on the Main Street parking meter but no ticket yet. It was almost noon. Perhaps he should stop and see if the prosecutor was in his office. But what good would that do?

There was no way he could make it back to the office before everyone left for the day. Perhaps a hamburger. He fed the meter another quarter and walked down Main Street toward a cafe that he had noticed near the courthouse. Before he got there Trooper Keadle went by in a state police cruiser.

When he finished his lunch Jake drove east on the road back to Washington. Somewhere off one of these side roads, between here and the accident site, Harold Strong had had a cabin. He wished he had thought of finding the cabin and stopping by before he went to town.

Who are you kidding, Jake? What would you look for? A long golden hair on the bedspread? Perhaps a sterling silver cigarette case bearing Mata Hari's initials? You're no murder investigator. Keadle has undoubtedly been through the cabin with a fine-tooth comb. If there were clues he has them.

Thoroughly disgruntled, Jake drove at forty miles an hour along the two-lane highway toward Virginia. He didn't want to see Trooper Keadle in the rearview mirror with his red light flashing. Not too likely, of course. The odds were that Keadle was sitting in his cruiser right now in sight of Strong's cabin, hoping against hope that Jake would drop by and enter without using a key.

Keadle was no hick cop, even if he liked to play the role. He undoubtedly knew a murder when he tripped over one, and then the very next morning a man appeared – by the Lord Harry a vice admiral in the US Navy – who wanted the investigation of the very recent death of a captain in that very same navy put on the back burner. And Keadle and the prosecutor went along. Or did they? And how did the FBI get involved?

But if it didn't happen like that, why did Henry tell that fairy story?

He glanced at the map he had jammed over the passenger's sun visor. The report said the accident happened four miles west of Capon Bridge, that little village Jake had stopped in this morning to get gas. The Shell station.

When he topped the mountain west of Capon Bridge he slowed and looked for the scenic overlook. There. On a whim he parked his car beside the trees so he could examine whatever marks remained after two months. As he got out of his car and surveyed the muddy gravel he knew it was hopeless. Two months of rain and snow and traffic pulling off to look at the valley had totally obliterated the marks that Keadle's report said were here after Strong's wreck.

He walked over to the edge. Some of the guardrails were obviously newer than the others. He looked down the embankment. Beer can, trash, bare dirt, washed-out furrows. Well, it sure looked like a car might have been dragged up that slope some time back. The ground was soft and no plants had yet had a chance to hide the scars. No sense going down there and getting muddy.

Harold Strong died here. Jake had lied to the office girl – he had never met Strong. He stood now feeling foolishly morbid and half listening to a car laboring up the grade from Capon Bridge. The engine noise carried through the trees budding with spring green and echoed off the mountainside.

Henry had been telling the truth about one thing anyway: Harold Strong had been murdered. Not even a race car could come up that grade and around that curve fast enough to skid completely across this pull-out and go over the edge. Not without help.

Jake glanced up as the car climbing the mountain went by. It was going about thirty miles per hour. The driver was watching the road. And the driver was Smoke Judy.

The commanding officer of Attack Squadron 128 (VA-128) nodded at Rita Moravia and Toad Tarkington, then picked up his phone. A yeoman appeared almost immediately to collect their orders for processing and a lieutenant commander was right behind. He led them into another office and gave each of them a manual on the A-6E and introduced them to their personal mentors, two lieutenants. 'These two gentlemen are going to teach you to be credible A-6 crewmen in one week, starting right now. We'll get your luggage over to the BOQ and these guys will drop you there when they get finished tonight.'

Toad's teacher was a prematurely bald extrovert from New England named Jenks, who began talking about the A-6E's electronic weapons system – radar, computers, intertial nav, forward-looking infrared and laser ranger-designator – in the car on the three-block trip to the building that housed the simulators. Toad listened silently with growing dread.

Jenks continued his monologue as he led Toad across the parking lot, lectured on at the security desk while Toad filled out a form to obtain a temporary visitor's pass, and didn't pause for breath as they climbed the stairs and went through a control room and across a catwalk inside a huge room to the simulator, a cockpit mounted on hydraulic rams. 'So just make yourself comfortable here in the hot seat,' Jenks said in summary, 'and we'll move right on into the hardware.'

Toad looked slowly around the cavernous room at the three other simulators. Then he looked into the cockpit. Like every military cockpit in the electronic age, it was filled with display screens, computer controls and information readouts in addition to all the usual gauges, dials, knobs, switches and warning lights. 'I have a question.'

'Shoot.'

'How long is the normal syllabus to train a bombardier-navigator?'

'Eight months.'

'And you're going to cram all that info into me in *one week*?'

'You look like a bright guy. That captain in Washington said you were motivated as hell.'

'Grafton?'

'I didn't talk to him. The skipper did. Sit down and let's get at it.'

Jenks turned and shouted to the technician in the control room, 'Okay, Art, fire it up.'

People were streaming out of Jefferson Plaza at 4:30 when Jake passed through the main entrance on the way in. He was still in civilian clothes. He waited impatiently for the tardy elevator.

The secretary was still in the office along with several officers. What was her name? 'Hi. What's happening?'

'Hello, Captain. Didn't expect to see you today.'

'Yeah. Didn't think I'd make it back. Seen Commander Judy?'

'Oh, he was in for a little while this morning, then he said he had a meeting. Said he'd probably be gone the rest of the day.'

Jake paused near the woman's desk. 'Did he say where the meeting was?'

'No, sir.'

'Was he here when you arrived this morning?'

She tried to remember. 'Yessir, I think so. Oh, by the way, the computer wizard stopped by this afternoon to give you your brief on the office system. He said he was going to be working late, so if you're going to be around a while, I'll call him now and see if he can come over and do the brief.'

'Sure. Call him.'

Jake greeted the other officers and walked across the room to his office door. Two of his new subordinates stuck their heads in for a few pleasantries, then shoved off.

A pile of documents sat in the in basket. Jake flipped through the stuff listlessly. There was enough work here to keep him chained to his desk for a week, or maybe a month since he didn't know anything about most of the matter the letters and memos referred to. He would have to use the staff heavily.

The secretary appeared in his door. 'The computer man will be here in a little while. His name is Kleinberg. Good night, Captain.'

'Did you lock up everything?'

'No, sir. I thought you might want to look through some files.'

'Sure. Good night.'

Jake waited for the door to click shut, then went out into the room. He found Judy's desk and sat down. He stirred through a small pile of phone messages, just names and numbers. A thin appointment book with a black cover. He flipped through it slowly. The days up until now were heavily annotated. Today's page was blank. He held the book at arm's length over the desk and dropped it. It fell with a splat.

Damn! He felt so frustrated.

Well, at least he knew most of Henry's once-upon-a-time story was true, though where that got him he had no idea. And he knew that Judy made a trip to West Virginia today. Why? To see Trooper Keadle or the prosecutor? To search Strong's cabin? Well, Judy was certainly going to be surprised to hear that Jake knew he was there. Or was he? Maybe he would tell Jake himself in the morning.

Jake turned on the office copy machine and while it was warming up stood and read the entries in Judy's calendar again carefully. Smoke seemed to have made a lot of notes about Karen. Karen who? Karen 472-3656, that's who. Why did he write her phone number down so often? Aha, because she had different phone numbers – at least four of them. And this guy Bob – lunch, tennis on Saturday, reminders that he called, to call Bob. Call DE. Call from RM. Drop car at garage. Commode broke. Smoke Judy seemed to jot down everything out of the ordinary. He was a detail man in a detail business.

When he had his copies Jake put the appointment book back on Judy's desk and went back to his little office. In a few moments he heard a knock on the door, so he heaved himself up and walked across the room to admit the visitor.

The man in civilian clothes who came in was slightly below medium height, built like a fireplug and just as bald. 'Hi. Name's Kleinberg. From NSA Computers.' His voice boomed. Here was a man who could never whisper. In his left hand he carried a leather valise.

'I'm Grafton.'

'Beg pardon,' the man said as he reached out and tilted the bottom of Jake's security tag. He stared at it a few seconds, then glanced again at Jake's face. 'Yep, you're Grafton, all right. Can't be too careful, y'know.'

'Uh-huh.'

'Let's look at the patient.'

Jake led the way to his desk. 'I don't know much about computers.'

'No sweat. I know enough for both of us. When we're through, you're going to be able to make this thing sing and dance.' Kleinberg turned on the computer. 'See this prompt here? That's the sign-on prompt and you have to type in your secret password. This is a code that identifies you to the machine, which allows you access to certain files and only certain files. Security, y'know. Here's your password.' He used a pencil on a sheet of paper and wrote, 'Reverberation.'

'How come I can't pick my own word?'

'We tried that on the second go-around. Everyone wanted to come up with something cute, except for the aviators, who all wanted to use their nicknames. You'd have thought they were ordering vanity license plates. So . . . Now type in your password.'

Jake did so. The computer prompt moved from left to right, but the letters failed to appear.

'Now hit "enter." Uh-oh the computer won't take it. So type it again and spell it right.' This time the computer blinked to the next screen. 'You only get two tries,' Kleinberg advised. 'If you are wrong both times, the computer will lock you out and you'll have to see me about getting back in.'

'How can it lock me out if I haven't told it exactly who I am?'

'It locks out everyone who has access from the bank of monitors in this office.' Kleinberg wrote another password on the paper: 'Fallacy.'

'This is the password that allows you access to files relating to the ATA, which is what I understand you are working on here in this shop. Type it in and hit "enter".' Jake obeyed. 'Now, to call up the directory of the files you have access to due to your security clearance and job title, you have to type one more password.' He wrote it down. 'Matriarch.'

After Jake entered his code, a long list of documents appeared on the screen. 'Of course, if you already have the document number, you can type it right in and not bother calling up the directory with the matriarch code word. Got it?'

' "Reverberation," "fallacy" and "matriarch." What was the first go-around on the code words?'

Kleinberg laughed. 'Well, we used computer-generated random series of letters. They weren't words, just a series of letters. But people couldn't remember them and took to writing them down in notebooks, check-books and so forth. So we tried plan two. This is plan three.'

Kleinberg took a lighter from his pocket and held the flame under the piece of paper on which he had written the code words. It flared. Just before the fire reached his fingers, he dropped the paper on the plastic carpet protector under the chair and watched the remnant turn to ash, which he crushed with his shoe. Kleinberg rubbed his hands and smiled. 'Now we begin.' He spent the next hour showing Jake how to create, edit and access documents on this list. When he had finished answering Jake's questions, he flipped the machine off and gave Jake one of his cards. 'Call me when you have a question, or ask one of the guys who's been around a while.'

'Uh-huh.'

'Welcome to Washington.' Kleinberg shook hands, hoisted his leather bag and left.

Jake began to lock away the papers on his desk. While he was here he might as well look again at that two-year-old book of Harold Strong's.

He opened the upper left drawer. The matchbooks and rubber bands and other stuff were still there, but the book wasn't. He looked in every drawer in the desk. Nope. It was gone.

Henry Jenks dropped Toad at the BOQ at 11 p.m. After he filled out the paperwork at the desk, Toad went up to his room and crashed.

The following day was a copy of the previous afternoon: an hour in the simulator, an hour at the blackboard, then back to the simulator. By noon he was navigating from one large radar-reflective target to another. In midafternoon he ran his first attack.

During all his hours in the simulator the canopy remained open and Jenks stood there beside him talking continuously, prompting him, pointing out errors. Running the system in the simulator wasn't too difficult with Jenks right there.

Toad wasn't fooled.

At five hundred feet above hostile terrain on a stormy night with the tracers streaking over the canopy and the missile warning lights flashing, this bombardier-navigator business was going to be a whole different ball game. The pilot would be slamming the plane around, pulling on that stick like it was the lever to open heaven's gate. And the BN had to sit here delicately tweaking the radar and infrared and nursing the computer and laser while trying not to vomit into his oxygen mask. Toad knew. He had been there in the backseat of an F-14. The best way to learn this stuff was by repetition. Every task, every adjustment, the correction for every failure – it all had to be automatic. If you had to think about it you didn't know it and you sure as hell wouldn't remember it when you were riding this bucking pig up the devil's asshole.

At five in the evening Jenks drove him back to the BOQ. 'Tonight you study the NATOPS.' NATOPS – Naval Air Training and Operating Procedures – was the Book on the airplane, the navy equivalent to the air force Dash One manual. 'Learn the emergency procedures. Tomorrow you and Moravia will be in the simulator together. We'll run some attacks and pop some emergencies and failures. The next day you fly the real airplane. Study hard.'

'Thanks, sadist.'

'You're all right, Tarkington, even if you are a fighter puke.'

Toad slammed the car door and stomped into the BOQ. He was whipped, drained. Maybe he ought to go jogging to clean the pipes. In his room he changed into his sweat togs. The wind coming in off Puget Sound had a pronounced bite and the sun was already setting, so he added a second heavy sweatshirt.

He was leaning into a post supporting the roof over the walkway leading to the officers' club when a gray navy pickup pulled up in front of the BOQ and dropped Rita Moravia. She was wearing an olive-drab flight suit and flight boots.

'If you're going running,' she called, 'will you wait for me?'

'Sure.' Toad continued to stretch his right leg, the one with the pins in it. He hopped around and trotted in place a few steps. The leg was ready. On the grass was a bronze bust: Lieutenant Mike McCormick, A-6 pilot killed over North Vietnam. The BOQ and officers' club were named for him.

Toad was standing beside the bust watching the A-6s in the landing pattern overhead and listening to the throaty roar of their engines when Moravia came out. She had her pair pulled back into a ponytail. 'Which way do you want to run?' she asked.

'I dunno. How about north along the beach?' They started off. 'Were you flying today?'

'Yes. Twice.' She picked up the pace to a fast trot.

'How'd you like it?'

'Old airframe, not as fast and agile as the Hornet, of course, but with better range and more lifting capacity. More complex.' An A-6 went over and she waited for the roar to fade. 'It's a nice plane to fly.'

On the western side of the road was a beach littered with driftwood and, beyond, the placid surface of the sound. Just visible in the fading glow of the sunset was an island five or six miles away – it was hard to tell. Silhouettes of mountains stood against the sky to the southwest. 'It's pretty here, isn't it?'

'Oh yes. Wait till you see it from the air.'

'Why'd you get into flying anyway?'

She shot him a hard glance and picked up the pace. He stayed with her. She was going too fast for conversation. The paved road ended and they were on gravel when she said, 'Four miles be enough?'

'Yep.' Well, he had stepped on it that time, got it out and dragged it in the dirt and tromped all over it. What's a pretty girl like you doing in this dirty, sweaty business anyway, sweetie? Ye gods, Toad, next you'll be asking about her sign.

On the inbound leg they stopped running several blocks short of the BOQ and walked to cool down. 'I got into flying because I thought it would be a challenge,' Rita said, watching him.

Toad just nodded. In the lobby she asked, 'Want to change and get some dinner?'

'Thanks anyway. I gotta study.'

As he showered Toad realized that somewhere on the run he had jettisoned his nascent plan to bed Rita Moravia. The Good Lord just doesn't have any mercy for you, Toad, my man. Not the tiniest pinch.

6

'The admiral can see you in thirty minutes, sir.'

'Thanks.' Jake Grafton cradled the phone and doodled on his legal pad.
It was almost 10:30 and Smoke Judy was at his desk. He had said good
morning to Jake and spent an hour on the phone, and now seemed to
be busy on the computer with a report, but he hadn't mentioned his
sojourns of yesterday. Jake had toyed with the idea of questioning Judy
about where he was yesterday, then decided against it. Whatever answer
Judy gave, truth or lie, what would that prove? Would a lie incriminate
him? In what? A murder? Espionage? If Judy told the truth, what would
the truth be? That he went to West Virginia yesterday – so what? And if
he denied it – what then? No, Jake didn't know enough to even ask an
intelligent question.

Vice Admiral Henry, however, was in a more interesting position. His
fairy tale about deflecting a murder investigation left him vulnerable.
Vulnerable to what? To more questions. He would have to answer
reasonable questions or . . . ? Or?'

I can't recognize truth when I hear it, Jake mused. What the hell kind
of job is this? Can I trust the admiral?

Do I have a choice? He tossed the pencil on the desk and rubbed his
eyes. He knew the answer to that one. He had no choice at all. He stood
and stretched. His doodles caught his eye. Airplanes. Gliders. Long wings.

In front of the breezeway between JP-1 and JP-2, he caught the shuttle
bus and rode it over to the Pentagon. The chief offered him a cup of
coffee, which he accepted. Then he was waved in to see Henry, who was
busy locking his desk and office safe.

'Good morning, sir.'

'Morning. Don't sit. We're going to a meeting with SECNAV.'

'Okay.' Jake had never met F. George Ludlow, but he had heard a lot
about him. Scion of an old New England family – was there any other
kind? – Ludlow was in his early forties, a Vietnam vet with a B.S. from
Yale and a business doctorate from Harvard. He had spent ten years
knocking around the gray-suit defense think tanks before being tapped

as Secretary of the Navy three years ago by his father-in-law, Royce Caplinger, the Secretary of Defense. Nepotism, fumed the Senate Democrats, but they confirmed the nomination anyway: Ludlow's credentials were as blue-chip as his family connections and dividends from the family investment trusts.

'What's this meeting about, sir?' Jake asked as he and the admiral walked the outer ring of the Pentagon – the E-ring – toward Ludlow's office.

'Don't know. When Ludlow wants you, he summons you – now.'

It was common knowledge that Ludlow had vigorous hands on the throttle and helm of the navy. He had firm ideas about what ships and weapons systems the navy needed, how they should be acquired, how they should be employed. With his insider's knowledge of Washington and the upper reaches of the defense establishment he outargued most admirals. Those he couldn't win over he shuffled off to sinecures or retirement. Unlike the usual dilettante who spent a year or two as a service secretary on his way to a bright political future or the vice presidency of a major defense contractor, Ludlow behaved exactly like a man whose present job was the fulfilment of a lifelong quest. If Ludlow had any other political or business ambitions, no hint of them had percolated down to Jake's level. His saving grace, or so it appeared to the rank and file, was his strong commitment to the navy as an institution, to its people and its traditions. This was probably one of the reasons for unease at the flag level, since the admirals were unwilling to defer to anyone as keeper of the faith, the role in which they cast themselves.

The corridor in which the secretary's office was located was decorated for the general public. Large oil portraits of naval heroes of the past were prominently displayed; Farragut, Dewey, Halsey and many others. The old admirals stared dourly at Jake and Vice Admiral Henry as they went to their appointment to discuss the navy of the future.

Ludlow's large office was paneled in dark wood, the real thing, not veneer, Jake noticed as he took his first, curious look – and nautical memorabilia were everywhere, on the desk, the credenza, the little sitting desk. Oil paintings of famous naval scenes – also original, Jake noted – adorned the walls. The chairs were black leather. One of them was occupied by a fat gent in his mid-sixties whose skin looked as tough as the chair covering. Jake recognized him from his picture – Senator Hiram Duquesne, chairman of the Senate Armed Services Committee. Ludlow was behind his desk and didn't rise from his chair.

'You gentlemen know the senator,' Ludlow said after Admiral Henry had introduced Jake.

Duquesne eyed Jake speculatively. 'Aren't you the pilot that strapped on El Hakim last year?'

'Yessir.'

'Sit down, gentlemen. Please.' Ludlow gestured to the chairs. Jake ended up on Henry's left, Duquesne on the admiral's right. Ludlow's executive assistant sat on the sofa with a legal pad on his lap, ready to take notes.

The senator and the two naval officers faced the secretary across his massive mahogany desk strewn with paper. Ludlow had one leg draped over his chair arm, revealing hairy skin in the gap between the top of his sock and his trouser leg. In his hands he held a rifle cartridge that still contained a bullet. He worked the cartridge back and forth between his fingers as he spoke to Jake. 'Senator Duquesne wanted to meet you when I informed him you would be doing the testing and evaluation of the ATA prototypes.'

'Now, as I understand it, George, you people are not going to do your usual T and E routine,' Senator Duquesne said. T and E was Test and Evaluation.

'No way to keep the lid on or meet our time goals if we did it the usual way.'

'You a test pilot?' Duquesne shot at Jake.

'No, sir.'

Ludlow's leg came off the arm of his chair. 'He's an attack pilot,' the secretary said mildly, 'one of the very best we have. He knows carrier aviation as well as anyone in uniform.'

'What d'ya know about stealth?' the senator demanded.

'Very little, sir, but I'm learning.'

'Horse puckey! What does the navy need for an attack plane at the turn of the century? What about range, payload, survivability, maintainability? How much should the navy pay?'

'I—' Jake began, but Ludlow was also talking: 'Senator, *policy* is my—'

Senator Duquesne raised his voice. He thundered at Ludlow: 'I'll say this again with these gentlemen present. I'm not happy about this whole thing, George. Not happy. You have a program here that you will want funded for three hundred and fifty airplanes at about fifty million each, seventeen and a half billion dollars' worth, and you intend to make the decision on which prototype to buy based on Captain Grafton's quick and dirty recommendation?'

'You overstate it, Senator. We – being me, CNO, Vice Admirals Henry and Dunedin – we propose to make a recommendation to SECDEF based on the needs of the navy. We will look closely at Captain Grafton's evaluation to help us determine which of the two prototypes best meets those needs. And his evaluation will be quick but it won't be dirty.' The senator twisted in his chair. The secretary continued, relentless. 'No captain determines the needs of the navy, Senator. I do that. The President and SECDEF—'

Duquesne stopped him with an upraised palm. 'Don't lecture me,

George. And don't patronize me! Major weapons systems procurement gets shrouded in secrecy, taken out of the normal channels where Congress can look things over, and major decisions get made on the basis of one document generated by one of your junior subordinates which no one can confirm or refute. And you tell me to *relax*? Seventeen *billion* dollars for a plane that may or may not be adequately tested, that may or may not do what we're buying it to do? Plus ten more billion for spare parts and simulators and all the rest of it. No dirt, huh? Goddamnit, Ludlow, I don't trust you any further than I could throw a scalded cat! You're trying to make Congress a goddamn rubber stamp!'

Ludlow leaned forward in his chair. 'I never said for you to relax! You people *agreed* to the classification level of these black stealth projects! You people *understood* the problems involved and approved the administrative shortcuts! Now you—'

'I said *don't patronize me*! And quit *pointing* that fucking bullet at me!'

Henry rose hastily and Jake followed. 'Talk to you later, Mr Secretary,' he said, and Ludlow nodded as he fired another volley at the senator.

'Jesus,' Jake muttered when they reached the hallway and the door closed behind them.

'Yeah,' the admiral agreed.

'How come Duquesne is so upset when the decision hasn't been made?'

'That's just it. One of the prototypes was manufactured in his home state. He's fought hard on the Hill for stealth and he wants his plane to be chosen and the air force didn't buy it. Now, if the navy doesn't . . . Well, you get the idea.'

'Uh-huh,' Jake said as the full dimensions of his new position came into much better focus. So Henry had asked for him to run the ATA project, eh? No doubt his name had been discussed with Ludlow and the Chief of Naval Operations as well as Vice Admiral Dunedin – NAVAIR. They could praise him to the skies for his report or ease him right out of the navy. They needed a man they could dispose of if necessary. And they found me, Jake thought bitterly. A gilt-edge reputation, my ass!

In Henry's office, Jake said calmly, 'Better make sure your antibugging devices are on.'

The admiral did so while eyeing Jake. When he was seated, Jake said, 'I took a little drive yesterday, sir. Saw a state trooper up in West Virginia named Keadle. Read an accident report.'

'So?'

'Passed one of the guys from my shop on my way back here yesterday afternoon. He was on his way to West Virginia.'

'Oh?'

'Admiral, why don't you tell me what really happened in West Virginia after Harold Strong was killed?'

'Are you suggesting I haven't?'

'I can't do my job, sir, unless you play straight with me. I play straight with you, you have to play straight with me.'

Admiral Henry looked out his window a while, examined his finger-nails and finally directed his gaze back to Jake. 'I think you had better discuss any concerns you have with Admiral Dunedin.' He picked up a sheet of paper and began to scan it. The interview was over.

'Aye aye, sir,' Jake said, and left the room. He retrieved his hat in the outer office and caught the shuttle back to Crystal City.

As the little bus wound its way from the parking lot, Jake looked back at the Pentagon. It appeared low and massive from this perspective. Endless rows of windows. It also looked gray under this overcast.

Admiral Dunedin was in conference. Jake didn't get in to see him until almost 3 P.M. He got right to it. 'I went to West Virginia yesterday to see what I could find out about Harold Strong's death. On the way back here I passed one of the people from my shop heading the other way.'

'Who?' said Dunedin, apparently genuinely curious.

'Smoke Judy.'

'How about that,' Dunedin muttered.

'Admiral, I'm a little baffled. Vice Admiral Henry briefed me on some of the events surrounding Strong's death, but this morning when I mentioned this incident to him, he didn't even ask who it was from my office that passed me. I get the distinct impression I'm being mush-roomed.'

Dunedin lifted an eyebrow, then apparently thought better of it and went back to deadpan. He apparently knew about mushrooms: you kept them in the dark and fed them shit. 'I guess everyone is a little baffled,' he said carefully. 'Strong's death was a tragedy. Nothing *we* can do about it, though.'

'Well, I could sure use a little more infor—'

'Who couldn't? But I don't have any information I can share with you. Sorry.' His tone made the apology a mere pleasantry. Before Jake could reply, he said. 'There's a meeting at sixteen-thirty hours in the Under Secretary of the Navy's office on next year's budget. We've got a billion dollars for ATA buried in there under carrier modernization and enhancement. You go to the meeting and represent me. If they try to cut that line item or slice it down in any way, you call me.'

'Yessir.' The admiral selected a report from his in basket and began to read. Jake left.

After he told the secretary that he was going to a meeting, he walked to the officer personnel office, where he had to wait until two other officers had finished before he could talk to the chief petty officer. 'Do you have my service record in here?'

'Last four digits of your social security number, sir?'

'Oh-six-oh-seven.'

It took the chief just half a minute to pull it from the drawer.

'Chief, how about you ginning up a request for retirement for my signature?'

The chief yeoman's eyes showed his surprise. 'Okay, sir, if that's what you want. It's gotta be effective on the first day of a month between four and six months from now.'

Jake eyed the wall calendar. 'September first. When can I sign it?'

'Monday okay?'

'See you then.'

'Any particular reason you want stated, sir?'

'The usual. Whatever you usually say.'

Dashing the four blocks to Dr Arnold's office after her eleven o'clock class on Friday was always a hassle for Callie. A student or two usually buttonholed her to clarify a point or comment made during class and it took several minutes to satisfy them without being rude. Then came the four-block march which crossed two avenues hub to hub with noon traffic.

She was perspiring slightly when Arnold's receptionist nodded at her. Two minutes early. Of course, a few minutes late wouldn't hurt, but Arnold ended the session precisely at ten minutes before the hour and the fee was $105 regardless. She sank onto the couch and once again tried to decide if the fifty minutes was worth the cost.

Forget the money. What are the most important things to discuss during this session? She was trying to arrange her thoughts when the door opened and Dr Arnold beckoned. He was of medium height, in his late thirties, and wore a neat brown beard. 'He looks like Sigmund Freud before he got old and twisted,' Jake had grumped once. Above the beard this morning was a small, thoughtful smile.

'Good morning, Callie.' He held the door open for her.

'Hello.' She sank into the stuffed armchair across from him, the middle of the three 'guest' chairs. When he used to come Jake always sat on her left, near the window, while she always used this chair. For a brief moment she wondered what Arnold made of her continued use of this chair although Jake wasn't here.

After a few preliminary comments, she stated, 'Jake went back to work this Monday,' and paused, waiting for his reaction.

Arnold prompted. 'How has that gone this week?'

'He seems enthusiastic, and somewhat relieved. They have him working on a new airplane project and he hasn't said much about it. If that's what's he's working on. I think he's disappointed, but it doesn't show. He's hiding it well.' She thought about it. 'That's unusual. He's always been stoic at work – his colleagues have told me that he usually shows little emotion at the office – but he's never been like that at home. I can read him very well.'

Dr Arnold, Benny to all his patients, looked up from his notes. 'Last weekend, did you threaten him?'

Callie's head bobbed. 'I suppose.' She swallowed hard and felt her eyes tearing up. She bit her lower lip. 'I never did that before. Never again!' She moved to the chair near the window, Jake's chair, and looked out. Trees just budding stood expectantly in the pale spring sun. Jake had sat here all winter and looked at the black, bare, upthrusted limbs. And now spring was finally here.

She should never have said those things, about leaving him. She could never do it. She loved him too much to even consider it. But it was so hard last fall, after she thought him dead and her life in ashes. When she heard he was still alive the euphoria swept her to heights she didn't believe possible. The subsequent descent from rapture to reality had been torturous.

An officer from the CNO's office had escorted her to Bethesda Naval Hospital the morning after Jake was flown back from Greece. She had expected – thinking about it now, she didn't know just what she expected. But her hopes were so high and the officer who drove her tried gently to prepare her.

His face was still swollen and mottled, his eyes mere slits, his tongue raw from where he had chewed on it. His eyes – those piercing gray eyes that had melted her a thousand times – they lay unfocused in the shapeless mass of flesh that was his face as IVs dripped their solution into his arms. A severe concussion, the doctor said gently. Jake had taken a lot of Gs, more Gs than any man could be expected to survive. Capillaries had burst under the tremendous strain. And he was grossly dehydrated, unable to take water. Slowly Callie began to understand. Brain damage. Bleeding in the frontal lobe, where memory and personality resided. Oh, she assured herself a hundred times that he would be the same – that life would never play them a dirty, filthy trick like that, that God was in his heaven, that the man who loved her and she loved with all her soul would get well . . . He had gotten well. Almost—

He's quieter, more subdued, as if he's someplace else . . . or thinking of something he can't share.

'Do you think he has forgotten?'

The words startled her. She had been musing aloud.

'I don't know. He says he can't remember much about it, and that's probably true. But he stops there and doesn't say what he does remember.'

Arnold nodded. For three months in this office Jake had said nothing of the flight that led to his injury. What of his decision to die?'

Callie stared at the psychologist. 'You think he made that decision?'

'You know he did.' Arnold's eyes held hers. 'He decided to ram the transport. The odds of surviving such a collision were very small. Jake knew that. He's a professional military aviator; he had to know the probable outcome of a ramming.' The doctor's shoulders moved ever so slightly. 'He was willing to die to kill his enemies.'

After a moment Callie nodded.

'*You* must come to grips with that. It was a profound moment in his life, one he apparently doesn't wish to dwell on or try to remember. The complex human being that he is, that's how he chooses to live with it. Now you must come to grips with his decision and you must learn to live with it.'

'Don't many men in combat come to that moment?'

'I think not.' Benny tugged at his beard. 'The literature – it's hard to say. Most men – I suspect – most men facing a situation that may cause their death who do go forward probably do so without thought. The situation draws them onward, the situation and their training and their own private concept of manhood. But in that cockpit – Jake evaluated the danger and saw no other alternative and decided to go forward. Willingly. To accept the inevitable consequences, one of which would be his death.' He continued to worry the strands of hair on his chin.

'There's a verse in the Bible,' Callie said, her chin quivering. ' "Greater love has no man than this, that a man lay down his life for his friends." '

'Aha! If only you believed that!'

'I do,' she said, trying to convince herself, and turned back to the window. Other husbands went off to work every morning, they had regular jobs, they came home nights and weekends and life was safe and sane. Of course, people die in car wrecks and you read about airliner crashes. But those things don't happen to people like me!

Why couldn't Jake have found a safe, sane, regular job, with an office and a company car and a nice predictable future? Damn him, she had waited all these years for the sword to drop. Those memorial services whenever someone was killed – she always went with Jake to those. The widow, the kids, the condolences, the organ music. But it wouldn't happen to Jake – oh no! He's a good pilot, real good, the other men say, *too good* to ever smear himself all over some farmer's potato field, *too good* to ever leaver her sitting alone in the chapel with the organ wheezing and some fat preacher spouting platitudes and everyone filing past and muttering well-meaning nonsense. Damn you, Jake. *Damn you!*

Arnold passed her a Kleenex and she used it on her eyes. He held out the box and she took several and blew her nose.

'Next week, perhaps we can talk about that little girl you want to adopt?'

Callie nodded and tried to arrange her face.

'Thank you for coming today.' He smiled gravely. She rose and he held the door for her, then eased it shut as she paused at the receptionist's desk to write a check.

He opened her file and made some notes. After a glance at his watch, he picked up his phone and dialed. On the third ring a man answered. One word: 'Yes.'

'She was here today,' Arnold said without preliminaries. 'He's going to be working on a new airplane project, she says.' He continued, reading from his notes.

It wasn't until the A-6 was taxiing toward the duty runway for takeoff that the incongruity of the whole situation struck Toad Tarkington. The plane thumped and wheezed and swayed like a drunken dowager as it rolled over the expansion joints in the concrete. He had been so busy with the computer and Inertial Navigation System while they sat in the chocks that he had had no time to look around and become accustomed to this new cockpit. Now as he took it all in a wry grin twisted his lips under his oxygen mask.

Rita Moravia sat in the pilot's seat on his left in the side-by-side cockpit. Her seat was slightly higher than his and several inches further forward, but due to her size her head was on the same level as his. Not an inch of her skin was exposed. Her helmet, green visor and oxygen mask encased her head, and her body and arms were sheathed in a green flight suit, gloves, steel-toed black boots. Over all this she wore a G suit, torso harness and survival vest, to which was attached an inflatable life vest. Toad wore exactly the same outfit, but the thought that the beautiful Rita Moravia was hidden somewhere under the flight gear in the pilot's seat struck him as amusing. One would never even know she was a woman except for the sound of her voice on the intercom system, the ICS. 'Takeoff check-list,' she said crisply, her voice all business.

Toad read the items one by one and she gave the response to each after checking the appropriate switch or lever or gauge as the plane rolled along. The taxiway seemed like a little highway going nowhere in particular; the concrete runways on the right were hidden by the grassy swell of a low hill. To the left was a gravel road, and paralleling that the beach, where the Puget Sound waves lapped at the land. The water in the sound appeared glassy today. Above them was blue sky, a pleasant change from the clouds that had moved restlessly from west to east since Toad and Rita arrived on the island. Even Mother Nature was cooperating. The background noise of the two idling engines, a not unpleasant drone, murmured of latent power. They promised flight. Toad breathed deeply and exhaled slowly. He had been on the ground too long.

Clearance copied and read back. Toad asked the tower for clearance to take off. It was readily granted. The traffic pattern was momentarily empty. Rita Moravia rolled the A-6 onto the runway and braked to a stop. With her left hand she advanced the throttles to the stops as Toad flipped the IFF to transmit. The IFF encoded the plane's radar blip on all air control radars.

The engines wound up slowly at first, then quick-ended to a full-throated roar that was loud even in the cockpit. The nose of the machine dipped as the thrust compressed the nose-gear oleo, almost as if the plane were crouching, gathering strength for its leap into the sky. Moravia waggled the stick gently, testing the controls one more time, while she waited for the engine temperatures to peak. Outside the plane, Toad knew, the roar of the two engines could be heard for several miles. No doubt the flight crewmen on the ramps near the hangars were pausing, listening as the roar reached them, their attention momentarily captured by the bird announcing its readiness for flight. Finally satisfied, Rita Moravia released the brakes.

The nose oleo rebounded and the A-6 began to roll, gathering speed, faster and faster and faster. The needle on the airspeed indicator came off the peg . . . 80 . . . 100 . . . faster and faster as the wheels thumped and the machine swayed gently over the uneven concrete . . . 130 . . . 140 . . . the nose came off the ground and Moravia stopped the stick's rearward movement with a gentle nudge.

As the broad, swept wings bit into the air the main wheel left the ground and the thumps and bumps ceased.

Moravia slapped the gear handle up and, passing 170 knots, raised the flaps and slats. Climbing and accelerating, the Intruder shot over the little town of Oak Harbor bellowing its song. Upward they flew, upward, into the smooth gentle sky.

He was flying again. It seemed – somehow it was strange and bittersweet all at once. He hadn't thought about this last flight in months, but now as the engines moaned and the plane swam through the air, memories of his last flight with Jake Grafton in an F-14 over the Med flooded over Toad Tarkington. There was fear in those memories. He fought to push them out of his mind as he twiddled the knobs to optimize the radar presentation and checked the computer readouts. He glanced outside. The peaks of the Cascade Mountains were sliding by beneath the plane. The steep crags were gray in those places where the clouds and snow didn't hide their naked slopes.

Rita Moravia had the Intruder level at Flight Level 230 – 23,000 feet. Toad concentrated on the equipment on the panel in front of him. As he tried desperately to remember all that his instructor had told him, he sneaked a glance at Moravia. She sat in her seat calmly scanning the sky and the instrument panel. She had engaged the autopilot and was watching it fly the plane. Now she adjusted the bug on the HSI, the rotating compass ring. She had the Yakima TACAN dialed in. Now she toggled the switch that moved her seat up a millimetre and stretched lazily. 'Nice plane, huh?' she said when her left hand once more came to rest on the throttles, where her ICS button was.

Toad fumbled with his ICS button, which he keyed with his left foot. 'Yeah. Fucking super.'

'How's the system?'

'Looks okay to me, as if I knew.'

'Found Yakima yet?'

He ignored the question as he studied the radar. The city was still seventy miles away according to the TACAN. There it was on the radar, right under the cursor cross hairs, just a blob of solid return amid a whole scopeful of return from hills and ridges and houses and barns.

Yeah, Toad, you better figure out how to find a city in all this mess or this little flight is gonna be a disaster. The whole essence of the bombardier's art was interpreting this jumble of return on the radar scope. And Jake Grafton and those other A-6 perverts demanded he pick it up in just a week! Well, he'd show them! If those attack weenies can figure out this shit in eight months, a week will be about right for the old Horny Toad. After all, this worn-out flying dump truck—

Moravia was asking Seattle Center if they could proceed direct to the start of the low-level route. Toad cycled the steering to that point and examined the radar carefully. Thank God the guys at VA-128 had picked a town on the Columbia River to start the route. Even a blind fighter RIO – Radar Intercept Officer – could find that. Or should be able to find it with the aid of the radar-scope photographs that were included in the navigation package for this route. He arranged the stack of photographs on his kneeboard and compared the first one to the live presentation on the radar scope. Yep!

They had passed the third checkpoint on the navigation route and were somewhere in central Oregon flying at 360 knots true, 335 indicated, 500 feet above the ground, when Toad's savage mood began to improve. He was identifying the checkpoints without difficulty, no doubt because they were ridiculously prominent features in the landscape ahead, but he was finding them. The system seemed to be working as advertised and the INS was tight, tight as a virgin's . . .

For the first time he became aware of Moravia's smooth, confident touch on the controls. She flew the plane with a skill that belied her inexperience. Toad watched her handle the plane. The stick barely moved as the plane rose and fell to follow the ground contour and her thumb flicked the trim button automatically. She was good. The airspeed needle seemed glued to the 335-knot tic on the dial. 'You're a pretty good pilot,' he said on the ICS.

'Just navigate,' she replied, not even glancing at him.

Another casual slap in the chops. Goddamn women! He placed his face against the black hood that shielded the radar scope and studiously ignored her.

The plane approached the Columbia River again from the south down a long, jagged canyon that ran almost straight north out of central Oregon. Stealing glances from the radar, out the right side of the airplane Toad saw a harsh, arid landscape of cliffs and stone pillars, spectacular monuments to the power of wind and water and the vastness of time. The almost vertical rock surfaces produced crisp, sharp images on the radar screen. He examined the infrared display. The infrared images were from a sensor mounted on a turret on the bottom of the aircraft's nose, immediately in front of the nose-gear door. The sides of the rock toward the sun looked almost white on the IR scope, which was mounted above the radar scope and was also shielded from extraneous light by the black flexible hood projecting from the instrument panel.

The navigation checkpoint to enter the navy's target range at Boardman, Oregon, was a grain silo and barn on top of a cliff near the lower reaches of this canyon. The cursors – cross hairs positioned by the computer on the radar screen – rested near a prominent blip. Toad turned up the magnification on the infrared as he moved the cursors to the blip. Yep. That was the barn all right.

Over the barn he cycled the steering to the initial point for the run-in to the target and called the range on radio.

'November Julie 832, you're cleared in.'

Rita let the plane drift up to 1,500 feet above the ground. They had left the cliffs and canyons behind them and flew now over almost flat, gently rolling terrain that was used for dry-land farming. Following a printed checklist on his kneeboard, Toad set the switches in the cockpit for bombing. Six blue twenty-five-pound Mark 76 practice bombs hung on a rack under the right wing, Station Four. Each of these little bombs contained a smoke charge that would mark the spot of impact. The A-6 crossed the initial point, the IP, and Rita swung it toward the target ten miles east.

The target lay on the south side of the Columbia River in flat, dry, treeless country. The run-in line was marked by a dirt road on the ground, but neither Toad nor Rita paid any attention. During the minute and forty seconds it took the Intruder to traverse the ten miles from the IP to the target, Toad was absorbed in getting the cursors precisely on the radar reflector that marked the target bull's-eye, checking the computer and inertial readouts, using the infrared for visual ID, locking up the target with the laser ranger-designator, then checking the information the computer received to make sure it was valid. Finally he put the system into attack. Even though the practice bombs lacked laser seekers, the laser in the nose turret would give the computer more precise range and angular information than the radar could. Rita was equally busy flying the plane and centering the steering commands on the Analog Display Indicator, the ADI, immediately in front of her.

The infrared and laser stayed locked to the radar reflector on the little tower that constituted the target bull's-eye even after bomb release as the nose turret rotated. In the cockpit Toad watched the picture on the infrared display change as the plane passed over the target. He was looking at an inverted picture of the tower when he saw the puff of smoke near the base sent up by the practice bomb. An excellent hit.

On the downwind leg Toad raised his helmet visor and swabbed his face with his gloved hands. This was work. The plane was headed west parallel to the Columbia River. Rita scanned the sky for light aircraft.

'832, your hit twenty-five feet at six o'clock.'

'Roger.' Toad made a note on his kneeboard. 'On the next run,' he said to Rita, 'let's do 500 knots.'

'Okay.'

At the increased speed Toad had only about sixty-five seconds from the IP to bomb release, so he had to work faster. The plane bounced in the warm afternoon thermals. In wartime the plane would race in toward its target at full throttle. The air could be full of flak and enemy radar signals probing the darkness to lock them up for a missile shot. Today over this Oregon prairie under a brilliant sun, Toad could visualize how it would be. Sweat trickled down his forehead and into his eyes as he manipulated the switches and knobs of the equipment. He got the bomb off but he was struggling. He would need a lot of practice to gain real proficiency, and today the equipment was working perfectly, no one was shooting.

'A thousand feet this time, as fast as she'll go.'

'Roger,' Rita said.

As fast as she'll go turned out to be 512 knots indicated. On the next run they came in at five hundred feet, then four hundred, then three.

On the downwind leg before their last run. Toad flipped the radar switch from transmit to standby. The picture disappeared from the scope. A stealth bomber that beaconed its position with radar emissions would have a short life and fiery end. The infrared was passive, emitting nothing.

As they crossed the IP inbound, Toad found the infra-red was still on the bull's-eye tower. With the help of the inertial, the computer had kept the cursors there and the infrared was slaved to the cursors. He turned the laser on early and stepped the computer into attack.

Yes, it could be done, and with practice, done well. Moisture in the air would degrade the IR, of course, but you couldn't have everything.

As they crossed the Columbia climbing northwest, the spotting tower gave them a call. 'We didn't spot your last hit. Maybe the smoke charge didn't go off.'

Toad checked the computer readouts. Rita had been eleven mils off on steering at the moment of weapon release. Toad couldn't resist. He informed her of that fact. She said nothing. 'Still,' Toad added magnanimously, 'an okay job.' He was feeling rather pleased with himself.

'For a woman.'

'I didn't say that, Miss Thin Skin. I said an okay job.'

'Look at the ordnance panel, ace.' Toad did so. He had inadvertently selected Station Three instead of Station Four for the last bomb run. The practice bombs were on Station Four, and the last bomb was undoubtedly still there. Station Three – the belly station – had been empty, thank God! Oh damn. And good ol' Rita had sat there and watched him do it and hadn't squeaked a word! 'Call Center and get our clearance back to Whidbey,' she said now, her voice deadpan.

Toad reached for the radio panel.

Terry Franklin was watching television when he heard the telephone ring. He listened for the second ring, but it didn't come. He sat staring at the TV screen, no longer hearing the words or seeing the picture.

His wife had taken the kids to the mall. She had left only a half hour ago. How long would she be?

He was trying to decide just how much time he had when the phone rang again. He felt his muscles tense. Only one ring.

He turned off the TV and got his coat from the closet. He felt in his pocket for the keys to the old Datsun. They were there. He snapped off the living-room lights and peered between the curtains at the street. No one out there.

Ring, pause, ring, pause, ring . . .

Three rings. The drop on G Street. He would have to hurry to beat Lucy and the kids home. He remembered to lock the door behind him.

Matilda Jackson was sixty-seven years old and she was fed up. Five years ago she retired from the law firm where she had worked as a clerk-typist for twenty-six years. Seventeen months ago she had made the last payment on her mortgage. The house wasn't much – a run-down row house in a run-down neighborhood – but by God it was hers. And it was all she could afford on her social security income and the $93.57 she got every month from the law firm's pension plan.

The house had been something when she and Charlie bought it in 1958, and Charlie had been a good worker inside and outside, keeping everything painted and nice and the sidewalk swept. But he had died of diabetes – had it really been sixteen years ago? – after they amputated his feet and his liver got bad.

Poor Charlie, thank God he can't see this neighborhood now, it'd break his heart. Everything gone to rack and ruin, trash everywhere, and those kids selling dope in the house right across the street, the house where ol' lady Melvin, the preacher's widow, used to live. Some old man from New Orleans was in there now: she didn't know his name.

Mrs Jackson heard a car stop outside and peered through the window. Four young men dressed fit to kill stood on the sidewalk looking around.

Mrs Jackson reached for her camera, an ancient Brownie, but she had loaded it with some of that new film the man at the drugstore said would take pictures without a flash. When she got the camera ready and pointed through the gap in the drapes she could see only two men. The other two must have gone inside.

Damn those cops anyway.

She had told those detectives that Melvin's was a crack house and nothing had happened. They weren't going to pay much attention to a fat old black lady, no way. She had seen that in their hard eyes as they looked up and down the street at the boarded-up windows and the trash and that worthless, shiftless Arnold Spivey sitting on Wilson's stoop drinking from a bottle in a paper bag.

She was going to get pictures. They would have to do something if she had pictures. And if they didn't do anything, she would send the photos to that neighborhood watch group or maybe even the newspapers. Leaving old people to watch their neighborhood rot and the dope peddlers take over – they would have to do something about pictures.

She snapped the camera at the two men on the sidewalk, slick loose-jointed dudes with sports coats and pimp hats with wide brims and flashy hatbands. The license plate of that big car would be in both photos.

Here comes someone. A white man, walking bold as brass after dark in a neighborhood as black as printer's ink, a neighborhood where the kids would rip off your arm to get your Timex watch. She squinted. Late fifties or early sixties, chunky, wearing a full-length raincoat and a little trilby hat. Oh yes, he went by earlier this evening, just walking and looking. She hadn't paid much attention then, but here he is, back again. She pointed the camera and clicked the shutter. The two dudes on the opposite sidewalk by the big car were watching him, but he was ignoring them.

Now what did he just do? Stuffed something in that hollow iron fence post as he walked by.

Why did he do that? My God, the street is full of trash; why didn't he just throw it down like everyone else does?

The two men who had gone into the crack house came out and they and their compatriots piled in the car and left, laughing and peeling rubber. Mrs Jackson got more photos of them, then busied herself in the kitchen making tea since the street seemed quiet now.

She was sipping tea in the darkened living room and looking through the curtain gap when a haggard black woman in dilapidated blue jeans and a torn sweatshirt staggered around the corner and along the sidewalk to the crack house. She struggled up the steps to the stoop. The door opened before she even knocked. Mrs Jackson didn't bother taking her picture; she was one of the regulars, a crack addict who Mrs Jackson suspected didn't have long to live. Mrs Blue next door had said her name was Mandy and she had heard she was doing tricks under the Southeast Freeway.

Nobody gave a damn. About Mandy or Mrs Jackson or Mrs Blue or any of them. Just a bunch of poor niggers down in the sewer.

Wonder what that white man stuffed in that fence post? Something to do with that crack house, no doubt. Maybe he's a judge or police on the take. Not getting enough. Maybe it's money, a pay-off for someone.

Well, we'll just see. We've got some rights too.

She pulled her sweater around her shoulders and got her cane. Her arthritis was bothering her pretty badly but there was no help for it. She unbolted the door and lowered herself down the steps. As she approached the hollow iron post two houses down she glanced around guiltily. Her frustration was fast evaporating into fear. No one looking. Quick! She reached into the post. Only a crushed cigarette pack. Disappointed, she felt around in the hollow cavity. There was nothing else. With the cigarette pack in her pocket, she slowly made her way back to her house, steeling herself to look straight ahead, Oh God, why had she done this?

She locked and bolted her doors and sat at the kitchen table examining her find. Writing on the back, block letters. Numbers and such. Code of some sort. Payoffs, most likely. We'll see what the police make of all this. Not that they'd ever tell an old black woman what it's all about. No matter, if they'd just close that crack house, that'd be something.

But should she go to the police? They've been told about that crack house and they've done nothing. What if the police have been paid off? What if they tell the dopers about her?

Mrs Jackson had lived too long in the ghetto not to know the dangers associated with interfering in someone else's illegal enterprise. As she stared at the cigarette pack she realized she had crossed the invisible line between officious nuisance and enemy. And she knew exactly what happened to enemies of dope dealers. They died. Fast and bloody. Those four punks on the sidewalk in their fancy clothes would smile as they cut off her ears, nose and tongue, then her arms.

She turned off the kitchen light and sat in the darkness, trying to think. What should she do? My God, what had she *done*?

Mrs Jackson was still sitting in the darkness of her kitchen thirty minutes later when Terry Franklin walked past the front of her house toward the hollow post. He had parked the car three blocks away. Normally he was very circumspect and drove around for at least an hour to make sure that he had lost any possible tails, but tonight he was in a hurry. He had to get home before Lucy and the kids got back from the mall. So he had driven straight from Annandale to G Street.

The block appeared empty. No, there was someone sitting in a doorway, across the street. Some black guy with a brown bag. A wino. No sweat. What a shitty neighborhood! He had never understood why the Russians had picked a drop in a run-down black neighborhood, but since he hadn't talked to them after he had found the described drops, he had had no opportunity to ask.

It would be just his luck to get mugged down here some night.

He walked at a regular pace toward the post, not too fast and not too slow. Just a man who knows where he's going. He would just reach in while barely breaking stride, get the cigarette pack and keep on walking, right on around the block and back to his car. Piece of cake.

He slowed his pace as he reached into the post.

It was empty!

Dumbfounded, he stopped and looked in. There was just enough light coming from the streetlight up on the corner and the windows of the houses to see into the hole. It was about four inches deep. *Empty!*

He walked on. What had happened? This had never happened before. What in hell was going on?

He turned and walked back to the post. He looked in again. The hole was still empty. He looked around on the sidewalk and the grass behind the fence for anything that might be an empty cigarette pack.

Nothing!

It *must* be here, somewhere, and he just wasn't seeing it.

He was living one of those cold-sweat gibbering nightmares where you are stuck in quicksand and going to die and the rope is forever just inches out of reach. Finally he realized the cigarette pack truly wasn't there.

Maybe he was being set up. Maybe the FBI was going to grab him.

Franklin looked around wildly, trying to see who was watching. Just blank windows. The wino – still there, sucking from his bottle. He reached into the hole again, trying to understand. Someone had gotten it. God, it must be the FBI. They *must* be on to him. Even now, they're *watching* from somewhere, ready to pounce. Prison – he would go to *prison*. The wino – an agent – watching and laughing and ready to arrest him.

Terry Franklin panicked.

He ran for the car, a staggering hell-bent gallop down the sidewalk as he tried to look in every direction for the agents closing in. To *arrest* him.

He careened into a garbage can and it fell over with a loud clang and the lid flew off and garbage went everywhere. He kept running. At the intersection a car slammed on its brakes to the screeching of tires, barely missing him. He bounced off a parked car but he didn't slow.

He almost broke the key getting it into the door lock. The engine ground mercilessly and refused to start.

He smacked his head against the steering wheel in rage, and frustration. He tried the ignition again as he scanned the sidewalks, searching for the agents that must be coming.

The engine caught. Franklin slammed the shift lever into drive and mashed on the accelerator.

Bang! Into the car ahead. *Holy . . . !* Reverse. Then forward, out of the parking space.

Cranking the wheel over at the corner, he slewed around with tires squalling and stomped on the gas.

Toad Tarkington stared glumly at the remains of a beer in the glass in front of him. Across the table Rita Moravia was chattering away with the peckerhead attack pilot who had spent the last three days initiating her into the mysteries of the A-6. Beside Toad sat the bombardier who had been coaching him, ol' Henry Jenks. Both these mental giants were hanging on every word from Moravia's gorgeous lips. There she sat, smiling and joking and behaving like a real live normal woman-type female, as she never did around him, damn her! And these two attack weenies were eating it with a spoon!

The pilot, Toad decided, had a rather high opinion of himself. He looked and acted like a lifelong miser who has just decided to spend a quarter on a piece of pussy that he knows will be worth two dollars. His smile widened every time Moravia glanced into his little pig eyes. If he wasn't careful his face would crack.

This BN, Jenks, wasn't any better. He obviously hadn't had a good piece of ass since his junior year of high school. Jenks was telling a funny to the pilot as he watched Rita's reaction out of the corner of his eyes. 'Do you know a fighter puke's definition of foreplay?' After the obligatory negative from his listeners, Jenks continued. 'Six hours of begging.' Rita joined in the ha-ha-has.

Watching these two cheap masturbators in action was a thirsty business. The waitress caught Toad's hi sign and came over. 'Four double tequilas, neat,' Toad said, and looked around to see if there were any other orders. The attack weenies were still drooling down Moravia's cleavage as she told an anecdote about something or other. 'That's it,' he told the waitress, who regarded him incredulously.

'Four?' she asked.

'Yeah.'

She shrugged and turned away.

The club was still crowded with the remnants of the Friday-night Happy Hour gang. The married guys had left some time back and a bunch of reservists were drifting in. Altogether forty or fifty people, ten or twelve of them women, three of whom were still in uniform. Canned rock music blared from loudspeakers that Toad didn't see. Only one couple was dancing.

When the waitress brought the drinks she sat them in the center of the table. Jenks looked at the drinks with raised eyebrows. 'I'll have another beer,' he said. 'Perrier with a twist,' Moravia chirped. 'Diet Coke,' intoned the lecher beside her.

Toad drank one of the tequilas in two gulps. The liquor burned all the way down. Ah baby!

Another song started on the loudspeakers, a fast number. Toad tossed off a second drink, then climbed up on his chair. He straightened and filled his lungs with air. *'Hey, fat girl,'* he roared.

Every eye in the place turned his way. Toad picked the nearest female and leaped toward her with a shout. 'Let's dance!' Behind him his chair flew over with a crash.

And oh, that woman could dance.

7

The bedroom lights were on in the second story of the town house when Terry Franklin parked the car. He turned off the ignition and headlights and sat behind the wheel, trying to think.

He had driven around for an hour and a half after his panicked departure from the drop, craning to spot the agents he felt sure were tailing him. At one point he had pulled over and looked at the damage to the front of his car. The left front headlight was smashed and the bumper bent from smacking into that car when he tried to get out of that parking space too quickly.

A dozen times he thought he spotted a tail, but the trailing vehicle usually went its own way at the next corner or the one after. A blue Ford with Pennsylvania plates followed along for half a mile until he could stand it no longer and ran a red light. His panicky wanderings back and forth through the avenues and traffic circles of downtown Washington seemed like something from a drug-induced nightmare, a horrible descent into a paranoid hell of traffic and stoplights and police cars that refused to chase him.

Franklin sat now behind the wheel smelling his own foul body odor. His clothes were sodden with sweat.

Lucy and the kids were home. He tried to come up with a lie for Lucy as he scanned the street for mysterious watchers and people sitting in cars.

How long could he live like this? Should he take the money he had and run? Where could he run with the FBI and CIA looking for him? He didn't have enough money to evade them forever. Should he go to Russia? The very thought nauseated him. Freezing in some gray workers' paradise for the rest of his days was about as far from the good life as a man could get this side of the grave.

He wasn't feeling well and went to the dispensary, that was what he would tell Lucy. God knows he must look like he was in the terminal stages of AIDS. No good. No prescription. A beer. Yeah, he went out for a beer. He got out of the car wishing he had really stopped for one. After another look at the broken headlight and grille, he plodded toward the front door.

She came out of the kitchen when she heard the door open. 'Where have *you* been?' She stood rigid, her face pale.

Uh-oh. He kept his voice calm. 'Hey, babe. I went out for a beer. Did you all get anything at the mall?'

'I *know* where you've been. Cindy across the street has told me all about your little expeditions when I'm out for the evening. I know *all* about you, you son of a bitch.'

He stared, thunderstruck. This isn't happening. No, not to me. For the love of – 'How?'

'Who is she? I want to know. Who is she?'

'Who is who?'

'Who is the goddamn bitch you're tomcatting with, you son of a fucking bitch. Who *is* she?'

At last he understood. As the relief washed over him he was suddenly too weak to stand. He sank into a chair. 'Lucy, there's no other wo—'

'*Don't* give me that *shit*! *I* know! Cindy *told* me!' She was a quivering, shouting pillar of hysterical righteousness. 'You're *cheating* on me.' Tears were flowing now. 'Oh God. I tried so hard . . .'

'Lucy, calm down. Please, for the love of— The kids will hear. Honest to God, there's no other woman.' He got to his feet and approached her. 'Babe, I love you. There's nobody—'

'Don't you touch me, *liar*. I'm getting a divorce.' She spun and made for the stairs. 'I'm locking the bedroom door. If you try to get in, I'll call the police. Liar. Cheat. Bastard.'

He lost it. It had been that kind of evening. 'You crazy cunt,' he roared. 'You don't know shit. I went down to the corner for a goddamn beer and when I get home you're fucking *loony* crazy. I haven't cheated on you! I haven't fucked another woman since that night I knocked you up at the drive-in. You don't have any goddamn evidence at all, you crazy lunatic.'

He heard the bedroom door slam and the kids sobbing. He threw himself onto the living-room couch. Some days – it's absolutely crazy how some days just go bug-fuck nuts. You almost get arrested, smash up the front of the car, your wife demands a divorce because you're cheating on her when you're not. What else? What else can fucking happen before midnight?

The drop was empty. He stretched out on the couch and contemplated that fact. He closed his eyes and tried to relax. He could hear Lucy putting the kids to bed upstairs. Finally the noises stopped.

He would have to call them. In Miami they had given him an emergency telephone number that he had memorized and a verification code. He would call. He looked around for the evening paper. On top of the TV. He flipped to the sports section. The code was simple; the location and opponent in the next scheduled game of the Bullets, Orioles or Redskins, whichever was in season. They had been insistent; he was never to call except in an emergency and then only from a pay phone. Well, this was sure as hell an emergency. But he wasn't going back out onto those streets tonight, no way. Even if he could work up the courage, Lucy would use a butcher knife on his crotch when he got back.

He went into the kitchen and dialed the phone. On the third ring a man's voice answered with a recitation of the telephone number. The voice was tired, the English perfect. 'Six-six-five, oh-one-oh-five.'

'This is Poor Richard.' He had picked his code name himself. Easier for him to remember, they said. 'It wasn't there. It wasn't at the dr—'

'Verify please.' The voice was hard, exasperated.

'The Bullets play the Celtics tomorrow night at Capital Centre.'

'I'll call you back. Where are you?'

'Seven-two-nine, seven-four-oh-one.'

'You're at *home?*' The voice was incredulous, outraged.

'Yeah, I—' He stopped when he realized he was talking to a dead instrument.

Shit. He would have to call again. He had to find out what the hell was going on. A pay phone. Lucy was going to come sweet-Jesus holy-hell screaming unglued. What a night! He picked up his jacket and eased the front door shut behind him.

From her seat on the top of the stairs, Lucy heard the door close. She had started to come down earlier but stopped when she heard him enter the kitchen and pick up the phone. She had heard his side of the conversation and she sat now trying to figure it out. 'Poor Richard' he had called himself. It wasn't there. The Bullets play the Celtics? A code of some sort?

What is he into? she asked herself, her horror growing. He had looked so stunned when she said she knew. That look was the verification she needed that he was cheating on her. But how did that fit with a code and nonsense sentences? Was he placing bets with a bookie? No, he wasn't spending money she didn't know about. Something to do with his job at the Pentagon? Could he be spying, like those Walkers several years ago? No, that wasn't possible. Or was it? He would do it if he could get away with it, she decided. In their eleven years of marriage she had found him a man who always put himself first.

What else could it be? My God, what other possibilities were there?

The sun was still embedded in the gray scud over the ocean on Saturday morning when Jake and Callie walked through the gap in the low dune on their way to the beach. Callie trailed along behind him on the narrow path, her hands tucked into the pockets of her windbreaker.

He strolled as he always did, his eyes moving restlessly across the sky and the sea and the naked sand and coming to rest often on her. Whenever she was with him she drew his eyes. It had been that way since they first met, one of the little unconscious things he did that told her without words what she meant to him. This morning walking beside him she was acutely aware of his glances.

'How did your little interview with the soul stripper go yesterday?'

'He says I have to come to grips with your decision to ram that transport in the Med last fall.'

Jake stopped and turned to face her. He looked bewildered. 'What the hell are you worrying about that for?'

'For a week I was a widow.'

He turned away and looked out to sea. It was a moment before he spoke. 'You may be again someday.' He faced her. 'Women live longer than men these days. I don't have a crystal ball, Callie. *Jesus*, we can't stop living because we're mortal.' He gestured angrily. 'I may get hit by a meteor ten seconds from now. I may get run over by some drunk when I step off the curb at—'

He stopped because she was walking away from him, along the beach, her arms wrapped around her chest.

He hurried after her. 'Hey—'

'For a whole week you were *dead*! You had killed yourself chasing those damned Arabs and I was left here all alone!' He put his hand on her arm and she jerked away, whirling to face him. 'You *knew* how much I loved you and . . . and . . . when they called and said you were alive, the memorial service was scheduled for the *next* morning. I was going to *bury* you. You were *dead*!' He enveloped her in his arms and she pressed her face against his shoulder.

After a while she stopped trembling and he murmured, 'Still love me?'

'Yes.'

'A little bit or a whole lot?'

'I haven't decided.'

With his arm around her shoulder, he started them walking north again. In a moment he paused and kissed her, then they resumed their journey with their arms locked together.

Something while. Whatever it was that blocked Toad's gaze, it was white. He closed his eyes and the pain and nausea washed over him, enveloping him. Ye gods . . . Something hard and cold against his cheek – he opened his eyes again – and white. Lotta light . . . He moved. Shit! He was lying in a fucking bathtub.

He raised himself slowly. His head felt like it was coming off. He was still dressed in his khaki uniform, but it was wrinkled and had vomit on it. He still had his shoes on. Oh god, he felt worse than he had ever felt in his entire twenty-eight years, felt like he had been dead for a week or two. He sat up slowly. His head was being hammered on by an angry King Kong. After a moment he grasped the shower handles and faucet and hauled himself erect. He swayed as the blood pounded in his temples with every beat of his heart. Then he tried to step out of the tub. He tripped and sprawled heavily on the floor, striking his head against the bottom of the sink cabinet. He lay there, too sick and dazed to move.

Amid the pain he heard the door open. 'Good morning.' A woman's voice.

Toad flopped over and squinted against the ceiling light. Rita Moravia!

What had he done to deserve this? It's true, life is all misery and pain.

'I'd appreciate it if you would transport yourself to your own room, Tarkington. Now. I don't want anybody to get the wrong idea about you and me.'

He tried to speak. His mouth was dry and tasted of sour vomit. He cleared his throat and licked his lips. 'How'd I get here?'

'Four men carried you in here last night. We thought someone should keep an eye on you during the night. I volunteered.'

'Aren't you a sweetie.'

'I want you out of here, Tarkington.'

He hoisted himself up and staggered past her. He was going to have to find another bathroom pretty damn quick. He went through the little sitting room and got the door open and was hustling down the hall when he heard her voice behind him. 'We're flying at two this afternoon. Meet you in the lobby at ten till twelve.'

Jake sat on the crest of the low dune and watched the glider moving north, away from him above the dune. He had its nose pointed obliquely forty-five degrees out to sea, but the velocity of the incoming wind was such that the plane stayed more or less over the dune. He was holding her low, only eight or ten feet up, to take advantage of the upward vector of the breeze as it cross the low sand hill.

'Better turn her back this way,' advised the eleven-year-old aviation expert from up the street.

Jake banked the plane. 'Keep the nose up,' David urged, his voice rising. Jake fed in back stick. Too late. The right wingtip kissed the sand and she cartwheeled. David was up and running instantly.

The boy was examining the wreckage when Jake reached him. The rubber bands that held the wings to the fuselage had popped off, which undoubtedly minimized the damage. 'A hole in the wing Monokote and a busted spar in the right horizontal stabilizer,' the youngster advised cheerfully. 'Not bad. Yippy skippy! You gotta remember to feed in a little back stick on the turns.'

'Yeah. Let's take it over to my house and fix it.'

'What kind of planes do you fly in the navy?' David asked as they walked down the beach with the pieces of the glider in their arms.

'A-6s mostly. Last year I flew the F-14 some.'

'Wow, those fighters! Did you see *Top Gun*?'

'Uh-huh.'

'My dad bought that movie for me. I must have watched it a couple dozen times. When I grow up I'm gonna fly fighters.' He paused, apparently considering the implications of this bold statement. 'What's it really like?' he asked, not quite so confident.

Jake was still trying to explain when they rounded the corner and he saw the strange car in the driveway. When he saw the blue Department of Defense bumper sticker with the three stars on it, he knew. Vice Admiral Henry. He led the boy inside.

The admiral was wearing jeans and a heavy jacket today. He and another man in a coat sat at the dining room table with Callie drinking coffee. David marched over to her and held the wing so she could see it. 'He let the nose fall in a turn and crashed. We can fix it, though.'

'Good morning, Admiral.'

'Jake, I'd like you to meet Luis Camacho.'

'Hi.' Jake leaned across the table and shook hands. Camacho was in his early fifties with no tan, a man who spent his life indoors. Even though he wore a jacket his spare tire was evident, but his handshake was firm and quick. He didn't smile. Jake got the impression that he was not a man who smiled often.

'Nice place you have here,' Camacho said.

'We like it,' Callie said. 'Would you like a quiet place to talk?'

The admiral stood. 'I thought we could take a walk along the beach. Be a shame to drive all the way over here from Washington and not walk on the beach.'

The three men left David working on the glider at the kitchen table. He was telling Callie about servos and receivers when they went out the door.

'Nice day,' Admiral Henry muttered as they walked toward the beach trail at the end of the street.

'They're all nice here,' Jake said. 'Raw and rainy at times, but nice.'

'Luis is from the FBI.'

'Got credentials?' Camacho produced them from a pocket and passed them to Jake, who looked the ID card and badge over carefully and returned them without comment.

Henry stopped at the end of the little path that led through the waist-high dune and looked right and left, up and down the beach. He turned right, south, and walked with his hands in his pockets toward the area with the fewest people. He didn't even glance toward the ocean. Out on the horizon a large containership was making its way north, perhaps to round Cape Henlopen and go up the Delaware.

'Yesterday you wanted to know what really happened in West Virginia after Harold Strong was killed.'

'Yessir.'

'I told you the truth, but I left a few things out. Camacho here was with me that morning. We met with Trooper Keadle and the local prosecutor, guy named Don Cookman. They weren't happy campers. They knew murder when they saw it and cooperation smacked of cover-up. So Luis got on the phone to Washington and the director of the FBI drove up along with the forensic team. We got cooperation with a capital C from then on.'

'Go on,' Jake prompted when the admiral fell silent.

The admiral turned to face him. 'You're asking too damn much, Jake.'

'I'm not asking for anything other than what I need to know to do my job.'

'Like shit.'

'Would you let yourself be led along by the nose if you were me? Jesus Christ, Admiral, my predecessor was murdered! I got a wife over there' – he pointed back toward his house – 'who would like to have me alive for—'

'What do you want to know?'

'Why was Strong killed? What did you tell those people in West Virginia? Why the silence on a murder? Who and what are you investigating?' He looked at Camacho. 'Who the hell *are* you?'

Camacho spoke first. 'I'm special agent in charge of the Washington-area FBI group that handles counter-espionage. *That's* why the locals in West Virginia cooperated. That's why Trooper Keadle called me when you left his office Thursday. That's why he called me when Commander Judy showed up that afternoon to search Harold Strong's cabin.' He turned and started down the beach, still talking. Admiral Henry and Jake Grafton trailed along. 'Why was Strong killed? If we knew that we would be almost there. It wasn't personal or domestic. No way. It was a hit, a contract. He got taken out by someone who knew precisely what they were doing, a cool customer. So the hypothesis that seems most likely is that he knew something he shouldn't. That leads us to his job – The ATA program.'

'That sea story about a Minotaur – that was true?'

'Yeah, that's the code name. But we don't know if it's one guy or several,' the agent said, with a glance at Tyler Henry, who picked that moment to look out to sea.

'I thought,' Jake said, 'that these spy things usually get broken when you get somebody to talk.'

'That's the history. It'd be nice if we knew who to put the screws to to clean up this little mess. But we don't. So right now we're busy doing it the hard way.' He led the two naval officers along the beach as he talked and answered questions. When Jake remembered to glance out to sea, the containership was no longer in sight.

'Let's transfer Smoke Judy,' Jake suggested to the admiral.

Henry just stared at him.

'Dunedin said if I got goosey, I could get rid of him.'

'I'd rather you left him in place,' Camacho said. 'I've already made that request to Admiral Henry and now I'll make it to you.'

'Going to be real tough to pretend I don't know anything.'

'You don't *know* anything,' Henry growled. He jerked his thumb at Camacho. 'If he talked to you for a week, you still wouldn't know anything. I sure as hell don't.'

An hour later, as they came single file through the dune trail, Henry said, 'Now you know as much as I do, which is precious little. On Monday you tell that chief in officer personnel to tear up your retirement papers.'

'Yessir.'

'Don't ever pull that stunt on me again, Grafton.'

'Or . . . ?'

'Don't you abandon ship and leave me and Dunedin up to our necks alone in this sack of shit.'

After the two men had departed in the admiral's car, Jake went back into the house. Callie was sitting on the couch reading a book. 'David got your plane fixed, but his mother called and he went home for lunch. He said he would come back later and help you fly it.'

Jake nodded and poured a cup of coffee.

'Want to tell me about it?'

'Huh?'

'Jake . . .' Her voice had that time-to-come-clean, no-more-nonsense tone. That tone in her voice always got his attention, perhaps because his mother had used it so effectively some years ago.

'Admiral Henry's my boss's boss. Camacho's a civilian. They drove over here to talk about a problem at the office. A classified problem. That's all I can say. You want coffee?'

She nodded yes. When he handed it to her she said, 'So you *are* working on the ATA program?'

'Callie, for Christ's sake. I told you I was. I don't lie to you.'

She sipped her coffee for a bit. 'David likes you,' she said.

It made him nervous when she shifted subjects like that. 'He's a great kid,' he said noncommittally. 'Honest, Callie. I tell you the truth. If something's classified and I can't talk about it, I just say so. You know that! You know me!'

She nodded her agreement and picked up the book. He waited a moment, slightly baffled, then wandered outside with his coffee cup in his hand. Women! Any man who thinks he's got them figured out should be declared incompetent and incarcerated to protect himself.

*

The cursors were running all over the scope when it occurred to Toad to check the velocities in the inertial. They were all gone to hell. 'Hold this heading,' he growled at Rita as he consulted his kneeboard cards. He pushed the buttons to take the inertial out of the system, then typed in a wind he thought would work.

'Okay,' he told her. 'This run, no inertial and no radar. Computer dead reckoning and the IR – that's all we'll use. We'll even leave the laser off. Go in at a hundred feet and let's see if we can hit anything.' Below two hundred feet system deliveries in the A-6 were degraded, probably, Toad suspected, due to the trigonometry of low grazing angles.

She lowered the left wing and let the nose sag down into the turn. When she leveled the wings they were on the run-in line at a hundred feet, throttles against the stops, bouncing moderately in the turbulence as the engines moaned through their helmets.

He got the reticle, or cross hair, on the IR display onto the tower. The cross hairs started drifting. The wind he typed into the computer was wrong. He pushed the velocity correct switch, then held the cross hairs on the tower bull's-eye.

'Master Arm on, in attack, and in range.'

'I'm committed,' she said. This meant she had squeezed the commit trigger on the stick, authorizing the computer to release the weapon.

Toad glanced out his side window. The desert was right there, close enough to touch, racing by beneath them. He came back to the IR scope. All okay. If Moravia got distracted and let the nose fall just a smidgen, they would be a fireball rolling across the desert so quickly they would never even know what happened. 'Release coming,' he advised. The cursors started to drift in close and he held them on the base of the tower.

When the release came she eased back on the stick and Toad felt the G press him down even as he watched the tower on the IR scope – now going inverted – for the hit. Pop. There it was! Almost dead-on.

That was the last bomb. He glanced at the panel in front of her. They were climbing and heading north for Yakima. He flipped the radar to transmit and began to adjust the picture.

'Your hit forty feet at seven-thirty.'

'Boardman, thanks a lot. We're switching to Center.'

'Have a safe flight.'

'Yo.' Toad dialed in the Seattle Center frequency.

'Pretty good bombing for a fighter puke,' Moravia said.

'Yep. It was that,' he agreed smugly, relishing the role and willing today to play it to the hilt. Moravia had had her fun last night. His head was still thumping like a toothache. 'Ain't anybody better than the ol' Horny Toad.'

'Or anyone more humble.'

'Humble is for folks that can't,' he shot back. 'I *can.*'

Rita called Center and asked for a clearance to the military operating area over Okanogan. She leveled the plane at Flight Level 220. Toad played with the scope.

Entering the area, Rita disengaged the autopilot and looked about expectantly. She and her pilot instructor of the previous week, Lieutenant Clyde 'Duke' Degan, had agreed to and briefed an ACM engagement. She was right on time. Now if she could just find him first. She dialed in the squadron tactical frequency and gave him a call.

'I'm here,' Degan replied.

Toad caught the first glimpse of the other A-6. It was high, near the sun. Ol' Duke didn't intend to give Moravia any break at all. 'All right,' Toad enthused. 'Now, by God, we're playing my game!' Toad pointed over her left shoulder. 'Up there. Better turn under him and get the nose down for some airspeed.'

Rita knew Toad had just recently finished a three-year tour in the backseat of F-14 Tomcats. He had ridden through literally hundreds of practice dogfights. Fighter crews lived for Air Combat Maneuvering (ACM), the orgiastic climax of their training and their existence. So she knew Toad Tarkington undoubtedly knew a thing or two about dog-fighting. She took his advice. 'Think he's seen us?' The A-6's radar had no air-to-air capability.

Toad kept the other plane in sight. Immediately above them – maybe two miles above – it rolled inverted, preparatory to a split S. 'Looks like it,' Toad murmured. 'Already you're at a serious disadvantage, assuming he's smart enough to cash in.'

With the throttles on the stops, she began a climbing right turn holding 340 knots indicated, the best climb speed. Toad glanced across the panel, then cranked his neck to keep the other plane in sight. 'He's coming down like a ruptured duck,' Toad advised. 'If you had guns you could get a low-percentage deflection shot here. Shake him up some.'

The other plane came rocketing down with vapor pouring off its wingtips. Now his wingtip speed brakes – boards – came open. 'He's trying to minimize his overshoot.' The other Intruder went dropping through their altitude with the boards still open, vapor swirling from his wings. 'Work the angles,' Toad advised. 'Turn into him and get the nose down.'

Rita Moravia did just that in a workmanlike four-G pull. 'Not too much nose-down,' Toad grunted against the G. Duke Degan would undoubtedly use his energy advantage to zoom again and try to turn in behind her, but he should not have left the boards out as long as he did. That was his second mistake. His first was the split S; he should have spiraled down to convert his energy advantage to a lethal position advantage.

Degan zoomed. Moravia smartly lifted her nose into a climb, still closing, then eased it to hold 340 indicated. 'Very nice,' Toad commented. Inexperienced pilots would just yank on the stick until they had squandered all their airspeed. Moravia had better sense. Patience, Toad decided. She was patient.

Degan was above them now, spread-eagled against the sky, maybe a mile ahead and four thousand feet above. And he was running out of airspeed.

'You got him now,' Toad said, excitement creeping into his voice.

Apparently Degan thought so too. He continued over the top of his loop and let the nose fall through as he half-rolled. He was going to try to go out underneath with a speed advantage and run away from her, then turn and come back into the fray on his own terms. Moravia anticipated him; as he committed with his nose she dumped hers and slammed down the left wing and honked her plane around.

'You get another deflection shot here,' Toad advised. 'You're kicking this guy's *ass*! What a clown! He should never have come back at you out of the loop.'

She was dead behind him now, both diving, but Degan lacked the speed advantage to pull away cleanly.

'Fox Two,' Toad whispered over the radio. Fox Two was the call when you were putting a heat-seeking missile in the air. 'You're dead meat.'

'Bull.' Degan's voice did not sound happy.

'Go ahead, try something wonderful and Rita will get a guns solution.'

'I have enough gas for one more series of turns,' Rita told the instructor.

A long pause. Degan wasn't liking this a bit. Part of the pain, Toad suspected, was Rita's well-modulated feminine voice on the radio and the ribbing Duke knew he would have to take in the ready room about getting whipped by a woman. Toad would have wagered a paycheck the guys back in the ready room at Whidbey were crowded around the duty officer's radio this very minute. Toad whacked Rita playfully on the right arm with his fist. He was having a hell of a good time. 'Okay,' Degan said at last, 'break off and we'll start again with a head-on pass at twenty-two grand. I'll run out to the west.'

Rita dropped her wing to turn east. Toad cackled for her benefit over the ICS. Then he keyed his radio mike switch. 'Hey, Duke, this is Toad. I got ten bucks to put on ol' Rita if you can spare it.'

'You're on, asshole.'

Toad chuckled over the radio. On the ICS he said, 'We got him now, Rita baby. He's mad, the sucker.'

'Don't *Rita-baby* me, you – you—'

'Goddamn, cool off, willya?' Toad roared. 'I don't give a damn if you're the lesbo queen of Xanadu – but right fucking now you're a fighter pilot.

This ain't for fun.' He paused for air, then muttered, ' "Fight to fly, fly to fight, fight to win." There ain't no other way.'

'You didn't just make that up.'

'That's the Top Gun motto. Now what're you gonna do on this high-speed pass?'

'I thought a turn in the same direction he turns.'

'He'll probably make a horizontal turn as hard as he can pull. No imagination. Wait to see which way he turns, then nose up about forty degrees and roll hard into him, the rolling scissors. If he's not too sharp you'll get a winning position advantage, and this guy hasn't impressed me.'

The two Intruders came together out of the emptiness at a combined speed of a thousand knots. At first the other plane was just a speck, but it grew larger quickly until it seemed to fill the wind-shield. Toad had been there before, in a head-on pass with Jake Grafton in a F-14 that resulted in a collision. Involuntarily he closed his eyes.

His head snapped down and the floor came up at him. She had the G on. He opened his eyes and used the steel handgrip on the canopy rail to pull himself around to look behind. 'Which way?'

'Left. I got him.' She was holding herself forward in the seat with her left hand on her handgrip as she craned back over her shoulder and applied the G.

'Get the nose up higher.' Enough advice. Either she could hack it or she couldn't.

The left wing sagged to the vertical and the nose fell toward the horizon. G off as she slammed the stick all the way to the right and the plane rolled two hundred degrees in the blink of an eye. Back on the stick with the nose coming down. Pull, pull, pull that nose around.

Degan was in front of them now and below, but Rita was on the inside of his turn going down at him. Relax the stick and build up your speed, close on him; Toad silently urged her on.

'Degan lost sight,' Toad said as he fought the vomit back in his throat. The hangover had caught up with him. He ripped off a glove and jerked the mask aside. His stomach heaved once. She was set up perfectly for a downhill Sidewinder shot.

'Fox Two,' he called over the radio. 'You owe me ten bucks, Degan.' Then he puked into the glove again.

Rita lifted the nose and reversed her turn until she was headed west. 'Fuel's going to be a little skosh,' she murmured to Toad, then called Degan and told him she was leaving this frequency for Seattle Center.

After the debrief the duty van dropped them at the BOQ. 'Thanks,' Rita said.

'For what?'

'Coaching me during the ACM.'

'No sweat. They're attack guys. ACM ain't their bag.'

'Are you going to get some dinner?' she asked.

'Naw. I'm going to bed.'

'I hope you aren't coming down with something,' she called after him.

Jake Grafton sat in the attic beside the pile of boxes that contained the miscellaneous junk he had collected through the years and had never been able to throw away. Everything from high school year-books to souvenirs from half the world's seaports was tucked away in some box or other. He examined the boxes and tried to remember which was which. Perhaps this one. He opened it. Shoetrees, almost empty bottles of aftershave, buttons, spools of thread and some paperback novels. Three worn-out shirts.

It was in the fourth box. He removed the pistol from the holster and flipped the cylinder out. The chambers were empty. He held the weapon up so the light from the bare forty-watt bulb on the rafter shone full upon it. No rust. Good thing he had oiled it before he put it away. He looked into the box to see if there was any ammo. Yep, one box of .357 magnum, a couple dozen shells in the box. He closed the cylinder, worked the action several times, then loaded the weapon.

With his back against one of the boxes, he extended his legs, crossed his ankles and thoughtfully stared at the holstered pistol on the floor beside him. Camacho said it had probably been a professional hit. Harold Strong would be just as dead if he had had a pistol. Still, a pistol nearby would make a nervous man feel better, sort of like an aspirin. Or a beer.

A large-frame revolver like this couldn't be hidden under a uniform. Perhaps in an attaché case? Then he would be the slowest draw in the East. In the car it could go in the glove compartment or under the seat, but it would be too far away if someone opened fire while he was sitting at a traffic light or driving along the freeway. And he rode the Metro to and from work anyhow. Maybe he should keep the gun in the bedroom or kitchen here at the beach and in the apartment in Arlington.

How would he explain the gun to Callie?

The hit man nailed Strong as he was driving to his weekend cabin. Probably the same route every Friday night. Predictable. Predictability was vulnerability. Okay. So what do I do routinely every day, every week? He reviewed his schedule in light of his new job. Boarding the Metro, driving to and from the beach, what else?

Strong was divorced, lived alone. What about Callie? Would she be a target?

Smoke Judy – had he put out the contract on Strong?

George Ludlow . . . Admiral Henry . . . Senator Duquesne was the tip of the congressional iceberg . . . Seventeen billion dollars, how many jobs did that mean, how many people supporting families and raising children? Seventeen . . .

'Jake.' Her voice seemed distant. 'Jake, are you still up here?'

He shook himself awake. 'Hmmm.'

Her head appeared in the attic access hole. She was standing on the ladder. 'What are you doing up here?'

'Drifted off.' He stirred himself. Rain was smacking against the roof, a steady drumming sound. He glanced at his watch: 1 A.M.

She came on up the ladder and sat down beside him. She touched the leather of the pistol holster. 'Why do you have this out?'

'Looking through the boxes.' He laid the holstered pistol in the nearest open box.

They sat holding hands, listening to the rain. 'Jake,' she said, 'I want to adopt that little girl.'

'Won't be easy, Callie. An eleven-year-old veteran of how many foster homes? She's had more rocky experiences and picked up more scars in her short life than you have in yours. Won't be easy.'

'You're having problems at work, aren't you?'

'Yes.'

'Bad?'

'I suppose.' He picked up her hand and examined it carefully, then looked her straight in the eye. 'I may be in over my head.'

'Won't be the first time.'

'That's true.'

'You've always managed to come out in one piece before.'

'That's the spirit. Good of you to point that out. I see you've taken our talk this morning to heart.' He tried to keep the sarcasm out of his voice, but some crept in anyway.

She took her hand back. 'Jake. Our lives are slipping by. I want that little girl. I want her now.'

'Okay, Callie.'

'You're doing what you want to do. I want that little girl.'

'I said okay.'

'Thursday. Thursday morning we see her, then that afternoon we go to the Department of Social Services for an interview.'

'Okay. I'm leaving town Monday, but I should be back Wednesday. I'll take Thursday off. Just for the record, though, last week I asked the personnel people to fill out retirement papers for me. I'm going to tell them to forget it before I leave on Monday.'

'Retirement? Is that what the admiral's visit today was about.'

'Not really. The retirement thing was the catalyst, maybe. No kidding, Callie, this may be the worst mess I've ever been in. Worse than Vietnam, worse than the Med last year.'

'You haven't done anything wrong, have you?'

'Not that I know of. Not yet.'

She got up and moved toward the ladder. 'I'm not going to wait any longer. I want that little girl,' she said, then went down.

Toad Tarkington was sound asleep when the phone rang. He was still groggy when he picked it up. 'Yeah.'

'Tarkington, this is Grafton.'

The cobwebs began to clear. 'Yessir.'

'How're you doing on the flying?'

'Pretty good, sir.'

'Flown any full-system hops yet?'

'Yessir.'

'How's Moravia doing?'

Toad checked his watch: 12:15 in the morning. It was 3:15 in Washington. 'She's doing great, sir. Good stick.'

'You doing okay dropping the bombs?'

'Yessir. It's a little different, but—'

'How many more hops are you going to get?'

'Six, I think. Two each Sunday, Monday and Tuesday. We come home Wednesday.'

'Stay Wednesday and fly two more hops. Do eight. And Toad, leave the radar off. I want you to fly all eight without the radar. Use the IR and the laser and nothing else. You understand?'

'Yessir. Leave the radar off.'

'See you this Friday in the office. And give me a written recommendation Friday on what we can do to the system to make it easier to use without the radar. Night.' The connection broke.

Toad cradled the dead instrument. He was wide awake. He got out of bed and went to the window. Raindrops were smearing the glass. What was that all about? Grafton didn't seem to be getting much sleep these days. Shore duty sure wasn't cracking up right.

He cranked the window open a couple inches. The wind whistled through the crack and chilled him. It would be a miserable night to try to get aboard the ship. The meatball would be dancing like a crazed dervish while the fuel gauge told its sad tale. 'Thank you, Lord, that I ain't at sea flying tonight,' he muttered, and went back to bed.

The phone rang again. Toad picked it up. 'Tarkington, sir.'

'Grafton again, Toad. Leave the Doppler off too. It radiates.'

'Aye aye, sir.'

'Good night, Toad.'

'Good night, Captain.'

8

The plane carrying Jake and Helmut Fritsche landed at San Francisco International Airport, where the two men rented a car and ventured forth upon the freeways. Fritsche drove since he had made this trip several dozen times.

'I guess a fair appraisal of Samuel Dodgers would include the word "crackpot," ' Fritsche said as they rolled south toward San Jose. 'Also "religious fanatic," "sports fanatic" and a few more.'

Jake eyed Fritsche, with his graying beard and bushy eyebrows. 'Crackpot?'

'Well, he's a man of outrageous enthusiasms. Got a PhD in physics from MIT in one of his prior incarnations, before he got religion or changed his name to that of his favorite baseball team. He grew up in Brooklyn, you know.'

'No,' said Jake Grafton through clenched teeth. 'I didn't.'

'Yeah. Anyway, he's dabbled in computers and radar for years and patented this technology for suppressing reflected radiation. He came to me with some technical problems. I used my influence with the navy to get him a good radar to work with. Had it delivered in a moving van.' He chuckled. 'I'll tell you that story sometime.'

'Henry says he's a genius.'

Fritsche nodded his agreement between drags on his cigar. Smoke filled the interior of the car. Jake cracked his window an inch to exhaust the thick fumes. 'He'll probably be in the running for a Nobel when his achievements get declassified.'

'Somebody said he's greedy.'

'Samuel wants some bucks, all right. I can't condemn him for that, not after a few years of reading about the pirates of Wall Street. Dodgers is the founder and only benefactor of his church and he wants to take it nationwide, with TV and radio and a hallelujah choir, the whole schmear. I think he realizes that since he's so heavy into hellfire and damnation, contributions are going to be light. The feel-good, be-happy ministries are the ones rolling in the dough. Dodgers is going to have to keep his afloat out of his own pocket.'

Jake Grafton arranged the collar of his civilian jacket around his neck and lowered the window another inch. 'What did George Ludlow say when he heard about Dr Dodgers?'

'Amen,' Fritsche said lightly.

'I believe it,' Jake muttered. His companion tittered good-naturedly.

The car rolled on into the farm district south of San Jose. Eventually Fritsche turned up a dirt driveway and parked in front of a ramshackle wooden structure. A large sign amid the weeds proclaimed 'Faith Apostolic Gospel Tabernacle.'

'I think we ought to get down on our knees inside and pray that GAO never get wind of this,' Jake said as he surveyed the weeds and the fading whitewash on the old structure. The last coat of thin whitewash had been applied over a still legible Grange hall sign.

'You'll see,' Fritsche assured him.

Samuel Dodgers was a stringy man in constant motion. He stood in the small, dusty chapel and tugged at this, gestured at that, reset the Dodgers baseball cap on his balding dome for the hundredth time, pulled at his trousers or ear or nose or lower lip, moving, always moving. 'So you fellows wanta see it again, huh, and see what progress looks like in the late twentieth century? When do I get some money?'

'You got your last check two weeks ago.'

'I mean the next one.' He hitched up his pants and reset his cap and looked from face to face expectantly. The sunlight coming through a dirty windowpane fell on a long, lean face. His chin jutted outward from almost nonexistent lips. Above the grim mouth was a sharp nose and two restless black eyes. 'The next check – when?'

'I think it's a couple months away,' Fritsche replied gently.

'If I weren't a Christian I'd cuss you government people. Your tax people squeeze the juice right out of a man – a man who's sitting on the biggest advancement in military technology since the horseshoe – but the giving hand is so all-fired parsimonious, stingy, miserly. You people are just *cheap!*'

'You're being paid according to the contract you agreed to, Dr Dodgers.'

'Get a man over a barrel and squeeze him. It's a sin to take advantage of a man trying to do the Lord's work like I am. A *sin.*'

Jake glanced at Helmut Fritsche. He appeared unperturbed.

Dodgers led them between a doze or so folding chairs toward the door near the altar. 'Praise the Lord and pass the ammunition,' Fritsche muttered just loud enough for Jake to hear above the tramping and scraping of heavy feet on the wooden floor.

The back half of the old Grange hall was a well-lit workshop. Several strings of naked hundred-watt bulbs were woven through the joists and cast their light on a crowded jumble of workbenches, tools and junk. The visitors picked their way through it behind Dodgers, who approached the only person in the place, a young man of about twenty with carrot-red hair and acne to match.

'My boy Harold,' Dodgers said to Jake, who shook the offered hand and introduced himself. 'Harold was at Stanford, but they weren't teaching him anything, so he came back here to work with me. Learn more here with me than he would in that Sodom of little minds. Those fools with their calculators, always saying that something won't work . . .' He continued to fulminate as he opened the large doors at the back end of the building and began stringing electrical cords. 'Well, Helmut, you seen this done before. Don't just stand there like a tourist.'

Dodgers drew Jake aside as Fritsche and Harold hooked up electrical cords and moved a workbench outside. 'Okay.' He cleared his throat. 'Over there on that little bench below those trees' – he pointed at the side of a hill about a half mile away – 'is the radar. Harold will run that. That's the radar the navy loaned me. Got it up there in a old two-holer that used to be here behind the tabernacle.' He stopped and showed Harold exactly how he wanted the power cables connected.

Jake joined him at a workbench. 'Now this little radar suppressor – it picks up the incoming signal on these three antennas here and feeds it into this computer over there. Got four of the fastest chips made in this thing – Harold did most of the computer design. Computers are his bag. Little hobby of mine too. Anyway, the computer analyzes the incoming signal: strength, frequency, direction, PRF – that's Pulse Repetition Frequency – and so forth, and generates a signal that goes out through these companion antennas to muffle out future signals. That's why these antennas are twins. You have a receiver and a transmitter.'

'But you can't suppress the first signal coming in?'

'Nope. They get one free look. The very first incoming pulse will not be muffled. Nor, in this generation of this device, will the second. See, you can't get a pulse repetition frequency until you have received at least two pulses, which you must have to time your outgoing pulses, the muffling pulses. But with existing radars, the return from one pulse will be treated like static. The cathode-ray tubes need a lot more pulses than that.'

'And when the guy painting you stops transmitting, you beacon one more time?'

'That's the problem Harold and I are working on right now. You see, after the first pulse comes in, and the second, the computer then has to figure it all out and start transmitting. Right now we've got the computing time down to about ten billionths of a second. That's not enough of a clean chirp to let any existing radar get a definable return. If the next pulse doesn't arrive right on time, we'll stop the muffling pulses ten nanoseconds later. Just need to fix the software, the XY dipole and . . .' His voice fell to an incoherent mumble.

'Why wouldn't a second radar that is in a receive-only mode see you beaconing to the first radar?'

'Bistatic radar? It would,' said the genius in jeans, 'if all we were doing was pulsing straight back at the transmitter. But we aren't. We're pulsing from a series of antennas all over the place to neutralize the reflected signal. Knowing how much to radiate, precisely enough yet not too much, that's where the computer really makes this thing work. First you must know the exact reflective characteristics of the object you are trying to protect – that's your airplane – and put that data into the computer's memory. Then the computer calculates the scatter characteristics of the incoming signal and tells each of the two hundred transmitters positioned over the fuselage and wings and tail just how much to radiate. All of the transmitters have to radiate in all directions. And this whole thing has to work very, very quickly. No computer was fast enough to handle this until superconductivity came along. See, to make the electrical signals move along fast enough to make this work, I've had to super-cool my computer in a tank of liquid hydrogen and encase the wires to each of the antennas in this special sheathing. That lowers the resistance just enough.' He gestured to a row of pressure bottles that stood in one corner of his workshop. 'Still, there's so much computing involved we had to go to a distributed system with multiple CPUs.'

Jake felt like a schoolboy who hadn't done his homework. 'But how does the outgoing radar signal cancel the incoming one?'

Dodgers stepped over to a blackboard standing in the corner. He looked around – 'Where's the rag?' – then used his shirt sleeve to erase a spot. 'Harold, where's that blasted chalk?'

'Here, Dad.' The young man picked up a piece from a nearby bench.

Dr Dodgers drew a sine wave on the board. 'Do you know *anything* about radiation?' he asked Jake gruffly.

Jake nodded hesitantly as he traced a sine wave in the air with his finger. He knew from experience that claiming knowledge in the presence of a physicist was not a good idea.

'It moves in waves,' Dodgers agreed dubiously. He drew another sine wave over the first, yet the peaks of the second were where the valleys of the first one were, and vice versa. 'The first line is the reflected signal. The second line is our outgoing signal. They cancel each other.'

Jake turned to Fritsche with raised eyebrows. Fritsche nodded affirmatively. 'This principle has been known for a century. Dr Dodger's real contribution – breakthrough – has been in the area of superconductivity at higher temperatures than anyone else has been able to achieve. So he asked himself what computer applications were now possible that had been impossible before.'

'And came up with this one,' Jake muttered, for the first time seeing the intelligence and determination in that face under the bill of the cap.

'Let's fire it up,' Dodgers suggested. 'Helmut, if you will be good enough to take Captain Grafton and Harold up to the outhouse, I'll do the magic down here.'

As Harold drove the rental car along a dirt track through a field, Jake asked, 'How's security out here?'

'Security?' the young man said, his puzzlement showing. 'The neighbors are all Presbyterians and Methodists and they think Dad's a harmless loony. Their kids get curious and come around occasionally when they're out of school or in the evenings, but we don't tell them anything and they wander off after a while. Just got to keep them away when we're radiating. Been having some troubles with the power company from time to time. We sure pull a lot of juice when we're cooling down that hydrogen and they've dropped the load hereabouts a time or two.'

'We had the head of the Federal Power Commission call the president of Pacific Gas and Electric,' Fritsche told Jake.

'The district engineer still comes around occasionally, though,' Harold continued. 'I think he's harmless. Dad's been feeding him a line about experimentation with electromagnetism, and he bought it 'cause he's local and knows Dad's a dingbat.' The youngster goosed the accelerator to take them through a mudhole in the road. 'Nice car, I'd sure like to have a car, but Dad – with the church and all . . .'

The radar was mounted in the old outhouse on the bench where the seats once were. It radiated right through the open door. Harold Dodgers removed a padlock from a flap door at the back of the structure to gain access to the control panel and scope. 'This is an Owl Screech radar,' Fritsche told Jake. 'We borrowed it from the EW range at Fallon.' The Electronic Warfare range at NAS Fallon, Nevada, provided realistic training for fleet aircrews.

'Wonder where the US Navy got this thing.' Owl Screech was a Soviet-made gunfire-control radar.

'From the Israelis, I think. They had a few to spare after the 1973 war.'

The drone of a jet somewhere overhead caused Jake to scan the blue sky. It was high, conning. An airliner or a bomber. A row of trees higher on the hill waved their leaves to the gentle breeze. So warm and pleasant here. Jake sat down in the grass while the red-headed youngster worked at the control panel and Helmut Fritsche observed.

'We're not getting any power,' Harold announced. 'Can I borrow the car and run back to the shop?'

'Sure. You have the keys.' Harold eased the car around and went bumping down the dirt road. Fritsche joined Jake in the grass.

Jake tossed a pebble at the outhouse. The stone made a satisfying thunk. 'What's the plan to get this gizmo into production?'

'Normally we would do engineering drawings and blueprints and take bids, but due to the time constraints and secrecy requirements, we'll have to select a contractor on a cost-plus basis. The government will retain title to the technology and we'll pay Dodgers royalties.'

'What contractor will get it?'

'One with the staff and manufacturing capacity to do it right and do it quickly. Probably an existing radar manufacturer.'

'Cost-plus. Isn't that beltway French for "can't lose?" And the contractor's engineers will see all the technology and have a leg up on bids for second- and third-generation gear.'

'Yep.'

'And if they can dream up ways to do it better, they can get some patents of their own.' Jake tossed another pebble at the outhouse. 'Gonna be a nice little plum for somebody.'

'Yep.'

'Good thing all the guys in our shop are honest.'

Fritsche sat silently, weighing that remark, Jake supposed. 'I guess our people are like everyone else,' Fritsche said at last, without inflection. 'People are pretty generally alike all over.'

'Why was Strong killed?'

'Don't know.'

'Any ideas?'

'Some. But I keep them to myself. I try not to gossip. There are laws against slander.'

Jake Grafton stood and brushed off the seat of his trousers. 'A river of money flowing along in front of a bunch of guys on middle-class salaries, a bunch of guys all humping to keep their bills paid until they get middle-class pensions and form letters of appreciation from the government. Everybody's honest. Nobody's tempted. Makes me want to salute the fucking flag and hum a march.' He looked down at Fritsche.

'I have no facts, Captain,' the scientist said. 'None.'

Jake looked around, trying to think of something to say. He gave up and strolled up the hill to the trees, where he relieved himself. Somehow aboard ship things had been simpler, more clear. On his way back to the wooden building he saw the car returning with Harold at the wheel.

The redhead had the radar fired up in less than a minute. With Fritsche and Jake looking over his shoulder, he flipped switches. 'This is its target-acquisition – its search – mode. And that blip right there is the tabernacle.' He pointed. Jake stared at the return a moment, then stepped a few paces to his right and looked around the shed at the scene. The radar in the shed made a variety of mechanical noises and he could hear the antenna banging back and forth against its stops. Now he referred again to the radar scope, which was American, not Soviet. Okay, there was the tabernacle, the house beyond and to the right, the trees on the left . . .

'Now,' said the young Dodgers, 'step over there again and wave your arms at my dad. Then he'll fire up the suppressor.' Jake did as requested and returned to the scope. Even as he watched, the blip that was the tabernacle faded from the screen, along with the ground return in the area beyond. Where the blip had been was merely a blank spot with no return at all.

'Try the frequency agility,' Fritsche suggested. Harold flipped another switch and then turned a dial. The tabernacle became faintly visible as a ghost image. 'As he changes frequency on the Owl Screech, the computer on the suppressor is trying to keep up,' Fritsche explained to Jake, 'so he sees this ghost image, which is not enough to lock on to. And remember, this is an American scope, more sensitive than Soviet scopes.'

'I'm impressed.'

'Go to a higher PRF and try to lock on the spot where we know the tabernacle is,' Fritsche said to Harold. 'Try the expanded display.'

Nothing. The radar failed to lock. The center of the presentation was an empty black spot.

After a long silence, Fritsche spoke softly, almost as if he were afraid of his own thoughts. 'If we could implement this technique at optical wavelengths you wouldn't even be able to see that building down there with the naked eye.'

'You mean you could see right through it?'

'No, it would look like a black hole. Nothing would come back from it. But no one is going to have that kind of technology until well into the next century.'

'For heaven's sake,' said a stunned Jake Grafton, 'let's just get the bugs worked out of this and get it to sea. That's more than enough for you and me.'

The phone on Luis Camacho's desk rang at noon on Tuesday as he was eating a tuna salad sandwich. He had mayonnaise on his fingers and managed to smear it on the telephone. 'Camacho.'

'Luis, this is Bob Pickering. Could you take a few minutes now and come down to my office? I have some folks here I would like you to meet.'

Camacho wrapped the half sandwich that remained and stuck it in his lower desk drawer, which he locked without thinking. Every drawer and cabinet in his office was always locked unless he was taking something out or putting something in. It was a habit.

Camacho knew Pickering, but not well. Pickering worked the District of Columbia and routinely handled walk-ins. 'Luis, this is Mrs Matilda Jackson and Mr Ralph Barber. Luis Camacho.' As they shook hands, Pickering added, 'Mr Barber's an attorney with Ferguson and Waithe.' Ferguson and Waithe was one of the District's larger firms, almost two hundred lawyers, and specialized in federal regulatory matters.

Pickering summarized Mrs Jackson's adventures of the previous Friday evening while Camacho glanced at the visitors. He concluded, 'Based on past experience, Mrs Jackson felt that the District police may not be sympathetic to a complaint from her, so she went to Mr Barber, her former boss, yesterday, and he thought she should come see us.'

Barber was in his fifties, still wearing his topcoat and white silk scarf. Apparently he hoped this interview would be brief. Mrs Jackson still had her coat around her too, but its faded cloth contrasted sharply with the blue mohair that kept the spring winds from the lawyer's plump frame.

'The neighborhood used to be someplace a person could be proud of,' Mrs Jackson said slowly. 'But those crack houses and dealers on the corners . . . The police have *got* to do something!'

'We felt that the information and evidence Mrs Jackson has would probably receive a more dispassionate look from the FBI.' The counselor gestured toward the edge of Pickering's desk, upon which lay a roll of film and a clear plastic Baggie containing a crumpled cigarette packet.

'I thought you might want to send these to the lab,' Pickering told Luis. 'I'll do the report and send you a copy. We'll get back to you in a few days, Mrs Jackson. One of us will. Right now we need to get a set of your fingerprints to compare with whatever is on that cigarette pack. Just in case, you understand.'

Camacho jotted the report number on a piece of paper from Pickering's desk, then excused himself. Curious about the two items he carried, he walked them straight to the lab and logged them in. Tomorrow afternoon, he was told. After three.

The Consolidated Technologies prototype had a hangar all to itself in Palmdale. As Jake stood and looked about the cavernous interior, he was surrounded by engineers and vice presidents, at least twenty people all told. The vice presidents all wore business suits, but the engineers seemed fond of short-sleeved white shirts with dark ties. If that garb didn't announce their profession, they all sported nerd buckets – plastic shirt-pocket protectors full of pens and pencils, from which dangled their building passes. Solar-powered calculators rested in belt holsters on engineers and vice presidents alike.

The black airplane had a conventional dual nose wheel with the nose tow bar that enabled it to be launched by catapult, but that was about the only feature Jake found familiar. The rounded wings were situated well back on the fuselage and a canard protruded under each side of the canopy. Two vertical stabilizers canted inboard rose from the rear of the fuselage. The engine air intakes were on top of the plane, behind the cockpit, which seated two crewmen in tandem.

The senior vice president, a tall woman in her late forties whom Wilson had said rose from the accounting department to her present position on sheer raw talent, led the group toward the machine and explained major features to Jake. 'The aircraft's shape is optimized to reduce the aircraft's Radar Cross Section. We've used radar-absorbent materials in all the leading and trailing edges – laminated layers of glass fiber and plastic with carbon coating . . .'

'Uh-huh,' said Jake Grafton.

'For low frequencies that put the plane into the Rayleigh region, we've tried to lower the overall electro-magnetic susceptibility . . . carbon-epoxy laminate for wing skin, coatings of multilayer absorbers – mainly Schiff base salts and honeycomb composites. The goal was to reduce resonant microwave frequency scattering, magnetic waves and even surface waves before they escape from the edges.'

'I see,' he lied. The canopy was open and the boarding ladder down, so Jake climbed up and peered into the forward cockpit. The control stick was a small vertical handle on the right side of the cockpit. Two power levers were installed on the left console. The forward panel contained two Multifunction Displays, MFDs, arranged on either side of the control panel for a Heads-Up Display, a HUD, which sat on top of the forward panel so as he flew the pilot could look straight ahead through the tilted glass. Under the HUD control panel was another screen, similar to the MFDs, but without the frame of buttons that circled the upper two. All of the screens looked like eleven-inch color television screens with the power off: they were larger than the five-inch displays to which Jake was accustomed. But the weirdest thing – there were no engine instruments. Oh, the panel had a conventional gear lever, a standby gyro and even a G meter, but of engine instruments there were none.

'Go ahead. Climb in and sit down,' the woman urged. Jake glanced again at her name tag. Adele DeCrescentis.

'Okay.' As he arranged himself in the pilot's seat, Ms DeCrescentis mounted the ladder. 'Where's the ashtray?' he asked.

'Captain, I don't think—'

'Sorry. Just kidding.' The look on her face implied that levity was inappropriate. Here in the high-tech cathedral, Jake thought. Or the new-car showroom.

Down below, the entourage was making small talk among themselves and casting many glances at the cockpit and vice president DeCrescentis, who probably didn't look very vice presidential perched on the boarding ladder. 'What's going to happen to engine airflow in high-angle-of-attack maneuvers?'

'That was one of the trade-offs,' said DeCrescentis, shifting her weight gingerly. Even the medium heels she was wearing must be mightily uncomfortable on the rungs of that ladder. 'Each intake has a flap that is raised hydraulically to funnel more air into the intake when the FCC – Flight Control Computer – senses an increase in G or angle of attack which correlates with a decrease in compressor inlet pressure, but those flaps can only do so much. The concept is angle-of-attack-limited, so it made sense to design to a five-G limit. That enabled us to lighten the airframe and increase the use of honeycomb composites, which made it even more stealthy. And we achieved better fuel economy.'

'I bet spins will be exciting.'

'The engines will compressor-stall in an upright spin and have to be shut down, but they can be restarted once a normal angle of attack is achieved. Inverted spins shouldn't be a problem.'

'Hmmm.' Jake moved the control handle experimentally. It looked like a joystick for a computer game. 'Fly by wire?'

'Of course.'

'Ms DeCrescentis, I appreciate all you folks taking the time this morning to show me this plane, but what say I sort of look it over with my staff? They've been involved in this project for quite a while and no doubt can answer any questions I know enough to ask.'

'I suppose,' she said reluctantly, glancing again at the crowd below. She maneuvered her way down the ladder and two men below reached up to help her to the floor.

Fritsche scrambled up and seated himself on the cockpit coaming. Commander Rob Knight, the project coordinator, came up behind him and stood on the ladder. 'What d'ya think?' Dr Fritsche asked.

'Pretty stealthy, I guess.'

'About the same RCS as a bird.'

'How big a bird?'

'You aren't impressed, are you?'

Jake Grafton took his time answering. He examined the panels on each side of the seat, then fingered the switches experimentally. 'You guys tell me if I'm wrong: what we have here is one of the air force stealth-fighter prototypes, a version the blue-sky boys decided not to buy. It's subsonic, shoots only smart weapons, has limited maneuverability and carries a nonstealthy belly tank for training purposes that can't be carried in combat. Combat radius unrefueled is about six hundred nautical miles. Now, that is. To make this plane carrier-suitable it needs a beefed-up structure, tail-hook and folding wings, all of which will add at least a thousand pounds of weight – probably fifteen hundred pounds – and cost us speed and range. This killing machine will lighten Uncle Sugar's wallet to the tune of about sixty-two million bucks a pop. *If*, and only *if*, it can be acquired on the most economic – the optimum – production schedule. Is that right?'

'Well, the cost factors are a lot more complicated than you've indicated, but your summary is fair.'

'Due to the likelihood that the five-G limit will be routinely exceeded by fleet aircrews in training situations, the design needs further modification to prevent compressor stalls. That involves more structural strengthening, computer-operated secondary intakes, loss of some stealthiness. That will cost an additional . . . ?'

'Five million a plane, assuming an optimum production schedule. Ten million more per plane if we buy new engines.'

'Five million a plane,' Jake continued. 'And if we don't buy that mod, we'll have the compressor-stall problem that plagued the F-14 the first ten years of its life, which will mean a higher attrition rate than we would experience otherwise.' Attrition meant crashes, planes lost in training accidents. 'Yet to go the new-engine route will take ten years because the engines don't even exist; all we have is an engineers' proposal saying they could build them sooner or later for about so many dollars apiece, subject to all the usual caveats about buy rates, research, inflation, etc.'

'Hiram Duquesne likes this plane.'

'Ah yes, Senator Duquesne. Another great American.'

'We didn't get the senior vice president this morning because she likes your nose,' Knight shot back. 'Consolidated has about two hundred million dollars of their own funds tied up in this prototype. They employ twenty thousand people. Consolidated is *big* business. They've bet their company on getting a stealth contract.'

'Yeah. Stock option and bonuses and company cars for the executives, jobs for the little people, and votes for the big people in Washington. I got the picture.'

'Don't be so damned cynical,' Rob Knight said. 'Listen, Jake, it may well come down to buying this plane to replace the A-6 or doing without. Ludlow and Royce Caplinger have to be goddamn sure they have the votes in Congress before they go up to Capitol Hill with their hats in their hands.'

'That's their problem, not mine, I'm just a worn-out, washed-up attack pilot. I didn't understand two words that DeCrescentis woman said.' He twiddled some knobs. 'I didn't ask for *this* job,' he roared. 'I'm not going to be responsible for whether twenty thousand people keep *their* jobs! Don't lay that *crap* on *me!*'

Knight retreated down the ladder. Fritsche followed, his face averted. Jake sat alone in the cockpit. He tried to imagine how this plane would feel to fly. With his right arm in the rest and his hand on the stick and his left curved over the throttles, he thought about how it would feel to look through the HUD at a Soviet ship. This plane had to be able to take on Soviet ships in the Med and the Indian Ocean and the Arctic in winter. But it also had to be able to fight in brushfire wars in places like Lebanon and North Africa, Afghanistan, Iran, Korea, Vietnam. Maybe China. Could it? With million-dollar missiles and five-G restriction?

When he had recovered his temper, he motioned to Knight and Fritsche, who ascended the ladder again. 'What would Sam Dodgers' gizmo do for this plane?'

'Lower the RCS from a bird to a June bug.' Fritsche frowned. 'It's so stealthy now that making it more so wouldn't be cost-effective, at least not in the lifetime of this machine. That's just my opinion, of course.'

'On the other hand,' Knight said, 'this plane wouldn't be junk if Dodgers' suppressor can't be made to work in a real airplane. Dodgers knows the reflective characteristics of that tabernacle wall precisely when viewed from the old outhouse by one radar. Protecting a shape as complex as an aircraft from numerous transmitters and God knows how many receivers situated in all three dimensions – that's another thing altogether.'

'Tell me what all this stuff is,' Jake said. 'This doesn't look like any cockpit I ever saw.'

'Both prototypes have exactly the same layout. This is all the stuff that was going into the A-6G. What these television-screen things are are Multifunction Displays. This lower middle one is a map that moves as the plane moves. The plane always stays in the center. This should do away with the necessity for the crew to always carry awkward charts in the cockpit.

'Now these upper two MFDs present literally all the information the pilot might wish to know, or the info can be presented on the HUD. A touch of the button calls up engine information, another button calls up the radar presentation from the rear cockpit, still another the presentation from either one of the two IR sensors, and so on. Then there's a variety of tactical displays . . .' He droned on.

Jake was astounded. This was several generations beyond the A-6 cockpit. It was technically as far beyond an A-6 as an A-6 was from a World War II B-17. 'I had no idea,' he muttered, awed.

Knight showed him the rear cockpit. It was equally futuristic. Instead of the HUD control panel, it possessed a third MFD, so three of them were arranged in a row right across the panel. Under the center one was the map display. 'This moving map – didn't James Bond have one like this in one of the movies?'

'Yep. But this is better.'

'*Mamma Mia!*'

The BN in an A-6 had one cursor control stick. The BN in this plane had two, one on each side panel, and instead of just a couple of buttons sticking out, each stick was festooned with buttons, like warts. 'The idea is that the BN won't have to reach for controls. Everything he needs is on those controls sticks.'

After Jake spent another half hour walking around the airplane and looking at every inch, he asked each of the commanders what they thought. One complained about range and payload, another about the intake problems, a third about the difficulty of maintenance. All were aghast at the cost. 'But five years from now we'll all probably think sixty-two million dollars for a plane was a hell of a buy,' Smoke Judy commented.

'You know,' Jake said later as he stood in the doorway with Helmut Fritsche and looked back at the all-black airplane. 'I had an uncle who went to the car dealer one morning to buy a station wagon for the family, and that evening he went home with a little red convertible coupe.'

'High tech *is* sexy.'

Jake thought about it. 'It's so damn neat that you try to convince yourself that you need it. All the bells and whistles and doohickeys and thingamajigs. And the day you have to bet your ass on these gadgets, they don't work.'

'Shapes and absorbers work.'

'I suppose. But how is Sam Dodgers' superconductive computer with multiple CPUs going to work after five hundred catapult shots and five hundred arrested landings when some kid racks the plane through a six-G pull to evade an optically aimed missile? How are all these MFDs and IR sensors and ring-laser gyros going to hold up? Is this techno-junk gonna work then?'

9

Terry Franklin stood with his back against a pillar and tried to keep his face pointed at Lincoln's Second Inaugural Address. The pillar was the second one on the right after you came through the main entrance. The man on the phone had been very precise about that. Second pillar on the right, on the side toward the Inaugural Address.

His eyes kept moving. He was nervous, so nervous. He had vomited up his breakfast an hour ago . . . Not that person, a teenage girl. Not that old fat woman with the cane and the two kids. Maybe that man in the suit over there . . . *he* could be FBI. Was he looking this way? Why was he turning? That long-haired guy in jeans . . .

He had been here ten minutes and had already spotted five men who could be FBI. Maybe they all were. What if they had him staked out, like a goat? Maybe he should just leave, walk away and forget all of this. He had plenty of money. Enough. He had enough. If they weren't on to him he could live carefully and comfortably for years with no one the wiser. But what if they *knew*?

'It's one of the world's great speeches, isn't it?'

He turned and stared. A man, in his fifties with a tan face, stocky, wearing a short jacket, looking at the speech carved in the marble. On his head a brimmed hat. What's the response? Holy . . . *think!* 'Yeah . . . uh, but I think the Gettysburg Address is better.'

'Stay twenty feet or so behind me.' The man turned and walked for the entrance, not fast, not slow, just walking. After he had gone three paces Terry Franklin could wait no longer and followed.

The man was only ten feet ahead going down the wide, broad steps in front of the Memorial. Franklin forced himself to slow down and lag behind. The distance had increased to fifteen feet by the time they reached the sidewalk, but it narrowed again as Franklin strode along. He stood right behind the man as he waited for a tour bus to roll by.

On the other side of the street the man said, 'Walk beside me.' He led Terry along the north side of the Reflecting Pool until he found an empty bench. 'Here,' he said.

'Can't we go somewhere private?' Franklin asked, still on his feet and looking around in all directions.

'This is private. Sit!' The petty officer obeyed. 'Look at me. Stop looking around. You're as nervous as a schoolboy smoking his first cigarette.'

'Something went wrong. Really wrong. Why in hell did you people have a drop in the black ghetto? Some nigger doper could have torn my head off over there.'

'The drops were selected in Moscow, from a list. That drop was originally chosen for another agent.' The man shrugged, resigned. 'Bureaucrats. These things happen.'

'So who got the message? Answer me that! Who saw me there? The cops? The FBI? NIS?' The pitch of his voice started rising. 'What am I supposed to do now? Wait until—'

'No one saw you. Some child or derelict probably removed the cigarette pack, or it was blown out of the hole by the wind. If you had been observed they would be tailing you now.'

Franklin couldn't help himself. He turned his head quickly, scanning.

'Sit still! You only call attention to yourself by doing that, and believe me, there is nothing to see. You are clean. I wouldn't be here if you weren't.'

Franklin stared at his feet. He was so miserable. 'I called in sick today.'

'And you rode the subways just as we instructed, and we checked you all the way. No one followed. No one pulled up to Metro stations to see if you got off. No one made phone calls or ran for a car after you passed by. You are clean. You are not being watched.'

'So who are you?'

'You don't need—' He took a deep breath and exhaled slowly. 'My name is Yuri.' The man extracted a pack of cigarettes from an inside jacket pocket and lit one. Marlboro Gold 100s, Franklin noticed. The fingers that held the cigarette were thick, the nails short. No rings.

'So what do you want me to do?'

'I'm here to evaluate you, to see if you are capable of going on, of continuing to serve.'

Franklin thought about it. Lucy hadn't spoken to him for four days now. God only knows what that bitch will do. Still, ten thousand bucks a disk was damn good money. And if . . .

'If you wish to continue, you must calm down. You must get a grip on yourself.' Yuri's voice was low and steady. 'Your greatest asset is that no one suspects you, and if you become nervous, irrational, irritable, not your usual self, then you call attention to yourself and *make* yourself suspect. Do you understand?'

'Yes.' He glanced at the man, who was looking at him carefully with inquisitive, knowing eyes. Franklin averted his gaze.

'We'll give you a rest,' Yuri said. 'We'll wait a few months before we give you another assignment. Will that help?'

Terry Franklin was torn. He wanted the money, quickly, but as he sat there on this bench knowing *they* could be watching he knew just how close he was to the end of his emotional rope. For the first time in his life he realized how little real courage he had. But for this kind of money maybe he could screw up enough stuff to keep going, for a while at least. If he had some time. He rubbed his eyes, trying to quell the tic in his left eyelid. 'Yes,' he said slowly, 'perhaps it would be better to let things cool off, settle down.'

'Okay. So tomorrow you go back to work as usual. Do all the usual things, all the things you normally do. Keep to your routine. Do nothing out of the ordinary. Be pleasant to your colleagues. Can you manage that?'

He considered it, visions of the office and the chief flashing before his eyes, fear welling up.

'Yes?'

'Yes.' He got it out.

'Do you want to talk about anything else?'

He shook his head no.

'You are doing important work. You have made a great contribution. Your work is known in Moscow.'

Terry Franklin said nothing. Of course his work was known in Moscow. Just as long as no one here found out about it, everything would be fine. Ensuring that that didn't happen was the whole problem.

'To show you how valuable your work is, we are raising your pay. To eleven thousand a disk.'

Franklin just nodded. The enormity of the risks he was running to earn that money had finally sunk in the last four days. He no longer thought of it as easy money. He was earning every goddamn dime.

'You may leave now. Walk up Twenty-third Street to the Foggy Bottom Metro station and board there. Goodbye.'

Terry Franklin rose and walked away without a backward glance.

'How long you guys gonna be in town?' the driver of the rental car shuttle bus asked George Wilson as they circled Terminal C at Dallas-Fort Worth to pick up more people.

'Oh, a day or so.'

'Going home then?'

'No. We've got a couple more cities to visit.' Inquisitive devil, Jake thought, sitting beside George and watching people board.

'Did you come here from home?' Maybe the driver was working for a tip. Or maybe he was just bored. He got the bus in motion again as the people who had just boarded tried to store their bags in the bin and hold on too.

'Nope. Came from L.A. Been on the road a while.'
'I knew it! You're a traveling salesman, huh?'
'Yep.'
'I can always tell.'

At TRX Industries the six men were passed from person to person until they reached the program manager. His ample gut hung over a wide leather belt secured with a Budweiser buckle. At least it appeared to be a Budweiser buckle, but it would be impossible to know for sure unless you checked while you were shining his cowboy boots. His name was Harry Franks.

After the introductions and how-are-yous, he said, 'Do you guys want to see it right now, or go to the conference room and watch the video presentation first?' He eyed Jake.

'I'd just as soon see the plane now.'

'For sure. Maybe see the presento during lunch. We worked real hard on it. You fellas follow me.'

As they strolled along he bantered with Wilson and the commanders, whom he called by name. Just a bunch of good ol' boys.

The plane was in the hangar. The design seemed to Jake Grafton to be more conventional than Consolidated's. This plane had a tandem cockpit and twin vertical stabilizers canted in at the top, toward each other, but there the similarity to the other prototype stopped. This bird was tactical navy gray, with engine intakes in the wing roots and no canards. Instead of a plenum chamber and fairings to cool the exhaust, the tailpipes were arranged above a fairing that might shield the worst of the heat signature from a ground observer. There were no afterburners. 'The Soviets are doing a lot of work on air-to-air IR sensors for the latest generation MiG's,' Smoke Judy said.

'Yeah, probably stole ours,' somebody grumbled.

Jake walked slowly around the plane, the chief engineer at his elbow. On the left side of the fuselage, just behind the nose radome, was a place from which a twenty-millimeter-cannon barrel peeked out. 'Vulcan?'

'Yep. Six hundred fifty pounds capacity, five hard points for missiles and bombs faired in underneath. This baby'll carry, shoot or drop anything in the US inventory or anything any NATO country's got.'

'Range?'

'Combat radius is projected at six hundred nautical miles unrefueled.'

'How stealthy is this thing?'

'Well,' said Harry Franks with his thumbs in his belt, 'it's got a head-on RCS of about a half of a square meter. That reduces its detection range compared with an A-6 Intruder by about forty-five percent. That's naked, as she sits. Hang bombs and a belly tank and the RCS rises, though it's still down about sixty percent from an A-6 loaded for bear. Our design concept was to be as stealthy as possible and still come up with a mission-capable attack plane with good range and flying characteristics. This prototype was optimized for aircraft-carrier operations. It seemed to us that if you guys couldn't get it aboard ship and keep it there for a reasonable cost, it didn't matter how stealthy it was.' He sighed and scratched his head and checked the shine on the toe of his boots. 'That logic didn't impress the air force, of course. Not stealthy enough for them by a long shot.'

'What's this thing gonna cost Uncle Sam?' Jake already knew this answer, but he wanted to hear Franks say it.

'Well, there're a ton of variables.' Franks's hands went into his pockets and he looked Jake straight in the eyes. 'Optimum production rates, as is, fifty-three mil.'

'When did you stop selling used cars and go to work for TRX?'

Franks chuckled good-naturedly.

'If it were something under fifty, I could probably bring my wife over and let her drive it.'

The engineer's grin disappeared. 'I hear you. You'll get some votes in Congress under fifty that you won't get over that number. But we already scraped and cut and chopped like hell to get down to fifty-three.'

'Uh-huh. Just a suggestion – we're a long way from a decision – but were I you, I'd be sweating that number again and trying to shrink it. Sweating it real hard.'

Later Jake managed to draw Dalton Harris aside. Harris had spent most of his career in electronic warfare. By definition he was an expert on Soviet radars, their capabilities and their usage. 'Tell me,' Jake asked, 'what a forty-five percent reduction in the detection range of an A-6 means to the Soviets. Over fifty percent reduction carrying weapons.'

'It means that all the Soviet fire-control radars are obsolete.' He shrugged. 'They would have to redesign and replace everything they have. Or – and this is a big or – they would have to double the number of existing radars.'

'At what cost?'

'Replacement would be astronomical. Their whole system involves using proven technology that can be manufactured in quantity at low cost by low-skilled workers with inexpensive equipment and techniques. They need a lot of everything since the Soviet military is so big. Has to be big because the country is; distances are mind-boggling. So they rarely declare anything obsolete until it's worn out completely. Yet in a mass obsolescence like this low-observable technology threatens, they have to come up with new cutting-edge designs or fixes for over a dozen types of front-line radars, manufacture huge quantities and get them all in service quickly.' Harris raised his hands and dropped them in a gesture of defeat. 'I don't think they can do it. It'll cost too much. Their best bet is to merely make a lot more of what they have, but that will cost them the farm and the family cow. All of which is why Gorbachev has become a good guy.'

'You think?'

'Look at it this way. The Soviet economy is on its ass. They don't even have money over there. The ruble is non-convertible. They've been spending at least an eighth of their gross national product on defense. The barrel is empty. They hate Star Wars because the research and development costs to match or counter it are prohibitive. Now comes stealth: the B-2, the F-117. Those are threats against land-based targets. If that wasn't enough bad news, now the US Navy wants a stealth bird to threaten their fleet – the A-12. I'll bet if we were on the Politburo and heard what countering this low-observable technology was going to cost, we'd think about converting to Christianity.'

'They must be looking hard for a way to do it on the cheap,' Jake suggested.

'Wouldn't surprise me,' Dalton Harris replied.

'Why not build their own stealth birds?'

'They will someday. Right now they can't afford it. When they do, though, we'll have to upgrade all our radars.'

'Hell, we can't afford it either,' Jake Grafton said. Franks was walking this way. When he was close enough Jake said to him, 'Let's sit down and talk about the flight-test schedule.'

'Oh, Mom,' Lucy Franklin sobbed into the telephone. 'I didn't want to call you, but I've got no place else to turn.'

'You did the right thing, Lucy. Has he hit you?'

'Oh no. It's nothing like that. It's . . .' She bit her lip. It was all so bizarre. Her neighbor, Melanie, hadn't believed her and neither had the minister. Her mother was her last hope. 'I think Terry is a spy.'

Silence on the other end of the phone. Finally: 'Tell me about it.'

Lucy explained. She went over the events of last Friday night in great detail.

'Well,' her mother said. '*Something* is going on. He's probably cheating on you.'

'*Mother!* Please! This is more serious. I'm scared stiff. I can't eat. I can't talk to him. I'm afraid of what he'll do to the kids. Mother, I'm petrified. I'm at the end of my rope.' She began to sob.

'Do you want me to come out there?'

'Oh, I don't know. What good would that do?'

'He wouldn't hurt you while I was there. We could confront him.' More silence. 'Let me talk to your father and call you back.'

'Not Daddy!' Lucy wailed. 'He won't *understand.*'

'I know you and he don't see eye to eye. He didn't think Terry was the right man for you.'

'He's never let me forget it.'

'Do you want to come home? Bring the kids?'

If she went home her father would be there. She was genuinely afraid of her father. He just had never been able to cope with a daughter . . . 'Can you come out here?'

'I'll call your dad at work, then call you back. Okay?'

'Mom, I really need you to help me through this one.'

They said their goodbyes and hung up. Lucy drank more coffee and chewed her fingernails. Mom would be such a help. Terry wouldn't do anything with her here. Oh, please, Daddy, let her come.

'Looks like gibberish, of course. What it is is two computer access code words and a file name.' The man from the lab laid an eight-by-ten color photo of the inside of the cigarette pack on Camacho's desk. 'No prints on the pack except for Mrs Jackson's.'

Camacho studied the print. The words and numbers were:

Interest   Golden.TS 849329.002EB

'And the photos?'

'They didn't come out so good. She used a miserable camera with a fixed focus.' The lab man handed Camacho the stack. He looked at each one and laid them across the desk. He stood and bent over to study them, moving slowly.

'This one.' He selected a photo of a man in a trilby hat wearing a full-length coat. Only the bottom half of his face was visible, and it was fuzzy. Yet obviously a white man. The other men in the pictures were black. 'Blow up the face and see what you can do with computer enhancement.'

The lab man checked the back of the photo for the number of the negative. He excused himself and left. Camacho sat in his chair and stared at the face. Thick cheeks, rounded chin, the suggestion of a fleshy nose. He had seen that face before. He picked up the phone: 'Dreyfus, bring in the mug book of Soviet embassy personnel.'

It took twenty minutes, but Camacho and Dreyfus finally agreed. The man in Mrs Jackson's photo was Vasily Pochinkov, assistant agricultural officer at the Soviet embassy.

'These black dudes,' Camacho tapped the stack. 'Take these over to the DC police and go through the mug books. They'll be in there.'

'Your father agreed that under the circumstances I should come.'

'Thank you, Mother. Thank you,' Lucy said.

'You should thank your father too. He was going to use this money for a down payment on a new car.'

'Yes.' Lucy said, trying to hold back the tears.

'He loves you too, Lucy. He always wanted what was best for you.'

'I know, Mom.'

'I'll be there day after tomorrow at one o'clock. Dulles.' She gave Lucy the flight number. 'Can you meet me?'

'The kids and I'll be there. Thanks so much, Mom. I really need you.'

'I know, baby. I know. Just don't tell Terry I'm coming.'

From his window seat Jake stared at the mountains and forests through the gaps in the cloud cover as the Boeing 727 descended into the twilight. The mountain ridges ran off to the northeast between valleys now dark and murky, enlivened only by the twinkling jewels of towns and villages.

Over the Shenandoah Valley the 727 pilot broke his descent. Jake felt the gentle adjustment in nose attitude and power addition. Now the left wing rose and the pilot eased to a new heading, still in a descent. This long glide back to earth was the best part, Jake decided, the best part of the flight after hours in the stratosphere. He closed his eyes and became one with the plane as the pilot leveled the wings and made another power adjustment. He could feel the controls, the stick and throttles in his hands, the—

'Is your seat belt fastened, sir?'

'Oh yes.' Jake moved the newspaper on his lap so the stewardess could visually check. She smiled automatically and moved on.

Your return from the sky should be gentle and slow so that all the bittersweet flavor can be savored. The airspeed and altitude that held you so high above the earth should be surrendered gradually, not – Arggh! What's the use? Why long for things that cannot be again? Stop it. Grafton! Stop wishing and longing and tasting the things of the past.

Power back, almost to idle. He heard the high-pitched whine of the flap motor and checked the wing. The pilot was milking them out as he turned yet again, no doubt following instructions from Air Traffic Control. The earth was only three or four thousand feet below and headlights of cars and trucks were visible. Farmhouses, towns, highways, dark woodlots, all slipped past beneath as the pilot in the cockpit of the airliner milked the flaps out further and eased left in a long sweeping turn that would probably line him up for the approach into Dulles. Jake waited. He was rewarded with a thunk and a hum as the gear doors opened and the main mounts were lowered into the slipstream.

You miss it too much, he told himself. Too much.

Callie was waiting when Jake stepped out of the shuttle bus onto the concourse. He saw her and grinned, and walked right into the fat lady ahead of him. She had stopped dead and bent over to scoop two children into her arms. The children piped their welcome to their grandmother as the line of people behind came to a jerky halt. Callie watched with a wide grin on her face.

'Hi, Mom,' Jake said as he put his arm over her shoulder.

The grin got even wider and her eyes sparkled. 'Hi, Dad.'

'We're not really going to do that, are we? Call each other Mom and Dad?'

'Maybe. Every now and then.'

'Miss me?'

'A teeny tiny little bit. I'm getting used to having you around.'

10

The plane to Washington was full. By some quirk, Toad was assigned a window seat and Rita was given the middle seat beside him. She asked about an aisle or window seat and was told by the harried agent that there were no more seats. Rita looked up and down the counter at the lines of people waiting to check baggage and get seat assignments, then turned back to the clerk and grinned. 'That'll be fine, thank you.'

Moravia had her hair pulled back and rolled tightly. Her white boater hat sat squarely, primly on the top of her head. She had used some makeup this morning, Toad noticed, and a glob of it showed on her right cheek where she had failed to feather it in. It was the only imperfection he could see. Her navy-blue blouse and skirt showed off a healthy figure in a modest yet sexy way. Toad took a deep breath and trailed along as they left the ticket counter. He had to stride to get up beside her.

'Let's get something to read,' he suggested. 'We have time.'

She was agreeable. At the newsstand Toad looked longingly at the *Playboy* and *Penthouse* magazines with their covers hidden under a piece of black plastic to keep from titillating schoolboys or heating up old ladies. Maybe he should buy one and read it on the plane. That would get Moravia all twitchy. He glanced over to where she stood looking at newsmagazines and slicks for upscale women. No. He devoted his attention to the rack of paperbacks and finally selected one by Kurt Vonnegut. *Slaughterhouse-Five* was Toad's favorite book. Vonnegut knew life was insanity, just as Toad did, deep down, in the place where he lived. Today he chose one called *Galápagos*.

When the boarding announcement came, the seats near the gate emptied as everyone surged toward the stewardess guarding the entrance to the jetway. Toad took his time and held back. Two people sandwiched themselves between him and Moravia as they ambled toward the door; a guy in a business suit with shoulder-length hair and a woman in her fifties with bad knees. Yet somehow when Toad turned in his boarding pass he ended up right behind Moravia going down the jetway. There was another line waiting to get through the airplane's door. He queued behind her. The people behind him pressed forward. His nose was almost in her hair. She was wearing a delicate, heavenly scent. He inhaled it clear to his toenails.

They inched down the crowded aisle toward their seats. The air was stifling; too many people, Toad felt the walls closing in on him. There was a woman already in the aisle seat in their row, and when Toad finished stuffing his attaché case and hat into the overhead bin, he found Moravia was already in her seat. The woman on the aisle ignored him. Toad muttered his excuses and edged in front of their knees. Rita looked up from the operation of removing her hat and for the first time since he had known her gave him a warm smile. 'Sorry.'

'No problem,' Toad said as he settled in beside her, acutely aware of her physical presence. Too aware. He adjusted the air nozzle in the overhead and turned hers on too. 'Is this okay?'

'Thank you. That helps a lot.' She smiled again, beautiful white teeth framed by lips that . . . Toad looked at his novel a while, couldn't get interested, then scanned the airline magazine from the seat pocket. Her skirt had inched up, revealing her knees. He obliquely examined her hands. Nails painted and trimmed, fingers long and slim. God! He caught her glancing at him and they both grinned nervously and looked away. He turned the overhead air vent full on and glued his face to the window.

They were somewhere over Montana and Toad was deep into Vonnegut's vision of humans evolving into seals in the millennia to come when Rita spoke again. 'Toad,' she said softly.

'Yeah.' She was looking straight into his eyes.

'Why can't you and I be friends?'

He was thunderstruck. 'Uh . . . aren't we?'

'You know what I mean.'

Toad Tarkington glanced around desperately. No one was apparently paying any attention. Those eyes were looking straight at him. Just what does she mean? There are friends and there are *friends*. He had been floating along footloose and free and – whap! – suddenly here he was, smack in the middle of one of those delicious ambiguities that women work so hard to snare men in. For the first time he noticed that her right eye was brown and her left was hazel, a brownish green. Why not just tell her the truth? One good reason, of course, is that truth rarely works with women. Ah . . . the hell with it! Pay the money and see all the cards.

He leaned into the aura of her. 'Because I like you too much to ever just be your friend, Rita Moravia. You are a beautiful woman and—' He reached up and smoothed the makeup in the caked buildup near her right ear. Then he lightly kissed her cheek. 'That's why.'

Those eyes were inches from his. 'I thought you didn't like me.'

'I like you too damn much.'

Her hands closed around his. 'Do you really mean that?'

He mumbled something inane.

Her lips glided into his. Her tongue was warm and slippery and the breath from her nostrils hot upon his cheek. Her hair brushed softly against his forehead. When she broke away he was breathing heavily. She had a trace of moisture on her upper lip. Out of the corner of his eye Toad saw the woman in the aisle seat scowling at them. 'Rita . . .'

She glanced over her left shoulder, then back at Toad. She straightened in her seat while holding tightly to his hand with her right. She gave the woman beside her a frozen smile. She gripped his hand fiercely.

'Will you excuse us?' she said, and stood, still holding his hand as she moved past the knees that guarded the aisle, dragging Toad along in her wake.

She marched aft, past the kitchen and the stews loading the lunch cart, and got behind a girl in jeans waiting for the rest rooms. She turned and flashed Toad a nervous smile, then stood nonchalantly, still gripping his hand with hers. He squeezed and got a quick grin over her shoulder.

They made room for a woman who came out of one lavatory and then stood between the little doors shoulder to shoulder. A boy of eleven or twelve joined them. He examined their uniforms like they were dummies in a store window. Rita studiously ignored the inspection, but Toad gave him a friendly wink. Meanwhile the stews maneuvered the luncheon cart into the aisle.

When the other lavatory door opened and the occupant was clear, Rita stepped in and pulled Toad along. 'Better get your mom to help you too,' Toad told the wide-eyed boy. As he got the door closed Rita slammed the lock over and wrapped herself around him.

When they finally broke for air, she whispered, 'I really thought you didn't like me.'

'Fool.'

'I wanted you to like me so much, but you were so distant, as if you didn't care at all.' Her arms were locked behind his back, crushing them together. With his hands against the side of her head, he eased her head back. Her lipstick was smeared. He kissed her again, slowly and deeply.

Matilda Jackson peered through the peephole in the door. A man. 'Luis Camacho, Mrs Jackson. We met yesterday. Don't you remember?'

Oh yes. One of the FBI agents. She unfastened the chain lock and shot the dead bolt. When she opened the door, he said in a low voice, barely audible, 'Special Agent Camacho, Mrs Jackson. May I come in?'

'Please'. She looked across the street at the crack house. No one in sight, though Lord knows, the lookout was probably watching out the window. Sometimes she caught a glimpse of him. She shut the door quickly.

Now he produced his credentials. 'I have a few follow-up questions and—'

'Let's talk in the kitchen.' She led the way. 'Would you like a cup of coffee?'

'That would be nice.'

The kitchen was warmer than the living room, and well lit. This was her favorite room in the house. Charlie had enjoyed sitting here watching her cook, the smell of baking things heavy in the air.

Camacho sat at the table and waited until she had poured coffee for both of them and sat down across from him. 'Perhaps we can go over the whole thing again, if you don't mind?'

'Oh, not at all.' She explained again about the crack house, about Mandy and Mrs Blue and the dudes who delivered the crack and picked up the money. He led her into the events of last Friday night, the photos and the man who left the cigarette pack in the iron post two doors up the streets.

'So you never saw anyone reach into that post?'

'No. I didn't. God, I didn't even think about that. If I had thought that somebody was going to come along any second and look for that thing I probably wouldn't have gone out there and gotten it. No. I know I shouldn't have done it, but I just wasn't thinking.'

'We're pleased that you did. It's concerned citizens like you that enable law enforcement to function. When the time comes, and it's months – even years – away, would you be willing to testify?'

'Well . . .' Those dopers, if they knew who she was . . .

'We'll need your testimony to get the photos introduced as evidence.'

'I'll . . .' She swallowed hard. She would be risking her life. 'I'll think about— Can't you do it without me? You don't know what you're asking.'

'We'll try, Mrs Jackson. We won't ask unless we really need you.' He sipped his coffee. 'How long has the crack house been there?'

'Three, maybe four months. I called the police—'

'Have you been watching the place since it opened?'

'Yes. On and off. You know how it is. I just look over there occasionally. Try and keep an eye on what's going on.'

'Have you seen the black men there before?'

'Oh yes.' She thought about it. 'At least a dozen times, I guess. I think they come almost every day to collect the money and such, but a lot of times I miss them. They don't come at the same time every day. And sometimes I think they skip a day.'

'Have they seen you watching?'

'I don't think so. My God, I hope not.' She sat back and smoothed her hair. 'I've tried to stay out of sight . . . I've seen them so often . . .'

'How about the man who put the cigarette pack in the hollow fence post? Have you seen him before?'

She thought about it. 'I – I don't think so. But really, I just can't remember.'

'Have you ever seen anyone retrieve anything from the post?'

'Well, I – I just can't remember. Maybe I saw somebody and didn't pay much attention. Is it important?'

'At this point I don't know.'

'Would he be white?'

'Probably.'

She thought about it. There were so many people, up and down the street, all day long, week in, week out. Yet not that many were white. 'I'll have to try and remember.'

'Okay.' He scooted his chair back and stood. 'I appreciate your taking the time to talk to me. Is there anything else you think we should know?'

'Oh, I guess not. But when are you all going to get that crack house closed down?'

'We'll talk to the District police. I hope it's soon.'

She accompanied him to the door and carefully locked it behind him. If only they would shut those people down. Get them out of the neighborhood.

'I got lipstick all over you,' Rita Moravia said, and used a wet paper towel to wipe Toad's face. This lavatory was certainly not designed for two adults. He perched on the commode with the top down and she sat on his lap, humming softly as she worked on his face and he swabbed hers.

He carefully wiped away all the mascara and makeup. 'You shouldn't use this stuff,' he said. 'You don't need it.'

'Why did you get drunk last Friday?'

'I wanted you and couldn't have you.' He lifted his shoulders and lowered them. 'It seemed like a good idea at the time.'

She laid her forehead against his and ran her fingers through his hair.

Someone pounded on the door.

'Maybe we should get back to our seats,' he suggested.

'I suppose,' she murmured, but she didn't move.

More knocking. 'Hey, in there!'

Toad helped her to her feet and straightened her uniform. He ran his hands across her buttocks and hips as he stood. She kissed him again to the accompaniment of the pounding on the door.

She stepped out first, her head up, still holding his hand. Three stews stood in the kitchen area staring at them. Rita Moravia smiled. 'We're newlyweds,' she announced simply and stepped past.

The women applauded wildly and the passengers joined in.

They parked the cars in the lot outside of Rita's apartment complex and Toad carried her bags in. He had followed her home from Dulles. They kissed in the elevator and they kissed in front of the door. A giggling, happy Rita used her key.

When the door swung open a young woman on the couch in front of the television shrieked. She had her hair in curlers and was wearing only bra and panties. Toad got an eyeful of skin as she scurried for the bedroom.

'Don't mind Harriet,' Rita said. 'I do the same for her on alternate Saturdays when she brings her boyfriend by.'

Toad grinned and nodded. He stood in the center of the living room and glanced about while Rita lugged her bags toward the bedroom. 'Need any help?'

'No, I'll manage. Make yourself comfortable.' In a moment she called from the bedroom, 'There's probably Coke in the fridge.'

Toad sagged comfortably into the couch the roommate had recently vacated. Aha, a remote control for the TV. He flipped around the dial until he found a basketball game and settled his feet upon the settee. Knowing women as he did, he knew he had a while to wait.

'Who's the hunk?' Harriet demanded of Rita in the bedroom.

'A friend.'

'What about Ogden? He's called twice this week wanting to know when you'd be home. I told him you'd call him this evening.' Ogden was an attorney at a large Washington law firm whom Rita had been dating.

Rita opened her suitcase on the bed and began to empty it. She separated her dirty clothes from the clean ones, working quickly. 'I'll call Ogden tomorrow.'

Harriet eased the bedroom door open and peeked at Toad sprawled on the couch. 'He's a live one, all right,' she said after she had eased the door shut again. 'Navy?'

'Yep.'

Harriet sat cross-legged on her bed. 'Are you sure about this, Rita? Ogden's a pretty great guy. He's athletic, rich parents, good future, madly in—'

'He wasn't the one. I'm sure.'

Harriet pounced. 'And this guy? Is he the one?'

'Maybe.' Rita removed the pins that held her hair against the back of her head and shook it out. 'He might be. He almost got away.' She grinned and attacked her hair with a brush. 'Reeled him in on the plane this afternoon.'

'*This* afternoon?'

'And I'm going over to his apartment to spend the night.'

Harriet flopped back on her bed and pointed her legs at the ceiling, toes extended. 'Well, no one can say you're just jumping right into bed with him. My God, you've stifled your hormones and female appetites for an entire afternoon . . . it's positively Victorian. This will set the sexual revolution back a hundred years if it gets out.' She lowered her legs and propped her head on one arm. 'Why not let it cool off a quarter of a degree, Rita? A week . . .'

Rita Moravia shook her head.

'You've got it bad, huh?'

'Yep.'

'Luis,' his wife called from the top of the stairs. 'Harlan is here.'

'Send him down.'

Mrs Camacho smiled at her next-door neighbor and said, 'He's in the basement watching a basketball game. As usual.'

'I thought he might be,' Harlan said, smiled and descended the staircase.

'Hey, Harlan. Great game. Boston College and West Virginia. BC's ahead by a bucket.'

'Do you men want a beer?' Mrs Camacho calling down from the kitchen.

'Thanks anyway, honey.' They heard her close the door at the top of the stairs.

Harlan Albright sank into a chair near Camacho. He extracted a pack of Marlboros from his pocket and lit one. 'Catching any spies?'

'Got Matilda Jackson's photos back from the lab yesterday afternoon. She's got one of Vasily Pochinkov, the assistant agricultural whosis at the embassy. So we've burned him. I'm trying to get surveillance approved. And sure enough, Mrs Jackson had Franklin's drop message. The computer guys should decide it's the Pentagon by tomorrow.'

'Better tell me all of it.' Albright stared at the television as Camacho went through the initial interview with Mrs Jackson and her attorney, the lab report, the interview with Mrs Jackson today at her house. When Camacho was finished, Albright lit another cigarette. 'Is there a crack house across the street?'

'Apparently. One of my men was going to check the DC police mug books. We'll have names and rap sheets by tomorrow, probably.'

'But there's no way to tie this in with the crack gang?'

'You know there isn't.'

'Did Mrs Jackson ever see Franklin?'

Luis Camacho rubbed his chin thoughtfully. 'I'm not sure. She may have and doesn't remember. She said she'd think about it.'

'What do you think?'

'How many times has he been to that drop?'

'Five.'

He considered. 'I think she's probably seen him,' he said at last. 'Whether she could pick him out of a lineup or mug book, I don't know.'

'Where will you be if your boss asks you why you haven't tried that, once the Pentagon angle is nailed down?'

'I'll look like an incompetent. I'll have to bring her in to go over the photo books to cover myself.'

'When?'

'Maybe next week. Maybe the week after. They'll want to evaluate. At first they're going to be interested in Pochinkov. For a day or two. Then they'll get interested in Mrs Jackson again.'

'Pochinkov is a dead end.'

'They'll come to that conclusion. Bigelow, my boss, has no background in counterespionage, but he's a smart man. He'll drool over Pochinkov for a day or two, toy with the idea of trapping and turning him, then eventually decide that we can't spare the manpower to watch him day and night forever. Of course, the National Security Council could decide to try to catch him servicing a drop just so we can kick him out of the country, but you probably have a better feel for that than I.'

A wry grin twisted Albright's lips. The implication was that Albright knew whether or not the Soviets were going to pick up an American diplomat in Moscow anytime soon, knowledge that Camacho well knew Albright would never have. So even here, in the safety and comfort of his own den, Camacho was stroking the ego of his control. He did it unconsciously, without even thinking. No wonder Luis Camacho had done so well in the FBI.

'How come you guys had a drop in that neighborhood anyway?'

'It was on the approved list.' Albright shrugged. The paper pushers in Moscow had no appreciation of the dynamics of an American neighborhood, how fast it could evolve or erode. The approval of drop sites was one method Soviet intelligence bureaucrats used to justify their salaries, but Albright wasn't going to explain that to Camacho. He had learned early in his career that a wise man never complains about things he can't change, especially to an agent he needed to keep loyal and motivated.

Still, Luis Camacho wasn't like other agents. Albright had been running him now for over ten years, but it was only in the last few years, when the source the Americans called the Minotaur had surfaced and within months Camacho had had the serendipitous good fortune to be assigned to head the Washington DC, FBI counterespionage department, that Camacho had become a Soviet treasure.

Tonight as he stared at the ballet of black men on the television screen, Albright reflected again on that chain of events. After a high-profile black-tie affair in the ballroom of a Washington hotel, the Soviet ambassador had discovered a picture postcard in his coat pocket as his limousine returned him to the embassy. On the front of the card was a photo of the Pentagon at night. On the back were two words and a series of numbers and letters – a computer file name – all written in block letters. Below that were ten words; not a message, just words. Nothing else. No fingerprints except the ambassador's.

It had been enough. Using Terry Franklin, the Soviets had obtained engineering and performance data on the new US Air Force stealth fighter, the F-117A, from the Pentagon computer system. The information appeared genuine. So who was the source? Unmasking the source would undoubtedly reveal why the information was passed and enable the Soviet intelligence community to properly evaluate its authenticity. But the official guest list for the black-tie reception ran to over three hundred names and was almost a Who's Who of official Washington. The names of spouses and girlfriends in attendance were not on the list, nor were the names of at least a dozen officials who had been seen there. The lists of hotel and caterer personnel were also inaccurate and incomplete.

The upper echelons of the Soviet intelligence community were stymied. The first rule of intelligence gathering – know your source – had been violated. Yet the information appeared genuine and revealed just how far ahead of the Soviets the Americans were with stealth technology.

Three months after the ambassador had received the postcard, an unsigned letter in a plain white envelope arrived at the Soviet embassy addressed to the ambassador. The letter, in neat block letters, was a commentary on the rights of minorities in the Soviet Union. In accordance with standard procedure for unsolicited mail, the letter was sent to Moscow. There the code was broken. The writer had constructed a matrix using the first random word on the original postcard as the key word. The message was three random words, the first two of which proved to be computer access words. The third word wasn't a word at all, but a series of numbers and letters. From the bowels of the Pentagon, Terry Franklin produced a fascinating document concerning the development of a land-based anti-satellite laser about which Soviet intelligence had known absolutely nothing.

Further letters followed, each encoded on the basis of a key word which appeared on the original postcard, the ambassador's. The information was golden: more stealth, Trident missile updates, SDI research breakthroughs, laser optics for artillery, satellite navigation systems . . . the list was breathtaking. The Soviets were seeing hard data on America's most precious defense secrets. And they didn't know who was giving it to them. Or why.

So Harlan Albright was told to use Mother Russia's most precious agent to find out. And here he sat, Luis Camacho, FBI special agent in charge, Washington, DC, office of counterespionage. Camacho hadn't found a sniff.

Damn, it was frustrating. And now the Terry Franklin tool to exploit the unknown source was unraveling.

'Do you believe in the entropy principle?' Camacho asked. There was a commercial on the television.

Albright shifted his gaze and tried to clear his thoughts. 'Entropy?'

'Disorder always increases in a closed system.'

'I suppose.'

'Will Franklin hold up?'

'I don't know. I doubt it. And he knows too much.' He felt a chill as he contemplated the wrath of his superiors if Franklin should ever list his thefts for the Americans.

'Can you get him to the Soviet Union?'

Albright shrugged and stood. 'I'd better go home and get some sleep.'

'Yeah.'

'Drop over tomorrow evening.'

'Sure'.

Rita Moravia's worst moment came when she preceded Toad into his apartment. 'I've only been here a month or so,' Toad said behind her. Open cardboard boxes brimming with books and towels and bric-a-brac sat everywhere. She stepped into the kitchen. The sink was full of dishes. Something hideous was growing in a saucepan on the stove. The refrigerator contained half a case of beer and a six-pack of Coke – nothing else. At least it was clean. But how in the world had this man managed to get all these dishes dirty? Aha, the freezer was chock-full of frozen vegetables and TV dinners. Even some meat.

She dumped the contents of the saucepan into the sink and ran the pan full of water, then let the water from the faucet flush the putrid mixture past the trap.

Toad was fidgety. 'I'm not much of a housekeeper,' he mumbled. 'Been trying to get unpacked and all but I've been so busy.'

Rita went into the bedroom and snapped on the lights. The bed was a rumpled mess. She ripped away the spread and blanket and tossed them on the floor, then began stripping the sheets. 'Get out clean sheets.'

'Uh . . . y'see, that's the only set I have. Why waste money on extra sheets when you can only use one set at a . . .' He ran out of words when she glanced at him as she removed the pillows from their cases. 'Why don't I take the sheets and pillowcases down to the basement and run them through the washer?' He grabbed them from the floor where Rita had thrown them and charged for the door. It closed behind him with a bang. Rita Moravia smiled and shook her head.

She tackled the bedroom first. Dirty clothes were piled in one corner of the closet. She used a T-shirt for a dustrag. No cleanser in the bathroom. He had never cleaned the commode. She was swabbing it when she heard the apartment door open. In seconds he appeared.

'Hey, Rita, you don't—'

'Is there a convenience store nearby that's still open?'

'I suppose . . .'

'I want cleanser, dishwashing liquid, something to clean these floors with . . . a mop and some sponges. And an air freshener.'

'Tomorrow I—'

'*Now*, Tarkington.'

He turned and left without a word.

In twenty minutes he was back with a bag full of supplies. She handed him the laundry from the closet. 'You go wash these and then clean up the living room and kitchen.'

When she got the sheets back on the bed she locked the bedroom door. Toad was making noises in the kitchen. She washed her face, brushed her teeth and hung up her clothes from the overnight bag. She put on a frilly negligee Harriet had given her for Christmas when it looked as if her anemic romance with Ogden might finally blossom.

Poor Ogden. His town house always looked as if the maid just left five minutes before you arrived. Appearances were so important to him. He would be devastated if he could see her in this slum. Oh well. Toad had something that Ogden would never have. She thought about it as she brushed out her hair again. Tarkington had guts as well as brains, and he knew what was important and what wasn't. He believed in himself and his abilities with a profound, unshakable faith, so he wasn't threatened by what she was, what she accomplished. Any way you looked at it, Toad Tarkington was a man.

And a man was precisely what Rita Moravia wanted in her life.

She turned off all the lights except the one on the nightstand, then opened the bedroom door.

Toad was up to his elbows in soapsuds in the sink. He had used too much dishwashing liquid. Too much water too. Water and suds were slopped over half the counter. Damn. He shouldn't have brought Rita here with the apartment in such a mess. He had been meaning to unpack and clean it up, but the chore always seemed one that could wait. He had been seeing that secretary over in Alexandria but they always went to her place. It just hadn't occurred to him how Rita might react until it was too late – like when he was fishing for the key to open the door.

Doggone, Toad, you find a really nice girl for a change and you screw it up right at the start. More water slopped over the edge of the sink. He felt it soaking the front of his pants. Oh poop.

He heard a laugh and turned. Rita was standing in the kitchen door laughing with her hand over her mouth. He grinned at her and worked blindly on the dishes. He couldn't take his eyes off her.

'You used too much water,' she said.

'Uh-huh.' With her hair down around her shoulders she looked like a completely different woman – softer, more feminine. And that frilly little nothing she was wearing!

'Do you have any dish towels?'

'Of course I have—'

'Where?'

'Where?' He forced his eyes to look at the likely places while he considered. 'Oh yeah, in that box over there behind the table.'

She swabbed the counter while he hurriedly finished the dishes and stacked them in the drainer. He pulled the plug in the sink and she wiped his hands and arms.

'I'm sorry this place is such a mess. I—'

She put her arms around his neck and kissed him. He never did get to finish that apology.

'What's your first name?'

'Robert.'

'Why do they call you Toad?'

'Because I'm horny all the time.'

'Umm,' Rita Moravia said. 'Oh yes, I see. Lucky me.'

11

'We got something,' Dreyfus said with a grin as he leaned in Luis Camacho's office door.

'Well, don't keep me waiting.'

After entering and closing the door, Dreyfus approached the desk and handed Camacho a photocopy of the message from the cigarette pack that Mrs Jackson had supplied. 'Interest Golden.TS 849329.002EB.'

'What I did,' Dreyfus said, 'was to have the computer wizards in the basement assume this message came from one of those letters that have been going to the Soviet embassy.' Camacho nodded. All mail addressed to the Soviet embassy was routinely examined and interesting items photocopied. So the FBI had copies of messages from sixty-three letters that looked suspicious.

'And sho nuff, it did. This little dilly right here.' From a file he pulled another photocopy. The message was a vitriolic screed on Soviet support of the Afghan puppet regime.

'What's the code word?'

'Luteinizing.'

'What the heck kind of word is that?'

'Some medical word.'

'Will that break any of the other messages?'

'These four.' Dreyfus laid four more photocopies on the desk before his boss. On the bottom of each was penciled the code word and the message, and the initials of the computer technician.

'How about that?' Camacho said. 'Very nicely done, Dreyfus.'

Dreyfus sagged into a seat across the desk. He was tall and angular and liked his pipe, which he extracted from a sweater pocket and charged. 'We're still short a whole bunch of code words.'

Camacho eyed his colleague as he drew deeply on the pipe and exhaled clouds of smoke. 'So now we know how the code is constructed?' he prompted.

'Yeah. It's a matrix.'

'And?'

'And if we could tie up the mainframe for a couple weeks, we could construct a matrix for each and every word in the dictionary and compare them with every message. Given enough time on the computer, we can crack them all.'

'And then we'll know what was stolen.' Camacho turned to the window. There was little to see. It was a windy, cold day out there. 'Two weeks? Jesus, that's a hell of a lot of computing time. You should be able to find the Grand Unified Theory with two weeks on a Cray computer.'

'Well, from looking at this word he used – "luteinizing" – it's obvious that some of the words are probably verb participles, past tense, etc. It's possible – probable, since this guy's pretty damn cute – that some of the code words are the names of persons or places. The number of possible English code words is in the millions, and the computer must construct a matrix for each and every one of them and test each matrix against all the suspected messages. So what is that – a couple million repetitions of the program times sixty? Assuming he used real words or names. But if he made up random combinations of letters, say a dozen letters . . .' Dreyfus shrugged.

On a scratch pad Camacho wrote, '26^{12}.' 'Point made,' he muttered.

'Oh, I know, I know. Even after we have all the messages cracked, we won't have the Minotaur. But we'll have his scent. Once we know which files he's been in, we can trot over to the Pentagon and glom on to the access sheets for those files. Our boy has seen them all.'

'Maybe. But not very likely. Probably he got the access codes during an unauthorized peek in the main security files. But the document key words and numbers—' He sighed. 'I would bet my last penny he hasn't seen all the files he's given away. I'll bet there isn't a man alive who's had authorized access to all those files.'

'It's worth a try.'

'Agreed. But we'll never get the Cray mainframe for two weeks. The fingerprint guys would cry a river. So let's get started with what we have. Get the access sheets for those five files we know about and let's see who's on them. And for Christ's sake, keep your head down. Don't let anyone know what you're after. We don't want to spook our man.'

'Okay,' Dreyfus agreed. 'While we're at it, why don't we just pick up Terry Franklin and sweat the little bastard?'

'Not yet.'

Dreyfus' pipe was dead. He sucked audibly, then got out his lighter. When he was exhaling smoke again, he said, 'I think we're making a mistake not keeping Franklin under surveillance.'

'What if the little shit bolts? What then? Is Franklin the only mole Ivan has over there? Is he?'

Dreyfus threw up his hands and gathered up his papers.

'Get somebody to tackle this decoding project with the mainframe when it's not in use. The front office will never give us two weeks, but let's see what they can do with a couple hours here and there.'

'Sure, Luis.'

'Again, nice work, Dreyfus.'

Camacho stared at the door after Dreyfus left. He had slipped and made a mistake; he had lied to Dreyfus. The only way to keep two separate lives completely, safely separate was to never tell a lie. Never. You often had to leave out part of the truth, but that wasn't a lie. A lie was a booby trap, a land mine that could explode at any time with fatal results. And this lie had been a big one. He sat now staring at the objects on his desk with unseeing eyes as he examined the dimensions of the lie and its possible implications. Stupid! A stupid, idiotic lie.

He rubbed his forehead again and found he couldn't sit still. He paced, back and forth and back and forth, until finally he was standing in front of the Pentagon organization chart. If there were forty files or sixty-three or any number, there would be a small group of people who would have access to all of them, if you constructed just one more hypothesis – that all the files concerned classified projects in research or development. Tyler Henry the admiral suspected they did. Albright the spy already knew and had told him so. Camacho the spy catcher must verify or refute that hypothesis soon, or Dreyfus and Henry and Albright and a lot of the others are going to think him incompetent, or worse.

He stood staring at one box on the complex chart. Inside the box was printed: 'Under Secretary of Defense for Acquisition.'

He sat at his desk and unlocked the lower right drawer and removed a file. Inside were photocopies of all sixty-three letters. They were in chronological order. All had been written on plain white copy machine paper in #2 lead pencil, which had been a wise precaution on the part of the person or persons who wrote them. Ink could be analyzed chemically and the sellers of pens could be interviewed, but a #2 lead pencil was a #2 lead pencil. And copy machine paper – the stuff was everywhere, in every office of the nation.

On an average day the Soviet embassy received several dozen casual cards and letters mailed from all over the United States. Most of the messages were short and to the point. Many were crude. 'Eat shit, Ivan,' seemed to be popular. The Chernobyl disaster and the Armenian earthquake had elicited thousands of pieces of mail, much to the chagrin of the postal inspectors and FBI agents assigned to screen it.

Over the last three years these letters in this file had been culled for further scrutiny. All the messages were printed in small block letters, all were long enough to contain an internal code and all of them had been written in English by someone with a fairly decent education. Some were signed and some weren't. Interestingly, about 80 percent of these letters had been mailed in the Washington metropolitan area. Not a one had been mailed from over a hundred miles away. All had been enclosed in cheap, plain white envelopes available in hundreds of bookstores, convenience stores, supermarkets, etc., all over town.

Camacho looked closely. It was easy to see that the same person had written them all; the penmanship was so careful and neat, the style of the writer so consistent from letter to letter. And every now and then, maybe once in every other letter, the syntax was tortuous, not quite right. It was as if the writer purposefully chose a difficult sentence construction. The conclusion that these letters, or at least some of them, contained an internal code was inescapable.

The mechanics of the matrix demanded a reasonably long letter if one were going to encrypt a long message, say three dozen characters. If it took an average of three words to signal one character, then the message must run to at least nine dozen words, too many for a postcard.

The sheer number of letters was daunting. Some of them were probably dross. The Minotaur knew these letters would arouse suspicion, so he wrote lots of them. And it was impossible to tell which contained a code and which didn't. He was hiding in plain sight.

Maybe that was the key. Maybe the Minotaur wasn't just some career civil servant, some clerk. Maybe he was a man in plain sight, out in the open, known to one and all. But why? Why was he committing treason? That's what the Soviets wanted to know.

Camacho picked up the phone and punched numbers. 'Dreyfus, pull the files on all the political people in the Defense Department and put them in the conference room.'

'All of them? Again?'

'All.'

'Yessir,' Dreyfus said without enthusiasm.

Even a blind hog finds an acorn occasionally, Camacho told himself as he cradled the phone. And if there's an acorn in those files, this time I'm going to find it.

The youngest child, a four-year-old boy, threw a fit as Lucy Franklin drove toward Dulles. The nine-year-old, Karen, had been deviling him all morning, and apparently he decided he had had enough. He wailed at the top of his lungs and punched at his sister. One of his swings connected with her nose. Blood spouted and she screamed too. Lucy pulled off the freeway and put the car in neutral.

'Shut up!' she roared. 'Both you kids, *stop it!*'

Satisfied with the outcome of the battle, the boy sat back and stared at the blood dripping on his sister's dress as she sobbed uncontrollably.

'Look at you two. Fighting again. Now Karen's hurt. Aren't you sorry, Kevin?'

He didn't look a bit sorry, which made Karen cry harder. Lucy got her into the front seat and held a tissue on her nose until the bleeding stopped. She cuddled the child. Karen had vomited twice during the night, so this morning Lucy had kept her home from school.

The traffic roared by. 'Say you're sorry, Kevin.'

'I'm sorry.' His hand came over the seat and touched Karen's hair. The sobbing gradually eased. Holding a tissue against Karen's nose with her left hand, Lucy leaned over the seat and cuddled the boy. This week had been tough on them. Terry was so distant, saying little, shouting at the children as they ran through the house and made their usual noise.

He was a volcano about to erupt. His tension and fear were tangible, visible, frightening to the children, terrifying to Lucy. Even as she sat here on the freeway, the unreasoning panic that Terry caused washed over her again. What had he done? What would he do? Would he hurt the children? Would he hurt her?

'Mommy, don't cry.'

'I'm not crying, sweetheart. I just have something in my eye.'

'I'm okay now,' Karen said, casting an evil glance across the seat back at her brother.

'No more fighting. You two love each other. No more fighting. It makes me sad to see you two trying to irritate each other.'

Now Kevin's hand touched her hair. 'Let's go get Grandma.'

'Yes. Let's do.' She started the engine and slipped out into traffic.

At lunch Toad and Rita shared a table, just the two of them. From a table fifty feet away Jake Grafton watched the body language and gestures as he listened to George Wilson and Dalton Harris talk baseball. So Toad Tarkington had fallen in love again! That guy went over that precipice with awe-inspiring regularity. The impact at the bottom was also spectacular.

You really had to tip your hat to the guy. He arrives, takes in the female situation at a glance, then immediately makes a fool of himself over the best-looking woman in sight. Jake allowed himself a grin. The ol' Horny Toad.

Back in the office after lunch, Jake called Tarkington over to his desk. 'I've been looking over this memo about the A-6 system. How did it go when you turned off the radar and Doppler?'

'Well, sir, without the Doppler to dampen the velocities, the inertial tends to drift somewhat. But without the radar all you have is the IR and it's tough. When it isn't raining or snowing you can run attacks okay once you've found the target. The nav system just isn't tight enough to let you find the targets without the radar. The IR doesn't have enough field of view. With a global positioning system to stabilize the inertial you might have a chance, but not now.'

'It looks to me like you've got a handle on the major problems. This evening how about jumping a plane and flying up to Calverton, New York? With Commander Richards. The guys at Grumman are expecting you two. I want you to look over the A-6G system and play with it and let me know what you think. Come back Monday. Tuesday you and I are going to take a little trip out West.'

The lieutenant's face reflected his dismay.

'That's not going to put you out or interfere with anything, is it?' Jake tried to appear solicitous.

'Geez, CAG. The whole weekend—'

'You didn't have anything going, did you? I mean, you haven't been around here long enough to—'

'Oh no, sir. I just thought I'd do my laundry and all. Maybe take in a movie. Write a letter to my mom.'

Jake couldn't hold back a smile. 'Running out of clean underwear, huh?'

Toad nodded, trying to maintain a straight face.

'Buy some more. See you Monday, Toad.'

'Yessir. Monday.'

At four o'clock Jake received a call from Commander Rob Knight. 'Could you come over to my office?'

'Well, I was getting ready to go home.'

'On your way?'

'Sure.'

Jake locked the files, turned off the lights and snagged his hat on the way out. Smoke Judy was still there. 'Lock up, will you, Smoke?'

'Sure, Captain. Have a good weekend.'

'You too.'

Jake walked to the Pentagon. He was getting very familiar with this route. The parking lot was emptying as he crossed it and he had to do some dodging.

On the fourth-level corridor the pile of used furniture was still gathering dust. Jake turned right on the D-Ring and walked down three doors. He knocked.

Rear Admiral Costello opened the door. 'Ah, Captain, please come in.'

The room was packed. People were sitting on desks. Everyone had a beer can in his hand. Vice Admiral Henry was there, Costello's three aides – all captains fresh from carrier commands and waiting for the flag list or new orders – together with the four office regulars and two admirals Jake didn't know. He accepted a beer and found himself talking to Henry. 'Glad you could join us, Captain.'

'Delighted, sir.'

It was Happy Hour. These men who had spent their lives in the camaraderie of ready rooms needed two hours at the end of the week to review the week's frustrations and reduce them to manageable proportions. Soon the subject turned from shop to mutual friends, ships, ports, and planes they had flown.

Just before six Jake excused himself. He and Callie were going to the beach this evening. Tyler Henry grabbed his hat and started with Jake for the door. As Jake opened it, Henry paused and took a long, smiling look at the bulletin board. He was looking at a photo. It was a black-and-white eight-by-ten of singer Ann-Margret holding a microphone in her hand and singing her heart out, wearing a sleeveless shorty blouse and no pants at all.

'I was there,' Henry said. '*Kitty Hawk*, '67 or '68. That woman . . .' He pointed at the picture. 'She's *all* lady. She's my favorite entertainer.'

The photo was autographed and signed. 'To the guys of OP-506.' Yes, thought Jake Grafton, remembering those days. No doubt that was a great moment for her, performing before five thousand screaming sailors, but it was an even greater moment for them, a moment they would remember and cherish every day of their lives, each and every man jack of them. Of course, bombing North Vietnam twelve hours a day, some of them didn't have very many days left. The loss rate then was almost a plane a day. No doubt Ann-Margret had known that.

'Mine too,' said Jake Grafton, and together with the admiral walked into the corridor where he said goodbye. The admiral went back toward his office as Jake set off alone for the subway.

At six o'clock, as Jake Grafton was boarding the subway at the Pentagon station, Luis Camacho closed the last of the files piled up on his desk. It was hopeless: 218 files, 218 political appointees in the Department of Defense, including the service secretaries and unders and assistants. He had selected just eighteen files: the Under Secretary of Defense for Acquisition, his political aides, and the assistants and under secretaries in SECDEF's office. And SECDEF. All these men had held their positions for at least three years. But it was still hopeless.

If one of these men was the Minotaur, no hint of it came from the FBI background investigations that had been completed for the Senate confirmation process. The common thread was that they were pillars of the establishment, the kind of men generations of mothers prayed their daughters would marry. All eighteen were white, well educated, leaders in their local communities, respected by all those similarly situated. Several had previously held elected or appointed office. Most were family men or divorced family men. Thirteen of them had graduated from an Ivy League school. Tennis was the most popular sport and golf a close second. Several were yachtsmen. Every single one of them could be labeled independently wealthy, most from old family money, a few from small fortunes they had made themselves.

It was sickening. Wealth, privilege, power, spelled out in these files in black and white. Oh, they had a few little peccadillos. One man had flunked out of three colleges before he had completed his education in a fourth. Three drunken-driving convictions. One illegitimate child. One man had been known to frequent prostitutes in his younger days, and one had been accused of being a closet homosexual by a disgruntled soon-to-be-ex during a messy divorce. Luis Camacho, career cop, thought it pretty tame stuff.

For several seconds he sat and stared at the piles of folders spread over the table. No cop, he told himself, ever looked seriously at a more unlikely group of suspects. There wasn't even one man with a family or background that might be vulnerable to intense scrutiny. Not here. These men had had every advantage that birth, wealth, and social position could confer. Sadly he shook his head.

If the key to the Minotaur's behavior was in his past, it was going to remain buried unless a small army of agents with a lot of time were told to dig deep. The agents Camacho could get. What frustrated Camacho was his suspicion that he was running out of time. What infuriated him was his conviction that no matter how deep they dug, the investigators could come up dry. And without something . . . some artifact . . . something tangible, how could he sell a man to Albright as the Minotaur? Albright would want a man he could understand, with a motivation that could be reduced to writing and passed from the Aquarium to the Kremlin and would explain. The committee should have thought this problem through two years ago.

He went back to his office and found a photo of Terry Franklin in the file. Actually there were four of them. The one he selected was a full-figure shot taken with a hidden camera. Franklin was looking just to the right of the camera, perhaps waiting for a car to pass the parked van the photographer had used. This picture he placed in an inside pocket of his sports coat. He glanced at his watch. If he went to the Pentagon, he could probably still catch Vice Admiral Henry, who rarely left before 7 P.M.

Terry Franklin stopped at a neighborhood bar after he got off the bus from work. On the Friday evening of the longest week of his life, he deserved a few drinks. Waiting for the ax to fall was squeezing the juice right out of him. He had been a bumbling fool all week, botching one job after another, having to ask the chief for help with several problems that were so minor he had been embarrassed. The chief was solicitous, asking if he was having problems at home.

The problem was he couldn't think about anything else. He could no longer concentrate on his job, his wife, the kids, anything. He *had* to get his mind off it and he just couldn't! Sitting here at the bar, he glanced warily at the other customers, then bit his lip. A panic-stricken scream was just beneath the surface. He was losing it. It was like one of those nightmares he had as a kid – he was fleeing from a hideous monster and his legs went slower and slower and the monster was reaching out, within inches of catching him – and he woke up screaming with pee soaking his pajamas.

He was going to have to get all this crap stuffed into one sock, going to have to wire himself together so he could get from one end of the day to the other. He had all of tonight, all day Saturday, all day Sunday – three nights and two whole days – before he had to face his demons on Monday.

He ordered another CC on the rocks. Sure, he could do it. No one knew. No one was going to arrest him. No one was going to toss him into prison with a bunch of homo thieves and killers. After all, this is *America*, land of the gullible, home of the foolish.

He would deliver and collect on another dozen floppies or so. Then he would empty his safe-deposit box and be on his way to a new life. Perhaps Rio. He would lie on the beach all day and fuck beach bunnies at night.

He sipped on his drink and thought about how it would be. The life he had always wanted was right there within his grasp, so close, within inches. But he was going to have to be realistic about the monsters, going to have to keep trotting. No urine-soaked pajamas. No screaming fits. Amen.

He paid the tab and left two quarters on the bar. Outside he forced himself to pause and examine the headlines on the newspaper in the vending stand. Same old crap. The world was still turning, things were burning down, trains were still crashing . . .

He walked the two blocks home with his head up, breathing the spring air. It seemed just yesterday that it was so cold and miserable. Spring is here. And I've got a fortune in the bank and no one knows but me.

His neighbor was washing his car in the driveway. 'Hey, Terry, how's it going?'

'Pretty good. And you?'

'Just fine. Say, I've been meaning to ask you. How's the spy business?'

Terry Franklin froze.

The asshole tossed his sponge into a bucket and wiped his hands on his jeans. He grinned as he reached for his cigarettes. 'Lucy has been telling Melanie that you're a spy. I laughed myself sick. So . . .'

Terry didn't hear any more. He lurched for the front door.

'*Lucy!*' He slammed the door behind him and charged for the kitchen. '*Lucy,*' he bellowed, 'you *stupid*—'

Lucy was sitting with her mother drinking coffee at the counter. Both women stared, openmouthed.

'What – what does Jared mean – about Melanie? *What* did you tell Melanie?' He thought he was doing pretty well under the circumstances, staying calm and keeping the legs going. But it came out as a roar.

'Now listen here, Terry—' Lucy's mom began.

'Lucy, I need to talk to you.' He grabbed her arm and half lifted her from the stool. 'Now, Lucy.'

'Let go of her, Terry!'

'Mom Southworth, *please*! I need to talk to—'

'*No!*' The old lady had a voice like a drill instructor.

'Lucy, what did you tell that moron Melanie?'

'I told her that—'

'Get your hands off her, Terry. I know all about you. You stupid, greedy—' The older woman was fat, with two chins. Just now Terry Franklin thought her the ugliest woman he had ever laid eyes on.

'Shut up, you nosy old bitch! What the hell are you doing here anyway? Lucy, I want to talk to you.' He grabbed her arm and dragged her from the stool toward the downstairs half-bath. He pulled her inside and slammed the door. 'What in the name of God have you been saying to Melanie?'

Lucy was scared witless. 'Noth—'

'Did you tell her I was a spy?'

Terry didn't need an answer; it was written all over her face. The mother-in-law pounding on the door and shouting. Something about calling the police.

'You – you—' he whimpered as his legs turned to wood and the monster's fetid breath engulfed him.

Lucy opened the door and slid out as he sagged down onto the floor and covered his face with his hands. His whole life was shattered, smashed to bits by that silly, simple twat!

It was 8:30 P.M. when Luis Camacho parked in front of Mrs Jackson's house and locked his car. It was a delightful spring evening, still a nip in the air, but almost no wind. The foliage was budding. Summer was coming and the earth was ready.

As he walked down the street Camacho glanced at the crack house. Someone was peering through a curtain on the second floor; he saw it move. No one on the sidewalk. Mrs Jackson's gate was ajar, but not a light showed through the curtains.

He mounted the stoop and rapped on the door. As he waited he glanced around. Street still empty. Such a beautiful evening. He knocked some more. Perhaps she had gone to the store, or to a neighbor's?

Suddenly he knew. He tried the knob. It turned. He pushed the door open several inches and called into the darkness, 'Mrs Jackson? Mrs Jackson, are you here?' He gingerly pushed the door open wider and reached under his jacket for the butt of the .357 magnum on his right hip.

All the lights were off. Camacho closed the door behind him and stood in the darkness listening with the revolver in his hand.

Nothing. Not a sound. Not a squeak, not a creak, nothing.

He waited, flexing his fingers on the butt of the gun. All he could hear was the thud of his own heart.

Slowly, carefully, he groped for the light switch on the wall.

She was lying near the kitchen door with her right leg twisted under her, staring fixedly at the ceiling. In the center of her forehead was a small red circle. No blood. She had died instantly.

With the revolver ready he went from room to room, turning on lights and glancing into closets. Everything was neat, clean, tidy. Satisfied that the killer was gone, he came back to the living room and stood looking at Mrs Jackson. He stooped and touched her cheek. She had been dead for hours. Around the bullet hole in her forehead was a black substance. A powder burn.

The phone was in the kitchen. Her purse sat beside it, the catch still latched. Camacho wrapped his handkerchief loosely around the telephone receiver before he picked it up. He dialed with a pen from his shirt pocket. As he waited for the duty officer to answer, he idly noticed that the fire under the coffeepot had been turned off. A professional hit. With any luck the body would not have been discovered for days and the time of death would have been problematic.

'This is Special Agent Camacho.' He gave them the address. 'I've discovered a corpse. Better send the forensic team and the DC police liaison officer. And call Dreyfus at home and ask him to come over.'

Back in the living room he tried to avoid looking at Mrs Jackson. Something shiny in a candy dish on the sideboard caught his eye. He stepped carefully over the body and bent to look. A spent .22 caliber Long Rifle cartridge. The killer hadn't bothered to retrieve the spent casing! And why should he? Twenty-two caliber rimfire ammunition was sold everywhere and was virtually untraceable. But how had this shell got here?

He went back to the corpse and stood near it. Then he stooped down and felt her head carefully. Another bullet hole in the back of her head. Okay, where is the second shell?

The FBI agent got down on his hands and knees and looked under everything. He found it in a corner, half hidden by the edge of the carpet, bearing the Remington 'U.' Camacho didn't touch it.

So Mrs Jackson had opened the door and admitted her killer. Locks not forced or scratched up. She had started back toward the kitchen, the killer behind, and he had shot her in the back of the head. She had died on her feet and collapsed where she stood. He had walked over to her and fired a second shot into her brain with the pistol held inches from her face. That shell casing was ejected by the pistol into the candy dish. The killer had then proceeded on through the house, checking for other people, turning off lights, turning off the stove, making sure nothing would cause a fire or call attention to the house. Then he had left and closed the door carefully behind him. He hadn't bothered to lock it.

Even that was smart. No doubt the assassin had worn gloves, so he left no fingerprints. If the local punks tried the knob and came in to see what they could steal, they would probably not be so sophisticated, and they would automatically become the prime suspects in Mrs Jackson's murder. All very slick.

The bastard!

Camacho was standing by the front window looking at the crack house when the lab van pulled up, followed immediately by a sedan with city plates and two sedans with US government tags. Two hours later the forensic team and the other people departed with the body. Dreyfus and a lieutenant from the DC force remained with Luis Camacho.

'When are you going to raid that crack house, shut it down?' Camacho asked the question of the plainclothes lieutenant as he jerked his head at the building across the street.

'Who says it's a crack house?'

'What're you afraid of? Think the mayor might be in there?'

'Listen, asshole! If you've got any evidence that dwelling is being used for illegal purposes, I'd like to see it. We'll do some affidavits, find a judge and get a warrant. Then we'll raid the place. Now are you all hot air or do you have some *evidence*?'

'We have a statement from a woman now dead. We sent a copy over to you guys three days ago.'

'I saw that statement, then routed it to the narcs. All it said was that there was suspicious activity over there. A little old woman thought something nasty was going on in her neighborhood. Big fucking deal! No judge in this country would have called that probable cause and issued a warrant, even if that statement had been sworn, which it wasn't. Now where's the goddamn *evidence*?'

'Whatever happened to "usually reliable sources"?'

The lieutenant didn't reply.

'All you guys must belong to the ACLU.' Camacho stood looking at the house, the peeling paint, the mortar missing from the brick joints, the trash in front of the place, the light leaking around drawn blinds. Just then a large old Cadillac hardtop came around the corner and drifted slowly to a stop at the curb. Four young black men got out. One went up the steps toward the door of the house, which opened before he reached it and closed behind him.

'Just follow me,' Camacho said. 'I'll get you some evidence.' Even before he finished speaking he was out the door and going down the stairs to the sidewalk two at a time.

He went across the street toward the Cad at a brisk walk. The three men were staring.

'Hi.' He reached into his jacket pocket with his left hand and pulled out his credentials. 'FBI—'

One of the men was moving, going sideways and reaching under his shirt. Camacho rammed his left shoulder into the nearest man and fell on top of him as he drew his revolver. He heard a shot, then two more in quick succession. The man who had gone for his gun fell backward against the car, then slid to the sidewalk as Camacho jammed his revolver against the teeth of the struggling man under him.

'Don't!' The man opened his mouth and Camacho jammed the gun in up to the trigger guard. 'Freeze, shithead!'

On the other side of the car someone was pleading, 'Don't shoot, don't shoot.'

'You even hiccup, I'm gonna blow your brains out.' Camacho felt the man for a weapon as he stared into his wide eyes. There was an automatic in his waistband. The agent extracted it and turned the man so he could look over his shoulder at the house.

Dreyfus was checking the man on the sidewalk and the police lieutenant was cuffing the third one.

Camacho pulled the barrel of the revolver clear of his man's lips. 'Is there a back way outta there?'

The lips contorted. Camacho cocked the revolver and placed the barrel right between his eyes. 'Answer me, or so help me God . . .'

'Yeah. The alley.'

Camacho pulled the man from the sidewalk and shoved him behind the Cad. 'Quick, on your belly, hands behind your back. Assume the position, fucker, right *now*.' As the man obeyed, Camacho tossed his cuffs to the lieutenant, then began to run for the corner.

He rounded the corner at a run just as a car was coming out of the alley in the middle of the block, its engine howling. He dived onto his face. An automatic weapon roared as the rear of the car slewed and smoke poured from the tires. Scrambling behind a parked car, Camacho managed to fire one shot at the fleeing car, although he knew that the hollow-point +P .38 slug had no chance of penetrating the body of the car. Someone leaning out a rear passenger window hosed another burst in his general direction as the car ran the stop sign at the next corner. The bullets slapped the concrete and parked cars. Luis Camacho huddled behind a car and listened to the engine noise fade away.

When he walked back to the Cadillac, Dreyfus was watching the cuffed men lying in the street and lighting his pipe while the police lieutenant used his car radio. Camacho looked at the man who had been shot. He was dead, with two holes in his chest about four inches apart. A cocked nine-millimeter Beretta automatic lay on the street near him.

'Was it you that got this guy?' Camacho asked Dreyfus.

'Yeah. After he took a shot at you.'

'No shit.'

'You are a goddamn hopeless romantic, Luis.'

The lieutenant came over at a trot. His face was livid. 'You fucking *idiot*! Are you tired of living? You almost got one of us *killed*! We're the *good* guys, or haven't you keyhole peepers heard?'

'I'm sorry. I just didn't think it through.'

'The FBI, the fearless band of idiots.' The lieutenant said the words softly, a benediction, a sublime pronouncement of irrefutable truth. He looked up and down the street, breathing deeply. The red tinge in his cheeks subsided slowly. Finally he said, 'Okay, Rambo. How do you want this to read?'

'Hell, just tell it straight. This car came along and parked in front of a crime scene. I approached them and identified myself and one of them pulled a weapon.' He shrugged.

The police officer nudged one of the prone men with his foot. 'A real smart bunch of punks. Drive right up and park across the street from two cars with government plates. You shitheads deserve to be in jail. Just in case you haven't figured it out, you're under arrest.'

The wail of an approaching siren caromed from the fronts of the delapidated houses.

'See you around, Lieutenant,' Camacho said.

'Leaving? Some congressman fucking his secretary tonight?'

'You city guys can handle this. Mrs Jackson's my problem.'

'The old lady can cool off without you, Rambo. I'm gonna go get a search warrant for this house, and you're gonna have to sign an affidavit. A couple of them. You and your sidekick here, J. Edgar Earp, are gonna be working with me for the next eighteen hours. Now get your cute little ass over here and start searching this car. Let's see what these hot shooters were driving around.'

The lieutenant was right. It did take eighteen hours.

Terry Franklin never knew how long he stayed in the bathroom. The flowers on the wallpaper formed a curious pattern. Each had a petal that joined to an offset flower, all of them; it was very curious how they did that. He thought about how the flowers joined and about nothing at all for a long, long time.

When he came out of the bathroom the house was dark and silent. He flipped on the kitchen light and drank milk from the carton in the refrigerator. He was very tired. He climbed the stairs and lay down on the bed.

The sun was shining in the windows when he awoke. He was still dressed. He used the toilet, then went downstairs and found something to eat in the refrigerator. Cold pizza. He ate it cold. It was left over from a week or more ago when he had taken the whole family to Pizza Hut. He thought about that for a while, trying to recall just when it had been, remembering the crowd and the kids with the cheese strings dangling from their mouths and hands. The memory was fresh, as if it had happened just a short while ago, yet it was all wrong. The memory was from the wrong perspective, like when you remember a scene from your childhood. You remember it as you saw it as a child, with everything large and the adults tall and the other children just your size. That's the way he remembered Pizza Hut.

He sat the empty plate in the sink and ran some water into it, then went into the living room and lay down on the couch. He was tired again. He slept most of the day.

12

At four o'clock Saturday afternoon an exhausted Luis Camacho arrived home with a raging headache and went straight to bed. When he awoke the house was quiet and dark and his wife was asleep beside him. He checked the luminous display on the clock-radio on the bedside stand: 12:47. Slipping on his robe, he padded downstairs to the kitchen, where he raided the refrigerator. He got a plate from the dishwasher and helped himself to some leftover meat loaf and a couple of big spoonfuls of tuna casserole. He nuked it for a minute in the microwave while he poured a glass of milk.

From the kitchen table he could see Albright's bedroom window across the waist-high cedar fence, just twenty feet or so away. The window was dark. Good ol' Harlan Albright. Peter Aleksandrovich Chistyakov. Yuri.

Matilda Jackson had unlocked her front door and opened it for her killer, then turned her back on him. So it was someone she thought she had no reason to fear. A small-caliber automatic with a good silencer, the point-blank coup de grace, the methodical search of the house for possible witnesses and the turning off of the lights and appliances; certainly he was no thief or teenage drug guard-turned-gunman. No, Mrs Jackson had been the victim of a trained, experienced assassin who convinced her it was safe to admit him into her house. Perhaps he told her he was with the FBI? Then he put two bullets into her brain.

Not to protect Pochinkov, who had diplomatic immunity and could not be arrested or prosecuted. The Americans needed no testimony from Mrs Jackson or anyone else should they decide to declare Pochinkov persona non grata. Camacho thought about the picture of Terry Franklin in his jacket pocket, which he had hoped Mrs Jackson might recognize. He had discussed the possibility of Mrs Jackson identifying Franklin with Harlan Albright.

And Albright had lost no time. Why take a chance? Why risk endangering a valuable agent? He probably had not pulled the trigger himself. Just a quick call from a pay phone and Mrs Jackson was on her way to the graveyard.

436

The ability to kill people with a telephone call – that's the ultimate manifestation of power, isn't it? And those ignorant charlatans in the Caribbean are still sticking pins into dolls. If only they could comprehend how far mankind had progressed with the wondrous aid of modern technology, developed from the triumphant findings of rigorous, unbiased science. Two thousand years *anno domini* murder is no longer uncertain, affected by mysterious forces and mystic symbols and the position of the moon and planets. We civilized moderns just let our fingers do the walking . . .

Camacho rinsed the dirty dish, glass and fork and placed them in the dishwasher. Somewhere here in the kitchen his wife had cigarettes hidden. They had both quit smoking six months ago, but she still liked to savor a cigarette in the afternoon over a cup of coffee while a soap blared on the television. And she thought he didn't know. A cop is supposed to know things, lots of things, and occasionally he finds he knows too much.

The pack was on the top shelf in the pantry, behind a box of instant rice. After a couple of puffs, he poured himself a finger of bourbon and added water and ice. He sat at the kitchen table and opened the sliding glass door to the backyard a few inches to exhaust the smoke.

Beyond the back fence the houses facing the next street over were silhouetted against the glare of the streetlights. The shapes cast weird shadows in his backyard. He smoked two cigarettes before he finished the whiskey and put both butts in the garbage under the sink. In the family room he lay down on the couch and pulled the throw blanket over him.

As he tried to relax the faces and images ran through his mind in a disjointed, unconnected way: Albright, Franklin, Matilda Jackson with her obscene third eye, Admiral Henry, Dreyfus with his pipe and files, Harold Strong blunt and profane, all the letters with their penciled block words that said nothing at all and yet whispered of something, something just beyond his understanding . . . It was a long time before Luis Camacho drifted off to sleep.

He awoke to the smell of coffee and bacon. Breakfast was strained, as usual. In a crisis of identity last fall, their sixteen-year-old son had transformed himself into a punk all in the course of one sunny Saturday at the mall. The boy sat sullenly at the table this morning with his remaining hair hanging over his forehead and obscuring his eyes. The shaved place above his left ear, clear up to where his part used to be back in those old, 'normal' days, looked extraordinarily white and obscenely naked, his father thought, rather like a swatch of an old maid's thigh. Luis Camacho sipped coffee and studied the tense, quivering lips visible below the cascading hair.

When the boy had left the table and ascended the stairs, Luis remarked, 'What *is* his problem?'

'He's sixteen years old,' Sally said crossly. 'He's not popular, he's not a good student, he's not an athlete, and the girls don't know he's alive. The only thing he does have is acne.'

'Sounds like an epitaph.'

'It's his whole life.'

Camacho was just starting on the Sunday paper when the phone rang. His wife answered. 'It's for you,' she called.

It was Dreyfus, calling from a car phone. 'Luis, it's Smoke Judy. He's out driving this morning. Left his house in Morningside ten minutes ago. Maybe a meet.'

'Where is he now?'

'Going north on the beltway. We just passed the Capital Centre arena.'

'You guys got the van in standby?'

'Nope. It's back at the shop.' The shop was headquarters, the J. Edgar Hoover Building. 'Nobody thought we'd need it today.'

'Get it. I want a record this time. Any idea where he's going?'

'Not a glimmer.'

'I've got to get dressed and shaved. I'll be in the car in fifteen minutes. Call me on the car phone then.'

'Sure.'

Sally came into the bathroom while he was shaving. 'You're in the paper today.' She showed him the story and the photo. 'You didn't tell me there was a shooting.'

'Friday night. Dreyfus shot a guy.'

'It says here the dead man had already shot at you.'

He eyed her in the mirror, then attacked his upper lip.

'Luis, you could have been killed.'

'Then Gerald could shave his head as bare as his ass and run around in a loincloth.'

She closed her eyes and shook her head. 'Weren't you scared?'

He hugged her. 'Yeah. I seem to be spending more and more time in that condition.'

Camacho was driving south on New Hampshire Avenue past the old Naval Ordnance Lab, now the navy's Surface Weapons Center, when the car phone buzzed. It was only 9:30 on Sunday morning, but already a good volume of traffic was flowing along the avenue. It seemed as if all the Silver Spring suburbanites had big plans for this spring day, which was partly overcast. He wondered if it would rain as he picked up the phone. 'Camacho.'

'He turned off the beltway and is headed north on I-95 toward Baltimore.'

'How many cars do you have?'

'Seven.'

'Stay loose. He'll be looking.' A car would be in front of the suspect vehicle and another well behind, but in sight. The additional cars would be at least a mile back. Every four or five minutes the car behind would pass Judy as the lead car accelerated away and got off at the next exit, where it would watch the cavalcade pass and join as the last car. The third car would assume the position immediately behind Judy. If this was done properly, Judy would never notice he was being followed. Had the agents had a helicopter or light plane this morning, none of the cars would have even been in sight of the suspect.

Camacho drove onto the beltway eastbound and went down two miles to the I-95 exit, where he merged with a string of cars and trucks headed north. He eased the car up to five miles per hour over the speed limit and stayed in the right-hand lane.

In the two weeks that Camacho's men had had Commander Smoke Judy under surveillance, he had gone driving on only one occasion. That time he had gone to a mall and spent forty-five minutes in an electronics store watching college basketball on television, eaten two slices of pepperoni pizza and swizzled a medium-sized Sprite, and gawked for five minutes in a store that specialized in racy lingerie. Just another debonair von vivant out on the town.

As he passed the Fort Meade exit rain began to fall. Dreyfus called once. The subject was still headed north. Dreyfus had had the lead car take the Route 32 exit in case Judy was on his way to Baltimore-Washington International Airport, but Judy passed it by. After a U-turn the FBI car was back on I-95 chasing the cavalcade. Camacho hung up the telephone and listened to the wipers. Since this was his personal car, he didn't have a radio to monitor the surveillance.

In a few minutes the rain ceased. The clouds still looked threatening with patches of blue here and there. The car ahead flung up a spray from the wet road that kept Camacho fiddling with his wiper control and wishing he had taken the intermittent wiper option.

Following the ribbon of interstate highways, Smoke Judy circled Baltimore and headed north toward York. Just short of the Pennsylvania line he began to slow in the left lane. Dreyfus was in the car immediately behind and used the radio to call the trailing car, which was three miles back. When Judy swung through an emergency vehicle turnaround and accelerated south, the trailing car was already southbound at fifty miles per hour, waiting for Judy to catch up. Dreyfus and the drivers of the other car waited until Judy was completely out of sight before they gunned across the median throwing mud and turf and resumed the pursuit. One of the cars almost got stuck.

'He thinks he's being cute,' Dreyfus told Camacho, who took the first exit he came to and crossed over the highway, then sat at the head of the on-ramp to wait.

'Think he's spotted you?'

'I don't – we'll see. He'll go straight home if he has.'

Smoke Judy didn't go home. He went to the inner harbor of Baltimore and parked in an outlying lot, then walked unhurriedly past the aquarium and the head of the pier where the three-masted frigate *Constellation* was berthed and sat in front of the giant indoor food mall, near the water. He sat for almost twenty minutes watching the gulls and people as a gentle wind blew in from the bay.

Camacho and Dreyfus watched him through one-way glass mounted in the side of a Potomac Power van parked on a yellow line near the frigate pier. From the outside of the van the glass appeared to be a sign unless one inspected it from close range. A man wearing jeans and a tool belt had rigged yellow ropes around the vehicle as soon as it came to a stop to ensure that no one got that close.

The distance from the van to where Judy sat was a little over a hundred yards. Camacho aimed a small television camera mounted on a pedestal while Dreyfus snapped photos with a 35mm camera with a telephone lens. Beside them an agent wearing earphones huddled over a cassette recorder. A parabolic microphone on top of the van was slaved to the video camera, but right now the audio was a background murmur, like the background noise of a baseball radio broadcast.

'He isn't saying anything,' Camacho muttered to reassure the audio technician.

'I'll bet he goes inside,' Dreyfus said.

'More than likely. Too chilly to sit outside for long.'

'He's looked at his watch twice.'

Camacho turned the pedestal camera over to the second technician and helped himself to coffee from a thermos. 'Appreciate you guys coming out this morning.'

'Sure.'

As he sipped his coffee, Camacho glanced at his watch. 11:47. The meet was probably scheduled for twelve o'clock. Albright? If not, then who?

'Have we got the camera and audio units inside?'

'Yes, sir. The guys are already in the food court.'

Camacho took another large swig of coffee, then tapped the man at the camera on the shoulder. He moved aside. The camera had a powerful zoom. Camacho could see the expression on Judy's face. He looked like a tourist until you studied his face – alert, ready, in absolute control.

The agent backed off a tad on the zoom and scanned the camera. The crowd was large, lots of families and young couples. With the earpiece in his left ear he picked up snatches of conversation as the camera moved along. Feeling a bit like a voyeur, he aimed the camera at a stream of people coming from the dark interior of the huge, green-glass building into the light. A stringy youth in a black Harley shirt held hands with a vacant-eyed girl with large, unrestrained breasts and a slack jaw. Adenoids? '. . . that AIDS is bad shit. Had a hell of a time shaking it last time.'

A tight-faced gray-haired woman spoke to her male companion in a polished whine: '. . . too far to walk. My feet hurt and it's been just a terrible . . .' Camacho moved on, sampling the faces and polyglot sounds.

'I'm not hooked, I tell you. I just like the rush . . .' In her mid-thirties, she wore a one-piece designer outfit and a windblown coiffure and was speaking to a man in gray slacks and camel-colored cardigan who was chewing on his lower lip. Not wishing to hear more, Luis Camacho swung the camera away.

'He's moving,' Dreyfus said. 'Toward the door. He's looking at some-one. Do you see him?'

Camacho searched for the door to the mall and saw only backs. He waited. The light was fading noticeably now as a dark cloud choked off the sunlight. In a few seconds Smoke Judy entered his range of vision from the left and joined the crowd streaming into the interior gloom. Camacho released the camera and rubbed his eyes.

Dreyfus was on the radio, talking to the watchers inside. 'Here he comes,' one of them said, and launched into a running commentary on Judy's direction of travel for the benefit of his comrades stationed throughout the building.

'I'm going inside,' Camacho said. Judy had never met him, so that wasn't a concern. Depending on who it was, Judy's contact might recog-nize him, but even so he wanted to see – see now, with his own eyes – the person Smoke Judy did not want to be seen with. He would try to stay out of sight. Just in case.

A spatter of drops came in at an angle, driven by the strong breeze, as Luis Camacho walked across the head of the quay. A solid curtain of rain over the water moved rapidly this way. The crowd around two jugglers on unicycles dissolved as people began to run. The FBI agent reached the double doors and hurried through just as the deluge struck. A crowd was gathering by the exit, looking out and chattering nervously, but audible above the babble was the drumming of the rain on the glass windows of the building.

Camacho put the earpiece on his radio in place and rearranged his cap. The radio itself was in an interior jacket pocket. The microphone was pinned inside his lapel: he merely had to key the transmit switch and talk.

A voice on the radio reported that Judy was upstairs, on the second floor, wandering from booth to booth. That meant the person he had come to meet was still unknown, still moving through the crowd looking for watchers. Camacho stood near the door and looked at faces, an ocean of faces of all ages and colors and sizes. Could one of them be the Minotaur? No chance. The Minotaur was too careful, too circumspect. This wasn't his kind of risk. He didn't need men like Smoke Judy for his treason. Or did he?

'He's in line at the taco joint.'

Camacho was tempted to move. Not yet! Not yet.

'There's a man behind the subject, Caucasian male about fifty-five, five feet nine or so, about a hundred ninety pounds, wearing dark slacks, Hush Puppies and a faded blue windbreaker. No hat. Balding.'

Camacho shifted his weight and examined the people on the stairs. Families. Youngsters. Five black teenage boys with red ball caps and scarves. No one was looking at him.

'Guy in the windbreaker said something to the subject.'

'Get pictures.' That was Dreyfus in the van.

'Camera's rolling.' The lawyers at Justice loved these portable video cameras with automatic focus and light-level adjustment. Jurors raised in the television age thought prosecutors should have a movie of every ten-dollar back-alley deal. At last technology had delivered. The government's shysters could show each greedy, grubby, loving little moment in living color on the courtroom Zenith – and play it over and over again until even the stupidest juror was firmly convinced – while the defendants writhed and the defense shysters planned their appeals.

'Subject paying for his grub.'

Camacho swiveled his eyes again, looking at no one in particular, seeing everyone.

'Windbreaker paying, just dropped a coin. Kid retrieving it for him. He's nervous, looking around . . . Now he's following subject . . . They're gonna share a table. That's our man. That's him!'

He moved for the stairs, climbing slowly, listening to the running commentary from the observer. Pausing with his eyes just at the level of the second-story floor, Camacho scanned to his left, toward the taco stand. The observer said they were near there at a two-person table. He climbed carefully, watching, peering through moving legs and around bodies. He glimpsed Judy's face. Another step. He was at the top of the stairs. He moved left, keeping a fat woman between himself and Judy. Against the far wall he saw a man from the power company up on a step ladder, bending over a toolbox on the ladder's little platform. The video camera was in the tool box. Judy's face was panning again, examining the crowd.

Camacho turned his back. A pretzel stand was right in front of him. He pointed one out to the girl and asked for a soft drink. As she thumbed the dispenser he checked the mirror on the back wall. There was Judy again. And *there* was the man across from him.

Luis Camacho studied the face in the mirror. Fleshy, cleanshaven, pale.

He paid the girl and turned to his right, back toward the stairs, as he sipped the drink through a straw. Descending the stairs he kept his eyes glued on the back of the teenager in front of him in a conscious effort to avoid any possibility of eye contact with a nervous Smoke Judy. He threw the pretzel and nearly full cup in a trash hamper by the main door and pushed on through, out into the rain.

The wind threatened to blow his cap off. He held it with his hand as the wind whipped his trouser legs.

'So?' said Dreyfus as Camacho wiped the water off his face with a handkerchief when he had gained the shelter of the van.

Luis Camacho shrugged. 'They'll probably bus their own table. Put their trash in a receptacle. Have one of the guys take the whole bag.'

'Fingerprints?'

'Uh-huh.'

'Think it's the Minotaur?'

'What in hell would the Minotaur have to say to Smoke Judy?'

'How're they hanging down in your shop? How'd you like to ski Moscow? Quit fucking my wife. The possibilities—' The radio speaker squawked to life with another report from the food court and Dreyfus closed his eyes to listen.

Camacho took off the radio he was wearing and handed it to one of the technicians. 'See you tomorrow at the office,' he said to Dreyfus during a silent moment, then let himself out of the van and walked through the drizzling rain toward his car.

Harlan Albright came over to Camacho's house after supper. He accepted a cup of coffee and the two of them went to the basement. The boy was there, and he got up with a wounded look on his face and took the stairs two at a time. His father watched him go, then settled onto the couch and picked up the television remote control and began flipping channels.

'I see in the paper that Matilda Jackson is dead.'

Camacho grunted. Two of the channels had those damned game shows, people answering trivial questions to win flashy, useless consumer goods.

'Who killed her?'

'Someone who knew exactly what he was about.' Camacho stared at the sex goddess flipping answer cards on Channel 4.

'Too bad. Had you had a chance to show her Franklin's picture?'

'No.'

'Well, she was an old woman, had lived a long life. It would have come soon anyhow.'

Camacho jabbed the remote savagely. The television settled on the educational channel. Some Englishman was talking about cathedrals.

'Listen, asshole. I'm not in the mood for that shit tonight. It's been a long goddamn weekend.'

'Sorry. I read about the shooting incident in front of Jackson's house. That must have been touch and go.'

He examined the Russian's face. 'I know you probably dropped a dime on her, so don't waste the hot air on me. You don't give a damn about that old woman or anybody else.'

'Sometime—'

'Shut up!'

The Englishman was explaining about flying buttresses. He used a computer model to graphically depict the forces transferred through the stone.

Albright stood up. 'I'll drop over some night this week when you're in a better mood.'

'Ummm.'

Camacho listened to the footsteps climbing the stairs and the noises of Sally letting him out the front door. He stared at the television without seeing it, lost in thought.

When Luis Camacho returned to his office from his usual Monday-morning conference with his boss, he was in a foul mood. The boss had made several candid remarks about Camacho's conduct Friday night.

'Look at this shit,' he roared, waving a section of the Sunday *Washington Post*, 'the special agent in charge of counterespionage standing on a street corner with two punk dopers, in front of a fucking crack house, for Christ's sake! What in hell has busting dopers got to do with catching spies?'

Camacho remarked that he had asked the newspaper photographer not to take his picture.

'Ha! Apparently you haven't read the Constitution lately, mister.'

'That's what he said.'

'And I'm saying it too. I don't ever want to see your sweet little puss in the public press again, mister, or you're going to wind up in Pocatello chasing Nazis through cow shit up to your armpits. Those crackpots are probably the only nut cases around who never read the goddamned paper!' The boss had been irked for months by press coverage of the FBI investigation of the Aryan Nations white supremacy fanatics, and ridiculed it and them every chance he got. Sometimes he made up chances. 'If you wanta be famous, get a lobotomy and become a rock star.'

After he'd calmed down, he wanted a complete oral report on Matilda Jackson and Smoke Judy. That had taken an hour. Then the boss had asked questions for a half hour and discussed tactics and strategy for another thirty minutes. When he signaled the discussion was over, Luis Camacho was tired and needed to go to the rest room.

Now Camacho slumped in his office chair and shuffled through the paper in his in basket. He was rereading a new administrative procedure for the third time when Dreyfus tapped on his door, then stuck his head in. Pipe smoke swirled into the room. 'Wanta watch the tape of Smoke Judy we made yesterday?'

'Sure.'

'Got it on the VCR.'

The two men went to the little conference room next door and Dreyfus pushed buttons. 'The plates and glasses they used are at the lab. Should have some good prints.'

'Terrific.'

'The lab wizards synched up the sound from one of the mikes with the video.' Judy and the beefy man in the windbreaker appeared on the television screen. Dreyfus twiddled the color knob and adjusted the volume.

'. . . not happy with all the media on procurement problems down there.' The beefy man had a well-spoken baritone voice, but his nervousness was evident.

Judy replied, but his back must have been to the parabolic mike that picked up this sound track, because his words were indistinct. Dreyfus punched the pause button and said, 'We have two other audio tracks and think we got it all, but it'll take a few hours to come up with a complete transcript.'

Camacho nodded and the tape rolled on.

'. . . big risks. Some people will be going to prison,' Judy's companion said, 'after they've been drawn and quartered in a public trial that will take six months.'

Judy leaned forward and spoke earnestly. Snatches of his remarks came through: '. . . you people . . . a life-time building the company . . . literally millions at stake. You guys really need this because . . . You'll make tens of millions in the next twenty years and I'll get a little stock and a paycheck and a pension . . . not much . . .' The rest was too garbled to follow.

'That's enough,' Camacho said after another five minutes. 'Let me see the transcript when it's finished.'

Dreyfus stopped the tape and pushed the rewind button. 'I think that guy's gonna buy what Judy's selling.'

'When you get that rewound, come on back to my office.'

In his office Luis Camacho took a sheet of scratch paper and printed one word: 'Fallacy.' He handed it to Dreyfus when he came in. 'See if this is in any of the Minotaur's letters.'

Dreyfus dropped into a chair and began to fiddle with his pipe. He put the paper in his shirt pocket after a glance. 'Where'd you get it?' he asked when he had his pipe going again.

'Ask me no questions and I'll tell you no lies.'

'Vice Admiral Henry, huh?'

'I found it in the john.'

'Why can't we get a list of all the code words from NSA?'

'We've been all through this before.'

'So I'm not too bright. Tell me again.'

'NSA won't give us the code words without the approval of the committee. The committee has not approved.' The committee was slang for the ultrasecret group that formulated intelligence community policy and coordinated the intelligence activities of all US agencies. Some of its members included the directors of the FBI and CIA, the Secretary of Defense, the Secretary of State, the National Security Agency chief, and speaking directly for the President, the National Security Adviser.

'So what does that tell you?' Dreyfus asked, his voice sharper than usual.

Camacho rubbed his eyes, then his face. 'You tell me.'

'If it walks like a duck, quacks like a duck, and leaves duck shit all over, it probably is a duck.'

'Umm.'

'I think those assholes already know what the Minotaur has given away. So they're in no rush for us to put a list together.' Dreyfus flicked his lighter and puffed several times. 'Somebody in Moscow has gotta be telling them.'

'Maybe,' said Luis Camacho, weighing it. 'Or maybe they're hoping this whole thing will crawl into a corner and die quietly without becoming a major embarrassment. Budgetary blood feuds in Congress, some big-ticket military programs on the chopping block, Gramm-Rudman – hell, they'd be less than human if they didn't try to play ostrich for a while.'

'So what are we gonna do about Smoke Judy?'

'What would you suggest?'

'That shithead is shopping secrets to defense contractors. He wants more than a military pension. What'd the boss say when you told him this morning?' His voice had a belligerent, bitter edge.

'Hang loose. Keep an eye on him.'

'Fuck us! The same old story. No matter what we turn up, we get the same answer from ol' brass ass. Be cool, guys!'

'Calm down, Dreyfus. You've been around long enough—'

'How much shit you gonna eat, Luis, before you decide you don't like it? Right now the Minotaur is busy figuring what secrets to give away next and scribbling another little love letter to the Russian ambassador. Terry Franklin is still running around loose, you're sneaking code words from friends in the Pentagon – we're doing some dynamic drifting but our investigation is going nowhere. You know that! And the sickening thing is the committee is quite comfortable with that state of affairs.' His voice had risen to almost a shout. 'I'll tell you what *I* think – *I* think the guys on that committee are laughing themselves silly. *I* think they're tickled pink that the fucking Russians are seeing this stuff. That's what the hell *I* think.'

'*I* think you're an idiot, Dreyfus, with a big mouth and a piss ant's view of the world. I've heard enough. Now get back to work.'

Dreyfus bounced to his feet and rammed his right hand out in a Nazi salute. '*Ja wohl*—'

'You son of a—'

'Don't bullshit yourself, Luis. I know you're doing the best you can. But, goddamn, I'm sick of this fucking around!'

Camacho jerked his head at the door and Dreyfus went.

13

The Naval Weapons Center, China Lake, lies in the desert of southern California east of the range of mountains that form the eastern wall of the San Joaquin Valley. The air at China Lake is clean, hot, and dry. Tuesday afternoon Jake Grafton dragged in lungfuls of it as he walked across the baking concrete toward the air terminal with Helmut Fritsche and Samuel Dodgers. Behind them, still trading quips with the female crew of the T-39 that had flown them here from Andrews AFB in Washington, via NAS Moffett Field where they had collected Dodgers, Toad Tarkington and Rita Moravia supervised the loading of the luggage into a navy station wagon.

An hour later Dr Dodgers lifted his ball cap and scratched his head. He was standing with Grafton and Fritsche in a hangar that was empty except for an A-6E Intruder. Sentries were posted on the outside of the doors with orders to admit no one.

The men were examining grease-pencil marks placed on the plane by Fritsche. These were the locations he recommended for the special antennas of Dodgers' Athena system. And Sam Dodgers was scratching his head as he surveyed Fritsche's artwork. 'Well,' he said unenthusiastically, 'I guess these spots will work today, after we tweak the output of each antenna. But . . .' His voice trailed off. Jake glanced at him without curiosity. He had already discovered that Dodgers' enthusiasm came in uneven dribbles.

'It's the left side of the airplane only,' Fritsche said firmly. 'Fourteen antennas. Side of the tail, fuselage, left outboard pylon, under the cockpit rail, forward on the nose . . . and one on the left wingtip in place of the position light.'

'You really need one in front of the left intake, where that flat plate is. That plate is probably the biggest single contributor to the plane's RCS when viewed from this side – makes up maybe half of it.'

'Can't put one there. Might get broken off by the airflow and go down the intake. It'd destroy the engine.'

'How about in front of that plate?'

They discussed it. Yes.

'This jury rig is just for test purposes,' Fritsche told Jake. 'And operational Athena system for an aircraft will have to have conformal antennas, "smart skin" in the jargon of the trade. Literally, the antennas will be part of the aircraft's skin so they won't contribute to drag or ever be broken off.'

'How much is that going to cost?'

'Won't be cheap. Conformal antennas are under development, but they'll be new technology and aren't here yet.'

'Forget I asked.'

Jake wandered over to where Tarkington and Moravia stood with Commander L.D. Bonnet, the commanding officer of the A-6 Weapons System Support Activity, which owned the airplane. All three saluted Jake as he approached and he returned the gesture with a grin. 'So, L.D., are you going to let these children fly your plane?'

'Yes, sir. They appear sober and reasonably competent.'

'I appreciate your letting us borrow the plane and hangar for a few days.'

'Admiral Dunedin's very persuasive.'

Jake flashed a grin. L.D. must have hesitated a few seconds before he agreed to the Old Man's requests. 'Here's what I'd like to do. Fritsche and Dodgers are going to take a day or two to install some little antennas on the left side of the plane. They'll use glue and drill a few holes, then install a tiny fairing in front of each antenna. They're going to need the help of a couple of good, capable airframe technicians who can keep their mouths shut.'

Bonnet nodded.

'Then Rita and Toad will fly the plane up to the Electronic Warfare range at Fallon since the EW range here at China Lake is out of service this week. Fritsche and I will fly up there ahead of them. Dodgers will stay here to work on the gear in the plane. Rita, I want you to keep the plane under three hundred knots indicated to minimize the airflow stress on these antennas. They're going to be jury-rigged on there with a little bubble gum and Elmer's glue.'

'Aye aye, sir,' she said.

'L.D., I need you to loan me a couple of young officers with at least ten pounds of tact each. They'll alternate duty, so that one of them will be with Dodgers day and night. They're to escort him to work, stay with him all day, escort him to the head, take him back to the BOQ, eat with him, see that he talks to no one but them. And I mean no one.'

After discussing the details, Commander Bonnet departed. Jake Grafton explained to Rita and Toad exactly what he expected of his flight crew. He finished with a caution. 'This device, the project name, everything, is classified to the hilt. Admiral Dunedin tells me he has cells reserved at Leavenworth for anyone who violates the security regs. I don't want you to even whisper about this in your sleep.'

'I love secrets,' Toad said.

'I know. Just my luck, I get one of the world's great secret lovers. Keep it zipped, Toad.'

Jake went back to watch the installation process, so Toad and Rita set out on foot for base ops to plan their flights to and from Fallon, Nevada. As they walked along, Rita asked, 'What was it that Captain Grafton wanted you to keep zipped, Toad? Your mouth or—'

'Never ask a question if you think you might not like the answer. That's Tarkington's Golden Rule for survival in Uncle Sam's navy.'

They grinned at each other. Her hand slipped into his for a fleeting squeeze. Instinctively they both knew to play it cool. No hand-holding or huggy-squeezy or deep eye contact during duty hours. No winks or sighs or casual touching. If Captain Grafton saw any of that, the roof would fall in.

As Toad walked his shoulders were back and his head up. He was acutely conscious of how good he felt, how pungently vigorous and healthy. Takes a woman to do that for you, he told himself, and began whistling a lively little tune that seemed appropriate. Life *is* good.

Toad's feeling of euphoric bonhomie lasted precisely one hour and thirty-seven minutes, just the length of time it took to plan the flights to and from the Electronic Warfare Range near Fallon, Nevada, fill out the flight plans, visit casually with the weather briefer about the long-range forecast for the next three or four days and make a pit stop in the head. On the walk back to the hangar where Grafton and the wizards labored, Rita was quieter, more subdued than she had been the last few days.

'Do you like me?' she asked finally, wearing a gentle semi-serious look that Toad Tarkington, man of the world, recognized as trouble.

His jovial mood returned to earth with an unpleasant splat. Commitment time! It's their hormones, biology maybe, something to do with genes. 'Sure. You're a very nice lady who's fun to be with.'

'Oh.'

'You know what I mean. You're not one of those girls who write poetry until two in the morning and read Albert Camus in the cafeteria.'

'Uh-huh.'

'You're' – and here Toad grinned broadly and arranged his features in what he always thought was his most sincere, let's-fuck-tonight look – 'you're the kind of girl a guy likes to be around.'

'I understand,' Rita said, nodding. 'You like girls who open zippers with their teeth and wear crotchless panties.'

He didn't like the way she said that, with lips parted but almost immobile, her eyes narrowing ever so slightly.

'Rita, I try to avoid discussing serious relationships at midafternoon in parking lots.'

'Maybe if I shave my pussy and put four or five earrings in my left ear?'

Oh, so she wanted a little blood, huh! 'Right ear. Left ear is for lesbi—'

'You *asshole*!' She stalked away, her head down, braced against the hurricane.

'Hey, Ginger . . .' Ginger was her nickname, what the other aviators called her. She even had it on the name tag of her flight suit.

She spun around to face him, her hands clenched at her sides.

'Don't you *ever* call me that, Tarkington. Not *ever*. Not *you*.'

'Hey—' he said, but he was talking to her back. He raised his voice and shouted, 'I'd like to get to know you. But I'm not getting engaged in a parking lot, not even if you're the Queen of Sheba.'

When she was fifty feet away, she turned to face him. 'I wasn't asking you to get engaged,' she shouted back.

'Oh yes you were! Crotchless panties, shaved pussies, what the hell is wrong with you?'

She was walking away again. Toad turned back toward base ops. Ten feet away a lieutenant commander stood looking at him, shaking his head.

'You know, Lieutenant, when I discuss intimate apparel or personal hygiene with a lady friend, I usually try to find a slightly more private place.'

Toad turned beet red. 'Yessir,' he mumbled through clenched teeth and stalked by with his head down.

Samuel Dodgers forked his food without wasting an erg of precious energy. The utensil bit into the mashed potatoes and peas in one swift, brutal motion, then soared aloft by the most direct route to the waiting depository, where it was wiped clean in the blink of an eye and dispatched down for another load. A man working this hard should devote his attention to the job at hand, and Dodgers wisely did so. If he heard the conversation around him, he gave no sign.

Toad Tarkington gave Rita a hopeful wink when her eyes shifted to him from Dodgers and his rapidly emptying plate. Her eyes snapped down to her food. She pressed her lips firmly together and inhaled deeply through her nose, which strained the cloth and buttons on her khaki shirt. Toad sourly noted that the younger Dodgers shared his interest in the physics of Rita's bust expansion. It wasn't that she was extraordinarily endowed, but rather that she was so perfectly proportioned. Her gorgeous breasts formed symmetrical mounds that seemed . . . just so exactly, perfectly right, with the gentle swelling just visible in the deep V formed by the neckline of her shirt. Toad gave those twin masterpieces yet another glance as he sliced more meat from his pork chop and pondered the vicissitudes of love.

'Well, Toad,' he heard Jake Grafton say, 'are you satisfied with this tour of duty?'

'Yessir. You bet.' The captain was looking at him with an amused expression on his face. 'Just challenging as hell, sir.'

This remark drew a grunt from the gourmet at the other end of the table, who appeared to be finished anyway. Dodgers laid down his fork and used his napkin on his mouth. As far as Toad could see, he hadn't missed with a single gram. 'The road to hell may be challenging, sir, but the road to heaven is more so.'

'Uh-huh,' Toad Tarkington said, and attacked the remnants of his chop.

'The pathway of the righteous is narrow and difficult, and many there are who find the way too treacherous, too steep, too rigorous.' Dodgers was rolling, his phrases sonorous and heartfelt. 'The pathway of the righteous is strewn with the temptations of the flesh, of the spirit and of the heart, all exits from the difficult, righteous way, all exits to that short, smooth road that leads down straight to *hell.*'

'A soul freeway for the pink Cadillac. Amen,' Toad muttered, and didn't even glance at Rita when she kicked him in the shin.

'The pathway of the wicked is that straight, steep ro—'

'I'm sure,' Jake Grafton interrupted firmly. Looking at Rita, he asked, 'Have you got the flight to Fallon planned?'

'Yes, sir.' She described the route, mentioning navigation aids, time en route and her estimate of what her fuel state would be when she arrived over the Electronic Warfare range. Jake asked everyone present if they have been to NAS Fallon, and proceeded to tell anecdotes of his many visits there throughout his career. Toad Tarkington knew Grafton was going to monopolize the conversation through dessert just so he wouldn't have to listen to Dodgers' preaching. Apparently no one had ever told the physicist that three things were never discussed at a wardroom table – women, politics and religion.

Grafton was going easily from anecdote to anecdote when Rita finished eating and excused herself. Toad lingered, engrossed in the captain's tales. The younger Dodgers ordered dessert and asked several questions: even his old man seemed somewhat amused by Grafton's tales of ten-cent craps in Mom's saloon and midnight motorcycle rides through the desert by half-drunk fliers trying to sober up so they could fly at 5 A.M.

Dr Fritsche lit a cigar and sighed contentedly. He too seemed to find Grafton's tales of his younger days very pleasant this warm evening in a navy wardroom a hundred miles from the sea.

Like Jake Grafton, I love this life, Toad found himself thinking. As he listened he recalled his first two-week weapons deployment with his squadron to Fallon, before his first cruise. It was in Fallon that the ties to wives and girlfriends were temporarily broken and the twenty-four-hour-a-day camaraderie began to weld friendships among the junior officers that would last a lifetime. The challenge was to fly the planes as weapons, two or three flights a day, and on liberty to play as hard as they flew. As Jake Grafton described it and Toad remembered it, it was a gay, carefree, exciting life, the perfect existence for a youngster growing into manhood.

When Jake wound down, Toad smiled at everyone and excused himself. Walking toward the BOQ he found himself whistling again. I'm doing a lot of that lately, he thought, and laughed aloud. He was spending his life wisely and well. He liked the thought so much he roared heartily, and then chuckled contentedly at his own foolishness, his animosity toward Rita this afternoon forgotten.

There was no answer when he tapped on Rita's door. Perhaps she was in the head or down in the laundry room. Oh well, he would try to call her later.

When he opened the door to his room the lights were on and Rita was sitting in the chair by the small desk. Her hair was down over her shoulders and she was wearing only a teddy, a filmy little thing that . . . Toad gawked.

'Well, close the door before everyone in the building stops by to visit.'

'How'd you get in?' Toad asked, still staring.

'Just asked for a key at the desk.'

He got the door closed and latched and sat down on the end of the bed, close to her. The furniture was early Conrad Hilton, and there wasn't much of it.

He cleared his throat as she stared straight into his eyes.

'I was writing a letter,' she said, her eyes never wavering from him. 'To you.'

'Uh-huh.'

'I can finish it later.'

'What's it going to be about?'

'I'm sorry about the scene today in the parking lot. I just wanted – oh, I – let's forget it, shall we?'

'Sure,' he said. 'It was only a little pothole on the hard, righteous road.' His gaze was drifting lower and lower. 'Not enough to get us sidetracked onto that short, steep road that leads down . . . down straight . . .' Her nipples were visible through the lace of the teddy, ripe, red . . .

Rita stood in one smooth, fluid motion. 'I want to make love to you,' she murmured as she peeled off the teddy, 'but I don't want to be too forward.'

He pursed his lips and nodded. 'Uh-huh.' He reached out and she slid into his arms, her skin all silky and smooth.

'Should we turn off the lights?' she suggested as he caressed her breasts with his lips.

'You're pretty enough for lights,' he said, and pulled her down on the bed beside him.

'I don't want you to get the idea that I just want you for sex,' she said tentatively.

His mouth was full of breast, so the best he could manage was a reassuring noise.

'The sex is great, of course, but I want us to have something else.' She ran her fingers through his hair, then smoothed the stray locks. 'You're a pretty terrific guy, and it's more than sex. That's what I was trying to get at this afternoon in the parking lot.'

Toad reluctantly took a last lick at that swollen nipple, then shifted his body until his eyes were inches from hers. 'Are you trying to tell me you're in love with me?'

She frowned. 'I suppose. It hasn't happened quite the way I always dreamed it would. Girls have their fantasies.' She took a tiny little nip on her lower lip. 'I hope I'm saying this right. You don't mind, do you?'

'I'm delighted. I'm falling in love with you and I'm glad you feel the same way.'

'I love you,' Rita Moravia said softly, savoring it, then gently pulled his mouth onto hers.

When she was asleep, Toad eased out of bed and peered through the curtain. He was restless. Why had he said that – that falling-in-love stuff? Only a cretin tells a woman that just before he beds her. He sat in a chair and worried a fingernail. He was getting in over his head again and he had his doubts. Was he just scared? Nah, a little frightened maybe, nervous, but not scared. Why is it all women want to fall in love? He wondered what Samuel Dodgers would say on that subject.

Dreyfus laid it on Camacho's desk and sat down to light his pipe. Camacho knew what it was: his boss had called him. It was a copy of a letter. The original was at the lab.

He opened the folder that the lab technicians used for copies and glanced at it. There was no date. The envelope was postmarked Bakersfield, California, three days ago. The message was in florid longhand, yet quite legible.

Dear Sir,

I think it's my duty to inform you that my daughter's husband, Petty Officer First Class Terry Franklin USN, is a spy. He works at the Pentagon. Computers, or something like that. I don't know how long he has been a spy, but he is. My daughter Lucy is sure he is and so am I. He got a funny phone call once that Lucy overheard and he got really

really mad when he found out Lucy mentioned her suspicions to a neighbor. Lucy is afraid of him and so am I. He is crazy. He is a spy like that Walker fellow.

We are good citizens and pay our taxes and know you will do what has to be done. We are sorry for him but he did this himself. Lucy had absolutely nothing to do with this spy thing, and that's why I am writing this letter. I wanted her to write it but she said she just couldn't, even though she knows it has to be this way. Please arrest him and keep Lucy and the kids out of it. Please don't tell the newspapers he is married. His name is Terry Franklin and he works at the Pentagon and he is a spy. And PLEASE, whatever you do, don't tell Terry we told on him. He is crazy.

Sincerely,
Flora May Southworth

'Can you get a divorce in California if your spouse is a spy?'

Dreyfus snorted. 'You can get a divorce in California if your spouse farts in bed.'

'Progressive as hell.'

'Right out front.'

'Better call out there and have an agent go interview them. Tell him to stay all afternoon and take lots of notes.'

'You don't want them going to the press?'

'Do you know what the committee is going to want to do about this?'

'Well, they sure are gonna have to do something. Now we got the mother-in-law writing us letters. They probably talked to their minister and a lawyer and every neighbor in a five-block radius.'

'Not letters. A letter. One letter with no hard facts and a variety of unsubstantiated allegations. We get two dozen letters like this every month from people out to get even with someone in a sensitive job. I repeat, do you know what the committee—'

'No.' He spit it out.

'So we had better do our best to convince Mrs Southwood we are going like gangbusters on this hot tip. Pledge confidentiality. Better send two agents. Tell them to be thorough. Then two days later go back for a follow-up interview with more questions. New questions, not repeats.'

'A major break like this, maybe you want to send me out there to see that they do it right? I could go by bus, get there in a week or so.'

Camacho ignored him. He picked up the letter and read it again. Then he pulled a legal pad around and began making notes. Dreyfus got the message and left in a swirl of smoke, closing the door behind him.

Camacho threw the legal pad at the door.

14

With its twin engines bellowing a roar that could be heard for several miles, the Intruder departed the earth with a delicate wiggle, a perceptible rocking of the wings that Rita Moravia automatically smoothed with the faintest side pressure on the control stick. She had let the takeoff trim setting rotate the plane's nose to eight degrees nose-up and had stopped it there with a nudge of forward stick in that delicious moment when the weight of twenty-five tons of machine and fuel was transferred from the main landing gear to the wings. This was the transition to flight, a shimmering, imprecise hesitation as the machine gathered its strength and the wings took a firm bite into the warm morning air.

Now safely airborne, Rita slapped the gear handle up with her left hand. Her right thumb flicked at the coolie-hat button on the top of the stick, trimming the stick pressure to neutral as the twin-engined warplane accelerated.

She checked to make sure the landing gear were up and locked. They were. Temps, RPMs, fuel flow normal. Oil and hydraulic pressure okay. Using her left hand again, she raised the flap handle as she caressed the stick with her right to hold the nose steady through the configuration change. Accelerating nicely. Flaps and slats up and in and the stabilizer shifted, she isolated the flight hydraulic system and continued to trim. At 290 knots indicated she pulled the nose higher into the sky in order to comply with Jake Grafton's directive not to exceed 300 knots.

Toad had activated the IFF and was talking to Departure. Now he switched to Los Angeles Center. The controller asked him to push the identification button on the IFF – 'squawk ident' – and he complied. 'Xray Echo 22, radar contact. Come left to a heading of 020. Passing Flight Level 180, proceed on course.'

Rita Moravia dipped the left wing as Toad rogered.

When she leveled the wings on course, still climbing, he was humming and singing over the ICS as he turned the radar presentation and checked that he had properly entered the computer way-points. 'Hi-ho, hi-ho, it's off to work we go, with a hi-hi-hee and a fiddly-dee, hi-hi, ho-ho . . .'

Rita grinned behind her oxygen mask. Flying with the Toadman was an experience. No wonder Captain Grafton's face softened every time he saw Tarkington.

She leveled the plane at Flight Level 310 – 31,000 feet – and engaged the autopilot. Just above them a thin, wispy layer slid across the top of the canopy, so close it seemed they could almost reach up and let the gauzy tendrils slip around their fingers. Rita looked ahead and tried to find that point where the motion of the ropy filaments seemed to originate as they came racing toward the cockpit, accelerating as the distance closed. It was like flying just under an infinite, flat ceiling – some Steven Spielberg effect to give the audience a rush of speed and wonder as the woofers oomphed and the seats throbbed, before the credits came on the screen.

After a moment she disengaged the autopilot and let the nose creep up a smidgen. Almost imperceptibly the plane rose a hundred feet, where the cloud layer literally sliced around the cockpit. Toad picked that moment to withdraw his head from the radar scope and look slowly around. After a moment he glanced at her and caught her eye. She saw him wink, then readjust the hood and devote his attention to the computer and radar.

A lifetime of work, all for this.

She had been an outstanding student at an excellent suburban high school, one of those bright youngsters who applied themselves in a frenzy of self-discipline and diligence that separated her from her class-mates, who were more interested in boys, music and peer acceptance than school. She had shocked everyone, including her parents, by her announcement that she wanted to attend a military academy. In due course an appointment to the Naval Academy came from a congressman who knew better than to echo her mother's surprise or horror in an era when socially correct posturing was more important than his voting record.

So she set forth bravely that summer after high school, at the age of eighteen, set off into the unknown world of plebes at the Naval Academy, this girl who had never set foot on a military installation, this girl who knew only that she wanted to make her own way in life and that way would be much different from those of her mother or the friends of her youth.

It had been worse than different. It had been horrid, a humiliating nightmare beyond anything she had imagined in her worst moments of trepidation. All the sly taunts of her friends, bound for sororities and, they hoped, excellent marriages, hadn't even hinted at the emotional trauma she experienced those first weeks. During the day she braced and marched and ran and endured the hazing and shouting to the point of exhaustion, and at night she sobbed herself to sleep wondering if she had made the right choice. Finally one day she realized that she hadn't cried in a week. Her second, more important revelation occurred one morning at breakfast when an upperclassman had demanded to know the name of the Soviets' chief arms negotiator. She had answered the question correctly, and as he turned his attention to a gawky boy from Georgia seated beside her, she realized that these people were demanding nothing from her she could not accomplish. From then on she had cheerfully endured, and finally excelled.

She thought of those times this morning as the Intruder flew out from under the thin cloud layer into a crystal-clear desert sky and Toad Tarkington, the professional who had been there and back, caressed the system with a loving touch. She had made the right choice.

Sixty miles out she once again disengaged the auto-pilot and lowered the nose slightly, then slowly pulled the throttles aft as her speed crept up toward 300 knots indicated. She always liked the feel of the plane as it descended in these long, shallow, power-on glides, gravity helping the engines drive the plane down into the thicker, denser air near the earth. She could feel every knot of the airspeed the engines didn't generate – free airspeed it seemed, though of course it wasn't. Because she was the airplane and it was her, the energy was hers: the speed and the life and the power, she absorbed and possessed and became all of it.

Wingtip speed brakes cracked, but not enough. She flicked them out some more and felt the buffeting of the disturbed air, a gentle shaking that imparted itself to her through the stick and throttles and the seat in which she sat. Satisfied, she slid the speed-brake switch forward with her left thumb. The boards closed obediently and the buffeting ceased.

The desert below was baked brown and red and grayish black unleavened by the green of life. As she came down she could see sand and dirt in valleys and washes and rock the color of new iron in jagged cliffs and ridges.

Toad was chatting with Jake Grafton on the radio. 'Never fear, the pros are here.'

'Amen,' Grafton replied. It's a good thing Dodgers is back in China Lake, Rita thought.

'Okay, Misty, I have you in sight. Drop to about 8,000 on the pressure altimeter' – the land here was 4,000 feet above sea level – 'and come north up the valley until you see the van. It's red and has a yellow cross on the top.'

'What kind of a cross?' she asked curiously.

'Dodgers' son painted it. Three guesses.'

'I see it.' At this height it was just a speck amid the dirt and boulders.

'Okay, circle the van at a distance of three miles or so and I'll tell you when to turn on your gadget.'

'Roger that,' Toad said, and Rita flew away from the van, then turned to establish herself on the circle with her left wingtip pointed at the van.

Toad again examined the little box that had been taped to the top of the glare shield in front of him. The box wasn't much. It had a three-position power switch which he had had in the middle, or standby, position for the last five minutes. While in standby the coolant was circulating around the Athena computer. Beside the power station was a little green light that would come on to verify that the computer was receiving electrical power, and another light, yellow, to show when the system was detecting signals from an outside source. When that yellow light was on, the Athena system was doing its thing. Three was a red light too, but that would illuminate only when the temperature of the super-cooled computer exceeded a level that endangered it. If that light came on, Toad was to turn off the system.

Down on the ground Jake watched Harold Dodgers and Helmut Fritsche at the radar control panel. 'Got 'em,' Fritsche said after a bit, speaking loudly over the steady snoring of the engine of the generator mounted on the trailer behind the van. The engine noise muffled the moan of the Intruder's engines except when it had passed almost over-head. Jake looked at the green display. 'Tell 'em to turn it on.'

Jake did so. In less than two seconds the blip faded from the scope. Magic! Involuntarily he looked toward that spot in the sky where the plane had to be. Yes, there it was, just now a flash as the sun glinted from the canopy, then fading to a dull yet visible white spot in the washed-out blue. He looked again at the scope. Nothing.

'Maybe if they tightened the circle, flew closer,' Fritsche suggested.

The plane was still invisible. However, at five miles from the radar the strength of the emissions from Athena was too much: it beaconed and a false blip appeared at two miles and another at five.

'Dad's gonna have to tweak it,' Harold Dodgers said, his voice con-fident and cheerful. 'But by gum, it works.'

'Sure enough does,' Jake Grafton said, and wiped the perspiration from his forehead. Hard to believe, but that crackpot and his genius son had invented a device that would revolutionize warfare. Just as Admiral Henry had known it would.

After another twenty minutes, during which the Intruder flew back and forth in straight lines tangent to the five-mile circle so that Fritsche could chart the Athena's protection envelope, Jake told Rita and Toad to go on back to China Lane, where Dr Dodgers would tweak the computer. Then Rita and Toad would bring the plane back here for another session. Jake would have preferred to stage the plane from NAS Fallon, just a few miles west, but Admiral Dunedin had vetoed that on the grounds that base security there would be inadequate.

'Helmut, you better drive over to the range office and call Dodgers on the scrambler and tell him how it went. Then call Admiral Dunedin in Washington.'

'Sure.' Fritsche trotted over to the gray navy sedan parked near the van and left in a cloud of dust. Harold Dodgers killed the generator, which backfired once and fell silent. Now the Intruder's engines were plainly audible, the moan echoing from the rocky ridges and outcrops.

'CAG,' said a male voice on the radio. 'Are we sweet or what?'

'You're sweet, Misty. See you this afternoon back here.'

Jake watched the white dot shrink to nothing in the blue sky as Rita climbed away to the south. When even the engine noise was gone and all he could hear was the wind whispering across the sand, he walked over to the shade by the side of the van and sat down.

Anyway you looked at it, Athena was mind-boggling. A religious crackpot working in a shop that looks as if it should be full of broken-down cars comes up with an invention that will instantly obsolesce all conventional radar technology. But perhaps it wasn't as wild as it appeared. After all, without the benefit of budgets, bureaucrats, and MBA supervisors worried about short-term profitability, Thomas Edison had single-handedly electrified the world and along the way fathered the recording and motion-picture industry. With the same advantages Samuel Dodgers had made junk of all existing military radar systems and the tactics and strategy built around those systems. And if you're keeping score, he also just blew the B-2 program out of the sky. Why buy stealth bombers for $516 million each when you can make an existing plane invisible with a $250,000 device and some superglue?

A lot of people were going to be seriously unhappy when they heard. Powerful people, the kind that had both their senators' unlisted Washington numbers on their Rolodex.

Jake Grafton picked up a handful of dirt and let it trickle through his fingers. Tyler Henry, Ludlow, Royce Caplinger – they were sitting on a bomb. No doubt they'll let Jake Grafton go it alone for a while, stand out there by himself in front of the crowd as the duty expert. After he had run the bloomers up the flagpole and they had precisely measured the direction and velocity of the wind, then and only then would they decide what to do.

They must have been ecstatic when they realized that Jake Grafton was just the man they needed: a genuine, decorated live hero whom they could stand with shoulder to shoulder or disavow as a crazed maverick, whichever way the cookie crumbled. They would throw him to the sharks without a second thought if they concluded that course looked best. *Too bad, but he always was an officer who couldn't take orders, not a team player. And after that El Hakim thing, a bad concussion, psychiatrists; he was never right in the head. Too bad.*

These powerful people whose boats would start leaking when the Athena secret came out, what would they do? Fight. How? What would be their weapons?

The dirt escaping his fingers made a sculpted pile. The wind swirled away a portion of each handful. The slower the dirt trickled from his fingers, the more of it the wind claimed.

The most probable argument, Jake decided, was that Athena would destabilize the existing East-West military balance. This argument had finesse. Athena was too cheap to argue the dollars. So argue the consequences. Argue that Athena pushes Russia closer to a first strike. Argue nuclear war and radioactive ashes and the Four Horsemen. If you can't dazzle them with logic or baffle them with bullshit, then scare the bejesus out of them.

Jake stood and stirred the pile of dust with his toe. The wind carried it away grain by grain.

It was late afternoon, on the third flight of the day, and Rita was flying straight legs north and south, each leg one mile farther west of the radar site. Toad was bored. He was using the navigation system to ensure she stayed precisely where Captain Grafton wanted her to be. That was the hard part. After he had turned on the Athena system there was nothing to do but monitor its 'operating' light. He did keep an eye on the Athena temp light, so if it came on he could turn off the system in a smart, military manner. For this the US Navy was using its best Naval Flight Officer, a professional aerial warrior. Peace is hell.

Off to the west, down on the desert, was a long shadow cast by the two-story black windowless building that constituted the only structure in the town known as Frenchman's. That building was a whorehouse. Presumably it also contained the office of the mayor and the rest of the municipal employees. From this distance it appeared to be just a tiny box on the desert. He knew it was painted black and had two stories and no windows because he had once inspected it from the parking lot in front. Just a tourist, of course.

He keyed his ICS mike to call Rita's attention to this famous landmark, but thought better of it.

Rita was checking the fuel remaining in the various tanks. He pressed his head against the radar hood and examined the cursor position.

He heard a whump, a loud, loose whump, and instantaneously the air pressure and noise level rose dramatically. Something struck him. He jerked his head back from the hood and looked around wildly.

The wind howled, shrieked, screamed, even through his helmet. Rita was back against her seat, slumped down, covered with gore, her right hand groping wildly for her face.

A bird! They had hit a bird.

He keyed the ICS without conscious thought and said her name. He couldn't hear the sound of his own voice.

The plane was rolling off on one wing, the nose dipping. He used his left hand to grab the stick between Rita's knees and center it.

Slow down. They had to slow down, had to lessen the velocity of the wind funneling through that smashed-out left quarter panel. The bird must have come through there and crashed against Rita as she bent over the fuel management panel on the left console.

He pulled back on the stick to bring the nose up into a climb and concentrated on keeping the wings level. Higher. Higher. Twenty degrees nose-up. Airspeed dropping: 250 indicated, 240, 230 – he should drop the gear and flaps, get this flying pig slowed way down – 210 knots.

The gear handle was on the left side of the instrument panel, right under the hole where the plexiglas quarter panel used to be, right under that river of air that was pressurizing the cockpit.

He tried to reach it. Just beyond his fingertips. Harness release unlocked. No go. Juggling the stick with his left hand, he used his right to release the two Koch fittings on the top of his torso harness. If the seat fired now he wouldn't have a parachute. He reached again. Nope. He was going to have to unfasten the Koch fittings that held his bottom to the ejection seat. With fingers that were all thumbs he released the two catches, then attacked the bayonet fittings on his oxygen mask. Might as well get it off too. He jerked loose the cord that went to the earphones in his helmet.

Damn he was stalling. He could feel the buffet and the nose pitch forward. He let it go down and got some airspeed, then eased it back.

He was having difficulty holding the wings level. Power at about 86 percent on both engines. That was okay. But the smell – Jesus God!

The overpowering odor made his eyes water. He tried to breathe only through his mouth.

No longer restrained by the inertia reel in the ejection seat, he grasped the stick with his right hand and stretched across with his left to the gear handle and slapped it down.

Now for the flaps. He was lying across the center console, trying to keep his head out of the wind blast as he felt for the flap lever beside the throttle quadrant. Leave the throttle alone. Get the flaps down to thirty degrees. Fumbling, he pulled the lever aft.

Toad was overcorrecting with the stick as he fought to keep the wings level, first too much one way, then too much the other. Goddamn, those peckerhead pilots do this without even thinking about it.

There! Gear down and locked. Flaps and slats out, stabilator shifted. Hallelujah.

He glanced up at Rita. She had shit and blood and gore all over her face and shoulders. Feathers. They were everywhere!

Her helmet – it was twisted sideways. Using glances, he tried to wipe off the worst of the crap with his left hand as he concentrated on holding the plane straight and level: 140 knots now, 8,300 feet on the altimeter. Conditions in the cockpit were a lot better.

Were there any mountains this high around here? He couldn't remember, and he couldn't see over the top of the instrument panel, bent the way he was.

First things first. He twisted her helmet back straight. The face shield was shattered, broken, but it had protected her face and eyes from the worst of the impact.

She was dazed. She damn well better come out of it quick, because he sure couldn't land this plane.

Her right eye was covered with goo, whether hers or the bird's he couldn't tell. He wiped at it with his gloved fingers. The bird's.

Her left eye was clear but unfocused, blinking like crazy. 'C'mon, Rita baby. I can't keep flying this thing!' In his frustration he shouted. She couldn't hear him.

Back to the panel: 135 knots. Maybe he could engage the autopilot.

Yeah, the autopilot. If it would work. He jabbed at the switches and released the stick experimentally. Yeah! Hot damn! It engaged.

He devoted his attention to her. Cuffed her gently, rubbed her cheeks. She shook her head and raised her right hand to her face.

He got himself rearranged in his seat and held his mask to his face. 'Rita?' Nothing. No sound in his ears. Now what? He had forgotten to plug the cord to his helmet back in. He did so. '*Goddammit, Rita,*' he roared. 'Snap out of it.'

Someone was talking on the radio. He listened. He could hear the words now. It was Grafton. Toad keyed the radio mike. 'We took a bird hit. Rita's a little dazed. We're going to land at Fallon when she comes around.'

'Understand you took a bird. Where?'

'Right in the cockpit, CAG. Hit Rita in the head. We're going to Fallon when she comes around. Now I'm leaving this freq and calling Fallon on Guard.' Without waiting for a reply, he jabbed the channelization switches and called Fallon tower. 'Fallon tower, this is Misty 22 on Guard. Mayday. We're fifteen or twenty miles out. Roll the crash truck.'

Which way are we heading? 120 degrees. He tugged the stick to the right and settled into a ten-degree turn, which the autopilot held. Fallon was off to the west here somewhere. He craned to see over the instrument panel in that direction.

'Misty 22, Fallon tower on Guard. Roger your Mayday. Come up . . .' and the controller gave them discrete frequency.

Hey, stupid, look at the radar. He examined it. Be patient, Toad, be patient. You're doing okay, if only Rita comes around. And if she doesn't, well, screw it. You can figure out some way to eject her right over the runway, then you can hop out. Too bad those penny-pinchers in the puzzle palace never spent the bucks for a command ejection system for the A-6. But you can get her out somehow. It's been done before. There –

that must be the base there, just coming onto the screen from the right. He waited until it was dead ahead, then pushed the stick left until the wings were level. Now he dialed in the Fallon tower freq and gave them a call.

Rita was using her right arm to get her left up to the throttle quadrant. 'Toad?'

'Yeah. You okay?'

'What—'

'Bird strike. All that goo on you is bird shit and gore. Relax, it ain't you. Can you see?'

'I think – right eye's blurred. This wind. Left is red – blood – can't see . . .'

'Okay. I got the gear and flaps down and we're on autopilot motoring toward Fallon. After a while or two you're gonna land this thing. Just sit back right now and get yourself going again.'

She rubbed at her face with her right hand.

The autopilot dropped off the line. Automatically she grasped the stick and began flying.

'See,' exclaimed Toad Tarkington triumphantly, 'you *can* do it! All fucking right! We're almost home. Raise your left wing.' She did so and he resumed his monologue, only to pause occasionally to answer a question over the radio.

Rita Moravia flew by instinct, her vision restricted to one eye, and that giving her only a blurred impression of the altitude instruments on the panel before her. It was enough. She could feel the plane respond to her touch, and confirmation of that response was all she needed from her vision. Needed now. She would need to see a lot better to land. The wind – it was part of the problem. The wind wasn't coming into the plane through the shattered quarter panel at 140 knots – the closed cockpit prevented that – but it was coming in at an uncomfortable velocity and temperature.

Cold. She was cold. She should slow some more.

She tugged at the throttles with her left hand. Her arm was numb: her fingers felt like they were frozen. The power levers came back, though the engine RPM and fuel-flow tapes were too blurred to read. Still she turned her head and squinted with her good eye. She could make out the angle-of-attack spotlight indexer on the glare shield and trimmed to an on-speed condition.

For the first time she looked outside, trying to see the ground. Just a blurred brown backdrop. But Toad could get her lined up.

She tried to make her left thumb depress the ICS button, and after a few seconds succeeded. 'Where are we?'

'Come left about twenty degrees and start a descent to . . . oh, say, six thousand. Can you see?'

'I can see to fly. Can't see outside very well. Get me lined up and all and I think I can do it.'

Toad got back on the radio.

She made the heading change and only then retarded the throttles slightly and let the nose slip down a degree or so. One thing at a time. She had once had an instructor who liked to chant that to his students, who were often in over their heads. When it's all going to hell, he used to say, just do one thing at a time.

The plane sank slowly, the altimeter needle swinging counterclockwise with about the speed of an elevator indicator. So they had all day. Go down slow and you have an easy transition at the bottom. Go down too fast and . . . As she sat there she continued to blink and flex her left arm. Doesn't feel like anything's broken, just numb. Maybe the world's most colorful bruise on my shoulder, some orange-and-purple splotch that will be the envy of every tattooed motor-cyclist north of Juárez.

She was hurting now. As the numbness wore off she was hurting. Her face felt like someone had used a steak hammer on it. Like she had slid down the sidewalk on her cheekbones for a couple hundred yards.

'Come right about fifteen degrees or so and you'll be lined up,' Toad said. 'You got fourteen thousand feet of concrete here, Rita, but I think we should try for a wire.' He reached up with his left hand and pulled the handle to drop the tailhook. 'Just keep it lined up and descending wings level and we'll be in fat city.'

'Fuel? How's our fuel?'

'About ten grand or so. Just a little heavy. Let's dump the fuel in the wings.'

Rita reached with her left hand, up there under the blown-out quarter panel, for the dump switch on the fuel management panel. 'I can't get it,' she said finally.

'I'll get it.' Toad leaned across and hunted until he had the proper switch.

'Landing checklist.'

'Okay, you got three down and locked, flaps and slats out, stab shifted, boards?' She put them out and added some power. It took a while to get the plane stabilized on speed again.

'Pop-up?' Toad murmured when she once again had everything under control. 'Can you check the flaperon pop-up?' The switch was on her left console. She had to lower her head and look as she fumbled with numb fingers. 'Watch your wings,' Toad warned.

She brought the wings back to level.

'Screw the pop-up,' Toad announced, figuring that she just couldn't ascertain the switch position. 'It's probably still on. Check the brakes.'

This also took some doing. She had to lift both feet free of the deck where her heels rested and place the balls of her feet on top of the rubber pedals, then push. She had never before realized what a strain that put on her stomach muscles. She was weak as a kitten. She struggled and got her feet arranged and pushed hard. They met resistance. 'Brakes okay.' She would have to do this again on the runway if the hook skipped over the shirt-field arresting gear or she landed long. For now she let her feet slide down the pedals until her heels were once again on the deck.

'My mask.' She gagged. 'Get my mask off!'

Toad got her right fitting released just in time. She retched and the vomit poured down over her chest.

Seeing Rita vomit and smelling that smell, Toad felt his own stomach turn over. He choked it back and helped her hold the plane level until she stopped heaving.

'Okay,' she said when she finally got her mask back on, 'check your harness lock and we're ready to do it.' She took her hand off the stick and locked the harness lever on the forward right corner of the ejection seat.

'Oh, poo,' Toad said. She glanced his way. He was reconnecting his Koch fittings. 'Sort of forgot to strap myself back in,' he explained.

She ran her seat up as far as she could and yet still reach the rudder pedals. This put her face a little higher out of the wind, and in seconds she could see better, but only out of her right eye. Her left was still clogged with blood.

'Your'e coming down nicely, passing six thousand MSL, eighteen hundred above the ground. Let's keep this sink rate and we'll do okay. Come left a couple degrees, though.'

She complied.

'A little more. And gimme just a smidgen more power.'

When she squinted and blinked a few more times, she could make out the runway. There was a little crosswind and Toad had her aimed off to the left slightly to compensate.

The approach seemed to take forever, perhaps because she was hurting and perhaps because she was unsure if she could handle it at the bottom. She would just have to wait and see, but it was difficult waiting when she was so cold, and growing colder.

She let the plane descend without throttle corrections, without wiggling the stick or trying to sweeten her lineup. With three hundred feet still to go on the radar altimeter, she made a heading correction. She was going to have trouble judging the altitude with only one eye, and she thought about that. She could do it, she decided. There was the meatball on the Optical Landing System. She began to fly it, working mightily to move the throttles. Still coming down, on speed, lined up, across the threshold. Now! Throttles back a little and nose just so, right rudder and left stick to straighten her out . . . oh yes!

The mainmounts kissed the concrete.

The pilot used the stick to hold the nose wheel off as she smoothly closed the throttles. She had no more than got the engines to idle when she felt the rapid deceleration as the tailhook engaged the short-field arresting gear. The nose slammed down. As the plane was jerked to a rapid stop, she applied the brakes.

She got the flap handle forward with her left hand, but knew she wouldn't be able to tug hard enough to pull the parking brake handle out. Toggling the harness lock release by her right thigh, she got enough freedom to reach it with her right.

Toad opened the canopy. As it whined its way aft a fire truck came roaring up and screeched to a halt with firemen tumbling off.

Canopy open. Rita checked that the flaps and slats were in. Her left shoulder was aching badly now and it was difficult to make her fingers do as she wished. One of the firemen ran out from the wheel well and made a cutting motion across his throat. He had inserted the safety pins in the landing gear.

Both throttles around the horn to cutoff, engine-fuel master switches off as the RPMs dropped. Then the generators dropped off the line with an audible click and everything in the cockpit went dead. Exhausted, she fumbled with the generator switches until they too were secured.

It was very quiet. She got the mask loose and, using only her right hand, pried the helmet off. The compressor blades tinkled steadily, gently, as the wind kept them turning, like a mobile on the porch of your grandmother's house when you returned after a long absence.

A man was standing on the pilot's boarding ladder. He looked at her and drew back in horror.

'A bird,' she croaked.

She heard Toad give a disgusted exclamation. 'Wipe it off her, man! It's just bird guts. It ain't her brains!' They were loading Rita into an ambulance and the crash crew was filling out paperwork when a gray navy sedan screeched to a halt near the fire truck. Jake Grafton jumped out and strode toward Toad as white smoke wafted from the auto's engine compartment.

'Looks like you were in a hurry,' Toad said, and managed a grin. He was sitting, leaning back against the nose wheel, too drained to even stand. He felt as if he had just finished a ten-mile run. The crash chief tossed the captain a salute and he returned it even though he wasn't wearing a hat. He obviously had other things on his mind.

'How's Rita?'

'Gonna be okay, I think. When they looked at her they thought she had brains and eyeballs oozing out everywhere, but they got most of it cleaned off. Never saw so much shit. Must have been a damn big bird. They're taking her over to the hospital for X-rays and all.'

Jake Grafton deflated visibly. He wiped his forehead with a hand, and then wiped his hand on his trousers, leaving a wet stain.

'How come you didn't answer me on the damned radio? I about had heart failure when you started doing whifferdills.'

'I'm sorry, sir. I disconnected my plugs and got a little unstrapped so I could reach over the fly the plane. Rita was sorta out of it there for a little while.'

Jake climbed the pilot's ladder and surveyed the cockpit. He examined the hole left in the plexiglas quarter panel by the late buzzard or eagle or hawk. 'She come around okay?'

'Came to and landed this thing like it was on rails. Real damn sweet, CAG. Never saw a better landing.'

A sailor drove up aboard a yellow flight-line tractor. He swung in front of the plane and backed a tow back toward the nose wheel. 'Well,' said Jake Grafton as he made a quick inspection of the Athena antennas, all of which seemed to be firmly in place, 'you better zip over to the hospital and let them check you over too. I gotta get the plane put someplace private.'

'Uh, CAG, you're still gonna let us fly the prototypes, aren't you? I mean, it wasn't like we tried to hit that bird or anything.'

Jake looked at Toad, slightly surprised. 'Oh,' he said, 'you two are my crew. If the doctors say you can fly. Now get over to the hospital and find out. Better get cleaned up too. You look like you've been cleaning chickens and the chickens won.'

'Yessir. You bet. But, uh, I don't have a ride. Can I take your car?'

'Aw, Toad, you're gonna get that bird goo all over the seat.' He glanced at the car. Smoke was still leaking out. It was junk. 'Keys are in it. But be careful – it's government property.'

Amazingly enough, the car engine actually started after Toad ground on it awhile. Jake had driven about forty miles at full throttle, about a hundred miles per hour, so he shook his head in wonder when the transmission engaged with a thunk and Toad drove away trailing smoke.

15

The base dispensary contained an emergency room, but no other hospital facilities. After Rita Moravia was cut out of her flight gear, cleaned up and examined by a doctor, she was taken to a hospital in Reno, seventy miles away. Toad Tarkington arrived at the dispensary as the ambulance was driving away.

'Oh, Doctor,' the corpsman called when he saw Toad coming through the door, 'here comes the other one.'

The doctor was only a year or two out of med school, but he had already acquired the nuances of military practice. 'In here.' He gestured to an examining room. A corpsman followed them in and closed the door. 'Strip to the skin,' the doctor said. 'How do you feel?' He grasped Toad's wrist and glanced at his watch.

'Okay, Doc. The pilot took the bird hit. I just got splattered.'

'Did you become hypoxic, pass out, inhale any feathers or anything like that?'

'No, sir. I just peed my pants.'

The doctor checked his watch again, then looked at Toad with raised eyebrows.

'Not really,' Toad said, suddenly aware that he was no longer in the company of his peers. 'Sorry. How's Moravia?'

The doctor was still all business. 'Blurred vision in her left eye, some bruises and cuts, nothing serious. But she's an excellent candidate for a major-league infection. I gave her a large dose of penicillin and sent her to the hospital in Reno for X-rays and observation. She can stay there until we're sure she's okay.'

'And her eye?'

'I think it'll be okay. They'll look at that in Reno.'

The doctor spent the next five minutes examining Toad. He peed in a bottle and gave a blood sample. The corpsman gathered up his flight gear. Toad insisted it all be put in a duffel bag. He stood holding his flight suit, which already had a hen-house smell. 'What am I going to do for clothes?'

'Got any money?'

He dug his wallet from the chest pocket. 'Fifty-three dollars.'

The doctor added fifty dollars of his own money to Toad's fortune and sent the corpsman to the exchange for underwear, trousers, shirt, and tennis shoes. 'Should be open until nineteen hundred hours. You can make it if you hurry.' Toad gave the enlisted man his sizes and expressed a few opinions about color and style. The corpsman flashed Toad a wicked grin as he headed for the door.

An hour later Tarkington had talked the doctor into loaning him one of the navy sedans belonging to the dispensary. He was on his way to the parking lot in his new duds when he met Jake Grafton coming in.

'You okay?' the captain said.

'Yessir. Just fine. Thought I'd grab a little liberty.' Toad gave Jake back the keys to the sedan he had used to get to the dispensary, and displayed the keys to his borrowed vehicle. 'I think your car's had it. Want to come with me?'

'Where you going?'

'Reno. That's where they took Rita.' He told Jake what the doctor had said.

Jake begged off. He still had security arrangements and phone calls to make. 'Call me from the hospital and tell me how she is. I'll be at the BOQ. Leave a message at the desk if I'm not there.'

Jake watched Toad drive away toward the main gate, then went into the dispensary to see what the doctor really thought about Rita's left eye. She needed two great eyes to fly. Better than the doctor or even Toad, Jake Grafton knew what flying meant to Lieutenant Rita Moravia, US Naval Aviator.

They had her in a semi-private room with a beautiful white-haired lady who was fast asleep. Toad spent ten minutes talking to the floor nurse and the internist before he went in. 'They say you're gonna be okay,' he told Rita with a grin. She had a patch over her left eye. Scratches and small cuts were visible on her cheek.

She raised a finger to her lips. 'Mrs Douglas went to sleep a few minutes ago,' she whispered. Toad stood at the end of the bed glancing uneasily at the shiny, stark hospital equipment. Just being in a hospital made his leg ache.

'Here,' she said, still whispering, 'pull this chair and sit down. Have you had any dinner?' It was almost 10 P.M.

'Uh'uh. How you doin'?' He sat gingerly on the forward portion of the seat.

She shrugged. 'Thanks for saving my bacon.'

He waved it away. 'What's wrong with her?' he asked, glancing at the sleeping Mrs Douglas.

'Broken hip. She fell in her kitchen this morning. They're going to pin it tomorrow evening. She's been in a lot of pain today.'

Toad nodded vaguely and examined the sheets that covered Rita. Hospital sheets always looked so perfect, even with a body between them. Her hair was a mess. They had cleaned it and made no attempt to pretty it up. That's what's wrong with hospitals – your dignity is left at the front door on the way in.

'That shirt you're wearing is the most *horrid* garment I have – What are those colors? Chartreuse and mauve?'

'Beats me.' Toad muttered, glancing at his torso with distaste. 'One of the corpsmen picked it out at the exchange. He thought I would cut a dashing figure in it, I guess.'

'Dashing is not the word I would use.'

They sat for a while, each trying to think of something to say. 'Guess your helmet visor saved your eyes,' he said at last. 'Cushioned the impact.'

'It's amazing, when you stop to think about it. I thought about it all the way over here in the ambulance. The ambulance only goes ten miles over the speed limit, so everything on the road passes it. Light flashing, and everyone whizzing by. So I had plenty of time to think about the odds. It's amazing.'

'What is?'

'How with the whole wide sky to fly in, all those thousands of cubic miles, that bird and I tried to fly in exactly the same little piece of it. A foot further left, that bird would have missed the cockpit, a foot to the right and it would have hit the nose, a foot higher—'

'Life's like that. No guarantees. You never know.'

'Is that what combat is like?'

'I wouldn't know.'

'Weren't you and Captain Grafton – over the Med?'

Toad shrugged and slid further back into the chair. He crossed his leg with the pin in it over the good one and massaged it gently. 'One fight. A couple minutes of being scared stiff and too busy to even sweat it. That wasn't combat. Combat is day in and day out knowing they're going to be shooting and being scared before you go and going anyway. I've never done that. Hope I never have to.' He grinned wryly and cocked his head to better match the angle of hers against the pillow. 'I'm a peacetime drugstore cowboy. Didn't you know? Make love not war.'

'The Silver Star fooled me.'

'Medals don't mean shit. Over the Med CAG had the guts and determination, enough for him and me both with a lot left over. He's a balls-out fighter. Those Arab fighter jocks were hopelessly outclassed – at least that's what I kept telling myself then. Still tell myself that on nights when I wake up thinking about it. I'm even beginning to believe it.'

She smoothed the sheets with her right hand.

'How's your left shoulder?'

'Just bruised. Hurts now. If this eye clears up . . .'

'It will.'

'Got some cuts on the eyeball. Lots of bird flesh and even the stem of a little feather.'

'It'll be okay.'

'I suppose.'

'You'll fly again. Just wait and see. You're too good to stay on the ground. A person with your talent belongs in a cockpit.'

'Ummm.'

He put his feet on the floor, leaned forward and captured a hand. 'Listen, Rita – Ginger – I know how you feel. The fickle finger of fate just reached out and zinged you a little one and reminded you that you're mortal clay. We all are. But – you know all this – you've got to live every day the best you can, put the throttles against the stops and fly. Flying is what it's all about. And when that final flight comes, that last day, as come it will, then look the Man straight in the eye and tell Him it's been a hell of a great ride. And thank Him. *That's* the way you have to live it. That's the only way it can be done.'

She took her hand from his and touched her cheek.

'Get a good night's sleep. Get well. You got a lot of flying left to do.' He stood. 'I'll look in on you tomorrow afternoon. Hang tough.'

'Thanks for coming by.'

He paused at the door and winked. 'We fly together. Remember?'

'Kiss me, lover.'

He glanced at Mrs Douglas. Her eyes were closed and she seemed to be asleep. He bent over Rita and gave her his best effort.

It was 1 P.M. the next day when Luis Camacho pulled into his driveway in Silver Spring and let himself into his house. His wife was at work and his son was in school. The house felt strange on a weekday with both of them gone. He walked slowly through the downstairs, looking it over, listening to the refrigerator hum, looking out the windows.

He found his leather driving gloves in the hall closet, the pigskin ones his parents had given him two Christmases ago that he never wore because they were too nice. The batteries in the flashlight stowed in the catch-all drawer in the kitchen still had some juice, amazingly enough. He tucked the light into his hip pocket and let himself out the kitchen door into the backyard. The wooden fence between his house and Albright's had a gate with a rusty latch, no lock. The Labrador wanted to come with him, but he shooed it back and latched the gate behind him.

He opened his packet of lock picks on Harlan Albright's picnic table.

He stared at them a moment, trying to decide. It had been a while. Let's see, the lock is a Yale.

Opening it took ten minutes. The Lab finally quit whining next door. Probably he went back to his favorite spot in the sun and lay down. Camacho was beginning to think he wasn't going to get this lock when it clicked.

Albright had no fancy alarms, or none that Camacho had ever seen. Service manager at a local garage, he couldn't afford the visibility that a Fort Knox security system would give him. But no doubt he had some little doodads here and there to let him know if he had any unwanted visitors.

Luis Camacho stood in the door and carefully examined the interior. It looked precisely as he remembered it, exactly the way he had seen it for years. He stepped inside, eased the door shut and listened.

Albright's house was similar to his, one of four variations on the same basic floor plan the tract builder had used in half the houses in this subdivision. Other than minor interior adjustments, most of the differences were in the front façades.

As he stood there the faint hum of the refrigerator shut off. Albright's fridge was quieter than his. Probably newer too. He closed his eyes and concentrated, trying to shut out the faint sound of a car passing on the side street. Only a few creaks and groans as the house continued to warm in the early afternoon sun.

He moved slowly through the kitchen and into the family room. A bachelor. Albright spent his evenings here, watching TV or reading. Camacho moved slowly, checking the walls and looking behind pictures – O'Keefe prints – and tugging at the carpet edges. He inspected the books in the built-in bookcase, then randomly removed a few and checked the integrity of the wall behind by rapping with a knuckle. He didn't know what he hoped to find, but he would recognise it when he saw it. If there was anything to find, which was doubtful.

The garage was next, then the basement. It was still unfinished, no ceiling or drywall to cover the unpainted cinder blocks. Damp. Only two naked bulbs overhead, plus the one on the stairs. He glanced at the accumulated junk and the layers of dust and grime, and decided Albright cleaned his basement on the same schedule used by every other bachelor who owned one – never. There were some tools piled carelessly in one corner: a drill, a saber saw, a hammer, a box of hand tools. They were covered with the same thickness of dirt that covered everything else. Some cans of paint that looked like they had never been opened. Perhaps he had had a fit of enthusiasm which had waned on the way home from the hardware store. Camacho went back upstairs, consciously reminding himself to flip off the light switch at the head of the stairs.

He stopped dead in the kitchen. He turned and went back to the basement door. He opened it. Light switch on. What was that? Was it a noise? Lights off. Yes, there was a noise, some kind of faint grinding, just for a half second or so. He repeated the procedure. He wasn't imagining things. He could hear *something*.

In the slanted ceiling of the stairway, down about three feet from the bulb, was a dusty screen. Several of the strands had been pushed aside, perhaps by a careless jab from a broom handle, leaving a hole. He flipped the light several more times. He could just barely hear it, the most minute of noises, hard to recognize.

The screen was held on with four screws. Bare metal could be seen on the screw slots. When he got them out and lowered the screen he could see the camera lens. Rubber padding held on with rubber bands covered the camera body. A wire led to it. He stood on the stairs and examined it with his flashlight, then reached up and removed the camera, excess wire following along.

The wire was connected to a gadget on top with a small alligator clip. With the stairwell light off, he unclipped it and carried the camera to the kitchen table. Unwrapping the rubber padding with gloves on was difficult, so he took them off.

The gadget on top was some kind of an electromagnetic doohickey with a lever. When the current was turned on by flipping the light switch, the magnet was energized and caused this steel pin to push the camera shutter button, tripping the shutter. When the current ceased, the spring reset the lever, which released the shutter button and allowed the film to be automatically advanced by the camera.

It was a nice camera, a Canon. The little window said that it was on its ninth exposure. How many times had he turned that light on and off. He tried to count them. Six. No, five. So the film counter should be on four.

He opened the camera and removed the film, then pulled the celluloid completely from its cartridge and held it up to the window. Rewinding the film back onto the cartridge was a chore, but he managed, and after wiping the cartridge carefully, he reinstalled it in the camera. He used a dry dishcloth on the camera and wrapped it carefully. Working by feel with the overhead stair light off, he returned the device to its hole and screwed the screen back on. He flipped the light switch three times and was rewarded each time with that faint noise.

There were three bedrooms upstairs, exactly the same floor plan here as in his house next door, but only two of them were furnished. The largest was obviously lived in, but the middle-sized room was ready for a guest. Luis Camacho tried to remember if Harlan Albright had ever had an overnight guest that he knew about. No.

He checked the carpet. Albright might have some kind of pressure device under there, or perhaps heat-sensitive paper. Nope. Another camera? Apparently not.

There was a little trapdoor in the hall ceiling that led to the unfinished attic. An upholstered chair sat just inside the guest bedroom. He put his nose almost to the seat and scrutinized it carefully. Yes, a few smudges of dirt were visible.

Luis Camacho pulled the chair under the trapdoor, took his shoes off and stood on it. He eased the door up. It was dark up there. A few flakes of dust drifted down. He stood on tiptoe and used the flash. He felt between the joists.

Several items. One was a soft leather baglike thing, a zippered pistol rug. The other was a large, heavy metal toolbox that just fit through the trapdoor. He almost dropped the toolbox getting it down.

The pistol rug contained a Ruger .22 autopistol with black plastic grips and a partially full box of Remington ammunition. Bluing was worn off the pistol in places. The front sight and its sleeve were amputated, and threads were machined into the outside of the barrel to take the silencer, which was also in the rug. This was strictly a close-range weapon: with no front sight, it would be useless at any distance.

He sniffed the barrel of the pistol. Cleaned since last use. He pushed the catch and the magazine dropped out of the grip into his hand. It was full. He shoved it back in until it clicked. No doubt the cleaning rod and patches and gun oil were up there in the joists somewhere. He replaced the items in the rug and zipped it closed.

The toolbox wasn't locked. Neatly packed in and padded to prevent damage were fuses, a roll of wire and a two-channel Futaba radio transmitter for radio-controlled models. Lots of servos, ten of them. A little bag containing crystals to change the frequency of the transmitter. Four miniature radio receivers, also made by Futaba. A bunch of nickel-cadmium batteries with a charging unit. Four six-cell batteries wrapped with black plastic. There was even a manual alarm clock.

But the pièce de résistance, the item that impressed Luis Camacho, was a radio receiver with a frequency-adjustment knob, volume knob, ear-piece and spike meter. This device would allow the careful craftsman to check for possible radio interference in the area in which he intended to do his bit to improve the human species, before he armed his own device. Better safe than sorry.

All in all, it was an impressive kit. Everything recommended by *Gentleman's Quarterly* for the well-heeled professional bomber was in there, including a case containing a set of jeweler's screwdrivers and wrenches.

Camacho repacked the items carefully, trying to put everything back exactly as he found it. After much straining he got the toolbox back through the trapdoor into the attic.

He checked carefully in the joists as far as he could reach and see, then replaced the pistol rug. He was meticulous in restoring everything to its proper place, wiping a few flecks of dust from the chair arms and retrieving a larger piece from the carpet. When he had given everything a last look, he went down to the kitchen and seated himself at the table.

Where was the plastique? It had to be here someplace. Using his flashlight, he descended again to the basement and examined the paint cans. He hefted them, shook them gently. They contained something, but it probably wasn't paint. Oh well.

He locked the kitchen door behind him and crossed through the back gate to his own yard.

Standing in his own kitchen with a pot of coffee dripping through the filter, he thought about Albright's treasure as he maneuvered a cup under the black coffee basket to fill it. With the Pyrex pot back in place, he sipped on the hot liquid as he dialed the phone.

After talking to three people, he was connected with the man he wanted, an explosives expert. 'Well, the material's ability to resist the effects of heat and cold and humidity depends on just what kind of stuff it is. Semtex is a brand real popular right now, made in Czechoslovakia. Heat won't do it any good, but if the heat is not too severe or prolonged, it shouldn't take much of its punch away.'

'How about storage in an uninsulated attic?'

'Here, in this climate?'

'Yes.'

'Not recommended. Best would be a place slightly below room temperature, a place where the temp stays pretty constant.'

'Thanks.'

'I keep mine in the wine cellar.'

'Sure.'

Camacho finished the cup of coffee, dumped the rest of the pot down the sink and turned off the coffee maker. He wiped the area with a dishrag and threw the wet grounds into the garbage. He didn't want his wife noticing he had been there.

It was three o'clock when he locked the front door and drove away.

At about the same instant that Luis Camacho was starting his car to return to his office, Toad Tarkington was parking at the Reno hospital. When he arrived in the room, Rita was sitting in a chair talking with Mrs Douglas, her roommate. After the introductions Toad pulled up the other chair, a molded plastic job made for a smaller bottom than his.

'When are they going to let you go?' he asked as he tried to arrange himself comfortably.

'Probably tomorrow. The doctor will be around in an hour or so.'

'Did you get a good night's sleep?'

'Not really.' She smiled at Mrs Douglas. 'We had a series of little naps, didn't we?'

'We did.' Mrs Douglas had a delicate voice. 'I don't sleep much anymore anyway.' She bit on her lower lip.

'Perhaps we should go for a little walk,' Rita suggested. She rose and made sure her robe belt was firmly tied. 'We'll be back in a little bit, Mrs Douglas.'

'Okay, dear.'

Out in the hall Toad said, 'I see you fixed your hair.'

'Wasn't it a fright? A hospital volunteer helped me this morning. She said it would help how I felt, and she was right.' She walked slowly in her slippers, her hands in his pockets. 'Poor Mrs Douglas. Here I've been so concerned about my little half-acre and her two daughters came in this morning and told her she had to go to a nursing home. She's very upset. Oh, Toad, it was terrible, for all of them. They're afraid she'll fall again with no one there, and the daughters work, with families of their own.'

Toad made a sympathetic noise. He had never given the problems of elderly people much thought. He really didn't want to do so now either.

Rita paused for a drink from a water fountain, then turned back toward her room. 'I just wanted you to know the situation. Now we'll go back and cheer her up.'

Toad put his hand on her arm. 'Whoa, lady. Let's run that one by again. Just *how* are we going to do that?'

'You cheered me up last night. You make me feel good just being around you. You can do the same with her.'

Toad looked up and down the hall for help, someone or something to rescue him. No such luck. He looked again at Rita, who was absorbing every twitch of his facial muscles. 'Women my own age I don't understand. Now it's true I've picked up a smattering of experience here and there with the gentle sex, but eighty-year-old ladies with busted hips are completely out of—'

'You can do it,' Rita said with simple, matter-of-fact faith, and grasping his hand, she led him back along the hallway.

In the room she nudged him toward the chair near Mrs Douglas. He started to give Rita a glare, but when he realized Mrs Douglas was watching him, he changed it to a smile. It came out as a silly, nervous smile.

Women! If they didn't screw there'd be a bounty on 'em.

'Rita says you're facing some very significant changes in your life.'

The elderly woman nodded. She was still chewing on her lip. At that moment Toad forgot Rita and saw before him his own mother as she would be in a few years. 'Pretty damned tough,' he said, meaning it.

'My life now is my garden, the roses and bulbs and the annuals that I plant every spring. I do my housework and spend my time watching the cycle of life in my garden. I wasn't ready to give that up.'

'I see.'

'I have most of my things planted now. The bulbs have been up for a month or so. They were so pretty this spring.'

'I don't suppose any of us are ever ready to give up something we love.'

'I suppose not. But I had hoped that I wouldn't have to. My husband – he died fifteen years ago with a heart attack while he was playing golf. He so loved golf. I was hoping that someday in my garden I . . .' She closed her eyes.

When she opened them again Toad asked about her garden. It was not large, he was told. Very small, in fact. But it was enough. That was one of life's most important lessons, learning what was enough and what was too much. Understanding what was *sufficient*. 'But,' Mrs Douglas sighed, 'what is sufficient changes as you get older. It's one thing for a child, another for an adult, another thing still when you reach my age. I think as you age life gets simpler, more basic.'

'I'm curious,' said Toad Tarkington, feeling more than a little embarrassed. He shot a hot glance at Rita. 'Do you pray much?'

'No. It's too much like begging. The professional prayers always want things they will never get, things they just can't have. Like peace on earth and conversion of the sinners and cures for all the sick. And to prove they really want all these things that can never be, they grovel and beg.'

'At least they're sincere,' Rita said.

'Beggars always are,' Mrs Douglas shot back. 'That's their one virtue.'

Toad grinned. Mrs Douglas appeared to be a fellow cynic, which he found quite agreeable. Perhaps the age difference doesn't matter that much after all. A few minutes later he asked one more question. 'What will heaven be like, do you think?'

'A garden. With roses and flowers of all kinds. My heaven will be that anyway. What yours will be, I don't know.' Mrs Douglas waggled a finger at him without lifting her hand from the bed. 'You are two very young people, to spend time with an old woman to cheer her up. When are you going to marry?'

Toad laughed and stood. 'You tell her, Mrs Douglas. She absolutely refuses to become an honest woman.' He said his goodbyes and Rita followed him into the hall.

'Thanks. That wasn't so hard, was it?' She had her arms folded across her chest.

'Hang tough, Rita. If they let you take a hike tonight or tomorrow, give me a call at the BOQ. Captain Grafton or I will come get you and bring you some clothes.'

She nodded. 'You come if you can.'

'Sure.' He paused. 'What do you want from life, Rita? What will be sufficient?'

She shook her head. He winked and walked away.

16

In an era when the average American male stood almost six feet tall, Secretary of Defense Royce Caplinger towered just five feet six inches in his custom-made shoes with two-inch heels. Perhaps understandably, his hero and role model was Douglas MacArthur, of whom he had written a biography ten years before. The critics had savaged it and the post-Vietnam public had ignored it. Caplinger, said one wag, would have won MacArthur sainthood had the book been even half true.

How deeply this experience hurt Caplinger only his family might have known. The world was allowed to see only the merciless efficiency and detached intellect that had made him a millionaire by the time he was thirty and president and CEO of one of the twenty largest industrial companies in the nation when he was forty-two. Now worth in excess of a hundred million dollars, he was a man who believed in himself with a maniacal faith; in the world of titanic egos in which he moved he saw himself as a giant and, to his credit, others saw him the same way.

Rude and abrasive, Caplinger never forgot or forgave. He had never been accused of possessing a sense of humor. He won many more battles than he lost because he was *right*, often terrifically right, as his many enemies freely acknowledged. He often won when he was wrong too, because he could play major-league hardball with the best of them. Years ago his subordinates had labeled him 'the cannibal,' whispering that he liked the taste of raw flesh.

Caplinger had the brain of Caesar and the soul of a lizard, all housed in the body of a chimpanzee, or so one of his more daring victims had groused to *Time* magazine. This quote crossed Jake Grafton's mind just now as he watched the secretary's gaze dart back and forth across the faces of the men at the luncheon table as they were served pear halves in china dishes bearing the seal of the Navy Department by a steward in a white jacket.

Jake was back in Washington for a week while the China Lake crowd fixed their A-6, Rita Moravia recovered, and Samuel Dodgers tinkered with the Athena device. This was Jake's first meal in the Secretary of the

Navy's dining/conference room, so today he was playing tourist and taking it all in.

The room was spacious and paneled with dark wood, perhaps mahogany. Deep blue drapes dressed up the windows. A half dozen oil paintings of sailing ships and battles, with little spotlights to show them to advantage, were arranged strategically between the windows and doors. Gleaming brass bric-a-brac provided the accents. Sort of early New York Yacht Club, Jake decided, a nineteenth-century vision of a great place for railroad pirates and coal barons to socialize over whiskey with nautical small talk about spankers and jibs and their latest weekend sail to Newport. He would describe the room for Callie this evening. He sipped his sugarless iced tea and turned his attention to the conversation.

In keeping with his temperament, Caplinger was doing the talking: '. . . the Congress has ceased to exist as a viable legislative body since Watergate. They can't even manage to give senior leaders or the judiciary a pay raise without making a hash of it. Without strong, capable leaders, Congress is a collection of mediocrities drifting . . .'

Jake used his knife to slice the fruit in his dish, two whole halves, to make it go further. Already he suspected this wasn't going to be much of a meal.

At the opposite end of the table from the Secretary of Defense sat today's host, Secretary of the Navy George Ludlow. He was nibbling at pieces of pear he nicked off with his fork and listening to Caplinger. No doubt he was used to these monologues; he had married Caplinger's second daughter, a modestly pretty young woman with a smile that looked vacuous in news photos. Jake Grafton had never met her and probably never would.

'. . . five hundred thirty-five ants on a soapbox drifting down the Potomac, each of them thinking he's steering.' Caplinger chuckled and everyone else smiled politely. Jake had heard that old saw before.

Across the long table from Jake sat Tyler Henry, Under Secretary of Defense for Acquisition Russell Queen, and the Chief of Naval Operations, Admiral Jerome Nathan Lanham.

Lanham was a submariner, a nuke, with all the baggage that term implies: team player, risk minimizer, technocrat par excellence in the service of the nuclear genie. His patron saint was Hyman Rickover, the father of the nuclear navy, whose portrait hung in Lanham's office. Like Rickover, Jerome Nathan Lanham was reputed to have little use for nonengineers. Just now he sat regarding Jake Grafton, A.B. in history, with raised eyebrows.

Jake nodded politely and speared another tiny hunk of pear. The dish was half full of juice. He wondered if he should go after it with a spoon and surveyed the table to see if anyone else was. Nope. Well, hell. He used the spoon anyway, trying to be discreet, as Caplinger ruminated upon the current political situation in Japan and the steward began serving a tiny garden salad. '. . . wanted to hang Hirohito after the war, but MacArthur said no, which was genius. The Japanese would never have forgiven us.'

'If we conquered Iran today, what would you do with Khomeini?' Helmut Fritsche, seated to Jake's right, asked the question of Caplinger, who grinned broadly.

'Such a tiny hypothetical – he should have been a lawyer,' Ludlow muttered sotto voce as the others laughed.

'Make Khomeini a martyr? No. I'd ensure he didn't get any older, but the autopsy – and there would be one – would read "old age".'

After the salad came small bowls of navy bean soup accompanied by some tasteless crackers. Even Caplinger thought they were insipid. 'George, these crackers taste worse than some of my old predictions.'

When the soup was gone, the steward filled coffee cups and whisked away the dishes, then retired. Jake watched incredulously. Apparently they had just had the entire meal. At least Ludlow wasn't blowing the whole navy budget this year on grub.

'Well, Grafton,' Caplinger said, 'will Athena work?'

'Yessir. It's the biggest technical advance in naval aviation since I've been in the navy.'

'If it works' – the Secretary of Defense eyed Jake across the rim of his coffee cup – 'it'll be the biggest leap forward for the military since the invention of radar. The air force is going to want this technology yesterday. It'll save their strategic bomber program.' Jake understood. The air force would be able to use much cheaper bombers than the B-2, which they would never get any significant number of at a half billion dollars each.

'I want it right now,' Admiral Lanham said. 'These devices will make surface ships invisible to radar satellites and cruise missiles. The entire Soviet naval air arm will be obsolete. I want a crash program that puts Athena in the fleet *right now*, and *damn* the cost!'

Caplinger shifted his gaze to Helmut Fritsche, on Jake's right. 'Will it work? Can it be made to work?'

'Anything's possible given enough time and money.'

'How much?' demanded Under SECDEF Russell Queen. In civilian life he had been president of a large accounting firm. White skin, banker's hands, bald, Queen had long ago lost the battle of the bulge. He was a humorless man with thick glasses. Jake decided it would require prodigious faith to believe Russell Queen had once been young or ever loved a woman. 'How much do you think will be enough?'

Fritsche's shoulders rose a quarter inch and fell. 'Depends on how you go about it – how you structure the contract, how many units you buy annually, how big a risk you're willing to take on unproven technology. We didn't test a full-up system. All we did was prove the concept, and we have some more work to do on that next week. We're a long way from an operational system that will protect just one tactical airplane.'

'How long?'

Helmut Fritsche took out a cigar and rolled it thoughtfully between his hands. He didn't reach for a match. 'Two or three years – if you can make all the paper pushers keep hands off. Four or five if it's business as usual.' Every head at the table bobbed its owner's concurrence.

'Humph,' snorted Caplinger, who sucked in a bushel of air and sent it down as far as it would go, then exhaled slowly. 'I can try to put – maybe slip it under the stealth stuff – but . . .' His enthusiasm wouldn't fill a thimble. Even the Secretary of Defense couldn't control the legions of bureaucrats with rice bowls to protect. They were too well armed with statutes and regulations and pet congressmen. 'Russell, you'll have to make this work, find some dollars in one of your little hidey-holes, keep it too small for anyone to get curious about. And no fucking memos.'

Queen nodded slowly, his smooth round face revealing his discomfort. He looked, Jake thought, like a man staring into a dark abyss that he has been told to lower himself into.

'I don't think that's the way to do it,' Ludlow said. 'Admiral Lanham wants it now and the air force will too. We're going to have to fund Athena as one of our highest-priority items. We're going to have to throw money at it and hope the technology works.'

'Do you agree, Admiral?'

'Yes, sir. I'd rather have Athena than a whole lot of projects I can name, including the A-12.'

'We need them both,' Caplinger said. 'So we'll keep Athena in with the ATA and request funding for them both.'

'What about Congress?' Ludlow murmured. When no one replied, he expanded the question. 'How will Athena be seen by the liberals dying to chop the defense budget? Will they think it gives us such a large qualitative technical advantage over the Soviets that they can chop our capital budget? Shrink the navy?' To maintain a navy, worn-out, obsolete ships must be constantly replaced with new ones. New ships are expensive and require years to construct. A decision not to build as many as necessary to maintain current force levels was a decision to shrink the navy. Insufficient ships to fulfill continuing worldwide commitments forced planners to delay ship overhauls and keep sailors at sea for grotesquely long periods, which wore out ships prematurely and devastated enlisted retention rates It was a cruel downward spiral. This was the post-Vietnam nightmare from which the navy was just recovering.

'No democracy will ever buy enough ships,' Jake Grafton said. 'Not over the long haul.'

'You're saying we can't maintain a six-hundred-ship navy,' Lanham said, frowning.

'We don't have six hundred ships now, sir, and we're not likely to ever get them,' Jake shot back, suddenly sure he didn't want Lanham to think he could be cowed.

'Lessen the primary threat and we won't need as many ships. That's the argument,' said Ludlow.

'Politicians never understand commitments,' Royce Caplinger said dryly, 'perhaps because they make so many of them. The federal deficit is totally out of control due to mandated increases in social program expenditures. They borrowed money and never asked if they could afford the interest. They approved treaties and never weighed the cost in defense expenditures.'

The CNO made a gesture of frustration. 'We have more practical concerns. The air force is facing institutional death. They gave up the close air support mission to the army a generation ago. The strategic bomber mission is on the ropes. All they have left are ICBMs – which the army could run – and tactical air and airlift. Their bases are fixed, vulnerable to ICBMs and political upheavals. The world is passing them by. They're panicking. And they have a *lot* of friends. If they don't get Athena and get it now . . .'

'It'll get ugly,' Ludlow agreed.

'*I* am the Secretary of Defense,' Caplinger said, his voice hard. '*I* will take care of the air force. You people take care of the navy.'

The heavy silence that followed was broken by Tyler Henry. 'No one has mentioned the Minotaur.' All eyes turned to the vice admiral. An uncomfortable look crossed his face, as if he had just farted in church.

'What about him?' Caplinger asked.

'He hasn't gotten Athena yet, but the minute we start bringing defense contractors into the loop, he will.'

Caplinger leaned forward. 'Where will we be if he gives Athena to the Russians?'

Henry had recovered his composure. 'We'll have lost our advantage,' he said with a trace of irritation in his voice. 'They outgun us two to one. We need the technological edge to stay in the game.'

Caplinger got to his feet and reached for the jacket draped over the back of his chair. 'Thanks for lunch, George. Russell, you talk to these people and get this Athena business on track. I want it in production as soon as possible. We'll include it with the ATA in the budget. Black all the way.' He paused and surveyed the faces at the table. 'The navy can develop this. Keep it under wraps. Security as tight as a miser's money belt. Develop it for planes *and* ships. But the air force must be brought into this as soon as we have to start talking to Congress. This may kill the B-2, but it'll save the B-1.'

'But what about the billions we're pouring into stealth planes now?' Russell Queen the bean counter asked his boss.

'Heck, Russell, this Athena gizmo may not work. Probably won't. Sorry, Tyler, but after all! A religious crackpot in a backyard workshop? It's too good to be true. Sounds like something Tom Clancy dreamed up after he had a bad pizza.'

An hour later as Tyler Henry and Jake Grafton walked along the E-Ring back toward the admiral's office, Jake remarked, 'At lunch, Admiral, you said we need a technological edge to stay in the game. What if the game has changed?'

'You mean Gorbachev reforming the Kremlin, converting the commies? Bull fucking shit.'

'The Soviets packed up and pulled out of Afghanistan. They helped get the Cubans out of Angola. They're relaxing their hold on Eastern Europe. They're even talking to the Chinese. *Something's* going on.'

'So the sons of Uncle Joe Stalin have given up their goal of world domination? The fucking thugs who murdered twenty million of their *own* people? My aching ass. That's all big-lie propaganda that liberal half-wits *want* to believe. Twenty *million* men, women and children! They make Adolf Hitler look like a weenie waver. We'd better have the edge when the shit splatters, because we'll never get a second chance.'

'So you're keeping an open mind on the question.'

'You've been hanging around with that loose-screw Tarkington too long, Grafton. You're beginning to sound like him.' Dunedin must have mentioned Tarkington to Henry, Jake surmised. He was sure Henry had never met the lieutenant.

'But what if Royce Caplinger and the politicos in Congress *think* the game has changed?'

'Caplinger isn't a fool.' Two paces later Henry added, ' "Thinking politician" is an oxymoron.'

After Jake parted from the admiral he walked to the cafeteria, where he bought a packet of Nabs and washed them down with a half-pint of milk. Humans are unique animals, he reflected. What other species has man's ability to see the world as he wants it to be, rather than as it actually is? He couldn't think of any. The worst of it is that this human trait deprives you of the ability to recognize reality when you see it. On this gloomy note his thoughts turned to Callie.

'What d'ya think's wrong with it?' Camacho asked nervously as he and Harlan Albright stood listening to Luis' car. It had a ragged, sick sound, most likely because Camacho had taken out one of the spark plugs and pounded the little arm against the core until there was no gap at all, then reinstalled it.

'Sounds to me like you got a cylinder missing, but I'm no mechanic,' Albright said, and made notations on the service form. 'We'll have a guy look at it this afternoon and give you a call. I can't give you an estimate or tell you how long it'll take to fix until we find out what's wrong.'

'What neighborhood of finance are we talking here? Checking, savings, or second mortgage?'

Albright grinned and slid the form across the counter for Camacho to sign. 'We'll call you.'

'Well, poo. How about running me back downtown?'

The service manager glanced at the wall clock. 'I get off for lunch in about thirty minutes. You wait and I'll take you. Go browse in the show-room or get some coffee.'

Albright was driving a new car with dealer plates. Camacho settled into the passenger seat and fastened the seat belt as Albright pulled out into traffic. 'Thought I oughta drop by and fill you in. Sally and I have to go to a church dinner tonight. The only thing wrong with my car is a bad spark plug. Don't let your mechanical wizards screw me.'

'So what's happening?'

'We've got a letter from Terry Franklin's mother-in-law. She says he's a spy and wants us to bust him.'

Albright glanced at the FBI agent. 'You must get letters like that all the time.'

'We do. And we check them out. Which is precisely what we're going to do with this one. Sometime toward the end of next week we'll have to interview Franklin. Thought you ought to know.'

'I appreciate that. And the search for the Minotaur?'

'We need a letter from *his* mother-in-law.'

'Maybe you already got it. Maybe Franklin is the Minotaur.'

'Yeah. And I'm Donald Trump. I just live like this because I think money is vulgar. Jesus, you know damn well that little shit doesn't have the balls or the brains.'

'I've been thinking about it.' He coasted the car up to a stoplight and waited until it turned green. 'It's possible he could be hacking the codes from the computer, mailing them to the embassy, then waiting for us to pay him to copy the files. Maybe he's slicker than anyone suspected. Maybe being a schlep is his idea of secondary cover.'

'Seriously, I thought of that some time back. But I can't find a shred of evidence. And this stuff you're getting – I thought you said it was good.'

'Excellent.'

'So the Minotaur knows quality. It's not Franklin or any other com-puter clerk. It's somebody so high they know what you need.'

Albright acknowledged this logic. In the world of espionage, need determines value. He spotted a Burger King and turned in. With the engine off, he leaned back in his seat and adjusted his testicles to a more comfortable position. 'You're stringing me along, Luis.'

Camacho already had his door open, but he pulled it closed. 'Say that again.'

'I think you're a lot closer to the Minotaur than you're telling me. You may even know who he is. That leads me to some interesting speculations.'

Camacho had been expecting this, but now that it was here he still didn't know how to play it. 'So I'm a double agent. Is that it?'

Harlan Albright raised an eyebrow, then looked away.

'Start the fucking car. Take me to the office. I don't have time to sit around and shoot the shit with you over a greaseburger.'

Albright turned the key. The engine caught. Two blocks later he said, 'You going to deny it?'

'Why bother? You have never given me a list of the stuff you got from the Minotaur. Now today you give me this crap about Franklin being the Minotaur and I'm supposed to go charging off like Inspector Clouseau. Why don't you go back to Moscow and tell Gorby you screwed the pooch? Mail me a postcard when you get to Siberia. I hear it's lovely in the snow.'

'I don't know the file names. Even if I did, I don't have the authority to give them to you.'

'Go tell it to somebody who gives a shit. I don't.'

'What about Smoke Judy?'

'What about him?'

'What's he up to?'

'He's trying to peddle inside knowledge of defense contracts. So far without much success, as far as I can tell. Apparently he doesn't think money is vulgar.'

'Are the fraud people onto him? IG or NIS?' IG was the Inspector General. NIS meant Naval Investigative Service.

'If somebody's opened a file on him, I don't know about it.'

'Don't turn him over to them.'

'Why not?'

'Because I'm asking you not to.'

'Well, kiss my ass. You're taking a big chance, asking a double agent for a favor. Stop up here at the corner.' They were going west on Constitution Avenue. 'This is close enough. I need some air.'

Albright pulled over to the curb and braked to a stop. 'Don't turn him over.'

'Up yours.'

'I was trying to motivate you. You know I don't doubt your loyalty.'

'If I was a double agent we would have pulled in Terry Franklin a long time ago and squeezed him for the name of every file that you don't want me to know. He'd sing like a canary.'

'I know,' Albright replied as Camacho opened the car door and stepped out.

'You don't know shit. You don't know how many anonymous fraud, waste and abuse hot lines there are over at the Pentagon. The damn numbers are posted everywhere. Don't like your boss? Nail him to the cross on your coffee break. Busybodies and prissy fat ladies are burning up the wires. Somebody could drop a dime on Judy any minute. Then I'll be your fall guy, the double agent.'

'Find the Minotaur.'

'That mechanic screws me, I'll break your nose.' Luis Camacho shut the door firmly and walked away.

As he trudged through the tourists and secretaries on lunch break he tried to decide if he had handled it well or poorly. The lies were plausible, he concluded, but he was suspect. Peter Aleksandrovich was nobody's fool. And 'schlep' – what an interesting word for a commie to use. Underestimating this man could be fatal.

The new Amy Carol Grafton frowned at the peas on her plate. She glowered at the carrots. She carved herself a tiny chunk of meat loaf and put it in her mouth, where she held it without chewing as she stared at the offending vegetables.

'What's the matter, Amy?' Callie asked.

Amy Carol sat erect in her chair and tossed her black pageboy hair. 'I don't like vegetables.'

'They're good for you. You need to eat some of them.' Amy's brand-new mom was the soul of reason. Jake Grafton took another sip of coffee and the last bite of his meat loaf.

'I don't like green food.'

'Then eat your carrots, dear.' Callie smiled distractedly. If the child didn't eat her peas, what would be her vitamin count for vegetables today? Callie had spent the past week researching diets for diabetics. Right now she was swamped with strange facts.

'I don't like orange stuff either.'

'Amy,' said the new father with a glint in his eye. 'I don't care what you like or don't like. Your mom put this stuff on the table, so you're going to eat it. Now start.'

'She isn't my mom. And you're not my dad. My parents are dead. You're Callie and Jake. And I don't like you, Jake, not one little bit.'

'Fine. But you're going to sit there until you finish those vegetables and I say you can get up.'

'Why?' Her lower lip began to quiver and her brows knitted. Callie thought Amy looked so cute and helpless when she clouded up. Jake thought Callie had a lot to learn.

'Because I said so.' Jake picked up the newspaper, opened it ostentatiously and hid behind it.

Callie got up and went to the sink, rinsing dishes. Jake reached around the paper every so often for a sip of coffee. Their second meal with their new daughter. Another disaster.

The youngster was trying to establish who's in charge, Jake told his wife. He thought Callie was making the same mistake Neville Chamberlain did. He used precisely those words to the new mother last night, after the first, opening-day debacle at the dinner table, when the youngster was finally in bed, and had been told in no uncertain terms that he was a lout.

Lout or not, 'I am wearing the trousers,' he said with his right trigger finger pointed straight up, 'and we are going to establish very early that I have the last say on junior-senior relations around here. Somebody has to be in charge and it's not going to be an eleven-year-old.'

'Just because you wear trousers, huh?'

'No. Because when I was growing up my father was the head of his family, and I intend to be the head of mine. It's a tried and true system with ancient tradition to commend it. We're going to stick with it.'

'You can't issue orders here, Captain Grafton. Amy and I don't wear uniforms.' She raised a finger, mimicking his gesture.

This evening was also off to a rocky start.

Jake put down his newspaper and examined the vegetable situation. The child apparently hadn't touched a pea or a carrot. She was staring fixedly at her plate with a sullen, defiant look.

'How was school today?' Jake asked.

No answer.

'I asked you a question, Amy.'

'Okay.'

'Tell me about your teachers.'

'What do you want to know?'

'Their names, what subjects they teach, what they look like, whether you like them. That kind of stuff.'

'Wellll,' Amy said, her gaze flicking across Jake's face, 'some of them are nice and some aren't.' And away she went on a five-minute exposition that covered the school day from opening to closing bell. Jake tossed in an occasional question when she paused for air.

When she had exhausted the teacher subject, Jake asked, 'What subjects do you think you're going to like best?'

Away she went again, debating the merits of math versus English, social studies versus science. This time when she ran down, Jake asked if she had any homework.

'Some math problems.'

'Need any help with them?'

'The division ones,' she said tentatively.

'Eat some of those peas and carrots and we'll clear the table and work on the problems.'

'How many do I have to eat?'

'Two spoonfuls of each.'

She made a face and did as she was bid. As he carried the dishes to the sink, Jake asked, 'Just what vegetables *do* you like?'

'Not any of them.'

'Well, do you have some that you don't hate as much as others?'

'Corn. Corn is okay. But not the creamed kind.' She squirmed. 'And I like lima beans.'

'No kidding? So do I. Maybe we can have some tomorrow night. How about it, Callie?'

His wife was standing by the little desk that served as a paper catchall, looking once again at the diet book. She turned to Jake and nodded. She had tears in her eyes. He winked at her.

'Amy, better get your school books. And, Callie, don't we have some sugarless dessert around here for little girls who eat their dinner?'

17

A woman from the garage called at 10 A.M. and said his car was ready: $119.26. Camacho told her he would stop by after work. She hung up before he could even ask what the problem had been.

Dreyfus gave him a ride and dropped him in front of the showroom.

The new cars gleamed shamelessly and flashed their chrome with wanton abandon as he walked by. Light, easy-listening music sounded everywhere. Two salesmen asked if he needed help.

He paid for the repairs at a window where a harried young woman juggled two phones as she pounded numbers into a computer. He surrendered his driver's license for her scrutiny before she asked. Without even glancing to see if his puss matched the photo, she copied the number onto the check and slid it back at him.

His six-year-old car sat amid twenty or so others of its vintage on a gravel lot out back. Dingy and coated with road grime, it hadn't seen wax since . . . not since he gave his son twenty dollars that Saturday two years ago and the kid let the wax dry like paint all over the car before he tried to wipe it off.

Camacho unlocked the door, rolled down the windows and tossed the yellow card dangling from the rearview-mirror bracket onto the floor. The car started readily enough and ran sweetly. He examined the invoice. Diagnostic test. Defective spark plug. Defective lead cable? Ouch – they got him there! Labor. How is it a garage can charge $55 per hour for a mechanic's time?

About two miles from the garage was a shopping center with a large parking lot, most of which was empty except for light poles and a couple of cars that looked as if they had sat in those spots all winter. One even had two flat tires.

He parked near it and got his jack from the trunk. The rear end went up first. He had an old army blanket in the trunk and spread it under the car so he wouldn't get too filthy.

With coat and tie on the back seat, flashlight in hand, Luis Camacho slid gingerly under the car. He knew exactly what he was looking for, but it might be hard to spot.

Five minutes later he stood beside the car and scratched his head. If Albright had put a bomb in this thing, where was it?

After a thorough scrutiny of the engine compartment and the trunk cavity, he attacked the door panels and rockers with a Phillips-head screwdriver. How many possible places were there? The backseats? Could he get them loose and look under them? The odds of a bomb being there were small, of course, but there was a chance. Just how big a chance, Camacho didn't know. Peter Aleksandrovich Chistyakov was not a man to take unnecessary risks. That double-agent discussion yesterday had frightened Camacho, coming as it did from a man who owned an assassin's pistol and had enough gadgets in his attic to blow up half the cops in Washington.

To assess just how likely it was that good ol' Harlan Albright had decided to eliminate a possible threat, one would need to know just what it was that was being threatened. How many other agents was he running? What kind of information were they getting?

Of course, Albright could slip a bomb under the car any night while Camacho snored in his own bed. Risky, but feasible. But perhaps he had planted a bomb with a radio-actuated device as insurance, hoping he wouldn't have to use it, but with it already in place should the need arise. A careful man might do something like that, right?

Apparently, Albright was a careful man. The bomb was in the driver's door, behind the panel, below the window glass when it was rolled completely down. It had been carefully taped in place so it wouldn't rattle.

At a glance it appeared to contain a couple pounds of plastique. One fuse stuck out of the oblong mass. A wire ran from the fuse to a servo and from the servo to a six-volt battery. A little receiver was wired to the servo and four AA batteries were hooked up to power it. A tiny wire attached to the receiver was routed all along the inside of the door. It was a simple, radio-actuated bomb. Simple and effective.

Luis Camacho pulled the fuse from the bomb and used a penknife to cut the wire. The plastique and the rest of it he left in place.

Sweating in spite of the fifty-five-degree weather and fifteen-mile-per-hour wind, he replaced the jack in the trunk. The door panel he put in the back seat.

Had he figured it right? Was this merely insurance? Or had Albright-Chistyakov already decided to push the button?

Standing there beside the car, he looked around slowly, checking. A lot of good that will do you, Luis. Cursing under his breath, he got behind the wheel and started the car.

There was a little hardware store in the shopping center, right between a gourmet food store and a factory fabric outlet. Inside Camacho bought a small flashlight, a coil of insulated wire, and some black electrician's tape.

Out in the parking lot he used the knife and screwdriver to disassemble the flashlight. The bulb he mounted with tape on a hole he carved in the door panel. Fifteen minutes later he had the last screw back in place and the crank for the window reinstalled.

There! Now if Albright pushes the button, instead of a big bang, this flashlight bulb will illuminate and burn continuously until that six-volt ni-cad battery in the door is completely discharged. Assuming he sees the illuminated bulb – and the unsoldered wire connections don't vibrate loose – our saintly hero Luis Camacho, FBI ace spy catcher, will then have time to bend over and kiss his ass goodbye before the bullets from the silenced Ruger .22 send him to a kinder, more gentle world.

What more could any man ask?

He sat behind the wheel staring at the storefronts. After a moment he got out of the car and walked back across the parking lot to the gourmet store, the Bon Vivant. The place smelled of herb and flower leaf sachets. The clerk, a woman in her forties with long, ironed hair, was too engrossed in a book to even nod at him. He wandered through the aisles, looking at cans and jars of stuff imported from all over the world. Nothing from Iowa here. If it's green or purple and packed in a jar from Europe or the Orient, with an outrageous price, you know it's got to be good.

He selected a jar of blue French jam, 'Bilberry' the label said, paid $4.32 plus tax to the refugee from Berkeley, and walked back across the empty, gray parking lot to his car.

The flight surgeon at the China Lake dispensary pronounced Rita fit to fly on Friday afternoon. Jake Grafton spent Saturday in the hangar with Samuel Dodgers and Helmut Fritsche going over the computer program and modifications to Athena that were needed.

As he worked Jake became even more impressed with Dodgers' technological achievement and even more disenchanted with Dodgers the human being. Like every fanatic, Dodgers thought in absolutes which left no room for tolerance or dissent. On technical matters his mind was open, inquiring, incisive, leaping to new insights regardless of where the leap took him or the hoary precedents shattered by the jump. On everything else, however, every aspect of the human condition, Dodgers was bigoted, voluble, and usually wrong. It was as if his maker had increased his scientific talents at the expense of all the others, thus creating a mean little genius who viewed the world as a collection of wicked conspiracies hatched by evil, godless agents of the devil. His opinion of most of his less gifted fellow men was equally bleak. And he *did* believe in the devil. He waxed long and loud on Satan and his works whenever he had a half minute that was not devoted to the task at hand.

How Fritsche tolerated this diatribes Jake couldn't fathom. He found himself increasingly irritated, and retreated to the head or the outside of building when he had had all he could stomach.

'How can you listen to that asshole without choking him?' Jake asked during a brief interlude when nature called Dodgers to the head.

'Whatszat?' Fritsche asked, raising his eyebrows curiously.

'Those endless scatterbrained rantings,' Jake explained patiently. 'In the last hour he's slandered every racial and ethnic group on the planet and denounced everyone in government as thieves and liars and worse. How can you listen to this?'

'Oh. That. I never listen. I'm too busy thinking about Athena. I shut out all that other stuff.'

'Wish I could.'

'Hmmm,' said Fritsche, obviously not paying much attention to Jake either.

'If he doesn't cool it some, I'll probably strangle him by dinner-time. Better learn all you can this afternoon.'

'Uh-huh,' said Fritsche, who was bending and re-examining the cooling unit that kept the computer temperature down. It was certainly a marvel of miniaturization and engineering. 'How this man made this in a backyard workshop just boggles the mind. Look here, the craftsmanship of these welds, the way he polished this forging with acid to minimize heat loss. Look here! See how he built this to maximize cooling and shorten the wire runs. And he didn't even use a computer to design this!'

'Instinct. The troll's a genius,' Jake Grafton admitted reluctantly.

The other shoe fell on Sunday morning, when Jake received a telephone call from Washington. George Ludlow was on the other end of the wire. 'Royce Caplinger's flying out to see you this afternoon. He's bringing Senator Hiram Duquesne with him. Each of them will have an aide along. Get them rooms in the BOQ.'

'Jesus, Mr Secretary. This project's got a security lid tight as a virgin's twat. We don't need any godda – any senator—'

'Duquesne *had* to be told, *Captain*. He's the *chairman* of the Senate Armed Services Committee. I'm not asking your opinion. I'm *informing* you. Got it?'

'Yessir. I got it. Have you also informed Admiral Dunedin?'

'Yes.' The connection broke. Jake cradled the phone. He soon learned there were but two empty rooms in the BOQ, so he sent the two junior members of his party to a motel off base. Those two were Toad and Rita, neither of whom looked very distressed when they tossed their bags into the back of a navy station wagon and drove away.

He wore his only clean white uniform and was standing in the sun in front of the terminal when the T-39 taxied up and Royce Caplinger stepped out. The CO of the base was standing beside Jake. Both officers saluted smartly. They also snapped a salute to Senator Duquesne, who was dressed in slacks and pullover shirt and looked like he had had a couple snorts on the trip. As Duquesne blinked mightily at the bright light, a woman descended the little stair from the plane.

Jake recognized her even as Caplinger said her name. 'Ms DeCrescentis. She's a guest of Senator Duquesne.'

'Consolidated Technologies. She's a vice president, isn't she?'

'Yep,' said Duquesne. 'Good to see you again, Captain,' he said in a tone that implied just the opposite.

'Hitchhiking today, Ms DeCrescentis?'

'She's here to take the tour with us,' Caplinger said.

'Could I talk to you privately for a moment,' Jake said, not a question, and walked away from the group.

Twenty paces or so away Jake turned around. Caplinger was right behind. Jake let him have it: 'Ludlow said you were coming for a briefing with a senator, even though this project is classified to the hilt. But I'm not about to let a vice president of a defense contractor that is going to be bidding on the ATA have a look at Athena or be a party to any conversation on the subject. She has no bona fide need to know at this stage of the game. She doesn't have access. Not only no, but hell no. Sir.'

'My responsibility,' Caplinger said, then clamped his lips into a thin line.

'No, sir. Ludlow didn't mention any defense contractors, and even if he had, I'd have to clear this with Admiral Dunedin. I take orders from him. He'd probably have to talk to CNO. Her presence would violate a couple dozen reg—'

'Call him.'

'Now?'

'Yews, goddamnit, right fucking now. We'll wait in the lounge.' Caplinger stalked for the blue carpet that led inside, followed by Jake Grafton. The base CO led the others inside.

Jake used the phone in the operations officer's office on the second deck.

He reached Dunedin at his office in Crystal City on the first try and outlined the situation. 'Fuck!' said the admiral.

'Yessir.'

'I'll call Ludlow. If that goes sour I'll call CNO.'

'Okay.' Jake gave him the phone number where he could be reached.

'You're really sticking your neck out, Jake.'

'So fire me.'

'I'll call you back.'

Thirty minutes went by. Jake stared out the window at the little passenger jet and watched the men with the gas truck refuel it as heat waves rose off the tarmac. Blue mountains lay on the horizon. Not a single airplane stirring this Sunday morning. After a while he examined the photos and mementós the ops boss had arranged on his walls. He recognized some of the names and faces in the group pictures.

He was sitting behind the desk with his feet propped on it and doodling on a scratch pad when the phone rang. 'Captain Grafton.'

'George Ludlow. Admiral Dunedin tells me there's a problem.'

'Yessir. Caplinger and Duquesne arrived here a while ago with a vice president of Consolidated Technologies tagging along. They want her to see Athena. It's classified special access, above top secret, and she's getting an unfair advantage over the other contractors. I said no.'

'What did Caplinger say?'

'He wasn't happy.'

'Do you understand that Hiram Duquesne is chairman of the Senate Armed Services Committee? We have to have his support if we're going to get a replacement aircraft for the A-6. Without it we're pissing up a rope.'

'I understand that. And I understand that you chose me for this job because I can wear a Medal of Honor on my shirt and because I'm expendable. You're going to have me make a recommendation on which plane to buy based on a short operational evaluation fly-off, and if you like it, I'll have to go over to Congress and defend it. You can disavow me anytime. I understand all of that. I took the job anyway. Now I'm telling you, I can't go over to the Hill and make a recommendation if five or six senators and congressmen are out to cut my balls off with a scalping knife because I let Consolidated in on the ground floor in violation of the law and DOD regulations. I won't be able to hide behind Royce Caplinger over there. That little shit is too goddamn small to hide behind.'

Ludlow chuckled, a dry sound that lasted three or four seconds. 'So get Caplinger. I'll talk to him.'

Jake left the phone lying on the desk and went downstairs to the VIP lounge. 'Mr Secretary, you have a phone call upstairs.'

Duquesne's face was still red and mottled. DeCrescentis looked like she could chew up all of them and spit hamburger. The base CO was nowhere in sight. He had probably attacked in another direction, maybe toward the golf course.

Jake followed the Defense Secretary back up the stairs.

As soon as Caplinger recognized his son-in-law's voice, he shooed Jake from the office. Jake could hear his voice booming through the door. It wasn't just the Advanced Tactical Aircraft he was concerned about – it was the entire defense budget. As he roared at Ludlow: '. . . you and I both know that Grafton will probably recommend the TRX plane. With Athena, it's the obvious choice. But that leaves Duquesne in political trouble at home and we *need* his support. Jesus fucking Christ, George, you people have an aircraft carrier up for funding, three Aegis cruisers, two boomer boats, the air force wants more F-117s and some B-2s, the army wants more tanks. SDI is desperate for money. And Congress is trying to cut the deficit! Don't tell *me* to tell Duquesne to *fuck off*!'

He was silent for a moment, and when he spoke again his voice was low and Grafton couldn't hear the words. He knew Ludlow well enough to know how it was going, however. Let Grafton take the heat, the Secretary of the Navy was probably saying. Make Grafton the villain.

And that was how it went. When Caplinger came out of the office he buttonholed Jake. 'You're going downstairs and explain to the senator that *you* personally must put DeCrescentis back on that plane. You will brief me and the senator this afternoon on Athena and we'll see it in operation tomorrow. But *you* are going to insist that woman goes home *now*, and *you* are going to make Duquesne like it. Got it?'

'Aye aye, sir.'

The senator didn't like it, of course, and DeCrescentis liked it even less, but when Grafton made it clear that the law was going to be obeyed regardless and he was the man insisting, both of them gave ground with what grace they could muster. Duquesne had more of it than the corporate vice president did, perhaps because he knew that even Caesar had to retreat occasionally.

After an hour with Samuel Dodgers in the hangar, it appeared Hiram Duquesne wished he had joined DeCrescentis on the plane.

Dodgers gave Athena no more than half his air and used the rest to blast away at Congress, corporations and the communist-Jew-nigger conspiracy. Finally Jake told him to shut up. It didn't take. Jake told him again in terms and tones that would have stopped a rock band in full screech. Dodgers stormed off, leaving Caplinger and Duquesne gaping foolishly at each other.

Jake Grafton took a deep breath, made his excuses to the two politicians, and left them in the care of a stunned Helmut Fritsche.

In the parking lot, he caught up with Dodgers, trembling with outrage. 'You owe me an apology,' the scientist spluttered, holding himself rigid, his fists clenched.

'No, sir,' Grafton said in a normal voice. 'You owe me one. And you owe apologies to all three of those men in there.'

Dodgers was speechless.

'You have inflicted yourself on everyone within earshot since the day I met you. Now there's not going to be any more of that while I'm around. Do you understand?'

'How *dare* you talk to *me* like this!' When Dodgers got it out, it came out loud.

Jake lowered his voice still more. 'I'm the officer responsible. That's *it* as far as you're concerned. You do your work and keep your personal opinions to yourself, and you and I will get along.'

The scientist spluttered. 'I don't want to get along with you, *you . . .*' He couldn't find the word.

'You'd better reconcile yourself to it if you want this project to go anywhere.'

'. . . sinner. Agent of Satan.'

'You want money for your church, right? *I'm the man.*' With that Jake turned his back on Samuel Dodgers.

The little neighborhood bar was fairly well lit and not very fancy, with cheap furniture and oilcloth table covers. A television high in one corner was tuned to a ball game, one of the NCAA tournament semifinals. Smoke Judy slid into an empty booth and ordered a draft. The waitress flirted for a moment when she brought it, then skipped away.

Smoke sipped his beer and watched the body posture of the men leaning against the bar and sitting on the stools. Some were absorbed in the game, some were talking to a buddy. Most of them were doing a little of both.

This was Smoke Judy's favorite weekend beer spot, only a mile from his place. He knew the bartender casually and they often exchanged pleasantries on slow days. There were a lot worse ways to make a living, Smoke decided, than running a neighborhood bar where the guys could stop in after work or take a break from lawn mowing and garage cleaning. The crowd was nice and the work pleasant, although the money wouldn't be great.

Maybe he would get a place like this when he retired next year. He had dropped a hint to the bartender – who also owned the place – a few weeks back, trying to find out if he had ever thought of selling, but the man didn't get his drift, or pretended he didn't.

He was going to retire next year, with twenty-two years in. By law, as a commander he could stay in the navy until he had completed twenty-six years of service, but he wasn't going to endure the hassle of staff job after staff job with no chance of promotion.

The end of the line had been a tour in command of a training squadron in Texas. Four of those damn kids had crashed, three fatally. Hard to believe. He had worked hard and flown hard and done it by the book, and still those goddamned kids just kept smashing themselves into the ground like suicidal rats. The accident investigators had never said or even implied he was at fault. Yet every crash had felt like God whacking him on the head, compressing another two vertebrae. He had gotten punchy toward the end, a screamer in the cockpit, afraid to certify any student safe for anything. He left that for the lieutenants.

The admiral had been sympathetic, of course, but he had no choice. He said. He had to rate Judy the lowest of all his squadron commanders. After all, four accidents? Nine million dollars' worth of airplanes and three lives? That had been God's final whack. Judy would never be promoted or given another command. All that remained was a decision on when to retire.

He had seen it coming, like something from a Greek tragedy, after that second kid augered in on a night instrument solo. A fucking Canoe U grad no less! Then the third one, that kid punched out of a perfectly good airplane on a solo acro hop after he flew into the only cloud for fifty miles in any direction for ten whole seconds and got the plane into a high-speed spiral and panicked. But he stood there in the CO's office afterwards and said he was sorry! The fourth one, that shithead – Judy had personally given him a down once already – one clear, cloudless day that spastic bastard failed to get the nose up to the horizon on a pullout from a simulated strafing run and pancaked in, smearing himself and his airplane across a half mile of cow pasture. The commanding officer is always responsible. And so it had been, like a judgment from the Doomsday book.

Next year. With twenty-two in. That would give him 55 percent of his base pay, and if one or two of these little deals he was working with hungry contractors came through, he would do all right. Not rich, but okay.

He paid for the beer and left two quarters for a tip. His car was parked just fifty feet down the street, but as he walked toward it, the car in front backed right into it!

'Awww . . .'

The driver got out and walked back to examine the damage.

'Awww, shit!' Smoke Judy exclaimed when he saw the broken grille, the smashed headlight and the bowed-out fender. 'Get your goddamn driver's license yesterday?'

'Jesus, mister, I am sorry! My foot just slipped off the brake. Don't know how it happened.'

'Awww, damn. The second time this year somebody has smacked it when it was parked. Look at this fender, willya? Those Japs must make these things out of recycled beer cans. Look how this thing's sprung? And this headlight socket!'

The other driver turned from examining his own bent fender and smashed taillight and surveyed Judy's damage. He was chunky, fifty or so, flecks of gray in his hair. 'Don't worry. I got insurance. They'll fix it good as new. But honest, I am really sorry.'

'I suppose.' Smoke Judy shook his head.

'Maybe we'd better exchange information.'

'Yeah.' Judy unlocked his car and fished the registration and insurance certificate from the glove box while the other driver rooted in his.

'Maybe we should go inside and do this,' the chunky man suggested. 'Can I buy you a beer?'

'Why not.' Smoke turned and led the way back into the bar he had just come out of. 'My name's Judy. Smoke Judy.'

'Sorry we had to meet like this. I'm Harlan Albright.'

Dodgers kept his opinions to himself at dinner Sunday evening, partially because he was too busy with his food to waste effort on small talk, and partially because he could not have gotten a word in edgewise against Caplinger's verbal flow. There were just the four of them around a table in an empty dining room – empty because the officers' club was usually closed on Sunday evening and Secretary Caplinger declined to go off-base to eat – Dodgers, Caplinger, Senator Duquesne, and Jake Grafton. Caplinger discussed the budget deficit, Third World debt, global pollution, and the illegal drug industry with a depth of knowledge and insight that amazed Jake and even quieted the senator, who was the only person at the table who tried to participate in the conversation. It was obvious that Royce Caplinger not only had read widely but had thought deeply about all these issues. Less obvious but equally impressive was the way he wove the strands of these mega-issues into one whole cloth.

After the steward placed a coffeepot in the center of the table and departed, closing the door behind him, Caplinger eyed Jake speculatively. 'Well, Captain, it seems to me that now would be a good time to sound you out.'

'I'm just an O–6, Mr Secretary. All I see are the elephant's feet.'

Caplinger poured himself a cup of coffee and used a spoon to stir in cream. He surveyed Samuel Dodgers as if seeing him this evening for the first time. 'Good of you to share your Sabbath with us, Doctor. We're looking forward to seeing your handiwork tomorrow.'

Dodgers wiped his mouth and tossed his napkin beside his plate. 'Tomorrow.' He nodded at everyone except Grafton and departed.

When the door had firmly closed behind the inventor, Caplinger remarked, 'Senator, what will happen on the Hill if it becomes common gossip that the father of Athena is a fascist churl?'

'You'll be in trouble. That man couldn't sell water in Death Valley on the Fourth of July.'

'My thought exactly. We'll have to make sure he stays out of sight and sound. Little difficult to do in America, but not impossible.' He grinned. When he did his face twisted. It didn't look like he made the effort very often. 'So how do the elephant's feet look, Captain?'

Jake Grafton reached for the coffeepot. 'I confess, sir, that I'm baffled. Seems to me that these new weapons systems under development, with the sole exception of Athena, are going to be too expensive for the nation ever to afford enough of them to do any good.'

All traces of the smile disappeared from Caplinger's face. 'Go on.'

'As the cost goes up, the quantity goes down. And every "technical breakthrough" seems to double or triple the cost. If anything, Athena will be the exception that proves the rule. Athena should be a fairly cheap system, all things considered, but it'll be the only one.'

'And . . .' prompted the Secretary of Defense.

'Well, if our goal is to maintain forces which deny the Soviets any confidence in a favourable outcome in any probable nuclear war scenario, we seem to have reached the treadmill. We can't maintain forces if we can't afford them.'

'You made a rather large assumption.'

'So what is our goal?'

'The general public regards nuclear war as unwinnable. That's the universal popular wisdom, and like anything that almost everyone believes, it's wrong. The Soviets have invested heavily in hardened bunkers for the top leadership. They've built underground cities for the communist elite. *Somebody* over there thinks they can win! Now their idea of victory and ours are two very different things, but as long as they think they can win, the likelihood of a nuclear war increases. Nuclear war becomes *more likely* to happen.'

Caplinger glanced at the senator, then turned his attention back to Jake. He seemed to be weighing his words. 'Our goal,' he finally said, 'is to prevent nuclear war. To do that we must make them *think* they can't win.'

'So you are saying that any method of denying the Russians confidence in a favorable outcome – however they define favorable – is acceptable?'

Caplinger tugged at his lower lip. His eyes were unfocused. Jake thought he seemed to be turning it over in his mind yet again, examining it for flaws, looking . . . Slowly the chin dipped, then rose again. 'We need . . .' His gaze rose to the ceiling and went slowly around it. 'We need . . . we need forces that can survive the initial strike and respond in a flexible manner, forces that are controllable, programmable, selective. It can't be all or nothing, Captain. It can't be just one exchange of broadsides. If all we have is that one broadside, we just *lost.*'

'Explain,' prompted Senator Duquesne.

'We'll never shoot our broadside. That's the dirty little secret that they know and we know and we will *never* admit. No man elected President of the United States in the nuclear age would order every ICBM fired, every Trident missile launched, every nuclear weapon in our arsenal detonated on the Soviets. Not even if the Soviets make a massive first strike at us. To massively retaliate would mean the end of life on the planet Earth. No rational man would do it.' Caplinger shrugged. 'That's the flaw in Mutual Assured Destruction. No sane man would ever push the button.'

Royce Caplinger sipped his coffee, now cold, and made a face. 'We must deny the communists the ability to *ever* come out of those bunkers. We need the ability to hit pinpoint, mobile targets on a selective, as-needed basis. That's the mission of the F-117 and the B-2. If we can achieve that, there will never be a first strike. There will never be a nuclear war.'

Caplinger pushed his chair back away from the table. 'Life will continue on this planet until pollution ruins the atmosphere and sewage makes the seas a barren, watery desert. Then life on this fragile little pebble orbiting this modest star will come to the end that the Creator must have intended when he made man. Watching our Japanese televisions, listening to our compact laser disks, wearing our designer clothes, we'll all starve.'

He rose abruptly and made for the door. Jake Grafton also got to his feet. When the door closed behind Caplinger, Jake shook the senator's hand and wished him good night.

'He's a great man,' the senator said, trying to read Jake's thoughts.

'Yes.'

'But he is not sanguine. The political give-and-take – it depresses him.'

'Yes,' Jake Grafton said, and nodded his farewell. Suddenly he too needed to be alone.

On Monday morning Jake put Secretary Caplinger, Senator Duquesne, and their aides on a plane to Fallon with Helmut Fritsche and Harold Dodgers. He had decided to stay at China Lake and supervise the good doctor.

Sam Dodgers was in a foul mood, muttering darkly about money and conspiracies. Jake managed to keep his mouth shut. When the Athena device was ready and installed in the A-6, he helped strap Rita Moravia and Toad Tarkington into the cockpit. Toad was whistling some tune Jake didn't recognize.

'No birds today. Okay?'

'Whatever you say, boss.' Toad was in high spirits. Higher than usual. He must be screwing Moravia, Jake decided, trying to catch some hint between them. The pilot was all business.

'Work the long distances today. Start at thirty miles and let Fritsche call you closer when he has the info he wants. Just keep the radar he's using on your left side.'

'Sure, CAG. We understand.' He resumed his whistling as Jake helped him latch his Koch fittings.

'You know who whistles in the navy, Toad?'

'No, sir.'

'Bosun's mates and damn fools.'

Toad grinned. 'I'm in that second category, sir. Enjoy your day with Dr Dodgers.'

Jake punched him on the shoulder and climbed down the boarding ladder.

As the Intruder taxied out, Jake climbed into the yellow ramp truck that the base ops people had loaned him. He had no desire to return to the hangar and watch Dodgers tinker with a computer.

He drove down a taxiway and parked near the duty runway. He got out and sat on the hood. Already the morning was warm, growing hotter by the minute as the sun climbed higher and higher into the deep blue sky. Singing birds were audible here, away from the hustle and bustle of the ramp. A large jackrabbit watched him from the safety of a clump of brush.

He could hear the faint murmur of engines in the distance, and assumed that was Rita and Toad. The minutes passed as he sat there in the sun with the breeze in his hair. He had joined the navy those many years ago to fly, and now he was reduced to sitting beside a runway waiting for younger people to take off. Yet this was the world he knew. The world Royce Caplinger had spoken of last night – nuclear deterrence, global strategy – that was an alien environment, as foreign to him as the concerns of headhunters in the jungles of the Amazon.

He saw the tiny tail of the warplane moving above the swell in the runway. It turned and became a knife edge. Still at least a mile away, the visible tail came to a stop and remained motionless for several minutes.

Caplinger's pessimism troubled him. Sure, the world had its problems, but every generation had faced problems: problems were the stuff life was made of. A man as brilliant as Caplinger, he shouldn't be so . . . so *bitter*.

He heard the engines snarl, yet the tiny white speck of tail did not move. No doubt Rita was standing on the brakes, letting the engines wind up to full power and the temps stabilize before she let it roll. Now . . . now the tail began to move, slowly at first, then faster and faster.

The Intruder came over the swell in the runway accelerating quickly. A river of hot, shimmering air poured down and away behind the bird.

He pressed his fingers in his ears as the sound swelled in volume and intensity. The nose wheel rose a foot or so above the concrete. With a delicate wiggle the bird of prey lifted itself free of the earth and continued toward him in a gentle climb as the wheels retracted into the body of the beast. The howl of the engines grew until it was intolerable.

Now the machine was passing just overhead, roaring a thunderous song that enveloped him with an intensity beyond imagination. He glimpsed the helmeted figure of Rita Moravia in the cockpit with her left hand on the throttles, looking forward, toward the open sky.

He buried his face in his shoulder as the plane swept past and waves of hot jet exhaust and disturbed air cascaded over him.

When the gale subsided the noise was fading too, so he looked again for the Intruder. It was climbing steeply into the blue ocean above, its engine noise now a deep, resonant, subsiding roar.

He got down from the truck hood and seated himself behind the wheel.

The birds in the scrub were still singing and the jackrabbit was still watching suspiciously.

Grinning to himself Jake Grafton started the engine of the pickup and drove away.

18

The day Terry Franklin died was a beautiful day, 'the finest day this year' according to a TV weatherman on one of Washington's local breakfast shows. The sun crept over the edge of the earth into a cloudless sky as a warm, gentle zephyr from the west stirred the new foliage. The weather reader promised a high temperature of seventy-four. Humidity was low. This was the day everyone had dreamed of while they endured the cold, humid winter and the wet, miserable spring. Now, at last, it was here. And on this day sent from heaven Terry Franklin died.

He certainly didn't expect to die today, of course, or any other day in the foreseeable future. For him this was just another day to be endured, another day to live through on his way to the life of gleeful indolence he was earning with his treason.

He awoke when his alarm went off. If he heard the birds singing outside his window he showed no sign. He used his electric razor on his face and gave his teeth a very quick pass with the cordless toothbrush he received for Christmas from his kids, whom he hadn't seen or heard from for three weeks and, truthfully, hoped he wouldn't hear from. If he heard from the kids he would also hear from Lucy, and she would want money. He assumed that she was back in California with her mother, the wicked witch of the west. If so, Lucy didn't need any money: her father the tooth mechanic could pay the grocery bill and buy the kids new shoes.

He put on his uniform while the coffee brewed. The coffee he drank black, just the way he had learned to like it on his first cruise, which he had made to the Med aboard a guided-missile frigate.

He paused automatically on the front stoop and looked around for the morning newspaper, then remembered that there wouldn't be one and pulled the door closed and tried to ensure it was locked. He had canceled the paper a week after Lucy left. He never read it and Lucy only scanned the front page and read the funnies. She always wanted it for the crossword puzzle, which she worked every morning while watching Oprah. Twenty-five cents a day for a fucking crossword puzzle. He had relished that call to the circulation office.

The Datsun started on the first crank. He backed out of the drive and rolled down his window as he drove toward the stop sign at the corner. He fastened his seat belt, punched up the Top 40 station on the stereo and rolled. He only had three miles to go to the Park 'N' Ride, but still he enjoyed the private little world of his car. These few minutes in the car, with the music he liked adjusted to the volume he liked, he cherished as the best part of the day.

He hadn't heard from the Russians since his talk with that Yuri fellow, and he had mixed emotions about that. In a way it was quite pleasant not sweating drop trips or clandestine computer time or the slim chance of being searched leaving the Pentagon. Yet every day that went by without a call was another day he had to waste on his dreary, humdrum job, on this humdrum bus ride, on this humdrum colorless suburb. Every day he spent here was a day he wasn't *there*, lying in the sun, fucking the beach bunnies, drinking Cuba Libres and enjoying life.

His fantasy was *there*, waiting, and he was firmly and hopelessly planted *here*. What made the waiting so frustrating was the money he already had in the bank. That he had committed a variety of serious crimes to obtain the money troubled him not a whit. He had never given it a moment's thought. In fact, he felt exactly like all the other people who see a large sum of unearned money come their way – lottery winners, traffic accident victims, legatees, swindlers, personal injury lawyers and so on – the money was his by divine right. Somehow, some way, the rulers of the universe had decreed that he deserved the good things and good times that big money will buy because he wasn't like all those schmucks who flog it eight to five. He was different. Special. The money *made* him special. The unique and wonderful emissions given off by large quantities of money made him tingle.

Perhaps because he felt so good about himself, Terry Franklin took the time this morning, the last morning of his life, to smile at the bus driver as he boarded and to nod at a woman he recognized as he went down the aisle.

As the bus threaded its way through rush hour traffic, he watched the scenery roll by without seeing a thing. He rode lost in reverie, already enjoying his fantasy.

The morning was spent cleaning and repairing a computer keyboard on which a secretary had spilled coffee. She also had a taste for doughnuts and potato chips, he noted with a sneer as he worked with a toothbrush to rid the mechanism of soggy crumbs. He could just picture her: still young but overweight, always dieting or talking to her fellow airheads about dieting as she munches yet another doughnut and swills yet another cup of coffee loaded with sugar. She must have had at least three lumps in this stuff she spilled. Lucy's clone.

He almost decided to tell the chief to trash this keyboard, then changed his mind. The chief had cut him a lot of slack these past three weeks: he should try to prove to the chief that he could still carry his share of the load. He put more WD-40 on the keyboard and reattacked the sticky mess with the toothbrush.

Terry Franklin's last meal was a hot dog with mustard, catsup and relish, a small order of fries and a medium Sprite. He ate it with another sailor from his section in the main cafeteria. They discussed the new secretary in the division office – was she really a blonde, would she or wouldn't she, was it worth trying to find out, and so on.

The afternoon went quickly. The chief sent him with one other man to work on a balky tape drive in the enlisted manpower section, and the afternoon flew by. They had found the problem but had not yet repaired it when quitting time rolled around.

So he carried his tools back to the shop and exchanged guffaws with his shipmates, then walked to the bus stop outside and found a place in the usual line.

Had he known what was coming, one wonders what he would have done differently. No doubt a larger man who knew the end was nigh might have lived his last day pretty much as he had all his others, but Terry Franklin was not a big man in any sense of the word, and he had come to realize that in the last three weeks, since the fiasco of the bungled drop. He knew he was a coward, a weakling without backbone or character, but, he thought, only he knew, and so what? Superman lives in Metropolis and Batman lives in Gotham. The rest of us just try to get along.

Yet, given who he was and what he was, should he have known he might be approaching the end of his string? The signs were certainly there if he had thought it through dispassionately, with some detachment. He didn't, of course.

He used most of his last hour on earth to stare out of the bus window and think about the feel of the sun on his back and sand between his bare toes, and to daydream of a hard young female body under him mingling her sweat with his. She didn't have a face, this girl in his dreams, but she had firm brown tits and a flat stomach and long brown legs with taut thighs.

When he turned the key in the car ignition the radio boomed to life as the engine caught. '. . . like a bat outta *hell*, ba-dupe, ba-dupey . . .'

He rolled the window down and fastened his seat belt and patted the steering wheel with his hands in time to the music.

The car in front of him turned right after four blocks, and the one behind turned left a block later. Terry Franklin paid no attention. He drove out onto an old boulevard now lined with small strip businesses and proceeded about a mile before he swung the car onto a side street. He liked to drive through these quiet residential streets because they had so little traffic and he thought he made better time, though he had never clocked it.

At the first stop sign he came to, a little girl was crossing the street pushing a miniature baby carriage containing her doll. That she had chosen to cross the street at just this time and place probably gave Terry Franklin another minute of life.

One minute was just about the time it took for him to wait until the little girl was clear, depress the accelerator and cruise down to the next cross street. He glanced both ways, no traffic, and took his foot off the brake to roll on through. '. . . like a bat outta *hell* . . .'

That's when the bomb underneath the vehicle, directly under the driver's seat, exploded.

Terry Franklin felt a concussive impact as his knees came up to smash into his chin, but that was the only sensation that he was conscious of in the thousandth of a second he had left to live. The floor of the car came apart and the seat springs and fabric and padding were all forced explosively upward. His skull popped like a ripe melon when this rising, accelerating column on which he sat smashed into the roof of the car and bowed it upward. The windows exploded outward as the fireball continued to expand, showering the area with glass. Fragments of springs and plastic and fabric were forced deep into Terry Franklin's now lifeless corpse, which began to sear from the intense heat.

The car, still in gear and torn almost in two, moved like a wounded crab diagonally across the intersection and lightly impacted a parked vehicle. Then the engine quit from fuel starvation. The severed fuel line dumped its liquid into the molten mess in the center of the vehicle and the smoldering wreckage became an inferno. In ten seconds the fire was so hot the fuel tank exploded.

Coming around the corner four blocks away, FBI agent Clarence Brown saw the rising fireball from the exploding gas tank. He grabbed the dash-mounted mike. 'Holy shit, his car blew up. It blew up! The subject's car blew up!'

The voice on the telephone had a hollow, metallic sound, like it was coming through a long pipe. 'Little development I thought you would want to know about, Luis. Probably nothing important. Terry Franklin just went out with a bang. His car blew up.'

'Anybody else hurt, Dreyfus?'

'Not another soul. We had an agent following him, keeping tabs per your instructions, and he saw the gas tank go poof. The lab guys are on the way. The agent at the scene, Brown, says it looks like a bomb.'

'What time, exactly?'

'Sixteen fifty-seven.'

Camacho looked at his watch. Seventeen minutes ago. 'Get a search warrant for his house.'

'Already doing the affidavit.'

'Send a man over to the house to watch it. And you'd better alert somebody out in California that they'll have to do a next-of-kin notification when we get a positive ID from the medical examiner.'

'The ID's gonna take a while. The corpse is still in the car, roasted like a Christmas turkey.'

'Have the people in California quietly check to see that his wife and in-laws are physically there.'

'You *knew* this was going to happen, didn't you?'

'I just follow orders, asshole,' Camacho snarled. 'Why don't you do the same?' He slammed the phone onto its cradle.

Two minutes later it rang again. 'Yes.'

'Dreyfus again. Already we're getting calls from TV stations. There's a chopper overhead now. It's real visual with the smoke column and all. Evening news for sure, distraught housewives and sobbing kids, the whole bit. What's the official hot screaming poop?'

'We're investigating, cooperating with the local police. Off the record, hint at drugs.'

'Roger hint.'

'Is local law on the scene?'

'Yeah. Couple cruisers and a big red fire truck.'

'Don't let 'em touch anything.'

'Roger Wilco, over and out.'

Luis Camacho pulled into his driveway at five minutes after midnight and checked the jury-rigged bulb in the hole in the door panel. Still off. Amen.

The night air retained some of the heat from the day. The FBI agent stood in his shirt sleeves beside his car and breathed the deep, rich scent of the earth.

The neighborhood was quiet. He could hear crickets.

All the lights were off in Harlan Albright's house. Only a gleam of the hall light was visible through the window of his own door. Camacho picked up the package on his front seat and locked his car, then used his key on the front door. He shot the bolt behind him.

There was a note by the phone. Albright had called.

Camacho poured himself a bourbon and added three ice cubes from the tray in the freeze. He opened the kitchen door and stood there sipping his drink and looking at the shadows in the backyard. The dog whined and wagged its tail.

Taking his time, Camacho strolled the length of the yard and seated himself in the tire swing hanging from the old oak. He absently petted the dog and made comforting noises as he sipped the liquor and let the alcohol take effect.

It would be interesting to see how many of those servos were still in Albright's mad bomber kit. And the batteries and fuses.

You sure had to take your hat off to Peter Aleksandrovish, a.k.a. good ol' Harlan. Terry Franklin's sudden end had been a nice tidy job. No loose ends. No secondary casualties that might fester into an eventual murder indictment that would make a spy swap impossible, should the worst happen and he get arrested by the FBI. Terry Franklin had been very neatly and permanently silenced. Scratch one asset-turned-debit. Clean up that balance sheet. Wipe off the red ink, and, *voilà!* we have a profitable enterprise, as anyone can plainly see.

Good ol' Harlan's house was as dark as a tomb. The big maples in front shielded it from the streetlights and the oaks and beeches here in back performed a similar service with that little alley light. So the house was just a looming black shape.

Camacho thought about the stairs up to the bedroom, pictured himself once again slipping up there, careful as a mouse, looking for booby traps, prying open the trapdoor to the attic – he shivered as he thought about it. Good ol' Harlan would probably rig some more unpleasant surprises, like plastique that goes boom when the someone coming into a room steps in the wrong place, or forgets to turn the light on and off three times in three seconds. Good ol' Harlan would be just the man for a little rig like that.

Wonder if Harlan's found the blank film in the camera? Had Camacho been careful enough with the operation? Had he tripped a camera he didn't find? If so, that bulb in the door would come on very soon.

His fatigue hit him all at once. It was all he could do to walk back to the house, lock the door, and ascend the stairs. He stripped off his clothes and fell into bed.

'I don't want to ever get married,' Rita said.

'Me neither,' Toad Tarkington agreed fervently. 'Half the marriages fail, kids in single-parent households, everybody broke – who needs it?' It was a pretty Saturday morning and they were on their way to a restaurant for breakfast, with Toad at the wheel.

'People should be free to have a relationship without being *bound*,' she said.

'When two people break up they shouldn't have to hire lawyers to fight over the dog.'

'Marriage is an obsolete institution.'

'It's doomed,' Toad pronounced, sounding a good bit like Samuel Dodgers denouncing sin, which was probably unintentional. But to prove he wasn't a bigot he added, 'Of course, my parents are happily married. Thirty-five years this July. It's a lot tougher nowadays, though. My sister was only married three years, one kid – the divorce was real messy. My dad had to help her with the legal fees.'

'Did she get custody?' Rita asked.

Toad told her about it. Both of them shook their heads sadly. Truly, modern marriage was a misery.

'Two people who love each other don't need all that,' Rita sniffed. 'I want a man who loves me and wants to be with me, not because he had to, but because he wants to.'

'It's the has-to part that turns me off,' Toad explained. 'You know, I think it's terrific that you and I think so much alike.'

'Well, we're very similar. We both have middle-class backgrounds, good educations, we're naval officers, we fly. You're only a year older than I am. It's no wonder.'

'I guess.'

Toad wheeled her Mazda into the restaurant parking lot and found a space. He opened the door for Rita and she smiled her thanks, a gorgeous little grin that he returned. She rested her fingers lightly on his arm as they walked across the macadam. He held the door for her and she preceded him through. He had never felt better in his life – so alive, so *into* all of it. They loved each other without strings. And the best part, he told himself, was that they could be so forthright, so frank with each other. Wouldn't the world be a better place if everyone's relationships were so open and honest?

They were married that afternoon in Oakland, Maryland.

The glider wheeled and soared six feet above the dune, the sun flashing on its wings. Jake Grafton sat in the sand with the wind at his back. David and Amy sat beside him, hugging their knees. He manipulated the levers on the radio control box without taking his eyes from the free-flying bird.

'Remember to keep the nose up in the turns,' David reminded him as the glider reached the tuft of sea grass a hundred feet north along the dune where Jake had been turning. He had the technique now, he hoped. He hadn't crashed in ten minutes. He thought he could stay aloft as long as the wind remained steady.

Back the glider came, crossing silently above their heads. 'Totally awesome,' David murmured.

'Awesome' seemed to be *the* word this year in the sixth grade. What had it been when Jake had been twelve years old? He tried to remember and drew a blank.

Amy Carol stretched out in the sand on her stomach, her chin on her forearms. Her figure was still a collection of straight lines. Callie said she would start to fill out soon. David matched her position, his big feet incongruous beside Amy's petite ones. No doubt his growth would also spurt in the next year or so; he already had the feet of a good-sized man, though the rest of him had a lot further to go.

'Your dad's gonna be a pretty good pilot,' David told her.

'He isn't my dad. He's Jake.'

'He's gonna be good,' David insisted.

'That's not so tough to do,' she said, sitting up.

'Oh no? Why don't you try it.'

'Can I, Jake?'

'Yeah. Come over here and watch me for a minute.' He explained the controls and demonstrated how they worked. After two passes up and down the beach with Amy watching intently, he turned the box over to her. She overbanked and nosed the plane in on the very next turn.

David smacked his hands together in exasperation. ' "Nothing to it." Girls!' He pronounced the last word as if it were spelled 'gurls.'

The left wing had torn and a broken spar. The three aviators collected their gear and trudged for the house. 'Don't worry, Cap'n,' the boy said with a disgusted glance at Amy. 'I can fix it good as new.'

'I'm sure you can,' Jake told him, grinning.

'Girls don't know nothin' about flyin'.'

'Don't bet on it, Dave. There's a woman pilot working for me, and she's real darn good.'

Amy squared her shoulders, threw her head back and marched proudly before them, at long last assuming her rightful place among the exalted sisters.

'You're *what*?' exclaimed Harriet. Rita's horrified roommate. It was Sunday evening and they were in the bedroom. Out in the living room Toad had settled in to watch a Knicks game.

Rita held up her left hand and waggled it proudly. 'Here's the ring. I'm married.'

'My *God*! How long have you known him? A month? How long were you engaged?'

'A little over an hour. We were driving to Deep Creek Lake for the weekend and around Frostburg we decided to get married. So Toad drove off the next exit and into Oakland. We found the most delightful minister. He knew a lady in the county clerk's office – she was a member of his church – and she drove downtown and opened up the courthouse just to issue us a license. Wasn't that sweet?'

Harriet lowered herself onto the bed and covered her face with her hands.

'The minister's wife gave me some flowers from her garden. Some paper-white narcissus and tulips and multicolored butterfly daffodils, all accented by bridal wreath in a beautiful bouquet. I cradled them in my right arm when we said our vows.' She sighed, remembering. 'I have the best ones down in the car. I thought you and I could press them.'

'A *one-hour* engagement! Rita, Rita, Rita, you poor poor child. What do you know about this man? What?' Harriet opened the bedroom door a crack and looked with loathing at the groom sagged out in front of the TV with a beer in his hand. No wonder they called him Toad.

'My God, Rita, how could you?' she hissed. 'What do you *know* about him? He could be AC-DC or a closet pervert, or even a Republican? What *will* your mother say?' Harriet spun like a lioness ready to pounce. 'Have you told her yet?'

'Wellll—'

'I *knew* it! When are you going to tell her? After all, Rita, she is your *mother*. She once told me that after buying a thousand wedding presents for all of your friends, she was so looking forward to inviting every one of them to your wedding. You're her *only* daughter!' Harriet threw herself backward onto her bed and bounced once. 'How *could* you!' she moaned.

'It was easy,' Rita Moravia Tarkington said lightly. She dearly enjoyed Harriet's tantrums. 'It was so romantic. Just like I always wanted it to be. He's so handsome, so . . . We're going to be so very happy all our lives. He's . . . he's . . .' She sighed again and smiled.

'One thing's for sure,' Harriet said acidly, 'he's all yours now.'

On Monday morning Lieutenant Toad Tarkington and Lieutenant Rita Moravia entered Jake's office together, side by side. They stopped in front of his desk and waited at parade rest until he looked up from the report he was working on.

'Yeah.'

'We have some news for you, Captain,' Rita said.

Jake carefully surveyed their expectant faces. He scowled. 'Why have I got the feeling I'm not going to enjoy this?'

Rita and Toad both grinned broadly and glanced at each other. 'We're married,' Toad said.

Jake Grafton clapped his hands over his ears. 'I didn't hear that. Whatever it was, I didn't hear it. And I don't want to hear it.' He stood and leaned slightly toward them, his voice low: 'I have enough problems around here without people sniping at me about the romantic status of my test crew. What you two do on your own time is your business. But until we get the prototype testing completed and I submit the report, you two puppies are going to walk the line for me. All business. No kissy-facey or kootchy-koo or groping or any of that other goofy hooey. No glorious announcements. Strictly business.'

'Yes, sir,' Rita said.

'I warned you about this, Tarkington. No romances, I said. And look at you! It's disgusting, that's what it is.'

'Yessir,' Toad said.

'I can't let you out of my sight for a minute.'

'I just couldn't control myself, sir.'

'You two are going to be very happy someday. But not today or tomorrow. Right now you're serious, committed, dedicated professionals. Pretend. Try real hard.'

'Yessir,' they both said.

'Congratulations. Get back to work.'

'Aye aye, sir.' They came to attention like plebes at the Naval Academy, did a smart about-face and marched out. Rita leading. Jake Grafton bit his lip and resumed work on his report.

19

'Somebody explain how this airplane is going to be used.' Jake Grafton looked from face to face. He had his staff gathered around while he stood at the office blackboard with marker in hand. 'Who wants the floor?'

'Captain, there's been two or three studies on that written during the last three or four years,' said Smoke Judy.

'I know. Somebody dug them out for me and I read them. I want to hear your ideas.'

'Seems to me,' said Toad Tarkington, 'that the first thing it has to do is land and take off from a carrier. Must be carrier-compatible.'

Jake wrote that down. Obvious, but often overlooked. Any navy attack plane must have a tailhook, nose tow, strong keel, routinely tolerate a six-hundred-foot-per-minute sink rate collision with the deck on landing, fit into allotted deck space and accept electrical power and inertial alignment information from the ship's systems. It had to be capable of being launched from existing catapults and arrested with existing machinery. In addition, it would have to be able to fly down a 3.5-degree glide slope carrying enough power to make a wave-off feasible, and with a low enough nose attitude so that the pilot could see the carrier's optical landing system. Amazingly enough, in the late 1960s the navy was almost forced to buy a plane that wasn't carrier-compatible – the TFX, which the air force called the F-111 and immediately began using as an all-weather tactical bomber with a system identical to the A-6's.

'Corrosion-resistant,' Tarkington added as Jake made furious notes. 'Has to be able to withstand long exposure to salty environment without a lot of expensive maintenance.'

'Maintenance,' muttered Les Richards. 'Got to have easy main-tainability designed in. Easy access to engines, black boxes and so forth, without a lot of special equipment.'

The requirements came thick and fast now, as quick as Jake could write. Range, speed, payload and a lot of other parameters. After ten minutes he had filled up most of the board and his staff paused for air.

'How're we going to use this thing?' he asked again. 'What I'm getting at is this: these stealth designs appear to be optimized for high-altitude ingress over heavily defended territory. Presumably at night. Are all our missions going to be at night?'

'We can't afford to give away the day,' someone said.

'What's that mean in the way of aircraft capability? Daytime means enemy fighters and optically aimed surface-to-air missiles. They'll see our plane. Do we have to be able to engage the fighters and dodge the missiles? How much G capability do we need? Sustained turning ability? Dash speed? Climb speed? Will we go in low in the daytime? If so, how about ability to withstand bird strikes and turbulence?'

The staff spent an hour on these questions. There was no consensus, nor did Jake expect one. No plane in the world could do everything, but any design must meet most of the major requirements for its intended employment. Shortcomings due to design trade-offs would have to be overcome or endured.

'Weapons.' The ideal plane would carry and deliver every weapon in the US and NATO inventory, and a lot of them. Was that a realistic goal with the stealth designs under consideration?

After four hours of brainstorming, the staff reexamined the proposed test program for the prototypes. In the five flights of each airplane that SECDEF had budgeted money and time for, they needed to acquire as much information as possible to answer real questions. Company test pilots had already flown both planes. These five flights of each plane by the navy would have to produce data that verified or refuted the manufacturers' claims. More importantly, the flights would determine which plane was best suited to fill the navy's mission requirements, or which could be made so by cost-effect modifications.

'We really need more than five flights per plane, Captain,' Les Richards said.

'Five flights are enough for what we want to find out, if we do it right. This little evolution is just a new car test drive with us doing the driving. Five flights are enough for what we want to find out if we do it right, which is precisely what we're going to do. Henry and Ludlow and Caplinger want a fast recommendation and a fast decision.'

'Don't they always? Then the paper pushers in SECDEF's office will spend a couple of years mulling it over, sending it from in basket to in basket.'

'Ours is not to reason why . . .'

The pace accelerated relentlessly in the office. Working days lasted twelve hours now, and Jake ran everyone out and turned off the lights himself at 7 P.M. He insisted that no one work on Saturday and Sunday, believing that the break would make people more productive during the week.

The weeks slid by, one by one.

Jake spent less than half his time in the office and the rest in an endless series of meetings with people from everywhere in government: SECNAV, SECDEF, OPNAV, NAVAIR, NAVSEA, the FAA, the EPA, the air force, the marines, and a host of others. Most of the time he attended these conferences with Admiral Dunedin or Commander Rob Knight.

The meetings went on and on, the paper piled higher and higher. The same subjects kept cropping up in different meetings, where they had to be rehashed again and again. Government by committee is government by consensus, and key players from every office high and low had to be listened to and pacified.

Jake felt like the sorcerer's apprentice as he tried to pin people down and arrive at final resolutions of issues. Meetings bred more meetings: the final item on every agenda was to set the times and places for follow-up meetings.

He discovered to his horror that no one person had a complete grasp of the tens of thousands of regulations and directives that covered every aspect of procurement. At every meeting, it seemed, someone had another requirement that needed to be at least given lip service. He finally found where all this stuff was stored, a library that at last measurement contained over 1,152 linear feet of statutes, regulations, directives, and case law concerning defense procurement. Jake Grafton looked at this collection in awe and disgust, and never visited the place again.

The silent army of faceless gnomes who spent their working lives writing, interpreting, clarifying, and applying these millions of paragraphs of 'thou shalts' and 'thou shalt nots' took on flesh and substance. They came in all sexes, shapes, and colors, each with his or her own coffee cup and a tiny circle of responsibility, which, no matter how small, of course overlapped with that of three or four others.

The key players were all known to Jake's staff: 'Watch out for the Arachnid,' someone would say before a meeting. Or 'Beware of the Sewer Rat. He'll be there this morning.' 'The Gatekeeper will grill you on this.' The staff named these key players in the procurement process because of their resemblance to the characters in the game Dungeons and Dragons. When he returned from battle Jake had to contribute to the office lore by recounting the latest exploits of the evil ones.

'It's a miracle that the navy even owns a rowboat,' Grafton remarked one day to Admiral Dunedin.

'True, but the Russians are more screwed up than we are. They manage every single sector of their economy like this, not just the military. You can't even buy toilet paper in a store over there.'

'The bureaucrat factor is a multiplier,' Jake decided. 'The more people there are to do paperwork, the more paper there is to be worked and the slower everything goes, until finally the wheels stop dead and only the paper moves.'

'The crat factor: it's a law of physics,' Dunedin agreed.

Jake took a briefcase full of unclassified material home every night, and after Callie and Amy were in bed he stayed awake until midnight scribbling notes, answering queries, and reading replies and reports prepared by his staff.

He spent countless hours on the budget, trying to justify every dollar he needed for the next fiscal year. He had to make assumptions about where the ATA program would be then, and then he had to justify the assumptions. Athena was still buried deep, outside the normal budgetary process. Still he would need staff and travel money and all the rest of it. He involved everyone he could lay hands on and cajoled Admiral Dunedin into finding him two more officers and another yeoman. He didn't have desks for them. They had to share.

But things were being accomplished. A Request for Proposal (RFP) on the Athena project was drafted, chopped by everyone up and down the line, committeed and lawyered and redrafted twice and finally approved. Numbered copies went by courier to a half dozen major defense con-tractors who were believed to have the technical facilities and staff to handle development of a small superconducting computer for aviation use. The office staff had to be informed, and this had been done by the admiral.

Inevitably the number of people who knew about Athena and what it could do was expanding exponentially. Access was still strictly need-to-know, but the system ensured that a great many people had the need, or could claim they did, citing chapter and verse of some regulation or directive no one else had ever read or even seen.

Callie was understanding about the time demands Jake faced. She had spent enough years as a navy wife to know how the service worked. Amy was less so. She and Callie were still going round and round, and she found Jake a pleasant change. He made rules and he enforced them, and he tucked her into bed every night. She wanted more of his time and he had previous little to give. The weekends became their special time together.

'Why do you spend so much time at work, Jake?'

'It's my job. I have to.'

'I'm not going to have a job like yours. I'm going to get a job that gives me plenty of time to spend with my little girl.'

'Are you my little girl?'

'No. I'm Amy. I'm not anybody's little girl. But I'm going to have a little girl of my own someday.'

'Do you ever think much about those somedays? What they'll be like?'

'Sure. I'll have lots of money and lots of time and a very nice little girl to buy stuff for and spend time with.'

'How are you going to get lots of money if you don't spend much time earning it?'

'I'm going to inherit it. From you and Callie.'

'Guess we'd better work hard then.'

One day in early May, Special Agent Lloyd Dreyfus made an appointment to see Luis Camacho's boss, P. R. Bigelow, without telling Camacho. He had thought about it for a week before he made the appointment with the secretary, and then he had two more days to wait. Jumping the chain of command was as grievous a sin in the FBI as it was in the military, yet he had decided to do it anyway and to hell with what Camacho or anyone else thought. As the day and hour approached, however, the enormity of his transgression increased with each passing hour. Surely Bigelow would understand. Even if he didn't, he must realize Dreyfus had a right and duty to voice his concerns.

Dreyfus rehearsed his speech carefully. It wasn't technically a speech: perhaps a better description would be 'short, panicky monologue.' He had to justify himself as soon as he opened his mouth, get Bigelow's sympathetic attention before he had a chance to start quoting the regulations, before he lost his cool and went ballistic. Was Bigelow a ballistic kind of guy? Dreyfus couldn't recall Camacho ever saying.

He tried to recall everything he had ever heard about P. R. Bigelow, and that wasn't much. Strange, when you stopped to think about it. Camacho *never* mentioned his superior officer, never said, 'Bigelow wants this,' or 'Bigelow is pleased' or 'Bigelow says blah-blah.' Come to think of it, Camacho *never* talked about *anyone*. If the Director himself told Luis Camacho to do thus and so, Camacho would just tell Dreyfus, 'Do this' or 'Do that.' He sometimes said what he hoped to find or achieve, but he *never* even hinted who had told him to cause something to happen, or why it was to happen. He *never* expressed a personal opinion. Curious as hell. Camacho was one weird duck, beyond a reasonable doubt.

Sitting in Bigelow's reception area with the secretary checking him out surreptitiously as she did her nails, Dreyfus went over his list one more time. He wanted everything right on the top of his tongue. It would be worse than disastrous to think of the clincher on the way to the surgery in the dungeon. Once again he assured himself he was doing the right thing. *The* right thing. Doing the *right* thing. He fondled his pipe in his pocket as if it were a set of worry beads.

The ten-button phone on the nail polisher's desk buzzed to attract its owner's attention. After listening a moment and grunting into the instrument in a pleasant, respectful way, she hung up and said to Dreyfus, 'He'll see you now.' Her painted eyebrows arched knowingly, condescendingly.

P. R. Bigelow was eating a large jelly doughnut at his desk. He mumbled his greeting with his mouth full, a glob of red goo in the corner of his mouth.

Dreyfus took a chair and launched into his prepared remarks. 'I've asked for this time, sir, to ensure you know what is going on with the Minotaur investigation. The answer is almost nothing. For months now we've been spinning our wheels, begging computer time to try and crack the Minotaur's letters to the Soviet ambassador, following a few people hither and yon all over Washington, monitoring some phone lines, wasting an army of manpower and bushels of money, and we are going essentially nowhere. I thought you should know that.'

Bigelow wiped the jam from his lips with a napkin, sipped coffee from a white mug labeled 'World's Best Dad', and took another bite of doughnut.

His attitude rattled Dreyfus, who got out his pipe and rubbed the bowl carefully. 'Our best lead was a navy enlisted computer technician in the Pentagon, a guy we thought was tapping the computer for some of this stuff. Name of Terry Franklin. Yet Camacho never let us pick the guy up. So we sat and watched him do his little thing, and we were diligently following him, right on his tail, in March when his car blew up with him in it.'

Bigelow finished the doughnut and used a moist finger to capture and convey the last few crumbs to his mouth. Then he dabbed his lips a final time and used two napkins to scrub the powered sugar and flecks of jelly from his oak desk. He put his trash in the wastebasket and, sighing contentedly, rearranged his bottom in his chair.

'And . . . ?' said P. R. Bigelow.

'A hit man wiped a walk-in witness to a drop with Franklin. Camacho talked to her a couple times, but she got eliminated before we could get her to look at any photos. A professional hit. Two twenty-two caliber slugs in the skull. We've got the autopsy and lab reports and we've talked to neighbors up and down the street. We've got nothing at all. We're absolutely dry on this one.'

'Anything else?'

'Yes,' said Lloyd Dreyfus with an edge in his voice. He was beginning to lose his temper and didn't care if it showed a little. 'One of the staff officers in the navy's ATA project – a Commander Judy – is trying to peddle classified inside info to interested defense contractors. We got interested in this officer when the project manager was murdered over in West Virginia one Friday evening in early February. That murder is unsolved – no one is doing anything on it – and Camacho doesn't appear to be doing any follow-up on Judy's contracts. He hasn't even turned the file over to the fraud investigators or NIS. We know some of the people Judy's talked to and . . .' Dreyfus threw up his hands in frustration.

'Finished yet?'

'Yes, I think that about covers it.'

'So you asked for this appointment on the off chance that Camacho has been lying to me about the activities of his office, purposely bungling the search for this mole, wasting millions of dollars and thousands of man-hours on wild-goose chases.' Dreyfus opened his mouth to interrupt, but Bigelow held up a hand. 'I grant that you can probably phrase it more tactfully. You notice I did not suggest that you came up here to tattle and gain some personal advantage. You are a better man than that.' He sighed heavily, almost a belch. 'Of course there is another possibility. Perhaps you just wanted to see if I was so stupid as to be satisfied with the progress of the investigation to date.'

'I—' The upraised palm stopped him again.

'I *am* satisfied. Camacho has kept me fully informed of the activities of his subordinates, of which you are one, by the way. His lines of inquiry have been initiated with my knowledge and, where necessary, my approval. He has discussed his concerns with me and I have informed him of mine. He has followed orders to the letter. I am completely satisfied with his performance. He is one of the most talented senior officers in the bureau.'

Dreyfus just stared.

'Before you go back to work, do you wish for me to arrange a meeting for you with the Director?' Bigelow managed to make his face look interested and mildly amused at the same time. Yes, Lloyd, you miserable, disloyal, alarmist peckerhead, you jumped from the top of the cliff, but you seem to have had the luck to strike a bush a few feet below the edge, which arrested your downward progress. Do you wish my help in completing your suicidal plunge?

Dreyfus shook his head no.

'I suggest that you not mention this little conversation to any of your colleagues.'

'Yessir.'

'I don't want to see you in this office ever again, Dreyfus, unless you have your supervisor with you, or unless I send for you.'

'Yessir.'

'Let's both get back to work.' P. R. Bigelow nodded toward the closed office door and Dreyfus took the hint.

By mid-May the dance of the dwarves at the Pentagon had reached a critical frenzy. A thousand details were beginning to come together for a trip into the desert with the prototypes in June. The airplanes had been moved weeks earlier to the Tonopah Test Range in Nevada, the same secret field where the air force had tested its stealth prototypes. Also known as Area 58, or Groom Lake, the field lay about a hundred miles northwest of Las Vegas on a huge government reservation with excellent physical security. Here the contractors' field teams readied the planes in separate hangars and installed telemetry devices.

Toad and Rita would leave for Nevada two weeks before Jake and the rest of the staff. They had intensive sessions planned with company test pilots and engineers to learn everything they could about the planes and how they flew. The Saturday night before they left, Jake and Callie had them to dinner at the house in Rehoboth Beach.

'How do you like being married?' Callie asked Rita in the kitchen.

'I should have had a brother,' Rita confided. 'Men are such sloppy creatures. They don't think like we do.'

On the screened-in porch, Jake and Toad sipped on bourbon and Amy slurped a Coke. 'So how's married life, Toad?'

'Oh, so-so, I guess. Isn't exactly like I thought it would be, but nothing ever is. Ol' Rita can think up stuff for me to do faster than I can do it, and we only live in an apartment. If we had a town house or something with a basement and a lawn, she'd have worked me to death by now.'

Amy Carol thought this remark deliriously funny and giggled hugely.

'Why don't you go visit with Mom and Rita?'

She stood regally and tossed her hair. 'I do believe I will join the ladies, but she isn't my mom. I wish you'd stop calling her that.' She flounced off toward the kitchen.

'The day she' – Jake pointed after the departing youngster – 'gets married, I am going to get down on my knees and give thanks.'

'That bad, huh?'

'She's about driven Callie over the edge. That poor woman had no idea what she was getting into. No matter how much love she pours on Amy, the kid still does exactly as she chooses. She intentionally disobeys and cuts up just to get her goat. And Callie never gets mad, never pops off, never gives her anything but love. She's gonna go nuts.'

'Maybe she should get angry.'

'That's what I think. And Callie insists she doesn't want my help or advice.'

'They're all alike,' Toad said, now vastly experienced.

Amy was back in five minutes, hopping from foot to foot, so excited she bounced. 'Can we fly the glider now, so I can show Rita? She's a *pilot*.'

Toad gasped. 'She is?'

'You're teasing me,' Amy said, stamping her foot.

'The wind's wrong,' Jake pointed out. 'It isn't coming in from the sea. This evening it's a land breeze.'

'David said we might be able to fly the glider above the house in a land breeze. He said the wind just goes right up and over our house.'

'I never thought of that. Well, run down the street and see if he can spend a half hour consulting with us.' As Amy scampered off, Jake told

Toad, 'There's an aviation expert right down the street who is kind enough to offer advice from time to time.'

The aviation expert was apparently unoccupied at the moment. He showed up wearing a monster-truck T-shirt bearing the legend 'Eat Street'. His shoelaces were untied, his cowlicks fully aroused, and his grin as impish as ever. He listened carefully to Jake's plan. 'Sounds to me like it might work, Cap'n,' he said with a sidelong glance at Toad. 'Might ding up your plane a little, though.'

'I'll risk it if you'll fix the damage.'

'Callie! Rita!' Amy called excitedly. 'We're going to fly.'

Jake readied the plane for flight in the front yard under David's supervision. Eight rubber bands were stretched to hold the six-foot wing to the fuselage. Batteries were tested and inserted, the cover closed, switch on, controls waggled to the full extent of their travel using the radio control box: Amy checked each item after Jake performed it while David briefed Toad on proper launch procedure. In five minutes they were ready for the sky.

Toad climbed the ladder from the garage and scaled the sloping roof until he sat perched on the ridgepole with the plane in hand. 'Pretty good breeze up here,' he informed the crowd below, which now included Callie and Rita.

'Don't you jump off there, Darius Green,' Rita called as Toad sucked on a finger and held it aloft.

'As you can plainly see, dear wife, I'm not wearing my wings tonight,' Tarkington replied lightly. He flapped his elbows experimentally. ' "I'll astonish the nation and all creation, by flyin' over the celebration! I'll dance on the chimneys, I'll stand on the steeple, I'll flop up to winders and scare all the people," ' quoteth he, striking a precarious pose, or trying to, up there on the ridge of the roof with an airplane grasped carefully in his right hand.

'Maybe I'd better alert the emergency room at the hospital,' Callie said, laughing.

'Oh, Callie,' Amy groaned. 'He's not going to jump! Really!'

Toad finished his recitation with a flourish: ' "And I'll say to the gawpin' fools below, What world's this here that I've come near?" '

Jake Grafton handed the radio control box to David. 'You're up first. Whenever you're ready.'

The youngster centered the control levers and shouted to Toad, 'Let 'er go!'

With the gentlest of tosses, Toad laid the glider into the rising air currents. The boy immediately banked left and raised the nose until the aircraft was barely moving in relation to the ground. As it reached the end of the house, he reversed the controls and flew it back the other way. The ship soared upward on the rising current of air. It floated above Toad's head, back and forth along the peak of the roof, banking gently to maintain position and rising and falling as the air currents dictated.

'All right!' Toad shouted and began to clap. On the ground the spectators all did likewise.

'There's just enough wind,' Jake told David, grinning broadly. 'Now, by god, that's *flying!*'

'Awesome,' David agreed, his pixie grin spreading uncontrollably.

After a few minutes, David handed the control box to Jake. He overbanked and the plane lost altitude precipitously, threatening to strike Toad straddling the roof's ridge. 'Keep your nose up,' David advised hurriedly. 'You can fly slower than that.' As the glider responded, he continued. 'That's it! She's got plenty of camber in those wings and good washout. She'll fly real, real slow, just riding those updrafts. That's it! Let 'er fly. Just sorta urge 'er along.'

He was right. The plane soared like a living thing, banking and diving and climbing, seeking the rising air and responding willingly. The evening sun flashed on the wings and fuselage and made the little craft brightly lustrous against the darkening blue of the sky above.

'Let Rita try it,' Amy urged.

'Don't you want to?'

'No. Let Rita.'

'Come over here, Rita Moravia.' The pilot did as she was bid. She watched the captain manipulate the controls as he explained what each was. 'The thing you gotta watch is that the controls work backwards as you look at the plane head-on. Turn around and fly it by looking over your shoulder. Then left will be left and right will be right.'

Rita obediently faced away from the house and looked back over her shoulder. Toad waved. Jake handed her the radio control box. As David and Amy tried to offer simultaneous advice, Rita clumsily swung the plane back and forth and worked the nose hesitantly. She overcontrolled as David groaned, 'Not too much, no no no.'

But the wind was dying. She got the nose too high trying to maintain altitude: the plane stalled and the nose fell through. David scrambled, but Rita stalled it again and the left wing and nose dug into the sandy lawn before the running boy could reach it. The rubber bands let loose and the wing popped free of the fuselage, minimizing the damage.

'Nasty,' David declared.

'My dinner!' Callie exclaimed, and charged for the door.

'You did great for a first solo,' Amy assured Rita. The pilot pulled the girl to her and gave her a mighty hug and kiss on the cheek. She got a big hug in return.

'She ain't banged up too bad, Cap'n,' David called.

Up on the roof Toad was laughing. He blew Rita a kiss.

*

After dinner Callie shooed Jake and Toad off to the screened-in porch while she cleaned up the dishes. Rita and Amy helped.

'So what did your parents think of Toad when they met him, or have they yet?' Callie asked Rita.

'We went to visit them two weekends ago. Mother invited a few of their closest friends over to meet the newlyweds. Then she cornered Toad, and making sure I was in earshot, she asked him, "Now that you're married, when is Rita going to give up flying?"' Rita laughed ruefully, remembering. 'How well do you know Toad?' she asked Callie.

'Not very well. I met him for the first time last year in the Mediterranean.'

'Well, he looked at Mother with that slightly baffled, Lord of the Turnip Truck expression of his, and said, "Why would she do that? Flying is what she does." I could have kissed him right there in front of everyone.' Rita chuckled again.

'Doesn't your mom want you to fly?' Amy piped, her chin resting on a hand, her eyes fixed on her new heroine.

'My mother is one of these new moderns who have elevated the elimination of risk to a religious status. She serves only food certified safe for laboratory rats. She writes weekly letters to congressmen urging a national fifty-five-mile-per-hour speed limit, helmets for motorcyclists, gun control – she has never been on a motorcycle in her life and to the best of my knowledge has never even seen a real firearm. Her latest cause is a ban on mountain climbing since she read an article about how many people per year fall off cliffs or die of hypothermia. This from a woman who regards a walk across a large parking lot as a survival trek.'

'I'm not afraid of things,' Amy assured Rita.

'It's not fear that motivates Mother. She thinks of government as Super-Mom, and who better to advise the politicians than the superest mom of them all?'

'Flying is risky, inherently dangerous. I can understand your mother's concern,' Callie said as she rinsed a pot. 'Flying is something I've had to live with. It's a part of Jake and his life, a big part. But I've had very mixed emotions about his being grounded.' As she dried the pot she turned to Rita. 'You or Toad may be killed or crippled for life in an accident. After it happens, if it happens, it won't matter whose fault it is or how good you are in a cockpit. I know. I've seen it too many times.'

'*Life* is risky,' Rita replied. 'Life isn't some bland puree with all the caffeine and cholesterol removed. It doesn't just go on for ever and ever without end, amen. For every living thing there is a beginning, a middle, and an end. And life is chance. Chance is the means whereby God rules the universe.'

The flier thought a moment, then continued, choosing her words carefully. 'I have the courage to *try* to live with my fate, whatever it may be.'

'Do you have enough?' Amy asked, dead serious.

'I don't know,' said Rita. She smiled at the youngster. 'I hope so. I haven't needed much courage so far. I'm healthy, reasonably intelligent, and I've been lucky. But still, I gather courage where I find it and save it for the storms to come.'

20

Through the years Jake Grafton had become a connoisseur of air force bases. Visiting one was like driving through Newport or Beverly Hills. With manicured lawns, trimmed trees, well-kept substantial buildings and nifty painted signs, air force bases made him feel like a poor farm boy visiting the estate of a rich uncle. In contrast, the money the admirals wheedled from a parsimonious Congress went into ships and airplanes. The dedication of a new cinder-block enlisted quarters at some cramped navy base in the industrial district of a major port city was such a rare event that it would draw a half dozen admirals and maybe the CNO.

The Tonopah facility, however, didn't look like any air force base Jake had ever seen. It looked like some shacky, jerry-built temporary facility the navy had stuck out in the middle of nowhere during World War II and had only now decided to improve. Perhaps this base was just too new. Bulldozers and earthmovers sat scattered around on large, open wounds of raw earth. No trees or grass yet, though two trenchers appeared to be excavating for a sprinkler system. When the wind blew, great clouds of dust embedded with tumbleweeds swept across the flat, featureless desert and through the stark frames of buildings under construction, and the wind blew most of the time.

Security was as tight as Jake had ever seen it in the military. Air policemen in natty uniforms with white dickeys at their throats manned the gates and patrolled chain link fences topped with barbed wire while they fought to keep their spiffy blue berets in place against the wind. The fences were woven with metal strips to form opaque barriers. Signs every few yards forbade stopping or photography. You needed a pass to enter any area, and prominent signs vibrating in the wind advised you of that fact.

The place reeked with that peculiar aroma of government intrigue: *Important, stupendous things are happening here. You don't want to know! We who do also know that you couldn't handle it. Trust us.* In other words, the overall effect was precisely the same gray ambience of don't-bother-us superiority that oozes from large post offices and the mausoleums that house the departments of motor vehicles, social services, and similar enterprises throughout the land.

Even the sergeant at the desk of the Visiting Officers' Quarters wanted to see Jake Grafton's security documents. He made cryptic notations in a battered green logbook and passed them back without comment as he frowned at Helmut Fritsche's facial hair. After all, didn't Lenin wear a beard?

As he escorted Jake and Fritsche down the hall towards their rooms, Toad Tarkington said, 'This place is really dead, Captain. The nearest whorehouse is fifty miles away.'

Fritsche groaned.

'Tonopah makes China Lake look like Paris after dark,' Tarkington told the physicist with relish. 'This is as far as you can get away from civilization without starting out the other side.' He lowered his voice. 'There's spies everywhere. The place is crawling with 'em. Watch your mouth. Remember, loose lips sink—'

'Loose lips sink lieutenants,' Jake Grafton rumbled.

'Yessir, them too,' Toad chirped.

That evening Jake inspected the Consolidated Technologies airplane. Under the bright lights of the cavernous hangar, it was being tended by a small army of engineers and technicians who were busy checking every system, every wire, every screw and bolt and rivet. Adele DeCrescentis watched a man fill in a checklist. Each item was carefully marked when completed. Rita Moravia walked back and forth around the aircraft, looking, probing, asking more questions of the company test pilot who stood beside her. Toad Tarkington was in the aft cockpit, going over the radar and computer one more time as a nearby yellow cart supplied electrical power and cooling air.

At 9 P.M. they gathered in a large ready room on the second deck of the hangar's office pod. The room was devoid of furnishings except for one portable blackboard and thirty or so folding chairs.

The meeting lasted until midnight. Every aspect of tomorrow's flight was gone over in detail. Consolidated's people approved the test profile and agreed on the performance envelope Rita would have to stay within on the first flight. The route of the flight was laid out on a large map which was posted on one wall and briefed by Commander Les Richards. He pointed out the places where ground cameras would be posted. Real-time telemetry from the airplane would be supervised by Commander Dalton Harris. Smoke Judy would fly the chase plane, an F-14 borrowed from NAS Miramar, and a carefully briefed RIO would film the Consolidated prototype in flight from the F-14's backseat.

After the meeting broke up, Jake Grafton spent another thirty minutes with his staff, then went down to the hangar deck. Only a dozen or so technicians were still on the job.

The overhead floods made little gleaming pinpoints where they reflected on the black surface of the Consolidated stealth plane. As he walked, the tiny pinpoints moved along the complex curved surfaces in an unpredictable way. With his face only a foot or so from the skin of the plane, he studied it. The dark material seemed to have an infinite depth, or perhaps it was only his imagination.

The outer skin, he knew, was made of a composite that was virtually transparent to radar waves. Underneath, carrying the stresses, was a honeycomb radar-absorbent structure made of synthetic material formed into small hexagonal chambers. The honeycomb was bonded to inner skins of graphite and other strong composites. He touched the airplane's skin. Smooth and cool.

From this angle the curves and smooth junctions of the skin became art. No wonder the Consolidated people were so proud of their creation.

But how would it hold up aboard a ship? Could it stand the rough handling and salt air and the poundings of cat shots and traps? Thousands of them? Would it be easy to fly, within the capabilities of the average pilot – not just a superbly trained, gifted professional like Rita Moravia, but the average bright lad from Moline or Miami with only three hundred hours of flight time who would have to learn to use this Art Deco sculpture as a weapon?

Five flights. He needed a lot of answers in just a short time. Rita and Toad would have to get them.

He walked away musing about Rita's lack of test experience and wondering if he had made a mistake giving her this ride.

Tomorrow. He would know then.

But the following day problems with the telemetry equipment kept the prototype firmly on the ground. The engineers were still laboring in the sun on a concrete mat where the temperature exceeded a hundred and ten when Jake glanced at his watch and ordered the plane towed back into the hangar. The Soviet satellite would soon be overhead. The hangar's interior was shady and cool. And since the air force owned it, it was air-conditioned.

The next morning, Wednesday, the F-14 took off with a cracking roar that seemed to split the desert apart. Smoke Judy pulled the power off when he was safely airborne and made a dirty turn to the downwind leg. He came drifting down toward the earth paralleling the runway and stabilized at one hundred feet just as Rita began to roll.

The prototype was noticeably quieter, so quiet that its noise was barely audible above the howl of the Tomcat's engines as Smoke used his throttles to hang the heavy fighter just above the runway as the stealth bird accelerated. When Rita lifted off and retracted her gear, Smoke added power to stay with her and the sound of the stealth plane was entirely muffled.

'Damn quiet,' George Wilson remarked. 'About like a Boeing 767, maybe less.' The low noise level was a direct by-product of burying the exhaust nozzles and tailpipes in the fuselage, shielded from the underside, to reduce the plane's infrared signature.

In the cockpit Rita concentrated on maintaining the selected test profile and getting the feel of the controls. She had spent hours sitting in the cockpit the last few weeks memorizing the position of every switch, knob, and gauge, learning which buttons she needed to press to place information where she wanted it on the MFDs, and so even now, minutes into her first flight in the plane, it was familiar.

In the backseat Toad was busy with the system. He checked the inertial; it seemed okay. With ring laser gyros, it had not a single moving part and was more accurate than any conventional inertial using electro-mechanical gyros. It would need to be. To keep the stealth plane hidden, it would be necessary to fly with the radar off most of the time, and the ring laser inertial would have to keep a very accurate running tally of the plane's position.

The computer was also functioning perfectly. He had encoded the waypoint and checkpoint information onto optical-electronic – optronic – cards on the ground and loaded them into the computer after engine start. The two-million-dollar pocket calculator, he called it. It hummed right along, belching readouts of airspeed, groundspeed, altitude, wind direction and velocity, true course, magnetic course, drift angle, time to go to checkpoint, etc., over fifteen readouts simultaneously. He had this information on the right-hand MFD, roughly the location on the panel where it would be in an A-6E.

Some of the displays were not yet hooked up since development work was not yet complete. Consequently the three-dimensional information presentations on the pilot's holographic Heads-Up Display could not be tested.

The phased-array radar in the nose received Toad's attention next. The antenna was flat and fixed, it did not rotate or move. Actually it was made up of several hundred miniature antennas, individually varying their pulse frequencies to steer or focus the main beam. A conventional radar dish would have acted as a reflector to send the enemy's radar signals back to him. Toad tuned the radar to optimize the presentation and dictated his switch and dial positions on the ICS, which, like the radar presentation, was being recorded on tape for later study.

The next major pieces of gear he turned on and integrated into the system were, for him, the most interesting. Two new infrared search and tracking systems that were able to distinguish major targets as far away as a hundred miles, depending upon the aircraft's altitude and the relative heat value of the target. One could be used for searching for enemy fighters while the other was used to navigate or locate a target on the ground. The range of these sensors was a tenfold improvement over the relatively primitive IR gear in the A-6E. Since a stealthy attack plane would fly most of its mission with its radar off, these new gizmos would literally be the eyes of the bombardier-navigator.

Toad took a second glance to his left. Smoke had the F-14 about a hundred feet away in perfect formation. The backseater's helmet was hidden behind this camera, which was pointed this way. That videotape would show every twitch of the flight control surfaces. Toad turned back to the task at hand.

He felt the plane yawing as Rita experimented with the controls and advanced and retarded each throttle independently. She was talking on the radio, telling Smoke what she was doing, reading the engine perform-ance data to the people on the ground so it could be coordinated with the telemetry data, giving her impressions of the feel of the plane.

'Seems responsive and sensitive in all axes,' she said. 'Engine response is good, automatic systems functioning as advertised. Got a hundred feet a minute more climb than I expected. Fuel flow fifty pounds per hour high. Oil pressure in the green, exhaust gas temps are a hundred high. I like it. A nice plane.'

She leveled the plane at Flight Level 240 at .72 Mach, 420 knots true. Toad checked the range and depression angles of the radar and IR sensors, and ran checks on the inertial and computer.

Thirty minutes later, after hitting three navigation checkpoints, Rita dropped the nose two degrees and began a power-on descent back toward Tonopah. She leveled at 5,000 feet at 550 knots and raced toward the field. Smoke Judy was a hundred feet away on the right side, immobile in relation to the stealth bird.

In the backseat Toad ran an attack. His target was the hangar that had housed the plane. The system gave Rita steering and time and distance to go to a laser-guided bomb release. Everything functioned as advertised. No weapon was released because the plane carried none, but a tone sounded on the radio and was captured on all the tapes, and it ceased abruptly at the weapons-release point, interrupted by the electronic pulse to the empty bomb rack cunningly faired into the airplane's belly.

After three attacks at different altitudes, Rita slowed the plane with speed brakes and dropped the gear and flaps. She entered the landing pattern.

Two fleet Landing Signal Officers that Jake had borrowed from Miramar – they had flown the F-14 to Tonopah – stood on the end of the runway in a portable radio-equipped trailer that a truck had delivered. They had spent the last three days painting the outline of a carrier deck on the air force's main runway and rigging a portable Optical Landing System – OLS – which the truck had also delivered. Now they watched Rita make simulated carrier approaches flying the ball, the 'meatball,' on the OLS. Jake Grafton stood beside them.

'Paddles has you,' the senior man told Rita as she passed the ninety-degree position. One other LSO wrote while the first watched the approach with the radiotelephone transceiver held to his ear and dictated his comments.

'On speed, little lined up left, little too much power . . .' The plane swept past and its wheels whacked into the runway, right on the line that marked the target touchdown point. The nose wheel smacked down and the engines roared and Rita flew it off the runway. The LSO shouted to his writer, 'Fair pass.'

Jake Grafton stared at the plane in the pattern. It just looks weird, he told himself. The lifting fuselage and invisible intakes and the canards and the black color, it didn't look like a real airplane. Then he knew. It looked like a *model*. It looked like one of those plastic planes he had glued together and held at arm's length and marveled at.

'You're carrying too much power in the groove,' the LSO told Rita after the second pass.

'I'm just floating down with the power way back,' she replied. 'And we're hearing a little rumble. Maybe incipient compressor stall. I'll use the boards next time around.'

The Consolidated engineers had thought the speed brakes would be unnecessary in the pattern. Yet with the intakes on top of the plane, behind the cockpit, maybe the air reaching them was too turbulent when the plane was all cocked up in the landing configuration. Jake Grafton began to chew on his lower lip. The air force doesn't land planes like this, he reminded himself. They wouldn't have tried these maneuvers when they flew the plane.

With the boards out the plane approached at a slightly higher nose attitude, its engine noise louder. The speed brakes allowed – required – Rita to come in with a higher power setting. 'This feels better,' she commented. 'But I'm still hearing that rumble. Little more pronounced now, if anything.'

'Looks better,' the junior LSO told Jake. 'I think the boards give her more control.'

'Six-hundred-feet-a-minute sink rate,' Rita reported. Once again the main mounts smacked in with puffs of fried rubber from each tire as it rotated up to speed. The main oleos compressed and the nose slapped down, then she was adding power and pulling the nose right back up into the sky.

After the sixth pass she pulled the throttles back to idle and the plane stayed on the deck. The engine noise was really subdued.

'Quiet bugger, ain't it?' one LSO said, grinning. 'We'll have to call this one the Burglar. First we had the Intruder, now the Burglar.'

'I think it ought to be called the Penetrator,' the senior man said. ' "Yeah, baby, I'm a Penetrator pilot." '. He cackled at his own wit.

When Rita cleared the runway, Smoke Judy called the LSOs. 'Since you guys are all set up, how about giving me a couple?'

'If you got the gas, you get the pass,' the LSO radioed.

The debriefing took until 9 P.M. with an hour break for dinner. The telemetry data and the videotapes were played and studied. Rita and Toad were each carefully debriefed as a dozen engineers gathered around and the naval officers hovered in the background.

The plane was then thoroughly inspected by a team of structural engineers. The simulated carrier landings had placed stresses on the structure that the air force had never anticipated when it developed the specifications for this prototype. No one expected visible damage, and there was none, but if the plane were to be put into production, strengthening would inevitably be needed. Just where and how much was the concern, and the telemetry data would pinpoint these locations.

And some minor equipment problems had surfaced. The Consolidated technicians would work all night to fix those as navy maintenance specialists watched and took notes. The intake rumble in the landing pattern was the most serious problem, and Adele DeCrescentis discussed it on the phone with the people at the Consolidated factory in Burbank for over an hour.

All in all, it had been a fine day. Rita and Toad were still going a mile a minute when Jake loaded them all into the vans at 9 P.M. for the two-mile trip to the VOQ, the Visiting Officers' Quarters.

Jake and his department heads gathered in his room that evening. Someone produced a cold six-pack of beer and they each took a bottle.

'The day after tomorrow. It'll all be decided then,' Les Richards, the A-6 bombardier, told the assembled group. 'Day after tomorrow we pull some Gs, and I don't think we can live with a five-G limitation. I don't think the navy needs an attack plane for a low-level mission that is that G-limited. It'll get bounced around too much down low, and if a fighter ever spots it or someone pops an IR or optically guided missile, this thing is dead meat.'

'What if they beef it up?' someone asked. 'Strengthen the spars and so on?'

'Cut performance too much. More weight. We don't have a whole lot of performance to begin with. And what if the compressors stall?'

'Could they enlarge the automatic flaps on the intakes that raise up and scoop more air in when the engines need it?'

'It'd be turbulent air. We learned today that those two engines like a diet of smooth, undisturbed air.'

'Oh no we didn't.'

So it went. Jake ran them all out at midnight and collapsed into bed.

The following day was spent in further intensive review of the videotapes and telemetry data, and planning the second flight.

Glitches developed. Under the usual ground rules for op-eval fly-offs, the manufacturer cleared various areas of the flight performance envelope for the navy test pilots to explore. Rita wanted to examine the slow-flight characteristics of the aircraft before she proceeded to high-angle-of-attack/high-G maneuvers. Consolidated's Chief engineer did not want her below 200 knots clean and 120 knots dirty.

When Jake joined the conversation, Rita was saying, 'I flew the plane at 124 knots yesterday, three o'clock angle of attack. Now, is that 1.3 times the stall speed or isn't it? How are we supposed to verify the stall speed if we can't stall it?'

Jake merely stood and listened.

'We've told you what the stall speed is,' the engineer explained patiently, 'at every weight and every altitude and every configuration. Those speeds were established by *experimental* test pilots.'

'Well, I'm an engineering test pilot – all navy test pilots are trained to that standard – but I can't see how we can do a proper operational evaluation of your airplane if we don't explore the left side of the envelope.'

The civilian appealed to Jake. 'Listen, Captain. This is the only prototype we have. If she drills a deep hole with it, we have big problems. It'll be goddamn hard to sell an airplane when all we have is the wreckage.'

'What makes you think,' Jake asked, 'that she can't safely recover from a stall?'

'I didn't say that. You're putting words into my mouth.'

'Get DeCrescentis over here.' The chief engineer went off to find her.

'We have to stall that plane, Captain,' Rita told him. 'If those rumbles in the landing pattern yesterday were incipient compressor stalls, we'll get some real ones if we get her slowed down enough. I think that's what Consolidated doesn't want us into.'

Adele DeCrescentis backed her engineer. Jake heard her out, then said, 'I don't think you people really want to sell this plane to the navy.'

The vice president set her jaw. 'We sure as hell want it in one piece to sell to somebody.'

'Well, I'll tell you this. We're going to fly that plane the way *I* want it flown or we'll stop this show right now. The navy isn't spending ten million bucks for a fly-off if all we can do is cruise the damn thing down the interstate at fifty-five. We're trying to find out if that plane can be used to fight with, Ms DeCrescentis, not profile around the Paris Air Show.'

She opened her mouth, but Jake didn't give her a chance. 'I mean it! We'll fly it my way or we won't fly it. Your choice.'

She looked about her, opened her mouth, then closed it again Finally she said, 'I'll have to think about it for a bit.' She wheeled and made a beeline for the Consolidated offices and the phones, the chief engineer trailing after her.

'Maybe you had better make a phone call too,' Rita suggested.

'Nope.' He looked at Rita and grinned. 'Captains have to obey orders, of course, but George Ludlow and Royce Caplinger shoved me out in front on this one. They want me to make a recommendation and take the heat so they sort of have to let me do it my way.' He shrugged. 'Generally speaking, doing it your way is not very good for your career, but I've been to the mat once too often anyway. That's *why* I got this job. Ludlow's a pretty good SECNAV. He understands the navy and the people in it. He wouldn't send a guy with a shot at flag over to Capitol Hill to get his balls cut off, not if he had any other choice.'

Rita looked dubious.

'Are you right about this, Miss Moravia?'

'Yes, sir. I am.'

'I think so too. So that's the way we'll do it. As long as I'm in charge.'

When Adele DeCrescentis returned, she agreed with Jake. Apparently the president of the company could also read tea leaves.

'Go find that Consolidated test pilot,' Jake told Rita when they were alone. 'Take him over to the club and buy him a drink. Find out everything he knows about stalling this invisible airplane, off the record.'

'Aye aye, sir,' Rita said, and marched off.

Cumulus clouds and rain squalls moving through the area from the west delayed the second flight another day, but when she finally got the plane to altitude, Rita attacked the performance envelope with vigor while Smoke Judy in the F-14 hung like glue on first one wing, then the other.

Stalls were first.

They were almost last. With the nose at ten degrees above the horizon and the power at 70 percent, she let the plane coast into the first one, but didn't get there because the pitty-pat thumping began in the intakes and increased in intensity to a drumming rat-a-tat-tat played by a drunk. The EGT rose dramatically and RPMs dropped on both engines. She could feel vibrations reaching her through the seat and throttles and rudder pedals.

Compressor stalls! Well, that mousy little test pilot for Consolidated hadn't been lying. She pushed the nose over, which incidentally worsened the thumping from behind the cockpit, and held it there while her speed increased and the noise finally abated, all the while reading the numbers from the engine instruments over the radio.

With the engines back to normal, she had another thought. If a pilot got slow and lost power in the landing pattern, on final, this thing could pancake into the ground short of the runway. Aboard ship the technical phrase for that turn of events was 'ramp strike.'

She smoothly pulled the nose to twenty degrees above the horizon and as her speed dropped began feeding in power until she had the throttles forward against the stops. The airspeed continued to decay. This was 'the back side of the power curve,' that flight regime where drag increased so dramatically as the airspeed bled off that the engines lacked sufficient power to accelerate the plane.

The onset of compressor stall was instantaneous and dramatic, a violent hammering from the intakes behind the cockpit caused the whole plane to quiver. Before she could recover, the plane stalled. It broke crisply and fell straight forward until the nose was fifteen degrees below the horizon, then the canard authority returned. Still the engine compressors were stalled, with EGT going to the red lines and RPM dropping below 85 percent.

Rita smartly retarded the throttles to keep the engines from over-temping. The pounding continued.

Throttles to idle. EGT above red line.

She chopped the throttles to cutoff, securing the flow of fuel to the engines.

The pounding ceased. The cockpit was very quiet.

Toad remarked later that all he could hear as Rita worked to restart the engines 'was God laughing.'

This time as Rita approached touchdown, she flared the plane and pulled the throttles aft. Sure enough, the pounding of turbulent air in the intakes began just before the main wheels kissed the runway. She held the nose off and watched the EGT tapes twitch as the plane decelerated. When she was losing stabilator authority, she lowered the nose to the runway and smoothly applied the brakes.

'Another day, another dollar,' Toad told her on the ICS.

Removing the engines from the airplane, inspecting them, inspecting the intakes and reinstalling the engines took three days, mainly because Jake Grafton demanded that a factory rep look at the compressor and turbine blades with a borescope, which had to be flown in.

Consolidated's chief engineer was livid. He was so furious that he didn't trust himself to speak, and turned away when anyone in uniform approached him. Adele DeCrescentis was equally outraged, but she hid it better. She listened to Rita and reviewed the telemetry and videotapes and grunted when Jake Grafton spoke to her.

The navy personnel left the Consolidated employees to their misery.

'We're wasting our time flying that bird again,' Les Richards and George Wilson told Jake. 'It's unsat and there is no possible fix that would cure the problem. The whole design sucks.'

'How do you know they can't fix it?'

'Well, look at it. At high angles of attack the intakes are blanked off by the cockpit and the shape of the fuselage, that aerodynamic shape. How *could* they fix it?'

'Goddamn, I'm not an aeronautical engineer! How the hell would I know?'

'Well, I am,' Wilson said, 'and they *can't*.'

'Never say never. Regardless, we're going to fly this bird five times. I don't want anyone to say that we didn't give Consolidated a fair chance.'

'We're wasting our time and the navy's money.'

'What's a few million?' Jake asked rhetorically. The real objective was to get money for an acceptable airplane from Congress. So he was philosophical.

Toad Tarkington slipped down the hall to his wife's room when he thought everyone else was in bed. They had been running a low-profile romance since they arrived in Tonopah.

'Tell me again,' Toad said, 'just what that Consolidated test pilot said about stalls when you pumped him. What's his name?'

'Stu Vinich. He just said they had had some compressor-stall problems at high angles of attack.'

'Nothing else? Nothing about how serious they were?'

'He couldn't, Toad. The company was downplaying the whole subject. People who talk out of school draw unemployment checks.'

'We were damned lucky that thing didn't spin. And we were lucky the engines relit.'

'Luck is part of the job,' Rita told him.

'Yeah. If we had punched and our chutes hadn't opened, Vinich would have just stood at our graves and shook his head.'

'He said enough. I knew what to expect.'

Toad turned out the light and snuggled down beside her.

Jake Grafton was poking and prodding the plane, trying to stay out of the technicians' way, when he noticed Adele DeCrescentis watching him. He walked over. 'You know,' he said, 'this thing reminds me of a twelve-ton Swiss watch.'

'A quartz watch,' the vice president said.

'Yeah. Anyway, I was wondering. Just how hard would it be for your folks to put a twenty-millimeter cannon on this plane?'

'A gun?' She appeared dumbfounded, as if the idea had never occurred to her.

'Uh-huh. A gun. A little Gatling, snuggled inside the fuselage with five hundred rounds or so. What do you think?'

'When we were designing this plane, not a single, solitary air force officer ever even breathed the word "gun." '

'Somehow that doesn't surprise me. But would it be feasible?'

'With some fairly major design changes, which will cost a good deal of money, I suppose it might be. It would take a full-blown engineering study to determine that for sure. But why? A machine like this? You want it down in the weeds dueling with antiaircraft guns? Shooting at tanks?'

'When tanks are the threat, Ms DeCrescentis, we won't be able to shoot million-dollar missiles at all of 'em. The Warsaw Pact has over fifty *thousand* tanks. A nice little twenty-millimeter with armor-piercing shells would be just the right prescription.'

Senator Hiram Duquesne was not philosophical when he telephoned George Ludlow. 'You keeping up on what's going on out in Tonopah?' he thundered.

'Well, I get reports from Vice Admiral Dunedin. Captain Grafton reports to him several times a day.'

'I want to know why the officer in charge out there insisted on performing maneuvers that the manufacturer did not feel the plane was ready for, or safe to perform.'

'He's doing an op-eval. He knows what he's doing.'

'Oh does he? He's got a twenty-five-year-old woman with no previous test experience flying that plane, *a four-hundred-million-dollar prototype!*'

'She's not twenty-five. She's twenty-seven.'

'Have you seen her?'

'What do you mean?'

'I mean what the hell is going on over there, George? A lot of people have a lot riding on the outcome of this fly-off. And you got Bo Derek's little sister out there flying the planes! Is she the best test pilot you people have? My God, we've been spending millions for that Test Pilot School in Pax River – is she the best you've got?'

'If you have any information that implies she's incompetent, I'd like to hear it.'

'I hear she intentionally shut down both engines while she was up in the sky. Now Consolidated is spending a ton checking them for damage. I'll bet Chuck Yeager never shut down both engines on a test flight at the same time!'

'I wouldn't know. You'd have to ask the air force.'

'Don't get cute. I'm serious. Dead serious. Don't let that hero fly-boy Grafton and his bimbo test pilot screw this up, George. I'm warning you.'

'Thanks.'

'By the way, the authorization for reactors for that new carrier you guys want to start? My committee voted this morning to delete it. Maybe next year, huh?'

The senator hung up before Ludlow could respond.

Jake Grafton changed Rita's test profile for the last three flights. He had her avoid all high-angle-of-attack maneuvers, though he did let her ease forward the advertised five-G limit, where the airflow to the engines once again became turbulent and began to rumble.

The three flights took another ten days. When they were finished the navy crowd spent three more days correlating their data and talking to Consolidated engineers, then packed up for the return to Washington. It would be three weeks before they came back to fly the TRX prototype.

On their last night in Tonopah the navy contingent threw a party in the officers' club for a very subdued group from Consolidated. Adele DeCrescentis didn't attend, which was perhaps just as well. Along toward midnight, after Toad Tarkington had enjoyed the entire salubrious effect of alcohol and had begun the downhill slide, he spotted Stu Vinich in a corner putting the moves on some woman from Consolidated's avionics division. He strolled over, tapped Vinich on the shoulder, and as the test pilot turned, flattened him with one roundhouse punch.

21

Jake Grafton was amazed when he saw Amy at the passenger terminal at Andrews Air Force Base. In the three weeks he had been gone the child had visibly grown. 'Hi, Jake,' she warbled, and ran to throw her arms around him.

'Miss me?' he asked.

'Not as much as Callie did,' was the sophisticated reply.

As he and Callie waited for the luggage to be off-loaded from the airplane, Callie visited with the other officers who had ridden the DC-9 from Tonopah. Jake made a fuss over Amy and teased her a little, causing her cheeks to redden. But she stayed right there beside him, saying hello to everyone and smiling broadly when spoken to.

'So how'd it go?' Callie asked him as they walked to the car.

Jake shrugged. Everything was classified. 'Okay, I guess. And you?'

'I stopped going to Dr Arnold. Last Friday was my last appointment.'

Jake set his luggage on the pavement and gave her a tight squeeze as Amy skipped on ahead, her black hair bobbing with every bound. Callie looked happier than Jake had seen her in a long, long time.

The next morning, a Tuesday, he spent closeted with Admiral Dunedin going over the test results. They watched videotapes and looked at numbers, and began writing down tentative conclusions.

'So how did Moravia do?' the admiral asked at one point.

'Fine. Good stick, keeps her wits about her, knows more aeronautical engineering than I even knew existed.'

'So you want to keep her for the TRX bird?'

'No reason not to.'

The admiral told him about the conversation Senator Duquesne had had with George Ludlow. 'The secretary didn't tell me to fire her, or keep her, or anything else,' Dunedin concluded. 'He just relayed the conversation.'

'Let me see if I understand this, Admiral. Duquesne's committee deleted the appropriation for reactors for the new carrier from this year's budget. Is he implying that if we get another test pilot he'll put it back in?'

'No. I think the message is that unless the navy buys the Consolidated plane, he's not going to be – he'll be less enthusiastic about navy budget requests.'

'Sir, I don't think Consolidated's plane can be modified enough to meet the mission requirements for a new attack plane. And you have to factor Athena into the equation. With Athena we won't need to buy all that expensive stealth stuff on every airplane.'

'Fly the TRX plane. Then we'll see.'

'Do you want me to get another test pilot?'

'I just wanted you to understand what's going on. The temperature is rising. Ludlow and all the politicos in SECDEF's office are playing politics right along with everyone else in this town. The admirals and generals are parading over to the hill for hearings. It's that merry time of year.'

'I think we have to keep Moravia. After she's flown both planes she cam make point-by-point comparisons that can't be questioned for extraneous reasons. Consolidated will beat us to death with Rita's corpse if we use another test pilot to fly the TRX plane, and then recommend it instead of theirs. They'll claim they got shafted by an incompetent, inexperienced pilot. You and I will look like blundering idiots, or worse.'

'I agree,' the admiral said.

Proposals from contractors were arriving based on the navy's Request for Proposal (RFP) on the Athena project. The afternoon was devoted to examining these documents, which were as thick as metropolitan telephone directories. 'How come these guys can't just say what they want to say and leave it at that?'

'Lawyers wrote these.'

'I can't make head or tail of some of this stuff. They've used every acronym in the book and made up a bunch more. These things look like dispatches from Babel.'

One morning several days later Dreyfus stuck his head in Luis Camacho's office door. 'The Minotaur mailed the Russians another letter.'

Dreyfus handed Camacho a copy and sank into a chair while his boss perused it. Addressed to the Soviet ambassador, the letter was a commentary on Gorbachev's recent visit to Cuba. The last paragraph contained some advice on how the Soviets should handle Castro.

'On generic copy paper, as usual. Just like all the others.'

'Has the original been through the lab yet?'

'Nope. I just took it down.'

'Go get it. I want to see it.'

'What for? That's an accurate copy.'

'Please. Now'.

With a shake of his head, Dreyfus complied.

Camacho opened his desk drawer and pulled out a pair of rubber gloves, which he worked onto his hands without the benefit of baby powder. Then he extracted a jar from the lower left drawer. He opened it and used a letter opener to smear a little of the blue jelly on his desk. Oops, too much. He used a piece of paper from a legal pad to blot the mess, then stared at the stain on the back of the paper. After firmly closing the jar, he stowed it back in his desk.

When Dreyfus returned with the letter, Camacho was at the window idly watching the pedestrians on E Street. He gingerly opened the plastic bag and extracted the letter while Dreyfus watched openmouthed. He laid the fully opened letter on the desk and pressed. Then he turned it over and examined the blue smear on the back. Satisfactory. Not too much, yet enough for the lab to get a sample. He refolded the letter and replaced it in the see-through plastic bag.

'Take it back to the lab.'

'Did I see that?'

'No. You are as ignorant as you look.'

'You're the boss.'

'Indeed. And while you're at it, see if this word is encoded in the text.' Camacho seized a piece of scratch paper and carefully printed a word. 'Kilderkin.' He passed the paper to Dreyfus.

'Anything else?' Dreyfus asked hopefully.

'Like what?'

'Oh, I dunno. I've got the feeling that neat and wonderful wheels are turning like crazy, though I haven't the foggiest idea why. Or where the wheels will take us.'

'What do you want? A Tuesday-morning miracle?'

'It doesn't have to be a miracle. A tiny little sleight of hand would be welcome. Or a very brief explanation.'

Camacho shot his cuffs. 'See. Nothing up my sleeves. No hat, so no rabbit.'

Dreyfus stood and ambled toward the door. 'Kilderkin, huh? You know, I get the impression that—'

'Never trust your impressions. Wait for evidence.'

'So what do we do with the original letter when the lab's through with it?' The agent fluttered the plastic bag gently.

'The usual. Stick it back in its envelope and let the post office deliver it. I'm sure the ambassador will convey the writer's advice to the members of the Politiburo at his earliest opportunity. This may be the great watershed in US-Soviet re—' He stopped because Dreyfus was already out the door and had closed it behind him.

At ten o'clock Dreyfus was back. He waited patiently until Camacho was off the phone, then said, 'Okay, how'd you know?'

'Know what?'

'That that antique word from merry ol' English would crack it?'

'Kilderkin?'

'Yeah.'

'Elementary, my dear Watson. A kilderkin is a barrel or cask. It contains something, as that letter did.'

'Shit.'

Camacho extended his hand. Dreyfus passed him a small piece of white paper containing the three words from the message and waited while he examined it. The second word was 'kilderkin.'

'That's all,' Camacho said, looking up as he folded the small page and stuck it into his shirt pocket. 'Thanks.'

'Always a pleasure, Holmes.'

When he was again alone, Camacho dialed a telephone number from memory and identified himself to the woman who answered. In a moment the person he wanted was on the line and he said, 'Let's have lunch.'

'Can't today. Pretty busy.'

'Appointments?'

'Yep.'

'Cancel them.'

'Where and when?'

'On the mall, in front of the Air and Space Museum. Twelve or so.'

The line went dead in Camacho's ear. He cradled the instrument. He leaned back in his chair and looked out his little window at the buildings on the other side of E Street. He pursed his lips and, breathing deeply in and out, gently massaged his head with one hand.

An hour later he was out on the sidewalk in his shirt sleeves, striding along. He had left his pistol locked in his desk drawer, his jacket and tie over the back of his chair. He was violating FBI policy but so be it. The summer heat was palpable, a living, breathing monster no doubt goaded by the sheer numbers of humans who were defying it this midday. Where did all these people come from? The streets were packed with cars, taxis, snorting buses and trucks, the sidewalks covered with swarming humanity.

Overhead the summer haze made the sky appear a gauzy, indistinct white, but it failed to soften the sun's fierce glare. Camacho's shirt wilted swiftly and glued itself to the small of his back. He could feel the perspiration soaking into his socks. Little beads of sweat congealed around the hairs on the back of his hands, and he automatically wiped the palms on his trousers as he walked.

Every shady circle under the mall trees was home to office workers and tourists who could no longer stay on their feet. Children sprawled and played on the hard-packed dirt. The grass that had grown under the trees so profusely this spring had succumbed weeks ago under the impact of infinite feet. An endless stream of joggers and serious runners pounded up and down the gravel paths of the mall, little dust spurts rising from the thud of each foot. The combined effect was a thin brown curtain of dust that rose into the air and tilted away toward the monolithic art museums that lined the northern side of the open expanse.

The street in front of the Air and Space Museum was bumper to bumper with tour buses. As he came closer, Luis Camacho threaded his way through the hordes of teenagers and middle-aged pink people in shorts and cutesy T-shirts.

The great American sightseeing excursion was in full swing. Herds of Japanese tourists clad in the requisite button-down short-sleeved shirts clustered near some of the buses and busily snapped their cameras at each other, the huge windowless museums to the north, the distant Washington Monument and the dome of the Capitol rising in the east like a corpulent moon. In spite of the oppressive heat, the mood was cheerful, gay.

Camacho found a spot in the shade near a tree and sat down gratefully. Cigarette butts and candy-bar wrappers littered the ground. He didn't care. To his left a souvenir stand was doing a land-office business in film, soft drinks and ice-cream bars. Squalling youngsters and frisky youths queued like soldiers in the sun as they waited for their turn to surrender their money to the happy merchant.

Derelicts shuffled slowly through the human forest. They were blithely ignored as they mined the trash bins for pop cans. A couple of alkies snoozed further away from the street in the shade cast by the treetops, out where the grass still survived: their day had apparently ended some hours ago when the critical intoxication level had been reached and surpassed.

He had been there no more than five minutes when he spotted the man he had come to meet feeling his way through the crowd, looking about him. Camacho stood and walked toward him.

'Morning, Admiral.'

'Let's get the hell out of this crowd,' Tyler Henry growled. 'Next time pick a quieter spot.' Henry was clad in beige slacks and a yellow pullover with a little fox on the right breast. His eyes were hidden behind the naval aviator's de rigueur sunglasses.

'Aye aye, sir.'

The two men walked east, toward the duck pond at the base of Capitol Hill. When they were out of earshot of the tourists and drunks, Henry said, 'Okay. I haven't got much time today. What d'ya want?'

'We intercepted another letter from the Minotaur this morning. Thought you'd be interested. Here's the coded message it contained.'

The FBI agent passed him the little square of paper with the three words penciled on it.

Admiral Henry stopped dead and stared at the words on the paper. 'Kilderkin. Holy fuck! The damned Minotaur is giving away *Athena!*'

'Yes.'

'Awww, *goddamn!* Awww . . .'

Camacho gingerly removed the paper from the admiral's fingers, refolded it and put it in his pocket.

'And I suppose you assholes with badges just stuffed the fucking letter back in the envelope and gave it to the postman?' When he saw Camacho's silent nod, Henry scuffed angrily at the dirt. He indulged himself in some heavy cussing.

'Do you know what Athena is? Do you silly half-wit peepers have *any* idea what the hell Athena is all about?'

'Well, you said—'

'I *know* what I told you! I'm asking if any of your superiors have even the slightest glimmer how valuable Athena is.'

'I don't know.'

The admiral gestured hugely in exasperation. 'Just what in the name of God is going on, Luis?'

They had reached the edge of the duck pond. Camacho stood with folded arms and gazed across the placid surface, past the statue of US Grant on horseback, at the imposing edifice of the Capitol building. 'I can only guess,' he said softly.

'But do they have any idea what Athena is – just what the hell they are giving away?'

'I don't know what they know.'

'This isn't fiber optics, or ring laser gyros, or any of that other magic shit they've been letting the Minotaur cart out of the vault. Athena is the Hope Diamond, the mother lode, the most precious, priceless treasure in the vault. Do those stupid, ignorant, incompetent, half-wit political pimps have even the faintest glimmer what it is the Minotaur just laid his filthy hands on?'

'*I don't know!*'

'*Athena will make radar obsolete.* Inevitably it will become cheaper and we'll be able to miniaturize it, get it so small and cheap we can use it to hide tanks and jeeps, not just ships and airplanes. We can hide satellites with it. In ten years or so we can probably hide submarines with it. Athena will revolutionize strategy, tactics, weaponry. And *we've* got it! The Russians don't! Yet! If we can keep them from getting it for just a couple years – just a couple years – I tell you, Luis, Athena will give America such a huge technological edge that war will become a political and military impossibility. *War will be impossible!*'

'I believe you.'

'Then *why*? Tell me that? *Why?*'

Camacho shrugged.

'What could be so goddamn valuable that they would bet the ranch, the nation, the future of mankind?'

'I don't know for sure, and I couldn't tell you if I did.'

The admiral exploded. Thirty-some years in the navy had really taught him how to swear. Camacho didn't think he had ever heard such a virtuoso performance.

Finally Henry stopped spluttering. Bitterness had replaced his exasperation. 'I think there's some treason going on over in your shop, Camacho. That's all it could be.'

'Better go easy with that word.'

'Treason.' Henry spit it out. 'Don't like it, huh? By God, if Congress gets hold of this, that may be the kindest word those slimy spook bastards ever hear. People will go to prison over this. You wait and see.'

Camacho lost his temper. 'I showed you that piece of paper so you could take some reasonable steps to protect Athena, you swabbie,' he snarled. 'Like change the code or empty the file. Not so you could shoot your mouth off about things you know nothing about, things that will ruin you and *me*. Now I've heard all the crap from you that I'm gonna listen to. I've heard *enough*. One more crack out of line and I'll come get you with a national security warrant and you can sit in a padded cell at St Elizabeth's until I think it's safe to let you out. That may be when you're a corpse. Is *that* what you want?'

'No,' said Tyler Henry contritely, aware that he had gone too far.

'Just one word, Admiral, just one little slip by you, and I'll come after you with that goddamn warrant. You'd better believe it! You and John Hinckley can spend your declining years together.'

Camacho wheeled and walked away, leaving Henry standing there staring at his retreating back.

22

Tyler Henry accompanied the ATA project crew when they returned to Tonopah in July. The admiral shook hands with the TRX engineers and spent three hours inspecting the plane, which occupied the hangar where the Consolidated bird had rested, and asking questions. At his request Rita Moravia and Toad Tarkington remained beside him. Many of his questions were directed at Rita, but when he wanted to know something about the navigation/attack system, he asked Toad.

'Is that right, Franks?' the admiral growled at the TRX program manager after he had listened carefully to one of Toad's answers.

Harry Franks nodded his assent. It looked to Jake as if Franks had lost ten pounds or so, but the cotton of his colorful sport shirt still seemed loaded near its tensile strength where it stretched over his middle. Franks rolled the stump of a dead cigar from one corner of his mouth to the other and winked at Jake.

With his shoulders thrown back and his genial air of self-assurance and command, Franks reminded Jake of the salty chief petty officers he had grown to respect and admire when he was a junior officer. Franks certainly was no modern naval officer or chief in mufti, not with that gut. In today's navy even the chief petty officers were slimmed down or retired, victims of rigid weight standards enforced with awesome zeal. The senior admirals liked to think of their service as a lean, mean fighting machine, which of course it was not. More accurately, the navy was a host of skinny technocrats. Not only were most sailors technicians, most of the officers spent the vast majority of their professional lives as administrators, experts on instructions, notices, regulations, and budgets. The bureaucracy was mean but certainly not lean.

Confusing, Jake mused, glancing once again at Frank's portico, very confusing.

Unlike the trendy and not so trendy humans who stood admiring it, TRX's prototype was exquisite functionality. The mission was all-weather attack. The plane would be launched from the deck of an aircraft carrier, in any weather day or night, to penetrate the enemy's defenses, find and destroy the target without outside aid, and return to the tiny ship in the vast ocean from whence it came, there to be refueled and armed and launched again. Every form and feature had been carefully crafted for the rigid demands of this mission, and no other.

As he stood listening to the engineers describe their creation, Jake Grafton's eye fell on Rita Moravia and Toad Tarkington, two intelligent young people in perfect health with good educations. They and others like them would have to use this machine as a weapon, when and if. The technocrats would build it and take it to sea. Yet the plane would never be anything but a cunning collection of glue, diodes, and weird alloys. The attack must come from the hearts of those who rode it down the catapult into the sky.

The important things in war never change. As always, victory would go to those who prepared wisely, planned well, and drove home their thrusts with a grim, fierce determination.

When the F-14 chase plane was safely airborne, Rita Moravia smoothly advanced the throttles to the stops and let the two improved F404 engines wind up to full power as she checked the trim setting one more time. The cockpit noise level was higher than in the Consolidated plane, and no doubt the roar of the engines outside was also louder. The exhausts had not been as deeply inset above the wing and cooled as extensively with bypass air from the compressors; consequently more of the engine's rated power was available to propel the plane through the atmosphere. And the noise was not the only clue: she could feel slightly more vibration and a perceptibly greater dip of the nose as the thrust of the screaming engines compressed the nose-gear oleo.

'Anytime you're ready,' Toad announced.

After dictating all the engine data onto the audio recorder wired into the ICS, Rita released the brakes. The nose oleo rebounded and the plane rolled smartly, picking up speed.

The little thumps and bumps as the wheels crossed the expansion joints in the concrete runway came quicker and quicker. The needle on the airspeed indicator came off the peg. On the holographic Heads-Up Display – the HUD – functioning in this prototype, the symbology came alive. The sound of the engines dropped in volume and pitch as the machine accelerated.

Now the weight came off the nose wheel as the stabilator and living wing controls took effect and began to exert aerodynamic force on the nose, trying to lift it from the runway. Oh yes. With the joystick held ever so lightly in her fingers, she felt the nose wheel bobble, skip lightly, then rise from the concrete as the wings gripped the air.

The master warning light illuminated – bright yellow – and beside the HUD the right engine fire warning light – brilliant blood red.

She smoothly pulled both throttles to idle, then secured the right one. Nose held off until the main mounts were firmly planted, decelerating nicely, speed brakes and flaperon pop-up deployed, five thousand feet of concrete remaining, slowing . . .

'Ginger aborting,' she broadcast on the radio. 'Fire light, right engine, roll the truck.'

Nose wheel firmly on the concrete, Rita applied the brakes with a firm, steady pressure. She rolled to a stop and killed the remaining engine as she opened the canopy. The fire truck charged toward them.

Rita pulled her helmet off. 'Any fire?' she shouted at the man on the truck as the engine noise died. Without conscious effort, her fingers danced across the panels turning off everything.

'Not that we can see.'

'Let's get out anyway,' Rita told Toad, who had already toggled his quick-release fittings and was craning out of the rear cockpit, looking for smoke.

Standing beside the runway, perspiring profusely as the summer desert sun cooked them, Rita and Toad heard the news five minutes later from Harry Franks. A swarm of technicians already had the engine bay doors open. 'Electrical problem, I'm sure. We'll tow it into the hangar and check it out. Nice abort,' he added with a nod at Rita. 'You two want to ride back in the van? It's air-conditioned.'

'Yep,' said Tarkington. 'Nothing like air force hospitality.'

They flew the plane for the first time the following day. Rita came back from the flight with a large smile on her face. 'Captain,' she told Jake Grafton as she brushed sweat-soaked hair from her forehead and eyes, 'that's one sweet machine. Power, handling, plenty of G available, sweet and honest. A *very* nice airplane.'

Before Harry Franks's grin could get too wide, she started detailing problems: 'Controls are oversensitive. Twitchy. Flying the ball is a real challenge. The left generator dropped off the line twice, which was maybe a good thing, because we found the power relay works as advertised; the inertial stayed up and humming. Toad got the computer running again without any problem each time. And the rudder trim . . .'

When Rita paused for air, Toad chimed in. 'I'd like to go over how those fiber optic data buses work with someone, one more time. I'm still trying to figure out how . . .'

The routine was exactly like it had been a month before. Telemetry, videotapes and the Flight Data Recorder info were carefully reviewed and the data compiled for a later in-depth analysis. Those problems that could be fixed were, and major problems were carefully delineated for factory study.

Jake Grafton demanded all his people quit work at 9 P.M. He wanted them rested and back at the hangar at six each morning. Harry Franks worked his technicians around the clock in shifts, although he himself put in eighteen-hour days and was on call at night.

Toad tried to get out of the hangar as often as possible. The air force was using this field for stealth fighters – F-117s – and several other low-observable prototypes, including the B-2. Every so often if he was outside he would hear a rumble and there, before his very eyes, would be some exotic shape that seemed to defy the laws of gravity and common sense as it cleaved the hot blue desert air. He felt vaguely guilty, and slightly naughty. To satisfy his idle curiosity he was seeing something that the Powers That Be – Those Who Knew – the Appointed, Anointed Keepers of the Secret – didn't think his little mind should be burdened with. So he stood and gawked, curious and mystified, a little boy at the knothole watching the love rites of the groping teenagers. He would go back to work shaking his head and trot outside again, hopefully, several hours later.

He bumped into Jake Grafton on one of these excursions. The captain stood with his hands in his pockets watching a pair of F-117s come into the break.

'Amazing, huh?' Jake said.

'Yes, sir.'

'I've been flying for twenty-five years,' Grafton said, 'and reading everything I could about planes for ten more. And all this time I never even *dreamed* . . .'

'I know what you mean. It's like science and technology have gone crazy in some kind of souped-up hothouse. The technology is breeding, and we don't recognize the offspring.'

'And it's not just one technical field. It's airframes and engines, composites and glues, fabricating techniques, Computer-Assisted Design, avionics and computers and lasers and radars. It's everything! In five years everything I learned in a lifetime will be obsolete.'

Or less than five years, Jake told himself glumly as the bat-winged B-2 drifted quietly overhead. Maybe everything I know is obsolete *now*!

When Toad Tarkington thought about it afterwards, he remembered the sun. It was one of those little details you notice at the time and don't think about, yet remember later.

He had seen the sun many times before in the cockpit, bright and warm and bathing everything in a brilliant, clean light, its beams darting and dancing across the cockpit as the plane turned and climbed and dived. A clean light, bright, oh so bright, warming bodies encased in Nomex and sweating inside helmets and gloves and flying boots. This was part of flying, and after a while you didn't notice it anymore. Yet for a few seconds that morning he did notice it. The memory of it stayed with him, and somehow, looking back, it seemed important.

He was deep into the mysteries of the radar and computer and how they talked to each other, acutely aware of how little time aloft he had. The radar's picture was automatically recorded on videotape, but he muttered into the ICS – the audio track of the tape – like a voodoo priest so he would know later just what the gain and brightness had been for each particular presentation. He worked fast. These flights were grotesquely short.

Rita concentrated on flying the plane, on keeping it precisely on speed and on altitude, exactly where the test profile required. She was extraordinarily good at this type of flying, Toad had discovered. She had the knack. It required skill, patience and self-discipline as one concentrated on the task at hand to the exclusion of everything else, all qualities Rita Moravia possessed in abundance. The airspeed needle stayed glued on the proper number and all the other needles did precisely what they were supposed to, almost as if they were slaves to Rita's iron will.

Toad also kept track of their position over the earth, and every now and then wasted three seconds on a glance over at the chase plane. Still there, precisely where it should be. Smoke Judy was a no-nonsense, Sierra Hotel pilot who had almost nothing to say on the radio; he knew how busy Rita and Toad were.

Periodically Toad reminded Rita of which task was next on the list. He could just see the top of her helmet, partially masked by the top of her ejection seat, if he looked straight ahead. He could also see the upside-down reflection of her lap and arms in the canopy, weirdly distorted by the curvature. Her hand on the stick – he could see that because in this plane the control stick was where it should be, between the pilot's legs.

And the sun. He saw the brilliance of the sun's gaze as the sublime light played across the kneeboard on his right thigh and back and forth across the instruments on the panel before him.

'How's control response?' he asked.

'Better.' In a moment she added, 'Still not right, though.'

He would never have known it from the sensation reaching him through the plane. The ride was smooth as glass. 'I told Orville and Wilbur they were wasting their time. They wouldn't listen.'

'What's next?'

She already knew, of course. She had prepared the flight profile. To humor her, Toad consulted his copy. 'High-G chandelles.'

'Okay.'

He felt the surge as the power increased. Rita wasted no time. He saw her glance at Smoke Judy, assuring herself the F-14 was clear, then the left wing sagged gently as the nose began to rise and the G increased. The G came on in a steadily rising grunt as the horizon tilted crazily. Rita was flying the G line on the holographic HUD. Toad temporarily abandoned his radar research and strained every muscle in the classic M–1 maneuver, trying to retain blood in his head and upper body as he forced air in and out past his lips. The inflatable pads in his G suit had become giant sausages, squeezing his legs to keep the blood from pooling there.

This maneuver was designed to allow Rita to explore the limits of G and maneuverability at ever-changing airspeeds. Toad felt the nibble of the stall buffet, and for the first time felt the wings rock sloppily, almost as if Rita were fighting to control their position.

'I'm having some troub—' she said, but before she could complete the thought the plane departed.

The down wing quit flying and the upper wing flopped them over inverted. The plane began to gyrate wildly. Positive Gs mashed them for half a second, then negative Gs threw them up against their harness straps, but since the airplane was inverted, it was upward toward the earth. The airplane spun like a lopsided Frisbee, bucking up and down madly as the Gs slammed them, positive, negative, positive, negative. The ride was so violent Toad couldn't read the MFDs on the panel before him.

'Inverted spin,' he gasped over the ICS.

'The controls – it won't—' Rita sounded exasperated.

'You're in an inverted spin,' Toad heard a hard, calm male voice say. Smoke Judy on the radio.

'I'm – the controls—'

'Twenty-nine thousand . . . twenty-eight . . .' By a supreme effort of will Toad made himself concentrate on the altimeter and read the spinning needles.

'Spin assist,' he reminded her. This switch would allow the horizontal stabilator its full travel, not restricted by its high-speed limited throw. The danger was if the pilot pulled too hard at high speed without the mechanical limit, the tail might be ripped away. Right now Rita needed all the help she could get to pull the nose down.

'It's on.'

'Twenty-five thousand.' He was having trouble staying conscious. The ride was vicious, violent beyond description. His vision closed in until he was looking through a pipe. He knew the signs. He was passing out. 'Twenty-two,' he croaked.

Miraculously the violent pitching action of the nose decreased and he felt as if he were being thrown sideways. As the G decreased, his vision came back. Rita had them out of the spin and diving. She had the power back, about 80 percent or so. She rolled the plane upright and the G came on steadily as she pulled to get them out of their rocketing dive. 'Okay,' she whispered, 'okay, baby, come to Mama.'

The wings started rocking again as the G increased, and Toad opened his mouth to shout a warning. Too late. The right wing slammed down and the plane rolled inverted again. 'Spin,' was all he could get out.

He fought the slamming up and down. 'Seventeen thousand . . .'

'Rita, you'd better eject.' The hard, fast voice of Smoke Judy.

'I've got it,' Rita shouted on the radio. 'Stay with me.' That was for Toad. She had the nose coming steadily down now, that yawing sensation again as she fed in full rudder.

'Fifteen grand,' Toad advised.

They were running out of sky.

'It's the control! I've—'

'Thirteen!'

She was out of the spin now, upright, but the nose was still way low, seventy degrees below the horizon. Power at idle, she deployed the speed brakes and began to cautiously lift the nose.

'Eleven thousand.'

'Come on, baby.'

'Ten.'

The ground was horribly close. Their speed was rapidly building, even with the boards out and engines at idle. The ground elevation here was at least four thousand feet above sea level, so they were within six thousand feet of the ground, now five, still forty degrees nose down. They would make it. Rita added another pound of back pressure to the stick.

The left wing snapped down.

Toad pulled the ejection handle.

The windblast hit him like the fist of God. He was tumbling, then he wasn't, now hurling toward the earth – an earth so close he could plainly see every rock and bush – and cursing himself for the fool that he was for waiting so long. Lazily, slowly, as if time didn't matter, the seat kicked him loose with a thump.

The ground was *right there*, racing up at him. He closed his eyes.

He was going to die now. So this is how it feels . . .

A tremendous shock snapped through him, almost ripping his boots off. The opening shock of the parachute canopy.

The ground was right there! He swung for another few seconds, then smashed into a thicket of brush. Too late he remembered he should have protected his head. He came to rest in the middle of an opaque dust cloud.

He was conscious through it all. He wiggled his limbs experimentally. Still in one piece, thank the Lord!

Rita! Where was Rita!?

He was standing before the dust had cleared, ripping his helmet off and trying to see. He tore at his Koch fittings. There! Rid of the chute.

Striding out of the brush, almost falling, looking.

Another dust cloud. Several hundred yards away and down the hill slightly. Something had impacted there. Rita? But there was no chute visible.

Mother of God!

He began to run.

23

'You still here?' the doctor asked when he saw Toad leaning against the counter at the nurses' station. The doctor was about forty and clad in a loose green hospital garment with tennis shoes on his feet.

'How is she?'

'Unconscious.' The doctor swabbed the perspiration from his forehead with his sleeve. 'I don't know when she'll come around. I don't know if she ever will.'

'What's wrong with her?' Toad demanded, grasping the doctor by the arm.

'Everything.' He patiently pried Toad's hand loose. 'Her spleen exploded. Fractured skull with severe concussion. Blood in her urine – kidney damage. Broken ribs, busted collarbone, two fractured vertebrae. That's just the stuff we know about. We're still looking.'

'She hit the ground before her parachute opened,' Toad explained. 'The drag chute was out and the main chute must have been partially deployed. She just needed another hundred feet or so.'

'Her status is extremely unstable.' The doctor took out a pack of cigarettes and lit one. 'I don't know how she's made it this long.' He flipped the ash on the floor, right in front of the No Smoking sign. 'The average person wouldn't have made it to the hospital. But she's young and she's in great shape, good strong heart. Perhaps, just perhaps . . .' He took a deep drag and exhaled the smoke through his nose, savoring it.

'Is she gonna be able to fly again?' Toad wanted to know.

The doctor took a small portable ashtray from his pocket and stubbed out the cigarette in it after a couple more deep drags. He looked Toad over carefully before he spoke. 'I don't think you heard what I said. She'll be lucky if she lives. Walking out of this hospital will be a miracle. There's nothing you can do for her. Now why don't you go back to the Q and take one of those sleeping pills the nurse gave you. You need to get some rest.'

The doctor turned away from Toad and leaned his elbows on the counter of the nurses' station. 'When you get Lieutenant Moravia's emergency data sheet from the navy, let me know. We'll have to notify her next of kin. They may want to fly out here to be with her.'

Toad smacked the waist-high counter with his hand. 'I am her next of kin. She's my *wife*.'

'Oh,' he said, looking Toad over again, then rubbing the back of his neck. 'Sorry. I didn't know that.'

'I want to be in the room with her. I'll sit in the chair.'

The doctor opened his mouth, closed it and glanced at the nurses, then shrugged. 'Sure, Lieutenant. Okay. Why not?'

Thirty minutes later Jake Grafton stuck his head into the room. He looked at Rita, the two nurses, the doctor, the IV drips and the heart monitor, then motioned to Toad, who followed him out into the hall.

'How is she?'

'She's in a deep coma. She may die.' Tarkington repeated what the doctor had told him.

Jake Grafton listened carefully, his face expressionless. When Toad finally ran down, he said, 'C'mon. Let's go find a place to sit.' They ended up in the staff lounge in plastic chairs at the only table, between a microwave oven and a pop machine. 'What happened out there today?'

Toad's recapitulation of the flight took thirty minutes. After he had heard it all, from takeoff to loading Rita into the meat wagon, Jake had questions, lots of them.

They had been talking for over an hour when a young enlisted man opened the door and stuck his head in. 'Captain Grafton? There's an Admiral Dunedin on the phone for you.'

'Tell him I'll be right there.'

On the way down the hall he told Toad, 'You go check on Rita. I'll see you in a bit.'

The phone was in the duty officer's office. Jake held it to his ear as the air force officer, a woman, closed the door on her way out. 'This is Captain Grafton, sir.'

'Admiral Dunedin, Jake. We got your message about the crash. How's Moravia?'

'In a coma. It's an open question whether she'll pull through. She ejected too low and her chute didn't fully open before she hit the ground. She's got a fractured skull, damaged spleen and a variety of other problems. Five or six bones broken.'

'And Tarkington?'

'Not a scratch.'

'So what happened?'

'Well, sir, the way it looks right now, the fly-by-wire system is suspect. We were having troubles with the control inputs – they were too much at low speeds – so we went with new E-PROMs. Now, all those parameters are supposed to be trouble-shot and double-checked on the bench test equipment and all that, but something went wrong somewhere. The plane got away from Rita in a high-G maneuver and went into an inverted spin. She recovered, then it departed again when she pulled G on the pullout. Coming out of the second spin, she just ran out of sky. It flipped on the pullout and Toad punched.

'Hindsight and all, they should have ejected on the second departure, but . . . They were trying to save the plane. Now it looks like Toad may have punched too late for Rita.'

'How's Tarkington taking it?'

'Blaming himself. I might as well tell you, if you didn't know, they're married.'

There was a pregnant silence. 'I didn't know.'

'Yeah.'

'Did that have any bearing on this accident?'

'Not that I can see. They stayed with the plane because it was a prototype and they were trying to save it. Rita thought she could save it all the way down. The last departure at five thousand feet above the ground made it a lost cause, so Toad punched them both out while they still had a little room left in the seat performance envelope. Apparently they were closer to the edge of the envelope than he thought.'

'TRX doesn't have another prototype.'

'I know. We're going to have to go with the data we have. I'll get started on the report as soon as I get back to Washington. But I would appreciate it if you would get a team of experts from the company that made that fly-by-wire system out here, like tomorrow. Have them bring their test equipment. We need some instant answers.'

'You have the box?'

'One of them, anyway. It's a little mashed up, but all the circuitry and boards appear intact. I'm hoping they can test it.'

'Why not just put it on a plane to the factory?'

'I want to be there when they check it out. And just now I can't leave here.'

'I understand.'

They talked for several more minutes, then hung up. Both men had a lot to do.

Toad wandered the corridors, looking in on Rita from time to time. A nurse was with her every minute. The evening nurse was a woman in her thirties, and she never gave him more than a glance. Rita was in good hands, he told himself. But she didn't move. She just lay there in the ICU cubicle with her eyes closed, her chest slowly rising and falling in time with the mechanical hissing and clicking of the respirator. The IVs dripped and the heart monitor made its little green lines on the cathode-ray tube. What he could see of her face was swollen, mottled.

So after looking yet again at Rita and her bandages and all the equipment, he would wander off down the hall, lost in his own thoughts.

Hospitals in the evening are dismal places, especially when there aren't many visitors. The staffers rush on unknown errands along the waxed linoleum of the corridors. In the rooms lay the sick people with their maladjusted televisions blaring out the networks' mixture of violence and comedy and ads for the consumer trash of a too wealthy society. The canned laughter and incomprehensible dialogue float through open doors and down the clean, sterile corridors, sounding exactly like the insane cackling of a band of whacked-out dopers. No one in the captive audience laughs or even chuckles at the drivel on the screens. It's just noise to help survive a miserable experience. Or background noise while you die.

Toad hated hospitals. He hated all of it – the pathetic potted plants and cut flowers, the carts loaded with dirty dinner trays, the waiting bedpans and urine bottles, the gleaming aluminum IV frames, the distant buzzer of someone trying to summon a nurse, the moans of some poor devil out of his head, the smell of disinfectant, the whispering – he loathed it all.

He relived the final moments of the flight yet again. It didn't matter that he was in a hospital corridor with the TV noise and the nurses talking in the background: he was back in the plane with the negative Gs and the spinning and Rita's voice in his ears. In his private world the events of seconds expanded into minutes, and every sensation and emotion racked him more powerfully than before.

He found himself in the staff lounge. He hadn't eaten since breakfast, but he wasn't hungry. He got a pop from the machine and sipped it while he inspected the bulletin board. Apparently management was having the usual trouble keeping the staff lounge clean. And the bowling league still needed more people. Come on, people! Sign up and roll a few lines on Thursday nights and forget all these bastards here in the hospital for a little while. They'll still be here on Friday.

He thought about calling Rita's parents, and finally decided to do it. He tried for three minutes to persuade the long-distance operator to bill the call to his number in Virginia, and when she refused, called collect. No one answered.

Back down the corridor to check on Rita. No change. Another glance from the nurse.

He walked and walked and flew again, spinning wildly, out of control, the altimeter winding down, down, down, out there on the very edge of life itself.

'So what are the possibilities?' Jake addressed the question to George Wilson, the aerodynamics expert. The group had watched the videotape made by the chase plane flown by Smoke Judy.

'It's an inverted spin, no question,' Wilson said.

'Why?'

'The plane has negative stability. All these low-observable designs do. The fly-by-wire system is supposed to keep it from stalling and spinning, and obviously it didn't.' Everyone there knew what the term 'negative stability' meant. If the pilot released the controls, a plane with positive stability would tend to return to a wings-level, stable condition. Neutral stability meant that the airplane would stay in the flight attitude it was in when the controls were released. Negative stability, on the other hand, meant that once the plane was displaced from wings-level, it would tend to increase the rate of displacement if the controls were released.

'So the fly-by-wire system is the first place to look,' Jake Grafton said. 'Smoke, you saw this whole thing up close and personal. Do you have anything you want to add?'

'No, sir. I think the movie captured it, got even more of it than I remember seeing at the time. We could sit and niggle over her decision to recover from the second spin instead of ejecting, but I doubt that would be fair. It was a prototype and she's a test pilot.'

Jake nodded. He agreed with Smoke, as he usually did. He had tried keeping Smoke Judy at arm's length after that night he saw him in West Virginia, yet except for that unexplained sighting, he had nothing else against the man. Judy was proving to be a fine officer and an excellent pilot, a man whose opinions and judgment could be trusted. Which was precisely why Jake had assigned him to fly the chase plane.

They discussed the test results they had and decided how to proceed. As Jake had told the admiral, his report was going to be written with the data the group had gathered. The reason for the crash would have to be included, if it could be established by the time he was ready to submit the document. So this evening he assigned the bulk of his staff to compiling test results and the rest to investigate, or monitor the contractor's investigation of, the crash.

'Except for the people who are working with TRX, the rest of you need to get back to Washington and dig in. Admiral Dunedin and SECNAV will want the report ASAP.'

Jake Grafton came back to the hospital about ten that night to look in on Rita and talk to the doctor on duty. When he was finished, he dragged Toad off to the VOQ. 'If you're blaming yourself about this, you'd better stop,' he said when they were in the car.

Tarkington was glum. 'She fought it all the way down. The controls were just too sensitive. The plane was out there on the edge of the envelope – high G, high angle of attack – and every time she thought she had it under control she lost it again. She kept saying, "I've got it this time."'

'She's not a quitter,'

'Not by a long shot.' Toad looked out the passenger's side window. 'A hundred and twenty pounds of pure guts.'

'So now you're telling yourself you should have ejected on the second departure.'

'Only a thousand times today.'

'Why didn't you?'

'I should have.'

'Why didn't you? Because she is your wife?'

'Naw,' said Toad Tarkington, swallowing hard. 'That wasn't it. For just a few seconds there I was flying with you again, over the Med, and you were telling me to hang in there, Toad-man, hang tough. So I hung tough. I wanted to give Rita that chance. She was asking for it. So I sat there and watched the altimeter unwind and waited for her to perform her miracle, and look – I may have killed her, or crippled her for life.'

'It's all your fault, is that it?'

'Aw, Christ, CAG.'

'Well, if you'd been in the front seat and she'd been in the back, what would you have done?'

'About what Rita did. If I were as good a pilot as Rita.'

'I've been around these planes for a few years, Toad, and let me tell you, there are no *right* answers. Some answers are better than others, but every option has unforeseen twists. If you had jumped when the plane departed the second time, with fifteen or sixteen thousand feet of altitude, you and Rita would have spent the rest of your lives thinking you jumped too soon, that you might have saved it if you had hung in there just a little longer. My father always called that being between a rock and a hard place.'

Toad shook his head.

'Years ago, in Vietnam, I learned that you can't second-guess yourself. You have to do the best you can all the time, make the best decision you can in the time you have to make it – which is always precious little – and live with the consequences regardless. That's the way flying is. And occasionally you're going to make a mistake, fuck it up. That's inevitable. The trick is to not make a fatal mistake.'

Jake Grafton's voice hardened. 'Flying isn't chess or football or checkers! Flying isn't some *game*! Flying is life distilled down to the essence – it's the straight, two hundred-proof stuff. And Rita *knows*; she's a US Naval Aviator. She chose this line of work and worked like a slave to earn that ride today. She *knows*.'

'Yes,' Toad admitted. 'She knows.'

At 3 A.M. Rita's mother answered her phone in Connecticut. She had obviously just awoke. 'This is Toad Tarkington, Mrs Moravia.' You know, the guy who married your daughter? Sorry to bother you this time of night. I tried to call earlier—'

'We were at a party. Is everything okay?' She was wide awake now and becoming apprehensive.

'Well, not really. That's sorta why I'm calling. I thought you should know.'

She went to battle stations while Toad tried to collect his thoughts.

He interrupted her torrent of words. 'What it is – Rita and I jumped out of an airplane today, Mrs Moravia. Rita's over in the hospital now.'

He could hear her talking to Mr Moravia. The pitch in her voice was rising.

'Anyway, Rita's banged up pretty good and I thought you should know.'

'How bad is it?'

'She's in a coma, Mrs Moravia. She hit the ground before her parachute had time to open.' Silence. Dead silence. Toad continued, 'Anyway, I'm with her and she's getting the best medical treatment there is and I'll call and let you know when anything changes.'

Mr Moravia spoke now. Perhaps his wife had handed him the phone. 'What's the prognosis, son?'

'She could die, Mr Moravia. She's in bad shape.'

'Should we come out there?' He didn't even know where Toad was calling from.

'Not now. When she comes out of the coma, that might be a good idea. But not now. I'll keep you advised.'

'Are you okay?'

'Fine, sir. No injuries.' Nice that he should ask, Toad thought.

'We'll pray for her.'

'Yes. Do that. I'm doing some of that myself.'

Harry Franks, the program manager for TRX, stood in the middle of the hangar issuing orders. A small army of workmen were placing wreckage in piles as he directed. They had been working since dawn.

He greeted Jake Grafton without enthusiasm. 'Give me five more minutes and we'll go upstairs,' he said, then pointed to a pile for a forklift operator with a piece of what looked like outboard wingtip.

Jake and the commanders wandered toward the door, trying to get out of the way. The plane had exploded and burned when it hit, so the pieces that were left were blackened and charred.

In an office on the second floor, the engineers from the company that had manufactured the fly-by-wire system, AeroTech, were completing the setup of their equipment. An AeroTech vice president sat on one of the few chairs, sipping coffee and watching the final installation of the network of wires that powered and connected the test boxes. He didn't look very vice presidential. He and the engineers had flown in early this morning and had had only a few hours' sleep. He stood up to shake hands with Jake.

After the introductions, they got right to it. The only surviving processor from the crashed prototype was carefully removed from its bent, damaged box and its innards exposed. It was physically examined by the assembled experts with all the curiosity of a group of med students examining a man with a new disease.

Jake backed off to let the experts have room. He found himself beside Harry Franks. 'Tell me again how the fly-by-wire system works.'

'The aircraft had negative stability,' Franks said, hooking his thumbs behind his belt and warming to the subject. 'Most high-tech tactical aircraft today have negative stability.' Jake nodded.

Franks continued. 'A human cannot fly a negatively stable machine. It would be like trying to keep a barn door balanced on top of a flagpole. So computers actually do the flying. In that way we could build a highly maneuverable aircraft and optimize its low-observable – stealth – features without worrying that we were compromising or negating the ability of the pilot to control it. Now, the way it works is pretty neat.'

Jake allowed himself a small smile. All engineers think elegant solutions to technical problems are neat.

'There are three computers,' Harry Franks continued. 'They each sample the aircraft's attitude and all the other raw data – like air density, temperature, airspeed and so on – forty times a second. Then they see what control input the pilot has made. The pilot's control input merely tells the three computers what the pilots wants the plane to do. The computers then figure out what control throws are necessary to comply with the pilot's order, and they compare their answers. They take a vote. Any two computers can overrule the third. After the vote, the agreed electrical signal is sent to the hydraulic actuators, which move the controls. This little sequence takes place forty times a second. You understand?'

'Yep. I think so. But how does the computer know how much to move the controls? That's what the pilot does in a conventional airplane.'

'Well, obviously, the computer has to be told. So the data that it uses is placed in a Programmable Read-Only Memory, a PROM. Since it's electrical, we call it an E-PROM. There are other types, like UV-PROMS and—'

Jake halted him with his hand. 'So what you guys did when Rita complained of control sensitivity was to change the E-PROMS?'

'Yeah. Exactly. They come on chips. The data is just fried into the little beggars. We called AeroTech and they cooked us some more and flew 'em down. That's all there was to it.'

'But the plane crashed.'

'Yeah,' said Harry Franks defensively, 'but we don't know yet—'

'Something went very wrong. We know that much,' Jake Grafton said. 'The plane went into three inverted spins. Rita was trying to get it out and succeeded twice.'

'Maybe she—'

'Uh-uh. Nope. She knew exactly what she was doing. She recovered from more inverted spins at Test Pilot School than you've even seen.'

The vice president of AeroTech had a cherubic, round face. The face looked like it had spent two days in the tropical sun when he faced Jake an hour later and said, 'I don't know how it happened, but the data is wrong on this chip.'

'How's that?'

He gestured futilely. 'I mean we've run the data three times, and I don't know how the heck it happened, but the E-PROM data on this chip is just flat wrong. Look here.' He flipped open a thick computer printout. 'See this line here?' He read off the number, which was all it was, a number. 'Now look here. This is the data on this chip.' His finger moved to another computer printout, one Jake had just watched running through the printer. Jake looked. It was a different number.

'How could this happen? I thought you people checked these things.'

'We *do* check the data. After the chip is cooked, we check every damn number. I don't know what – I'm at a loss what to tell you.'

'This is only one box,' Harry Franks said. 'There were three of them. Maybe this is the only one that was defective.'

'We'll never know,' Jake Grafton said slowly, surveying the faces around him and trying to catalogue their reactions. 'The other boxes got smashed and burned. This is the only one left in one piece.'

'I don't know what to say,' the AeroTech executive said.

Jake Grafton walked out of the room, looking for a phone.

Luis Camacho listened to Admiral Henry's voice on the telephone and doodled on a legal pad. Today he was drawing houses, all with the proper perspective of course. He had the roofline and baseline right, he decided.

'Okay, so AeroTech sold you a defective E-PROM chip. Or two or three of them. Sue the bastards. What do you need the FBI for?'

'I had the aircraft's control data base printed out from our computer. It's wrong. Now, I don't know if the AeroTech chip has this data on it or not, but the stuff in the Pentagon computer is *wrong*. So I got on the phone to that National Security Agency computer doctor who tends our stuff, Kleinberg. Fred Kleinberg. He played with his top secret programs that I'm not supposed to know jack about, and tells me the last guy who made a change on that data base was Harold Strong.'

Camacho extended the lines of the roof, eaves, and base of the house until they met at the perspective convergence point. Of course, Albright's house had more shrubs around it, and with the fence and all you would never see it looking just like this.

'You still there, Luis?'

'Yeah. I'm still here.'

'I want you and your guys to look into it.'

'You called NIS?' NIS was the Naval Investigative Service.

'Nope. Since you are apparently the only guy inside the beltway who knows what the fuck is going on, I want you to investigate this.'

'Investigate what?'

'This computer screw-up, you spook asshole. A four-hundred-million-dollar prototype airplane that's *supposed* to be black as the ace of spades just made a smoking hole in the ground and the pilot is at death's door. The data on the computer chips that fly the plane is wrong. The last guy who messed with the data is dead, murdered. Somebody, someplace is bound to have committed a federal crime. Now get off your fat ass and figure out if the Minotaur or some other bastard is screwing with my program! Goddamn, what have I got to do? Call the Director? Go see the President? Maybe I should put an ad in the *Post*?'

'I'll be over in a little while.'

The admiral slammed the phone in Camacho's ear. The agent cradled his instrument and went to the door. 'Dreyfus? Come in here.'

At three o'clock Eastern Daylight Time that afternoon Lloyd Dreyfus and two other FBI agents boarded a plane at National Airport for a flight to Detroit, where a man from the local field office would meet them. They planned to drive straight to AeroTech's headquarters in the suburbs.

The agents were airborne somewhere over Pennsylvania when Toad Tarkington arrived at the hospital at the air force's Tonopah facility. He stopped at the nurses' station. 'How is she?'

The nurse on duty had been there yesterday when they brought Rita in. She was an air force captain. She looked at Toad with sympathy. 'No change, Lieutenant. I'm sorry.'

'The doctor around?'

'He's eating a late lunch. He'll be back in a half hour or so.'

'Can I see her?'

'Sure.'

The ICU nurse nodded and Toad pulled a chair over near Rita's bed. Her chest was still rising and falling rhythmically, the IVs were dripping, the green line on the heart monitor was spiking – she lay exactly as he had seen her yesterday and this morning when he looked in.

The IV needles were in her left arm, so he picked up her right hand and massaged it gently. In a moment he wrapped her fingers around two of his. 'Rita, this is Toad. If you can hear me, squeeze my hand a little.'

The hand stayed limp.

'Try real hard, Rita.'

Nothing.

'Harder.'

He gave up finally and continued to lightly knead her fingers.

There was a window there by her bed. When he pulled the curtains back he could see the distant blue mountains. Clouds were building over the peaks.

Life is not fair. Good things happen to bad people and vice versa, almost as if the goodness or badness of those who bear the load was not factored into the equations for that great computer in the sky. Toad stood facing out the window and ruminated about it. Somehow he had survived this last ejection all in one piece and Rita hadn't. It wasn't because he was a good person, or because of his pious rectitude or exemplary morals or conspicuous faith. He was physically okay because he had been lucky, sort of. And Rita was smashed up because her luck deserted her. Yet perhaps the ejection had cost him something more valuable than his life.

Your luck won't last forever, Tarkington. The day will come, Toad-man, the day will come. Regardless of how you live or the promises you keep, on that day to come your luck will desert you. You won't recognize the morning, you won't recognize the noon, but that *will* be the day. And on that day you'll lose her forever.

He slumped into the chair. Looking at Rita in her bandages was hard, looking at the IV racks, respirator, and heart monitor was harder. He twisted, trying to get comfortable.

Somehow, someway, the E-PROMS in the fly-by-wire computers were screwed up. He had heard them talking this afternoon. How could it happen? How could TRX and AeroTech's checks and double checks and Quality Assurance programs all go south at precisely the same time?

Someday hell! She might die today, or tomorrow. Or the day after. You could lose her any day.

He picked up her hand again and massaged it slowly and gently. Finally he placed it carefully back on the covers. He leaned over Rita and kissed the two square inches on her forehead not covered with a bandage. 'Hang tough, Rita. Hang tough.'

24

The corporate offices and manufacturing facilities of AeroTech sat in a manicured industrial sub-division of a Detroit suburb in a low, sprawling, windowless building among a dozen similar buildings carefully arranged amid the lawns and pruned trees. A gardener was laboring in a flower bed as the FBI car swung into the parking lot.

Agent Lloyd Dreyfus decided that the goddess of the post-industrial revolution had come, conquered, and already departed this corner of Michigan. Smokestacks now belonged only to the intercity poor and wretched Third World peasants. Not a single one of the antique structures blighted the skyline in any direction.

After a display of credentials to the wide-eyed receptionist, the agents were ushered in to see the presidents of the company, who had trouble understanding just why the FBI were here at the AeroTech facilities. No, Dreyfus did not have a search warrant. He had not thought one necessary since AeroTech was a defense contractor with annual billings in the millions and the agents were here to investigate, not to search. But he could, of course, get such a warrant if the official thought it necessary. Did he? No. Company employees examined security clearance documents with care and led the government men to an empty conference room.

The investigation took time. At 9 P.M. the FBI team had established that the data contained on the E-PROM chip from the TRX prototype that crashed in Nevada did not correspond to the data that AeroTech had used to manufacture its chips. Yes, a call had been received last week from a TRX engineer in Tonopah, and yes, he had updated the data base via computer modem. The company had manufactured new E-PROM chips based on the revised data. The new chips had been taken to the mail room for overnight shipping. Yes, the records in the mailroom showed three chips sent by a bonded commercial overnight courier.

So at 9 P.M. Dreyfus sat in the conference room and scratched his head. He had been making notes all evening on a yellow pad, and now he went over them again, placing a tick mark by each item after he considered it carefully. One of the agents had gone out for burgers, and now

Dreyfus munched a cold cheeseburger and sipped a Coke in which all the ice had melted.

He decided he had two problems, and he decided to tackle the one that he thought would be the simpler first. He asked to see the company president, who was shown into the conference room and motioned into a chair beside Dreyfus.

'Sorry we're taking so long,' Dreyfus said as he wadded up the cheeseburger wrapper and tossed it at a waste can.

'Quite all right,' the president said cheerfully enough. His name was Homer T. Wiggins. The company prospectus, which Dreyfus had thumbed through earlier in the evening at a slow moment, said he was the largest shareholder of AeroTech and one of its four founders.

'It appears we have a little problem that necessitates a search. Now, when we got here this afternoon I told you we were here to investigate, not search. Now we want to search. We can do so with your permission, or we can go get a warrant. It's your choice.' Dreyfus got out his pipe and tobacco and began the charging ritual.

'Why do you want to search?' Wiggins asked.

Dreyfus shrugged. 'I can't tell you. I should tell you, though, that I believe I have enough information to persuade a judge to find probable cause and issue a search warrant.'

'On what grounds? Just what is it you're investigating?'

Dreyfus took his time lighting his pipe. He puffed experimentally to ensure it was lit and drawing properly. Finally satisfied, he tucked his lighter into a pocket and took a deep drag on the pipe. 'I can't tell you.'

Homer T. Wiggins had the look of a very sick man. 'Just what is it you want to search for?'

'Oh! Didn't I tell you? E-PROM chips.'

Bewilderment replaced the pain on Wiggins' face. 'Go right ahead. Search to your heart's content.'

After escorting the president out of the conference room and posting an agent to guard the paper spread out on the table, Dreyfus led the other two down the hall and round the corner to the mail room. 'Okay,' he said. 'I want computer chips. Start looking.'

It took an hour. One agent found three chips in a package without an address within fifteen minutes, but it was an hour before Dreyfus decided those were the only chips in the room. Back he went to see the president with the chips in hand. The president's eyes expanded dramatically.

'Okay. Now I want one of your engineers to put these on your testing machine and let me know what these chips are.'

With a glance at the clock, Wiggins picked up his phone. A half hour later a rumpled, unhappy engineer with long hair and the faint odor of bourbon about him appeared in the door. 'Sorry, Tom, but these men want some tests run this evening. Apparently it can't wait until to-morrow.' He held out the bag with the chips in it.

'Go with him, Frank, and explain what we want,' Dreyfus told one of the agents, then resumed his exploration of an industry magazine that resided on a side table.

The agent appeared in the door at five minutes before midnight and motioned to Dreyfus, who joined him in the hall. 'Okay, Dreyfus. Those were the chips that they manufactured last week with the new data from TRX. The engineer is printing out the data now, but it's exactly the same.'

'Good. The guy in the mail room just sent the wrong chips to Tonopah.'

'But when the chips reached Tonopah, wouldn't TRX test them before installation?'

'No doubt they should have, but I suspect someone will admit that there was a mistake, human error, and somehow or other the chips that did get installed didn't get checked.' After all, Dreyfus knew, mistakes made the world the happy place it is today. What should have happened and what did happen were usually vastly different things.

'Then where the hell did the bad chips come from?'

'From here. Right here.' The question was, how did AeroTech get the erroneous data that was burned into the bad chips? That data was the stuff Admiral Henry said was in the Pentagon computer, stuff that Harold Strong had been the last man to revise. A phone call from Camacho earlier in the afternoon had given Dreyfus that fact. And the bad data had been cooked onto chips at AeroTech.

'Well, Frank, it looks like it's going to be a long night. I want you to go back to the local office and wake up someone in the US Attorney's office. Have him get cracking. I want a search-and-seizure warrant for all AeroTech's travel, long-distance-telephone and expense-account records and all the data-base files. Until we have the warrant, we'll lock this place up and post a guard. Someone around here has a nasty little secret. If we can find the smoking gun, we'll know how and when and can save ourselves the trouble of listening to a lot of lies.'

'You'll need to come down to the office and write the affidavit.'

'Yeah.' He was going to have to call Camacho at home. No doubt Luis Camacho could think of a plausible story for the judge.

The phone call came at 2 A.M. and woke Camacho from a sound sleep. He listened to Dreyfus' recitation of the events of the evening as he tried to move noiselessly around the bedroom and put on his robe and slippers. When Dreyfus had completed his summary, Camacho told him to call back in five minutes. He was down in the kitchen sipping a glass of milk when the phone rang again.

'Dreyfus again, boss. What do I put on the affidavit?'

'The truth. Suspected illegal sale of classified defense information. Don't name any names.'

'I don't have any names to name yet.'

'Don't give me that, you pilgrim!'

'Oh, you don't want me to use Smoke Judy's name? Oh! Okay, John Doe strikes again. Anything else?'

'Bye.'

'Night, Luis.'

The lights were off over at Albright's house. Camacho checked from the backyard as he walked out to the swing. It was a hot, still, muggy night. He didn't stay on the swing long. The gnats and mosquitoes were still hunting for rich, red blood. Cursing, Camacho swatted furiously until he regained the safety of his kitchen and got the sliding glass door closed behind him.

Wide awake now, he flipped on the radio and twiddled the dial. They were still playing a ball game out on the Coast. Baltimore versus Oakland. Eleventh inning, three runs apiece.

José Canseco was coming to the plate. The A's announcer was all atwitter. Camacho searched through the cupboard for something to eat. Didn't she have some crackers in here? Cookies? Or did the teenage food monster eat every crumb?

He heard a rapping and turned. The sliding glass door was opening.

'Hi, Harlan. Come on in.'

'Saw your light. Couldn't sleep. The air conditioning crapped out today and that place is too stuffy to sleep in.'

'It'd be better if there was a breeze.'

'What a climate!'

Canseco took the first pitch. Strike one. 'Want some milk?'

'Yeah. That'd be good. Got any cookies?'

'I'm looking.' Up here, behind the flour. Half a package of Fig Newtons. He carried them over to the counter where Albright sat and took one from the package and bit into it. 'Little stale, but edible.'

The radio audience sighed. Foul tip up toward the press box. Strike two. Harlan Albright helped himself to a cookie while Camacho poured him a glass of milk.

Another foul tip. The sound of the bat on the ball was plainly audible.

Both men nibbled a cookie and sipped milk as they listened. The announcer was hyping the moment for all it was worth. Men on first and second, one out. Two strikes on José Canseco.

Another foul tip.

'Guy ought to quit fouling the ball,' Albright said. 'Sometimes you want them to either hit it or strike out, it doesn't matter, as long as the game goes on.'

'Yeah,' Camacho mumbled with his mouth full. He swallowed. 'But the guy keeps swinging to stay alive.'

The Baltimore pitcher swung around and threw to second. Too late.

'Now the pitcher's doing it.' Albright helped himself to another Fig Newton.

Camacho finished his milk and set the glass in the sink.

'Here's the pitch,' the radio blared. The crack of the bat started the crowd roaring. 'Through the hole, looks like it's going to the wall. Man rounding third is trotting home. And that's it, folks. The A's win it in the eleventh inning on an RBI double by José Canseco.' Camacho flipped the radio off.

'A good player,' Albright told him.

'Good kid,' Luis agreed.

'Gonna be a superstar.'

'If he lasts.'

'Yeah. They all gotta last. Everyone has high expectations, then for some reason, sometimes the kid sorta fizzles. Know what I mean?'

Camacho nodded and put Albright's glass in the sink.

'We had high hopes for you—'

'Why don't you go home and swelter at your house, Harlan. It's two-thirty in the morning and I have to work tomorrow.'

'I don't. Got the air conditioner guys coming in the morning. I'll call in sick. Tomorrow night my place is going to be like Moscow in winter.'

'Terrific.'

Albright heaved himself off the stool and reached for the sliding glass door. As his hand closed on it, he paused and looked at Camacho. 'Anything new?'

'Yeah. One or two little things, since you mentioned it. The Soviet ambassador got a letter several weeks ago. For some reason there was a stain on it, a jelly stain. We analyzed it. Looks like a French brand of blueberry. Imported. We have a dozen agents on it.'

'Amazing.' Albright shook his head like a great bear. He brightened. 'That might lead to something, eh?'

'It might. You never know.'

'Amazing. All those letters, over three and a half years! The Minotaur has never made a mistake, not even one tiny slip. And now he sends a letter with a jelly stain on it? It's too good to be real.'

'You take your breaks where you find them. If it is a break. We'll find out if I can keep enough people working on it. Another development just cropped up.'

'Like what? Peanut butter on the envelope?'

'Nothing to do with the Minotaur.'

'What?' Albright was no longer amused.

'Crash of the navy's ATA prototype. Augered in yesterday out in Nevada.' He glanced at the wall clock. 'Day before yesterday, actually. Seems somebody has been peddling erroneous information to a defense contractor. AeroTech. So the smelly stuff has hit the fan, so to speak.'

'Keep your people on the Minotaur.' His tone was flat.

'What am I supposed to do now? Salute?'

Albright slid the door open. 'I'm not kidding, Luis. We need some progress.' He stepped through the door and pulled it shut behind him. Then he disappeared into the darkness.

A minute or so later, Luis Camacho locked the door and pulled the drapes.

After Jake Grafton and the rest of the staff left for Washington, the atmosphere at the base at Tonopah took on the ethereal silence of a graveyard, or so it seemed to Toad Tarkington. He divided his time between the hangar, where a TRX crew was mocking up the remnants of the airplane he and Rita had abandoned, and the hospital, where Rita remained in a coma.

Toad drove the two miles back and forth between the two locations in an air force sedan that one of the commanders had assumed he would return to the motor pool. He would, eventually, but he was in no hurry. After all, the commander had signed for the car and hadn't really *ordered* him to return it.

The lounge in the VOQ was empty. The other guests apparently were too busy to hang around the pool table and bet dimes and swap lies while the TV hummed in the background, as the naval aviators had. The camaraderie was an essential part of naval aviation. Those who flew the planes gave and demanded this friendship of each other.

That first evening alone Toad tossed the cue ball down the table and watched it carom off the rails. He looked at the empty seats and the blank TV screen and the racks of cue sticks, and trudged off to his room to call Rita's parents yet again. He was talking to them twice a day now.

He was also calling his own folks out in Santa Barbara once a day, keeping them updated on Rita and talking just to hear their voices. Likely as not his parents were slightly baffled and secretly pleased by this attention from the son who usually phoned once a month and never wrote because he had said everything in the phone call.

It's funny, he mused, that now, *now*, with Rita in such bad shape, the sound of his mother's voice was so comforting.

After the second day alone, it finally occurred to him that the problem was that he had almost nothing to do. He was standing in the hangar watching, listening, but he had no people to supervise or reports to write or memos due, so he merely observed with his mind in neutral. At the hospital he sat beside Rita, who was moved to a private room, and did a monologue for her or stared at the wall. And thought. He pondered and thought and mused some more.

That evening on the way to the hospital he stopped by the exchange and bought a spiral notebook. In Rita's room he began to write. 'Dear Rita,' he began, then sucked on the pen and looked out the window. He dated the page. Dear, dear Rita: 'Someday you will wake, and when you do, I will give you this letter.'

He wrote, sometimes for several hours at a sitting. He started out writing about Toad Tarkington: growing up in southern California with the beach and surf just down the road, baseball and football in the endless summer, the hard-bodied bimbettes chased and wooed and sometimes conquered. He described how he felt about his first true love, and his second and third and fourth. He devoted page after page to college and grades and all-night parties.

Finally he decided he had squeezed the sponge pretty dry on his youth, so he turned to the navy. Without even realizing it, his style changed. Instead of the light, witty, listen-to-this style he had adopted for tales of his youth, he wrote seriously now, with no attempt at humor. Facts, impressions, opinions, ambitions, they came pouring from his pen.

In four days the TRX crew finished their work and mysteriously vanished. Several days later a group of officers and civilians from Washington arrived unannounced. They poked and prodded the dis-membered, blackened carcass and photographed everything, then climbed back into the waiting planes parked on the baking ramp in front of base ops. Toad was left with his solitude and his writing.

So the days passed, one by one, as Rita slept.

In Washington, Jake Grafton was also writing, though he went about it in a vastly different manner than Tarkington. He dictated general ideas into a recording machine and gave the tapes to his subordinates, who expanded the ideas into smooth, detailed drafts which Jake then worked on with a pencil. Flight test data and observations were marshaled, correlated and compiled. Graphs were drawn and projections made about performance, maintenance man-hours, mean time between failures and, of course, costs. Money dripped from every page. Every officer in the group had an input, and conclusions and recommendations were argued and reargued around Jake's desk, with him listening and jotting notes and occasionally indicating he had heard enough on one subject or another. All of it went into a mushrooming document with the words 'top secret' smeared all over.

Vice Admiral Tyler Henry spent some unhappy hours with Luis Camacho. It had been quickly established that the data contained on the E-PROM chip from the crashed prototype was identical to the erroneous data contained in the Pentagon computer file that had last been changed by the deceased Captain Harold Strong. TRX's latest, correct batch of E-PROM data was also in the computer, but under another file number.

Three days and a dozen phone calls after he had sent Lloyd Dreyfus to Detroit, Camacho went himself. On Thursday at noon he rode the Metro out to National Airport and was sitting in the president of AeroTech's office in Detroit at 3:50.

Homer T. Wiggins had gotten himself a lawyer, a manicured, fiftyish aristocrat in a Brooks Brothers suit and dark maroon tie. His stylish tan and his gray temples and sideburns made him look like something sent over from central casting. 'Martin Prescott Nash,' he pronounced with a tiny nod at Camacho, then pointedly ignored the proffered hand. Camacho retracted his spurned appendage and used a handkerchief to wipe it carefully as he sized up Wiggins, who was apparently trying his best to look like a pillar of outraged rectitude.

'My client is one of the most respected leading citizens of this state,' Nash began in a tone that might come naturally to a feminist activist lecturing a group of convicted rapists. He had it just right – the slight voice quaver, the distinct pronunciation of each word, the subtle trace of outrage. 'He is active in over a dozen civic organizations, gives over half a million dollars a year to charity and provides employment to six hundred people, every one of whom pays the taxes that provide salaries for you gentlemen.' He had just the slightest little bit of difficulty pronouncing the word 'gentlemen.'

Nash continued, listing the contributions Homer T. Wiggins had made to the arts, the people of the great state of Michigan and the human race. Camacho settled into his chair and let him go, occasionally glancing at his watch.

Dreyfus waited until he had Camacho's eye, then winked broadly. Wiggins saw the gesture and winced.

Finally, as Nash paused for breath, Camacho asked, 'Are you a criminal lawyer?'

'Well, no,' admitted the pleader. 'I specialize in corporate law. My firm has advised Homer for ten years now. We handled his last stock offering, over ten million shares on the American Exchange, and the subordinated debenture—'

'He needs a criminal lawyer.'

Deflated, Nash looked to his left, right at the pasty, perspiring face of leading citizen Homer T. Wiggins, who was staring at Camacho and licking his lips.

'Read him his rights, Dreyfus.'

Both agents knew this had been done on one prior occasion, yesterday, and Wiggins had declined to answer questions unless his lawyer was present. Dreyfus removed the Miranda card from his credentials folder and read it yet again, slowly, with feeling. The warning usually had a profound effect on men who had never in their lives thought of themselves as criminals. All the color drained from Wiggins' face and he began to breathe in short, rapid breaths. It was as if he could hear the pillars crumbling and see the plaster falling from the ceiling of that magnificent edifice of position, responsibility and respect that had housed him so well all these years.

As Dreyfus put the card away, Wiggins squeaked, 'You going to arrest me?'

'That depends.'

'On what?' said Martin Prescott Nash, who was looking a little pale himself.

'On whether or not I get some truthful answers to the questions I came here to ask.'

'Are you offering immunity?'

'No. I have no such authority. I am here to question Mr Wiggins as a principal about bribery of a government employee and illegally obtaining classified defense information. Both charges are felonies. If you want to talk to us, Mr Wiggins, we'll listen. We may or may not arrest you today. I haven't decided. Anything you say will be included in our reports and will be conveyed to the Justice Department. The attorneys there may or may not use it as evidence against you. They may take it into account when they are trying to decide if prosecution is warranted, or they may not. They may consider your cooperation when they make a sentencing recommendation after your conviction – if there is one – or again, they may not. I have nothing to offer. You have the right to remain silent, but you've heard your rights and your attorney is here with you. Or you can decide to cooperate with the government that you and your six hundred employees support with your tax dollars by telling us the truth. It's up to you.'

Nash wanted to talk to his client in private. The agents went into the hall and walked toward the cafeteria.

'Have you really got it?' Camacho asked Dreyfus.

'Chapter and verse. He turned in expense-account reports for every trip to Washington, including credit-card receipts for dinners with the name Thomas H. Judy on the back as a business guest in his own handwriting. Apparently he didn't want any more trouble with those IRS troglodytes about his expense account.'

'Can you tie him personally to the data?'

'Yep. An engineer here got the computer printout about seven months ago – Wiggins himself handed it to him. Told him to make up some experimental chips to see if they could validate the method and their computer stuff, and to develop a cost projection. All of which he did. Other people swear to that. I've got a sworn statement in writing from this engineer burning Wiggins and a cassette recording of him telling it to me originally. And the NSA computer records show Judy as one of the officers who had routine access to the E-PROM data. We've got Homer T. cold as a frozen steak.'

'Is this the right time?' Camacho muttered, thinking aloud.

'Well, shit!' Dreyfus hissed. '*I don't know!* I just dig this stuff up. You—'

Camacho silenced him with a glance. Dreyfus lit his pipe and walked along with smoke billowing.

'So why the big screw-up with the chips?' Camacho asked when they reached the cafeteria, which housed three microwaves and a wall full of vending machines.

'Oh, AeroTech got in four or five different data dumps from TRX and even one from the Pentagon, all in the last three months. The first three chips just sat there on the engineer's desk. No one is sure how or when they went to the mail room. No one knows how they got mixed up with an outgoing shipment. The mail-room guy is from Haiti, with a heavy accent. He denies everything. Rumor has it he used to be a medical doctor in his former life.' Dreyfus shrugged. 'Looks like human error, that plus the usual carelessness and a tiny pinch of rotten luck. *Voilà!* Anything that can go wrong, will. Isn't that the fourth or fifth law of thermo-dynamics or Murphy or the Georgia state legislature?'

'Something like that.' Camacho removed a plastic cup full of decaffeinated coffee from the vending machine and sat on a plastic chair at a plastic table beneath a fluorescent light with a faulty igniter – the light hummed and flickered.

'I think the doctor in the mail room is an illegal.'

'You asked to see his green card?'

'Nope.'

'Going to?'

'Not unless you tell me to.'

'Let's go see if Wiggins wants to talk.'

Dreyfus stoked his pipe again on the stroll down the hall. Wiggins' secretary glared at them. Dreyfus gave her a sympathetic grin, which she ignored.

They sat silently and flipped through the magazines on the stand. It was five more minutes before the buzzer sounded and they were waved into the inner sanctum.

'My client,' said the counselor, 'wishes to cooperate. With the understanding, of course, that he can cease answering questions at any time.'

Wiggins had met Smoke Judy on five different occasions. Judy knew that AeroTech needed contracts and offered to help in return for a small cash payment and some stock. On two occasions he talked about a job after he retired. Wiggins had been noncommittal about the job, but had agreed to the money and the stock. Five thousand dollars cash and a bearer certificate for a thousand shares of AeroTech – currently worth $12.75 each – had bought the company an advance peek at the flight control data for the TRX prototype. The navy was just floating a Request for Proposal (RFP) for the fly-by-wire system. AeroTech bid for the chip business and won the contract.

All this Wiggins admitted, but he stoutly denied any wrongdoing. 'This company, it needs the business. And we underbid every other contractor for those chips. We *saved* the government *a lot of money*. We didn't do *anything* that other defense contractors don't routinely do. It's a cutthroat business.'

The FBI agents seemed unimpressed.

'Listen, if I hadn't agreed to Judy's offer, he would have peddled that information to my competitors. Then where would I have been? No contract. I have a duty to this company.' Color returned to Homer Wiggins' cheeks.

'Of course,' Dreyfus said, 'you could have called us when Judy first approached you.'

'I've spent fifteen years building this business. I did it with my bare hands, with no money, with a ton of sweat, taking risks that would scare the wits out of a Vegas gambler. *I built it!*' Camacho found himself staring at Wiggins' gold wedding ring and gold class ring. Was that Yale?

'Now the navy wants me to make E-PROMs cheaper than anyone else. So I do. And *this* is the gratitude, *this* is the reward! *I am treated like a criminal!*' He sprayed saliva across the desk, and for the first time Camacho saw the drive and determination that had built a successful corporation.

'*I am treated like a criminal for doing what everyone else does and for making E-PROM chips cheaper than anyone else can.*'

Camacho looked at his watch: 5:30. Maybe he was still in the office. 'Do you want to go to jail tonight?'

Wiggins gaped. The blood drained from his face, and for a moment Camacho thought he had stopped breathing.

'No,' he whispered.

'Now see here—' the lawyer began, but Camacho cut him off with a jab of his hand.

'Have you talked to Judy this week?'

'No. No!'

'I want you to call him for me. I'll tell you what to say. I'll listen on an extension. You will say precisely what I tell you and nothing else. Will you do it?'

'What choice do I have?' Wiggins was recovering. This man's recuperative powers were excellent. He could handle it.

'You don't go to jail this evening. I make my report to the Justice

Department and they take it from there. If they indict you, that's their business. My report will show that you cooperated.'

'I'll make the call.'

'Homer,' said Nash, 'maybe—'

'I'll make the call. And you go on home, Prescott. Thanks for being here this afternoon. I'll call you.'

'Are you sure you— ?'

Wiggins was examining his hand. Martin Prescott Nash rose from his chair and went out the door. It swung shut behind him.

'Smoke, this is Homer Wiggins.'

'I told you never to call me—'

'Something's come up. The FBI are here, in Detroit. They're checking out the chips. I'm just letting you know.'

Smoke Judy was silent for several seconds. 'Have they talked to you?'

'Yes.'

'What— ?' His voice fell. 'Do they know?'

'About you? I don't know. I think – they might. Definitely.'

'Did you— ?'

'I've got to go now, Smoke. I just wanted you to know.' Wiggins held the instrument away from his ear, and at a nod from Camacho, Dreyfus simultaneously depressed the buttons on both telephones, severing the connection.

When they were alone in the car on the way back to the airport, Camacho said, 'I got a little job for you tomorrow, Dreyfus. We're going to need all our people, and you'll probably have to borrow a bunch.'

Dreyfus fished out his pipe and tobacco and merely glanced at his boss.

'I want to keep track of a man. We'll need discreet surveillance teams, couple of choppers and the electronics boys.'

'Anyone I know.'

'Nope. It's my next-door neighbor, guy named Harlan Albright.'

'You know, in my fifteen years in the FBI I have never felt more like a mushroom than I have working for you. You've kept me in the dark and shoveled shit at me for eighteen months now. If you got croaked tomorrow, I couldn't even tell the old man what the hell you were working on. I don't know.'

Camacho, behind the wheel, kept his eyes on the road. 'The electronics guys already put listening devices in his house, three days ago when his air conditioning went out. It was too good an opportunity to pass up.'

Dreyfus got his pipe going strongly and rolled down his window. The car's air conditioning was going full blast. 'Think he's screwing your wife?'

'Read the security regulations lately, Dreyfus?'

'Listen, boss. And listen good. You want good solid work from me but you don't want me to know anything. Now I am just about one day away from submitting my resignation. I don't need this shit and I'm not gonna keep taking it! Not for you, not for the old man, not for the Director, not for any of you spook dingdongs. And you can put that in my final evaluation!'

Camacho braked the car to a stop at a light. He just sat there behind the wheel, watching the light, waiting for it to change. When it did, he glanced left and hesitated. An old junker car was going to run the red. As it hurled by, Dreyfus leaned out his window with his middle finger jabbed prominently aloft.

Camacho took his foot off the brake and fed gas.

'Okay,' Luis Camacho said. 'You want to know what's going on. I'll tell you.' And he did.

25

On Saturday the sun rose into a clean, bright sky, a pleasant change from the haze that had been stalled over the Potomac River basin for a week. The morning weatherman credited a cold front that had swept through during the night and blessed the metropolitan Washington area with some much-needed showers.

Commander Smoke Judy absorbed the weather information while he scraped at his chin. He had acquired the habit of listening to the morning forecast during his twenty years in naval aviation, and it was hard to break. Yet he wasn't paying much attention. His mind was on other things.

After finishing at the sink and dressing, he poured himself a glass of orange juice and opened the sliding glass door to his apartment balcony. The view was excellent, considering he was only six floors up. From out here he could see the gleam of the Potomac and, on the horizon, the jutting spire of the Washington Monument. As usual, the jets were droning into and out of National Airport. Even with that cold front last night today would be hot. Already the sun had a bite to it.

He sat on the little folding chair in the sun and thought once again about Harold Strong and the flight control data and Homer T. Wiggins of AeroTech. Nothing in life ever works out just the way you think it will, he told himself bitterly. They should put that over the door of every public building in Washington.

Strong had gotten suspicious. Judy had spent one too many evenings in the office, asked one too many questions about that TRX fly-by-wire system. So Strong had doctored the data, rendering it worthless unless one knew exactly how and where it had been changed.

When Smoke found out, it was too late. He had already given the data to AeroTech, to Homer T. Wiggins. Oh, even defective it was good for what Homer wanted it for, to check the AeroTech manufacturing capability and cost out the manufacturing process. Heck, he could have written Homer a purely fictitious report that would have allowed AeroTech to accomplish the same thing. So it wasn't like he had stiffed

Homer. And both he and Homer *knew* that the preliminary data would be changed, probably many times, during the course of development. There was no possibility that the erroneous stuff would end up in an airplane that someone was going to try to fly.

And still, it happened! It happened. All the checks that were supposed to be done, the fail-safe, zero-defects program, all of it went down the crapper in an unbelievable series of coincidences. *Now* TRX was going to fire a couple of clowns who each thought the other guy had done the checks. So neither did them.

He tossed off the last gulp of orange juice and wiped his mouth with his fingers. He sat the empty glass on the concrete beside his chair and sat looking at the city.

Nothing he had ever attempted in his whole life had worked out right. What was it the hippies called it? Karma?

Funny, killing Harold Strong had been easier than he thought it would be. Probably too easy. No doubt someway, somehow, he had fucked that up too.

Looking back, it had been a bad decision. Strong probably had nothing but a few baseless suspicions that he couldn't prove.

Ah well, what was done was done. You signed for the plane and flew it as best you could and if today was your day to die, you died. That was life.

He had wanted something besides a pension, and now he had his savings – about $56,000 – and the cash from five little deals – $30,000 – and some stock he probably couldn't sell. Plus his pension, a lousy 55 percent of his base pay if he lasted twenty-two years. Yet if he cut and ran, his pension would evaporate like a gob of spit on a hot steel deck. If he didn't run, well . . . he would have to give his savings and the cash to a lawyer to try to stay out of prison.

FBI agents were probably watching him this very minute. Sitting somewhere in one of these apartments or in a vehicle down in the lot, watching him. If Wiggins had been telling the truth . . . But there was really no reason for him to lie. What did Wiggins have to gain by lying?

Judy had gone to work yesterday, though he had been sorely tempted to call in sick. That little conversation Thursday evening with Wiggins, just before he walked out of the office, that had shaken him. He had locked up his papers, bid everyone a pleasant good evening and walked out sweating.

That evening he had convinced himself there really wasn't any hurry. It might be six months or a year before they got around to arresting him, if they ever did, and he could get out on bail. And where could he run? What with?

He pushed himself up, out of the chair, and went inside. He drew the curtains. Rummaging through the bottom drawer of his dresser, he found the .38 he always wore in his flight gear. He flipped out the cylinder.

Empty. Did he have any cartridges? He sat on the bed and tried to remember. There should be six in the left, radio pocket of his survival vest, which was piled in a corner of the closet. He had put them there when he emptied the pistol after his last flight in that F-14 at Tonopah.

He found the brass cartridges and dropped them into the cylinder holes.

The pistol was old, with the bluing completely gone in places. Nowadays they issued the kids nine-millimeters, but he had always liked the old .38. Amazingly enough, this was the one they issued him twenty years ago when he checked into his first fleet squadron.

The money was in a gym bag on the other side of the closet floor. He spread it on the bed and examined the miserable pile. Fifteen bundles of a hundred twenties each. Three weeks' take for a twelve year-old crack salesman. For this he had wagered his pension and risked years in prison?

He went into the kitchen and poured himself the last of the bourbon, added some ice and water and went back out onto the balcony.

'Here's to you, Smoke Judy, you stupid, unlucky bastard.'

He sipped the liquor and watched the shadows shorten as the sun rose higher into the sky. Already it was hot. It was going to be a scorcher.

Twenty miles north of where Smoke Judy sat, Luis Camacho was trying to get his lawn mower started. He diddled with the choke and jerked the starter rope repeatedly. The plug fired a few times, then gave up. He decided he had flooded it. He could take out the plug and pull it through a few times, but no.

He sat in the shade on the concrete of his driveway, with his back against the wall, and waited for the recalcitrant device to purify itself. He was trying to work up the energy to stand and again assault the machine when Harlan Albright came out of his house, saw him, and crossed the grass toward him.

'Hey,' Albright said.

'Hey yourself. Know anything about lawn mowers?'

'Cars are my bag. I pay a kid to cut mine.'

'Why didn't you hire my kid?'

'You must be kidding! He doesn't even cut *your* grass.'

'He needs a better offer than I can make.' Camacho stood, flexed his arms a few times experimentally, then grasped the rope. Choke off. He yanked. The engine spluttered.

Albright bent and adjusted the needle valve. 'Now try it.'

It started on the next jerk of the lanyard. Albright played with the needle valve until the engine ran smoothly.

When Luis finished the front and back yards and put the machine back in the garage, Albright had a beer waiting. Ten o'clock. 'What the heck, it's Saturday.'

They sat on Albright's front steps, in the shade of the big maple.

'What's new in the glamorous, dazzling world of counter-espionage?'

'Our people visiting the gourmet food stores had a nibble. A store over in Reston. Not much of anything, but it was all we got. One of the clerks got to talking about how many famous people buy their stuff at that store. She had a name, but she couldn't remember if he had ever bought any jam. She said he or his secretary come in there once a month or so.'

'Who?'

'It isn't evidence. The clerk was a dingbat. The agent said she looked like she had terminal anorexia. Didn't look like she weighed ninety pounds. Obviously been eating her own stuff.'

'Who?'

'Royce Caplinger.'

Albright's eyebrows rose once, then fell back into place. 'She sure?'

'I told you, she was bragging. She also said she had three senators, five congressmen, two ex-congressmen, a dozen flag officers from all services, and three high-class hookers that buy stuff from her on a regular basis.'

'Hookers, huh? What's the name of the store?'

'The Gourmet Market.'

'You going to follow up?'

'Yeah. Sure. I've got a SWAT team sitting on the place twenty-four hours a day. A cockroach couldn't get in or out without us knowing it. If Caplinger ever shows up again and buys French blueberry jam, we'll bust him on the spot.' He drained the beer can and stood. 'Still, it's a lead. Someplace to look.'

'How's the ATA crash investigation going?'

'So-so. The usual. Dazzle. Glamour.'

'Why are you in that investigation anyway?'

'The admiral in charge is scared to death of the Minotaur. And he knows I'm the best; he won't talk to anybody else. No shit.' He tossed the empty can at Albright. 'I gotta go. Taking Sally to the mall. Thanks for the beer.'

When he held the door open for Sally, Camacho automatically glanced across the car at the little bulb he had inset in the driver's door. It was dark.

He got into the car and started the engine and backed out onto the street.

'I want to run by the Richards house and pick up Gerald.' The boy had spent the night with a friend.

'Why? He can walk home this afternoon and he has a key to the house.'

'I'm taking you two to the airport. I want you to go visit your mother for a week or two.'

'But I'm not packed! The PTA has a benefit on Thurs—'

'I want you both out of town for a while. Don't argue. I mean it.'

'What about our clothes?' his wife protested. 'We can't—'

'Oh yes you can! Buy some more clothes. You have your checkbook.'

'Luis, what is this all about?'

He pulled over to the side of the street and put the car in neutral. He turned in the seat to face his wife. 'I'm working a case. The people we're after know where I live. I'd just feel a whole lot better if you and Gerald weren't home until I wrap this up. Now there's no danger, but why take a chance?'

'You're really serious, aren't you?'

'Yes. I am.'

'Mother – how will I explain dropping in on her and Dad like this?'

'Tell them we had a fight and you want some time alone.'

'Mom won't believe that! She knows you too well to—'

'You think of something. Tell them we're redoing the downstairs and you've developed an allergy to paint. I don't care. Just don't tell the truth. Your mother'll spill it to every one of her friends, and it's a very small world.' He put the car in gear and rolled.

Sally chewed on her lip and twisted the strap of her purse. 'I don't like this, Luis.'

'I don't either, but this is the way it has to be.'

Smoke Judy was sipping beer in a booth at his favorite bar when he saw Harlan Albright come in and ask for change for the parking meter. Judy waited several minutes, paid his tab and left.

Albright was behind the wheel of his car. Judy opened the passenger door and sat down. 'Hi.'

'Want to take a little ride?'

'Sure. Why not?' Smoke took his sunglasses from the neck of his shirt, where they hung suspended by an earpiece, cleaned them on a shirttail, then put them on. He tossed his gym bag onto the backseat.

After several blocks, Albright glanced at Judy and asked, 'How's things at the office? Hear you guys had a crash.'

'Where'd you hear that?'

'Oh, people talk.'

Judy shrugged.

'Got anything on today?'

'Not really.'

'Want to go over on the Eastern Shore and get some dinner? I know a great little place that serves the best crab in Maryland.'

'They'll serve us like this?' Both men were in jeans. Albright was wearing a pullover shirt that sported a Redskins logo.

'I think so.'

'Why not?'

Albright drove to the beltway and got on it headed east. Traffic was heavy, as usual. He took the exit toward Annapolis and engaged the cruise control. Judy turned on the radio and found a ball game. The Orioles, only the second inning.

Judy noticed that Albright kept checking the rear-view mirrors, but he quit after a while and drove with his left elbow out the window. 'Can't stand air conditioning,' he muttered, and Judy nodded.

Luis Camacho sat in his backyard with a beer in his hand. He had carried out the portable TV that Sally normally watched in the kitchen, and rigged up the extension cord. He had the Orioles game on.

When he returned from the airport, Albright's car was missing. He had called the office and got Dreyfus. 'Where is he?'

'On the beltway heading east. Picked up a guy at a bar in Alexandria, but we don't know who. Couldn't get close enough.'

'Okay. Any idea where they're going?'

'He made no phone calls before he left the house. Didn't say anything. About thirty minutes after you left for the airport, he got in his car and drove off. He went over to Reston and stopped by the Gourmet Market.'

'Heard from Susan yet?' Susan was the wife of an FBI agent. She and her husband owned the market, and Camacho had enlisted their help. Susan was the skinniest woman Camacho had ever met, but to the best of his knowledge she was not suffering from anorexia.

'Yeah. Said he came in and bought some things, stood and chatted, said he was new in the neighborhood. Spent about fifteen minutes in the store. She says he never asked about Caplinger or anyone else, and she didn't volunteer. She wants to know if you think he'll be back.'

'Tell her probably not. I think Albright just wanted some tangible verification of my little tale.'

'Okay. I'll call you back when he gets to wherever he's going and let you know.'

'Dreyfus, I meant what I said yesterday. Under no circumstances, *none*, do I want him to burn the tail. Lose him if you have to, but *don't* give him a chance to figure out we're watching.'

'Gotcha, boss.'

Now Camacho sat in his backyard with the TV going. He nursed the beer and paid no attention to the game.

Everything that could be done had been done. Nothing had been rushed. The situation had been allowed to ripen naturally, and now all was in readiness. Including Dreyfus, he had sixty-five agents on this case. They were in the main telephone exchange in case Albright used a pay phone, Albright's house was wired and continuously monitored, a fleet of unmarked cars was at this very minute preceding and following Albright as he drove the highways, two vans full of cameras and parabolic listening devices trailed the caravan, two helicopters were airborne, Dreyfus had a stack of signed John Doe warrants in the desk. What else? Oh yes, all the top lab technicians were on call.

He sipped his beer and tried to think of something else that should be done, some contingency that he had not foreseen. He could think of nothing. Well, that wasn't really true. This whole operation could fizzle, any operation could, but it wouldn't be because he hadn't prepared as well as possible. His worst handicap was the requirement to stay loose on Albright, to remain completely hidden. Well, that was the only way it could be, so no use worrying.

But he was worried. When he could sit still no longer, he got the lawn rake from the garage and set to work on the grass clippings as the ball-park announcer chanted the summer myth yet again and the afternoon heat continued to build.

Smoke Judy was impressed. The building wasn't much, but the prices on the menu were reasonable and the seafood heaped on the plates of the early diners looked scrumptious and smelled the same. Didn't they call this decor 'rustic'? Unfinished boards on the interior walls, with fishing nets and crab pots hanging from the ceiling. Subdued lighting. 'The food's great,' Albright assured him. 'Deviled crab is the house specialty.'

They had ordered their dinner and were sipping the foam off frosty glasses of beer when Albright said, 'Got a little proposition for you, if you're interested.'

Judy wiped off his foam mustache with a finger. 'Depends.'

'Did you ever hear the term "kilderkin"?'

Smoke set the beer mug down and straightened in his chair. He looked around at the other guests with interest. Two or three looked like they could be the right age and level of fitness. His eyes swung back to Albright. 'Let's go to the john.'

He rose and led the way.

It was a one-seater with a urinal and a sink. Not the cleanest rest room he was ever in, but better than most. And it was empty. Judy turned and set his feet, the right slightly behind the left. He got his weight up on the balls of his feet and bent his knees sightly. 'Hands on the door, feet back and spread. The position, man.'

Albright stood with his hands on his hips a moment, then did as he was told.

'I'm not wearing a wire.'

'Uh-huh.' He felt Albright all over, including his crotch. He inspected his belt and his shoes and his pen. He examined his sunglasses. He looked at the patch on his jeans. Then he removed Albright's wallet and moved back against the sink. 'You can turn around now.'

Albright watched him go through it. He looked at the driver's license carefully, the library card, the automobile registration and insurance cards, the receipts from the food store and the laundry, the credit cards. He counted the cash. It was in hundreds, twenty of them. 'Gonna play poker tonight?'

'I like to pay in cash.'

'Why the credit cards then?'

'You never know.'

Judy passed the wallet back. 'You want to talk to me, then you walk out there and cancel our dinner orders and pay the tab. Leave a tip. We'll go to a place I pick. You drive, but I don't want you to say one word in the car. Not a word. Got it?'

'Okay.'

In the car Judy pointed in the direction he wanted Albright to go. Meanwhile he watched the other cars. They weren't being followed. He had Albright make a series of random turns, then take the road leading east. Fifteen miles later they came to a big roadhouse at a crossroads. Judy gestured and Albright drove into the lot and killed the engine.

They went to a booth in the back and Judy seated himself so that he could watch the door.

'You were saying?'

'Kilderkin.'

'What about it?'

'Kilderkin is the access word for a file in the computer at the Pentagon. It's a file held in the office where you work. The Athena file. I can supply you with the code words to get to it. I want you to copy the Athena file onto a floppy disk and give it to me.'

'All of it? All the documents?'

'Yes. It might take more than one disk.'

'Might. What do I get out of it?'

'A hundred grand.'

Commander Smoke Judy stared at him a while, then looked around the room thoughtfully. In a moment the waiter came over. They asked for beers and menus.

'What do you know about that file?' Judy asked.

'I'm not going to tell you. Let's just say I want it.'

'Why?'

'All you need to know is I want it a hundred thousand dollars' worth.'

'You don't want it bad enough.'

'How badly do I have to want it?'

'If you ever decide you want it for a quarter million reasons, you come talk to me. Half up front and half on delivery. Cash. Used twenties.'

'No. That's not – No!'

Judy picked up his menu. 'I think I'll have the bacon cheeseburger. What about you?'

'Maybe a plain hamburger.'

Judy nodded and waited patiently for the waiter.

When they had finished their greaseburgers and were drinking a cup of coffee, Albright said, 'If I pay you fifty tonight, fifty on Monday, when could you have the disks?'

'When will you have the rest of the money?'

'A week from Monday.'

'Then that's when you get the disks.'

At seven o'clock Luis Camacho called his in-laws. Sally answered.

'Hey. You made it.'

'Oh, Luis. It's going to be a nice visit. The folks are a little baffled, but they're delighted to have us.'

'Great. It'll go okay.'

'What did you do this afternoon? What did you have for dinner?'

They discussed the condition of the larder for three or four minutes, then Camacho wished her good night.

An hour and a half later the phone rang. 'He's headed home,' Dreyfus reported.

'Who was with him?'

'Don't know. We got an infrared photo as they crossed the Chesapeake Bay Bridge. The photographer isn't very optimistic. They came on into the metro area and stopped at a storage place in Bladensburg for a bit. Then the subject dropped the passenger at a Metro station and he was gone by the time we could get a man into the station. Subject is heading your way now. He'll be there in about five minutes.'

'Get someone over to Smoke Judy's place. See if they can spot him coming home. And get a list of the license numbers of the cars parked around that bar where the subject picked up his passenger. Run them through the computer.'

'Okay, boss. Anything else?'

'When will the photo be ready?'

'Tomorrow.'

'Okay.'

'And I put a stakeout on the storage lot. Thought we might get a warrant tomorrow and search it.'

'The subject will be making some phone calls tonight or tomorrow. Be ready.'

'You really think he's going to move?'

'He's got to. He's got to go for checkmate or concede.'

'Keep your gun handy.'

On Sunday morning Luis Camacho was painting the yard furniture when Harlan Albright hailed him across the back fence. He came through the gate and settled himself on one of the chairs waiting for its spring coat.

'I have another brush in the garage if you want to help.'

Albright grinned and sipped his coffee. 'Who said Tom Sawyer is dead? Sorry. I gotta go run some errands this morning.' He looked at the house. 'Where's Sally?'

'Went to visit her mother.' Camacho was working on a table leg and didn't look up.

'Oh.'

'Women,' Luis muttered.

'Yeah. Gonna stay a week or two?'

'Dunno.'

'Like that, huh?'

'Yeah.'

'And the boy?'

'He went too. It's been years since he spent time with his grandparents. He didn't want to go, of course.'

Albright watched Camacho work on the table. The paint ran down the brush onto his fingers, which he wiped on the grass. 'May rain this afternoon, you know,' Albright said.

'Just my luck.'

'What would you say to packing it in and going home?'

Camacho put the paintbrush in the can and stood up. He looked carefully at Albright, trying to read his expression.

'You mean Russia?'

'Yeah. You been here what? Twenty-eight or -nine years?'

'Thirty-one.'

'Yeah. Are you ready to go home?'

'I can't even speak the language anymore. When I hear it I have to concentrate real hard to get the drift, and then I can't think of the proper response. I been dreaming in English for over twenty-five years. Want some more coffee?'

'Okay.'

Luis took his cup and went inside. He returned in a moment with Albright's coffee and a cup for himself. They both sampled the brew, then sat in silence. Birds were squawking vigorously in the tree behind them. Camacho took a deep breath and exhaled slowly. How could he leave? He liked this place and these people.

Albright broke the silence. 'You really think Caplinger is the Minotaur?'

Luis considered. 'He could be,' he said at last. 'It fits. He has the necessary access, he was on the official guest list of that party three years ago when the first letter was stuck in the ambassador's coat. He's an egomaniac, likes the power trip. It's possible.'

'But why?'

Camacho shrugged. 'List all the possibilities and look at them. Pick the one you like.'

'I've done that. And you know what? I got the sneaking suspicion that the real reason wasn't on my list.'

'Why does a happily married man start buying tricks on a street comer? Why does a man in his fifties steal a few hundred from the petty-cash drawer?'

'That was the shortest reason on the list. Nut case. But I don't think so.'

'Happens all the time.' Camacho drained his cup, set it out of the way and got back to the painting.

'Royce Allen Caplinger,' Albright said, pronouncing the name slowly. 'Sixty-three years old. Estimated net worth, $132 million. Son of a druggist. Grew up in St Paul. Married twice. Second wife died of a heart attack six years ago. Hasn't remarried, though he's screwing his secretary who's worked for him for fifteen years. He's been doing that about once a month for ten years. She's forty-two, never married, modestly attractive, had a hysterectomy eight years ago. Caplinger collects American Indian art, pays too much, sometimes gets good stuff, sometimes bad. Buys what he likes and to hell with the experts. Has a copy of every book ever written about MacArthur and the best MacArthur memorabilia collection in existence. *Time* said he has every piece of old junk Mrs MacArthur ever threw out. What else? Oh yeah. He has two grown children, two dogs, and drives a fifteen-year-old Jaguar. Owns an estate in Virginia near Middleburg, Gives his entire government salary to charity.'

'Was involved in a panty raid when he was in college and was suspended for a semester,' Camacho said without taking his eyes from his work.

'That too. The rattling bones from his youth.' Albright tossed the dregs of his coffee into the grass and laid the cup on his lap. 'So, Dr Freud, has Caplinger gone over the edge? Is he copulating with Mother Russia?'

Albright rose and, dangling the cup from a finger, ambled through the gate. Thirty minutes later Camacho heard his car start out front and drive away.

Albright drove to a Wal-Mart store near Laurel. After browsing for ten minutes, he used the pay phone in the entryway. No one answered at the number he tried. He waited exactly one minute and tried again. The third time someone picked up the phone.

Albright talked for almost a minute. The other party never spoke. Then Albright hung up and went back into the store, where he wandered the aisles and handled merchandise for another half hour.

When he left the store he drove aimlessly for an hour. At Burtonsville he stopped for gas and bought a can of soda pop, a Dr Pepper. He drank the contents as he drove north on Route 29 and used a rag in the car to carefully wipe the fingerprints from the can.

Approaching the outskirts of Columbia, he took the off-ramp for Route 32, made an illegal left turn at the top and a sweeping right down onto Route 29 headed south as he scanned the mirrors. No one followed. No choppers or light planes in sight. At Route 216 he turned right from the through lane at the very last instant, just as the stoplight turned green.

He was on two-lane blacktop now, a local county road. He watched the mirror. A car turned from 29 onto this road, but it had been traveling north. He didn't recognize it. Local traffic passed him going the other way.

Fulton was a tiny village – just a few farms, a church and a small post office with a few nearby shops – 1.1 miles west of Route 29. Albright angled left onto the Lime Kiln Road. This asphalt ribbon was more narrow and twisty as it followed the natural descent of a creek. He was in an area of beautiful homes set in huge meadows well back from the road. Trees lined the fences and horses grazed on the lush grass. The car that had followed him from Route 29 turned left at Reservoir Road and went up a little hill into a sprawling subdivision.

A half mile past Reservoir Road Albright slowed the car. There it was, right beside the road – a stone drinking fountain fed by a pipe from a spring. He eased to a stop and slammed the gear shift lever into park. From the floor of the backseat he selected a 7-Up can, grasping it with a rag. He slid across the seat, opened the passenger door and set the can at the base of the fountain so it was visible from the road. Back into the car, door shut, and rolling again. Twenty seconds.

He glanced left, up a long sloping meadow at a huge house set on top of the hill in a grove of trees. No one in sight.

Three hundred yards farther on he came to a T intersection. This was Brown Bridge Road, another strip of two-lane asphalt with a double yellow line down the center and no berms. He sat at the intersection and looked both ways. No traffic. Nothing in the rearview mirror.

He turned right. The road wound up a wooded draw and came out into rolling, open country. A mile from Lime Kiln Road came to another stop sign at a T intersection. This was Route 216 again. To the right, east, was Fulton; 1.1 miles to the west was Highland Junction. He knew, because he had spent many a Sunday driving these suburban county roads, learning their twists and turns, looking for likely drop sites. Directly across the road was a Methodist church. Three or four cars in the lot, no people in sight.

He turned right, toward Fulton. He went through the village and out to Route 29, which he crossed and continued on through Skaggsville, across I-95 and into Laurel, where he turned around in the parking lot of a convenience store and began retracing his route as he watched for vehicles he had seen before and scanned the sky for airplanes.

Exactly thirty minutes later, at 2:47 P.M, he again passed Reservoir Road on Lime Kiln. Someone was changing a flat tire on a van fifty yards up the hill on Reservoir. He hadn't seen that van before. Maybe. It could be the FBI. Or it could be anybody. He continued past and slowed for the stone fountain.

The 7-Up can was still there. No vehicles in sight. No people on the hills that he could see. No choppers or planes overhead. He kept rolling past the fountain and dropped down to the Brown Bridge Road intersection.

He stopped at the stop sign and looked both ways. No traffic. He looked back over his shoulder, thinking about the van with the flat tire, weighing it.

He turned left. The road ran along a creek that was dropping toward the Patuxent River. The little valley was heavily wooded. Houses sat amid the trees off to his left, but the steep bank on his right was a forest.

Two-tenths of a mile from the intersection a gravel road branched off to the right. 'Schooley Mill Road,' the sign read. He took it.

The road was narrow, no more than ten feet wide. It ran just along the north side of the creek, parallel to the asphalt road, which was twenty-five feet or so above him at the top of a steep embankment on his left. This was a secluded lovers' lane, for a few hundred yards invisible from the paved road above. Apparently, when the teenagers weren't screwing here, the locals used this lane as a trash depository. Green garbage bags, beer and soda-pop cans lay abandoned alongside the gravel.

There was one paved driveway leading north from this road, and it had a mailbox on a wooden post. He passed the box and stopped at the first large tree. He bolted out the passenger door, set the Dr Pepper can at the base of the tree and jumped back in the car.

A tenth of a mile later Schooley Mill Road rejoined Brown Bridge Road. Two-tenths of a mile after he was back on the asphalt he crossed Brown Bridge, a modern low concrete highway bridge across the Patuxent River, which was several hundred yards wide here. Now this highway became Ednor Road. He continued the two miles to New Hampshire Avenue, Maryland Route 650, and turned left. He had to be back at the drop in twenty-five minutes. He checked his watch.

Eight thousand feet overhead in a Cessna 172, Agent Clarence Brown laid his binoculars in his lap and rubbed his eyes as he keyed the mike. 'Subject went down that Schooley Mill fuck road and was hidden by the trees for about two minutes. He might have stopped in there. You better check it.'

Sitting in the van with the wheel off on Reservoir Road, Lloyd Dreyfus turned to the man beside him. 'That can down at the spring wasn't the drop. The subject was just testing the water.'

'You sure?'

'Hell no.' But Dreyfus felt it in his gut. He looked at his map. The drops were close together, too close really. Albright should have been more careful. He's getting careless.

'Think he's spotted the plane?'

'No,' Dreyfus said. 'Brown's too high. He flew right over us a couple minutes ago. You can't hear him at that altitude and you can't see him unless you know where to look.'

Dreyfus keyed the radio mike. 'Stay on him, Clarence. I want to know when he's coming back.'

'Roger.'

To the man beside him Dreyfus said, 'Have the guys get the wheel back on. Get ready to roll fast.' Then he switched frequencies and began moving his agents.

Ten minutes later when Vasily Pochinkov passed the Methodist church on Route 216 and turned onto Brown Bridge Road, he was photographed from a station wagon parked in the church parking lot amid four other cars. He never noticed. His eye was captured by the svelte figure of a woman in shorts walking toward the church door.

He glanced at his wife in the passenger seat as she hunted for a glove on the floor. She had dropped it and was feeling blindly. She was too fat to bend over and look for it.

Why is it, he wondered, not for the first time, that all Russian women have figures like potato sacks while American women keep their figures well past middle age? You wouldn't know it to look at her, but this potato bag was only thirty-four years old and had had the figure of a ballerina when he married her just twelve years ago. It took a lot of vodka these days to prime himself for an expedition between those padded pillars she called thighs.

'Get ready, Nadya. Get the gloves on.'

The road began to twist and descend as it dropped toward Brown Bridge. Pochinkov slowed to twenty-five miles per hour, watched the odometer and looked for Schooley Mill Road.

There!

He saw the Dr Pepper can when he was fifty yards away. He glanced around as he braked to a stop. The glen was empty. Nadya stepped out, a green garbage bag in hand, and placed it fifteen feet west of the tree. While she was doing that, Pochinkov walked over to the Dr Pepper can, glanced around once and placed a second one beside it.

They got back in the car, closed the door and rolled.

The Buick was climbing the hill on the south side of the river when the van shot out of Lime Kiln Road and roared the thousand feet to the entrance to Schooley Mill. The driver braked to a halt and two men wearing gloves jumped out. One opened the green trash bag while the other took flash photos.

Inside the van Lloyd Dreyfus was listening to Agent Brown in the Cessna. 'Subject is about a half mile south of Ednor Road, north-bound on New Hampshire. I'd say you have no more than six or seven minutes . . . He just passed the drop car, which was southbound.'

The two men piled back into the van within a minute. The agent at the wheel fed gas when he heard the rear door slam. When he reached the asphalt of Brown Bridge, he made a hard left and headed east, back up the road, toward Lime Kiln.

The lane was empty when Harlan Albright entered four minutes later. He didn't even get out of the car. After a glance at the soda cans, he merely braked to a stop beside the trash bag and picked it up. He set it on the floor in front of the empty passenger seat as he pulled the door shut with his left hand and took his foot off the brake.

Glancing in he could see trash: a wadded-up bread wrapper, a couple empty vegetable cans, three squashed soda-pop cans and an old meat wrapper. They had, he knew, been carefully washed so they would not attract dogs. Under the trash was the money, $200,000 in used twenties, one hundred bundles of a hundred twenties each.

It was 5 P.M. when he pulled into his driveway in Silver Spring. The Sunday *Post* was still lying by the mailbox. He took it into the house with him, turned on the television, and settled back with the newspaper.

26

Toad Tarkington awoke at four-thirty Monday and went to the bathroom. He got back into bed, but he wasn't sleepy. Still dark outside. Wide awake and irritated because he couldn't sleep, he went to the window and peered out. Some clouds with stars visible between them. Not too many stars, though. Funny, but early in the morning, just before dawn, the stars seem to fade, almost as if the weaker ones grow tired of shining and are sent home early.

He prowled the little room, restless. He pulled on jeans and a sweatshirt and was sitting in the easy chair when the light began to spread on the eastern horizon.

The telephone rang.

'Tarkington.'

'Lieutenant, this is the shift supervisor at the hospital. Your wife is awake and she asked for you.'

'I'll be right over. You tell her!' He dropped the instrument onto the hook and grabbed for his shoes.

The sedan refused to start. He jabbed at the accelerator and held the key over. The engine ground and ground and didn't fire. Too late he realized he had probably flooded it.

Heck. It was only three-quarters of a mile or so over there. He slammed the door behind him and began to trot. Awake! Asking for him! He picked up the pace.

The sun was about ready to come over the earth's rim. The clouds above were blue, turning pink. Above them was blue sky.

The last three blocks he sprinted, down the street and across the windswept dirt that would someday be a lawn and across the empty parking lot with its tumbleweeds and right through the front door.

The nurse at the desk was grinning as he charged by. He skidded around the corner and lunged down the hall for the ICU.

A doctor was there beside her bed, talking to her as a nurse took her pulse. The doctor stepped back as Toad skidded to a halt inside the door and walked forward, into Rita's line of sight.

She tried to grin.

'Hey, babe.' He bent over and kissed her.

'Yeah, Mrs Moravia, she's out of the coma. And she recognizes me! She's asleep right now, real tired, but she's out of the coma!'

'Oh, *thank God*!'

'I really think she's gonna be okay, Mrs Moravia. It's like a miracle. She doesn't remember anything about the flight or the ejection, but she remembers me and being in Nevada and the other flights, and she kept asking how long she's been in the hospital. The doctor and the nurses are excited! I'm excited!' That was an understatement of major proportions. He was so worked up he felt like he could fly by merely flapping his arms.

After promising to call again after his next visit with Rita, Toad called his parents. He called his sister to give her the news. He called Harriet, Rita's best friend. Due to the time difference on the East Coast, Harriet was at work. And he called Jake Grafton.

Captain Grafton was also at the office and he could hear the activity in the background, but Toad could almost see Grafton leaning back in his chair and propping his feet on his middle desk drawer as if he had all the time in the world. The captain kept him on the phone almost twenty minutes, making him tell of Rita's every word and gesture, listening as long as Toad wanted to talk. Finally Toad realized the captain must have something else to do, and said a reluctant goodbye.

'You tell her I said to get well quick.'

'I will, sir.'

'And tell her Amy asks about her every day. Amy and Callie have been pulling real hard for her.'

'I'll tell her.'

'Keep the faith, shipmate,' Jake Grafton said, and was gone.

'Yeah,' said Toad Tarkington, hanging up the receiver and wiping his eyes. The tears wouldn't stop. So he laughed and cried at the very same time.

Monday evening after work Commander Smoke Judy went home, changed clothes, then drove to a bar in Georgetown. He had trouble finding the place, then he had to park six blocks away and hike back. The streets were packed with the trendy and the chic. Poodles anointed lampposts and fire hydrants as their ladies gazed away with a studied casualness.

Judy had to stand by the door until a stool opened at the bar. He perched there and studied the beer list. The bartender paused across the polished mahogany bar and said, 'On draft we have Guinness, Watney's, Steinlager—'

'Gimme a Bud. In a bottle.'

He saw Harlan Albright come in about fifteen minutes later and grab an empty stool on the far end. Albright was carrying a gym bag.

Nice touch that, Judy decided. Half the people in the place, men and women, had a gym bag with them or were wearing exercise clothes. Not sweaty tank tops and grungy snorts, mind you, but stuff that looked like it came from Saks and routinely visited a dry-cleaning plant.

When the man beside Judy left to visit a woman who had just slipped into a booth, Albright came over and sat on the vacant stool.

'Ever been here before?'

'Nope. Gonna come back, though. This is a real meat market. And on a Monday evening too!'

'Next Monday. A week from today, same time, right here.' Albright signaled the bartender, laid a five on the wood and left.

Smoke nursed his second beer. The mirror behind the bar gave him an excellent view of the Lycra thighs and hungry eyes of the female patrons, most of whom seemed to be drinking white wine or Perrier with a twist.

Smoke Judy, fighter pilot, took a last swallow and counted his change. He left a dollar tip. With a final glance around, he hoisted the gym bag and walked out, right past some sweet little piece in spandex on her way in.

Tuesday evening Rita grinned as Toad entered her room. She had been moved from the ICU and was in a semiprivate room, but the other bed was empty. The respirator and heart monitor had not accompanied her.

Toad closed the door behind him and kissed her. 'How you feeling?'

'Like I got hit by a truck.' Her voice was soft, almost a whisper.

'I've been talking to the doctor. They're going to medevac you to Bethesda on Thursday if you keep improving. Being as how I'm next of kin, I get to ride along.'

'Good,' she said, and continued to grin with her eyes on him.

'So,' he said, returning her smile. 'So.'

'I've read a little bit.' Her grin broadened.

'I thought you couldn't focus very well yet.'

'I can't. Read a little here, a little there. *The Adventures of Tarkington.* You're a pretty good writer.'

'You're a poor critic.'

'I'm glad I married you.'

'I'm damn glad you did.'

The air force medevac plane, a C-141, landed at Andrews AFB. Rita traveled the rest of the way to Bethesda in an ambulance. That evening, when she awoke from her nap, Toad was waiting with her parents, whom he had driven straight to the hospital from National Airport.

Mrs Moravia was teary but determined to maintain a stiff upper lip.

Five minutes after she arrived she launched into a speech that she had apparently been rehearsing for weeks:

'It's time, Rita. It's *time*. You've got a fine husband and it's time you stopped this flying business. Why, Sarah Barnes – you remember Sarah, the cheerleader who went to Bryn Mawr? Such a sweet girl! I can't think of her new married name . . . Sarah just had her second baby, a perfectly darling little boy. Her husband's a med student who's going into pediatrics. And Nancy Stroh, who married that new dentist from Newport – you knew about that, a perfectly gorgeous wedding in May – her mother told me just last week that Nancy's practically pregnant. And Kimberly Hyer . . .'

Mr Moravia slipped out into the hallway and Toad followed.

'She looks very tired.'

'She's had a long day,' Toad said.

'Is she going to recover completely?'

'No way to tell. The physical therapy will start in a few weeks and we'll know more then. Right now she's pretty desperate to get out of that lower-body cast. The itching and all is driving her nuts. That's a good sign, I think.'

Ten minutes later, as they finished coffees from a vending machine, Toad suggested, 'Maybe we'd better go get your wife and say good night to Rita. She wears down pretty quickly and she'll need some sleep.'

'We can visit some more in the morning,' the older man agreed.

Walking back toward the room, Toad said, 'Rita turned out a little different than her mom.'

'Different generations.' Mr Moravia shrugged. He was a philosopher.

'They want different things,' Toad said, probing gently.

'Every generation does.'

'Rita'll keep flying if the doctors let her.'

'I believe you. Madeline's just blowing off steam. Rita knows that. Where are we going to eat tonight?'

The next morning, a Friday, Toad accompanied the Moravias to the hospital, then had Mr Moravia drop him at a Metro station. They were going to the National Gallery. Toad went to the office.

Even the subways were stifling in the August heat. Toad's white uniform shirt threatened to melt before he reached the air-conditioned sanctuary of the lobby in Crystal City.

The elevator took forever to respond to the call button. He waited impatiently. For seven weeks now he had been speculating on the cause of the accident, and Jake Grafton and Helmut Fritsche and Smoke Judy had all refused to enlighten him on the telephone. They had been non-committal. 'We're investigating.' That was the party line. Toad jabbed the up button again. He wanted some answers.

He gave the secretary the hi sign and marched straight for Grafton's office. The door was closed, so he knocked, then opened it and stuck his head in.''Lo, Captain.' Two men he didn't know were sitting in the guest chairs.

'Be with you in a few minutes, Toad. Good to see you back.'

Tarkington went to his desk and impatiently pawed the stuff in his basket. Routine read-and-initial crap. He threw his hat on his desk and sat staring at Grafton's closed door.

The secretary came over to his desk. 'How's Rita?'

'She's up at Bethesda. I think she's gonna be okay.'

'It was big news around here that you two were married.' She grinned and leaned forward conspiratorily. 'None of us had any idea! It's so romantic.'

'Yeah,' said Toad Tarkington.

'We're all just delighted that she's doing so well. We've had her in our thoughts and prayers every day.'

'Thank you,' Toad said, finally pulling his eyes from Grafton's door and giving the woman a smile. 'Know anything about that accident? Why it happened?'

'It's all very hush-hush,' she confided, her voice low. She glanced around. 'I just haven't seen anything on it, but it was *so terrible!*'

After he assured her he would convey her good wishes to Rita, she went back to her desk. She was sitting there sorting the mail when Smoke Judy came in. Toad went over to him. 'Commander, good to see you.'

'Hey, Tarkington. How's your wife?'

'Gonna be okay, I think, Commander. Say' – Toad drew the senior officer away from the secretary's desk – 'what can you tell me about the accident investigation? What went wrong?'

'Toad, all that is classified special access, and I don't know if you have access. All I've seen is the confidential section of the report. You'll have to talk to Captain Grafton.'

'Sorta off the record, it was the E-PROMs, wasn't it? I figure EMI dicked them up.' EMI was Electromagnetic Interference.

Judy grinned. 'Ask Grafton. Give my best to your wife. And congratulations!'

'Thanks.'

Grafton's door opened and Toad stood. He watched the two men in civilian clothes who came out. Their eyes swept the office as they exited, casually, taking in everything at a glance. Toad forgot about them as soon as they were out of sight. He was walking toward the door when Jake Grafton stuck his head out and motioned to him.

'How's Rita?'

'Settled in at Bethesda, sir. The reason I wanted to see you' – Toad carefully closed the door – 'is that I want to know why that plane went out of control. What have you guys found out?'

Jake Grafton stood with his back to Toad, facing the window. In a moment he rubbed his nose, then tugged at an earlobe.

'What have you found out, sir?' Toad asked again.

'Huh? Oh. Sorry. The E-PROMs were defective.'

'EMI, I'll bet.'

'No. The chips were defective. Won't happen, can't happen, not a chance in a zillion, but it did.' Grafton shoved both hands into his pockets and turned around slowly. He stared at a corner of his desk. 'Defective when installed.'

Something was amiss. 'When did you learn this?' Toad said.

'Uh, we knew something was wrong with the chips when we saw the telemetry, but . . . ah . . .' He gestured vaguely at the door. 'Those guys who were just here . . .'

'Who were they?'

'Uh . . .' Suddenly the wrinkles disappeared from Jake Grafton's brow and he looked straight at Toad's face, as if seeing him for the first time. 'Can't tell you that,' he said curtly. 'Classified.'

'CAG, I've got a wife who may be crippled for life. I *need* to know.'

'You *want* to know. There's a hell of a difference. Glad you're back.'

Toad tried to approach the subject from another angle, only to be rebuffed and shown the door.

Jake Grafton went back to the window and stared without seeing. Agents Camacho and Dreyfus had been informative, to a point. No doubt it was a rare experience for them, answering the questions instead of asking them. And all those looks and pauses, searching for words! A performance! That's what it had been – a performance. Produced and acted because Vice Admiral Henry demanded it. Well, as little satisfaction as they gave, they were still virgins.

So what did he know? The E-PROMs were defective. The data on the chips was that of preliminary engineering work done several years ago. Somehow . . . No. Someone in this office or at TRX had given that data to the manufacturer. The agents had skated around that conclusion, but they didn't challenge it. They couldn't. 'Who?' was the question they had refused to answer. He had run through names to see if he could get a reaction, but no. They had just stared at him.

'Does this having anything to do with Captain Strong's death?' He had asked them that and they had discussed the possibilities, in the end saying nothing of substance. They should have been politicians, not federal agents.

The only fact he now had that he hadn't had before was that the data on the chips matched preliminary engineering work. For *that* they had come at Henry's insistence?

'Why in hell,' Jake muttered, 'does everything have to be so damned complicated?'

At 2 P.M. Smoke Judy decided to do it. The desk beside him was empty. Les Richards was at a meeting and would be for another hour, at least. Most of the people in the office were busy on Captain Grafton's report or were in a meeting somewhere.

He inserted a formatted disk in the a-drive of his terminal and started tapping. The code word for the file he wanted was 'kilderkin.' He didn't legally have access to this file. The code word that Albright had supplied was a word he had never heard before. Before he typed it, he wiped his hands on his trousers and adjusted the brightness level of the screen.

He had been debating this all week. He had a hundred grand of Albright's money plus the bucks he already had. He could walk out of here this evening, jump a plane at Dulles tomorrow and by 7 A.M. Monday be so far from Washington these clowns would never find him. Not in fifty years, even if he lived to be ninety-three.

He would be stiffing Albright, of course, but the man was a spy and wasn't going to squeal very loudly. And what the hey, in the big wide world of espionage, a hundred thousand bucks must be small change.

Or he could copy this file and give it to Albright on Monday night. Roll the dice, pass Go and collect another hundred and fifty. Then he would have a total of almost three hundred thousand green American dollars, in cash. Now, for that kind of money you could live pretty damn good in one of those little beach villages out on the edge of nowhere. Get yourself a firm, warm something to take to bed at night. Live modestly but well, loose and relaxed, as light as it's possible to get and keep breathing.

If he copied this file he would not be able to ever come back. If he walked without it, the heat would dissipate sooner or later over that E-PROM chip flap and he could slip back into the country.

Do you pay a hundred and fifty grand to keep your options open? Without the money he would eventually go broke and have to come back.

He typed the word. 'Kilderkin.' There was the list. Three dozen documents. He looked at the list carefully. Something caught his eye. He studied the column of numbers that listed how many bytes each file was composed of. Boy, these were short files.

Then he understood.

He opened one of the files. The title page came up. He hit the page advance key. The second page was blank. Nothing!

The title page was the whole document! He tried a second document. Just a title page.

The Athena file was empty!

Smoke Judy stared at the screen, trying to think. Possibility Three leaped into his mind. It hadn't even occurred to him until this moment. No wonder you never went up the ladder, Smoke. You just don't think like those snake charmers, those greasy dream merchants who slice off a couple million before they're thirty and spend the rest of their lives pretending they are somebody. Okay, my slow, dim-witted son, this is your chance to butcher the fat hog. Albright isn't going to have a computer in that singles bar to check the disk. Give him an empty disk, take his fucking money, and run.

But no. The joke will be on him. He'll get exactly what he paid for. It's Albright's tough luck the file is empty, not yours.

Judy punched the keys. The disk whirled and whirred.

The file was quickly copied. No wonder, short as it was. Judy put the disk in a side pocket of his gym bag, exited the program and turned off the terminal. He spent another ten minutes cleaning up his desk, locking the drawers, watching the other people in the office.

At the door he used the grease pencil to annotate the personnel board hanging on the wall. Back at 4:30. 'I'm going to work out,' he called to the secretary, snagged his cover from the hat rack and logged out with the security guards. That easy. *Sayonara*, mothers.

The elevator took a while to arrive. It always did. The navy had a dirt-cheap lease on this space, so the building owner refused to update the elevators. The thought made Smoke Judy smile. This was the very last time he would ever have to put up with all the petty irritations that came with the uniform. He was through. When he took this uniform off tonight, that would be the very last time.

Thank you, Commander Judy. Thank you for your twenty-one years of faithful service to the navy and the nation. Thank you for eight cruises, three of them to the Indian Ocean. Thank you for your devotion, which ruined your marriage and cost you your kids. Thank you for accepting a mediocre salary and a family move every two years and the prospect of a pissy little pension. Thank you for groveling before the tyrannical god of the fitness report, your fate dependent upon his every whim. Commander Smoke Judy, you are a great American.

The signal above the elevators dinged. Judy glanced at it. The up light illuminated on the elevator at the far left.

The door of that elevator opened. Vice Admiral Tyler Henry stepped out. Automatically the commander straightened.

'Good afternoon, Ad—'

The look on Henry's face stopped him.

'*You!*' the admiral roared. He turned to the civilian who had accompanied him on the elevator as he pointed a rigid finger at Judy. 'That's *him*! *That's* the fucking traitor!'

Judy turned and banged open the door to the stairs. With his last glimpse over his shoulder he saw the civilian reaching under his jacket for something on his belt.

He went down the staircase like a rabbit descending a hole, taking them three at a time.

'Stop! NIS!' The shout came from above, a hollow sound, reverberating in the stairwell.

Your luck's running true to form, Smoke.

He groped into the gym bag as he ran. The pistol was under the gym clothes.

Seventh floor. Sixth. Noises from above. They were after him. Fourth.

He kept going down.

Second floor. As he rounded the landing Vice Admiral Henry came through the fireproof door on the first floor. He rode the damn elevator!

Smoke shot at the man behind Henry through the door opening and threw his weight against the door, slamming it shut. In this enclosed space the report deafened him. The admiral grabbed for him, so he chopped at his head with the gun barrel.

Tyler Henry went to his knees. Smoke reversed the gun in his hand and hit him in the head with the butt, using all his strength. The admiral collapsed.

With ears ringing, he wiped his forehead, trying to think. If he could get into the parking garages under the building quickly enough, he might have a chance. He could hear running feet above. Galvanized, he leaped over the admiral's body and charged downward.

Level G1. Smoke went out the door and looked wildly around as he ran for the nearest row of cars. No one in sight. He had beaten them down here, but he had mere seconds.

He ran along looking for keys dangling in the ignition, frustration and panic welling in him.

Hang tough, Smoke. You've been in tight spots before and you've always gotten yourself out in one piece.

He loped down the row, searching desperately.

Ah, there ahead, some guy was unlocking his door. A civilian. Smoke went for him on a dead run.

The man heard Judy coming at the last moment and looked back over his shoulder, just in time to see the gun barrel chopping down.

Smoke picked up the keys from the concrete and tossed his gym bag through the open driver's door. He pulled the man out of the way and got behind the wheel. As he started the car he could see men pouring out of the elevator and stairwell. They were searching, spreading out, hunting for him.

The engine caught. Smoke backed out carefully, snicked the transmission into drive and headed for the exit. Someone was coming this way, shouting.

A shot!

He stepped on the gas.

He went around the last pillar with tires squalling and shot up the exit ramp.

The street at the top of the ramp was one-way, from right to left. Smoke looked right. One car coming. He swerved that way and jammed the accelerator down. The driver of the sedan swerved to avoid him, then decided to try to ram. Too late!

Down the street a half block to the intersection, then left through a hole in traffic, almost grazing an oncoming truck, which skidded to avoid him with its horn roaring.

Right again, then left. He ran a red light and swung right onto the bus-only ramp, which led up onto the freeway. Merged with traffic and scanning the rearview mirror, only then did Smoke Judy begin to try to sort out what had happened.

'He's dead.' The ambulance attendant covered the body of Vice Admiral Tyler Henry with a sheet. 'You people give us some room.'

Jake Grafton walked out into the elevator lobby, dazed. A half dozen FBI agents were talking on their hand-held radios and listening to the words coming back. There was still a bloody spot on the floor where one agent had gone down with a bullet in his shoulder. Who would have believed . . . Smoke Judy?

Toad Tarkington blocked his path.

'Judy. He's the guy who sold the E-PROM data, wasn't he?'

Jake nodded.

Toad turned and walked away.

'Tarkington! Tarkington!'

Jake caught up with the lieutenant in the plaza. 'Where do you think you're going?'

Tarkington didn't look at him. 'For a few lousy bucks that bastard damn near killed my wife. She'll never fully recover. She'll carry the scars *all her life.*'

'The FBI'll get him. They're the pros at this.'

'They'd better,' Toad muttered. 'If I get to the cock-sucker before they do, they can quit looking.'

Tarkington walked away and Jake stood and watched him go. What the hell, he needs some time off anyway. He'll never find Judy. The FBI will scoop him up in a day or two. And maybe the time off will do Toad some good.

Back inside he ran into an agent he recognized, Lloyd Dreyfus. 'What the hell happened, Dreyfus?'

'Well, Captain, it seems that the National Security Agency was monitoring the terminals, and when Judy got into the Athena file, they called Vice Admiral Henry right after they called us. Henry beat us here by about a minute.'

Jake started to speak and Dreyfus held up a hand. 'I know, I know. They shouldn't have done that. And now some poor schnook will probably lose his job. But Tyler Henry was Tyler Henry. Very few people ever managed to say no to him and make it stick.'

'That's true,' Jake acknowledged. 'Who was the civilian upstairs with Henry?'

'Guy from the Naval Investigative Service. We got all this from him.'

'Where's Luis Camacho?'

'Working.'

'I want to talk to him.'

'I'll pass that along.'

'No. You tell him he'll talk with me or I'm going to raise holy hell. When somebody kills a vice admiral in a navy building, the lid is gonna get ripped off pretty damned quick. Right now I know a lot more than my boss, and I don't know much. When I start answering his questions he is not going to be a happy camper. He's a vice admiral too, by the way. I *will* answer his questions. He's another one of those guys who doesn't take no for an answer. George Ludlow, the Secretary of the Navy, he hasn't even heard the word since he got out of diapers. And CNO . . .' Jake snorted.

'Camacho—'

'He won't be able to wave his badge over on the E-Ring and stuff this shit back into the goose . . . You *tell him!*'

As Commander Smoke Judy drove across the George Mason Memorial Bridge into Washington, he stripped off his white uniform shirt with the black shoulder boards and threw it onto the floor of the backseat. He was still wearing a white T-shirt, but that would attract less attention than the uniform. His cover was gone, lost somewhere back in the stairwell.

He needed a change of clothes, he needed to get rid of this car and he needed a place to hide.

He took the Fourteenth Street exit on the east side of the bridge and went north, rolling slowly with the traffic between tour buses and out-of-state cars laden with tourists. A motel? No – they would be checking motels and hotels and bus stations and . . .

He crossed Constitution Avenue and continued north into the business district.

Three blocks north of New York Avenue he was stopped in traffic inching through a single-lane construction choke point when he saw a drunk stagger into an alley, a derelict, or in the language of the social reformers, a 'homeless person.'

It took him five minutes to go halfway around the block and enter the alley from the other end. There was just room to get the car by a delivery truck. The drunk was collapsed beside a metal Dumpster, his wine bottle beside him. His head lay on a blanket roll. Beside him sat a green trash bag. After checking to make sure there was no one in sight, Smoke stopped the car and stepped out.

The drunk was semiconscious. Smoke examined the trash bag. It contained an old coat, some filthy shirts.

'Sorry, buddy. This is the end of the line.' Judy throttled him with both hands. The bum, who looked to be in his sixties, with a two-week growth of beard, kicked some and struggled ineffectually. In less than a minute he was gone.

Judy stripped the shirt from the dead man and put it on over his T-shirt. The trousers were next. Sheltered between the Dumpster and the delivery truck, Smoke took off his white trousers and white shoes and socks and pulled the derelict's grime-encrusted trousers on. Perhaps this garment had once been gray, but now it was just dark, blotchy. And a little big. All the better. He even took the dead man's shoes. They were too small, but he put them on anyway.

Judy loaded the trash bag and blanket roll in the car. He helped himself to the wine bottle too, wedging it between the stuff on the backseat so it wouldn't fall over and spill.

He rolled out of the alley and, with the help of a courteous tourist, managed to get back into traffic. He discarded all his white uniform items in a Dumpster near RFK Memorial Stadium, then parked the car in the lot at DC General Hospital.

With his blanket roll over one shoulder and the trash bag – which now contained his gym bag – dangling across the other, he shuffled across the parking lot toward the Burke Street Metro stop. He didn't get far. His feet were killing him. The shoes were impossibly small. He sat on a curb with a little hedge behind it and put on his running shoes from his gym bag. The car keys he buried in the soft dirt. He stuffed the drunk's shoes under the hedge, sprinkled some wine on himself and smeared it on his face and left the bottle beside the shoes after wiping it of prints. There was an old cap in the trash bag, which he donned.

He sat there on the curb, considering. A car drove into the lot. A woman and her two teenage youngsters. She glanced at him, then ignored him. The teenagers scowled.

This just might work, Judy told himself. He shouldered his load and set off again for the Metro stop.

Harlan Albright was in the car dealer's snack area, feeding quarters into the coffee machine, when FBI agents arrived at 4:30 to arrest him. He extracted the paper cup from the little door in the front of the machine and sipped it experimentally as he glanced idly through the picture windows at the service desk. Three men in business suits, one of them black, short haircuts, their coats hanging open. One of them had a word with Joe Talley, the other service rep, while the other two scanned the area.

As he looked at them, Albright knew. They weren't here about a car. When Talley pointed in his direction, Albright moved.

On the back wall of the snack area was a door marked 'Employees Only.' It was locked. Albright used his key and went through into the parts storeroom. The door automatically locked behind him.

He walked between the shelves and passed the man at the counter with a greeting. Out in the corridor he walked ten feet, then turned left and went through an unmarked door into the service bay.

Halfway down the bay, one of the mechanics was lowering a car on the hoist. 'You about finished with that LTD, Jimmy?'

'All done, Mr Albright. Was gonna take it out of here.'

'I'll do that. The owner is out at the service desk now. She's impatient, as usual.'

'Starter wire was loose,' the mechanic said. 'That was the whole problem. Keys are in it. But what about the paperwork?'

'Go ahead and walk it over to the office.'

'Sure.' As Albright started the car, the mechanic raised the garage door and kicked the lifting blocks out of the way of the tires.

Albright backed out carefully and drove down the alley toward the area where customers' cars were parked.

Yep, another guy in a business suit hustling this way, and another going around the building toward the front entrance. Albright turned left and drove by the agent walking toward the main showroom. That agent looked at him with surprise. As Albright paused at the street, he glanced in the rearview mirror. The agent was talking on a hand-held radio and looking his way.

Albright fed gas and slipped the car into traffic.

They would be right behind him. He jammed the accelerator down and shot across the next intersection just as the light turned red.

He went straight for three more blocks, then turned right for a block, then right again.

He entered the dealership lot from the back and coasted the car toward the service parking area, watching carefully for agents. His trip around town had taken five minutes. Yes, they all seemed to be gone.

He parked the car and walked back inside.

Joe Talley saw him coming. 'Hey, Harlan, some guys were here looking for you.'

''S'at right?'

'Yeah. Didn't say, but they were cops. Had those little radios and charged outta here like their tails were on fire. Just a couple minutes ago. Say, what've you done anyway? Robbed a bank?'

'Nah.' Albright quickly sorted through the rack of keys of cars that were awaiting service. 'Forgot to put a quarter in the meter.' This one, a new Taurus. In for its first oil change.

'Sons of bitches came after me two years ago,' Talley said. 'My ex swore out a warrant.'

'I sent her the fucking check last week,' Albright growled. He walked back toward the parking area. 'They come back, you tell 'em I went out to feed the meter,' he called. 'See you after a while.'

'Yeah, sure, Harlan.' Talley laughed.

'Do my time card too, will ya, Joe?'

'You're covered.' Talley went back to annotating a service form.

Albright never returned to the dealership, of course. Less than two hours later he abandoned the Taurus in a parking garage in downtown Washington and walked four blocks to a KGB safe house.

'Just like that, cool as ice, he went back and traded cars?'

'Yessir.' Dreyfus tried to keep his eyes on Camacho's face. It was difficult.

'Two guys in two hours go through our fingers! What is this, Keystone Kops?' Camacho sighed heavily. 'Well, what are we doing to round up these public enemies?'

'Warrants for them both, Murder One for Judy and Accessory Before the Fact for Albright. Stakeouts. Briefings for the DC, federal, airport and suburban police – every pistol-packer within fifty miles of the Washington Monument. Photos on the eleven o'clock news and in tomorrow's papers. The cover story is drugs.'

'We really needed Albright, Lloyd.'

'I know, sir.' Dreyfus was stunned. Luis Camacho had never before called him by his first name in the five years they had known each other.

Camacho sat rubbing his forehead with the first two fingers of his left hand.

'Drugs in the Pentagon is going to get a lot of press,' Dreyfus volunteered. 'Already Ted Koppel wants the Director for *Nightline*. Some nitwit on the Hill is promising a congressional investigation. Everybody on the west side of the Potomac is probably going to have to pee in a bottle on Monday morning.'

If Camacho heard, he gave no sign. After a moment he said softly, 'We'll never get him unless he comes to us.'

27

A Saturday in August is a terrible time to be in Washington. The heat and humidity make any trip outdoors an endurance trek. The summer haze diffuses the sunlight, but doesn't soften it. Perspiration oozes from every square inch of hide and clothes become sodden rags.

By eleven o'clock Saturday morning, Smoke Judy felt as if he had lived on the street for six months. He had managed only two hours' sleep the night before, most of it in fifteen-minute spurts. The alley he now called home housed three other derelicts, all of whom were comatose drunk by 9 P.M. They had no trouble at all sleeping.

At 7 A.M., or thereabouts – Judy had stowed his watch in his gym bag – his companions stirred themselves and collected their traps. He followed them as they staggered the five blocks to a mission. Two of them vomited along the way. The little neon sign over the door proclaimed: 'Jesus Saves.'

Breakfast was scrambled eggs, toast and black coffee. Judy carefully observed the men and four women, maybe five – he wasn't sure about one – who ate listlessly or not at all. The alcoholics in the final stages of their disease drank coffee but didn't touch the food. Almost everyone smoked cigarettes. A man across from him offered him an unflltered Pall Mall, which Smoke Judy accepted. He hadn't smoked a cigarette since he was twenty-four, but when in Rome . . .

'I see you been to the barber college,' his benefactor said as he blew out his match.

'Yeah.'

'Go there myself from time to time.'

Judy concentrated on smoking the cigarette until the man beside him lost interest in conversation. Behind the screen of rising smoke he studied the people around him. He was apparently the only one who showed any interest in his companions. Most of them sat with vacant eyes, or stared at their plates, or the wall, or the smoke rising from, their cigarettes.

By eight o'clock he was back on the street. The humidity was bad and the heat was building. Already the concrete sidewalks had become griddles. His companions wandered off in twos and threes, looking for shady spots to snooze, spots near areas of heavy pedestrian traffic that later in the day could be mined by panhandling for enough money to purchase the daily bottle.

Deciding the street was too dangerous for a man with only a day's growth of beard. Judy ambled back toward the alley where he had spent the night. He concentrated on the derelict's shuffle, the head-down, stoop-shouldered, eyes-averted gait that characterized so many of the defeated wanderers.

His eye caught a headline in a newspaper rack. The photo – that was him! He walked along, wondering. Up ahead was a trash bin with a paper sticking out. He snagged it and took it back to the alley.

Drugs. Cocaine trafficking. The photo of him in uniform was that service-record shot he had submitted last year. The picture of Harlan Albright was a candid street shot, almost as if he had been unaware of the camera. Still, it was a good likeness. With his back to the Dumpster, sitting on the asphalt, Smoke Judy read the stories carefully. Vice Admiral Henry was dead, according to the *Post*, killed by a drug dealer resisting arrest. Well, was the *Post* ever wrong?

When he finished the story he threw the paper in the Dumpster.

Now he lay in the heat, his head on his blanket roll, watching an old dog search for edible garbage. A slight breeze wafted down the alley, but it wasn't much. The place was a sauna. After the dog left, the only creatures vigorously stirring were the flies.

Jesus, who would have believed things could go so wrong so fast? The feds must have been monitoring access to that file, and the instant he opened it, jumped in the car to drive over and arrest him. From commander in the US Navy to hunted fugitive killer all in one fifteen-minute period – that had to be a new record for the fastest fall in the history of the navy.

As he thought about it, Smoke Judy did not agonize over the split-second decisions he had made or torture himself with what-ifs. He had spent his adult life in a discipline composed of split-second decisions, and he had long ago learned to live with them. You made the best choice you could on the information you had and never wasted time later regretting the choice. He didn't now.

Still, as he looked back, he couldn't really pinpoint any specific decision that he could say had been the perfect choice to make when he made it. So here he was, lying in an alley ten blocks northeast of the White House. Hell must be like this, dirty and hot, all the sinners baking slowly, desperate for a beer. God, a cold beer would taste so good!

The money. After that phone call from Homer T. Wiggins, he had felt it unsafe to leave the money in his apartment when he wasn't there, so he had put it in a duffel bag in the trunk of his car. His passport was in the bag too. The car was undoubtedly in the police impound lot by this time and the money and passport were in the evidence safe. He had been tempted yesterday to try to get it, but that temptation he had easily resisted. Smoke Judy, fighter pilot, knew all about what happened to guys who went back to a heavily defended target for one more run.

Man, the bumper sticker is right – shit happens. And it happens fast. The real crazy thing is it all happened to him. The great sewer in the sky dumped it all on him. Fuck! He said it aloud: 'Fuck.'

'*Fuck!*' He shouted it, liking the sound of his voice booming the obscenity at the alley walls. The word seemed to gain weight and substance as it echoed toward the street. He filled his lungs with air and roared. '*Fuck fuck fuck fuck fuck!*'

'Hey, you down there.' He looked up. Some guy was leaning out a window. 'You stop that damn shouting or I'll call a cop to run you out of there. You hear?'

'Yeah. Sorry.'

'Goddamn fucking drunk psychos,' the man said as he closed the window, probably to keep in the cool, conditioned air.

Okay, Judy told himself, going through the whole thing one more time. He was in the smelly stuff to his eyes. Okay. How was he going to get the hell out of this mess?

Well, this alley was as good a place as any to spend the weekend. If he tried to check into a motel or hotel, or tried to buy clothes or steal a car, he might be recognized. The cops wouldn't be looking for him in an alley, at least not for a few days. No doubt they were watching the airports, train station and bus depot. And looking for that car he drove away from Crystal City.

So sitting here in this shithole for a few days looked like a pretty good idea. Of course, selling the E-PROM data to Homer T. Wiggins had looked good too, as did killing Harold Strong, copying the Athena file . . .

Ah me.

Well, he still had a card. One chance. $150,000. Boy, did he ever need that money now. Monday evening, Harlan Albright, that meat market in Georgetown. One way or the other. Albright was parting with the cash, he told himself grimly. There were still five live cartridges left in the pistol.

Jake Grafton sent his family to the beach Friday evening. Saturday he was back at the office finishing his report on the testing of the prototypes. He had already circulated a draft to his superiors and now he was incorporating their comments.

The senior secretary had volunteered to work on Saturday, and she was making the changes on the computer when the telephone rang. 'Jake, this is Admiral Dunedin. I have a couple FBI agents here with me. Could you come up to my office?'

'Yessir. Be right there.'

The agents turned out to be Camacho and Dreyfus. They shook his hand politely. Jake sat in a chair against the wall, facing the side of the admiral's desk.

'Captain,' the admiral said to get the ball rolling, 'these gentlemen said you had some concerns that you wished to discuss.'

Jake snorted and rearranged his fanny on the chair. 'I suspect my concerns are minor and worlds away from the FBI's, but they're real enough. I've read the morning papers. Apparently the ATA program is some kind of cover for drug dealers who are supplying all the addicts in the Pentagon, and one of them went bug-fuck crazy yesterday and beat an admiral to death.'

'Now, Captain—' Camacho began.

'Let me finish. Presumably this boondoggle operation is run by some airhead who is unable to recognize the nefarious character of his subordinates, who have been engaged in subverting the national defense establishment from within. Moral rot and all that. And who is the airhead who commands this collection of criminals in uniform? Why, it's the navy's very own Jake Grafton, who next week is going to be testifying before various committees of Congress about the necessity to fund a new all-weather, carrier-based, stealth attack plane. No doubt this Captain Bligh will be questioned closely by concerned congressmen about his inability to see beyond the end of his nose. So my question is this – just what the hell do you gentlemen suggest I tell the congressmen?'

The agents looked at each other, then the admiral.

'We need this airplane,' said the admiral. 'Any suggestions?'

'This would be a great place for the truth,' Jake observed.

It was Camacho who spoke. 'The truth is this is a national security matter. Any additional comment will jeopardize an ongoing investigation.'

'You expect me to go over to the Hill and say that?' Jake asked incredulously. 'See this uniform? I'm a naval officer, not a spook. How about the directors of the FBI and CIA go over there and make a little statement behind closed doors, ahead of time?'

Camacho considered it.

'They can swear on Bibles or cross their hearts, or whatever it is you spooks do on those rare occasions when you're really going to come clean.'

'I suppose we could ask the Director,' Camacho said with a glance at Dreyfus.

'While you're mulling that, how about explaining to me and the admiral just what is going on? I'd like to know enough to avoid stepping on my crank, and I don't think that's asking too much.'

'This matter should be resolved in the next few weeks,' Camacho murmured.

Grafton just stared. The admiral looked equally frosty.

'Judy was selling information to defense contractors. He—'

'We *know* that,' the admiral said testily. 'Tell us something we don't know.'

'He was recruited by a Soviet agent to copy the Athena file. Apparently he agreed to do so. He attempted it Friday afternoon, NSA called us and Henry, Henry beat us here.' He shrugged.

'How did Admiral Henry learn that there might be an attempt to copy the Athena file?' Dunedin wanted to know.

'I told him,' Camacho said.

'Oh.'

'Yes.'

'Why?'

'I can't go into that. Obviously, I had authority to tell him.'

'Did Henry know that?'

'Know what?'

'Know that you had authority to tell him.'

'I don't know what he knew. Or thought or suspected. Perhaps.'

Dunedin's eyebrow was up. He looked skeptical.

'What do you want to hear, Admiral? That Henry thought he was getting unauthorized information from a confidential source? Okay, that's what he thought. Henry was Mr Naval Aviation. Honest, loyal, brilliant, he had an immense ego. Perhaps that's why he was Assistant Chief of Naval Operations for Air. He had the habit of sticking his nose in where it didn't belong, of wanting to know more than the law allowed. For example, we found this notebook in his desk drawer yesterday afternoon.' Camacho took a small spiral notebook from an inside coat pocket and tossed it on the desk.

Dunedin examined it for a moment, turning the pages slowly. He glanced up at Camacho several times, but each time his eyes quickly returned to the pages before him. Without comment, he slowly closed the book and passed it across the table to Captain Grafton.

'A, B, C . . . who are these people?'

'The letters stand for people that Henry wanted information about. Some of the information was supplied by psychotherapists, some by police agencies, some by people in government in sensitive positions who talked out of school. One of those letters apparently stands for Callie Grafton. I believe she was seeing a psychologist, wasn't she, Captain?'

Jake Grafton began ripping pages from the notebook. A handful at a time, he deposited them in the classified burn bag by Dunedin's desk.

As he watched, Camacho continued. 'Henry was very worried about the Minotaur. He feared the unknown. So he did what he could to protect his trust. It's hard to condemn him.'

'These little pieces of the cloth that you let us see, they're tantalizing.' The admiral leaned back in his chair and made a tent of his fingers.

That comment drew no response from the agents. Dreyfus examined his fingernails as Camacho watched Grafton complete his job of destruction.

'Why did this Soviet agent approach Judy?' the admiral asked. 'Why did he single him out?'

'I told him about the commander's troubles,' Camacho replied.

'*You* told *him?*' The admiral's eyes widened. 'Good God! Who are you working for, anyway?'

'I'm on your side, Admiral.'

'Hallelujah! I hate to think of the mess we'd be in if you weren't.'

'Why my wife?' Jake asked.

'You'd been given guardianship of the holy grail, Athena. You, a captain. Smoke Judy worked for you. Admiral Henry knew Judy was a bad apple, and he knew I knew.'

'It's a wonder he slept nights,' Dunedin muttered.

'Are you saying he didn't trust me?' Jake said doggedly.

'Tyler Henry didn't trust anyone. He didn't just cut the cards, he insisted on shuffling every time. But I don't think it was you he was really worried about. It was me. He didn't want you corrupted by me.'

'Say again?'

'He thought I might recruit you, so he was looking for clues in the only place he could.' Camacho stood. Dreyfus got to his feet a second later. 'Gentlemen, that's the crop. That's all you get.'

'Not so fast, Camacho,' the admiral said, pointing toward the chairs. 'You can hike when I finish this interview. I have a few more questions to ask, and so you sit right there and I'll do the asking.'

Camacho obeyed. Dreyfus remained erect. 'You can wait outside,' the admiral said.

'He can stay,' Camacho said. Dreyfus sat.

'Who approved this operation?'

'My superiors.'

'Who are?'

'The Assistant Director and the Director. And the committee.'

'What I want to know is this; who gave you the green light to screw around with the US Navy? As if we didn't have enough troubles.'

'My superiors.'

'I want *names*, mister! I want to know the names of the idiots who authorized a covert operation that resulted in the death of a vice admiral and jeopardized congressional approval of the A-12. I want some ass! The

CNO is going to want blood. George Ludlow, Royce Caplinger, if they don't know about this—'

'Ask them. Any more questions?'

'Ludlow? Caplinger? *They* knew?'

'The people who have to know, know. You said those names, I didn't. Now if *you* will excuse me, I've said all I can say and I have work to do.' Dreyfus reached the door before Camacho got completely out of his chair.

'The FBI Director better be there pouring oil on the water when I get to those hearings, Camacho,' Jake said.

'And if he isn't?' Dreyfus asked with exaggerated politeness.

'Then you'd better be there with a warrant if you want me to keep quiet. I have this nasty little habit of answering questions by telling the truth.'

Camacho just nodded and strolled for the door, which Dreyfus opened and held. 'Thank you both,' he told the naval officers, then stepped through.

When the door was shut behind them, Dunedin said, 'Too bad we don't know any truth to answer questions with.'

'We know a little.'

'You've still got a lot to learn, Jake. Truth isn't something you can extrapolate from a tiny piece. And believe me, those two have given us the tiniest piece they could. If it was a piece of the truth at all, which is debatable.'

On Monday morning Jake signed his report, which recommended the TRX prototype as the plane the navy should buy, and hand-carried it to Admiral Dunedin's office. The admiral flipped through it to see that the changes he wanted were made, then he signed the prepared endorsement. From there Jake carried it over to the program coordinator's office. Commander Rob Knight was tapping a letter on his word processor when Jake came in.

'This is it, huh?'

'Yep,' Jake pulled up a chair. Knight reviewed the changes, then signed the routing slip. 'Congratulations. Another milestone passed.'

'Think we'll get this plane?'

'Looks good. Looks good.' Knight grinned. He spent a large portion of his time talking to congressional staffers on behalf of the CNO's office. 'They know we need it. They know it's a good buy. The only really iffy thing is the choice of prototypes. Duquesne knows this is coming and he's loading his guns.'

'What's he going to come at me with?'

'I'll know more by tomorrow. I'll be over at nine with a guy from the Office of Legislative Affairs to brief you on expected questions, suggested answers, how to keep your cool – all the good stuff. You'll be testifying with Admiral Dunedin and he'll go first. But you're the guy they'll try to rip. You originated the recommendation. If they can get you to admit you're an incompetent, lying idiot, then Dunedin, CNO, SECNAV, SECDEF, they all have to reconsider. So wear your steel underwear.'

Jake's next stop was CNO's office. He had to talk to the executive assistant – the EA – and wait an hour, but with the CNO's blessing on his document, he walked it down to the Secretary of the Navy's office. After the obligatory half hour wait while the EA reviewed the document, Ludlow invited him in.

'How close is this to the draft I saw?'

'Pretty close, sir. Vice Admiral Dunedin and CNO wanted some changes, and they're incorporated.'

'Are you prepared to defend this report on the Hill?'

'Yessir.'

Ludlow quizzed him for an hour on the technical aspects of the report. Apparently satisfied, he accompanied Jake to the door. 'Just don't get cute with the elected ones. Be open, above board, a good little sailor.'

Smoke Judy changed into his running clothes and stowed his rags behind a Dumpster in a Georgetown alley. God, he smelled ripe. But what the hell – they sold this stink in a bottle now didn't they? He would probably have women crawling all over him. Everyone would think he just ran five miles and dropped by for a tall, cool Perrier. Just as trendy as a pair of Gucci shoes.

He walked the four blocks to the bar carrying the gym bag in his right hand. The place was packed, just like last week. If anyone noticed his aroma, they didn't show it.

He made his way through the crowd and into the men's room, where he washed his face and neck and arms as thoroughly as possible. He even used a paper towel on his armpits without taking his shirt off.

Whew! He felt better.

He stepped out of the men's room and stood looking. A two-person booth opened up at the back of the room, so he immediately slipped into it. Holding the gym bag under the table, he extracted the pistol from the bag and laid it on his lap.

The waitress didn't give his four-day beard a second glance. 'Gimme a Bud.'

He drank the first one quickly, then nursed the second. Twenty minutes passed, then thirty.

What if Albright doesn't show?

Judy got a sick feeling in the pit of his stomach. The beer felt like it was going to come up. He stared at the door, scrutinizing every face.

When Albright came in, Judy almost shouted.

He walked the length of the room and slid into the booth. Only then did Judy realize his hands were empty.

'Jesus,' Albright said, 'You look bad.'

'Had a little trouble.'

'I guess you did. I read about it. Dealing, are you?'

'A crock.'

'Yeah.' Albright ordered a Corona. He sat looking around.

'Where'd you spend the weekend?'

'In an alley.'

'Smart.'

'They haven't caught me yet.'

'You wired?'

'What?'

'Are you wearing a wire?'

'Hell no. Where's the fucking money?'

'You got it?'

'Yeah, right here. You wanna see it?'

'Okay. Show me.'

Judy passed him the gym bag. 'The side pocket. Look but don't take it out.' Albright did as requested.

'So, you got it?'

'What's it look like?'

'What it looks like, my friend, is a five-and-a-quarter-inch floppy disk, which could have anything under the sun on it. It could even be empty. You didn't think I was just going to take it on faith that you're an honorable gentleman and hand you all that lettuce, did you?'

'Something like that.'

The Corona came. Albright took his time squeezing the lime slice and dropping it down the neck of the bottle. 'Your good health,' he said, and took a sip.

'Where is it?'

'Where is what?'

'The bread, asshole.'

'Out in my car.'

'You want the disk, you go get it.'

'I need to see what's on the disk first. What say we both go out there and I'll check the disk on my laptop. I brought it along, just in case.'

'Uh-uh. No money, no disk.'

'You make me very suspicious, my friend. Your refusal to come outside indicates there is a very good possibility you are wearing a wire. The possibility is even higher that the file I want is not on this disk.' Albright grinned. 'You see how it is.'

'What I see is this: I've got it and you aren't leaving here with it until I see the money.'

'When did you copy this disk?'

'Friday afternoon.'

'When did the admiral come by?'

'About ten minutes later.'

Albright looked at the faces around him, then turned back to Judy. 'Even if you think you have the file – I will grant you your good faith – I doubt seriously if it is the information I want. Not on Friday afternoon, with NIS and the FBI just ten minutes away. They were waiting for you. It was a trap.'

'I got the file,' Judy insisted.

'No. I think not.' Albright started to slide out of the booth. Something hard hit his leg, and he stopped.

'Is that what I think it is?'

'I don't know what you think. Use your hand, gently, and feel.'

Albright did so. 'I see.'

'Turn back around. Face me.'

Albright obeyed. He took another sip of beer. 'Now what?'

'Now I want that money.'

'How do you propose to get it?'

'You had better think of something I like real fucking quick or you aren't walking out of here. I'm going to blow your cock off with the first one, then I'm going to put one right in your solar plexus. Who knows, an ambulance could get here so fast you might live. But you'll be in a wheelchair for the rest of your life and you're going to do all your peeing sitting down.'

Albright wasn't fazed. 'Do you have any suggestions?'

'You do the suggestions. You have one minute.'

'Hmmm.'

'I got nothing to lose, Albright. I *will* pull this trigger. Believe it!'

'You'll be caught.'

'Probably, but they're going to try me for killing a vice admiral, not for blowing the cock off a commie spy. Who knows, with you on my record, I may get probation. You got forty seconds.'

'Who knows. Indeed, who knows,' Albright considered.

'Thirty seconds.'

'Quiet. I'm thinking.' He took a deep breath, then exhaled slowly. 'Look to your left. Against the bar. There is a man there wearing a UCLA sweatshirt. Look at his hand.'

Warily, Smoke glanced left, then back at Albright. The man across the booth was watching him with an amused look. Judy looked again. The man at the bar had a pistol, and it was pointed straight at him.

'I didn't come alone. You pull that trigger and he will kill you before you pull it again.'

In spite of himself, Judy looked again. It sure looked like a real pistol, an automatic, held low, shielded by the body of the man beside him. The gunman was looking straight into his eyes.

'So,' said Harlan Albright. 'Here is how it will be. You will put your gun back in the gym bag. We will walk out to my car – oh yes, I do have a car. We will put the disk in the laptop and check it. If indeed it contains the Athena file, I will give you the money. If not, we'll shake hands, and you'll go your way, I mine.'

'I oughta just shoot you, here and now.'

'As you say, I may live. You most certainly won't. Your choice.'

'I'm busted. I got nothing. They—' He swallowed hard. Tears were obstructing his vision. 'They emptied the file. It was a setup. Nothing there but the title pages of thirty documents, each document just one page. Honest. I got what you wanted to buy. I'm desperate! I *need* the money.'

Albright nodded. 'I'm sorry.'

'C'mon, mister,' he pleaded. 'I'll do you a deal. The title pages must be worth something. I got fifteen bucks to my name. That's it! Fifteen lousy bucks.' He was sobbing.

'I think not.' Albright looked around. Spectators were watching Judy. It was past time to go. Albright took out his wallet and tossed all the currency he had on the table. 'There's something over a hundred and forty there. You take it.'

Judy seized the bills. He scooped them up with his left hand, then fumbled below the table with the gun. 'I need the gym bag. Here' – he held out the disk. 'You take it. I don't want it.'

'Good luck,' Albright said, and then rose and walked toward the entrance, leaving Judy holding the disk and staring after him. When Albright was through the door, the gunman on Smoke's left followed him.

Judy lowered his head to the table.

'Mister,' he heard someone saying. 'Mister, you're going to have to leave. Please, mister,' urged the hard, insistent voice, 'you can't stay here.'

28

'Senator Duquesne has a copy of your service record.'

'What? How'd he get that?'

Commander Rob Knight shrugged. 'God only knows, and he won't tell. What's in your service record that would do him any good?'

'I don't know,' Jake Grafton said.

'He may not use any part of it. Probably won't. But he told some colleague's aide, figuring you'd hear about it and get worried.'

'What a guy.'

'This is major-league hardball, Grafton. And he's got that crackpot Samuel Dodgers scheduled to testify before you get on the stand, after SECDEF and Dunedin finish.'

'He's playing Russian roulette. Dodgers is a genius with the personality of a warthog.'

'His strategy, apparently, is to get the A-12 defeated. The story I hear from a couple aides is that Athena is such a revolutionary new technology, it needs to be produced and evaluated before the navy buys any stealth airplanes – i.e., neither prototype will be purchased. Then Consolidated can participate in another competition for a more conventional design that makes full use of Athena's capabilities. The argument is that a more conventional airplane that uses Athena exclusively for stealth protection will save the government several billions.'

'Is he going to try this out on Caplinger?'

'Nope. He's going to let Caplinger and Dunedin testify, then wring the juice out of Dodgers and dump it all in your lap in the hope you'll blow it.'

'Has he got the votes?'

'Not yet. There are enough fence sitters so that the issue is very much up in the air. We had the A-12 sold to the Senate and the House committees until Athena came along, but with the headlines lately – and the budget deficit – any way they can save money looks better and better.'

Jake knew the headlines Knight was referring to. The Soviets under Mikhail Gorbachev had renounced world domination, and the aftershocks were being felt in capitals around the world. Gorbachev was well on his way to becoming the most popular and overexposed human on the planet, eclipsing rock stars, athletes, and, in some places, even God. The Cold War was over, according to some commentators and politicians with their own agendas. True or not, the perception of great change taking place in the 'evil empire' had profound consequences for the foreign and domestic policy of every Western democracy, and none more so than the United States.

The two officers spent the morning going over the cost projections of the A-12, which were based on an optimum purchase schedule. Any proposal that kept the A-6 in service for more years than already planned would also have to include the escalating costs of maintaining and repairing this ageing airframe. These costs were also calculated. Finally, any new proposal for another design would incur huge upfront costs, as the A-12 program had, and to kill the A-12 now would mean all the money spent to date would be wasted.

After lunch Knight, an officer from the Office of Legislative Affairs, and Jake's staff gathered in the conference room and pretended to be a congressional panel. They spent the afternoon grilling him. By five o'clock he was drained and hoarse.

Callie was reading Amy a bedtime story when the telephone rang. The girl leaped for the phone, then held it out to Jake.

'Captain Grafton.'

'This is Luis Camacho. Do you have a Robert E. Tarkington working for you?'

'What's he done now?' Tarkington had been on the mock panel this afternoon and had done a terrible job. His heart had obviously not been in it.

'Well, he's not at home, for one thing. His car is sitting outside an apartment building in Morningside and we think he's in it. It's the building that Commander Judy lives in. He's right smack-dab in the middle of our surveillance.'

'So run him off.'

'Well, that might produce sticky complications. I understand he has reason to bear Judy a grudge concerning his wife's injuries a couple of months ago. He might be armed. If so, he might be arrested on a concealed weapons charge, which I suppose wouldn't do his navy career much good.'

'It wouldn't. What if I ran him off?'

'Would you? Here's the address.' Camacho gave it, said goodbye, then hung up.

Callie looked at Jake with raised eyebrows. 'Would you ladies like to go for a ride before bedtime? Maybe get some frozen yogurt?'

After five minutes of furious activity, the females were ready. Jake drove through the heart of monumental Washington and ended up on the Suitland Parkway. Callie gave him directions with the aid of a map. They got lost once but eventually found the right street.

Although it was after 9 P.M., it had been totally dark less than half an hour. Heat still rose from the streets and children still ran through yards. Here and there stickball games were being conducted under streetlights. 'This is the best time of the day,' Jake told Callie as they sat at a stoplight listening to pop music pouring from the open windows of a car full of teenagers.

Six blocks later Callie said, 'That's the building, I think, up there on the left.'

'Keep your eyes peeled for Toad,' Jake advised Amy. 'He's sitting in one of these cars.'

'Why?' Amy asked.

'You'll have to ask him. Now look.'

His car was parked a half block beyond the apartment building. Only the top of his head was visible as Jake drove by with Amy squealing and pointing. Jake turned around again and this time double-parked just past his car. With the engine running and the transmission in park, he got out and walked back.

Toad's window was down. He stared blankly up at Jake's face.

'We're going out for a frozen yogurt, Wanta come?'

'How'd you—'

'Lock your car and climb in with us.'

'Jesus. CAG, I—'

Jake opened the driver's door and held it. 'Come on. That's an order.'

Toad pulled up the windows and locked the car. 'You can ride in back.' Toad obediently slipped in beside Amy. She greeted him like a long-lost friend. 'How's Rita?' she demanded.

'Doing okay,' Toad said. 'And how are you, Mrs Grafton?'

'Just fine, Toad. What kind of frozen yogurt do you like?'

'Any kind,' Tarkington said, still bewildered.

'Why were you parked out here?' Amy asked, hanging her arms around Toad's neck. 'You don't live here, do you?'

'Waiting on a man. He hasn't shown up.'

'Oh!' Amy thought about it. 'When can we see Rita?'

'Anytime you want.'

'Well, it's only nine o'clock,' Jake said to Callie. 'No school tomorrow for you aristocrats. What say we drive over to Bethesda and see if Rita's still awake? That okay with you, Toad?'

'Sure, Captain, sure.'

They stopped at a mall near the beltway entrance and bought cones of frozen yogurt. Everyone got one. As Amy skipped back toward the car and the adults followed, Toad asked Jake. 'How'd you know where I was?'

'FBI called me. They don't want you there.'

The younger man bristled. 'It's a public street. And I didn't see them lurking around waiting on anybody.'

'Oh, they're there. They saw you, got your license number, ran the plate and called me. They really didn't want to arrest you on a felony weapons charge.'

Toad's shoulders sagged.

'You must get on with your life,' Callie said gently, 'yours and Rita's, for you are part of her.'

'Let's go see her,' Jake suggested, and led the way toward the car.

Tarkington rode silently as Amy chattered between licks on her cone. He put his tongue in motion in the hospital reception room after the woman at the desk said, 'It's after visiting hours, Lieutenant.'

'I know, but I'm her husband. These are my folks, just in from the Coast. We'll be quiet and not stay long.' Toad winked at her and gave her his most sincere lying smile.

'I don't suppose a short visit after hours will do any real harm. For such close relatives.'

'Toad,' Amy asked in the elevator, 'why did you tell that lady a lie?'

'I didn't *really* lie,' Toad explained. 'See, I winked at her and she knew you weren't my relatives, that I was just giving her a good reason to bend the rules a tiny bit. If I tell you a story about fairies and frogs and passionate princesses, you know it isn't true and so it isn't a lie, is it? It's a story.'

'Well . . .' Amy said as she scrunched up her brows and tried to follow Toad's logic.

'I knew you'd understand, sis,' Toad said as the elevator door opened. He led them off and along the corridor toward Rita's room.

Rita was asleep when they tiptoed into the room. 'Maybe we should let her sleep,' Callie suggested.

Toad bent over and whispered her name. Her eyes fluttered. Then he kissed her cheek. 'You've got company, dearest.'

'Oh, Callie! Amy! Captain Grafton. What a pleasant surprise. How nice of you to come by.'

'Toad brought us,' Amy said. 'He lied to the lady downstairs. Said we were his family.' She winked hugely while Callie rolled her eyes.

Thirty minutes later Jake insisted they had to go. He led his family down the corridor while Toad said a private goodbye to Rita. Amy was tiring and talking too loud, so Callie tried to hush her, which made her whine. Jake picked her up and carried her.

In the car Callie chided Toad. 'You sitting in that car in Morningside while your in-laws are at your house. You should be ashamed.'

'Well . . .'

'When Rita gets out of the hospital, you must bring her over to the beach some weekend.'

'Sure. You bet, Mrs Grafton. I will.'

Back in Morningside, Jake double-parked across the street and walked with Toad over to his car. Jake waited until Tarkington had the car unlocked, then said, 'You have a beautiful wife, a good job, and all of life before you. Don't fuck it up by sitting here waiting to kill a man.'

'You saw what he did to Rita.'

'Yeah. And if you get lucky and get a bullet into him, the stuff that will happen to you afterwards will hurt her a lot worse than the airplane crash did. You'll be the one who twisted the knife. *Don't do that to her.*'

'Yessir.' Toad shook Jake's hand, then climbed into the car and cranked the window down.

'Thanks, CAG . . .'

'It's a good life, kid. Don't throw it away.'

'. . . for the frozen yogurt.' Tarkington started his car and snapped on the headlights.

'Night, Toad.'

'Good night, sir.'

As soon as Jake got his car rolling. Amy stretched out in the backseat. In a few minutes he checked that she was asleep, then said to Callie, 'Admiral Henry had a notebook.' He told her what he had learned from Camacho, that Callie's psychologist was telling Henry what she said in her therapy sessions.

'Oh, Jake.' She bit her lip. 'I've half a mind to write a letter to the Medical Board.'

'He was just trying to help Henry.'

'Damn him.' He looked at her. She was rigid, with both fists clenched.

He began to talk. He told her about the Minotaur, about Smoke Judy and Luis Camacho and the Russian spy. Crossing the Anacostia River, going north on South Capitol Street, creeping through the cooling evening along Independence Avenue by the Air and Space Museum, he told her everything he knew.

She listened carefully. They were parked facing the Lincoln Memorial on Twenty-third Street and watching the crowd still going to and from The Wall when she said, 'Camacho told the spy about Judy?'

'That Judy was corrupt? Yes. So he says.'

'He wanted something to happen.'

'What do you mean?'

'He was trying to make something happen.'

'Something *has* happened. Judy tried to steal the Athena file and killed Henry getting away.'

'That wasn't it,' she said, speaking with conviction. 'Henry had ordered the file changed, the documents moved. You knew – everyone with access knew. Camacho must have warned Henry.'

'But if Camacho knows a Soviet spy and talks to him, why doesn't he arrest him?'

'Something is *supposed* to happen. Something involving the spy and the Minotaur. And it hasn't happened yet.'

On Friday morning at 7 A.M. Jake met Rob Knight in a bagel joint on Independence Avenue, two blocks east of the Capitol. As they huddled at a tiny table in a corner munching bagels smeared with cream cheese and sipping coffee, Knight filled Jake in on the testimony of Royce Caplinger and Vice Admiral Dunedin before the joint subcommittee of the Senate and House Armed Services Committees the previous day. Neither had been asked about Vice Admiral Henry's death or Smoke Judy, perhaps because the Director of the FBI had spent thirty minutes with the committee before Caplinger went on.

'Dodgers will go first this morning. Duquesne will be done with him in an hour or so. He's going to question him very lightly on just the technical aspects of Athena, then praise him to the skies as the intellectual heir of Edison, Bell, and Einstein. That's his plan, anyway.' Knight grinned impishly.

'You really enjoy this, don't you?'

'It's the ultimate theater. The stakes are money, the mother's milk of politics, great heaping mountains of it. And the actors are politicians, without a doubt the lowest form of animate life. Charlatans, mountebanks, liars, hypocrites – they'd cut off your nuts for another term in office, or even a favorable article in a hometown newspaper. If you rendered the whole lot of 'em, you couldn't skim enough scruples to fill a thimble.'

'They're not all like that,' Jake protested.

Knight made a gesture of frustration. 'I suppose not.'

'When do they want me there?'

'Well, you're going to watch Dodgers' performance. You go after him. Normally these things are closed-door, but I got some members to sign two passes.' He displayed them, then handed one to Jake.

They wandered outside, then across to the Library of Congress. On the second floor of the giant anteroom they found a wooden bench in a corner and reviewed the documents Jake would refer to if necessary during his testimony.

After thirty minutes, Jake announced he was ready and stowed the documents in the briefcase he had chained to his wrist.

'Nervous?'

'Yeah. My stomach feels like . . .'

'Well, that's normal. I've seen vice admirals preparing for these soirees sweat like they were going to the gallows.'

'Too bad about Admiral Henry.'

'Yeah. Think they'll ever catch Judy?'

'Oh, he'll turn up, sooner or later.'

'What are you going to say if they ask you about him?'

'The truth. Just watch.'

'Don't get rattled. If you can't remember something, just say so. And don't feel bad about fumbling for a document. I'll be right there with you, and I'll help you find it.'

They chatted for another five minutes about this and that, about their careers, about mutual friends, about ships they had been on. Finally Knight announced that it was time.

They crossed the street and walked past the limos and congressmen's cars parked in the Capitol's back lot. They went up the marble steps and into the rotunda.

The place was packed with tourists standing in knots of thirty or more, cameras clicking, guides roaring their patter over the hubbub, the noise echoing in the huge open space above. The two naval officers in service-dress blue uniforms threaded their way through and turned right, passing between the statues into the main corridor.

They went up one flight of stairs and stopped finally beside a door manned by armed security guards, where they showed their passes. The guards consulted a list and said they could go in.

'You ready?' Knight asked again.

'Let's go to the head first.'

'Good idea.' Knight asked a guard for directions to the nearest men's.

Standing shoulder to shoulder at the urinals, Knight said, 'Think of all the great men who have relieved themselves here – senators, congressmen, generals, tycoons, kings. Makes you humble, doesn't it?'

The hearing room was a disappointment to Jake. He had expected some spacious room richly decorated in a courtroom motif, but what they got was another drab, windowless hearing room that needed paint and more lights. He and Knight took a seat against the back wall and watched the elected persons make their way in. They conferred with one another and found chairs on the dais that dominated the room. Duquesne came in, nodded at Jake and placed his briefcase at the speaker's stand in the center of the dais. Then he went from political person to political person shaking hands, murmuring softly.

'It never stops, does it?' Knight whispered.

'They'll be shaking hands and kissing babies at their own funerals,' Jake agreed.

Dodgers didn't even glance around when he was led in by two men that Jake assumed were senatorial aides. They placed him at the little witness table and sat down on either side of him.

With a glance at the clock, Duquesne took his seat. 'By mutual agreement, this is a meeting of the Senate and House Armed Services Committees' joint subcommittee on stealth projects. Dr Dodgers, I understand you are here by subpoena. Please pass it to the clerk, and state your full name.'

'Samuel Brooklyn Dodgers.'

'Is that his real name?' one of the congresswomen asked Duquesne, who repeated the question to Dodgers.

'Yes. I had it legally changed some years back.'

'Do you wish to make a statement to the subcommittee?'

'Yes, I do.'

Duquesne looked surprised. 'Is it written? Do you have copies with you?'

'No, sir. I just have a few preliminary remarks.'

'Go ahead then. You have five minutes.'

'As you know, I am the inventor of a radar supression device that the US Navy has licensed and is putting into production under the code name Athena. I have been working closely with the navy on my invention, and I must, say, they are very enthusiastic, as I am. My invention renders radar obsolete, makes it useless, which will revolutionize warfare as we know it. I feel my invention is the greatest instrument for God's peace ever invented. It will give the United States an insurmountable military advantage that will allow us to lead the world to God's new kingdom here on earth. We can once and for all demand that the heathen nations—'

Senator Duquesne interrupted as his colleagues began whispering among themselves. 'Please limit your remarks to the subject at hand, Dr Dodgers.'

'Yessir. Athena will allow us to convert the Jews and Moslems and pagans to God-fearing, righteous Christians who won't start wars or—'

'Dr Dodgers,' Duquesne said, 'I must insist. Your invention is not the only matter before this joint subcommittee. We are short of time. We have another witness to follow you.' Duquesne gestured at Jake. For the first time Dodgers turned and saw him. 'We could get right to the questions, if you don't mind.'

'One more point, sir. The naval officer who is in charge of Athena is here today, Captain Jake Grafton. I see him sitting back there against the wall. I wish to say here and now that he is a godless sinner, a mouther of obscene blasphemies, an agent of Satan. I have complained to the navy and various members of Congress to no avail. I am a man of God and a man of peace. I cannot continue to work with this—'

Duquesne whacked his gavel. 'Time! Thank you, Dr Dodgers. We'll get right to the questions.'

The aides whispered fervently in Dodgers' ear. Duquesne gave them the time. When Dodgers seemed to be settled down, Duquesne led him through a set of simple questions about Athena: what it was, how it worked, what Dodgers projected its capabilities as being.

'Dr Dodgers, does the Athena device have to go on a stealth airplane?'

'No, sir. It would work on any airplane, stealth or not. It would work on a ship, on a building, on a tank, a truck – anything that has a fixed set of radar-reflective properties that the computer can be programmed to nullify.'

When Duquesne had finished, he opened the floor to questions from other members. The chairman of the House Armed Services Committee, Representative Delman Richardson, from California, went first.

'I take it, Doctor, that you are convinced your device can be put into production cheaply and in a timely manner?'

'Yessir.'

'And it will work? It will do what you and the navy say it will do?'

'Yes. That is correct. It will prevent the object that it is placed upon from being detected by radar.'

'Yet, if I understand your earlier statement correctly, you think we should use this military advantage to convert the peoples of the world to Christianity?'

An uproar ensued as Duquesne tried to rule the question out of order and various members all tried to talk at once. The issue seemed to be whether the members from the House could ask the questions they could have asked had they not agreed to a joint hearing to save time. While all this was going on Rob Knight nudged Jake. 'Best show in town,' he whispered.

On the threat of being abandoned by the House subcommittee members, Duquesne caved in. Dodgers was given free rein to state his views on religion, sin, and conspiracies by each and every minority he could readily recall. Duquesne took it like a man, Jake thought. He should have known better. Other committee members took it less well, seeming to take offense that they had to sit through a recitation of Dodgers' poisonous inanities.

Dodgers was finally silenced by mutual consent and shown the door. After a ten-minute recess, it was Jake's turn. Gazing upward at the legislators on the dais, he immediately understood the psychological advantage the raised platform conferred on his interrogators.

'Do *you* have a statement to make?' Duquesne asked him when the preliminaries were completed.

'No, sir.'

A chuckle swept the room. That's a good start, Jake thought.

A committee staffer passed out copies of Jake's report and led him through it, page by page, conclusion by conclusion. It took the rest of the morning. When Duquesne announced a lunch break, Jake was surprised at how much time had passed.

He and Knight walked back to the bagel place for a tuna salad sandwich.

'How am I doing?'

'They haven't even started on you yet. Ask me at five o'clock.'

'Are we going to be here that long?'

'Maybe. Depends on Duquesne.'

After lunch the senator resumed his questioning. 'Tell me, Captain, just what were your orders when you were given your present assignment?'

'I was told to evaluate the two prototypes and prepare a recommendation as to which one I believed the navy should select for production as the A-12, medium attack bomber.'

'Did Vice Admiral Henry or Secretary Ludlow tell you – let me rephrase that – did either of them suggest which prototype you should recommend?'

'No. They didn't.'

'They didn't even hint at which one they wanted?'

'They discussed the navy's requirements for a new medium attack bomber on numerous occasions with me, sir, and they did make it clear to me that the plane had to be able to meet the needs of the navy. But they did not tell me which plane they thought would best meet those needs. Determining that was the whole purpose of the fly-off.'

'So the conclusions stated in this report and the recommendations made are yours?'

'Yessir. And the admirals wrote endorsements, and the Secretary of the Navy wrote one when he forwarded the report to SECDEF.'

'Did you tell your superiors what the substance of your report would be before you wrote it?'

'Yessir. I kept them fully informed about my activities and my opinions as I reached them.'

'Did you suggest changes to the draft document?'

'Yessir. That is normal practice. We were under a time crunch, and I circulated a summary of the report and they commented upon it and I made certain changes to the report that I felt were necessary based on their comments. But this is *my* report. I could have refused to make a suggested change and they could have commented on the matter in their endorsement. That, too, would be normal practice.'

'Did you refuse to make any changes?'

'No, sir.'

'So this report is now the way your superiors in the chain of command want it to be?'

'I believe the endorsements speak for themselves, sir.'

'You recommended the navy purchase the TRX plane in spite of the fact that the prototype crashed during evaluation and you failed to complete all the tests you had planned?'

'That is correct.'

'Why?'

'Senator, I think the report addresses that point much better than I could orally. I felt that the TRX plane had fewer technical problems than the Consolidated prototype and was a better compromise of mission capability and stealthiness. I also felt it was better suited to carrier operations. I thought that it would require fewer preproduction modifications to achieve the performance goals. All this is in the report. In short, I thought this plane gave the navy the most bang for its bucks.'

'Did you personally fly either plane?'

'No, sir. A test pilot did.'

'How much experience did this test pilot have?'

'I believe she has about sixteen hundred hours total flight time.'

'That isn't much, is it?'

'Everything is relative.'

'How much flight time do you have, Captain?'

'About forty-five hundred hours.'

'Do you have any previous experience testing prototypes?'

'No, sir.'

'Did your test pilot have any previous prototype testing experience?'

'No, sir.'

'Yet you used her anyway. Why is that?'

'She had an outstanding record at the Test Pilot School at Patuxent River. She finished first in her class. My predecessor was on the staff at TPS and picked her for this project. I saw no reason to fire her and get someone else.'

'Yet she crashed the TRX prototype?'

'It crashed while she was flying it. The E-PROM chips in the fly-by-wire system were defective.'

'Would the plane have crashed with a more experienced pilot at the controls?'

'Well, that's impossible to say, really.'

'You, for instance?'

'Senator, any answer I gave to that question would be pure speculation. I feel Lieutenant Moravia did a fine job handling that plane before and after it went out of control. There may be a pilot somewhere on this planet who could have saved it, but I don't know.'

Duquesne led him into the buy-rate and cost projections for the A-12. 'I see here that you recommend a total buy of three hundred sixty planes: a dozen the first year, twenty-four the second, then forty-eight each year subsequently.'

'That's correct.' Jake went into the cost equations. Before he could get very deep into the subject, Duquesne moved on.

Finally Duquesne got down to it.

'Captain, you have also been in charge of the Athena program, have you not?'

'Yes, sir.'

'This morning Dr Dodgers testified that this device would be cheap to build' – he gave the figures – 'could be in production in a year or fifteen months and could protect any object it was placed upon. In view of that, why does the navy want a stealth attack plane?'

'Athena can be made to work, with enough research, time and money. But it's not going to be easy. Right now the only way to determine the radar-reflective characteristics of an object is to test the entire object on a specially constructed range. And these characteristics change based on the frequency of the radar doing the looking. So every frequency must be tested. Consequently the data base that the Athena computer must use is very, very large. That's why we need a super-conductive computer to perform all the calculations required in a minimum amount of time. Still, it is impossible to build a system that could effectively counter every conceivable frequency. Athena will counter every frequency the Soviets are known to use. Yet if they shift frequencies quickly enough, with a semi-stealthy aircraft design we would not lose all our airplanes before Athena could be modified.

'Secondly, Athena will *not* be ready for the fleet in a year. More like three or four. Third, new technology may be developed to counter Athena. We believe, based on what we know now, that we need an attack plane with at least A-6 performance and payload capabilities, state-of-the-art avionics, and stealthy characteristics. That's the A-12. The TRX plane is the best that American industry can give us now, and now is the time when we need to put this airplane into production.'

'Why not kill the A-12 program and build a conventional attack plane that uses Athena to hide?'

'As I mentioned, Athena is added protection for our aircraft, but not the sole source, due to the limitations inherent in the technology. Quick change is the rule in electronic warfare, not the exception. The Israelis almost lost their 1973 war with Egypt due to advances in electronic warfare made by the Soviets and supplied to Egypt of which the West was not aware. The United States cannot afford to lose a war with the Soviets, Senator.'

Jake reached for his briefcase. Knight had it ready. 'My staff has done some calculations. To kill this program now and start all over again on another one, writing off all the development money spent to date and adding the inevitable inflationary factor, I figure it will cost just about the same per plane. Assuming Athena works well enough to become operational. If it doesn't, we'll have a brand-new, obsolete airplane. Regardless, in the interim we'll have to make do with the A-6, which is not ageing gracefully. We may even need to fund the A-6G program, just to keep the A-6s in the air until the follow-on airplane arrives.'

An aide passed a copy of Jake's figures to every member. Jake spent the next hour defending the methodology and the numbers.

Duquesne opened the floor to questions from other members, who had a variety of concerns. One of them asked, 'I understand you were awarded the Medal of Honor by this Congress, Captain?'

'That's correct, sir.'

'Why aren't you wearing it now?'

'It's a little gaudy, don't you think?'

Another congressman asked, 'Why is the navy going to name the A-12 the Avenger?' The propeller-driven Grumman TBF Avenger was the plane the President flew during World War II.

'In a survey of A-6 flight crews conducted navy-wide, that was the most popular suggestion. The people in the navy are very proud of the navy's tradition and history.'

'The choice of that name looks a little like bootlicking, don't you think?'

'Sir, I happen to like that name. The Avenger torpedo-bomber was a fine airplane in its day, with a proud name and a great combat record. We've named other jets after prop planes – Phantom and Corsair are two – so it's a choice popular with the people in naval aviation. Should Avenger get derailed somewhere along the way, my personal second choice would be Hellcat, another good old navy name.'

'That choice wouldn't be popular with Dr Dodgers,' the congressman said dryly.

'I doubt if it would,' Jake agreed.

And then it was over. He was excused. It was 4 P.M. Out on the steps Knight said, 'One down, two to go.'

That was right. Assuming the Armed Services Committees authorized some airplanes and the full House and Senate agreed, then the battle would begin to convince the appropriations committees to provide the dollars to pay for them.

Jake groaned.

'Relax. You did very well.'

'C'mon. Let's go get a beer somewhere. I'm dying of thirst.'

On Sunday morning as they walked on the beach and Amy played in the surf, Jake and Callie talked again about the Minotaur. 'As I understand it,' Jake said, 'he's not a mole in the usual sense of the word. He's not a Russian who slipped in years ago and worked his way into a position of trust. He's an American. A traitor.'

'This world of espionage and counterespionage,' Callie said, 'it reminds me of Alice in Wonderland. Nothing is ever as it seems.'

'What made you think of that?'

'If you lose something and look for it in all the usual places and you don't find it, what conclusions do you reach?'

'It isn't in a usual place.'

'Precisely. And if the FBI has been looking for a mole for three years, then the mole is not in the usual place.'

'But the usual places are positions where a person would have access to the information being passed.'

'Perhaps the mole was never there at all.'

Jake stared at her.

'How do you know the FBI has been looking?' she asked.

'Henry said so. Camacho said so.'

'Henry merely repeated what he was told. Camacho told you what he wanted you to hear. What if there is no mole at all? What if the Minotaur is merely a character, an actor assigned to play a part?'

Amy called her to look at something that had washed up on the beach during the night, and she went. Jake stood and watched them. The surf broke and swirled around their ankles as the seabirds circled and called.

'You are a very smart woman,' he told her when she rejoined him.

'Oh, I'm glad you noticed. What did I say that was smart?'

On Monday morning at the office Jake stopped by the copy machine and helped himself to twenty or so sheets of paper. In his office he closed the door and pulled on a pair of gloves he had brought from home. Spreading the pile of paper gingerly, he selected a sheet from the middle of the pile and slid it away from the others. It should be free of fingerprints. From his pocket he took a black government pen. He clicked the point in and out a few times as he stared thoughtfully at the paper.

In block letters in the center of the page he wrote: 'I KNOW WHO YOU ARE.' He put the words all on one line.

He inspected it carefully, then folded the sheet and placed it in a blank letter-sized envelope he had removed from a box at home this morning.

There was a pair of tweezers in his desk, in that vanity case Callie got him for Christmas a year or so ago. He found them and dropped them in his pocket.

He took the gloves off. With the envelope inside his shirt, he went to the men's head. There he used the tweezers to put the envelope on the counter. Holding his shirt pocket open, he used the tweezers again to fish a stamp from the interior. He moistened it on a damp place on the sink, then affixed it to the envelope.

Back in the office, trying hard not to touch the envelope at all, he dug through the classified Department of Defense directory until he found the address he wanted. This he copied onto the face of the envelope in block letters.

He put the envelope back into his shirt, put on his hat and told the secretary in the outer office he would be back in ten minutes.

He dropped the envelope in a mailbox on the plaza near the entrance to his building, then retraced his steps back to the office.

29

Vice Admiral Henry's funeral was on Wednesday in Arlington National Cemetery, held outdoors on the grass at the request of his eldest daughter. Everyone who was anyone in the Department of Defense was on hand, so Jake Grafton ended up seated among the rank and file. The politicians who ruled the armed forces sat on the right-hand side of the aisle, while on the left were the admirals and generals, who had been carefully seated in order of seniority as protocol demanded. A band played funeral airs and Royce Caplinger, George Ludlow, and CNO delivered short eulogies.

From where he sat Jake could see the backs of the heads of some of the heavyweights. Off to his left were the rows and rows of white monuments, marching across the green rolling terrain with faultless precision.

To his right was the low bulk of the Pentagon, only the top of it visible between the heads of the people and the uniformed ushers at parade rest.

Tyler Henry had spent his adult life in uniform, and Jake had no doubt that interment at this cemetery, with all those who had also served, would have met with Henry's approval. After all, Henry had died in combat, fighting for something he believed in.

Half listening to the speeches, Jake Grafton once again considered all he knew about the Minotaur affair. It was precious little, yet it seemed to him he could see the underlying structure. Perhaps, he mused, even that was an illusion.

The funeral was real enough. Henry was truly dead. The people involved were real, the information passed to the Soviets was real, Smoke Judy's attempt to steal the Athena file was real. And yet . . .

When he got back to the office, he made another trip to the copy machine for paper. This time he wrote: 'I KNOW YOU ARE THE MINOTAUR.'

He addressed the envelope as before and deposited it in the plaza mailbox when he went down to catch the shuttle to the Pentagon for another round of meetings.

*

On Thursday the announcement was made that the various committees of congress had authorized the navy to purchase the TRX plane as the A-12. Although the buy schedule was lower than planned, which would raise the cost of each plane by five million dollars, a general celebration was in order. That afternoon Jake and Admiral Dunedin treated everyone in the office to a beer bash at Gus's Place, a beanery on the lower floor of Jefferson Plaza 1.

'If you had any class, Grafton,' Rob Knight told him, 'you'd have taken us to Amelia's in the Underground.'

'No class. You got that right.'

'Two more hearings to go,' Rob said. 'Without an appropriation of money, all we have is a piece of paper to frame.'

Dunedin was in a cheerful mood. He laughed and joked with the troops, seemingly glad to once again, if only for a little while, be just one of the guys. He never could be, of course. The officers he had spent his career with were all retired, except for those precious few who were also vice admirals. All the others were playing golf in Phoenix and Orlando, selling insurance in Virginia Beach or boats in San Diego, or were working for defense contractors.

At one point Dunedin ended up at Jake's table. When they were temporarily alone, he said, 'Really a shame about Tyler Henry. He was going to retire in three months, you know.'

No, Jake didn't know.

'Had a little cottage up in Maine, right near the beach. Owned it for years. Was going to spend the rest of his life there, he told me, and if he never heard the sound of freedom again he thought he could live with that.' 'The sound of freedom' was a public relations euphemism for jet noise.

'I guess you burn out after a while,' Jake said.

'I guess. You win some, lose some, hope for the best. Even the politicians, they try to do that.'

Jake remembered that comment the following week after he watched Royce Caplinger sweat in front of a Senate Appropriations subcommittee. They kept him going over numbers for most of the day. Although he was subpoenaed, Jake never took the stand. He was delighted.

Caplinger stayed afterwards for private conversations with the senators. Jake left with Toad Tarkington, who had accompanied him. As they were leaving, Caplinger and Senator Duquesne were shaking hands. It was then that Jake remembered Dunedin's comment.

A week later the House Appropriations Committee held their closed-door hearing. Caplinger spent three hours on the stand, Ludlow two hours. After lunch came Jake's turn on the hot seat. Three hours later Congresswoman Samantha Strader cleared her throat.

Strader was in her early fifties, her hair permed, her eyes screwed up in a characteristic squint. One of only two Democrats in her state's congressional delegation, she represented a district carved from the core of her state's capital city, the only area of the state with a significant minority population. She had one of the safest Democratic seats in the country and had been elected pro forma a dozen times, yet until the last election she had been almost unknown outside her state. Prior to that election she had publicly entertained the idea of entering the presidential primaries as the only woman in the field. Her short-lived quest came to grief on the shoals of political and financial reality, but not before her name and face had been splashed coast to coast by the media. She had jabbed and pricked the real contenders during her moment in the spotlight, had a delightful time, and squinted all the while.

Sam Strader's avowed passion was the military. Every officer in the Pentagon knew what that meant. She hated them. With an excellent mind, a quick wit, and a tongue to match, she was a formidable opponent.

Today, at this closed hearing of the black projects subcommittee of the House Appropriations Committee, she adjusted the microphone in front of her and gazed at Jake Grafton as though looking through a dense smoke screen. 'Captain, please justify, if you can, the acquisition of another very expensive major weapons system by the US Navy when Chairman Gorbachev is cutting the Soviet military budget drastically, reducing manpower levels by ten percent, slashing new ship construction, cutting navy steaming time.'

'Congresswoman,' Jake said, trying to digest the question. 'I don't think I'm qualified to address that. I'm here to testify about the merits of the prototypes evaluated by the Advanced Tactical Aircraft program for production as the A-12.'

'Didn't Secretary Ludlow send you over here to testify?'

'Yes, ma'am. He did. And this panel questioned him for two hours this morning.'

'Now it's your turn. Answer the question, if you can.'

'As I've already said, we need the A-12 because the A-6 is wearing out. The A-6 has an airframe designed in the 1950s, and is already past the end of its service life. The carriers must have a viable all-weather attack capability or they are obsolete and—'

'But what about the Soviet initiative?'

'Congresswoman, he's trying to answer your question.' The chairman of the House Appropriations Committee was a Texas Democrat. Just now he looked bored. No doubt he was faking. Rumor had it he had underestimated Sam Strader once too often in the past. That was a mistake Jake Grafton had no intention of making. He was sitting at attention, listening carefully.

Strader ignored the chairman. 'Captain Grafton, I want to know when the navy is going to realize that the Soviet threat is diminishing and accordingly lower its requests for funds from this Congress.'

'The navy doesn't make budget requests of Congress. The administration does. Be that as it may, you assume the Soviet threat is diminishing significantly. I disagree. And the Soviets are only one of our possible adversaries. They still have four million men under arms. They have a formidable, capable navy. We are buying the A-12 to provide an all-weather attack capability for our aircraft carriers for the next thirty years. We must provide a strong Sunday punch for our fleet regardless of the twists and turns of Soviet policy or the ups and downs of this or that communist politician.'

'If the threat is diminishing, can we then scrap a carrier or two and cut back the A-12 buy order?'

'Congresswoman, the Warsaw Pact still has over fifty thousand tanks, four times as much artillery, and twice as many planes as NATO can muster. The Soviet army is three times larger than ours. We are a sea power. Over fifty percent of our oil is imported. I think any reduction of our naval capability when faced with these realities would be very unwise.'

'Captain, it seems to me that both we and the Soviets have spent more money on the military than either nation can afford, and now we have a perfect opportunity to reduce that expenditure. If we deterred them with what we had before they made a ten percent reduction, we can deter them just as well in the future if we make a ten percent reduction.'

'You persist in assuming the Soviet Union is our only possible opponent in a world in which we have global commitments. In the last forty years the navy has seen action in Korea, Vietnam, Grenada, and Libya and Lebanon several times. We've had to meet those commitments and deter the Soviets *too*.'

'And more gadgets are going to enable the navy to continue to do that?'

'I wouldn't characterize the A-12 as a—'

'I would! You people are gadget-happy. The attitude in the Pentagon seems to be that gadgets will keep us free. In the meantime our schools are atrocious and our bridges and highways are disintegrating. We desperately need a nationwide child-care system for working mothers and a long-term, healthcare system for the elderly. The damage that drugs are doing to the children of America is a national disgrace. We need to greatly expand our drug education and law enforcement efforts. Yet we can afford none of this because we keep borrowing money to buy grotesque gadgets to kill people with. And this at a time when the Cold War is *over*!'

'I'm not testifying to that,' Jake said tartly, and felt Toad Tarkington kick him under the table. 'The choices are difficult,' he added. 'I don't envy you your responsibilities.'

'Congresswoman Strader,' the chairman rumbled. 'This is a closed hearing. Your remarks will not leave this room, so I am at a loss as to why you are making a stump speech to Captain Grafton, who, unless I am mistaken, doesn't vote in your district.'

Strader shifted her squint back to Grafton. 'Just when will the navy's budget requests reflect the new geopolitical realities?'

Jake answered carefully. 'The navy's budget requests *to the administration* are based on the needs of the navy in light of the commitments the government has assigned the navy. As for geopolitical realities, I think the political ferment that is occurring in the Soviet Union is the most hopeful development in that nation in this century. But who knows if Gorbachev will prevail? He may be assassinated. There may be a coup. He may just be booted out by his colleagues. We can't sink the US Navy this year and hope for the best.'

'Time will tell. Is that your testimony? We should let the real human needs of our citizens go unmet so we can continue to fund a military establishment that is a travesty in a world seeking real peace?'

'Your admiration for Chairman Gorbachev is in many ways reminiscent of Neville Chamberlain's warm regard for Adolf Hitler. I hope you don't have reason later on to regret your enthusiasm, as Chamberlain did.'

Toad's shoe smacked on his shin again as Strader snarled, 'I deeply resent that remark, Captain. I—'

The chairman cut her off. 'Congresswoman Strader, this is not the time and place for a political colloquy with Captain Grafton. Please address your questions to the issue at hand. I must insist.'

Strader stared at Grafton. She was furious. 'Why is the A-12 a black project?'

'The technology involved is—'

'*No!* I reject that. The air force used that explanation for the B-2 bomber – $516 million each – and going higher – and the F-117A – $62 million each. They're acquired unproven airplanes with limited capabilities, airplanes that must be operated from paved runways that will be the Soviets' first nuclear targets in the event of war. No, Captain Grafton. *Public debate* is what the administration and the Pentagon seek to avoid.' Her gaze shifted to the chairman. 'Public debate is what you wish to avoid, Mr Chairman, so that your state can secure another bloated, outrageous defense contract for technology that may well not do what those hogs at the Pentagon—'

'Time's up.' The chairman smacked his gavel.

Strader was just getting up steam. '. . . that those money-hungry swine at the Pentagon have carefully steered to your state so that—'

'You're out of *time*, Congresswoman,' the chairman said, his voice rising, 'and out of *order*. Thank you for your testimony, Captain Grafton. You're excused.'

Strader kept talking. Jake packed his briefcase and handcuffed it to his wrist. '. . . these machines are being purchased to fight wars that everyone knows will *never* occur. Billions of dollars down the sewer! It's *obscene*.'

Jake rose and walked for the door with Tarkington at his elbow. Behind him Strader and the chairman were shouting at each other.

'You ever kick me again, Tarkington, and you'll need a proctologist to surgically remove that shoe.'

'Yes, sir.'

When the door closed behind them and they were walking down the corridor, Jake said, 'I really lost it in there, didn't I?'

'Yes, sir. You did.'

'Well, if they'll just vote the funds now, we've done the navy a pretty good job.'

'I suppose.'

As they went down the outside steps of the Capitol, Jake said, 'I hope she's right. I hope the wars never occur.'

'Yeah. And I hope I live forever,' Toad Tarkington said, and signaled to the transportation pool driver, who was standing beside the car a hundred yards away.

As the car pulled up, Toad climbed into the front seat, Jake into the back. They had just pulled the doors shut when the rear door opened again. Jake looked up. The man standing there had a pistol pointed at him. 'Slide over, Captain.'

Jake hesitated for just a second and glanced into the front seat. The driver had a gun pointed at Toad, Jake scooted.

The man outside took a seat and pulled the door shut.

'Gentlemen, as you can see, we are both armed. You are going to be our guests for a little while. Mr Tarkington?'

When Toad didn't respond, the man beside Jake nudged Toad in the neck with the barrel of his gun. 'Mr Tarkington?'

'Yeah.'

'I have a gun too, and it is pointed at Captain Grafton. The gentleman behind the wheel is going to put his gun in his pocket and drive. If you twitch, if you shout, if you open your door or reach for the wheel or ignition key. I will first shoot Captain Grafton, then I will shoot you. Do you understand?'

'Yeah.'

'Do you feel heroic?'

'Not especially.'

'That is very good. You and your captain may live through this experience if you do exactly as I say, when I say it.'

Tarkington said nothing.

'Put on your seat belts and lock your doors.'

Jake and Toad obeyed.

'Okay, if everyone understands the ground rules, we go.'

The driver put the transmission in drive and fed gas.

The gunman in the backseat was in his fifties, with short hair. He was tanned, stocky, and wore a well-fitting dark suit.

'Where is the sailor who was driving this car?'

'Captain, I warn you for the last time. You will sit absolutely quiet. One word, just one more word, and I will hurt you very badly.'

Jake Grafton looked at the gunman, then at the back of the driver's head. Toad sat rigid, staring straight ahead.

The car went out onto Independence Avenue and crept west in stop-and-go traffic. Jake eased the briefcase on his lap and felt the gun dig into his side. He sat very still and eventually the gun went away.

Okay, so he wasn't going to whack this guy with the briefcase and bail out of the car. That stuff only works in movies. He was going to sit very still and hope this guy didn't blow his brains out, or Tarkington's.

In spite of the air conditioning, Jake was perspiring profusely. He felt the moisture form rivulets on his face.

He tried to think. Here he was in the backseat of a navy Ford Fairmont sedan rolling through the streets of Washington. At the curbs buses were loading and unloading tourists, hordes of people from Nashville and Little Rock and Tokyo. People in cars with plates from the Midwest and South rubbernecked, and the drivers ignored the traffic signs, seeming to delight in suicidal lane changes and illegal turns onto one-way streets. Kids were running and shoving and demanding pop, mothers were calming squealing infants, and everyone was waiting in line or looking for a restroom. Yet in the middle of it all Jake Grafton and Toad Tarkington had guns in their ribs.

Maybe this guy was the Minotaur. Maybe he was an Ivy League political appointee who had sold out for some reason only a psychiatrist would understand. Yet the way he handled that pistol – Jake knew competence with a weapon when he saw it.

The driver swung left on Fourteenth Street and began to accelerate as he jockeyed with traffic. He crossed the Potomac on the George Mason Memorial Bridge and took the ramp down onto George Washington Parkway northbound.

'You can drop us anywhere along here,' Toad said, 'and we'll walk back to the office.'

Jake winced at the sound of his voice. The gunman beside him paid no attention.

'Glad we could give you guys a—' The driver's right hand flicked into

Toad's face with a sickening smack, which knocked his hat off. The car didn't even swerve.

Toad sagged against the window, then slowly raised his head.

The car continued up the parkway. The river was visible between the trees on the right. They passed the entrance to the CIA complex at Langley and continued on at fifty-five miles per hour, the traffic flowing around them at least ten miles over the speed limit.

Traffic on the beltway was thickening as the first surge of rush hour emptied from the city. The man at the wheel kept the car in the middle lane. On and on they rolled, past the Frederick cutoff, east now across the northern edges of the city.

Jake Grafton was bitterly regretting the impulse that had made him mail two letters to the Minotaur when the driver finally edged into a gap in the right lane and took the ramp down to New Hampshire Avenue, where he caught the green light and turned left, northward. They passed the Naval Surface Weapons Center and turned left, into a residential area. After four or five turns down shady streets with cars parked at the curbs and in driveways, the man at the wheel slowed. From a pocket he produced a garage-door opener. He aimed it as he swung left into a driveway. The door rose obediently. The car coasted to a stop inside the garage and the driver triggered the remote-control device again. The garage got very dark as the closing door shut out the light.

'Okay, gentlemen. We are here. We will sit here very quiet and still while the driver checks out the house.' The driver was already out of the car. He fiddled with the knob on the inside door, used a key or pick, and had it open in a few seconds. Before he entered he took out his pistol. In about a minute he was back. He nodded.

Toad went first, walking around the car while the driver in the doorway held a pistol on him.

Then it was Jake's turn. From the garage he entered a kitchen. Through the sliding glass door he could see a backyard swing.

'The basement.'

Jake went down the stairs. The slanted ceiling was so low he had to tilt his head.

The older of the two men, the man who had ridden in the backseat with Jake, held out his hand toward Toad. 'The handcuff key.'

Toad extracted it from his pocket and passed it across. The man used it to unlock the briefcase from Jake's wrist and cuff him to a chair. The driver produced a set of cuffs from a trouser pocket and cuffed Tarkington to a table.

As the driver sat on the couch with his pistol on his lap and lit a cigarette, the older man examined the lock on the briefcase. He glanced at jake. 'The combination?'

'Fuck you.'

'Ah, Captain. Do you honestly think I couldn't open the case without it? I merely wished to save myself several minutes of effort.'

Jake told him the combination. The man had it open in thirty seconds, scooped out the documents, and after glancing at his watch, sat down on the couch to read them.

'Who are you?' Toad asked.

'Does it matter?' the reader asked without looking up.

'Not right now. But I'd like a name to give to the FBI.'

The man just chuckled dryly and continued reading.

After a while – Jake wasn't sure how long, since he couldn't see his watch – the man said, 'This Athena device, a superconductive computer with multiple CPUs, do you think it can be successfully produced in three years?'

Jake said nothing. His stomach felt like he had swallowed a stone.

'Oh well, I don't have the time to get the answers, and I doubt that you would be forthright in any event. But it certainly is an interesting technological development. You Americans! A nation of tinkerers. What will you think of next?'

He went back through the documents slowly, taking his time, studying them. His pistol lay on the table beside him, within easy reach. Twice he glanced at his watch.

Jake looked around the room. The driver kept his eyes on him or Toad all the time. His pistol lay in his lap. Toad had both wrists cuffed together around the leg of a rather large table. Still, given a few seconds, he could lift the leg and be free of the table. Obviously that possibility did not concern the two gunmen very much. If Toad tried it, he would be shot or pistol-whipped within seconds.

Jake's cuffs went through the arm of a chair. Beside the chair sat a floor lamp, but to reach it with his right hand, he would need to stick his left hand under this chair arm. It was temptingly close, but he would need an opportunity. And if he got it, what then?

What did those instructors always say at SERE – Survival, Evasion, Resistance, and Escape – school? Never give up. Stay ready. Your chance will come.

These guys were waiting for someone. That much was obvious. Who? The Minotaur?

They had been in the basement for almost an hour when the stocky man spoke to the driver. 'Upstairs now, I think. Be sure to unplug the garage-door opener.'

'Yes, sir.' The driver went.

'Are you the Minotaur?' Toad asked.

The stocky man threw back his head and laughed. 'That is good. Very good. You are a real comedian.'

'He's not the Minotaur,' Jake said.

'Ah, Captain. What makes you say that?'

Jake didn't answer.

'A captain in the US Navy knows the identity of the Minotaur. Or at least knows who he is not. Interesting. Instructive. I'll bet you are a fount of interesting information, Captain. No doubt we'll have time later this evening to elicit some of it.'

He walked toward Jake with his back toward Toad. Jake tried to keep his eyes on the gunman, yet still he saw Toad bend down and grasp the table leg. It came off the floor. Even as it did the gunman whirled with his pistol at arm's length, leveled in both hands, pointed straight at Toad's face. 'What makes you think,' he asked easily, 'that I need you alive?'

Toad let the table leg go back down to the floor. 'Oh,' he said lightly, trying to smile and not succeeding. 'I thought you liked my witty repartee.'

'I *do* like you. With a mouth like yours you should be in Hollywood in the movies, not pushing paper at the Pentagon.' The gunman lowered the gun and took the seat on the couch that the driver had vacated, a place where he could watch both men with a minimum of effort. 'Now I think we will sit silently, not saying a word. Like mice.'

'You're a cocksucker,' Toad said.

The gunman looked at him and pursed his lips slightly.

'A genuine cocksucker. A cheap dick-sucking spook with a gun, a man who thinks everybody should faint dead away when he pulls out his weapon. Is that what they do when you whip out your dick? Is that—'

The gunman was very quick. He was moving and chopping with the pistol all in one motion.

Toad Tarkington was just as quick. He came off the chair and kicked mightily with his right leg. It caught the man in the knee and he lost his balance. Toad was erect now, the table hanging from his cuffs, his leg swinging again. This kick hit the gunman in the arm. The pistol went flying.

Jake leaped from the chair, dragging it. The lamp fell over. He dragged the heavy chair toward the pistol on the floor. Toad was still kicking.

He was almost to the gun when he heard the shot and saw a chunk fly from the carpet just in front of him.

He froze. The driver came down the stairs with the gun leveled. 'Get back.' He gestured threateningly at Toad, who seemed to shrink as his muscles relaxed. Tarkington exhaled convulsively, then turned slightly to find the chair he had been sitting on. At that moment the driver hit him a vicious blow in the back of the head with the gun and he fell heavily, overturning the table.

The second man helped the stocky man to the couch. He was still holding his stomach. He had blood on the corner of his mouth. Apparently one of Toad's kicks had taken him in the face.

'Upstairs. Get back upstairs. Get me my gun first.'

The second man obeyed, then went back up the stairs.

'Sit in the chair, Captain, right where you are. Sit! One move, just one, and I'll kill you and the lieutenant. Understand?'

Jake made the smallest of head nods. He sat.

Time passed. Minute by minute. The gunman on the couch massaged his arm and leg. Toad had really connected. Twice the man wiped the sweat from his face with his shirttail.

Toad stirred once. The table was on end beside him, He lay amid the magazines and newspapers that had gone flying when he jerked the table off the floor. Toad seemed to be breathing easily.

Jake heard the shuffling on the floor above him, and faintly the sound of a door closing. In seconds he heard someone walking above, then steps on the stair. He turned his head. Legs descending.

Luis Camacho walked into the room with the driver behind him, his gun in Camacho's back. 'Hi, Harlan. Didn't know if I was going to see you again.'

Camacho walked over to the couch and seated himself next to Albright. 'Jesus, what have you idiots done to my basement?'

Albright gestured at Tarkington, who was stirring again. 'That fucker thought he was a hero.'

'Looks like that table has a busted leg. My wife isn't going to be happy.'

The driver stood near the bottom of the stairs where he could watch everyone. He kept the pistol leveled at Camacho.

'Well, Captain,' Camacho said. 'You've had an eventful afternoon.'

'Yeah,' Jake replied. 'Who are those guys?'

'Well, the man beside me goes by the name of Harlan Albright. His real name is Peter Aleksandrovich Chistyakov. And this gentleman with the pistol at the bottom of the stairs – though I have never before had the pleasure – is, I think, Major Arkady Yakov of the Soviet Army.'

'Okay,' Albright said, 'thanks for the introductions.' He rose from the couch and turned Toad's table upright, then pulled a chair around and sat on it, facing Camacho.

'You know why I'm here. I thought since I was going to drop by, I might as well help myself to some Athena information on the way. It was very interesting. But it is you I want.'

'How droll. I wanted to talk to you too. You should have called.'

'You're going to give me some answers, Luis. Now. If you don't, I'm going to kill the lieutenant. Then the captain. Then you. I want answers.'

'What will you do with them if you get them?'

Albright's eyes widened. He took three steps across to the telephone at the end of the couch, picked it up and held it to his ear. He jiggled the button on the cradle, then replaced the instrument. 'Upstairs, Yakov. Check the front and back.'

The major took the stairs two at a time.

In about a minute he was back. He spoke to Albright in a foreign language, one that sounded to Jake like Russian.

'This is a setup.'

Camacho shrugged. 'My people saw you drive in. I thought you might be by to see me sooner or later. Didn't know who you brought with you, though. Sorry, Captain.'

Jake nodded.

Camacho stood and shook out his trousers. 'Tell you what, Harlan. Let's you and I go downtown. We can talk there. No sense keeping these fellows any longer.'

Albright took his pistol from his pocket. 'Sit.'

When Camacho obeyed, Albright followed suit, back at the table. He rubbed his eyes. 'So.' He spoke a sentence in Russian.

Camacho waved a hand irritably. 'You know I can't handle that language anymore. English or nothing.'

'You've been stringing me right along, haven't you, Luis?'

Camacho's shoulders moved a quarter inch up, then subsided.

'That name you gave me. That was bullshit, wasn't it?'

'No. That was the name.'

'Why?'

'You have something we want. At least, we think you have it. You're going to give it to me, Harlan. Hard or easy, you're going to give it to me.'

'Tell me what you want and maybe I'll give it to you now.'

Camacho threw back his head and laughed. 'You want to defect?'

Albright's eyebrows went up. 'Maybe.'

'Then shoot the major.'

'Just like that?'

'Then we'll talk. That would be the easy way. The hard way will be more strenuous, but equally productive, I think.'

Albright glanced at the major, who was looking straight at Camacho. Still, Jake saw the major's eyes flick sideways to catch Albright's glance.

'You can't get out of here, Harlan,' Camacho said, and stretched lazily, 'The place is completely surrounded, with helicopters and light planes overhead. Why don't you two give me the guns and we'll go upstairs and wave at Dreyfus. Then you and I can go downtown to the office. I'm sure the two of us can work something out.'

'I may not know the fact you want, Luis.'

'I think you do.'

'You've gone to an extraordinary lot of trouble for nothing if I don't know it.'

'Life's like that.'

'Maybe I could just give it to you here and now. If I know it.'

Camacho sat silently looking at Albright. 'Three names,' he said at last.

Albright laughed, a long, loud guffaw. 'All of this – for that?'

'Yes.'

'My hat is off to you. I salute you. Never did I suspect. Not even once.' Albright shook his head and chuckled silently as he examined his pistol.

Camacho sat motionless, watching Albright.

'You do know,' the FBI agent said finally, when all the laughing had stopped.

'You found the bomb?'

'Yes.'

'It was a warning. I needed that name.'

'I know. Hard or easy. Your choice.'

'You mean it?'

'Yes.'

'We'll take you and Captain Grafton as hostages,' Albright said, rising from the chair. He glanced toward Yakov and jerked his head at Jake. As Yakov stepped in that direction Albright shot him.

Yakov spun, firing at Albright. The bullet hit Albright square in the chest and his pistol sagged, exploding again pointed at the floor. At almost the same instant Toad Tarkington lashed out with his feet, and Albright went sideways as a foot was kicked out from under him. Yakov's second shot hit his shoulder and he spun from the impact as he fell.

Yakov's third shot came as he was falling. It was aimed at Camacho, who was still sitting on the couch. He hadn't moved.

Camacho doubled over as Yakov hit the floor.

Jake toppled his chair going for Yakov's pistol. He wrestled the gun from the major's weak grasp and crouched beside the chair, on top of the Russian major as he watched Albright.

The whole sequence hadn't taken five seconds.

Toad got to his feet. He was free of the table. He bent down shakily and retrieved the pistol that Albright had dropped. 'This one's still alive.'

'Quick,' Jake said. 'Check Camacho.'

Jake held the gun on the major's head as Toad stretched Camacho on the couch. 'He's hit lower down,' Toad said. 'Dead center. Still alive, though.'

'Go upstairs. Get the agents.' Toad made for the stairs. 'Put the gun in your pocket,' Jake called after him. 'Don't let them shoot you.'

Camacho sat up on one elbow.

'Is he dead?' he whispered hoarsely, looking at the major.

'No,' Jake said. 'He's hit in the right side, but he isn't dead. He may make it.'

'Kill him.'

'Why?'

'He heard too much. Kill him!' Camacho coughed, a bubbly gurgle.

Jake moved toward Camacho, dragging the chair. Behind him Major Yakov began to crawl.

'Give me the gun,' Camacho said.

'No.'

'This isn't a game, Grafton! *Give me the gun!*'

Jake tossed it.

The pistol landed on the couch. Camacho groped for it while Yakov struggled for the stairs.

Yakov jerked as the first shot hit him. He tried again to crawl. Taking his time, Camacho shot him four more times. A red stain spread across the back of Yakov's shirt and he lay still.

Camacho dropped the pistol and sagged down onto the couch.

'Albright! Albright, can you hear me?'

'Yeah.'

'Give – me – the – names,' Camacho dragged himself along the couch so he could see the Russian's face.

'I—' Albright's lips were moving but no sound came out. Then he ceased to move at all.

Camacho's head went down to rest on the couch.

'Who is the Minotaur?' Jake demanded. With a heave he got the chair over to the couch and shook Camacho. 'Tell me! *Who is the Minotaur?*'

'You don't want – No! It's not what you – he's not . . .'

Camacho went limp. Jake turned his head so he could see his face. His eyes were open, staring fixedly at nothing.

Jake sagged down beside the bloody couch. He heard the sound of running feet upstairs.

30

The sky was crystal-clear, a pleasant change from the late-summer haze. From this infinite sky a bright sun shone down on a day not hot and not yet cold, a perfect late-September Sunday. The trees along the roads where Jake Grafton drove had just begun to lose their green and don their autumn colors. Their leaves shimmered and glistened in the brilliant sun.

Most of the radio stations were broadcasting music, but it was public-service time on the others. He listened a few moments to two women discussing the nuances of breast-feeding, then twirled the selector knob. The next station had a preacher asking for donations for his radio ministry. Send the money to a PO box in Arkansas. He left the dial there. The fulminations filled the car and drifted out the open window. Samuel Dodgers would have liked this guy: hellfire for sinners, damnation for the tempters.

Toad Tarkington was leaning against the side of his car at the Denny's restaurant when Jake pulled into the lot.

'Been waiting long?'

'Five minutes.' Toad walked around the front of Jake's car and climbed in. In spite of the sun and seventy-five-degree temperature, he was wearing a windbreaker.

'How's Rita?'

'Doing okay.'

Jake got the car in motion.

'Where're we going?'

'I told you on the phone. To see the Minotaur.'

'Yessir. But where is that?'

'You'll see.'

Toad lapsed into silence. He sat with his hands in his lap and stared straight ahead at the road. On the radio the preacher expounded on how Bible prophecy had predicted the popularity of rock music.

Passing through Middleburg Toad said, 'I think we ought to kill him.'

Jake held out his right hand, palm up. Toad just looked at it.

'Let me have it.'

'What?'

'Your gun. The one you have under that jacket.'

Toad reached under the left side of his jacket and extracted a pistol from his beltline, which he laid in the captain's hand. It was a navy-issue nine-millimeter automatic, well oiled but worn. Jake pushed the button and the clip fell out in his hand. This he pocketed. Holding the gun with his right hand, he worked the slide with his left. A shiny cartridge flipped out and went over his shoulder into the backseat. The gun he slipped under the driver's seat.

'Who is he?'

'You'll see.'

'Why are we going if we aren't going to kill him?'

'You've been watching too many Clint Eastwood movies. And you ask too many questions.'

'So why did you call me?'

'I didn't want to go alone. I wanted a witness. The witness had to be someone who is basically incorruptible, someone beyond his reach.'

'I'm not beyond anyone's reach.'

'Oh, I think you are, Tarkington. Not physical reach. I'm talking about moral reach. None of his weapons will get to you.'

'You make me sound retarded. How do you know this guy we're going to see is the Minotaur?'

'I wrote him three letters. Notes. Then this morning I called him and said I was dropping by to chat.'

'Just friendly as fucking shit.' Toad thought about it. Jake waited for him to ask how Jake learned the Minotaur's identity, but the lieutenant had other things on his mind. 'If it weren't for this turd, Camacho would have arrested Judy months ago and Rita wouldn't have got whacked up. Camacho would still be alive.' He reached for the radio and snapped it off. 'Goddamnit, Captain, this man is *guilty.*'

'You don't *know* anything, Toad. You don't know who, you don't know why. Since Rita did get hurt, since that little mess in Camacho's basement, I thought you had a right to know. That's why I called you. So you're going to find out this afternoon.'

'Do you know?'

'Why, you mean?'

Toad nodded.

Jake thought about it. 'I've made some guesses. But they're only that. Guesses are three for a quarter. Facts I don't have. Camacho, though, he knew.'

'And he's dead.'

'Yes.' Jake turned the radio back on.

'Are we going to turn him in, call the cops?'

'You ask too many questions.'

In a moment Toad said, 'Why do you listen to this crap?' He gestured toward the radio.

'It's refreshing to hear a man who knows precisely where he stands. Even if I don't share his perch.'

The leaves of the trees alongside the road had the deep green hues of late summer. Cattle and horses grazing, an occasional female rider on a groomed horse in the manicured meadows, glimpses of huge two- or three-story mansions set back well away from the public road at the end of long drives; this countryside was fat. The contrast between this rich and verdant world of moneyed indolence and the baked, potholed streets of Washington jarred Jake Grafton. He could feel his confidence in his assessment of the situation ebbing away as the car took them farther and farther from the Pentagon and the navy.

Five miles north of Middleburg he began to watch the left side of the road. He found the tree and mailbox he had heard about. The box merely had a number, no name. He turned into the hard-packed gravel drive and drove along it. Huge old trees lined the north side of the road, a row that ended in a small grove around a large brick house almost covered with ivy.

Jake Grafton parked right in front.

'Ring the bell,' he muttered at Toad, who gave several tugs on a pull. The sound of chimes or something was just audible through the door.

Tarkington's eyes darted around.

The door opened.

'Did you get lost?' Royce Caplinger asked, and stood aside to let the two men enter.

'Little longer drive than I figured, Mr Secretary.'

Toad gaped.

'Close your mouth, son. People'll think you're a politician,' Caplinger muttered and led the way down the hall. They passed through a dining room furnished with massive antique tables and chairs and accented with pewter tankards and plates, and on through a kitchen with brick walls and a huge fireplace with an iron kettle hanging in it. A refrigerator, sink, and conventional stove sat against the far wall, on the other side of a work island.

'Nice place you have here,' Jake Grafton said.

'Rustic as hell. I like it. Makes me feel like Thomas Jefferson.'

'He's real dead,' Toad said.

'Yeah. Sometimes I feel that way too, out here without the traffic and airplane noise and five million people all scurrying . . .' They were in the study now, a corner room with high windows and ceilings. The walls were covered with books. Newspapers scattered on the carpet, some kind of a red-and-blue Oriental thing.

Caplinger waved his hand toward chairs and sank into a large stuffed chair with visibly cracked leather.

He stared at them. Toad avoided his gaze and looked at the books and the bric-a-brac tucked between them. By Toad's chair was a pipe stand. In it was a corncob pipe, blackened from many fires.

'I wasn't sure, but I thought it might be you, Captain,' Caplinger said. 'Didn't recognize your voice on the phone this morning.'

Jake Grafton rubbed his face with his hands and crossed his legs.

'We were just driving through the neighborhood, Royce,' Toad said, 'and thought we'd drop by and ask why you turned traitor and gave all those secrets to the Russians. Why did you?'

Jake caught Toad's eye. He moved his head ever-so-slightly from side to side.

Jake addressed Caplinger. 'Mr Secretary, we have a problem. We know you're the Minotaur and we have some ideas, probably erroneous, about the events of the last few months. Four or five people have died violently. Mr Tarkington's wife, Rita Moravia, is a navy test pilot who was seriously injured, almost killed, because various law enforcement agencies failed to properly investigate and make arrests on information they had had for some time. To make a long story short, we came here to ask if you would like to discuss this matter with us before we go to the authorities and the press. Would you?'

'Are you going to the press?'

'That depends.'

'You notice I didn't ask about the authorities. That doesn't worry me, but for reasons – well!'

Caplinger slapped his knees and stood suddenly. Toad started. 'Relax, son. I only eat lieutenants at the office. Come on, let's make some coffee.' He led the way into the kitchen.

He filled a pot with water. The pot went on the stove, after he lit the gas jet with a match. He put a paper filter in a drip pot and ladled three spoonfuls of coffee in. 'You two are entitled to an explanation. Not legally, but morally. I'm sorry about your wife, Lieutenant. So was Luis Camacho. We had too much at stake to move prematurely.' He shrugged. 'Life is complicated.'

Caplinger pulled a stool from under the counter and perched on it.

'Three years ago, no, four, a KGB colonel defected to the United States. It wasn't in the papers, so I won't tell you his name. He thought he was brimming with useful information that we would be delighted to have in return for a ton of money and a new life in the West. The money he got and the new identity he got. But the information wasn't worth much. He did, however, have one piece of information that he didn't think much of but we found most interesting.'

Caplinger checked the water on the stove.

'It seems that one day about three years before he defected he paid a visit to the Aquarium, the Moscow headquarters of the GRU, which is

Soviet military intelligence. His errand doesn't really matter. During his two or three hours there he was taken into the office of a general who was not expecting company. On the desk was a sheet of paper with four names. The colonel read the names upside down before the general covered the paper with a handy file.'

The water began to rumble. Caplinger checked the pot as he continued. 'Under hypnosis the defector could remember three of the four names. We recognized one of them. V. Y. Tsybov.'

The coffeepot began to whistle. As he reached for it Caplinger said, 'Vladimir Yakovich Tsybov was the real name of Luis Camacho.'

He poured the hot water into the drip cone and watched the black fluid run out the bottom. 'Luis Camacho was a Soviet mole, a deep illegal sent to this country when he was twenty years old. He was half Russian and half Armenian, and with his olive skin and facial characteristics, he seemed a natural to play the role of a Mexican-American. He knew just a smattering of Spanish, but what the hey. His forefathers, so said his bio, had been in this country since Texas became a state.

'Tsybov, now Camacho, attended a university in Texas and graduated with honors. He obtained a law degree at night while he worked days. The FBI recruited him.

'It's funny' – Caplinger shook his head – 'that J. Edgar Hoover's lily-white FBI needed a smart Mexican-American. But at the time Hoover was casting suspicious eyes on the farm-labor movement in California, which was just being organized, and needed some Chicanos to use as undercover agents. So Luis Camacho was investigated and approved and recruited.'

Caplinger laughed. 'Hoover, the paranoid anti-communist, recruited a deep Soviet plant! Oh, they tried to check Camacho's past, and the reports to Washington certainly looked thorough. But the agents in the field – all good, white Anglo Protestants with dark suits and short haircuts – couldn't get much cooperation from the Chicano population of Dallas and San Antonio. So rather than admit failure to the Great One, they sort of filled in the gaps and sent the usual reports to Washington. And the FBI got themselves a new agent.

'How do you like your coffee?'

Royce Caplinger got milk from the refrigerator and let Toad add some to his coffee. They carried their cups back to the study.

'Where was I?'

'Camacho was a deep plant.'

'Yes. Anyway, being smart and competent, he rose as far as the racial politics of the FBI would allow, which really wasn't very far. Still, amazingly enough, Luis Camacho liked America. But that is another story.' Caplinger set his coffee beside him. 'Maybe I should fill it in, though. Luis was a very special human being. Luis—'

'There were three other names on the list,' Toad said irritably. His whole manner told what he thought of Caplinger's tale.

'Ah yes,' Caplinger said, looking at the lieutenant thoughtfully. 'Three more names, two of which the defector could remember, one which he could not. The problem was we didn't know who any of the other three were. Tsybov was Camacho, whom the Soviets thought was still a plant under deep cover, a sleeper, available for use if the need arose. They didn't know that Camacho had revealed himself to us voluntarily almost ten years before.'

Caplinger looked from face to face. 'You see the problem. The Soviets had three more agents in America planted deep. And we didn't know who they were!

'Naturally the intelligence coordinating committee took this matter up. What could be done?'

'So you became the Minotaur.' Jake Grafton made it a statement, not a question.

'We needed bait, good bait. We wanted those three deep agents. Or two or one. Whatever we could get. Someone had to become the Minotaur, so the President chose me.'

'The President?' Toad said, incredulously.

'Of course. Who better to choose what military secrets the Soviets would find interesting? Who better to reveal the aces?' Caplinger sipped his coffee.

'So you . . .' Jake began. 'You wrote the letters and mailed them?'

'Yes. The National Security Agency gave me the computer codes I needed and helped with the encryptions. But I had to sit down and write each letter. The human touch, you see. Each letter would reveal something of the man who wrote it, so they all had to be written by one man.

'Much to our dismay, the instrument the Soviets chose to exploit the gifts of the Minotaur was a traitor-for-hire who had already approached their embassy a year or so before. Terry Franklin. What Terry Franklin didn't know was that the National Security Agency has special programs that reveal when each selected classified document is accessed. He wrote a trapdoor program that got him by the first security layer, but there was another that he didn't know about. So we were immediately on to him. And immediately faced with a dilemma.'

'If you arrested him too soon, the Soviets might just ignore the Minotaur.'

'Precisely, Captain. For this to work, the information had to be very good stuff, the best. And we had to give them enough so that they would become addicted to it. Then, and only then, would they feel the potential profit was enough to risk deep plants that had been in place for twenty to thirty years.' The secretary looked from face to face. 'Don't you see? These sleepers were assets! They belonged to someone in the GRU who had built his career on the fact that he had these assets, which would someday, at the right moment, be of incalculable value. Our task was to convince him or his superiors that now was that moment.'

'So you let Franklin do his thing.'

'Precisely. And we gave them excellent information. We let them see the best stuff that we had. We got them addicted, and curious. So one day Franklin's control approached Camacho, Tsybov.' He lifted a finger skyward for dramatic effect. 'That was a very important event. *The Soviets had gone to one of the names on the list.* Now we knew we were on the right track. We were heartened.'

Caplinger rose quickly from his chair and began to pace. He explained that Harlan Albright, the control, was a GRU colonel. He made contact with Camacho, moved into the house beside him, insisted on biweekly briefings. 'What the Soviets wanted, of course, was the identity of the Minotaur. So the game began for Luis Camacho. We didn't authorize him to reveal the Minotaur's identity. But he knew. He had to know. He knew from the first. He was the man who was actually going to uncover the sleepers.'

He was silent for a moment, thinking it over yet again. 'Once Camacho was in the game, he became the key player. It was inevitable. He had to appear to be a double agent and yet he had to force the Soviets to act. *To act* as we wanted them to. He was playing a dangerous role. And to appreciate how good he was at it, you would have to have known Luis Camacho very, very well. I didn't, but I got the flavor of the man. In his own way, in his own field, he was a master.'

Caplinger stopped at the window and looked out at the meadows and distant blue mountains, which were a thin line on the western horizon. 'Inevitably, and I do not use that word lightly, people were going to get hurt. Smoke Judy was an information peddler. He killed Harold Strong – your predecessor, Captain – when Strong found out about his activities. Camacho learned his identity, but we thought he might be of use later, so the committee ordered him left alone. Certainly no one could foresee that an indirect result of that decision would be the loss of the TRX prototype and your wife's injuries, Lieutenant, but . . . there were reasons that looked good at the time why it was handled the way it was.' He finished lamely and turned to face Tarkington. 'I am sorry.'

Tarkington was examining his running shoes. He retied one of the laces.

'Anyway, there were several other deaths. A woman was killed who witnessed a drop set up by the Soviets to give Terry Franklin information, a Mrs Matilda Jackson. Harlan Albright killed her, after *we* ordered Camacho to reveal her identity to Albright as proof of his bona fides, his commitment. Camacho refused at first, but we convinced him. This was the way it *had* to be. Better to sacrifice one to save the many.' The secretary went back to his chair and sat heavily. He shook his head slowly. 'Too often,' he said softly, 'we must assume some of God's burden. It is not light.'

'Too bad,' said Toad Tarkington, now staring at the secretary, 'that after you gave an innocent civilian the chop, this whole thing fizzled.'

'Did it?' Caplinger's voice assumed an edge, a hard flinty edge. 'Did it now?'

When Toad didn't respond, Caplinger went on, his voice back to normal. 'So after three years and some damn tragic risks, the stage was set. After a few carefully chosen facts were fed to Albright, he killed Terry Franklin. That was a masterpiece of cunning, well set up by Camacho. Of course Luis didn't like it, not he, but he played his part to perfection. Albright personally eliminated the Soviets' only access to the Pentagon computer. He had to find another. Because now the Minotaur offered the richest gift of all: Athena.'

'Smoke Judy,' said Jake Grafton, unable to keep silent.

'Yes. Smoke Judy, a bitter little man who had killed once and found how easy it is. Of course, that was the crisis. When Judy failed, as fail he surely would with Luis Camacho watching him, Albright would have no other choice. He would have to go to another deep plant on the list! And he would make this inevitable choice of his own free will, unpressured by anyone. That was our thinking, at least. Didn't work out that way. Camacho thought Albright was onto him and made a decision on his own to warn Vice Admiral Henry about the risk to Athena.' He gestured to the heavens. 'It was all downhill from there. Henry took it upon himself to apprehend Judy. You know how that turned out. The jig was up. Camacho had no choice. He sent men to arrest Albright.'

'You were willing to give away Athena?' Jake's horror was in his voice.

'We on the committee were willing to take the risk Albright would get it, which isn't precisely the same thing, Captain. By now the Minotaur's credentials were impeccable. We thought that surely, for this exquisite technical jewel, the Soviets would brush the dirt off one or two deep agents.'

'But they didn't?'

'No. Perhaps Albright was suspicious. Probably was. Camacho knew that Albright saw the whole operation too clearly, so he revealed the Minotaur's actual identity to save the game. It wasn't enough. With Judy and Albright in hiding, the Minotaur wrote one more letter, giving the access codes for the new Athena file. Then we waited for the Soviets to activate one of the sleepers. They didn't. What happened next was Albright kidnapped you, swiped all the Athena information he could readily lay hands on, then went to Camacho's house to kill him. Camacho had been expecting Albright to try something, but we didn't know exactly what it would be. When Luis Camacho came down those stairs and saw you there that afternoon – then he knew. The Soviets weren't going to invest any more major assets in this operation. His sole hope of getting the sleepers' names was Harlan Albright, who *might* know.'

Jake said, 'I wondered why the Athena file was suddenly re-named, all the access codes changed.'

'Henry shouldn't have done that. Camacho shouldn't have warned him. But Camacho was worried he didn't have all the possible holes covered and he knew Athena's real value. Still, it would have worked if Henry hadn't interfered.' Caplinger sounded as if he was trying to convince himself.

'We had to let the Russians work at it. If they succeeded too easily, they would have smelled the setup. No, our mistake was giving them the real Minotaur. Perhaps they found his identity too troublesome once they knew.'

Caplinger shrugged. 'After Judy failed, we wanted Albright badly. Our thinking then was that perhaps we could get the names from him, willingly or with hypnosis and drugs. We thought the odds about three to one that he knew the names *then*. If the GRU was even contemplating using a sleeper, the controller had to be briefed in advance, before the possibility became the necessity. Yet Albright evaded the clowns sent to pick him up. The agents thought they were going to arrest a mail-fraud suspect.' Caplinger spread his hands, a gesture of frustration. 'So we waited, hoping against hope a sleeping mole would awaken. It didn't happen.'

'So you failed,' Toad said.

'Oh no, Mr Tarkington. The Minotaur succeeded beyond our wildest dreams. Not exactly in the way we expected, of course, but the benefits are real and tangible. This operation was one of the most successful covert intelligence operations ever undertaken by any nation. Ever.'

'Please explain, sir.'

'I see the disbelief written all over your face, Captain.'

'My impression is that you people gave away the ranch, sir. Just how many top secret programs *did* you compromise?'

'We showed them the crown jewels, Captain. We had to. They would never have taken the bait otherwise. The three buried moles are very valuable.'

'Pooh.' Tarkington shook his head. 'I'm not buying it. Those three agents may have turned, exactly like Camacho. If the Soviets ever try to use them, those guys may run straight to the FBI. The Russians may not even know where they are now.'

'You are a very young man, *Lieutenant*.' Caplinger was scathing. 'You have a *lot* to learn. The deep plants are valuable to the Soviets as chips in the Cold War poker games, at home and abroad. They are valuable in exactly the same way that thermonuclear weapons are valuable, ICBMs, boomer submarines – I could go on. Those three buried agents are *hole cards*, Lieutenant. They may even be dead. *Yet we can never afford to ignore them.* Do you begin to understand?'

'Yessir.' Toad looked miserable. 'But—'

'There are layers and layers and layers.'

'But listen,' Toad objected reasonably. 'We didn't even know these men existed until four years ago. What if they don't?'

'*Aha!* The light becomes a glow!'

Caplinger leaped from his chair, galvanized. 'Perhaps they don't exist! Perhaps the defection of a mid-level KGB officer was a ploy, and the list was bait to make us think they had three agents. They write the list, they leave it where a man of dubious professional accomplishments, a man of dubious loyalty and dubious value, will see it. Very convenient, you must admit! And in the fullness of time he is given an opportunity to defect which he, no fool, takes as the best of a poor range of options.'

Caplinger's voice rose to a shout. 'And he gets here and tells us his little tale. We give it credence. *We must!* We have no other choice.'

'I'm slightly baffled, Mr Secretary,' Jake said dryly. 'Just how did the Minotaur succeed, if that word can even be used in these kinds of – what the hell are they? – games?'

Royce Caplinger began to walk back and forth, lost in thought. 'The Soviet Union today is a nation in transition. Their system is against the wall. The Soviet people want good wages and housing and food to eat. The generals want to maintain their privileged positions. The politicians want to stay in power. (That's human enough. Ours will sell their soul for another term in office.) To do all of this the Soviets need money, vast quantities of it, money that does not exist.

'So the government is scrambling for money. What the Minotaur did was prove beyond a shadow of a doubt that the amount they have been spending for defense was nowhere near enough. The Soviets have spent as much money in real terms as we have for defense over the years, but it's a much larger percentage of their Gross National Product. Only a dictatorship can maintain that level of defense spending.' He stopped his pacing and spread his arms. 'The Minotaur put the spotlight on the Soviet system's failings. The Soviet economy, if it can be called that, is an abject debacle: food must be purchased from abroad, there is nothing in the stores to buy, the prosperity of the other industrial nations has eluded them. And now the military needs many more billions to replace hardware it has spent billions to obtain which is now obsolete, years and years before the Soviets planned to replace it.'

He examined the faces of his listeners. 'Don't you read newspapers? Where have you been? Gorbachev has been talking *perestroika* and *glasnost* for years. Why? The threat of Star Wars technology was a major impetus. There was no way they could match it. Under no conceivable circumstances could enough rubles be printed or squeezed from the people to fund such a program. The generals lost power. The politicians gained it. Through diplomacy the threat of Star Wars could be blunted, perhaps even eliminated. Soviet foreign policy changed course dramatically; arms reduction treaties were agreed to and signed, mutual verification was at last swallowed with good grace. Then came the Minotaur's revelations.'

'I see,' Jake said, rubbing his chin and glancing at Toad.

'Yes, Captain. We are having a major technological revolution in America just now. The research of the space programs has borne fruit. Ever smaller, ever more powerful computers, lasers, missiles, fiber optics, new manufacturing techniques that allow us to build structures and engines with capabilities undreamed of ten years ago: *last year's cutting-edge designs are obsolete before we can get them into production!* It's like something out of science fiction. This must have struck you these past six months?'

'Yes.'

Caplinger nodded as he seated himself behind the desk. He just couldn't stay still for any length of time, Jake thought. 'It struck me five years ago when I became SECDEF. I listened to the briefings in awe. This black magic was *real*. It's not just Star Wars; it's everything. Jet engines with over three times the thrust per pound of Soviet engines are *real*, ready for deployment. Stealth obsoletes their radar systems. America is preparing to deploy a new generation of weaponry that will make obsolete everything the Russian generals have bled the Soviet Union to get for the last forty years. They have reached the end of their string. If this is table stakes, they have bet their last ruble, and we have raised.'

'The Minotaur,' Jake said slowly, 'gave them the awful truth.'

'Chapter and verse. Imagine the horror in Moscow as the true dimensions of their dilemma sank in. The rumors and hints they had heard were *all true*! The United States was even farther ahead technologically than the worst pessimists predicted. It was a nightmare.'

'They could have ordered a first strike,' Tarkington said. 'Started World War III before their military situation became hopeless.'

'Yes. But they didn't. They are, after all, sane.'

'Jee-sus!' Tarkington came out of his chair like a coiled spring. He planted himself in front of Caplinger's desk. 'What if they *had*?'

'Then none of us would be alive now, would we, Lieutenant? Please sit down.'

'Who commissioned you to play God with the universe, Caplinger? Where does it say in the Constitution that you have the right to bet the existence of every living thing on this planet, for whatever reason?'

Caplinger rose from his chair and leaned across the desk, until his face was only a foot from Toad's. 'What ivory tower did you crawl down from? You think we should just strum our banjos and sing folk songs and *pray* that nuclear war never happens? Sit down and *shut the fuck up!*'

Tarkington obeyed. The cords in his neck were plainly visible.

'What is he, Captain?' Caplinger jerked a thumb at Toad. 'Your conscience that you drag around?'

'He's a man who cares,' Jake Grafton said slowly. 'He sincerely cares.'

'We all do,' Caplinger replied, cooling down and taking his seat again. He rubbed his hand across his balding dome several times. 'We all care, Tarkington. You think I enjoy this?'

'Yep. That's precisely what I think.'

Caplinger rubbed his face. 'Maybe you're right.' He toyed with a pen on his desk. 'Yeah. I guess "enjoy" isn't the right word. But I do get satisfaction from it. Yes, I do.' He looked at Tarkington. 'This is my contribution. Is that so terrible?'

'That retired woman that Albright killed – I'll bet she enjoyed her little walk-on role in your drama. Didn't she have any rights?'

Caplinger looked away.

Toad pressed. 'You just chopped her like she was nothing. Is that what we are to you? Pawns? Rita – you have the right to stuff my wife through the meat grinder for the greater good? You asshole!'

After a while Caplinger said. 'We took big risks, but the reward was worth it.' He set his jaw. 'It was worth it,' he insisted.

Neither officer replied.

Caplinger examined both their faces. 'Come, gentlemen. Let's have another cup of coffee.' Toad didn't get out of his chair. He had the corncob pipe in his hands as the other two men left the room.

In the kitchen Jake said, 'Somebody's liable to shoot Gorbachev, you know. He's threatening to break a lot of rice bowls. Revolutions from the top rarely work.'

'Even if Gorbachev dies, the Soviet union will never be the same. If the old guard tries to clamp down, sooner or later there'll be another Russian Revolution, from the bottom next time. There's going to be another revolution in China, sooner or later. The communists can't go backwards, though they can sure try.'

'Why were they so concerned about the Minotaur's identity?'

' "They" is a very broad term. The GRU wanted evidence that the Minotaur's revelations were false, to discredit them. When Camacho gave them the name of the Secretary of Defense, they were left with an empty bag. The men in the Politburo realized that it was entirely possible the United States government was providing the information as a matter of policy. That possibility had to be weighed.

'The implications are difficult,' he added, searching for words. 'Perhaps the best way to say it is this: Some of the Soviet decision makers saw America, maybe for the first time, as we see ourselves – strong and confident, with excellent reasons for being confident. Frightened men start wars, and we aren't frightened.'

Back in the den, Jake asked, 'So we still don't know the identity of the three deep moles, the sleepers?'

'Let's say we're resigned to the fact that, if the agents exist, they will probably not be revealed. But we achieved so much! The changes in the Soviet Union the last three years have been profound.'

'You play your fucking games,' Toad murmured, 'and the little guys get left holding the bag. Like Camacho.'

'Ah, I hear the voice of the eternal private complaining because the generals are willing to sacrifice him to achieve a military objective.'

'Sorry, I didn't read about your little war in the papers. And I didn't volunteer to fight it.'

'America was Luis Camacho's adopted home. He loved this country and he loved its people. He knew exactly what he was doing every step of the way. Like you and your wife when you fly, he knew the risks. You think his job was *easy*? Having Albright right next door? Camacho had a wife and kid. You think he had no nerves?'

Toad sat silently with his arms folded across his chest, staring out the window. Jake and Caplinger talked a while longer. It was almost 4 P.M. when Caplinger said, 'By the way, Captain, you did an excellent job presenting the TRX plane and Athena to Congress. I'm looking forward to getting a ride in an A-12 someday.'

'That makes two of us.'

Toad picked up the corncob pipe from the pipe stand again and examined it idly. 'Why did Camacho admit his past?'

Caplinger smiled. 'Who knows the human heart? His explanation, which I read very carefully after Albright approached him a year or so ago, was that America is a country that cares about people. You see, he was a cop. A cop in J. Edgar Hoover's FBI. But in spite of Hoover's paranoid insanities, Luis saw that the vast majority of the agents there were trying their best to enforce the laws in an even, fair manner, with due regard to the rights of their fellow citizens. Camacho came from a country where the police have no such mission. The police there are *not* honest, honorable men.' He shrugged. 'Luis Camacho instinctively understood Hoover. He had grown up in a nation ruled by such men. But Camacho came to see himself as a public servant. He became an American.'

'Thanks for your time today, Mr Secretary.'

'I'll walk you to your car.'

He led them through the kitchen to the door that led to the parking area. As he walked, he asked Jake, 'How'd you learn I was the Minotaur?'

'I didn't. I guessed. Your seeing us today was the proof.'

'You guessed?'

'Yes, sir. My wife suggested that perhaps the Minotaur was a role played by an actor, an intuitive insight which seemed to me to explain a great deal. Then I remembered that comment you made one evening at dinner in China Lake this past summer, something to the effect that the perception of reality is more important than the facts. Camacho had said that the people who had to know about this operation did know. By implication that comment included you. So I decided you were probably the Minotaur.'

'I thought your notes meant blackmail, until I saw you this afternoon.'

'I thought you might.'

Jake stepped to the car ten feet away and opened the door.

'All our scheming,' Caplinger mused. 'So transparent. No wonder Camacho thought Albright saw through it. Albright was no fool.'

Royce Caplinger stopped at the end of the walk to look at the clouds building above the mountains to the west. He started as something hard dug into his back.

In his ear Toad said, 'You miscalculated once too often, Caplinger.'

Catching the tone but not the words, Jake Grafton turned with a puzzled look on his face.

The lieutenant had his arm on Caplinger's shoulder. He jerked the older man sideways until he was between him and Grafton. 'Don't move, Captain! I swear I'll shoot him if I have to.'

'What—?'

'That's right, Caplinger,' Toad hissed in the secretary's ear. 'I'll pull this trigger and blow your spine clean in half. This time it isn't Matilda Jackson or Rita Moravia or Luis Camacho. It's you! You thought you had everything figured, didn't you? Minotaur! *You were wrong!* The decision has been made. It's time for you to die.'

The secretary tried to turn. 'Now listen—'

'Tarkington!' Jake Grafton roared.

Toad twisted the man's arm, squeezing as hard as he could. 'The decision has been made! *They* decided. It's over for *you.*'

'Please *listen*—' Caplinger began as Jake strode toward the two men, his face a mask of livid fury.

'*Tarkington!*'

'So long, asshole!' Toad stepped to one side, raised his arm and pointed right into Caplinger's face, 'Bang,' he said, and let the corncob pipe fall from his hand.

Caplinger stood staring at it.

'Tarkington,' Jake said softly, his voice as ominous as a gathering storm.

Toad walked away down the drive. He stumbled once, caught himself and kept walking. He didn't look back.

Caplinger lowered himself into the gravel. He put his head on his knees. After a bit he whispered, 'I really . . . I really thought . . .'

'His wife . . .'

'He's right, you know.' Jake turned and looked down the long, straight driveway. Tarkington was still going, marching for the road, his head up and shoulders back. 'Yeah.'

'Go. Take him with you. Go.'

'You going to be okay?'

'Yes. Just go.'

Jake started the car, turned it around and went down the driveway. He slowed to a crawl alongside Toad, who kept walking. 'Get in.'

Tarkington ignored him. He was chewing on his lower lip.

'Get in the car, Lieutenant, or I will court-martial you, so help me God!'

Tarkington stopped and looked at Grafton behind the wheel. He hesitated, then opened the passenger door and climbed in.

As Jake started the car rolling again he glanced in the rearview mirror. In front of the huge mansion covered with ivy, Caplinger was still sitting in the gravel with his head down.

Three miles down the road Toad spoke. 'Why did you stay in the navy?'

'Some things are worth fighting for.'

Toad sat silently, his eyes on the road, for a long time. Finally he said, 'I'm sorry.'

'Everyone's sorry.' We're born sorry, we spend our life apologizing, and we die sorry. Sorry for all the guys with their names on the Wall. Sorry for the silly bastards who sent them there and stayed home and aren't sorry themselves. Sorry for the 230 grunts killed in Lebanon by a truck bomb. Sorry for the simple sonuvabitch who wouldn't let the sentry load his rifle. We're sorry for them all.

'Forget it,' Jake added.

'I should've killed the bastard.'

'Wouldn't have done any good.'

'I suppose not.'

31

Rita was released from the hospital on a Wednesday in November. She wore a cervical collar and a blue uniform that Toad had had dry-cleaned. He picked her up at noon. 'Where to, beautiful?'

'Straight to the beauty shop, James. I'm going to treat myself to a cut, shampoo and perm, then home to bed.'

She was very tired when he got her home to their apartment. After a nap, that evening she walked around slowly, looking at this, touching that. Harriet came over for a gabfest and left at nine when Rita visibly wilted.

On Friday, Rita insisted on going to the office with Toad. The crowd paraded by the desk one at a time to welcome her back. She greeted each of them joyfully, with genuine enthusiasm. Her delightful exhilaration was contagious. She seemed the incarnation of the promise and hope of life. Yet by noon she was tired, so Toad drove her home, then he returned to the office alone.

Saturday morning arrived crisp and clear. 'How do you feel today?' Toad asked as he helped her into the collar.

'Good. I'll need a nap this afternoon, though.'

'Want to go on an expedition? I promise a nap.'

'Where?'

He wouldn't tell. So, suitably dressed, they went down to the car, where Toad announced he had forgotten something upstairs. He rode the elevator back up to the third floor and made several quick phone calls, then returned smiling.

He drove out to a small civilian airport in Reston, all the while refusing to answer questions, parked the car in front of the flying service's little building, and came around to help her out.

' "Just as lovely a morning as ever was seen, for a nice little trip in a flying machine," ' quoteth Toad.

'What is this? Toad! I can't fly!'

'I can. You can watch me.'

'*You?* You've been taking lessons?'

'Got my license too. Last weekend. Now we're both pilots.' He grinned broadly and hugged her gently.

Toad took her inside and introduced her to the owner of the flying service, who visited with her while Toad preflighted the plane and taxied it to the front, where he killed the engine. The machine was a Cessna 172, white with a red stripe extending horizontally along the fuselage, back from the prop spinner. Toad thought it looked racy.

Rita was standing in the door, watching him. He couldn't resist. He bowed deeply from the waist. 'Come,' he said. 'Come fly with me.'

He helped her strap into the right seat, then walked around the machine and strapped himself into the left.

'This feels funny,' she giggled.

'Come fly with me, darling Rita. We'll fly the halls of heaven, watch the angel choir. We'll soar with the eagles and see where the storms are born. Fly with me, Rita, all your life.'

'Start the engine, Toad-man.'

With a half inch of throttle, the engine spluttered to life again. He pulled the throttle back to idle and the Lycoming ran smoothly, the propeller a blurred disk. Out they went down the narrow asphalt taxiway with Toad monitoring the Unicom frequency and checking the sky. He paused at the end of the taxiway, ran the engine up to 1,700 RPM and checked the mags, carb heat and mixture control, all the while acutely aware of Rita's scrutiny.

He was trying very hard to do everything right and not to laugh at the incongruity of the situation. When he glanced at Rita, she quickly averted her gaze. She was biting her lip, no doubt to keep from smiling. She had that scrunched-up look around her eyes. Trying hard to keep a straight face himself, Toad got back to the business at hand.

He wiped the controls through a cycle and ran the flaps out and in with an eye on the voltage needle. Satisfied, he announced his intentions on Unicom and took the runway.

The engine snarled as he smoothly pushed the throttle knob in all the way. With his feet dancing on the rudder pedals, the plane swerved only a little as it accelerated. At fifty-five knots he pulled back on the yoke and the plane came willingly off the runway. He trimmed the plane for a seventy-knot climb and said, 'You've got it.'

She took the wheel gingerly and waggled it experimentally. 'Oh, Toad! It's *terrific*! It flies great.'

'Anything that gets you off the ground is a great airplane.' He gave her the course he wanted and checked that the IFF was properly set.

Upward they climbed. They circled south of the metropolitan Washington area and headed eastward across the Chesapeake at 5,500 feet, 105 knots indicated. The engine was loud, but not unpleasantly so.

Rita flew with a smile, occasionally waggling the wings or kicking the rudder, just to see how it felt. She made gentle coordinated climbing and descending turns as Toad monitored the engine instruments, swept the sky for other airplanes, and kept track of their position with the VOR needles. Still, 105 knots was not warp speed, so between all these tasks he had time to watch the boats on the Chesapeake a mile below. They were small, trailing short wakes on the great blue water, under the great blue sky.

The wind helped the plane eastward. About fifteen knots of wind from the northwest, Toad figured. Approaching the eastern shore of Maryland, he could see smoke rising skyward from odd smokestacks and bending with the wind as it drifted aloft.

Rita signaled that he should take the controls, and he did. She sat back in her seat and watched him fly. Somewhere over eastern Maryland she began to laugh.

What began as a giggle quickly became an eye-watering gut buster. Toad joined in. Together they laughed until they had tears in their eyes. When they had melted themselves down to wide grins, she ran her fingers through his hair as he continued his impersonation of Orville Wright, Glenn Curtiss and Eddie Rickenbacker, David McCampbell and Randy Cunningham, Jake Grafton and Rita Moravia and all the rest, all those who were only truly alive when they had a stick in their hand and the airplane was a part of them.

Finally she devoted her attention to the sky and the green earth spread out below. When he next looked at her she wore a gentle, contented smile. She seemed very much at peace.

I must always remember her this way, he thought, with the sun on her face and the blue sky behind her, happy and content.

The field at Rehoboth was grass. Toad held the plane off until the stall warning sounded, and after the main mounts kissed, he held the weight off the nose with full back elevator until he had slowed to the speed of a man walking.

Jake Grafton was leaning on the fence, watching them taxi in. Toad flapped a hand. The captain waved back.

'Have a good flight?' Jake asked after Toad killed the engine and climbed out.

'The best. No lie, sir, this was the finest flight of my life.'

' 'Lo, Rita. Was he safe?'

She laughed and grasped Toad's hand. 'I'll fly with him anytime.'

At the Graftons' house Callie led Rita upstairs, where she stretched out in Amy's bed, at Amy's proud insistence. Callie seized the girl's hand and led her from the room, closing the door behind them. 'You can visit with her all you want when she wakes. She's very tired right now.'

'I'm going to be just like her when I grow up,' Amy announced, not for the first time.

'You already are, Amy. I think you're sisters at heart.'

They had finished dinner and Jake and Toad were sipping coffee as Callie, Rita, and Amy rinsed the dishes and arranged them in the dishwasher when the phone rang. Callie answered it in the kitchen, then struck her head around the corner and said, 'It's for you, Jake.'

He took the call on the phone in the living room.

'Captain, this is George Ludlow. Sorry to disturb you at home.'

'Quite all right, sir.'

'Just wanted you to know. We have a new man ordered in as the prospective program manager. Rear Admiral Harry Church. He'll arrive Wednesday. I want you to do the turnover by December 15.'

'Aye aye, sir. But this is pretty quick, isn't it? I've only been at this job nine months or so and am not due for orders for another—'

'You're going to the staff of the Chairman of the Joint Chiefs. From your record, it looks as if you've never had a joint staff tour. CNO wants you to get one now so they can send you to a task group when you make rear admiral.'

'Rear admiral? I thought—'

'CNO thinks you're flag material. For what it's worth, two senators and three congressmen have mentioned you to me this past month. They want to see your name on the flag list next year or the year after. I concur. Wholeheartedly. So does Royce Caplinger. The CNO personally picked this billet for you.'

After a few pleasantries, they said goodbye. Jake hung up, slightly stunned. Callie glanced at him and raised an inquisitive eyebrow, but he shrugged and grinned. He would tell her later, when they were alone.

The phone rang again. 'Is Amy there?' The voice was high, well modulated. David, from down the street.

'Amy, it's for you.'

Jake resumed his seat at the table. He was only half listening when he heard Amy say, 'I'll have to ask my dad.' She held the phone at arm's length and said loudly, 'Jake, can I go over to David's?'

'Sure. Be back in about an hour or so and you can go with us when we take Rita and Toad back to the airport.'

'Can David come too?'

'Yep.'

She held the phone to her ear. 'My dad says I can come over. And you can go with us to the airport. See you in a sec.' She threw the instrument roughly onto its cradle and bolted, elbows flying.

'Wear your coat,' Callie called.

The youngster snagged the garment from the peg and charged for the door, yelling over her shoulder, 'See you later, Rita.' The door slammed shut behind her.

'You get that?' Toad asked Jake with a grin. 'Dad?'

'Yeah,' said Jake Grafton. He stretched hugely. 'It's a nice sound, isn't it?'

One Thursday in February, Admiral Church, the new project manager, called Toad to his office. Tarkington was one of only three officers in the office this day: everyone else was somewhere in Texas or Nevada or over at the Pentagon. The first production A-12 was due to roll out next week and everyone was swamped with work. Although Washington was suffering one of its rare blizzards, the navy was steaming as before. The Metro wasn't running and all nonessential government employees had the day off. Only one of the civil service secretaries had made it to the office.

'You wanted to see me, sir?'

'Yes, Lieutenant. We got a call from the DC police. They would like one of the officers to drop by DC General this afternoon. If you can spare the time, would you go, please.'

'Yes, sir. Did they say what this is all about?'

'No, they didn't. But they wanted an officer from this unit. Ask for a Dr Wagner. And brief me in the morning, will you?'

'Aye aye, sir.'

As Toad approached the reception desk at DC General Hospital, he brushed the snow from his coat and shook the moisture from his cover. He explained his errand to the receptionist. She busied herself with the telephone buttons and he watched the flakes fall outside the front door while he absently pulled off his black leather gloves and placed them in the left pocket of his navy-blue bridge coat. The white scarf around his neck he folded and tucked into the other pocket. Finally he removed the coat and hung it over his arm. His hat he retrieved from the counter and held in his left hand.

'A navy officer . . .' the receptionist was telling someone. '. . . Dr Wagner.'

The snow had been falling for two days. The sailor from Minnesota who had driven him here had had numerous pithy comments about the locals' ability to drive on icy, snow-packed streets. The hospital staff, Toad noted with a trace of satisfaction, was apparently as indifferent to the edicts of the transportation authorities as Admiral Church was.

'Take the elevator on that wall. Third floor, turn left, then left again, forth or fifth door on the right. I think.'

'I'll find it.'

She smiled and fielded another phone call. Toad went to the bank of elevators and jabbed a button.

Wagner was in his early fifties, with thin, iron-gray hair and an air of nervous energy. He seemed fit and agile in spite of the rather prominent tummy he sported.

'You from the A-12 program?'

'Yessir.'

'Know why we asked you to come over?'

'Haven't the foggiest.'

'Put your coat and hat on this chair. And do sit down.' Dr Wagner hefted a pile of files to make room, then quickly surveyed the office for an empty spot. He placed the files on a corner of his desk, then took the remaining unoccupied seat. The chair behind the desk already contained a heap of paper a foot thick.

Wagner glanced at Toad's uniform, then spoke. 'Terrible weather. Plays havoc with the street people. Police and charities are scooping them up as fast as they can and bringing the ones in need of medical attention here.'

Toad nodded politely, wondering what this had to do with the navy.

'Got a case in last week during that terrible cold snap, those nights when it got down almost to zero. Just terrible.' He shook his head. 'Wreck of a man. Had to amputate all his fingers and toes. Did save the stump of one thumb. He was dying of hypothermia, gangrene, and alcohol poisoning when the police found him. And we had to amputate his ears, the tip of his nose, and a portion of his lower lip. They were gangrenous when we got him, probably from damage during that storm at the end of January.'

Seeing the look on Toad's face, the doctor added, 'Amazingly enough, I think he's out of danger now. His liver – well, usually these alcoholics have a liver the size and consistency of a football, but this one doesn't. Damaged, of course, but not yet fatally so.'

'Amazing.'

'Yep. Anyway, this man is, of course, incoherent most of the time, but he has lucid moments occasionally. We thought you might be able to identify him.'

Toad smiled his doubt. 'We have our share of party animals in the navy, but we haven't misplaced any from our office lately.'

'No fingerprints to match, of course,' the doctor said. 'No fingers. No wallet, no ID, no jewelry, but he is *somebody*. It's a long shot, I know.'

'Has he given a name?'

'No. He keeps talking about a woman, probably a wife or daughter. Judy. Never gives her last name. And this only during coherent moments. There aren't all that many of those.'

Toad Tarkington felt hot. He tugged at his tie.

'You must see quite a few of these folks,' he managed.

'Yes. Schizophrenics, most of them. Mental illness complicated by alcoholism and drug addiction. What say we go look? You're busy and I don't want to keep you. Not a chance in a thousand, I know.'

Toad lurched to his feet and arranged his coat and hat on his arm.

'How do you know,' he asked as they walked the corridor, 'that these derelicts aren't criminals?'

'No doubt some of them are. Petty thieves and whatnot. But the prosecutors have bigger fish to fry. And even if we found a man they wanted to prosecute, he'd probably be incompetent to stand trial.'

'I see.'

'We'd have to send them to St Elizabeth's for treatment and evaluation, hoping they could get well enough to understand the charges against them and assist in their defense.'

'Very civilized,' Toad said.

'I detect a note of irony there.' The medical man paused at the fire door of a staircase with his hand on the knob. 'Actually all these derelicts should be in an institution. They are completely incapable of looking after themselves. The lawyers and judges – they are such asses.'

'What d'ya mean?'

'Unless someone is being held for trial, we must go to the courts and seek an involuntary commitment order. We must prove the person we wish to commit is a danger to himself or others. Assuming the judge agrees, we can hold the man for six months. Then there is another hearing on precisely the same issue. And a group of public-interest lawyers have dedicated themselves to representing these people for nothing. The attorneys, all with the best of intentions, do their absolute damnedest to get these sick people out of the institutional setting and right back onto the streets, where they can drink and starve themselves to death.'

'What a great country,' Toad muttered.

The doctor opened the door and led the way down the stairs. 'In America these days, freedom for those who are functionally disabled, incapable of keeping body and soul together, means the freedom to commit suicide with a bottle on a public sidewalk while the world walks around them. The politicians ignore the problem: these people don't vote. There is no problem, the lawyers say. Vagrancy and alcoholism aren't crimes, the judges say. Nothing can be done.'

'This man we're going to see – is he dangerous?'

'Only to himself. And the lawyers and judges would disagree.'

They were in a corridor now, proceeding past double swinging doors with little windows that opened onto wards. Toad could see the patients in the beds, smell the disinfectant. Nurses hustled by. He could hear people moaning, and from somewhere a man roaring common obscenities in a mindless chant, the mantra of the insane.

'What will become of him?'

'When the bandages come off? Oh, we'll ship him over to St Elizabeth's and they'll try for an involuntary commitment, and who knows, they may get lucky. But in six months, or a year, or a year and a half, the judge will turn him loose. He'll drink himself to death in an alley. Or die some winter night when the police are late coming by.'

The doctor turned left and went through a door.

The patient was staring at a spot on the ceiling over the bed. Both arms were bandaged to the elbows. Lumps, bandages probably, under the covers where his feet were.

A chunk of his lower lip was missing. The cavity had stitches at the bottom of it. Bandages on both ears and nose; a strip of tape went completely around his head to hold them in place. He was secured to the bed by a cloth harness.

'You have to get over here, where he will see you. I think the alcohol has destroyed a lot of his peripheral vision.' The doctor led the hesitant lieutenant to where he wanted him, then waved his hand in front of the patient's eyes.

The eyes moved. They traveled up the hand to the doctor's face. Then they moved to Toad, focusing on the dark, navy-blue uniform.

The man in the bed tried to speak.

'Take your time,' the doctor said. 'Tell us who you are.'

'Uh . . . uh . . .'

'What is your name? Please tell us your name.'

'Uh . . .' He stared at the uniform, at the ribbons, at the wings, at the brass buttons, at the gold rings on the sleeves. 'Ju-dee. Ju-dee.' His gaze was fixated on the gleaming wings.

'There he goes again,' the doctor said to Toad. 'Sometimes he mumbles about A-12. That could be an apartment, of course, but I remembered seeing all that stuff in the papers about the navy's new airplane, so I decided to call you. A long shot.' The doctor sighed. 'I do wish I knew who his Judy is. Maybe a daughter who'd like to take care of him, or at least know where he is. She's obviously someone he cares about.' His voice became brisk, business-like: 'So, do you recognize him?'

Toad Tarkington stared at the man in the bed as he weighed it: three squares a day in a nice warm cell for thirty or forty years, or an alcoholic's death in a frozen alley.

At last he said, 'I never saw him before in my life.'

Under Siege

To my parents,
Gilbert and Violet Coonts

Government is not eloquence. It is
not reason. It is a force. Like fire,
a dangerous servant and a fearful master.

– *George Washington*

Of all the tasks of government, the
most basic is to protect its citizens
from violence.

– *John Foster Dulles*

1

Walter P. Harrington was eastbound on the inner loop of the beltway around Washington, DC, this December evening, in the leftmost lane. He kept the speedometer needle rock-steady at fifty-five miles per hour. Traffic swirled past him on his right.

Harrington ignored the glares and occasional honks and upthrust fingers from drivers darting into the middle lanes to get around and kept his eyes firmly on the road ahead, though he did occasionally glance at the speedometer to ensure the needle was on the double nickel. It usually was. Maintaining exactly fifty-five was a point of pride with him. He often thought that if the speedometer ever broke he could nail fifty-five anyway. He had had plenty of practice.

He also ignored the car that hung three feet behind his rear bumper flashing its lights repeatedly from low to high beam and back again. His rearview mirror had been carefully adjusted to make such shenanigans futile.

Walter P. Harrington had absolutely no intention of moving into the middle or right-hand lane. He *always* drove in the left-hand lane. Walter P. Harrington was obeying the law. *They* weren't.

The car behind him darted past him on the right, the driver shaking a fist out his window. Harrington didn't even glance at him. Nor did he pay any attention to the next car that eased up behind him, a white four-door Chevrolet Caprice.

In the Chevy were two men wearing surgical gloves. The driver, Vincent Pioche, muttered to his passenger, 'It's him, all right. That's his car. A maroon Chrysler. License number's right and everything.'

The passenger, Tony Anselmo, swiveled his head carefully, scanning the traffic. 'No cops in sight.'

'What'cha think?'

'Well, we could just pass him and be waiting for him when he gets home.'

'Neighbors, kids,' Vinnie Pioche said disgustedly.

Both men sat silently staring at the back of Walter P. Harrington's balding head. 'Little jerk driving fifty-five in the left lane,' Tony said.

'Yeah, he's an asshole, all right. The problem is, he may swerve right and nail us before we can get by.'

'He won't,' Tony Anselmo said thoughtfully. 'He'll go out like a light. Won't even twitch.'

'In his neighborhood, there may be a cop two blocks away and we won't know. Or some broad looking out the window ready to call nine-one-one. A kid screwing his girl under a tree. I hate the fucking suburbs.'

They followed Walter P. Harrington for a mile, weighing the risks.

'I dunno, Vinnie.'

'In a right-hand curve, with him turning right, when he goes out the car will tend to straighten and go into the concrete median. I'll floor this heap and we'll be by before he smacks it and rebounds.'

'If he comes right he'll clip us,' Tony objected.

'Not if you do it right. Stick it in his ear.' When Tony didn't move, Vinnie glanced at him. That moved him.

Tony Anselmo crawled across the passenger seat back and flopped onto the rear seat. He paused to catch his breath. He was getting too old for this shit and he knew it.

Under a blanket on the floor were two weapons, a twelve-gauge sawed-off pump shotgun and a Remington Model Four Auto Rifle in .30–06 caliber. Both weapons were loaded. After he rolled down the left rear window, Tony Anselmo picked up the rifle and cradled it in his arms. He flicked the crossbolt safety off. The shotgun would be easier, but the buckshot pellets might be deflected by the window glass. It would take two or three shots to be sure, and they didn't have that kind of time.

'Okay,' he told Vinnie. 'Get in the next lane, pull up beside his rear bumper, and sit there until you see a right curve coming. Try to let some space open up in front of you.'

'Got it.' Vinnie used his blinker to ease into a space in the traffic on his right. That stream was flowing along at sixty-five to seventy miles per hour but he was still doing fifty-five, so a space quickly opened as the car in front pulled away.

Tony scanned the traffic for police cars. He saw none, nor did he see any cars that might be unmarked cruisers. Harrington was plainly visible, his head about twenty to twenty-five feet away, his hands in the ten-and-two position on his steering wheel. He was concentrating on the road ahead, looking neither left nor right.

'Looks good. Any time.'

'Curve coming up. Fifteen seconds. Get ready.'

Anselmo scooted to the right side of the car, then leaned left, resting the barrel of the rifle on the ledge of the open window. 'I'm ready.'

'Five seconds.'

Anselmo concentrated on the open sights of the rifle. This was going to be a shot at a bouncing, moving target smaller than a basketball at a range of about a dozen feet, from a bouncing, moving platform. Not a difficult shot, but tricky. An easy shot to miss and wonder why.

'Here we go.' Anselmo felt the engine rev. Out of the corner of his eye he saw they were gaining on Harrington's Chrysler.

Then they were there, right alongside, passing with a three or four mile-per-hour edge, Harrington's head plainly visible. Tony could feel the centrifugal force pushing him toward Harrington's car, feel the Chevy heel slightly.

Tony swung the rifle gently, adjusting for the jolts of the car. His finger tightened on the trigger.

Harrington's head exploded as the rifle bellowed.

Vinnie floored the accelerator and the Chevy began to pull away. As expected, with a dead hand at the wheel, Harrington's car eased left, toward the concrete median barricade.

'Get by, get by,' Tony shouted.

In the car immediately behind Pioche, the horrified passenger screamed at her horrified husband behind the wheel. He swerved right as far as he could and still stay in his lane. It wasn't enough. The rear end of Harrington's decelerating Chrysler swung ponderously into the traffic lane as the front ground spectacularly on the concrete barrier. The left rear fender of the maroon Chrysler kissed the left front corner of the swerving vehicle, a gentle impact that merely helped the Chrysler complete its 180-degree spin.

The wife screamed and the husband fought the wheel as their car swept past the Chrysler, which, with its entire right side in contact with the barrier, rapidly ground to a smoking halt as pieces of metal showered the interstate.

In the backseat the two teenagers cursed and looked back at the receding Chrysler. The wife's screams died to sobs. 'Did you see that man shooting, Jerry? *Jerry? My God!*'

Behind the wheel of his car Jerry McManus of Owosso, Michigan, strove manfully to keep the vehicle going down the highway in a straight line as he began to feel the full effects of a massive adrenal shock. In front of him the white sedan that contained the gunman accelerated and pulled away. A moment later another vehicle, a van, swung left into the widening gap and McManus lost sight of the gunman.

Jerry McManus had just been driving down the road on the way back to the motel, comfortably following these two cars at fifty-five miles per hour while all the locals played NASCAR in the right lanes and the kids in the backseat hassled each other and his wife gabbled on about her rich great-aunt who lived in Arlington or someplace.

Owosso, Michigan, didn't have any freeways, and even if it had McManus wouldn't have driven them, living as he did immediately behind the gas station that he owned. But now, on the *big* annual vacation, the pilgrimage to the tourist traps of Washington, DC, that his wife had insisted upon – 'it will *broaden* the children, make them understand what America's all about, make them *appreciate* their heritage' – out here on these goddamn racing strips they call beltways, these maniacs are murdering each other with guns. Why in hell can't they do it downtown, around those marble monuments to dead politicians? And to think we took the kids out of school for two weeks for this!

'We're going home,' Jerry McManus told his wife grimly.

She looked at him. He had his jaw set.

Behind them the teenagers resumed their interrupted argument. The youngsters had been bickering at each other for the entire week. When in Washington . . .

'We're going home,' Jerry said again. 'Today.'

'Okay,' Tony Anselmo said as he rolled up the rear window to staunch the flow of fifty-degree air into the vehicle. 'Nobody's following us.' He turned his attention to the rifle. 'Let's get off at the next exit.'

He flipped the box magazine from the weapon and jacked the bolt to clear it. Then he broke it into two pieces and placed it in a shopping bag that also lay on the floor. The magazine, the loose cartridge, and the spent brass all went into the bag.

Vinnie steered the Chevy down the off-ramp and turned right, toward the District. After two blocks he turned into a narrow side street and pulled to the curb in the middle of the block. No vehicles followed.

Tony got out of the car carrying the shopping bag and went around to the trunk. In fifteen seconds he had the license plate slid from its holder and another in place. The original plate, stolen, went into the shopping bag. From the trunk Tony took two cartons of eggs wrapped in plastic. After taking the plastic off, he dumped the eggs into the shopping bag, then threw the plastic wrap on top. Holding the bag shut, he broke the eggs. These were old, old eggs that had never been refrigerated. They would make the bag and its contents stink to high heaven.

Holding the bag firmly shut, he climbed back into the passenger seat, beside the driver.

A half mile from the beltway they saw the tops of a large apartment complex. Vinnie Pioche steered slowly through the parking lot. The dumpster was in back. No pedestrians were about.

Tony Anselmo hopped out, tossed the shopping bag into the dumpster, then got nimbly back into the car. The vehicle was stopped for only fourteen seconds.

*

Out on the beltway traffic had ground to a halt. A Maryland state trooper arrived within three minutes and blocked the eastbound fast lane with his cruiser. After a quick glance into the remains of the maroon Chrysler, he used his radio to call for an ambulance and the crime lab wagon. Soon another trooper stopped his car behind the first one and began directing traffic.

A curiosity slowdown developed in the westbound lanes, but traffic was still getting through until a third cruiser with lights flashing parked immediately beside the concrete barrier westbound. Traffic on the beltway around the northern edge of Washington, DC, stopped dead.

Pioche and Anselmo took the Baltimore Parkway into the heart of Washington and found a spot in a parking garage. They had dinner at a small Italian restaurant where they were known. The headwaiter insisted they try a fine red wine from northern Italy, compliments of the house. After the uncorking ceremony, they sipped the cool, robust liquid and languidly studied the menu. They had plenty of time.

Outside on the streets the evening dusk became full darkness and the temperature began to drop. It would get down into the thirties tonight.

The reporter and photographer for *The Washington Post* entered the beltway jam-up from the east, westbound. The police scanner had warned them. After thirty minutes of stop-and-go creeping, the reporter, who was driving, eased the car to a stop in front of the police cruiser halted against the median barrier. The two men exited through the driver's door and stood for a moment staring at the wreckage of the maroon Chrysler on the other side of the barrier. A television chopper was hovering overhead, just high enough so that its downwash created a gentle breeze and cut the fumes from the idling vehicles creeping by.

The reporter approached the plainclothes detective who was in charge, Detective Eddie Milk, who was standing to one side watching. Milk had a meaty face, a tired face, noted the reporter, who wasn't feeling so chipper himself after a long day.

'Hi, Eddie. Some fucking mess, eh?'

Even though Milk knew and tolerated reporters like this young one from the *Post*, he had other things to do at the moment. Milk concentrated his attention on the ambulance attendants, who were placing the remains of Walter P. Harrington on a stretcher. They were in no hurry.

The reporter got a good look. The head was gone from the torso: all that remained was a bloody fragment of tissue on top of the neck. There was no face at all. The photographer had his equipment out and began snapping pictures. He even got a close-up of the corpse, though he knew the editors would never use it.

Milk finally opened up. 'At least one shot, maybe more, from the right side of the vehicle. One of them hit the driver smack in the right side of the head. Killed instantly. Can't give you his ID yet. Get it downtown.'

'Any witnesses?'

'You kidding?'

'Dope or guns in the car?'

'Not so far.'

Jack Yocke, the reporter, was twenty-eight years old, two inches over six feet tall, and he still had a flat stomach. He silently watched the ambulance crew carry the corpse to their ambulance, then pile in and roar away with lights and sirens going.

The *Post* photographer, a dark man clad in jeans and tee-shirt and wearing a ponytail, stood atop the median barrier and aimed his camera down into the front seat of the Chrysler. From where Yocke stood he could see that the left side of the vehicle's interior was covered with blood and tissue. Sights like this used to repulse him, but not now. He thought of them as surefire front-page play in an era when those boring policy stories out of State and the White House and overseas usually had top priority on 'the Front.'

In the cars creeping past, faces stared blankly at the smashed car, the police, the photographer. Slowly but perceptibly, the speed of the passing vehicles began to increase. The body was gone.

Yocke looked around carefully, at the traffic, at the huge noise fences on the edge of the right of way, and at the tops of the trees beyond. To the west he could just see the spire of the Mormon cathedral.

'An assassination?'

'How would I know?' the cop grunted.

'Rifle or pistol?'

'Rifle. You saw what's left of the driver's head.'

'Color of the car that impacted the victim's car?'

'You know I can't tell you that. Check downtown.'

'What do we know about the victim?'

'He's dead.'

'Gimme a break, Eddie. It's all got to come out anyway and I'm close to a deadline.'

The cop regarded Yocke sourly. 'All right,' he grunted. 'Victim's driver's license says he was a male Caucasian, fifty-nine years old, Maryland resident.'

'How about his name and address, for Christ's sake! I won't print it until you guys release it. I won't bother the family.'

'Don't know you.' That was true.

And Yocke didn't know the cop, but the reporter had seen him twice and learned his name and had made the effort to associate the name and face. 'Jack Yocke.' He stuck out his hand to shake, but the cop ignored it and curled a lip.

'You kids are ignorant liars. You'd screw me in less than a heartbeat. No.'

Jack Yocke shrugged and walked past Harrington's car, looking around the technicians into the bloody interior. The photographer had finished shooting pictures and radioed in to the *Post*'s photo desk. Now he was standing beside the *Post*'s car.

Yocke walked west, back along the way the victim had come. He could sec where the car had impacted the concrete barrier, scarring it and leaving streaks of paint and chrome. Fragments of headlight and the colored glass of blinkers lay on the pavement amid the dirt and gravel and occasional squashed pop can. He kept his head down and his eyes moving.

He walked on up the road another hundred yards, still looking, past the cars and trucks, breathing the fumes.

The motorists regarded him curiously. Several of them surreptitiously eased their door locks down. One guy in the cab of a truck wanted to question him but he moved on without speaking.

Facing eastward, Yocke could just see the crash site. He looked to the right, the south. Nothing was visible but treetops. Where was the rifleman when he pulled the trigger? He walked back toward the curve, carefully inspecting the naked, gray upthrust branches of the trees.

This was crazy. The guy wasn't up in a tree! Only military snipers did that kind of thing.

Yocke slipped through the standing vehicles to the south side of the road and walked along scanning the terrain which sloped steeply downward to the noise fence. The rifleman could have stood here on the edge of the road, of course, and fired through a gap in traffic. Or – Yocke stopped and looked at the cars – or he could have fired from another vehicle.

Somewhere in this area, then the Chrysler impacted the median barrier in that curve.

Yocke took a last look around, then trudged back toward the officials around the wreck.

Milk glanced at him. Yocke thanked him, was ignored, motioned to the photographer, then vaulted the barrier.

The photographer got behind the wheel. Looking back over his shoulder, he put the car in motion as Yocke pulled his door closed.

Yocke extracted a small address book from a hip pocket, looked up a number, then dialed the cellular phone.

'Department of Motor Vehicles.'

'Bob Lassiter, please.'

'Just a moment.'

In a few moments the reporter had his man. 'Hey Bob. Jack Yocke. Howzit going?'

'Just gimme the number. Jack.'

'Bob, I really appreciate your help. It's Maryland, GY3-7097.'

Silence. Yocke knew Lassiter was working the computer terminal on his desk. Yocke got his pen ready. In about fifteen seconds Lassiter said, 'Okay, plate's on a 1987 Chrysler New Yorker registered to a Walter P. Harrington of 686 Bo Peep Drive, Laurel.'

'Bo Peep?'

'Yeah. Cutesy shit like that, probably some cheap subdivision full of fat women addicted to soap operas.'

'Spell Harrington.'

Lassiter did so.

'Thanks, Bob.'

'This is the third time this month, Jack. You promised me the Giants game.'

'I know. Bob. I'm working on it.'

'Yeah. And try to get better seats than last time. We were down so low all we could see was the asses of the Redskins standing in front of the bench.'

'Sure.' Yocke broke the connection. Lassiter wouldn't get tickets to the Redskins-Giants game: Yocke had already promised those to a source in the mayor's office.

The reporter made another call. He knew the number. It was *The Washington Post* library where researchers had access to back issues of the paper on microfilm. The indexes were computerized.

'Susan Holley.'

'Susan, Jack Yocke. Helluva accident on the beltway. Guy shot in the head. Can you see if we have anything on a Walter P. Harrington of 686 Bo Peep Drive, Laurel, Maryland.'

'Bo Peep?'

'Yep. Harrington with two r's. Also, remember that epidemic of freeway shootings out in California a couple years ago? Can you find out if we ever had any of that around Washington?'

'Freeway snipers, you mean?'

'Well, yes, anything we have on motorists blazing away at each other on the freeway.'

'I'll call you.'

'Thanks.'

Yocke hung up. He had a gut feeling Harrington had not been a sniper victim since the terrain offered no obvious vantage point for sniping. Sitting a long distance away and potting some driver was the whole kick for the sniping freaks, Yocke suspected.

Yet the freeway shootouts, didn't those people usually use pistols? He tried to imagine someone using a high-powered rifle on another driver while he kept his own vehicle going straight down the road. That didn't seem too likely, either.

So what was left? The rifleman in another vehicle with a second person driving. An assassination? Just who the hell was the dead man, anyway?

The story for tomorrow morning's paper would be long on drama but short on facts. Getting your head shot off on the beltway was big news. But the following stories would be the tough ones. The who and the why. He was going to have to try to get hold of Mrs Harrington, if there was a Mrs, find out where the dead guy had worked, try to sniff out a possible reason someone might have wanted him dead.

'Drugs, you think?' the photographer asked.

'I don't know,' Jack Yocke replied. 'Never heard of a killing like this one. It had to be a rifle, but there's no vantage point for a rifleman. If it was close range, why didn't he use a pistol or submachine gun?'

'Those heavy drug hitters like the Uzis and Mac-10s,' the photographer commented.

'If it had been one of those the car would look like Swiss cheese.' Yocke sighed. 'It's weird. I've seen quite a few corpses over the last three years. Who did it and why has never been a mystery. Now this.'

The photographer had the car southbound on Connecticut Avenue. Yocke was idly watching the storefronts. 'In there,' he demanded, pointing. 'Turn in there.'

The photographer, whose name was Harold Dorgan, complied.

'Over there, by that bookstore. I'll be in and out like a rabbit.'

'Not again,' Dorgan groaned.

'Hey, this won't take a minute.' When the car stopped, Yocke stepped out and strode for the door.

It was a small, neighborhood bookstore, maybe twelve hundred square feet, and just now empty of customers. The clerk behind the register was in her mid-to-late twenties, tallish, with a nice figure. She watched Yocke's approach through a pair of large glasses that hung a half inch too far down her nose.

The reporter gave her his nicest smile. 'Hi. You the manager?'

'Manager, owner, and stock clerk. May I help you?' She had a rich, clear voice.

'Jack Yocke, *Washington Post*.' He held out his hand and she shook it. 'I was wondering if you had any copies of my book, *Politics of Poverty*? If you do, I'd be delighted to autograph them.'

'Oh yes. I've seen your byline, Mr Yocke.' She came out from behind the counter. She was wearing flats, so she was even taller than Jack had first thought, only two or three inches shorter than he was. 'Over here. I think I have three copies.

'Only two,' she said picking them up and handing them to him. 'One must have sold.'

'Hallelujah.' Jack grinned. He used his pen to write, 'Best Wishes, Jack Yocke,' on the flyleaf of each book.

'Thanks, Ms . . . ?'

'Tish Samuels.'

He handed her the books and watched her put them back on the shelf. No wedding ring.

'How long have you lived in Washington, Mr Yocke?'

'Little under three years. Came here from a paper in Louisville, Kentucky.'

'Like the city?'

'It's interesting,' he told her. Actually he loved the city. His usual explanation, which he didn't want to get into just now, was that the city resembles a research hospital containing one or more – usually a lot more – specimens of every disease that affects the body politic: avarice, ambition, selfishness and self-interest, incompetence, stupidity, duplicity, mendacity, lust, poverty, wealth – you name it, Washington has it, and has it in spades. It's all here in its purest form, on public display for anyone with the slightest spark of interest in the human condition to muse upon or study. Washington is El Dorado for the sly and the bold, for every identifiable species of pencil thief and con artist, some in office, some out, all preying on their fellow man.

'Say, Tish,' Jack Yocke said, 'I've got a party invitation for tomorrow night. How about going with me? I could pick you up after work, or . . .'

She walked back behind the register and gave him an amused half smile. 'Thanks anyway. Mr Yocke. I think not.'

Jack lounged against a display case and looked straight into her eyes. 'I've been taking a class at Georgetown University and the instructor is throwing an end-of-semester class party. The people in the class hardly know each other, so it's sort of a get-acquainted thing for everyone. Low key. I really would enjoy the pleasure of your company. Please.'

'What's the class?'

'Spanish.'

Tish Samuels' grin widened. 'I close the store at five on Saturday.'

'See you then. We'll get a bite somewhere and go party.'

Yocke actually was taking Spanish. He had hopes of breaking out of the cop beat and getting sent to Latin America by the foreign desk. This, he hoped, would be a way to leapfrog over endless, boring years on the metro staff where there were too many reporters covering too few stories – few of them worth the front page.

Out in the car Dorgan asked him, 'How many books did you sign, anyway? A couple dozen?'

'Naw. She only had two.'

'If it takes that long to sign just two, you better never write a best-seller.'

By eight P.M. Jack Yocke had learned several things. The *Post* had never before mentioned the late Walter P. Harrington in any of its articles, and the police had brought in the victim's wife to make an identification. She had recognized his wallet and wedding ring, so the victim's name and address were officially released to the press.

Ruing the impulse that had made him tap his Maryland DMV source and renew the man's claim on a pair of Redskins' tickets, Yocke wrote as much as he knew, which wasn't much, and padded the story with all the color he could remember. After he had pushed the right keys to send it on its electronic way to the metro editor, he spent a moment calculating just how many ducats he was in debt. Two pairs for every home game should just about cover it, he concluded. He had a source for tickets, a widow whose husband had bought season tickets years ago when the Redskins weren't so popular. She kept renewing them to maintain the connection with her husband but almost never went to the games herself.

He was getting his assignments at the metro editor's desk when one of the national reporters rushed in with a printout of wire service copy he had read on his computer terminal. 'Listen to this, you guys. The Colombians just captured Chano Aldana, the big banana of the Medellín cartel. They're going to extradite him tonight.'

Yocke whistled softly.

'Where are they going to hold him?' the editor asked.

'An "undisclosed" place. The Air Force has a plane on the way down to Bogotá now. Going to bring them back to Miami and turn them over to US marshals. After that, they're all mum.'

'I guess the lid's off, now,' Yocke said to no one in particular as the national reporter hurried away. 'It'll blow off,' he added, scanning the big room for Ottmar Mergenthaler, the political columnist with whom he had been having a running argument about the drug issue. Mergenthaler was nowhere in sight.

Just as well, Yocke concluded. The columnist believed, and had written ad nauseam, that traditional law enforcement methods adequately funded and vigorously applied would be sufficient to handle the illegal drug epidemic. Yocke had argued that police and courts didn't have even a sporting chance against the drug syndicates, which he compared to a bloated, gargantuan leech sucking the blood from a dying victim.

The verbal sparring between the talented newcomer, Yocke, and the pro with thirty years of journalism experience had not prevented a friendship. They genuinely liked each other.

As Yocke marshaled his arguments yet again to fire at the man who wasn't there, he took stock of the *Post* newsroom. It was populated by literate, informed, opinionated people, every one of whom subconsciously assumed that Washington was the center of the universe and the *Post* was the axis on which it turned.

This newspaper and *The New York Times* were the career zeniths that every journalist aimed for, Yocke thought, at least those with any ambition. Yocke knew. He had ambition enough for twenty men.

Jack Yocke and the photographer were headed for Laurel to interview the Harringtons' neighbors – and, if possible, the widow herself – when Vinnie Pioche and Tony Anselmo finished their meal and strode out into the gloom of the Washington evening.

They took their time walking toward the parking garage. A lady of the evening standing on one corner watched them come toward her, took a step their way, then abruptly changed her mind after a good look at Vinnie's face. Tony knew Vinnie pretty well, and he knew that look. It would freeze water.

Once in the car they drove to a garage in Arlington and beeped the horn once in front of the door, which began to open within seconds.

The fat gent inside was smoking a foul cigar. He handed them a pair of keys to a ten-year-old Ford sedan. Tony used one of the keys to open the trunk. Inside was a sawed-off twelve-gauge pump shotgun, a box of twenty-five buckshot cartridges, latex surgical gloves, and two nine-millimeter pistols. They pulled on the gloves before they touched the weapons or the car.

Vinnie stared at the pistols, then ignored them. Tony helped himself to one and made sure the clip was full and there was a round in the chamber while his companion carefully loaded the shotgun, then placed five more cartridges in his right jacket pocket.

Tony slid behind the wheel and started the car. The engine started on the first crank and the gas gauge read full. He let it idle while Vinnie arranged himself in the passenger seat and laid the sawed-off on his lap, the barrel pointed toward the door.

Anselmo nodded at the cigar smoker, who pushed the button for the garage door opener.

'Nice car,' Tony said to Vinnie, who didn't reply. He had used up most of his conversational repertoire at dinner, when he had grunted and nodded to acknowledge Tony's occasional comments on the food or the weather.

Vinnie Pioche had the personality of a warthog, Tony reflected yet again as he piloted the car across the Francis Scott Key Bridge back into Washington. Still, a more workmanlike hitter would be hard to find. Through the years, when somebody had a contract and wanted it done just right, with no repercussions, they sent for Vinnie. He was *reliable*. Or he used to be. These days he was getting . . . not goofy . . . but a little out of control, out there on the edge of something that sane men rarely see. Which was precisely why Tony was here. '*Make sure it goes okay, Tony.*'

They found a parking place a hundred feet from the row house they wanted, just a block east of Vermont, a mile or so northeast of downtown. Tony killed the lights and the engine. The two men sat silently, watching the street and the occasional car that rattled over the potholes.

Streetlights cast a pale, garish light on the parked cars and the row houses with their little stoops and their flowerpots on second-floor windowsills. This neighborhood was much like home. Here they felt comfortable in a way they never would in the sprawling suburbs with huge lawns and tree-shaded dark places and the winding little lanes that went nowhere in particular.

Tony checked his watch. Thirty minutes or so to wait. Vinnie fondled the shotgun. Tony adjusted the rearview mirror and his testicles and settled lower in his seat.

Twenty-six minutes later a yellow cab slowly passed. Tony watched in the driver's door mirror as the brake lights came on and the cab drifted to a stop in the middle of the block.

'It's them,' he said as he started the engine. 'Remember, not the woman.'

'Yeah. I'll remember.'

Vinnie got out of the car and eased the door closed until the latch caught. He held the shotgun low against his right leg, almost behind it, and waited.

Tony watched a man and a woman get out of the cab and the cab get under way. Vinnie started across the street.

No one else on the street. The wind was beginning to pick up and the temperature was dropping. Tony turned in the seat and watched Vinnie cross the street and stride toward the couple, now standing on the stoop, the woman digging in her purse.

Vinnie stopped on the sidewalk fifteen feet away from the couple, raised the shotgun, and as the man turned slightly toward him, fired.

The man sagged backward. Vinnie shot him again as he was falling. The victim fell to the sidewalk, beside the stoop. Vinnie stepped around the stoop and shot him three more times on the ground.

The shotgun blasts were high-pitched cracks, loud even here. The woman stood on the stoop, watching.

A pause, then one more shot, a deeper note.

Now Vinnie was walking this way, replacing the .45 in his shoulder holster, the shotgun held vertically against his left leg.

Anselmo eased the car out of its parking place and waited.

Vinnie Pioche just walked. Lights were coming on, windows opening, a few heads popping out. He didn't look up. He opened the car door and took his seat, and Tony drove away, in no hurry at all.

Just before he turned the corner, Tony Anselmo glanced in the driver's door mirror. The woman was unlocking the door to her town house and looking down off the stoop, down toward the dead man. Well, she had been paid enough and she knew it was coming.

2

On the flight from Dallas–Fort Worth, Henry Charon sat in a window seat and spent most of his time watching the landscape below and the shadows cast by cumulus clouds. Sitting in the aisle seat, a young lawyer with blow-dried hair and gold cufflinks occupied himself by studying legal documents. He had glanced at Charon when he seated himself, then forgotten about him.

Most people paid little attention to Henry Charon. He liked it that way. People had been looking around and over and through him all his life. Of medium height, with slender, ropey muscles unprotected by the fat layers that encased most other forty-year-old men, Henry Charon lacked even one distinguishing physical feature to attract the eye. As a boy he had been the quiet child teachers forgot about and girls never saw, the youngster who sat and watched others play the recess games. One teacher who did notice him those many years ago had labeled him mildly retarded, an unintentional tribute to the protective shell that, even then, Henry Charon had drawn around himself.

He was not retarded. Far from it. Henry Charon was of above-average intelligence and he was a gifted observer. Most of his fellow humans, he had noted long ago, were curiously fascinated by the trivial and banal. Most people, Henry Charon had concluded years ago, were just plain boring.

Although the lawyer in the aisle seat had ignored his companion, Charon surveyed him carefully. Had he been asked, he could have described the young attorney's attire right down to the design on his cufflinks and the fact that the end of one shoelace was missing its plastic protector.

He had also catalogued the lawyer's face and would recognize him again if he saw him anywhere. This was a skill Charon worked diligently to perfect. He was a hunter of men, and faces were his stock in trade.

He hadn't always been in this line of work, of course, and as he automatically scanned the faces around him and committed them to memory, in one corner of his mind he mused on that fact.

He had grown up on a hard-scrabble ranch in the foothills of the Sangre de Cristo Mountains of New Mexico. His mother had died when he was three and his father had died when he was twenty-four. The only child, Charon inherited the family place. Weeks would pass without his seeing another person. He did the minimum of work on the ranch, tended the cattle when he had to, and hunted all the rest of the time, in season and out.

Since he was twelve years old Henry Charon had hunted all year long. He had never been caught by conservation officers although he had been suspected and they had tried.

Sagging cattle prices in the late '70s and a thrown rod in the engine of his old pickup changed his life. A banker in Santa Fe laid reality on the table. Unless he devised a way to earn additional income Charon was eventually going to lose the ranch. That fall Henry Charon became a hunting guide. He advertised in the Los Angeles and Dallas newspapers and had so many responses he turned people away.

In spite of his taciturn manner and introspective personality, Henry Charon enjoyed immediate success at his new venture. His gentlemen nimrods always saw trophy animals, sometimes several of them. When one of the corporate captains with his shiny, expensive new rifle needed a little help bringing down his deer or elk, the crack of Charon's .30-30 was usually unnoticed amid the magnum blasts. Stories of successful hunts spread quickly through the boardrooms and country clubs of Texas and Southern California. Charon jacked his rates from merely high to outrageous and was still booked for years in advance.

The event that changed his life came in 1984, on the evening before the last day of elk season, as he drank coffee around the camp-fire with his client, who this year had come alone and paid without quibble the entire fee for a party of four. That was the client's third season.

The client was looking for someone to kill a man. He didn't state it baldly but that was the drift of the conversation. He didn't ask Charon to undertake the chore, yet somehow in the oblique conversation it became unmistakable that the demise of a certain board member at the client's savings and loan would be worth fifty thousand dollars cash, no questions asked.

The client got his elk the next morning and Charon had him on the plane in Santa Fe by six P.M.

Intrigued, Henry Charon thought about it for a week. Really, when one thought about it objectively, it was hunting and hunting was the one thing that he was extraordinarily good at. Finally he packed a canvas bag and headed for Texas.

The whole thing was ridiculously easy. Three days of observation established that the quarry always took the same route to work in his black BMW sedan. Charon went home. From a closet he selected a rifle that one of his clients from the year before had brought along for a backup gun and had left behind.

Three mornings later in Arlington, Texas, the quarry died instantly from a bullet in the head as he drove to work. The police investigation established that the shot must have been fired from a salvage yard almost a hundred and fifty yards away as the victim's car waited at a traffic light. There were no witnesses. A careful search of the salvage yard turned up no clues. Asked to assist, the FBI identified several dozen ex-military snipers as possible suspects. These men were all discreetly questioned and their alibis checked, to no avail. The crime remained unsolved.

Two weeks later the money arrived at the ranch in the Sangre de Cristo in a cardboard box, mailed first class without a return address.

The savings-and-loan man came to the ranch on two more occasions. He was stout, in his late fifties, and wore custom-made alligator-hide cowboy boots. He sat on the porch in the old rocker and looked at the mountains against the blue sky and talked about how tough times were in Texas since the oil business cratered. On each visit he mentioned the names of men connected with the savings and loan industry in the Dallas–Fort Worth area. The first man subsequently drowned on a fishing trip in Honduras and the other apparently shot himself with a Luger pistol, a family heirloom his father had brought back from World War II, one evening when he was home alone.

The last time Henry Charon saw the original client he brought another man with him, introduced him, then got back into his Mercedes and drove off down the dirt road, dust swirling. The new man's name was Tassone. From Vegas, the savings-and-loan man said.

Tassone was as lean as his chauffeur was fat. He looked over the house and grounds with a deadpan expression and made himself comfortable on the porch. 'Awful quiet out here,' he observed.

Charon nodded to be sociable. He scanned the hillsides slowly, carefully.

'I hear you got a talent.'

Charon again examined the draw where the ranch road went down to the paved road. He shrugged. Tassone had his feet on the rail.

'A man with talent can make a good living,' Tassone said. When Charon made no reply, he added, 'If he stays alive.'

Charon seated himself on the porch rail, one leg up, his hands on his leg. He turned his gaze to Tassone.

'If he's smart enough,' the man in the chair said.

Charon stared at the visitor for a moment, as if he were sizing him up. Then he said, 'Why don't you take the pistol out of that holster under your jacket and put it on the floor.'

'And if I don't?'

Charon uncoiled explosively. He drew the hunting knife from his boot with his right hand and launched himself at the man in the chair, all in the same motion. Before Tassone could move, the knife was at his throat and Charon's face was inches from his.

'If you don't, I'll bury you out here.'

'What about Sweet?' Sweet was the Texas savings-and-loan man. 'He knows I'm here.'

'Sweet will go in the same hole. He'll be easy to find. He just drove about a mile down the road and stopped. He's sitting down there now, waiting for you.'

'Reach under my coat and help yourself to the gun.'

Charon did so, then moved back to the rail. The pistol was a small automatic, a Walther, in .380 caliber. He thumbed the cartridges from the clip, jacked the shell from the chamber, then tossed the weapon back to Tassone.

With his eyes on Charon, Tassone holstered the gun. 'How'd you know Sweet didn't leave?'

'The road goes down that draw over there.' Charon jerked his head a half inch. 'I was watching for dust. There wasn't any. There's a wide place under a cottonwood where the creek still has water in it this time of year. He's sitting there in the shade waiting for you.'

'Maybe he's circling around on foot to get a shot at you. Maybe he thinks you've outlived your usefulness.'

'Sweet isn't stupid. I took him hunting. He knows he wouldn't have a chance in a hundred to kill me at my game, on my own ground. Now you may have dropped off someone on your way up here, someone who's a lot better than Sweet. So I've been looking. Those cattle out there on that hillside in front of the house are three-quarters wild, and they're not edgy. Behind the house – that's a possibility, but there's a flock of pheasants up there. Saw 'em fly in before you drove up.'

Tassone looked carefully around him, perhaps really seeing the setting for the first time. In a moment he said, 'Cities aren't like this. Ain't no spooky cows or cowshit or pheasants. Think you can handle that?'

'The principles are the same.'

The visitor crossed his legs and settled back into his chair. He took out a pack of cigarettes and lit one. 'Got a little business proposition for you.' An hour later he walked down the road toward the car where Sweet was waiting.

That was the last time Charon saw Sweet, the savings-and-loan man. Three years had passed since then, busy years.

This afternoon, when the plane landed, Henry Charon joined the throng in the aisle and eased his one soft bag from the overhead bin. As usual, the stewardess at the door of the plane gave him her mindless thank-you while her eyes automatically shifted to the person behind him. Anonymous as always, Henry Charon followed the striding lawyer into the National Airport concourse.

Taking his time, his eyes in constant motion. Charon moved with the crowd, not too fast, not too slow. He avoided the cab stand in front of the terminal and started for the buses, only to change his mind when he glimpsed the train at the Metro station a hundred yards away.

He studied a posted map of the system, then bought one at a kiosk. Soon he was in a window seat on the yellow train.

The second hotel he tried had a vacant single room. Charon registered under a false name and paid cash for a four-day stay. He didn't even have to show his false driver's license or credit card.

With his bag in his room and the room key in his pocket. Henry Charon set forth upon the streets. He wandered along looking at everything, reading street signs and occasionally referring to a map. After an hour of strolling he found himself in Lafayette Park, across the street from the White House.

Comfortable in spite of the sixty-degree temperature, he sat on a bench and watched the squirrels. One paused a few feet away and stared at him. 'Sorry,' he muttered with genuine regret. 'Don't have a thing for you today.'

After a few moments he strolled toward the south edge of the block-sized park.

Four portable billboards stood on the wide sidewalk facing the White House. ANTINUCLEAR PEACE VIGIL the signs proclaimed. Two aging hippies in sandals, one male, one female, attended the billboards.

Across the eight-lane boulevard, surrounded by lush grass and a ten-foot-high, black wrought-iron fence, stood the White House, like something from a set for *Gone With the Wind.* The incongruity was jarring amid the stone-and-steel office building that stretched away in all directions.

Along the sidewalk curb were bullet-shaped concrete barricades linked together at the top by a heavy chain. Henry Charon correctly assumed they had been erected to impede truck-bomb terrorists. Similar barricades were erected around the White House gates, to his left and right, down toward the corners.

Tourists crowded the sidewalk. They pointed cameras through the black fence and photographed each other with the White House in the background. Many of the tourists, at least half, appeared to be Japanese.

On the sidewalk, parked back-in against the fence, sat a security guard on his motorcycle, a Kawasaki CSR 350, doing paperwork. Charon walked closer and examined his uniform; black trousers with a blue stripe up each leg, white shirt, the ubiquitous portable radio transceiver, nightstick, and pistol. The shoulder patch on his shirt said US PARK POLICE.

Another man standing beside Charon spoke to the guard: 'Whatever happened to the Harleys?'

'We got them too,' the guard responded, and didn't raise his eyes from his report.

Charon walked on, proceeding east, then turned at the corner by the Treasury building and walked south along the fence. Looking in at the mansion grounds he could see the guards standing at their little kiosks, the trees and flowers, the driveway that curved up the entrance. A black limo stood in the shade under the roof overhang, waiting for someone.

He strolled westward toward the vast expanse of grass that formed the Ellipse. Tourists hurried by him without so much as a glance. Never a smile or a head nod. The little man who wasn't there found a spot to sit and watch the people.

Inside the White House the attorney general was passing a few minutes with the President's chief of staff, William C. Dorfman, whom he detested.

Dorfman was a superb political operator, arrogant, condescending, sure of himself. An extraordinarily intelligent man, he had no patience for those with lesser gifts. The former governor of a Midwestern state, Dorfman had been a successful entrepreneur and college professor. He seemed to have a sixth sense about what argument would carry the most weight with his listeners. What Dorfman lacked, the attorney general firmly believed, was any sense of right and wrong. The political expedient of the moment always struck Dorfman as proper.

The real flaw in Dorfman's psyche, the attorney general mused, was the way he regarded people as merely members of groups, groups to be manipulated for his own purposes. Over at Justice the attorney general referred to Dorfman as 'the Weathervane.' He had some other, less complimentary epithets for the chief of staff, but these he used only in the presence of his wife, for the attorney general was an old-fashioned gentleman.

Others in Washington were less kind. Dorfman had racked up an impressive list of enemies in his two years in the White House. One of the more memorable remarks currently going around the cocktail-party circuit was one made by a senator who felt he had been double-crossed by the chief of staff: 'Dorfman is a genius by birth, a liar by inclination, and a politician by choice.'

Just now as he listened to Will Dorfman, the senator's remark crossed the attorney general's mind.

'What happens if this guy gets acquitted?' Dorfman asked, for the second time.

'He won't,' the attorney general, Gideon Cohen, said curtly. He always found himself speaking curtly to Dorfman.

'There'll be a dozen retired crocks and out-of-work cleaning women on that jury, people who are such little warts they've never heard of Chano Aldana or the Medellín cartel, people who don't read the papers or watch TV. The defense lawyers won't let anyone on that jury who even knows where Colombia *is*. When the jurors finally figure out what the hell is going on, they're going to be scared pissless.'

'The jury system has been around for centuries. They'll do their duty.'

Dorfman snorted and repositioned his calendar on the desk in front of him. He glanced at the vase of fresh-cut flowers that were placed on his desk every morning, one of the White House perks, and helped himself to a handful of M&Ms in a vase within his reach. He didn't offer any to his visitor. 'You really believe that crap?'

Cohen *did* believe in the jury system. He knew that the quiet dignity of the courtroom, the bearing of the judge, the seriousness of the proceedings, the possible consequences to the defendant – all that had an effect on the members of the jury, most of whom, it was true, were from modest walks of life. Yet the honest citizen who felt the weight of his responsibilities was the backbone of the system. And ten-cent sophisticates like Dorfman would never understand. Cohen looked pointedly at his watch.

Dorfman sneered and hid it behind his hand. Gideon Cohen was one of those born-to-money Harvard grads who had spent his adult life waltzing to the top of a big New York law firm, a guy who gave up eight or nine hundred thou a year to suffer nobly through a tour in the cabinet. He liked to stand around at parties and cluck about the financial sacrifices with his social equals. Cohen was a royal pain in a conservative's ass. Even worse, he was a snob. His whole attitude made it crystal dear that Dorfman couldn't have gotten a job polishing doorknobs at Cohen's New York firm.

When Cohen looked at his watch the third time, Dorfman rose and stepped toward the door to check with the secretary. As he passed Cohen, he farted.

Alone in the chief of staff's plush, spacious office, Gideon Cohen let his eyes glide across the three original Winslow Homer paintings on the wall and come to rest on the Frederick Remington bronze of a bronc rider about to become airborne, also an original. More perks, gaudy ones, just in case you failed to appreciate the exalted station of the man who parked his padded rump in the padded leather chair. The art belonged to the US government, Cohen knew, and the top dozen or so White House staffers were allowed to choose what they wanted to gaze upon during their tour at the master's feet. Unfortunately the art had to go back to the museums when the voters or the President sent the apostles back to private life.

Ah, power, Cohen mused disgustedly, what a whore you are!

Behind him, he heard Dorfman call his name.

Three minutes later in the Oval Office Dorfman settled into one of the leather chairs as Cohen shook hands with the President. George Bush had on his Kennebunkport outfit this afternoon. He was leaving for Maine just as soon as he finished this meeting, which Cohen had pleaded for.

'The dope king again?' the President muttered as he dropped into a chair beside Cohen.

'Yessir. The drug cartels in Colombia are issuing death threats, as usual, and the Florida senators are in a panic.'

'I just got off the phone with the governor down there. He doesn't want that trial in Florida, anywhere in Florida.'

'You seen this morning's paper?'

George Bush winced. 'Mergenthaler's on his high horse again.'

Ottmar Mergenthaler's column this morning argued that since the drug crisis was a national crisis, the trial of Chano Aldana should be moved to Washington. He also implied, snidely, that the Bush administration was secretly less than enthusiastic about the war on drugs. 'I detect the golden lips of Bob Cherry,' Bush said. Cherry was the senior senator from Florida. No doubt he had been whispering his case to the columnist.

'I think we should bring Aldana here, to Washington,' Cohen said. 'We can blanket the trial with FBI personnel, convict this guy, and do it without anyone getting hurt.'

Bush looked at his chief of staff. 'Will?'

'Politically, it'll look good if we do it right here in Washington in front of God and everybody. It'll send a message to Peoria that we're really serious about this, regardless of Mergenthaler's columns. Stiffen some backbones in Colombia. *If* – and this is a damn big if – we get convictions.'

'What about that, Gid?' the President asked, his gaze shifting to the attorney general. 'If this guy beats the rap, it sure as hell better happen down in Florida.'

'We can always fire the US attorney down there if he blows it,' Dorfman said blandly and smiled at Cohen.

'Chano Aldana is going to be convicted,' Gideon Cohen stated forcefully. 'A district jury convicted Rayful Edmonds.' Young Rayful had led a crime syndicate that distributed up to two hundred kilos of crack cocaine a week in the Washington area, an estimated thirty per cent of the business. 'A jury'll convict Aldana. If it doesn't happen, you can fire your attorney general.'

Dorfman kept his eyes on Cohen and nodded solemnly. 'May have to,' he muttered. 'But what will a conviction get us? When Rayful went to jail the price of crack in the District didn't jump a dime. The stuff just kept coming in. People aren't stupid – they see that!'

'This drug business is another tar baby,' the President said slowly, 'like the damn abortion thing. It's political dynamite. The further out front I get on this the more people expect to see tangible results. You and Bennett keep wanting me to take big risks for tiny gains, yet everyone keeps telling me the drug problem is getting worse, not better. All we're doing is pissing on a forest fire.' He sent his eyebrows up and down. 'Failure is very expensive in politics, Gid.'

'I understand, Mr President. We've discussed—'

'What would we have to do to solve this drug mess, and I mean *solve* it?'

Gideon Cohen took a deep breath and exhaled slowly. 'Repeal the Fourth Amendment or legalize dope. Those are the choices.'

Dorfman leaped from his chair. '*For the love of* – are you out of your *mind*?' he roared. '*Jeez-us H.*—'

Bush waved his chief of staff into silence. 'Will convicting Chano Aldano have *any* effect on the problem?'

'A diplomatic effect, yes. A moral effect, I hope. But—'

'Will convicting him have any direct effect at all on the amount of drugs that comes into the United States?' Dorfman demanded.

'Hell, no,' Cohen shot back, relieved to have a target for his frustration. 'Convicting a killer doesn't prevent murder. But you have to try killers because a civilized society cannot condone murder. You have to punish it whenever and wherever you can.'

'This war on drugs has all the earmarks of a windmill crusade,' Dorfman explained, back in his seat and now the soul of reason. 'Repealing the Fourth Amendment, legalizing dope . . .' He shook his head slowly. 'We have to take positive steps, that's true enough, but the President cannot appear as an ineffectual bumbler, an incompetent. That's a sin the voters won't forgive. Remember Jimmy Carter?' His voice turned hard: '*And he can't advocate some crackpot solution.* He'd be laughed out of office.'

'I'm not asking for political hara-kiri,' Cohen said wearily. 'I just want to get this dope kingpin up here where we can try him with enough security so that we don't have any incidents. We need to ensure no one gets to the jurors. The jurors have to *feel* safe. We *will* get convictions.'

'We'd better,' Dorfman said caustically.

'Will, you've argued all along that what was needed here was more cops, more judges, and more prisons,' Cohen said, letting a little of his anger leak out. ' "Leave the rehab programs and drug-prevention seminars to the Democrats," you said. Okay, now we have to put Aldana in prison. This is where that policy road has taken us. We have no other options.'

'I'm not suggesting we let him go,' Dorfman snarled, his aggressive instincts fully aroused. 'I'm wondering if you're the man to put him in the can.'

The President waved his hands to cut them off and rose to his feet. 'I don't fancy having to apologize to this asshole and buy him a plane ticket back to Medellín. Bring Aldana to Washington. But announce this as your decision, Gid. I've got a plane to catch.' He paused at the door. 'And Gid?'

'Yessir.'

'Don't make any speeches about repealing the Fourth Amendment. Please.'

Cohen nodded.

'Everybody's getting panicky. Ted Kennedy says cigarette smoking leads to drug abuse. That dingy congress-woman – Strader – wants to put a National Guardsman on every corner in Washington. Somebody else wants to put all the addicts in the army. A columnist out in Denver wants us to invade Colombia – I'm not kidding – as if Vietnam never happened.' Bush opened the door and held it. 'Maybe we should put all the addicts in the army and send *them* to Colombia.'

Dorfman tittered.

'You're a good attorney general, Gid. I need you to keep thinking. Don't panic.'

Cohen nodded again as the President went through the door and it closed behind him.

Henry Charon took twenty minutes to circle the White House grounds. On the west side of the executive mansion he found himself across the street from a gray stone mausoleum that his map labeled the Executive Office Building.

He was standing facing it with his hands in his pockets when he heard the sound of a helicopter. He turned. One was coming in from the southeast, lower and lower over the tops of the buildings, until it turned slightly and sank out of sight, hidden by the trees, on the grounds behind the White House.

Henry Charon retraced his steps south along the sidewalk, looking for a gap in the trees and shrubs where the helicopter would be visible. He could find no such gap. Finally he stopped and waited, listening to the faint tone of the idling jet engines. The sound had that distinctive whop-whop-whop as the downwash of the rotors rhythmically pulsed it.

The chopper had been on the ground for four and a half minutes by Charon's watch when the engine noise rose in pitch and volume. In a few seconds the machine became visible above the trees. The nose pitched down and the helicopter began to move forward. Now it laid over on its side slightly and veered right as it continued to climb, its engines apparently at full power. The mirage distortions that marked the hot jet exhausts were plainly visible.

The machine finished its turn to the southeast and continued to climb and accelerate. Finally it was hidden by one of the buildings over beyond the Treasury. Which one? Henry Charon consulted his map.

With his hands in his pockets, Charon walked past the White House on Constitution Avenue and proceeded east.

*

Six blocks north, in the *Washington Post* building on Fifteenth Street NW, Jack Yocke had asked to attend the afternoon story conference of editors. At the meeting an editor from each of the paper's main divisions – metro, national, foreign, sports, style – briefed the lead stories that his staff wanted run in tomorrow's paper. The *Post*'s executive or managing editor then picked the stories for the next day's front page.

Arranged on the table in front of every chair were stacks of legal-sized papers, 'slug' sheets, containing brief paragraphs on each of the top stories for tomorrow's paper. On weekdays the *Post*'s executive editor, Ben Bradlee, routinely attended Page One meetings. Weekends, Yocke knew, Bradlee would escape to his Maryland west shore hideaway unless his wife, Sally, was throwing a dinner or the Redskins were playing at home.

Yocke took his seat and studied the slug sheets. The beltway killing yesterday afternoon was in there, as was last night's 'stoop murder.' Both stories had unusual twists. The beltway killing looked like a wire-service story from Los Angeles, the city of rage, yet it had happened here in Washington – Powerville USA – and the killer had used a rifle. The victim was one Walter P. Harrington, head cashier of Second Potomac Savings and Loan. The neighbors had told Yocke that Harrington was a prig, a martinet, married to an equally offensive wife, yet for all of that respected as an honest, hard-working citizen who kept to himself and never disturbed the neighborhood.

The stoop murder appeared to be a garden-variety mob rubout, but the victim, Judson Lincoln, apparently had not been associated with the mob in any way. Yocke had spent two hours this morning working the phones and hadn't heard a hint. Lincoln owned a string of ten check-cashing establishments scattered through the poorer sections of down-town DC. He had been mentioned in stories in the *Post* at least seven times in the last twelve years, always as a prominent local businessman. Twice the *Post* had run his photo.

How would one handle that in a news story? '*Judson Lincoln, prominent District businessman who was not a member of any crime family, was professionally assassinated last night on the stoop of his mistress's town house as the lady looked on.*' Great lead!

Black, honest, respected, sixty-two-year-old Judson Lincoln had enjoyed the company of young women with big tits. If that was his worst sin he was probably sitting on a cloud strumming a harp right now. Lincoln had just returned from the theater with one such woman when he was gunned down. Had his outraged wife arranged his murder?

Jack Yocke was musing on these mysteries when the framed lead press plate mounted on the wall, the *Post*'s very own trophy, captured his attention. It was Bradlee's favorite *Post* front page: NIXON RESIGNS.

Yesterday's news, Yocke sighed to himself as he surveyed the ranks of the fashionably disheveled men and women taking seats around the table. Most of them were young, in their late twenties or early thirties. These aggressive, mortgaged-to-the-hilt graduates of prestigious colleges had replaced the overweight cigar chompers of yesteryear for whom murders were bigger news than presidential pontifications. Whether the new journalism was better was debatable, but one thing was certain: trendy cost more, a lot more. The new-age journalists of *The Washington Post* – always three words with the definite article capitalized, intoned the style manual – were paid about twice the real wages of the shiny-pants reporters of the manual typewriter era.

Some of this new breed dressed like fops – white collars atop striped shirts, with carefully uncoordinated padded coats and pleated trousers. How the old *Front-Page* style reporters would have hooted through their broken teeth at these dandies of the nineties!

And here was their leader, the deputy managing editor, Joseph Yangella, making his entrance. He was nattily dressed, fashionably gray-ing, socially concerned, a man you would never see half potted at a prizefight with a floozie on his arm. He nodded right and left and settled into his seat at the head of the conference table. His shirtsleeves were rolled up and his tie was loosened, as usual. Why did he wear a tie, anyway? He got right to business.

'This Colombian doper – where is he going for trial? Ed?' Yangella looked over his glasses, which he habitually kept perched precariously on the end of his nose.

The national editor said, 'We're getting all kinds of rumblings. Senator Cherry doesn't want him tried in Florida and is throwing his weight around. Justice isn't saying anything. The governor of Florida is having a fit. Nothing from the White House, although we hear the attorney general went over there about an hour ago.'

'Any announcements coming?'

'Maybe later today. Nothing for sure.'

'What's your lead right now?'

'Cherry and the governor.'

The editor nodded. He perused the slug sheet. 'Another airliner bombing in Colombia?'

'Yes,' the foreign editor told him. 'Seventy-six people dead, five of them Americans. The Medellín cartel is taking credit. Retaliation for the extradition of Aldana. It's the fifth or sixth one they've blown up in the last couple of years. They also blew up a bank yesterday and killed another judge. We've got some pictures.'

The paper's pollster spoke. 'We've got a poll conducted by a newspaper in Miami coming in over the wires. Seventy-three percent of those polled don't want Aldana tried in south Florida.'

'Can we get a poll here in Washington?' Yangella asked him.

'Take some time.'

The conversation moved to international affairs; political events in Germany, Moscow, and Budapest, and a flood in Bangladesh. They spent a minute discussing the efforts to rescue a child trapped in an abandoned well in Texas, a story that the TV networks were feasting on. Forty-five seconds were devoted to a new study on the reasons high schools gave diplomas to functional illiterates.

The managing editor didn't say a word or ask a question about Jack Yocke's murder stories. A murder is a murder is a murder, Yocke told himself. Unless you have the good fortune to be spectacularly butchered by a beautiful young woman from a filthy rich or politically prominent family, your demise is *not* going to make the front page of *The Washington Post.*

Joseph Yangella was clearing his throat to announce his decisions when the door opened and a woman from national stuck her head in.

'News conference at Justice in forty-five minutes. Rumor has it Cohen will announce that Aldana is being brought back to Washington for arraignment and trial.'

Yangella nodded. The tousled head withdrew and the door closed softly.

'All right then,' Yangella announced. 'On the front page we'll go with the doper to Washington.' He put a check mark beside each story as he announced it. 'The poll in Miami, airliner bombing and violence in Colombia, flooding in Bangladesh, the kid in the well, illiterate graduates. Photos of the airliner bombing and the rescue team in Texas. Let's do it.'

Everyone rose and strode purposefully for the door.

After dinner that evening Henry Charon bought copies of the *Post* and the *Washington Times* and took them to his room. It was after nine P.M. when he finished the papers. The assassin stood at the window a moment, looking at the lights of the city. He stretched, relieved himself in the bathroom, and put on a sweater and warm coat. The paper said the temperature might drop to forty tonight. He made sure the room door locked behind him on his way out.

3

Jack Yocke and his date could hear the voices through the door. When he knocked the door was immediately opened by a black-haired, gawky colt of a girl, about twelve years old or so. She smiled, flashing her braces, as she stood aside to allow them to pass.

'Hi,' said Jack.

'Hi. I'm Amy. My folks are here somewhere. Drinks are in the kitchen.' She spoke quickly, the words tumbling over each other.

'Jack Yocke.' He stuck out his hand solemnly. 'This is Tish Samuels.'

The youngster shook hands with her eyes averted, blushing slightly. 'Pleased to meet you,' she murmured.

They found their hostess in the kitchen talking with several other women. When she turned to them, Yocke said, 'Mrs Grafton, I'm Jack Yocke, one of your students. This is Tish Samuels.'

'I remember you, Mr Yocke. You had such a terrible time with your pronunciation.' She extended her hand to Tish. 'Thanks for joining us. May I fix you a drink? Snacks are in the dining room.'

'What a lovely apartment you have, Mrs Grafton,' Tish said.

'Call me Callie.'

His duty done, Yocke left Tish to visit with the women and wandered into the dining area. He surveyed the crowd with a professional eye. His fellow students he knew, and their spouses and dates he quickly catalogued. But there were some other guests he didn't know. He was greeting people and reminding them of his name when he saw the man he wanted to meet lounging against a wall, beer in hand, listening to a shorter man wearing a beard. Jack Yocke nodded and smiled his way through the crowd.

The bearded man was monopolizing the conversation. Yocke caught snatches of it: '. . . The critical factor is that real communism has never been tried . . . commentators ignore . . . still viable as an ideal . . .'

The trapped listener nodded occasionally, perfunctorily. Steel-rimmed glasses rode comfortably on a prominent nose set in a rather square face. His thinning, short hair was combed straight back. Just visible on his left temple was a jagged scar that had obviously been there for years. As his gaze swung across Yocke, who grinned politely, the reporter got a glimpse of gray eyes. Just now the man's features registered polite interest, although when his eyes scanned the crowd, the expression faded.

The reporter broke in, his hand out. 'Jack Yocke.'

'Jake Grafton.'

Grafton was a trim six feet tall, with just the slightest hint of tummy sag. He looked to be in his early forties. According to the people Yocke talked to, this man was destined for high command in the US Navy, assuming, of course, that he didn't stumble somewhere along the way. And Jack Yocke, future star journalist, needed access to those on their way to the high, windswept places.

'Our host,' Yocke acknowledged, and turned to the other man.

'Wilson Conroy.'

'Ah yes. Professor Conroy, Georgetown University. You're something of a celebrity.'

The professor didn't seem overjoyed at that comment. He grunted something and took a sip of his drink, something clear in a tall glass.

'Political science, isn't it?' Yocke knew that it was. Conroy was a card-carrying communist with tenure on the Georgetown faculty. A couple of years ago the paper had a reporter attend several of his classes, during which Conroy vigorously championed the Stalinist viewpoint in a one-sided debate with his students, few of whom could defend themselves from the professor's carefully selected facts and acid tongue. The resulting story in the Sunday edition of the *Post* had ignited yet another public drive to have the professor fired. The encrusted layers had been thoroughly blasted from the pillars of academic freedom with columns, editorials, and a flood of letters to the editor, all of which sold a lot of newspapers but accomplished nothing else whatever. A half dozen congressmen had gotten into the act for the edification of the folks back home, on the off chance there might be a couple of votes lying around loose in their districts.

Conroy had relished the villain's role, reveled in the notoriety, right up until the fall of 1989, when communist governments in Eastern Europe had begun collapsing like houses of cards. Since then he had been keeping a low profile, refusing to grant interviews to the press.

'Yes. Political science.' The academic's eyes flicked nervously over the crowd of people, who were chattering in the usual cocktail-party hubbub.

'Tell me, Professor, what do you make of the latest moves in the Soviet Politburo?'

The professor turned to face Yocke squarely. As he did Jake Grafton lightly touched Yocke's arm, then slid away from the wall and moved toward the snacks.

'They're abandoning the faith. They're abandoning their friends, those who have believed and sustained them.'

'Then, in your opinion, communism hasn't failed?'

The professor's lips quivered. 'It's a great tragedy for the human race. The communists have become greedy, sold their souls for dollars, sold their dream to the American financial swashbucklers and defrauders who have enslaved working people . . .' He ranted on, becoming more and more embittered.

When he paused for breath, Yocke asked, 'What if they're right and you're wrong?'

'*I'm* not wrong! We were *never* wrong!' Conroy's voice rose into a high quaver. '*I'm not wrong!*' He backed away from Yocke, his arms rigid at his sides. His empty glass fell unnoticed to the carpet. 'We had a chance to change mankind for the *better*. We had a chance to build a true community where all men would be brothers, a world of workers free from exploitation by the strong, the greedy, the lazy, those who inherit wealth, those . . .'

All eyes were on him now. Other conversations had stopped. Conroy didn't notice. He was in full cry: '. . . the exploiters have triumphed! *This* is mankind's most shameful hour.' His voice grew hoarse and spittle flew from his lips. 'The communists have surrendered to the rich and powerful. They have sold us into *bondage*, into *slavery!*'

Then Callie Grafton was there, her hand on his shoulder, whispering in his ear. Wilson Conroy's eyes closed and his shoulders sagged. She led him gently from the silent room and the startled eyes.

Subdued conversations began again.

Jack Yocke stood there isolated, all eyes avoiding him. Tish Samuels was nowhere in sight. Suddenly he was desperately thirsty. He headed for the kitchen.

He was standing there by the sink working on a bourbon and water when Jake Grafton came in.

'What'd you say your name was?'

'Jack Yocke, Captain. Look, I owe you and your wife an apology, I didn't mean to set Conroy off.'

'Umm.' Jake opened the refrigerator and took out a bottle of beer. He twisted off the cap and took a sip. 'What kind of work do you do?'

'I'm a reporter. *Washington Post.*'

Grafton nodded once and drank beer.

'Your wife is a fine teacher. I really enjoyed her course.'

'She likes teaching.'

'That comes through in the classroom.'

'Heard anything this afternoon about that Colombian druggie, Aldana? Where is he going to end up?'

'Here in Washington. Justice announced it three or four hours ago.'

Jake Grafton sighed.

'Think there'll be trouble?'

'Wouldn't surprise me,' Yocke's host said. 'Seems every age has at least one Caligula, an absolute despot absolutely corrupted. Ours are criminal psychopaths, and we seem to have a lot more than one. I hear Chano Aldana has a net worth of four billion dollars. Awesome, isn't it?'

'Is the American government ready to endure the problems the Colombian government is having?'

Jake Grafton snorted. 'My crystal ball is sorta cloudy just now. Why'd you take a Spanish class, anyway, Jack?'

'Thought it would help me on the job.' That was true enough, as far as it went. Jack Yocke had taken the course so he could get bargaining chips to talk his way onto the foreign staff where reporters fluent in foreign languages had a leg up. Still, he wasn't about to pass up an opportunity to meet anybody who might help him later in his career, so he had come to the end-of-semester party to meet Jake Grafton. 'Maybe I can get a jail-cell interview with Aldana.'

That comment made Grafton shrug.

'I understand you're in the Navy?'

'Yeah.'

'On the staff of the Joint Chiefs?'

Those gray eyes behind the steel-rimmed spectacles appraised Yocke's face carefully. 'Uh-huh.'

Yocke decided to try a shot in the dark. 'What do you think will happen when they bring Aldana here for trial?'

Jake Grafton's face registered genuine amusement. 'Enjoy the party. Jack,' he said over his shoulder as he went through the door.

Oh well, Yocke reflected. Creation took God six days.

He heard someone knocking on the hall door and stepped to the kitchen door, where he could inspect the new arrival. The daughter, Amy, passed him and pulled the door open.

'Hey, beautiful.' The man who entered was about thirty, five feet ten or so, with short brown hair and white, even teeth. He presented Amy with a box wrapped in Christmas paper. 'For you, from some ardent admirers. Merry yo ho ho and all that good stuff.'

The girl took the box and shook it enthusiastically.

'I wouldn't do that if I were you,' the newcomer said seriously. 'That thing breaks, the world as we know it will cease to exist. Time and space will warp, everything will be twisted and grossly deformed and sucked right in – rocks and dirt and cats and kids and everything.' He made a slurping sound with his mouth. 'The moon'll probably go too. Maybe a couple planets.'

Smiling broadly, Amy shook the box vigorously one more time, then threw her arms around the man. 'Oh, Toad! Thank you.'

'It's from me *and* Rita.' He ran his fingers through her hair and arranged a lock behind an ear.

'Thank her too.'

'I will.'

As Amy trotted away. Jack Yocke introduced himself.

'Name's Toad Tarkington,' the newcomer informed him.

Another navy man. Jack Yocke thought with a flash of irritation, with another of those childish buddy-buddy nicknames. He wondered what they called Grafton. 'Toad, eh? Bet your mother cringes when she hears that.'

'She used to. The finer nuances, sometimes they escape her.' Tarkington gestured helplessly and grinned.

Jack Yocke suddenly decided he didn't like the smooth, glib Mr Tarkington. 'Most civilians don't understand the subtleties of male bonding, do they? But I think it's quaint.'

The grin disappeared from Tarkington's face. He surveyed Yocke with a raised eyebrow for two or three seconds, then said, 'You look constipated.'

Before he could reply, Jack Yocke found himself looking at Tarkington's back.

A half hour later he found Tish in a group on the balcony. The view was excellent this time of evening, with the lights of the city twinkling in the crisp air. Washington had enjoyed an unseasonably long fall, and although there had been several cold snaps, the temperature was still in the fifties this evening. And all these people were outside enjoying it, even if they did have to rub their arms occasionally or snuggle against their significant other. To the left one could catch a swatch of the Potomac and straight ahead the Washington Monument rose above the skyline.

'Everybody, this is Jack Yocke,' Tish told the five people gathered there.

They nodded politely, then one of Yocke's fellow Spanish students resumed a monologue Yocke's appearance had apparently interrupted. He was middle-aged and called himself Brother Harold. 'Anyway, I decided, why all the fasting, chanting, special clothes, and mantras to memorize? If I could reduce meditation to the essentials, make it a sort of subliminal programming, then the balance, the transcendence, could be made available to a wider audience.'

'You ready to leave?' Yocke whispered to his date.

'A minute,' she whispered back, intent on Brother Harold's spiel.

Yocke tried to look interested. He had already heard this tale three times this fall. Unlike Jake Grafton or Wilson Conroy, Brother Harold thought it would be a very good thing for Yocke to do a story about him for the newspaper.

'. . . So I introduced music. Not just any music of course, but carefully chosen music of the soul.' He expounded a moment on the chants of ancient monks and echo chambers and the spheres of the brain, then concluded, 'The goal was ecstasy through reverberation. And it works! I am *so* pleased. My followers have finally found quiescence and tranquility. The method is startlingly transformative.'

Yocke concluded he had had enough. He slipped back through the sliding glass door and waited just inside. Toad Tarkington was standing alone against a wall with a beer bottle in his hand. He didn't even bother to look at Yocke. The reporter returned the compliment.

In a moment Tish joined him. 'What is quiescence?' she asked as she slid the door closed behind her.

'Damned if I know. I bet Brother Harold doesn't know either. Let's say good-bye to the hostess and split.'

'He's so sincere.'

'Crackpots always are,' Yocke muttered, remembering with distaste his scene with Conroy.

Callie Grafton was at the door saying good-bye to another couple, her daughter Amy beside her shifting from foot to foot. Callie was slightly above medium height with an erect, regal carriage. Tonight her hair was swept back and held with a clasp. Her eyes look tired, Jack Yocke thought as he thanked her for the party and the Spanish class.

'I hope Professor Conroy is all right, Mrs Grafton. I didn't mean to upset him.'

'He's lying down. This is a very trying time for him.'

Yocke nodded, Tish squeezed her hand, and then they were out in the corridor walking for the elevator.

'I really like her,' Tish said once the elevator doors had closed behind them. 'We had a delightful talk.'

'She has strange friends,' Yocke remarked, meaning Wilson Conroy.

'Since the collapse of communism in Eastern Europe and the Soviet Union,' Tish explained, 'people have been laughing at Conroy. He never minded being hated, reviled—'

'Never minded? The poisonous little wart *loved* it!'

'—but the laughter is destroying him.'

'So Mrs Grafton feels sorry for him, eh?'

'No,' Tish Samuels said patiently. 'Pity would kill him. She's Conroy's friend because he has no others.'

'Umph,'

In the parking lot she asked, 'Did you meet Toad Tarkington?'

'Uh-huh.'

'He and I had a nice chat. His wife is out of town, so he came by himself. He's very nice.'

'Navy, right?'

'Golly, I'm not sure. I didn't ask.'

'The military is what's wrong with this town. Every other guy you meet is in the service.'

'So?'

Yocke unlocked the car and helped her into the passenger seat.

'I don't like the military,' he said when he was in the driver's seat. He stuck the key into the ignition and engaged the starter. 'I don't like the simplistic way they look at the world, I don't like the rituals, the deference to seniority, the glorification of war and suffering and death. I don't like the demands they make on the public purse. The whole gig irritates me.'

'Well,' said Tish Samuels tentatively, 'I'm sure that basically the people in the service are pretty much like the rest of us.'

Yocke continued his train of thought, unwilling to let it lie. 'The military is a fossil. Warriors are anachronisms in a world trying to feed five billion people. They cause more problems than they solve.'

'Perhaps,' said the date, looking out the window and apparently not interested in the reporter's profound opinions.

'Did you meet Mrs Grafton's husband?'

'Oh, I said a few words to him. He seems very nice, in a serious sort of way.'

'Want to go get a drink someplace?'

'Not tonight, thank you. I'd better be getting home. Maybe the next time.'

'Sure.' Jack Yocke flicked the car into gear and threaded his way out onto the street.

After he dropped Tish Samuels at her apartment building, Jack Yocke drove downtown to the office. As he had expected, Ottmar Mergenthaler was working late. The columnist was in his small glassed-in cubicle in the middle of the newsroom tapping away on the word processor. Yocke stuck his head in.

'Hey, Ott. How's it going?'

Mergenthaler sat back in his chair. 'Pull up a chair, Jack.' When the reporter was seated, the older man asked, 'How did it go this evening?'

'Okay, I guess.'

'Well, what do you think of him?' Mergenthaler had been the one who suggested he try to meet the husband of Callie Grafton, the Spanish instructor.

'I don't know. I asked him for a simple opinion and he grinned at me and walked away.'

'Rome wasn't written in a day. It takes years to develop a good source.'

Yocke worried a fingernail. 'Grafton doesn't give a hoot in hell what anybody thinks, about him or about anything.'

Mergenthaler laced his fingers behind his head. 'Four people whom I highly respect have mentioned his name to me. One of them, a vice admiral who just retired, had the strongest opinion. He said, and I quote, "Jake Grafton is the most talented, most promising officer in the armed forces today." ' Mergenthaler cocked an eyebrow and pursed his lips.

'Another senior official put it a little differently. He said, "Jake Grafton is a man of war." '

Jack Yocke snorted. 'We really need guys like that with peace breaking out all over.'

'Are you a natural-born cynic, or are you trying to grow into one?'

'These military people – a damned clique of macho knotheads worshiping the phallic gun. Grafton is just like all of them – oh, he was pleasant enough – but I could feel it.'

Mergenthaler looked amused. 'My very young and inexperienced friend, if you have to like the people you write about, you are in the wrong line of work.'

Yocke grinned. 'What're you writing tonight?'

'Drugs again.' Mergenthaler turned back to the screen and scrolled the document up. He tapped the cursor position keys aimlessly while he read. Yocke stood and read over his shoulder.

The column was an epitaph for three young black men, all of whom had died yesterday on the streets and sidewalks of Washington. All three had apparently been engaged in the crack trade. All three had been shot to death. All three had presumably been killed by other young black men also engaged in the crack business. Three murders was slightly above the daily average for the metropolitan area, but not significantly so.

Mergenthaler had obviously spent most of the day visiting the relatives of the dead men: the column contained descriptions of people and places he could not have acquired over the phone.

When Yocke resumed his seat, he said, 'Ott, you're going to burn yourself out.'

The older man spotted something in the document he wanted to change. He punched keys for a moment. When he finished he muttered. 'Too sentimental?'

'Nobody cares about black crackheads. Nobody gives a damn if they go to prison or starve to death or slaughter each other. You know that, Ott.'

'I'll have to work some more on this. My job is to make people give a damn.'

Yocke left the columnist's cubicle and went to his desk out in the newsroom. He found a notebook to scribble in amid the loose paper on his desk and got on the phone to the Montgomery County police. Perhaps they had made some progress on the beltway killing.

Jack Yocke had murders of his own to write about, whether anyone gave a damn about the victims or not.

After all the guests had left, Toad Tarkington was washing dishes in the Graftons' kitchen when Amy came in and posed self-consciously where he could see her. She had applied some eyeshadow and lipstick at some point in the evening. Toad noted with surprise. He consciously suppressed a grin. This past year she had been shooting up, developing in all the right places. She was only a few inches shorter than Callie.

'Little past your bedtime, isn't it?'

'Oh, Toad, don't be so parental. I'm a teenager now, you know.'

'Almost.'

'Near enough.'

'Grab a towel and dry some of these things.'

Amy did as requested.

'Nice party, huh?' she said as she finished the punch bowl and put it away.

'Yeah.'

'Is Rita coming for Christmas?'

'I hope so.' Rita, Toad's wife, was a navy test pilot. Just now she was out in Nevada testing the first of the Navy's new A-12 stealth attack planes. Both Toad and Rita held the rank of lieutenant. 'Depends on the flight test schedule, of course,' Toad added glumly.

'Do you love Rita?' Amy asked softly.

Toad Tarkington knew trouble when it slapped him in the face. His gaze ripped from the dishes and settled on the young girl leaning against the counter and facing him self-consciously, her weight balanced on one leg and her eyes demurely lowered.

He cleared his throat. 'Why do you ask?'

'Well,' she said softly, flashing her lashes, 'you're only fifteen years older than I am, and I'll be eighteen in five years, and . . .' She ran out of steam.

Toad Tarkington got a nice chunk of his lower lip between his teeth and bit hard.

He took his hands from the water and dried them on a towel. 'Listen, little one. You've still got a lot of growing left to do. You'll meet Mr Right someday. Maybe in five years or when you're in college. You've got to take life at its natural pace. But you'll meet him. He's out there right now, hoping that someday he'll meet you. And when you finally find him he won't be fifteen years older than you are.'

She examined his eyes.

A blush began at her neck and worked its way up her face as tears welled up. 'You're laughing at me.'

'No no no, Amy. I know what it cost you to bring this subject up.' He reached out and cradled her cheek in his palm. 'But I love Rita very much.'

She bit the inside of her mouth, which made her lips contort.

'Believe me, the guy for you is out there. When you finally meet him, you'll know. And he'll know. He'll look straight into your heart and see the warm, wonderful human being there, and he'll fall madly in love with you. You wait and see.'

'Wait? Life just seems so . . . so *forever!*' Her despair was palpable.

'Yeah,' Toad said. 'And teenagers live in the now. You'll be an adult the day you know in your gut that the future is as real as today is. Understand?'

He heard a noise. Jake Grafton was lounging against the doorjamb. Jake held out his hands. Amy took them.

He kissed her forehead. 'I think it's time for you to hit the sack. Tell Toad good night.'

She paused at the door and looked back. Her eyes were still shiny. 'Good night. Toad.'

'Good night, Amy Carol.'

Both men stood silently until they heard Amy's bedroom door click shut.

'She's really growing fast,' Toad said.

'Too fast,' said Jake Grafton, and he hunted in the refrigerator for a beer, which he tossed to Toad, then took another for himself.

Ten minutes later Callie joined them in the living room. The men were deep into a discussion of the Gorbachev revolution and the centrifugal forces pulling the Soviet Union apart. 'What will the world be like after the dust settles?' Callie asked. 'Will the world be a safer place or less so?'

She received a carefully thought-out reply from Toad and a sincere 'I don't know' from her husband.

She expected Jake's answer. Through the years she had found him a man ready to admit what he didn't know. One of his great strengths was a complete lack of pretense. After years of association with academics, Callie found Jake a breath of fresh air. He knew who he was and what he was, and to his everlasting credit he never tried to be anything else.

As she sat watching him tonight, a smile spread across her face.

'Not to change the subject, Captain,' Toad Tarkington said, 'but is it true you're now the senior officer in one of the Joint Staff divisions?'

'Alas, it's true,' Jake admitted. 'I get to decide who opens the mail and makes the coffee.'

Toad chuckled. After almost two years in Washington, he knew only too well how close to the truth that comment was. 'Well, you know that Rita is out in Nevada flying the first production A-12. She's going to be pretty busy with that for a year or so, and they have a Test Pilot School-graduate bombardier flying with her. So I'm sort of the gofer in the A-12 shop now.'

Jake nodded and Callie said something polite.

'What I was thinking,' Toad continued, 'was that maybe I could get a transfer over to your shop. If I'm going to make coffee and run errands, why not over at your place? Maybe get an X in the joint staff tour box.'

'Hmmm.'

'What d'ya think, sir?'

'Well, you're too junior.'

'Oh, Jake,' Callie murmured. Toad flashed her a grin.

'Really, Callie, he is too junior. I don't think they have any billets for lieutenants on the Joint Staff. It's a *very* senior staff.'

'Then it needs some younger people,' she told her husband. 'You make it sound like a retirement home, full of fuddy-duddies and senior golfers.'

'I am *not* a fuddy-duddy,' Jake Grafton told her archly.

'I know, dear. I didn't mean to imply that you were.' She winked at Toad and he laughed.

The lieutenant rose from the couch, said his good-byes, and after promising to tell Rita the Graftons said hello, departed.

'Really, Jake,' Callie said, 'you should see if he could transfer to the Joint Staff.'

'Be better for his career if he cut his shore tour short and went back to sea in an F-14 squadron.'

'Toad knows that. He just thinks very highly of you and wants to work nearby. That's quite a compliment.'

'I know that.' A smile spread across Jake Grafton's face. 'The ol' Horny Toad. He's a good kid.'

Henry Charon stood leaning against an abandoned grocery store in northeast Washington and watched the black teenagers in the middle of the street hawk crack to the drivers of the vehicles streaming by. Some of the drivers stopped and made purchases, some didn't. The drivers were white and black, men and women, mostly young or middle-aged. Knots of young black men stood on the corners scrutinizing traffic, inspecting the pedestrians, and keeping a wary eye on Charon.

The wind whipped trash down the street and made the cold cut through Charon's clothes. Yet he was dressed more heavily than most of the crack dealers, who stayed in continual motion to keep warm. Somewhere a boom box was blasting hard rock.

He had been there no more than five minutes when a tall, skinny youngster detached himself from the group on the corner across the street and skipped through the cars toward him.

'Hey, man.'

'Hey,' said Henry Charon.

'Hey, man, you gonna buy this sidewalk?'

'Just watching.'

'Want some product?'

Charon shook his head. Four of the teenagers on the corner were staring at him. One of them sat down by a garbage can and reached behind it, his eyes glued to Charon and his interrogator. Charon would have bet a thousand dollars against a nickel that there was a loaded weapon behind that garbage can.

'A fucking tourist!' the skinny kid said with disgust. 'Take a hike, honkey. You don't wanta get caught under the wheels of commerce.'

'I'm curious. How do you know I'm not a cop?'

'You no cop, man. You ain't got the look. You some little booger tourist from nowhere-ville. Now I'm tired of your jive, honkey. You got ten seconds to start hiking back to honkey-town or you'll have to carry your balls home in your hand. You dig?'

'I dig.' Henry Charon turned and started walking.

The intersection two blocks south was covered with steel plates and timbers. Under the street, construction was continuing on a new subway tunnel.

Using his flashlight, Charon looked for the entrance. He found it, closed with a sheet of plywood. He had it off in seconds.

The interior resembled a wet, dark, dripping cavern. Henry Charon felt his way along, inspecting the overhead when he wasn't looking for a place to put his feet. The tunnel continued ahead and behind him as far as he could see.

He began walking south, stepping over construction material and dodging the occasional low-hanging electrical wire. He inspected the sides of the tunnel and the overhead, looking for the ventilator shafts he knew would have to be there. He found three.

It was warmer here than it had been on the street. There was no wind, though a match revealed the air was flowing gently back in the direction from which he had come. Actually quite pleasant. Charon unbuttoned his coat and continued walking.

In several places the workmen had rigged forms to pour the concrete floor. The precast concrete shells were already in place on the arched top and sides of the tunnel, probably installed as the tunnel was dug.

After what he judged to be four hundred yards or so of travel, he came to a giant enlarged cavern. His flashlight beam looked puny as he examined the pillars and construction debris. When finished, this would no doubt be a subway station. Another tunnel came in on a lower level. Charon descended a ladder and walked away in the new direction.

This was his third exploratory trip to Washington in the past four weeks and the second time he had been in these tunnels. If the construction crews were making progress, it was not readily visible to Charon's untutored eye.

Tassone had visited him a month ago at the ranch in New Mexico, and he had had a list. Six names. Six men in Washington he had wanted killed. Was it feasible? Would Charon be interested? Charon had looked at the list.

'George Bush?'

'Yeah.'

'You're asking me to kill the President of the United States?'

'No. I'm asking you if it can be done. If you say yes, I'll ask you if you're interested. If you say yes, I'll ask you how much. If all those questions are decided to the satisfaction of everyone involved, then we will decide whether or not to proceed, and when.'

'These other names – all of them?'

'As many as possible. Obviously, the more you get, the more we'll pay.'

Charon had studied the names on the list, then watched as Tassone burned it and crumbled the ashes and dribbled them out onto the wind.

'I'll think about it.'

So after three trips to Washington, what did he think?

It was feasible to kill the President, of course. The President was an elected officeholder and had to appear in public from time to time. The best personal security system in the world could not protect a working politician from a determined, committed assassin. All the security apparatus could do was minimize the possibility that an amateur might succeed and increase the level of difficulty for a professional.

The real problem would come afterward. Charon had no illusions on that score. Successful or not, the assassin would be the object of the most intensive manhunt in American history. Every hand would be against him. Anyone found to have knowingly aided the assassin would be ruthlessly destroyed – financially and professionally and in every other way. In addition, accused conspirators would face the death penalty if the government could get a conviction, and God knows, the prosecutors would pull out all the stops. Before the hit the assassin would be on his own. Afterward he would be a pariah.

For the assassin to walk away from the scene of the crime would not be too difficult, with some careful planning, but as the full investigative resources of the federal government were engaged, the net would become more and more difficult to evade. The longer the killer remained at large, the greater the efforts of the hunters.

Yes, it would be a hunt, a hunt for a rabid wolf.

As Henry Charon saw it, therein lay the challenge. He had spent his life stalking game in the wild mountain places and, these last few years, in the wild city places. Occasionally a deer or elk or cougar had successfully eluded him and those moments made the kills sweeter. After assassinating the President, he would be the quarry. If he could do the unexpected, stay one jump ahead of those who hunted him, the chase would be – ah, the chase would be sublime, his grandest adventure.

And if he lost and his hunters won, so be it. Nothing lives forever. For the mountain lion and the bull elk and Henry Charon, living was the challenge. Death will come for the quick and the bold, the slow and the careful, the wise and the foolish, each and every one.

Death is easy. Except for a moment or two of pain, death has no terrors for those who are willing to face life. Henry Charon's acceptance of the biologically inevitable was not an intellectual exercise for a philosophy class, but subconscious, ingrained. He had killed too often to fear it.

Now he reached that place in the tunnel he had found on his last visit. It was in a long, gentle curve, halfway up the wall. As he had been walking along he had momentarily felt a puff of cooler air. Investigation had revealed a narrow, oblong gap just wide enough for a wiry man to wriggle through. On the other side was an ancient basement, the dark home of rats and insects.

After checking the area with his flashlight, Henry Charon squirmed through the gaping crack, which was lined with stones at odd angles. He was now in a room with a dirt floor and walls of old brick. The ceiling was a concrete slab. Above that, Charon had concluded after an afternoon of discreet pacing, was dirt and an asphalt basketball court.

This basement was at least a century old. The house which had stood above it had apparently been demolished thirty or forty years ago during a spasm of enthusiasm for urban renewal. The ceiling slab had not been poured here: the edges were not mated to the brick walls in any way. No doubt the demolition contractor had thought it cheaper to just cover the hole rather than pay to haul in dirt to fill it.

There was no way out of this room except through the subway tunnel. That was the bad news. The good news was that the subway tunnel was the only entrance. A man would be reasonably safe here for a short while if he could get in without being observed.

Air entered this subterranean vault from several cracks in the brick walls and around the large stones that choked the opening through which coal had once probably been dumped into the basement. Charon suspected that nearby were other basements, other century-old ruins of nineteenth-century Washington, and the dark air passages were used by rats to go back and forth.

He checked the supplies he had brought here on two evenings last week, on his last trip to Washington. Canned food, a sterno stove, a first-aid kit, two gallons of water, three blankets, and two flashlights with extra D-cell batteries. It was all here, apparently undisturbed. He examined one of the blankets more carefully with his flashlight. A rat had apparently decided it would make a good nest. He shook out the blanket and refolded it.

He picked up a handful of dirt from the floor and sifted it through his fingers. It was dry, the consistency of dust. That was good. This would not be a safe place to be if water in any quantity ever came in.

Charon turned off the flashlight and sat in the darkness near the exit hole, listening. The sounds of traffic on the street twenty to thirty feet over his head were always there. Faint but audible. There was another sound too, of such low frequency as almost to be felt rather than heard. He eased his head out into the tunnel for a look, then crawled out.

Now he heard it, a faint rumble. It seemed to be coming down the tunnel.

Standing in the subway tunnel he reinspected the hole with the flash. He wanted to leave no obvious evidence that anyone had been in there. Satisfied, he walked south as the rumbling noise faded again to silence. Not total silence, of course. He could still hear the street sounds from the world above.

If Tassone just wanted George Bush assassinated, that would be a large enough challenge to satisfy anyone, Henry Charon mused as he walked along. Make the hit, ride out the manhunt that would immediately follow, then leave Washington several weeks later for the ranch. Sit at the ranch for several years enduring the agony of waiting for the FBI to come driving up the road, and hoping they never came.

But Bush was merely the first name on the list. The other five, they would have to be killed after the presidential hit. That was the rub. The sequence was dictated by logic. If he first shot the Chief Justice of the Supreme Court, or the attorney general, the Secret Service would surround Bush with a security curtain that one man could not hope to penetrate. So Bush had to be the first target.

That sequence inevitably created an escape problem of extraordinary complexity. He had to move in spite of the dragnet and find his targets. And escape without revealing his identity. Again and again.

Could it be done? Could he do it?

He glimpsed light ahead and doused the flashlight. Two hundred yards of careful walking brought him to a steel mesh. Here the new tunnel joined an existing one. He stood in the darkness and waited.

Yes. Here comes the rumble again, much louder, swelling and growing, rushing toward him.

He stood watching as a subway train rushed by with a roar, the passengers plainly visible in the windows, standing, sitting, reading, talking to each other. And as fast as the train had come, it was gone, the sound fading.

Henry Charon extracted a subway map from his hip pocket and consulted it in the dim glow of the flashlight. He traced the lines and looked again at the layout of the system, committing the routes to memory. The avenues and streets and subway lines, they had to be as familiar to him as the ridges and mesas of the Sangre de Cristos.

With the map back in his pocket, he examined the steel fence carefully and the padlocked mesh door in the middle of it. He could cut that lock if he had to. A Yale. He would buy one just like it, just in case.

It felt strange here in this tunnel, walking through the darkness with just the glow of the flashlight and the smell of earth in his nostrils. In fifteen minutes he arrived at the cavern that would someday be a subway station and picked his way around and through the scaffolding.

He found the opening to the outside world, kicked the plywood off, then reset it.

It was chilly on the street. After buttoning his coat, Henry Charon walked along absorbing the sights and sounds, looking, examining the terrain yet again, searching for cover, committing everything to memory.

Could it be done? Could *he* do it?

Even if he pulled it off, did everything absolutely right and fate had no nasty little surprises for him – like a cop at an unexpected place or a tourist snapping pictures at the wrong time – Tassone and his unknown masters were still the weak links.

Who did Tassone work for? How many people in Tassone's organization knew of the New Mexico hitter, Tassone's trips, the cash in the suitcases? Were any of these people government informers? Would they become so in the future? Were any of them alcoholics or drug addicts? Would someone whisper to a mistress, brag at a bar?

All who knew the identity of the assassin of the President of the United States were serious threats for as long as they lived. They would always carry this immense, valuable secret. If they were ever arrested or threatened, the immense, valuable secret could always be sold or traded.

The project tempted Henry Charon. The preparations, the anticipation that would grow and grow, the kill, the chase afterward, just thinking of these things made him feel vigorously alive, like the first glimpse of a bull elk against a far ridge on a clear, frosty morning. Yet the unknown, faceless ones could ruin him at any time. If he successfully escaped he would have to live with the possibility of betrayal all the rest of his life.

Yet you had to weigh everything, and the hunt was what really mattered.

Henry Charon walked on, thinking again of the hunt and how it would be.

4

On Sunday, T. Jefferson Brody woke up alone in his king-sized bed in his five-bedroom, four-bathroom, $1.6 million mansion in Kenwood. After a long hot shower, he shaved and dressed in gray wool slacks and a tweed sports coat that had set him back half a grand.

Ten minutes later he eased the Mercedes from the three-car garage and thumbed the garage-door controller as he backed down the drive.

T. Jefferson Brody should have felt good this morning. Friday he had deposited another fat legal fee in his Washington bank and shuffled another equally fat fee off to the Netherlands Antilles on the first leg of an electronic journey to Switzerland. He had done some calculations on an envelope last night, then burned the envelope. The sums he had managed to squirrel away were significant in any man's league: he had over four million dollars in cash here in the States on which he had paid income taxes and six million in Switzerland on which he hadn't. That plus the house (half paid for) and the cars, antiques, and art (cash on the barrelhead) gave him a nice, tidy little fortune. T. Jefferson was doing all right for himself.

The fly in the wine of T. Jefferson Brody was that he wanted a lot more. He knew there was a lot more to be made, a whale of a lot more, and it just didn't seem that he was getting a share commensurate with his contribution. The things he did – the things only he could do – enabled his clients to make mountains of money, yet he was left with the crumbs that dribbled from their napkins. Just fees. Never a percentage of the action. Of course, lawyers traditionally have received fees for their services, but T. Jefferson Brody's services weren't traditional.

As he drove down Massachusetts Avenue into the District this morning for breakfast with the representative of his oldest, though certainly not richest, client, T. Jefferson tried to decide if he should announce a fee increase or something equally nebulous that would put more money into his pocket. He would wait, he decided, to hear what the client wanted.

These people were going to have to realize that T. Jefferson Brody was a very valuable asset to have in their huddle. T. Jefferson delivered. Always.

Money talks and bullshit walks. Somehow he would have to make that point. Professionally and unobtrusively, of course.

He checked his car with the valet at the Hay Adams Hotel and walked purposefully through the lobby to the elevator. Whenever Bernie Shapiro came to town he always stayed in the same suite, a huge corner job with an excellent view of Lafayette Park and the White House.

Bernie opened the door, grunted once, and closed it behind the visitor. 'When's it gonna get cold down here?'

'Weird weather,' T. Jefferson agreed as he took off his topcoat and laid it on a handy chair. 'Maybe the climate is really getting warmer.'

'Like hell. Nearly froze my ass off in New York these past two weeks.'

Bernie Shapiro was a bear of a man. He had been fearsome in his youth; now he was merely fat. The years, however, had added no padding to his abrasive personality. He sank into an easy chair and relit the stump of cigar that protruded from his fleshy jowls. 'Breakfast'll be here in a few minutes,' he muttered as he eyed his visitor through the thick smoke.

The attorney found a chair and took in the luxurious room and the White House, just visible from this angle through the naked tree branches.

Classical music played on the radio beside the bed a tad too loud for comfortable conversation. This was a normal precaution. The music would vibrate the window glass and foil any parabolic mikes that might be pointed in this direction by inquisitive souls, such as FBI agents.

The men discussed the Giants' and Redskins' chances this year as they waited for breakfast to be delivered. The knock of the room-service waiter came precisely on the hour. After all, this *was* the Hay Adams.

When the white-jacketed waiter had wheeled the serving cart back into the hall and closed the door behind him, Bernie opened his briefcase and extracted a device artfully crafted to look like a portable radio. This device detected the electromagnetic field created by microphones. Bernie pulled out the antenna, then walked around the room, paying careful attention to the needle on the dial as he paused at light switches and electrical outlets, swept the antenna over the food and slowly down Brody's back and front. The operation took, about two minutes. Finally satisfied, Bernie nodded toward the conference table laden with food as he collapsed the antenna and flipped switches.

The lawyer seated himself and poured a cup of coffee while Bernie put the device back in his briefcase. Only when both men were seated and had their food on their plates did the serious conversation begin.

'We've decided to expand our business. What with everybody making acquisitions and expanding their profit potential, it seemed like the thing to do.'

'Absolutely,' T. Jefferson agreed as he forked into the eggs benedict.

'We thought we would get into the check-cashing business at several likely places around the country. We've located a little business here in Washington and want you to buy it for us. You'll do all the negotiating, set up some corporations, front the whole deal.'

'Same as the DePaolo deal?'

'Pretty much.'

'What's the name of the company you want to buy?'

'A to Z Checks. The owner ran into some trouble Friday evening and the business now belongs to his widow. I want you to make her an offer. Better wait until Tuesday. The funeral's tomorrow. The business is ten outlets. We'll pay a flat four hundred thousand, but if you can get it for less you keep the difference.'

'Okay.'

Bernie got to work on his sausage as Jefferson Brody turned the project over in his mind and decided it offered few problems. A couple of dummy corporations and some negotiating. Assignments of the leases on the outlets – he knew from experience that these storefront operations were always leased – and the usual business papers. All very straightforward.

'If the widow won't take our offer, you let me know.'

'What's the business make in profit?'

'About a hundred grand a year.'

'Your offer sounds reasonable. But if you don't mind my asking, why do you want this business?'

'That's the second half of the project. The crack business here in Washington is turning some hefty dollars. Six organizations here in the area have all the trade. Anyone else tries to get started, they shut them down. These organizations are all getting along and turning decent money, with the usual friction at street level for turf.' Bernie waved that away as a problem not worthy of discussion. 'The real problem is washing the dough after they got it. That's the service we'll provide. We'll take the cash and trade it for government checks – welfare, ADC, Social Security, and so on – and the usual private checks, deposit the checks in a business account, then run the money through dummy corporations which will feed it to legit businesses owned by us. Other real businesses with absolutely no connection to the first set will feed money back to our crack friends. They'll get a nice legit income from a corporation they own and nobody can ever prove a thing. I think they'll really like this operation when it's explained to them. We won't need you for that though.'

'What will you charge for this service?'

'Twenty percent.' Bernie grinned.

Brody felt his eyebrows struggling to rise. He made an effort to control his face.

'They're paying ten to fifteen percent now. So they'll be less than enthusiastic at first. They'll change their minds, though, and see the benefits of our proposal.'

'Will ten outlets do enough business to handle the volume you'll need?'

'I doubt it,' Bernie said. 'We'll probably double the number of outlets within a month, then open other outlets in other cities. A to Z is going to enjoy an explosive expansion.'

They discussed the intricacies of it. The key to staying in business was having a bulletproof cover story. 'You'll need a bank, maybe two,' Brody told his client as they pushed their plates toward the center of the table and poured coffee.

'Yeah. There's a savings and loan in Bethesda that should become available in the next week or so. The head cashier had a bad accident on the freeway Friday. Guy named Harrington.' Bernie grinned. 'Fridays are not good days around here, apparently.'

The lawyer chuckled his agreement.

Bernie continued: 'This Harrington was washing money for Freeman McNally.' McNally was the largest crack dealer in Washington and also one of T. Jefferson Brody's clients. Bernie Shapiro may or may not have known that. Brody survived by *never, ever* mentioning one client's affairs to another client. He had absolutely no intention of breaking that rule now.

Bernie continued: 'A guy on the inside figured out what Harrington was up to and talked to a guy who knew somebody. One thing led to another, and now we got a deal with this guy on the inside. Tomorrow or the day after the regulators will be called in. Three or four days after that, the place will probably be for sale cheap. You're going to buy it for us.'

T. Jefferson Brody grinned this time. "Okay. But we'll need some front people for this one. Little tougher to buy an S and L.'

'Our guy inside will get a piece, and he'll come up with three or four names. We put up all the money and he'll run it for us. You'll do the legal work, of course.'

They discussed it for over an hour. When they had ironed out the details, T. Jefferson Brody thought it time to broach the subject of his fee. 'Bernie, this new enterprise should be very profitable for you.'

'Should be.' Bernie lit a fresh cigar.

'I want to raise my fee.'

Bernie puffed serenely on the cigar and stared through the smoke at the lawyer. 'We pay you fifty a month, Tee.'

'I know. And I do excellent work that enables you to make really major money. In good conscience, Bernie, I think my fee should be higher.'

'You're a fixer,' Bernie Shapiro said, his eyes on the attorney. 'If we go down the tubes, you'll still be standing there high and dry. You take no risks, you invest no money, you're shielded by client confidentiality. Fifty a month is enough.'

Brody tried to interrupt but Bernie raised his palm. 'We never expected you to do our work exclusively. If we thought you'd violated a confidence, Tee, tried to shave a little for yourself from one of our deals, or played both ends against the middle, we'd find another lawyer. We'd even send flowers to your funeral. But you don't do things like that. So we pay you a fifty-thousand-dollar monthly retainer for whatever little chores you do, regardless.'

T. Jefferson Brody opened his mouth, then closed it again. Bernie Shapiro smiled. He had a good smile. 'Think of it this way, Tee. You don't even have to go to the trouble of billing us. We send the check on the first of the month even if you spent the previous month on vacation in the Bahamas. Isn't that so?'

Brody nodded.

'Thanks for dropping by this morning, Tee. Tuesday you start with the widow.' Bernie stood and held the lawyer's coat. 'Stay in touch.'

'Sure.'

'Remember, Tee. Greed is bad for your soul.'

As T. Jefferson Brody drove away from the Hay Adams in his Mercedes coupé, Henry Charon left his hotel, a significantly more modest establishment than the Hay Adams, and set forth upon the sidewalks. This morning his course took him toward the Supreme Court building, immediately behind the Capitol. He circled the building slowly, examined the tags on the parking spaces, and stood looking at buildings across Second Street. Then he wandered in that direction.

Assassinating people was exactly like hunting deer. The hunter's task was to place himself to take advantage of a momentary opportunity. The skill involved was to get to the right place at the right time with the right equipment and to make the shot when fate and circumstances offered.

He should have been a military sniper, Charon thought, not for the first time. He would have been good at the work and he would have enjoyed it. Yet snipers need wars to employ their skills. An assassin is in demand all the time.

He came back to the unsolved problem of potential informers in the organization or group that wanted to hire him. He had no idea who these people were, though he supposed that with a reasonable effort he could find out. If he found out, what then?

Perhaps the thing to do was to plan now for a permanent disappearance, a permanent change of identity. The drawback was time. He didn't have enough time to do it right. And if done incorrectly, such a move would be worse than doing nothing at all.

Afterward, could he devote six months to proper preparation, then vanish? Would he have six months?

Mulling these and similar questions, in the alley behind the buildings facing Second Street Henry Charon found a dumpster sitting directly beneath a fire escape. He moved the large metal trash box and pulled on rubber gloves. Apparently no one was watching. Vaulting to the top of the dumpster, he curled his fingers around the lowest rung of the ladder and pulled it down. With one last glance around, Charon was on his way up.

The building didn't even have a burglar alarm. It was old, with wooden-frame windows. He used a credit card on a latch and was inside in seconds. The elevator worked. He took it to the top floor. The offices on this floor were empty and dark this Sunday afternoon. Henry Charon went looking for the stairs.

The door to the roof had a lock that yielded to a set of picks. Charon stepped out on the roof and took in the scene at a glance. The view down into the Supreme Court parking lot was partially obscured by defoliated tree branches. That didn't bother him. He had made many a shot through much thicker brush and foliage and at much longer ranges. The Supreme Court building was about a hundred yards from here and the Capitol about five hundred. The adjacent buildings were of the same height as this one. An eighteen-inch-high combing provided cover around the edge of the flat roof. Excellent.

Thirty seconds after opening the door, Charon had it closed and locked. Back down the stairs he went, out through the top-floor office window to the fire escape, down the ladder to the top of the dumpster. He was walking briskly toward Constitution Avenue a minute and nine seconds after he closed the door on the roof.

Jack Yocke carefully proofed his follow-up story on Friday's beltway murder. He scrolled it slowly up the screen as he checked every word and comma.

The heart of the story was a speculation by a Montgomery County police lieutenant that some frustrated speeder might have potted Walter P. Harrington in a moment of rage because he was a sadistic jerk who always drove at fifty-five miles per hour in the fast lane. Yocke had dressed it up some for the *Post*, but that was the essence of the story. No new evidence. The bullet that killed Harrington had not been recovered. No witnesses to the killing had come forward. The widow was devastated. The funeral was Monday.

Off the record, the Montgomery County police had admitted that the killing would probably never be solved unless the killer got drunk and talked too much. Jack Yocke had passed that information to the editor so he would not expect follow-up stories.

As he punched keys to send the story of Walter P. Harrington on its electronic way, Yocke saw Ottmar Mergenthaler stroll through the newsroom on his way to his cubicle. Mergenthaler waved him over.

'Hey, Jack, you busy right now?'

'Nothing that can't wait.'

'That Colombian drug kingpin is having a press conference. Want to go with me?'

'Sure.'

'Gotta get a tape recorder, then we'll do it.'

In the car Jack asked, 'How'd you get this plum, anyway?'

Mergenthaler chuckled. 'I know the lawyer representing Aldana. Guy name of Thanos Liarakos, big criminal defense mercenary. Known him for years. He always represents mob guys and dopers. They're the only crooks who can afford him. Gets one off the hook just often enough to be able to charge outrageously and still have all the work he can handle. Anyway, he called and said Aldana was demanding a jail-cell press conference with a network TV crew, but I could come if I wanted.'

'What's he going to say?'

'Liarakos didn't know. He strongly advised Aldana against talking to the press, but the client insisted.'

'There goes his claim that media hype has prejudiced possible jurors – prevented any possibility of a fair trial.'

'Yep. Looks like Aldana isn't the type to take advice from lawyers, no matter what they cost to keep around.'

'Has he really got a net worth of four billion dollars?'

'Who the hell knows? I'll bet even Aldana doesn't.'

Four billion! What is that . . . ? *Four thousand million?* The sum was beyond comprehension. Oh, the government throws around numbers like that, but not individuals. Four billion was more than the gross national product of Iceland. You could buy Arkansas for that amount, own your own state. You could hire every whore in North and South America and keep them as your private harem in the state you owned on the Mississippi. And if the feds didn't like it, you could hire every lawyer in New York and Washington to raise hell in every court in America. 'That's a lot of money,' Jack Yocke muttered.

'Too much.'

Yocke snorted. 'That's heresy, Ott! There's no such thing. Bite your tongue.'

There was a mob at the district jail. Reporters and cameramen crammed the entryway. After Yocke and Mergenthaler elbowed their way to the desk, they found the desk sergeant engaged in a shouting match with a local TV anchorman as the cameras rolled.

'You can't keep us out. We're the press!'

'I don't give a fuck who you are. The only people who get in are people on this list.' The sergeant stabbed the sheet of paper on the counter in front of him with a rigid finger. 'You ain't on it. Now get the hell outta here or we'll find a cell for you. And turn off that fucking spotlight!'

'This is *America*!'

'Read my lips, asshole! *Out!*'

'Mergenthaler, *Washington Post*.' The reporter slid his credentials across the dark wood at the sergeant, who consulted his list while the TV anchorman made yet another eloquent protest.

'You're on the list. Through that door over there.'

'I have another guy with me from the *Post*.'

Yocke displayed his credentials and was waved through as the sergeant addressed himself to the still spluttering TV man: 'No. No! *No!* What part of no don't you understand?'

Two policemen searched them for weapons while a third checked Mergenthaler's tape recorder. Then they were led down a long corridor that had decades worth of dirt caked on its dark, once-green walls. Up a flight of ill-lit stairs, through another security checkpoint, through steel doors that slid open as they approached and closed behind them, and past rows of brimming cells. The occupants jeered and shouted obscenities.

The reporters were led through another steel door into a booking room of some sort where a camera crew was busy setting up lights and two cameras. This room had several steel doors besides the one they had entered. One was partially open and Yocke peeked. Beyond was a suite of four cells, padded, cells for psychos. Apparently the cops didn't want Aldana out in the multiple-occupancy cells with the common criminals.

The network correspondent, whom Yocke recognized but didn't know, nodded at Mergenthaler, then consulted a notebook while a woman worked on him from a portable makeup box. She combed his hair and squirted hairspray. One of the technicians tested a pin-on microphone as a uniformed cop watched without expression.

Mergenthaler found a spot where he could observe and not be caught by the cameras. Yocke leaned against the wall beside him.

The minutes passed. Five, then ten.

Occasionally someone coughed, but mostly they stood silently. Waiting.

What kind of man was this Aldana? Jack Yocke tried to picture the man he thought would appear, based upon what he knew about him. A thug, he decided. Some sort of hate-filled Latin American barrio bastard who thought Adolf Hitler was the prophet of how to win and rule in the coming chaos. Sounds like the title of a self-help best-seller. Yocke wondered if there was a big book in Chano Aldana's future.

A darkly handsome man in a gray suit came out of one of the doors. He squinted against the floodlights, then said hello to the TV talker and Mergenthaler.

'My client will be out in a moment. Here are the rules. He has a statement to make, then the TV people get five minutes to ask questions. After they finish, Mergenthaler gets five minutes.'

'I don't want Mergenthaler here while we're filming,' the correspondent said.

'When will you run your interview?' Thanos Liarakos asked.

'Tonight probably, and on the morning show tomorrow.'

'I don't see any problem.' The lawyer frowned. 'He isn't going to scoop you. And you can film while he asks questions, if you wish.'

No, the TV people weren't going to do that. Under no circumstances were they going to take the chance that Mergenthaler might ask more perceptive questions on camera than their man.

'Show business,' Mergenthaler whispered sourly to Yocke. Speaking louder, he asked, 'Mr Liarakos, do you know what Aldana will say?'

'No.'

'Has he discussed it with you?'

'No.'

'Did you recommend to your client that he hold a press conference?'

'No comment.'

'If the prosecutors ask the judge for a gag order, will you fight it?'

'I never speculate in that manner.'

'Can Aldana get a fair trial here in Washington?'

'I don't think that he can get a fair trial anywhere in the United States.'

'How much longer do we have to wait?' grumped the TV man.

'I have one question, Mr Liarakos,' Yocke said. 'Jack Yocke of the *Post*.'

'He with you, Ott?'

'Yes.'

'Okay. Shoot.'

'Are you satisfied that your client has arranged to pay your fee, which reportedly is very high, with money that is not the proceeds of any criminal activity?'

Liarakos frowned. 'No comment,' he said crisply, and disappeared through one of the steel doors.

The TV man grinned broadly at Yocke. A trace of a smile flickered across Mergenthaler's lips.

Time passed slowly. The TV man kept glancing at his watch.

After seven minutes, the door opened and two uniformed cops came out, then two men Jack Yocke took to be US marshals. Liarakos followed them, then a Latin-looking man of medium height wearing a trim mustache. Other cops and marshals followed, but this was the man who captured Yocke's attention.

As he arranged himself in the chair and the television lights came on, Yocke stared. The man was pleasantly plump, with full cheeks that would turn into saggy jowls in a few more years. He looked like a middle-aged banker who hadn't raised a sweat since his school days. He was clad in slacks and a short-sleeved white shirt, no tie. He blinked at the glare of the lights and looked around warily as a technician hooked up the lapel mike.

When the technician was out of the way and one of the marshals had been waved out of camera-shot, the correspondent began. 'I understand you have a statement to make, Señor Aldana.'

Aldana looked straight at the camera.

'I am Chano Aldana,' he said with a noticeable Spanish accent. 'I am your worst nightmare come to life. I am the faceless, starving masses whom you refused food. I am the slave you delivered in chains to the merciless altar of the moneylenders. I am the sick you refused to heal. I am the beggar you turned away from the feast. To me has been given the key to the bottomless pit. And I have opened it.'

The network correspondent stood for several seconds with his mouth ajar, his face slack.

'Señor Aldana, are you guilty of the crimes of which you are accused?'

'*You* are the guilty ones. Not I.'

'Are you the head of the Medellín cocaine-smuggling cartel?'

'I am a Third World businessman.'

When it became obvious that was the whole answer, the correspondent persisted, 'Are you a cocaine smuggler?'

'I have never smuggled cocaine.'

'Your statement seems to imply that people working for you will cause violence if you are not released. Is that what you mean?'

'I meant what I said. Precisely. The people who know of my reputation will tell you that I am a man of my word.'

When Mergenthaler's turn came and the TV lights were off, he asked, 'What did you mean, "To me has been given the key to the bottomless pit"?'

'I am He who was thrown out of Heaven. I am He you have kept away from the feast. *To me has been given the key to the pit and I have opened it.*'

'How about one straight answer. Are you or are you not involved in the cocaine-smuggling business?'

'I have never smuggled cocaine.'

'Do you really have a net worth of four billion American dollars?'

'I am a wealthy man. I do not know just how wealthy.'

'At last, a straight answer.'

Aldana's upper lip curled into a sneer and his eyes narrowed. His gaze locked on the journalist, he rose from the chair. As the marshals led him through the door that led back to his cell, he kept his eyes on Mergenthaler until the door cut off his view.

'He's crazy as a bedbug,' Yocke said in the car.

Ottmar Mergenthaler sat motionless behind the wheel, the ignition key in his hand. 'Too bad Geraldo Rivera missed this one.'

'He didn't scare you with that staring act, did he?'

Mergenthaler glanced at the younger man. 'Yeah. He did.'

The columnist examined the key and carefully placed it in the ignition switch. 'He's insane and has armies of hired killers that have murdered hundreds of politicians, judges, and police in Colombia. They've blown up airliners, bombed department stores and newspapers, and assassinated dozens of journalists who refused to be quiet. They don't care who they kill. They truly don't.'

The columnist started the car and engaged the transmission. 'Yeah, Jack, that man scared me.'

5

An American's enthusiasm for law and order is directly proportional to the degree to which he believes his personal safety or his livelihood is threatened. When the perceived threat recedes, so does his willingness to be policed.

America is the most underpoliced nation on earth. The average American spends his life without any but casual contact with policemen – except for the ubiquitous traffic cops enforcing ridiculously low speed limits that Americans insist are necessary and yet almost universally ignore. Many law-abiding citizens have never in their lives spoken to a policeman, and the vast majority have never suffered the indignity of contact with policemen performing their duty.

No paramilitary police patrol American streets. No secret police monitor telephone conversations or scrutinize mail or hire neighbors to tattle. No policeman calls an American to account for slandering the government or the president or writing scurrilous letters to editors or politicians.

Regardless of the degree of his paranoia or hatred, an American will be left undisturbed unless and until his conduct crosses the threshold into violence, in which case he can expect to reside in a cell for a relatively short time, there to contemplate the error of his ways. No firing squad. No political prison. No gulag. Though he be mad as a March hare, no permanent commitment to an insane asylum. In America a man's right to hate his neighbor is protected as it is nowhere else on earth.

In spite of repeated influxes of immigrants from every hate-soaked, war-torn corner of the earth, America has institutionalized personal freedom. The courts have zealously fostered it, perhaps unintentionally, by acting vigorously and self-righteously on the oft-stated and highly dubious assumption that for every wrong there is a remedy. Not a remedy in the next life, but here, in America. Now! Never in all of the tragic, bloody course of human history has such a radical, illogical concept been routinely accepted and acted upon by so many supposedly rational beings.

So the social fabric remains intact. No group of any size sincerely believes no one will listen to its grievance. Everyone will listen. Newspapers will spill *ink, the idle sympathize and donate money, politicians orate, judges fashion a remedy.*

And America will go on.

Jack Yocke stared at the words on the screen as he worried a fingernail. This was America as he saw it, a deliciously mad, pragmatic place. Americans want justice, but not too much. They want order, but not too much. They want laws, but not too many. Now, into this cauldron of free spirits had been introduced Chano Aldana and his four billion dollars.

$4,000,000,000. The amount of murder, mayhem, treachery, and treason that four billion dollars would buy was almost beyond comprehension. And Aldana was just the man to make the purchase. What did he care if the foundations cracked and the house came down? He had his. And he had served notice.

'Your style is atrocious.' Ott Mergenthaler was reading over his shoulder.

'Not right for the *Post*, eh?'

'Definitely not.'

'Aldana can't win.'

'You know it and I know it, but apparently he doesn't.'

'A little licentiousness, Americans enjoy that. A little illicit pleasure to apologize for on Sunday morning, what's the harm? But Aldana will sooner or later be crushed like a gnat if he tries to intimidate people here like he did in Colombia.'

'No doubt Liarakos tried to tell him that.'

'His best defense is to play the underdog. David versus Goliath.'

'Chano Aldana *is* Goliath,' the columnist said dryly and pulled a nearby chair around. 'He made that pretty plain this afternoon.'

'We're going to have to legalize dope, Ott. Right now nobody wants to make it legal, yet nobody wants to live in an America that is so well-policed that it can't be sold.'

'If more-efficient police are what it takes, I'm for it,' Mergenthaler said.

'Aww, bullshit. You haven't thought this through. You despised J. Edgar Hoover. You thought the House Un-American Activities Committee was a cancer on the body politic.' When Mergenthaler tried to reply, Yocke raised his voice and overrode him. '*I've* read some of your old columns. Don't try to change your spots now.'

After making sure Yocke had really shut up, Mergenthaler said, 'I've been to Holland and seen the kids lying in the public squares, whacked out on hash, scrambling their brains permanently while the police stand and watch, while the world walks around them. I've been to the Dutch morgues and seen the bodies. *I've been to the DC morgue and seen the bodies there too.* This shit ain't tobacco and it ain't liquor. Two crack joints will make an average person an addict. Legalize it? *No! A thousand times no.*'

Jack Yocke threw up his hands. 'Medellín had four thousand and fifteen murder victims delivered to the morgue in 1989. Those were the bodies they found. Medellín has a population of two million. That's a murder rate of over two hundred per hundred thousand people.' Yocke's eyes narrowed. 'Our rate here in the District is around eighteen or nineteen. That's four hundred and thirty-eight murders in 1989. When our murder rate is ten times worse than it is now, Ott – *ten times worse* – then I'll ask you how much sympathy you feel for all those addicts who knew better and took their first puff anyway.'

'It won't get that bad here.'

'You think the black militants and liberals who run this town are gonna fix things? You met Aldana this afternoon. Like hell it won't get that bad!'

'Didn't you just say that Aldana would get his sooner or later?'

'It isn't Aldana I'm worried about. It's all the other flies that kind of money will attract.'

When Mergenthaler left and went back to his office, Jack Yocke tried to write some more and found he couldn't. He was fuming, irritable. His eye fell on the front page of today's paper with its photo of George Bush sailing off Kennebunkport, Maine. Bush was waving, wearing a wide grin. Jack Yocke threw the paper into the wastepaper basket.

Rock Creek Park is Washington's attempt at Central Park. Unlike that vast expanse of trees and grass in New York City, Rock Creek Park is not a pedestrian's paradise. Part of the reason is geography.

The park begins a dozen miles north of the Potomac River in Montgomery County, Maryland, as an undeveloped stretch along a modest creek meandering southward toward the river.

For several hundred yards after the creek flows under the eight-lane beltway, houses and yards come right to the edge of the water. The gentle trickle soon reaches the grounds of the Walter Reed Army Hospital, however, with its vast expanse of lawns. South of the hospital grounds the park is about a quarter mile wide for several miles. Here it is a pleasant oasis of trees and greenery on the steep banks of the creek ravine.

Crossing into the District, the green belt finally assumes parklike dimensions. For the next four miles the park is about a mile wide and provides a site for a golf course and numerous scenic stretches of two-lane blacktop that wind through the wooded, boulder-choked ravines of aptly named Rock Creek and its tributaries.

The park narrows at the National Zoological Park, which occupies its entire width. South of the zoo, the park along the creek drainage is only several hundred yards wide, merely the sides of the steep Rock Creek ravine, and is crisscrossed by bridges that carry the major streets and avenues of Washington.

Two miles south of the zoo the creek deposits its saline solution of street and lawn runoff into the Potomac. The creek mouth is directly across the Georgetown Channel from Theodore Roosevelt Island. The park there provides a modest accent of green near the water, a mere foreground for the vast urban skyline behind it.

For most of its length the park consists of uncomfortably steep, rock-strewn hillsides densely covered with hardwood trees. In spite of the mild autumn, by early December the trees had lost all their leaves and transformed themselves into a semi-opaque wilderness of gray branches and trunks that gently muffled some of the city noise.

Henry Charon automatically adjusted the placement of his feet to avoid fallen branches and loose rocks, yet the thick carpet of dead, dry leaves rustled loudly at every step. A good soaking rain, he knew, would leave the leaf carpet sodden and allow a man to walk silently across it. Not now, though.

Below him, on his right, cars hummed along Ross Drive, one of the scenic lanes along Rock Creek that functioned as an alternate commuter route during rush hour. Charon strode along the hillside in a tireless, swinging gait with his eyes moving. He paused occasionally to examine major outcrops of rock, then resumed his northward movements.

This type of terrain he knew well. It would be a wonderful area in which to hide, if he could find the right place. These sidewalk warriors would be on his turf if they hunted him here.

He consulted his map again, then changed course to top the ridge. This ridge wasn't high, only a hundred feet or so, but it was far too steep for casual urban walkers and hikers. Accustomed as he was to scrambling up slopes in the Rockies, Henry Charon didn't even draw a deep breath as he climbed to the top of the narrow ridgeline and paused to examine his surroundings.

Just before dusk he found it. He was exploring along the foot of an outcropping from the formation that formed the caprock of the ridge. A gap in the rock led into a small sheltered cave, more of an overhang, really. A large boulder obscured most of the opening. In the gloom he could see several pop cans and cigarette butts. The dirt of the floor was packed hard, no doubt from the feet of teenagers or derelicts. Many footprints and shoe marks. This place would do nicely, if he ever needed it.

He examined the place carefully, paying particular attention to the cracks and crevices that rose off to one side. He pulled some loose rock from one. Yes, he could put a gun and some other supplies in there and pile the rock back in, just in case.

Henry Charon left the cave and paused outside to examine the setting again. He was sure he could find it again. After a last look around in all directions, Henry Charon set off down the hillside.

About a half hour later Thanos Liarakos arrived at his home in Edgemoor and parked the Jag in the garage.

His wife, Elizabeth, was in the kitchen putting the finishing touches on the canapés. The guests were supposed to arrive at seven. She gave him a buss on the cheek as he poured himself a drink. 'How'd it go today?'

'You wouldn't believe it. The man is certifiably insane. At the press conference he claimed he was the devil.'

She looked at him to see if he was kidding. 'An insanity defense?'

'I suggested it, and he didn't say anything one way or the other, until I mentioned the psychiatrists and psychologists, then he just said no. That's it, one word. "No." End of discussion.'

'Your mother called this afternoon.' Elizabeth had her back to him and was spreading cream cheese on the celery.

'Umph.' Elizabeth's birthday had been last week. She had just turned thirty-nine. As he stared at her trim waistline and the way her buttocks shaped her dress, Liarakos decided she could pass for ten years younger.

'She just heard on the news that you're representing Aldana.'

'And she was unhappy.'

'She had a fit. Wanted to know how you could defend scum like that. "All those years . . . my little boy . . . no honor." It wasn't a pleasant conversation.'

Liarakos turned his attention to the backyard. They had almost an acre here. The hired man had raked the leaves three times this fall but at least a bushel had collected on the top of the pool cover and in the hot tub. He would have to clean up the leaves again when he had time.

'I told her,' Elizabeth was saying, 'that every man is entitled to a defense, but you know her.'

'Yeah.'

'I tried to be nice to her, Thanos, I really did. But I am so sick of hearing her whine and bitch. Honest to God, I have completely had it with her ethics lectures.'

'I know.'

'Why don't you explain it to her one more time?' She turned to face him. 'It's not fair that I have to be the one who keeps explaining the Constitution and the American legal system to her. When she starts that how-can-my-Thanos-do-this crap, I just cringe. She doesn't listen, she won't listen.'

'I'll talk to her again.'

'Promise?'

'Yeah, promise.'

She turned back to the celery.

'Where are the girls?' he asked.

'Upstairs. They're going to be doing homework while the guests are here. And I bought them a new CD today. They're listening to that for the eleventh time.'

Liarakos wandered into the living room. Elizabeth had the crystal out, the wine open, and the cheeses and crackers already arranged on the white damask tablecloth. At least she understood what he did professionally. She had been a new associate, a Harvard Law grad, when they started dating. Six months later they spent a long ski weekend in Aspen and returned home married. She had had to resign her position with the firm of course, but he had just made junior partner.

It had been rocky along the way, but they were still trying, still hanging in there.

His mind turned to his new client, turning over possible defense tactics, reviewing the charges yet again. Aldana's case was going to be difficult. The government had two turncoat witnesses and enough circumstantial evidence to sink the *Titanic*. Aldana's little press conference performance this afternoon hadn't helped.

He would tape the network news at six. Tomorrow he would put the associates to researching pretrial publicity issues. Perhaps the press conference hadn't precluded such a motion, considering the overwhelming publicity Aldana's extradition had received.

He checked his watch. The network evening news would come on in ten minutes. He should probably set up the VCR now.

When that chore was completed, he wandered back to the kitchen for another drink. 'When did the maid leave?'

'About five. She helped me with all of this.'

'You want me to help?'

'No. Go relax. I've got everything under control.'

Everything under control. A defense lawyer never had everything under control. The concept was foreign to him. About all you could do was anticipate the thrusts and jabs of the prosecution and attempt to parry them. And have a few surprises of your own up your sleeve. The name of the game was damage control.

How could he control the damage the government witnesses would do? And the client, Aldana? Could he be controlled? Would he listen to good advice? Liarakos snorted. He already knew the answer to that. Oh well, it was Aldana's ass on the line, not his. Still, he hated to lose. He never fought gracefully in a losing cause, which was why his defense team was bringing in two million dollars a year in fees to the firm.

He snapped the television on in the living room and stood watching it as Elizabeth set the last of the hors d'oeuvres on the table.

Aldana's press conference was the lead story. 'Come watch this, Elizabeth.'

The anchor said Aldana's statement spoke for itself. He fell silent and looked off to one side, at the monitor no doubt, waiting. Aldana came on the screen. As his voice filled the living room – '*To me has been given the key . . .*' – Liarakos heard his wife's sharp intake of breath. 'My God!'

'He has an effect, doesn't he?'

After the questions, the network replayed the statement three times. The consensus of the 'experts' – a lawyer, a psychiatrist, and a college instructor in South American voodoo culture – was that Aldana was a criminal megalomaniac.

The phone rang and at the same time the door chimes sounded. As Elizabeth went to the front door to admit the guests, Liarakos went to the study to take the call. The firm's senior partner was on the line:

'I just saw our newest, most famous client on the news.'

'Yeah, I watched it too.'

'Thanos, you've got to figure out a way to shut him up. In one performance he managed to convince half the people in America that he's guilty as hell. And that was the half that was undecided.'

'I strongly urged him not—'

'Thanos, he's one man. Our firm has fifty-two partners and one hundred twelve associates who represent over a dozen Fortune five hundred companies and about a hundred fifty smaller ones. The heart of our business is regulatory matters and commercial litigation. Now it's one thing to represent run-of-the-mill criminal defendants, but it's quite another to represent a man who's out to prove he's the Antichrist, beyond a reasonable doubt.'

'He's innocent until proven guilty.'

'You know that and I know that, but the general public may not. I'm laying it right on the line, Thanos. We have never told you whom you could or couldn't represent. But this firm is not going to bankrupt itself for the privilege of representing the most notorious criminal since Al Capone. Now you shut that man up or tell him he'll have to get another lawyer. Have I made myself clear?'

'You have, Harvey.'

'Stop by my office tomorrow.' The connection broke.

Thanos Liarakos sat for a moment with the telephone receiver in his hand, then slowly lowered it onto its cradle.

Harvey Brewster was something of an ass. If he thought the firm could get rid of Chano Aldana by just throwing his file at him and filing a notice with the clerk of the court, he was in for a rude surprise. The judge would not let Liarakos or the firm out of the case unless and until another competent, experienced attorney had agreed to represent Aldana and not delay the proceedings. The pressure on the judge to proceed expeditiously would be excruciating, and the judge had the tools to transfer that pressure squarely onto the counsel for both sides.

Liarakos knew the judge would not hesitate to use his authority. Liarakos knew the judge. Gardner Snyder was in his early seventies and had been on the bench for over thirty years. He was the frostiest curmudgeon wearing a judicial robe that Liarakos had ever run into. No doubt that was why the Justice Department had maneuvered so adroitly to ensure that this case went onto Snyder's calendar.

Perhaps tomorrow the prosecutor would move for an order gagging both sides. Liarakos suspected that just now the prosecutor's phone was also ringing. Perhaps he should make the motion himself. It was indisputable that Aldana would have to be silenced one way or the other or the man wouldn't get a fair trial.

The door opened. Elizabeth's head appeared. 'Thanos, come visit with our guests.'

The guests were buzzing about Aldana's news conference. Those who hadn't seen the news show were being briefed by those who had. Liarakos was bombarded with questions, all of which he shrugged off with a smile. The smile was an effort.

He had finished his third drink of the evening and was telling himself he didn't need and probably couldn't handle a fourth, when he saw Elizabeth motioning to him from the kitchen.

'Your mother's on the phone. She's really revved.'

'I'll take it in the study.'

Jefferson Brody and a woman Liarakos knew only vaguely were in a serious discussion in the study, but he made his excuses and closed the door firmly behind them.

'Hi, Mom.'

'Thanos, Thanos, what have you done?'

'Well, I—'

She wasn't interested in his answer. She steamrollered on: 'I saw that horrible man – *your client* – on the news this evening. I meant to call you immediately but my friends have been on the phone for over an hour. I called you as soon as I had a chance.'

'Mom, I'm a lawyer. I—'

'You don't have to make a living representing dope-peddling scum like that! My God, your father and I scrimped and saved and did without to put you through college and law school so you could represent filth like Alda . . . Alda-something. Have you no honor? Have you no morals? What kind of man are you, Thanos?'

'Mom, I'm a lawyer – no, *let me finish*! I'm a lawyer and this man is entitled to be represented by a lawyer no matter what crimes he is accused of.'

'But he is *guilty*!'

'He isn't guilty until a jury says he is. And guilty or not, he must have a lawyer.'

'I hope to God you lose and this man pays for his crimes, Thanos. He has murdered and assassinated and bribed and done God knows what-all and he must be put somewhere so he can't keep hurting innocent people. *Thousands* of innocent people. Thanos, you pervert your talents and your religion by helping such a man.'

'Mom, I'm not going to keep arguing this.'

'He says he has the key to hell. And he *does*. You are helping this scum stay in business. You are helping him murder innocent people. How in the name of your dead father do you sleep nights?'

'I've heard all of this I'm going to listen to.'

'No, you haven't! You are going to listen to your mother who loves you and wants to save your soul. You are going to stop helping these people. Thanos! My Thanos. You are breaking my heart.'

'Mom, we have a houseful of guests. I'm not going to insult them by staying here in the study listening to you rant about something you don't understand. Don't you have any faith in me?'

'Faith in you? When you prostitute yourself for criminals such as Aldana? You make me nauseous.' She slammed her phone down.

Is there anybody who didn't watch the news tonight?

His baseball glove was lying on the table. He picked it up and kneaded the soft leather. He smacked the pocket with his fist. Damn! Damn, damn, damn.

He turned off the lights and sat in the darkness. After a moment he loosened his tie and stretched out on the couch. The hum of voices through the door, the gentle background of the furnace fans, the noises reached him and he listened for a while, then didn't listen. The noises became background, like an evening crowd in the grandstand at Tinker Field in Orlando, buzzing and sighing in rhythm with the game.

The crowds were never large, maybe fifteen hundred people on a good evening. But all the hot, muggy evenings were very good, regardless of how many people came to watch. The fastballs only came in about eighty miles per hour, plenty fast if you were forty-one years old and trying to get the bat around on one of them. On those all-too-rare occasions when you slapped the ball with good wood you strained every tendon charging for first. Occasionally you even surprised yourself and beat the throw.

That summer now seemed like a dream time. Liarakos could still smell the sweat, still feel the earth under his spikes, still see the ball leave the bat and float toward him as he charged it. Even then he knew he was living a fantasy, the sublime pinnacle of his life. The sun and the sweat and the laughter of his teammates . . .

Someone was shaking him. 'Daddy. Wake up. Daddy.'

The lights were on. 'Huh?'

It was Susanna, his twelve-year-old. 'Daddy, it's Mommy. She's locked herself in the upstairs bathroom and won't come out.'

Thanos Liarakos uncoiled and rushed from the room. Through the living room and the guests staring, up the stairs two at a time with Susanna in her nightie running behind him, trying to keep up.

He tried the handle on the door. Locked! He pounded on the door with his fists. 'Elizabeth? *Elizabeth, can you hear me?*'

Nothing.

Not again! Please God, not again!

'Elizabeth, if you don't open this door *now*, I'm going to break it down.'

Susanna and her younger sister were standing there in the hallway, watching. They were sobbing.

'You girls go to your room. Do as I say.' They went.

He kicked at the door. The girls were standing in their doorway, watching and crying. He braced himself against the wall and smashed at the door with his right foot. It splintered. Another kick and the lock gave.

She was on the floor. A trace of white powder around her nostrils. Some powder on the counter. A rolled-up dollar bill clutched in her hand. Her eyes unfocused, the pupils huge. Her heart going like a racehorse.

Damn!

'Where did you get it, Elizabeth? Who gave you the cocaine?'

He shook her vigorously. Her eyes swam.

'Can you hear me, woman? *Who gave you the coke?*'

'Jeff, uhh, Jeffer . . .'

He lowered her to the floor and went to the girls' bedroom. 'Susanna, call an ambulance. Dial nine-one-one. Your mother's sick.'

The child was crying freely. He held her at arm's length and stared into her face. 'Can you do this?'

She nodded and wiped at her tears.

'Good girl. Dial nine-one-one and give them our address and tell them to send an ambulance.'

Down the hall past the bathroom to the staircase, and down them two at a time. T. Jefferson Brody was standing by the far wall.

Brody put up his hands as Liarakos charged at him. 'Now, Thanos—'

'Get outta my house, you son of a bitch.' He hit him with all he had. Brody went down and two men grabbed Liarakos' arms.

'Out! All you people get out!' He jerked his arms free. 'Party's over. Everybody get the fuck outta my house.'

He gestured toward Brody, who was sitting on the floor rubbing his jaw. 'Drag this piece of dog shit out with you or I'll kill him.'

6

At six o'clock the alarm rang beside Thanos Liarakos' bed. He silenced it and rolled out. He had been asleep less than an hour. He had gotten home from the hospital at three A.M., checked on the kids and the maid, who had graciously agreed to return and spend the night when he called her at midnight. The lady and the kids were all asleep in the same bed. Tired as he was, Liarakos couldn't sleep. The last time he remembered glancing at the clock it had been almost five A.M.

He showered and shaved and dressed. In the kitchen he wrote a note for the kids:

> Your Mom is okay. She is in the hospital and was asleep when I left her.
> You may stay home from school with Marla today if you wish.
> I love you both,
>
> > Dad

When he backed the car out of the garage there was a television reporter and a cameraman at the end of the driveway, on the sidewalk. They shouted questions at him as he backed down the drive right at them. Two cameramen. One refused to get out of the way. Liarakos kept the car creeping backward. The reporter, a woman, held a microphone against the driver's window glass and shouted: 'Is Aldana threatening Americans? Is he sane? How much money has he paid you?'

She expected no answers in this theater of the absurd, Liarakos knew. Asking rhetorical questions was the whole show. *This* was award-winning television journalism.

The rear bumper lightly contacted the camera tripod. Then the man moved.

Liarakos kept the car drifting backward into the street, flipped the transmission into drive, and accelerated away.

The morning was overcast and gloomy. A wind drove the dry brown leaves along the streets in waves. Here and there whirlwinds built little columns of leaves that spun crazily for a few seconds in the gray half light, then flowed on.

His wife was still asleep. The blinds were closed and the lights off in her private room. Still wearing his topcoat, Thanos Liarakos sank into the padded visitor's chair.

In a few moments his breathing rhythm matched hers. He felt himself relaxing and drifting and didn't fight it.

He had been in his late thirties when he realized that he could see his entire life, all of it, as if he were a detached observer and his life were a play that he had seen several times before. The whole of it was being acted out before him daily, scene by scene. Yet he knew how it had been and how it would have to be.

Staring at his face in the mirror as he shaved every morning, he could see how the lines would deepen, how the jowls would continue to sag, how the hair would gray and thin. He stared at a face not young and soon to be old.

In nursing homes, he knew, a portion of the daily routine for the elderly is reminiscence therapy. The staff encourages the fragile people waiting to die to look back, to savor the events in their life as if they were great feats woven into a tapestry to instruct generations yet unborn.

Thanos Liarakos was seeing it as it would be, looking back while he was still living it. All his achievements and accomplishments that he had previously thought so important shrank mercilessly from the vantage of this curious double perspective. Court victories lost their sweetness and disasters lost their sting. He had found a way to live with life, or perhaps a merciful God had given him the way. Whichever. Only the perspective mattered.

Drifting now, half asleep, Liarakos swirled the colored glass inside his kaleidoscope of past and future, looking for the pattern. His father had stepped off the boat from Greece with fifty dollars in his pocket and one extra shirt, and parlayed that into five submarine sandwich shops which had sent three sons through college. His mother had raised the sons while his father worked twelve to fifteen hours a day. Those bittersweet days were irretrievably gone. They were as far from the present as the day Odysseus sacked the stronghold on the proud height of Troy. Yet when he talked to his mother he was listening to a voice from the past that would soon be lost to him. So soon, so soon, he would be standing by her grave and his father's grave, remembering, feeling the life escaping like a handful of sand flowing through his fingers. So he tolerated her diatribes and cherished her.

His daughters – they were his offerings to the human race, to the future and its infinite potential, to God and whatever great and incomprehensible thing He had in mind for the human species. The girls were not special, not gifted – they were just people. They and their children would work and love and marry and have children, long after Thanos Liarakos and the Greek of the sandwich shop were dust. So he loved them desperately.

Elizabeth. Ahh, gentle Elizabeth, with your mother's heart and your empty desires and your cravings . . .

You love a woman for many reasons. A goddess she seems when you are young. But finally you see she is of common clay, the same as you, with faults and fears and vain, foolish dreams and petty vices. So you cherish her, love her even more. As she ages you cling closer and closer, holding tighter and tighter. She becomes the female half of you. The roughening of her skin, the engraved lines on her face, the thickening waistline and the sagging breasts, none of it matters a damn. You love her for what she is not as much as for what she is.

Elizabeth, your vices aren't so petty. You are selling your soul for that white powder. It will lay you in your grave, devastate your husband who loves you, deprive two girls of the mother that you promised to be when you gave them life.

Two nurses entered the room and flipped on the light over the bed. Thanos Liarakos came fully awake and squinted at the two white-clad figures bending over Elizabeth. They pried open her eyes and checked her pulse. The stouter nurse rigged a blood-pressure cuff. Elizabeth groaned but said nothing. She was still intoxicated.

'Lucky,' one of them muttered as she checked the IV drip. 'She was lucky this time.'

Liarakos looked at his watch. Almost eight o'clock. The sounds of the staff chattering in the corridors and moving tray carts and equipment came through the open door. He levered himself out of the chair and stood swaying while his heart compensated for the sudden change of position.

He was still standing at the foot of the bed when the nurses bustled out.

She looked old. With no makeup and her hair a mess, Elizabeth looked finished with life. No more warm moments with the children, no more sensuous I-love-yous, no more evenings with the fire crackling and the children laughing. She looked used up. Burned out.

Thanos Liarakos rubbed his face and wondered why he wasn't crying. Ah, it was that crazy double perspective. He had lived this play before.

But he should be crying. He really should. This was the place he was *supposed* to cry.

The lead headline in this morning's *Post* was THE KEY TO HELL. The bold black letters spanned the width of the top of page one. The editor had run a photo of Aldana getting off the plane at Andrews Air Force Base wearing handcuffs and a fierce scowl. Ottmar Mergenthaler and Jack

Yocke had shared the byline on the story. Beside the story was Mergenthaler's column.

Jack Yocke read the four inches of Ott's column that was on the front page and flipped to page A-12 for the rest of it. The federal government and the American people, Mergenthaler said, shouldn't let themselves be intimidated by Chano Aldana, who was obviously going to try the same tactics here that he had used with mixed success in Colombia. If he thought the American people would respond like frightened sheep to terrorism and extortion, Aldana didn't understand the American people.

Yocke snorted and tossed the paper on his desk. Maybe he should give Ott a soapbox for Christmas.

His phone rang. 'Jack, there's a reporter from a Dallas paper on the line. He wants to talk to you about your interview yesterday with Aldana.'

'I don't answer questions. I ask them.'

'Does that mean no?'

'Yep.'

Yocke tucked a notebook and pencils in his jacket pocket as he stirred through his message slips and the unopened mail. He would have to return these calls later, maybe this evening. With his coat over his arm, he went looking for his editor. Maybe he could go down to the courthouse with the rest of the newsroom crew and mill around smartly while Aldana was arraigned.

In a dingy office two doors from the courtroom, Thanos Liarakos arranged his fanny in a chair across a desk from the US attorney for the District, William L. Bader.

Bader was known as an aggressive prosecutor who meticulously prepared his cases. Rumor with the hard tang of truth had it that Bader had judicial ambitions. Liarakos didn't hold that against him. Bader was a damn good lawyer.

'I dropped in to have a little chat about the shenanigans your people used to get my client on Judge Snyder's calendar.'

'What shenanigans?' Bader's eyebrows rose a sixteenth of an inch.

'You can wipe off the innocent look. You're wasting it on me. The people in the clerk's office have whispered in the wrong places.'

'So you'd rather be in front of Maximum John or Hanging Jack?'

'Well, you know how these things are. My client might have lucked out with Judge Worth if the deck hadn't been so neatly stacked against him.' Judge Worth had the reputation, probably exaggerated, of bending over backward to help defense counsel and screwing the prosecution at every opportunity.

'So why are you in here complaining? The hearing in front of the magistrate starts in twenty minutes. Complain to her.'

'I don't think opening this can of worms will do you any good in the newspapers, Will. People might get the idea the government is conducting a vendetta against Aldana, trying to make him a scapegoat. I thought you might do something for me, and I'll live with Judge Snyder.'

'What?'

'Make a motion for a gag order. Both sides. Including the defendant.'

Bader's eyes went to a copy of the *Post* on the corner of the desk. He spent several seconds looking at it. Then he sat back in his chair and rubbed his nose. It was a big nose, but it was well arranged in a large, square, craggy face.

'You want a trial or a circus?' Liarakos asked.

'That fool is putting the noose around his own neck. I don't give a damn if he holds press conferences twice a day and threatens to butcher everybody east of Pittsburgh.'

'You don't know how that will cut and neither do I,' Thanos Liarakos shot back. 'What we *both* know is that we're officers of the court. Let's have a fair trial and not let this deteriorate into some kind of Geraldo Rivera spectacular.'

Bader snorted derisively.

'We gotta stopper this asshole before he poisons the well,' Liarakos said softly. 'What if no one with an IQ above fifty is willing to serve on the jury? What if one or two jurors become afraid to convict him?'

'I'll worry about that when and if it happens. He's *your* client, dammit! You want him quiet, *you* shut him up.'

'Gimme a fucking break, Will.'

Bader's lips twisted and he massaged an eyebrow. He was, Liarakos suspected, trying to decide how Judge Snyder would view the prosecutor's failure to ask for a gag order if the defendant kept grabbing headlines with veiled threats. Thanos Liarakos sensed that he had won. He sat back in his chair and crossed his legs.

'All right, all right.'

Bader called for a secretary and dictated the motion. When he finished, he asked Liarakos, 'Is that satisfactory to you?'

The defense lawyer suggested a change that strengthened the requested order. He cited a case from memory. Will Bader nodded and waved the secretary toward a typewriter.

'I might as well tell you now,' Bader said, 'while you're in a good mood and feeling full of bonhomie – I'm filing a motion today to seize all of Aldana's assets. Everything he has, including the money he used to pay your fee, is proceeds of criminal activity. Every dime.'

Both men were well aware of the implications of such a motion. If he were stripped of all his assets, an accused individual could no longer pay his attorney's fee. Of course, the court could then appoint an attorney to represent him, but the defense that could then be mounted was severely restricted by the limited funds that were, by law, available from the government to pay defense counsel. In effect, by confiscating the defendant's assets in a civil action the government could greatly increase its odds of ultimately convicting the defendant in the criminal case, where the burden of proof was so much higher. These motions were fair, the judges reasoned, because in good conscience a criminal should not be allowed to use the proceeds of his crime to avoid being punished for committing it.

Critics – mainly defense attorneys – argued that the government had the can before the horse: stripping assets from a defendant before he had been convicted of anything seemed to shrink the presumption of innocence to the vanishing point. The problem was that the profits of crime were real – you could touch the money – but the presumption of innocence was a legal fiction, and ninety-nine percent of the time it was just that, fiction. The defendant was guilty and everybody knew it except the jurors. So the government grabbed the bucks.

Liarakos, of course, had been expecting just such a motion. The only question was when. The arguments pro and con he knew well, for he had fought these motions in other cases. Some he won, some he lost.

He cleared his throat. 'I might as well tell you now, my client has engaged another firm to represent him in any civil confiscation action. Off the record, no doubt you'll get some assets. But you'll not get them all.'

'Every little bit helps,' Bader said grinning. 'What with the deficit and all, it's nice to see guys like Aldana contributing their mite. We'll be serving interrogatories next week, and maybe depositions the following week?'

'Not up to me. Serve them on him and he'll send them to the firm he's hired.'

If Chano Aldana thought he had problems now, Liarakos told himself, wait until he read the interrogatories. Any answer he supplied could be used against him in the criminal trial. Most of these asset confiscation actions went uncontested for this very good reason. Regardless of how the criminal action went, Aldana was going to return to Colombia a much poorer man.

Which somehow didn't break Liarakos' heart.

Jack Yocke stood against the back wall of the courtroom shoulder to shoulder with three dozen other reporters and made notes on his steno pad. 'Courtroom packed . . . crowd hushed, expectant . . .'

Defense attorney Thanos Liarakos' assistant, Judith Lewis, was already at the defense table, which was marked with a small sign. To her far right, with an empty chair between them, sat a man in a brown sports coat and slacks. Yocke murmured to the man beside him and pointed.

'The interpreter.'

At the prosecutor's table sat another woman, whom Yocke assumed was an assistant. He whispered another question to the man beside him. Wilda Rodriguez-Herrera. The man spelled the name as Yocke wrote it down. Why is it, the *Post* reporter wondered, that most high-powered lawyers these days have female factotums? Both women were in their middle-to-late twenties or perhaps early thirties – it was impossible to tell at this distance – and were dressed for success in conservative getups that must have set each of them back a week's pay. Yocke jotted another note.

Aldana entered in company with two US marshals. He was wearing a dark suit and a deep maroon tie. His hands were cuffed in front of him. As one of the marshals took the cuffs off, Aldana looked quickly around the room, scanning each face. Every eye in the room was on him. The room was so quiet Yocke could hear the clink of metal as the cuffs were removed from Aldana's wrists.

The defendant sat down at the defense table between Judith Lewis and the interpreter. One of the marshals took a chair immediately behind him, inside the barricade, while the other moved to a chair against the wall where he could watch the defendant and the crowd without turning his head.

Lewis whispered something to Aldana. He made no reply, didn't look at her, kept his face impassive. Now the interpreter whispered in his ear. Aldana replied, a few phrases only, and didn't look at him. He surveyed the bailiff, who averted his eyes; then Aldana turned his head, leaned forward slightly in his chair, and stared for several seconds at Assistant Prosecutor Rodriguez-Herrera, who was busy with a sheet of paper that lay on the table in front of her.

Now his eye caught the *Post* courtroom artist in the far corner, who was studying him through a pair of opera glasses mounted on a tripod. For the first time Aldana's features moved – the upper lip rose into a slight sneer and his eyes became mere slits.

The moment passed and the face resumed its impassive calm. Aldana looked back toward the front of the room, at the magistrate's bench with the flags behind it. He leaned back in his chair, sat loosely, comfortably, staring at the flags. He crossed his legs. In a moment he uncrossed them.

He's nervous, Yocke decided, and scribbled some more in his notebook. He's trying not to show it, but he is nervous. Maybe he's human after all.

Minutes passed. Coughs and hacks and muttered comments from the audience. Aldana poured himself a cup of water from the pitcher on the table and spilled some. He ignored the spill. After several sips he placed the cup on the table in front of him and didn't touch it again.

As he stared at Aldana, Jack Yocke reviewed what he had heard about the defendant. A barrio brat from Medellín, Chano Aldana reputedly had worked his way to the top of the local cocaine industry by outthinking and murdering his rivals. He was smarter than the average sewer rat and twice as ruthless. Rumor had it he had personally executed over two dozen men and had ordered the murders of hundreds more by name, including a candidate for president of Colombia. A vicious enemy of the law-and-order forces battling the cartels for control of Colombia, he had ordered airliners and department stores bombed, judges murdered, and policemen tortured.

Yet this monster had a human side: he liked soccer and controlled several teams in the central Colombian league. Referees and star players on rival teams had been assassinated on his order. Finally the government had suspended league play because of organized crime's corrosive influence on the games.

The last two years Aldana had allegedly spent hiding somewhere in the Amazon. He had been captured by the Colombian government when he decided in a weak moment to visit a prostitute of whom he was fond. Somehow he had survived the ensuing shootout, although six of his bodyguards hadn't. Sewer rat's luck.

By all accounts Aldana was an amazing man, a Latin Al Capone with several of Hitler's worst traits thrown in for seasoning. Yet staring at this slightly overweight, middle-aged Latin male with the black curly hair and the modest thin mustache, Jack Yocke found this tale of unadulterated evil hard to believe. It was incredible, really. Even Aldana's performance at yesterday's news conference couldn't overcome one's natural inclination to accept the man as a fellow human being. Yocke tried to picture him eating snake and monkey meat in the jungle – and gave up.

US Attorney William Bader had a herculean task ahead of him to convince twelve working-class Americans that Chano Aldana was *el padrino*, the godfather.

Yocke was furiously scribbling notes when the door to the hallway opened and a man entered, a man wearing a naval officer's blue uniform. Captain Jake Grafton. His ribbons and wings made a splotch of color on his left breast. Those and the four gold rings on each sleeve looked strangely out of place among all these civilians.

Jack Yocke stared as Grafton surveyed the seating arrangements, apparently concluded the place was full, and took up a station against the wall, near the door. His eyes met those of the reporter. He nodded once, then his gaze settled on Chano Aldana, who had turned to examine the newcomer. Aldana turned back toward the bench.

Several of the spectators looked the captain over, whispering back and forth, and finally dismissed him.

Jake Grafton? Why is he here? Yocke scribbled down the name in his notebook and put three question marks after it.

A few minutes later the door behind the bench opened and Bader came in, followed by Thanos Liarakos. Bader glanced at Aldana and the audience and sat down beside Rodriguez-Herrera.

Judith Lewis moved to the chair at the far left of her table and Liarakos took the one she had vacated. He spoke to the defendant, got something in reply, then spoke to Lewis.

He looks tired, Yocke thought, and studied the attorney. Dark, trim, of medium height with black hair streaked with gray at the temples, Liarakos habitually wore thousand-dollar tailor-made wool suits. He was wearing one today, if Yocke's eyes could be trusted. Liarakos normally looked every inch the successful criminal lawyer. Yet Mergenthaler had said that Liarakos had spent the summer of 1989 playing baseball in a professional senior league in Florida. At the age of forty-one he had tried out for a team composed almost exclusively of former major leaguers and made it. Jack Yocke didn't know exactly what to make of that.

This morning, the reporter thought, the honest, sincere face that juries loved looked softer, less on stage. Then the explanation occurred to him – there was no jury.

'All rise,' the bailiff announced. The lawyers rose respectfully as the audience shuffled noisily to its feet. Aldana hesitated a second, and Liarakos pulled almost imperceptibly on his sleeve.

The magistrate, enshrouded in her judicial robe, entered and took her seat behind the raised bench.

The bailiff chanted the incomprehensible incantation that opened every court session and ended with a curt 'Be seated.'

Jack Yocke kept his attention on the defendant. Aldana was leaning forward in his chair staring at the magistrate, a fifty-ish woman with her hair pulled back severely, wearing a stylish pair of large glasses. He didn't take his eyes off her as she read the indictment handed down by a grand jury in Miami several years ago and the interpreter spoke in a low tone in his ear. Yocke could just hear the rat-a-tat-tat of the Spanish, although he couldn't make out the words.

'How do you plead?'

Liarakos half rose from his chair. 'Not guilty, your honor.'

The magistrate ordered a not guilty plea entered in the record, then addressed the prosecutor. 'I understand you have a preliminary motion in this matter, Mr Bader?'

'Yes, your honor. May I approach the bench?'

She nodded and he walked up and handed the clerk a paper, which the clerk stamped and passed to the magistrate white Bader handed a copy to Liarakos.

'The prosecution is asking the court for a gag order in this case, your honor. The order is to apply to attorneys for both sides and the defendant.'

'Any argument, Mr Liarakos?'

'No, your honor. We will have some motions of our own, and I understand you have set a date next week to hear them?'

'That's correct.' She gave him the date and time. 'Without argument, Mr Bader, your motion is granted.' She consulted the proposed order. After a moment, she read, ' "Counsel for the government and the defendant, and the defendant, are enjoined from discussing this case, the facts, legal theories, possible witnesses, testimony to be introduced at trial, and any and all other matters connected therewith with the press or any of the representatives thereof. They shall not do, say, or write anything for publication or broadcast that might in any way prejudice possible jurors or interfere with the orderly administration of justice." Is there a motion for bail, Mr Liarakos?'

'Not today, your honor.'

'Mr Bader?'

'We have filed a motion, your honor, to confiscate the defendant's assets as proceeds of criminal activity.' The courtroom buzzed and the magistrate looked stem. She raised her gavel but the noise ceased before she could tap the anvil. Bader continued: 'We'd like you to set a date for a hearing.'

The attorneys and the magistrate discussed the scheduling and checked their calendars and settled on a Monday in January.

'This matter is adjourned until next Thursday.' The magistrate rose from the bench as the bailiff intoned 'All rise,' and the reporters gathered their coats for the dash to the phones.

As the marshals put the cuffs on him, Aldana got in a heated discussion with his attorney. Yocke edged as close as he could.

'Why didn't you argue against this?'

Liarakos spoke too softly to hear, although Yocke tried.

'But she can't make me be silent!'

More whispers.

'No one can gag me up. No one.' His voice was loud, but the sharp edge of command was there too. The crowd stopped dead, captivated by this drama. 'That woman can't gag me up while they send me up the railroad for a crime of which I am not guilty. This is *supposed* to be America! Not the Germany of the Nazis or the Russia of the Stalinistas.'

'This is not the time or place—'

'Are you *my* lawyer or *their* lawyer?' The voice was a brutal snarl.

'*Shut the fuck up.*' Although Liarakos' voice was low, it cut like a whip. The lawyer turned to the nearest marshal. 'Clear these people out of here, please, and give me a moment alone with my client. You may wait in the hallway. Ms Lewis will knock on the door, when we need you.'

'Everybody out.' The crowd began to move.

Just before he went through the door, Jack Yocke glanced back at

Chano Aldana. The defendant was glaring at Liarakos, his face dark with fury, his lips pressed together. His body was tense, coiled.

In the hallway Yocke sprinted to catch up with Jake Grafton. 'Captain, wait! Please! Jack Yocke of the *Post*. I was at your party the—'

'I remember you, Jack.' Grafton had his dark bridge coat over his arm and held his white hat with the scrambled eggs on the bill in his left hand. Yocke glanced at his chest to see if the blue-and-white ribbon of the Congressional Medal of Honor was displayed there. It wasn't. Maybe Mergenthaler was correct: he had said that Grafton never wore the decoration he received several years ago for ramming El Hakim's plane with his F-14 over the Med.

'I'm curious, Captain. You were the last man in town I expected to see here today. Why'd you come?'

'Wanted to get a look at Aldana.'

'Officially?'

For a fraction of a second Grafton looked annoyed. 'What's an official look?'

'I mean is this personal or does the Joint Staff have some interest in Aldana?'

'No comment.'

'Aw, come on, Captain! Gimme a break. Why is the military interested in Chano Aldana?'

A grin spread slowly across the captain's face. He settled his white hat on his head, nodded, and turned away.

Jack Yocke watched him go, then remembered he needed to find a phone.

'You should have seen him come unglued, Ott. That man is something else!'

'Jack, you need to stop using those banal phrases. People will get the idea you're a semiliterate bum.'

'I'm telling you, Ott, you should have seen him! Oh, he never really lost his temper. He didn't actually threaten Liarakos, but that look! This man *could* order the murder of hundreds of people. He could kill them himself. I was ten feet from him and I could literally feel the energy.'

'Maybe you should write a letter to Shirley MacLaine.'

'Listen to me, Ott. Aldana is *criminally insane*.'

'He's behind bars and guarded night and day. What should we do about it?'

Yocke lost his temper. 'Okay, go ahead and snicker like a retarded hyena. I'm telling you we've got a rattlesnake in our pocket and the pocket is cloth. Dammit, Aldana scared the hell out of me!'

'He scared the hell out of me too,' Ott admitted.

The telephone rang. Yocke reached for it without looking.

It was his editor. 'Jack, the feds just closed a savings and loan over in Maryland. Please go up there and interview everyone you can lay hands on. Try to find some depositors this time.'

'You want some brain surgeon who'll miss his ski Christmas in Aspen?'

'I was hoping that with some diligent effort you might find some little old white-haired lady who's got five bucks in her purse and no access to her checking account.'

'What's the name of this place?'

'Second Potomac Savings and Loan.'

Where had he heard that name before? Yocke asked himself as he pocketed his notebook and checked his pocket pencil supply. Oh yes, that Harrington guy who was killed on the beltway – he'd worked there, hadn't he?

The wind made the bare tree limbs wave somberly back and forth under the gray sky. Sitting under an ancient oak just inside the tree line, Henry Charon listened intently to the gentle rattling and tapping as the limbs high above him softly impacted those of other trees. The noise of traffic speeding by on the interstate eighty yards away muffled all the lesser forest noises, the rustle of the leaves, the sound of a chipmunk searching the leaf carpet for its dinner, the chirping of the birds.

The hunter tried to ignore the drone of the cars and trucks. He paid close attention to the gusts and swirls of the wind, subconsciously calculating the direction and velocity.

The rest area in front of him was almost empty. At the far end sat a ten-year-old pickup with Pennsylvania plates and sporting a camper on the back. The driver was apparently asleep inside. Closer, facing the highway, sat the rental car that Charon had driven to this rest stop halfway between Baltimore and Philadelphia. He had rented it using one of his fake driver's licenses and a real Visa card in that name.

A station wagon chock-full of kids and pillows and suitcases came off the highway and pulled to a stop in front of the rest rooms. Youngsters piled out and ran for the little brick building. New Jersey tags. Three minutes later the station wagon accelerated past the pickup toward the on-ramp.

Henry Charon adjusted the collar and fastened the top button on his coat. The wind had a chill to it, no doubt due to its moisture content. Yet it didn't smell of snow.

What if snow came while he were still in Washington? How would that affect his plans?

Charon was still considering it when another car came off the interstate and proceeded slowly through the parking area. One man at the wheel. Tassone. He drove slowly through the lot, looked over the rental car, and braked to a stop beside the pickup. After a moment Tassone's car, a sedan, backed the hundred feet to the rest room building, where he turned off the ignition and got out.

Tassone glanced around as he walked toward the rest rooms. In a few moments he came out and strolled over to where Charon was sitting.

'Hey.' Tassone lowered himself to the ground and leaned back against a tree trunk six feet or so from Charon. 'How's everything?'

'Fine,' Charon said.

'Gonna snow,' Tassone said as he pulled his coat collar higher and jabbed his hands into his pockets.

'I doubt it.'

Tassone wiggled around, trying to find a soft spot for his bottom. 'Wanta sit in the car?'

'This is fine.'

'What d'ya think about the job?'

'You'll have to make a list.'

Tassone fumbled inside his coat for a pencil. From an inside jacket pocket he produced a small spiral notepad. 'Shoot.'

Charon began to recite. He had not committed the items to paper since the possession of such a list would inevitably be incriminating. Tassone could write it down in his own handwriting and take the risk of the list being discovered on his person. Charon could still deny everything.

It took five minutes for Tassone to list all the items. Charon had him read the list back, then gave him two more items, with careful descriptions.

Tassone looked over the list carefully and asked a few questions, then stored the notebook in his pocket.

'So it's feasible?' he asked the hunter.

'It can be done.'

'When?'

'When could you deliver everything on the list?'

'Take about a week, I think. Some of these things will take some work and some serious money. I'll call you.'

'No, I'll call you.' Charon gave him the number of a pay phone in Union Station. 'A week from today, at precisely this time.' Both men glanced at their watches.

'Okay.'

'No names.'

'Of course. You'll do it then?'

'How many people know about me, counting yourself as one?'

'Two.'

'Only two?'

'That's right.'

Something was stirring in the leaves behind them. Henry Charon came erect in one easy motion and, with a tree for cover, stood looking carefully in that direction. Then he saw it, a flash of brown. A red squirrel.

'Ten million, cash, in advance.'

Tassone whistled. 'I—'

'That's for the first name on your list. One million for each of the others, if and when. No guarantees on any of them. You pay a million for each one I get. Take it or leave it.'

'You want the bread sent to Switzerland or what?'

'Cash. In my hands. Used twenties and fifties. No sequential numbers.'

'Okay.'

'You have the authority to make this commitment?'

Now Tassone stood. 'You ain't going to pop anybody until you get paid, are you?'

'No.'

'Well, I'm telling you you'll get paid. How long before you get started?'

'A week or ten days after I get the stuff on that list. Two or three weeks would be better.'

'Better for you. Not for me. We want you started as soon as possible.'

'Let's see how you do getting the equipment I requested.'

'Okay,' said Tassone, and dusted off his trousers. 'Okay. You call me in a week.'

When Jake Grafton returned to his office in the Pentagon, there was a message waiting. The chairman wanted to see him. He called the chairman's office and reached an aide. They agreed he could probably get in to see the general in fifteen minutes or so.

This would be only the fourth occasion on which Jake had met General Hayden Land. For most of the officers on the Joint Staff a meeting with the senior officer in the American military, even with all the Joint Chiefs present, was a rare occurrence. As he walked out of the office this morning the other six officers in the antidrug section appeared and formed a line of sideboys at the door that Jake would have to walk through. They did some pushing and shoving, then came to rigid attention and saluted with mighty flourishes as Jake walked between the rows.

'You guys!'

The other naval officer in the antidrug section whistled, imitating a boatswain's pipe.

'Carry on,' said Jake Grafton with a wide grin and headed for the corridor.

Grafton was the senior officer in the group, which spent its time doing the staff work required to allow the Joint Chiefs to make informed decisions about military cooperation with antidrug law-enforcement efforts. When Jake reported to the Joint Staff a year ago he came to this billet for the simple reason that the O-6 who held it was completing his tour and leaving. Grafton had no special training for the job – indeed, he spent the first two months simply trying to understand what it was the military was doing to assist the various law enforcement agencies – but no matter. Learning on the job went with the uniform. And this past year the job had grown by leaps and bounds as an increasingly alarmed public demanded every federal resource be harnessed to combat the narco-terrorists, and the reluctant Joint Chiefs had finally turned to face the pressure. So Jake Grafton had been busy.

The first black man to hold the top job in the military, General Hayden Land was reputed to be as sharp as they come, an extraordinarily fast study on the intricacies of military policy. He was also, rumor said, very politically astute. He had come to his current post from the National Security Council where he had personally witnessed the meshing of politics and national security issues and the resultant effects on the military.

As he walked out of the Joint Staff spaces just ten minutes after he had entered, Jake was again hailed by name by Mr James, the portly door attendant who had been greeting members of the Joint Staff for over twenty years. He seemed to know everyone's name – quite a feat considering that there were 1,600 officers on the Joint Staff – and shook hands right and left when they streamed past him into the secure spaces in the morning. 'Short day, eh, Captain Grafton?'

'Some people have all the luck,' Jake told him.

The foyer of General Land's E-Ring office was decorated with original paintings that depicted black American servicemen in action. As the aide informed the general that he was there, Grafton examined them again. One was of union soldiers in the crater at Petersburg, another was of cavalrymen fighting Indians on the western plains, and a third was of Army Air Corps pilots manning fighters during World War II.

'He'll see you now,' the aide said, and walked for the door. That was when Jake's eye was captured by the painting of a black sailor defiantly firing a machine gun at attacking Japanese planes. Dorrie Miller aboard USS *West Virginia* at Pearl Harbor.

'I like the general's taste in art,' he muttered to the aide as he passed into the chairman's office.

'Captain Grafton, sir,' the aide said to the general behind the desk, then stood to one side. The general carried his fifty or so years well, Jake thought as he scanned the square figure, the short hair, the immaculate uniform with four silver stars on each shoulder strap.

'Come in, Captain, and find a chair. I called down to your office this morning to suggest you go see Aldana, and they said you had already left.'

'Yessir, I went over there.' Jake sank into a chair with the general's gaze upon him. 'Just curious, I guess,' Jake added. 'The prosecution asked for a gag order and got it. That might help keep the lid on, at least for a little while.'

General Land turned his gaze toward the window, which looked out across the Pentagon parking lots at the skyline of Arlington. 'You really think it'll come out?'

'If only American soldiers knew, sir, I'd be more hopeful. They know what classified information is. But with all those Colombian cops and Justice Department lawyers in on it, there's just no way. The press is going to get this and probably pretty soon. Who knows, Aldana's lawyer, Liarakos, may want to make a motion to have the court consider the legality of the arrest. I'm not a lawyer and I don't know any to ask, but Liarakos looks like the type of guy who will throw every stone he can lay hands on.'

'Oh, but surely it's got to be legal,' the general said. 'The attorney general is the one who requested our help.'

'All I'm saying, sir, is that Liarakos may raise the issue with the court. In fact, the press may have already caught the rumblings of this. This past weekend a reporter, one of my wife's language students, was at a party at my house. He saw me today in court and buttonholed me afterward.'

'Reporter for whom?'

'*The Washington Post*, sir.'

Land grinned. 'God,' he said, 'I feel like Dick Nixon. Think Deep Throat's been whispering?'

Jake laughed. 'I don't think Gideon Cohen is going to have a heart attack if he reads in the newspapers that American Special Forces troops captured Aldana with the cooperation of Colombian police. I told him that it would come out eventually and he shrugged it off. He knows.'

'What about this Aldana?'

'A psychopath.'

'Umm. When he was captured he told the major leading the raid he was going to see them all dead.' General Land showed his teeth. It was not a nice smile. 'I was against us getting into this mess. The military has no business in law enforcement. Won't work, can't work, isn't good for the military or the country. But when I heard that scum threatened our men, my doubts got smaller. Maybe Cohen's right. Maybe we need to go in there and kick some ass.'

'General, if you want my opinion, you were right the first time. These cartel criminals have bribed, threatened, bullied, and occasionally subverted the Colombian authorities. They haven't gotten to our men yet, but now they're going to try. We're not set up to investigate our own people. We take any eighteen-year-olds who can pass the written test and the physical and turn them into soldiers, sailors, and marines. Background checks and loyalty investigations are messes we shouldn't get ourselves into.'

'We may have to,' General Land said. 'The world's changing and we may have to change with it.'

7

When the attorney general walked into William C. Dorfman's White House office, the morning paper was on the desk, open and folded, displaying Mergenthaler's column. Gideon Cohen sighed and sat while he waited for the chief of staff to finish a telephone call.

'No, we are not going to release a text of the indictment. It's sealed. And no, we are not going to ask Mexico to hand over any of its citizens. We have no extradition treaty with Mexico.'

He listened for several seconds, then spat into the phone, 'Fuck no!' and slammed it down.

'That bubble-brain wants to know if we are really offering rewards for these guys' – Dorfman stabbed the newspaper with a rigid finger – 'and paying bounty hunters to bring them to the US for trial.'

Cohen pursed his lips and crossed his legs. Ottmar Mergenthaler's column in the *Post* this morning had revealed, for the first time, that a federal grand jury in Los Angeles had handed down a secret indictment several weeks ago bringing charges against nineteen former and present members of the Mexican government for drug smuggling and complicity in the kidnapping and murder of US Drug Enforcement Administration undercover agent Enrique Camarena, whose body had been discovered near Guadalajara in March 1985, over five years ago. One of those indicted was the former director of the Mexican Federal Judicial Police – the Mexican equivalent of the FBI – and another was his brother, the former head of the Mexican government's antidrug unit. And one of those indicted was a medical doctor who had been arrested just yesterday in El Paso. It seemed that several unknown men had accompanied the good doctor on a plane trip from Mexico, turned him over to waiting federal agents, then immediately reboarded the plane for the flight back to Mexico.

'Are you going to pay bounties?'

'Why not? It's perfectly legal to pay rewards to people who deliver fugitives to lawful authority. That principle has been firmly embedded in the common law for hundreds of years.'

'Oh, spare me the lecture. What in hell are you trying to do, anyway?'

Two years ago Cohen would have bristled. Not anymore. 'Enforce the law,' he said mildly. 'That's still one of the goals of this administration, isn't it?'

Dorfman sat back in his chair and stared at Gideon Cohen. Dorfman's eyes looked owlish when magnified by his hornrim glasses. 'It won't be news to you that I don't like you.'

'Do you mean that personally or professionally?' Cohen asked, and tried to look interested.

Dorfman continued as if he hadn't heard. 'I've suggested to the President that he ask for your resignation. In my opinion you are not loyal to this administration. You don't seem to appreciate the political realities that the President has to face every day, for every decision. With you every decision is black or white.'

'Frankly, Dorfman, I really don't give a damn about your opinion. Are you informing me officially that the President wants my resignation?'

The chief of staff took his time answering. He played with a pen on the table, scrutinized a coffee cup, examined the framed photograph of his family that sat on his desk. 'No,' he said when he had squeezed all the juice from the moment that it could conceivably yield, 'I'm not. I'm just letting you know where you stand.'

'Thanks.' The disgust Cohen felt showed on his face. Dorfman's petty grandstanding was so typical of the man.

Dorfman and Cohen went into the Oval Office as a Boy Scout troop came out. The official photographer was still there, snapping pictures of the President behind his desk. This morning, Cohen thought, George Bush looked more harried than usual. He obviously was not paying much attention to the photographer's directions.

'Come on over here, Gid. Let's get some of the two of us.'

When the photo session was over, the photographer closed the door behind him on the way out. Dorfman flopped the morning paper on Bush's desk.

'Where did Mergenthaler get this information?' the President asked curtly.

'I don't know.'

'This administration has more leaks than an antique rowboat. Anybody who's caught chopping any more holes in the bottom without the permission of a cabinet officer is to be fired on the spot.'

'If we catch anyone.'

Bush nodded, his mind already on something else. In the age of telephones leaks were an inevitable fact of government life, although that didn't make them any easier to swallow. Still, the Bush White House had been remarkably tight under Dorfman's iron hand.

'When's the Mexican ambassador coming over?' the President asked his chief of staff.

'Two-thirty.'

'What should I tell him about this indictment?' he asked Cohen. 'And this bounty business?'

'That we have good solid evidence against these nineteen individuals. Tell him we want Mexico to sign an extradition treaty.'

Dorfman exploded. '*They will never—*'

Bush chopped him off. 'Mergenthaler says the DEA wants to kidnap a couple of these men and bring them here for trial.'

'That's accurate. The whole column is accurate. The way the DEA presented it to me, they want to escort one or two of these men into United States territory and arrest them here.'

President Bush picked up the paper and let it fall to the desk. He pushed his chair back and sat staring at Gideon Cohen. 'No.'

'Yes.'

'*No*, and that's final. The Mexicans owe us 50 *billion* dollars.' He repeated the figure sourly. 'Nine years into the longest economic expansion in American history and we're in debt to our eyes. Trillions of dollars in federal debt, savings-and-loan fraud, farm credit disasters, credit card debt at an all-time high, the junk bond market ready to implode, and the Third World tottering on the brink of bankruptcy – no, no, they're beyond that – they went beyond the brink years ago and are dancing as fast as they can on thin air. They're paying the interest on old loans with the proceeds from new loans, *in exactly the same way that the federal government finances the federal deficit.* The same kind of funny money shenanigans that sank the American S-and-L industry. It's fraud. Outright, government-approved fraud. And now, on top of everything, the Soviet Union wants foreign aid. I feel like a poor man with twelve sick kids and one aspirin.'

'How do we know Mexico would default?'

'That is precisely what they would do. Try to imagine the howl that would go up if agents for the Mexican government kidnapped a few prominent citizens here in the United States and dragged them off to Mexico City for trial. Half of Texas would grab the ol' thirty-thirties and head for Nuevo Laredo to teach the chili peppers some manners.'

Dorfman added, 'I can name a dozen senators who would demand a declaration of war.'

'We'll never get the money back regardless,' the attorney general pointed out with impeccable logic.

'I'm not going to argue, Gid.' This said, the President continued anyway: 'Right now foreign investors are financing about thirty percent of the federal deficit by buying Treasury bonds. If Mexico defaults on its foreign debt, the rest of Latin America probably will too. The American banking system will then collapse unless the federal government bails it out, which it will be forced to do since all deposits are insured by the government up to a hundred thousand dollars. The only way to bail out the banks will be with more bonds, and to sell more bonds interest rates *must* rise. This will only work for a short period, then the government *must* raise taxes, which will suck even more money from consumers' pockets. The net effect of all this will be to send the economy of the United States – and the rest of the world – into a deep recession, further decreasing the nation's ability to service existing debt. Get the picture?'

'And if the Fed lowers interest rates drastically to save the economy, the Japanese and Europeans will stop buying bonds.'

'You got it.'

Cohen ran his fingers through what was left of his hair. He was reminded of a remark by a Soviet politician: 'The Soviet Union is on the edge of the abyss.' Here in the Oval Office he was hearing a different version of the same thing. Only this time it was the United States. Gideon Cohen shivered involuntarily.

'We'd have to devalue the dollar,' Cohen said slowly.

George Bush flipped his hand in acknowledgement.

'So why not devalue right now and go after these dope smugglers who are murdering us with slow poison?'

A sneer crossed Dorfman's face as the President rubbed his eyes with the heels of his hands. 'Get serious,' Dorfman muttered.

The President said, 'Congress would never approve it. If I even publicly suggested devaluing the currency, you wouldn't see another Republican in this office in your lifetime. For God's sake, Gid, I didn't run for this job just so I could become the most hated man in America. I'm *supposed* to be doing what the people want. That's what I'm trying to do. Surely you see that?'

'Mr President, your good faith has never been in question. Not with me, at least. My point is that the American people want an effective solution to this dope business. A lot of past and present Mexican government officials –including cops, especially cops – are in it up to their eyes. We're not talking about just looking the other way while a load of marijuana goes by – we're talking about the torture and murder of US law-enforcement officers by Mexican police officials. *The voters in this country want it stopped!*'

'The voters have got long shopping lists, and they elect congressmen to get the goods for them. They elected me to mind the store. The American people aren't stupid: they know that government can't be all things to all people. I'm supposed to do what's in the best interests of the United States as a nation, as an ongoing concern. *And I will!*'

'Mr President, I'm saying that drugs are our number-one domestic problem. Mexico is a large part of that problem. We can't ignore that simple, fundamental fact.'

'Mexico, land of *la mordida*, the bite,' Bush said, the fatigue evident in his voice. 'Everybody who's ever been there has had to bribe some petty functionary or other. Five bucks here, a ten-spot there. And no doubt big bribes are taken for big favors. I recall one time when Barbara and I—'

'Are you implying that there's no drug corruption here?' Cohen asked ingenuously. 'In America?'

The President and the chief of staff looked at each other.

'What are you saying?' Dorfman asked.

'Mexicans are no different from anybody else. The amounts of money that are right there for the taking – it's a rare man who can say no. The DEA has been swarming over Mexico for years, so we have a pretty good feel for who, when, and how much. We're years behind here.'

'The FBI is working on cases against highly placed American officials? Not just county sheriffs and border patrolmen?'

Cohen nodded.

Dorfman sighed. 'That really wouldn't be so bad,' he told the President. 'Exposing bad apples is good politics.'

'There are exceptions to that rule. This will probably be one of them.' Cohen leaned forward in his seat and spoke to the President. 'A fistful of indictments against some highly placed officials, very high. Think about it. Dorfman can manage the PR impact until hell won't have it, but the "war on drugs" is going to look like those little red, white, and blue WIN buttons – all show and no attempt to tackle the underlying problems, the *real* problems. We're going to get it all thrown back in our faces unless we take effective steps to meet the drug problem head-on.'

The President got out of his chair and stepped to the window behind him. He stood looking out into the Rose Garden. 'We aren't just sitting on our thumbs. I approved the bounty on that Mexican doctor. I approved the use of US soldiers to arrest Aldana. That hasn't come out yet but it will. When it does the hue and cry will be something to hear. I don't give a damn what anybody says, we're doing a lot, all we can, and the voters will see that.'

Cohen spoke. 'Mr President, I'm not questioning your commitment. But the public doesn't see enough of it. What the public sees is slogans and presentations to sixth-graders. "Just say no" is an obscene joke. Hell, the mayor of Washington couldn't say no. The chief of the Mexican federal police couldn't say no. The president of Panama couldn't say no. Professional athletes and movie stars can't say no. Cops can't say no. Congressmen can't say no. *That list is going to grow like a hothouse tomato in radio-active soil irrigated with steroids.*'

'Who?' George Bush asked.

'I haven't asked,' Cohen replied. 'I don't want to know.'

'You don't?' The President turned slightly and looked at Cohen with raised eyebrows.

'It's come to that,' the attorney general said woodenly. 'If I don't know I can't be accused of tipping anyone off, of inadvertently or intentionally warning a suspect under investigation. You don't want to know either. Believe me, some of them will find out one way or another that they are under suspicion and try to throw their weight around. It's human nature.'

With the possible exception of journalism students in a university some-where, no one reads every single word in any edition of *The Washington Post*. Even if the classified ads were ignored and one were a fast reader, reading all the stories would take hours. Your twenty-five cents usually buys you two and a quarter pounds of paper, ten or more sections full of news, features, articles and ads aimed at different tastes and interests. Statecraft, politics, murders, rapes, disasters, business, sports, science, gardening, celebrity gossip and gushings, book reviews, movie hype, music tripe, opinions from every hue of the political spectrum, television listings – the entire world was captured every day on thirty-six ounces of newsprint. Or as much of the world as any civilized being at the very center of the universe – Washington – could possibly care to learn about.

Jack Yocke had a secret ambition to be the first human to read the whole thing. He had it on his list for some morning when he was in bed with the flu. But not today. Sitting at his desk he flipped through the paper scanning the headlines and speed reading the stories that looked interesting.

The Soviets' formal request for foreign aid from the United States was the hottest topic of the day. Senators and representatives were having a field day, as were most of the political columnists. No one denied that the Soviets needed real money – all they could get – but the hard fact mentioned only by the hopelessly practical was that the United States government had no money to give. The cookie jar was empty. There weren't even any crumbs.

Most pundits and politicians were making lists of things the Soviets would have to do to qualify for American largesse, confidently assuming that if America wanted to badly enough, some largesse could be found somewhere. After all, do we really need a military in this brave new world? Surely the nations now receiving foreign aid, together with welfare recipients and Social Security retirees, would be willing to share their mite with the Russians, for the greater good.

In any event, to qualify for the American dole the Soviets would need to free the Baltic states, release all their remaining political prisoners, and open borders for US trade and investment. Of course the Russians would also have to permanently cease all financial and military aid to Cuba and

Libya and Vietnam and Afghanistan and Angola and every other Third World manure pile where the godless commies had opposed the holy forces of capitalism and democracy. They would also have to disband the KGB and the GRU, quit spying on the US and everybody else. And – this almost didn't need to be mentioned – while they were at it the Russians would have to disband the entire Soviet military and sell their ships, tanks, and artillery for scrap. If they did *all* this, well, they would certainly be entitled to some bucks if and when we found some.

Today Jack Yocke scanned the wish lists and moved on. He found a couple of interesting columns by two pundits who had solved the foreign aid issue yesterday. The price of coca leaves in Bolivia and Peru was down from one hundred US dollars to just ten dollars per hundredweight. One columnist opined that this fact meant that George Bush was winning the war on drugs. Another, who had probably stayed awake during his freshman economics class, thought the price drop meant that Bolivian and Peruvian farmers had a bumper crop this year and all the millions spent on eradication efforts had been wasted.

Jack Yocke checked his Rolodex. He found the number he wanted under a code he had made up himself. He called it.

'Yeah, man.'

'Hey, this is Jack Yocke. How's it going?'

'Too smooth, dude. What's on your mind?'

'You seen this morning's paper?'

'I never read that honkey shit. You know that.'

'Question. What's the street price doing right now?'

'What d'ya mean?'

'Is it going up or down?'

'Steady, man. Five bucks a pop. Some talk about dropping it to four, but nobody wants to do that. Not as much juice for everybody, you know?'

'Any supply problems?'

'Not that I heard.'

'Thanks.'

'Be cool, dude.'

The man that Yocke had been talking to, Harrison Ronald Ford – he had taken to using his full name since that actor became popular – cradled the telephone and went back to his coffee.

The newspaper that he had just told Yocke he never read was spread on the kitchen table in front of him. The story he had been reading when the phone rang had Yocke's byline. Second Potomac Savings and Loan taken over by the feds, the headline shouted. Recently murdered cashier Walter P. Harrington apparently involved in money laundering, according to an unnamed source. Second Potomac officials aghast. Massive violations of record-keeping requirements. The rank-and-file staff knew something fishy was going on, but no one wanted to speak out and risk his job and pension rights. So now they had neither.

Harrison Ronald poured himself another cup of coffee and lit another cigarette. He glanced out the dirty window at the building across the alley, then resumed his seat at the kitchen table and flipped to the comics. After he scanned them and grinned at 'Cathy,' he picked up a pencil and began the crossword puzzle.

Harrison Ronald liked crossword puzzles. He had discovered long ago that he could think about other things while he filled in the little squares. Today he had much to think about.

At the head of his list was Freeman McNally. He knew that McNally had been laundering money through Harrington's S-and-L. What would McNally do now? McNally's operation was taking in almost three million cash a week. About a fourth of that amount went to the West Coast to pay for new raw product, and a big chunk went to salaries and payoffs and other expenses. Still the operation produced a million a week pure profit – a little over four million a month – cash that Freeman McNally had to somehow turn into legitimate funds that he and his immediate cronies could spend and squirrel away.

It was certainly a pleasant problem, but a problem nonetheless. It would be interesting to hear Freeman's solution.

In the year that Harrison Ronald had spent working for the organization he had acquired a tremendous respect for Freeman McNally. A sixth-grade dropout, McNally had common sense, superior intelligence, and a cat's ability to land on his feet when the unexpected occurred, as it did with a frequency that would have appalled any legitimate business-man.

Many of McNally's troubles were caused by the people who worked for him: they got greedy, they became addicted, they liked to strut their stuff in front of the wrong people, they became convinced of their own personal invulnerability. McNally was a natural leader. His judgments were hard to fault. Those people that he concluded were a danger disappeared, quickly and forever. Those errant souls whom he believed trainable he corrected and trusted.

Like every crack dealer, McNally was in a never-ending battle to protect his turf, the street corners and houses where his street dealers sold his product. This was combat and McNally had a natural aptitude for it. He was ruthless efficiency incarnate.

And like every crack dealer, McNally was in a cash-and-carry business that demanded constant vigilance against cheaters and thieves. Here too McNally excelled, but he had been blessed with a generous dollop of paranoia and a natural talent for larceny. To Harrison Ronald's personal knowledge, poorly advised optimists had attempted to swindle Freeman McNally on two occasions. Several of these foolish individuals had received bullets in the brain as souvenirs of their adventure and one had been dismembered with a chain saw while still alive.

But although Freeman McNally had many attributes in common with other successful crack-ring leaders, he was also unique. McNally intuitively understood that the most serious threat to the health of his enterprise was the authorities – the police, the DEA, the FBI. So he had systematically set about reducing that threat to an acceptable level. He found politicians, cops and drug enforcement agents who could be bought and he bought them.

Consequently Harrison Ronald Ford was in Washington undercover instead of riding around Evansville, Indiana, in a patrol car. He wasn't known as Harrison Ronald Ford here though, but as Sammy Z.

Mother of Galahad, 23 Across. Six letters, the last of which is an E.

Ford had arrived in Washington a year ago and rented this shithole to live in. After two weeks of hanging around bars, he got a job as a lookout for one of McNally's distributors. He had been doing that for about a month when who should come strolling down the street one rainy Thursday night but his high school baseball buddy from Evansville, Jack Yocke.

He had leveled with Yocke – he had no choice: Yocke knew he was a cop – and the reporter apparently had kept the secret. Ten months had passed, Harrison Ronald was still alive, with all his arms and legs firmly attached, and he was now personally running errands and delivering product for Freeman.

He was close. Very close. He knew the names of two of the local cops on Freeman's list and one of the politicians, but he had no evidence that would stand up in court.

It would come. Sooner or later he would get the evidence. If he lived long enough.

Elaine. Elaine was the mother of Galahad.

If that fox Freeman McNally didn't catch on.

Damn that Yocke anyway. Why did that white boy have to pick today to call? Oh well, if worse came to worst. Jack Yocke would write him one hell of an obituary.

The late Judson Lincoln had lived in a modest three-story town house in a fashionably chic neighborhood a mile or so northeast of the White House. T. Jefferson Brody wheeled his Mercedes into a vacant parking place a block past the Lincoln residence and walked back.

He was expected. He had telephoned the widow this morning and informed her of his interest in discussing the purchase of the business that had belonged to her deceased husband. She had apparently called her attorney, then called him back and proposed this meeting at two P.M.

Mrs Lincoln had sounded calm enough on the phone this morning, but that was certainly nothing to bank upon. This would in all likelihood be a tense afternoon with the sniveling widow, probably some brainless, ill-mannered brats, and for sure, one overpaid fat lawyer anxious to split hairs and niggle ad nauseam over contractual phrasing. Looming like a thunderstorm on the horizon would be the question of who had killed Judson Lincoln, prominent black businessman and civic pillar to whom we point with pride. And police. They would be in constant contact with the widow, asking every question they thought they could get away with.

Oh well, T. Jefferson could handle it.

After pushing the doorbell, Brody adjusted the twenty-dollar royal-blue silk hanky in his breast pocket. He hoped he wouldn't need to offer it as a repository for the contents of the widow's nose, but . . . He straightened his tie and made sure his suit jacket was properly buttoned and hanging correctly under his knee-length mohair topcoat.

The door was opened by a black woman in a maid outfit that was complete right down to the little white apron. He handed her his card and said. 'To see Mrs Lincoln, please.'

'I'll take your coat, sir.' When Brody had shed the garment, the maid said. 'This way, sir.'

She led Brody fifteen feet down the hallway to the study.

Mrs Lincoln was a tall woman with chiseled features and a magnificent figure. Her waist, Brody noted appreciatively, wouldn't go over twenty-two inches. Her bust, he estimated, would tape almost twice that. Judson Lincoln must have been out of his mind to go chasing floozies with this magnificent piece waiting for him at home!

Then she smiled.

T. Jefferson Brody felt his knees get watery.

'I'm Deborah Lincoln, Mr Brody. This is my attorney, Jeremiah Jones.'

For the first time Brody glanced at the attorney. He was about twenty-five with slicked-back hair, miserable teeth, and a weasel smile. 'Yes, yes, Mr Brody. Deborah has told me of your client's interest in her husband's business. Such a tragedy that took him from her so early in life.'

As Brody feasted his eyes upon the widow, it occurred to him that she seemed to be weathering her husband's unfortunate demise very well. Just now she made eye contact with Jones and they both smiled slightly. She turned back to Brody and, it seemed to him, made a real effort to arrange her face.

'A tragedy,' Brody agreed after another look at gigolo Jones. 'Ahem, well, life must go on. Sorry to disturb you so soon after . . . ah, but my clients are anxious that I speak to you about their interest in your husband's business before you . . . ah, before you . . .'

The beautiful Deborah Lincoln took her attorney's hand and squeezed it as she gazed raptly at Brody.

'. . . They want to buy the business,' Brody finished lamely, his thoughts galloping.

Yes, indeed, Deborah Lincoln. Yes, indeed, you need a man to comfort you in your hour of need. But why this pimp in mufti? Why not T. Jefferson Brody?

'I have an excellent offer to lay before you.' Brody gave the widow Lincoln his most honest, sincere smile.

Negotiations with Deborah Lincoln and attorney Jones took all of an hour. Brody offered $350,000, the attorney demanded $450,000. After some genteel give-and-take, Mrs Lincoln graciously agreed to compromise at $400,000. Her attorney held her hand and looked into her eyes and tried to persuade her to demand more, but her mind was made up.

'Four hundred thousand is fair,' she said. 'That's about what Judson thought the business was worth.'

She gave Jones a gentle grin and squeezed his hand. When they weren't looking his way, T. Jefferson Brody rolled his eyes heavenward.

It was agreed that tomorrow afternoon Mrs Lincoln and Mr Jones would come to Brody's office to look over the lease assignments, bill of sale, and other documents. Brody would have the check ready.

After shaking hands all around, Brody was escorted from the room by the maid, who helped him with his coat and held the door for him.

Down on the sidewalk, with the door firmly closed behind him, Jefferson Brody permitted himself a big smile as he walked toward his car.

The door was opened by a young woman with a scarf around her head. 'Yes.'

'I understand you have an apartment for rent?' Henry Charon raised his eyebrows hopefully.

'Yes. Come in, come in. It's too cold out there. What is it, forty-five degrees?'

'Nearer fifty, I think.'

'It's upstairs. A bedroom, bath, living room, and kitchenette. Fairly nice.'

They were standing in the hallway now. The New Hampshire Avenue building was old but fairly clean. The woman wore huge glasses in brown, horn-rim frames, but the optical correction in the glass was so large that her eyes were comically enlarged. Charon found himself staring at those brown eyes, fascinated. She focused on one thing, then another, and he could plainly see every twitch of the muscles around her eyes.

'I'd like to see the apartment, please.'

'The rent's nine hundred a month,' she apologized. She had a pleasant voice and spoke clearly, articulating every word precisely. 'Really obscene, I know, but what can we do?'

Charon grimaced for her benefit, then said, 'I'd like to see it.'

Her eyes reflected her empathy, then she turned and made for the stairs. 'Just moving to town?'

'That's right.'

'Oh, you'll like Washington. It's so vibrant, so exciting! All the great ideas are here. This is such an intellectually stimulating city!'

The apartment was on the third floor. The living room faced the street, but the bedroom looked down on an alley that ran alongside the building. The grillwork of a fire escape was visible out the bedroom window, and he unlocked the sash, raised it, and stuck his head out. The fire escape went all the way to the roof.

He closed the window as his guide explained about the heat. Forced-air gas, no individual thermostats, temperature kept at sixty-five all winter.

'You must come look at the kitchen.' She led him on. 'It's small but intimate and reasonably equipped. Perfect for meals for two, but you could do food for four quite easily, six or eight in a pinch.'

'Very nice,' Henry Charon said, and opened the refrigerator and looked inside to humor her. 'Very nice.'

She showed him the bathroom. Adequate hot water, he was assured.

'The neighbors?' he asked when they were standing in the living room.

'Well,' she said, lowering her voice as if to tell a secret. 'Everyone who lives here is so very nice. Two doctoral students – I'm one of those – a Library of Congress researcher, a paralegal, a free-lance writer, and a public-interest attorney. Oh, and one librarian.'

'Ummm.'

'This is the only vacancy we've had in over a year. We've had five inquiries, but the landlord insisted on a hundred and fifty a month rent increase, which just puts it out of so many persons' reach.'

'I can believe it.'

'The previous tenant died of AIDS.' She looked wistfully around the room, then turned those huge eyes on Charon. He stared into them. 'It was so tragic. He suffered so. His friend just couldn't afford to keep the apartment after he passed away.'

'I see.'

'What kind of work do you do?'

'Consulting, mostly. Government stuff.'

He began asking questions just to hear her voice and watch the expression in her eyes. She was studying political science, hoped to teach in a private university, got a break on her rent to manage the building, the neighborhood was quiet with only reasonable traffic, she had lived here for two years and grown up in Newton, Massachusetts, the corner grocery on the next street over was excellent. Her name was Grisella Clifton.

'Well,' Henry Charon sighed at last, reluctant to end the conversation, 'You've sold me. I'll take it.'

A half hour later she walked out the door with him. She paused by her car, a weathered VW bug. 'I'm delighted you'll be living here with us, Mr Tackett.'

Henry Charon nodded and watched her maneuver the Volkswagen from its parking place. She kept both hands firmly on the wheel and leaned toward it until the moving plastic threatened to graze her nose. On the back of the car were a variety of bumper stickers: ONE WOMAN FOR PEACE, CHILDCARE BEFORE WARFARE, THIS CAR IS A NUCLEAR FREE ZONE.

On Wednesday afternoon Jefferson Brody concluded that Jeremiah Jones wasn't much of a lawyer. While Mrs Lincoln examined the original oil paintings on the paneled mahogany and the bronze nude that Brody had paid eleven thousand dollars for, Jones looked over the legal documents, asked two stupid questions, and flipped through the two full pages of representations and warranties that Mrs Lincoln was asked to make as seller of the business without taking the time to read them carefully. Jones was a sheep, Brody decided. A black sheep, he chuckled to himself, pleased at his own wit.

Mrs Lincoln signed the documents while Brody's secretary watched. Then the secretary notarized the documents, carefully sealed them, and separated them into piles, one pile for Mrs Lincoln and one for Brody's clients, whose identities were, of course, still undisclosed. The documents merely transferred the business to the ABC Corporation, which was precisely one day old.

'You understand, I'm sure,' Brody commented to Jones, 'why my clients have not given me the authority to reveal their identities.'

'Perfectly,' Jones said with a wave of his hand. 'Happens all the time.'

Brody produced the cashier's check of a New York bank in the amount of four hundred thousand dollars. After Jones had examined it, it went to Mrs Lincoln, who merely glanced at it and folded it for her purse.

Jones glanced at his watch and stood. 'I'd better run. I have an appointment at my office and I think I'm going to be late. Deborah, can you get home in a taxi?'

'Of course, Jeremiah. Oh, why don't you take this check and have your secretary deposit it for me? Could you do that?'

'If you'll make out a deposit slip.'

'Won't take a minute.' Mrs Lincoln got out her checkbook, carefully tore a deposit slip from the back, and noted the check number on it. Then she turned the check over and endorsed it. This didn't take thirty seconds. She handed both pieces of paper to Jones. 'Thank you so much.'

'Of course. I'll call you.'

Jones shook hands with Brody and left.

'Well, Mr Brody, I've taken up enough of your time,' Deborah Lincoln said. 'I'll ask your secretary to call me a taxi.'

T. Jefferson stood. 'I've enjoyed meeting you, Mrs Lincoln.'

'Please call me Deborah.'

'Deborah. It's such a shame that the tragedy to your husband . . . I hope the police weren't too rough.'

'Oh,' she said with a slight grimace, 'they certainly weren't pleasant. Almost suggested I'd hired it done. They said it was a professional killing.' She tried to grin. 'It certainly didn't help that Judson was killed on the stoop of his bimbo's house, if you know what I mean.'

'I understand,' Brody said gravely and reached for her hand. She let him take it.

'You know, I'm not sure how to say this, but I have the feeling that things will go well for you from now on.'

'Well, I hope so. With the business sold and all. That certainly is a load off my mind. I know nothing at all of Judson's business, Mr—'

'Jefferson, please.'

'Jefferson, and your people paid what the business was worth, I believe.' She took her hand back and looked again at the paintings and the sculpture. 'Such a nice office.'

'What say – how about I buy you dinner? Could I do that for you?'

She looked at him with surprise. 'Why, Mr – Jefferson. So nice of you to ask. Why, yes, I'd like that.'

Brody looked at his watch, a Rolex. 'Almost four o'clock. I think we've done enough business for today. Perhaps we might go to a little place I know for drinks, then dinner afterward, when we're hungry?'

'You're very thoughtful.'

The evening turned out to be one of the most pleasant that T. Jefferson Brody could remember. The beautiful black woman with the striking figure was a gifted conversationalist, Brody concluded, a woman who knew how to put a man at ease. She kept him talking about his favorite subject – T. Jefferson Brody – and drew from him a highly modified version of his life story. Professional triumphs, wealthy clients, vacations in Europe and the Caribbean – with a few drinks in him Brody waxed expansive. As he told it his life was a triumphant march ever deeper into the palace of wealth and privilege. He savored every step because he had earned it.

After dinner – chateaubriand for two of course – and a $250 bottle of twelve-year-old French wine, Jefferson Brody seated the widow Lincoln and her magnificent rack of tits in his Mercedes and drove her to his humble $1.6 million abode in Kenwood.

He led her through the house pronouncing the brand names of his possessions as if they were the names of wild and dangerous game he had stalked and vanquished in darkest Africa while armed only with a spear. Majolica plates from Rosselli, trompe l'oeil paneling, Italian leather sofas and chairs, Jesurum lace table and bed linen, two original Chippendale chairs, Faberge eggs – they were trophies, in a way, and it would not be overstatement to say that he loved them.

After the tour, he led her back to the den where he fixed drinks. She had a vodka tonic and he made himself a scotch and soda. With the lights dimmed and the strains of a Dvorak CD floating from the Klipsch speakers, T. Jefferson Brody ran his fingertips along the widow's thigh and kissed her willing lips.

Three sips of scotch and three minutes later he went quietly to sleep. The remains of his drink spilled down his trouser leg and onto the Kashan carpet.

Mrs Lincoln managed to lever herself out from under Brody's bulk and find a light switch. She refastened her brassiere and straightened her clothes, then made a telephone call.

When Jefferson Brody awoke sunlight was streaming through the window. He squinted mightily against the light and rashly tried to move, which almost tore his head in half. His head was pounding like a bass drum, the worst hangover of his life.

'My God . . .'

His memory was a jumble. Deborah Lincoln, with the sublime tits . . . she was in – no, she was here. Here! In his house. They were kissing and he had his hand . . . and nothing! There was nothing else. His mind was empty. That was all he could remember.

What time is it?

He felt for his watch. Not on his wrist.

The *Rolex*! *Not on his wrist!*

T. Jefferson Brody pried his eyes open and gritted his teeth against the pain in his head. His watch was missing. He looked around. The TV and VCR were gone. Where the Klipsch speakers had stood only bare wires remained. His wallet lay in the middle of the carpet, empty. *Oh my God . . .*

He staggered into the dining room. The doors to the china cabinet were ajar, and the cabinet was bare! The Spode china, the silver and crystal – gone!

'I've been robbed!' he croaked. '*God fucking damn, I've been robbed!*'

He lurched into the living room. The Fabergé eggs, the engravings, everything small enough to carry, all gone!

The police! He would call the police. He made for the kitchen and the phone on the counter.

A newspaper was arranged over the phone. He tossed it aside and picked up the receiver while he tried to focus on the buttons.

Something red on the newspaper caught his eye. A big red circle around a photo, a photo of a fat, frumpy black woman. The circle – it was *lipstick*! He bent to stare at the paper. Yesterday's *Post*. The picture caption: 'Mrs Judson Lincoln, at National Airport after her husband's funeral, reflected on the many civic contributions to the citizens of Washington made by the late Mr Lincoln, a District native.'

'Lemme get this straight, Tee, You paid this woman you thought was Mrs Lincoln four hundred grand. You took her to dinner. She slipped you a Mickey last night and cleaned out your house?'

'Yeah, Bernie. The papers she signed are worthless. Forgeries. I don't know who the hell she is, but I'm sitting here looking at a photo of Mrs Judson Lincoln in yesterday's paper, and the broad who signed the papers and took the money ain't her.'

'Did she have nice tits, Tee?'

'Yeah, but—'

Bernie Shapiro had a high-pitched, nasal he-he-he laugh that was truly nauseating if you were suffering from the aftereffects of a Mickey Finn. Brody held the telephone well away from his ear. Shapiro giggled and snorted until he choked.

'Listen, Bernie,' Brody protested when Shapiro stopped coughing, 'this isn't so damned funny. She's got your money!'

'Oh, no, Tee. She's got four hundred grand of *your* money! We gave you *our* four hundred Gs to buy that goddamn check cashing company, and you had better do just precisely that with it. You got forty-eight hours, Tee. I expect to see documents transferring title to that business on my desk within forty-eight hours, and they goddamn well better be signed by the real, bona fide, genuine Mrs Judson widow Lincoln. Are you on my wavelength?'

'Yeah, Bernie. But it would sure be nice if you helped me catch up with this black bitch and get the money back.'

'You haven't called the cops, have you?'

'No. Thought I oughta talk to you first.'

'Well, you finally did something right. I'll think about helping you catch up with the broad, Tee, but in the meantime you had better get cracking on the Lincoln deal. I'm not going to tell you again.'

'Sure. Sure, Bernie.'

'Tell me what this woman looked like.'

Brody did so.

'This lawyer with her, what'd he look like?'

Brody described Jeremiah Jones right down to his shoelaces and bad teeth.

'I'll think about it, Tee, maybe ask around. But you got forty-eight hours.'

'Yeah.'

'Don't do nothing stupid.' The connection broke.

Jefferson Brody cradled the receiver and picked up the ice bag, which he held carefully against his forehead. It helped a little. Maybe he should take three more aspirins.

He needed to lie down for a few hours. That was it. Get his feet up.

But first he wandered through the house, cataloguing yet again all the things that were missing. If he ever caught up with that cunt, he'd kill her. Maybe after he'd closed the Lincoln deal he could talk Bernie into putting a contract on her black ass.

In the hallway, as he passed the door to the garage, a sense of foreboding came over T. Jefferson Brody. He opened the door and peered into the garage. Empty. Hadn't he parked the Mercedes in here last night? Or had he left it in the driveway?

He hit the button to open the garage door. The door rose slowly, majestically, revealing an empty driveway.

Oh no! She'd stolen the damned car too!

8

'Why? Tell me why.'

'Because I wanted it,' Elizabeth snarled. 'Is that too difficult for you to understand?'

Thanos Liarakos pinched his nose and stroked an eyebrow. His associates had seen him do this many times in the courtroom, and they knew it was an unconscious mannerism to handle stress. If his wife knew the significance of the gesture, she ignored it now. She hugged her knees and stared at the hospital's stenciled name on the sheets.

After a moment he said, 'That stuff will kill you.'

She sneered.

'What am I supposed to say to you? Should I talk about the kids? Should I tell you how much I love you? Should I tell you once again that you're playing Russian roulette? And you are going to *lose*.'

'I'm not one of your half-witted jurors. Spare me the eloquence.'

'You're prostituting your soul for this white powder, Elizabeth. Prostituting your dignity. Your intelligence. Your humanity. You are! You're trading everything that makes life worth living for a few minutes of feeling good. God, you are a fool.'

'If that's the way you feel, why don't you get out of here? I'm not going to sit quietly while you call me a whore. You bastard!'

'What *do* you want, Elizabeth?'

She glared at him and wrapped her arms around her chest.

'Do you want to come home?'

She said nothing.

'I'm going to lay it out for you in black and white. You're a cocaine addict. When they discharge you in a few days you're going back to that clinic. I've already made the phone calls and sent them a check.' This would be her third trip. 'You are going to sign yourself in and stay until you are cured, finally, once and for all. You are going to learn to live without cocaine for the rest of your life. *Then* you may come home.'

'Jesus, you make it sound like I've got a nasty virus or a pesky little venereal disease. "When the pus in your vagina drys up—"'

'You can kick it, Elizabeth.'

'You're so goddamn certain! *I'm* the one that's in here living it. What if I *can't?*'

'If you *don't*, I'll file for a divorce. I'll ask for custody and I'll get it. You can whore and steal and do whatever else you have to to maintain your addiction, and when the people from the morgue call, the kids and I will see that you get a Christian burial and a nice little marble slab. Every year on Mother's Day we'll put flowers on your grave.'

Tears ran down Elizabeth's face. 'Maybe I should just kill myself and get it over with,' she said softly. But too late. Her husband missed this histrionic fillip. He was already halfway through the door.

Before she could say anything else he disappeared down the corridor.

Henry Charon was at the apartment on New Hampshire Avenue at nine A.M. when the truck from the furniture rental company came. Grisella Clifton wasn't home, and Charon felt vaguely put out. He showed the truck crew where to put the bed, the couch, the dresser, the chairs, and the television, then tipped the driver and his helper a ten-spot each.

At eleven o'clock he was at the apartment he'd rented in Georgetown when the truck from the furniture rental company in Arlington arrived, A-to-Z Rentals. The deliverymen had the furniture inside and arranged by eleven-forty. He tipped both those men and locked the door behind him as he left.

At one he was at the apartment near Lafayette Circle. The telephone company installation person – a woman – showed up a half hour late. She apologized and Charon waved it aside. She had almost finished when the furniture arrived, this time from a rental company in Chevy Chase.

At four P.M. he bought a car from an elderly lady living in Bethesda. He had called five people with cars for sale in the classified section of the newspaper and settled on her because she sounded like an elderly recluse.

She was. Even better, she peered at him myopically. At her daughter's insistence, she explained at length while he nodded understandingly, she was giving up the car, a seven-year-old Chevrolet two-door sedan, brown. The plates were valid for three more months. He paid her cash and drove it straight to a Sears auto service center where he had the oil and plugs changed, the radiator serviced, all the belts and hoses replaced, and a new battery and new tires installed. While he was waiting he ate a hamburger in the mall.

As he strolled through the evening crowd toward the auto service center at the north end of the mall, he passed an electronics store. In he went. Fifteen minutes later he came out with a police band radio scanner.

That evening at the Lafayette Circle apartment he read the instruction book and played with the dials and switches. The radio worked well whether plugged into the wall socket or on its rechargable batteries. He stretched out on the bed and listened to the dispatcher and the officers on the street. They routinely used two-digit codes to shorten the transmissions. Tomorrow he would go to the library and try to find a list of the codes. And he would visit more electronics stores and buy more scanners, but only one at each store.

Tomorrow the telephone people were installing phones in the other two apartments. And tomorrow he would have to shop for food and first-aid supplies. Then tomorrow night he would begin moving food, water, and medical supplies to the subway hideout.

Maybe the following night he could put some dried beef and bandages in the cave in Rock Creek Park.

So much to do and so little time.

As he listened to the scanner he mentally went through the checklist one more time.

The real problem was afterward, after the hunt. He did not yet have a solution and he began to worry it again. The FBI would have his fingerprints – that was inevitable. Henry Charon had no illusions. The fact that the fingerprints the FBI acquired would match not a single set of the tens of millions they had on file would eventually cause the agents to look in the right places. They would have plenty of time – all they needed, in spite of exhortations by politicians and outraged pundits – and the cooperation of every law-enforcement officer in the nation.

Eventually, inevitably, the net would pull him in. Unless he was not there. Or unless the FBI stopped looking because they thought they already had their man. The false clues would not have to hold up forever; indeed, every day that passed would allow the real trail to get colder and colder. A month or so would probably be sufficient.

Why not a red herring?

At three the following afternoon Jack Yocke was finishing a story on the collapse of Second Potomac Savings and Loan. His editor had told him earlier to keep the story tight: space was going to be at a premium in tomorrow's paper. The Soviets had just announced an immediate cessation of foreign aid to Cuba and Libya. Both nations would be permitted to continue to purchase goods from the Soviet Union but only at world market prices, with hard currency.

Yocke hung up the telephone without looking and kept right on tapping on the computer keyboard. The authorities were fully satisfied that the late Walter P. Harrington had been using Second Potomac to launder money for the crack trade. Local crack money or from somewhere else? No one was saying, not even off the record.

And someone had used a high-powered rifle to blow his head off while he drove the left lane of the Beltway at fifty-five miles per hour – his widow fervently insisted that he *always* drove fifty-five.

It certainly had not been a motorist enraged over Harrington's highway manners. Not using a rifle.

Money, money, money. Hadn't the other man killed the evening Harrington died also had something to do with money? Didn't he own some kind of check-cashing business?

The phone rang.

Still tapping the Second Potomac story, Yocke cradled the receiver against his shoulder and cheek. 'Yocke.'

'Jack, there's been a shooting at the day-care center in the Shiloh Baptist Church, next door to the Jefferson projects. About thirty minutes or so ago. Would you run over there? I'm also sending a photographer.'

'Yo.'

Yocke looked over his story, pushed RECORD and then left the terminal to turn itself off.

The Jefferson projects was not the worst public housing project in the city, nor was it the best. It was simply average. Ninety-eight percent black and Hispanic, the tenants existed in a netherworld of poverty and squalor where the crack trade boomed twenty-four hours a day and men sneaked in and out to avoid jeopardizing their girlfriends' welfare eligibility.

All the legitimate merchants in a five-block radius of the projects had long ago gone out of business, except for one sixty-year-old Armenian grocer who had been robbed forty-two times in the last sixty months, a record even for Washington. Yocke had done a story on him six months or so ago. He had been robbed four times since then.

'One of these crackheads is going to kill you some night,' Yocke had told the grocer.

'Where am I gonna go? Answer me that. I grew up in the house across the street. I've never lived anywhere else. The grocery business is the only trade I know. And they never steal over a day's receipts.'

'Some strung-out kid is going to smear your brains all over the back counter.'

'It's sorta like a tax, y'know? That's the way I look at it. The scumbags take my money at gunpoint and buy crack. The city takes my money legally and pays the mayor a salary he doesn't earn and he uses it to buy crack. The feds take my money legally and pay welfare to that crowd in the projects and they let their kids starve while they spend the money on crack. What the hell's the difference?'

Still pondering the crack tax, Yocke slowed the pool car as he went by the Armenian's corner grocery and looked in. The old man was bagging groceries for an elderly black lady.

He parked the car two blocks from the project and walked. As he rounded a corner, there they were, long three-story gray buildings, four to a block, decaying without grace under a cold gray sky.

Something about the scene jarred him. Oh yeah, the place was deserted. The teenage boys who manned the sidewalks and sold crack to the white people who drove in from the suburbs were gone. The cops were here.

Yocke veered onto a sidewalk between the buildings and strode along purposefully, his steps echoing on the cinderblock walls and the gray, vacant window.

White man, white man, the echoes said, over and over. White man, white man . . .

The church was across the street from the projects, on the western edge. Police cars in front, lights flashing. An ambulance. One cop keeping an eye on the vehicles.

Yocke showed the cop his ID. 'Understand there's been a shooting?'

The cop was a black man in his fifties with a pot gut. The strap that held his pistol in its holster was unlatched. The gun could be drawn in a clean, crisp motion. The cop jerked his thumb over his shoulder and grunted.

'Can I go in?'

'After they bring the body out. Be another ten minutes or so.'

Yocke got out his notebook and pencil. 'Who is it?'

'Was.'

'Yeah.'

The woman who ran the day care. I don't know her name.'

'What happened?'

'Well, near as I can figure, from what I've heard, a couple squad cars stopped over on Grant.' Grant was the street bordering the west side of the projects. 'The dealers ran through the projects. A cop chased one guy. He went charging into the church, through the day-care center toward the playground door, and when the victim didn't get out of his way fast enough, he drilled her. One shot. Right through the heart.'

The radio transceiver on the cop's belt holster crackled into life. He held it to his ear with his left hand. His right remained near his gun butt.

Other cops were searching the abandoned buildings and tenements to the west of the church. The cryptic transmissions floated from the radios of the parked cruisers.

When the radio fell momentarily silent, Yocke asked the patrolman, 'Where were the kids when the shooting occurred?'

'Where the hell do you think? Right there. They saw the whole thing.'

'When?'

'About two-forty or so.'

'You haven't got the killer yet?'

The cop spit on the sidewalk. 'Not yet.'

'Description?'

'Black male, about eighteen or so, five feet ten to six feet, maybe a hundred fifty or sixty. Medium-length hair. Was wearing a red ball-cap, black leather coat, white running shoes. That's the description from the cop chasing him. All the kids say is that he had a big gun.'

Big gun, Yocke scribbled. Yeah, any pistol vomiting bullets into real people, with real blood flying, it's a big gun when you remember it. Big as your nightmares, big as evil personified, big as sudden death.

'How old are the kids?'

'Youngest's a few weeks. Oldest is almost six.'

'Name of the cop chasing the shooter?'

'Ask the lieutenant.'

'Why was the cop chasing the shooter?'

'Ask the lieutenant.'

'Is there anything else you can tell me?'

'Your newspaper sucks.'

Yocke put the notebook in his pocket and rolled his collar upright. The wind was picking up. Dirt and trash swirled around the cars and funneled between the barracks of the projects. A chilly wind.

'May rain,' the cop said when he saw Yocke looking at the gray sky.

'Might.'

'Been a dry fall. We need the rain.'

'How many years you been on the force?'

'Too fucking many.'

The minutes passed. Yocke fought the chill wind as the police radio told its story of futility. The man who had done the shooting was nowhere to be found.

The *Post* photographer showed up. He burned film as Yocke shivered.

Finally, after twenty minutes, the ambulance crew brought the body out on a wheeled stretcher covered with a white sheet, which was strapped down to keep it from blowing away. It went into the vehicle and the crew followed. One man got in the driver's seat, turned off the flashing overhead lights, and drove away.

'You can go in now,' the cop beside Yocke told him.

The church foyer was dirty and dark and needed paint. The sounds of children sobbing were plainly audible.

On the wall a small announcement board gave the title of this Sunday's sermon: 'The Christian's Choice in Today's World.' Beneath the sermon board was a faded poster with a girl's picture: 'Missing since 4/21/88. Black female, 13, five feet two.' Her name was there, what she had been wearing that evening nineteen months ago, a phone number to call.

A stairway led up to the left. To the sanctuary, probably. Yocke continued along the hallway, toward the sobbing. At the end of the hall the door stood open.

A young woman had the children huddled around her. About a dozen of them. God, they're so small! Talking softly among themselves were three policemen in uniform, two in plainclothes. Two lab technicians were repacking their cases. And curiously, no one stood on or near the ubiquitous chalk outline on the floor.

The *Post* photographer, Harold Dorgan, followed Yocke in. He began taking pictures of the children and the young woman trying to comfort them.

The lieutenant was in his forties. His shirt was dirty and he needed a shave. He also needed a breath freshener Yocke soon discovered. After Dorgan had taken a dozen pictures, the lieutenant told him that was enough and shooed him out.

The victim's name was Jane Wilkens. Age thirty-six. Unmarried. Mother of three children. Killed by one .357-inch-diameter slug that had gone through her entire body, including her heart, and buried itself in the wall near the rear door. Wilkens had started shouting as the gunman burst through the door with the pistol in his hand. As he came at her he pointed the weapon and fired one shot from a distance of perhaps five feet. She was still falling when he ran by her. He jerked open the door to the playground and ran out.

No one saw which way he went after he went through the door. The playground was surrounded by a five-foot-high fence that an agile man could vault anywhere he wished.

The pistol had not been found, so searching officers had been advised to proceed with caution. 'Maybe a thirty-eight Special,' the lieutenant said, 'but more likely a three fifty-seven Magnum. Damn bullet went through plaster, a layer of drywall, and shattered a concrete block. Almost went through it.'

'A cop was chasing this guy,' Yocke murmured.

'Yeah. Patrolman Harry Phelps.'

'Why?'

'Because he ran.'

'What do you mean?'

'I mean a couple cruisers pulled up over on Grant and a bunch of those kids took off like jackrabbits. Officer Phelps ran after this guy. The suspect pulled a weapon, looked back over his shoulder several times at the officer, and charged into this church. Officer Phelps kept coming, heard the shot, and stopped by the victim to administer first aid. She lived for about fifteen seconds after he reached her.'

'So Jane Wilkens would still be alive if Phelps had not elected to chase this guy?'

'Whatever you're implying, I don't like it,' the lieutenant snarled. 'And I don't like your face. Phelps – Officer Phelps – was doing his job. We're trying to police this shithole, Mr *Washington* fucking *Post*!'

'Yeah, but—'

'Get outta my face!'

'Listen. I—'

'Out! This is a crime scene. Out!'

Jack Yocke went.

Dorgan was sitting on the curb in front of the church. Yocke sat down beside him. The overweight cop attending the door ignored them.

'What d'ya think?' Dorgan said.

'I don't think. I gave that up years ago.'

'I'm going to walk over to Grant and snap a few, then head back downtown. I think I got some good shots of the kids. Really tough on them to see that.'

'Yeah.'

'Try not to get mugged.' With that Dorgan rose, adjusted his camera bags, and trudged away. Yocke watched him go.

The curb was cold on his fanny. He stood and dusted his seat, then walked back and forth on the sidewalk.

After a while the kids came out. Each of them was carrying a little brown paper bag. Yocke watched them disappear into the projects.

A few minutes later the cops began dribbling out. When the lieutenant came out he ignored Yocke and climbed into the passenger seat of a cruiser. The uniformed officer with him got behind the wheel.

Yocke saw the man coming a block away. With his hands in his jacket pockets, his head up, he walked rapidly in this direction.

He's coming here, Yocke decided, and watched him come. About forty-five, he had short gray hair. His chocolate skin was stretched tight over his cheekbones and jaw.

The man looked at the cop and Yocke and went up the three steps and through the door without pausing.

Yocke leaned on the little railing that protected what had once been grass. The temperature had dropped at least five degrees and the sky was grayer. He was wondering whether he should return to the office or try to get back inside when a drop of rain struck him.

He set off through the projects, back toward the car. Droplets of rain raised little puffs of dirt beside the empty sidewalks. He met a policeman coming the other way. The officer had his pistol in his right hand, down by his leg, and was talking on his hand-held radio. He ignored Yocke.

The pool car was still intact. All four wheels still attached, the windshield unbroken, the doors still locked and closed. Another miracle.

Yocke drove slowly through the projects as rain spattered the windshield. On impulse, he went back to the church and parked in front.

All the cops were gone.

Yocke locked the car and went inside.

In the foyer he paused and listened. The door to the day-care center was still open and he could hear voices. He walked toward it.

The young woman who had comforted the children was crying on the shoulder of the man Yocke had seen enter, the man with the gray hair and the skin stretched tight across his face.

'You a reporter?' the man asked.

'Yes.' Yocke looked at the children's chairs, decided they were too small, and lowered himself into a cross-legged position on the floor.

'I want you to write this down. Write it down and write it good. It's all the writing that Jane is ever gonna get.'

Yocke got out the notebook.

'Jane Wilkens was the mother of my children. Had two kids by her. We never lived together. Asked her to marry me years ago but she wouldn't. She knew I used to be on heroin and if I lived around these damn projects, I'd go off the wagon. But she couldn't live anywhere else. This was where her work was, these kids. These kids were her work. She was trying to save some of them.

'She grew up in the Jefferson projects, but got herself out. Got an education. Got a scholarship to George Washington and got a degree in biology. Went to Pennsylvania and got a masters. She worked for a couple years as a microbiologist, then gave it up and came back here to this church to run the day care. Work with the kids.'

'Why?'

'You been in those projects? Really looked? Try to imagine living in there. No privacy, walls paper thin, kids abused and hungry, trash everywhere, light bulbs out, doors kicked in, liquor sales out of one apartment and crack out of another, the white women from the suburbs buying theirs down on the streets, the smell of shit and piss and filth and hopelessness. Yeah, it stinks. It gets in your nose so bad you'll never get it out. I smelled it again coming down the street this evening.

'So the kids are growing up in this manure pile, growing up like little rats, without love, without food, without anybody to hug them. Jane wanted to give them what their mamas couldn't. She wanted to give them a little love. Maybe save a couple. Can't save 'em all, but maybe save a few. Their mamas – all strung out, head nursing, whoring, whatever will turn a dollar to get the stuff from the number-one man.'

'She took two kids to the emergency room last week,' the young woman said. 'One was starving to death even though she was eating – eating here, anyway – and the other had a bacterial infection of the lungs. Jane did things like that all the time.'

The man shook his head, faintly irritated. 'But Jane never tried to shut down the trade,' he said slowly, 'never interfered with anybody's addiction, never passed judgment, never talked to the police. She just tried to save the kids. The kids . . .'

'What's your name?'

'Name's Tom Shannon. I work for the city. Drive a street sweeper. I'm president of a chapter of Narcotics Anonymous. Biggest chapter in the city. Me, I try to do what I can to help the people who want to help themselves. I tried to get a chapter started over here in the Jeffersons, but there wasn't no interest. You gotta want to help yourself.

'Maybe that's what's wrong. Jane was trying to save a few little kids and I was trying to save the grownups that wanta save themselves, and nobody was doing anything for all these people who are locked in the cycle. Nobody was attacking the trade. So the trade killed Jane.'

'A man killed Jane.'

'No, the crack trade killed her. That guy who pulled the trigger, he was an addict and a dealer. He had it on him. So he ran from the cops. And he shot Jane because she was standing in front of him screaming. No other reason. She was just there. All the people who are making money from the crack business killed her as sure as if they pulled the trigger. They don't give a damn who they hurt. They don't give a damn if the world blows up, as long as they get theirs. *They* killed Jane.'

The young woman was sitting by herself now, drying her eyes, listening to Tom Shannon. He was looking straight into Yocke's eyes.

'Now I'm telling you and you can write it any way you want, but I'm not going to be a victim anymore. Jane was a victim and I was a victim. No more! *I'm not going to be a victim anymore!*'

9

'Bernie, this is Jefferson Brody. I got it! The widow signed.'

'Glad to hear it, Tee.'

'She was reluctant but—'

'Yeah. Ya did good. I thought you would. That's what I told the guys. Tee screwed the pooch but he'll make it good. Wait and see.'

'I appreciate—'

'Send me the papers. I'll be talking to you in a few days.'

'Bernie, have you found that woman? I'd—'

'Working on that, Tee. I'll be in touch.'

The phone went dead on T. Jefferson Brody. He cradled the receiver and sat staring at the dark cherry paneling on his office walls. He had had to pay Mrs Lincoln $450,000 for the check-cashing business but now didn't seem to be the time to lay that on Bernie. Although Bernie was a good client, he had his rough edges.

The black bitch with the big tits who had conned him and robbed him – she was going to pay. T. Jefferson Brody intended to teach her a lesson she would never forget. And that little weasel ambulance chaser who helped her. He rubbed his hands together as he contemplated his revenge.

But that would have to wait.

He buzzed his secretary on the intercom. 'Hilda, get me Senator Cherry's office, please.'

'Yes, Mr Brody.'

Thanos Liarakos completed the paperwork at the hospital's administration office, then took the suitcase to his wife's room on the third floor and helped her select an outfit from it. She made only one or two swipes at her hair with a comb and didn't bother with makeup or lipstick, although they were in the case. Liarakos said nothing. She was dressed and nervously pacing the room when a nurse arrived with a wheelchair for the grand exit.

'Where are we going?' Elizabeth asked, finally, when they were in the car.

As if she didn't know. Liarakos muttered. 'To the airport.'

'You mean we're not even going by the house so I can say good-bye to the children?'

'Oh, can it, Elizabeth! You talked to them this morning on the telephone and they're both in school right now.'

'Well, I just wanted to see my home again for a few minutes. And I need some other outfits.'

'I packed exactly the outfits you told me to pack.'

'I forgot a few.'

'You're going to the clinic *now. Right fucking now!*'

'You are a bastard.'

He pulled over to the curb. The driver behind honked and gestured as he went by. Liarakos paid no attention.

'You can get out here or you can go to the clinic. Your choice.'

'I don't have any money.'

He put the transmission in park and stared out the window.

'Oh, Thanos, you know how much I love you. You know how much I love the children. I'll leave the stuff alone. I *promise*! Tell you what, darling. Let's go home and put on some soft music and I'll put on that gorgeous negligée you got me for my birthday. I'll show you just how much I love you.' She caressed his arm, then his hair. 'Darling, it'll be just like it was when we were first married, on those Sunday mornings when there were just the two of us. Oh, Than—'

'You don't know what this costs me, Elizabeth. You really don't.'

'Darling, I—'

'You don't have *any* idea!' He pushed her hands away.

'You don't love *me*,' she snarled, 'You're just thinking of your precious practice, what your boss might think. Well, by God, I—'

Liarakos reached across her and opened the passenger door.

'Out.'

She began crying.

He sat watching the traffic flow by, his face averted, his right hand on the wheel and his right shoulder up.

She was still sobbing uncontrollably when a police cruiser pulled up alongside. The officer twirled his finger. Liarakos rolled down his window. 'Move it, Mac.'

He pulled the lever down into drive and got the car into motion. Beside him Elizabeth blew her nose on tissues and continued to sob.

Traffic on the expressway to Dulles rolled along at slightly illegal speeds all the way to the airport. Liarakos parked and got the suitcase out of the trunk. He came around the car and opened the door for Elizabeth. She made a production out of blowing her nose one last time and stuffing the tissue paper into the trash bag hanging from the cigarette lighter.

He took her arm and guided her toward the terminal.

'I've got five dollars and seventy-two cents in my purse.'

'You don't need money at the clinic.'

'But what if I want to get my hair done somewhere else? And I may need to take a taxi to the clinic.'

'They'll meet you at the airport. They have all the other times. Remember?'

'But Thanos, what if they don't? I'll be stranded. Give me a hundred to cover incidentals.'

'Elizabeth, for Christ's sake! You're just making it harder on both of us.'

'*You* have no idea how difficult this is for *me*. That's the problem. You only think of yourself. If you love me, think about *me*! I'm your *wife*, or have you forgotten?'

'I haven't forgotten.'

He gave the ticket to the agent and checked the bag. 'Window seat, please.'

'Just Mrs Liarakos?'

'Yes.'

The agent gave them the gate number. 'Boarding in fifteen minutes.'

'Thanks.'

They waited near the gate. Liarakos stood by the windows where he could see the shuttle buses going back and forth to the airplanes. Elizabeth walked away and found a seat by herself.

He watched her reflection in the glass. Every movement she made was like something from an old memory that you remember with pain. In the past when she had a moment she would remove her compact from her purse and check her reflection, touch up her hair, see that her eye shadow and lipstick were just so. Not today. She just sat there with her purse in her lap, her hands resting upon it, while she idly scanned people coming and going and sitting and reading.

When they called the plane Liarakos escorted her to the gate agent and handed him the ticket. He leaned toward her and whispered in her ear. 'Get well.'

She glanced at him, her face neutral, then went through the door into the shuttle bus.

He went back to the glass and watched her through the bus windows. She didn't look back at him. She sat staring straight ahead. She was still sitting like that when the passenger door closed and the bus pulled away.

That evening Captain Jake Grafton informed his wife that Lieutenant Toad Tarkington was getting orders to the staff of the Joint Chiefs, just as he desired.

'That's very nice,' Callie told Jake. 'Did you have to twist many arms to make it happen?'

'A couple.'

'Does Toad know yet?'

'Not yet. I think they'll tell him in a day or two.'

'You'll never guess who stopped me after class today to chat.'

Jake Grafton made an uninterested noise, then decided to humor her and take a stab at it. 'That commie professor, ol' what's-his-name.'

'No. It was that *Washington Post* reporter, Jack Yocke. He thanked me for the party and . . .'

Jake went back to today's newspaper think-piece on Soviet internal politics. For generations the forces at work inside the Communist Party had been Soviet state secrets and the subject of classified intelligence summaries that circulated inside the US military. Those summaries had been more guesses made by analysts based on poor, fragmentary information. Now the Soviets were baring all with an abandon that would make even Donald Trump blush.

As he mused on this curious miracle, Jake Grafton became aware of a questioning tone in his wife's voice, which had risen in pitch. 'Say again, dear?'

'I said. Jack suggested you and he have breakfast some morning. Would you like to do that?'

'No.'

The captain scanned the column to find his place.

'Well, why not?'

He lowered the paper and scrutinized his wife, who was poised with a ladle in one hand, looking at him with one eyebrow raised aloft. He had never been able to figure out how she got one eyebrow up but not the other. He had tried it a few times in the privacy of the bathroom with no success.

'We are not friends or social acquaintances. We haven't said two dozen words to each other. And I have no desire to know him better.'

'Jack is a brilliant, socially concerned journalist whom you should take the trouble to get to know. He's written an excellent book that you would enjoy and find informative: *The Politics of Poverty*.'

'He wants to pump me on what's going on inside the Pentagon. And there's absolutely nothing I can tell him. It'd be a waste of time for both of us.'

'Jake . . .'

'Callie, I don't *like* the guy. I'm not about to waste an hour listening to him try to pump me. No.'

She sighed and went back to stirring the chili. Jake rustled the newspaper and raised it ostentatiously.

'I've been reading his book,' she said, undaunted. 'He gave me a copy.'

'I saw it on the nightstand.'

'It's excellent. Well written, lots of insights that—'

'If I ever become CNO and get an overpowering itch to leak something to the newspapers, Jack Yocke will be the first guy I call. I promise.'

Callie changed the subject. Her husband grunted once or twice, then she abandoned conversation. Jake didn't notice. He was engrossed in an account of Fidel Castro's latest speech, in which the dictator announced that the rice and meat ration of the Cuban people had been cut in half. Again. To two ounces of meat and a pound of rice per week. In addition, Cuba would henceforth purchase its oil from Mexico, not the Soviet Union, and it would cost more, a lot more. This meant more sacrifices, which Castro was confident the Cuban people would take in their stride. The Cuban comrades had been betrayed by their Soviet brothers in socialism, but *viva la Revolución!*

The socially concerned journalist of whom Callie spoke was thinking impure thoughts. He had picked up Tish Samuels at the apartment that she shared with a mousy girlfriend and they had gone to a postwedding party at the home of a fellow reporter who had eloped several weeks ago with an oral surgeon. Earlier in the evening Yocke had been miserable company, but now, several drinks and two hours later, he was feeling fairly chipper and more sociable. Perhaps it was the cheerful bonhomie of his colleagues, who were ribbing the newly weds unmercifully. Whatever, in spite of himself Jack Yocke had absorbed some of the glow.

Just now he stood half listening to one of the sports columnists expound on the coming NFL playoffs while he watched Tish Samuels on the other side of the room. She had glanced this way several times and was aware of his scrutiny.

The next time she looked, he gave her a wide grin. She returned it. He raised his glass at her and took a sip. She gestured with her glass in reply and nodded.

Yes indeed, in spite of everything, life goes stumbling on. And Jack Yocke did like life.

So he sipped his drink and listened to the sportswriter and assessed Tish's womanly charms as she moved along talking to everyone. She was a tall woman, but she certainly had it in all the right places. Jack Yocke took a deep breath and exhaled slowly as he waited for her to turn his way again.

The sportswriter rambled on. The most interesting events in the world were happening in the NFL. *This* was the Redskins' year. Hallelujah!

Tish turned. She smiled broadly and blew him a kiss. Jack Yocke grinned foolishly, exposing every tooth in his head.

An hour later in the car, she hummed softly while he kissed her. He kissed her again and she returned it with a fervor that he found most pleasant.

Finally, reluctantly, he inserted the key in the ignition and brought the engine to life. 'Where to?' he asked.

'Your place?'

'Got a roommate too. He's home tonight.'

'The bookstore.'

He put the car in motion. In the empty parking lot in front of the strip shopping center, he parked and sat staring at the blank windows.

'Come on,' Tish said, reaching for the door handle. 'Let's.'

Jack Yocke dug in the glove box and pulled out something red and frilly. 'Would you wear these?' he asked hesitantly.

There were two of them. She held the soft cloth up so the light caught it. 'What are these? *Garters?*'

'Yeah.' He shrugged and grinned hopefully.

His grin was sort of cute, in a pathetic sort of way, Tish decided. 'A little kink, eh?'

'Well, they're just—'

'You're kidding, right?'

'No, I just thought . . .'

'Garters.' She sighed. 'Jesus, I haven't worn garters since the senior prom.' She took a good look at his face. 'Oh, all right, you pervert.'

She fumbled for the seat belt release. He reached down to help. She pushed his hands away. 'I'm not going to put them on here in the car, for Christ's sake!'

'I—'

'Oh, shut up! Garters!'

Really, Tish thought as she walked toward the door of the bookstore, feeling in her purse for her keys. Is this my fate at thirty-one? Sex with oversized adolescent boys whose ideas of erotica came straight from a whorehouse?

'Are there no men left?' she murmured.

Jack Yocke missed that comment. He was furtively scanning the parking lot.

If he weren't so good-looking and so thoroughly nice . . .

She opened the door and held it for him, then relocked it. The only light in the store was that coming through the display windows from the big lights in the parking area. She walked by the light switches without touching them and led the way between the book racks toward the little office by the back door. Behind her she heard Yocke stumble over something.

The second time he stumbled she heard books fall. She took his hand and led him around the racks to the office. Yocke helped her with her coat. The scruffy couch held a half dozen cartons of books, which they set on the floor.

As they undressed in the darkness, she couldn't resist. 'Why garters?'

'You don't have to wear them if you don't want to.'

'Then why'd you ask?'

'Well—'

He touched her bare skin and all her doubts dissolved.

Afterward, with him on top and panting, she said, 'We forgot the garters.'

He caressed her thighs. 'It doesn't matter.'

'You're a pretty good lover, y'know. For a pervert.'

He kissed her.

'Really, be honest about the garters. I want to know.'

'You mean that?'

'Yes.'

'Well, I've found that women sometimes change their minds. Yet if I give them something innocuous to think about, it takes their minds off *sex* and I get laid more often.'

'Oooh . . . youuu . . .'

'Now admit it, you were so busy thinking about the garters that you forgot to have second thoughts. Isn't that so?'

Tish bucked once and pushed and he flopped off onto the floor with a thud. She closed the office door and flipped on the lights. It took several seconds for her eyes to adjust. Yocke was on his back amid the boxes, looking a little dazed.

She found the garters and pulled them on. Then she stood beside him on one leg and used the other foot to rub his chest and stomach.

'Do you like?'

'Gawd almighty,' Jack Yocke said.

Evansville, Indiana, patrolman Harrison Ronald Ford, alias Sammy Z, watched the fat white man stroll down the sidewalk looking neither left nor right. Watching him, you would have thought he owned the sidewalk and all the houses and was out collecting rent. Everything about him said he was *the man*.

Harrison Ronald shifted his buttocks on the cold concrete stoop where he was perched and watched the man check house numbers. When he arrived in the dim glow of the nearby streetlight, he glanced at Ford, then started up the steps on which Ford was sitting.

'Going somewhere, Fatty?'

'Got an appointment.'

'Great. I'll bet you got a name too.'

'Tony Anselmo.'

'Why don't you wait down there on the sidewalk and I'll check inside. Okay?'

As Anselmo retreated to the sidewalk, Harrison Ronald checked the street again. No traffic. No one in the parked cars. No strollers or tourists other than the guards posted on each of the corners. Although the guards weren't armed, each of them was within ten feet of a concealed Uzi.

Except for the guards, this appeared to be a typical lower-middle-class black neighborhood. No crack was sold here.

Everything appeared normal to Ford's practiced eyes.

Harrison rapped on the door and disappeared through it when it opened.

Inside the hallway sat another guard with an Uzi on his lap. He nodded as Harrison walked by. The second man locked and bolted the door behind him.

Freeman McNally was in the kitchen eating cake, drinking milk, and reading a newspaper. He was twenty pounds or so overweight and had a hairline in full retreat. Still, encased within the fat was muscle. When he moved he was light on his feet. As Ford entered he looked up from the paper.

'Guy named Tony Anselmo says he has an appointment.'

'What's he look like?'

'Fat honkey, about fifty or so. Prosperous.'

'Let him in. After you frisk him, go on back out front.'

'Sure, Freeman.'

Out on the sidewalk, Ford said, 'They heard of you. Go on in.' He followed Anselmo up the stairs.

Inside, the guard with the Uzi centered it on Anselmo's ample middle. 'Against the wall and spread 'em.'

Ford quickly patted him down, checked his belt front and back, his crotch, and his ankles. 'You do that like a cop,' Anselmo rumbled.

'He's clean,' Ford told the guard, then went back out onto the stoop and resumed his seat.

Harrison Ronald had heard of Fat Tony Anselmo. Sitting on the stoop smoking a cigarette and listening to the noises of the city at night, he tried to recall what he had read in the police intelligence briefing books. Anselmo was a soldier for a New York crime family, the Zubin Costello outfit. Bernie Shapiro was one of the three or four key lieutenants, and Anselmo was supposed to work for him. Suspected of a dozen or so hits in his younger days, Tony Anselmo had once plea-bargained a murder charge down to carrying a concealed weapon and was back on the street after six months in the can. That was the only time he had ever been in jail.

It would have been nice, Ford mused, if Freeman had invited him to remain. Sooner or later, if he lived long enough, but not yet.

As he sat on the stoop smoking, Ford speculated on whether Anselmo had asked for this meeting or Freeman had. And he formed various tentative hypotheses about the business being discussed. Certainly not the purchase of raw product: Freeman got all he could handle from the West Coast.

Money, Ford decided. They were probably doing a deal to wash or invest money. Ford assumed the Costello family had a lot of experience in both activities.

Or perhaps bribery of public officials. That was certainly a possibility.

When the glowing tip of the cigarette reached the filter, Ford lit another one from the stub. He automatically checked the street-corner guards yet again, then watched the smoke swirl on the gentle breeze.

Cold. Tonight was going to be cold. Harrison Ronald turned up the collar of his leather jacket and glanced at his watch.

'Why a bookstore?' Jack Yocke asked.

He and Tish were lying on the couch in the bookstore office in the darkness with Yocke's coat thrown over them. She was still wearing the garters.

'It sounds silly now,' she said. 'But I had to make a living at something, and I like books, so I drove around until I found a spot without a bookstore for two miles in any direction, and I rented that spot.'

'Sensible approach.'

'I thought I was very conservative. I love books. I was so certain the store would be a surefire hit. Ha! I'm barely eating. Still, two years in the business and I'm current on all my bills. That's something.'

'Indeed it is. A lot of people can't say that.'

'Now tell me, why a newspaper?'

'Oh, amazingly enough, in spite of the hours, in spite of the deadlines and the editors, I thought I'd like it. Talk about optimism! Sometimes I feel like a mortician. Or a minister. All the shattered lives. I spend my days galloping from tragedy to tragedy. "Who what when where why, ma'am, and can you spell the perpetrator's name one more time?" I see as much blood as an ambulance driver. I ask the kinds of questions the morticians and chaplains don't have to ask. "Why do you think your husband stabbed you, Ms Butcher?" "What did the gunman say before he shot you, Mr Target?" "After he raped, mutilated, and murdered her, why do you keep insisting he's such a good boy, Mrs Spock?" '

'It must be challenging.'

'It would be,' Jack Yocke agreed, 'if you had enough time to do it right, to write it right. You never do. You look at the blood – when you can get to the scene before they cart out the bodies – telephone everyone you can think of, then write six hundred words for the first edition which the editor chops in half or doesn't like at all. Then wait, wait, check, check. Up one blind alley after another. Finally you get a good story, only to get buried under a human wave attack of other reporters as some editor finally decides that there really is a good story here on Yocke's supposed beat but Yocke can't cover it all by himself.'

'So why do you do it?'

'I don't know.' He really didn't. At night he went home to his apartment either completely drained or completely frustrated. The stories, when he got some, were never good enough. The black ink on the newsprint never captured the insanity, the fear, the terror, the grief, the desperation of the people who live the lives that make police news. The waste, the future smeared all over the floor – he could never get that into the stories.

'People just read the paper while they drink their morning coffee,' he told her, 'then throw it away. Or wrap the garbage in it. Or use it to line the cat box. Then, hi-ho, off to work or aerobics class or luncheon at the club.'

'What else could you do?'

'I've never been able to think of anything. And this police beat can't last forever.'

She got up off the couch and turned on the light. She took off the garters as he watched and handed them to him. Then she began putting on her clothes.

'Get dressed and run me home. I have to get a little sleep, then be down here scrubbed and cheerful to open this place at nine. That's when the little old ladies like to come in to see if we have any new "spicy" books.'

' "Spicy"?'

'Bodice rippers. Soft-core porn. That's what pays the rent around here.'

'You're kidding.'

'I wish I were. I sold three Amy Tans last year and just one Fay Weldon. It's enough to make you cry.'

'Maybe you need a better location.'

'What I need is to write a sizzling world-class fuck book, one so hot it'll melt an old maid's panties.' She eyed him as she buttoned her blouse. 'That's what I'm scribbling on. You want to see it?'

'Sure.'

Tish opened the desk drawer and pulled it out. She had about a hundred pages of manuscript that she had whacked out on the old typewriter on the corner of the desk. He flipped through the pages, scanning.

'The rule is no four-letter words. His cock is always his love member.'

'Looks fine to me,' Yocke said, and handed it back. He bent down to retrieve his trousers.

When he straightened up she was reading carefully. After a moment she tossed the pile of paper back in the drawer. 'It's shit, I know, but that's what sells. And goddamn, if shit sells, that's what I'm going to write.'

Twenty minutes later, in front of her apartment building, she said, 'Don't get out. I can make it to the door.'

He bussed her on the cheek.

'Are you going to call me again, or was this just a one-night stand?'

'I'll call you.'

'Promise?'

'Yeah.'

After he drove away he felt grubby. Oh well, what's one more lie in a world full of them.

Harrison Ronald – Sammy Z – got off work at five A.M. One of his colleagues dropped him at the apartment house he called home. He went upstairs and made a pot of coffee. Then, at the kitchen table, he tackled the crossword puzzle in the early edition of the *Post*.

After Tony Anselmo left Freeman, Sammy Z and one of the other lieutenants were sent to a crack lab in a sleazy motel on New York Avenue. There they picked up a bundle, watched the chemists at work, and flirted with a saucy nineteen-year-old with strawberry-sized nipples – and an aversion to brassieres – while they waited for their escort car to arrive. When it did and the three gunmen it contained had leered over the upthrust nipples, the group set out to deliver the crack to street rings at two locations. There the distributors had turned over the night's receipts, about sixty grand by the looks of it. And Freeman was currently selling at eleven locations in the metro area!

Sammy Z drove the money to Freeman's brother in a little house he was using for three or four nights. The elder McNally was the treasurer and accountant and payroll man. His office changed regularly and randomly. Freeman always knew, and he gave Sammy the location as he walked out the door.

Delivering dope or money was tricky. The lieutenant rode in the backseat of the car with the Uzi loaded and ready on his lap. The guard car behind always contained two or three men also armed with Uzis and pistols. The lead driver kept the two-car motorcade well within the speed limit, obeyed all the traffic laws, and never sped up to make it through a yellow light. The routes were agreed on in advance and snaked through the city without pattern. The same vehicle was never used two nights in a row.

The whole operation reminded Harrison Ronald of those old black-and-white *Untouchables* TV shows, with Al Capone and Frank Nitty delivering beer in Chicago and all the hoods packing Thompson sub-machine guns. Big guns and big bucks. White hoods and white cops – well, maybe things are a little different today.

The sky was graying nicely through the dirty kitchen window when Harrison Ronald finished the crossword puzzle and his third cup of coffee simultaneously. He turned off the coffeepot, got a conservative cloth coat out of the closet, and locked the door behind him.

Right now he was driving a fifteen-year-old, rusted-out Chrysler that belonged to Freeman McNally. It had once been royal blue. Now it was just dirty and dark. The seats were trashed. Damage to the left front fender and hood had been repaired with a sledgehammer by an ignorant enthusiast. The windshield was chipped and cracked. The only feature that might capture the eye of a careful observer was the new Michelin radials, mounted backward to hide the manufacturer's name on the sidewalls. All in all, the car looked like a typical DC heap.

As an observer might suspect, the Chrysler was difficult to start – damn near impossible on cold mornings. This particular December morning Harrison Ronald ground and ground with the starter while he played with the manual choke.

Eventually the engine fired. It strangled when he pushed the choke off too soon. With a sigh he engaged the starter again. Finally, with coaxing, the engine rumbled to life and gave signs of sustained combustion.

Still, she idled rough and spewed a gray haze that was visible in the rearview mirror. That, however, was because the original six-cylinder mill had been replaced with a huge old V-8 hemi that had been breathed upon by someone who knew exactly what he was about. Under the crinkled hood was a work of art, complete with racing cams, valves, and pistons, hogged-out valve ports, a high-capacity fuel pump, and a four-barrel carb. To handle the extra power the go-fast man had added a four-speed transmission and beefed up the suspension and brakes. This car could lay rubber for two hundred feet.

When the engine had warmed and the idle smoothed somewhat, Harrison Ronald slipped the clutch to get out of the parking place.

He couldn't resist: he goosed it once on the street and the tires howled and smoked. With a little paint and bodywork, he told himself, this would be a *nice* car.

He checked his rearview mirrors constantly and darted through lights as they turned red. Finally satisfied that no one was following, he headed for the beltway. Rush-hour traffic was still flowing into the city, so the trip outbound was unimpeded. Once on the beltway, he followed the signs for I-95 south, toward Richmond.

The morning was gray and windy. The rain of a few days ago had soaked into the thirsty earth and settled the dust. Still, as dry as the fall had been, the earth needed more.

He exited the interstate at Fredericksburg. Five minutes later he drove past the office of a motel and went around to the back side, which faced a hill, and parked.

Harrison Ronald stood in the nearly empty lot and stretched. He should have been in bed two hours ago. Get a good job, his grandmother had said, something regular, with a future.

He knocked on the door of room 212.

'Just a minute.'

The door opened. 'Come on in.'

The white man was tall and lean, with a prominent Adam's apple and a nose to match. He grinned and shook Ford's hand. His name was Thomas F. Hooper. Special Agent Hooper was in charge of the FBI's drug enforcement division. Hooper had recruited Ford from the Evansville police department. A little temporary undercover work, he said, that will do wonders for your police career. Both lies, he now cheerfully acknowledged.

'Want some breakfast?'

'I could eat something.'

'Great. Freddy's over at McDonald's getting a bagful. He'll be back in a bit.'

Ford fell into a chair and stretched out full-length.

'So how's it going?'

'Freeman's a busy fellow. Making money like he owned the mint.'

Hooper got a cassette recorder from his leather valise and plugged it into the socket under the desk. He dictated his name and the date and Ford's name, then played it back to make sure it was working.

Harrison Ronald watched this operation with heavy eyelids.

'You're tired.'

'Amen.'

'Coffee will perk you up. You want to start now?'

'Okay.'

It had been a week since Ford had talked to Hooper. So Ford covered the past week minute by minute – names, descriptions, addresses, drug quantities, estimated amounts of money, everything Ford could recall. He had taken no notes. Written nothing down: that would have been too dangerous. Still, after eight months, he knew exactly what Hooper and the Justice Department wanted, so it flowed forth without prompting.

Freddy, Hooper's assistant, came in ten minutes after they started. Ford kept on talking as the men shared coffee and breakfast biscuits stuffed with eggs, cheese, and sausage.

Ford talked for almost an hour. When he finished Hooper had questions, lots of them. That went on for another hour with only two short pauses to change cassettes. When they were through Hooper knew what Ford had observed this past week almost as well as Ford did.

Finally Hooper said, 'So what do you think?'

Harrison Ronald held out his coffee cup for a refill, which Freddy provided from a thermos. 'I think there's too much crack in the city. They can't move the stuff fast enough. And I think Freeman is getting, or is about to get, a lot of pressure from the Costello mob to wash his money with them, probably at a higher cost. Somebody removed Walter Harrington and Second Potomac from the game. Freeman and his fellow dealers got some problems.'

'What do you think Freeman'll do?'

'I don't know. I haven't been able to get a hint. I do know this: the guy is sharp as a razor. He didn't get where he is by letting people cut themselves in on his action, by taking less and liking it. I think Freeman might fight back. He's definitely the man for it.'

Freddy disagreed. He was in his late forties, also white, and had chased dopers since he joined the FBI. 'I think Freeman and the others will cut back on the amount of coke they're bringing in. They have to do that or expand, the market by fighting each other. They all have a real good thing here and they've made a lot of money. A *lot* of money. They won't be able to retire and live the good life if they get into heavy ordnance.'

'There's no love lost between the big hitters,' Harrison Ronald objected.

'Business is business and money is money,' Freddy said.

'What do you guys want me to do if the shooting starts?'

'Run like hell,' Hooper muttered.

'For Christ's sake, don't kill any civilians,' Freddy added.

'Cut and run?'

'Yep,' said Hooper. 'You're no good to anybody if you're dead.'

'Do you guys have enough?'

'We got enough to lock up Freeman for thirty years, and most of the people he works for.'

'And the cops and politicians on the take?'

Hooper turned off the recorder and removed the cassette. He marked it with a pen from his shirt pocket.

'And the cops and politicians?' Ford prompted.

'You got a lot. More than we hoped for. But if someone puts you in the cemetery we got nothing. Oh, we know a ton, but we won't have a witness to get it into evidence.'

'I don't think I'll get into the inner circle anytime soon. Freeman's got four lieutenants, and two of them are his brothers. They're all millionaires many times over and each of them would go to the grave for Freeman McNally.'

'Maybe that can be arranged,' Freddy said.

'What d'ya mean by that?'

'Nothing to worry about. Gimme some particulars on each one.' Freddy pulled out a pencil and a pocket notebook.

'Now wait just a fucking minute! We're cops. I'm not going to ice any of these guys, except in self-defense.'

'We're not asking you to kill anybody and we're sure as hell not going to. Jesus! This isn't Argentina! But maybe we can get one of these guys off the street for a while and leave a vacancy at the trough for you.'

The undercover officer talked for ten minutes. He told them everything he knew; the names of the wives, the mistresses, the kids, what they ate, what they laughed at, how they liked their liquor, and how often they used their own products.

In the silence that followed his recitation, Hooper asked, 'How's that car running?'

'Real sweet.' Ford smiled faintly. 'You gotta go for a ride sometime. It's the hottest thing I ever sat in.'

'Stay alive, Harrison. Please.'

'I'll do my best.' Harrison Ronald's smile broadened into a grin. 'That's a promise.'

'You can quit anytime, you know.'

'Yeah.'

'I mean it. We've got a lot more than we ever thought we'd get. If you want to go back to Evansville, just say so and you'll be on your way today.'

'I'll stick a while longer. I confess, I'm curious about Tony Anselmo and how he fits in.'

'Curiosity has killed a lot of cops.'

'I know that.'

On the way back to Washington the thought occurred to him, not for the first time, that he should have stayed in the Marines. At the age of twenty, after two years of college, he had joined the Corps. He had done a four year hitch, the last two on Okinawa where he had been an instructor in unarmed combat. He had grown to love the Corps. But his girl was in Indiana and she wouldn't leave. So he took his discharge and went home and took the test for the police while he was trying to talk her into marrying him.

He got accepted by the police the afternoon before she ditched him. The oldest story in the world. She had dated other men while he was gone. He was a great guy but she wasn't in love. She hoped they'd always be friends.

He had learned a lot in the Corps, things that would keep him alive now, like managing stress and self-confidence. And unarmed combat. As a rule street gangs didn't contain experts at fighting with their hands. Oh, occasionally you ran into a karate guy who thought he was pretty tough. But while he was getting ready to give you one of those lethal kicks, you went for him in an aggressive, brutally violent way and broke his leg, then crushed his windpipe. And these Uzi toters never practiced with their weapons. Murder was their game, not combat.

He thought about murder for a while. His murder.

When this was over, he might go back to the Corps. Why not?

10

Jake Grafton had no more than walked through the door Wednesday evening when the telephone rang. Callie answered it. After exchanging pleasant greetings with whoever was on the other end, she offered the instrument to Jake. 'It's for you.'

'Hello.'

'Captain Grafton, this is Jack Yocke, *Washington Post.*'

'Hi.'

'Sorry to bother you at home, but we just got a story from a stringer in South America that perhaps you can help me with. It seems that the US Army sent some people to Colombia and they shot it out with Chano Aldana's bodyguards and arrested him. Apparently there were some Colombian police along, but the word we get is that it was a US Army operation all the way.'

'Why do you think I can help you with that story?' Callie was standing there watching him, futilely trying to push her hair back off her forehead. She must really like this jerk, though Jake hadn't the foggiest idea why.

'I've been doing some checking,' Yocke said, 'since I saw you at Aldana's arraignment. Apparently you're the senior officer in the anti-drug operations section of the Joint Staff. So this little matter had to cross your desk.'

'You haven't answered my question, Mr Yocke. Why do you think I can help you with your story?'

'You're saying you won't?'

'Mr Yocke, I drink coffee in the morning and go to lunch every day. Everything else I do at my office is classified. I cannot help you.' Callie frowned. Jake turned his back on her. 'I suggest you try the Pentagon's public information office.'

'Do you have that number handy, Captain?'

'Try the phone book.' Jake cradled the receiver without saying good-bye.

'Jake, that was rude.'

'Oh, Callie!'

'Well, it was.'

'That damned kid calls me at home and asks me to give him classified information? Bullshit! You tell him the next time he's conjugating some verbs for you that he had better never pull this stunt on me again or I'll rearrange his nose the next time I meet him.'

'I'm sure he didn't know the information was classified,' Callie said, but she was talking to herself. Her husband was on his way to the bedroom.

Well, she told herself, Jake was right. A reporter should know better. Yocke's young. He'll learn. And fast, if he spends much time around Jake.

That evening when Harrison Ronald arrived at Freeman McNally's house for work, Ike Randolph met him at the door.

'Freeman wants to see you.'

Ike grinned. It was more of a sneer, Harrison thought, and he had seen it before, whenever someone was about to lose a pound of flesh. Ike enjoyed the smell of fear.

In spite of himself, Harrison Ronald felt his heart accelerate. For some reason his armpits were instantly wet.

Ike patted him down. That was routine, but this evening Ike was more thorough than usual – on purpose, no doubt.

Ike Randolph, convicted armed robber, convicted child rapist – you had to have the milk of human kindness oozing from your pores to like Ike. He had, Harrison knew, grown up in the same cesspool that spawned Freeman. Mom McNally had fed them both and paid bail when they got arrested for shoplifting and, later, stripping cars. She hadn't had the money to bail them out when they were caught mugging tourists. Ike had had the gun and taken the felony fall; Freeman had pleaded guilty to a misdemeanor. Yet after his plea Freeman spent ten more days in jail while Ike walked on probation. The two of them still liked to laugh about that when they were drinking.

Several years later a judge decided to let Ike do a little time after a six-year-old girl required surgery on her vagina and uterus following Ike's attentions. He had had a couple of minor possession convictions since – nothing serious.

This evening Ike gave Harrison a little shove after he finished frisking him.

'Hey!'

'Shut up, motherfuck! Go on. Freeman's waiting.'

McNally was sitting on a sofa in the living room at the back of the house. Both his brothers were there too. Ike closed the door behind them.

'Called you this morning,' Freeman said.

Harrison Ronald concentrated on managing his face. Look innocent!

'Where were you?'

'Out. I do that every now and then.'

'Don't gimme no sass, Z. I don't take sass from nobody.'

'Hey, Freeman. I just went out to get some tail.'

'What's her name?' This from the eldest of the brothers, Ruben. He was the accountant.

'You don't know her.'

Freeman stood up and approached Ford, who was still trying to decide if he should break McNally's arm and use him for a shield when Freeman slapped him. 'You weren't at your pad last Wednesday either. You're gonna tell me the truth, bro, or I'm gonna unscrew your head and shit in it. *What's her name?*'

This appeared to be an excellent time to look scared, and Harrison did so. It was ridiculously easy. The fear was boiling. 'Her name's Ruthola and she's married. We got this little thing going. I sneak over on Wednesday morning when the kid's at day care. Honest, Freeman, it's just a piece of ass.'

Freeman grunted and examined Ford's eyes. Ford forced himself to meet his gaze. McNally's deep brown eyes looked almost black. The urge to attack was almost overpowering: Harrison flexed his hands as he fought it back.

'Call her.'

'Christ, her ol' man might be home.'

'So this'll be the end of a good thing. A piece of ass ain't worth your life, is it?'

'Not to me.'

'Call her.'

Freeman McNally picked up the phone on the table by the couch and motioned to the one on the other side of the room. Ford lifted the indicated instrument from its cradle and dialed.

It rang on the other end. Once. Twice. Three times. Harrison held his breath.

'Hello.' It was a woman's voice.

'Ruthola, this is Sammy.'

Silence. At that instant Harrison Ronald Ford knew he was a dead man. A chill surged through him. Then her voice came in a hiss. 'Why'd you call? You *promised* you wouldn't!'

'Hey, babe, I won't be able to make it next week. Gonna be out of town. Just wanted you to know.'

'Oh, honey, don't call me when he's *home*!' The words just poured out. 'You *promised*! Call me tomorrow at ten, lover.' She hung up.

Harrison Ronald cradled the phone. He felt a powerful urge to urinate.

Freeman snickered once. He rubbed his fingers through his hair while everyone in the room watched. 'She a nice piece?' he said, finally, the corners of his lips twitching perceptibly.

Harrison tried to shrug nonchalantly. The shrug was more of a nervous jerk.

'Where's her ol' man work?'

Ford's stomach was threatening to heave. This, he decided, would be a good place for the truth. He got it out: 'He's FBI.'

They stared at him with their mouths open, frozen. Harrison tried another grin, which came out, he thought, like a clown leering.

'You *stupid*—' Ike roared from behind him. '*Of all the*—'

Freeman giggled. Then he laughed. The others began laughing. The laughter rose to a roar. Freeman McNally held his sides and pounded his thigh.

Harrison turned slowly. Even Ike was laughing. Harrison Ronald joined in. The relief was so great he felt a twinge of hysteria. The tears rolled down his cheeks as his diaphragm flapped uncontrollably.

Eight months ago, when Hooper had told him that someday he might need an alibi and introduced him to Ruthola, he hadn't anticipated it would be like this, hadn't understood that he would be so taut he almost twanged.

Ruthola Barnes, wife of Special Agent Ziggy Barnes, she had known. 'I've done this before,' she told him then. 'Trust me. Just say you're Sammy and talk to me like we just got out of bed, like we're both still naked and standing in the kitchen making coffee. I'll do the rest.'

That was eight months ago. He hadn't seen her since. Yet when he needed her, she was there.

Ah, Ziggy Barnes, you are a lucky, lucky man.

The key to success for a trial lawyer lies in preparation, and no one did it better than Thanos Liarakos. Thursday morning he began to submerge himself in the reams and reams of witness interrogation transcripts that were spewing from the prosecutor's office just as fast as the folks over there could run an industrial-size copy machine.

There were going to be a lot of transcripts, tens of thousands of pages, the prosecutor had told the judge. The people answering the questions were drug dealers, wholesalers, smugglers – pilots, guards, boat crewmen, drivers, lookouts, and so on – people from every nook and cranny of the drug business. At some point in their interrogation by police or FBI or DEA they were asked where they got the drug, when, how much, and of course, from whom.

Liarakos' associates had spent the last two days going over this pile and placing small squares of yellow sticky paper at every passage that they thought might be of interest. The difficulty, of course, was that at this stage of trial preparation the prosecutor still had not decided on a list of witnesses. So a lot of the material being read by the defense attorneys would be superfluous, unless Liarakos wanted to try to subpoena a witness himself and introduce testimony he hoped would be exculpatory.

Exculpatory, a nifty little word that meant confuse the hell out of the jurors.

Confusion and deceit were at the very heart of the trial process. The theory that comfortable law professors and appellate judges liked to cite stated that in the thrust and parry of adversarial combat – somehow, for reasons only a psychiatrist would find of interest, these legal thinkers still believed in medieval trial by combat – the truth would be revealed. Revealed to whom was a question never addressed. Perhaps it was best for everyone that the philosophical questions were left to mystics and the tactics and ethics to the trial lawyers. 'The American legal system isn't going to be reformed anytime soon, so we're stuck with it' – Thanos Liarakos had made this remark on several occasions to young associates appalled at their first journey into the morass.

The meat of the defense lawyer's job was to ensure that the truth revealed in the courtroom melodrama was in the best interests of his client. Thanos Liarakos was very good at that.

He had already come to the conclusion that the point of his attack had to be on the jury's perception of Chano Aldana. He had assumed all along that the prosecution had sufficient evidence to convince any twelve men and women that Chano Aldana was imbedded to his eyes in the drug-smuggling business. Yet there was more to it than that. The whole thrust of the government's case was that Aldana was the kingpin of the entire Medellín cartel, some Latin American ogre who bought men's souls and terrorized and murdered those he couldn't buy. Liarakos wanted the jury to believe that the prosecutor, William C. Bader, had to prove that Aldana *was* the devil incarnate or they could not convict.

Everything Liarakos did or said at trial would be designed to force the jury to the question, Is Chano Aldana the personification of evil? Is this man sitting here with us today Adolf Hitler's insane bastard? Is this slightly overweight gentleman in the sports coat from Sears the spiritual heir of Ivan the Terrible? If Liarakos could induce the jury to raise the bar high enough, the prosecutor's evidence would fall short.

Liarakos' primary asset was Aldana himself. He looked so average, so normal. He would be dressed appropriately. He would smile in the right places and look sad in the right places. And regardless of the testimony of the prosecution's witnesses, Chano Aldana would continue to look like an underdog. Even the sheer weight and number of the prosecution's witnesses would be turned against the government – Liarakos would ask, After all these years, after all the money spent and hundreds – nay, thousands – of people questioned, is this *all* the government has? *Is this all?*

The difficulty was going to be controlling Aldana. He appeared to be pathologically adverse to taking direction from anyone and he had all the charm of a rabid dog. Yet there must be a way . . .

He was musing along these lines when Judith Lewis, his chief assistant, brought in another stack of transcripts festooned with yellow stickies.

She put the pile on his credenza, then sat down. When Liarakos looked up, she said, 'I don't think they've got it.'

'Explain.'

'If this sample of transcripts is representative of the government's evidence, they don't have enough to get a conviction. Most of this stuff is inadmissible hearsay. They might get it into evidence if we were stupid enough to make Aldana's character an issue, but not otherwise. In this whole pile there is not one possible witness who had direct contact with Aldana.'

'They must have better stuff. They just haven't given it to us yet.'

'No, sir. I'll bet you any sum I can raise they don't have it.' She swallowed hard. 'Chano Aldana is going to walk.'

Liarakos examined her face carefully. 'That's our job, Judith. We're *trying* to get him acquitted.'

'But he's guilty!'

'Who says?'

'Oh, don't give me that crap. He's guilty as Cain.' She crossed her legs and turned her head toward the window.

'He isn't guilty until the jury says he is.'

'You can believe that if it makes you feel any better, but I don't. He's taken credit for arranging the murders of at least three Colombian presidential candidates. I spent thirty minutes with the man yesterday.' She sat silently for a moment recalling the meeting, then shuddered. 'He did it,' she said. 'He had them killed, like they were cockroaches.'

'Colombia didn't choose to try him for murder, Judith. Colombia extradited him to the United States. We're not defending him from a murder charge.'

'Colombia *couldn't* try him. Get serious! In 1985 forty-five leftist guerrillas drove an armored car into the basement of the Colombian Palace of Justice. They held the place for a day and executed all the justices. Aldana hired them. Over a hundred people died – were murdered – that day. Try Aldana in Colombia? My God, wake up! Listen to yourself!'

'Judith, you don't *know* he did that! We're lawyers. Even if he committed a thousand crimes, he isn't *guilty* until a jury convicts him.'

'Semantics,' Judith Lewis muttered contemptuously. 'I spent my child-hood learning the difference between good and bad, and now, all grown up and wearing two-hundred-dollar dresses, with an expensive educa-tion. I sit here listening to you argue that evil is all in the label. *Bullshit! Fucking bullshit!* I *know* Chano Aldana is guilty as charged on every count in the American indictment, and on probably another two thousand counts that haven't been charged. He is a dope smuggler, a terrorist, an extortionist, a man killer, a murderer of women and unborn babies. He deserves to roast in the hottest fire in hell.'

'Only if the government can prove it,' Thanos Liarakos pleaded. 'Only if the jury *says* the government proved it.'

'The government hasn't got it.'

'Then they shouldn't have indicted him.'

'I quit,' she said simply.

She walked for the door, opened it, and passed through. She left the door standing open.

Liarakos sat for a moment thinking about what she had just said. Then he went after her. She was in her office putting on her coat. 'Ms Lewis, would you come back to my office, please, and discuss this matter further?'

Wearing her coat, she followed him past the secretary's workstation and, when he stood aside, preceded him into his office. He closed the door and faced her.

'What do you mean you quit?'

'I quit. That's plain English. It's exactly what I mean.'

'Do you mean you wish to work on some other case or perhaps for another partner?'

'No. I mean I quit this firm. I quit the legal profession. *I quit*! I am through trying to be a lawyer. I don't have the stomach for it.'

She brushed past him. She paused at the door. 'You can mail my last check to the Salvation Army. There's nothing in my office I want to come back for.'

'Take a few days off and think this over. You spent three years in law school and three years in practice. That's six years of your life.'

'No. I know you're doing what you think is right. But I don't think it's right. I don't *want* to think it's right.'

'Judith—'

'No, Mr Liarakos. I'm not going to squander another minute of my life arguing about a dope dealer's constitutional rights. I'm not going to touch another dollar earned by helping a dope dealer escape justice. No.'

This time when she left he didn't go after her.

He sat in his chair and stared at the transcripts.

A ball glove wrapped around a scruffy baseball lay on the credenza. He pulled on the glove and tossed the ball into it. The impact of the ball meeting the leather made a satisfying 'thock' which tingled his hand. The thumb of the glove was sweat stained. He had habitually raked it across his forehead to wipe away the perspiration. He did that now, enjoying the cool smoothness of the leather, then placed the glove back on the polished mahogany.

He kept a bottle of old scotch in the bottom drawer of his desk. He got it out and poured a shot into an empty coffee cup.

He was pouring a second when the phone rang.

'Yes.'

'There's a lady on the phone calling from California. She won't give her name. Says it's a personal matter.'

'My wife?'

'No, sir. I know her voice.'

'I'll take the call.'

The phone clicked.

'Hello,' he said. 'This is Thanos Liarakos.'

'Mr Liarakos, this is Karen Allison with the California Clinic?'

'Yes.'

'Your wife apparently left the clinic during the night, Mr Liarakos. We can't find her on the grounds. She took her suitcase with her.'

'Yes,' he said.

'I'm sorry, Mr Liarakos. We did what we could.'

'Yes,' he said, and gently cradled the telephone.

On Friday morning Henry Charon drove to Baltimore to find a pay telephone. He parked at a mall and located a bank of three phones near the men's room. Since he was early, he ate lunch in the food court, lingered over coffee, then strolled the mall from end to end. Finally, with five minutes to go, he walked to the pay phones and waited. A woman was busy explaining to her husband why the new sheets on sale were a bargain. She hung up a minute before the hour and walked away briskly, apparently the winner of the budget battle. She had glanced at Charon once, for no more than a second, and had not looked at him again.

Charon dialed. The number he was calling, according to Tassone, was a pay phone in Pittsburgh. The area code – 412 – was right, anyway. Charon had checked. When the operator came on the line he fed in quarters from a ten-dollar roll.

Tassone answered on the second ring. 'Yes.'

'You got my shipment?'

'Yes. Where and when?'

'Truck stop at Breezewood, Pennsylvania. Tomorrow at three.'

'Got it.' The connection broke.

Charon walked out of the mall and got in the car. Before he started it he carefully studied a map, then folded it neatly and stuck it above the visor.

Four hours later in Philadelphia he bought a ticket for tomorrow's seven-fourteen A.M. bus to Pittsburgh. He ate dinner in a fast-food restaurant, then drove around north Philly until he found a cheap motel, where he paid cash.

He was up at five A.M. He parked the car at a twenty-four-hour garage a half block from the bus station and was in the waiting room thirty minutes early.

The bus left right on the minute. Charon's luggage consisted only of a backpack, which rested on the seat beside him. There were eleven passengers. Charon sat near the back of the bus where the driver couldn't see him in his mirror.

Two seats forward, on the other side of the aisle, sat a couple that lit a marijuana cigarette thirty minutes into the trip, just after the bus had reached cruising speed on the Pennsylvania Turnpike. The odor was sickly sweet and heavy. Charon cracked his window and waited for the driver to see the obvious smoke cloud and stop the bus. The bus never stopped. After a second cigarette the man and woman drifted off to sleep.

Henry Charon watched the countryside pass and wondered what it would be like to hunt it.

Four people got off the bus at Harrisburg and three got on. The couple across the aisle lit more marijuana. One of the new passengers cursed, which drew laughter from the smokers. The bus driver ignored the whole affair.

The driver pulled into the bus parking area at the Breezewood truck stop a little after noon. He announced a thirty-minute lunch stop, then darted down the stairs and headed for the restaurant. Most of the passengers trailed after him.

Taking his backpack, Henry Charon went to the men's room in the truckers' section of the building. He found a stall, dropped his trousers, and settled in. When he came out an hour later the bus was gone.

Charon bought a newspaper, then went into the restaurant and asked for a menu and a booth by the windows.

Senator Bob Cherry had the reputation of being an old-time politician. Now in his early seventies, he had been a US naval aviator during World War II and had shot down seven Japanese planes. After the war and law school, Bob Cherry had gone into politics. He had served four years in the Florida legislature, four years in the United States House of Representatives, and then run for the Senate. He had been there ever since.

Tall, gaunt, with piercing eyes and a gravel voice, he mastered the rules of the world's most exclusive gentlemen's club and set out to make it his own. He had. He had passed up chances to run for majority leader and whip: he preferred to lend his support to others, more ambitious than he and perhaps less wise, and use his influence to dictate who sat on the various committees that accomplished the work of the Senate. As chairman of the Government Oversight Committee and patron of the party leaders the power he wielded was enormous. Cabinet officers invited him to breakfast, presidents invited him to lunch, and every socialite in

Washington invited him to dinner. When Bob Cherry wanted something, he usually got it.

His wife had died ten years ago, and ever since he had had a succession of tall, shapely secretaries. Each lasted about two years. His current helper was approximately twenty-six and was a former Miss Georgia.

Today, at lunch, T. Jefferson Brody had trouble keeping his eyes off her. He wasn't trying very hard. He knew Bob Cherry well enough to know that the old goat got a kick out of younger men drooling down the cleavage of the sweet piece who was screwing him afternoon and night. So T. Jefferson Brody, diplomat that he was, ogled Miss Tina Jordan appreciatively. When she walked across the dining room on her way to the ladies', he made a point of admiring her shapely ass as it swayed deliriously from side to side.

Brody sighed wistfully. 'She's something else.'

'That she is,' Bob Cherry agreed with a tight grin. 'What's on your mind, Jefferson?'

Brody took a check from his inside jacket pocket and passed it to the senator. It was for five thousand dollars. 'A donation to your voter-registration PAC.'

Cherry stared at the check. 'The FM Development Corporation. Never heard of 'em.'

'They're nationwide. Build shopping centers and stuff all over. They've contributed to your PAC before.'

'Oh. Forgot. And they say the memory is the first thing to go.' Cherry folded the check and slipped it into a pocket. 'Well, thank you and FM Development. Any donation on behalf of good government is deeply appreciated.'

'What's the government going to do about foreign aid to Russia?'

Cherry took a sip of his wine, then said, 'Probably arrange tax credits for corporations that do joint ventures with the Soviets. Something like that. American business could teach the Russians a lot, provide capital, management expertise, inventory control, and so on. Our companies wouldn't have to make much of a profit, if any, with tax credits as an incentive. It might work pretty well.' He went on, detailing some of the proposals.

Jefferson Brody didn't pay much attention. He was thinking about PACs – political action committees. PACs were a glaring loophole that had survived the latest get-naked-and-honest bloodletting over election reform. Members of Congress could have private war chests with which they could pretty much do as they pleased as long as the money wasn't spent for direct reelection efforts. So the war chests were for voter-registration efforts, political education of constituents, presidential exploratory efforts, that kind of thing.

The niftiest thing about the noncampaign PACs though, and Brody felt his chest expand as he contemplated the genius of the guy who had thought of this, was that the elected person could put wife, son, daughter, and two or three girlfriends on the PAC payroll, thereby supplementing the family income. He could also use the donated loot to pay his own expenses if those expenses were related, in even a vague, hazy way, to the purposes of the PAC.

Consequently congressional PACs were slush funds, pure and simple. In private the politicians scrambled desperately to avoid the hardship of trying to make ends meet on a salary four times larger than the average American's, while in public they orated endlessly about all they had done to improve the lot of those said average working stiffs. Harsh and heavy, they told their constituents, were the burdens of public service.

Not that T. Jefferson Brody was put off by the hypocrisy of many politicians – Brody would have recoiled in horror at the mere thought of trying to survive on ninety thousand dollars a year. On the contrary, their greed was a real plus. Some needy soul on Capitol Hill always had a hand out. And T. Jefferson Brody was making a fine living counseling clients to fill those empty palms.

As Miss Tina Jordan returned from the powder room, Brody glanced at his watch. He had a dinner engagement this evening with another senator, Hiram Duquesne, who wanted a campaign contribution. Hiram was one of those lucky dogs who had gotten into office before January 8, 1980, so by law when he retired he could pocket all the campaign contributions he had received over the years and hadn't spent. Needless to say, with the most recent election only six weeks past and Duquesne once again a winner, he was still soliciting. Luckily FM Development had a campaign contribution PAC to help those pre-1980 incumbents, the Hiram Duquesnes of the world, who wanted their golden years to be truly golden.

Bob Cherry was in that blessed group, too, Brody remembered with a start. No doubt he would have Miss Jordan call him next week and remind him of that fact. Brody had that to look forward to. He glanced again at his watch. He was going to have to get back to the office and transfer some funds before he delivered Duquesne's check.

Still, he didn't want to rush Bob Cherry and his piece. He suggested dessert and Cherry accepted. Miss Jordan sipped a cup of cappuccino while the senator ate cheesecake and Brody admired the scenery.

When the luncheon bill came, Brody expertly palmed it. Cherry pretended he hadn't seen it.

After an hour Henry Charon got up, paid his bill at the truck stop's restaurant – it was a *lot* less than Brody had just put on his gold plastic – and went to the gift shop-convenience store. He spent twenty minutes there, then another twenty in the men's room. By a quarter to three he was once again seated in a booth by the windows in the restaurant. So at five minutes before three P.M. he saw the van pull in and Tassone get out. He stood beside the truck and pulled off a pair of driving gloves while he looked around. He stuck the gloves in his pocket and walked toward the building.

Tassone came into the restaurant right on the hour. He looked around casually and came over to Charon's booth in the corner.

'Hi.'

'Want some coffee?' Charon muttered.

'Yeah.' When the waitress came over Tassone ordered.

'It's all there.'

'All of it?'

'Everything.'

Henry Charon nodded and again scanned the parking area.

'So how many people know about this?' Charon asked after Tassone's coffee came and the waitress departed.

'Well, it took some doing to get what you wanted. Obviously, the people that supplied it know I took delivery. But they aren't going to be shooting their mouths off. Most of this stuff is hot and they were paid well.'

'Who else?'

'The guy fronting the dough. He knows.'

'And all the people working for him?'

'Don't make me laugh. He and I know, but nobody else. And believe me, I'm not about to tell you who he is. Another thing, after you get the bread, you won't see me again. If you're entitled to any more money under our deal, someone else will deliver it.'

'I don't want to see you again.'

'You might as well know this too: Tassone ain't my real name.'

A flicker of a grin crossed Charon's lips. He watched the other man sip his coffee.

Charon passed a yellow slip of paper across the table. 'You'll need this to get the truck back. Wednesday of next week. At a garage in Philadelphia.' He gave Tassone the address.

'The money? When and where.'

'My place in New Mexico. A week from today. Just you.'

'I understand.' Tassone sighed. 'You really think you can do this?'

'Yeah.'

'When? My guy wants to know.'

'When I'm ready. Not before.' Tassone started to speak but Charon continued: 'He won't have to wait too long.'

The truck wore Pennsylvania commercial plates. Charon drove out of the parking area and followed the signs toward I-70 east. The truck was new – only 326 miles on the odometer – and almost full of gas. Charon wore his own driving gloves. Twenty-five miles after leaving Breezewood he crossed into Maryland.

He kept the truck at fifty-five miles per hour where he could. Laboring up the low mountain east of Hagerstown the best he could do was thirty-five in the right-hand lane. Crossing the crest he kept the transmission in third gear to keep the brakes from overheating.

At Frederick he took I-270 toward Washington. Traffic was light and he rolled right along in the right lane.

The storage place he had rented was in northeast Washington. Charon's worst moment came as he backed the truck between the narrow buildings and nicked the corner of one. He inspected the damage – negligible, thank God – and tried it again. This time he got the truck right up to the open garage door of the storage bin he had rented last week.

The extra key on the ring fit the lock on the back of the truck. Charon unloaded the vehicle carefully but quickly. It wasn't until he had the garage door down that he stood and took inventory.

Four handguns, rifles, ammo, medical supplies, food, canned water, clothes, and those green boxes with US ARMY stenciled all over them. Charon opened each box and inspected the contents. He went through all the other items, examining everything.

Thirty minutes later he got into the truck and maneuvered it carefully out of the alley between the storage buildings.

It was going well, he decided. Everything was there, just as it should be. Getting everything done in time and in sequence, that was the difficulty. Still, it was do-able. Now to get this truck to Philly and pick up the car.

Henry Charon grinned as he came off the entrance ramp onto I-95 north. This was going to be his best hunt ever.

11

Jack Yocke was pecking randomly and morosely on his computer keyboard when Ott Mergenthaler walked by, then sat on the edge of the desk as he played with a piece of paper. 'I read your story,' Ott said, 'on the Jane Wilkens murder over in the Jefferson projects.'

'Umph.'

'It's good, real good.'

'They aren't going to run it now. Going to save it for some Sunday when they need some filler. If they run it at all.'

'It's still a good story.'

'Too many murder stories are bad for a paper, y'know? The matrons in Bethesda don't want to read that crap. The White House and political reporters take all the space anyhow. What could possibly be more important than Senator Horsebutt's carefully staffed and massaged opinion about what the Soviets ought to do to qualify for American foreign aid?'

'So what are you working on today?'

'Oh, just trying to get someone in the police or the DEA or the FBI or the Federal Home Loan Bank Board to say that there is a connection between the Harrington murder – he was the cashier at Second Potomac S-and-L – and the Judson Lincoln murder. Lincoln ran a chain of check-cashing outlets here in the metro area. Apparently they've just been sold to some outfit nobody ever heard of.'

'What makes you think the killings are connected?'

'The men were shot about four hours apart, apparently by professionals. Both were in finance. Harrington, at least, was laundering money for someone. Coincidence, maybe, but I got this feeling.'

'What do the pros say?'

'They aren't saying anything. Absolutely nothing. They just listen and grunt "no comment." '

'So what else is new?'

'The world just keeps on turning.'

'That's page one news.'

'This rag needs some real reporters. Not blood-and-guts guys like me, but some dirt sniffers who will get the *real* news, like who Senator Horsebutt is fucking on Tuesday nights and an opinion from his doctor on how he manages. Perhaps a think-piece listing the names and vital statistics and track records of all of America's top bimbos. Why are we scribbling stories about problems at the sewage farm when we could be picking on rich and famous assholes and selling a lot more papers?'

'Lighten up. And quit feeling sorry for yourself.'

'I'm maudlin, I know.' Yocke stretched and grinned. 'But self-pity soothes a tortured soul, Ott. You ought to try it sometime.'

'I gave it up when I quit smoking.'

'What windmill are you tilting at today?'

'I don't see my columns quite that way, Sancho. My literary efforts, short and sweet as they are, are really the beating heart of this newspaper that you so irreverently called a rag, the newspaper that pays your generous and unearned salary, by the way.'

Ott hoisted his cheeks off the desk. He tossed the paper he was holding in Yocke's lap and walked away. Yocke unfolded it. On the sheet was Ott Mergenthaler's column for tomorrow's paper, printed in three columns.

Unnamed sources in the Justice Department were quoted as saying that the evidence against Chano Aldana was weak. An acquittal was a definite possibility. Ott chided, gently and eruditely, as was his style, the prosecutors and Justice Department officials who had induced a grand jury to indict on weak, hearsay evidence. He also carved off a polite piece of the administration officials who had moved heaven and earth to extradite a man from Colombia that they probably couldn't convict.

Yocke refolded the paper and tossed it on top of one of his piles.

Mergenthaler's column in the *Post* the following morning should have caused a two-kiloton explosion in William C. Dorfman's office, but amazingly, no one on the White House staff saw it that morning. No staffer had time to read anything in the newspaper until early afternoon, because at seven A.M. a thunderbolt arrived from Havana: another Cuban revolution was in full swing.

The evening before in Havana army troops had fired upon a mass rally of over forty thousand people protesting the government's food rationing policies. Some reports said over a hundred people had been killed and several hundred wounded: the casualty figures varied wildly from source to source. This morning half the army was locked in combat with troops loyal to Castro. A group of students had seized Radio Havana and were proclaiming a democracy.

The *Washington Post* staff, with better sources than the White House or the State Department, knew about the revolution at six-thirty A.M., only an hour after the students went on Radio Havana chanting, '*Comunismo está muerto.*' Communism is dead.

Jack Yocke heard the news at eight-oh-five at police headquarters. He charged out of the building and headed for the *Post*.

Breaking into a conference of editors in the newsroom, he blurted, 'I speak Spanish.' None of the editors discussing how to cover the Cuba story seemed to hear him. He danced from foot to foot. This was his break, the one he had been waiting for. He *knew*!

He scurried off to find Ottmar Mergenthaler. The columnist was not at his desk. There he was, coming out of Bradlee's office. Yocke intercepted him.

'Ott, I got to talk to you. You gotta help me. I gotta go to Cuba.'

'Sure, Jack. Sure.'

'I speak Spanish. I've been taking a class. *You're not listening, Ott!* I write good blood-and-guts. *Great* blood-and-guts. I've paid my dues covering cops. I deserve a shot. Ott, you ancient idiot, *I speak Spanish!*'

'I'm listening. Jack. But I just write columns around here.'

'Be a pal. Go in and see Bradlee. Hell, call Donnie Graham if you have to. But get me to fucking Cuba!'

Mergenthaler stopped, took a deep breath, and rolled his eyes. Then he turned around and walked back toward Bradlee's office. 'Wait here, goddammit!' he growled when Yocke tagged along immediately behind him, threatening to step on his heels.

Ooooh boy, what a break this would be, Jack Yocke told himself as he waited. His big assets were that he was young, single, low salaried, and spoke Spanish . . . sort of. Callie Grafton would probably give him a C for his first semester. No reason to burden Ott or Bradlee with those trivial details, of course. As far as they were concerned he had no nervous family to bug the editors if he went and might even speak a little Spanish, like he claimed.

Every writer needs a war, at least one good one, to get famous in a hurry. You mix the blood and shit and booze together and anoint yourself and then, by God, you're Ernest Hemingway.

There are just so damn few good wars anymore! A revolution in Cuba wouldn't be a zinger like Korea or Vietnam, but Castro wouldn't go quietly, without a fight. Whatever happened, it would be better than covering cops. Jack Yocke assured himself of that. He had the talent to make it something big if he got the chance.

Two minutes later Ott returned.

'Okay, Ben is going to talk to foreign. Better get your passport in case they decide to request a visa for you. But you'd be helping out the regulars. Remember that, Junior.'

Yocke grabbed the older man by his ears, pulled his head down and kissed him soundly on his tan, bald pate.

'Thanks, Ott,' Yocke called as he trotted away. 'I owe you.'

That day Jack Yocke took the problems as they came. He encountered the first one when he got back to his apartment to throw some clothes in a bag.

What do you take to a revolution? Some underwear, sure. A suit and tie? Well, maybe. Why not? Tennis shoes would be good, some slacks and pullover shirts. Cuba's in the tropics, right? But it might get chilly at night this time of year. Maybe a sweater or sweatshirt. Socks. He wadded all this stuff into a soft, fake-leather vinyl bag and tossed in a razor and toothbrush and toothpaste.

Cuba. In Latin America. Cuba's bacteria have undoubtedly been recycled through fifty generations of immune natives and have probably grown virulent enough to disembowel a gringo, like the bacteria the Mexicans are so proud of. Yocke added all the antidiarrhea medicine in his bathroom to the bag.

His passport was in the top left drawer of his dresser, under the hankies. He didn't bother packing any hankies.

With the encased laptop computer that he had signed for from the *Post* dangling from a strap over his shoulder and the fake-leather bag banging against his leg, he hailed a cab – hey, he was on the expense account – and rode with nervous anticipation back to the *Post*. He kept the cab waiting while he trotted into the building and rode up to the travel office.

Trying very hard to conceal his nervousness, he stood in line until he had his tickets and money. They were *really* going to let him go!

He didn't feel safe until he was on his way to the airport. Then he sat back and grinned broadly. This was his chance! All the writing he had ever done had been mere preparation for this story. And he felt confident. He was *ready*.

After he had checked his bag at the ticket counter and gotten his seat assignment, Jack Yocke wandered into a newsstand and bought a carton of Marlboros. He took the cigarette packs out of the carton and stuffed them around the computer inside its case. Fortunately there was room. Then he went to the bar and watched the latest news on the Cable News Network.

While Yocke was sipping coffee from a paper cup, one of the CNN White House correspondents assured the audience that President Bush was closely monitoring the situation in Cuba.

That statement had been given out by the White House press flacks upon the order of William C. Dorfman.

Actually the President was at that very moment discussing with Dorfman and the chairman of the national Republican party a matter more weighty than a revolution in Cuba. The American people had recently elected a larger Democratic House and Senate majority, and two of the loyal Republican congressmen who would be unemployed in January wanted government jobs.

Dorfman suggested ambassadorships: he named several possible small nations in sub-Sahara Africa. The national chairman thought the two Republican legislators might prefer to be assistant secretaries of something or other. 'Who the hell wants to go to equatorial Africa?'

The men in the Oval Office had their feet up and were in no hurry. Dorfman had canceled most of the President's regular schedule today so he would have plenty of time to closely monitor the Cuban thing.

At noon the President went down to the White House situation room for a briefing. He was back at twelve-fifteen and when lunch was brought in turned on the television to see what the media were saying. Various loyal army units in the provinces had capitulated to mobs that had besieged their barracks shouting for food. Fidel Castro had appeared on Havana television – the show ran thirty seconds of poor-quality tape – and blamed the 'riots' by 'counterrevolutionaries' on Yankee imperialists. He announced that the traitors who had seized Radio Havana that morning had been captured and shot.

'There's no organized opposition,' Bush informed his guests. 'The lid just blew off.'

CNN then ran a story about several dozen major corporations buying up huge tracts in West Virginia to open landfills for the entire eastern seaboard's garbage. The President watched while he ate a BLT on whole wheat with a double shot of mayo. The governor of West Virginia, a Democrat, was outraged, but the yokels in the legislature refused to forbid landfills or even regulate them. Apparently a lot of West Virginians thought their children and grandchildren wouldn't mind living on top of New York City's garbage and drinking the effluvia in their water so long as they got jobs driving the bulldozers.

'Makes you wonder about democracy, doesn't it?' the national chairman muttered. 'If the Russians and Cubans only knew.'

Bush finished off the last bite of the BLT and jabbed the remote control, turning off the television. He asked the national chairman what the Democrats thought about foreign aid to the Soviets.

They were deep into that subject when an aide motioned Dorfman from the room and showed him Mergenthaler's column.

Dorfman ate three Rolaids as he read. When he finished he snapped, 'Get Cohen on the phone,' and went to his office to take the call.

'I'm calling about Mergenthaler's column, Gid.'

'What about it?' Cohen was equally brusque.

'Somebody over in your empire told him you guys can't convict Aldana.'

'That's somebody's opinion. I don't know whose. It isn't mine.'

'You gonna call a press conference and deny it?'

'Deny what?'

Dorfman held the phone away from his ear and looked at it dis-tastefully. If the man was as stupid as he sounded, he wasn't qualified to prosecute a traffic ticket.

'Are you or are you not going to convict Chano Aldana?'

'I'm not a psychic.'

'You want me to tell the President that?'

'If the President wants to talk to me about the case against Aldana, I'll be delighted to brief him. We have evidence. Mountains of it. We're still sifting through it page by page. We think Aldana's guilty and we'll try to prove it.'

'The President will want you to say that in a press release.'

'Have you talked to him about it?'

'Not yet, but—'

'If the President wants a press release, we'll do one. I don't advise it. If we start issuing press releases to deny leaks we're going to be as busy as the sorcerer's apprentice. Call me back when you find out the President's decision.' The attorney general hung up.

The President did want a press release. Dorfman had his youngest, most junior aide call the attorney general and deliver the message.

When Jack Yocke had collected his bag from the luggage carousel at Miami airport, he found a pay phone with a Miami telephone directory still attached. He looked up an address, then hailed a cab in front of the terminal.

2422 South Davis was smack in the middle of the Cuban section of town. The business signs were in Spanish. Latin rhythms floated from passing cars. Yocke paid the cab driver and stood on the sidewalk for a moment watching the passing swarms of humanity.

The storefronts looked Mexican. Maybe that's what Cuba looks like, sort of Matamoros East without the tourists, whores, and sex shows.

The black lettering on the glass of the door between a dress store and what he took to be a laundry had been painted freehand by someone in a hurry. CUBA LIBRE, it said, like the rum drink. 'Free Cuba.'

Jack Yocke opened the door and went inside. He walked along a hall, then began climbing a flight of stairs. The worn steps creaked as they took his weight. At the top of the stairs was another door, one with no glass. He tried the knob. It turned.

The small office was empty. Two closed doors against the back wall presumably led to offices that overlooked the back alley. He could hear people, men and women, arguing in Spanish behind one of the doors. Yocke took a seat and arranged his bag and computer on the chair beside him.

He crossed his legs and tried to figure out what the conversation was about. No soap. These people didn't speak Spanish like Mrs Grafton. They should have taken her course.

The phone rang. And rang. And rang, while the argument continued unabated.

It stopped, finally. Shortly thereafter a woman opened the door and started. 'Who are you?'

'Name's Jack Yocke. You the receptionist?'

'How long have you been sitting here?' She had a definite accent and her skin was a warm brown.

'Just a couple of minutes.' About fifteen, actually. 'Your door was unlocked and . . . I hope you don't mind.'

'We're closed.'

A man came from the inside of the office and stood in the doorway looking at Yocke. 'I don't know him,' he told the woman. His accent was less pronounced than the woman's, but noticeable. He was a slight man without a trace of excess flesh. His skin stretched tightly across his face; his eyes were deeply set.

Yocke took out his wallet and removed his press card. He handed it to the woman and smiled broadly. 'Jack Yocke, *Washington Post.*'

The man snatched the card and looked at it incredulously. 'You, reporter?'

'Yes. I—'

'Out! Take your card.' The man threw it at him. 'Beat it! Scram! Right now, *hombre.*'

Yocke pocketed the card. He slowly arranged the strap of the computer case over his shoulder and hefted the vinyl bag. 'Could I get your name for my story? I don't know much Spanish, but I know *bote* and *viaje por mar* and a couple more words. I know that Santa Clara is a city in Cuba. And I can add two and two.'

'*Tienes las orejos grandes y la mala lengua.*'

'Yep. Big ears and a bad mouth. That's me.'

They stared at him openmouthed. The phone started ringing again. They let it ring.

'What you want?' Back in English.

'Same as you. To go to Cuba.'

'Why?'

'I'm a reporter. They're having a revolution.' Jack Yocke grinned.

The phone was still ringing. The man and woman looked at each other.

'No,' she said.

'*Sí.*' The man stood partially aside. 'Come in.'

'Why don't you answer your phone?'

'Reporters.' He spit out the word. 'They have treated us as cracked pots – that is the words, no? – for years, ignored us, and now they drive us *loco.* "A story, *now* give us a story! Tell us of Cuba and Fidel!" *Now* you want to spill on us some of the ink you use for your football and your stories of foolish rich men and silly women with the big tits, eh? Truly, *señor*, yours is a miserable profession.'

There were two other men in the room. Cubans. In their thirties, lean and wiry, they were sitting in straight-backed chairs and they didn't rise. They did, however, scrutinize Yocke's face with the coldest stares he could remember.

The cadaverous man who had admitted him closed the door carefully and said, 'But first let's establish just what your real profession is, *señor*.'

Yocke turned to face him. 'What do you think my profession might be, if I'm not a reporter?'

The man went behind the desk and opened a drawer. He extracted a large revolver and pointed it straight at Yocke. 'Oh, let me think. What a puzzle! Can you help me?'

The revolver looked like as big as a cannon. The black hole in the muzzle looked large enough to drive a car through. Jack Yocke grinned nervously. No one else smiled.

'Perhaps you are of Fidel. Perhaps you are CIA. Those possibilities leap immediately to my mind. Sit!'

Yocke sat.

'Now. Put that thing over your shoulder on the floor there beside you. Place your hands on the table in front of you, *señor*, and remain still as the most dead man you ever saw, or *Holy Mother*! I will make you very very dead very very quickly.'

The two spectators came over and, carefully staying out of the possible line of fire, emptied Yocke's pockets, turning them inside out. The contents they put on the desk.

'Stand in the corner, *señor*, facing the wall.'

Jack Yocke obeyed.

He heard the door open, then fifteen seconds later close again. He heard the sounds of zippers being opened. His computer case. Maybe his suitbag.

'You could call my editor at the *Post* and ask him what I look like.'

'I know I look like a fool, *señor*. For that I blame my father. But a fool I am not. If you are a *Fidelista* or a CIA, you have a wonderful cover. I expect no less. *Por favor*, *señor*, do not twitch like that! The noise of this pistol is distressing in such a small room.'

After several minutes the cadaverous man, who was the only one who had spoken, told Yocke, 'Turn around.'

The reporter did so. The contents of his wallet were spread all over the desk. One of the Cubans was punching the buttons of the computer, slowly, randomly, absorbed, while he watched the screen. The third man was pawing through Yocke's clothes and underwear, which were piled on the floor.

With his gun just under his right hand, the man at the desk was ripping open cigarette packs. He crumbled the cigarettes into piles of tobacco and paper and randomly ripped apart filters with his fingernails. It took two more minutes. Satisfied at last, he raked the mess into a trash can beside the desk. Most of it went into the trash, anyway: the rest went onto the wooden floor.

Now the man wiped his hands together to get rid of the tobacco crumbs, then picked up the revolver. He pointed it at the reporter's belly button.

'*Ahora bien*, we will come to Jesus, as you say. The truth.'

'My name is Jack Yocke. I'm a reporter for the *Washington Post*. I left Washington this morning to go to Cuba. I figured that none of the other correspondents trying to get there would think of going over to Cuba with the exiles. So I flew into Miami Airport and looked in the telephone book. I looked under "Cuba" and found an address for Cuba Libre. I hailed a taxi. Here I am. That's the truth.'

The man stared. The other two finished their explorations and joined in the scrutiny.

'We don't have time for your games. We have things to do.'

'Take me with you to Cuba, please. I'm asking you as nice and polite as I know how.'

'What makes you think we are going to Cuba?'

'Please, mister, don't jerk my chain! Some of the Cubans *must* be going! If you guys aren't, who is? I need to get to Cuba one way or the other. What the hell you want me to do – hire an airplane and parachute out of it? Goddammit, my paper wants stories from Cuba and sent *me* to get them. I won't write a story about you or mention your names without your approval. Is that what you're worried about? You can be a confidential source. I'm just asking for your help. But with or without you, I'm going to Cuba.'

The three men glanced at each other. Nothing was said.

After several seconds, the man behind the desk put the pistol back in the drawer and gestured. 'Your things.' He shook his head. 'Only in America . . .'

His name was Hector Santana. He didn't introduce the other two, but Yocke later learned their names: Jesús Ruiz and Tomás García. The three conferred briefly in whispers in the far corner, then Santana faced him again.

'You must understand the danger. There is much danger. We will go by boat. We will have to avoid your Coast Guard, which will be alert for boats going to Cuba, and we will have to avoid the Cuban Navy, which will be even more alert. If we are caught by the Americans, we will be in serious trouble. If we are caught by the Cubans, we will be dead.'

'I understand. I want to go.'

'You say it so easily, so lightly. A ride in a pedal-boat on a park lake! You would risk your life for your employer's sake, to write a story for a newspaper?'

'Well, it does sound sort of stupid, when you put it like that. But yes, I—'

'You are a *fool.*'

'You'll be just as dead as I.'

'Ahh, but we are fighting for our country. For *Cuba.* You, you risk your life for money, for glory. And those things they are as nothing. They are as smoke. You are a very great fool.'

'You've told me the risks. You've given me your opinion. I still want to go if you'll take me.'

Santana shrugged grandly. 'You must stay with us and make no calls. You may telephone anyone anywhere, if the telephones work, when we get to Havana. Not before.'

'That's reasonable. Sure.'

'And we, of course, accept your offer of professional secrecy. No stories about us. No names. Ever. You must swear it.'

'I swear. When do we get to Havana?'

Around midnight the three men, with Jack Yocke wedged in the backseat, drove through a steady rain to a marina. Yocke never knew where the marina was because the Cubans made him wear a blindfold. He was led from the car to a slick gangplank which he stumbled up carrying the computer. Only when he was in a little cabin below decks was he allowed to remove the blindfold. His escort tossed the vinyl bag on the deck, then left, closing the door behind him.

The engine on the boat was already running, a muffled throbbing that pulsated the deck and bulkheads. After sitting in the darkness a few minutes Yocke tried the door latch. Locked. There was a tiny porthole but the view was only of black water and shimmering lights.

Within minutes the boat got under way. The deck tilted and the vibration changed and the noise level rose. Yocke checked his watch: twelve forty-six.

Yocke tried to decide how large the boat was. It wasn't little, he concluded. But it wasn't a ship. It turned too quickly. He stretched out on the couch bunk in the darkness and tried to sleep.

After a half hour or so the motion of the vessel changed. She began to roll and pitch with authority. Sometime later the motion changed again as the growl of the engine rose. Now the motion was more vigorous, the roll and pitch moments sharper and quicker.

The day had been a long one. Jack Yocke slept.

He awoke sometime later. The vessel was pounding in the sea, the engines throbbing heavily. They were pushing her hard. He wedged himself into the bunk and in minutes was again asleep.

Hector Santana shook him awake at five A.M. 'You may come up on deck now.'

The boat was still pitching enthusiastically. Worse than when he went to sleep, but not so badly as it had several hours ago. Above the engine noise Yocke asked, 'Where are we?'

'Just off Andros Island.'

'Are we in the Gulf Stream?'

'We've crossed it. The ride was much worse.'

On deck the only illumination was from several little red lights above the chart and binnacle in front of the helmsman. The rain had stopped. The boat appeared to be a giant cabin cruiser. This high above the water the motion was even more pronounced. Yocke found a handhold.

A ghostly white wake stretched away behind the boat straight as a highway into the vast, total darkness. Not a star or other light in the entire visible universe.

He could hear a radio, the announcer speaking in Spanish. When his eyes became better adjusted, he could just make out the figures of four or five men huddled around it.

'How goes the revolution?'

'Fighting in the cities. Much of the army is still loyal to Fidel.'

'Where will we land?'

'Caibarién.'

'When?'

'Tomorrow morning, before dawn.'

'How fast are we going?'

'Twenty-eight knots.'

After a few moments, Yocke asked, 'This your boat?'

'Belongs to a friend.'

'Nice of him to let you use it like this.'

'He will report it stolen this evening.'

'Why are you going to Cuba?'

'It's my country.'

Yocke eased himself to another handhold. His eyes were fairly well adjusted now and he could just make out Samaria's face. 'Uh-uh. Nope. Yesterday evening I told you why I wanted to go, but you didn't bother to tell me why you and your friends were going. And I didn't ask.'

'We noted the omission. Very good manners for a reporter. Tomás thought too good. I said no. He is *diplomático*, I said. Finally Tomás agreed.'

'Perhaps you can tell me now.'

'Maybe later. We'll see. If you're still alive.' With that Santana went below.

12

At dawn the blackness faded to slate gray. A gray, indefinite sky above a gray sea. Visibility about a mile in fog. There were no other vessels to be seen, no land, nothing but gray in every direction.

The helmsman slowed the boat to two or three knots and it began to roll and pitch sloppily. On the low fantail, behind the raised bridge, the other passengers baited fishing rods with small fish and rigged them to troll. One man went up on the high fish platform. Jack Yocke had no desire to join him. The motion of the boat would be much worse there.

Sandwiches and coffee were brought up from below. Yocke had had two bites before he realized he had made a mistake. He puked over the rail and the wind sprayed some of it over the men sitting on the fantail watching the fishing rods. They were angry at first, then they laughed.

'Go below and lie down,' Santana told him.

Yocke was back on deck in two minutes, heaving again. The motion of the boat was impossible to endure in the confined spaces below.

He ended up lying on the deck forward, crawling to the rail to puke, then lying on his back waiting.

Hours passed. He was reduced to dry heaves.

Oh God, he was sick. Every now and then he could hear the Cubans on the bridge laughing. He didn't care. He didn't care if he died here and now. Nothing was worth this.

Once he heard a plane. A jet. Oh, to be up there, sitting in a comfortable, stable seat, one that didn't bob and roll and go endlessly up and down, up and down . . .

Since there was absolutely nothing in his stomach at this stage, he merely curled into the fetal position and retched until he gagged, then retched some more.

He resolved never again to travel by water, anywhere. To never again set foot on boat, ship, ferry, scow, schooner, sloop, anything that floated. If he couldn't go by air or rail, he wouldn't go.

When Jack Yocke finally felt better it was after twelve o'clock on his watch. He sat and stared at the sea. The visibility had improved – maybe three or four miles – and the clouds were broken, with sunlight shining through in places, making the sea a brilliant blue. The sunlight on the sea hurt his eyes. He got up and staggered along the deck edge, holding on like grim death, to the bridge area. How had he managed to get to the forward deck when he was so sick?

'Drink this. It's water,' Santana said, and he obeyed.

His stomach was still queasy, but nowhere near as bad as it had been.

For the first time he seriously examined his companions, of whom five were visible above decks. Santana, the two from yesterday – Jesús Ruiz and Tomás García – and two more whose names he never learned. Ruiz was the helmsman while García spent his time listening to a shortwave radio. Yocke got a chance to observe García closely for several minutes, and he seemed to be monitoring the VHF band.

Santana saw him looking over García's shoulder. 'That jet two hours ago was US Coast Guard. They saw us with this radar but never got a visual identification. They reported our position, course, and speed to their headquarters in Miami, which presumably passed it to the two cutters that are somewhere out here.'

'Where?'

'I wish I knew.'

'Did we change course after the jet passed?'

'Yes. We are now headed northeast, toward Andros Island.'

'What are we worried about? We're just out here fishing.'

'Fishing,' Santana agreed. Automatically he checked the rods and the angle of the lines.

'No luck, huh?' Yocke said, also looking.

'We had a tuna strike this morning, while you were sick. I had them take the baits off. We are just trolling bare hooks.'

'Maybe we should try to catch something.'

'We don't have the fuel to waste on a fight. And the fish would be killed for no reason. That,' Hector Santana added with a glance at the reporter, 'would be a sin.'

Jack Yocke listened to the news, sometimes in Spanish, sometimes in English from a US station, and watched the men. He avoided drawing them into conversation, and none of them except Santana approached him to talk.

All afternoon the Cubans huddled near the radio and chafed, each man in his own way. The revolution was in full swing, people they knew and cared deeply for were risking everything, including their lives, yet here they sat on a fifty-foot boat on a vast, empty sea, going nowhere at three knots.

Yocke was as impatient as the rest. He reminded himself that his interest was strictly professional. Well, sporting too, in that he was rooting hard for the underdogs, yet somehow this thought tweaked from him a pang of guilt, which annoyed him. It wasn't his fault he wasn't a Cuban or that Cuba had become a poor, starving bucolic workers' paradise under the magnificent benevolence of the 'maximum leader.' For thirty-one years Fidel Castro had been the Cuban saint, a sugarcane version of George Washington, Marx, Lenin, Stalin, and St Paul, togged out in army fatigues and spouting revolutionary bullshit that the vast majority of Cubans believed or at least tolerated. It wasn't until the Soviets had cut them off the dole and starvation threatened that the Cuban people had finally held up a yardstick to see how tall Fidel really was.

Yocke vomited again in late afternoon, but afterward the queasiness seemed to leave him. Weak and dehydrated, he still felt better.

As evening came the visibility lifted significantly. Just before dark Yocke could see land off the northeast and east, a dark line on the horizon perhaps ten miles away. It was difficult to judge and he didn't ask. As the light faded the two men on the fantail reeled in the fishing lines and stowed the rods.

When the night enclosed them completely and the only lights in the universe were the red glow from the binnacle and chart table, Santana spoke to the helmsman. He spun the wheel and pushed the twin throttles forward. The fantail descended and the bow rose as the screws bit into the sea.

With Santana bending over the chart and Ruiz at the helm, the boat glided through the night. García played with the Loran and the other two acted as lookouts.

Yocke stood on the left rear corner of the bridge, out of whispered earshot and out of the way, and watched. He was the first to see the weak flashes of light off in the darkness a little to the left of their course, and pointed them out to Santana.

Ruiz cut the throttle. The boat rose and fell gently on the swell, enveloped by darkness. Santana pointed a flashlight with a cone of paper taped around the head in the direction of the first light and keyed it several times. At the answering light, Ruiz advanced the throttles.

After five minutes or so and another hurried conference over the chart, the Cubans killed the engine. One man went forward to lower the anchor.

Rocking in the night, they waited. Jack Yocke could just faintly hear breakers crashing on a beach. Or perhaps against rocks.

Santana came over for a moment beside him. 'Be very quiet. Stay here on the bridge,' he whispered. 'If there is any trouble, lie down and do not move.' To reinforce his message, he tapped the reporter's arm gently with a revolver.

Yocke looked. García came up from below decks with a rifle of some kind. He moved forward of the bridge. The man on the fantail also had a rifle or perhaps a submachine gun. It was very difficult for Yocke to see clearly in the haphazard starlight coming through gaps in the cloud cover overhead.

Twenty minutes passed. Thirty. Ruiz muttered something in Spanish to Santana about the time.

Yocke didn't realize they had company until the other boat bumped against theirs. Other men came aboard. After a quick conference on the fantail, everyone except Ruiz went to the fantail to help.

The job took about fifteen minutes, as close as Yocke could tell. Box after heavy box was handed from the smaller boat to this one, then carefully carried below. Over thirty boxes, perhaps three dozen.

Then the other boat was pushed away into the darkness. Ruiz started his engines, waited just a moment to ensure that the other boat would drift clear, then engaged the screws and advanced the throttles. He brought them up slowly and steadily as the speed built until the two throttles were against the forward stops and the bow was leaping off sweils and whacking into others. Yocke found a handhold.

After a while Santana and the others came up from below and stood joking and laughing on the bridge. They were in a jovial mood. They passed a bottle around, then Santana brought it over to where Yocke sat and offered him a swig.

Yocke declined. 'My stomach.'

'I understand. Perhaps when we reach Cuba.'

'What do you guys have in those boxes?'

'You don't really want to know. You're just an uninvited hitchhiker, remember?'

'Amazing how your accent goes and comes.'

'Accents are useful. They are like clothes. One dresses the part. Always.'

'Watching you load those boxes, I finally realized how big a fool I've been.'

Santana tilted the bottle. He wiped his mouth on his sleeve. 'Well, perhaps. If so, that is progress. Most fools live their entire lives without ever knowing wisdom.' He belched. 'I think there's one swallow left. You never know, it might be your very last.'

Yocke took the bottle and drained it. The rum burned all the way down. He wound up and threw the bottle as far out into the wake as he could. He didn't see it splash.

'None of us ever know, do we?'

'That is right,' Santana agreed cheerfully enough and left him to examine the chart and fiddle with the Loran and confer in a low voice with Ruiz and García.

In a few minutes García made himself comfortable across from Yocke. He still had the rifle. He rested it across his knees.

The hours passed. Sometimes the ride would grow rougher or smoother for a time, but the throttles stayed against the stops. Ruiz worked the helm only to hold his course. He did have to work at it. After a few hours Santana relieved him and he went below. García smoked cigarettes and never moved.

When Ruiz came back on deck at midnight, Yocke asked Santana if he could go below and get his gear. Santana got it for him.

Yocke donned a sweatshirt and pulled a sweater over it. Using the vinyl bag for a pillow, he stretched out on the deck.

When he awoke he was aware that the boat was not rolling as before. She was now moving directly across the swells and pitching heavily, the engine still at full cry.

All the men were on deck, looking away to port. Yocke joined them and peered into the darkness. Beside him García pointed.

A white masthead light was just visible, another light under it. 'Cuban patrol boat.'

'Has he seen us?'

'*Sí.* I think so.'

Yocke moved over to where Santana stood, beside the helmsman. He was looking at the chart.

'Where are we?'

'Here.' Santana jabbed with his finger. The spot he indicated was ten miles or so north of the Cuban coast. 'The patrol boat has us on radar.'

'You could run east away from him.'

'No. We have been picking up radar signals from the east. There is a patrol boat over there too, though farther away. We were trying to go between them.'

'You have a radar detector?'

'Yes. One of your American ones for detecting police radar. We have modfied it to receive different frequencies. It works quite well.'

'So what are you going to do?' Yocke looked again at the lights on the horizon. Was the Cuban boat visibly closer or was that his imagination?

'We can try for shallow water. We don't have many options.'

'You could turn around and go north.'

Santana was looking at the chart.

'Surely that's better than getting killed?'

'Go sit down. Stay out of the way.'

Yocke didn't have to be told twice.

After a quick conference around the helm, everyone except Santana went below. He took the wheel.

Yocke was watching the lights, which were truly closer, when he saw the flash. Santana saw it too and spun the wheel. The nose of the boat slewed to port. Yocke heard the rumble as the shot went over and, after a moment, the splash. Then, finally, he heard the boom of the shot.

Santana spun the wheel again, turning starboard, then steadied up after thirty degrees or so of heading change. The next shot was short, though much closer.

The stars seemed to be brighter. Yocke checked his watch. A few minutes after five A.M. He looked down toward the south. Lights. Town, perhaps. Or villages. Cuba. God, it would be a long swim! And sharks – these waters were full of sharks.

He was thinking of sharks and wondering about the current when he saw the third flash. The gunboat was definitely closer.

This time the shot fell just in front of the bow.

'The next one'll be the charm,' Yocke said loudly enough for Santana to hear.

'Pray,' was the response.

The other Cubans rushed up from below. Two of them went forward and two settled on the port side of the bridge. They each had a dark pipe on their shoulder, something like a World War II bazooka.

'Get over here, Yocke! By me!' Santana ordered.

'Ready?' Santana shouted.

'*Sí, Adelante!*'

Santana spun the wheel and the boat heeled to starboard as her nose came port. She had completed forty-five degrees or so of heading change when the gunboat fired again. Santana held in his turn until he was heading only ten or fifteen degrees south of the gunboat, running toward her at full throttle. 'Not yet,' he shouted.

The swells were smaller and farther apart here in the lee of Cuba and the boat rode more steadily on the step.

Jack Yocke peered through the bridge glass trying to estimate the distance. Ahead of him, on the deck, the two men lay prone, on their elbows, each with a tube across his shoulder and pointed toward the charging gunboat.

The gunboat fired again. Santana swerved port, bringing the gunboat onto the nose. Just when Yocke concluded the Cuban Navy had again missed, the platform above the bridge exploded, showering the fantail with debris.

Santana chopped the throttle and slammed the transmission into neutral.

'They're gonna hit us with the next one,' Yocke shouted.

'Everybody down. Take cover!'

'They'll kill us,' Yocke shouted at Santana, infuriated at the man's composure.

'They're not in range yet.'

'Oh, damn,' Yocke muttered, and got facedown on the floor.

The seconds passed. Miraculously, the next explosion didn't come. Yocke lay on his belly waiting, sweating profusely, and when it finally seemed that the shooting was over, he got up on his knee for a look. The gunboat was closer, much closer.

Another flash. This time the bridge glass to Yocke's right exploded. He felt the sting of something hitting his face and instinctively raised his arm.

'Fire!' Santana shouted.

One of the men behind fired first. A whooshing crack and a great flash of light and the rocket shot forward, illuminating the surface of the black sea with the fire from its exhaust.

Then the man beside him fired. Another report and flash.

The men up forward fired no more than a second apart.

Half blinded by the flashes, Jack Yocke tried to look anyway.

One of the missiles hit a swell and detonated. Well short.

Another hit the gunboat with a flash. A second impacted almost in the same place. The fourth must have missed.

Yocke turned. The two men behind him were going down the ladder, heading below. Santana shoved the transmission lever forward and firewalled the throttle. As the stern bit into the sea he cranked the helm over.

In thirty seconds they were back, carrying more rocket launchers.

They squatted and waited.

The gunboat was obviously hit badly. Her bow turned northward and the smear of fire was visible.

Santana veered off to the south, to pass under the gunboat's stern, perhaps a quarter mile away, Yocke guessed.

As they approached to almost abeam, tracers reached from the gunboat. The man behind Yocke fired another missile. This one impacted the Cuban gunboat just above the waterline.

Then they were by, the distance increasing.

'What the fuck are those things?' Yocke asked.

'LAW rockets.' Yocke had heard of these, though he had never seen one. Light antitank weapons.

'How many you got down there?'

'Not as many as we started with.'

'Where'd you get 'em?'

'You never stop asking fool questions, do you?'

'Sorry.'

The gunboat was on fire, dead in the water, rapidly falling astern when Yocke saw her last. His face was stinging. It was blood.

The back end of the port side of the bridge was a mess. The shell had blown out the window and passed through the supporting structure that held up the roof. Luckily the stuff offered too little resistance to activate the fuse or everyone on the bridge would have been cut to bits by the shrapnel of the exploding warhead. And the fiberglass had been cooked by the exhaust of the missiles getting under way.

To hell with these idiots!

Jack Yocke went below and found the cabin he had slept in leaving Miami and turned on the light. He was shaking like a leaf. He sat on the bunk and tried to get his breathing under control while blood dripped off his chin onto his shirt and trousers.

Ten minutes later he was looking in the mirror above the washbasin and using a towel to extract the glass shards from the cuts in his face when Hector Santana came in.

'How do you feel?'

'You want the truth or some macho bullshit from a B movie?'

'Whatever pleases you.'

'I damn near shit myself.'

Santana grinned. The grin looked wicked on that tight, death's-head face.

Yocke averted his eyes and concentrated on raking a glass splinter from a cut over his eye. When he got it out, he said, 'Why'd you let me come along?'

'Tomás and Jesús wanted to kill you in Miami. You were obviously a plant. Even if you were a reporter, you might talk, talk far too much, much too soon. I don't like to kill unless it is required. So we brought you.'

'A great bunch of guys you are! What would you have done earlier this evening if you had run into a US Coast Guard cutter? After you picked up the weapons?'

'Probably scuttled.'

'My ass! You'd have shot it out.'

'Think what you like.'

'If we had survived that encounter, you would have killed me.'

Santana shrugged. 'A lot of time, effort, and money went into acquiring these weapons. Three men lost their lives. We desperately need these weapons to fight the *Fidelistas*. Much is at stake. Many lives. Yet you came to our office and stuck your nose in where it didn't belong. You wanted a free ride to the revolution, as if a revolution against Castro would be some kind of a Cuban circus that you had improvidently forgotten to buy a ticket for. You wanted to sneak in under the tent flap!'

Santana snorted. 'You Americans! You persist in thinking the world is a comfortable little place, full of comfortable, reasonable people, despite all the evidence to the contrary. If only everyone would buy a Sunday edition of the *Post* and read it carefully, perhaps write a thoughtful, well-crafted letter to the editor, then everything would be *okay*.'

Hector Santana sucked in a bushel of air and sighed audibly. 'Have a *nice* day,' he said over his shoulder as he went through the door.

Jack Yocke stared at his face in the mirror. Blood was still trickling from several of the deeper cuts.

The boat glided gently through the shallow waters of an inlet behind an island as the daylight came. The remains of the fishing tower above the bridge listed at a crazy angle. The back end of the bridge didn't look any better in the gray half light of dawn than it had an hour ago. The plexiglass fragments were charred a sooty black.

As Yocke watched, Santana ran the boat into a cut on the bank sheltered by several trees. A half dozen men came aboard and carried the LAW rockets, still in their olive-drab boxes stenciled US ARMY, over a plank to a truck barely visible amid the vegetation.

When the job was complete, the men piled into the truck and drove away. Everyone went with them except Santana. He stood on the bridge with Yocke. 'Well,' he said, 'that's done.'

'What next?'

'Unless you're in the mood for a swim, I suggest you go ashore. Better take your stuff with you. Oh, and take my bag from the galley ashore with you. And this.' Santana drew his revolver from his waistband and tossed it at the reporter, who barely caught it.

With Yocke standing on sand trying to readjust his muscles to the absence of motion, Santana maneuvered the boat from the cut and slowly eased her several hundred yards out into the inlet, where he killed the engine. He went forward and heaved the anchor overboard.

He worked on the boat for ten or fifteen minutes while Yocke sat on the vinyl suitbag watching. The quiet was uncomfortable after two nights and a day listening to the engines. Yocke could hear birds singing somewhere and the slap-slap of water lapping at the shore, but that was about it. No engine noise, no jets overhead, no barely audible radio or television babble. Just the chee-cheeing of the birds and the water.

The pistol felt strange in his hand. Yocke examined it. A Smith & Wesson .357. It wasn't a new gun or even in very good condition. He could see bare metal in places where the blueing was gone. But the thing that struck Jack Yocke was the weight. This thing was heavier than he thought it would be. He knew very little about firearms and had handled them on only a few occasions. Looking into the chambers from the front, he could see the bullets. Shiny little pills of instant death. Ugliness. Everything he didn't like about the world and the people in it was right here in his hand.

He carefully laid the pistol on top of the computer case and wiped his hands in the sand.

Santana came off the boat in a clean dive and began swimming. The sun was up now and the water was a pale, sandy blue. The man swam efficiently, without wasted effort.

He was standing beside Yocke taking off his wet clothes when a dull 'crump' reached them and the remains of the fish tower toppled slowly into the water. Ten seconds later another explosion, more powerful but still strangely muffled.

Santana stripped to the skin and opened his bag. He had his underwear and trousers on when he next looked at the boat. She was down visibly at the head and listing.

'How deep's the water there?'

'Sixty or seventy feet, maybe. That's the channel.'

'Clear as this water is, she'll be visible from the air.'

'No one will look from the air for a few days. Then it won't matter. We'll be in Havana.'

'Or dead,' Jack Yocke added.

'You are very intuitive. Your grasp of the situation is really remarkable.'

'Fuck you very much.'

The forward deck was completely awash when Santana stood and dusted the sand from his trousers. He tucked the revolver into his waistline and let the loose shirt hang over it. 'Come on,' he said, slung his bag over his shoulder and began walking as Yocke hurried to pick up his gear.

From a low dune a hundred yards or so inland Yocke paused and looked back at the inlet in time to see the water close over the bridge of the boat. Hector Santana kept walking. He didn't bother to look.

'Campaigning with Cortés,' Jack Yocke muttered under his breath. He shifted the computer strap to ease the strain on his shoulder and hefted the vinyl suitcase. 'Or perhaps, *Walking Across Cuba* by Jack Yocke, ace reporter and world-class idiot.'

An hour passed as they walked. Yocke got thirsty and said so. Santana didn't say a word.

They were on a dirt road leading through sugarcane fields. The cane was knee high or so and green, rippling from air currents that never seemed to reach the two hikers. Away off to the south, the direction they were walking, Yocke could see clouds building over low hills or perhaps mountains. 'Are there mountains in Cuba?' he asked.

They passed several empty shacks. One had an ancient, skinny chicken wandering aimlessly in the yard. No other living thing in sight.

'Where is everybody?' he asked. 'Maybe we ought to look around for some water, huh? I'll bet they got a well or something.' Santana kept walking without replying. 'What's wrong with that idea, Jack?' Yocke muttered loud enough for the Cuban to hear.

'Hey, Hector,' Jack Yocke said five minutes later. 'Wanta tell me where we're going? If we're going to walk clear to Havana maybe I should lighten the load. What d'ya think?'

When Santana didn't reply, Yocke stepped near his ear and yelled, '*Hey, asshole!*'

'Did it ever occur to you,' Santana said patiently, 'that if we are stopped by Cuban troops, the less you know the better? For you, for me, for everyone?'

They walked for another hour. A small group of shacks came into sight and Santana headed for them. He went into the yard and motioned for Yocke to stay. Then he went up to a porch and looked through the screen. 'María? Carlos?'

Santana went inside. Yocke sat on his vinyl bag and took his shoes off and massaged his feet. A skinny chicken came over to watch. Does Cuba have any chickens that aren't skinny?

An old car, almost obscured by grass and weeds, sat rotting in a shed beside the house. Yocke went over and examined the car as murmurs of Spanish came through the window. An ancient Chevrolet sedan. Forty years old if it was a day. There wasn't enough paint even to tell what the original color had been. The back window was missing. Several chickens had obviously been raising their families on the rear seat.

At least he wasn't seasick. That was something. He was hungry enough to eat one of those scrawny chickens raw. He was watching one and trying to decide if he could catch it when Santana and a young woman came out of the house. The woman stood by Yocke as Santana went over to the car, got in, and ground on the engine.

Amazingly enough, a puff of blue smoke came out from under the car and the engine caught.

Santana backed the car into the yard. The woman opened the rear door and raked the chicken shit and straw out onto the ground. Santana got out of the car, leaving the engine running. 'This is it. This is our transportation to Havana.'

'You gotta be shitting me!'

'Put your stuff in the trunk.'

'Can I have some water?'

'In the house. They don't have any food, so don't ask.'

The young woman took him inside. There was an old woman in a rocker, and she nodded at him. His escort dipped him a glass of water from a pail that sat in the kitchen. He drained it and she gave him another.

'You speak English?'

'A little,' she said.

'What's your name?'

'María.'

'You know Santana?'

'Who?'

Yocke jerked his head toward the yard. 'Santana.'

'Oh. Pablo.' She smiled. 'He's my brother.'

Yocke handed back the glass. 'Thanks. *Gracias.*'

'*De nada.*'

Santana was waiting in the car. Yocke walked around and opened the front seat passenger door. 'You ride in back,' Santana told him. 'María's coming with us.'

Yocke dusted the rear seat as best he could and sat. The odor of chicken shit wouldn't be too bad at speed if they kept the windows down. Maria came out of the house with three or four plastic jugs filled with water. She put them in the trunk and climbed in beside her brother.

As they rolled out of the farmyard, Yocke could hear the transmission grinding. Or the differential. Perhaps both. 'This thing'll never make it to Havana.'

'Beats walking,' Santana said.

They had gone just a mile or so when they came to a two-lane asphalt road running east and west. Santana turned right, west.

For the first few hours the car made good time, rolling along at twenty-five or thirty miles per hour, Yocke estimated. The speedometer needle never moved off the peg. The few vehicles on the road were all west-bound. The flatbeds of cane trucks were packed with people, the old cars similarly stuffed and riding on their frames. Occasional knots of people walked west alongside the road.

Cane fields swept away to the horizon to the north and south across the flat, rolling fields, under a bright sun. Here and there shacks near the roads stood deserted and empty, with not even a chicken or pig in sight.

After two hours they came to a town. It was a real town, with streets and throngs of people in the streets. The car took an hour to creep through as Santana leaned out and shouted to knots of people in doorways, huddled around radios, '*Que pasa?*'

'The prisons have been emptied,' Santana told Jack Yocke at one point. 'The guards refused to fire on the people, who liberated the prisoners.'

On the west side of town the road was jammed with walking people: men, women, children, the elderly, the lame. The western pilgrimage grew denser at every crossroads, every village.

The Chevy proceeded little faster than the walking people, who gently parted in front of it to let it past and closed in again behind, like water in the wake of a boat's passage.

The radiator boiled over around noon. The three of them piled out and sat beside the car in a little shady strip as the human stream trudged by. Some of the people carried chickens and ducks with their feet tied together. Every now and then a man passed with a pig arranged around his shoulders.

Yocke mopped his face with his shirttail and relieved himself beside the road. Everyone else was doing likewise. There was no embarrassment: there was nowhere else to do it. He stood there with his back to the road looking out across the miles of growing cane and breathing deeply of the sweet odor, and made a wet spot on the red earth.

An army truck came by, also headed west. In addition to the troops packed willy-nilly in the back, civilians had clambered aboard, poultry, kids, and all. Yocke thought the truck looked like Noah's ark as it slowly breasted the human sea, trailing diesel fumes. He caught a glimpse of a goat amid the people and protruding rifles.

Eventually the steam from the Chevy's tired engine subsided. Water from bottles in the trunk was added, the worn-out radiator cap was replaced and carefully wired down, then Santana got behind the wheel and cranked the engine. It caught. For Santana's benefit, Yocke raised his hands in thanksgiving, then took his place amid the chicken dung.

In late afternoon the radiator failed catastrophically. Clouds of steam billowed from around the hood.

They pushed the car off the road, into the cane, and took what they could carry from the car. Yocke had to have the computer. He took the toothbrush and razor from the vinyl bag and put them in his pocket. His passport and money were already in his pocket. He changed shirts and socks. The rest of it was left.

As Yocke stood on the road beside the car waiting for the others, another army truck approached. A young woman sat on the left front fender facing forward with her blouse open breast-feeding a baby, her long, dark hair streaming gently in the shifting air currents. Her attention was concentrated on the child. She appeared golden in the evening sunlight. Yocke stood transfixed until the truck was far up the road and the young madonna no longer visible.

His companions were already walking westward with the throng. Jack Yocke eased the strap of the computer on his shoulder and set off after them.

At dusk, with the sunset still glowing ahead of them, they came to a burned-out Soviet-made armored personnel carrier – APC – sitting fifty feet or so off the road in a drainage ditch. Jack Yocke walked over to look.

A missile had punched a neat hole in the side armor; explosion and fire had done the rest. Burned, mutilated bodies lay everywhere, perhaps a dozen. Several reasonably intact bodies lay on the side of the ditch. These men had been shot by someone who had gotten behind them. The holes in their backs were neat and precise. Very military. The bodies had begun to bloat, stretching the clothing on the corpses drum-head tight.

One of the men was very young, just a boy really. He had been dead a while, perhaps since this morning. Flies crawled around his mouth and eyes and ears. A shift in the breeze gave Yocke a full close of the stench.

He staggered out of the ditch retching.

Santana and the young woman were waiting for him. Together they rejoined the human river flowing westward in the gathering dusk.

They reached the outskirts of Havana about nine P.M.

The streets were packed. People everywhere. Water could be had but no food. Those who had poultry or the carcasses of dogs built a fire out of anything that would burn and roasted them. The smoke wafted through the streets and between the buildings: the shadows it cast under the flickering streetlights played wildly over the crowd. Some people were drunk, shouting and singing and scuffling.

Government warehouses had been looted earlier in the afternoon, Santana learned, but the food had been eaten by those who carried it off. *Mañana*, tomorrow, the Yankees would send food. That was the rumor, oft-repeated, as hungry children wailed endlessly.

Castro was being held by the revolutionary committee, according to the radios, which were being played at maximum volume from every window. Fidel and his brother and the top government officials would be shot tomorrow in the Plaza de Revolution. *Viva Cuba! Cuba Libre!*

People stretched out in the street to sleep. Whole families. The crowd swirled and eddied and flowed around them, flowed toward the center of the city and the government offices around the Plaza de Revolución. Yocke followed Hector Santana and his sister.

The American was exhausted. The endless walking, the lack of sleep and food – these things had taken their toll. He wanted to slump down on the first vacant stretch of pavement he came to and sleep forever.

On he trudged, following Santana, following the crowd through the smoke and noise and dim lights.

When he reached the plaza he stopped and gaped. It was huge, covering several acres, and was packed with people. There wasn't room to lie down. People stood shoulder to shoulder, more people in one place than Jack Yocke had ever seen in his lifetime. The crowd was alive, buzzing endlessly with thousands of conversations. As he stood and looked in awe, chants broke out. 'Cu-ba, Cu-ba, Cu-ba,' over and over, growing as tens of thousands of voices picked it up. The sound had a low, pulsating thud to it that seemed to make the building walls shake.

Then Yocke realized he had lost Santana. He didn't care. He had to sleep.

He turned and retraced his steps, away from the plaza. Several blocks away he found an alley. It was full of sleeping people. He felt his way in, found a spot, and lay down. The chanting wasn't as loud here, two blocks from the square, but it was clear, distinctive, sublime. 'Cu-ba, Cu-ba,' repeated endlessly, like a religious chant.

Jack Yocke drifted into sleep thinking about dead soldiers and madonnas on army trucks and listening to that relentless sound.

They shot Castro around ten o'clock the next morning. He was shot first. The dictator was led out onto the platform where he had harangued his fellow countrymen for thirty-one years. Behind him were arrayed his lieutenants. All had their hands tied in front of them.

Yocke listened as a speaker read the charges over a microphone that blasted his voice to every corner of the square. Yocke understood little of it, not that it mattered. He elbowed and shoved and fought his way through the crowd, trying to get closer.

Ten men and women were selected from the crowd and allowed to climb up to the platform. Castro was led to a wall and faced around at the volunteers, who were lined up and given assault rifles by soldiers who stood beside them.

The speaker was still reading when someone opened fire. Three or four shots, ripping out. Castro went down.

He was assisted to his feet. The speaker stopped talking.

Someone shouted an order and all ten rifles fired raggedly.

The dictator toppled and lay still.

The soldiers took back their rifles and the members of the firing squad were sent back into the crowd. More leaped forward, too many. Ten men and women were selected and the rest herded back, forcibly, as three of the dictator's comrades were led over to stand beside his body. A jagged fusillade felled all three.

The scene was repeated four more times. Then a man with a pistol walked along and fired a bullet downward into each head. After six shots he had to stop and reload. Then six more. And finally four more.

'*Viva Cuba! Viva Cuba! Viva Cuba!*'

For the first time since the drama began, the reporter tore his gaze from the platform and looked at the faces of the people around him. They were weeping. Men, women, children – on every face were tears. Whether they were weeping for what they had lost or what they had gained, Jack Yocke didn't know.

About two that afternoon he was wandering along a mile or so from the square, by the front of a large luxury hotel on a decently wide street that had obviously been built in the bad old days BF – Before Fidel – when he heard his name called.

'Jack Yocke! *Hey, Jack! Up here!*'

He elevated his gaze. On a third-floor balcony, gesturing madly, stood Ottmar Mergenthaler. 'Jesus Christ, Jack! Where the hell you been?'

13

Three hours into his first day as a junior – *very* junior – weenie on the Joint Staff of the JCS, Lieutenant Toad Tarkington was wondering if perhaps Captain Grafton hadn't been right. Maybe he should have asked to have his shore tour cut short and gone back to sea. Sitting at a borrowed desk in an anonymous room without windows deep in the Pentagon, Toad was working his way through a giant hardbound manual of rules and regulations that he was supposed to be reading carefully, embedding permanently in the gray matter. He glanced surreptitiously around the large office to see if there was a single other 0-3 in sight.

He was going to be the coffee and paperclips guy. He knew it in his bones. Rumor had it there were other peasants with railroad tracks on the staff, although he hadn't yet seen a live one.

At the next desk over a female navy lieutenant commander was giving him the eye. Uh-oh! He turned the page he had been praying over for five minutes and examined the title of the next directive in the book. Something about uniforms, shiny shoes, and all that. He initialed it in the stamped box provided, sneaked a glance at the lieutenant commander – she was still looking – and pretended to read.

Without moving his head he checked his watch. Ten thirty-two. Oh, my God! He would be dead of boredom by lunchtime. If his heart stopped right now he would not fall over, he would just remain frozen here staring at this page until his uniform rotted off or they decided to buy new desks and move this one out. Maybe some of these other people sitting here at the other twenty-seven desks were already dead and nobody knew. Perhaps he should get a mirror and check all the bodies for signs of respiration. Maybe – the telephone buzzed softly. His first call!

He grabbed it and almost fumbled the receiver onto the floor.

'Lieutenant Tarkington, sir.'

'Is this Robert Tarkington?' A woman's voice.

'Yes it is.'

'Mr Tarkington, this is Nurse Hilda Hamhocker, at the Center for Disease Control?'

He glanced around to see if anyone was eavesdropping. Not noticeably so, anyway. 'Yes.'

'I'm calling to ask if you have known a woman named Rita Moravia?'

'Let's see. Rita Moravia . . . a short, squatty woman with a Marine Corps tattoo and a big wart right on the end of her nose? I do believe I know her, yes.'

'I mean, have you *known* her? In the biblical sense, Mr Tarkington. You see, she's one of our clients and has given your name as an "intimate" partner.'

The lieutenant commander was all ears, surveying him from beneath a droopy bang.

'That list of partners is modestly short, I trust.'

'Oh, no. Tragically long, Mr Tarkington. Voluminous. Like the Manhattan telephone directory. We've been calling for three months and we're only now getting to the Ts.'

'Yes. I have *known* her, Nurse Hamhocker.'

'Would you like to know Miss Moravia again, Mr Tarkington?'

'Well, yes, this very minute would be just perfect. Right here on my clean borrowed desk while everyone watches. But you see, the dear little diseased squatty person is never around. Not *ever*!'

'Oh, my poor, poor Horny Toad. It's that bad, is it?'

'Yes, Rita, it's that bad. Are you ever coming home?'

'Christmas leave starts in a week, lover. I'll be coming into National on United.' She gave him the flight number and time. 'Meet me, will you?'

'Plan on getting known again in the parking lot.'

'If you'll make that a backseat, I'll say yes.'

'Okay, the backseat.'

'I'll hold you to that, Toad. Bye.'

''Bye, babe.' He cradled the instrument and took a deep breath.

The lieutenant commander arched an eyebrow and raked her errant bang back into place. Then she concentrated on the document on the desk in front of her.

Toad took another deep breath, sighed, and resumed his study of the read-and-initial book. Ten minutes later he found a memo that he read with dismay. 'Staff is reminded,' the document said – rather too officially and formally for Toad's taste – 'that classified information shall not be discussed over unsecure telephones. [Numerous cites.] To ensure compliance with this regulation, all telephones in the staff spaces are continuously monitored while in use and the conversations taped by the communications security group.'

'Stepped in it again, Toad-man,' he muttered.

His stupor had returned and was threatening to become terminal ennui when Captain Jake Grafton entered the room, scanned it once, and headed in Toad's direction. Toad stood as the captain walked over and pulled a chair around. As usual, both officers wore their blue uniforms. But, Toad noticed with a pang, the two gold stripes around each of his sleeves contrasted sharply with the four on each of the captain's.

'Sit, for heaven's sake. If you pop up every time a senior officer comes around in this place, you'll wear out your shoes.'

'Yessir.' Toad put his bottom back into his chair.

'Howzit goin'?'

'Just about finished the read-and-initial book.' Toad sighed. 'What do you do around here, anyway?'

'I'm not sure. Seems to change every other week. Right now I'm doing analyses of counternarcotics operations from information sent over by the FBI and DEA. What can the military do to help and how much will it cost? That kind of thing. Keeps me jumping.'

'Sounds sexy.'

'Today it is. And it has absolutely nothing to do with training troops and aircrews or sustaining combat readiness.'

'Exciting, too, eh?'

Jake Grafton gave Tarkington a skeptical look.

'Well, at least we're pentaguys,' Toad said earnestly, 'ready to help chart the future of mankind, along with a thousand or so equally dedicated and talented Joint Staff souls. Makes me tingle.'

'Pentaguys?'

'I just made that up. Like it?' The lieutenant's innocent face broke into a grin, which caused his cheeks to dimple and exposed a set of perfect teeth. Deep creases radiated from the corners of his eyes.

The captain grinned back. He had known Tarkington for several years; one of Toad's most endearing qualities was his absolute refusal to take anything seriously. This trait, the captain well knew, was rare among career officers, who learned early on that literally everything was *very important*. In the highly competitive world of the peacetime military, an officer's ranking among his peers might turn on something as trivial as how often he got a haircut, how he handled himself at social functions, the neatness of his handwriting. For lack of a neat signature a fitness report was a notch lower than it might have been, so a choice assignment went to someone else, a promotion didn't materialize . . . There was an acronym popular now in the Navy that seemed to Jake to perfectly capture the insanity of the system: WETSU – We Eat This Shit Up. One battleship captain that Jake knew had even adopted WETSU as the ship's motto.

Toad Tarkington seemed oblivious to the rat race going on around him. One day it would probably dawn on him that he was a rodent in the maze with everyone else, but that realization hadn't hit him yet. Jake fervently hoped it never would.

'So what am I gonna be doing around here to thwart the forces of evil?' Toad asked.

'Officially you're one of thirty junior officer interns. For a while, at least, you'll be in my shop assisting me.'

'How about them apples!' Toad's eyebrows waggled. 'I'll start by drafting up a memo for you to fire off to the Joint Chiefs: "Shape up or ship out!" Don't worry, I'll make it more diplomatic than that, take the edge off, pad it and grease it. Then memos for the FBI and DEA. We'll—'

'We'll start in the morning at oh-seven-thirty,' Jake said, rising from his chair. He looked around again, taking it all in. 'What do you think of this place, anyway?'

'All these different kinds of uniforms, it looks like a bus drivers' convention.' Toad lowered his voice. 'Don't you think the Air Farce folks look like they work for Greyhound?'

'I'll give you the same advice my daddy gave me, Tarkington, when he put me on a bus and sent me off to the service. Keep your mouth shut and your bowels open, and you'll do okay.' Jake Grafton walked away.

Toad grinned broadly and settled back into his chair.

'I couldn't help overhearing your insensitive remark, Lieutenant,' the lieutenant commander at the desk across the aisle informed him.

Toad swiveled. The lieutenant commander reminded him of his third-grade teacher, that time she caught him throwing spitballs. She had that look.

'I'm sorry, ma'am.'

'Our friends in the Air Force are very proud of their uniform.'

'Yes, ma'am. No offense intended.'

'Who was that captain?'

'Captain Grafton, ma'am.'

'He was very informal with you, Lieutenant.' The way she said 'lieutenant' made it sound like the lowest rank in the Guatemalan National Guard. 'Here at Joint Staff we're much more formal.'

'I'm sure.' Toad tried out a smile.

'This is a *military* organization.'

'I'll try to remember,' Toad assured her, and stalked off toward the men's head.

Henry Charon eased the car to a stop in front of the abandoned farmhouse and killed the engine. He rolled down his window and sat looking at the overgrown fields and the stark leafless trees beyond. The dismal gray sky seemed to rest right on the treetops. The crisp air smelled of snow.

He had followed the dirt road for four miles, just a rut through the forest, and made it through a mudhole that he had explored with a stick before he tried it. There were tire tracks that he thought were at least a month old, left by deer hunters. Nothing fresh. That was why he had selected this dirt road after he had examined three others.

He was deep in the Monongahela National Forest, four hours west of Washington in the West Virginia mountains. Henry Charon took a deep deep breath and smiled. It was gorgeous here.

He pulled on his coat and hat and locked the car, then walked back along the road in the direction from which he had come. He inspected the remnants of an apple orchard and the brush that had grown up on a two-acre plot that had once been a garden.

When he had walked about a mile, he left the road and began climbing the hillside. He proceeded slowly, taking his time, pausing frequently to listen and look. He moved like a shadow through the gray trees, climbing steadily to the top of the ridge, then along it with the abandoned farm somewhere below him on his left. He intended to circle the abandoned farm to ensure that there were no people nearby. If there were he would hear or see enough to warn him of their presence.

As he moved Henry Charon examined the trees, noting the places where deer had browsed, feeling the pellet droppings and estimating their age. This was his first outing in the hardwood forests of the eastern United States. He felt like a youngster again, exploring and greeting new things with delight. He saw where the chipmunks had opened their acorns and he spent five minutes watching a squirrel watching him. He examined a groundhog hole and ran his fingers along the scars in a young sapling that a buck had used to rub the velvet from his antlers earlier this autumn. He heard a woodpecker drumming and detoured for a hundred yards to glimpse it.

He had been in the fourth grade when he found a biography of Daniel Boone in the school library. The book had fascinated him and, he admitted now to himself as he glided silently through the forest, changed his life. The years Boone spent alone in Kentucky hunting wild game for furs and food and avoiding hostile Indians had seemed to young Henry Charon to be the ultimate in adventure. And now, at last, he was in the type of forest Boone had known so well. True, it wasn't the virgin forest of two hundred and fifty years ago, but still . . .

He was thinking of Boone and the hunting years when he saw the doe. She was browsing and had her back to him. He froze. Something, instinct perhaps, made her turn her head and swivel her large ears for any sound that should not have been there.

Henry Charon stood immobile. The deer's eyes and brain were alert to movement, so Charon held every muscle in his body absolutely still. He even held his breath.

The gentle wind was from the northwest, carrying his scent away from her as she sampled the breeze. Satisfied at last, she resumed her browsing.

Slowly, ever so slowly, he stepped closer. He froze whenever her head position would allow his movement to be picked up by her peripheral vision.

He was only twenty-five feet or so from her when she finally saw him. She had moved unexpectedly. Now she stood stock still, tense, ready to flee, her ears bent toward him to catch the slightest sound.

Henry Charon remained motionless.

She relaxed slightly and started toward him, her ears still attuned, her eyes fixed on him.

Surprised, he moved a hand.

The deer paused, wary, then kept coming.

Someone tamed her, he thought. *She's tame!*

The doe came to him and sniffed his hands. He presented them for her inspection, then scratched between her ears.

Her coat was stiff and thick to his touch. He stroked her and felt it. He spoke to her and watched her ears move to catch the sound of his voice.

The memory must have been strong. She seemed unafraid.

The moment bothered him, somehow. Man had changed the natural order of things and Henry Charon knew that this change was not for the better. For her own safety the doe should flee man. Yet he had not the heart to frighten her. He petted her and spoke softly to her as if she could understand, then watched in silence when she finally walked away.

The doe paused and looked back, then trotted off into the trees. She was soon lost from sight. Thirty seconds later he could no longer hear her feet among the leaves that carpeted the ground.

An hour later he arrived back at his car. He opened the trunk and got some targets, which he posted on the wall of the ramshackle farmhouse.

The pistols were first. All 9 mm, he fired them two-handed at the target at a distance of ten paces. There were four pistols, all identical Smith & Wesson automatics. He fired a clipful through each. One seemed to have a noticeably heavier trigger pull than the others, and he set it aside. When he finished, he carefully retrieved all the spent brass. If he missed one it was no big deal, but he didn't want to leave forty shells scattered about.

After he posted a fresh target, he took the three rifles and moved off to fifty yards.

The rifles were Winchester Model 70s in .30-06, with 3 × 9 variable scopes. He squeezed off three rounds from the first rifle, checked the target with the binoculars, and adjusted the scope. All three bullets in his third string formed a group that could be covered with a dime. Charon carefully placed every spent cartridge in his pocket.

After repeating the process with the second and third rifle he moved back to one hundred yards. He fired three, checked the target, fired again.

The final group from each rifle formed a small, nickle-sized group about one inch above his point of aim. This with factory ammunition.

Satisfied, he wiped the weapons carefully and stored each in a soft guncase and repacked them in the trunk of the car.

The final item he carried several hundred yards up the hill. Then he came back to the car and backed it down the road past the first bend. From the floor of the backseat he took several old newspapers. He retrieved the targets from the wall of the house and added them to the newspapers.

On the side of the other hill, high up near the tree line, was a fairly prominent outcroppping of rock. Standing on the rock and using the binoculars, he could just make out the item he had left amid the trees and leaves on the other side of the little valley. At least three hundred yards, he decided. Closer to four hundred.

He used the targets and wadded up sheets of newsprint to build a small fire. To this he added sticks and twigs and a relatively dry piece of a dead limb. Then he walked back across the valley.

The weapon was in an olive-drab tube. Ridiculously simple instructions were printed on the tube in yellow stenciled letters. He followed them. Tube on right shoulder, eyepiece open, power on, crosshairs on the rock outcropping – listen for the tone. There it is! Heat source acquired.

Charon squeezed the trigger.

The missile left in a flash and roar. Loud but not terribly so. It shot across the valley trailing fire and exploded above the rock ledge, seemingly right in the fire.

Carrying the now empty tube, Henry Charon walked back across the valley. The weapon had gone right through the fire and exploded against the base of a tree on the other side. The shrapnel had sprayed everywhere. The bark of the trees was severely flayed: one small wrist-thick tree trunk had been completely severed by flying shrapnel. The tree the missile had impacted was severely damaged. No doubt it and several other trees would eventually die.

Satisfactory. Quite satisfactory. The other two missiles should work equally well.

He put the remnants of the fire completely out, scattered the charred wood, and dumped dirt on the site where it had been.

Fifteen minutes later Henry Charon started the car. The empty cartridges and spent missile launcher were all in the trunk. He had found a likely spot to bury them on the way in, about two miles back. There was enough daylight left.

Smiling, thinking about the doe, Henry Charon slipped the transmission into drive and turned the car around.

14

Harrison Ronald Ford drove McNally's old Chrysler that evening. Pure luck, he later decided. He picked up the guard at a Seven-Eleven at nine o'clock that night and together they drove to the old Sanitary Bakery warehouse on Fourth Street NE, on the edge of the railyard. The guard didn't say much – he never did. About twenty-five or so, he called himself Tooley.

The window openings in the lower two levels of the ancient bakery warehouse were blocked up with concrete blocks. The windows in the upper levels showed the ravages of rocks and wind. A high chain-link fence surrounded the property out to the Fourth Street NE sidewalk and the dirt street that ran along the north side. Inside the fence were about a dozen garbage trucks. Watching through the wire as Ford rumbled by were two Dobermans.

He pulled into the parking area on the south side of the building and walked toward the only door, which had steel bars welded over it, as Tooley trailed along. Two other cars sat in the empty lot.

Ford opened the door. Tooley never opened doors, preferring to let the driver do it. He was being paid to look tough and shoot, if necessary, and that was all he was going to do.

Ike Randolph was there supervising the cutting and packaging operation, as usual. McNally had used this warehouse for only three days now, and in a few more, anytime the whim struck him, he would change to another location. Not that Freeman was or had ever been within a mile of the building. That's what he hired Ike and the others for. If the cops raided the place, the hired help could take the fall.

'Okay,' Ike said and spread out a large map of the city. 'Here's the route tonight and where to take the stuff. Pay attention.' He traced the route he wanted Harrison Ronald to follow as Tooley and one of the guys from the chase car watched over his shoulder. Two deliveries. When Ike finished, Harrison then traced the route, calling out streets and turns, proving that he knew it.

'You got it.'

The gunnies from the chase car said little. In their early twenties, wearing expensive, trendy clothes, they looked, Harrison thought, exactly like what they were, drug guys with more money than they knew how to spend. Which was precisely the impression they hoped to create. In the world of the inner city these young men had spent their lives in, the druggies had the bucks and the choice ass – they had the *status*. Tonight, as usual, these two young gunnies stood around looking tough and with it.

The little sweet piece was also there, and Harrison Ronald flirted with her to keep up appearances. She flirted right back as Tooley watched, looking bored.

'She's a hooker, man,' he told Harrison as they walked through the empty lower floor of the warehouse toward the entrance, Harrison carried the stuff in a plain brown grocery bag. 'Uses so much of that shit she's cutting, Freeman *charges* her to work here.'

'So what's your bitch, Tooley? She won't go down on you?'

'Stick it in that, Z, and it'll rot right off. You won't have nothing left to piss through but some grotty ol' pubic hair.'

The guard at the door handed Tooley and the chase car crew Browning 9-mm automatics. As Harrison watched, Tooley popped the clip out, inspected it, then slid it home. He cocked the weapon, pulled back the slide just enough to glimpse brass, then lowered the hammer and put the pistol in his coat pocket. The other two men did the same, their evening ritual.

Now the guard handed Tooley an Uzi. He inspected the clip to ensure it was fully loaded, then pulled the bolt back into the cocked and ready position and engaged the safety. Then he reached for the grocery sack the guard offered him and inserted the weapon in it. After checking their Uzis, the two gunmen put them under their coats and walked to their car as the guard watched through the one dirty window. Satisfied, he opened the door again and motioned to Tooley and Harrison Ronald.

Tooley got into the backseat of the Chrysler while Harrison Ronald slid behind the wheel and put the dope on the floor on the passenger's side.

Two youngsters about ten years old were playing basketball on the street. The hoop was mounted on a backboard on a pole right by the edge of the pavement. They stood aside while Harrison eased the car past them and headed north, toward Rhode Island Avenue. The chase car, a dark Pontiac Trans-Am, followed four car lengths behind.

Ford glanced in the rearview mirror. Tooley had the Uzi out and was examining the safety.

'Put that fucking thing down where nobody can see it.'

'Just drive, mother.'

'And point it in some other direction.'

Tooley grinned. He didn't have a nice grin. He kept the gun aimed in the center of Ford's back. 'I told you to drive, motherfuck.'

At Rhode Island the light was red. Wailing, Ford checked the rearview mirror. Tooley was just sitting back there, watching the back of Ford's head, with his hand on the trigger and the gun pointed at Ford's back.

'Turn right here,' he said.

'You heard Ike.'

'Little change of plan.' He prodded Harrison in the back of the neck with the barrel of the submachine gun.

The light turned green.

'Now! Turn right.'

Ford kept his feet on the brake and clutch and sat staring into the rearview mirror, trying to read what was in Tooley's face.

'Do it, Z, or I'll blow your fucking brains right out the front windshield.' Tooley jabbed him with the barrel, hard.

Ford cranked the wheel and turned right.

'Now what?'

'Just do like I tell you.'

'Freeman'll kill you. Slow.'

'Who's gonna tell him, man? You?'

'He'll find out. He always does.'

'Your problem is your mouth. I've got a cure for that. Turn left up ahead on Thirteenth.' Tooley glanced behind to see if the Trans-Am was following. It was.

As they went around the corner, Tooley looked over his shoulder again to check the chase car. As he did so Harrison Ronald stiffened, rose, and half twisted in his seat. He used the bottom of his hand in a swinging backhand chopping motion that caught Tooley in the throat.

The gunman gagged, then choked. The Uzi fell to the floor as he clawed at his throat. Harrison applied the brakes moderately and brought the Chrysler to a swift halt. Then he turned and chopped again with all his strength at the hands around Tooley's neck. His larynx crushed, the gunman collapsed.

The rear window and front windows both popped as a bullet punched a neat hole in them and left them crazed, with radiating and circular cracks.

Harrison Ronald Ford popped the clutch and slammed the accelerator down, both in one fluid motion.

The tires squawled and smoke poured from the rear wheel wells as the big engine revved and Ford tried to keep the steering wheel centered.

He cranked it over and slid around the first corner, braking hard, then jamming on the gas halfway through the turn. The engine snarled and responded with neck-snapping power.

The Trans-Am stayed with him. Several more shots. Another bullet punched glass. In the backseat Tooley was still struggling to breathe, the tendons in his neck standing out like cords, his feet kicking spasmodically.

Ford took another right, then shot across oncoming traffic in a sweeping left turn, still accelerating, onto Rhode Island northeast-bound.

The fat was in the fire now. The two men in the chase car had to kill him. If they didn't. Freeman McNally would kill *them*, just as surely as the sun would rise tomorrow.

Fifty, sixty, seventy . . . he stayed on the gas and weaved around slower traffic. The engine was willing and the tires gripped well. The Pontiac was behind, still coming.

What to do? Think. Swerve to avoid a VW turning left, straight through a red light with horn blazing. Eighty . . . He backed off the gas, afraid to go faster.

Cops – where are the fucking traffic cops with their fucking speed guns and ticket books?

He was going to get the green light at South Dakota Avenue. Amen. At the last instant he slammed on the brakes and swerved right and went around the corner on two wheels.

Back on the gas. Around a truck, brakes on hard for a sedan just piddling, skidding some, then clear and in the right lane and back on the throttle.

They were still following. Flashes from the passenger side. Another bullet punched through the glass and he felt several more thump into the bodywork.

He was up to ninety approaching Bladensburg, crowding the center-line. Another green light. Hallelujah! Feathering the brake he dropped to about fifty and used the whole street to make the sweeping right onto Bladensburg southwest-bound.

Now he was heading into the heart of the city, toward the Capitol, which was still four miles or so ahead. The Capitol area would be crawling with tourists and cops. Right now Harrison Ronald wanted to see the flashing lights of a police cruiser more than he wanted anything else.

As he sawed at the wheel and tapped the brakes and swerved to avoid traffic, he realized he would never outrun the car behind. In spite of his car's capabilities, the gunmen in the Trans-Am had the telling advantage. Harrison Ronald was trying to keep from killing pedestrians and motorists while the men behind didn't care. They had bet their lives when they decided to rip off Freeman McNally. If some little old lady got run over, that was her tough luck.

Harrison Ronald held his horn down. He slammed the accelerator to the floor and went through a yellow light at the New York Avenue intersection at seventy-five.

The headlights of the dark Trans-Am were almost fifty yards back. In the rearview mirror he saw someone pull into the intersection in front of the speeding Pontiac and get lightly clipped. The left front fender of the Trans-Am disintegrated, the man at the wheel fought desperately to hold it on the road, and the black car kept coming.

With horn braying and the big hemi engine throbbing, Harrison Ronald straddled the painted centerline. He used his left foot to flash the low and high beams up and down.

His luck couldn't hold. It didn't. A yellow light ahead. It would be red when he got there.

He slowed. The Trans-Am grew larger in the rearview mirror.

More bullets spanged into the Chrysler. One buried itself in the dashboard.

He picked a gap between the cars crossing in front of him and aimed the Chrysier for the gap. Now – clutch out and on the throttle, skidding some, going through, pedal to the floor.

He checked the mirror. With luck the Trans-Am would hit somebody or stop to avoid a collision.

No luck. The Pontiac shot a gap and kept coming, but too far back to shoot.

Now he was on Maryland Avenue, a boulevard that went straight as an arrow toward the Capitol building. The lighted dome rose straight ahead above the trees.

The four lanes were crowded. Harrison Ronald straddled the median, which scraped the bottom side of the Chrysler, a ripping, grinding sound that sounded loud even above the engine noise. Something came off the car. The muffler and tailpipe. He ran over three traffic signs but had to swerve from the median to avoid the lightpoles.

Avoiding one lightpole his wheel clipped the curb and the Chrysler swapped ends and skidded backwards, straight into a delivery truck.

The engine was still running. He had trouble getting the shift lever into first but he made it, and with the wheel cranked over, did a wheel-spinning 180 and got under way as the Trans-Am came thundering down on him with the guy leaning out of the passenger window spraying lead.

Several cars crashed together getting out of the way. One car ran through a parking lot and buried itself in a plate-glass window.

Ahead was a park, one of those blocks from which the major avenues in the city radiated. Harrison Ronald went through it. If he didn't the Trans-Am might gain more ground than he could afford to lose.

The front end parted with mother earth as it bucked the curb, but the rear wheels impacting the obstruction brought the nose down with a crash that jammed the front bumper into the concrete in a shower of sparks.

Luckily the park was deserted on a December night. He braked hard and slid around the statue in the center and jam accelerated. The dome of the Capitol was dead ahead.

The front wheels were vibrating badly now and he gripped the steering wheel tightly to hold on.

A skidding right turn, doing about sixty or seventy, onto Constitution Avenue westbound. Okay, goddammit, where are the cops?

Almost on cue he heard a siren over the unmuffled roar of the engine.

Yet the Trans-Am was gaining.

The Mall – he would go across the grass of the Mall. Everybody and their brother would see them. Even as he considered it another burst of bullets came through the car.

Something stung his ear.

He swung right, hard, the car skidding out of control. It used the whole road and then some, bouncing off parked vehicles, but he ended up headed north on First.

The damned Pontiac was still with him.

He. swung left onto D Street. Aha! Ahead on the left was the Labor Department building and the ramp that went under it down onto I-395. If he could make that turn and get down onto the freeway . . .

A semitractor crept around the corner and filled the street. He slammed on the brakes. Skidding again. Off the brakes, just by the truck on the right, slamming over parking meters, then hard right, down a couple blocks, left, on the gas.

The Pontiac was gaining. Hadn't they had enough? The siren – was it closer?

Ahead was the mall on the south side of the National Collection of Fine Arts. He went for it.

And a bus.

A huge bus, coming from right to left. He braked hard. Another bus following. He could make the gap. He shot through.

Behind him he heard tires squealing, then the sound of a crash.

Harrison Ronald applied the brakes firmly. He avoided some drunks and trash cans, then turned left on Ninth, joining with traffic.

In the rear seat Tooley looked very very dead. His lips and tongue were swollen, protruding, as were his eyes, which were focused on nothing at all.

Sometime during the chase one or more of the bags holding the cocaine had split, and the white powder was all over the passenger seat floor.

Harrison Ronald got out a hanky and wiped the stick shift knob, the light switch, the dashboard, the mirror, the steering wheel. Jesus, his prints were all over this car. Still . . .

He turned some corners and pulled into the first vacant spot by the curb he came to. He wiped the door lever and took a last wipe of the wheel. Then he switched the ignition off and got out. Pocketing the key, he took two seconds to rub the handkerchief over the outside door handle, then walked away. On the sidewalk he took the car key off the ring which also contained the key to his apartment. After wiping it with the cloth, he dropped the car key into the first trash barrel he came to.

Three blocks later he found a pay phone that still worked. He dialed 911 and reported the car stolen. When the dispatcher asked his name, he hung up.

The wailing of the sirens echoed from the buildings and seemed to come from every direction. There was blood on his cheek and his left ear was burning fiercely. His left arm was burning too. Blood there on his jacket.

The second number Harrison Ronald Ford dialed was the home phone of FBI Special Agent Thomas F. Hooper. 'We have to talk. Now. A difficulty has arisen.'

Harrison Ronald Ford was sitting on the steps on the south side of the Lincoln Memorial when Hooper came around the corner and slowly climbed up toward him. The spot Ford had selected was in the shadow, out of the spotlights that illuminated the columns around him.

'You okay?'

'Fucking arm feels like it's on fire.'

The undercover man had removed his undershirt in a subway restroom and torn it into strips. He had his shirt and jacket unbuttoned now and sat holding one of the folded cotton strips against the groove in his left tricep.

'How bad is it?'

'Just a crease. Hurts like hell, though.'

'Want to go to a doctor?'

'Nah. After a while I gotta go see Freeman and they'll do the doctoring there.' Bullet wounds treated by a doctor had to be reported to police, so Ford didn't want to try and explain to Freeman how he had gotten away with a stunt like that.

In the dim light Hooper inspected Ford's face, then used one of the pieces of tee-shirt to swab the wound.

'You were lucky.'

'That's true.'

'You're gonna run out of luck.'

'Has to happen.'

'Why don't you quit now. We'll bust McNally, go with what we have.'

Harrison sat in silence, thinking about it. Fifty feet away a couple held each other close and sat looking at the lights of the city. From where they sat, off to the left, they could see the white obelisk of the Washington Monument against the black sky. 'How many casualties?'

'Ten dead, apparently. Plus that guy you killed in the car.'

'He was going to kill me when we got to where he wanted to go.'

'I understand. It was justified.'

'I had to do it.'

'I understand! Christ, don't sweat it. He was a shithead. He had it coming.'

Harrison removed the makeshift bandage from his arm and held it out where he could see it. Fresh blood. He was still bleeding. He refolded it and ran it back inside his shirt.

'I didn't know what to do. There's never any cops around when you need them.'

'All out on the freeway writing speeding tickets,' Hooper agreed. After a few moments, he asked, 'Who's the Chrysler registered to?'

'Some derelict. The address on the registration certificate is a vacant lot. Freeman McNally owns it but you'll never prove it. And my prints are all over it.'

'Any of his prints on it?'

'Not to my knowledge.'

'Too bad.'

Yeah, it was all too bad. Eleven people dead! Holy shit!

'C'mon. You've done enough. Let me take you to the doctor. We'll do a taped debrief tomorrow and I'll have you on the plane to Evansville tomorrow evening.'

'Got a cigarette?'

'No.'

'Reach inside my coat here and get one and light it for me, will'ya?'

Hooper did so.

'Y'know,' Harrison Ronald said after a bit, 'I think this little deal is gonna get me in tight with Freeman. Somebody tried to rip him off. He's gonna be curious as a cat about what I know and then he's going after somebody.'

'What do you know?'

'Nothing. Absolutely nothing.'

'Maybe we could dream up something for you to know.'

'Too dangerous, man. He'd check it out. If it doesn't check out, I'm dead. Just like that. Lying to Freeman McNally is like playing Russian roulette. You tell one and stop breathing while you wait to see if your brains are flying out the side of your head.'

'There's got to be a profit in this for us someplace,' Hooper said.

'A few more days. You'll see. Just a few more days.' Harrison Ronald sighed. 'C'mon, help me up. My ass is frozen and my legs are getting stiff. I gotta go see Freeman.'

'What if he decides that you might have been in it with the others and it just got fucked up?'

'There's that,' Harrison Ronald said sourly. 'But you didn't have to say it, man.'

'There's no telling,' Hooper insisted. 'It could go down like that.'

'If it does, it's been nice knowing you.'

'What about a wire? You could wear a wire. We could wait just a block away.'

'You gotta be shitting me!'

Hooper sat back down and watched Ford go down the steps and turn east to go around the front of the Memorial. It was too late for the subway so he had some walking to do. Maybe he would call Freeman from someplace.

Hooper felt cold. The steps were cold and the air was cold and he was cold. He pulled his coat tightly around him and sat looking at the lights of Arlington.

15

Eleven Dead in Drug Chase, the morning headline screamed.

In the backseat of his limo on the way to his office. White House chief of staff William C. Dorfman read the story with a growing sense of horror. Six passengers on a bus had been killed and five injured – three critically – at ten-eighteen P.M. last night when a 1988 Pontiac Trans-Am slammed into a busload of Japanese museum directors and their families on the street near the National Collection of Fine Arts. The Japanese had just attended a reception at the museum and were returning to their hotel when the Pontiac smashed into the side of the bus. Witnesses estimated the car was traveling at seventy miles per hour just prior to impact. The two men in the automobile had died instantly. Two Uzi submachine guns were found in the wreckage.

A husband and wife from Silver Spring died five or six minutes earlier when the same vehicle, chasing an older four-door sedan, precipitated a head-on collision at an intersection on Bladensburg Road. The driver of a large truck belonging to a wholesale grocer had swerved to avoid the Pontiac and had struck the car driven by the Maryland couple.

Finally, if all that weren't enough, the body of a black man in his midtwenties had been found in a bullet-riddled Chrysler abandoned on H Street, three blocks from the White House. Police believed this to be the car the Pontiac had chased. Ten pounds of cocaine and crack had been recovered from the car, which had also contained an Uzi submachine gun.

The story contained accounts by three or four witnesses who told of the passenger in the Pontiac blazing away with an automatic weapon at the Chrysler as it tore down Bladensburg Road and Maryland Avenue at speeds of up to ninety miles per hour. Eight vehicles had been reported with bullet damage and police expected to learn of more.

Two photos accompanied the story. One was of the Chrysler shot full of holes and the other was of a Japanese woman in a kimono drenched with blood being assisted toward an ambulance.

Before he finished the story, Dorfman snapped on the limo's small television. The morning show on the channel that came up was running footage of the wrecked bus with the nearly unrecognizable remains of the Pontiac buried in its side. Shots of ambulance attendants leading away crying, bleeding victims followed.

Oh, my God! Why did that woman have to be wearing a kimono?

As if the savings-and-loan insider fraud debacle and the crises in the Baltic republics and Cuba weren't enough! And to make life at the top truly perfect, George Bush had a press conference scheduled for this afternoon. *God!* The reporters would be in a feeding frenzy.

Dorfman turned down the sound on the television and dialed the car telephone.

'Why wasn't I informed of this bus incident last night?' he roared at the hapless aide who answered. He ignored the aide's spluttering. He knew the answer. Procedure dictated that the chief of staff be informed immediately of national security crises and international incidents, and a car-bus wreck had not fit neatly into either category. Still, he had to do something to blow off steam and the aide was an inviting target. The little wart never went beyond his instructions, never showed an ounce of initiative.

I'm going to have to get out of this fucking business before I have a heart attack, Dorfman told himself. I'm thirty pounds overweight and take those damn blood pressure pills and this shit is going to kill me. Sooner rather than later.

When he charged into his office, an aide started talking before Dorfman could open his mouth. 'The Japanese ambassador wants an audience with the President. This morning.'

'Get the Mouth in here.' That was the White House press secretary. 'And where's that memo Gid Cohen sent over here last week? The one that lists all the antidrug initiatives he recommends?'

Thirty seconds later the memo from Cohen was on his desk. Let's see, the AG wants to change the currency to make hoards worthless – we can do that. It'll piss off the bankers and change-machine manufacturers and little ol' ladies with mattresses full of the stuff, but . . . He wants special courts and more federal judges and prosecutors to handle drug cases: okay, bite the bullet and do it. He wants to fund a nationwide drug rehab program: we'll need hard dollar info on that. He wants to fold the DEA in with the FBI and make one superagency. Christ, that will drive the Democrats bonkers.

A national ID card? Dorfman wrote no and underlined it. More prisons, mandatory sentencing for drug crimes, changes in the rules of criminal procedure, a revision of the bail laws, an increased role for the military in interdicting smuggling . . .

Dorfman kept reading, marking yes, no, and maybe. When he had originally received this memo he glanced at it and discarded it as yet another example of Cohen's lack of sensitivity to political reality. Well, he told himself now, reality was changing fast.

When the press secretary came in, Dorfman didn't bother to look up. 'What're you going to say about the bus deal?'

'That the President will have a statement at his news conference. The government offers its condolences on behalf of the American people to the citizens of Japan who lost relatives last night. A quote from the President that says this accident was a tragedy.'

'Let me see the quote.' Dorfman scanned the paper, then passed it back. 'Okay. What is the President going to say at the news conference?'

'I've got two speechwriters working on it. Have something for you in about an hour.'

'Go. Do it.'

Two minutes later, with Cohen's memo in hand, William C. Dorfman headed for the Oval Office to see the President.

The secretary in his outer office called after him: 'The attorney general's on the phone. He wants to come over and see the President. He has the director of the FBI with him.'

'Okay.'

Dorfman and Bush had framed a strategy to respond to the public relations crisis posed by the death of six Japanese VIPs and were fleshing it out when the attorney general and the director of the FBI were shown into the Oval Office fifteen minutes later.

'What do you have on this bus thing?' President Bush asked the FBI director.

'For public consumption, we're working on it, following every lead. Doing autopsies on the people in the cars. When we know who they are we'll work backward. For you only, one of our undercover agents was driving the car being chased. He was delivering ten pounds of coke and crack for Freeman McNally's drug syndicate when the people who were supposed to be guarding the shipment tried to rip him off. Those were the three men who died, two in the Pontiac and one in the Chrysler.'

Dorfman couldn't believe his ears. He goggled. 'Say again. The part about the undercover agent.'

'Our man was driving the Chrysler.'

'FBI?'

'One of our undercover people, temporarily on loan to the FBI from his regular police job.'

'A cop drove like a freaked-out maniac through the heart of downtown Washington and got *eleven people killed*?'

'What the hell do you think he ought to have done?' the director demanded. 'Let them shoot him?'

'Well, Jesus, I think you ought to ask the Japanese ambassador that question. Maybe he can give you an answer. One escapes me just now.'

George Bush broke in. 'Our guy okay?'

'Got grazed by two bullets. But he's okay. Shook as hell.'

'You got enough to arrest Freeman McNally?'

'No, sir,' said Gideon Cohen. 'We don't. Oh, we have it chapter and verse from the undercover man, but we're going to need more than just the testimony of one man. And most of his testimony will be hearsay. He's had little personal contact with McNally.'

'When?'

'Soon. But not yet.'

The press is gonna crucify us,' Dorfman muttered.

'Had to happen sooner or later,' Gideon Cohen remarked to no one in particular.

'Explain.'

'We've got over four hundred murders a year here in the District, something like eighty per cent of them drug related. It was just a matter of time before some tourists or political bigwigs got caught in a crossfire.'

'I don't buy that. This drug chase in the downtown sounds like sloppy police work to me. Where were the uniformed police while these people were playing Al Capone and Dutch Schultz on Constitution Avenue?'

Cohen sneered. 'Jesus, Dorfman, get real! If four hundred middle-class white people had been slaughtered last year in Howard County, there'd have been a mass march on Washington before the Fourth of July. They'd have dragged you politics-as-usual guys out of the Capitol kicking and screaming and hung the whole damn crowd.'

'I think we're wasting our time pointing fingers at the cops,' George Bush said dryly and adjusted the trousers of his eight-hundred-dollar suit. 'The Japanese ambassador is coming over in a little while to hand me my head on a plate. The country is in an uproar. So what was politically impossible last week is possible now. That's all any politician can ever try to do, Gid – the possible. I'm not the Pied Piper. I can't take them where they don't want to go. And I'm not apologizing for that. I'm not Jesus Christ either.'

Bush picked up Cohen's wish list from his desk. 'A federal ID card for every man, woman, and child in the country? That'll never wash. The Supreme Court says they can burn the flag as political protest. They'll be using these cards for toilet paper.'

'That'd be nice to have, but—'

'A national, mandatory drug rehab program? For an estimated ten billion per year? Where are we going to get the money? For another federal bureaucracy that will be so big and bloated it won't help anybody.'

'It would—'

'And an overhaul of the criminal justice system,' the President continued. ' "Streamline and eliminate delay" you say. The procedures of the criminal justice system, obsolete and inefficient though they are, are mandated by the Bill of Rights according to the nine wise men on the Supreme Court. We'd need a constitutional convention to revise the Bill of Rights. Despite widely held opinions to the contrary, I am not damn fool enough to advocate opening that Pandora's box.'

Cohen said nothing.

'Some of this stuff we can do. I've marked the items. Now, Gid, you and Bill and the secretary of the Treasury get together and come up with specifics. You've got two hours. We'll get the Senate and House leadership over here and brief them, then we'll go to the press conference and see if I can get through that with a whole hide. I don't suppose they'll have many questions about Cuba or Lithuania or foreign aid to the Soviets, all subjects I've spent two days reviewing.' He threw up his hands. 'In the meantime the Japanese ambassador, one of the best friends America has in the Japanese government, wants to tell me what he thinks of American law enforcement. Mr FBI Director, you can sit here with me and sweat through that.'

This morning in his Pentagon cubicle Captain Jake Grafton read with professional interest the stories in the *Washington Times* and the *Post* about the chase and spectacular accident of the previous evening. As the senior officer in the Joint Staff counternarcotics section, he routinely read the papers to learn what the public press had to say about the drug problem. The press, he knew, defined the issues for the electorate, which in turn set the priorities for the politicians. The issues with which the government sought to grapple were those nebulous perceptions created by the passing of selected raw facts through these imperfect double filters: any public servant who failed to understand this basic truth was doomed to frustrated ineffectiveness. Despite the fact that he had spent his professional life in a military organization solving simpler, more clearly defined problems, Jake Grafton, farmer's son and history major, instinctively understood how things worked in a democracy.

At a cubicle behind him, Jake could hear one of his colleagues, an air force lieutenant colonel, explaining the operation of the computer terminals to Toad Tarkington. A terminal rested on every desk. Tarkington seemed to be soaking up the procedures with nonchalant ease. Jake glanced at the dark screen on his own desk and smiled wryly. He had struggled like Hercules to acquire computer literacy while Tarkington seemed to pick it up as naturally as breathing.

Beside the front-page story in the *Post* about the car-bus crash was another story that the captain read with interest. By Jack Yocke, datelined Havana, Cuba, it was, the tag line promised, the first in a five-part series.

The story was about a rural family and its trek to the capital to personally witness the downfall of Castro. Why they came, what they saw and ate, where they slept, what they wanted for themselves and their children, these were the strands that Yocke wove. The story was raw, powerful, and Jake Grafton was impressed. Perhaps there was more to Jack Yocke than—

The telephone interrupted his perusal of the paper. He folded it and laid it on his desk.

'Captain, would you come to my office, please.'

Four minutes later he stood in front of his boss, a two-star army general. When he had first reported to the Joint Staff Jake had studied the organization chart carefully and, after counting, concluded that there were fifty-seven flag officers between him and the chairman of the Joint Chiefs, a four-star army general. Major General Franks was the fifty-seventh down from the top. Jake Grafton had already discovered how short that distance really was.

'Captain, would you go to the chairman's office on the E-Ring. He is going over to the White House in a few minutes and he wants the senior officer in the counter-narcotics section to accompany him.'

'Yes, sir,' Jake Grafton said, and made his exit. He didn't ask General Franks what this was about because Franks probably didn't know.

Leaving the Joint Staff spaces, Jake Grafton was hailed by the door attendant. Jake returned Mr James' greeting with a preoccupied smile.

Hayden Land was brusque this morning. 'They're in a snit over at the White House. Dorfman ordered me to appear. Ordered me! That man has the personality of a cliff ape.'

The general's aide accompanied Hayden Land and Jake to the White House. As they rode through the streets in the chairman's limo, General Land briefed both the junior officers: 'The President is going to announce new initiatives to combat the drug business. The White House staff have two proposals that affect the military. They want to increase the number of army teams patrolling the Mexican border, and they want a carrier battle group put into the eastern Caribbean or the Gulf of Mexico.'

'The Caribbean?' Jake Grafton echoed, his surprise evident.

'The idea is that the carrier's aircraft can help intercept and track suspicious air and surface traffic.'

'We do that now with air force AWACS planes, sir. Nothing moves over the gulf that we don't know about. And to put a carrier in there will mean that it will have to be diverted from someplace else, probably the Med. We'll only have one boat in the Med.'

'I talked to CNO about it this morning,' General Land said. 'Those were the points he made. All you have to do today is listen. I just thought that seeing it and hearing it firsthand would help you do the staff work to make it happen if the President orders it, which he probably will. His staff believes that the incident last night with the busload of Japanese tourists requires an immediate response. Apparently they've sold that to the President.'

'Yessir,' Jake Grafton said and took off his white cover for a moment to run his fingers through his thinning hair. 'I don't think a carrier in the Gulf of Mexico is going to help them grab one more pound of cocaine than we are getting now. But putting a boat down there for any extended period of time will have a negative effect on our combat capability in the Med. It'll cut it in half.'

The aide spoke for the first time. 'Sir, I understand there's also a proposal to authorize the Air Force and Navy to shoot down planes that refuse to obey the instructions of interceptors?'

General Land nodded.

'That's been around a while,' Jake said. 'The general aviation pilots' organizations have squealed loudly. God only knows what some doctor putting along in his Skyhawk will do when he meets an F-16 up close and personal for the first time. Cessnas and Pipers going down in flames over the Florida beaches will make great television.'

'The doctors and dentists had better find someplace else to fly,' General Land said in a tone that ended the conversation. 'This drug mess just went from boiling to superheated. The administration is going to whale away with everything they can lay their hands on. Anybody that doesn't want to be hurt had better get the hell out of the way.'

That comment seemed to capture the essence of the atmosphere at the White House. Jake stood against the wall and obeyed General Land's order: he kept his mouth firmly shut. He listened to William C. Dorfman brief the senators and congressmen on the initiatives ordered by the President, and he watched the President explain his reasoning to the senior officials.

'Gentlemen, the American people have had enough. I've had enough. We're going to put a stop to this drug business. We can't allow it to continue.'

Senator Hiram Duquesne spoke up: 'Mr President, everyone's mad right now, but sooner or later they're going to sober up. I'm not about to sit silently and watch the rights of American citizens trampled by cops and soldiers on a witch hunt.'

'We're not hunting witches, Hiram,' the President said. 'We're hunting drug smugglers and drug dealers.'

A few smiles greeted this remark, but no chuckles.

'How long is this state of emergency going to last?' Duquesne pressed. Jake Grafton had met Senator Duquesne before, a year ago when he was working on the A-12 project. Apparently Duquesne hadn't mellowed any these past twelve months.

'I haven't declared a state of emergency.'

'Call it what you like,' Hiram Duquesne shot back. 'How long?'

'Until we get results.'

'It's going to cost a lot of money to change the currency,' another senator pointed out. 'You going to want to do it again next year?'

'I don't know.'

'This marriage of the FBI and DEA,' said Senator Bob Cherry. 'I think that'll go over like a lead brick with Congress. The last thing this country needs is a bigger, more powerful police bureaucracy.'

'It's efficiency I'm after.'

Bob Cherry raised his eyebrows. 'You won't get it with that move. More layers of paper pushers means less efficiency, not more. All you get when you add bureaucrats is more inertia. And a big police bureaucracy that can't be stopped is the last thing this country needs or wants.'

'I want to try it,' the President insisted.

'Good luck,' Cherry said.

'I need you on this. Bob. I'm asking for bipartisan support. I'm asking for your help.'

'Mr President, we in Congress are getting just as much, if not more, heat about that incident last night than you are. People want to know why tourists should have to run the risk of being slaughtered in the streets just to visit the capital of this country. My office this morning was a madhouse. We had to take the phones off the hooks. But Congress is not going to be stampeded. I can promise you this: we'll immediately look at your proposals, and those that have a chance of working we'll approve. Speedily. Those that don't . . .' He shrugged.

That evening at dinner Jake Grafton told his wife about his day.

'On television one of the commentators said the President has panicked,' Callie told him.

Jake snorted. 'And last year they said he was timid. The poor devil gets it from every side.'

'Will these proposals work? Can the drug crisis be solved?'

The captain took his time answering. 'There aren't any easy solutions. There are a lot of little things that will each have some effect on the problem. But there are no easy, simple, grand solutions just lying around waiting to be discovered. None.'

'You're saying drugs are here to stay.'

'At some levels, yes. We humans have learned to live with alcohol and tobacco and prostitution – we're going to have to learn to live with dope.'

'Even if it ruins people's lives?' Amy asked.

Jake Grafton chewed a bite of ham while he thought about that one. 'A lot of things can ruin lives. People get so fat their hearts give out. They literally eat themselves to death. Should we have a law that regulates how much you can eat?'

'Drugs are different,' Amy said.

'Indeed they are,' Callie said, and gave her husband a sidelong glance with an eyebrow ominously arched.

Jake Grafton wisely changed the subject.

Later Callie said, 'Did you read that terrific article in today's paper that Jack Yocke wrote about Cuba?'

'Yeah.'

'I'm inviting him and his girlfriend over for dinner Saturday night, if he's back from Cuba. I'll call him tomorrow at the paper.'

'Oh.'

'Now, Jake, don't start that. I had him in class all semester and he is a bright young man with a lot of talent. You should take the time to get to know him.'

'Doesn't look like I'm getting an option.'

'Now dear, you know better than that.'

'Okay, okay. Invite him over. If you think he's a nice guy, I'm sure he is. After all, look how right you were about me.'

'Maybe you should reevaluate, Callie,' Amy said tartly, and went off to her bedroom to do her homework.

16

The wind was out of the northwest at fifteen or twenty knots. Small flakes of snow were driven almost horizontally in against the sage and juniper that covered the sloping sides of the arroyo. Higher up on the hillsides the pines showed a tinge of white, but the dirt road leading down the arroyo was still free from accumulation.

From a window in his living room, Henry Charon scanned the scene yet again.

The snow would accumulate as the day wore on and deepen significantly during the night. How much depended only on the amount of moisture left in the clouds coming down from the San Juans. The air was certainly cold enough. It leaked around the doorsill and the edges of the window and felt cold on his face.

Charon inserted another chunk of piñon in the wood stove. Then he went into the bedroom and got out the old .45 Colt automatic he kept in the drawer by the dresser and checked to ensure it was locked, with a cartridge in the chamber. It was. He shoved it between his belt and the small of his back and pulled the bulky sweatshirt down so it couldn't be seen. Then he went back into the living room.

He liked sitting in the old easy chair here by the stove, with the window on his right. From it he could see the barn and the road, and against the sky, several tall hills. The mountains that were normally visible were obscured by clouds this morning.

Really, when you thought about it, it was a shame that life doesn't go on forever. To sit here and watch the winters, to spend the summer evenings on the porch listening to the meadowlarks and crickets, to step out in the morning with a rifle under your arm and walk off up the trail looking for deer and elk as the sky was shot with fire by the rising sun, he had done that all his life and it was very pleasant.

Very pleasant.

But this other hunt would be a real challenge, in a way that hunting deer and elk and bear had long ceased to be. And he would have to pay his dues. He had learned that in life. This might well be the last morning he was ever going to sit here feeding logs into the stove and watching the snow come down. So he let his eyes travel across the juniper and pines and took it all in, one more time.

About ten or so he saw the car coming up the road. The snow was beginning to stick. He pulled on his coat and went out onto the porch.

'Hey,' Tassone said as he climbed out from behind the wheel.

'Come on in.'

'Got some stuff here in the trunk. Help me with it.'

There was a suitcase and two army duffel bags. They left the suitcase and carried the duffel bags inside. The bags were green, with US ARMY stenciled on them, and they sported padlocks.

Inside, with the door closed, Tassone shivered involuntarily. 'Getting cold out there.'

'Winter's here.'

Tassone tossed Charon a key ring and went to stand with his backside toward the stove.

Charon used the key on the padlocks of the duffel bags. Each was full of money, bundles of twenties and fifties.

'Five million in each bag,' Tassone said. 'Count it if you want.'

Henry Charon felt deep into each bag, ensuring it was full of money. 'No need for that, I think.'

'It's a lot of money.'

'You want the job?'

'No, thanks. I want to keep on living. My life's worth more than that.'

'I hope to keep on living too.'

Tassone nodded and looked around the room, taking it all in. Charon replaced the padlocks and put the duffel bags in the bedroom. When he came back Tassone had his coat off and was in the easy chair.

'I got coffee if you want it.'

'Yeah. I'll take a cup. Black.'

They both got a cup of coffee and sat listening to the wind. The snow continued to fall.

'What you gonna do? Afterward, I mean.'

Henry Charon thought a moment. 'Live here, I hope. I like it here.'

'Lonely, I bet.'

Henry Charon shrugged. He had never thought so.

They drank their coffee in silence. After a bit Charon added a log to the stove.

'What do you think about the other names on the list?'

'I'll do what I can. I told you that.'

'A million each. I'll wait two or three months, then come up here with the money. If you aren't here, you want me to leave it?'

'Yeah,' said Henry Charon, thinking about it. 'Yeah. That would be good. I'll get here sometime.' He hoped. 'Leave the money under the porch. It's dry there. It'll be okay.'

'There's going to be a couple other hit teams in Washington while you're there.'

'You never told me that before.'

'Didn't know before. I'm telling you now. You can back out if you want.'

'I don't want out. But that does change things, of course.'

'I know.'

Change things! Henry Charon stared out the window at the snow. My God! They'll be searching every nook and cranny. Still, if he could evade long enough, one of the teams might get caught. This might be the red herring he had been thinking about.

'Well,' Tassone said, draining his cup and setting it on the windowsill. 'I don't want to get snowed in here. Got a flight from Albuquerque this evening. I'd better get going.' He stood and put on his coat.

'Be careful going down. The road will be slick in places.'

'Yeah. It was starting to get that way coming up.'

'Keep to the high side and take it easy.'

Charon followed Tassone out on the porch and stood watching him as he walked for the car. Then he put his right hand under his sweatshirt behind his back and drew the automatic from his belt. He leveled it, holding it with both hands.

As Tassone reached for the car door Charon shot him, once.

The big slug sent Tassone sprawling in the mud.

With the pistol ready, Charon went down the three steps and walked over to the man on the ground.

Tassone was looking up at him, bewilderment on his face. 'Why?' Then all his muscles relaxed and he stopped breathing.

Charon put the muzzle of the pistol against the man's forehead and felt for a pulse in his neck. He felt a flutter, then it ceased. The bullet had hit him under the left shoulder blade and exited from the front of his chest.

The assassin carefully lowered the hammer of the weapon and replaced it between his belt and the small of his back. Then he went back inside to get his coat and hat and gloves.

Why? Because Tassone was the only link between whoever was paying the freight and Henry Charon. With him gone, the evidential link could never be completed. He had to die, the fool. And he *had* been a fool. The FBI would inevitably pick up the trail of the Stinger missiles and the guns. And that trail would lead to Tassone, who was now a dead end. Why, indeed!

He had shot Tassone in the front yard because he didn't want any blood or bullet holes in the house. The rain and snow would take care of any blood outside.

Charon fished Tassone's wallet from a pocket and took it inside to the kitchen table. There was very little there. A little over three hundred dollars in bills, some credit cards and a Texas driver's license for Anthony Tassone. Nothing else.

He carefully fed the credit cards and driver's license into the stove. Even the money. The wallet he put into his pocket.

Outside he pulled the pickup around and placed the body in the bed. He got the suitcase from the trunk and inspected the car carefully. As he suspected, it was a rental from one of the agencies at the Albuquerque airport. He would drive it down there himself tomorrow and park it at the rental car return and drop the paperwork and keys in the express return slot. At that moment Tassone would cease to exist. Then Charon would board the plane to Washington.

There was a candy wrapper on the floor of the car, and Charon pocketed that too.

The contents of the suitcase were as innocuous as the wallet. Several changes of clothing, toilet articles, and a paperback novel by Judith Krantz. He put everything back and tossed it into the bed of the truck.

It took him twenty minutes to travel the five miles up the mountainside to the old mine. He had the pickup in four-wheel drive, but still he took it slow and easy. The higher he climbed on the mountain the worse the snow was and the poorer the road. Tomorrow he might not even have been able to get the truck up here.

Visibility was poor at the mine, less than a hundred yards. The dilapidated, weather-beaten boards and timbers that formed a shack around the shaft were half rotted, about to fall down. The mine had been abandoned in the late fifties. Henry Charon walked up on the hill, then around the mountain, then back down the road. Fifteen minutes later, satisfied that no one was around, he pulled the corpse out of the pickup and dragged it across to the mine shaft and dropped it in. The suitcase followed.

He then tied a rope around the front bumper of the pickup and lowered that into the shaft. He got a reel of coated wire from the tool chest behind the truck cab, and unwound a hundred feet or so and lowered that down the shaft. Finally, he put a flashlight, four sticks of dynamite, and a blasting cap into his pocket, took a last look around, and, using the rope, lowered himself down the shaft.

He worked quickly. He dragged the body fifty feet down one of the two drifts that led off from the bottom, then brought the suitcase and put it beside the body. He left the wallet and candy wrapper.

The dynamite he wedged between the rock wall and a six-by-six oak timber that helped hold up a weak place in the roof. He stripped the insulation from the wire he had lowered into the shaft and twisted the raw wire to the blasting cap, which he then inserted into one of the dynamite sticks. With the dynamite packed into place with dirt and small rocks, he took a last look around with the flashlight.

Had he forgotten anything?

The keys to the rental car. They were in his pocket. Okay.

Charon was not even breathing hard when he got to the surface. He pulled the rope out of the hole.

He had a little wind-up detonator in his toolbox. He attached the wire to the terminals, wound it up, and let it go. A dull thud that he could feel with his feet followed. Using his flashlight, he looked down into the shaft. It was all dust, impossible to see the bottom.

He got back into the pickup and started the engine. He turned the heater up. The visibility had deteriorated to less than a hundred feet. About four inches or so of snow on the ground.

Tassone was going to be missed, of course, but Charon thought that whoever wanted George Bush killed ten million dollars worth was not going to miss his messenger boy very much. And Charon would try to get as many of the other people on the list as he could. Of course, Tassone wasn't around to deliver additional money, and Charon didn't know who to go to to get paid, but so be it. Somebody was going to get his money's worth and that would be all that mattered.

And ten million was enough. More than enough, it was more money than Henry Charon could spend in two lifetimes.

Fifteen minutes later Charon tried to pull the wire up out of the shaft. It wouldn't come. Probably a rock lying on it. He dropped the rope back into the shaft and went back down. The dust had almost completely settled. The flashlight's beam revealed that the drift tunnel was blocked, with a huge slab pinning the detonator wire. Charon cut the wire, then came back up the rope hand over hand.

He coiled the rope and wire and stowed everything. Going down the mountain the pickup truck slid once, but he got it stopped in time. It took most of an hour to get back to the house. Only an inch of snow on the ground there.

Inside the cabin he threw another log in the stove and washed the cup Tassone had used and put it back in the cabinet. Henry Charon made a fresh pot of coffee. After it had dripped through, he poured some into his cup and stretched out in the easy chair.

'Your ten o'clock appointment is here, Mr Brody.'

The lawyer reached for the intercom button. 'Send him in.'

T. Jefferson Brody walked over to the door and met Freeman McNally coming through. Brody carefully closed the door and shook Freeman's hand, then pointed to the red leather client's chair. 'Good to see you.'

'Yeah, Tee. Howzit goin'?'

'Pretty good.' Brody went around his desk and arranged himself in his eighteen-hundred-dollar custom-made swivel chair. 'How's business?'

'Oh, you know,' McNally said and made a vague gesture. 'Always problems. Nothing ever goes right.'

'That's true.'

'You been watching the TV the last couple days?'

'You mean that car-bus crash? Yeah, I heard about that.'

'One of my drivers. Some of our guards tried to rip off his load. He was lucky he wasn't killed.'

'A lot of heat,' Brody said, referring to the President's press conference and the announced government initiatives. The papers were full of it.

'Yeah. That's why I came to see you. Some of those things The Man wants to do are going to hurt. I think it's time we called in some of those markers for donations we been making to those senators and congressmen.'

'I was wondering when you might want to do that.'

'Now is when. Putting the DEA and FBI together is not going to help us businessmen. Yeah, like they say on TV, it'll take 'em forever to decide to do anything, but some day they'll know too much. I mean, it'll all go into the same paper mill and eventually something will pop out that's damn bad for me.'

'What else?'

'Well, this new money proposal. Now that will hurt. I got about ten million in cash on hand to run my business on a day-to-day basis.'

'I understand.'

'Seems to me this whole thing is sorta antiblack, y'know? The black people don't use whitey's banks and they're the ones who'll lose the most. Shit, all the white guys got theirs in checking and investments and all that. It's the black women and poor families who keep theirs in cookie jars and stuffed in mattresses. Damn banks charge big fees these days for checking accounts unless you got a white man's balance.'

'That's a good argument. I'll use that.'

'Yeah. And this bail reform business. That's antiblack too. Whites got houses and expensive cars and all to post as bail. Black man's gotta go buy a bail bond. That takes cash.'

Freeman had two or three other points to make, then Brody asked, 'Who tried to rip you off the other night?'

'I don't know for sure, but I think Willie Teal's behind it. He's been getting his stuff through Cuba and that's dried up on him. So I think he put the word out he'd pay top dollar for supplies, and that sorta tempted my guys. No way to know for sure, though, as the three dips that tried to rip me all got killed.'

'Saved you some trouble,' Brody noted and smiled.

'It wouldn't have been no trouble. You gotta make folks want to be honest or you're outta business. That's part of it.'

The buzzing of the intercom caused T. Jefferson Brody to raise a finger at his client. 'Yes.'

'Senator Cherry's on the phone, sir.'

Brody looked at Freeman. 'You'll get a kick out of this.' He punched buttons for the speaker phone. 'Yes.'

'Bob Cherry. How's it going, Jefferson?' The sound was quite good, although a little tinny.

'Just fine, Senator. And you?'

'Well, I've been going over my reelection finances with my campaign chairman – you know I'm up for reelection in two years?'

'Yessir. I thought that was the date.'

'Anyway, those PACs that you represent have been so generous in the past, I was hoping that one or two of them might make a contribution to my reelection campaign.'

'Sir, I'll have to talk to my clients, but I'm optimistic. They've always believed that someone must pay for good government.' Brody winked broadly at Freeman McNally, who grinned.

'I wish more people felt that way. Talk to you soon.'

When the phone was back on the cradle, Brody smiled at Freeman McNally and explained. McNally threw back his head and laughed. 'They just call you up and ask for money?'

'You got it.'

'If I could do that, I could retire from business. You know, hire a few people to work the phones and generally take life easy.'

'Well, you're not in Congress.'

'Yeah. My business is a little more direct. Tell me, is Willie Teal one of your clients?' All trace of humor was gone from his face now.

'No.'

'I'm glad to hear that. How about Bernie Shapiro?'

'Wellll . . . I'll be straight with you. Freeman. My rule is to never discuss my clients' identities or business with anybody. Ever. You know that.'

Freeman McNally stood and walked around the room, looking at this and that. 'You got a lot of nice stuff here,' he said softly.

T. Jefferson Brody made a modest gesture, which McNally missed.

McNally spoke with his back to the lawyer. 'Bernie Shapiro is in with the Costello family. They're moving in on the laundry business. Gonna cost me. And I don't like to pay more money for the same service.'

Brody said nothing.

McNally came over to the desk and sat on the corner of it, where he could look down on T. Jefferson Brody. 'Tee, I give you some advice. You're a good lawyer for what I need done. You know people and can get in places I can't get into. But if I ever hear, ever, ever, ever hear that you told anybody about my business without me giving you the okay, you'll be dead two hours after I hear it.' He lowered his face to look straight into Brody's eyes. 'You understand?'

'Freeman, I'm a lawyer. Everything you say to me is privileged.'

'You understand me, Tee?'

'Yes.' Brody's tongue was thick and he had trouble getting the words out.

'Good.' Freeman got up and walked over to the window. He pulled back the drapes and looked out.

After ten or fifteen seconds Brody decided to try to get back to business. He had been successfully handling scum like McNally for ten years now, and though there were rough moments, you couldn't let them think you were scared. 'Are you and Shapiro going to do business?'

'I dunno. Not if I can help it. I think that asshole killed the guy who was washing my dough. And I think he killed the guy who owned the check-cashing business. Guy named Lincoln. Shapiro paid off a broad, a grifter named Sweet Cherry Lane who was servicing the guy, and she set him up.'

Bells began to ring for T. Jefferson Brody. 'What does this Lane woman look like?' he asked softly.

Freeman turned away from the window. He came back and dropped into the client chair. 'Sorta chocolate, huge, firm tits, tiny waist, tall and regal. A real prime piece of pussy, I hear tell.'

'If someone wanted this bitch taught a lesson, could you do a favor like that?'

A slow grin spread across Freeman's face. 'Lay it out, Tee.'

'She robbed me, Freeman.' Brody swallowed and took a deep breath. 'Honest. Stole my car and watch and a bunch of shit right out of my house – and she stole the $400,000 that Shapiro paid for that check cashing business.'

'Naw.'

'Yes. The goddamn cunt pretended to be the widow, signed everything, took the check, slipped me a Mickey and cleaned me out.'

'What the fuck kind of lawyer are you, Tee? You didn't even ask to see some ID before you gave her four hundred Gs?'

'Hey,' Brody snarled. 'The bitch conned me. Now I want to slice some of her. Will you help me?'

The grin on Freeman McNally's face faded in the face of the lawyer's fury. He stood. 'I'll think about it, Tee. In the meantime, you get busy on those senators and congressmen. I've paid a lot of good money to those people, now I want something. You get it. Then we'll talk.'

He paused at the door and spoke without looking at Brody. 'I try to never get personal. With me it's all business. That way everybody knows where they stand. When you get personal you make mistakes, take stupid risks. It's not good.' He shook his head. 'Not good.' Then he went out.

Brody stared at the door and chewed on his lower lip.

Ott Mergenthaler returned from lunch at two-thirty in the afternoon with a smile on his face and a spring in his walk. Jack Yocke couldn't resist. 'Back to the old grind, eh, Ott?'

Mergenthaler grinned and dropped into a chair that Yocke hooked around with his foot. 'Well, Jack, when you're the most famous columnist writing in English and you've been in the outback for a week or so, the movers and shakers are just dying to unburden themselves of nifty secrets and juicy tidbits. They can only carry that stuff so long without relief and then they get constipated.'

'A tube steak on the sidewalk?'

'A really fine fettucine alfredo and a clear, dry Chianti.' Ott kissed his fingertips.

'Who was the mover and shaker, or is that a secret?'

'Read my column tomorrow. But if you can't wait that long, it was Bob Cherry.'

'Cuba, right? Did you tell him to read my stuff?'

'That car-bus wreck and the Bush initiatives. God, what a mess! Half a country is screaming that Bush is overreacting and the other half is screaming that he hasn't done enough. He's getting it both ways, coming and going. Why any sane man gets into politics, I'll never know.'

'Any line on who the ten pounds of dope belonged to?'

'No, but funny thing. Cherry implied that the government knows all about it.'

'What do you mean?'

'Well, he's on the Oversight Committee and presumably has been briefed, and he just shrugged off the question of how the investigation is going. Muttered something like, "That's not an issue."'

'What d'ya mean, that's not an issue? They know and aren't telling?'

'Yeah. Precisely.' Ott Mergenthaler raised his eyebrows. 'Normally you gotta watch Cherry like a hawk. He likes to pretend he knows everything, has a finger in every pie. Sometimes he does, sometimes he doesn't. Now at lunch today he didn't say so directly, but he left me and the other two reporters with the impression that the feds had a man on the inside. And he *knew* that was the impression he was creating and he could see by our reaction that we thought this was very important.'

'On the inside. Undercover?'

Mergenthaler nodded.

'You're not going to print that, are you?'

'I have to. Two other reporters were there.' He named them. 'They'll use it. You can bet the ranch on that.'

'You can't attribute this to Cherry.'

'That's right. But this is an answer of sorts to a legit question. What is the federal government doing to bring to justice the people who indirectly caused eleven deaths in the heart of Washington? Cherry's answer – that's a nonquestion.'

'And if Cherry had said that to three reporters, who else has he said it to?'

'Precisely. Hell, knowing Cherry, he's . . . And I know him. What I can't figure out is, did he spill the beans on his own hook or was he told to?'

'If you knew that,' Jack Yocke mused, 'you might get a better idea of whether or not it's true.'

'Wonder what the government's told the Japs.'

'Call the Japanese ambassador and ask.'

'I'll do that.' Mergenthaler made a small ceremony of maneuvering himself out of the chair and strolling off toward his office.

Jack Yocke watched him go, then jerked the Rolodex around and flipped through it. He found the number he wanted and dialed.

One ring. Two. Three. C'mon, answer the damn phone!

'Sammy.'

'Jack Yocke. You alone?'

'Just me and Jesus.'

'Your phone tapped?'

'How the fuck would I know, man?'

'Ah, what an affable, genial guy you are. Okay, Mr Laid Back Bro, a US senator just hinted to one of our columnists that the government knows all there is to know about that car-bus wreck. Our guy was left with the clear impression that the feds got somebody undercover.'

'Give me that again, slower.'

Yocke repeated his message.

'That's all?'

'Isn't that enough?'

'Who was the senator?'

'Bob Cherry.'

'Thanks, man.'

'It'll be in tomorrow's paper. Just thought you'd like to know.'

'Thanks.'

Harrison Ronald Ford hung up the phone and went back to his crossword puzzle. He stared at it without seeing the words. Then he went over to the sink and vomited into it.

It's out! The word's out. *Hooper* – that *asshole*!

His stomach tied itself into a knot and he heaved again.

He turned on the water to flush the mess down the drain. Saliva was still dripping from his mouth.

He heaved again, dry this time. He looked at the telephone on the table, tempted. No way! That fucker McNally had too goddamn many people on his payroll.

When the retching stopped, he grabbed his coat and slammed the door behind him.

'Hooper, you fucking *shithead*! *What're you trying to do to me?*' Harrison Ronald roared the words into the telephone.

'Calm down. What're you talking about?'

Ford repeated his conversation of six minutes ago with Jack Yocke.

'Gimme your number. I'll call you back in eight or ten minutes.'

'This is a fucking pay phone, you shithead! Nobody can call this fucking number because Marion fucking Barry doesn't want fucking dope peddlers taking orders on this fucking phone.'

'So call me back in ten minutes.'

'In ten minutes I may well be as dead as Ma Bell, you blithering shithead. If I don't call the funeral will be on Wednesday. Closed casket!'

He slammed the phone onto its hook and looked around to see who had been listening to his shouting. No one, thank God!

Hooper used the government directory to look up the number, then dialed. 'Senator Cherry, please. This is Special Agent Thomas Hooper.'

'I'm sorry, sir,' the woman said. 'Senator Cherry is on the Senate floor. What is this about?'

'I'm not at liberty to say. When could I expect a return call.'

'Well, not today. Perhaps tomorrow morning?' The pitch of her voice rose slightly when she said 'morning,' making it a question and a pleasantry at the same time.

'I suggest you send an aide to find the senator. Tell the aide that if the senator does not telephone Special Agent Thomas Hooper at 893-9338 in the next fifteen minutes, I will send a squad of agents to find him and physically transport him to the FBI building. See that he gets that message or he is going to be grossly inconvenienced.'

'Would you repeat that number?'

'893-9338.'

The next call went to *The Washington Post* switchboard. 'Jack Yocke, please.'

After several rings, the reporter answered.

'Mr Yocke, this is Special Agent Thomas Hooper of the FBI. I understand we have a mutual friend.'

'I know a lot of people, Mr Hooper. Which mutual friend are we discussing?'

'The one you just talked to, oh, ten or fifteen minutes ago.'

'You say you're with the FBI?'

'Call the FBI building and ask for me.' Hooper hung up.

In half a minute the phone rang.

'Hooper.'

'Jack Yocke, Mr Hooper. Trying to be careful.'

'Our friend tells me that you discussed with him a conversation that one of your colleagues had over the lunch hour with Senator Cherry. Who is the colleague?'

'Ott Mergenthaler.'

'And who else was a party to that conversation?'

Yocke gave him the the names and the newspapers they worked for.

'Mr Yocke, is my friend a good friend of yours?'

'Yes.'

Then I suggest you not mention that luncheon conversation, this conversation, or his name to another living soul. You understand?'

'I think it's clear.'

'Good. Thanks.'

' 'Bye.'

Hooper walked from his office to his secretary's desk. 'Is Freddy back yet?'

'From Cuba? He got in about seven A.M. He's been over at Justice most of the morning.'

'See if you can find him.'

While Hooper was waiting he carefully and legibly wrote the three reporters' names and the newspapers they worked for on a blank sheet of paper. Freddy came in about five minutes later. 'How'd it go in Cuba?'

'We got Zaba. And enough evidence to fry Chano Aldana.'

'Great. But we have a more pressing problem. Senator Bob Cherry had lunch with these three reporters.' He shoved his note across the desk. 'Cherry hinted that the government knew everything it wanted to know about that car-bus crash the other night because it had an undercover agent in place.'

'Aww, damn,' Freddy said. 'He was just briefed on that this morning and he's spilled it already!'

'Go to the director's office, tell the executive assistant what the problem is, and see if the director will telephone the publishers of those newspapers and kill the story. Report back to me as soon as possible.'

'That may keep it out of the papers for a day or two, but that won't cork it. It's out of the bottle now, Tom.'

'I'll talk to Cherry.'

'Good luck. He's probably told a dozen people.'

Hooper rubbed his forehead. 'Go see the director.'

He was still rubbing his forehead, trying to think, when the phone rang again, the direct line. 'Hooper.'

'Okay, it's me. I've calmed down a little. Sorry.'

'Forget it, Harrison. Where are you?'

'Why?'

'I'm sending an agent in a car to get you. You're done.'

'How'd the word get out?'

'We told the President and briefed key members of the congressional Oversight Committees. One of the senators then had lunch with a team of reporters and dropped some hints.'

'Awww, fuck!'

'Where are you?'

'Now you calm down. Freeman patted me on the head after that incident. I'm in real tight now, man. He's got a meeting sometime tonight with Fat Tony Anselmo. Something heavy's going down. We're cunt-hair close, Tom. No shit.'

'You are *done*, Harrison. I don't want to see you a corpse. Not only would death be bad for your health, it'd leave me with no case. We've got enough to take Freeman and his associates off the street for a few years, and I'm not greedy. You're *done*.'

'Now look, Tom. I'm a big boy and I stopped wearing diapers last year. I'm not done until I say I'm done.'

'Harrison, *I'm* in charge of this case. We can maybe keep Cherry's little luncheon chat out of the papers for a few days, but he's probably already run off at the mouth all over town. I don't know. He'll probably lie to me about it. This is your life you're betting.'

'Two nights. Two more nights and then we bust 'em.'

'You are a flaming idiot.'

'That's what everybody says. Talk to you tomorrow.'

The phone went dead.

Hooper hung the instrument up and sat staring at it.

When it rang again he let the secretary in the outer office take it. She buzzed him. 'Senator Cherry, sir.'

He pushed the button. 'Senator, this is Special Agent Hooper. We need to have a talk. Immediately.'

'I understand you made some threatening remarks a few minutes ago to one of my staff, Hooper. What the hell is going on over there anyway?'

'I really need to see you as soon as possible on a very urgent matter. Senator. I'm sorry if your secretary felt I was threatening.'

The senator huffed and puffed a bit, but Hooper was willing to grovel, and soon the feathers were back in place. 'Well,' Cherry agreed finally, 'I'm going out to dinner before I attend a reception at the French embassy. You could come by about sixish?'

'Senator, I know the unwritten rules, but I just can't come over. You'll have to stop by here.'

The senator gave him a few seconds of frosty silence. 'Okay,' he said with no grace.

'The guard at the quadrangle entrance will be expecting you and will escort you to my office.'

Special Agent Hooper was staring at the classified file on this operation when his assistant, Freddy Murray, returned from the director's office. Freddy pulled up a chair and reported:

'The director made the calls. The publishers agreed to kill the story unless it runs elsewhere, then they'll have to run it. That leak's plugged, at least for a little while.'

'Thanks, Freddy.'

'We got to wrap this operation up, Tom, and make some arrests. The pressure is excruciating and it's gonna get worse. While I was in the director's office he was on the phone to the attorney general. The AG has been talking to the President. Did you see this morning's paper?'

Hooper laid three documents on the table. 'Why'd we start this operation, anyway?'

Hooper knew the answer to that question, of course, but he liked to think aloud. Freddy Murray thought this quirk of Hooper's a fortunate habit because his subordinates then knew where the boss's thoughts were going without having to ask. So he willingly played along. 'To find out who in the bureau is on McNally's payroll.'

'And what have we discovered?'

'Nothing.'

'Correct.'

'So.' Hooper used the eraser on a pencil to scratch his head. 'So.'

'We've got enough to put McNally out of business,' Freddy pointed out. 'It's not like this operation hasn't borne fruit. Ford has filled our stocking with goodies. And the people in the front office are getting more desperate by the hour.'

'Who are the three guys we thought might be dirty?'

'Wilson, Kovecki, and Moreto.'

'Aren't these documents still on the computer?' Hooper pointed to them. Freddy looked at them. They were weekly progress reports to the assistant director. Harrison Ford's name was contained on each.

'I think so.'

'Let's rewrite these reports. We'll construct four files, one for each of McNally's chief lieutenants, naming each of them in turn as our undercover operative. Then we let each man get an unauthorized peek at one of the files. What d'ya think?'

Freddy sat silently for a minute or so, turning it over and looking under it. 'I think we're liable to get somebody killed.'

'Listen, Harrison's dangling over the shark pit on a worn-out, fraying rope and blood is dripping into the water. The word is out – the feds have somebody inside. If McNally hears this rumor he'll be looking for the traitor – you can bet Harrison Ronald Ford's ass on that. Our first duty is to keep our guy alive, and our second is to find the rotten apples around here. We're about out of time, Freddy.'

'I don't like it.'

'You got a better suggestion?'

'Four files. Three suspects. Who's the fourth file for?'

'Bob Cherry.'

Freddy scratched his crotch and picked his nose. 'You're not playing by the rules,' he objected, finally.

'There ain't no rules in a knife fight,' Hooper growled. 'Ask Freeman McNally.'

'Why Cherry?'

'Why not? The shit started the rumor. Let's give him something to season it with. A name.'

'What if our little conversation this evening goes well and he shuts up?'

'You had any dealings with this guy? He thinks he's one of the twelve disciples.'

'Okay, so we let him get a sneaky peek at a bogus file. Then we talk to him? He'll come unglued – we call him in so we can bitch at him about his loose mouth and we leave secret files lying around unattended? He'll latch onto that like a pit bull with AIDS. He'll crucify us.'

Hooper swiveled his chair and looked out the window. 'Gimme something better.'

'So we forget the file for the senator,' Freddy said, musing aloud. 'Let's play to him. We'll just stroke him and when everything's copacetic, introduce the name into the conversation. After all, he's entitled to be briefed. Let's brief the son of a bitch.'

They got busy with the computer. The facts had to change on each report to fit the bona fides of the man they wanted to use. It took some serious brainstorming. They had two files constructed when Freddy said, 'What if two or more names get back to McNally? Where are we then?'

They discussed it. After batting it back and forth, they decided that McNally would probably conclude that the FBI was engaged in funny business, which would discredit not only the names but the undercover agent rumor as well. They went back to work on the last file.

At noon Hooper sent his secretary home for the rest of the day. She was aghast. Hooper was insistent. 'And don't mention this to anyone.'

'But the personnel regulations!'

'See you Monday.'

By three that afternoon Hooper and Freddy had drilled a hole through the plasterboard between the outer office and Hooper's office. They installed a one-way mirror on Hooper's side of the wall. The secretary's forgettable print was rehung on her side to cover the hole. Freddy trotted down the hall and borrowed a vacuum cleaner from a cleaning closet to clean up the dust and drywall fragments.

The suspects were called one at a time into Hooper's office to interview for the new positions in the division that Hooper had just yesterday recommended be created and filled in response to President Bush's recent announcements.

Wilson didn't look at the files on the desk in the fifteen minutes Hooper kept him waiting. When Hooper went into the office finally, Wilson flatly stated he wasn't interested in transferring from his present position. But he appreciated being considered.

They had better luck with the second man, Kovecki. He did glance at the target file. The name in his was Ruben McNally, the accountant. In fact, Kovecki looked at all three files on the desk. One of them was his personnel file, and he settled in to examine that closely. He was still looking at it when Hooper went in to interview him.

Moreto also looked. He selected the bogus file from the three on the desk and scanned it quickly. The name in his file was Billy Enright. Then Moreto went over to the window and stared out. He was at the window when Hooper entered the room.

In between interviews Hooper fielded a call from the director. 'I want you to take your man to the grand jury on Monday. The prosecutors are doing the indictments this weekend. Monday night you start picking these guys up.'

'Yessir.'

'Hooper,' the director said, 'this comes straight from the White House. I expect you to make it happen.'

At six-seventeen that evening the senator arrived. With the former Miss Georgia parked in the outer office visiting with a ga-ga young agent who was acting as the building escort, Tom Hooper and Freddy Murray gently cautioned the great man behind closed doors and gave him a fairly complete briefing on the operation, including the name of the undercover man, Ike Randolph. Most of the other things they told the senator were equally accurate but carefully tailored to fit the bare bones of the truth, which the senator already knew. They failed to mention the planned expedition to the grand jury Monday or the arrests they hoped to make within hours of obtaining indictments.

At seven thirty-two Hooper finally locked his office and he and Freddy headed for the Metro.

17

'Thanos Liarakos, please. This is Jack Yocke of *The Washington Post*.'

'I'm sorry, Mr Yocke,' the female on the other end of the telephone line told him briskly. 'Mr Liarakos isn't taking any calls from the press today.'

'Well, we're running a story in tomorrow's paper about the extradition of General Julio Zaba from Cuba. The FBI brought him in from Havana this morning. The spokeswoman at the Justice Department said he'll be placed on trial here in Washington. They have a secret indictment handed down just yesterday from the grand jury. According to her and the press folks over at the White House, General Zaba was personally paid big bucks by Mr Liarakos' client, Chano Aldana, to allow dope smugglers to use Cuban—'

'Really, Mr Yocke. Mr Liarakos is not—'

'Would he like to comment on this story?'

'If I say, "No comment," what will you say in the story you're writing?'

'I'll say that Mr Liarakos refused to comment on the story.'

The phone went dead. She had put him on hold.

Jack Yocke put his feet on his desk and cradled the phone between his cheek and shoulder. He cracked his knuckles. Aldana and Zaba. The A-to-Z connection. Too bad the *Post* wouldn't let him make a crack like that in print.

She came back on. 'Mr Yocke?'

'Still here.'

'You may say this: In view of the gag orders issued in the Aldana case by Judge Snyder, Mr Liarakos does not believe he is at liberty to comment on this matter.'

'Okay. Got it. Thanks.'

He was just finishing the story when the phone jingled. 'Yocke.'

'This is Tish. Sorry I couldn't get back to you earlier.'

'Hey. I was wondering if you would like to go to dinner with me at the Graftons' tomorrow night? I meant to call you last week, but I got called out of town unexpectedly.' The last sentence was a lie. He had intended never to call her again, but Mrs Grafton had specifically asked him to bring Tish Samuels. He wondered what Mrs Grafton's reaction would be if she heard Tish's little speech about her literary ambitions.

'I've been reading your Cuba stories. They're very good.'

'Thank you. I was down there and all and real busy.'

'You apologize too much, Jack. Yes, I'd like to go to the Graftons' with you. What time?'

You apologize too much. Only to women, Jack Yocke thought. Why is that?

Thirty minutes later he was in talking to Ott about General Zaba when he was summoned back to his desk by the telephone operator. 'Your Cuban call is ready.' He had a call in for Pablo Oteyza, formerly known as Hector Santana.

Yocke picked up the phone. 'Jack Yocke speaking.'

'Pablo Oteyza.'

'*Señor*, I'm the *Post* report—'

'I remember you, Jack.

'Congratulations on being named to the interim government.'

'Thanks.'

'I sent you my articles on Cuba. Did you get any of them yet?'

'Not yet. The mail is still very confused. And I haven't yet heard a megaton detonation from the north, followed by a tidal wave of reporters, so I assume you honored your promises to me about what you would and would not publish.'

'Yessir. I don't think you'll find anything embarrassing to you or the American government in the articles.'

'Or my American friends.'

'Right. *Señor*, I know you're busy. It's just been announced here that General Zaba was extradited and brought to Washington for trial. What can you tell me about him?'

'He was an associate of Chano Aldana. He used Cuban gunboats and naval facilities to smuggle cocaine. We gave the FBI agents all the evidence we have been able to assemble and let them interview Zaba's subordinates. Your people were very pleased.'

'Will there be any other extraditions?'

'Perhaps. It will take time for the FBI and the American prosecutors to evaluate what they have. And to see if Zaba wants to talk. If the American government gets indictments for drug trafficking against other Cubans, my government will evaluate them and decide on a case-by-case basis. We made it plain to the FBI that people who were just following orders will not be extradited.'

'Any truth to the rumor that Zaba's extradition was a quid pro quo for American economic aid?'

'Speaking for my government, I can say that the new government of

Cuba and the government of the United States will cooperate on many matters. Economic aid is very high on our list of priorities.'

'You sound like a politician.'

'I *am* a politician, Jack. I look forward to reading your stories.'

'Thanks for your time.'

'Yes.' Oteyza hung up.

Jack Yocke tapped keys on his computer to bring up the Zaba story, then began to make insertions.

To say that Harrison Ronald was apprehensive when he drove to work on Friday night would be an understatement. After his second telephone conversation with Special Agent Hooper, he had walked the streets for an hour, then reluctantly retraced his steps back to his apartment.

He had gotten out his slab-sided .45 Colt automatic and stuffed a full clip up the handle and jacked a round into the chamber. With the weapon cocked and locked and under the pillow, he tried to get some sleep.

He couldn't. He lay there staring at the ceiling and wondering who was saying what to whom.

Why in hell had he insisted on two more nights? Two more nights of waiting for someone to blow his silly brains out.

He had thought his nervous system had had all it could handle the other evening when he walked four miles from the Lincoln Memorial to McNally's northwest hidey-hole. He had told the tale of the evening's adventures to that little ferret Billy Enright, who left him sitting in a bedroom while he went to call Freeman.

He sat for an hour listening to every sound, every muffled footstep, waiting. Then Freeman had come in, inspected the bullet groove in his arm and cuts in his face and insisted that the wounds be cleaned and bandaged by a proper doctor. In the living room Billy had the television going, with the victims and blood and smashed car being shown again and again. When they had had their fill, Freeman and Billy drove him to some quack who had gotten himself banned for life from the practice of medicine by prescribing painkillers to rich matrons suffering from obesity and boredom.

All concern he was, Freeman that night. His face reflected solicitude, glee when he heard how Sammy Z had killed the guy in the backseat by crushing his larynx, laughter when he heard about the high-speed chase and the final, fatal crash. Keystone Kops stuff, slapstick. Ha ha ha.

'Ya' did good, Z, real good.'

'Sorry about your merchandise, Freeman, but I didn't think it was smart to go hiking down the street bleeding and all and carrying ten pounds of shit. And I had to ditch the car fast. It looked like Swiss cheese.'

'You did right, Z, my man. Don't sweat it.'

'Sorry about the car.'

'Fuck the car. I'll get another.' McNally snapped his fingers. 'That Tooley! I'd like to know who put that chickenshit cocksucker up to robbing me. No way that bubble-brain would dream that up by hisself.'

'I'll ask around,' Billy Enright promised. 'Put the word out. Maybe offer some bread for info.'

'Offer ten Gs,' Freeman said, taking a thick roll of bills from his pocket. He divided it without counting and handed half to Harrison Ronald. 'Here, I pay my debts. You were working for me, so I owe you. Here.'

Harrison glanced at the stack and pocketed it. 'Thanks,' he said, with feeling.

'Make it five Gs,' Freeman told Enright. 'If we offer too much, people'll be dreaming up tales. Five's enough.'

So Harrison Ronald was in tight with Freeman. Maybe. In any event, McNally had tossed him the keys to a four-year-old Ford Mustang, and that was what he was driving this evening. And that wad of bills, when he counted it back at the apartment, consisted of forty-three $100 bills.

In tight – maybe. Ford had no illusions about Freeman McNally. He would pay forty-three hundred dollars to see the look of surprise on his victim's face when he jammed a pistol up his ass and pulled the trigger.

If he had heard the rumor and decided Sammy Z was a cop, he would still be the same old Freeman McNally, right up until he grinned that grin and took care of business.

Take care of business. That was Freeman's motto. God, he took care of it all right!

Well, dealing coke and crack wasn't for the squeamish or indecisive. Nobody who knew McNally ever suspected he had either of those flaws.

As he threaded the Mustang through the heavy evening traffic – only seven shopping days left before Christmas – Harrison Ronald wrestled again with the why. Why had he demanded two more nights of this?

He had worried this question all afternoon and he still was not satisfied with the answer that fell out. He thought Freeman and the boys ought to be locked up for a serious stretch and he thought it was worth a big risk for somebody to accomplish that chore. But he had no personal ax to grind, other than the fact he loathed all these swine. Still, there were a lot of people in the world he would just as soon not spend time with. The discovery of another dozen or two wasn't earthshaking. No. The question was, Why did *he* want to risk his butt to put Freeman and friends and maybe one or two crooked cops where the sun don't shine?

Grappling with the why question made him uncomfortable. He wasn't a hero. The possibility that someone might see him as one was embarrassing.

Harrison thought that perhaps it was the challenge. Or some sense that he owed something. Payback. Something like that, probably. That wasn't too bad. But when he thought about it honestly – and he did do that: he was an honest man – he sensed a little bit of thrill at the excitement of it all. Living on the edge burned you out and scared the shit out of you and made you want to heave your guts at times, but it was certainly never dull. Every emotion came full blast, undiluted.

The thrill aspect made him slightly ashamed, coming as it did with a dollop or two of the hero juice.

Two more nights. Hang in there, Harrison Ronald, Evansville PD.

He parked the car in the alley and said hi to the guy standing in the shadows, hopping from foot to foot to keep warm. His name was Will Colby and he and Sammy Z had delivered crack on a half dozen occasions. Harrison rapped on the back door.

If they thought he was a cop, the reception inside was going to be very warm. As he waited for the door to open, he wiped the perspiration from his face with a glove and glanced again at Colby, who was looking up and down the alley. Colby seemed relaxed, bored perhaps.

Thirty degrees and a breeze, and he was sweating! Where's the thrill now, hero? He consciously willed his muscles to relax.

Ike Randolph opened the door and looked around.

'Hey, Ike.'

Ike jerked his head and Harrison Ronald went inside.

As they went through the kitchen, Ike said, 'Better get some coffee. You're out front tonight.'

Harrison filled a styrofoam cup with steaming liquid. 'When they coming?'

'Ten. Got a piece on you?'

'Nope.'

'Get something from the bedroom and go on out front.'

Harrison selected a .357 Smith & Wesson, checked the cylinder, then stuffed the weapon into the pocket of his pea coat. He had bought this coat because it was warm and had deep pockets and a large collar. There was sure a lot of standing around outside in this business. Just like police work.

With that irony in mind, he walked down the hall carrying the coffee, nodded at the guy with the Uzi, and went out the front door to the stoop.

Harrison had seen the guy out front before, but didn't know his name. 'I got it. Anything happening?'

'Just cold as holy hell,' the guy said, then went up the steps and inside.

So far so good. Another three minutes of life and fair prospect of more. Amen.

He was still standing there at nine fifty-five when a dark gray Cadillac wearing New York plates pulled up to the curb in front and the man in the passenger seat climbed out. Fat Tony Anselmo. The man at the wheel killed the engine.

Anselmo glanced at Ford, taking in every feature with one quick sweep, then climbed the stairs and pushed the doorbell button. The door opened in seconds and he went in.

The man at the wheel sank into the seat until only the top half of his face was visible under his dark, brimmed hat. At twenty-five feet the features were hard to distinguish in the glare and shadows of the streetlights, but Harrison Ronald knew who he was: Vincent Pioche, hitter for the Costello family in Brooklyn and Queens. According to Freddy Murray, the FBI thought he had killed over twenty men. No one knew for sure, including Pioche, who had probably forgotten some of his victims. Brains weren't his long suit.

If you were going to make your living in criminal enterprises, Ford mused, you should either be a rocket scientist or mildly retarded. The people between those extremes were the ones in trouble. The thinking they did was both too much and not enough. Like Tooley.

That line of thought led him to consider himself. He had a high school diploma and two years of college. He could balance a checkbook and write a report. Tooley probably could have too, if he had had any reports to write.

Was he as smart as Freeman McNally, the PhD of crack philosophy?

The very thought gave him goosebumps. The wind was cold and he had been out here over an hour. He began walking around.

Ike came out about ten-thirty and relieved him while he went inside for a break. He got another cup of coffee and hit the bathroom.

He was standing by the guard with the Uzi in the hallway sipping coffee when the door to the living room opened and Fat Tony came out. He already had his coat on. Freeman was behind him.

Freeman followed Tony to the door while Harrison trailed after.

Together they stood on the stoop and watched Tony Anselmo get into the car. As it drove off, McNally said, 'There goes the two guys who killed Harrington and Lincoln a couple weeks ago.'

Because he thought he ought to say something, Harrison Ronald asked, 'How'd you hear that?'

'You can find out anything if you know who to ask and you've got enough money.'

Freeman went back inside. Ike nodded and Harrison reluctantly descended to the sidewalk.

Yeah, with enough money to spread around you can find out anything, like who's the undercover cop in the McNally organization.

On Saturday morning at eight A.M. Harrison Ronald Ford met special agents Hooper and Murray in the motel in Fredericksburg. The first thing he did was give them the forty-three hundred dollars that Freeman had given him. The money, Hooper said, would go to a fund to finance antidrug operations.

As they sipped coffee, Harrison Ronald told them the news: 'Freeman says Fat Tony Anselmo and Vinnie Pioche killed two guys named Harrington and Lincoln several weeks ago.'

'How'd he find out?' Freddy asked.

'He says he asked the right person and used money.'

'We'll follow it up. Right now I think those murders are being investigated by local police. To the best of my knowledge, they're wide open.'

'Did he know why?' Hooper asked.

'Freeman didn't say specifically. Fat Tony spent an hour and a half with him last night. I think it's this money-washing business. It all fits.' Harrison Ronald shrugged.

'Monday you're going to the grand jury. If they indict McNally and his gang, we start busting them Monday night.'

Harrison Ronald nodded and inspected his hands. They were shaking.

'There's no reason for you to go back there tonight. Those clowns aren't going anyplace.'

'Last night I got this tidbit on Anselmo and Pioche. That may wrap up two unsolved killings. Who knows what I might pick up tonight?'

'It isn't worth the risk,' Freddy insisted, dragging his chair close to the undercover man. 'This undercover op rumor might land there today. Tonight they may decide to put a bullet into you for insurance.'

'May, may, might, might. *Are you crazy?*' Ford's voice rose to a roar. '*They could have killed me anytime in the last ten months. I've been living on borrowed time, you asshole.*'

Silence greeted that outburst. Eventually Freddy got up from his chair and went over to sit on the bed.

Hooper took the chair and dragged it even closer to Ford, less than two feet away.

Hooper spoke softly: 'Why do you want to go back?'

'Because I'm scared. I've been getting more and more scared every day.'

'You're burning out,' Freddy said. 'Happens to everyone. That's normal. You're not Superman.'

'Freeman McNally ain't gonna die or get religion when you arrest him, Freddy. Even in jail, he's gonna continue to be the same old asshole. And sooner or later, his lawyer is going to tell him my real name. I have to learn to live with that or I'm done.'

Hooper sighed. 'Look. If killing you would let Freeman walk, he'd do it in the blink of an eye. But when he finally finds out he's been had, he's done regardless. And your real name will *never come out*. That I can promise.'

The undercover man didn't seem very impressed. 'Used to be, I got over the fear after a shift,' he muttered. 'Did a crossword puzzle or two, got some sleep, maybe had a drink, I'd get back to normal. Doesn't happen now. I'm scared all the time. Had to give up whiskey or I'd get stinking drunk and stay that way.'

'There's no need to go back.'

'I *need* to. Don't you see that? *I'm fucking scared shitless.* If I don't go back I'll be scared all my life. Don't you see? How am I ever going to sit in a patrol car by myself in downtown Evansville at night? How am I gonna stop a speeder and walk up on his car? They send me in to arrest some drunk with a gun, how am I gonna do that? I am fucking scared shitless and I got to get a handle on it or I ain't gonna be able to keep going, man. It's that simple.'

18

President Bush left for Camp David in the mountains northwest of Frederick, Maryland, around nine A.M. for a weekend retreat to hash out foreign policy issues with the secretary of state and the national security adviser. Before he boarded the helicopter, however, he had another session with Dorfman and Attorney General Gideon Cohen.

'What does this Zaba character know?'

'More than enough to convict Chano Aldana,' Cohen told the President. 'He had at least half a dozen personal meetings with Aldana that we know of – four in Cuba and two in Colombia. He gave orders to his subordinates to assist in shipping cocaine from Colombia to Cuba. He personally supervised at least four transshipments on to the United States.'

'Is he talking?' Dorfman asked, a little annoyed that Cohen, as usual, was putting the cart before the horse.

'Not yet. Judge Snyder appointed him a lawyer yesterday. Guy named Szymanski from New York.'

'The shyster that got those S and L thieves acquitted last week?'

'Yes. David Szymanski. He's got a national reputation and Judge Snyder called him and asked if he would serve. He agreed.'

'Szymanski could dry up Niagara,' Dorfman said acidly. 'If Szymanski can't shut him up, this Zaba has a terminal case of motormouth.'

'I talked to the secretary of state about this matter. He felt it was important that we get top-notch counsel for Zaba. We may well want Cuba to send us some more of these people to try, and we need to show the Cubans that anyone extradited will get quality counsel and a fair trial. That's critical. I personally asked Judge Snyder—'

'Okay, okay,' George Bush said, breaking in. 'Will Zaba talk or won't he?'

'I think he will,' Cohen told him. 'The Cubans put it to him this way: If he cooperated with us he could eventually return to Cuba a free man. When he gets back there he can always blame Castro.'

'Who's conveniently dead,' Dorfman remarked.

'No doubt Cuba will publicize his testimony as an example of the corruption of the old regime.'

'No doubt,' George Bush said. 'You going to let him cop a plea?'

'If Szymanski asks, yes. Zaba will have to agree to testify against Chano Aldana. His sentencing hearing will be delayed until after the Aldana trial.'

'Won't that give Aldana's lawyer something to squawk about?' Dorfman asked.

'Yes.'

'How about this drug bust on Monday night? Is that on schedule?'

'Yessir.'

'You and I and the director of the FBI will have a press conference Tuesday morning. Schedule that, please, Will.'

'Yessir.'

'And Will, go see that the reporters are moved back far enough so that I don't have to hear any questions on the way out to the chopper.'

Dorfman departed. When they were alone, George Bush said, 'Gid, I know that you and Dorfman strike sparks, but I need you both.'

'The asshole thinks he was born in a manger,' Cohen said hotly.

The President was taken aback. He had never heard Cohen blow off steam before – apparently lawyers at blue-chip New York firms didn't often indulge themselves. 'That's true,' the President replied with a wry grin, 'but he's *my* asshole.'

Cohen's eyebrows rose and fell.

'There's no way in the world I can please everyone. Dorfman attracts the criticism. He takes the blame. He takes the heat I can't afford to take. That's his job.'

The attorney general nodded.

'This drug thing . . . We have to just keep plugging at it. We're trying and the voters will understand that. Only pundits and TV preachers expect miracles. And I don't want anybody railroaded. Our job is to make the damn system work.'

Harrison Ronald got back to his apartment around noon. He locked and bolted the door and fell into bed with the .45 automatic in his hand. He was instantly asleep.

At five o'clock he awoke with a start. Someone upstairs had slammed a door. The pistol was still in his hand. He flexed his fingers around it, felt its heft, and lay awake listening to the sounds of the building.

When this was over he would go home. Home to Evansville and spend Christmas with his grandmother. He hadn't talked to her in five or six months. She didn't even know where he was. Tough on her, but better for him. She was getting on and liked to share confidences with her friends and minister.

Oh well. It would soon be over. One more night. When he walked out of this dump in three hours, he was never coming back. The landlord could have it – the worn-out TV, the clothes, the bargain-basement dinnerware and pots and pans, all of it. Harrison Ronald was going straight back to the real world.

He had leveled with Hooper about why he wanted to go back. He was going to have to learn how to live with fear – not just the fear of Freeman McNally – but fear itself. He had learned in the Marines that the only way to conquer this poison called fear was to face it.

Ah me. Ten months in a sewage pond. Ten months in hell. And this time tomorrow he could be out of it.

He lay in bed listening to the sounds and thinking about the life he was going back to.

Thanos Liarakos was in the den when he heard the kids shouting. 'Mommy, Mommy, you're home!'

She was standing there in the front hallway with the kids around her, looking at him. Her hair and clothes were a mess. She just stood there looking at him as the girls squealed and pranced and tugged at her hands.

'Hug them, Elizabeth.'

Now she looked at their upturned faces. She ran her hands through her hair, then bent and kissed them.

'Okay, girls,' he said. 'Run upstairs a while and let Mommy and Daddy visit. No, why don't you go out to the kitchen and help Mrs Hamner fix dinner. Mommy will stay for dinner.'

They gave her a last squeeze and ran for the kitchen.

'Hello, Thanos.'

'Come in and sit down.' He gestured toward the den.

She selected her easy chair, the antique one she had had recovered – when was it? – a year ago? He sat in his looking at her. She had aged ten years. Bags under her eyes, lines along her cheeks, sagging pouches under her jaw.

'Why'd you come back?'

Elizabeth gestured vaguely and looked at the wall.

'You didn't stay at the clinic. They called and said you walked away.'

She took a deep breath and let her eyes rest on him.

'Still on the dope, I see.'

'I thought you'd be glad to see me. The girls are.'

'You can stay for dinner if you want. Then you leave.'

'Why are you doing this to me?'

'Don't give me that shit! You're doing this to yourself. Look at yourself, for Christ's sake. You look like hell.'

She looked down at her clothes, as if seeing them for the first time.

'Why don't you go upstairs, take a shower, wash your hair, and put on clean clothes. Dinner will be in about forty-five minutes.'

She gathered herself and stood. She nodded several times without looking at him, then opened the door and walked out. Liarakos followed her to the foot of the stairs and stood there for three or four minutes, then he slowly climbed the staircase. He stood in the bedroom until he heard the shower running, then left.

He had said she would stay for dinner on impulse; now he regretted it. Could he manage his emotions for two hours? He loved her and he hated her, both at the same time. The irresistible tidal currents tore at him.

Hatred. In her foolish weakness and selfishness she abandoned every-thing for that white powder. Abandoned the children, *him* – yes, *him* – was it hatred or rage?

Love. Yes. If there were no love there would be no hatred. Just sorrow.

And then he was outside himself, staring at this man from an angle above, watching him walk, seeing the meaningless gestures and the twitching of the facial muscles, knowing the pain and knowing too that somehow none of it really mattered.

It didn't, you know. Didn't matter. The kids would grow into adults and make their own lives and forget, and he would keep getting up every day and shaving and going to the office. Age would creep over him, then decrepitude, then, finally, the nursing home and the grave. None of it mattered. In the long run none of it mattered a damn.

Yet there he was, standing there imprisoned on this tired old earth, being ripped apart.

'Lisa, tell your mother what you've been doing in school.'

The child prattled about mice and gerbils and short stories. Elizabeth kept her eyes on her plate, on her food, concentrated on using the knife and fork at the proper time, on handling the utensils with the proper hands. She patted her tips with the napkin and carefully replaced it in her lap.

'Susanna, your turn.'

The child was deep into a convoluted tale of fish and frogs when Elizabeth scooted her chair back a moment and murmured, 'Excuse me.' She bent down for her purse.

Liarakos snagged it. 'I'll watch it.'

His wife stared at him, her face registering no emotion. Then it came. A snarl which began with a twitching of her upper lip and spread across her face.

Liarakos flipped her the purse. She caught it and rose from her chair and went along the hall toward the downstairs half bath.

'You girls finish your dinner,' he said.

'Is Mommy going to stay?'

'No.'

They accepted that and ate in silence. They finished and he shooed them upstairs. Minutes later Elizabeth came back to the dining room, gliding carefully, her face composed.

He sat in silence watching her eat. She picked at the food, then finally placed the fork on the plate and didn't pick it up again.

'Don't you want to know where I've been?'

'No.'

'Could you give me a ride or some money for taxi fare?'

'You can get wherever you're going the same way you got here. Good-bye.'

'Thanos, I—'

'*Good-bye*, Elizabeth. Take your purse and go. Now! Don't come back.'

'Thanks for—'

'If you don't go right now, I'll physically eject you.'

She stared at him for several seconds, then rose. After half a minute he heard the front door open, then click shut.

Harrison Ronald looked at his watch for the forty-fifth time. Two hours and three minutes until he had to be there.

He examined his face in the broken mirror over the cigarette-scarred dresser – would they read it in his face? *He* could see it written all over his kisser, plain as a newspaper headline. Guilt. That was what was there. Old-fashioned grade-A guilt, the kind your momma always gave you, shot through with cholesterol and saturated fats and plenty of salt and sugar. *I did it! I'm the snitch! I'm the stoolie!* Whitey sent this chocolate Tom to tattle on all you shit-shoveling niggers and pack your black asses off up the river.

If Freeman asked him the question his face would shatter like frozen glass.

Two hours and two minutes.

Coffee? He had had three cups this evening. That was more than enough caffeine. No booze. No beer. No alcohol, period.

God, he was going to get stinking drunk tomorrow night. He was going to go on a world-class bender and stay yellow-puke drunk for three whole days.

If he was still alive tomorrow night, that is.

Two hours and one minute. A hundred-and-twenty-one minutes.

He picked up the automatic and ran his fingers over it. He would take it with him tonight. In ten months he had never carried a gun, but tonight . . . Maybe it would give him an edge, since they wouldn't expect it.

Two hours flat.

*

Captain Jake Grafton was feeling expansive. He had had a delightful day with his daughter, Amy, and had finished most of his Christmas shopping. Callie had gone by herself to buy Amy's presents and presumably one for Jake. He had glimpsed her sorting through his clothes this morning, probably checking sizes. This evening the captain smiled genially and let his eyes rest happily on Amy Carol, then on Callie at the other end of the dinner table. Two beautiful women. He was a very lucky man.

The captain's gaze moved down the table to Toad Tarkington, who was paying no attention to anyone except his wife, Rita Moravia, who sat beside him. Tomorrow Toad would probably have a crick in his neck. Rita was also the object of Amy's undivided attention. Amy adored the navy test pilot, but this evening as she regarded Rita a curious expression played about her features.

When Callie's gaze met Jake's, he nodded toward Amy and knitted his brows into a question. His wife shook her head almost imperceptibly and looked away.

One of those femaie things, Grafton concluded, that men are not expected to understand or concern themselves about. He sighed.

Across the table from the Tarkingtons sat Jack Yocke and his date, Tish Samuels. Tish was a lovely person, with a pleasant smile and kind word for everyone. In several ways she reminded Jake of his wife, like the way she held her head, the way she listened, her thoughtful comments . . . Tish also listened intently to Rita as she finished telling a flying story. When Rita concluded, Tish smiled and glanced at Yocke.

Whether the reporter knew it or not, the woman was obviously in love with him. Yocke seemed mellow, more relaxed than he had been the first time he was at the Graftons'. Or perhaps it was just Jake's mood that made him seem that way.

As usual when he was relaxed, Jake Grafton said little. He nibbled his food and took sparing sips of wine and let the conversation flow over him.

Callie turned to Yocke and said, 'I've been reading your stories on Cuba. They are very, very good.'

'Thank you,' Jack Yocke said, genuinely pleased by the compliment.

Callie led him on, and in a few moments Yocke was talking about Cuba. Toad even tore his attention away from Rita to listen and occasionally toss in a question.

At first Yocke's comments were superficial, but it seemed as if the company drew him out. Even Jake began to pay attention.

'. . . the thing that impressed me was the sense of destiny that the people had, the common people, the workers. They were gaining something. And then I realized that what they were talking about, what they wanted, was democracy, the right to vote for the leaders who made the laws. You know, we've had it here for so long that we've become blasé. It's fashionable these days to sneer at politicians, laugh at the swine prostituting themselves for campaign money and begging shamelessly for votes. And yet, when you're up to your eyes in dictatorship, being ordered around by some self-appointed Caesar with big ideas in a little head, democracy looks damned good.'

His listeners seemed to agree, so Yocke developed the thought: 'It's funny, but democracy rests on the simplest premise that has ever supported a form of human government: a majority of the people will be right more often than not. Think about it! Errors are part of the system. They are inevitable as the political currents ebb and flow. Yet in the long run, a shifting, changing majority will be right a majority of the time.'

'Will these countries which are embracing democracy for the first time have the patience to wait for the successes and to tolerate the errors?' Jake Grafton asked, the first time during dinner that he had spoken.

Yocke looked down the table at the captain. 'I don't know,' he said. 'It takes a lot of faith to believe in the good faith and wisdom of your fellow men. Democracy will stick in some places, sure. I think it needs to get its roots in deep though, or it'll get ripped up by the first big blow. There's always someone promising instant salvation if he could just get his hands on the helm and throttle.'

'How about democracy in America? A fad or here to stay?'

'Jake Grafton!' Callie admonished. 'What a question!'

'It's a good one,' Yocke told her. 'One of the common errors is to get rid of the system. We've got a lot of problems in America and two hundred and fifty million people advocating solutions. I should know – I make my living writing about the problems.'

'You didn't answer the question,' Toad Tarkington said, and grinned.

'I don't know the answer,' Jack Yocke told him.

'I don't think anything could make us give up our republic,' Callie declared.

'What do you think, Captain?' Tish Samuels asked.

Jake snorted. 'The roots are in deep all right, but if the storm were bad enough . . . Who wants coffee besides me?'

As Callie poured coffee, Jake saw Rita speaking softly to Amy. The youngster listened, her face clouding heavily, then she abruptly fled the room.

Jake folded his napkin and excused himself. He didn't get past Callie. She thrust the coffeepot at him, then followed Amy into the bedroom.

'How do you want it, Toad?' Jake leaned over the lieutenant's shoulder.

'In the cup, if possible, CAG.'

'Rita, have you picked up any new lines to teach this clown? His act is getting real stale.'

Rita grinned at Jake. 'I know. I was hoping that since he works in your shop now you could give him some help.'

'You work for Captain Grafton?' Jack Yocke asked Toad.

'Maybe I should go visit with Callie and Amy for a minute,' Rita said, and rose from her chair. She came out of it supplely, effortlessly. Toad and Jake watched her until the bedroom door closed behind her.

'Yeah,' Toad said to the reporter. 'CAG can't get rid of me. Actually I have been of some small service to Captain Grafton in the past in his epic struggles to defend the free world from the forces of evil and all that. I suggested yesterday that he buy a Batmobile and I'd keep it over at my place until he needs it. He doesn't have a garage here.'

'What do you two do over in the Pentagon?' Yocke asked.

'It's very hush-hush,' Toad confided, lowering his voice appropriately. 'We're drafting top-secret war plans to go into effect if Canada attacks us. We figure they'll probably take out the automobile plants in Detroit first. Surprise attack. Maybe a Sunday morning. Then—'

'Toad!' Jack growled.

Tarkington gestured helplessly at Tish Samuels who was grinning. 'My lips are sealed. Anyway, it's a real dilly of a tip-top secret, which as you know are the very best kind. If the Canadians ever find out . . .'

As they cleared the table, Jake said to Toad, 'Rita seems to be fully recovered from that crash last year.'

'She's got some scars,' Toad said, 'but she's amazed the therapists. Amazed me too.'

They had the dishes in the washer and were in the living room drinking coffee when Amy and Rita came out of the bedroom holding hands. Both looked like they had been crying. Callie headed for the kitchen and Jake trailed after her.

'What was that all about?'

'Amy worships Rita and has a crush on Toad.' Callie rolled her eyes heavenward. 'Hormones!'

'Ouch.'

Callie smiled and gave Jake a hug. 'I love you.'

'I love you too, woman. But we'd better get back to our guests.'

'Aren't you glad we invited Jack Yocke?'

'He's a good kid.'

Fear increases exponentially the closer you get to the feared object. Harrison Ronald made this discovery as he drove toward Freeman McNally's northwest Washington house.

He could feel it, a paralyzing, mind-numbing daze that made him want to puke and run at the same time.

He was paying less and less attention to the traffic around him, and he knew it but couldn't do better. That was another thing about fear – a little of it is necessary, keeps you sharp, makes you function at peak efficiency in potentially dangerous situations. But too much of it is paralyzing. Fear becomes terror, which numbs the mind and muscles. And if the ratchet is loosened just a notch, the terror becomes panic and all the muscles receive one message from the shorted-out brain – flee.

He drove slower and slower. When the traffic lights turned green he had to will himself to depress the accelerator. A man in a car behind raced his engine and gunned by with his middle finger held rigidly aloft. Ford ignored him.

In spite of everything, he got there. He eased the car down the alley and into a parking place behind McNally's row house. The guard was standing in the shadow of a fence. Ford killed the engine. He was not going to retch, no sir. Under no circumstances was he going to let himself vomit.

'Now or never,' he said aloud, comforted by the sound of his voice, which sounded more or less under control, and opened the door. The guard walked toward him with his hands in his coat pockets.

Oh, damn! *This is it!*

'You Z?'

'Yeah, man.'

'Ain't nobody in there. You're supposed to go over to the Sanitary and pick up a load.'

He stood there beside the car staring at the man. It didn't compute. Think, goddamn it! Think! The Sanitary Bakery . . .

'The guard'll meet you there.'

Ford turned and reopened the car door. He seated himself, then tried to remember what he had done with the key. Not this pocket, nor this . . . here! He stabbed it at the ignition. Turn the key.

With the engine running a tidal wave of relief rolled over him. He pulled the shift lever back a notch and let the car drift backward, toward the alley.

Everything's cool. Everything's cool as a fucking ice cube.

Look behind you, idiot. Don't hit the pole.

As the guard returned to the shadows he backed out into the alley and fed gas.

The relief turned to disgust. He had sweated bullets all day, for what? *For nothing!*

Maybe he should just split. Why not? He had proved to himself he could make it through today. That was the main thing. Nothing's going to happen tonight, and why should he deliver another load of shit for Freeman McNally? The feds already had enough evidence for 241 counts on an indictment. Why add another?

What are you proving, Harrison? You've had no sleep, you've been scared shitless for ten months, you killed a guy, you got enough evidence to send McNally and friends up the river so long that crack will be legal when they get out, *but you have to be alive to testify.*

Why dick around with it another night? Don't lose sight of the main thing – *you've made it through today.*

But he knew the answer. He pointed the car toward Georgia Avenue and fed gas.

'How well do you know Captain Grafton?' Jack Yocke asked Toad Tarkington. It was about ten o'clock and they were standing on the balcony looking at the city. It was nippy but there was little wind.

'Oh, about as well as any junior officer can know a senior one. I think he personally likes me, but at the office I'm just another one of the guys.'

'By reputation, he's one of the best officers in the Navy.'

'He's the best I ever met. Period,' Toad said. 'You want paper shuffled, Captain Grafton can handle it. You want critical decisions wisely made or carefully defended, he's your man. You need a man to lead other men into combat, get Grafton. You want a plane flown to hell and back, nobody's better than he is. If you want an officer who will always do *right* regardless of the consequences, then you want Jake Grafton.'

'How about you?'

'Me? I'm just a lieutenant. I fly when I'm told, sleep when I'm told, and shit when it's on the schedule.'

'How does Captain Grafton always know what the right thing to do is?'

'What is this? Twenty questions? Don't you ever lay off?'

'Just curious. I'm not going to print this.'

'You'd better not. I'll break your pencil.'

'How does he know?'

'He's got common sense. That's a rare commodity inside the beltway. I haven't seen enough of it in this town to fill a condom, but common sense is Jake Grafton's long suit.'

Yocke chuckled.

'Better watch that,' Toad admonished. 'Your press card may melt if you crack a smile. Your reputation as an uptight superprick is on the line here.'

Jack Yocke grinned. 'I deserved that. Sorry about those cracks the first time I met you. I was having a bad day.'

'Had one of those myself one time,' Tarkington muttered. He stamped his feet. 'I'm getting cold. Let's go inside.'

Harrison Ronald stood by the side of the Mustang and stared at the right front tire. Flat.

Traffic whizzed by on Rhode Island Avenue. When he felt the wheel pulling and heard the thumping, he had pulled into a convenience store parking lot.

Fate, he decided, as he opened the trunk and rooted in it for the jack and lug wrench. On the way to his rendezvous with destiny, Galahad's horse threw a shoe. How come this stuff never happens in the movies?

He got the front end off the ground, but the lug nuts were rusted on. Damn that Freeman, he never had these tires rotated or balanced or aligned. Got so damned much money he never takes care of anything.

He needed a cheater bar or a hammer. Frustrated, he sat on the pavement and kicked at the end of the lug wrench. The wrench flew off, scarring the nut. He tried it again. And again. Finally the nut turned.

A police cruiser pulled into the lot and stopped in front of the store. Two white cops. They got out of the cruiser, stood for a moment or two silently watching Ford wrestle with the wrench, then went inside.

Jesus, didn't they see the outline of the automatic in the small of his back, under his coat? Those shitheads. A weapon was the first thing they should have been looking for.

As Ford kicked at the last nut, he glanced through the big plate-glass windows. The cops were sipping coffee and flirting with the girl behind the counter.

He skinned his knuckle and it started bleeding. Well, it wouldn't bleed long. The dirt and grease would get in the skinned place and stop the blood. His father's hands had always had chunks missing, cavities full of dirt and grease that slowly, ever so slowly, healed just in time to be ripped open again. As a kid he had looked at his father's thick, heavy hands and asked, 'Don't they hurt?'

Dad, wherever you are, my hands are cold and hurt like hell and my ass is freezing from the pavement and my nose is dripping.

He wiped his nose on his sleeve.

So what did'ya expect? The cops'd help? Get real!

Jack Yocke found himself staring at Tish Samuels. He had been watching her for several minutes when he realized with a start what he was doing. He glanced around to see if anyone had noticed. Jake Grafton met his eyes. Yocke smiled and looked away.

Okay, so she's not *Playboy* beautiful, she'll never be on the cover of *Cosmo*. In her own way she's lovely.

Standing there watching her move, watching her gestures and body language, he remembered the Cuban madonna on the hood of the truck with the baby at her breast. How long had he looked at that girl? Thirty seconds? A minute? That woman had been life going down the road. In spite of war, revolution, poverty, starvation, she rode with courage from the past into the future.

He looked at Tish and tried to visualize her on the hood of that truck. She could ride there, he concluded. She's a survivor.

He poured himself another drink and settled on the couch to watch Tish Samuels.

Maybe he was just getting older. His ambitions somehow seemed less important than they used to be and he was rapidly losing faith in his own opinions. How many of his colleagues truly believed in the ultimate wisdom of the voters? Opinionated, egotistical iconoclasts – Jack Yocke marching bravely among them – they believed only in themselves.

Okay, Jack. If your meager brains and wisdom won't be enough, what will be? What *do* you believe in?

Musing thus, he found himself contemplating his shoes and in his mind's eye seeing the people walking on the road to Havana, walking as the dust rose and the sun beat down, walking into the unknown.

In front of the Sanitary Bakery Harrison Ronald turned the car around on a whim and backed it up beside the others. Six other cars. A crowd tonight.

He went to the door and knocked.

The man inside shut the door behind him and bolted it and jerked his head. 'They want you upstairs, second floor, way down at the end.'

The interior of the warehouse was dark, no lights. The only illumination came from streetlights outside through the dirty windows high up in the wall. He knew what was in here though and went along confidently as his eyes adjusted.

Second floor, down at the end. God, there was nothing down there but some empty offices with six inches of dust, din, and rat shit, and some broken-down furniture that was so trashed the last tenant had left it.

He checked the position of the automatic in his waistband at the small of his back and pushed against the thumb safety to ensure that it was still on. Wouldn't do to shoot yourself in the ass, Harrison Ronald.

He went up the stairs and turned left, toward the east end of the building. He could hear moaning. A male voice.

He stopped dead. Someone groaning, a deep, animal sound.

Harrison Ronald stood frozen, listening. There! Again!

He slipped his hand under his coat and touched the butt of the automatic again, then pulled his hand away.

No one in sight. Just the windows and the dim light and the black shapes of the pillars that hold up the roof. And that sound.

The terror seized him then. He started shaking as the low animal sound curled around him and echoed gently down the vast, empty, dark room. Someone past screaming, someone who had screamed his lungs out, who was now past words and pleas and prayers, someone who was past all caring. Someone who moaned now only because he still breathed.

There was something else. A *smell*! He sniffed carefully. Burned meat. Yes, burned meat, the smell of fried fat, acrid and pungent.

Oh, my God!

Harrison Ronald Ford walked forward. Toward the door cracked open and the light leaking out.

The moans were louder, and the voice.

'You betrayed your brothers, your brothers of the *blood*. Sold out to the honkey fucks, sold out your flesh and blood, *sold out . . .*' Freeman McNally. Harrison Ronald recognized the voice. Freeman McNal – '*What did they pay you? Money? You'll never spend it. Women? You'll never screw 'em, not with what you got now. Ha!*'

McNally was insane. Crazy mad. His voice was an octave too high, on the verge of hysteria.

'Kill me.'

Silence.

A scream. '*Kill me!*'

Harrison Ronald Ford pushed open the door. The stench was overpowering.

A naked man was tied to a chair in the middle of the room and above him an unshaded bulb burned. At least, he had once been a man. Strips of flesh hung from his frame. His crotch was a mass of raw meat. His face – Harrison walked closer to see his face – only one eye left – the other socket was black and burned and empty. On his chest were more burns. Amazingly, there was very little blood.

'Put the gun away, Sammy.'

He looked around. Other men sat in chairs around the wall. On the floor was a laundry iron with bits of flesh still clinging to it, a wisp of smoke rising.

'Put the gun away, Sammy.' It was Freeman. He was standing against the window. He had a pistol out and was pointing it.

Harrison looked down. The Colt was in his hand. He lowered it, then looked again at the man in the chair.

'Kill me.'

'The shithead sold us out. He was whispering tales to the feds. He admitted it, finally.'

He could kill them all. The thought ran through Harrison's mind and he moved his thumb to the safety. Five of them, seven rounds. Freeman first, then the others. As fast as he could pull the trigger.

Freeman walked over to Ford and stood looking at the man in the chair with his arms crossed over his chest.

'Isn't that some heavy shit? I've known him as long as I can remember. *And he sold me out.*' Freeman snorted and shook his head. The sweat flew from his brow. 'And all this time I thought it was you, Sammy. Shee-it!'

McNally shook his head again and walked back to the window. There he turned and pointed his pistol at Harrison Ford. 'You got a gun. Kill him.' He said it conversationally, like he was ordering a pizza.

The tortured man was staring at Ford with his one eye. His hands were still tied behind the chair, or what was left of his hands. Traces of white showed through the seared flesh – bones.

'Shoot him,' Freeman said, making it an order.

Harrison took a step closer. The eye followed him. Now the badly burned lips moved. He bent down to hear. 'Kill me,' the lips whispered.

Harrison thumbed off the safety. He raised the Colt and pointed it above the raw, oozing hole where the man's left ear had been. The ear itself lay on the floor by the iron.

'Sorry, Ike,' Ford said, and pulled the trigger.

19

Ike Randolph's body was in the trunk of the car when Harrison Ronald parked it on E Street in front of the FBI building. Freeman had told him to get rid of it, dump the body in the street somewhere. The mutilated corpse would certainly be a little point to ponder for anyone who someday might entertain the notion of crossing Freeman McNally.

Yeah, Freeman. Whatever you say, man. Four of them had tossed the body in the trunk and Harrison had driven away. He hadn't waved good-bye.

And he pondered the point.

The sun was up.

Sunday. Eight A.M. The streets and parking places were empty. In a few hours the suburban malls would open and the last-minute Christmas crowds would pack the parking lots and surge through the sprawling temples of retailing. The shoppers would swarm over the downtown malls too, but that was two hours away. Right now the only people on the streets were alcoholics and derelicts. Paper and trash from overflowing cans swept by the car, carried by the wind.

Harrison sat behind the wheel with the engine off and listened to the silence.

He had made it. He was still alive.

His hands shook.

The relief hit him like a hammer and he began to sob.

He was tired, desperately tired. The tears rolled down his cheeks and he lacked the energy to move.

Done.

Well, hell, I gotta get to Hooper. Give him the keys to Ike Randolph's hearse, then get some sleep.

He remembered to lock the car, then climbed the stairs to the FBI building and walked through the open foyer to the quadrangle. He went down the stairs to the quadrangle plaza and crossed to the kiosk where the Federal Security guard stood. The uniformed man watched him approach.

'Tom Hooper. Call him.'

'And who are you?'

'Sam . . . Harrison Ronald Ford. Evansville, Indiana, police. He's expecting me.'

'If you want to stand over there, sir, I'll call up and see if he's here.'

He walked away so the rent-a-cop could watch his hands. He was too tired to stand. He sank down against the wall and crossed his arms on his knees and lowered his head to rest on them.

He was sitting like that, crying, when Thomas Hooper spoke to him six or seven minutes later.

'There's a corpse in the trunk of the car.'

'Who?' Freddy and Hooper stared at Ford.

'Ike Randolph. They tortured him. He's a real mess.'

The FBI agents looked at each other.

'We gotta ditch the body.'

'Why?' Freddy asked, incredulous.

'We gotta, man,' Harrison insisted.

'Now listen. We go to the grand jury on Monday. Monday evening or Tuesday they hand down murder indictments and we scoop up Freeman McNally and his lieutenants and lock them up. They won't get out on bail. There's no bail for murder. Then we give the grand jury all the rest of it and let them come up with a couple hundred counts.'

Harrison was tired. 'You listen. Freeman gave me tonight off. But if that body don't show up someplace, he'll smell a rat. The very first thing he'll do is check my apartment to see if I'm there. I won't be, man, I can guarantee you of that. I ain't ever going back there. Then Freeman'll *know.* Maybe he'll skip. Maybe he'll be waiting with heavy ordnance when you go to bust him. Maybe he'll put out a contract on me. *I don't want to spend the rest of my life looking over my shoulder!'*

'We can't just go dump a corpse in the public street and—'

'Why not?' Tom Hooper asked.

'Well, hell, we're the cops, for Christ's sake.'

'We dump the corpse and wait half an hour and call the police. Why not?'

Hooper was thinking of the grand jury and the lawyers. Just because the FBI wanted a quick indictment was no guarantee there would be one. It might take a week. And as he sat staring at Harrison Ford, he realized that he was going to play it Ford's way or the undercover man might go to pieces. Ford might not last a week.

'Where you parked?'

'Right in front of the building on E.'

'Come on, Freddy, Let's go get this over with.'

'At least let's pull the car into the basement and let the lab guys photograph the body.'

'Are you fucking out of your mind?' Harrison roared. 'The only reason, the *only reason*, I'm still alive after ten months of this shit is that nobody knew I was undercover. Now you're going to let the lab people see the car and the body and me? Do I look suicidal?'

'Forget it, Freddy,' Hooper said. 'We'll just be creative on our reports. Won't be the first time. Not for me, anyway.'

In the car they talked about it. They drove down toward Fort McNair. On the east side of the army post was a huge, empty parking lot. Weeds growing up through cracks in the asphalt. Beer cans and trash strewn about.

The parking lot was bounded on the west and north by an eight-foot-high brick wall. Across the wall were huge old houses, quarters for senior army officers stationed in Washington. To the east, sixty yards or so away, were small private houses, but brush and trees obscured the view. A power relay station surrounded by a chainlink fence formed the southern boundary of the two-acre parking area.

They didn't waste time looking the place over. Ford backed up toward the brick wall and popped the button in the glove box to release the trunk lid. He left the engine running. All three men got out and went around back.

Freddy took one look and heaved.

'For the love of—'

'Look at his hands! They burned his fingers off!'

'Come on, you shitheads,' Ford growled. 'Grab hold.'

They laid the corpse on the ground and got back in the car. Ford jerked the shift lever into drive and fed gas. Freddy retched some more.

'What I can't figure,' Harrison mused, 'is why Ike? Why'd he think Ike was the stoolie?'

'Remember Senator Cherry?'

'The mouth.'

'Yeah. We told him Ike was our man inside.'

Harrison Ronald braked the car to a stop and slowly turned to face Hooper, who was sitting beside him in the passenger seat. 'You mean Ike was a cop?'

'Naw. He was just a hood. But we figured that since Cherry was talking out of school and there was little chance we could shut him up, we'd better do something to cover your ass. So we gave him a name – Ike Randolph.'

Harrison faced forward. He flexed his fingers around the wheel.

'And Freeman killed him. That'll put him in prison for life. Too bad about Ike, but—'

'Freeman didn't kill Ike.' Harrison Ronald said it so softly Freddy in the backseat leaned forward.

'What say?'

'Freeman didn't kill Ike. I did. Oh, Freeman tortured him, mutilated him, but he wanted to spread the fun around. He's that kind of guy. *I* killed him.'

'*You?*' Freddy said, stunned.

'It was Ike or me, man. If I hadn't pulled the trigger, I'd be a hundred and eighty pounds of burned dead meat this very minute. Just like Ike.'

'Drive. Goddamnit, *drive!*' Hooper commanded. 'We can't sit here like three fucking tourists in the middle of the street. Everybody in town will get our license number.'

Harrison put the car into motion.

'*You* killed him,' Freddy said, still wrestling with it.

'What in hell did you think was gonna happen?' Harrison roared, sick of these two men and sick of himself. 'Fuckhead! You *white* fuckhead? You *knew* if Cherry talked Ike Randolph was a corpse looking for a grave to fall into. And now he's dead! Well and truly dead, dead as I would be if anybody had whispered my name.'

'Why didn't you dump the body before you came to us?' Freddy asked.

'I wanted you to see it. Ike was a pathological asshole, but he didn't deserve *that.* I wanted you coat-and-tie FBI paper pushers to see it and smell it and get it smeared all over your clean white hands. So sue me.'

The ceiling was at least five thousand feet, Henry Charon estimated as he drove up the interstate toward Frederick, Maryland. Hazy, five or six miles visibility. Not like out west where you can see for fifty miles on the bad days.

He knew where he was going, a little park along the Potomac. There should be no one there in December, a week before Christmas. The place had been deserted last week when he found it after consulting an aviation sectional map and a highway map. He had drawn some lines and done some calculating.

Just before he got to Frederick he exited the four-lane and turned south on a county road. The two-lane blacktop wound southward through fertile farming country of the Monocacy River valley. Neat homes and barns stood near the road and cattle grazed in the fields.

Henry Charon turned right onto a dirt road just past an abandoned gas station and proceeded west for 4.2 miles. The road he wanted was sheltered by a grove of trees. There!

No fresh tracks in the mud. And not too much mud. That was good.

He parked the car and pulled on his parka and gloves. Before he put his feet on the ground, he pulled a pair of galoshes over his hunting boots and buckled them.

It took him half an hour to check the area. No hunters or fishermen on the river, no one in the fields to the north.

The only house visible from the parking lot was a half mile or so away on the other side of the Potomac River, in Virginia. He checked the house with binoculars. No one about.

Occasionally a light plane flew over. Charon didn't look up. He was only sixteen nautical miles north of Dulles International and seven or eight miles north of Leesburg. Harper's Ferry was about fifteen miles to the west. So there were going to be planes.

He got the radios from the trunk of the car and went over to the pile of gravel near the bank, where he sat down. From this gravel pile he had an unobstructed view straight up and to the south and southeast from the zenith down to the treetops on the other side of the river, about ten degrees above the horizon. That was enough. More than enough.

He turned on each radio and checked the batteries. He had installed a fresh set in each unit this morning and he had others in the car, just in case. The needles rose into the green.

He selected the VHF frequency band on the first radio and dialed in the frequency for the northern sector of Dulles Approach, 126.1. With the antenna up and tweaked to the right just a little, reception was acceptable. On the other radio he selected UHF, and dialed in frequency 384.9. He was fairly confident they would be using VHF, but he wasn't taking any chances.

Both radios began spewing out the usual chatter between controllers and pilots. Charon arranged one radio on each side of the rock pile and adjusted the volume knob. They didn't need to be loud – he had excellent hearing in spite of the thousands of rifle shots he had listened to over the years without ear protection.

He got out the sandwich and coffee he had purchased at a fast-food emporium's drive-through lane this morning. He ate slowly, savoring each bite. The coffee cooled too quickly, but he drank it anyway. It was going to be a long afternoon.

Perhaps. Who knew?

All the preparation, all the planning was over. He was as ready as he would ever get. He thought about the past three weeks, about the plans he had made and contingencies he had provided for.

One chance in four. He had a twenty-five percent chance today, he concluded. As usual, the quarry had the advantage, which was just the way Henry Charon liked it.

Charon grinned. He finished the coffee and sandwich and carefully placed the paper and cup on the backseat of the car, where it couldn't blow out, yet where he could dispose of it the first chance he got.

Then he sat down again on the gravel and began listening intently to the radios.

He rose occasionally to scan with the binoculars, then resumed his seat.

This little park was on one of the two routes he thought it probable the helicopter carrying the President might take when flying from Camp David to the White House. He suspected that the helicopter would in all likelihood avoid the airport traffic area at Frederick and Gaithersburg. If so, it could pass those two airports to the east and enter Washington heading straight south for the White House, thereby overflying Silver Spring and Bethesda. On the other hand, if the chopper passed to the west of Frederick it would probably overfly this little park on the Potomac on its way straight down the river into Washington.

As he had studied the map Charon had come to favor the Potomac route. As the helicopter descended into the Washington area noise over populated areas would be minimized by flying down the river. That struck him as just the kind of consideration that a harried staffer would base a decision upon.

Still, he wasn't a pilot and he knew next to nothing about air traffic control. He hadn't had the time to monitor the route of other Camp David trips or to do the dry runs that would ensure success at the proper time. This whole thing was pretty shoestring. Yet the longer he spent in this area checking things out, the greater were the chances he would be seen and remembered.

So he would try this. If he got the opportunity, he would shoot. If not, he would look for another opportunity.

One chance in four. Maybe less. But enough.

He sighed and watched the birds and listened to the river when the radios fell momentarily silent. Occasionally he rose and used the binoculars to check the area. There were three picnic tables between the parking area and the riverbank. Near each table was a small stone barbecue grill. In the summer this would be a very pleasant spot for an outing, if you could get an empty table.

It was a few minutes after three P.M. when he heard the call he was waiting for. It came over the VHF radio.

'Dulles Approach, Marine One's with you climbing to three thousand out of Papa Forty enroute to Papa Fifty-six, over.' Charon knew those areas: Prohibited Area 40 was Camp David, Prohibited Area 56 was the White House – Capitol complex.

'Marine One, Dulles Approach, squawk four one four two ident.'

A Cessna pilot made a call to Approach now, but his transmission went unanswered. Henry Charon turned off the radio tuned to UHF and put it back in the trunk of the car.

'Marine One, Dulles Approach, radar contact. You are cleared as filed to Papa Fifty-six, any altitude below five thousand. Report reaching three thousand and any change of altitude thereafter, over.'

'Marine One cleared as filed. Report any change of altitude. We're level at three now.'

'Readback correct. Cessna Five One Six One Yankee, go ahead with your request.'

One last scan with the binoculars. He let them dangle around his neck. From the trunk he pulled out a roll of carpet. He put it on the ground and unrolled it. He took a second roll out and did the same.

Charon put one of the four-foot-long tubes carefully on the ground right by the gravel pile after he had inspected it for damage. The second he inspected and kept in his hands.

He arranged himself against the gravel so he had some support for his lower back, yet the exhaust from the missile would pass safely above the gravel. They would find this spot, of course, and the carbon from the missile exhaust would prove that it was fired here. He just didn't want the hot exhaust deflected onto his back. He put the missile launcher across his lap.

He sat there and waited, counting the minutes. If the chopper was cruising at a hundred and twenty knots, it was making two nautical miles a minute over the ground. He had figured the distance at twenty-four miles. Twelve minutes. With a tail wind or more speed, the time would be less. He would wait for eighteen minutes and if the chopper had not appeared it would have used a different route. And the wind was out of the northwest, so the chopper would have a tail wind today. Eighteen minutes, then he would leave and try something else.

The helicopter might not use this route. There was no way of knowing of course. He would soon see.

And the pilot of the helicopter didn't make the call to Dulles Approach from Camp David. He had lifted off a minute or two earlier and was climbing out on course when he called Approach. So less than twelve minutes.

The minutes passed as he scanned the sky. Six, seven, eight . . .

He heard the distinctive noise of a helicopter. He looked. The trees behind him would block his view until it was almost overhead.

He turned on the batteries in both launchers and grasped the binoculars.

There it was! High, to his left. Perhaps a mile east of his position.

He checked with the binoculars, thumbing the focus wheel expertly. Yes. A Marine VIP chopper, like the one he had seen on the White House lawn.

He lowered the binoculars and raised the missile launcher to his shoulder. Power on. Aim. Lock on. He squeezed the trigger.

The missile left with a roar.

Charon dropped the empty launcher and picked up the second one. Power on. Aim. Lock on. Shoot!

With the second missile on its way he tossed both launchers, the rugs, and the binoculars in the trunk of the car.

He looked up. The first missile had already detonated, leaving a puff of dirty smoke against the light gray overcast above. The chopper was falling off to the right, the nose swinging.

Whap! The warhead of the second missile exploded right against the chopper.

The helicopter's forward progress ceased and it began to rotate and fall, a corkscrewing motion.

Henry Charon picked up the remaining radio.

'*Mayday, Mayday! Marine One has had a total hydraulic failure and has lost an engine! We're going down!*'

'Marine One, Dulles, say again.'

The pitch of the voice was higher, but the pilot was still thinking, still in control. The words poured out. '*Dulles, we've lost an engine and hydraulics. The copilot's dead. Two explosions, like missiles. We're going down and . . . uh . . . roll the ambulances and emergency vehicles. We're going down!*'

Charon snapped off the radio and carefully placed it in the trunk of the car on top of one of the rugs. He closed the trunk lid firmly.

He scanned the area. Nothing left lying about.

The assassin paused by the driver's door and looked again for the stricken helicopter. Much lower, falling several miles to the southeast with the nose very low . . . rotating quickly, like once a second. The crash was going to be real bad.

Henry Charon seated himself in the car, started it, and drove away.

20

Henry Charon dialed the radio to a Washington news-talk station and pointed the car north, toward Frederick. A woman was debating with various callers the appropriateness of the federal response to the AIDS crisis. At Frederick he turned east on I-70. When he saw a rest stop, he pulled off.

He parked the car on the edge of the lot and removed the galoshes. These he put in the trunk. He carefully wrapped the spent missile launching tubes in the rugs and wound the rugs with gray duct tape. After closing the trunk and ensuring the car was locked, he walked fifty yards to the rest rooms and relieved himself.

Rolling again, he was listening to the radio when the announcer broke in with a bulletin:

'A United States Marine Corps helicopter carrying the President of the United States and several other high-ranking officials has crashed in northern Virginia north of Dulles Airport. Emergency crews from Dulles International are responding. We have no word yet on the condition of the President. No further information is available at this time. Stay tuned for further news as we receive it.'

The radio station stopped taking calls. In short order the woman guest was off the air and two newsmen began discussing and speculating about the bulletin. They mentioned the fact that President Bush had spent the weekend at Camp David and was presumably on his way back to Washington when the accident occurred. They called it an accident. They read the list of the officials that had spent the weekend with the President and speculated about the reasons the helicopter might have crashed. The reasons they advanced all concerned mechanical failure or a midair collision. It was obvious to Charon that neither man knew much about helicopters.

He turned the radio off.

So it had started. The hunt was on and he was the quarry.

He turned off the interstate and followed the twists and turns of a county road for several miles until he reached a landfill. He pulled up to the booth.

The woman inside had the radio on.

'Five dollars,' she said distractedly.

He took out his wallet and gave her the money. She pushed a small clipboard at him. On it was a form, a certification that he was not disposing of hazardous materials. False swearing, the form said, was perjury in the second degree.

'What's happened?' Charon asked as he scrawled something illegible by the printed X.

'President Bush's helicopter has crashed.'

'You're kidding? Is he dead?'

'They don't know yet.'

Charon handed the clipboard back and was waved on through.

More luck. His was the only vehicle there to dump trash. A snorting bulldozer was attacking a small mountain of the stuff while a huge flock of seagulls darted and swooped.

Henry Charon opened the trunk and got rid of the galoshes and the two missile launchers wrapped in carpet. He threw the cylinders down toward the base of a garbage pile that looked as if it would be next: Then he got the sandwich wrapper, bag, and coffee cup from the floor of the rear seat and added them to the garbage wasteland spread out at his feet.

He pulled the car out of the dozer's way, carefully avoiding the soft ground off the vehicle ruts. A pickup truck loaded with construction debris parked a little further down the cut and the driver began throwing off trash. He was still at it when the big dozer shoved a hill-sized pile of garbage and dirt over the rug-wrapped missile launchers.

Special Agent Thomas Hooper got the news at the FBI facility in Quantico. Hooper, Freddy Murray, and an assistant federal prosecutor were interrogating Harrison Ronald when the call came.

Prior to his assignment three years ago to the drug crimes division. Hooper had served for five years as special agent in charge of the FBI SWAT team. He was still on call. Use of the FBI for paramilitary operations was rare, but occasionally a situation arose. When the situation required more men than the SWAT team had available, the watch officer went down the standby list of qualified agents. He wanted Hooper to go to the crash site. He passed the news, the order, and the location in as few words as possible.

Hooper hung up the phone and found the other men were staring at him, no doubt in reaction to the look on his face. 'The President's helicopter just crashed,' he told them, 'with him in it. I gotta go.'

'Is he dead?'

'Don't know,' Hooper muttered to his stunned audience on his way out of the room.

Jake, Callie, and Amy Grafton were returning to their apartment from a shopping mall when they heard the news on the radio. The family carried the packages upstairs and Amy ran for the television. Regular programming had been interrupted and the networks were using their weekend news teams.

Like tens of millions of viewers all over America, the Graftons got the news as the networks acquired it. Four people were dead in the wreckage and four were injured, three critically. Both the pilots were dead, as was the secretary of state and the national security adviser. One of those critically injured was the President, who had been flown to Bethesda Naval Hospital by another helicopter. Mrs Bush, on vacation in Kennebunkport, was flying back to Washington.

Footage of the wreckage was shown, shot from about a hundred yards away.

Later in the evening witnesses to the crash were interviewed. One elderly woman working in her flowerbed had seen the craft fall. She unaffectedly searched for words as the camera rolled: 'I knew they were going to die. It was falling so fast, twirling around, I closed my eyes and prayed.'

What did you pray for?

'For God to take to Himself the souls of those about to die.'

Amy decided she wanted to sit beside her father on the couch. He wrapped his arms around her.

In the newsroom of *The Washington Post* Jack Yocke was assigned to assist a team of reporters in writing a story assessing the presidency of George Bush, a story that would not run unless he died. Two weeks ago Yocke would have chafed at not being sent off willy-nilly to the crash site. Not this evening. As he called up the major stories of the Bush presidency on his computer screen and perused them, he found himself trying to get a sense of this man chosen by his fellow citizens to lead them.

World War II naval aviator, Texas oil entrepreneur, self-made millionaire, politician, public servant – why did George Bush want the toughest job in the world? What had he said? How did he approach the job? Why did he avoid the spotlight's glare? Did he have a sense of where America should go, and if so, what was it? These questions Yocke wrestled with, though he occasionally took a moment to read the wire service ticker and listen to the television.

He also took a moment to call Tish Samuels.

'Heard the news?'

'Isn't it terrible?'

'Yes.'

'Oh, I feel for his wife,' Tish said. 'I admire her so. This must be extraordinarily tough on her, to be so frightened with the whole world watching.'

The helicopter had crashed in a pasture just a hundred yards west of the Potomac, which flowed south at this point. In the glare of portable floodlights Special Agent Tom Hooper caught a glimpse of at least three dead cows. One of them was ripped almost in half. He asked the Virginia state trooper escorting him toward the helicopter.

'Shrapnel from the rotor blades,' the trooper said. 'The forward blades were still turning when it hit the ground.'

The wreckage looked grotesque in the glare of the floodlights. The chopper had impacted nose low, so the cockpit was badly squashed. The crew hadn't had a chance. A team was cutting through the wreckage to get the last body out of the cockpit. Another team wearing army fatigue uniforms was examining the engines. The rest of the machine was almost as badly mangled as the cockpit, but not quite. Hooper marveled that four fragile human beings had survived the helicopter's encounter with the earth. Maybe.

The senior Secret Service agent was holding an impromptu meeting beside the machine. Hooper joined the group.

'The army experts are ninety-nine percent certain that this machine was struck by missiles. At least two. Probably heat seekers. We'll know for sure tomorrow when we analyze the warhead fragments.'

'You're saying that this was an assassination attempt?' someone asked, the disbelief evident in his voice.

'Yes.'

Hooper was stunned. He turned slightly to look at the wreckage, and now the evidence leaped at him – a hole and jagged tears in the right engine compartment, and another spray of small holes near the exhaust.

'When are you going to announce this?'

'That's up to the White House. None of *you* are going to say it to anybody. Now there's a ton of things that have to be done as soon as possible, so let's get at it.'

The Secret Service assigned the FBI the job of locating the place where the missiles had been fired. Hooper walked back toward his car and its radio with his mind racing. He would draw a circle with a ten-mile radius around this spot and seal it. Then he would search every foot of ground within the circle and interview every human being he could find. For that he would need people, as many as he could get. The local sheriffs and state police could help with roadblocks. But the searching, for that he would need a lot of people. Perhaps the Marines at Quantico could lend him some.

An assassin. He was out there somewhere. No doubt the Secret Service would redouble its efforts to guard the Vice-President and Mrs Bush, but he would check to see if they needed more people.

So he got on the radio and began. He knew he would be at it all night and into tomorrow, and he was. Understandably, Hooper completely forgot about the grand jury and Freeman McNally. They would have to wait.

Henry Charon settled into the New Hampshire Avenue apartment to watch television. He was munching a bag of chips and sipping a beer when someone knocked on the door.

He scanned the apartment. Nothing lying around that would incriminate him. Leaving the television on, he opened the door.

'Hello, Mr Tackett,' Grisella Clifton said. 'Remember me? The building manager?' She was wearing a frumpy housedress and a bulky sweater.

'Oh, sure. Grisella, right?'

She nodded. 'My television is on the fritz. May I watch with you?'

'Sure. Come in.'

She settled in on the couch. He offered her some potato chips and beer. 'I just couldn't. I'm not the least bit hungry. Isn't this whole thing so tragic?'

Henry Charon agreed that it was and plopped into the stuffed lounge chair.

'You're watching NBC? I've been watching CNN. They've been talking to some witnesses who saw the crash. What could have gone wrong with the helicopter?'

Charon shrugged. 'We can change the channel if you like.'

'If you don't mind. I think CNN is so . . . so newsy.' Obligingly, he rose and turned the dial. 'I just can't believe what happened to my set. The picture suddenly got all fuzzy. Just when there is something important on, it quits. Isn't that so typical?'

'Ummm.'

'I do hope you don't mind this intrusion. But I just needed to be around someone. In the midst of life . . . It really bothers me, y'know?'

He nodded and glanced at her. She prattled on. He found he could hear anything important said on TV and still catch enough of her remarks to make appropriate responses.

She ceased talking when a doctor at Bethesda Naval Hospital came on the show. He explained the extent of the President's injuries in detail to the dozens of reporters and used a pointer and a mannequin to answer questions.

What if he survives? Charon asked himself. He had been paid to kill Bush, not put him in the hospital.

Not a word had yet been said on TV about an assassination attempt, but no doubt the Secret Service and FBI knew. The physical evidence of the helicopter would shriek murder to the first professional aircraft accident investigator who looked. Getting to Bush for a second attempt would be a real neat trick.

Listening to Grisella Clifton's nervous chatter – why was she nervous, anyway? – watching the images on the screen, he began to examine the problem. The armor might have a crack somewhere. He would have to think about it.

All over America, in hamlets and cities and on farms, people gathered around televisions or sat in automobiles with the radios on. The President of the United States lay in a hospital close to death, and two hundred and fifty million Americans held their breath.

It didn't matter if you had voted for George Bush or against him, whether you liked his politics, whether you even knew what his politics were. You sat and listened and were deeply moved as the condition of the President became known. He was seriously injured, with a concussion, broken ribs, a damaged spleen and a seriously fractured leg.

The surgeon at Bethesda reappeared on the television and ignored all the shouted questions. 'We don't know. We don't know. We're running tests and we'll see.' He paused, listened to the cacophony a moment, then said, 'He's unconscious. His vital signs are erratic. We don't know.'

He was not a king, not a dictator, but a fellow American who had been chosen to lead the nation for a period of four years. Four years – long enough for a skillful politician who understood the mood and spirit of the people to accomplish something worthwhile, yet not enough time for a fool or incompetent to do irreparable damage.

The nation had had all kinds of presidents in the 201 years since George Washington had taken the oath of office. Yet each of them had understood that they spoke for their fellow citizens, and by doing so they created in the American people a deep, abiding respect for the office of the presidency and the men who held it that seemed, in a curious way, to have little to do with the individual merit or personal failings of each temporary occupant. Americans expected the president to weigh the interests of everyone when he made a decision, to speak for all of them. From their congressmen and senators they expected partisanship; from their president they expected leadership. This working politician, this common citizen they raised to the high place, he became the embodiment of their unspoken hopes and dreams. In some vague, slightly mystical way, he became the personification of America. And of all it stood for.

So on this Sunday evening in December, all over America people collected themselves and took stock. Churches were opened so that those so inclined could pray and hear words of comfort. Parents told their children where they were and what they had been doing when they heard that John F. Kennedy had been assassinated. Switchboards jammed as millions decided to call home and touch base with their roots. In airports, shopping malls, and bars from coast to coast, as they gathered around television sets strangers spoke to each other.

There were incidents, of course. In Dallas a man in a bar cheered when an announcer said the President's life was in grave danger; he was severely beaten and, had he not been rescued by hastily summoned police, would probably have been beaten to death. An Iranian with a long-expired student visa lost his front teeth at a shopping mall in suburban Chicago after he loudly announced that George Bush deserved to die. In San Francisco a waiter dumped a tray of food in the lap of a self-styled animal rights activist who expressed a similar opinion. The activist repeated her remark to the manager who had rushed to apologize, and he summarily ejected her and apologized to his other patrons, who applauded loudly.

At nine-thirty that evening one of the network correspondents informed the White House press secretary's office that his network had a story that the dead pilot of the President's helicopter had mentioned explosions – 'like missiles' – in his last transmission to Dulles Approach. The network was going with the story on the hour. Did the White House wish to comment?

Yes, it did. The press secretary said he would hold a news conference at ten-fifteen, and he asked the network to hold the story until after the conference. After a hurried consultation with New York, the correspondent agreed.

At ten twenty-two that night the White House press secretary appeared at the rostrum in the basement press room and squinted as his eyes adjusted to the glare of the floodlights. He held a paper in front of him and read from it. At his side were the directors of the Secret Service and the FBI.

'The Vice-President of the United States has authorized me to announce that the helicopter accident this afternoon which claimed the lives of five people was an assassination attempt. We assume—'

He got no further. People who knew better shouted questions at the top of their lungs.

The press secretary waited for the uproar to die. He swabbed his forehead with a handkerchief and continued to stare at the paper in his hand. Finally he resumed:

'We assume that the assassination attempt was directed at the President of the United States, although we have no direct evidence to support or refute that assumption. Apparently a party or parties unknown fired at least two heat-seeking missiles at the helicopter carrying the President, at least two of which appear to have inflicted major damage on the craft, rendering it unairworthy. The pilot immediately lost control. The crash occurred shortly thereafter. If you have questions, the directors of the Secret Service and the FBI are here to help me answer them.'

'How do you know about the missiles?'

'The shrapnel from the warheads punctured the fuselage in many places,' the director of the Secret Service said.

'Do you have any suspects?'

'Not yet.'

'Do you have any clues?'

'None that we're going to discuss in public.'

'Are arrests imminent?'

'No.'

'Is it true that the pilot of the helicopter told Dulles Approach about explosions, like missiles, in one of his last transmissions?' This was from the network correspondent who had agreed to hold this story.

'Yes, that is true.'

'Why wasn't this announced earlier?'

The press secretary was tired and had had a hell of a bad evening. He had little patience with questions like that. 'We had to check it out. There are a couple of thousand rumors out there, including one that the pilot was drunk. We will release information when we have verified it and believe it is true. Not before.'

'Was the pilot drunk?'

'Not to my knowledge. There will be autopsies on all the victims, of course.'

Across the nation the mood of those still watching television, and they were many, turned gloomy. An assassin. A killer. Not an ordinary killer, but one who had directly attacked the United States of America.

All four of the networks seized the assassin angle with both hands. Film clips were aired of the Kennedy assassination. Pictures of Lincoln, Garfield, and McKinley were shown. Profiles of past presidential assassins and would-be killers were hastily assembled and aired. One network sent a crew to the New York residence of Jacqueline Onassis, Kennedy's widow, and camped outside with the camera running. The lady didn't come out.

At the *Post* Ott Mergenthaler stopped by Yocke's desk. The television in the corner was showing footage of Jack Ruby shooting Lee Harvey Oswald. 'Wanta go get a sandwich?'

'Okay. I can take a break.'

They walked to the elevator and took it down to the cafeteria. Normally at this time of night it was closed, but not this night.

'What do you think?' Yocke asked. 'A nut like Oswald?'

'Not very likely. Crackpots don't shoot missiles.'

'Remember a few weeks ago when they extradited Chano Aldana? That "communiqué" from the Extraditables in Colombia? "We will bring the American government to its knees." '

'I remember. If this is their work, they've made a good start.'

'So what do you think?'

'I think nobody in Colombia has factored Quivering Dan Quayle into their calculations.'

'As I recall, you called Quayle Bush's biggest mistake.'

That's just one of the nicer things I've said about him. I also said he was impeachment insurance for Bush.'

They went through the serving line, helping themselves to cold sandwiches and hot coffee. When they were seated, Mergenthaler continued, 'Quayle's a genuine nice guy, never been accused of being a deep thinker, no ideological cross to bear although he can mouth the conservative line and appears at times to believe some of it. He's just the kind of guy you'd like to include in a foursome on Sunday morning. Pleasant, affable, likes the kind of jokes dentists tell and can probably tell a few himself. Never worried about money a day in his life. If you hit your last ball into the creek, he'll toss you one with a grin and refuse to take a dollar for it.'

Ott sipped coffee and munched some on his sandwich.

'Every observer who knows this guy says he grows into his job. People underestimate him – that's ridiculously easy to do – and he surprises them. He's got a modest amount of brains but never had to use them before he got into public office. So he learns how to be a congressman, how to be a senator, how to be a vice president. His staff feeds him lines to say and he says them. If Bush dies, Quayle will presumably learn how to be a president. Given enough time, enough good will by all concerned, he can probably learn how to do a mediocre job.'

'He isn't going to have any time at all,' Yocke said.

'That's my point. He's walking straight into a blast furnace. In addition to all the stuff Bush has been juggling, Quayle will have the drug crisis going full blast, hot enough to melt steel. People are going to want this kid who never made a tough decision in his life to *do* something. And you know what? I'll bet he will!'

Ott worked on his sandwich some more, then added, 'If I was a doper in Colombia, I'd crawl into a hole and pull the hole in after me. The biggest temptation any man in the White House faces is to overreact. You got all those generals who'll want to go kick ass. If the Extraditables claim Bush as a trophy, the public is going to howl for blood. We may have a real rootin', tootin' *war* on our hands, mister. The hell with the S-and-L crisis, the hell with federal aid to education, the hell with balancing the budget. We're going to blow the whole wad on a trip to Colombia to burn out that hornet's nest. You watch. You see if I'm right.'

'I don't think the Colombian dopers are behind this, Ott,' Yocke said.

'Oh, I know, Aldana blew a lot of smoke. But that terrorist gig they've been running in Colombia won't work here. Not in America.'

'I wish I had your optimism. If Quayle sends the Army and Air Force to Colombia to kick ass, *that* won't work. The people we're after will run and hide. We'd have to burn the damn place down and sift the ashes to get 'em. No, if the Colombians start murdering judges here and buying everyone who can be bought, America is going to change and change fast. *This will cease to be the America you and I grew up in.* I'm not sure what it will become. Frankly, I hope to God I never have to find out.'

'Let's pray that George Bush doesn't die.'

Ott snorted. 'More to the point, we'd better pray that the Colombians don't claim they shot him down.'

21

Sitting in his room in the FBI dorm at the Quantico Marine barracks, Harrison Ronald Ford flipped through the Monday morning *Post* looking for the story about Ike Randolph's body. Most of the paper was devoted to the assassination attempt. That and a minute-by-minute account of Bush's life, including interviews with people who knew him when.

At first Ford thought it wasn't there, but he finally found the story on page B-7, three whole paragraphs: Body of a severely burned unidentified black male shot through the head found Sunday morning by a military policeman on a routine check of the perimeter of Fort McNair. Well, that was better than the anonymous phone call idea, though Ford was sure that someone had told the MP to go look.

He was disappointed. Likely as not Freeman and the boys would never see this little piddley story, considering what great readers they were. The whole damn crowd didn't invest a dollar a month in reading material. If it wasn't on the top half of the front page and staring at them through the glass of the newspaper dispenser, they would never see it.

Maybe one or two of the TV stations had picked up the story and run it when they were momentarily out of George Bush footage.

He tossed the paper on the desk.

Nothing was going right. The grand jury appearance had been postponed. Hooper was out chasing assassins all over Maryland and northern Virginia, Freddy was unreachable at the J. Edgar Hoover Building. And he was sitting here stewing. Wondering what was going through Freeman McNally's agile little mind.

It wouldn't be anything good, that was certain. When he didn't show up for work tonight, no doubt someone would check his apartment. At least he had had the good sense to leave the Mustang parked in front of the joint. That simpleton Freddy had wanted to take it back to the FBI lab. Harrison had told Hooper and Freddy in no uncertain terms what he thought of their intellectual ability.

His disappearance would not be something Freeman McNally would ignore. What was it he had said about Fat Tony Anselmo – you can find out anything if you know who to ask and have enough money?

Harrison stared out the window at the manicured lawn and trimmed trees.

The day was dismal. Overcast, threatening to rain.

And he was sitting here in plain view of anybody out there with a set of binoculars. He lowered the window blind and pulled the string to shut the louvers.

Then he threw himself full-length on the bed.

Ten months of this shit and he was still sweating it. Would it ever end?

'Did you watch any TV this morning?' Mergenthaler demanded of Jack Yocke on Monday morning. The older man stood at the opening of the cubicle with a wad of newspapers in his hand. He always read the New York *Times*, the Chicago *Herald Tribune*, and the Los Angeles *Times* every morning when he arrived for work.

'Fifteen minutes or so.'

Those idiots are canonizing Bush and he hasn't even had the decency to die. I got NBC's eulogy with my morning coffee. If he lives we'll have our very first saint in the White House. The Democrats won't even bother to have a convention in '92.'

'Haven't you heard? The Democrats are talking about running Donald Trump and Leona Helmsley in '92.'

'Stop laughing! I'm not kidding! I don't care how maudlin and saccharin those television twits get after he dies, if he dies. But if he doesn't, we're going to have to live with a politician the public gets all weepy just thinking about. Saint George. Yuck! Turns my stomach.'

'Oh, I don't think it'll be that bad,' Jack Yocke said slowly. 'The public's memory is short. By '92 the Republicans will be spending millions trying to remind the voters that George almost gave his life for his country.'

'Humph! By God, I hope you're right. This damn country won't work if we gotta start being nice to the politicians. And it won't work if we have only one viable political party.' Mergenthaler stalked away toward his glassed-in office.

All across America this Monday morning the wheels of commerce turned slowly, if at all. Parents let children stay home from school and took a sick day themselves. The televisions stayed on. From coast to coast streets, stores, and factories were nearly deserted as everyone participated in the national drama by watching the talking heads on television.

Normal programming was preempted. Every fact, rumor, and tidbit about the shootdown and the President's condition was played and replayed, experts discussed the massive manhunt, politicians went from network to network for cameo appearances to assure the viewing audiences that the wheels of government were continuing to turn and to urge the public to remain calm.

Why these officials felt it necessary to urge the public to keep its wits was never explained. The only people who seemed outraged beyond endurance were a few elderly ladies who telephoned their local television stations to voice bitter complaint about the preemption of their favourite soap operas. Even so, there were fewer of these calls than television executives expected.

Amidst the speculation about the identity and motives of the assassins, a new element was slowly introduced. Tentatively, with circumspection at first, Dan Quayle began to get airtime.

He had appeared in the White House press room at seven-thirty A.M., in time to be carried live on all the morning shows, said a few carefully prepared words, then embarked in a heavily guarded motorcade for Bethesda Naval Hospital to see the President's doctors, since Bush was still comatose.

By midmorning the networks were heavily into Quayle. His wife, his kids, his parents, his school chums and former professors back in Indiana, all were paraded before cameras and all mouthed appropriate words. Those that didn't, didn't get on the air.

All the networks approached the subject in basically the same way. The popular perception that Quayle was a lightweight airhead was silently refuted by the carefully chosen words and pictures the network chose to air. Quayle was cast in a presidential light, spoken of with deference. Conspicuously absent this morning were the snide asides and giggles up the sleeves and lighthearted try-to-top-this reporting of his public misstatements and bloopers that had characterized media coverage of Dan Quayle since the day Bush chose him as his vice-presidential candidate.

In the *Post* newsroom Ott Mergenthaler noticed the collective corporate decision to polish Quayle's image and began making phone calls, trying to pin down producers and executives on why they made this decision.

Over in the Joint Staff spaces of the Pentagon, Toad Tarkington noticed it too. And when Toad noticed something, he quickly made everyone in earshot aware of it. Today, as usual in his new assignment, his listeners were all senior to him in years, rank, and experience, but that didn't seem to crimp the Toad-man's style in any significant way.

'Hoo boy, I'm telling you, they're grooming Danny the Dweeb for the big one. They ought to turn on the TV in George's room. If he saw this he'd leap out of bed and jog down to the White House.'

'Mr Tarkington,' the Air Force colonel said in a tired, resigned voice, 'please! Must you?'

'This is all a sick joke, right? Quivering Dan Quayle? The pride of the

Indiana National Guard? Somebody call me when the commercial comes on. I'm gonna go buy some popcorn.'

'Can it, Toad,' Jake Grafton said. 'Don't you have any work to do?'

'Yessir. As you know, I'm preparing a contingency plan to convert all the A-6s to Agent Orange spray aircraft so we can zap the South American cocaine fields. I figure if we mix the stuff with the gas, we can just fly over the fields with the fuel dumps on and—'

'Back to work.'

'Aye aye, sir.'

Judge Snyder was at least seventy, with thin hair and a thick waist and big, hamlike hands. He was tall, about three inches over six feet, but he appeared taller because he moved with that clumsy awkwardness that some big men have. Still, the word that came to most people's minds after they had met Judge Snyder was 'crusty'. Even his wife used that word when describing him to new acquaintances. The young lawyers with fashionably long, styled hair who practised in front of him would have added another word – 'profane' – although no one had ever heard him indulge in salty language in the presence of his wife. Clearly he was not of the generation of the buttoned-down, big-firm Mercedes drivers who constituted the majority of the lawyers who practiced in his courtroom.

When Thanos Liarakos entered the judge's office at ten o'clock on Monday morning, Snyder had a television going and was reading a newspaper. He held the paper up before him, spread wide, as he leaned back in his heavy swivel chair.

His office was full of books, with briefs and case files stacked everywhere. On the wall behind him was a framed piece of needlework. Inside delicate pink and yellow flower borders were the words SUE THE BASTARDS.

When the door closed Judge Snyder lowered one corner of the paper and frowned at his visitor. 'Why aren't you at home, Liarakos, watching the damned TV with everybody else?'

'Seen enough of it, your honor,' was the reply.

'Me too. Turn that damn thing over there off, will you?'

Liarakos did, then dropped into a chair. He took an envelope from his jacket pocket and extracted the contents, which he handed to the judge.

Snyder reluctantly folded the newspaper and laid it in front of him on the desk. He perused Liarakos' document.

'The prosecutor seen this?' the judge asked curtly.

'Yes, sir.'

'What'd he say?'

'Well, he didn't want a say. Said he would abide by your decision.'

'I *know* he'll abide by my decision. I want to know if he wants to argue before I make it.'

'No. He doesn't.'

'Well?' the judge said, holding the sheets between thumb and forefinger and waving them gently back and forth.

'It's a personal problem. I just don't think I can adequately represent Aldana and I want to be excused. There are dozens of competent, experienced criminal lawyers in this town and Aldana can afford any of them. Hell, he could hire 'em all.'

'Why?'

'It's personal.'

'Had some young puppy in here last week with a motion like this. It all came down to the fact he thought his client was guilty. This isn't any damned silly nonsense like that, is it?'

'No. It's personal.'

'You sick?'

'No.'

'In trouble with the law?'

'No, sir.'

'Motion denied.' Snyder tossed the paper back across the desk. It landed in front of Liarakos, who stared at it.

'It's my wife. She's a cocaine addict.'

'Sorry to hear that. But what's that got to do with this motion?'

Liarakos raised his hands, then lowered them. He opened his mouth, then closed it and stared at his hands. 'I want out. I can't in good conscience defend Aldana. He's entitled to a good defense and *I can't give it to him.*'

'Horseshit,' Judge Snyder said. 'How many lawyers are there these days who haven't had a friend become addicted to something? All these damn fools used pot in college. They go to parties and somebody has a sugar bowl full of powder for the guests who are "with it". I may be an old fart but I know what the hell goes on. Half the bar has your problem or some version of it.'

Seeing the look on Liarakos' face, Judge Snyder's tone softened, 'Now look. If I approve that motion, Aldana's new lawyer will think up fifty reasons why he needs a ton of extra time to study the government's case and file motions and I'll almost have to give it to him. Yet the government wants Aldana tried as soon as possible, for a lot of reasons that have to do with foreign policy and our relations with Colombia. Those reasons are good ones, in my opinion. I suggest you talk to your client. Tell him what you've told me. If he wants to get another lawyer, that's his business. It's *his* ass. But the new lawyer will get not one more day than you've got. Tell Aldana that too.'

'I've already talked to him,' Liarakos said. 'He wants me.'

'Did you tell him your wife was a cocaine addict?'

'Yes. I did.'

The judge very much wanted to ask what Aldana's reaction to that revelation was, but he refrained. Attorney-client privilege. He contented himself with readjusting his fanny in his chair and easing the pressure on his scrotum. He also raised an eyebrow.

'He just grinned,' Liarakos muttered. He stood up and walked around the room.

He was examining a law book when he said, 'I probably shouldn't say this, but I will. My impression is that it really doesn't matter to Chano Aldana who his lawyer is. Apparently the man thinks he'll never go to trial.'

'Had a dog like that once,' Judge Snyder said, and lazily stretched his arms out as far as they would go. 'Kept shitting on the carpet. His education was painful, but he finally got the message.'

At two o'clock that afternoon Vice-President Quayle held a news conference. Television rating services later reported that more people watched this news conference than any previous one in the history of television.

When Quayle first walked into the glare of the television lights and looked at the sea of faces of the waiting media, he handled it well, his aides offstage thought as they watched him on a monitor. He looked calm, properly somber, in charge. He began by reading a short statement that expressed the nation's outrage at the person or persons who had attempted to take the President's life and the government's resolve to bring the perpetrators to justice. The aides nodded with every phrase. The Vice-President had rehearsed this little speech for a quarter hour, and it came off just right, they thought.

The first question was unexpected, however, and horrified the aides and William C. Dorfman, who stood among them staring at the monitor with his tummy hanging over his belt and a sheen of perspiration on his forehead, 'Mr Vice-President, a group calling themselves the Extraditables, who are known Colombian narcotics traffickers, has just claimed credit for shooting down President Bush. Does the government have any evidence to support or refute that claim?'

It was here that the worldwide audience got another look at that blank, frozen, wide-eyed stare that an inspired reporter had once dubbed 'the deer in the headlights look.'

'I . . . I hadn't heard that,' Quayle said after a few seconds. 'Did it just come in?'

'Yessir. From Medellín, Colombia.'

'Well, I don't know,' Quayle said lamely. 'We are investigating – looking at evidence and all – I don't know. Ahh . . . of course, nut groups and criminals can say anything. We'll see.'

The same reporter had a follow-up question. 'What will be the United States government's response if the Extraditables' claim proves to be true?'

'Well, I don't know that it is true. As I said, criminals can say anything. If it's true, I don't know. We'll . . . ahh . . . I guess I don't want to . . . ahh . . . speculate about what we might do.'

Off-stage Dorfman nodded vigorously. He had impressed on the Vice-president the necessity of not committing himself or the government to any particular course of action on any matter. So far so good.

'Why,' another reporter asked, 'haven't the people who did this been apprehended?'

Quayle was ready for this one. 'The various law-enforcement agencies are doing everything within their power to find the people who shot down the President. I am satisfied with the manpower and methods they are using. We will announce results when we have some that can be publicized without jeopardizing the ongoing investigation.'

'Do you feel,' a woman reporter asked, 'that you are capable of properly fulfilling the heavy responsibilities that you have just assumed?'

'Well . . . I . . . I think I can do what needs to be done. I'm hoping right along with everybody else that George Bush recovers quickly and can reassume the responsibilities of his office.' Here the Vice-President spoke sincerely, and quite effectively, Dorfman thought. This response had been carefully rehearsed. 'No one wants George Bush to get well more than I do. I'm praying for him and I hope everyone else in America is too.'

When it was over Dorfman led the entourage back toward the office spaces as he snarled at his executive assistant, 'Get me a copy of that damned Extraditables press release. And get the CIA and State Department people over here on the double. I want to know what the fuck is going on and why the hell the press got it before we did. I want to know *now!*'

At the conference in the cabinet room that followed, Quayle sat at the center of the table where Bush normally sat and said little. Arranged around the table were the directors of the FBI, CIA, and DEA, the assistant secretary of state – the secretary had died in the helicopter crash that had injured the President – the attorney general, and the head of the Secret Service. Dorfman sat beside Quayle and did the talking. As usual, he was blunt.

'Are the Extraditables behind this?'

No one knew.

'By God, we'd better find out and damn fast.'

'We're squeezing our sources now. We'll hear something soon.'

'Squeeze harder. We've got to find out who is behind this attempted murder and get these people arrested. Right now the public is holding its breath. We can't get on with the business of government when ninety percent of the stuff in the newspapers and on the air is about assassins and victims. So the people who did this have got to be found. Find them.'

Afterward Dorfman had a private conference with Dan Quayle, a man whom he would have despised if he had ever taken the time to think about him, which he hadn't. Dorfman occupied the center of the universe and everyone else merely orbited his star. Still, while he had never had any patience with people who lacked his intellectual gifts, lazy rich people who floated effortlessly along enjoying life's bounties had always brought forth the darkest side of his aggressive personality. Just now he had to steel himself to treat Quayle with what he thought was deference.

'This Extraditables claim,' he muttered, 'is political dynamite. No doubt this very minute someone is advocating an invasion of Colombia. The least misstep and we could have Colombians publicly assaulted in our streets. Remember the hostage mess in Iran ten or eleven years ago?'

Quayle remembered.

'And yet, if we don't take measured, positive steps to handle this mess, people will say that you're incompetent. Anything you do will be too much for some people, too little for others.'

'I've been in politics for a while,' Quayle said, a little annoyed at Dorfman. He disliked being patronized and that was all he ever got from Dorfman. He had spent the last two years assiduously avoiding the man.

Dorfman continued, trying to sound reasonable. 'My role for the President has been to play the bad cop, the hard ass, the guy who says no. I suggest that until the President recovers enough to resume his duties, you continue to use me the same way. Let me play the heavy. When something positive comes along, you take the credit.'

'That might have worked for George Bush, but it won't work for me,' Dan Quayle said. 'Not over the long haul. People think I'm incompetent, a featherweight.' Dorfman tried to interrupt but Quayle kept going. 'I'm not going to let you be de facto President while I sit on my thumb. That won't work.'

'I know that, sir. I'm merely making a suggestion. You're the man in charge.'

Quayle's innocent blue eyes zeroed in and didn't blink. 'Governor, I'm going to lay it right on the line with you. Everyone knows that you wanted to be the vice-presidential candidate in '88 but Bush picked me instead. Everyone knows that you want the spot in '92. And everyone, including me, suspects that you've been lobbying the President to dump me from the ticket.'

'I haven't,' Dorfman said, his face reddening.

Dan Quayle continued as if he hadn't heard. 'Right now I don't think it would be a good idea to replace Bush's team, at least until we get some idea of when the President might be capable of resuming his duties. But,' Quayle added matter-of-factly, 'this team had better get some results.'

*

At four P.M. that afternoon Thanos Liarakos had a short visit with his client, Chanos Aldana, in a cell. The guard was outside and the two were alone. Liarakos had long suspected these visitation cells were bugged but this afternoon he never gave possible listeners a thought.

'Your colleagues in Colombia are taking credit for the attempted assassination of George Bush.'

Aldana merely grunted. Something like amusement played across his fleshy features.

'Well, did they do it? Or did you hire it done?'

'What's it to you, Mr American lawyer?'

'I'm your defense counsel. I want to know if you're responsible for the attempt on the President's life.'

Aldana snorted. Then his lips curled in a sneer. 'You've got two daughters, right? What are their names – let me think – oh yes! Susanna and Lisa. Now listen very, very carefully, Mr Thanos Liarakos, rich American lawyer with the clean white hands. You tell these people that if they don't send me back to Colombia, many more Americans will die. You silly people have been living in a dream world. I'm going to show you the hard, naked truth. And if you double-cross me, if you don't do exactly what I tell you, you won't have two pretty little daughters anymore.' Aldana snapped his fingers. '*Do you understand me, Mr Thanos Liarakos?*'

'Guard! Guard! I'm ready to leave.' Liarakos pounded on the door. He wiped his palms on his trousers.

'You had better pay attention, Mr Liarakos,' Aldana hissed. 'If you think I can't reach you or your daughters, that will be your last mistake. I got to George Bush. *I can get to anyone on this planet. Do you understand?*'

The door opened then and Liarakos went through, but not without looking back over his shoulder at the round, sneering face of Chano Aldana.

As he walked down the corridor he wiped his hands on his trousers again, then swabbed his face with his sleeve. He saw the sign on the door that said MEN and ducked in. Suddenly he had an overpowering urge to urinate.

The prosecutor, William Bader, and Thanos Liarakos twisted uncomfortably in their chairs across the desk from Attorney General Gideon Cohen. Liarakos had gone directly from the cell to the prosecutor's office, and the two of them had come here, to the Department of Justice. Liarakos had just finished his tale.

'What does he expect the American government to do?' Cohen asked, his eyebrows high in disbelief.

'Send him back to Colombia,' Liarakos said curtly. 'I told you that.'

'No.'

The attorney general leaned back in his chair and stared at Liarakos. Liarakos stared back.

'I want protection for my daughters,' Liarakos said at last.

'Send them to their grandparents.'

'Don't give me that crap! These people can reach anywhere! I *believe* the son of a bitch. I want *protection*!'

'Two FBI agents.'

'Around the clock. In school and in the head. Every minute of every day.'

'For a while, okay.' Cohen nodded. 'But we're going to hold Aldana incommunicado. You are the only human who talks to him.'

Liarakos snorted. 'You wish. The jailers will see him. We have to feed him. They'll tell him what's happening. He'll threaten and bribe them. How are you going to stop that?'

'Quantico,' Bader suggested. 'Let's let the Marines hold him in their brig down there. Move all the other prisoners out.'

'Any objection, counselor?' Cohen asked.

'Do it,' Liarakos stood.

'Not so fast,' Cohen said, straightening in his chair. 'I want you to talk to the FBI. He claims he's responsible for four murders and the attempted assassination of the President. He's threatened other people. You're going to repeat this word for word in a sworn deposition.'

'No, I'm not. Attorney–client privilege.'

'Waived,' Cohen shot back.

'Like *hell*! I do a deposition like that and you'll have to find another lawyer to defend the cocksucker and Judge Snyder will have a pound of my ass. I've told you what my client wanted me to say. *That's it.* You tell the FBI and the White House and anybody else you care to. This hot potato is all yours. I'm done. And I'm leaving.' Liarakos walked out.

Cohen was on the phone to the FBI before the door closed behind the defense lawyer.

At midnight Henry Charon locked the door to the New Hampshire Avenue apartment and went down the stairs to the street. He walked the block to his car, unlocked it, maneuvered it carefully from his parking place, and drove away.

The evening was chilly and humid. Much colder and it might snow. He was dressed for the weather. Long underwear, hiking boots, a sweater and warm coat. Under his thin leather gloves he wore a set of latex surgical gloves, just in case.

Scrupulously obeying the traffic laws, Henry Charon drove to National Airport and parked in the long-term lot. He put the entry ticket in his shirt pocket and sat behind the wheel scanning the lot. It took him about three minutes to decide on the vehicle he wanted. Just as he was about to get out of his car, another car drove in. He waited until the driver had exited the lot, then got out and carefully locked his door and put the keys in his trouser pocket.

The car he had selected was a Toyota. Getting in took about half a minute. Charon slid a thin, flat metal shim down between the driver's window glass and the felt seal and fished carefully until he got the notch in the shim in the right place. Then he pulled. The door lock button rose with a click.

Inside the car he felt under the mat. No luck. Not that he really needed a key, of course. He could hot wire the car with about five minutes of work, but a key would be nice. He looked in the ashtray and the glove box and the little compartment for cassette tapes. A spare key was wedged in there under a Grateful Dead tape.

The car started on the first crank. Half a tank of gas.

Charon gave the attendant the ticket from his shirt pocket and a dollar on the way out. The attendant had a portable radio going, a news-talk station. As the attendant glanced at the ticket and rang it up, Charon heard a voice on the radio mention Dan Quayle. As the wooden arm in front of the car rose, Charon fed gas. The attendant hadn't even looked at him.

It took an hour to find the house he was looking for in Silver Spring, set back among tall, stately maples and some really large pines. No cars on the street. He drove down to the corner and out to the main avenue, memorizing the turns, then turned around and came back.

As he eased the car down the driveway he examined the house for lights. One was on behind drapes in a downstairs room – he could just make out the glow.

Charon left the engine running and slipped the transmission into park. He pulled off the leather gloves and laid them on the seat beside him.

The automatic was in one coat pocket and the silencer in another. It took about six twists to screw the silencer into place. He didn't check the magazine or chamber – he knew they were ready.

He opened the car door and stepped out, then pushed the door closed until the interior light went out.

A brick stoop, a little button for the doorbell. He could hear the tinkle somewhere in the house.

The breeze was chilly and the wind in the pines made a gentle moan. It was a sound he had always liked. Now he shut that sound out and listened for others, car doors or engines or voices.

Nothing.

The door opened. A man about sixty, thick at the waist, in his shirt-sleeves. He looked like his photo last week in *Newsweek* magazine.

Well, Charon thought, this was luck indeed.

'Yes?' the man said, cocking his head quizzically.

Henry Charon shot him dead center in the chest. The gun made a popping noise, not loud, a metallic thwock. As he fell Charon shot him again. With the man lying in the foyer on his side, his legs twisted, Charon stepped over and fired a slug into his skull.

Then he pulled the door closed and walked for the car.

He heard voices now. 'Dad! Dad!' A woman calling.

Seated behind the wheel, Charon saw lights in the second story come on.

He pulled the shift lever one notch rearward, into reverse, then looked over his shoulder and backed down the driveway toward the circle of warmth from the streetlight. No cars coming.

Henry Charon backed into the street, put the car in drive, and drove at twenty-five miles per hour toward the avenue. He glanced at his watch. Two-nineteen A.M.

At three-oh-five he took a ticket from the automatic device guarding the parking lot entrance at National Airport and wheeled the car back into exactly the same stall he had taken it from. He replaced the key in the cassette tray, locked the car, then walked toward the terminal to get a cup of coffee.

He would let about an hour pass before he drove his own car past the attendant and handed him the ticket he had just acquired driving in. No use giving the man two short-time tickets in the same night. The second time he might look at the driver. Not that he would remember me, Charon thought, wryly amused. Nobody ever does.

During the night Harrison Ronald awoke with a start. He found himself fully alert, lying rigid in bed, listening to the silence.

And God, it was quiet. Nothing! He strained his ears to pick up the slightest noise.

Fully awake and taut as a violin string, he eased the automatic from under his pillow and slipped from the bed. He listened at the door. Nothing. He put his ear to the door and stood that way for several seconds, listening to the sounds of his breathing but nothing else.

The fear was palpable, tangible, right there beside him in the darkness. He could smell the monster's fetid breath.

Frustrated, listening to his heart thud, he glided noiselessly to the window.

He pulled the blinds back ever so slightly. The light on the pole between the trees cast weird shadows on the grass, which looked from this angle like the green felt on a pool table.

Too quiet. No wind. The tree limbs were absolutely still.

What had awakened him?

He held his wristwatch so that the dim glow coming through the gap in the blinds fell upon it. Three-fourteen A.M.

Not even a hum from the heating system. That was probably it. It was off.

In a moment the system kicked back on.

He felt the tension ebbing and walked back to the bed. He sat gingerly upon it and tossed the heavy pistol onto the blanket beside him. Rubbing his face, then lying full-length on the bed, Harrison Ronald tried to relax.

What was Freeman doing right now? Did he know?

Of course he knew. Or suspected. Freeman would be curious, with that alley dog asshole-sniffing curiosity that had to be satisfied, so he would take steps to learn the truth. He would talk to people and use money and sooner or later he would know. What then?

22

Tuesday the world came unglued. Those were the words a senator used later to describe the day, and those words stuck in tens of millions of minds as the perfect description.

It started whenever you awoke and turned on your television to check on the President's condition at Bethesda and found yourself staring at a stark image of a suburban two-story Cape Cod house surrounded by tall pines and lit by floodlights. In the gray dawn half light, the surreal image looked ominous.

The troubling thing about the picture was not the ambulances, the flashing blue-and-white beacons, the uniformed policemen and the clean-cut FBI types in Sears suits, nor was it the sobbing grown daughter and her two children home to visit Dad for Christmas. No. The troubling thing about the image was that the house looked like something from the set of an old *Leave It to Beaver* show. As you stared at it you could see that it looked exactly like the one in the ads for house paint for great American homes 'just like yours' – the perfect distillation of the American two-story dream house in Hometown, USA. And the owner had been assassinated, murdered, when he opened his door to a stranger.

The owner, of course, was Somebody, Congressman Doyle Hopkins of Minnesota, majority leader of the House of Representatives. He had been shot three times at point-blank range.

A better crime to push the panic buttons of middle-class America could not have been devised. The sanctity of home, neighborhood, and family circle had been savagely violated.

The television newspeople, no fools they, played that theme for all it was worth. 'Why did he open the door?' one of them asked rhetorically, as if every suburban householder had not done the same thing dozens of times, as if the evil intent of Hopkins' assailant had been written across his face so plainly it would have still been obvious in the stark shadows of the porch light.

But if you stayed glued to the tube long enough, eventually you were told that the President's condition was unchanged. The doctor in charge

928

of the President's medical team held a morning press conference, but only a few minutes of that got on the air. The story of the hour was the killing of the House majority leader.

That was the story of the hour until nine A.M. Eastern time, anyway. At eight fifty-eight five heavily armed men walked into the rotunda of the Capitol building wearing heavy, knee-length coats. They shot the four security guards on duty with pistols before the security men could get off a shot, then extracted Uzis from under their coats and ran along the corridors shooting everyone they saw.

A reporter-camera team setting up to interview the Speaker of the House was the first to get this atrocity on the air, at nine-oh-one A.M., just in time to capture a gruesome vignette of one of the gunmen mowing down the woman reporter, then turning the weapon on the cameraman. As he was hammered into a wall with five slugs in his body the camera fell to the marble floor and was smashed.

A uniformed security guard near the Senate cloakroom was running toward the noise of gunfire with his pistol drawn when he rounded a corner and almost careened into one of the Uzi-toting gunmen. They exchanged shots at a range of five feet. In the roar of the Uzi on full automatic fire the report of the guard's weapon was lost. Both men went down fatally wounded.

There were four gunmen left alive. One of them charged into a subcommittee hearing room where people were gathering and emptied a magazine into the crowd. The noise of the chattering automatic weapon was deafening, overpowering, in this room which had been recently renovated to improve the acoustics. Only when the triphammer blasts ended could those still alive hear the screams and moans, and then they sounded muffled, as if they were coming from a great distance.

The killer stood calmly amidst the blood and gore and groaning victims and changed magazines. He emptied the second magazine into the prostrate crowd and was inserting the third one into his weapon when a guard appeared in the doorway and shot him with a .357 Magnum.

The first two rounds from the revolver hammered the gunman to the floor but the guard walked toward him still shooting. He fired the sixth and last round into the gunman's brain from a distance of three feet.

Sixteen people in the room were dead and seventeen wounded. Only three people escaped without bullet wounds.

Another of the gunmen was shot to death in the House dining room after he sprayed the diners with two magazines and used the third on the chandeliers. His weapon jammed. He was crouched amid a shower of shattered glass trying to clear the weapon when two guards standing at different doorways opened fire with their revolvers. The man went down with three bullets in him and was shot twice more as he lay on the floor.

One of the gunmen somehow ended up in the old Senate chamber which, mercifully, was empty. Didn't matter. He stood near the lectern and sprayed two magazines of slugs into the polished desks and speaker's bench. Then he threw the Uzi down, drew a pistol, and blew his brains out.

The only terrorist taken alive was shot from behind as he ran down a corridor on the second level. He had killed over a dozen people and wounded nine others before a woman guard leveled him with a slug through the liver.

Watching the pandemonium on television – every station in town had a crew at the Capitol within twenty minutes and two of them had helicopters circling overhead – White House chief of staff William C. Dorfman took the first report from the FBI watch officer over the telephone in his office.

'How many of them were there?'

'We don't know.'

'Have you gotten them all?'

'We don't know.'

'Casualties?'

'Don't know yet.'

'Well, goddammit, call me back when you know something, you fucking idiot!' Dorfman roared and slammed down the phone so hard the plastic housing on the instrument cracked.

These temper tantrums were a character defect and were doing him no good politically. Dorfman knew it and was trying to control himself. Still . . .

One minute later the telephone rang again. It was Vice-President Quayle. 'I'm going over to the Capitol. I want you to go with me.'

'Mr Vice-President, I don't think that's a good idea,' Dorfman replied as he jabbed the button on the remote to kill the TV volume. 'The FBI just told me that they don't know if the guards got all the terrorists. The nation can't afford to lose you to a—'

'I'm going, Dorfman. You're coming with me. I'll be at the Rose Garden entrance in five minutes. Have the cars brought around.'

The line went dead.

'Yessir,' Dorfman said to nobody in particular.

The administration was sitting on a bomb with a lit fuse, Dorfman realized, and the fuse was dangerously short.

Terrorists! Not in the Middle East, not in some Third World shithole that nobody had ever heard of, but *here*! Washington, DC, the capital of the United States! The next thing you know wild-eyed lunatic ragheads will be blowing stuff up and slaughtering people in Moline and Columbus and Tulsa. My God!

At least Dan Quayle was smart enough to comprehend the gravity of the situation. That was undoubtedly why he wanted to personally view the carnage at the Capitol, console the survivors, and be seen by the American people doing it. That would help calm all those people from Bangor to LA who were right now beginning to feel the first twinges of panic.

Dorfman regretted his first impulse to advise Quayle not to go. Quayle's political instincts were sound. He was right.

Dorfman called for the cars and had a thirty-second shouting match with the senior Secret Service agent on duty, who didn't give a tinker's damn about politics but did care greatly about the life of the Vice-President that was entrusted to his care.

He also took the time to call Gideon Cohen and tell him to meet the Vice-President's party at the Capitol and to bring the director of the FBI along with him.

Dorfman shared the limo with the Vice-President, who had brought along his own chief of staff, one Carney Robinson, an intense blow-dried type who in his previous life had made a name for himself in public relations.

Dorfman apologized to Quayle for advising him not to go to the Capitol. 'This is wise,' Dorfman said. Neither Quayle nor Robinson replied. They sat silendy looking back at the people on the sidewalks looking at them.

After a bit Dan Quayle cleared his throat. 'Will, use the phone there. Call General Land at the Pentagon and ask him to meet us at the Capitol.'

Without a word Dorfman seized the instrument and placed the call.

Henry Charon woke up a few minutes after ten A.M. at the Hampshire Avenue apartment and made himself a pot of coffee. While he waited for it to drip through he took a quick shower, brushed his teeth, and shaved.

Then he dressed, even putting on his shoes and a sweater. Only then did he pour himself some coffee and turn on the television to see what the hunters were up to.

He stood in front of the screen staring at it, trying to understand. A group of terrorists? The Capitol?

He sat on the sofa and propped his feet on the chair while he sipped the steaming hot liquid in the cup.

Well, one thing was certain – the FBI and police were going to be thoroughly confused. That, Charon reflected, was more than he had hoped for.

It was also an opportunity.

He drained the cup and poured himself another while he thought about it. After a couple of sips he went to the window and stood looking down into the street. Not many people about this morning. A few empty parking places, though. Another gray day.

The FBI would be around before very long, either FBI or local police. They would be looking for terrorists and assassins, so they would be knocking on doors and asking questions. Nothing to fear there.

His mind went back to the Capitol. He remembered the office building just east of the Supreme Court. What was it, five or six hundred yards over to the Capitol?

Could he make a shot at that distance? Well, with the best of the rifles he had fired three shots into a one-inch group at a hundred yards, so theoretically at five hundred yards a perfect shot should hit within a circle five inches in diameter. Yet the impact point would be about fifty-six inches below the point of aim because the bullet would be dropping, affected by gravity. If he made a perfect shot. With no wind. And the distance was precisely five hundred yards.

With the wind blowing and a fifty-yard error in his estimate of the distance, all bets were off.

Henry Charon didn't have to review the ballistics – he knew them cold. And he knew just how extraordinarily difficult it would be to hit a man-sized target at 500 yards, especially since the target man would not be cooperating by holding absolutely still. It would be a real challenge.

He stood watching the passersby below and the bare branches being stirred by the breeze and tried to remember what the field of view looked like from the top of the office building.

He went back to the little living room and stood with the cup in his hand watching the television. The Vice-President was on his way to the Capitol, the announcer said. He would be there shortly. Stay tuned.

His mind made up, Charon snapped off the television. He turned off the coffeepot and the lights, grabbed his coat, and locked the door behind him.

'How many dead?' Dan Quayle asked the special agent who had greeted them and escorted them through the police lines into the building as reporters shouted questions and the cameras rolled. Quayle had ignored them.

'Sixty-one, sir. A couple more are in real bad shape and will probably die. Forty-three wounded.'

'Any idea who these people were?'

'Colombians, sir,' the agent said. 'On a suicide mission. One's still alive, barely, and he did some talking before he passed out from internal bleeding and shock. An agent who speaks Spanish took down what he could. Apparently these people were smuggled into the country this past weekend and told their target this morning.'

'Paid to commit suicide?' Dorfman asked in disbelief.

'Yes, sir. Fifty thousand before they left, and fifty more to the widow afterward.'

That stunned the politicians, who walked along in silence. The agent led them to a hearing room where seventeen men and women and the man who had killed them lay as they had fallen. The wounded had been removed, but photographers and lab men were busy. They didn't look up at the gawking politicos or the Secret Service agents who stood with pistols in their hands.

Quayle just stood rooted with his hands in his pockets, looking right and left. Spent brass casings lay scattered about, bullet holes here and there, blood all over, bodies contorted and twisted.

'Why?' Quayle asked.

'Sir?'

'Why in hell would anybody take money to commit murder and be killed doing it?'

'Well, this one guy – the one that's still alive – he said he has a wife and eight kids in Colombia. He used to have ten kids but two died because he couldn't feed them anything but corn and rice and he couldn't afford a doctor when they got sick. They live in a shack without running water. He had no job and no prospect of ever getting one. So when he got offered this money, he looked at the kids and figured it was the only way they were ever going to have a chance, so he took it. So he said, anyway.'

'Sixty-one people murdered,' Quayle muttered so softly Dorfman had to take a step closer to catch it. 'No, that's too nice a word. Butchered. Slaughtered. Exterminated.'

The agent led them from the room and down the hall toward the cafeteria. They passed several bodies in the corridors. Dorfman tried not to look at the faces, but Quayle did. He bent over each one for a second or two, then straightened and walked on. His hands stayed in his coat pockets and his shoulders sagged.

They were standing in the cafeteria when Gideon Cohen and General Land and several other military officers joined them. One of the officers was a navy captain, 'Grafton' his name tag said, who took it all in, his face expressionless.

'This guy who's still alive – he said he thinks there were other groups smuggled in.'

'How did they get here?'

'By airliner. They were met at the airport and taken somewhere and given food and weapons. This morning they were driven here in a van and dropped.'

'Where are the others? What are their targets?' Dorfman growled.

'He doesn't know.'

Attorney General Gideon Cohen spoke for the first time. 'Aldana's lawyer says Aldana told him yesterday afternoon that he was responsible for the attempt on the President's life. That's confidential, of course.'

'Bastard's lying,' Dorfman said forcefully.

'I wouldn't bet on it,' Cohen rumbled. 'Our people in Colombia are hearing rumors, too many rumors.'

Surrounded by Secret Service agents the group kept walking. 'Let's find a place to talk,' Quayle said. The Secret Service led them to an empty committee room – all the committee rooms were empty just now – checked it out, then stood guard outside the door.

Quayle dropped into a chair on the aisle. The others selected chairs nearby. As they were doing so the director of the FBI and another man came in.

'Did these people shoot down the President's helicopter?' Vice-President Quayle asked to get the ball rolling.

'You mean these very men killed here?' the FBI agent who had been escorting them asked. 'The survivor denied it, for whatever that's worth.'

The director of the FBI nodded at the agent who spoke. 'You may go back to your duties.'

The man rose, muttered, 'Gentlemen,' and left.

The director addressed Quayle. 'Mr Vice-President, I've brought with me today Special Agent Thomas Hooper. He's in charge of our antidrug task force and he's been working with the team that's looking for the people who shot down the President's helicopter. Before we came in we spent five minutes talking with the senior people who are working on this . . .' He gestured vaguely at the room around him. 'Hooper, tell them what you told me.'

Tom Hooper glanced around at the faces, some of which were looking his way, some averted. 'What we've got here is a classic narco-terrorist strike. It was committed by people with a minimum of training, people you would classify as apolitical amateurs. It didn't really matter how many people were killed or wounded here – the publicity the event would get would be precisely the same. This atrocity was a *political* act.

'The attempted assassination of the President was very different in several significant ways. That was meticulously planned, carefully prepared, all to take advantage of an opportunity if one presented itself. In other words, a professional assassin.'

'Just one?' someone asked.

'Probably,' Hooper replied. 'We've found the spot where the missiles were fired – a little picnic area beside the Potomac – and it appears that only one man spent the afternoon there. His tracks are all over. He wore some kind of rubber boots, but he appears to be of medium height, weight about one hundred sixty or so. Those are just tentative conclusions, of course.'

'Who hired the assassin?' Dorfman asked.

'No idea, sir,' Hooper said. 'Guesses are three for a quarter, but I wouldn't bet against you if you thought the same people are behind all of this.'

'Aldana,' Dorfman said as if the very name were poisonous.

Dan Quayle spoke slowly, seemingly feeling his way: 'The question is, what are we going to do to prevent any more of these slaughters?'

'We've got to find these other Colombians,' Dorfman said.

'Heavy guards around all public buildings and likely places,' somebody added.

'That won't stop these people,' The words were spoken quietly but with force. Everyone looked at the speaker. Captain Jake Grafton. He continued, 'All these people are after is an atrocity. They want publicity, fear, terror, to force the government to do their will. They'll find a target regardless. In Colombia they're blowing up department stores and banks and airliners. We've got all that plus shopping malls and these boutique emporiums, like the ones at the Old Post Office and Union Station. This close to Christmas . . .' His voice tailed off.

'I want to call out the National Guard,' Quayle said. 'We're going to have to guard the public buildings regardless, and as many of the shopping areas as we can find people for. And we can use the troops to search for these Colombians.'

'Are you talking martial law?' General Land asked.

'I don't care what you call it.'

'Troops will never find these terrorists, even if they're here,' the chairman of the Joint Chiefs protested. 'We can't have troops going door to door, searching every house. They aren't trained for that. That's what the FBI and police are for.'

'FBI, what do you say?' Quayle directed his question at the director.

'These aren't ordinary times. We need quick results. To get quick results we need a lot of people. Yet when this is over the American people are going to hold the FBI and the military accountable if innocent people's rights are trampled on, injustice done. That's inevitable.'

William Dorfman jumped in with both feet. 'The American people will hold *us* accountable if these murdering swine aren't caught and caught damn soon. We've got to move heaven and earth to stop this slaughter or this country will come unglued. That's the *first* priority. Better to jail some innocent people and turn 'em loose later than let the guilty stay free.'

'How about innocent people shot by nineteen-year-old kids with M-16s?' General Land asked Dorfman.

'Don't be a damn fool,' Dorfman retorted. '*Your* job is to make sure that doesn't happen. If you can't do the job we'll—'

Dorfman had the sense to shut up just then, for the look on Hayden Land's face would have boiled water. Jake Grafton doubted if there was another man living who had ever had the temerity to tell the general to his face that he was a damn fool.

The silence that followed Dorfman's outburst lasted for a long moment.

'Why not use regular troops?' Gideon Cohen suggested with a glance at General Land. 'Handpicked noncoms and officers? This is the federal district. I think that would be legal. Certainly justifiable. Even if it isn't legal it'll be a while before a judge says so.'

'No,' Dan Quayle said. 'National Guard.' He stood. 'When I get back to my office we'll announce it and prepare an order. In the meantime all nonessential government buildings should be evacuated, the employees sent home.'

Quayle left the room first, surrounded by Secret Service agents.

Walking the corridors of the Capitol with General Land, Jake Grafton felt profoundly depressed. General Land apparently was in a similar mood. They paused by a body draped with a sheet that the forensic people had yet to get to and stood for a moment. Holes and blood in the wall, pieces of plaster and plaster powder on the floor. The toe of a woman's shoe was just visible under the edge of the white cloth.

She had been somebody, with a family and a job, ambitions and a future. Now she was a hunk of meat to be diced and sliced, mourned and buried.

We're all victims, Jake mused, the living as well as the dead. The America that had given birth to this woman and made her what she was would soon be changed in unforeseeable, incalculable ways by the white-hot fury of the forces that had been unleashed here this morning. The transformations caused by war – make no mistake, this *was* war – would be irrevocable. And Jake knew that the changes so wrought would not be welcomed by most Americans, himself included.

God *damn* these terrorists. He said it to himself as a prayer.

He was walking down the sidewalk carrying the toolbox in one hand and a four-foot length of ducting balanced on his shoulder when he realized that there were men on the rooftops. Henry Charon stopped at the corner and took a quick look upward at the tops of the buildings while he shifted the duct pipe to his other shoulder.

He had driven in from the east and had no trouble finding a place to park. A lot of people hadn't come to work today.

Keeping his gaze on the sidewalk, he proceeded to the entrance of the old office building and climbed the stairs. In the lobby he set the toolbox on the floor and punched the elevator button. The lobby was empty. Now if that office still was . . .

In the elevator he pushed the button for the top floor. The contraption wheezed and moaned, then with a hum rose slowly for several seconds. It lurched to a halt and the door opened.

The woman standing there gasped when she saw him and started.

'Oh, my God!'

Henry Charon smiled.

Horror contorted her features. 'Oh, I'm *sorry*! Oh, my heavens, I am so sorry.' The door started to close, but she popped in, beating it.

'What floor?' he asked.

'Five, please.'

Charon pushed the button as she continued breathlessly, 'I just didn't expect anyone to be in here. I'm so jumpy. All these terrorists and murders! My God! I should have stayed home. I am *so* sorry. What you must think.'

'Forget it.'

She gave him a big, embarrassed smile and got off at the fifth floor. He grinned at her again as the door closed.

The top floor was the seventh, and Charon got off there. The hallway was empty. He walked over to the door labeled STAIR and pushed at it. It opened. Satisfied, he went to the door at the rear of the hallway and laid down the duct pipe and toolbox.

The lock took half a minute. He sat the box and pipe inside, surveyed the empty room, then locked the door behind him.

Through the tree branches he could see the northern half of the Capitol's grand staircase that led up to the main entrance, which led into the Rotunda. The marble steps were covered with people. That was the door those suicide pilots from Colombia went in this morning. But Charon could see only half the stair. The other half was obscured by the Supreme Court building.

The window was dirty. He wiped the inside of the glass with his sleeve. Some of the dirt came off. Out of the corner of his eye he picked up a man on the roof of the Supreme Court building.

This would have to do.

Luckily it was winter and all the trees on the Capitol grounds had lost all their leaves. In summer the vegetation would obscure the scene from here.

The scoped rifle was carefully packed inside the duct pipe and padded with bubble wrap. He removed the weapon and the three long sticks that were also there. These had a piece of rope carefully wrapped around all three sticks, near one end, so when he spread the sticks apart the contraption became a tripod.

He loaded the rifle and laid it on the floor. Then he used a squirt bottle of window cleaner and a rag on the inside of the window glass. He did the entire window as he scanned the Capitol parking lot and every roof he could see.

Four men in sight on the roofs. Hundreds of people over there around the Capitol.

He had one of the radios in the toolbox. With the earpiece in his ear, he turned it on and played with it until he found the audio broadcast frequency of a television station. In fifteen seconds it was plain that the announcer was on the Capitol steps.

Listening carefully, Charon rigged the tripod and braced the rifle upon it. He turned the scope magnification to its highest setting, adjusted the parallax ring, then settled the rifle on the tripod.

He stood well back from the window, near the middle of the room. Swinging the rifle through the narrow field of vision provided by the window sash, he was agreeably surprised at how much he could see. He was looking between tree branches though, and the breeze made them sway. The back-and-forth motion of the limbs made it more difficult to hold the reticle steady on target.

The announcer informed his audience that the Vice-President's party would soon be leaving the building. He didn't say how he knew.

If Charon made this, it would be one *hell* of a shot. Listening to the television audio, moving the crosshairs from person to person, he thought about some of the more memorable shots he had made. None of them had been this iffy, he decided. He wondered if he should really try this one. The images in the scope danced uncontrollably as the instrument's nine-power magnification exaggerated every twitch and tiny jiggle.

He settled the scope on a cop and took a deep breath, then exhaled smoothly and concentrated on holding the crosshairs of the reticle as steady as humanly possible on the center of the man's chest. Still, they moved around in a little circle, it was all he could do to keep the two filaments between the man's armpits. Just when he thought that was good enough, the man moved unexpectedly.

How long after he pulled the trigger would he have to clear the building. Sixty seconds? Less?

And the flight of the bullet would be affected slightly by the window glass. He couldn't open the window – an agent on a roof might see it and send someone to investigate. So he'd shoot through it. Impossible to say how much the glass would deflect the bullet. Maybe just enough to miss over this distance, a little more than a quarter mile. Maybe enough to throw the bullet ten or twelve feet off.

He thought about it as he turned the horizontal filament adjustment knob to compensate for bullet drop.

Okay. It's going to take a lot of luck to make this shot. A *lot* of luck.

What he really needed was a practice shot. Well, when you thought about it, he had had a lot of those. Thousands over the years. This one would have to do the trick.

Aha! The announcer: 'Here is the Vice-President now.'

Henry Charon straightened and worked the bolt, chambering a round. He snicked off the safety. He flexed his shoulders, set his feet, then settled the forearm of the rifle onto the tripod and grasped the junction with his left hand. He snuggled the butt into his shoulder and got the stock firmly in place under his cheekbone.

Now he swung the rifle toward the door of the Capitol. Someone had arranged a battery of microphones. The Vice-President ignored them and walked down the steps amid a phalanx of Secret Service agents carrying submachine guns in their hands. There was a corridor of sorts between the cameras and the people.

Behind Quayle – who was that? An army officer. And a naval officer, three or four civilians.

Charon tried to steady the rifle on the civilians, who were coming toward him down the steps. He couldn't shoot when they were moving: they were just too small at this distance. And until they stopped and stood still he couldn't even be sure who they were.

At the bottom of the stairs, right beside a limo, the Army officer stopped to talk to Dan Quayle. Okay, the civilians were joining the group. They were close together.

Who are they?

Dorfman! One of them is Dorfman. He's on the list. Who is the other? Aha! That's Cohen, the attorney general. Also on the list.

Quickly now. Breathe deeply, exhale slowly, relax and squeeze, slowly and steadily. Steady . . . steady . . .

Damn tree limbs – swaying around . . . Squeeze slowly, gently, allow for the wind, keep the crosshairs cen . . .

The rifle fired.

The report in the closed room was deafening, like two sticks of dynamite. Part of the window glass blew out.

23

Jake Grafton heard an audible thwock and turned, just in time to see Gideon Cohen spin half around and fall to the pavement.

The nearest Secret Service agent roared, 'Everybody down,' and the two agents closest to the Vice-President physically pushed him headfirst into the back seat of the limo. One of them dove in on top of him while the other slammed the door.

'*Get down! Everybody down!*'

Jake crouched, his eyes on Cohen. Was it just his imagination or did he really hear the report of a rifle several seconds after Cohen fell?

Cohen's groans were audible above the screams and shouts of the panicked onlookers, who were scattering or lying facedown on the steps and pavement. An agent was on top of the attorney general, bracing himself with his hands and knees so that none of his weight rested on the injured man.

'My God!' someone roared. 'They tried to kill the Vice-President!'

'Get that fucking car outta here!'

The Secret Service agents pointed their Uzis at the crowd, searching. They were still standing like this five seconds later when the driver of the limo stomped on the gas and made the rear tires squeal as he accelerated away.

Three or four men were examining Cohen. Jake tried to see but couldn't.

Where? Jake rose to his knees and tried to look for the spot where the shot had come from. All he could see was the backs of Secret Service agents. He stood.

'Goddammit, get back down here, Grafton,' General Land growled. 'Never stand up in a firefight. Were you born yesterday?'

As he came out of the stairwell into the lobby Henry Charon bumped into a woman. He reached out and caught her and steadied her on her feet.

'Sorry,' he said, and headed for the door to the sidewalk.

'Did you hear that explosion?' she called.

'Upstairs, it sounded like,' he told her over his shoulder and kept going for the door.

That's odd, she thought, staring after him. He's wearing surgical gloves.

Out on the sidewalk Henry Charon walked north at a brisk pace, but not too brisk. Just a man who knows where he's going and wants to get there. He reached the corner and crossed, then paused and watched an unmarked car with a blue light on the dash and a siren wailing round the corner and screech to a stop in the middle of the block, just fifty feet past the building he had just come out of.

Charon wheeled and walked east. He passed a man jogging in the other direction, toward the Capitol. 'Somebody tried to kill the Vice-President,' the man shouted, pointing at a small transistor radio he carried.

Charon nodded and kept going. Behind him he could hear more sirens.

At two that afternoon Billy Enright, one of McNally's lieutenants, who had been watching television, went into the next room and woke Freeman McNally. Freeman got out of bed and padded in to watch and listen. Someone had taken a shot at the Vice-President, and the feds were calling out the National Guard.

Freeman called T. Jefferson Brody at his office. Normally he never used the phone here for business, since it was probably tapped, but now he was calling his lawyer. 'It's me, Tee. You hear the news?'

'About the Capitol this morning? Holy damn! I heard all right.'

'The National Guard. Quayle's calling out the Guard.'

'Oh, that! Just to stand around at public buildings and stuff.'

The problem with Brody, McNally told himself, was that he had no understanding of how things worked. 'That's just the start,' he told the lawyer patiently. 'You talk to our friends, Tee. This Guard shit ain't good.'

'How heavy do you want me to get?'

'Lay the wood to 'em, man. This Guard shit is really bad. Those soldiers ain't going to spend all their time shining their shoes and strutting around in front of the public library. Once they're there, they're going to try to shut down the business. I can feel it.'

'You want me to go all the way if I have to?'

'All the way.'

McNally hung up and went back to the television. In a little while he went to the kitchen and made himself a cup of coffee.

When Billy Enright came in five minutes later and helped himself to an ice cream bar from the freezer compartment of the refrigerator, Freeman was sipping coffee at the table.

Freeman waited until Billy had unwrapped his ice cream and dropped into a chair at the table. 'Y'know,' he said, 'I think we got us a real window of opportunity here.'

'What do you mean?'

'If the soldiers show up tomorrow or the next day, what are they gonna be doin'?'

'Looking for terrorists and assassins. Gonna be everywhere. We'll have to cool it for a while, maybe take vacations.'

McNally waved that away. 'Think about it. For a week or two all these guys are going to do is search for these Colombians and this dude who tried to off Bush and Quayle. Now is the time to solve some of our little problems so when the Guard *leaves* we can get back in business. That's what I mean. We've got a little time here to fix things up and believe me, anything the cops get just now will go right through the cracks. The Guards ain't cops. They're mechanics and shoe salesmen. The priority is going to be on catching these big Colombian terror dudes. Dig?'

'Yeah,' said Billy Enright, lapping at a gob of ice cream that was threatening to run down the stick onto his fingers. 'I dig where you're coming from.'

Special Agent Freddy Murray was busy trying to coordinate the search for the assassin's trail when he got a call from one of his wiretap experts. 'Just recorded a tape I want you to hear.'

'Who?'

'Freeman McNally. Conversation with his lawyer.'

'We can't use that.'

'I know that. But you'd better listen to it. Pretty curious.'

'Bring it up.'

Murray got back to the task in hand. The FBI lab had identified the brand of tires on the vehicle the assassin had driven in and out of the picnic area on the Potomac that had been the site of the missile launching. Murray was assigning sectors in the Washington area, sending agents to interview every retail outlet for that brand of tire. If they had no success, he would expand the areas. And he expected no success.

This was classic police work, and given enough agents and enough time, would get results. The problem was that Murray had very little of either just now. Still, regardless of how loudly the politicians screamed and the deadlines they invented, the assassin would not be caught until he was caught. Sooner or later the elected ones would figure that out. Until they did, agents like Murray would have to just keep plugging.

He took three minutes to listen to the tape twice. Freeman McNally's voice, all right, Freddy would know that growl anywhere.

'What's that mean?' he asked the wiretap man. ' "All the way"?'

'I dunno. The bit about the friends is plain enough. I want to put a tail on this T. Jefferson Brody to find out who he thinks "our friends" are.'

'We don't have anybody.'

'One or two guys.'

'No! We don't have *anybody* available. Log the tape and file it and let's get back to work.'

'You're the boss.'

The wiretap man was no sooner out of the room than the direct line rang. 'Murray.'

'Harrison Ronald. What's happening?'

'Turn on the TV,' Murray snapped. He had no time for this.

'I don't mean that assassin shit! I mean the grand jury indictment, you twit.'

'It's been put on hold.'

'Remember me? The juicy little black worm that dangled on the end of your hook? For *ten fucking months*?'

'Maybe next week. I'll let you know.'

'You'll call me. *Ha!* I'm supposed to just sit here with my thumb up my ass until you get around to locking these people up?'

'Harrison, I—'

'Just how far down your friggin' list am I, anyway?'

'Harrison, I know where you're coming from. But I don't set the priorities around here. I'll call—'

Freddy stopped when he realized Harrison Ford had hung up on him.

Congresswoman Samantha Strader was in her early fifties and wore her hair stylishly permed. Representing a congressional district carved from the core of her state's capital city, she held one of the safest Democratic seats in the nation and, in effect, was in Congress for life. After twenty years in the Washington vortex, Sam Strader embodied the trendy prejudices of upper-middle-class white women. She was pro-choice, anti-military, fashionably leftist, and ardently feminist. She viciously attacked the professional hypocrisy of her colleagues in Congress because she was absolutely convinced that she herself was pure of heart and free of taint. Political cartoonists found her enchanting.

This woman, who was extraordinarily sensitive to the slightest whiff of male chauvinism, also possessed the chutzpah to tell the press, 'I have a uterus and a brain and I use both.' On detecting a slight, fancied or otherwise, she didn't cast aspersions – she hurled them, lobbed them like grenades, usually when reporters were around to hear the detonations. Her victims, most of whom possessed a brain and a penis but had never seen fit to brag about either, wisely kept their mouths shut and bided their time.

Still, Sam Strader had no trouble envisioning herself, acid tongue, uterus, and all, ensconced in the Oval Office as the first woman President of the United States. She campaigned more or less continuously to try to convince others to see her the same way. Seasoned political observers with a less-biased perspective thought she had no chance of becoming President unless the Republican party, in a suicidal frenzy, nominated Jim Bakker for the job.

One of the reasons Strader's mouth often got her into trouble was that she had little tolerance for people she considered fools, a trait she had in common with William C. Dorfman, whom she also despised. High on her list of fools who goaded her beyond endurance was Vice-President Dan Quayle, whose own particular brand of foot-in-mouth disease was of a different variety than Strader's but was, if anything, more debilitating.

This was the man who had said, 'I stand by all the misstatements.' There had been plenty of those, God knows. Once, when explaining why he would not be glad-handing around Latin America just then, he told reporters with a straight face, 'I don't speak Latin.' Quayle on the strategic significance of Hawaii: 'It is in the Pacific. It is a part of the United States that is an island that is right here.' He had spoken to the Samoans straight from the heart: 'Happy campers you are. Happy campers you have been. And as far as I am concerned, happy campers you will always be.'

Strader's very favorite Quaylism was this gem, from an address to the United Negro College Fund: 'What a waste it is to lose one's mind – or not to have a mind. How true that is.' On hearing this, Strader had sneered at the first reporter she met: 'That's the voice of experience if I ever heard it.'

On a visit to Chile ten months ago Quayle had purchased – in full view of a contingent of reporters – a souvenir doll with a flip-up dick. This light-hearted indulgence in the joys of crude male locker-room humor enraged feminists coast to coast, including Strader.

Dan Quayle was, in Strader's opinion, the living, breathing personification of all that was wrong with America. That the pampered, privileged son of a filthy-rich white man, one who had majored in 'booze and broads' in college and emerged so dismally ignorant that he failed an examination for National Guard enlisted public affairs specialist, could go on to become a congressman, a US senator, then Vice-President, and now, acting President, was enough to test the faith of even the most wildly optimistic.

Sitting here looking at Dan Quayle as William C. Dorfman explained why the presence of the National Guard was required in the District of Columbia, Sam Strader realized with a jolt what the future held. Quayle was stupid, practically retarded, and it was written all over his bland, expressionless face for anyone to see. And the whole world was looking! *She was going to be the next President of the United States.* The premonition gave her goose bumps.

Quayle sat in his chair beside the podium, Strader said later, like a neolithic about to receive an honorary degree from a bible college in

Arkansas. Spread at his feet were two dozen senators and congressmen and reporters from every major television network, wire service, and most of the nation's major newspapers. And Quayle looked bored with the whole proceeding.

As Dorfman explained it, the Guard would augment the federal security police charged with guarding public buildings and maintaining order, thereby freeing FBI and police to search for and apprehend the assassins who had killed the secretary of state, the national security adviser, and the House majority leader, and injured the President and the attorney general. In addition they would apprehend any Colombian narco-terrorists who might still be lurking about.

The press was restless. Too many questions remained unanswered.

The instant Dorfman opened the floor the questions were shouted: Who was behind the violence? How had these Colombian killers gotten into the country? What assurance could the government give the American people and citizens of Washington that the violence was over?

'We are doing our best,' Dorfman said, 'to preserve the public order. Obviously various criminal elements are at work here and we are proceeding vigorously, within the limits of the law, to apprehend those responsible. And to protect—'

Quayle interrupted. He got to his feet and went to the podium. 'Listen,' he said. 'If we knew who these people were and where they were we'd arrest them. Obviously we don't. We're doing everything we can. We will do everything we need to do. I promise.'

'Will you declare martial law?'

Quayle exchanged glances with General Land, who was standing off to one side of the platform. 'I will if I have to,' he said slowly. 'I'll do whatever has to be done to protect the public and preserve the Constitution.'

'What about people's constitutional rights?' Samantha Strader asked in a strident tone that carried over the reporters' voices.

Quayle looked at her. His expression didn't change. 'I'll arrest anybody who needs to be arrested and the courts can sort it all out afterward.'

The politicians looked queasy. The print reporters scribbled furiously while the television people waved their hands and shouted, 'Mr Vice-President, Mr Vice-President,' but the press conference was over. Quayle was leaving. Dorfman, General Land, and their aides all followed. The reporters waited only until Quayle passed out of the room, then they charged for the main doors.

Watching it all from a far corner, Jack Yocke shook his head and made a few notes in his small spiral notebook. Nearby Sam Strader cornered Ott Mergenthaler. 'Do you really think Dapper Danny made this decision, or was it good-buddy Jabba the Hut Dorfman?' she asked.

Ott mumbled something, and Jack Yocke grinned as he annotated his notebook. Ott hated it when people asked him questions – it nudged him off stride. But Strader's questions were pro forma: *she* was the elected one, following destiny's star.

'For five years,' she continued, apparently oblivious to whatever pearl Ott let slip, 'the Colombian druggies have used terrorism and murder against their government and their fellow citizens. They've blown up airliners, banks, slaughtered thousands. Everyone *knew* that someday narco-terrorism would come here.' That statement lifted Yocke's eyebrows a millimeter. 'Now the American people want to know. When it came, why were the macho muchachos in our government caught with their pants down?'

Yocke realized that someone wearing a uniform was standing beside him. He looked around into the face of Jake Grafton, who was apparently listening to Strader.

'Want to answer that one, Captain?' Yocke said, inclining his head an inch at the congresswoman.

'Off the record?'

'Way off.'

Grafton's shoulders rose and fell. 'They weren't unprepared. They just weren't ready, if you understand the difference. It's almost impossible for people who have known only peace to lift themselves to that level of mental readiness necessary to immediately and effectively counter a determined attack. The mind may say get ready, but the subconscious refuses to pump the adrenaline, refuses to let go of the comfortable present. We refuse to believe.'

'Pearl Harbor,' Yocke replied, nodding.

'Precisely.' Grafton looked around toward a crew breaking down the electrical cable network for a battery of television cameras. 'So what do you think?' Grafton added.

'I think Dorfman is finding out who's in charge.'

Jake Grafton nodded. A smile flickered on his lips, then disappeared.

'You were on the Capitol steps this afternoon when Cohen was shot. Why didn't you get down and stay down?'

Jake Grafton shrugged. 'I figured he'd only shoot once.'

'That was a rather large assumption.'

'As I said, the human mind works in strange ways. But what sane person would want to shoot me?'

'There's that,' Yocke acknowledged. 'But he shot at the Vice-President and missed. You could have collected another stray slug.'

'Did he miss?' Grafton asked. 'I got the gut feeling this guy hits what he aims at.'

Captain Grafton turned and left, leaving the reporter scratching his head. He had the feeling that Grafton had wanted to say something else but changed his mind.

*

Senator Bob Cherry was in a hurry when he got back to his office that afternoon. After the press conference he and a dozen of his colleagues had spent an hour grilling William C. Dorfman, and Dorfman had been insufferable, as usual. How George Bush tolerated the man's presence, Cherry told himself, was an enigma that only a shrink could explain.

And then there was Dan Quayle, a man with the intellect and personality to be a mediocre deputy sheriff. In a rural county, of course. Cherry had been convinced for years that Quayle had been chosen for VP instead of Senator Bob Dole because Bush and Dole, who had fought hard for the presidential nomination, personally loathed each other. As if personalities mattered.

As Cherry charged through the outer office, he spotted T. Jefferson Brody sitting at the guest's chair at his aide's desk. Brody rose. 'Evening, Senator.'

'You want to see me?' Cherry asked as he made for the door to his office. Brody noticed the senator gave Miss Georgia a quick smile in passing and got one in return.

'Just a couple of minutes, Senator.'

'Come on in. A couple of minutes is all I've got.'

Brody did as he was bid and closed the door behind him. Cherry stripped off his shirt and tie as he stirred through the phone messages on his desk.

'What's on your mind?'

'The aide said you were over at the White House?'

'Getting briefed. At least that's what they called it. Jesus, what a day!'

'The networks say that Quayle is calling out the National Guard.'

'Yep.' Cherry found a clean shirt in the closet beside the washroom and put it on.

'My clients were hoping that you might oppose that move.'

'Wouldn't do any good. Quayle's made up his mind. Not that I disagree with him. He's right about this, I think.'

Cherry selected a tie from the rack and looked at his image in a mirror as he worked on knotting it. 'Just out of curiosity, what's your people's beef?'

'My clients are the people who have contributed generously to your PAC and campaign fund, Senator.'

Cherry made a face. He had assumed that. His estimate of Brody's political sophistication went down a notch. 'What's their beef?' he repeated.

'Well, Senator, it's like this. They think it'll be bad for their business.'

'Pretty damn shortsighted of them, isn't it? I mean, tourism and business travel to Washington will fall like a chunk of blue ice with all these killers running around loose. The sooner they're behind bars the safer everyone will be.'

'That's just it, Senator. My clients don't feel that way. They think the FBI and Secret Service can find these people. Baldly, troops are bad for business.'

'Sorry. They'll have to live with their disappointment.'

Cherry selected a sports coat and pulled it on. He came back around to his desk and pushed a couple of the phone messages away from the others with a finger. 'I am in a hurry tonight, Jefferson. I have a couple of calls to make before I leave.'

'Senator, I don't think you understand.'

'Understand?'

'I'm not asking you for a favor. I'm telling you.' Brody grinned.

The senator straightened. His shoulders went back. 'Are you leaving or should I call my aide to throw you out?'

Brody sagged back in the chair and threw one leg over the other. 'It's funny, when you think about it. All those contributions, and you never once had anyone check to see who was actually giving you the money.'

'What . . . ?'

'FM Development, that's a real Florida corporation, and the sole stockholder is Freeman McNally, a prominent local businessman. Maybe you've heard of him? ABC Investments, that's . . .'

Cherry collapsed heavily into his chair. He stared at Brody.

'I'm sure the FBI could give you a fairly extensive dossier on Freeman McNally, Senator. You have really screwed the pooch this time.'

'What do you want?'

'I've told you. No National Guard. No troops.'

'No.' Cherry's face flushed scarlet.

Brody got out of his chair and sat on the edge of the desk. He leaned toward Bob Cherry. 'You just haven't thought this through yet. Senator. When it gets out that you've been flying around the country wining and dining and sixty-nining Miss Georgia and paying your campaign bills with *drug* money supplied by Washington's biggest crack dealer, your career will immediately hit the wall. Splat! You'll be *finished.*'

'I'll give the money back. *I didn't know!* I'll—'

'Get real! You politicians sold out to the country-club types who ran out and bought savings and loans. You let them shoot craps with government-insured money – five hundred *billion* dollars down the sewer. You've maneuvered like drunken snakes to get yourselves big pay raises. You've voted yourselves the best pensions in the nation while you've looted the Social Security trust fund. *You've damn near bankrupted America.* The *voters* have to *pay* for all that! Their *children* will have to pay for it! Their *grandchildren* will have to pay! *They* aren't going to believe that Bob Cherry was so senile, so abysmally stupid that he didn't check to see who was stuffing the money into his pocket!'

Brody stood. He buttoned his jacket and adjusted his tie. 'All you glad-handing backslappers do little favors for each other – a military base in this district, a sewer system there, a dam over here. Isn't that the way your exclusive little club works?'

Brody's voice dropped. 'You get busy and call in some markers. Raise some hell. I'd better be reading in the newspaper about your courageous stand to keep democracy *in* the District and the soldiers *out*, or come Friday you'll be reading about some very interesting contributions made by big-name dope dealers to a certain senator.'

Brody paused on the way to the door and turned around. 'One more word of advice, Senator. People who cross Freeman McNally rarely live to brag about it.'

T. Jefferson Brody's next stop was Senator Hiram Duquesne's office. He caught the senator on the way out of the door.

'If you don't mind, I'll walk along down to the garage,' Brody said.

He broached the subject of the National Guard troops.

'You know,' Duquesne said, 'if someone had suggested calling in the Guard this morning after the attack on the Capitol, I would have been against it. But after that shot at the Vice-President I'm for it.

'Gid Cohen's in bad shape. The doctor thinks he'll make it. Took that slug in the shoulder. Just missed his left lung by an inch.' Duquesne shook his head. 'The rifleman fired from a building five hundred and twenty-seven yards away. Left the rifle and a tripod and a toolbox. Just aimed, fired right through a closed window, dropped everything and walked away.'

'Amazing,' Brody agreed.

'I don't know what we're up against here, but this shit has got to stop. Quayle's doing the right thing. Didn't think that airhead had it in him.'

'My clients want you to oppose this move. They don't want the Guard in the District.'

'Sorry, Jefferson. This has gone too far for politics as usual. Quayle has the legal and moral responsibility and he is taking steps. The senate will back him up every way it can.'

Brody kept silent as they walked past the attendant at the entrance to the garage. He waited until they had reached Duquesne's car and the senator was fishing in his pocket for the key.

'My client is Freeman McNally. Perhaps you've heard of him?'

Senator Duquesne gaped.

'Freeman McNally. His reputation is a little unsavory, but he's a businessman. Pays his legal fees without a quibble. Contributes money to worthy causes. Gives freely to certain politicians. Like you, for instance. He's given you over twenty-five thousand dollars. Remember FM Development Corporation?'

'Why, you greasy, filthy son of a bitch!'

'Now, now. Senator, let's not get personal here. You were free to check to see where the money was coming from, and presumably you didn't bother. You were free to refuse the money. You never did.'

'What do you want from me?'

'I told you. My client doesn't want the Guard in the District. He's contributed generously to keep you in the Senate and he thought you should pull out all the stops and help him out on this.'

'And if I don't? Come on! Your kind of slime always has a stick handy if the carrot doesn't work.'

'My client wants to see you right out front, Senator, waving the banner to keep the military out of the District. If the parade leaves without you . . .' Brody shrugged. 'You're going to have a difficult time explaining away twenty-five thousand dollars in contributions from Washington's biggest crack dealer, Senator. Really tough.'

'Get out of my sight, you bastard.' Duquesne balled his right fist and took a step forward.

'Think it over, Senator.' Brody took a step backward. 'If I were you I wouldn't throw away my reputation and a Senate seat over this. I'd bend a little and go on down the road.'

Brody turned and walked quickly away.

'I'll see you roast in hell, Brody,' the senator called after him.

Brody kept walking.

Captain Jake Grafton and his staff spent the evening at the Pentagon. They had much to do. The National Guard had already begun mobilizing at the armory adjacent to RFK Stadium, but the usual chain of command was about to be radically altered. Grafton and his colleagues drafted an order for the signature of Vice-President Quayle that placed the Washington Guard unit under the immediate operational command of the chairman of the Joint Chiefs, thereby removing ten or so layers of generals and their staffs from the chain of command. This change had been requested by the White House. The order would be signed first thing in the morning.

After the order had been sent to the chairman's office for review, and probably for redrafting, Grafton and FBI special agent Thomas Hooper got themselves a cup of coffee and spread a street map of metro Washington over Grafton's desk.

Toad Tarkington, never one to be left out, pulled a chair around so he could see.

'I really don't have time for this,' Hooper muttered. Jake knew that well enough. Hooper looked exhausted. His shirt was dirty and he had spots on his sports coat. He needed a shave. He probably hadn't been home in several days. But his superiors had sent him over here anyway.

Jake got a yellow marker from his desk drawer and began putting yellow splotches on the map. He marked public buildings, the White House, the Executive Office Building, the Capitol, the Supreme Court, the FBI building, the Justice Department, the office buildings that were used by members of Congress.

Then he handed the marker to Hooper. 'Your turn.'

Hooper marked the courts, the jail, buildings used by various other government agencies. When he finished, he tossed the marker on the map.

'Twenty-six buildings,' Tarkington said, ever helpful.

'Around the clock, at least three armed men at every entrance.'

Jake pulled a scratch pad over and began figuring. 'Anybody want to guess the average number of entrances for each building?'

'Six or eight,' the Air Force colonel said from his seat on the adjacent desk.

They discussed it. They used seven.

'We don't have enough men. Nowhere near.'

'Get more,' Hooper said. 'Men are the one asset you guys got lots of.'

'Until we get more – and that will take some time – we'll have to put maybe one man at each entrance and keep mobile squads nearby to back them up.'

Hooper shrugged.

'You realize,' Grafton said, 'that all we're doing here is setting up a shootout if the Colombians or anybody else wants to start something. These troops will be issued ammunition and they'll shoot. They'll have to. There aren't enough of them to do anything else, and they aren't trained to do anything else. Some of them will be killed. Bystanders will be shot. It's gonna be real messy.'

'Better not be,' Hooper said. 'That's what you people are supposed to prevent.'

'Let's trim the list. Protect only key buildings.'

'No. I've got my orders. Protecting only key buildings merely sends the terrorists to unguarded buildings.'

'Not if what they're after is a confrontation.'

Hooper shook his head. 'The object of terrorism is to show the impotence of the government. Give them an opening and they'll take it.'

Toad Tarkington spoke up. 'What about a trap? Apparently unprotected buildings with a couple of squads of soldiers inside?'

'The buildings would have to be empty,' Hooper pointed out. 'But without a stream of civilians coming and going, any observer will immediately see that something is wrong.'

'You're telling us that this is a no-win situation,' Jake Grafton said.

Hooper raised his hands in acknowledgement.

'How did we get to this?' the colonel asked rhetorically. 'Again?'

'You can't *win* fighting terrorists,' Hooper said, trying to explain. 'The politicians – this is just my personal opinion – will *never* allow you to move fast enough to get the jump on these people. Politicians are reactive, always looking for consensus.'

'Bullshit,' said Jake Grafton. 'Politicians aren't stupid. *This is not a conventional war.* Every shot fired is a political statement. The politicos intuitively understand that and the guys in uniform had better learn it damn fast. Until we do, we're not even in the same ballgame.'

Hooper looked skeptical. He rubbed his face and drained the last of his coffee.

Jake Grafton picked up the phone and called the chairman's office. Anybody who thought Hayden Land was going to let the terrorists pick and choose their targets, he told himself, didn't know Hayden Land.

The final fillip of the evening for loyal slaves of the big eye made the eleven o'clock news coast to coast. The networks had spectacular footage.

At approximately ten P.M. Eastern Standard Time four cars drew up to a three-story row house in northeast Washington – two cars on the street in front, two in the alley. The men in the passenger seats of the cars used Uzi submachine guns on the men guarding the house, then sat in the cars and fired a total of twenty-four 40-mm grenades through the windows, totally destroying the interior of the structure and setting the place afire. Then the cars drove away.

None of the witnesses could, they said, describe any of the cars or the men in them. No one could remember a single license number.

Police theorized on camera that the killers had used M-79 grenade launchers. They said the house belonged to a suspected crack dealer, one Willie Teal.

The fire in the background behind the policemen and reporters played on screens nationwide. It was quickly out of control and burned out half the houses on the row.

The following morning when the fire was completely out, officials found fourteen bodies in the house where the fire had started, the one that had been assaulted with grenades. This total did not include the four men shot to death outside. Police also found the twisted remains of over a dozen pistols, three submachine guns, and five pump shotguns. A brief-case containing almost five hundred thousand dollars was in the rubble with most of the bills still intact. Five pounds of cocaine somehow escaped the fire and was discovered in a hiding place in the basement by a fireman searching for smoldering timbers.

Harrison Ronald Ford watched the conflagration on television as he lay in his bed in his room at the FBI dormitory at Quantico. He sipped a soda pop and rubbed his Colt automatic occasionally and listened to the commentators try to sum up the violence and horror of the day.

One earnest female was expounding eloquently when he rose from the bed and snapped the idiot box off.

So Freeman McNally had decided to permanently settle Willie Teal's hash. Another little lesson for those who thought they could cross Freeman McNally and get away with it.

M-79 grenade launchers, 40-mm grenades through the window. Like this window.

He pulled back the edge of the Venetian blind an inch or so and peeked out at the parking lot and the grass beyond.

What do you do when a grenade comes through the window into your bedroom at night? Do you huddle under the blanket? Pick it up and toss it back?

Hell no! You die, man! Bloody and perforated from hundreds of shards of steel, you die. Just like Willie Teal.

He was breathing hard. His heart was pounding and he was breathing too fast.

He turned off the light. In the darkness he got dressed, layering on sweaters and sweatshirts.

In the bathroom he tried to vomit and couldn't. His stomach felt like he had swallowed a stone. He closed the doors, stuffed a towel under it so light wouldn't leak, and turned on the light.

The .45 automatic was loaded and had a round in the chamber. The hammer was back and the thumb safety on. Cocked and locked, the DI had called this condition, way back when.

He put the muzzle in his mouth and tasted it.

Go ahead. Save Freeman the trouble. You know that he didn't decide to annihilate Willie Teal and not lift a finger to solve his biggest problem – you.

He saw himself in the mirror. So pathetic.

He put the gun in his waistband and sat on the commode and sobbed.

24

About two in the morning Harrison Ronald heard the fire door on the first floor of the stairwell being opened. It made a metallic noise that was clearly audible here on the third-story landing of the Quantico FBI dorm, where he sat in the darkness with the slab-sided Colt in his hand. Nobody had ever oiled the push-bars on the heavy doors, thank the Lord.

Harrison Ronald eased his head between the rails and stared downward into the darkness, trying to see. There was nothing. Not a glimmer of light. There should have been light, of course, but Harrison Ronald had unscrewed all the bulbs over two hours ago.

Somebody was down there.

He closed his eyes and concentrated on what he could hear. He even held his breath. Yes, a scraping sound. A shoe sole on the nonskid of the concrete steps.

Harrison Ronald pulled his head back and sat absolutely still, the automatic held firmly in both hands.

This is really it, he told himself. Anybody with a legit reason to use this stairwell would not try to be quiet.

This is really it!

He sat frozen. Any movement he made the other man was bound to hear. His feet were out of position and his butt was cold, ice-cold, on the hard concrete step. He sat listening, breathing shallowly.

A light! The man below was using a small pencil flash, looking things over. Now it was gone.

Somewhere outside a car horn honked. It sounded far, far away.

The man was at the second-floor fire door. The intruder would have to push down the thumb latch on top of the grip, then pull the door open. The thumb latch would require some serious pressure since it mechanically moved the push-bar on the other side.

The latch clicked and the sound echoed in the stairwell.

The man below stood for the longest time, also listening.

Harrison Ronald didn't even breathe.

Then the door opened and the intruder went through. He let the door swing shut but stopped it before the latch clicked.

Was that right? That's what it sounded like to Harrison Ronald. He eased himself upright, massaged his cold, stiff bottom, and still trying to make no noise, crept across the landing and down the stair to the second-floor door.

He felt the steel door, slid his fingers across to the jam. Yes, it was ajar.

He eased his eye to the window in the door and looked down the hallway. The man was outside his door. A thick figure, medium height, carrying a long weapon.

Harrison Ronald moved away from the window and stood in the darkness, trying to think.

The man might not come back this way although he had left the door ajar. Even if he did, he might be expecting Ford to be waiting here. If the man goes into the room. Ford asked himself, should I go down the hallway toward the room? Back up to the third-floor landing? Or down to the first floor?

He took another look.

The man was bent over, working on the lock.

What if there is more than one man?

That thought froze Harrison Ronald. No, not a sound here in the stairwell. Maybe another man coming from the lobby, using the elevator or the stairway beside it. If so, where was he?

He took another peek through the window. The stout man was going through the door. No one else in the hall.

The man would come out of there in seconds.

What to do?

Amazingly enough, the simple expedient of avoiding the man never occurred to Harrison Ronald Ford. He had lived with fear too long. He sought now to surprise his enemy, confront him in a way that maximized the slim advantage that surprise bestowed on the aggressor. For Harrison Ronald intended to be the aggressor. Growing up black in the blue-collar neighborhood of Evansville and as a young rifleman in the Marine Corps, he had learned the lesson well: attack – fiercely, ruthlessly, with iron-willed determination – always attack.

The door to Ford's room opened silently. A head peeped out and surveyed the dimly lit hallway. Now the stout figure emerged, moving lightly for a man so large, and came along the corridor toward the fire door standing ajar.

He opened the fire door and slipped through.

Crouching on the second step, Ford swung the edge of his hand with all his strength at the man's legs. The man pitched forward headlong. He made a sickening splat on the landing.

Ford was on him in seconds. His hands around the prone figure's throat, squeezing with all his strength. After a few seconds he stopped.

The man under him was absolutely limp. Sitting on his back, Harrison Ronald felt the carotid artery. Nothing.

He rolled the body over and felt gently in the darkness. The forehead was smashed in, pulpy. No blood, or at least no slick, smooth wet slimy substance.

Still breathing hard, still pumped with adrenaline, Ford grasped the dead man's arms and pulled the corpse up the steps. The weapon clattered away.

The body was heavy, at least two hundred pounds. Ford heaved and tugged with all his strength. He paused twice, but with one last mighty heave he managed to get the corpse to the second-floor landing.

He checked the hallway through the window in the door. Empty.

Wedging the door open, he tugged the body through and pulled it down the hallway, which, mercifully, was polished linoleum. He opened the door to his room and dragged the body inside, then raced back for the weapon on the stairs.

In his room, with the faint light from the parking lot coming through the window, he examined the man carefully. Even with his forehead smashed in, he was recognizable. Fat Tony Anselmo. There was a weapon in his coat pocket, a 9-mm automatic with a silencer as big as a sausage. The long weapon was a shotgun, a Remington pump with the barrel amputated just in front of the forearm. It was loaded.

Ford laid the shotgun on the bed and went through the man's pockets. A wallet containing cash, no credit cards. A lot of cash, mainly twenties. Ford put the wallet back in Anselmo's pocket. He quickly went through the other pockets. Cigarettes, lighter, a motel room key, some change, a small pocket knife, two wadded-up handkerchiefs. No car keys.

How had Anselmo gotten here?

Someone was outside waiting.

Ford checked the 9-mm. Loaded, with the safety on.

How long had Anselmo been in here? Five minutes? Four?

He stuffed the automatic in his belt. He was already wearing a jacket over a sweatshirt and sweater. The stairwell was unheated.

He opened the door slowly, checked the hallway, then slipped out. He headed for the stairs that led down to the lobby.

There was a man at the lobby desk, seated on a stool with his head down. Harrison Ford waited behind the fire door, watching him through the small window. The man was reading something on the desk in front of him. He turned a page. A newspaper.

A minute passed. Then another.

Come on! Don't just sit there all night, you knothead!

The desk man picked up his coffee cup and put it to his lips. He frowned, looked into the cup.

He rose from his stool and walked to his right. Ford's left.

The pot was in that little office across the hall. Quickly now!

Ford eased open the door, checked that the desk man was not in sight, then popped through and pushed the door shut behind him. He strode across the carpeted lobby and went through the outside door, closing it behind him.

He dropped behind the first bush he came to and looked around. Beyond this little driveway was the parking lot with the mercury-vapor lights shining down upon it.

Using the trees and shrubs for cover, he circled it as fast as he could trot, pausing and crouching several times behind large bushes for a careful scan.

He reached the vantage point he wanted, with all the cars between him and the entrance to the stairwell that Tony Anselmo had used. Crouching, staying low, he moved carefully parallel to the last row of cars with the 9-mm automatic in his hand.

Up there, on the second row. Wasn't that a head in that dark green car? Hard to tell. Perhaps a seat-back headrest. He moved slowly alongside a car, keeping it between him and the green sedan.

It took fifteen seconds to get to a place where he could look again.

Yes. A man.

He moved slowly now, going behind a line of cars working closer.

He also checked the other cars. There might be someone else out here.

The door to the green sedan opened. Ford realized it when the interior courtesy light came on.

Then it went off. The man was standing beside the car.

On his hands and knees, Ford crept across the back of the last car in this row, the third one, and looked forward. The green sedan was in the second row, and the man was standing beside the driver's door, about forty feet from where Ford was hunkered. He was doing something. A weapon. He was stuffing shells into a shotgun.

Ford heard the distinctive metallic snick as the man worked the action, chambering a round. He turned his back to Ford and started toward the stairwell door.

Harrison Ronald Ford rose into a crouch, braced his hand against the side of the car, and steadied the automatic. The damn thing had no sights.

He quickly aligned the silencer and squeezed off a round.

The man staggered, tried to turn. Ford squeezed again. Another pop. And another.

The man went down. The shotgun clattered as he hit the asphalt.

Ford ran to his right, all hunched over, down about five cars, then charged across the driving lane into the second row. Alongside a car he threw himself on his face and looked under the parked vehicles. He could see a dark shape on the asphalt, obviously not a tire.

Harrison Ronald Ford leveled the automatic with both hands, trying in the gloom to sight along the rounded top of the silencer.

Shit! This is crazy! He could not see well enough to really aim, even if he had had sights.

He lay there breathing rapidly, staring across the top of the weapon at the dark shape five cars over. The seconds ticked by.

He was going to have to do something.

If he went back to the spot that he had fired from, the man would have a clean shot between the cars at him. If he went along the first row, the same thing would eventually occur.

If the guy were still alive and conscious, that is.

Harrison Ronald wiped the sweat from his face with a sleeve.

Fuck!

He was sure as hell going to have to do something.

He got to his feet and rounded the front of the car he had been lying beside. The green sedan was plainly visible. Moving carefully, silently – he was wearing rubber-soled running shoes – he went toward it with the pistol grasped tightly with both hands, the safety off.

Kneeling on the asphalt, Ford tried again to see the fallen man between the tires. He saw a piece of him the second time, apparently still in the same place and position.

He rounded the front of the green car with the pistol ready and fired the instant it covered the man sprawled there on his side beside the front tire.

He needn't have bothered. Vinnie Pioche was already dead.

When Jake Grafton left the Pentagon, Callie was waiting out front in the car. The buses and subways didn't run at these hours of the night. Jake climbed in and sighed. 'I called home. Amy said you were here. How long have you been waiting?'

'Two hours.'

'I'm sorry.'

'Oh, Jake,' Callie said as they hugged each other. 'I was so worried about you today. Amy called me at school. She was distraught, almost hysterical. They've run film clips on TV, over and over, all evening. The attorney general getting shot, the Secret Service agents ready to blast the first person who twitched, and you're standing up and looking around like a damned fool.'

'Story of my life,' he muttered.

'Hug me again, Jacob Lee.'

'With pleasure,' he said and gave her another squeeze and a kiss. She drew away finally and looked at him with her arms around his neck. 'Your mother called.'

He nodded. There was nothing to say.

'Oh, Jake!'

Finally she released him and put the car in motion.

The radio was on. Something about a huge fire in northeast Washington.

'What's that all about?' he asked.

'Haven't you heard? Somebody attacked a row house. Set half the block on fire.'

'When?'

'About ten tonight. Have you been working on this National Guard thing all evening?'

Jake nodded and turned up the radio volume.

'What's happening, Jake? Assassinations, battles . . . it's almost like a war.'

'It *is* a war.' After listening a minute, he snapped the radio off. 'This is just the first battle. The have-nots versus the haves.'

'Have you eaten?'

'No, but I'm going to drop you at the apartment building. I need the car for a while. There's somebody I need to go see.'

'Oh, Jake! Not tonight! You need some sleep. Why, the sun will be up in a few hours.'

Jake Grafton grunted and sat watching the empty streets.

'Let me come with you.'

'You go home and stay with Amy. I'll be home in an hour or so.'

'They had Mrs Cohen on television tonight, coming out of the hospital after seeing her husband. And Mrs Bush. And Mrs Quayle. This whole mess, it's so *evil*!'

'Ummm,' Jake said, still watching the occasional passing car, wondering vaguely who was driving and where they were going at this hour of the night. The problem, he knew, was that the Colombian narco-terrorists knew exactly what they were fighting for and they wanted it very badly. They wanted a place in the sun.

'What I can't figure out is why Dan Quayle called out the National Guard instead of bringing in Army troops.'

'Who knows?' her husband replied. 'Maybe he got tired of all the flak he caught in '88 about joining the Guard to avoid service in Vietnam. Maybe he's going to show everybody what a fine fighting outfit the Guard is.'

'Doesn't that bother you, his avoiding Vietnam?'

Jake Grafton snorted. 'I seem to recall that back then most of the guys my age were trying to avoid going to Vietnam. In some quarters the quest took on religious status.'

'You went,' she said.

'Hell, Callie, half the country is still discriminating against Vietnam veterans. The US government says Agent Orange never hurt anybody.'

'You went,' she repeated.

Jake Grafton thought about that for a moment. Finally he said, 'I was always a slow child.'

His wife reached out and squeezed his hand. He squeezed hers in return.

Harrison Ronald Ford didn't hesitate. He wrestled the dead weight that had been Vinnie Pioche into the backseat of the green sedan. He tossed the shotgun into the front seat, then got behind the wheel. The keys were still in the ignition.

He started the car. Three quarters of a tank of gas.

How had two New York hoods gotten by the Marine sentries at the gate?

Leaving the car idling, he got out and walked around to look at the front bumper. Residing there was a nice blue Department of Defense officer's sticker. Clean and new.

Harrison got back behind the wheel. He closed the door and sat looking at the door that Fat Tony had gone through on his way upstairs to kill him as he waited for his heart to slow down and his breathing to get back to normal. His hands were still shaking from the adrenal aftershock.

These two worked for the Costello-Shapiro family in New York, the Big Bad Apple. Well, tonight they had been attending to a little chore for Freeman McNally.

Harrison had no proof of course, but he didn't need any. He *knew* Freeman McNally. Freeman had succeeded at an extremely risky enter-prise by killing anyone in whom he had the slightest doubt. Why Anselmo and Pioche had agreed to do this little job for Freeman was an interesting question, but one that would probably never be answered. A favor for a new business associate? Good ol' Freeman. A friend indeed.

Ford got out of the car again and closed the door. He looked for the spent shell of the last round he had fired into friend Vinnie. It had been flipped fifteen feet to the right of where he stood. He pocketed it and went back through the lot to find the others. The search took three minutes, but he found them.

Back behind the wheel of the car, he picked up the automatic and popped the clip from the handle. Still held six rounds. He slipped the clip back in place and put the safety on.

Other men would come after him, of course. If Freeman could reach him here in the FBI barracks in Quantico he could reach him anywhere – in a police car in Evansville, a barracks in Okinawa, a hut on a beach in Tasmania – *anywhere.*

It took Harrison Ronald about ten seconds to decide. Not really. It took him ten seconds before he was ready to announce the decision to himself.

It's the only choice I've got, he told himself.

He had actually made the decision before he stuffed Vinnie in the backseat and picked up the shells, but now it was official.

Harrison Ronald put the car in gear and fed gas. He coasted through the parking lot, avoiding the little driveway that went up by the office, and headed for the main gate and the interstate to Washington.

It was funny, when you thought about it. He had been scared silly for ten months, day and night and in between, and now he wasn't. He should have been, but he wasn't. As he drove along he even whistled.

Jake Grafton parked the car three blocks from what was left of Willie Teal's place and walked. Fire trucks and hoses were everywhere. Cops accosted him.

He showed them his military ID. Since he was still in uniform, he was allowed to pass.

Standing across the street from Willie Teal's, Jake Grafton marveled. The entire row from here to the corner was a smoking ruin. Six firemen played water on the wreckage by the light of three big portable flood-lights. Behind a yellow police-line tape, several hundred black people stood watching, occasionally pointing.

Jake turned to the nearest policeman and said to him, 'I'm looking for a reporter named Jack Yocke. Seen him around?'

'Young? Late twenties? Yeah. Saw him a while ago. Look over there, why don'cha?'

Yocke was interviewing a woman. He scribbled furiously in his note-book and occasionally tossed in a question. At one point he looked up and saw Grafton. He thanked the woman, spoke to her in a low, inaudible tone, then walked toward the naval officer.

'Somebody said the firemen had used enough water to float a battle-ship, but we certainly didn't expect to see the Navy show up to take advantage of that fact.'

'Who did this?'

Yocke's eyebrows went up. 'The police are right over there. They're working their side of the street and I'm working mine. My version will be in tomorrow's paper.'

'Gimme a straight answer.'

Yocke grinned. 'Prevailing opinion is that Freeman McNally just put a competitor out of business. Off the record, with a guarantee of anonym-ity, witnesses tell me four cars, eight men. They used grenade launchers. Just sat in the cars cool as ice cubes in January and fired grenades through the windows. The firemen and police are still carting bodies out of Teal's place. Ain't pretty.'

'You about finished here?'

Yocke shrugged.

'I want to have a little talk. Off the record, of course.'

'Is there any other way?'

Yocke led the way toward his car. Walking toward it he asked, 'You hungry?'

'Yeah.'

They went to an all-night restaurant, a Denny's, and got a seat well back from the door. The place was almost empty. After they had ordered, Jake said, 'Tell me about this town. Tell me about Washington.'

'You didn't come out here in the middle of the night to get a civics lecture.'

'I want to know how Washington works.'

'If you find out, you'll be the only one who knows.'

'Okay, Jack Yocke, *The Washington Post*'s star cynic, let's hear it.'

'You're serious, aren't you?'

'Yep.'

Yocke took a deep breath and exhaled slowly, then settled himself comfortably behind his podium. 'Metropolitan Washington is basically three cities. The first, and largest, is composed of federal government employees who live in the suburbs and commute. This is the richest, most stable community in the country. They are well paid, well educated, and never face layoffs or mergers or takeovers or competition or shrinking profit margins. It's a socialist Utopia. These people and the suburbanites who provide goods and services to them are Democrats: big government pays their wages and they believe in it with all the fervor of Jesus clinging to the cross.

'The second group, the smallest, is made up of the movers and shakers, the elected and appointed officials who make policy. This is official Washington, the Georgetown cocktail-party power elite. These people are the actors on the national stage: their audience is out there beyond the beltway. They're in the city but never a part of it.

'The last group are the inner-city residents, who are seventy percent black. This group only works in federal office buildings at night, when they clean them. The city of Washington is the biggest employer; forty-six thousand jobs for a population of about 586,000 people in the district.'

Jake whistled. 'Isn't that high?'

'One in every thirteen people works for the city. Highest average in the nation. But major industry dried up in Washington years ago, leaving only service jobs – waiters, maids, bus drivers, and so on. So the politicians create jobs, just like in Russia. The inner-city residents, like the suburbanites and the residents of every major inner city in the country, are also Democrats. They cling to big government like calves to the tit.'

'So what the hell is wrong?' Jake Grafton asked.

'Depends on who you ask. The black militants and the political preachers – that's *all* the preachers, by the way – claim it's racism. The liberals – you have to be rich and white to have enough guilt to fit into this category – claim it's all the fault of a parsimonious government, a government that doesn't do enough. I've never met a liberal yet who thought we had enough government. This even though the district has one of the highest tax rates in the country and the federal government kicks in a thousand bucks a head for every man, woman, and child every year.'

Jack Yocke shrugged grandly. 'To continue my tale, the schools in the suburbs are as good as any in the country. The schools in the inner city are right down there with the worst – fifty percent dropout rate, crime, drugs, abysmal test scores, poisonous race relations – by every measure abominable. The average inner-city resident is ignorant as a post, poor as a church mouse, paranoid about racial matters, and lives in a decaying slum. He collects a government check and complains about potholes that are never filled and garbage that is never hauled away while the local politicians orate and posture and play racial politics for all they're worth and steal everything that isn't nailed down. He'll vote for Marion Barry for mayor even though he knows the man is probably a drug addict and a perjurer because Barry uses the white establishment as a scapegoat for all his troubles.

'Speaking frankly, the District of Columbia is a Third World shithole. The local leaders are quacks, demagogues, and outright thieves. Public schools and hospitals are appallingly bad, tens of millions of dollars of public funds have been stolen or squandered, charges of racism are endemic. The *Washington Monthly* magazine said the District has "the worst government in America" which is probably true. A US senator called it the most corrupt *and* most incompetent urban government in America. With me so far?'

Their food came. The waitress asked if they needed anything else and they both shook their heads. When she was gone, Yocke continued:

'Except for tourism and government, the District has no other economic base, nothing to create middle-class jobs. Its people don't believe in self-help or education. They blame all their woes on the US government. If this place were in Central America or Africa, Barry would have proclaimed himself "maximum leader" or "president for life." Since they have the misfortune to be surrounded by the United States, however, they want this sixty-four-square-mile banana republic to become the fifty-first state.'

'Why?'

'Why not?'

With his mouth full of a bite of BLT, Jake said, 'Being a state won't help.'

'Of course not. But Marion Barry can be governor and Jesse Jackson can be a senator. The Democrats will get a bigger majority in the House and Senate and three automatic electoral votes. What more do you want, for Christ's sake?'

'You really are a cynic, aren't you?'

'Oh, come off it, you overpaid nincompoop in a sailor suit. I've been a reporter in this town for three years. I go out every night and look at the bodies. I spend evenings at the emergency room of DC General with the abused kids, the wives beat half to death, the overdoses, the gunshot victims who won't tell who shot them, the rape victims. I stand in the courthouse halls and watch the attorneys plea-bargain, selling their clients' constitutional rights for a reduced sentence or probation. I go to the jails and look at the same old faces again and again and again. I talk to the victims of muggings, robbery, burglary, auto theft. Human carnage is the name of my game, mister. Who the hell do you think you are?'

'Three years,' Jake Grafton sighed. 'It's too long, yet it's not long enough.'

The reporter suddenly looked tired. No doubt his day had been as long as Jake's. He said, 'You'd probably feel better if I had said ten years. Let's change it. Ten years' experience it is.'

'You're floating down a sewer in a glass-bottom boat, Yocke. Sooner or later you have to get in and swim.'

'You think *I'm* to blame for some of this?'

'I read the paper. I haven't seen any of this with your byline.'

'You ought to read the paper more carefully,' Yocke said. He rubbed the stubble on his jaw. 'There's a whole bunch of very talented people who think their mission in life is to write all of it – the good, the bad, and every subtle nuance in between. They put all of it in the paper. The hell of it is nobody pays any attention. It's like tossing pebbles into the Atlantic Ocean. Doesn't even disturb the fish.'

Jake took a sip of coffee, then helped himself to another bite of BLT. After he'd chewed and swallowed, he said, 'You've heard about the National Guard deal. How will that go, in this city you describe?'

Yocke took his time. He drank some coffee and slathered the remainder of his sandwich with more mustard. 'I don't know. If the troops are just going to stand around public buildings looking spiffy and the shooters stay home, everything will go swimmingly. Absent a charge of child molestation, Quayle will be our next president.'

'Why'd you say if?'

'You'd be home in bed, Captain, if that was all there was to it. Neither of us rode in yesterday on a hay wagon.'

Grafton caught the waitress' eye and held his cup aloft. She brought the pot and gave him a refill.

After swallowing his last bite of sandwich, Yocke continued: 'A lot of people in this town are fed up to here with these dopers and politicians. They've been demanding action and getting politics as usual. Something is going to give.'

'What're you saying? There's going to be a revolution?'

'Packed emergency rooms, innocent people slaughtered, children starving and neglected and abused, jails packed full as sardine cans, cops fighting for their lives. Now I'll tell you, a *lot* of little people are sick and tired of going to funerals. They've *had* it. And you know what? I don't think the political cretins have a clue. They're dancing between the raindrops blaming the big bad Colombians and the white establishment and the National Rifle Association.'

Jack Yocke threw up his hands. 'Ah well, even Fidel Castro got the message finally, just before they shot him.'

Jake nodded. 'Yeah.'

A few minutes later, Yocke asked, 'Why'd you stand up today when they shot at Quayle?'

'Stupid, I guess.'

'Captain, whatever you are, stupid isn't on the list.'

'Wondered where the shot came from. Took a look.'

Yocke's eyebrows went up and down once. 'Well, thanks for the sandwich.' He shoved the check across toward Grafton.

'Any time.'

Approaching Freeman's house, for the first time in a long time Harrison Ronald did not feel the dread. He didn't drive by, of course. After the fracas earlier this evening over at Teal's Freeman would have a squad of men in front and another squad of men in back, some of whom would inevitably recognize Sammy Z.

Harrison parked two blocks away and walked.

The streets were silent and empty. Amazingly quiet. A gentle breeze made the tree limb shadows cast by streetlights stir and shake.

He was behind a car, crouching, when he got his first look at the end of the alley. A streetlight was on the pole. But there was no one in sight. No guard.

Odd.

Using the cars for cover he worked his way to the alley and looked down it. He couldn't see anyone.

He went down the alley with the automatic in his hand, flitting from shadow to shadow, pausing occasionally to look and listen. Nothing.

Even Freeman's backyard was empty.

Nobody home. Okay, where would he be? Three or four possibilities suggested themselves, and as he mulled them Harrison Ronald tried the back door. Locked. He pounded loudly on the door with the butt of the pistol and stood to one side.

Thirty seconds passed, then a minute. He put the muzzle of the silenced pistol against the lock and pulled the trigger.

Inside the lights were off. He proceeded slowly, warily. The house was empty.

In the weapons room he wiped the prints from the automatic, even popped the magazine out and wiped that off on a handy cleaning rag, and tossed it into the box with the others. He selected another automatic with a silencer already attached, loaded it, and helped himself to a couple more loaded magazines. He was about to leave when a silenced Uzi caught his eye. Why not? He took it and four magazines of 9-mm ammo.

Leaving the Uzi inside the back door, he pulled the door shut behind him. He trotted down the alley and the two blocks to the car, then drove it back.

He maneuvered it into the parking area and dragged Vinnie from the car. God, the body was heavy! The corpse hadn't been this heavy when he loaded it into the car. Or perhaps he had been too pumped to notice.

He put Vinnie in the easy chair in front of the television, then turned the set on. The rest of the lights he unplugged.

Another trip to the car for Vinnie's twelve gauge, which he laid across the dead man's lap. The empty brass casings in his pocket he tossed around the room after wiping them.

When he started the car, he thought for a moment, trying to decide if there was anything else he wanted to do.

Yeah. Come to think of it . . .

Standing in the door to the living room, he sprayed a magazine of 9-mm slugs from the Uzi. Above the guttural buzzing of the silenced weapon the sound of the television shattering and the slugs slapping the plasterboard was plainly audible.

That magazine spent, he loaded another and went into the bedroom. Three bursts there, then into the kitchen where he finished out the magazine on the refrigerator and oven and dishes in the cabinets. He put another magazine in and emptied it in Freeman's bathroom into the toilet and the bathtub and the mirror and sink. The shattered porcelain and glass flew everywhere.

This was like pissing on Hitler's picture. Somehow it just wasn't enough.

He went back to the storeroom and got some more magazines for the Uzi. He looked around. Under the couch where the boxes of ammo were stored was a cardboard box half full of grenades. Harrison helped himself.

What would you have to do to make Freeman McNally pay enough? For what he did to the Ike Randolphs, for what he did to all the people he peddled his poison to, for all the unspeakable misery and pain this man gave the world so that he could line his pockets – *for what he did to*

Harrison Ronald Ford – what would you have to do to McNally to even the balance in the ledger?

The filthy fuck would have to scream until his soul shattered.

Seven cars were parked outside the Sanitary Bakery warehouse, including Freeman's big Mercedes. No guards in sight outside. Maybe they were all inside having a snort and a drink, still celebrating the big party at Willie Teal's.

Sitting here in the green sedan looking it over – this was *really* weird – Harrison Ronald wasn't scared. Not the least. He felt good, real good, like he had had a snort. He had never told the FBI agents of course, and would never tell anyone else, but he had had to snort the stuff in front of Ike and Billy Enright, and a couple times in front of Freeman and his brothers, just to prove his bona fides. Feds and cops would never touch the shit, according to street wisdom.

It had been tough leaving the stuff alone after he had used it more or less regularly for several months. Excruciatingly difficult. But that wasn't the hardest part. He had been nervous, scared, all along, but after doing the coke he had his first real attacks of paranoia, and they hadn't ceased, no doubt because he had plenty to be paranoid about. All he had to fight it had been grit and determination. They weren't enough.

But now all those waves of panic and loose-boweled terror were gone. He had made up his mind. He was going to attack. Maybe die.

And he felt good, real good.

He parked the car on the north side of the warehouse by the chain-link fence where the garbage trucks were kept and locked it after he got out.

The neighborhood was quiet enough – only traffic sounds coming across the railroad tracks from New York Avenue. That and the low guttural snarls of the two Dobermans on the other side of the fence. He stood looking between the garbage trucks at the slab-sided black bulk of the building. There was a door over there somewhere. He had seen it before during the daylight.

He used the silenced pistol on the dogs. Two shots each. The Dobermans went down like they were sledge-hammered.

The gate through the ten-foot-high fence was held together by a big chain with a padlock on it. Two shots for the padlock, then sixty seconds to unwrap the chain, squeeze through, then wrap it again.

The door was nailed shut with a two-by-six across it. No doubt there was other timber on the other side. He tried to remember if he had noticed this door in his many walks through the interior. If he had, he would remember, but he didn't. Still, there was undoubtedly concrete and steel in there somewhere for the bullets to ricochet from. The sound of the full-metal-jacketed 9-mm slugs spanging through the old ware-house would certainly announce his arrival. And his intentions.

Well, here goes nothing.

He sawed the board in half with half a magazine from the Uzi, then kicked at the center of it with all his strength. It gave.

He kicked three or four times. The noise was loud here. It was probably echoing all over that huge mausoleum. Yet apparently something was holding the upper part of the door on the inside. He used the rest of the magazine on the point of resistance and kicked some more. It sagged.

Empty magazine out, new magazine in, Uzi ready, he gave one last mighty kick and the door flew open. Harrison Ronald dived through and rolled sideways, right into a wall.

He lay there for a second, his eyes adjusting to the gloom. He was under a stair that led up to the second-floor balcony. The main stairwell that led to the upper levels was off to his left. The room that the guard was in – that the front door opened into – was off to his right on the other side of the building.

He heard someone running.

Up, moving to his right along the wall, the Uzi ready. He could see the light coming from the doorway to the guard room. The door was open. The only other light in the place came from a naked bulb on the third-floor landing on the east end of the building. But it was so high and far away the light seemed to get lost in the cavernous space.

A flash and a loud report came from behind a box against the far wall. The bullet hit near Ford's head. He scuttled toward the darkness, away from the open door.

Another shot. And another.

He used the Uzi. A three-shot burst. Little flashes against the masonry where the jacketed bullets hit. He fired again, not trying to aim in the semidarkness, just walking the slugs in. The third burst drew a scream.

Ford was up and running for the stair at the east end of the huge room when two wild shots from the screaming man sailed by. He kept going, running hard, and was in time to see the vague outline of someone coming down the stairs.

Harrison Ronald triggered a long burst at the stairway as he ran. The figure slumped and went down. From fifteen feet away he triggered a short burst into the body, then took cover beside the stairway, breathing hard.

His heart was thudding like a trip-hammer, yet he felt good, oh, so good. He should have done this six months ago.

The first man he had shot was still screaming. And cursing, the high-pitched wail of a man in agony. Like Ike Randolph in his final moments.

Someone above him on the balcony fired at him and a shard of something struck his face. It stung. He wiped at it. Wet. Blood.

Whoever was up there was moving – he could hear him.

Harrison dug a grenade from his coat pocket, got the pin out, and holding the Uzi in his left hand, came out of the darkness running and lofted the grenade upward with a basketball sky-hook shot.

The damn thing might come bouncing down before it popped, but what the hell. End it here.

It didn't. The grenade went off with a flash and boom that was painful in this huge masonry echo chamber. A big piece of the wooden balcony rail came crashing down, the gunman in the midst of it. He landed with a splat a dozen feet from Ford and lay where he had fallen as the dust and dirt settled around and on him.

'Hey, down there!'

The shout came from upstairs.

'I don't know who the hell you are down there but you'd better stop this shit, man!'

It sounded, Harrison decided, like Billy Enright. Maybe at the head of the stairs.

The stairs were pretty conventional. They went upward to a landing against the outer wall, then turned 180 degrees and went on up to the second floor, the balcony level. And so on, a landing between each floor, up to the fourth floor. If Ford could gain the balcony everyone above him was trapped. This was the only exit from the higher floors.

He tiptoed up the stairs and stopped on the step prior to the landing. He took out another grenade and pulled the pin. Then he stood, listening and waiting.

'There's five of us up here, man, and we're all armed.' It sounded like Billy was right around the corner at the head of the stairs, standing on the balcony. His voice was tense, wound tight. 'I think,' he continued, 'that you're only one—'

Ford leaned around the corner and tossed the grenade.

'*Fuck! You fuck—*'

The concussion of the explosion was intensely painful in this confined space. Some of the shrapnel ricocheted against the wall and bounced off Ford, too spent to penetrate.

Harrison Ronald rounded the corner with the IM spraying and charged up the stairs two at a time.

Billy Enright sat with his back to the waist-high balcony rail, trying to hold his guts in with both hands. In the center of his ripped-apart face his eyes widened in recognition. He opened his mouth, but only blood came out. Then he slowly toppled sideways.

Ford heard a laugh. From someplace. Where? He moved back into the stairwell and scanned the balcony, trying to see.

'You get him, Billy?'

Freeman McNally.

'Naw, Freeman. Billy's lying here trying to hold his guts in. Maybe you got a cheerful word for him. He could use it right now.'

Another laugh. 'Well, well, well. If it ain't our good buddy the fucking stoolie, Sammy Z.'

'I ain't a stoolie, Freeman. I'm a cop. The FBI put me in to get the goods on you. And I got 'em. Ten fucking months worth. They got it *all*. You're gonna be in jail until you're too old to get it up, Freeman, if you make it through tonight, which is very doubtful.'

McNally laughed again. It sounded like he was somewhere above, maybe on the fourth floor, talking out of one of the interior windows.

'This ain't your night, Freeman. You get lucky and kill me, you're going straight to the butt-fuck house. I hear all those homos got AIDS, man. They'll be delighted to see your tight little cherry ass.'

'Well, you got one thing right, Sammy. I am sure as hell gonna kill you.'

'It's already been tried tonight, Freeman. I hope you didn't waste any money on Vinnie and Tony. They won't ever be able to pay you back.'

Ford heard a noise above him, in the stairwell. Someone was coming down. 'I'm gonna kill you slow, real slow,' McNally said, 'like I did ol' Ike. You're gonna fucking beg for a bullet, boy.'

Ford ascended the stairs, both hands on the Uzi. He was four steps up when the top of a head peeped around the corner. Ford pulled the trigger and held it down.

The body plopped out from behind the wall onto the landing. Brains and blood were scattered all over the wall behind.

'Little hard to tell, Freeman,' Ford called, 'but I think you just lost a brother.'

He paused and changed magazines, then stepped over the corpse and kept going. Ahead of him was the glare of the naked bulb on top of the landing. He shot it out. The pieces of glass fell with a tinkle, leaving the stairwell in total darkness. All he could hear was the moans of the guard on the warehouse floor.

Harrison Ronald waited for his eyes to adjust.

Finally, when he realized he could see all he was going to see, he eased his head around the corner and looked. It was like looking into a coal mine at midnight. Nothing. Same the other way.

He got out two grenades. Pin out of one, he tossed it down the hall to his left, then the other one to the right. He had no more than got his hand back in when the first one went off. Then the second. Like two thunderclaps.

Silence.

Total silence. Like a tomb.

He wanted to talk, taunt Freeman about Ike, make the bastard suffer before he died. But he knew better. He stood silently, listening and trying to breathe slowly and noiselessly.

He was standing like that when he heard the explosion just behind him and felt the numbing shock of the bullet rip into him. Harrison staggered. He dropped the Uzi and went to his hands and knees.

Something grabbed his throat and squeezed violently. McNally had come down the staircase from above him.

'*I got him, Ruben, I got him!*'

His neck – he couldn't breathe . . .

Ford reached back, groping desperately. His hand found its target and he grabbed all he could get and pulled with all his strength.

Screaming, Freeman McNally released his neck hold as Ford twisted and squeezed and tore, trying to rip his balls off. Screaming high and loud in unbearable pain as Harrison Ronald filled his lungs and physically lifted the man with his right hand as he levered himself up.

Harrison got his left hand on McNally's neck and pushed him back against the wall, then smashed his head again as he tried to literally rip the man's testicles from his body.

The scream was choked off in McNally's throat. Another smash into the wall and Ford lost his grip. He spun the man to a better angle and drew back his right hand to smash his larynx, just as someone arrived and fired a weapon.

Ford threw Freeman aside and lunged. The weapon flew and his fist connected with something soft. He struck savagely, again and again and again as hard as he could until the man he was pummeling went limp.

He was losing blood. He could feel the wetness. And he was weakening.

Neither of the other two men moved.

He fumbled in his pocket for the little penlight he had taken from Tony Anselmo. When was that?

Ruben McNally was apparently dead, his nose bone rammed up between his eyes.

Freeman's eyes stared at nothing, refused to focus.

Harrison Ronald felt Freeman's carotid artery. No heartbeat.

Furious, he rolled him over. A bullet dead center in the back, right between the shoulder blades. Shot by his own brother!

'You . . . you . . . you . . .'

Ford was also hit in the back and he knew it. Unless he got medical attention quickly he would probably bleed to death, hemorrhage into a lung or something.

'You . . .' he told Freeman's frozen face, then couldn't think of anything to add. A wave of pain and nausea swept over him.

'Oh God, help me.'

He got to his feet and started down the stairs, then tripped and almost fell. The flashlight hit the concrete and broke. It wasn't much of a light anyway. He kept going.

'God, forgive me for . . . for . . . please forgive me.'

He tripped over a body and fell down the last flight of stairs. He lay there in the darkness with death creeping over him.

'No!'

Somehow he got to his feet and saw the light coming through the door to the guard's office a hundred feet away. He staggered in that direction.

The man behind the equipment box against the south wall was silent. Unconscious or dead. At least Ford didn't hear him as he shuffled by.

He got the phone off the hook and punched 911. 'Sanitary Bakery warehouse,' he told the operator as he threw the switch to electrically unlock the front door.

'The address and your name, please!' she said.

His legs were shaking and he was having trouble seeing. 'Send the FBI and an ambulance. Better hurry. FBI . . .'

The phone slipped out of his grasp and he was falling.

'I'm dying,' he said.

Then the blackness swept over him.

25

The subway and the buses didn't operate beyond the beltway on Wednesday morning, and tens of thousands of suburban commuters didn't hear the news on television or radio. Infuriated, many who normally rode to work on public transport tried to join the hordes who drove. This was a serious mistake. Troops and state policemen had blocked every beltway entrance to Washington and were making all vehicles attempting to enter or leave the district turn around. Only law-enforcement officers, people with military IDs, and emergency vehicles were being allowed to pass. Although many of those who normally worked in the city heard the news before they left their homes and consequently decided to stay home, the traffic jams that morning were monumental, even by Southern California standards.

All flights to and from National Airport were canceled. The trains and intercity buses were not running. Washington was isolated and troops patrolled the streets.

Not many troops at first. The National Guard was still mobilizing and had less than twenty-five percent of their men on duty. Regular army troops began arriving at three A.M. on C-141s and C-5s at Andrews Air Force Base. General Hayden Land had ordered in a division of infantry and two regiments of armored cavalry. It would take almost thirty-six hours to get all the men and their equipment to Washington.

During the night the Vice-President's original committment to guard major public buildings had evolved into a show of overwhelming force. The plan recommended to General Land by the Joint Staff had been approved by the White House. No White House staffer wanted to be the first to say 'enough,' not when the primary criticism that continued violence would stimulate would be that the government had not done enough to prevent it. So the more-is-better recommendations of Jake Grafton and his group had been adopted all the way up the line.

By ten A.M. tanks and armored personnel carriers were parked near the major government buildings in the downtown area. By noon they were in front of every hospital in town. By two P.M. every traffic circle in the

District had a tank parked in the flower beds beside the statue. The olive-drab monsters sat in pairs upon the Mall, the diesel engines idling in the chill December wind as the crews stood nearby drinking coffee from disposable cups and looking with wide eyes at the sprawling buildings bathed in the weak winter sun.

The men were dressed for the weather but they were still cold. Last night they had been in Georgia. They indulged themselves in a great deal of arm swinging and jogging in place.

At nine A.M. the Vice-President met with a delegation of two dozen congressmen and senators in the East Room of the White House. It was not a happy meeting. Legislators who lived outside the beltway were of course not present. Their colleagues demanded that representatives, senators, and members of their staffs have access through military lines.

Vice-President Quayle instantly agreed. 'This,' he explained, 'was a glitch no one thought of last night.'

'There's a hell of a lot of things you people never thought of last night,' Senator Bob Cherry thundered. 'Food – how are grocery trucks going to get into the city? How are sick people going to get in and out? Critical medical supplies? The radio says there are thousands of people stranded at National Airport and Union Station. Damn it, you can't just surgically remove this city from the rest of the United States and expect it to keep breathing. Won't happen.'

'It'll only be until we can thoroughly search the city for terrorists,' Quayle explained, looking from face to face. 'Surely everyone can see the necessity for extraordinary measures.'

'We gotta do *something*,' someone muttered.

'*Something* won't hack it,' Cherry boomed. 'This military idea is half-baked. Won't work. Why does anybody think a bunch of kids wearing uniforms and carrying rifles can do what the FBI can't?'

'This may not work,' Dan Quayle acknowledged. 'But we're going to try it for lack of something better. We've got to stop the terrorism and violence. Stop it dead, once and for all. That's what I'm trying to do.'

'But you can't just rip the Constitution into confetti,' Cherry groused. 'What about people's rights?'

'Senator,' Quayle began patiently, 'I'm well aware that Christmas is six days away and kids aren't out of school, and some people are being prevented from going to work and earning a living. I know this measure is a financial hardship on many and an outright disaster for others. My wife reminded me this morning that many employers cannot afford to pay their employees if they aren't working and a lot of those who can afford it won't bother. *I know* this measure is a real hardship on many. Still, it's necessary.'

'In *your* judgment,' Cherry said crossly.

'In *my* judgment,' Quayle echoed, irritated with Cherry and all of them. He had been in Washington long enough to learn that there was nothing fair about politics: if ordering in the National Guard and the Army turned out to be ineffective or a disaster, he would be blamed; yet if the measure worked and the terrorists were apprehended, the advisers and staff would get all the credit for convincing Dan Quayle, the bumbling fool, to do the right thing.

'You should have asked the advice of the senior members of Congress *before* you called in the military,' Cherry continued, not yet ready to let it lie. 'I, for one, am more than a little peeved that we get summoned like ladies in waiting to come over here and listen to edicts from the throne.'

Dan Quayle lost his temper. 'Goddammit, Senator, everybody in this room knew about this yesterday. *I* have assumed the President's responsibilities during his disability and *I* am *not* going to run the presidency by committee.'

'I'm not suggesting—' Cherry began, but Quayle ignored him and began talking into the microphone on the podium while referring to notes:

'I have appointed an independent nonpartisan presidential commission to oversee federal efforts to apprehend the people responsible for the atrocities of these past few days. This will be announced to the press as soon as we finish here. The commission will work closely with all the federal agencies involved to investigate all matters connected with these crimes. I want all the facts investigated and laid before the public. The commission will have the authority to pursue any line of inquiry it feels is germane. I will send a message to Congress today asking for a special appropriation so the commission can immediately hire staff and get to work. I certainly hope Congress will see fit to act quickly. I don't want anybody shouting cover-up when all the dust settles.

'Mr Dorfman, please read the names.'

Will Dorfman somehow didn't look his nasty, mean little self, Congresswoman Samantha Strader noted with a raised eyebrow. The troll actually looked human this morning – harried, a touch of exhaustion.

Dorfman read the list. The first name was that of the Chief Justice of the Supreme Court, Harlan Longstreet. That was fitting. Chief Justice Earl Warren had directed the inquiry into John F. Kennedy's assassination, but in spite of herculean efforts on the part of the investigators, nitpickers and conspiracy fanatics were still unsatisfied over twenty-five years later. Perhaps that was inevitable.

The eighth name Dorfman read was Sam Strader. When Dorfman had telephoned and asked her to serve she had been momentarily at a loss for words, a rare experience, not to be savored. 'Why me?' she asked.

'Quayle wants this commission to be nonpartisan, and the only way we know to do that is to get people from all across the political spectrum to serve.'

She mulled it for three seconds. Yes. Now, standing here watching

Danny the Dork prove that brains are not a prerequisite for public office, she was sure she had made the right decision.

She would have a delicious time tormenting those mate chauvinist fascists at the FBI who, God knew, richly deserved far worse. More importantly, she would be able to make the blind world see that emperor Quayle wore no pants – this military witch hunt for someone to pin the blame on had all the earmarks of a debacle in the making. Last, but certainly not least, tens of millions of voters who had never heard of Samantha Strader soon would.

There was no reason that she shouldn't be the next president. After all, Quayle had the charisma of a fish. The real problem was getting the Democratic nomination, and if she could show what a woman could do to clean up this terrorist mess, she would have a leg up.

All in all, this was going to be an enjoyable, interesting project. As usual, Samantha Strader had not a scintilla of self-doubt: she believed in herself and her opinions with a white-hot zeal that would have looked good on a messiah. Despite the seriousness of the occasion Strader indulged herself in a luxurious grin.

Special Agent Thomas F. Hooper found his colleague Freddy Murray lounging beside the nurse's station outside the intensive care unit. 'How is he?'

'Coming out of it. It'll be a few more hours. He surprised the surgeons. They thought he'd die on the table.'

'Seven dead men in the warehouse and one in his room at Quantico. The maid found the body an hour ago when she went in to change the sheets. The lab guys are trying to put it all together and figure out who everybody is.'

'I got ten bucks that says he killed them all.'

'No bet.'

Freddy Murray shook his head. 'Funny, isn't it? Ten months – wiretaps, depositions, surveillance cameras, the whole enchilada – and all we got to show for it are seven corpses.'

They stood silently, listening to the sounds of the hospital, the clicking, hissing, sucking, squeaking, groaning noises.

'The stiff in Harrison's room at Quantico is white. Not sure yet, but one of the agents thinks it's Tony Anselmo.'

'From New York?'

'Yeah.'

'We let this go on too long,' Freddy Murray said after a bit. 'We should've busted Freeman's bunch in September.'

'Don't give me that! We didn't have enough in September.'

Tom Hooper let it lie. 'Let's go sit down someplace. I only had three hours' sleep.'

They collapsed on the sofa in the ICU waiting room, two doors down the hall.

Hooper sighed, then extracted a sheet of paper from his pocket and passed it to Freddy. 'Ever seen this guy before?'

Freddy unfolded the paper. It was a copy of an artist's rendering of a face. A very plain face. At the bottom of the sheet this information appeared: 'White male, approximately forty years of age, five feet nine or ten inches, clean shaven, short dark hair, dark eyes.'

'Don't recognize him. Who is he?'

'The dude who shot Gideon Cohen yesterday. Maybe. A woman saw him in the lobby of the building as he was leaving. He was wearing surgical gloves.'

Freddy looked at the picture again, trying to visualize that face on a real man. He started to hand the paper back, but Hooper waved it away.

'Keep it. We're getting thousands made. It'll be on television nationwide in an hour or so and in the papers this evening and tomorrow.'

'It isn't that good a picture,' Freddy pointed out.

Hooper shrugged. 'You're a ray of sunshine.'

'So what are you going to do about Harrison?'

'Do?' Hooper muttered, donning a slightly puzzled look.

'You gonna arrest him or what?'

'What would I arrest him for? What charge? Is there any proof that he's done anything illegal?'

'I dunno. That's why I'm asking.'

'Get some cops up here – uniformed cops. I want a cop at the ICU door and one at the floor nurse's station twenty-four hours a day. And I want to hear immediately when Ford regains consciousness.'

Hooper summoned all his energy and extracted himself from the soft couch.

'Where you going?' Freddy asked.

'Over to see what the hell those guys have turned up on the Willie Teal murders. You oughta see that place! Fourteen bodies! And we figured out which one is Willie. He was sitting on the crapper with his pants around his ankles when the grenades started coming in. Boy, is he ever dead!' Hooper scratched his head and glanced at his watch. 'That search warrant for McNally's place ought to be signed by now. I'd sure like to find those grenade launchers.'

Hooper looked at Freddy. 'By the way, I haven't let them tell the press about these McNally killings. We'll hold onto that for a while and see what happens.'

'What could happen? The McNally brothers wiped out the Teal outfit. Now they're dead. End of story.'

Hooper grunted and walked out. Freddy watched him go, then headed for the pay phone. The police department was undoubtedly going to be delighted to furnish two officers around the clock.

There was a light. He could see the glare but his eyes wouldn't focus. Then the effort of holding his eyes open became too much and he closed them and drifted.

He had been dreaming and he tried to go back to the dream. It was July, that time of blue skies and hot, sticky days, and he was sitting on his grandmother's porch counting the squeaks as the swing went back and forth, back and forth.

He had the whole summer to loaf and play and yet the *only* thing he could think of to do was sit in the swing and listen to the chain squeak as it rubbed on the hooks in the ceiling.

His grandmother had been in the dream, sitting on the steps stringing beans, and it seemed important to see her again. Crazy as it seemed, with all the events of his whole life, the most important one, the memory that he treasured the most, was of a summer day when he was very young, swinging on the porch and watching his grandmother. So he tried to go back to the porch and the swing and the dry cracking sound as the beans snapped and. . .

But the light was back.

Someone was moving around.

'Harrison. Can you hear me?'

He tried to speak but his mouth was dry, like sandpaper. He licked his lips, then nodded a tiny bit. 'Yeah,' he whispered.

'It's me, Freddy. How you doing in there?'

'Where am I?'

'Hospital. You had a bullet in your back. You lost a lot of blood. They operated and got the slug and plugged up all the places you were leaking.'

He nodded again, which was difficult. He was having trouble moving. He had no place to go anyway.

'Harrison, can you tell me what happened?'

He thought about it, trying to remember. It was difficult. The warehouse, driving around, all jumbled out of order. After a while he thought he had it straight. He said, 'They came for me.'

'Anselmo?'

'And the other one. White guy. Pi . . . Pioche.'

That was right. He saw it clearly now. The stairwell. Fat Tony falling in the darkness. Freeman McNally screaming, the television shattering . . . No. Something was mixed up some . . .

That scream. It had been almost in his ear, painfully loud, the man in mortal agony. And Harrison had enjoyed it. He lay here now immobile, his eyes closed, remembering. Savoring that scream.

'What else can you tell me?'

Why was Freddy so insistent? 'He screamed,' Harrison said.

'Who?'

Who indeed! 'Freeman.'

'Why did you kill him?'

Why? Well, hell, you idiot, because . . . 'Because.'

'Hooper is gonna be over here in a few minutes to question you, Harrison. You killed eight guys. That's real heavy shit. Real heavy. I think you should think through what you're gonna say to Hooper very carefully. You dig me?'

Harrison sorted through it one more time. He felt like dog shit and he was getting sleepy again. 'Nine guys.'

'Nine?'

'Think so. It's pretty confusing.'

He was drifting again, back toward the porch and the swing and the bright, hot days when he heard Freddy say, 'You sleep now. We'll talk later.'

'Yeah,' he said, and tackled the problem of why his grandmother had white hair even back then. She was small and wiry and her hair was white as snow. It had been that way as long as he could remember.

'Senator Hiram Duquesne to see you, Mr Hooper.'

The secretary rolled her eyes heavenward and stepped clear so that Senator Duquesne could enter. He was fat – not plump, not overweight, but fat – in his middle sixties. His double chin swung as he walked. Embedded in the fleshy face were two of the hardest eyes that Tom Hooper had ever stared at. They swept him now.

The senator dropped into a chair and waited until the door was closed behind him. 'I've just come from a conference with the director,' he announced.

'Yessir. He called me.'

'I want to report an incident. I want a report made and an investigation done. I want it all in writing and dated and signed and I want a copy.'

Hooper grunted noncommittally. If FBI reports were going to be handed out the director would do the handing, not Hooper.

Just as Duquesne opened his mouth, the telephone rang. 'Excuse me a second, Senator.' He picked up the instrument. 'Yes.'

'Freddy is on the other line. Harrison is awake.'

'Tell him I'll be there as soon as I can.'

As he cradled the phone Duquesne said, 'You could ask her to hold your calls.'

'I don't have that luxury. Senator. Tell me about this incident.'

Duquesne told him. From the first approach by T. Jefferson Brody several years ago to the incident last night in the parking garage of the Senate office building, he gave Hooper every incident and the details on every check. Hooper made notes and asked questions to clarify points. It took fifteen minutes.

Finally Duquesne announced, 'There it is,' and Hooper leaned back in his chair and reviewed his notes.

'I want this pimp Brody arrested,' Senator Duquesne said. 'I'll take the heat.'

Hooper laid the legal pad back on the table. 'What do I arrest him for?'

'Attempted bribery, extortion, I don't know.'

'I don't know either. Assuming that all the contributions to the PACs he controlled were made according to law, and you have given me no information to suggest otherwise, there's nothing illegal about a notorious criminal making a political contribution. And people ask you to take positions on public issues twenty times a day.'

'Brody didn't ask. He *threatened* me. I'm sure you can grasp the distinction between a request and a threat.'

'Threatened you with what? *You* said *he* said he would call a matter of public record to the attention of the media if you didn't do what he wanted. I don't think that qualifies as a threat.'

Duquesne's face was turning a deep brick hue. 'Listen to me, you little badge toter. Don't give me one of those pissy nothing-can-be-done hog-crap sandwiches! I'm not going to listen to that!'

The expression on Hooper's face didn't change. 'Senator, you have been had by a pro. Now listen carefully to what I'm going to say. By your own admission the man has done nothing illegal. He was the only other witness to this conversation, and believe me, he will deny everything that even throws a shadow on him.'

Duquesne was taking it hard. His throat worked as he sat and stared at the desk between them.

'Now, here is what we *can* do. We can look into the accounting and see if he obeyed all the rules on his PACs and his contributions. That will take time but might turn up something. Brody sounds cute, but the law in this area is a minefield.'

'That asshole wouldn't slip up like that,' Duquesne said softly.

'The other thing we can do is put a wire on you and let you have another conversation with Brody. Maybe he'll say something this time that does compromise him.'

'And me!'

'Perhaps. That's a risk you'll have to take.'

'I don't like it.'

'Who else has this man approached? How many other members of Congress has he tried to influence?'

'I don't know. But I seem to recall that somebody said he was giving money to Bob Cherry and three or four others.'

'That'll be in their financial statements, right? We'll look and see if we can find these names.'

'Where does that get us?'

'I'll be frank, Senator. It may take someone someplace they don't want to go. Freeman McNally is dead. He was killed last night.'

Duquesne was speechless. 'Who did it?'

'We're investigating. This information is confidential. We have not released the news of McNally's death and would like to hold on to it for a while.'

Duquesne's color faded to a ghastly white. Out of the clear blue sky he had just supplied the FBI with a motive for the murder of a man who had just been killed.

Hooper watched the senator with an expressionless face. He well knew what Duquesne was thinking and it didn't bother Hooper a bit that he was thinking it.

'The good news,' the agent said after he had let Duquesne twist a while in the wind, 'is that Freeman has made his last political contribution. In the fullness of time, probably fairly soon, T. Jefferson Brody will hear of Mr McNally's unfortunate demise. Of course he will still have a hold on you, but I doubt that he'll be foolish enough to try to use it. He impresses me as a very careful fellow.'

'Cute. The bastard thinks he's cute.'

'Ah, yes, don't they all?'

Freddy was standing beside the nurses' station listening to a man sitting in a wheelchair with his head swathed in bandages tell the cop all about his recent hair transplant. 'You don't know how demoralizing it is to lose your hair. It's like you're visibly deteriorating, aging, you know?'

Hooper came through the door, took the scene in at a glance and led Freddy toward the waiting area, which was empty. Behind him the man was explaining, 'It was male pattern baldness all the way. My God, I felt so—'

'How is he?' Hooper asked as he pulled the door to the lounge closed.

'Sleeping again. The nurse said he'll probably wake up in a little bit and we can talk to him then. She'll come get me.'

'We found a body over at McNally's house. Vinnie Pioche, I think. And the place had been shot apart. Someone just stood inside the door of each room and sprayed lead everywhere. It's a real mess.'

'Probably Harrison. He said Pioche came with Anselmo to get him. And he said he thinks he killed nine men, but it's real confusing.'

Hooper fell into one of the chairs.

'Did he say why?'

'Because. He said he did it because.'

'That's real helpful. Just what I need to feed to the sharks in the US attorney's office.'

'He's still under the anesthetic, Tom. He doesn't know what the hell he's saying.'

Hooper grunted and stared at his toes. Then he took off his shoes and massaged his feet. 'We should have wrapped this one up in September.'

'We didn't have enough in September,' Freddy said.

Hooper eyed him without humor, then put his shoes back on.

Fifteen minutes later the nurse opened the door and stuck her head in. 'He's awake. Don't stay more than five minutes.'

Harrison Ronald had his eyes closed when the FBI agents stepped up to his bed, but the nurse nodded and left them. Freddy said, 'Harrison, it's me, Freddy. Tom Hooper is with me. How you feeling?'

Ford's eyes came open and slowly moved around until they found Freddy. After a moment they went to Hooper.

'Hey, Tom.'

'Hey, Harrison. Sorry about this.'

'It's over.'

'Yeah.'

Ford's eyes closed again. Hooper looked at Freddy, who shrugged.

'Harrison,' Hooper said, 'I need to ask you some questions, find out what happened. Why did you go to that warehouse anyway?'

The eyes focused on Hooper's face. They stayed there a while, went to Freddy, then back to Hooper. Harrison Ronald licked his lips, then said, 'I want a lawyer.'

'What?'

'A lawyer. I ain't saying anything without my lawyer's approval.'

'Aww, wait a goddamn minute! I'm not charging you with anything. You're the sole witness to a serious—'

The word 'crime' was right there on the tip of his tongue but he bit it off. He swallowed once. 'All this has to be investigated. You know that. You're a cop, for Chrissake!'

'I want a lawyer. That's all I have to say.'

Hooper opened his mouth and closed it again. He glanced at Freddy, who was standing with his hands in his pockets regarding the man in the bed.

'Okay. We'll get you a lawyer. I'll stop by tomorrow and see how you're doing.'

'Fine. See you then.'

'Come on, Freddy. We have work to do.'

Harrison Ronald Ford went back to sleep.

26

The first man the soldiers killed was Larry Ticono. At the age of sixteen he had dropped out of the seventh grade after failing it three times. In spite of the nine years he spent in the public school system, he was illiterate. On those rare occasions when he was asked to sign his name he used an illegible scrawl.

Larry Ticono had been arrested three times in his short life – twice for possession of illegal drugs and once for burglary – but he had spent a grand total of only five days in jail. After each arrest he was released on his own recognizance. He returned to court only when the police picked him up again. One of his possession arrests had apparently fallen completely through the cracks and been forgotten. He had pleaded guilty to the other two charges and had received probation.

The wonder was that he had lived so long. He had a two-hundred-dollar-a-day crack habit and his welfare check was only $436 a month. The shortfall he made up by stealing anything that wasn't welded in place. Cameras, radios, televisions, and car stereos were his favorite targets. He sold his loot to fences for fifteen to twenty percent of their market value – not retail value when new, but market value used. He tried to avoid muggings, which were dangerous, but did them when nothing else readily presented itself.

Larry Ticono's life defined the term 'hand to mouth.' He slept under bridges in good weather and in abandoned buildings in bad. He rarely had more than twenty dollars in his pocket and was never more than three hours away from withdrawal.

This afternoon Larry Ticono's three-hour margin had melted to zero. He was on the edge with only $17.34 in his pocket. The corner where he usually purchased crack was empty. Although Ticono didn't know it, his suppliers were the retail end of the distribution network of Willie Teal, who had been forcibly and permanently retired from the crack business the previous night. So the street-corner salesmen had no product and were not there.

Frustrated and desperate, Ticono walked a half mile to another neighborhood that he knew about and tried to make a deal with a fifteen-year-old in a pair of hundred-dollar Nike running shoes. That worthy had not received his morning delivery from his supplier, an employee of Freeman McNally. The streetwise dealers sensed that something was wrong although they had no hard information. They had seen the troops coming and going and had heard the news on television, and they were worried. Many of them were drifting away, back to the welfare apartments and ramshackle row houses they called home.

When Larry Ticono approached the fifteen-year-old, that youngster had only four crack bags left and no prospect of readily obtaining more. So that young capitalist demanded forty dollars a hit.

The thought occurred to Larry Ticono that he should just mug the kid, but it vaporized after one look at the corner boss, a heavyset man standing by a garbage can watching. Larry knew beyond a shadow of a doubt that the guard had a weapon within easy reach and would cheerfully kill him if he so much as touched the youngster.

After trying futilely to bargain, he reluctantly turned away.

Two blocks later Larry Ticono threw a brick through a window of an electronics store and grabbed a ghetto blaster. He was promptly shot by a convenience-store salesclerk wearing a National Guard uniform. The blaster was just too large and heavy to run with at any speed.

The fifty-five-grain .223 bullet from the M-16 hit Larry high up in the center of the back, a perfect shot, which was pure luck because the clerk was wearing a pair of fogged-up glasses and had barely qualified with the M-16 in training. Before he threw the rifle to his shoulder and pulled the trigger the clerk had never killed any creature larger than a cockroach.

Still traveling at over three thousand feet per second when it pierced Larry Ticono's skin, the jacketed bullet expended a major portion of its eleven hundred footpounds of energy shattering his backbone and driving the fragments through his heart, exploding it. The slug then exited his chest and buried itself in a parked car sixty yards away.

Larry Ticono, age nineteen, was dead before his body hit the pavement.

The convenience-store clerk vomited beside the body.

Jack Yocke took in the scene at a glance a half hour later when he arrived. He busied himself taking names and trying to think of something to say to the clerk-private, who was sitting on the tailgate of an olive-drab pickup staring at his hands.

'I shouted for him to stop, but he didn't,' the private said so softly Yocke had to strain to hear. 'He didn't stop,' he repeated wonderingly, amazed at the perverse ways of fate.

'No. He didn't.'

'He should have stopped.'

'Yes.'

'He *really* should have stopped.'

The reporter wandered over to a sergeant standing near the body smoking a cigarette. Some fifteen feet away a group of army or National Guard officers were conferring with a uniformed policeman. Yocke had yet to learn the nuances of the shoulder patches on the uniforms, which as far as he could see, were the only way to tell which service was which. The sergeant glanced at Yocke and continued to puff leisurely on his cigarette. He was thoughtfully surveying the faces of the watchers on the sidewalk across the street.

'I thought,' Jack Yocke said, 'that your people were supposed to fire their weapons only in self-defense.'

The sergeant appraised him carefully. 'That's right,' he said, then went back to scanning the crowd.

'Yet as I understand it, the victim was running away when the private shot him?'

'Something like that, I suppose.'

'So why'd he shoot?'

A look of disgust registered on the sergeant's face. 'Who *are* you, anyway?'

'Jack Yocke, *Washington Post*. I didn't mean—'

'Shove off, pencil pilot. Before I lose my temper and ram that notebook up your ass.'

'I'm sorry. No offense,' Yocke said, then turned away. He shouldn't have asked that question. Why had he done it? Now he felt guilty. It was a new experience.

Disgusted with himself, he looked again at the private slumped on the tailgate and the body covered with a sheet, then walked to his car.

He had always been so confident, so sure of himself and his perceptions. And now . . .

Six blocks away a group of people outside a closed liquor store – the military authorities had ordered them all closed – were throwing rocks at passing cars. One of them thudded into the side of the *Post*'s little sedan.

It's started. Jack Yocke decided. The supply of crack has dried up and the addicts are getting restless. He pointed the car toward the National Guard armory adjacent to RFK Stadium.

He didn't get very far into the building, of course. He showed his credentials and the soldier on duty let him into the press room, the first door on the right. There he found a half dozen government-issue steel desks, some folding chairs, and one telephone. And over a dozen of his colleagues, two of them from the *Post*. They were waiting for the press briefing scheduled for five P.M., fifteen minutes from now.

Yocke muttered at the people he knew – and he knew three or four of them – and found a corner to sit in. He sat there musing, thinking about the private who had killed a man when he shouldn't have, wondering if he, Jack Yocke, would have done any better. Maybe he wasn't really cut out to be a reporter. Stupid. He had made a stupid, insensitive remark, and now it rankled.

The reporters were waiting for Dan Quayle when he came out of Bethesda Naval Hospital. He could have avoided them but he didn't.

Ignoring the shouted questions, he stood still and waited until a battery of hand-held microphones were waving before him. 'The President regained consciousness this afternoon for a short period of time. Mrs Bush is with him. He is asleep now. The doctors believe his recovery will be rapid. He's in excellent health for a man his age and we have high hopes.'

'Did you discuss the hunt for the assassin with him?' someone shouted.

'No,' said Dan Quayle. Actually the President wasn't well enough to discuss anything, but he didn't say that. He thought about it and decided to let the monosyllable stand alone.

'Mr Vice-President, what about the claim that the Colombian Extraditables are making, that they are responsible.'

Quayle ignored that one. Then he heard a question he couldn't ignore.

'The Extraditables say that the terrorism will stop if you release Chano Aldana. Could you comment on that?'

'Said when?' Quayle asked, silencing all the other reporters.

'About an hour ago in Colombia, Mr Vice-President. It just came over the wires.'

Quayle thought about it. 'We're not going to bargain with terrorists,' he said. The crowd waited. The red lights on the fronts of the television cameras stayed on. 'Chano Aldana is going to get a fair trial. As long as I am acting for the President, I promise you, I will use the full might and power of the United States government to accomplish that come what may.'

'Are there any circumstances where you might release Aldana?' someone pressed.

'If the jury acquits him.'

'Before trial, I mean.'

'Not even if hell freezes over,' Dan Quayle replied, and turned away.

'You know,' Ott Mergenthaler said to Senator Bob Cherry, 'the man has the personality of a store dummy, but I do believe there's some steel in his backbone.'

Ott was in the senator's office and the two of them had just finished watching Quayle's performance. The senator reached for his remote control and killed the picture and sound after Quayle walked off camera and the network analysts came on.

Cherry sneered. 'He's a medical miracle. He's got the brain of a penguin and the jawbone of an ass.'

'Come off it, Senator. Say what you will, this crisis is not hurting Dan Quayle's reputation one whit. The public is getting a good look and I think they're liking what they see. I do, anyway.'

'Ott! Don't kid around! You don't really believe this National Guard move was wise? For God's sake, man, I thought you had some sense.'

'I do have, Senator, but I found out years ago that it does no good at all to proclaim the fact.'

Had Cherry known Mergenthaler better, he would have stopped right there. When the columnist retreated to dry, edged retorts, he had been pushed as far as he was willing to go. Cherry pressed on: 'Bush could control Dorfman, but Quayle can't. Dorfman is a shark and Quayle is a damn little fish. You don't seriously think that Dan Quayle is making the decisions over there, do you?'

'I hear he is,' Ott said mildly, cocking his head slightly.

'Don't you believe it! Dorfman's pulling the strings. And I guarantee you the last thing Will Dorfman cares about is the US Constitution. When is the Army going to leave? What about people's rights? Why hasn't the Congress been asked to authorize al! this extracurricular military activity? The legalities – they've got the troops outside the federal district, out in Maryland for God's sake. The government will get sued for—'

'What's your real bitch?'

Cherry looked blank. 'What do you mean?'

'You're blowing smoke. I've been writing a column in this town for fifteen years, Bob.'

Senator Cherry took a deep breath and exhaled. 'Okay, okay.' He shrugged. 'Quayle scares me. Real bad. If Bush dies we are in big big trouble.'

'Next presidential election is in two years. Look at it as the Democrats' big chance.'

Cherry writhed in his chair. 'This country can't afford to drift for two years with a clown on the bridge. The only damn thing Quayle knows how to do is play golf.'

'Bob, you're making a mountain out of a manure pile. True, Quayle's had a lot of bad press, some of it his fault, some of it because he's such an easy target to pick on and he's a darling of the conservatives. The man has an uncanny talent for saying the wrong thing. But this country is over two hundred years old! We can survive two years with *anybody* at the helm, be it Dan the Bogeyman or Hanoi Jane or my Aunt Matilda.'

Cherry wanted to argue. After a couple more minutes Ott Mergenthaler excused himself. Out in the corridor he shook his head sadly. Assassins and terrorists and wholesale murder everywhere you looked, and Bob Cherry wanted to mutter darkly about Dan Quayle. Worse, he expected Ott to print it.

Cherry looks old, Mergenthaler told himself. His age is telling.

Querulous – that's the word. He's become a whining, querulous old man absorbed with trivialities.

The news conference at the DC National Guard Armory had barely gotten under way when it was abruptly adjourned. A junior officer announced that someone had attacked the crowd at the L'Enfant Plaza Metro Station. The brass hustled out. Among them was Captain Jake Grafton.

Jack Yocke fought through the press crowd to get to the door and charged for the street at a dead run. He ran along the sidewalk toward the entrance to the Guard's parking lot, just in time to see a government car coming out. He bent and scanned the passengers. Nope. The next one? Nope again.

Grafton was in the third car. Yocke humped and waved his arms and shouted 'Captain Grafton! Captain Grafton!' at the top of his lungs. The uniformed driver locked the brakes. Yocke jerked open the rear door and jumped in.

As the car accelerated away Jake Grafton and Toad Tarkington looked the reporter over.

'Riding your thumb today?' Grafton asked.

'I'm really glad you stopped, sir. Thanks a lot. If you don't mind, I'd like to tag along with you.'

'The press regulations—'

'Yessir. Yessir. I know all about them. We have them stenciled on our underwear. Still, I'd like you to bend the rules a little and let me tag along with you for a few days. If you like, I'll even let you comment on the stories.'

Jake Grafton's brow wrinkled as he looked ahead at the traffic the driver was threading through. Toad Tarkington gave Yocke a big grin.

Grafton held a walkie-talkie in his hand. The instrument was spitting out words too garbled and tinny for Yocke to understand. Grafton held the device to his ear for a moment, then lowered it back to his lap.

'You'll have to agree,' Grafton said slowly, 'not to do any stories at all until this is completely over.'

Tarkington's grin faded.

'That's the *only* condition?' the reporter asked incredulously. 'You don't want to comment on the story?'

'No. Just don't print anything until this is all over.'

'No catch, eh?' Yocke said, still skeptical. Actually, all he wanted was a ride to L'Enfant Plaza. He sat now slightly stunned at Jake Grafton's willingness to go along with his spur-of-the-moment proposal. What was that old rule of thumb – if you ask ten girls to go to bed with you, you'll only get your face slapped nine times?

'We can always let you out at the next corner,' Toad told him sourly.

'Captain, you got a deal.'

'Umm.'

'What's happening now?'

'Some gunmen opened fire in the Metro Station at L'Enfant Plaza. Lot of people down, some of them soldiers. A real bloodbath.'

'Colombians?'

'I don't know.'

Yocke fished his notebook from an inside jacket pocket and flipped it open. As he scribbled and the car jolted, Toad said, 'It's T-A-R-K-I-N—'

'I got it, Frog. What's your hometown?'

'Intercourse, Pennsylvania.'

'Dry up, you two,' Jake Grafton said, and held the walkie-talkie to his ear.

He was going to have to mention this little arrangement to General Land at the first opportunity. But he thought the general would approve. Just this afternoon the subject of the presidential commission had arisen, forced to the fore by a request from Congresswoman Strader for a military district headquarters pass, which was granted. The career officers who had been watching Ms Strader's act for years suspected that she would be diligently searching for butts to kick at a postmortem later on, when both she and her colleagues would have the luxury of hindsight to enhance their wisdom. Alas, being second-guessed by Monday-morning quarterbacks went with the job.

When he saw Jack Yocke jumping up and down on the sidewalk, it occurred to Jake Grafton that it just might help to have an independent observer keep Ms Strader et al from playing fast and loose with the facts.

Jack Yocke was young and brash, but Jake Grafton had been reading the articles on Cuba and he was impressed. Yocke was a good reporter. He was observant and cared about people, and he could express himself well. He just needed seasoning. And a good reporter, Jake believed, would know a fact when he tripped over one. Yocke would do nicely.

These thoughts occupied Jake Grafton for about ten seconds, then he returned to the business at hand, a terrorist incident at a subway station. The general in charge was giving orders on the radio to the officer at the scene to storm the place as soon as possible. That struck Jake Grafton as logical. If these were suicide commandos like those who had shot up the Capitol building, the sooner they were killed the fewer the number of innocent people who would die.

The driver brought the car to a halt outside the main entrance to L'Enfant Plaza and the occupants jumped out and trotted toward a huddle of soldiers by the doors. The major general, Myles Greer, was conferring with a major. Jake could hear the sound of gunshots through the door, the ripping of automatic weapons fire. 'How long?' General Greer asked.

'Another two minutes. I've got three men at the west entrance and I want ten there.'

General Greer glanced at Grafton, who met his eyes. Greer had a tough decision to make and Jake Grafton knew it. And he was not about to use his position as General Land's liaison to influence that decision. The choice was simple and brutal: more soldiers meant more firepower, and the more firepower one accumulated, the fewer soldiers one was likely to lose. On the other hand, the shots they were hearing were being fired by the terrorists at unarmed civilians, and every second of delay meant that more of those civilians would die.

It took Greer about three seconds. 'Let's go now,' he said. The major gestured to the army lieutenant in battle dress and used the walkie-talkie.

Grafton spoke to the general, a question so soft that Jack Yocke almost missed it. 'You got the subways stopped?'

Apparently satisfied with the answer, Grafton turned to two soldiers who were standing to one side. 'You guys going to guard the doors?'

'Yessir.'

'Gimme your rifle.'

The young enlisted man looked toward his sergeant, who nodded. Toad Tarkington relieved another man of his weapon.

'I'm going with you,' Yocke said.

Grafton didn't argue. The soldiers were moving out, the lieutenant in the lead. 'Stay between me and Toad,' Grafton said over his shoulder to Yocke as he trotted after them.

The men ran along a corridor of shops empty of people. The Army had already evacuated them. The corridor twisted and made several ninety-degree bends. The running men spread out, their weapons at the ready.

The sounds of gunfire were louder. As the corridor came to another bend the men came upon a soldier lying prone, his rifle covering the blind corner.

The lieutenant used hand signals. When his men were ready he leaped around the corner and two men followed him. Then the others, cautiously.

They were facing an open double door, and beyond it, escalators down. The popping of gunfire was louder, made painful by the echos from the concrete walls.

At the head of the escalator the sergeant opened fire on an unseen target below. He was firing single shots.

A spray of bullets from below showered sparks off the overhead and shattered one of the neon lights.

The sergeant fired a fully automatic burst, then charged down the escalator. Two men followed.

The lieutenant eased up, took a quick look, and with a gesture to the men behind him, followed.

Jake Grafton and Toad Tarkington, with Yocke between them, followed the soldiers.

The first dead gunman lay twenty feet beyond the end of the escalator. An Uzi lay beside him. Around him were seven more bodies. Jack Yocke paused and watched as Jake Grafton went from body to body, checking for signs of life. Three men and four women. Several lay in little pools of blood. One of them had crawled for ten or twelve feet, leaving a bloody streak. As Grafton felt for the pulse of the last person he shook his head, then went off after the soldiers, keeping low. Yocke followed.

They were on a wide pedestrian walkway now, with the ceiling arching high overhead.

The walkway ended in a T-intersection, with walkways going right and left. The soldiers split up, running both ways. Jake Grafton looked over the edge, then ducked as bullets spanged pieces out of the chipped concrete.

Jack Yocke fell flat right where he was. The gunfire rose to a crescendo, then ceased. Yocke lay still in the sudden silence, waiting, his heart hammering.

Finally the reporter looked around. Toad was squatting nearby with his rifle at the ready. He was listening. Grafton was nowhere in sight.

Toad began to move.

Yocke followed him. They went to the rail and cautiously looked over. Grafton was below on one of the station platforms, listening to the Army lieutenant talk on the radio. Bodies lay scattered about. As they stood there looking at the carnage, Yocke heard the pounding of running feet behind him.

He dropped flat. Then he looked. Medics wearing white armbands displaying a red cross ran by carrying stretchers.

'Let's go down there,' Yocke suggested. Toad shrugged.

Jake Grafton was sitting on the concrete with his back to a pillar, his rifle across his lap. If he noticed Yocke he gave no sign.

'Any of your guys hurt?' Yocke asked the lieutenant, who was assembling his men.

'One. Flesh wound. But two National Guardsmen charged in when the shooting first started and they got zapped.'

'How many gunmen were there?'

'Five, I think.'

'And the civilians?'

'Seven wounded, forty-two dead.'

Yocke was poised to ask another question when the walkie-talkie squawked to life and the lieutenant walked away with the device to his ear.

The reporter looked around helplessly. Twisted and bloody bodies lay everywhere. Packages and attaché cases scattered about, here and there a shopping bag. He walked over to one woman and carefully picked up the wrapped Christmas presents that lay strewn randomly around her. There must be something, some gesture he could make to the arbiter of man's fate that would commend this woman's humanity. A prayer? But the grim god already knew. He placed the packages in a neat, pathetic pile beside the slack body.

She had been shot in the back, apparently as she tried to run from the obscene horror behind her.

Forty-two! My God!

Where will it end? Yocke wondered gloomily as a wave of revulsion and loathing swept over him. He averted his eyes and turned away.

Henry Charon stood in an empty third-floor office on L Street and scanned the traffic on the street below yet again. From where he stood he had an excellent view of the streetlight and the cars queuing there waiting for the light to turn green. And he could see the drivers.

The drivers sat behind the wheels of their vehicles waiting for the light to change with the look of distracted impatience that indelibly marked those who endured life in the big city. Some of them fiddled with the radios, but most just sat staring at the brake lights on the car ahead and occasionally glancing at the stoplight hanging above the intersection. When the light turned green they crept across the intersection and joined the block-long queue for the next light.

This was a good place. Excellent. A stand, like that one above the red-rock canyon where he had killed seven elk over the years. The elk would come up through the canyon from the aspen groves every evening about the same time.

He would be along soon. He was a creature of habit, like the elk. Regardless of traffic or weather, he always came this way. Or he had on the four evenings in the past that Henry Charon had watched. Yet even if he chose another route this evening – there was a chance that would happen, although slim – sooner or later he would again come this way. That was inevitable, like the evening habits of the deer and elk and bear.

Beside Charon was the rifle. This one was less than perfect; no doubt the stock was poorly bedded. But it would do. This would not be a long shot. No more than sixty yards.

A round was chambered in the rifle and the magazine contained three more. Henry Charon rarely needed more than one shot but he was ready, just in case. Although the habits of living things were predictable, random events happened to us all.

Henry Charon didn't move and he didn't fidget. He stood easily, almost immobile, watching. His ability to wait was one of his best qualities. Not waiting like the urban commuters, impatiently, distractedly, but waiting like the lion or the fox – silent, still, ever alert, always ready.

His eyes left the cars and went across the pedestrians and the people looking at headlines and making purchases at the sidewalk newsstand on the far corner beside the entrance to the Metro station. The vendor was warmly dressed and wore a Cossack hat with the muff down over his ears. His breath made great steaming clouds in the gloomy evening.

Charon's restless eyes scanned the cars yet again, then watched them creep across the intersection. One man blocked the crosswalk with his car when the light changed on him and he sat unperturbed staring straight ahead as pedestrians walked around the car, front and back, and glared at him.

Now he saw it – the car he was waiting for. Henry Charon lifted the binoculars to his eyes and adjusted the focus. Yes. It was *him*.

Charon looked at the cars ahead of his man with a practiced eye, estimating how many would get through the next green light. About six. That would bring this car down to third in line. Perfect.

Henry Charon laid the binoculars down and picked up the rifle. He checked the safety. Still on.

He looked again at the pedestrians, at the other cars, at the bag lady on the far side of the street rooting through a trash can.

The light changed and the traffic moved. One, two, three . . . six! Yes. The car he wanted was right there, third one back.

Henry Charon raised the rifle to his shoulder as he thumbed off the safety. The crosshairs came immediately into his line of vision without his even tilting his head. He put them on the driver, on his head, on his ear. Automatically Charon breathed deeply and exhaled. He was squeezing the trigger even before all the air had left his lungs.

The report and recoil came almost immediately. Charon brought the scope back into line and looked.

Good shot!

He laid the rifle down and walked briskly to the door, pulled it open and closed it behind him, making sure it locked. He passed the elevator and took the stairs downward two at a time.

Out onto the street – around the corner from where the victim sat dead in his car – and away at a diagonal. Charon stripped off the latex gloves from his hands and thrust them into the first trash can he came to. His car was in a garage five blocks away. He walked briskly, unhurriedly, scanning the faces of the people on the sidewalk with his practiced hunter's eye.

With all of the wounded and most of the dead removed from the underground Metro station, Jake Grafton, Yocke, and Tarkington went back the way they had come in. The chairman of the Joint Chiefs, General Hayden Land, was standing with the major general in the middle of a knot of people in uniform by the main entrance.

Grafton went over to the group and stood where General Land could see him and he could hear every thing that was said.

Toad Tarkington stood near the door to the mall. He pointed the rifle he was carrying at the sky and examined the action. His face was intense, grim.

A question popped to mind as Yocke watched Toad. Would the naval officer have used it? No, he had made the mistake of asking the wrong question once already today, and as he looked at Toad, he thought he knew the answer. Yocke was still feeling the aftereffects of the adrenaline. Somehow, for a reason he couldn't quite fathom, Toad seemed the proper person to tell. 'I was pretty pumped up back there.'

'Uh-huh,' Tarkington muttered and glanced at the reporter, then resumed his scrutiny of the weapon.

Yocke couldn't let it alone. 'You know, you can watch a hundred movies and see the carnage every night in the hospital, but nothing prepares you for that feding when the bullets are zinging by and you realize that every second could be your absolute last.' He snapped his fingers. 'Like that, life for you might stop right here. Like it did for all those folks down there on those subway platforms.'

Toad finished his inspection of the rifle and held it, butt on his hip, pointed at the sky. He surveyed the knot of senior officers and the smooth-faced soldiers in battle dress and glanced up at the steel-gray sky. 'I don't know how much life insurance you got,' Toad said, 'but if you're going to trail along behind Jake Grafton, you'd better get some more.' Without waiting for a reply Toad wandered off to find the soldier who had lent him the rifle.

Yocke watched him go.

The brass was still in conference. And here comes Samantha Strader, as I live and breathe. She marched over to the group and joined it. His reporter's juices flowing, Jack Yocke managed to squeeze between the shoulders of two aides.

One of the men talking was not in uniform, although he had that look. Yocke whispered to the man beside him, who whispered back, 'FBI. Guy named Hooper.'

That would be Special Agent Thomas F. Hooper. Yocke made a note as Hooper spoke to General Land. '. . . they came in on a freighter last week. At least twenty of them, armed to the teeth, paid to commit suicide.'

'So there's probably going to be more of this?' General Land said.

'Yes,' Hooper told him.

'Do your sources have any feel for their targets?'

That was Jake Grafton speaking.

'Anywhere there are people,' Hooper replied. 'The more people, the better for them.'

'Well, Captain?' General Land said.

'If we could just get everybody to stay home for a couple of days, sir, and use the time to search house-to-house – every building, every store, every apartment – a couple of days would do it. If we shut down all the public transportation and forbid everyone to use their cars, we could do it.'

'FBI?'

Hooper pulled at his earlobe. 'That's my recommendation too, General.'

'General Greer.'

Greer was the general in direct charge of the National Guard and army units, which had been integrated into one command. He considered for ten seconds. 'That's probably the only way, I think. We've got to find these people and keep crowds from congregating while we do it. Those are the priorities.'

'We're only four days away from Christmas,' Congresswoman Strader noted aloud.

Land glanced at her, then back to Greer and Hooper. 'Okay. You've got two days to find these people. Nothing moves inside the beltway unless it's a military or emergency vehicle. I want a concrete plan on how you're going to do this on my desk in three hours.'

'General, I suggest we shut everything down at midnight,' Jake Grafton added. 'Be a nightmare trying to do it any other way.'

'Midnight it is,' said General Land. He didn't get to be a four-star general by being indecisive. 'That'll give us eight hours to figure out how we're going to get this unscrewed.'

Jack Yocke scribbled furiously, bitterly aware of the irony of his position. He was hearing the scoop of the decade only because Jake Grafton had made him promise not to print anything.

Then he became aware that somehow he was no longer in the circle of people. Apparently the group had moved, almost ten feet, no doubt because General Land had moved. Wherever the chairman was was going to be the center of the action. Yocke rejoined the conference.

'. . . that negotiation is key to resolving situations like we had here today without bloodshed,' Strader was saying, her voice firm and businesslike. Lecturing to the anthropoids, Yocke thought, and jotted the impression down.

General Land's reply was inaudible.

Strader's voice carried. 'Why haven't you consulted with the FBI crisis-response team? They're expert at negotiating with terrorists and criminals in hostage situations.'

This time Yocke caught the reply. 'This was not a terrorist or a hostage situation, ma'am. These men were out to kill as many people as possible. This was an atrocity pure and simple and the men who did it knew they were going to die.'

'*You* don't know that!'

'I know a *war* when I'm in one, *madam.*'

'And I'm telling you that you don't know *what* those men wanted because General Greer didn't take the time to *talk* to them. Those men might be prisoners if General Greer had *talked* instead of charging in willy-nilly shooting everybody in sight.'

'Madam—' General Land began icily.

Strader chopped him off and bored in for the kill. 'The aggressive behavior of *your* troops may be the reason those men shot all these civilians.'

'General Greer did exactly the right thing. These people didn't *want* to talk,' Land's voice had a razor-sharp edge. 'They were too busy chasing down unarmed men and women and slaughtering them like rabbits. They might have laid down their arms, it's true, *after* they killed everyone in sight.'

'. . . lives at stake here.'

'When are you goddamn dithering fools gonna figure out *you can't negotiate with people who don't want to negotiate?*' The general's voice was a roar, the anger palpable. 'Now I've listened to all of the free advice I can stomach. I've got better things to do than stand here and shoot the shit with some civilian! Who the hell *are* you, anyway?'

'I'm Congresswoman Strader. I'm on the presidential commission to—'

'You can do your investigation later. Not now! Not here!'

'You wouldn't say that if I were a *man*! I've got a pass signed by—'

'*Major,*' the general barked, 'get her political ass out of my face, right fucking now.'

'Yes, *sir*!'

Infuriated, her face the color of a scalded lobster, Sam Strader was firmly escorted away.

When Jack Yocke had the last of it in his notebook in his private shorthand, he looked up, straight into the bemused face of Toad Tarkington.

'What we got here,' Tarkington said, 'is a total entertainment package. Write that down too.'

'Tarkington!' It was Grafton calling.

Yocke followed the young naval officer.

'Let's go,' Jake Grafton said. He began trotting toward the military sedan. 'Someone just shot the Chief Justice of the Supreme Court.'

'Is he dead?'

'Apparently.'

27

Henry Charon parked the car a block from the New Hampshire Avenue apartment and walked. The streetlights were on and the sky was dark Raindrops were beginning to splatter on the pavement and poing on the car roofs.

One of the cars near the apartment house was the green VW bug wearing its trendy bumper stickers. Ah yes, the sweater lady.

He paused in the entryway and used his key on the mailbox. As he suspected it contained the usual circulars and junk mail addressed to 'Occupant.' He put them in his pocket. He didn't want mail to accumulate in the box because very soon now someone would look through that little window. An FBI agent or police officer, or maybe a soldier, but *someone*. Someone hunting him.

He looked again up and down the street. The rain was getting heavier. Perhaps setting in for the night.

The cold felt good. When you live in the wild long enough you get used to the cold. You learn to endure it and never feel it. It's a part of everything and you fit in and adapt or you perish.

Henry Charon was good at that. He had learned to adapt. Becoming a part of his surroundings was his whole life.

So he stood for a few more seconds and let the cold and dampness seep over him as he listened to the tinny sound of the raindrops striking the cars.

Then he inserted his key in the doorlock and went inside.

The door to the first apartment was ajar and he could hear the television. This was where the apartment manager lived, the sweater lady, Grisella Clifton.

Wouldn't hurt to be seen for a moment. He paused at the door and raised his hand to knock.

She was seated in a stuffed chair in front of the television with a cat on her lap. Charon pushed the door open a few more inches. Now he could see the television. And hear the words:

'. . . an artist's conception of the man who shot and wounded attorney general Gideon Cohen yesterday at the Capitol in what may have been an attempt on the life of Vice-President Dan Quayle. This man is armed and very dangerous. If you see this man, do *not* attempt to apprehend or approach him, but notify the police immediately. At the bottom of the screen you will see a number to call if you think you might have seen this man. Please write this number down. And take a good, careful look.'

On the screen was an artist's line drawing. Charon stared. Yes, the artist had got him. Probably from that woman he had met in the lobby as he was leaving the building. Who would have thought she had gotten that good a look? Damn!

The cat saw him and tensed. Grisella Clifton turned and caught sight of him.

'Oh! You startled me, Mr Tackett.'

'Sorry. I was about to knock.'

She rose from her chair and turned toward him. The cat scurried away. 'I'm so sorry. I guess I heard the outside door open, but I was just so engrossed in this . . . this . . .'

She turned back toward the television. The artist's effort was still on the screen. She looked from the television to Charon, then back to the television.

He saw it in her face.

She drew her breath in sharply and her hand came up to cover her mouth. Her eyes widened.

'Oh! My *God*!'

He stood there trying to decide what to do.

'You're *him*! You tried to *kill* Vice-President Quayle!'

'No, I didn't,' Henry Charon said automatically, slightly irritated. He had been shooting at Gideon Cohen! And hit him too. That was one hell of a fine shot!

He saw her chest expand as she sucked in air. She was going to scream.

Without conscious thought he had balanced his weight on the balls of his feet, so now he pushed out toward her in one fluid motion with his hands outstretched.

Thanos Liarakos didn't know what made him turn his head to the right, but he did. She was sitting on a park bench there amid the naked black trees, the streetlight limning her.

He sat behind the wheel of the car staring, uncertain, yet at some level deep down very, very sure.

The man in the car behind laid on his horn.

Liarakos took his foot off the brake and let the car move. He went around the block looking for a parking place. Nothing. Not a single vacant spot. He jammed the gas pedal down and shot down the next street. Every spot full!

Around the corner, looking, the frustration welling rapidly.

He began to swear. The goddamn city, the goddamn traffic engineers and the goddamn planning board that let them remodel these goddamn row houses without driveways and garages – he cussed them all while he thought about Elizabeth.

There, a fireplug. He pulled in beside it and killed the engine. He hit the automatic door lock button on the door and was off and running even as the door slammed shut.

Elizabeth! Sitting out in the rain on a dismal cold night like this. Oh God – if there is a god up there – how could you do this to gentle Elizabeth? Why?

He jogged the last block and darted into the street to see around a tree that was in the way. In the process he was almost run over, but he dodged the delivery van and dashed across the traffic. Another Christian soul laid on his horn and squealed his brakes.

Liarakos paid no attention. On the edge of the park he halted and looked again.

She was still sitting there. Hadn't moved.

He walked forward.

As he passed a bench, still seventy-five feet from her, a derelict huddled there spoke: 'Hey man, I hate to ask this, but have you got any loose change you could . . .'

She wasn't looking around. She was sitting there staring downward, apparently oblivious of the cold and the cutting wind and the steady rain that was already starting to soak Liarakos.

'Some loose change would help, man.' The derelict was following him. He was aware of it but didn't bother to look behind him.

Her hands were in her coat pockets. The good coat she had worn to the clinic was gone, and in its place she wore a thin, faded cotton thing that looked as if it wouldn't warm a rabbit. Her hair was a sodden, dripping mess. She didn't look up.

'Elizabeth.'

She continued to stare at the ground. He squatted and looked up into her face. It was her all right. The corners of her lips were tilted up in a wan little smile.

Her eyes moved to his face, but they looked without recognition.

'Man, it's a damn cold night and a cup of coffee would do for me, you know? I had some troubles in my life and some of them wasn't my fault. How about some Christian charity for a poor ol' nigger. A little change wouldn't be much to you, but to me . . .'

He found his wallet and extracted a bill without taking his eyes off Elizabeth. He passed the bill back.

'God, this is a *twenty*! Are you—'

'Take it. And leave.'

'Thanks, mister.'

Her face had a glow about it. Aww, *fuck*! She was as high as a flag on the Fourth of July.

'I tell you, man,' the derelict said, ''cause you been real generous with me. She's in big trouble. She's strung out real bad, man.'

'Please leave.'

'Yeah.'

The footsteps shuffled away.

He reached out and caressed her face, pressed her hand between his.

The rain continued to fall. She sat with her thin, frozen smile amid the pigeon shit on the park bench among the glistening black trees, staring at nothing at all.

'So what can you tell me?' Jake Grafton asked the FBI lab man.

'Not much,' the investigator said, scratching his head. They were standing in the room from which the assassin had shot Chief Justice Longstreet. The rifle lay on the table. Everything in sight was covered by the fine dark grit of fingerprint dust.

'Apparently no fresh prints. We got a bunch, but I doubt that our guy left any. Be a fluke if he did.'

'Where did the bullet hit the Chief Justice?'

'About one inch above the left ear. Killed instantly. Haven't got the bullet yet. It went through the victim, through the upholstery and the sheet metal and buried itself in the asphalt of the street. Rifle is a thirty-oh-six, same caliber and make as the one that fired the bullet into the attorney general. Same brand of scope, and I suspect, the same brand of gun oil and so forth.'

The floor of the room in which they were standing had a fine layer of dust on it, and it showed tracks, a lot of tracks, so many in fact that the individual footprints ran together.

'Did you guys make all these?' Jake asked gloomily.

'No, as a matter of fact. Sort of curious, but the guy who did the shooting seemed to come into the room, go to the window, and stay there. He made some footprints, but not many, considering. He didn't have nervous feet.'

'Nervous feet,' Jake repeated.

The lab man seemed to be searching for words. 'He wasn't real excited, if you know what I mean.'

'A pro,' Toad Tarkington prompted.

'Maybe,' the FBI agent said. 'Maybe not. But he's a cool customer.'

The military curfew was announced at seven P.M., to take effect at midnight. Anyone on the streets between the hours of midnight and seven A.M. would be subject to arrest and prosecution by military tribunal for failure to obey emergency orders. Anyone on the streets *in a vehicle* between the hours of seven A.M. and midnight would also be subject to arrest. This curfew would be in effect for forty-eight hours, unless it was ended sooner or extended.

The order was news from coast to coast along with the murder of Supreme Court Chief Justice Harlan Longstreet and the subway massacre. The death toll continued to mount as two of the wounded succumbed to their injuries. One of them was a pregnant woman.

The mood of the nation, as reflected by man-on-the-street television interviews, was outrage. Politicians of stature were calling for an invasion of Colombia. Several wanted to declare war. Senator Bob Cherry was in the latter group. Ferried from newsroom to newsroom by limo, he abandoned his point-by-point criticism of Vice-president Quayle's efforts and lambasted the administration as unprepared and incompetent. He demanded the troops be pulled out of Washington and sent to Colombia.

On the other hand. Senator Hiram Duquesne and several of his colleagues journeyed to the Vice-President's office in the Executive Office Building that evening to offer their wholehearted support. They appeared before the cameras afterward and, in a rare show of unity, laid aside all partisan differences to praise the Vice-President's handling of the crisis.

Most of the people in the nation spent the evening in front of their televisions. One of those who watched was T. Jefferson Brody. He was sneering at Duquesne's image on the tube when the telephone rang.

The man calling he had never met, but he had heard his name several times and vaguely remembered that he did something or other for Freeman McNally.

'McNally's dead.'

The news stunned Brody. There were a hundred questions he wanted to ask, but since he didn't know where the man was calling from – the line might be tapped – he refrained.

After cradling the instrument, he used the remote control to turn off the television.

Freeman dead! First Willie Teal, now Freeman.

T. Jefferson pursed his lips and silently whistled. Well, it's a dangerous business, no question about that. That's why they made so much money at it.

What was he doing for Freeman? Oh, yes, the senators. Well, that was spilt milk. But it was a hook he might use later on somebody else's behalf. If and when. He would see.

And because his mind worked that way, Brody's thoughts immediately turned to Sweet Cherry Lane, the big-titted, cock-stroking bitch who had conned and robbed him. Freeman had been unwilling to assist in that little project, but now Freeman and his reasons – whatever they were –

were gone, leaving Brody in possession of the field. Bernie Shapiro hadn't been very enthusiastic either, but he would approach him again.

So T. Jefferson sat staring at the blank television screen and thinking graphic thoughts about what he would like to do to Sweet Cherry Lane. His lips twisted into a smile. This army curfew would be over in a few days, and then. . .

Ah, yes. And *then*!

At nine that night Toad Tarkington and Jack Yocke sat in a military pool vehicle with the engine and heater going, trying to stay warm. Yocke was behind the wheel. Since he knew the city so well Grafton had appointed him duty driver. Toad sat in the backseat.

The two naval officers had spent the evening at the Pentagon drafting the orders and plans for the chairman to sign and had picked up Yocke at the *Post* fifteen minutes ago.

Through the windshield they watched Jake Grafton and an army officer huddled over a map spread out on the hood of a jeep. The jeep was parked on the sidewalk under an apartment house entrance awning.

The rain continued to fall, drumming on the roof of the car in which Toad and Yocke sat.

'Grafton seems like an awful quiet guy for a successful military officer,' Yocke said just to break the silence.

Toad snorted. 'You're a reporter.'

'What d'ya mean?'

'The guy can talk your leg off. You haven't heard him at the office! What you gotta have to get ahead in the military is credibility. People have to pay attention when you voice an opinion, they have to believe that you know what you're talking about. Grafton's got credibility with a capital C.'

Yocke digested this information as he watched Grafton and the army officer. The army guy was wearing camouflage utilities, a thick coat, and a helmet. In contrast, Jake Grafton wore washed khakis, a green flight-deck coat, and a bridge cap with a khaki cover.

Yocke had had a good look at that green coat when Grafton got out of the car. It had grease stains on it in several places, no doubt souvenirs from one of the ships Grafton had been on. The trousers were no better. In spite of being washed so many times they looked faded, the grease stains were still visible. Sitting in the backseat, Tarkington was togged out about like Grafton, except that his heavy coat was khaki.

'Where do you navy officers get grease on your uniforms?'

'Flight deck,' Toad muttered, and declined to say anything else.

Yocke looked at his watch. He would like to find a few minutes to call Tish Samuels. Maybe after the next stop.

Grafton came back to the car and climbed into the passenger seat. His coat and hat were dripping. He left the door ajar, so the overhead courtesy light stayed on. The captain extracted a map from his pocket and studied it. After a few moments he held it so the other two men could see it.

'Okay. They are searching door to door in these grids here and here and here.' His finger rested on each in turn. 'This third one they'll finish in about a half hour. There's just time for that battalion to do one more before knocking off for the night. Which one do you think they ought to do?'

Toad and Yocke stared at the map. 'This is a little like roulette,' Toad remarked.

'Yep,' Jake Grafton said. 'Go ahead. Pick a winner.'

Yocke pointed. 'Why not this one? It has some warehouses and some public housing projects. Those are likely. These projects – you could run four or five Colombians who don't speak a word of English into a room and they could stay for weeks with no one the wiser. And even if the neighbors are suspicious, they won't call the cops. They know better.'

'Sold me.' Grafton sighed. He got out of the car and went back to the jeep with the radio equipment.

In about a minute he returned. 'Drive,' he said.

With the car in motion, Jake turned to Toad. 'Your wife home tonight?'

'Yessir.'

'Think she'd like to ride around with us?'

'Sure. If we swing by that way, I'll run up and get her.'

Toad gave Jack Yocke the address. When they pulled up in front, Jake said, 'Tell her to put on a uniform, as old and grungy as she's got.'

Toad nodded and walked quickly into the building.

'Nice of you to think of that,' Jack Yocke said.

'She's only got ten more days of leave left, and I can't spare him.'

'Off the record, way off, what do you do over at the Pentagon, anyway?'

Grafton chuckled. 'Well, I'm the senior officer in a little group of seven or eight people that do the staff work on military cooperation with antidrug efforts.'

'That doesn't tell me much.'

'Hmm. For example, we more or less have one carrier in the Gulf of Mexico and eastern Caribbean on a full-time basis now. That was one of my projects. I lost.'

'Lost? Isn't that a good idea?'

'That's just the trouble. Sounds like a terrific idea on the evening news or when some politician makes a speech in Philadelphia. Have a shipload of planes fly around over the ocean looking for boats and take pictures and call the Coast Guard when they see one. So a carrier home from six or seven months in the Mediterranean has to forgo maintenance and go sail around down there. The squadrons have money for a limited number of flight hours for each crew during the turnaround between cruises. With that money they have to train the new guys and keep the experienced crews sharp. Instead they spend the money to fly around in circles over the water. No one gets trained. The ships and planes don't get the proper maintenance. And when they're finished down south, we send them back to the Med.'

'But it sounds good in Philadelphia,' Yocke said. 'Honestly, that *is* important.'

'No doubt. But if we have to send untrained people into combat in Libya or the Middle East, they're going to *die*. They haven't had the necessary training. We'll lose airplanes we can't afford to lose. And even if we dance between the raindrops and don't have to fight, the ships will need more maintenance later, a lot more. Prophet that I am, I can tell you that when that day comes the money won't be available. Congress will say. Sorry about that. Haven't you heard about the savings-and-loan disaster and the deficit and the peace dividend?

'And our sailors and junior aviators don't want to spend their Jives at sea. So they get out of the service and we have to spend megabucks to recruit and train new people. It's really a vicious cycle.'

Grafton took a deep breath and exhaled slowly. 'My group documents the cost of the choices. We explain the options to the decision makers. That's what I do.'

Yocke wanted to keep Grafton talking. He changed the subject. 'I've been looking at these soldiers today. They look pretty young to be carrying loaded rifles through the streets of a city.'

'They *are* young. But they're good kids. They joined the Army to get a little piece of the American dream – a job, money for an education later, to learn a skill, to earn some respect. Young men have been joining the military for those reasons for thousands of years.'

'Can they fight?'

'You bet your ass. They're as good as any soldiers who ever wore an American uniform.'

'But they're not trained for the way you're using them.'

'Nope.'

The door to the apartment building opened and Rita Moravia and Toad Tarkington came out. Jack Yocke suppressed a grin. Moravia was a beautiful woman, but dressed in khaki trousers, a heavy coat, boater hat and flying boots, she didn't look the part.

'Hey, Rita,' Jake Grafton said.

'Captain. Mr Yocke.'

'Jack. Please.'

'Thanks for including me on your expedition. What's on the agenda?'

'Let's go watch the guys do a housing project.' Jake consulted the map. 'The Jefferson projects. You know where that is?' he asked Yocke.

'Yeah. I've been there before.' Yocke pulled the transmission lever into drive and got the car under way.

The supermarket parking lot was unexpectedly crowded. Charon walked between the parked cars and by the people pushing shopping carts to the pay phone mounted on the wall, beside a row of newspaper vending stands. He glanced around to ensure no one was within earshot. The shoppers were too busy with their own affairs. Charon peeled back the leather glove on his left wrist to reveal his watch. Then he removed the telephone from its hook. He read the instructions. No coin needed for emergency calls. Saved a quarter, anyway.

He dialed 911.

The phone rang three times before a woman said, 'Police emergency.'

He spoke quickly, as fast as possible. 'There's a woman being murdered in an apartment house on New Hampshire Avenue, I can hear the screams.' He gave the address. 'Better hurry.' He hung up quickly and walked back to his car, which was parked in the darkest corner of the lot with a fringe of trees and shrubs behind, blocking the view. Still, anyone in the lot could see him clearly if they only took the time to look. Predictably they didn't.

He removed his gear from the trunk and carried it twenty feet away. Then he got out the plastique and the timing device and put them on the floor of the driver's seat. He inserted the fuse in the plastique and very carefully set the timer. He watched it tick on the LCD display for several seconds. Satisfied, he reached into the backseat and got the one-gallon milk jug. He put that on the floor beside the plastique and unscrewed the lid. Between the lid and the jug he had used a piece of plastic wrap to ensure a good seal. Now he peeled it off and tossed it on the seat with the red plastic screw cap.

The vapors from the gasoline in the jug would fill the interior of the car. When the bomb went off in an hour the gasoline vapors would enhance the explosion and ensure that a very hot fire resulted. If everything worked as he thought it would, there would be no fingerprints left for the police. The confusion and uncertainty caused by the bomb would also slow the manhunt.

He had rigged up a half pound of plastique. That was a lot. Maybe too much. Too bad he hadn't had time to play with this stuff and get a better feel for the proper quantity to use.

The car keys were still in the ignition. Better remove those. No use tempting some kid to break the window before this thing pops. He put the keys under the seat.

What else?

That's it. He pushed down the door lock and carefully shut the door. It clicked. He then pushed hard until it closed completely with another click.

The first police officers on the scene double-parked. The driver locked his car door and stood on the sidewalk listening while his partner walked around the car as he checked to see if the shotgun was loaded. It was. He ensured the safety was on.

'I don't hear any screams.'

'Me either.'

They had just started up the stairs when the building literally blew apart. Both officers died instantly. As the fireball expanded it seared the paint on cars a hundred feet away.

The backup officers two blocks away on New Hampshire saw the explosion and called it in. As the seconds ticked away the rubble heap that had been a building became a roaring inferno.

The first fire truck arrived four minutes after the explosion. Fireman flaked out their hoses and opened hydrants. More police cars rushed to the scene and additional fire trucks were directed in.

Sixteen minutes after the initial blast a green 1968 Volkswagen beetle parked a hundred feet away from the apartment building blew up. Investigators later estimated the car contained four pounds of Semtex, a Czechoslovakian plastic explosive. Pieces of the vehicle were found on the roofs of buildings as far away as a hundred and twenty yards.

Seven firemen working on a pumping truck parked beside the VW were killed in the blast. Flying debris decapitated a policeman fifty feet away. The glass in every window on the block that faced the street was blown in, cutting one woman so badly she bled to death. Over a dozen people were injured by flying glass and debris.

The police had sealed the block when Jake Grafton and his junior officers arrived. They stood for a few minutes at the police line and watched the fire in the center of the block rage unchecked. They could just see members of the police bomb squad going down the rows of parked cars, checking each one.

Jake Grafton sent Toad to make a phone call. The military had better have some EOD teams – explosive ordnance disposal – nearby if needed.

Bombs. Terrorists? Or our shooter that lacked the nervous feet?

Nervous feet. What a silly thing to say. The assassin didn't have nervous feet.

'Captain Grafton?' A uniformed patrolman asked the question.

'Yes?'

'There's an FBI agent at police headquarters asking for you, sir. They want you to go down there, if you can.'

'Sure, Tell them I'm on my way.'

'Okay.'

Jake looked around. Yocke was talking to Rita. He would know where police headquarters were. Jake had no idea.

It wasn't a real forest, of course. Here on the side of the ridge in Rock Creek Park where Henry Charon stood the traffic noise was loud. Too loud. It would drown out the noises he needed to hear if anyone came along. Not that that was very likely on a winter's night like this. Rain, cold, wind. Perfect.

He continued slowly up the ridge, making no noise at all as he moved across the wet ground without a flashlight. On his back was a pack that contained his supplies. A sleeping bag on a string hung from one shoulder.

His weapons were in a long gym bag he carried in his right hand. Three grenades, a disassembled rifle, and plenty of ammunition. Under his coat he carried a pistol. The silencer was in his pocket.

He found the little notch in the rocks without difficulty. His woods sense led him unerringly to it. He felt around carefully. Good! The cache in the crack above his head was undisturbed.

He lowered the bags to the ground and slipped away from the cave. He circled it in the darkness, taking his time, pausing often to listen and look. In ten minutes he returned to the cave and began unpacking.

He fixed a can of hot stew on a Sterno burner, taking care that the light of the small flame was not visible from the slope below. When he had finished eating and had cleaned up, he got the radio down from the crack where he had cached it and inserted the earpiece. Then he pulled out the antenna and settled down cross-legged in the dry, sheltered area at the rear of the cave to listen.

First the television audio. Since they were covering the crisis on a continuous basis, the networks had a habit of summarizing the news every half hour. He didn't have long to wait.

The chaos on New Hampshire Avenue exceeded his expectations. No fingerprints, no evidence for the police to sift from the apartment. Henry Charon smiled. He didn't smile often and never for someone else's benefit. His smiles were strictly for himself.

The military curfew was news to him and he listened carefully, thoughtfully, trying to calculate what it all meant.

Obviously the troops were looking primarily for terrorists, armed Colombians. If they discovered him it would be solely by accident.

When he had schemed and laid his plans he had never considered the possibility of troops. But he knew there would be unexpected complications so he was not unduly worried. As he sat there in the darkness thinking about it, it seemed to him that the thing to do was to stay holed up until the troops found the terrorists and life on the streets returned to normal. Then once again he could melt into the crowds.

The fact that his picture had been widely disseminated didn't concern him. He had spent too many years as an anonymous face. He had dealt at the same gas station in New Mexico for five years before the owner began to recognize and greet him. And in a city the size of Washington the inhabitants studiously ignore the faces they see, avoiding eye contact. This was no small town. Human nature would protect him.

He tuned the radio to another frequency band, the police band, and experimented until he heard the dispatcher. He would listen for an hour. That would give him a feel for what was happening in the city.

Of course, he could walk out of the District tonight and steal a car in the suburbs and be on his way back to New Mexico when the sun rose, but no. There were two names left on that list Tassone had given him – General Hayden Land and William C. Dorfman. Which should he try first?

Or should he forget about those two and make another try at Bush? About the only way to get Bush now would be to blow up the whole hospital. That would be a project! Impractical to hope one man could successfully accomplish such a project on short notice of course, but interesting to think about. This was getting to be fun.

And once again Henry Charon, the assassin, smiled to himself.

'All calls to nine-one-one are recorded,' Special Agent Hooper explained. 'I thought someone from the military might want to listen to this, just for the record, since you guys are sort of in charge right now.'

'I like your delicate phrasing – "sort of in charge." '

'Anyway, I called over to the Pentagon and they suggested you. The people at Guard headquarters said you would be wherever something was happening.'

Jake let that one go by.

'Anyway, we'll have this tape analyzed by a computer for background noise, voice prints, all of it. We'll eventually get everything there is to get. But I thought you might like to give it a listen.'

'Where?'

'Up here.' Hooper led the way up a set of stairs. Toad, Rita, and Yocke trailed along behind Jake.

'*There's a woman being murdered in an apartment house on New Hampshire Avenue. I can hear the screams. Nineteen-fourteen New Hampshire. Better hurry.*'

Hooper played the tape three times.

'He's talking too fast.'

'He doesn't want to stay on the line very long.'

'He's from the Midwest.'

'He's white.'

'He sure as hell isn't Colombian.'

'Captain,' said Tom Hooper, looking at Grafton. He had sat silently while Toad and Yocke hashed it over.

Jake Grafton shrugged. 'He could have edited that down if he had wanted. Even talking fast, he stayed on the line longer than necessary.'

'What do you mean?'

'He could have said as little as this: "*Nineteen-fourteen New Hampshire. I can hear the screams.*" '

'So?'

'So. You asked what I think. That's what I think.'

'Maybe he's smart,' Jack Yocke said. 'Would the dispatcher have sent two officers over Code Red if all she had had was an address and reported screams?'

Hooper thought about it. 'I don't know. I'll ask. Maybe not.'

'So it's hurried and wordy and breathless. Unrehearsed, if you will. And it gets immediate action.'

'It did,' Hooper acknowledged. 'Officers were there in three minutes. The bomb exploded thirty seconds later.'

'Lot of fire,' Rita Moravia commented. 'I wouldn't have expected that.'

'Probably gasoline,' Hooper told her.

Jake Grafton checked his watch. He needed to get back to the National Guard Armory and talk to General Greer. And call General Land.

'You going to be in your office in the morning?' he asked Hooper.

'Yes.'

'Could you give me a rundown on what you have on the assassin at that time?'

'Sure. But it isn't much.'

'About ten.'

'Ten it is,' Jake Grafton said and turned his gaze to his entourage. 'Well, children, the night is young. Let's get busy.'

Henry Charon's sedan exploded right on schedule, just as Jake Grafton was leaving police headquarters. The glass in the huge windows of the nearby grocery store disintegrated and rained down on the unusually large crowd, people there to stock up on food for the next few days. Six people were injured, three critically. Miraculously, no one was near the sedan when it blew, but four parked cars were destroyed by the blast and the intense heat. The fire in the parking lot was burning so fiercely by the time the fire department arrived that the asphalt was also ablaze.

The assassin heard the calls on the police radio frequency. Satisfied, he turned the radio off and replaced it in the dry niche in the rock above his head, then slipped from the cave for another scout around. All he could hear were the sounds of vehicles passing below, and they were becoming infrequent.

The wind was cold, the rain still coming down.

As he undressed and crawled into his sleeping bag he reviewed the events of the last few days. Lying there in the darkness pleasantly tired, feeling the warmth of the bag, Henry Charon sighed contentedly and drifted off to sleep.

28

When Jake Grafton arrived at the National Guard Armory, over a dozen young men and three women were being led into the building in handcuffs. The troops escorting them pushed them roughly along with their rifle butts. One woman who refused to walk was being carried.

'Uh-oh,' Jake muttered as Jack Yocke pulled into a parking place in the lot reserved for government vehicles. As he got out of the car he could hear them cursing, loudly and vehemently. One woman was screaming at the top of her lungs.

The screams followed him down the hall as he headed for General Greer's office.

The soldiers searching the Jefferson projects had run into problems, the general said. People refused to open doors, some had illegal drugs in plain sight, and some verbally and physically attacked the soldiers. The officer in charge, Captain Joe White-Feather, had arrested sixteen of the most vociferous and truculent. He also had, the general said, another eight men on a truck coming in. Some residents of the projects had sworn that these men were drug dealers, and indeed, several pounds of drugs and a quantity of weapons had been recovered by the soldiers.

'We can't *not* arrest them,' the general said, and Jake Grafton glumly nodded his concurrence. In some complex, convoluted way, this whole mess was about illegal drugs and the people who sold and bought them. The soldiers were going to have to address the problem of the sellers and the users whether they or their superiors wanted to or not.

Captain Jake Grafton, naval officer, instinctively recoiled from the implications of the solution. Here was a law-enforcement function pure and simple, yet as the representative of the government on the spot, the soldiers had to do *something*. But what? A problem needing a surgeon's scalpel was going to be addressed with the proverbial blunt instrument, the US Army.

Jake Grafton reached for the phone.

Amazingly enough, no one on the Joint Staff had considered this possible complication. Career officers to a man, they had approached the problem from a purely military standpoint. The time crunch had demanded that logistics and the command, control, and communications functions – C³ – be addressed first. That was about as far as anyone had gotten. Yet the problem was reality *now*.

He got home that night at three A.M. Callie was waiting for him when he came through the door.

'Amy asleep?'

'For hours.'

'Got any coffee?'

She nodded and led the way to the kitchen. When both of them had a cup in front of them and were seated at the kitchen table, she asked, 'How is it going?'

He rubbed his face. 'We're locking up everyone who resists military authority and everyone in possession of drugs. Holding them down at the armory. The jails are full.'

'You're exhausted, Jake.'

'Without a doubt, this is one of the worst days of my life. God, *what a mess!* We're all in over our heads – General Land, General Greer, me, every soldier on the street.'

'Did you have any dinner?'

'Wasn't hungry.'

She headed for the refrigerator.

'Please, Callie, I don't want anything. I'm too tired. I'm going to take a shower and fall into the rack.'

'We saw you and Toad on television. Outside L'Enfant Plaza.'

'An atrocity, like something the Nazis did to the Jews. I wouldn't have believed it if I hadn't seen it with my own eyes. *Evil.* You could feel it. Wanton murder on a grand scale.'

She came over and put her arms around his shoulders. 'What kind of people would do that to other people?' she murmured.

Jake Grafton just shook his head and drank the last of his coffee.

The next morning he stopped by the armory before he went to the FBI building. The rain had slackened and become a mist, under a low ceiling. The streets and wide boulevards looked obscenely empty. Jake passed an occasional military vehicle, some government cars, and the usual police, but nothing else.

All the stoplights were working. He stopped at one, but his was the only car in all four directions. He looked, then went on through.

He was stopped at a roadblock on Constitution Avenue. A soldier standing forward of the door on the passenger's side of the car held an M-16 on him while a sergeant checked his ID card.

The sergeant saluted. 'You can go on now, sir.'

'Let me give you a word of advice. Sergeant. The people we're after will start shooting at the drop of a hat. I suggest you get a couple more riflemen to cover each car as you approach it. And you might park a couple of your trucks sideways in the street here so they can't go barreling through without stopping.'

'Yessir. I'll talk to my lieutenant.'

Ninety-one people were now being detained at the armory. They were being held in unused offices and in the corridors and along the sides of the giant squad bay. The soldiers had been busy. They had obtained chain and padlocks from a hardware store somewhere and were securing belligerent people to radiators and exposed pipes and anything else they could find that looked solid.

Some of the new arrivals cursed and screamed and shouted dire threats, but the ones who had been there a while tried to sleep or sobbed silently. Some of them lay in their own vomit. 'Withdrawal,' one officer told Jake as he walked by trying not to breathe the fetid stench. The soldiers had a couple of military doctors and corpsmen attending these people. Pairs of soldiers took prisoners to the heads one at a time.

Forty or fifty of the prisoners appeared to be just people who had ignored the order to keep their vehicles off the street. These people were sober and well dressed and were busy complaining loudly to an officer who was interviewing them one by one, checking addresses and driver's licenses and writing all the information down, then turning them loose to walk home. The cars stayed in the armory lot.

Jake paused and listened to one of the interviews. The man was doing his best to browbeat the officer, a major. Jake signaled to the major, who left his interviewee in mid-tirade and stepped into the hall. 'What are you doing with jerks like that?'

'Holding the worst ones,' the major said, smiling. He jerked his thumb over his shoulder. 'That one isn't too bad. He just can't get it through my head that the military order didn't apply to him.'

After a hurried conference with General Greer and a look at the map of the city, Jake drove off to FBI headquarters. He picked up Toad Tarkington en route.

Toad sat silently beside Jake and stared at the empty streets and rare pedestrians.

The federal guard at the kiosk at the main entrance of the FBI building telephoned upstairs. Two minutes later a junior agent arrived to take them upstairs. 'Not many people made it to work today,' the agent told them and gestured toward the empty offices. 'We have cars going around picking up people, but we'll only bring in about half of them.'

Hooper was expecting them. He took them into his office and poured coffee from a coffee maker on his credenza. His clothes were rumpled and he needed a shave.

'What's your job, exactly?' he asked Jake.

'The general sort of added me to his staff temporarily. I'm really on the Joint Staff, along with Lieutenant Tarkington here and sixteen hundred other people.'

Hooper had no reply. If the military bureaucracy were half as complicated as the FBI's, further questions would be futile. He glanced at his watch. 'I've got about a half hour. Then I have to give a presentation to the presidential commission, or the Longstreet Commission, which is what I understand they're calling themselves now that Chief Justice Longstreet is one of the victims.'

Without further ado he began: 'As you may know, the President's helicopter was shot down with a couple of Stinger missiles. American manufacture. We're inventorying the Stinger missiles in every ammo depot nationwide and looking at every theft report we have, but we haven't got anything solid yet. We've talked to everybody in a ten-mile radius of the little park on the river that the missiles were fired from, but so far nothing.

'Our best leads are the rifles that were left after the attorney general and the Chief Justice were shot. The rifles are identical, Winchester Model 70s, bolt action in thirty-oh-six caliber. We've tried to trace them both and we've gotten lucky. Ten years ago the rifle that fired the shot that hit the AG was sold by a gun store to a dentist in Pittsburgh. He sold it six weeks ago via a newspaper ad. A man called him about the ad, then showed up an hour later, looked the rifle over, and paid cash. No haggling and no name.

'But we got lucky again. Sometimes it goes like that and sometimes you can't buy a break. The dentist described the man and he had a distinctive tattoo on his forearm. That came up a hit on the national crime computer. Guy name of Melvin Doyle, who as luck would have it was arrested three days ago in Sewickley, Pennsylvania, for beating hell out of his ol' lady. Doyle's done time for grand larceny, forgery, and a variety of misdemeanors.'

Here he handed Jake a computer printout of Doyle's record. Jake glanced at it, then passed it to Toad, who read it through rapidly and laid it back on Hooper's desk.

'Our agents talked to Doyle last night. He was threatened with a charge of federal conspiracy to murder a public official, and he talked. He says he acquired three Model 70s for a guy he knew as Tony Pickle.' He dropped another sheet in front of Jake. 'This is Tony Pickle.

'Guy named Pasquale Piccali, also known as Anthony Tassone. Grew up in the rackets, moved to Dallas in the midseventies. Was involved in S-and-Ls in Texas. Lately been living in Vegas.'

He sat and stared at Jake.

'And,' the captain prompted.

'And that's it,' Hooper said. 'That's all the evidence we have.'

'The second rifle? Was it one of the three?'

'Don't know. Doyle didn't write down serial numbers.'

'Doyle get anything else for Tassone?'

'He denies it. We're looking.'

'Okay, now tell me what you think.'

'Our Texas office is very interested in Tony Pickle. Seems he was a sort of a Mr Fix-it for some real shady S-and-L operators, most of whom are being investigated or are under indictment. It seems that two or three may have stepped beyond the usual bank fraud, kickbacks, cooked books, and insider loan shenanigans. It looks like they got into money laundering. Extremely profitable. Perfect for an S-and-L that was watching a ton of loans go sour and rotten.'

'What does Tassone say about all this?'

'Don't know. We're looking. Haven't found him yet.'

'Who,' Toad asked, speaking for the first time, 'were these S-and-Ls washing money for?'

Special Agent Thomas F. Hooper eyed the junior officer speculatively. 'For the big coke importers. Maybe, roundabout, the Cali or Medellín cartels. That's the smell of it anyway. Lot of money involved,' He pursed his lips for a second. 'A *lot* of money,' he said again, fixing his eyes on the picture of Anthony Tassone.

'Forgive our ignorance,' Jake Grafton said. 'But how much money does the FBI consider to be a lot?'

'Over a billion. At least that.'

'That's a lot,' Toad Tarkington agreed. 'Even over at the Pentagon that's a lot.'

After using every minute of Hooper's half hour, Jake and Toad left the FBI building at about the same time that Deputy Sheriff Willard Grimes pulled his mud-spattered cruiser up to the pump at the gas station-general store at Apache Crossroads, New Mexico. The deputy swabbed the windshield in the wind and bitter cold as the gas trickled into the cruiser's tank.

When he had the nozzle back on the hook, Willard Grimes went inside.

The wind gusted through the clapboard building as he forced the door shut. 'Whew,' he said, 'think it'll ever get warm again?'

''Lo, Willard,' the proprietor said, looking up from the morning paper. 'How many gallons?'

'Sixteen point six,' Willard said, and poured himself a styrofoam cup full of hot, steaming coffee.

The man behind the counter made a note in a small green book, then pushed it over for Willard to sign. Willard scribbled his name with a flourish. He put twenty-six cents on the counter for the coffee.

'How's crime?' the man behind the counter asked.

'Oh, so so,' Willard told him. 'Gonna be trolling for speeders over on the interstate today. Sheriff told me to write at least five out-of-staters. Damn county commissioners are on him again to bring in some more fine money.'

'You know,' the proprietor said, 'the thing I like most about living out here is that there isn't any real crime. Not like those big cities.' He gestured toward the copy of the Sante Fe newspaper lying on the counter.

Deputy Grimes glanced at the paper. There was a drawing right below the headline. Someone's face. 'That the guy who supposedly took a shot at the Vice-President?'

'Yeah. The President, the Vice-President, and half the cabinet. Cutting a swath through Washington, this one is. Making Lee Harvey Oswald look like a goldfish. And you know something funny? When I first saw that picture on TV last night, I said to the wife, I said, "Darn if that don't look like Henry Charon, that lives up in the Twin Buttes area." Crazy how a fellow's mind works when he sees a drawing like that, ain't it?'

'Yeah,' said Willard Grimes, sipping the coffee and looking out the window at the lowering sky above the arrow-straight road pointing toward the horizon. He got out a cigarette and lit it as he sipped the coffee.

Oh yeah, now he remembered. Charon. Sort of a nondescript medium-sized guy. Skinny. Real quiet. Drives a Ford pickup.

Grimes ambled back to the counter and stared at the artist's drawing on the front page of the paper. He squinted. Naw.

'Couldn't be him, of course,' the proprietor said. 'Ain't nobody from around here going to go clear to Washington to gun down politicians. Don't make sense. Not that some of 'em couldn't use a little shootin'. The guy who's doing it is probably some kind of half-baked commie nut, like that idiot Oswald was. But Henry Charon? Buys gas and food here pretty regular.'

'Couldn't be him,' Deputy Willard Grimes agreed.

'Now if a fellow had it in for dirtball politicians,' the proprietor said, warming to his theme, 'there's a bunch that need shootin' a lot closer to home. Remember down in Albuquerque . . .'

Five minutes later, with another cup of coffee in his hand, Deputy Grimes was ready to leave for the interstate when a game warden drove up to the gas pump and parked his green truck. He came inside. Willard lingered to visit.

The game warden was eating a doughnut and kidding the proprietor when his eyes came to rest on the newspaper. 'Don't that beat all,' he exclaimed. 'If that isn't Henry Charon I'll eat my hat.'

'What?' said Willard Grimes.

'Henry Charon,' the game warden said. 'Got a little two-by-four ranch up toward Twin Buttes. I've chased that sonuvabitch all over northern

New Mexico. He's a damned poacher but we could never catch him at it. That's him all right.'

'How come you didn't say something yesterday?' Willard Grimes asked, his brow furrowing. 'That picture must have been on TV a hundred times already.'

'My TV broke a month ago. That's the first time I laid eyes on that picture. But I'll bet a week's pay that's Henry Charon. Sure as God made little green apples.'

The envelope containing the lab reports from the Sanitary Bakery warehouse case had lain in the in-basket for four hours before Special Agent Freddy Murray had the time to open it. He read the documents through once, then settled in to study them carefully. Finally he pulled a legal pad around and began making notes.

The corpse of one Antonio Anselmo, white male about forty-five years of age with a partial dental plate, had been found in Harrison Ford's locked room at the FBI barracks on the Quantico Marine Corps base. The forward portion of his skull had been crushed. Death had been instantaneous. When the field lab people saw the body at eleven A.M. Wednesday, they calculated that Anselmo had died between midnight and four A.M.

Hair, bits of flesh, and minute quantities of blood were found on the landing of the stairwell nearest to Ford's room. Blood type was the same as Anselmo's. Threads of clothing and one shirt button had been recovered from the stairs. Marks on the linoleum in the corridor that might have been made by a body.

Wallet – now this was interesting – both the wallet and a motel key bore partial prints of Harrison Ford.

A shotgun lay beside the body. It also had Ford's prints. And there was a minute oil stain on Anselmo's shirttail – a stain of gun oil. No other weapons in the room.

The second report went into great detail about the warehouse, with its six bodies and cocaine processing laboratory. Murray flipped through it uninterestedly.

He settled on the report concerning Freeman McNally's house. One body in the living room. Fifty-one-year-old white male named Vinnie Pioche. Shot three times, 9-mm slugs, two that entered the back and one that penetrated his right side, apparently while he was lying down. According to the coroner Pioche had been dead when the third shot struck him – no bleeding.

Then this ringer: the pistol that fired the slugs that killed Pioche was in the weapons room and contained no prints.

The report carefully detailed where each of eighty 9-mm rounds had struck in the lower floor of the house. Refrigerator, TV, bathroom – it was quite a list. There were diagrams and Murray referred to them several times as he read.

Cars outside the warehouse. One of them contained stains of human blood on the backseat. The blood matched Pioche's. The ignition key for this car had been recovered from Harrison Ford's pocket.

Now Freddy Murray went back to the report on the warehouse. He looked again at the coroner's detail of Freeman McNally's injuries. Scrotum partially ripped from the body, severe injury to the right testicle incurred just before death stopped the heart. Death caused by a bullet through the heart, a shot fired into his back from about four feet away.

Ruben McNally – half strangled and severely beaten, but the cause of death was internal bleeding in the brain caused when his nose bone was shoved into the cranial cavity.

Billy Enright . . .

Freddy sat back in his chair and whistled softly. Jesus. That was the only word that described it. Jesus!

He was still making notes an hour later when Tom Hooper came into the office and sagged into a seat.

'McNally?'

'Yeah.'

'What do you think?' Hooper asked as he took off his shoes.

'Well,' Freddy said slowly as he watched Hooper knead his right foot. 'I'm struck by the many points of similarity between the McNally mess and the massacre over at Teal's.'

Hooper didn't look up. 'Bullshit,' he said.

'No, I mean it, Tom.'

Hooper dropped his right foot and worked some on his left. Then he put them both flat on the floor and looked at Freddy. 'No.'

'I admit there are a lot of *dis*similarities too, but it really looks to me like another gang wipeout. We are just damned lucky our undercover officer survived with only *one* bullet in the back.'

Hooper pointed at the pile of reports. 'Look at the one for Ford,' he said. 'Read me the analysis of the clothes the emergency room people took off him.'

Freddy took his time. He found the passage, perused it, then said, 'Okay, there's some blood, three different types, some brain tissue—'

'Now where in hell do you suppose he got that on him?'

'Tom, in places in that warehouse it was on the walls and in puddles on the floor. He rubbed against it somewhere.'

Hooper put on his shoes and carefully tied the laces. That chore completed, he said, 'You and I both know that Ford went into that warehouse and gunned those men. He beat one to death with his bare hands. He went there to do it. No other reason.'

'Now you listen a minute, Tom. We got a ton of facts here but no story.

A clever man could string all these facts together to tell any story he wanted to tell. I guarantee you that the lawyer Harrison Ford ends up with will be a damn clever man. If he gets indicted, even *I* am going to contribute to his legal defense fund.'

Hooper said nothing.

Murray charged on. 'You think it isn't going to come out that the bureau sent him in undercover? *Ha!* The defense is going to make us out to be a bunch of incompetent paper pushers who couldn't prosecute Freeman McNally and are now trying to hang our own undercover operative. My God, Tom! The next hundred people we try to recruit to go undercover are going to laugh in our faces!'

'Cops and FBI agents gotta obey the law too. Harrison went over the edge.' The irritation was plain in Hooper's voice. 'Why are we having this conversation?'

'Ford's mistake was not being in bed sound asleep when Tony Anselmo came calling with his sawed-off shotgun. Then he could have just died in his sleep and none of this mess would have happened.'

'I know he killed Anselmo in self-defense,' Hooper growled. 'Nobody's suggesting charging him for that.'

'You think that fight at the warehouse wasn't self-defense? My *God*, Tom. *He's got a bullet in the back.*'

Hooper got out of his chair and went over to the window. He ran his fingers through his hair. 'So what are you suggesting?'

'I think Harrison Ford has done enough for his country. I'm suggesting we close the file on the McNally case and let Ford go back to Evansville.'

'Just like that?'

'Just like that.'

Hooper stood looking out the window.

'We should have busted McNally in September,' Freddy said, more to himself than to his boss.

Tom Hooper had spent twenty-six years in the FBI. He thought about those years now and the various tough choices he had had to make along the way. Freddy irritated him with all this crap about September. They had handled this case right all the way, and circumstances beyond everyone's control had intervened. His thoughts turned to Ford – the man was not a good undercover agent. Oh, sure, he could think on his feet and he was brave as a bull, but he had too much imagination. He thought too damn much.

He stood at the window tallying Ford's sins. Goddamn that asshole, anyway. 'Ford was planning to gun McNally and all the rest of them, then go back to his room at Quantico. He was going to call us and claim he and Anselmo had struggled and he had been knocked out. That's why he changed guns at McNally's house, We've got no proof that he killed Pioche. None! It's plausible that Anselmo killed him before he went to kill

Ford. If Ford hadn't been wounded at the warehouse we might not have been able to place him there. All we would have had is a bunch of corpses.'

'You think?' Freddy said behind him.

'I *know*! I can read that man's mind. He's no cop! He thinks like a goddamn jarhead. Attack! Always attack.'

Hooper turned around. Freddy was perusing the lab reports.

'You listening to me?' he asked Freddy.

'I heard.'

'Ford and McNally. They're just alike. Screw the law! The law is for those other guys, all those guys who can't get away with breaking it. They both think like that!'

Freddy folded the reports and stacked them neatly. He took his time with it and examined the pile to make sure it was perfectly aligned, with the files in proper numerical sequence. When he finished he spoke slowly, without looking at Hooper:

'McNally's out of business. Permanently. That, *I thought*, was our ultimate goal all along. And the government isn't going to have to spend a nickel trying him. No board and room in a heated cell for the rest of his life at the taxpayers' expense. No appeals. No claims of racial bigotry or oppression. It's all over.'

He picked up the stack of files and held it out for Hooper. 'Close the case,' he said.

Just then the intercom buzzed. 'Yes,' Freddy said into the box.

'There's a call for Mr Hooper from New Mexico. Another identification of that artist's drawing of the assassin.'

'Tell her I'll take it in my office,' Hooper told Freddy. He picked up the files and put them under his arm.

The first shots were fired at the soldiers in a poorer section of northeast Washington around two P.M. A detail had halted a beat-up '65 Cadillac containing two black youths and were marching them toward a truck when someone fired a shot. The soldiers dropped to the ground and began looking for the shooter. The two black youths ran. One of the soldiers in full combat gear ran after them. He had gone about fifty feet when there was another shot and he fell to the sidewalk.

His comrades sent a hail of lead into a second-floor window over a corner grocery, then kicked the door in and charged up the stairs. Inside the room they found a fifteen-year-old boy with a bullet-wound in his arm huddled on the floor. Beside him lay an old lever-action rifle.

'Why'd you shoot?' the sergeant demanded. 'Why'd you shoot that soldier?'

The boy wouldn't answer. He was dragged down the stairs and, in full view of a rapidly gathering crowd, was thrown roughly into a truck for the ride to the hospital. Beside him on a stretcher lay the man he had shot.

'Honkey pigs,' one woman shouted. 'Arresting *kids*! Why you honkies here in our neighborhood anyway? Out to hassle the niggers?'

A brick sailed over the crowd and just missed a soldier. It took the soldiers twenty minutes to run the crowd off.

While this incident was playing itself out, a dope addict in a public housing project two miles away fired a shotgun through a closed door, striking the soldier who was knocking on it full in the face.

The second shot splattered harmlessly against the wall.

The soldiers kicked in the door while the addict wrestled with the lever to break open the double-barrel. His wife was sitting nearby in a chair. She watched silently as two soldiers with their M-16s on full automatic emptied their magazines into her husband from a distance of eight feet. The soldiers were hasty and inexperienced. Some of their bullets missed. However thirty-two of them – the coroner did the counting later – ripped through the addict before his corpse hit the floor.

29

When darkness fell the number of incidents increased. The communications room at the armory became a beehive of activity as reports of shootings and angry crowds poured in over the radios.

At the Executive Office Building General Land conferred with the Vice-President. Lacking any other options, they agreed that more troops would be brought in and sent to each trouble spot. General Land ordered in a battalion that was on standby at Andrews Air Force Base.

Jake Grafton was at the armory poring over a map trying to learn which areas had been searched and which had not when he was called to the telephone.

'Captain, Special Agent Hooper.'

'Yes.'

'I thought you'd like to know. We've received over a dozen tentative identifications of the artist's conception of the assassin. Two in the Washington area and others from all over. We're checking all of them. But I thought you might want to swing by the local addresses. The agents are still there. You ready to copy?'

'Go ahead.' Jake got out his pen.

When the captain had copied and read back both addresses, Hooper said, 'I think the most likely ID is one out of New Mexico. Very definite. From a game warden and a gas station proprietor. They think the guy is a rancher out there and a suspected long-time poacher. Real good with firearms. Ran a guide service for out-of-state high rollers for the last seven or eight hunting seasons. A deputy sheriff went out to his ranch this afternoon and looked around. No one there. Doesn't appear to have been anyone there for a week or so.'

'What's the name?'

'Charon. Henry Charon. The New Mexico Department of Motor Vehicles gives his date of birth as March 6, 1952. We've already got a fax of the driver's license photo. I've seen it. This could be our guy. We've got agents showing it to our witness now.'

'Can I get some copies?'

'The agents checking out the local reports have copies. They'll give you one. We'll send some over to the armory as soon as we can.'

'Like maybe a couple thousand of them.'

'Well, we'll do what we can. Gonna take a little while.'

'As soon as you can.'

'Sure.'

'How about the national crime computer? This guy have a record or some warrants?'

'We tried. Didn't get a hit. We're checking.'

'Thanks for the call, Hooper.'

'Yeah.'

The nearest address was an apartment building in Georgetown. Jack Yocke drove. When they were stopped at a roadblock, he showed a pass signed by General Greer while Jake, Toad, and Rita displayed their green military ID cards. The sergeant examined the ID card photos and flashed a light in each of the officers' faces. Two men, both with M-16s leveled, stood where they could shoot past the sergeant.

'You may go on through, sir,' the sergeant said as he saluted. Jake returned the salute as Yocke fed gas.

There was no parking place in front of the building, so Yocke double-parked. 'A license to steal,' he gloated.

'Toad, write him a citation,' Jake said before he slammed the door.

The FBI agents were still talking to the apartment manager. Jake introduced himself. One of the agents took him out in the hall. He produced a sheet of fax paper with a picture in the middle. Much bigger than the little photo on a driver's license, the picture still had the same look: a man staring straight at the camera, his nose slightly distorted by the lens.

'The lady in here says this guy has been a tenant for about a month. We're waiting for a search warrant to arrive.'

'But I thought this was the New Mexico driver's license photo?'

'It is. It's the same guy.'

'Henry Charon.'

'Interesting name. But not the one he used here. Called himself Sam Donally. She asked to see a driver's license when he signed the lease. She thinks it was Virginia, but isn't sure. She didn't write down the number. We're running Virginia DMV now. Without a date of birth it'll take a little time.'

'Maybe he used the same date of birth. Easier to remember.'

'Maybe.'

'When did she last see him?'

'Four days or so ago. But she's only seen him about eight or ten times since he rented the apartment. He goes away for several days at a time. Says he does consulting work for the government. And – this is funny – of the ten other apartments in this building, six of the tenants are here – and not one can positively identify either the photo or the drawing. Three thought it might be him, but only after I suggested that it might be.'

'The manager expect him back at any definite time?'

'Whenever. He never says.'

'So he could just come waltzing in any ol' time?'

'It's possible.'

'Any chance he's upstairs now?'

'I went up on the fire escape fifteen minutes ago and peeked in. Place looks empty.'

Jake stared at the picture. The face was regular, the features quite average but arranged in such a way that no one would ever call the owner handsome. He looked . . . it was hard to say. He looked, Jake decided, like everybody else. It was as if the owner of that face bad no personality of his own. The eyes stared out, slightly bored, promising nothing. Not great intelligence, not wit, not . . . Nothing was hidden behind the smooth brow, the calm, unemotional features.

Wrong. *Everything was hidden.*

He took a copy of the artist's rendering from his pocket and held it beside the photo. Well, it was and it wasn't.

'Thanks,' Jake Grafton told the agent.

In the car he showed the picture to the others. They immediately whipped out their copies of the line drawing to compare.

'Oh yes,' Rita said. 'It's him. It's the same man.'

'No, it isn't,' said her husband. 'It could be, perhaps, but . . .'

'Let's go,' Jake told Yocke. 'The place on Lafayette Circle.'

With traffic practically nonexistent, Yocke made excellent time. He ran every red light after merely slowing for a look. They drove past the Lafayette Circle address. Toad pointed out the error, and Yocke circled the block.

There was a parking place clearly visible fifty feet down the street, but Yocke double-parked in front of the main entrance. He gave Grafton a bland, slightly smug smile.

The captain sighed and got out of the car. 'Toad, phone the armory and find out what's happening.'

While the lieutenant used the telephone inside, Jake conferred with another agent in the hall. He was back in the car waiting when Toad came down the steps.

'Riots,' Toad reported. 'The lid is coming off.'

'Any sign of the terrorists?'

'Nothing yet.'

'Let's go back to the armory,' Jake told Yocke and tapped the dashboard.

'Aye aye, sir. What did the manager say?'

'Wasn't the manager. He's gone for the holidays. It was one of the tenants. Identifies both pictures. Says the guy called himself Smithson. He couldn't remember the first name. Been here about a month.'

'Only one tenant?' Rita asked. 'What about all the others?'

'Just one. No one else is sure. The agents are going door to door.'

'You'd think if one person saw him and was sure, they all would at least recognize the photo.'

'You'd think,' Jake Grafton agreed.

Assume these people are correct. Assume Henry Charon–Smithson–Sam Donally were all one and the same man. He had two apartments. No, make that at least two. What if he had three? Or four?

Grafton looked up at the buildings the car drove past. He could be up there right now, watching the street. But why had so few people seen him?

Let's assume the man is really Henry Charon from New Mexico. He comes to town, takes several apartments. Why? Because the hotels and motels were the very first places the police checked. Yet the minute his picture ran in the paper, he would have to abandon all the apartments. Wouldn't he? But that was a bad break. Unexpected. He worked like hell to ensure there would be no witnesses. But he *was* seen. That was always a possibility.

Apartments. He rented apartments about a month ago. The conclusion was inescapable – the attempt on the President's life was very carefully *planned*. Most attempts to kill the President were made by emotionally disturbed individuals, Jake knew, screwballs who acted on a sudden impulse when an opportunity presented itself. Charon or Smithson or Donally had carefully planned, bided his time. And he should have succeeded. This was the nightmare the Secret Service worked to foil – the professional killer who stalked his prey, the hunter of men.

It fitted. Charon was a poacher and a professional hunting guide. He knew firearms. He could shoot.

A hunter. A man at home outdoors.

Well, there were the alleys and the railroad yards. Maybe the places under bridges and overpasses where the bums hang out.

No. He would be seen and remembered in all those areas unless he went to great pains to look like a derelict. And to pass freely in the world of working people and tourists that was the rest of Washington, he would have to be groomed and dressed appropriately.

A master of disguise, perhaps? A quick change artist?

Jake thought not.

Was he still in Washington? Well, the assumption was that all these long-range shootings were done by one man, and if so, there appeared to be no obvious reason why he should have left. Unless he's finished what he came to do or decided to abandon the rest of his plan. Questions – there were too many unanswered questions.

The car entered one of Washington's traffic circles. As Yocke piloted the car around Jake Grafton caught sight of the statue amidst the trees and evergreens. These little parks, he thought, were about as close to the outdoors as the residents of Washington ever get.

Perhaps a camper, mounted on a pickup bed. Maybe one of those vacation cruisers with the little toilet and the propane stove. Surely Henry Charon from New Mexico would be at home in something like that.

What else? He was missing something. Henry Charon, a hunter and small rancher from New Mexico. He comes to the big city and only *three* people see him? See and *remember*.

The problem, Jake thought, was that he himself had lived too long in cities. He didn't see the city as Charon did, as alien territory.

No, he had that wrong. Charon saw the city precisely as he saw the forests and mountains. A hunting ground.

But where did that fact take him? Jake Grafton didn't know.

The conversation among his fellow passengers caught his attention now. 'Why is it,' Rita asked Jack Yocke, 'that the newspapers and television give the impression that the whole city is in flames, with a million people rioting in the streets? My mother called me last night in a panic.'

'The television people are in show biz,' Yocke told her lightly.

'Have there been any more "communiqués" from Aldana's friends in Colombia?' Toad asked.

'Yeah,' said Yocke. 'They say they're going to blow up some airliners. They're going to bring this nation to its knees, they say. It's probably on TV right now. Be in tomorrow's paper.'

Jake Grafton sat in glum silence. The aftermath of all this . . . God only knew. But, he suspected, the plight of the desperately hopeless, all those people without the education or pluck to make it in America – the natural prey of the Chano Aldanas – would be ignored in the hue and cry. Not that the poor were the sole consumers of illegal drugs or even the majority. Oh no. But they were the core of the problem, the loyal consumer base unaffected by changing fashion or public education. The poor were the least likely to get treatment, the least likely to have the social and financial and spiritual assets to escape the downward spiral of addiction, crime, and early death.

'We're going to have to legalize dope,' Yocke said under his breath.

This comment produced an outburst from both Toad and Rita. Jake silenced them curtly. They were supposed to be fighting alligators: someone else was going to have to figure out a way to drain the swamp.

The situation room at the armory was packed with people, including General Land and his flag aides. Jake found time to quickly brief the chairman on the search for the assassin, then he got out of the way.

He stood there watching the brass do the math required to figure out how long it would take to search all the remainder of the city with the troops available. They knew as well as Jake that the people they were after might just walk a half block to a building that had already been searched.

General Land was acutely conscious of that possibility. He wanted street patrols to stop and examine the IDs of any suspicious characters. The DC police could help, but they had limited manpower.

The military presence was inexorably rising and would continue to rise until the terrorists were found. If they were here to be found. Score one for the narco-terrorists, Jake Grafton thought. If they had accomplished nothing else, the people inside the beltway were going to get a real taste of military dictatorship.

While these thoughts were going through Grafton's mind, Senator Bob Cherry and three other senators were voicing them on national television. Cherry dropped the bombshell toward the end of the program. Chano Aldana should be sent back to Colombia, he said, and then the terrorism would stop.

The people of Washington, the people of this nation, should not have to submit to being wounded, maimed, and murdered just so the administration can have the satisfaction of prosecuting Mr Aldana. The citizens huddle in their houses while the military makes war in the streets. We all admire persistence in the face of adversity, but at some point dogged insistence on observing all the arcane niceties of the law becomes foolhardy. Atrocities, bombings, assassinations – how much do we have to endure here in Northern Colombia? What price in blood and flesh does Dan Quayle think we should pay for Aldana's prosecution?'

Watching Cherry on a portable television in an armory office, Toad Tarkington muttered to Jack Yocke, 'He's got a talent for rhetorical questions, doesn't he?'

'It's taken him far,' Yocke replied.

Twenty minutes later Jake Grafton *saw* the map. It had been there for days and three enlisted men were diligently annotating it with pins and little symbols, but when someone stepped out of his way, suddenly it was hanging on the wall in his full view. And the thing he saw as he looked at it were all the areas that were not divided into blocks to be searched. For the first time he saw the open areas.

It was possible. Not very likely, but possible.

'General Greer, do you have a company I can borrow?'

The major general looked at him askance. 'A company?' he growled. He didn't think much of naval officers – the damned boat drivers usually had only the vaguest grasp of *real* war, the land war. Just now he swallowed his prejudices. Grafton, he knew, was different. Liaison with the Joint Staff, Grafton had never tried to tell him how to do his job. Unlike fifty or so flag officers of all services who had been wasting huge chunks of his time with unsolicited advice.

'Yessir. A couple hundred troops. I want to walk them through Rock Creek Park.'

The company commander lined his troops up in a parking lot of RFK Stadium across the street from the armory. As the sergeants counted noses and checked gear, Jake turned to Toad. 'Go get rifles and a couple extra magazines for me, you, and Rita. And three walkie-talkies.'

'What about Yocke?'

'He's a civilian.' Right now the reporter was inside in the command post taking notes. If he didn't get out here on the double he was going to be left behind. His problem.

'Aye aye, sir,' Tarkington said and trotted toward the armory.

The company commander, an army captain, asked Jake if he wanted to address the troops.

'No, you do it. Tell them we are going to be hunting a killer, the man who shot down the President's helicopter. They are to take their time, go slowly, use their flashlights. We'll do the Rock Creek Country Club first.'

'You want this man alive, sir?'

'I'll take him any way I can get him. I don't want any of your men killed trying to capture him. Anybody who fails to stop when challenged, they can shoot.'

'Your responsibility, sir?'

'My responsibility.'

The army officer saluted and went to talk to his men.

Ten minutes later, with the enlisted soldiers aboard the trucks, the officers consulted the maps. Just as Jake and the two navy lieutenants climbed into their car, Jack Yocke came running.

'Welcome to the party,' Toad told him.

The convoy moved slowly through the streets. Pedestrians were streaming in and out of the grocery stores, but the parking lots and streets lacked the usual glut of automobiles. The effect was jarring.

'I hear the stores are doing a land office business in liquor and contraceptives,' Yocke remarked.

'Can't watch television all the time,' Toad agreed.

'Oh, I don't know,' Rita said. 'The glare of the boob tube doesn't seem to affect your libido.'

Jake Grafton sighed.

Senator Cherry and his aide drove back to the Senate office building in Cherry's car. Like many of the senators and congressmen trapped in Washington this close to the holidays – Cherry had told the majority leader a week ago that the chambers should adjourn early for Christmas and had been ignored – he had been issued a vehicle pass by the White House staff.

Two FBI agents were waiting in the hall outside Cherry's office suite. Hooper he remembered. The other agent was named Murray. 'Your door's locked,' one of them noted.

'That's obvious,' Cherry thundered derisively. 'They gave me one lousy pass for one vehicle and *I* have to drive the damn thing. You think my receptionist is going to walk ten miles through the streets of this open sewer to unlock the door so you can have a nice place to wait?'

'No, sir.'

The aide unlocked the door and the agents followed the senator into his office. After he had flipped on the lights and settled behind his desk, Cherry boomed, 'Well?'

'Senator, we're trying to get a handle on the activities of a certain lawyer here in the District, fellow named T. Jefferson Brody.'

Bob Cherry stared at them.

'It seems he made some campaign contributions that—'

'Did the White House send you over here?'

'No, sir. As I said, we're—'

'You just got a call from Will Dorfman, didn't you? Dorfman is trying to shut me up. *That asshole!* Well, it won't work! I am going to continue to say what has to be said. If Dorfman doesn't like it he can stick—'

'I haven't talked to *anybody* at the White House, Senator,' Tom Hooper said with force. 'I'm asking you, do you know T. Jefferson Brody?'

'I've met him, yes. I've met a lot of people in Washington, Mister . . . I've forgotten your name.'

'Hooper.'

'Hooper. I'm a US senator. I meet people at parties, at dinners, they stream into this office by the hundreds. Just here in Washington I must have met ten thousand people in the last ten years. In Florida—'

'Brody. Jefferson Brody. He makes political contributions on behalf of people who want influence. Has he made any contributions to your campaign or any of your PACs?'

'I resent your implication, sir! You are implying that Jefferson Brody or someone owns a piece of me! You can haul your little tin badge right on out that—'

'I'm not implying anything, sir,' Hooper said without a trace of irritation. He had dealt with these elected apostles on numerous occasions in the past. It was one of the least pleasant aspects of his job. 'I'm trying to conduct an investigation into the activities of T. Jefferson Brody. If you don't want to answer questions or cooperate, your campaign finance statements are a matter of public record. We'll get them.'

'I'm perfectly willing to cooperate with the FBI,' Cherry said civilly. 'But your timing couldn't be more . . . curious, shall we say? I appear on network television and take a strong stand against the administration about a matter of public concern. An hour later when I get back to the office the FBI is waiting for me. Nobody from the White House called you, you *say*. But what about your superiors? Did Will Dorfman call the director?

'I'll be blunt, gentlemen. I think Dorfman is playing hardball, trying to use the FBI to silence someone who is speaking out against the administration's handling of this terrorism debacle. I know how Dorfman plays the game. Next he'll start telling *lies* about me. He's done it before. He's good at it. The slander, the invidious lie – those are Dorfman's weapons against Bush and Quayle's enemies.

'Now you go back and tell your superiors that Bob Cherry can't be muzzled. You tell the director to call Dorfman and tell him Bob Cherry didn't scare. No doubt that perverted little troglodyte will think of a filthy lie and find an ear to pour it into. *But I'm going to keep telling the truth about Dithering Danny and that parasite Dorfman until the day I die.*

'Now get out. *Get out of my office.*'

Hooper and Murray went.

With the door closed, Bob Cherry sat for a minute or two lost in thought. Automatically he reached out and rearranged the mementos on his desk, handling them and brushing off any specks of dust that might have come to rest on them. This altimeter mounted on a walnut stand – a presentation from a Florida veterans association. The gold doubloon from a Spanish treasure galleon, the baseball signed by Hank Aaron, the fifty-caliber machine-gun round on an alabaster base – all these things had been presented to him by groups of Florida citizens who appreciated his loyal service in the Senate, his sacrifices on their behalf.

He rose from his chair and went around the room looking at the photos on the wall, dusting an occasional frame with a finger and here and there straightening one. He was in every photo. He had posed with presidents, with movie idols, with famous industrialists and writers and athletes. Many of the photos bore handwritten inscriptions safely preserved forever behind nonglare glass: 'To Senator Bob Cherry, a real American,' 'To Bob Cherry, a friend.' 'To Senator Cherry, a true friend of the American working man.' 'To Florida's own Senator Bob Cherry, who believes in America.'

After he had looked at every picture and made sure it was hanging correctly on its private nail, he lay down on the couch and closed his eyes. He would rest a while.

Going down in the elevator, Freddy Murray said, 'You know, he might have gotten down off his high horse if you'd told him Freeman McNally was dead.'

'I was going to,' said Tom Hooper, 'but the jerk never gave me a chance.'

From a sound sleep Henry Charon came instantly awake. He lay in the darkness listening. He could hear the drip of water – the rain had begun again just as he drifted off to sleep – and the sound of branches rustling in a gentle breeze. Charon's eyes roamed freely in the dim half light that passed for darkness under that glowing overcast.

Something was not right. Something was out there in the night. Something that should not be there. It was very quiet. No traffic sounds at all from the road a hundred yards down the hilt. No sound of aircraft overhead.

Yes. There it was again. Very faint.

He slipped out of the sleeping bag and pulled his boots on, then his sweater and waterproof parka. He reached down into the sleeping bag and retrieved the pistol.

In less than a minute he was completely dressed, the pistol in his pocket and the rifle in his hand. He swung the rucksack containing the hand grenades and ammo and the duffle bag that he would need to hide the rifle over his shoulder. Everything else he left.

Only now did Henry Charon check the luminous hands of his watch. Eleven thirty-four.

He carefully left the little cave and moved with sure, silent steps twenty feet around to his right, to a prominence where he could look and listen. He sank to the ground at the base of a tree so he would not present a clear silhouette, motionless, a part of the rock, a dark, indistinct shape in a dark, wet universe.

The glow of the city lights reflecting on the clouds was only thinly dissipated by the naked branches of the trees.

And he heard the noise again. A man, moving slowly and carefully, but moving.

Charon saw nothing. His ears told him what he wanted to know. One man, sixty or so yards away, around the slope and down a bit.

And coming this way.

Henry Charon didn't form hypotheses about who this intruder might be or why he was here. Like the wary wild animal he was, he waited. He waited with infinite patience.

Now he got a fleeting look at the man. A soldier, judging by the helmet and the bulky shape, indistinct among the brush and trees. The man was moving slowly, warily, listening and looking.

But wait! Above on the ridge – another man. Two of them.

He turned his head ever so slowly to acquire the second man. He could hear him but that was all.

The second man was closer than the one lower on the slope. That he had gotten this close without Charon hearing him was a tribute to his skill. The first man was much clumsier.

Charon had a decision to make. Should he wait and see if these men would pass him without detecting him or should he move away? If they were hunting him, which was likely, they would check out this overhang of rock and, if they were halfway competent, find the cave and his gear.

He mulled these questions as an animal would, without consciously thinking about them, merely waiting for his instinct to tell him it was time to move.

The first man he had heard came closer, now plainly visible as he moved between the trees and rock outcrops. He was carrying a rifle in his hands.

The second man was right up the slope even with Charon, judging by the sound. Charon did not turn his head. Only his eyes moved.

'Psst. Pssst!' The hissing came from the lower man. He gestured in Charon's direction, then said in a stage whisper, 'There's some rocks to my left.'

Charon remained frozen. The man who had whispered moved behind the tree that sheltered Charon, but he did not move to reacquire him. The man was less than a dozen feet away.

At this distance Charon could hear every step the man took. He could hear him breathing deeply, as one does when one is trying to get plenty of air and be quiet too. He could hear his clothing rustle. He could hear the gentle, rhythmic swish of the water in his canteen. He even got a faint whiff of the odor of stale cigarette smoke.

The man moved away from Charon's back, toward the cave. Still Charon remained motionless. Slowly, ever so slowly, he rotated his head to try to acquire the man above him on the ridge. Nothing. The man was behind the trees or just over the rocky crest. In any event Charon couldn't see him from where he had made himself part of the earth.

A minute passed. The man behind brushed against the bushes, broke several branches.

'Billy! Billy! We got a cave here.'

Seconds passed.

'Billy! There's a bunch of stuff in the cave.'

'Say again.'

Now the soldier behind Charon spoke normally. 'There's a cave down here with a sleeping bag and some other stuff in it. Better report.'

As the metallic sounds of a walkie-talkie became audible, Henry Charon moved. He moved straight ahead, back in the direction the men had come from. He kept low yet moved surely and silently and used the brush and trees and rocks to screen himself from the men behind him.

The voices of the two men around the cave carried. They were still audible though the words were indistinct when Charon halted beside the base of a large tree and scanned the terrain.

Other men would be coming up this slope to check out the cave. He had to get well away but he didn't want to move onto someone who was sitting motionless. So he paused to scan and listen.

He could hear someone down the slope. The person slipped and fell heavily, then regained his feet. He moved steadily without pause, working his way upwards toward Charon. No doubt he was trying to find the cave.

Charon slipped along, staying low.

He froze when he heard the sound of a walkie-talkie. Below, to the left. Another one!

He kept going parallel with the ridge line. After several hundred yards the ridge began to curve. Perfect. The road below would also curve since it ran along the creek. Charon turned ninety degrees left and began his descent.

Through the trees he saw the glint of light reflecting on the asphalt when he was still twenty-five yards away. His progress was slow now, glacial. He flitted from tree to tree, looking and listening. It took him three minutes to get across the creek, which was small but full.

Then he got down on his stomach and crawled toward the road.

The roadside was brushy with dead weeds and briars. Charon lay prone, listening.

Nothing.

Ever so slowly he raised his head. He was beside a crooked little tree that had all its branches tilted toward the road. The bare branches formed a partial canopy that left him in deeper darkness. He scanned right and left, searching the shadows.

Another minute passed as he tried to satisfy himself that no one was nearby.

He rose to a crouch and trotted across the two-lane asphalt toward the brush beyond.

'Halt!'

The shout came from his right, a surprised, half-choked cry.

Henry Charon sprinted toward the waiting darkness.

The impact of the bullet tumbled him. He rolled once and regained his feet, his left side completely numb. He gained the brush and charged into it and kept going as a bullet slapped into a tree just above his head and the boom of a second shot rang out. He hadn't even heard the first one.

There was no pain. Just a numbness that extended from his armpit to his hip. He could still use his left arm, but not very well. The rifle was still in his right hand. He hadn't lost it. Thank God!

He attacked the hill in front of him, driving on both feet, fighting for air, not caring about how much noise he made.

They would be coming, that he knew. He had no illusions. No more than sixty seconds had passed before he heard the swelling noise of an engine coming down the road, then the squeal of its tires as the driver braked hard to a halt. Henry Charon went up the slope with all the strength that was in him.

The soldier was so nervous when Jake Grafton got out of the car that he couldn't stand still. He hopped from foot to foot, pointing up the slope.

'I shouted for him to halt but he didn't so I shot and he fell and got up and kept running and I shot again and dear God . . .'

'Show me.'

The soldier led him to the spot where the man had fallen. Jake used his flashlight. He followed the soldier's pointing finger.

Specks of blood on the brush. 'What's your name?'

'Specialist Garth, sir.'

'You hit him.'

Jake pointed his M-16 at the ground and fired three shots, spaced evenly apart. 'You stay here,' he told the soldier, 'and tell your lieutenant to get people on the streets up there.' He gestured toward the ridge he faced. 'I think there're streets and houses up there.'

'Yessir,' Specialist Garth said, still swallowing rapidly and wetting his lips. 'I hope—'

'You did right. You did your duty. Tell the lieutenant.' Jake strode back to the car and tossed his hat in. 'Toad, go down about fifty feet to the right. Rita, fifty feet left. We'll go up the hill. Keep your eyes peeled.'

'What about me?' Jack Yocke wanted to know.

'Stay here with the car.' The lieutenants were trotting to their assigned position. 'Better yet, drive the car around and meet us up on top.' And Jake turned and plunged into the brush.

Fifteen feet up the hill he regretted his impulse to have Yocke help. Having a car driven by an unarmed man waiting and ready for a desperate wounded man with a gun when he topped the hill wasn't the best idea Jake had had today.

Too late Jake Grafton turned around. Yocke was already driving away. 'Damn.'

Jake used his flashlight. He held it in his left hand and held the rifle by the pistol grip in his right, ready to fire. The trail in the wet earth was plain. Occasional splotches of blood.

If luck were a lady, this guy would be lying unconscious fifty feet up the hill bleeding to death. But Grafton had long ago lost all his illusions about that fickle bitch. The wounded man was probably tough as a man could be and would keep going until he died on his feet.

He's going to need a lot of killing, Jake Grafton told himself as he paused to scan the dark forest with his flash.

At the top of the hill was a chain-link fence topped by three strands of barbed wire. Behind it was a lawn and trees and a huge two-story house with lights in three or four of the windows. The fence was an impossible barrier for Henry Charon, who was bleeding and beginning to hurt.

He looked left and right, then went right on impulse. He moved quickly, still able to lope along although the shock of the bullet was wearing off.

The next house had a six-foot-high wooden fence, still too much for Charon. He kept going until he came to a small two-rail accent fence. He was across it and trotting across the lawn when he heard a car go by on the street.

Cars would mean police or soldiers. Charon went around the house and paused behind a huge evergreen to survey the area and catch his breath. He probed the wound with his hand. Bleeding. Behind him on the grass he could see the trail where he had come. Whoever followed would see it too.

The car that had gone by was not in sight, so Charon ran out onto the street and veered right. Pavement would show no tracks, although he was probably dripping blood.

He needed a place to hole up and dress the wound. Or to die if the wound was too bad. That was a possibility of course. He had seen it happen hundreds of times. A wounded animal would run for miles until it thought it had escaped its pursuer, then it would lie down and quietly bleed to death. Sometimes he had come upon them after they had lain down but while they were still alive. If they had lain too long they could not move. The shock and loss of blood weakened them, caused them to stiffen up so badly they couldn't rise. He wouldn't lie that long. He would be up and going before he got too weak or stiff.

But where?

He heard another vehicle, or perhaps the same one coming back, and darted down the first driveway he came to. The house was dark. Great.

He went around the garage and circled the house.

There might be a burglar alarm. Or a dog. He would have to take the chance.

He used the silenced pistol on the door lock. It took four shots, but finally it opened when he pushed against it with his shoulder and turned the doorknob.

He closed it behind him and stood listening. The darkness inside the house was almost total. He waited for his eyes to accommodate, then walked quietly and quickly from room to room.

Apparently empty. With the pistol in his hand he ascended the stairs.

The master bath was off the big bedroom. It lacked windows. He closed the door behind him and turned on the light.

His appearance in the mirror shocked him. The coat was sodden with blood. He stripped it carefully. God, the pain was getting bad! He had difficulty getting the sweater and shirt off, but he did.

The wound was down low, entry and exit holes about six inches apart, a couple of inches above his hip point and around on his back. He could only see the entrance hole by looking in the mirror. No way of telling what was bleeding inside. If his kidney or something vital were nicked, he would eventually pass out from loss of blood and die. And that would be that.

As it was, all he could try to do was get the external bleeding stopped. And it was a bleeder.

How much blood had he lost? Easily a pint, maybe more. He felt lightheaded. There was no time to lose.

He snapped off the light and went out into the bedroom where he stripped the sheets from the bed. Back in the bathroom with the light on he used his knife to cut the sheet, then tore it into strips which he painfully and slowly wrapped around his abdomen.

This would work. It he could get the bleeding stopped he could move.

Jake Grafton followed the trail to the street. He stood there with Toad and Rita and surveyed the wet asphalt with his flashlight. The blood drops were quickly dissipating as the rain intensified.

Jake began to trot.

Jack Yocke pulled alongside. 'Rita,' Jake said, 'go get the captain and the troops. Get them on trucks. Hurry.'

Obediently she jumped into the car, which sped away.

A hundred yards later the blood spots were gone. Jake Grafton stopped and stood panting as he looked around.

'Where do you think he went?' Toad demanded.

'I dunno.'

Jake used the flash again, shining it on the lawns and shrubs and tree trunks. 'Probably in one of these houses, but he could have kept going. We're going to have to get the troops to surround this area and search it. If we can get them in position quickly enough, we can bag this guy—'

Jake didn't answer. It was a possibility. One thing was for sure – whoever it was didn't want to stop and chat.

From the bedroom window Henry Charon saw the flashlight on the street as he searched the closet for clothes. He pulled out some men's shirts and tried one on as he watched the two figures on the street. Much to his disgust, the man of the house was a fatty.

The second bedroom down the hall bore evidence of a male presence. A radio-controlled plane hung from the ceiling, some large posters of scantily clad pinup girls adorned the walls. Charon checked the closets. Yep. And the shirt fit. He rooted until he found a sweater and added that. The jeans were a little big, but he had a belt.

And there was a decent coat. Not a parka, but a warm one with a Gortex surface.

When he had his boots back on, he went back to the master bedroom for the weapons and rucksack. Those two outside had walked fifty feet or so north and were obviously waiting.

Henry Charon had no doubt they were waiting for soldiers to arrive.

He went down the stairs and paused in the kitchen. The refrigerator. Pretty empty. Nothing but a loaf of bread and a half pack of baloney. The owners must be gone for the holidays. He stuffed the loaf in his pocket and wolfed down the baloney. The blood loss had made him ravenous. And food would help his body manufacture new blood cells.

He went into the front room and stood peeking through a crack in the drapes as he chewed and swallowed bread. He explored the bandage with his right hand. It wasn't sodden yet, but it would be after a while. He had extra sheet strips in the duffle bag.

Time to go.

Out in the backyard with the door pressed shut, he walked down the concrete walk to the swimming pool, which was covered for the winter. He was going to have to cross the grass.

He did so. The back fence was six feet high. He threw his bags over, then jumped and hooked a heel over the top. The pain in his side almost made him fall off. He struggled, then fell over the other side.

It was several seconds before he could move. It was so pleasant lying here on the soft ground, with the rain falling gently on his face. If he could just rest, sleep maybe, let this pain subside . . .

He struggled upright and got the bags positioned on his shoulders just as a dog in the nearby house began to yap.

He trotted past the left side of the house and got out on the street and kept going in a long, easy, ground-covering lope.

'What's that noise?'

'Dog barking somewhere,' Toad said. He still had perfect hearing, much better than Grafton's.

'You stay here. Get the troops spread around, maybe out ten blocks if you have enough men.'

Jake went down along the house they were in front of, trying to figure out where that dog was that was barking.

The backyard had a pool. He walked through the grass, looking for tracks with his flashlight. His boots sank into the soft earth. He went on toward the fence. That barking dog seemed to be across it and down a house.

He saw the tracks in the wet earth. Galvanized, Jake slung the rifle on his back and swung up. It occurred to him as he went over that he could have just made a fatal mistake.

The shot never came. He stood on the other side of the fence breathing hard, trying to listen. The dents in the grass went alongside the house.

Following, he stopped at the edge of the street and listened intently. He heard the faint sound of a man running, his boots hitting the pavement.

Jake Grafton ran in that direction. He was huffing badly, overheating from too many clothes. And he was sadly out of shape.

The street turned ninety degrees right in a wide sweeping turn. On both sides of the street were houses set well back from the pavement and partially obscured by yards full of huge bushes and evergreens.

As he rounded the curve Jake saw the man ahead. And the man glanced back over his shoulder and saw him. Jake tried to run faster.

The man ahead broke like a sprinter. And he's got a bullet in him!

He was going to have to shoot. No question. He would never catch him. As he ran he flipped the safety off and thumbed the selector to full automatic. The distance between them was growing.

The man ahead was coming to a streetlight. Now!

Jake stopped and flopped down on his belly in the street. Too late he realized a gentle crown in the road obscured the lower half of the fleeing man's body.

Panting desperately, Jake aligned the sights as best he could. He squeezed the trigger and held it down as he fought to hold the weapon on target.

He let the entire clip go in one long, thunderous three-second burst.

Half-blinded from the muzzle blasts, he rose into a crouch and stared, blinking his eyes desperately, trying to see.

The man he had been chasing was gone.

Disappointed beyond words, Jake sank into a sitting position in the middle of the street and tried to catch his breath. Oh God! Forty-five years old and tied to a desk. He still couldn't get enough air. His heart was thudding like he was going to die.

Three minutes later an army truck rounded the curve with a roar and squealed to a stop beside him. The sergeant on the running board leaped down and covered him with the M-16 while two men piled out of the rear of the truck and faced away with their weapons at the ready.

'Drop it.'

Jake let the rifle fall. 'I'm Captain Graft—'

'On your face, Jack, spread-eagle, or I'll cut you clean in half.'

He obeyed. Wearing khaki trousers and a green coat, he sure didn't look like a soldier. Rough hands searched him and found his wallet, which they extracted.

'Sorry, sir. You may stand up now.'

Jake rolled over and accepted an offered hand. When he was standing he asked, 'You guys with Bravo Company, Second Battalion?'

'No, sir. Charlie, First Battalion. Sorry about—'

'Forget it. Let me use your radio.'

Bravo Company was still assembling in Rock Creek Park. It would take another ten minutes or so, Rita estimated. She told him that the troops had removed all the equipment from the cave.

'Take it to the FBI. Special Agent Hooper.'

Jake deployed the Charlie Company soldiers in the truck and searched the neighborhood where the fugitive had disappeared.

Nothing. The man was gone.

At 1 A.M. Yocke came by with Toad and Rita, and Jake climbed into the car. He was exhausted.

30

Jake Grafton picked up Toad Tarkington at eight the next morning. They then drove over to the *Post* building to get Jack Yocke. He was wearing the same clothes he had had on last night.

'You sleeping up there?' Toad asked.

'You know how it is in the big city. Public transportation is the pits and if you drive you have to fight all the traffic.'

'Want to borrow a toothbrush?'

'Thanks anyway. A guy in the newsroom had one and we all shared. You won't believe who is up there right now talking to Ott Mergenthaler.' Without pausing, Yocke added, 'Sam Strader.'

That piece of news didn't seem to impress the two naval officers.

'And the powers that be have been on the phone more or less continuously with the White House. They want passes for our delivery trucks. Without them we can't publish.'

Jake grunted. He was thinking about a cup of coffee, wishing he had one. None of the fast-food, or corner delis were open; their people couldn't get to work. Banning cars had shut this town down.

'The thing that has our guys going is the authorities gave the TV people passes for their camera trucks.'

'Each station got passes for two trucks,' Jake said. 'The *Post* and the *Times* have hundreds of trucks.'

'Hey, I'm not arguing the case. I'm just filling you in on the news. That's my bag.'

The silence that followed was broken when Yocke asked Jake, 'How about a clarification of the ground rules between you and me. I agreed not to publish until "this is over." When will that be?'

'When all the troops leave and the civil government takes charge.'

'My editor wanted to know. I left him with the impression I'm getting red-hot sizzling stuff.'

'Are you?'

'Well, at least it's warm.'

'Body temperature?'

'Not quite that warm. Tepid might be the word.'

'What can we do,' Jake asked Toad, 'to give this intrepid lad some sizzle?'

'Let's think about that. I could tell you what Rita told me last night when I asked for some sizzle, but I doubt if it would help.'

'Probably not.'

Yocke was busy explaining what he meant by sizzle when the windshield popped audibly in front of the driver's seat and a neat hole surrounded by concentric lines appeared instantly, as if by magic.

Automatically Toad slammed on the brake.

'Floor it,' Grafton said. 'Let's get outta here.'

Tarkington jammed the accelerator down. The next bullet missed the passenger compartment and penetrated the sheet metal somewhere with an audible thud. The report followed a second later.

Toad swerved and kept going. The first comer he came to he went around with tires squealing.

'Anyone hurt?'

'Not me,' Grafton said and got busy brushing the tiny pieces of glass off the front seat. 'You can slow down now.'

'Someone's unhappy,' Yocke said. 'There's a lot of that these days.'

'That asshole could have killed one of us,' Toad groused.

'I think that was the idea,' Yocke said dryly.

Toad Tarkington raised his lip in a snarl. Yocke was still insufferable.

At the armory Jake spent a half hour in the command center. Random shootings were occurring at at least a half dozen locations in the city. Troops were being directed to the affected areas to find the snipers.

'We got over a hundred druggies back there locked up and more coming in all the time,' Major General Greer said. 'If it's just withdrawal or possession, I'm shipping them down to Fort McNair. We're putting them in the gymnasium there until somebody figures out what to do with them. But the people with weapons, the people that are actively resisting our guys or carrying significant quantities of drugs, I'm keeping them here. We have to separate the wheat from the chaff someway.'

'They're still carrying guns?' Jake asked.

'Oh yes. Apparently they're fighting each other *and* the soldiers. Just two hours ago we had a raging gun battle in the Northeast section. Seven civilians dead and wounded by the time the soldiers got there. They were using automatic weapons.'

'Any word on the terrorists?'

'Still looking. But even if we find them, my recommendation to General Land will be that we maintain martial law until this random shooting and gang warfare stops. We can't just walk out now and leave this mess to the cops.'

Jake went back to the office General Greer had made available and got on the phone.

'I have something I want to tell you,' Jack Yocke told Jake a half hour later when he and Tarkington finally got off the telephones.

Something about Yocke's tone caused Jake Grafton to raise his eyebrows. Toad caught it too. 'You want me to leave?' he asked the reporter.

'No. Maybe you both ought to hear this. You'll know what to do with it. Needless to say, it's not for public consumption.'

'Off the record?' Toad asked, horrified.

Yocke's lips twisted and he nodded.

Toad tiptoed to the door, opened it and peeked out, then closed it and wedged a chairback under the knob. 'Okay, fire away. But remember, even the walls have ears.'

'How do you stand him?' Yocke asked Grafton.

The captain rested his chin in his hand and sighed audibly.

'Three or four weeks ago they had a revolution down in Cuba.'

'We heard about that,' Toad said.

'I figured I'd avoid the mob of reporters and travel down there in a slightly unconventional way, a way that would generate a story. So I went to Miami and walked in on a group of Cuban exiles that might be planning on going back. I promised them I wouldn't do any stories on how I got to Cuba. They weren't too thrilled about having me but they took me with them to Cuba. As I said, I promised not to publish anything about them. But I didn't promise not to tell the US government.'

'Okay.' Jake nodded.

'At Andros Island in the Bahamas they loaded about three-dozen wire-guided antitank missiles aboard. That's where they said we were, anyway.'

'Maybe you'd better tell us the whole story,' Jake said, and pulled around a pad to take notes.

Yocke did. His recitation took fifteen minutes. When he was finished, both officers had questions to clear up minor points.

Finally, when everything seemed to have been covered, Jake asked, 'Why are you telling us this?'

Yocke just looked at him. 'Isn't that obvious?'

'You tell me.'

'I think the US government ought to look into where those anti-tank missiles came from. Maybe they were stolen from a government warehouse. Maybe – oh, I don't know. I'll bet they were stolen.'

'Why didn't you go to the FBI?'

'Because I'm a reporter. If it gets around that I tell tales to the FBI, I'm finished. People won't talk to me.'

'Why now?'

Yocke twisted. 'I wasn't going to tell. But I know you fellows and now seemed like a good time.'

'You could have been killed down in Miami,' Toad pointed out.

'Well, I'm still alive.'

'I'm trying to figure out why that is,' Jake told him, and leaned back in his chair and pulled out a lower desk drawer to rest his feet upon. 'Why are you still among the living?'

'I told you what they told me.'

'Hmmm. You think that was the real reason?'

'It sounded real good to me at the time.'

'How does it sound now?'

Yocke cleared his throat and rubbed his lips as he considered the question. 'It doesn't really hold water. Why should they trust me when a bullet would have solved their problem? They could have just dumped me out in the Gulf Stream. Nobody would have ever known and that would have been that. I don't know why they didn't, and I don't think the people in Cuba are going to give me any answer except the one they gave me then.'

'Surely you've got a theory or two?'

'Well, yes. This business about General Zaba got me thinking. You know, it's easy to assume that our government is made up of a bunch of boobs who never know what's going on and screw up anything positive they try to do.'

Jake's eyebrows rose a millimeter and fell.

'I've come to believe that most of the time you guys do your job right. It occurred to me that possibly one of the reasons General Zaba is in the US to testify against Chano Aldana is because the US government helped the rebels overthrow Castro.'

'Interesting,' Jake Grafton said.

'I think the reason I'm still alive is because the Cubans were CIA or knew that the CIA would not be pleased if American citizens got murdered.'

Jake shrugged. 'It's possible. But you haven't brought this up expecting me to find some answers, have you?' Jake asked.

'No. Just being a good citizen. I'm telling you on the off chance the US government lost some antitank missiles and wants to find out where they went.'

Jake Grafton laced his ringers behind his head. 'Rest assured, we'll report this to the right people, but the investigation will be classified and we won't be able to tell you anything. Sure, if someone gets prosecuted for stealing anti-tank missiles you'll hear about it, but that's if and when.'

Yocke raised a hand and nodded.

'Just passing the info along for what it's worth.' He got out of his chair. 'Now I have to go look in the command post room and call the office. If you guys go charging off, please come and find me.'

'Sure.'

After Yocke left, Toad went over to the door, waited about thirty seconds, then opened it and looked out. The hall was empty. He closed the door and stood with his back to it.

'I never thought he'd mention that to anybody.'

'Guess his conscience got him,' Jake Grafton said.

'Well, what do you think?'

'He's a pretty smart kid. I think he's ninety percent certain and is just making sure that Uncle Sam knows to cover the other ten. That's my feel,' Jake shrugged. 'But I don't know,' he added, and put his feet on the floor and closed the desk drawer. 'I guess we'll know what Yocke thinks if we see a story about it in the paper someday with his byline.'

He tore three pages of notes from the legal pad and held them out for Toad. 'Here. See these get to the CIA. Don't leave them lying around.'

'Should I do a cover memo?'

'Yep. Top secret.'

'The CIA guys are gonna think you raised this subject with him. They'll never believe he gave us this out of the blue.'

'It was a good operation,' Jake said after a moment. 'Yocke doesn't really know anything. He just suspects. But Castro's out and we have Zaba and Aldana is going to get what's coming to him. That's the bottom line.'

'Yocke's a pretty good reporter,' Toad said grudgingly.

Jake shooed Toad out with a wave of his fingers.

He called the telephone company and asked for Lieutenant Colonel Franz. The colonel was one of the officers from Jake's Joint Staff group. Jake had sent him to the telephone company yesterday morning.

'Colonel Franz speaking, sir.'

'Jake Grafton. What's happening over there?'

'We're doing our best, sir, but we only have three people counting me. It's like trying to sample the Niagara River with a beer can.'

'Uh huh.'

Franz sighed. Jake could hear him flipping paper, probably his notes. 'All we do is listen to calls at random. No method. But we have heard three that seemed to be discussing sniping at troops. One concerned "taking out" some rivals – I got that one. They must have had some kind of gear on the line that told them they were being monitored, because I only got ten or twelve words and one of them hung up while the other was talking.'

'Exactly what was said?'

' "With Willie out the field is open so we got to take them out before—" Really, it was over before I even realized what I was listening to.'

'Anything else?'

'One interesting thing. It seems there's going to be a rally this evening.

The others have heard calls on that. Five calls all together. You realize there could have been 500 calls on that subject and we've intercepted five.'

'A *rally*?'

'Yeah. That's the word they used. A rally.'

'Where?'

'I don't know.'

A rally? What in hell did that mean? Jake Grafton wrote the word on the pad in front of him.

'What d'ya think?'

'We could use some more people,' Colonel Franz told him.

'Look around. Find out how tough it would be to turn off the whole phone system. There's got to be some switches around there someplace that would shut the whole thing down.'

'Turn it off? Wow! Are you . . .'

'Just took around. I'll call you back.'

Jake put in a call to General Land at the Pentagon. The Chairman would be tied up for another quarter hour. His aide said he would leave him the message.

Jake doodled as he waited. Henry Charon. Apartments. Sleeping bags in caves. Poacher and small rancher.

Why is Henry Charon still in Washington? If he is. Jake wrote that question down and stared at it.

He called the FBI and asked for Special Agent Hooper.

'You had some excitement last night.'

'He got away,' Jake said. 'Any developments?'

'The people in New Mexico got a warrant and searched Charon's ranch and took prints. Most of them were of one person and they match the prints on the stuff your people brought us last night from that cave in Rock Creek Park. It's definitely the same person.'

'Any photos of this guy?'

'Nothing in the house in New Mexico. Not a one. We're looking.'

'We need those driver's license photos as soon as you can get them over here.'

'Be a couple more hours.'

'How about this Tassone guy that the fellow in Pennsylvania sold the rifles to?'

'Nothing on him yet. Apparently no one in Vegas has seen him for a couple weeks.'

'How about here in Washington?'

'We're working on it.'

'You going to put the Charon DMV photo on the air?'

'Be on the noon news.'

'Tell me, if we shut down the telephone system, would you all be able to keep operating?'

Hooper paused before he answered. 'Well, we have the government lines and dedicated lines for the computers and all. If those stay up, we'll be okay. And the local police have radios.'

'Okay. Thanks. Call me if you get anything, will you? I'm at the armory.'

'Found the terrorists yet?'

'You'll be the first to hear.'

He had no more than hung up when the telephone rang again. General Land's aide was on the line. In a moment Jake was talking to the Chairman.

'Sir, I'd like to recommend that we shut down the local telephone system. Apparently people are using it to plan attacks on the soldiers and on rival gangs. And somebody is trying to get up a rally for this evening.'

'A rally?'

'Yessir.'

'Bullshit. There'll be no rallys while we're trying to put a lid on things.'

'Yessir. I'll pass that to General Greer.'

'You talk to Greer about the telephone system. If he thinks shutting the system down is warranted, it's okay with me. Tell him I'll back him either way.'

'Aye aye, sir.'

Jake hung up the telephone and went off to find Major General Greer. He left the pad with his questions about Henry Charon lying on the desk.

His side hurt like fire. The pain woke him and Henry Charon lay in the darkness with his eyes open fighting it. He groped with his right hand until he found the flashlight and flipped it on.

The beam swung around the little cellar, taking in the supplies, the brick walls, the concrete slab, the ceiling.

He had gotten here at 3 A.M. after a four-mile trek through the alleys and back yards of Washington. He had successfully avoided the army patrols and a roving band of juveniles, but the effort had exhausted him. Never in his life had he been so tired.

With the pain of the wound and the cold and the wet and the exertion, he had wondered for a while if he would make it at all.

Now as he lay on the sleeping bag, still fully dressed in the damp clothes he had stolen last night, the pain knifed savagely through him and he wondered if he could move. Only one way to find out. He pulled himself into a sitting position.

Oh *God*! A groan escaped him.

But he wouldn't give in. Oh no. Using his right hand, he pulled the battery-operated lantern over and turned it on. It flooded the little room with light.

He eased himself around so he could examine the sleeping bag where he lay. A little blood, but not much. That was good. Very good. The bleeding had stopped.

The best thing would be to lay still for a few days until that bullet hole began to heal, but of course that was impossible.

In spite of the pain he was hungry. He tried to order his thoughts and prioritize what he needed to do. He seemed to be mentally alert. That was also good and cheered him.

First he needed to administer a local anesthetic. He got out the first aid kit and opened it. He could use his left hand if he didn't move his shoulder too much. The pain radiated that far.

It took three or four minutes, but he got a hypodermic filled and proceeded to inject himself in four places, above, below, and to the right and left of the wound. The contortions required caused him to break into a sweat and bite his lip, but the effect of the drug was immediate. The pain eased to a dull ache.

The roof of the old cellar was just high enough to let him stand, so he eased himself upright and stood swaying while his blood pressure and heart rate adjusted. He took a few experimental steps. He ground his teeth together.

He relieved himself into a bucket in the comer. He examined the urine flow carefully. Not even pink. No blood at all.

Food. And water. He needed both to replace the lost blood.

He rigged the Sterno can and lit it and opened a can of stew. While it was heating he munched on some beef jerky and drank deeply from the water can.

Still waiting for the stew to heat, he stripped off the clothes he was wearing. He pulled on dry trousers, but he left the shirt off. In a little while he was going to have to change this bandage. The wet clothes he hung on a convenient nail.

There! He felt better already.

After he had eaten the stew, he opened a can of fruit cocktail and consumed that. He finished it by drinking the last of the juice, then another pint of water.

Pleasantly full, Henry Charon lay back down on the sleeping bag. For the first time he looked at his watch. Almost 12 o'clock. Noon or midnight, he didn't know. But he couldn't have slept all day, clear through until midnight.

He pulled the radio over and turned it on. In a few minutes he had the television audio.

Noon. It was almost noon. He had slept for about eight hours.

He turned off the lantern to save the battery and lay in the darkness listening to the radio. He had the volume turned down so low it was just barely audible. He didn't want anyone passing in the subway tunnel outside to hear it – but that was unlikely. With the military in charge of the city all work on the tunnels had stopped.

So he lay there in the darkness half-listening to television audio on the radio and thinking about last night. He had heard that officer on the road talking to the soldier who shot him as he climbed the ridge away from them. Really, that had been a stroke of terrible luck. Shot crossing a road! He had damn near ended up a road kill, like some rabbit or stray dog smashed flat on the asphalt.

He sighed and closed his eyes, trying to forget the dull pain in his back.

Any way you looked at it, this had been the best hunt of his life. Far and away the best. Even last night when the soldiers were chasing him and he was hurting so badly – that had been a rare experience, something to be savored. He had been out there on the edge of life, living it to the hilt, making it on his own strength and wits and determination. Sublime. That was the word. Sublime. Nothing he had ever done in his entire life up to this point could match it. Everything up to now had been merely preparation for last night; for slipping down through the forest between the soldiers, for going up that ridge wounded and bleeding and digging like hell, for throwing himself down in the street and rolling clear with the bullets flaying the air over his head, then running and scheming and doubling back occasionally to throw off possible pursuers.

Most men live a lifetime and never have even one good hunt. He had had so many. And to top it off with last night!

He was going back through it again, thinking through each impression, reliving the emotions, when he heard his name on the radio. He fumbled with it and got the volume up.

'. . . has been tentatively identified as a New Mexico rancher and firearms expert. This man is armed and extremely dangerous. He is believed to have been wounded last night by troops in the District of Columbia as they tried to apprehend him. If you see this man, please, we urge you, do not attempt to approach him or apprehend him yourself. Just call the number on the screen and tell the authorities your name and address, and where and when you believe you saw him.

'Why Henry Charon undertook to assassinate the President and Vice-President is not known at this time. We hope to have more for you from New Mexico on Charon's background later this afternoon. Stay tuned to this station.'

Charon snapped off the radio. He lay in the darkness with his eyes open.

Not fingerprints. His prints were not on file anyplace. If they had his prints they had nothing. It must have been the drawing. Someone in New Mexico must have recognized it and called the police.

That conclusion reached, he dismissed the whole matter and began again to examine the events of last night in minute detail. After all, there was nothing he could do about what the police and FBI knew. If they knew, they knew.

Deep down Henry Charon had never really expected to make a clean escape. He knew the odds were too great. He had signed on for the hunt and it had been superb, exceeding his wildest expectations.

As the bullets had ripped over his head and the roar of the M-16 shattered the night, he had learned for the very first time the extraordinary thrill of coming face to face with death and escaping out the other side. The experience could not be explained – it defied words. So he lay here in the darkness savoring every morsel of it.

Eventually he would turn to the problem of what to do next, but not right now.

'These goddamn terrorists are in the District. You know it, I know it, everybody knows it. The question is what are they going to do next?'

Major General Greer stood with Jake Grafton looking at the map of the city that took up most of a wall. Greer was a stocky man, deeply tanned, with short iron-gray hair that stood straight up all over his head. He had made up his mind to be a soldier when he was nine years old and had seen no reason to change that decision from that day to this.

He glanced at Grafton. He expected a response when he asked questions aloud.

'They can wait for us to find them, sir,' Jake Grafton said, 'and shoot it out right there.'

'That's Option One,' Greer said, nodding. This thinking aloud was a habit with him, one his staff was used to. Jake was catching on fast. Over in the corner, Grafton noticed, Jack Yocke was taking notes.

'Or they can select a target and hit it. Or two targets. Possibly three depending on how many and how well armed they are.'

'Option two.'

'They can hope we don't find them and give up the search.'

'Three. Any more?'

'Not that I can think of.'

'Me either. I like number two the best. That's the one I'd pick if I were them. I suspect a bunch of civilians paid to get killed won't do well just sitting and waiting.'

Greer sighed. 'As if we knew. Anyway, if they take option two, what will be their target?'

Jake let his eyes roam across the map. 'The White House,' he suggested tentatively.

'I have two companies of troops and ten tanks at Bethesda Naval Hospital. One company of troops around the White House and four tanks sitting there, one on each corner. Another company with tanks at the old Executive Office Building. Same thing at the Naval Observatory, where the Vice-President lives. Also at the Capitol on the off chance they'd hit that again, and at the Senate and House office buildings. What else?'

'I don't know.'

'Join the crowd,' said General Greer.

'What about the marine base at Quantico?'

'Where they're holding Aldana? I think not. Chano Aldana doesn't strike me as the suicidal type. They'd never get him out alive. I've given orders to that effect. That's the last place they'd strike.'

Only half the city had been searched so far. It was going very slowly. The troops were being sniped at from locations throughout the city. Five soldiers had been wounded and two were dead so far. And the soldiers were shooting back. Eleven civilians were dead so far.

Greer turned away from the map and ran his hand through the stubble on his head. He sank into the nearest chair. 'Did you want something?' he asked Jake.

The captain told him about the eavesdroppers at the telephone exchange and what Lieutenant Franz had reported.

'A rally?' the general repeated.

'Tonight.'

'Damnedest thing I ever heard. If it happens we'll break it up.'

'I suggest we shut down the local telephone system. The people at the telephone company say it can be done. We know the people sniping at soldiers and other civilians are coordinating their activities by telephone. What this rally business means, I have no idea, but I don't like it. On the other hand, I'm told the television showed a photo of the guy the FBI believe is the assassin on the noon news, along with a telephone number to call if anyone sees him. They've been broadcasting similar appeals about the terrorists for two days. If we turn off the phones, we won't get any calls.'

'Have you discussed this with General Land?'

'Yessir. He says it's your decision. He'll back you up either way.'

'Haven't had any calls so far.'

'No, sir.'

'This rally business, that bothers me. The last thing we need is a bunch of innocent civilians wandering the streets en masse with all these criminals taking potshots at people. Hell, if something like that happens it could turn into a bloodbath.'

Greer sat silently rubbing his head. 'Turn the damn phones off,' he said finally. 'I'm going to screw this damn town down tighter and tighter until something pops.'

31

The Longstreet Commission later listed many factors that contributed to the violence that occurred in Washington that day. However nobody disputed the assertion that the black population's long-cherished, deep-seated belief that they were victims of intentional racist oppression aggravated the situation and brought it to a boil.

Young males in street gangs – black males, by definition in the inner city – began breaking windows and looting stores, and when soldiers showed up, they threw rocks and bottles and everything else they could readily lay their hands on.

At first the soldiers fired their rifles into the air. When that didn't work, they waded in pushing and shoving and dragging the most belligerent to trucks for transportation to the armory.

Automobiles were set ablaze by the mobs, which became larger and more violent as television broadcast the madness. Inevitably some of the people on the streets were killed by soldiers, most of whom were no older than those who were screaming insults at them and hurling rocks. A television camera caught one of these incidents and instantly it became a rallying cry.

General Land ordered the television cameras off the streets, but by then it was too late. A dozen buildings in the poorer neighborhoods were ablaze and fire trucks and emergency crews were unable to get their equipment to the fires because of the rioting mobs. Some of the army officers decided to use tanks to try to cow the rioters, but the immediate response was to fill bottles with gasoline and stick blazing rags down the neck. These the rioters threw. After one tank was disabled and two men severely burned getting out of it, an accompanying tank opened fire with a machine gun. A dozen people were mowed down. The rioters fled in every direction, setting fire to cars and smashing windows as they ran. The whole scene played on television to a horrified nation.

The smell of smoke and burning rubber wafted throughout the city under the gray sky. Although one could smell the smoke almost every-where in the city, the rioting was confined to the inner-city neighborhoods, the poor black ghettos, just as it had been during the major urban riots of the Vietnam War era. This did not occur by accident. Over half the twelve-thousand soldiers in the district were being used to protect the public buildings and monuments of official Washington. Still, the vast majority of rioters stayed close to home of their own accord, righting and looting and burning in their own neighborhoods.

Generals Land and Greer rushed troops to every corner. The only option they had was to continue to increase the troop presence until the situation stabilized. The search for the terrorists was abandoned.

As the sun moved lower on the western horizon, the temperature of the air began to drop quickly from the daytime high of fifty-six degrees. In the armory General Greer and the staff watched the falling mercury as closely as they did the incoming situation reports. Perhaps cold could accomplish what the soldiers couldn't. Someone prayed aloud for rain.

With darkness approaching General Greer committed the last of his troops to the inner-city neighborhoods. Gunfire and flames still racked the city, but the number of people on the streets was definitely decreasing.

'Captain Grafton. We have a problem out front.' The young army captain was apologetic. 'General Greer said he's too busy and asked if you would handle it.'

Jake laid down the pen he was using to draft a report for General Land. 'Yes.'

'It's out front, sir. If you would accompany me?'

In the hallway the junior officer told him, 'We've got some people out here, sir, who want their relatives released into their custody.'

'How many?'

'Only three. They had to walk to get here, and with the rioting and all . . .'

'Yeah. How many have you released so far?'

'We haven't released anybody, sir. We send the curfew violaters and simple possession cases over to Fort McNair, but the rioters and looters and shooters we've kept here.'

'These people the relatives want, what category are they in?'

'A looter, a shooter, and a possession case. The possession case is a woman. She was giving a guy a blow job in a car and since they weren't supposed to be in cars, our people searched them. The guy had some crack on him and she had some traces of powder and crack in her purse. So we brought them in.'

The civilians were standing by the desk near the entrance to the equipment bay. Two were black women and one was a white man. Jake spoke to the oldest woman first.

'I'm Harriet Hannifan, General. I want my boy back.' She was in her fifties, Jake guessed, stout, with gray hair. Her purse hung on her arm. Her shoes were worn.

'What's his name, ma'am?'

'Jimmy Hannifan.'

Jake turned to the sergeant at the desk, who consulted his notes. 'Looting, sir. He was throwing rocks through store windows. We caught him trying to run with a television. He dropped it and it broke all to hell and we caught him anyway.'

'Your son ever been in trouble before, ma'am?'

'He's my grandson. Lord, yes, he's been in trouble at school and he runs with a bad crowd. He's only sixteen and wants to quit school but I won't let him.'

'Bring him out here,' Jake told the captain.

'How far did you walk to get here?' Jake asked Mrs Hannifan.

'A couple of miles or so.'

'Pretty dangerous.'

'He's all I got.'

'And you, ma'am?' Jake said to the other woman, who was younger than Mrs Hannifan but not dressed as well.

'It's my boy. He shot at some people. I saw the soldiers take him away.'

Jake was tempted to refuse. But he hesitated. 'How far did you come?'

'From Emerson and Georgia Avenue. I don't know how far it is.'

'Five or six miles,' the sergeant said. 'Through all that rioting.'

Jake nodded at the captain.

'And you, sir?'

'My name's Liarakos. I'd like to see my wife. The sergeant says she's been detained for drug possession.'

'You mean you want her released?'

'No.' Liarakos spoke forcefully. 'I want to see her first. Then, maybe, but . . .' His voice trailed off.

Jake turned to the captain and said, 'Bring those men to my office. And take this gentleman back to visit his wife.' He asked the women to accompany him.

Back in his office with everyone seated, he sent Toad for coffee. Jack Yocke sat silently at the other desk.

The younger woman began to sob. Her name was Fulbright. 'I know it's not your fault,' she said, 'but it's more than a body can stand, what with the drugs and the unemployed and the schools that don't teach them nothing. How can they grow up to be men living in this? I ask you.'

'I don't know.'

The silence grew uncomfortable as Mrs Fulbright sobbed. Jake could think of nothing to say, and once he shot a glance at Yocke, hoping he would help. The reporter returned his look impassively and said nothing.

Toad brought the coffee just seconds before two soldiers escorted the men into the room in handcuffs. Men? They were just boys.

'You kids are leaving,' Jake said, 'because these women cared enough about you to risk their lives walking over here. You may not have much money, but you got something a lot of folks will never have – people that love you.'

Both the youngsters looked uncomfortable, embarrassed. Ah, what's the use? Jake wondered. But maybe, just maybe . . . 'Toad, when these ladies finish their coffee, drive these people home.'

'My God, Thanos, why did you come?'

'I—'

She held up a hand so he couldn't see her face. He pulled her hand away. She was crying.

'You shouldn't have come,' she whispered. 'Oh, my God, Thanos, look what I've done to myself.'

The room they had her in held five other women. It stank of vomit and urine. A half dozen bare mattresses lay scattered on the floor, but there was no other furniture. Elizabeth sat huddled on a mattress. Her clothes were filthy.

'I'm sorry, Thanos. I'm sorry.'

'That's the first step on the road back, Elizabeth.'

'I feel so dirty. So degraded! And I've crawled into this sewer all by myself. How can you even look at—'

'You want to go home? Without the dope?'

'I don't know if I can! But why would you – don't you know what I've done? Don't you know why I'm here?'

'I know.'

She tore her hand from his grasp and held it in front of her face. 'Please leave, for the love of—'

Liarakos rose and pounded on the door.

'Sir, I'd like to take my wife home.'

Liarakos stood in front of Grafton's desk. Jake Grafton forced himself to look up into the man's face. 'Fine,' he said. 'Where do you live?'

'Edgemoor.'

'Isn't that over on the other side of Rock Creek Park?'

'Yes.'

'Jack, go catch Toad. Tell him he'll have two more passengers. Go with him, Mr Liarakos.'

Liarakos turned to go, then looked back. 'Thanks, I—'

Jake waved him out.

In ten minutes Yocke was back. 'They all left with Toad,' he said and sat down in the chair in front of Jake's desk. 'Do you know who that man was?'

'Lee-something. I've forgotten.'

Thanos Liarakos. He's the lawyer representing Chano Aldana.'

'Everybody has their troubles,' Jake Grafton said, his eyes back on his report. The skin on his face was taut across the bones. His eyes looked like they were recessed even deeper into their sockets.

'You knew that when you first saw him, didn't you?'

'You're worse than Tarkington. Go find something to do someplace else, will you?'

Yocke rose uncertainly. He wandered aimlessly for several seconds, went out the door and down the hall, then out to the desk in the bay where the soldiers were checking in the prisoners. He waited until the sergeant finished logging in two more surly prisoners, then asked, 'Mrs Liarakos. Who was the man arrested with her?'

'Ah, I've got it here,' The sergeant flipped through his book, a green, hardbound logbook. He found the entry. 'Guy who refused to give his name. Stuff in his wallet says he is one T. Jefferson Brody, a lawyer if you can believe that. Three hours ago. He's in bay four if you want to talk to him.' The sergeant gestured vaguely to his left.

Some of the prisoners were still drunk and belligerent. They shouted and raved obscenities. The smell of urine and body odor made the air heavy and lifeless. Yocke tried to breathe shallowly.

He looked into bay four, a waist-high enclosure with a stained concrete floor normally used for the repair of vehicles. The bay now held several dozen men who were shackled in place. Immediately across the corridor was another bay which contained women. The women sat with their backs to the men.

Yocke didn't recognise Brody. Dressed in a filthy blue suit, the lawyer was standing and straining against the chain around his wrist, screaming at the top of his lungs at the women's area. '*You fucking cunt! I'll rip your fucking liver out with my bare hands. We won't be in here forever, you fucking bitch. Then you wait! I'll get out if it's the last thing I ever do!*'

One of the soldiers walked over with a look of disgust on his face. 'Hey *you*! Big mouth! I'm telling you for the very last time. Shut up!'

'That fucking cunt *robbed* me,' Brody howled. 'I'll—'

'Shut up, butt-face, or we'll gag you. You hear me!'

Brody fell silent. He stared fixedly across at the women's holding area. After a moment he sat down, but his gaze never wavered.

Jack Yocke turned away, slightly nauseated. Hell couldn't be any worse than this, he told himself, and shivered.

The first bomb exploded at six-thirty P.M. A truck packed with five tons of dynamite was driven through the fence at a huge electrical transmission substation on Greenleaf Point, near the mouth of the Anacostia River. The driver ran back through the hole in the wire as two soldiers chased him and fired their rifles. The driver disappeared into the low-income housing projects nearby. The soldiers were going back through the fence to examine the truck when its cargo detonated in a stupendous blast that was felt and heard for miles. The electrical substation was instantly obliterated. The lights went out in downtown and southeast Washington.

In the next fifteen minutes three more substations were attacked, effectively depriving the entire city of electricity.

'At least the damned TV stations are off the air,' Toad Tarkington told Rita Moravia, who had just arrived at the armory on the back of an army truck.

While General Greer was responding to these attacks, a major natural-gas pumping station in Arlington was bombed. The explosion resembled a small nuclear blast. Then the place caught fire. In the darkness that fell on the city when the lights went out the glare of the raging inferno could be seen from rooftops all over the city.

At the same time the explosions were racking the city, an army platoon was ambushed and wiped out on the Capital Beltway by twenty men carrying automatic weapons. Three men in uniform waved the truck to a halt, then shot the driver and sergeant as they emerged from the cab. Some of the men were machine-gunned as they exited the back of the truck. A dozen survivors, trapped in the truck bed and unable to see out, threw out their weapons and surrendered. They were led down into the drainage ditch beside the freeway and shot. The weapons, ammunition, and radios were collected and loaded into the truck.

The attackers climbed into the back of the vehicle under the canvas covering and took their seats. In the cab two men examined the controls of the truck, which was still idling, managed to get the transmission into gear, and drove away.

The truck left the beltway at Kenilworth Avenue and proceeded south toward the city at about twenty-five miles per hour. Anticipating the enthusiasm of teenage soldiers, the Army had long ago installed a governor to prevent the engine from over-revving, yet the inexperienced driver couldn't get the transmission into a higher gear.

The two headlights behind metal grilles put out little light, but it was enough. The huge tires rolled easily over the potholes and broken pavement that commuters had accepted as their lot for years.

On the front of the truck was a huge steel horizontal beam, painted olive-drab like the rest of the vehicle. This beam was intended by the Army to enable the truck to push other, disabled, military vehicles.

At the Kenilworth–New York Avenue interchange a half dozen National Guardsmen were manning a roadblock. The driver of the hijacked truck didn't even slow down. The steel beam on the front delivered a glancing blow to the bus parked crossways in the road, shoving it aside as the truck careened on with the engine roaring. The men in back opened up with automatic weapons at the soldiers in the road as the truck swept past.

A third of a mile later the truck thundered by the sign that marked the boundary of the District of Columbia. It was a large white sign with blue letters artfully arranged above and below the logo of the Capitol dome. The sign read: WELCOME TO WASHINGTON, A CAPITAL CITY, MARION C. BARRY, MAYOR.

Henry Charon soaked the old bandage with water from the jug, then slowly unwrapped it from around his waist. It hurt too much for him to twist around to try to see the wound, so he didn't bother. He merely wrapped strips of the stolen sheet around his middle and tied them in neat knots.

Then he put on a flannel shirt and over that a sweatshirt.

The coat he had appropriated last night from the college boy was fashionable but certainly not utilitarian enough for Charon's taste. He hung it on a nail and donned a spare water-resistant parka. His well-worn leather hunting boots went on his feet over two pairs of wool socks.

He threaded a scabbard for a hunting knife onto his belt and positioned it so it hung into his rear hip pocket. When the belt was fastened and adjusted just so below the makeshift bandage about his middle, he inserted the thin-bladed razor-sharp skinning knife he favored into the scabbard and snapped the restraining strap around the handle.

Lastly he put on his cap, a wool-lined billed affair with ear flaps folded around the sides, just in case. The cap was a dark brown and bore the dirt and stains of many winters.

The silencer attached smoothly, effortlessly to the 9-mm pistol. He checked to ensure the magazine was loaded and pulled back the slide until he saw the gleam from a round in the chamber. Flicking the safety on, he slipped the weapon behind his belt in the small of his back. The grenades and two loaded magazines for the pistol went into the pockets of the parka.

He opened the duffle bag and checked the Model 70 Winchester. Still secure, properly padded, with a box of .30–06 ammo wrapped in bubble wrap. He zipped the bag closed and slung it on his shoulder.

What else? Oh yeah, the pencil flash. He tried it, then turned it off and stowed it in one of the pockets of the parka.

Not the radio. It would be nice but was too bulky. Food, water? A handful of jerky and a plastic baby bottle full of water – that would have to do. And the street map.

Anything else?

Gloves. He pulled them on slowly, good pigskin gloves that fit perfectly.

True, this would not be a stalk of Rocky Mountain Bighorn above timberline in sub-zero cold and blowing snow. Yet the quarry would be the wariest, most difficult game of all – man. Henry Charon grinned in delicious anticipation and turned off the battery-powered lantern.

The hijacked truck drove slowly through the gate into the armory parking lot and came to a stop beside three other trucks. The driver turned off the lights, killed the engine, and climbed down. On the other side the sergeant walked back and watched his men disembark from the bed.

The men didn't line up in formation. They immediately wandered away in twos and threes.

The parking lot was lit by emergency lights mounted on poles and powered by portable generators, which were noisy. The light was adequate, but barely.

The sergeant and a half dozen men walked toward the open door of the armory and passed inside. Two of the men halted inside the huge open bay and stared a moment at the prisoners shackled to the south wall. In the dim glare of the emergency lights that had automatically illuminated when the electricity failed the bay was quite a sight. Over two hundred sobbing, cursing, crying men and women were chained there. The noise was like something from a nightmare about an insane asylum.

After several seconds of silent observation, the intruders turned their attention to the soldiers guarding them, the men coming and going, the ladder that led up to a catwalk and more offices.

Another two of the men walked the length of the bay to the door on the other end while the sergeant and his remaining companions left the bay and walked into the hallway. Although the sergeant knew no English and couldn't read the posted signs, he immediately headed for the large double door standing open at the end of the hall that seemed to have a large number of people coming and going. He passed several Americans on the way, but they didn't give him a glance. With his dark, Latin complexion he fit right into this multiracial army.

The fake sergeant, with his two companions immediately behind him, paused in the large open doorway. Maps covered every wall and radios and telephones stood on the desks. In the center of the room behind a large desk sat a stocky man with two silver stars on each collar.

With a nod to his companions, the sergeant unobtrusively removed a grenade from the webbing across his chest and pulled the pin while the two men beside him did likewise. The three of them each tossed the grenades underhanded toward the center of the room and dove behind nearby desks for cover.

'Grenades!'

The shout galvanized the soldiers. Men were leaping and running and diving when the little hand bombs exploded. The shrapnel destroyed the emergency lighting.

The darkness and silence that followed the explosions was broken only by the high-pitched scream of some poor soul in mortal agony. Then the three intruders opened fire with their rifles.

Out in the squad bay the explosions were muffled but plainly audible. As the soldiers reacted the two terrorists near each door began, in a very businesslike fashion, shooting uniformed men as fast as they could aim and pull the trigger.

But there were too many soldiers. In less than twenty seconds the four intruders were dead.

In the parking lot the gunfire and staccato blasts of grenades continued unabated. One of the men from the hijacked truck reached an M-60 machine gun mounted on a swivel on the back of a jeep and began spraying the soldiers indiscriminately. He was soon shot, but another man took his place. Over eighty soldiers went down in the first thirty seconds of the firefight.

Inside the command post, most of the soldiers had been unarmed. Not that it mattered. The only light was the strobing muzzle blasts. Those soldiers who survived the grenades lay huddled on the floor as the bullets lashed and tore through the furniture and radios. By some miracle, all three of the terrorists fired their weapons aimed too high.

One officer had a pistol. When the automatic bursts stopped – he thought the intruders had expended all the shells in their magazines and were changing them – he opened fire with the pistol at the spots in the darkness where the muzzle blasts seemed to have been coming from. He hit two of the gunmen, but the third one successfully reloaded and killed him with a burst of six slugs.

This man emptied his rifle and reached for another grenade. Just as he got the pin out, a private ran up to the door behind him and gave him a point-blank burst from his M-16. The grenade fell, unseeen by the private, who was killed in the explosion that followed a few seconds later. From the first grenade blast to the last, thirty seconds had passed.

Outside in the parking lot the battle lasted longer. Between the machine gun and bursts from M-16s on full automatic, the number of men who were down was staggering.

Still the soldiers who were unwounded or not wounded too severely fought back. In the confusion some of the Americans shot each other.

The shooting was still going on a minute later when someone began roaring, 'Cease fire, cease fire.' Then it stopped.

The sergeants were turning the bodies of the terrorists over and searching their pockets by the time that Jake Grafton got outside with his rifle. He had been in the head.

'They all look Latin, sir,' someone said to Jake.

'Here's one still alive.' The man the soldier was referring to was babbling in Spanish. He had a hole in the center of his stomach that was pumping blood. He was staring at the wound and repeating the rosary in Spanish.

'Colombia, *sí*?'

The wounded man continued his prayer. The soldier grabbed his shirt, half lifted him, and shook him violently. 'Colombia, *sí*?'

'*Sí. sí. sí . . .*'

'I hope you die slow, motherfuck!' The soldier dropped the man to the pavement.

'How many did we lose?' Jake asked the major beside him as he stared about at the carnage.

'We're counting. Sweet Jesus, I think a lot of our guys shot each other. Everybody was shooting at everybody,' The major's face wore an indescribable look of sadness. 'God have mercy.'

Jake Grafton felt a terrible lethargy. He wanted to just turn off his brain.

'General Greer's dead, sir.'

Jake nodded slowly. Somehow he wasn't surprised. Toad, Rita, where were they?

He found them inside administering first aid to wounded men. Rita was working on a man with a sucking chest wound and Toad was trying to get the bleeding stopped on a man with a bullet through the thigh.

Jake left them and went to find a radio that still worked.

The radio was in the command post, its metal cover scarred by shrapnel. All over the room the medics and volunteers worked feverishly in the light of battery-powered lanterns and flashlights to save the living. The dead lay unattended in their own blood and gore. Jake Grafton fought the vomit back and held the flashlight as the technician tuned the radio to the proper frequency and made the call.

Minutes passed. The saliva in Jake's mouth kept flowing and he kept swallowing. His eyes remained firmly on the radio.

After an eternity the chairman's voice came over the speaker. Jake picked up his mike.

'Captain Grafton, sir. The terrorists found us. They just hit the armory about six or seven minutes ago. We think about eighteen or twenty of them. We haven't got a good count yet, but we think we've got about fifty US dead and a hundred wounded.'

Silence. What was there to say? When the words came it was a question: 'Who's the senior army officer over there still on his feet?'

'Colonel Jonat, I think, sir. He's checking the wounded in the parking lot. General Greer and the two brigadiers that were here are dead.'

'I'll be over there by helicopter as soon as I can. Right now the Vice-President wants to see me over at the White House. Tell the colonel to hold the fort.'

'Yes, sir.'

Jake went outside to find Colonel Jonat and get some air. The emergency generators continued to hum and the lights made grotesque shadows.

After a brief conversation with the colonel, who was organizing the transport of the wounded to the hospital, Jake bummed a cigarette. He was standing beside the door savoring the bitter taste of it when Rita came out. 'I didn't know you smoked, sir.'

Jake Grafton took another drag.

The distance was six hundred yards if it was an inch. Little quartering crosswind. Maybe ten knots. Let's see – the bullet would be in the air for about a second. How much would the wind cause it to drift? He tried to remember the wind tables. Ten knots meant the air would move about seventeen feet in a second. Forty-five degrees off – call it twelve feet in a second. The bullet was stabilized by its spin and would tend to resist being displaced by the wind, but the wind would have an effect. How much? A couple feet over this distance. *If* he was right about the velocity of the wind and the direction, and *if* the wind was steady throughout the flight of the bullet, which it wouldn't be.

And the trajectory dip – about nine or ten feet at six hundred yards.

An impossible shot.

Only a damned fool would try a shot like that.

Henry Charon steadied the rifle on the concrete rail and stared through the scope at the armory. The average guy was six feet tall, so twice that distance would be twelve feet.

The people looked tiny in the scope, even with the nine-power magnification.

The assassin twisted the parallax adjustment ring on the scope to the infinity setting, then backed off a thirty-second of an inch. He settled the rifle again and braced it against his shoulder and studied the scene before the door of the armory.

He had come here because he knew that General Land would come to the armory eventually. Yet with all that shooting over there a while ago – the chairman of the Joint Chiefs should be coming shortly. All Charon had to do was wait. And make this shot.

Wait a sec – that guy standing there smoking near the door? Isn't that the officer from last night? Isn't *that* the man who was standing on the street outside the house under the streetlight?

It's him, all right. Same grungy coat and khaki trousers, same build, same shaped head.

That man hadn't fired the shot that had hit Charon, of course, but he had sprayed a clip full of .223 slugs within inches of his head. He had certainly tried. Wonder if he would try again, given the opportunity?

The thought amused Charon.

He backed away from the scope a moment, rubbed his eyes, then settled in with the rifle hard up against his shoulder. He thumbed off the safety and, just for grins, steadied the scope crosshairs about two feet to the right and nine feet above Jake Grafton's chest. That was the spot.

He filled his lungs, exhaled, and concentrated on holding the rifle absolutely motionless while he took the slack out of the trigger.

Releasing the pressure on the trigger, Charon breathed several times as he thought about last night, about the feel of being chased.

But now – now was *after*. He was looking *back*.

What was he, Henry Charon, going to do with ten million dollars if by some miracle he got away? Sit on a beach somewhere and sip fruit drinks? Perhaps Europe. He tried to picture himself strolling the Left Bank or touring castles on the Rhine. Who was he kidding? He had never expected to get out of this alive. Thirty or forty years of boring anticlimax would be the same as prison.

He exhaled and steadied the crosshairs and ever so gently caressed the trigger with firm, steady pressure. Like all superb riflemen he concentrated on his sight picture without anticipating the moment of letoff. So he was agreeably surprised when the rifle fired.

Something stung Jake Grafton's upper left arm and he jerked. He looked. A hole. There was a hole in his coat! What . . .

He heard the report, a sharp crack.

'*Take cover!*' he screamed. '*Take cover!*' He pushed Rita down and fell on the pavement beside her. '*Fire coming in!*'

Where? He looked around. Against the skyline he could just see the hulking shape of RFK Stadium. Jake scrambled to his feet and began to run. A flash from the stadium high on the structure. Something buzzed by his ear.

Luckily he had hung onto his rifle. It held a full magazine.

As he ran through the gate and turned right for the stadium Jake shrugged off his coat and let it fall. Out of the circle of light and into the darkness, running hard, his heart coming up to speed too quickly and his breath not quickly enough, running . . .

A goddamn sniper! Some nut or dope addict? Or a diversion to pull the troops out of the armory?

Someone was following him, running along behind. He didn't look back.

The stadium was surrounded by a huge chain-link fence topped by barbed wire. Everything in this goddamn city had a fence around it! He made for an arch in the structure that he thought should be a gate. The fence would have a gate outside that. It did.

It was padlocked. He shot the lock. Then jerked it. No. This time he put the muzzle right up against one of the links in the chain and pulled the trigger. Sparks flew and slivers of metal sprayed him, but the chain fell away.

He tugged at the gate. Rita pounded up. She was carrying a rifle. She helped him pull the gate open.

'Get men to surround this stadium outside the fence. Tell them to shoot anybody coming out unless it's me.'

'You think he's still in there?'

'I dunno. Keep moving. Don't be a stationary target.' He went through the gate and ran for the arch.

Ramps led away to the right and left. Jake turned left and trotted upward.

On the second level he stopped to catch his breath and listen. The place was dark as a tomb.

Madness. This was madness.

Rita met a squad of soldiers running toward the stadium with their weapons at high port. 'Surround it. Stay outside the fence. Captain Grafton's in there. Anybody else comes out, shoot them.'

'No warning first?'

'No. Shoot first. And take cover. This guy is a sniper. Try to get behind something in the darkness and lay very still.' She pointed to the sergeant. 'Go back to the armory and ask the colonel for a couple dozen more men. Spread them around.'

'What are you going to do?'

'I'm going in there too.' And with that she slipped through the gate in the fence and ran for the ramp.

Jake walked now, slowly and carefully with the rifle held in both hands and his finger on the safety. His eyes had adjusted all they were going to. He had had trouble the last few years with his night vision, but giving up smoking had helped a lot. His night vision was almost normal now. And he had just smoked a cigarette!

The place was so quiet. Black slabs of concrete, long corridors, huge doors that led out to the seats.

On the third level he turned and went out to the seats, where he could survey the interior of the stadium. There was a faint glow from the clouds, just enough to see the form of the place but not enough to see anyone on the other side of the playing field, if there were anyone there to see.

He hunkered down partially shielded behind a row of seats and scanned carefully, examining the geometric pattern of seats and aisles. After a minute he shifted position and began scanning in the other direction.

Nothing.

He was going to have to come up with a system. Something scientific. A plan.

Okay. He would go up to the top-level concourse and work his way completely around the stadium, occasionally taking the time to survey the seats. Then he would come down a level and repeat the procedure, and so on.

If the guy is in here . . .

But he probably isn't. Why would he stay?

Jake got up, staying low, and moved along the row. He would go out a different place than where he came an. No use being stupid about this.

He heard the bullet smack the seat near him and the booming echo of the report immediately thereafter. He fell flat and crawled, the rifle clunking against the seats.

Well, one thing's dear at least. He's still here.

Colonel Orrin Jonat sent a dozen more troopers to the stadium. With that dozen gone and the casualties and people to transport the wounded to the hospital and stack the dead, he was down to less than fifty men to guard almost four hundred *and* run the war.

First he took the time to arrange four teams of two men each around the armory. Not enough men, it was true, but all he could spare. It had also occurred to him that the sniper from the stadium might be a diversion. Still he had to balance that possibility against the other requirements. He was going to have to bring in a couple of companies from the streets. He didn't have enough men to get new radios in service and keep track of units on the streets.

Were these terrorists the last of them? he asked himself. If only he knew the answer to that!

The army lieutenant leading the squad across the vast, empty parking lots toward the stadium heard the shot from inside. When he got to the gate the sergeant there quickly briefed him.

'Maybe we should go in, sir?' the sergeant suggested.

'The navy people told us to stay out, right?'

'Yes, sir.'

'So we got two good guys and at least one bad guy in there in the dark. If we send more people in, we'll end up shooting the wrong folks. It's inevitable. We just did *that* over at the armory. Not again. Deploy the men around the stadium. Anybody tries to sneak out, drill 'em dead.'

Henry Charon was thoroughly enjoying himself. Standing at the mouth of one of the tunnels that led out from the concourse, he looked through the scope on the rifle. He could just make out the man on the other side of the stadium scuttling up the stairs toward the tunnel exit. This is a damn good scope, he told himself. It gathers the ambient light, allowing you to see better at night with the scope than you can with the naked eye.

Charon moved the crosshairs slightly to one side of the moving man and squeezed the trigger. The rifle set back against his shoulder with a nice firm kick as the roar filled the stadium.

He worked the bolt, then trotted back into the tunnel. He turned left at the concourse and jogged along.

He felt good. His side was hurting but not terribly so and he had adequate range of motion. He was fit. He could trot ten miles without breaking a sweat.

Henry Charon wondered if the other man was having as much fun as he was.

'Colonel, there's a bunch of people coming down the street.'

Orrin Jonat looked at the soldier disbelievingly. 'What?'

'A bunch of people. Not armed apparently. They're just walking this way.'

'How many is a bunch?'

'Hundreds. We can't tell.'

Colonel Jonat followed the soldier outside. He walked to the gate and looked down the street. Good lord, the street was filled with people.

He stepped back through the gate and got his people in. Then he had it closed. It was just a chain-link fence about six feet high. He asked the sergeant to install the padlock.

'I don't know where the lock is, sir.'

'Go find it,' Colonel Jonat said. 'Or get one of those locks we've been using for the prisoners. Hurry.'

He stood there waiting. The head of the column turned and a dozen people came toward the gate shoulder to shoulder.

'Open up.'

The crowd was mostly black. Some white people, but predominantly black men and women. They ranged from young to fairly elderly. Some of the people were supporting others. There, was even a man in a wheelchair. The man facing Colonel Jonat was about forty. He spoke. 'Open up.'

'This is a military installation. I'm the officer in charge, Colonel Jonat. I'm ordering you people to disperse. You may not come in.'

'We're not armed, Colonel, as you can see. There are about a thousand people here and nobody is even carrying a pocketknife. Now open this gate.'

'It's not locked, Tom,' the man beside him said, pointing.

Where in *hell* is that sergeant?

'Open the gate or we'll open it. I'll not ask you again.'

'What do you want here? Talk to me.'

The spokesman stood aside. 'Open the gate,' he said to the people beside him. They laid willing hands on the gate and pushed.

Jonat jumped back out of the way. He backed up ten feet or so and soldiers with their rifles ready surrounded him. 'Halt, goddammit, or we'll open fire!'

The crowd came through the gate and stopped two feet in front of the colonel. He could see more and more people gathering in the street. A thousand? He believed it.

'We want your prisoners.'

'You aren't going to get them. Now get the hell off government property or—'

'Or what? You would shoot unarmed civilians who are just standing here? What are you, some kind of Nazi?'

Jonat tried to reason with the man. He raised his voice so that more people could hear. 'Listen, folks. I don't know why you came, but I can't release these prisoners. They've shot at soldiers, killed some, looted, burned, sold drugs – you name it. I know Washington has been through hell the last few days, but these people will have to answer for what they've done. They will get a fair hearing and federal judges will treat them fairly. Please, go on home and let's get this city back to normal. Your sons and husbands will be treated fairly. I promise!'

'We want these people now.'

'Out! Get out. Or I'll order these men to shoot you where you stand.'

The crowd moved as one. They came forward, crowding, pressing. One woman walked up so close to the soldier beside Jonat that the muzzle of his M-16 was against her breast.

'Go ahead, Colonel,' she said. 'Tell him to shoot. He can't miss. I'll hold still.'

She was a black woman, about thirty or so, with a strong, proud face. Orrin Jonat stared at her, but she was staring at the soldier who held the rifle. He was black, too. He stared back, his jaw slack, his hand on the trigger of his weapon. 'Could you do it?' she asked softly. 'Could you murder me? Could you spend the rest of your life seeing my face and knowing that you killed me when I offer you no harm?'

The soldier picked the muzzle up, pointing the rifle safely at the sky, and took a step backward.

'Move back, Colonel. Move back.' The spokesman, also spoke softly, but with a hard edge to his voice.

Involuntarily the colonel retreated a step. As he did so the whole crowd moved silently forward. 'Order your men to stand back. Colonel. You don't want to be the Reinhard Heydrich of Washington. Order them back.'

'We *know* who these people are. We'll find them and arrest them again. They *will* answer for their acts. As *you* will.'

'As God is my judge, I know you speak the truth, Colonel. Now stand back.'

To his credit, Orrin Jonat knew when he was beaten. He spoke loudly: 'Hold your fire, men. No shooting. Now back up.'

The spokesman led the way through the door. He paused inside and looked at the bodies arranged in rows on the floor as people swarmed in behind him. Then he looked at the prisoners shackled to the wall. He motioned to his companions and they started forward.

Toad Tarkington was making a list of the dead from the information on their dogtags when the civilians came through the door, and now he positioned himself between the obvious leader and the prisoners. 'Stop right there,' he shouted. 'Not another fucking step, buddy.'

'Get out of the way.' The man spoke calmly but with an air of authority.

The crowd surged past the man who faced Toad. Men, women, old people, they just kept coming.

Toad reached inside his coat and drew a pistol. He pointed it at the man in front of him and cocked the hammer.

'I can't shoot everybody, Jack, but I can sure as hell shoot you. Now stop these people or I blow your head clean off.'

Out of the corner of his eye he saw something coming. He pulled the trigger just as the lights went out.

Jake Grafton stood in the third-level concourse listening. He was in total darkness, a spot so black he couldn't even see his hands. He closed his eyes and concentrated on what he could hear.

Some background noise from over toward the armory, but in here, nothing. Quiet as King Tut's tomb.

He opened his eyes and felt his way along the wall. Ahead he could see the glow where a ramp along the exterior wall came up. He paused. He would be an excellent target when he entered that faint glow. If there were anyone around.

He took a deep breath to steady himself, then moved forward.

Up a level. He would climb up a level.

Five minutes had passed since that second shot had spanged into the seat beside him as he scurried up the stairs for the safety of the tunnel. Too long. He should have moved more than the hundred yards he had come.

He should have set up an ambush. As long as this guy doesn't know where I am, Jake told himself, I've got the advantage.

But there was the ramp. Should he go for it or stay here?

His mouth was dry. He licked his lips and wiped the sweat from his forehead. Okay. To do it or not? The entrance to the ramp was only fifteen yards or so away.

He went for it as fast as he could. He rounded the corner and halted with his back against the wall, breathing hard. Then he heard it. A faint laugh.

Someone laughing!

'This is really too easy. You're not using your head, mister.'

Jake ran up the ramp. As hard and fast as he could go. He came out on the top level and trotted along the concourse. After about a minute had passed he found a real dark spot and came to a halt. He stood there gripping the rifle tightly with both hands and listening.

Ambush. He needed to find a spot. Needed to sit and let this psycho come to him. Needed to wait if it took all night. But where?

He kept going. Fifty yards further along he came to another place where two ramps came up from below. There seemed to be more light than usual. Aha, the armory was down there and the emergency lights in the parking area were reflecting up here. Jake looked around. If he went along this corridor to the north, he could look back this way. If and when, bang.

His mind made up, he went down the corridor seventy-five feet or so and lay down against the exterior concourse wall, facing back toward the ramp area.

Of course his back was vulnerable, but if the sniper came that way, he would hear him coming. Maybe. The main thing was to stay put and stay quiet.

Who was this sniper, anyway? Could he be Charon? Naw, Charon was an assassin, out to shoot the big trophy cats. He wouldn't waste a bullet on a mouse.

Toad Tarkington was spinning. He was sitting in a cockpit of a violently spinning airplane and the Gs were pushing him forward out of the seat. The altimeter was unwinding at a sickening rate. He couldn't raise his arms or move. His eyes were redding out and he could feel the pain of the blood pooling in his head. Spinning viciously, violently, dying . . .

He opened his eyes. He was looking into the face of Jack Yocke.

Yocke pried open an eyelid and looked with interest. 'You're going to be okay, I think. Your head's as hard as a brick. If I were you I wouldn't try to sit up yet though.'

'What happened?'

'Well, a man hit you on the head with an ax handle. And you shot a man, fellow named Tom Shannon.'

'He dead?'

'No. You got him in the shoulder. He's sitting right here beside you. If you turn your head you can visit with him.'

Toad tried. The pain shot through his head so badly he felt himself going out again. He lay absolutely still and the feeling passed.

After a moment he opened his eyes and swiveled his head a millimeter, then another. Yocke was applying a bandage to a man who was naked from the waist up. They were on the floor of the armory bay.

Toad held his head and turned it. All the prisoners were gone! The three of them were the only ones in the whole room.

'How long I been out?'

'Fifteen, twenty minutes. Something like that.'

'Damn you, Yocke.'

'Hey, Toad.' The reporter came over and stared down at him. 'You could have killed Shannon.'

'If he was the asshole in front, I was trying to. I'm damn sorry I didn't.'

Yocke looked tired. 'I didn't know you were carrying a pistol under that coat.'

'I told you, being around Grafton, you gotta . . .'

'Lie still. You probably have a concussion.'

'Jerk. Reporter jerk. *Spectator*.' Toad tried to sit. The effort nauseated him and made him so dizzy he had to steady himself with his hands on the floor.

When he opened his eyes he was looking straight at Shannon. 'So you took 'em, huh? We'll get 'em back. Those fucking dirtballs won't get away with killing soldiers and all that shit just because a damn mob turns 'em loose.'

Shannon just stared at him.

Yocke came over and used his fingers to part the hair on the back of Toad's head. He looked carefully. 'You got a real bad goose egg, Toad.'

'We'll find those assholes, Shannon, even if we have to flood this damn town and comb all the rats with a wire brush.'

'Toad,' Yocke said gently. 'They didn't let those people go.'

Toad Tarkington gaped. It didn't compute. He looked again at the maintenance bays where the prisoners had been held. It was empty. 'What d'ya mean?'

'They didn't turn them loose, Toad. They're hanging them. All of them.'

By some ironic quirk of fate, they brought Sweet Cherry Lane to the same light pole where they were hanging T. Jefferson Brody.

'Bitch, cunt, nigger slut! I hope we end up in the same furnace in hell so I can kick the shit out of you for a million years!'

The man in front of him put the noose around his neck while two women and two men held his arms. He struggled. *They couldn't do this to him! He was a member of the bar!*

'I got money. I'll pay you to let me go. Please! For God's sake.'

He could feel the noose tightening as eight people in front of him pulled the rope. Holy shit! It was going to happen! They were *really* going to do it.

T. Jefferson Brody peed his pants.

Sweet Cherry Lane was standing there silently, watching him, as two men held her arms immobile and a third draped a noose around her neck.

'Why?' he croaked at her. 'Why did Freeman McNally protect you?'

'I'm his half-sister,' she said.

Before he could reply the people holding his arms let go and the rope around his neck lifted him clear of the ground. He grabbed the rope and held on with both hands as it elevated him higher and higher and the merciless pressure on his neck began to strangle him. He was kicking wildly, which caused him to spin slowly, first one way, then the other. His vision faded. Can't breathe, can't see, can't . . .

He heard a step. Lying there against the curved wall, he could hear a soft sound, followed by another. The sounds weren't like leather heels clicking on a wooden floor, but like something soft brushing against something that . . . The sound carried well against the wall. They were footsteps. That was all they could be.

Jake Grafton tightened his grip on the rifle and thumbed the safety off. He had it pointed at the ramp opening. As soon as this dude stepped into that square of faint light . . .

Another step. He was coming slowly, methodically, step by step. But how far away was he? How far would sounds carry around this curved concrete wall? Maybe a hundred yards, he speculated. Maybe twice that. Naw. Fifty was more like it.

The steps paused, then resumed.

He's coming.

Sweat dripped into Jake's eyes but he didn't move. He merely blinked and tried to ignore the stinging.

Suddenly he realized what a damn poor position he had chosen. He should have picked the doorway to a rest room to lie in, something that would have allowed him to look both ways. For the thought came in all its horror that the man he sought was probably behind him in the darkness.

Jake started to turn around.

'No, friend,' the voice said softly. 'Just hold it right there.'

Jake froze.

'Well, we had ourselves a nice little hunt, didn't we? We stalked and stalked and now we are at the end.'

'You'll never get away, Charon.'

The man laughed. 'I'll outlive you by quite a while.'

He was behind Jake. But which side of the concourse? Probably near the exterior wall or his footsteps wouldn't have carried so well.

Jake tried to decide what to do. He knew to the depths of his soul that anything he tried would be futile. But he couldn't let this guy just shoot him like a dog! If he spun, he would have to rise to his knees and swing the rifle.

Jake thumbed the selector to full automatic fire. He turned his head, looking.

'You're thinking about turning and trying a shot, aren't you? Go ahead. I'll put the first one up your ass.'

'Who hired you?'

Another soft laugh. 'Would you believe I never asked? I don't know.'

'How much did they pay you?'

'A lot of money. And you know something funny? I do believe I would have done it for nothing.' Another chuckle.

The next time the guy spoke. While he was speaking Jake would spin and let this guy have a magazine-full of hot lead. 'You really don't have to kill me, do you? You've had your fun.'

'That's an interesting—'

A burst of gunfire strobed the corridor. Jake had just started to spin. He completed the maneuver and flopped down with the rifle aimed into the darkness in front of him.

In the silence that followed he heard something soft and heavy fall to the concrete. And he heard a sigh.

'Captain, don't shoot! It's me.'

Rita!

He got up slowly, almost falling. Then a light came on. She had a small flashlight and she was shining it down on Henry Charon. He lay on his back, the rifle just out of reach of his right hand.

Jake walked up and stood looking down. He kept his rifle pointed at Charon and his finger on the trigger.

'How . . . ?' Charon said. He had been hit in the chest by at least three bullets. The red stain was spreading rapidly.

Rita seemed to understand. She flashed the light on her feet. They were bare. 'I took my shoes off.'

When she put the light back on Charon's face he was grinning. Then he died. The smile faded as the muscles went slack.

Jake bent down and felt for Charon's pulse. He straightened slowly.

'Come on,' he said. 'Let's go.'

Rita extinguished the penlight. Together they walked along the concourse toward the light.

*

The bodies hung from every pole. Jake Grafton stared, trying to comprehend. Some poles had one, some had two. But they all hung lifelessly, stirring only as the cold night breeze moved them.

Inside the armory he found the soldiers gathered around Toad Tarkington, who was sitting on the concrete floor nursing his head. Jack Yocke was beside him talking to a civilian.

'You want anything in the paper about why you did it, Tom? You know they'll try you for a dozen felonies, perhaps even a dozen murders?'

The middle-aged, balding black man sitting on the floor was being worked on by a medic, who was strapping tape around a bandage arranged on his chest. Blood was smeared on his chest and trousers.

The same man on the floor ignored the audience. He stared at Yocke. 'Will you write it true? Write it the way I say it?'

'You know I will. You've read my stuff.'

'The Jefferson projects. You remember?'

Yocke nodded. Oh yes, he remembered. The murder of Jane Wilkens by a crack dealer running from the cops. Another life lost to the crack business. 'Jane,' he said.

'Yeah. Jane.' Shannon took a deep breath and grimaced at the pain. 'It was my idea. We're all victims. We all lost somebody – a son, daughter, wife, maybe even our own souls. We *lost* because we expected someone to fight the evil for us and we waited and waited and they never did. Oh, they *talked*, but . . .'

He lifted his good hand and pleaded, 'Don't you see, if we don't fight evil, we *become* evil. If you ain't part of the solution you're part of the problem – it's *that* simple. So we decided to take a stand, all of us victims.

'Then this terrorist stuff started. And the dopers started looting and shooting and trying to wipe out their competition so they could have a competitive advantage when it was all over.

'Now I tell you this, Jack Yocke, and you gotta write it just like this: I *hope* the talkers try me. I *hope* I get prosecuted. The people who don't want to be victims anymore wilt see how it *has* to be. We can't wait for George Bush or Dan Quayle or the hot-air artists. We can't wait for the police. *We* have to take *our* stand.

'I've taken mine. You kill my woman, you kill my kids, don't hide behind the law 'cause it ain't big enough. Justice *will* be done! *Right* will be done. There are just enough people like me. Just enough. You'll see.'

The medic finished and spread a blanket on a stretcher. Four men lifted the wounded man onto it.

'I'm not good with words,' the man told Yocke. 'I never had much education. But I know right from wrong and I know which side I'm on. I've planted my feet. *Here* I am.'

'What can one man do?' Jack Yocke asked.

'Lead an army, part the Red Sea, convert the world. Maybe not me. But here *I* stand until the world takes its place beside me.'

The medics carried him away.

The chairman of the Joint Chiefs arrived by helicopter fifteen minutes later. Ten minutes after that the Vice-President arrived. Together they walked through the parking lot looking at the dangling corpses.

Jake Grafton went over to where Toad and Rita were sitting in chairs. 'Come on. Let's go home. You got the car keys. Toad?'

'In my pocket.'

'Rita, take the keys and bring the car up to the door.'

'What about Yocke?' Toad asked as Jake helped him into the front seat.

'He's over with the heavies getting a story. Let's go home.'

As the car exited the armory parking lot. Toad pointed toward the official party in the parking lot across the street. 'Wonder what they're thinking?'

'They're politicians. Tom Shannon and the other citizens here tonight just delivered a message. They're reading it now.'

32

People heard the news of the hangings on portable battery-operated radios then ran next door to tell their neighbors. The news seemed to drain whatever energy remained from the wounded city. The next morning it lay stunned, exhausted, its citizens cold and without power.

There was no rioting, no looting, no fires. The soldiers walked the streets without incident as crews worked feverishly to restore power to the residential neighborhoods. The bombed substations would require weeks to repair or rebuild, but emergency repairs began to restore power to a few areas by nightfall. In the areas still without power, people were evacuated to schools and auditoriums where the Army installed portable generators. The people of Washington began to reach out to help each other.

Jake Grafton spent the day in a round of meetings as the federal authorities devised ways to thwart the terrorist threat from the Extraditables in the short term. Over the long term, the problem was the cocaine industry in South America.

The next day the ban against motor vehicles was lifted and people swarmed the city in a monumental traffic jam. That evening, after conferring with the directors of the FBI, DEA, and CIA and being advised that those organizations knew of no additional terrorists in the country, General Land started pulling out the troops.

He had Jake Grafton, Toad, and Rita come to his office and make a complete report. An hour later when the chairman signaled the interview was over, Jake asked for leave for himself and Toad. Rita was already on leave. The request was granted.

Out in front of the Pentagon Jake asked the two lieutenants, 'You want to come over to the beach house and spend Christmas with Callie and Amy and me?'

They glanced at each other, then accepted.

All the troops were out of the city on the twenty-ninth of December. The following day George Bush was discharged from Bethesda Naval Hospital and returned to the White House.

He held a news conference that afternoon that was carried live nation-wide. Attorney General Gideon Cohen sat beside him.

Bush said he felt good and was getting better every day. He wanted to take this opportunity to publicly thank Vice-President Quayle for his excellent stewardship during his incapacity, and he did so with the leaders of the House and Senate and all of the surviving Supreme Court justices in attendance. And he announced the formation of a presidential commission to study the nation's illegal drug problem and make recommendations on what needed to be done to solve it. Gideon Cohen was appointed chairman.

'I have asked the attorney general to chair this commission because he has been one of the harshest critics of our efforts to date. I know we can rely on him to give us a thorough, honest evaluation of our shortcomings. I promise you, we will ask the Congress to turn the commission's recommendations into legislation.'

Then the President got down to brass tacks. 'The drug problem is a complex social issue that is not going to go away by itself. Its causes include everything from poverty in Colombia and Peru to poverty and rotten schools in this country. The crux of the problem is that so many people have been left out of the world's evolving economy, people in the Third World, people right here in America. I don't know that there are solutions – certainly no easy ones – but I promise you this: we are going to face the problem.'

Intended by the President to help calm the political atmosphere, which was rife with accusations and recriminations, the news conference had no such effect. It was too little too late.

Critics like Congresswoman Samantha Strader attacked the Army's handling of the crisis and damned Tom Shannon as a psychotic vigilante. He would have been stuffed into the same crack that held Bernard Goetz had he not been black. Unable to hurl the racist stink bomb, those who opposed tougher drug laws and tougher law enforcement and those with their own political agendas and ambitions united to demand that Shannon be tried, convicted, and hurried on his way to perdition.

Those who believed that the government hadn't done enough to combat illegal drugs rushed to Shannon's defense. It was wrong, they claimed, to martyr Shannon on the altar of the white man's guilt.

Jack Yocke's articles in the *Post* merely drew the lines for the comba-tants. Saint or sinner, Tom Shannon stood at the vortex of the developing firestorm. Curiously, he stood alone. After a quiet conference with his chief adviser, Will Dorfman, George Bush decided not to have the FBI or police attempt to discover the identities of the people who had accompanied Shannon to the armory. Those seeking to destroy Shannon were likewise not interested in having the stories of a thousand victims of the drug trade paraded before the public one at a time, night after night, ad infinitum. So Tom Shannon was the only man charged, for conspiracy with a person or persons unknown to lynch 382 people.

When Jack Yocke went to see him in the hospital, Shannon grinned. 'Nobody wants to try us all, but they think if they try just me all the other victims will go away. Won't happen. Those people buried too many kids, buried too many husbands.'

'What about legalization of dope?' Jade Yocke asked toward the end of the interview. 'There's a lot of talk about that since Christmas. What do you think?'

'Personally I'm against it,' Shannon said. 'There's too many fools who'll get addicted. Off the record, though, I think that's what will have to be done. We've got to get the big money out of the business. If the money is gone the criminals will go. That'll stop the recruitment of kids just out of diapers to a life of using and abusing, a life of crime and ignorance and squalor. A whole generation of black kids is going down the toilet. It's an obscenity that's got to stop.'

Remarkably, in spite of the hurricane-velocity winds building inside the beltway, life elsewhere in America returned quickly to normal. The soaps went back on television during the day and the sitcoms returned at night. Critics complained of the sexual innuendo that passed as humor this winter on the tube. A network executive said the critics didn't know what was funny.

The ball fell in Times Square on New Year's Eve and a great many people awoke the next morning with a hangover, but not as many as in past years, some pollster said in a headline story, because people these days were drinking less. Southern Cat won another Rose Bowl.

During the first week of January two former executives of a large Texas savings and loan pleaded guilty to twenty-eight counts of bank fraud and asked the court to put them on probation.

The wife of a well-known movie star sued her husband for divorce and claimed he was having an affair with his latest leading lady. The betrayed wife went from one syndicated morning talk show to the next idling her story and explaining to the sympathetic hosts the financial hardships that loomed as she tried to survive on half a million a month and keep the kids in school.

Iran had a little earthquake. Another ayatollah died while a blizzard stranded airline passengers in Denver, and Whitefish, Montana, reported record low temperatures.

The Democrats wanted to know when the administration was going to get serious about raising taxes and the Republicans wanted to know when the Democrats were going to get serious about cutting government spending.

Another congressman announced he was gay.

And the network that had rights to televise the Super Bowl officially kicked off the hype with a show in which millionaire football players explained how their teams had overcome adversity this past year.

While all this was going on Senator Bob Cherry quietly resigned from the US Senate. He told the Florida newspapers that he was tired and had done all he could for his country. Guessing who the governor would appoint to fill Cherry's seat became the diversion of the hour in Florida.

A fine wet rain, almost a mist, fell almost continuously in Washington that first week of the new year. Then the wind picked up and blew the clouds eastward out to sea.

Thanos Liarakos glanced again at the street sign and once again consulted his map. He drove slowly for several more blocks, then found the street he wanted. The trees in this suburban tract development were small and stick-like in the anemic sunlight. They would grow larger of course, but it would take twenty or thirty years for these neighborhoods to look settled, permanent.

He found the building he wanted and drove another half block looking for a parking place, then walked back. The sprawling one-story brick structure was surrounded on three sides by a chain-link fence. Inside the sturdy wire were sandboxes and swings and child-powered merry-go-rounds. And children. Lots of them, squealing, running, laughing.

Liarakos went in the front door and down the empty hallway. He paused outside the door marked office, squared his shoulders, then went in. 'Miss Judith Lewis, please. Is she around?'

The owlish-looking young woman with a heavy sweater and shiny pink lips sitting behind the desk noted his suit and tie, grinned perfunctorily, and said, 'She has playground duty. Might be in back.'

'And how . . . ?'

'Down the corridor to the first left and straight on out. You can't miss it.'

'Thank you.'

Judith Lewis was standing with her arms folded across her chest listening to a young boy tell a tale of woe, with much pointing and gesturing. She bent down and wiped his face and stroked his hair. As she did so the lower edge of her coat dragged in the dirt. That, Liarakos suspected, was not a detail that would bother Judith Lewis very much.

The child grinned finally and ran off to join his friends.

'Hello, Judith.'

She turned and saw him, then rose to her feet. 'Hello,' she acknowledged without enthusiasm. She half turned away so she could watch the children. He approached and stood beside her, also watching the children.

'How was your holiday?' he asked.

'Fine.' Her voice was hard and flat. She checked her watch.

'Beautiful youngsters.'

'Recess is over in three minutes. Say what you came to say.'

'Okay. That Cuban general, Zaba, knows enough to convict Chano Aldana. And he's talking, singing his heart out. I've been reading transcripts of his interrogations. If the prosecutors can get Zaba on the stand they can get a conviction.'

'Why are you telling me all this?'

'Isn't it obvious?'

'I'm not going back to work for you, Mr Liarakos. I thought I made that plain.'

'What you made plain, Ms Lewis, is that you thought Chano Aldana was the devil incarnate and ought to be locked up so he can't continue to murder and terrorize and sell poison to ruin the lives of children like these.'

'You were equally definite in your opinion, Mr Liarakos, as I recall,' Her voice was acidic. 'Like every wealthy, successful criminal, Aldana deserves the best legal defense money can buy, and that of course is *you*. And if you can hoodwink and bamboozle the jurors, it's your sworn duty to do so. Then you go home to your beautiful wife and children and eat a gourmet dinner and rest your weary soul, your duty well and truly done. Isn't that the spin you want on it? Oh, I haven't forgotten our last conversation, Mr Liarakos. I doubt that I ever will. It brought into very stark relief all the doubts I've had through the years of law school and practice.'

The bell rang. All the children charged for the door.

'If you'll ex—' she began, but he interrupted:

'I came to ask you to come back to work.'

She stared at him as the schoolyard emptied and the last of the children disappeared inside.

'Listen, there's more to the legal profession than the Chano Aldanas of the world. Someone has to be in a position to help all these people who need someone to speak for them. Someone has to represent Jane Roe and Karen Ann Quinlan and John T. Scopes and all the rest of the folks who can't speak for themselves. That's why you went to law school, isn't it?'

'Yes, it is.' She said it softly, almost inaudibly. She lifted the hem of her coat and brushed at the loose dirt that clung there.

'Where do you think you get the experience to help that one client in a hundred? You get it by going to court every day, wrestling with the prosecutors and the judges and the system. *Someone* has to know how to work the system.'

She turned and faced the school.

'Someone has to care. Someone has to fight it every blessed day and do the best they can. If someone doesn't, the little people are going to go down the slop chute. Now I ask you, if *you* won't do it, who will?'

'You keep asking these goddammed rhetorical questions, Mr Liarakos,' she said bitterly. 'And you're representing Chano Aldana.'

'He paid the fee. The firm needs the money. I need the money. I'll do my level best for the bastard.'

'Why?'

'Ms Lewis, if you have to ask, you'd better stay here with the grade-school kids.'

'Aldana is going to walk.'

Liarakos snorted. 'No, he isn't. Zaba knows enough to convict Aldana. I've been reading the transcripts of the interrogations. He's singing like a bird. They got everything chapter and verse. Names, locations, dates, amounts, quantities – everything. Zaba was the Cuban connection and he personally met with Aldana at least seven times. He even arranged for a couple of murders of DEA agents by Cuban intelligence. The prosecutors have got it.'

'So. What are you going to do?'

'Me? I'm just going to give Aldana a hundred percent of my best efforts and the prosecutors are going to nail his guilty hide to the wall. Clarence Darrow couldn't get the sonofabitch off. There's no way. I've been doing this for a lot of years and I *know*. Aldana's guilty and the jury will see that and he'll go up the river for the rest of his natural life.'

'And you?'

'I'll go home afterward, Ms Lewis, and pour myself a stiff drink and give thanks that God created the jury system.'

'But what if the jury *won't* convict Aldana?'

'Judith, you have got to believe in your fellow man or you'll have no hope at all. If the ordinary men and women on the jury won't convict him, why try to get him off the streets? If they won't convict him, they *deserve* him.'

She kept brushing at the coat.

'You made a fine little speech in my office a few weeks ago, Judith. Something about the law existing to protect those who can't protect themselves. And here they are.' He gestured toward the school building. 'I thought you meant it.'

She ran her hand through her hair.

She grimaced. 'Are you sure?'

'I'll see you tomorrow at the office,' he said, 'or the next morning. Whenever you can get there.'

She kept brushing at her coat.

'Oh, and you and I have a new client. Guy name of Tom Shannon. A *pro bono* case.'

'Shannon? Isn't he the man who led the lynch mob to the armory, the scapegoat they want to hang?'

'That's the man,' Liarakos agreed. 'You and he have a lot in common. He also says he knows the difference between good and evil.'

He turned and walked toward the door to the school and went through it, leaving Judith Lewis in the middle of the empty playground staring after him, flipping at her coat hem automatically.

'God damn you,' she whispered. 'God damn you.' And she began to cry.

She had thought she was out of it. And now this! The principal and the school officials – when they hired her she promised to stay. They were going to think her such a terrible liar.

She went over to the bench against the wall and tried to compose herself.

Well, tomorrow was impossible. She would call the school officials this afternoon, but she should give them at least one more day so that they could find someone else.

She used the hem of her skirt to wipe the tears from her eyes.

The doctor had a breezy manner. He radiated confidence and self-assurance. Apparently he had picked up the patois in Patient Relations 101.

'You're going to be fine. Every third day we'll change the dressing and inch the drain out. But I think you're well enough to go home.'

Harrison Ronald Ford nodded and swung his feet back and forth as the doctor examined the surgical incisions in his back. He was perched on the side of the bed, which was too far above the floor for his feet to comfortably reach. Normally the nurse had a little stool placed just so.

'Hold still please.'

Harrison obeyed. Since the doctor couldn't see his face, he grinned.

'Yes indeedy. Looking very fine. Gonna be a dilly of a scar, but maybe you can get a big tattoo back here and no one will notice. I have a rather extraordinary picture of a naked woman on a stallion I can let you look at if you want to consider classical artwork.'

'Big tits?'

'Melons.'

'Bring it in.'

'Now if you have any trouble at all, you call me. Any time, day or night. And the people downstairs want you to continue in physical therapy every day. Make those appointments before you leave this afternoon.'

'Sure.'

The doctor came around to face him. 'The nurse will be in in a moment to put a new bandage on you. I just wanted to check you one last time and shake your hand.'

'Thanks, Doc.'

They took him in a wheelchair to the administration office to finish the paperwork. The administrator asked for his address and telephone number and he gave them the apartment he had used as Sammy Z. 'We'll see you tomorrow at ten in the morning.'

'Sure.' The doctor popped in and Harrison shook hands all around, one more time.

At his request they called him a taxi. It was waiting out front when he scribbled his name for the final time. With the nurse holding grimly to his elbow, he maneuvered himself out of the wheelchair and into the back-seat. She supervised the cabbie as he placed the two bags that Freddy Murray had brought up from Quantico in the trunk. Harrison waved at her as the cabbie put the car into motion.

She gave him a distracted smile and charged back inside pushing the wheelchair.

'Where to, Mac?'

'National Airport.'

'What airline?'

'Oh, I dunno. Don't have reservations yet.'

'Well, you won't have no problem. Holiday rush is all over. Where you heading?'

'Evansville, Indiana.'

'Go through Chicago or Cleveland?'

'One of those.'

'Maybe US Air.'

'Fine.'

Harrison Ronald sat back and watched the cars gliding along under the winter sky. He had been in Washington, what? Almost eleven months. Seemed like forever.

The cab driver whistled for a redcap to handle the bags and Harrison gave him a two-dollar tip. The driver was right. He had no trouble getting a ticket on the next plane, which was scheduled to leave in an hour.

Harrison Ronald strolled to the boarding area and sat watching the businessmen and mothers with children. The men in suits were reading or writing reports, darting over to the pay phones and making credit card calls. The kids were hollering and scurrying about and demanding their mothers' attention. He sighed. It was so normal – so . . . almost like another world after all the stuff he had been through these last few months. He shook his head in wonder. Life does indeed go on.

Amazingly enough the airplane actually left on time. Most of the seats were empty. Harrison Ronald moved from his aisle seat to the window and took his last look at Washington as it fell away below.

It was over then. Really and truly over. No more terror, no more waiting for the ax to fall, no more sleepless nights wondering what Freeman McNally was hearing and thinking. Over.

What would he do now? He had been avoiding the issue but he examined it now as Washington slipped behind and the Alleghenies came into view like ribs.

The Corps – maybe. After he was healed up completely. He would go find a doctor to do all the therapy and bandage changing and drain pulling that the folks in Washington were worried about. Or perhaps he should go back to the cops. Maybe that. He would have to think about it some more. But now he felt so good, almost euphoric. It was hard to envision himself back on the street dealing with the would-be Freeman McNallys, all the lazy losers who thought that everyone should hold still while they carved off a chunk without earning it.

He was tired so he reclined the seat and closed his eyes. The important thing was that he was going back to the front porch. Spring would come eventually, then the summer with its muggy heat. He would sit in the swing and watch his grandmother string beans and shuck corn for canning. Maybe go to the ballpark on hot summer evenings. Paint the house for her – that was what he would do. He thought about the paint, the smell of it with the heat on his back. It would be very good. And there would be plenty of time – all the time he would ever need. With these images in his mind he dozed off.

He awoke on the descent into Chicago. The plane to Evansville was a four-engine turboprop which entered the clouds as it left O'Hare and stayed in them until it was on final approach into the Evansville airport. Harrison was glued to the window looking at the Ohio River looping by the downtown and the streets and neighborhoods all neatly, perfectly square. He saw the high school he had graduated from and he saw the minor league ballpark where he had sold hot dogs all those summers growing up.

He took a cab from the airport.

The little house looked exactly the same. The swing was put away for the winter and the trees were bare, but the grass had been mowed just before the cold stopped all growth. The house still needed painting. And the soffit under the eaves – he would fix those rotten places too.

The doctor had told him not to lift anything, so he had the cabbie put the bags on the porch. Then he tried the door. Unlocked.

He stepped in.

'Grandmom! It's me, Harrison.'

'Who?'

Her voice came floating down the hallway from the kitchen.

He walked that way. He saw her before he got to the kitchen door. She was old and small and her hair was white. She didn't move too quickly anymore, but he thought he had never seen a more beautiful woman.

'Oh, Harrison! What a wonderful surprise! You're home!'

'Yeah, Grandmom. I'm home.'

He took her gently in his arms.